Forever

KINDLE ALEXANDER

TRADEMARK ACKNOWLEDGEMENTS

The author acknowledges the trademarked status and trademark owners of the following trademarks mentioned in this work of fiction:

Acura: Honda Giken Kogyo Kabushiki Kaisha (Honda Motor Co., LTD)
Advil: Wyeth, LLC
Amazon: Amazon Technologies, Inc.
Aston Martin: Aston Martin Lagonda Limited Company
Audi R8 Coupe: Audi Aktiengesellschaft Corporation
Bud Light: Anheuser-Busch, Incorporated
Cadillac CTS-V Coupe: General Motors LLC
Captain America: Marvel Characters, Inc.
Disney and Frozen: Disney Enterprises, Inc.
Emily Post: The Emily Post Institute, Inc.
GQ: Advanced Magazine Publishers, Inc.
Hilton: HLT Domestic IP LLC
H&M: H & M Hennes & Mauritz AB
Kawasaki Ninja: Kawasaki Jukogyo Kabushiki Kaisha
Ken and Barbie: Mattel, Inc.
Lamaze: Lamaze International, Inc.
La-Z-Boy: La-Z-Boy, Inc.
Mack Truck: Mack Trucks, Inc.
Motrin: Johnson & Johnson Corporation
Nordstrom: NIHC, Inc.
Patrón: Patrón Spirits International AG
Reddit: Reddit, Inc.
Skype: Skype Corporation
Starbucks: Starbucks Corporation
Styrofoam: The Dow Chemical Company
The Walking Dead: AMC Film Holdings LLC
Uber: Uber Technologies, Inc.
Vogue: Advance Magazine Publishers Inc.
Williams-Sonoma: Williams-Sonoma, Inc.
YouTube: Google, Inc.
Wayne's World
WhatsApp
Max Steele
Grand Theft Auto
Echo Show
Amazon Alexa
Sony Productions
QuickBooks
Star Wars Solo
J.Crew
The National Culinary Review
Barney's

DEDICATION

Kindle, you're forever in our hearts.

Perry, you're missed every day.

Daddy, you're the best father a daughter could have. You will always be my hero and you will live forever in my heart. I love you. I hope I made you proud.

NOTE FROM AUTHOR

Creative license was taken with this story. It's a work of fiction.

A SPECIAL THANKS

We'd like to give a special **thank you** to the **brilliant and talented, Author Kris Michaels**. In crafting our stories, we go to great lengths to research the lives of our characters. Landon's specific military career as outlined in Always became a complication. Although we took a few liberties, Kris Michaels, who retired from the United States Air Force, spent weeks, maybe months with us to ensure Landon's character was as Air Force authentic as possible. We appreciate her time so much, and Landon *loves* her. He was worried we'd get it wrong.

About Kris Michaels

USA Today and Amazon Bestselling Author, Kris Michaels is the alter ego of a happily married wife and mother. She writes romance, usually with characters from military and law enforcement backgrounds.

Kris was born and raised in South Dakota. She graduated many years ago from a high school class consisting of 13 students (yes that is thirteen, eleven girls and two boys...lucky boys). She joined the military, met her husband, and traveled the world. Today she lives on the Gulf Coast and writes full time.

Kris is an avid people watcher and dreamer. The stories she writes are crafted around the hopes and dreams of a true romantic. She believes love is essential, people are beautiful, and everyone deserves a happy ending.

When she isn't writing Kris enjoys a full life revolving around family, friends, laughing, whiskey, and cold red wine. (Yes cold...don't judge.)

Find more about Kris Michaels here: https://amzn.to/2vUsWU5

Chapter 1

July 2014—Landstuhl, Germany

"Damn, Doc! You're a machine. You've gotta be exhausted."

Robert Adams glanced from reading the chart in his hand to the tall blond nurse who had come to a stop beside him. He'd met the guy weeks ago and had seen him around the hospital dozens of times since. Robert winced internally. If he hadn't become such a self-absorbed ass and been the better person he was raised to be, he'd have made it a point to remember the man's name. This was just another reminder of how he hadn't even tried to fit in socially with the hospital staff.

If he'd learned anything from the past eight or so months, self-beratement didn't help adjust his rotten attitude. Robert had given up on any hope of absolution and had let this funky, fucked-up mood consume his entire life.

Yet another thing his fathers would have been disappointed in him for.

"I think that's preaching to the choir," he said, giving up on the guy's name but remembering the nurse was always around the hospital too. For the past month, Robert had been placed on limited duty at the Landstuhl Regional Military Hospital in Germany. From the janitorial staff all the way to the top brass, the whole team seemed to have a great respect for one another. They were solid professionals who genuinely got along, and they had had no problem welcoming Robert—a civilian—into their circle with open arms. He'd been the one to purposefully keep his distance.

Another point in the hospital staff's favor was that not one person had referenced either one of his fathers. They offered no awkward condolences on their untimely deaths. There was no talk of his dad, Avery Adams, being a great patriot of their country or the loss of his other father, his daddy, Kane Adams, so quickly after Avery's death. Robert didn't have to listen to all the ridiculous theories of soul mates—a perfect love intertwined with a connection so deep that death couldn't break his fathers' bond. Here at LRMC, Robert was just a man immersing himself in work.

The scalpel hadn't felt right in his hand for a good while now, and he refused to jeopardize any surgical patient until it did again. After pulling political strings to gain special permission, he'd come to LRMC in merely a support capacity. He took every shift offered in order to keep his plate so full there wasn't time to dwell on what had happened in his personal life. Especially his responsibility in his beloved daddy's sudden decline and ultimate death. Pain lanced his heart so sharply it forced the air from his lungs as the weight of what he'd done sat heavily on his chest. And just like that, the overwhelming feeling returned, threatening to drag him under.

He'd heard time eased loss, and perhaps it might, but he doubted the guilt would ever fade. If he'd done things differently, he wouldn't be here in Germany chasing mystical signs, searching for anything to give purpose to his pain. Robert scrubbed a hand down his face.

"You okay, buddy?" the nurse asked, interrupting his pity party.

Robert glanced over, surprised to see the man still standing beside him. Apparently, this depression he fought robbed him of any reasonable thought. How could he move forward when his head and heart couldn't get past how badly he'd handled things?

"Yeah, I'm fine, just a little tired. I'm doing rounds then heading out." Forcing a grin, Robert tried for upbeat, hoping to hide the pain silently drowning him. And it seemed to work. The nurse gave an easy nod, accepting his answer.

"I'm on duty tonight. Let me know what you need." The guy squeezed his shoulder then gave him a reassuring pat on the back before leaving Robert standing there alone.

"Right," he muttered and forced himself back to the patient chart in his hand, refusing to wallow in the murky pit of regret that the conversation had stirred. He stared at the notes, not remembering a single thing he'd read from just moments ago. He had to do better.

"Fuck my life!" Landon Russo bit the words out in complete frustration, letting the paperback in his hand drop to his chest in surrender. In every possible way, he was totally screwed. Being trapped in this hospital bed for days on end had taken its toll. He was antsy and bored lying there, staring at a dingy ceiling that had certainly seen better days.

He'd seen better days too.

Honestly, if he'd planned to go down in a blaze of glory, at least his injuries could have happened in a more honorable way. Of course, he didn't have that kind of luck. Even his supposedly stupidly high IQ hadn't helped override his general cockiness.

Somehow, Landon had allowed his dumbass buddies to goad him into playing chicken with an old abandoned tower. The tall structure had been built a few years after the military base opened in 1953 and had been abandoned long ago. It had no use today other than the fact it had become a distraction from boredom and offered bragging rights to the ones brave enough to accept the challenge. They had boasted it to be a rite of passage, playing a game of double dare with the old wooden structure known as The Tower, or *Der Turm* as they called it there. Hell, the name alone—so ominous sounding—had caused him to want to climb the thing. Fueled by the fact that he'd never been one to pass up a dare, Landon had somehow agreed with their fearless stupidity. In hindsight, his agreement might have had more to do with the alcohol coursing through his blood than anything else. What a dumbass move on his part.

His moment of glory sure as hell had bit him on the ass. He had an arm filled with pins and screws holding it together and a deeply bruised body as his reward for being the bravest of his squadron. He'd scrambled his way to the top of the old rotting tower. The fucked-up part? Even now, he had a small amount of pride in the fact he had made it all the way up those rickety old steps as far as they went before climbing the rest of the way on a decaying wood ladder. Landon had proudly carved his name alongside those of the other brave soldiers who had conquered the tower before him.

Heights had never been a fear for him. And even drunk, he'd had no issue climbing so high. The complication came from the hard, unforgiving earth below—German dirt had no give, and the pain radiating through his bones was a testament to that fact.

Lying on this hospital bed, Landon still refused to take full responsibility for the situation. Maybe he was being arrogant, maybe he wasn't. One thing he knew for certain, though, was that he wouldn't be laid up in the hospital if the guys hadn't feared disciplinary action by calling for help. After carving his name at the top, he'd made it about halfway down when the steps gave out underneath his weight. His instincts automatically kicked in and he'd grabbed onto a somewhat sturdy support beam. He had dangled there for a good long time waiting to be saved. His buddies had fucked it all up. Helpless bunch of pansy-asses. Every last one of them had tried to be the hero and climbed up after him.

He shook his head as memories of that night flooded his thoughts. Of course, the old decayed structure couldn't hold all their combined weight and shimmied and shook as they attempted to ascend the structure. He'd tried to stop them, but they'd ignored his warnings. The beam he was hanging on snapped. He swore he hit every single board holding that tower together on his way down. How he'd been the one to hit the ground first was beyond him, but somehow those dumb motherfuckers had even found a way to use his body to break their falls.

Idiots. And he was supposed to trust his life to those men? Only a few days had passed since the accident. Irritation with the whole incident still burrowed deep under his skin. Now, instead of him walking away with a reprimand, he was stuck in the hospital, feeling helpless, hurting like a motherfucker, and to add insult to injury, they were all going to be disciplined anyway.

He wasn't sure what bothered him the most, the multiple injuries that were going to require extensive physical therapy to get him back on his feet or the fact he literally couldn't wipe his own ass without help. He guessed neither of those superseded his bruised ego. These things didn't happen to Landon Russo. He always found a way to land on his feet, but not this time.

He clenched his jaw in frustration and tightened his hold on the paperback weighing on his chest—the same book he couldn't quite manage to turn the pages of in order to read. This was seriously some fucked-up shit. What he wouldn't give for a distraction.

"Hello, I'm Dr. Adams."

From the first syllable uttered, Landon knew exactly who the voice belonged to, which was damn odd because he'd never expected to hear it again, especially not in a German military hospital thousands of miles away from the United States. That deep rich timbre had been imprinted on his heart almost a year ago while performing an honor that would remain in the forefront of his memories for the rest of his life.

When Landon glanced toward the door, his gaze locked on Dr. Robert Adams, world renowned heart surgeon and son of a

United States vice president.

The doctor stood about six foot two, thick blond hair, and just as handsome as Landon remembered. He scanned the man's face and his heart began to race as his stomach filled with uncertainty. As much as Landon admired Vice President Adams, he could find no good reason for Dr. Robert Adams to be standing in front of him right now. The smile that had automatically lifted the corners of his mouth, fell as he wondered if the heart surgeon's presence indicated something far worse about his condition. How much damage had the fall caused?

He quickly ticked off his known injuries, trying to remember a mention of anything remotely close to a heart complication. They said surgery had gone well. His arm would require healing time and some intensive physical therapy, but he'd been told he was lucky he hadn't been hurt worse. He could expect a full recovery. What hadn't they told him?

The blood pumping through his veins was the only sound he could hear as he watched Dr. Adams's mouth move. His fist tightened around the paperback still on his chest as he interrupted whatever the doctor was saying, "Just give it to me straight."

Wait. If he did have some untold heart problem, he certainly didn't rank high enough on the food chain for someone of Dr. Adams's caliber to fly here and look after him. He wasn't even a military doctor.

It still took a second to rein in his runaway imagination. Judging from the look on Dr. Adams's face, he was still processing Landon's sudden outburst.

"Give you what straight?" Dr. Adams asked, crossing his arms over his chest, a small spark of amusement lighting his eyes.

Well hell, now Landon didn't want to answer that question. He'd jumped to conclusions, a stupid side effect of being confined to a hospital bed for so many days, but he was still completely confused. He figured it was best to just keep quiet. He didn't want to embarrass himself any more than he already had. Silence filled the next few seconds. Neither man looked away from the other.

Landon noticed the fine lines of worry and the deep look of exhaustion etched on Dr. Adams's face. The lines deepened when the doctor furrowed his brow. Landon knew that look—he himself had worn it many times throughout the years.

Landon's heart did a twist for an altogether different reason.

Dr. Adams glanced over at the monitor next to the bed when the steady beep suddenly grew faster. "What just happened?"

This time the doctor gave him a practiced smile, cocking his head to the side as he studied Landon. The scrutiny had Landon instantly wanting to pass whatever inspection he was under and earn a real grin. This smile was only meant to encourage Landon to explain himself.

The strange tension running through his body intensified as the weight of Dr. Adams's gaze moved down his body, then quickly back up before stopping at the paperback on his chest. Dr. Adams lowered his hand, using a single finger to edge the book over to get a better look. The doctor eased the book from Landon's fingers and lifted it to scan the cover. This time when their eyes met there was genuine curiosity staring back at him. "*A Game of Thrones*. You're doing some light reading, are you?"

That comment weirdly lifted Landon's mood. It was his first time to tackle a George R. R. Martin novel. Yes, he got the books were all engrossing, but that was kind of the point. He needed something to fully occupy his overactive mind—absurdly over-imaginative based on all the scenarios he'd conjured in the last few minutes. It still took him a second to say, "I have an uncle who works in a library. He sends me books he thinks I'll like."

"It's a good choice." Dr. Adams crossed his arms over his chest as he stared down at Landon.

"You've read it?"

"No, not yet. It's long and the author's known to be very descriptive. My dad had a small library and encouraged me to read *A Game of Thrones* several times over the last few years. He met Martin once—" Dr. Adams's tone changed before he abruptly stopped speaking midsentence. For the briefest of moments, the doctor seemed lighter, the lines around his eyes easing before he reached down again and ran a finger across the cover. "Martin left an impression on my father. He felt like once this series was complete, it would be a great tale for the ages." Silence sat between them again as Dr. Adams seemed lost in thought until he lifted a hand and rubbed his eyes. "So you haven't gotten very far?"

"No, I'm having trouble. It's a struggle turning the pages." Landon confessed with a sudden deep need to offer comfort and he wasn't certain why.

Dr. Adams looked down at the immobilizer holding Landon's bandaged arm and hand in place before nodding. "I'm sure it's difficult. We have volunteers who can read to you. I can request one for you."

"Yeah, they offered that to me today, but I was being my normal stubborn ass self and turned it down because I thought I could fucking manage." He immediately stopped the train of thought and said, "Sorry about the language."

"No problem. So, you don't like to accept help. You'd rather figure it out on your own. I get it." Dr. Adams nodded in perhaps unspoken agreement. "How're your pain levels?"

"Hey, Landon." Holly, a med tech he knew stepped inside the room. "Hey, Dr. Adams."

Landon watched the good doctor slip back into professional mode. His face became blank and guarded again.

He didn't acknowledge Holly's greeting, but said to Landon, "I'm here because I've heard you're rejecting your pain medication. There's no sense in suffering, not right now."

Landon wanted to make the doctor happy, so he gave a nod and Dr. Adams did too. A smile broke the stern look on the doctor's face. The man seemed relieved, like he'd been expecting Landon to put up a fight.

"As long as we've got that straight. I'll leave you to it. Goodnight."

Landon kept his gaze glued on the doctor until he left the

room and disappeared from his view. He couldn't have been more than a few feet down the hall when Holly sighed loudly. "He's so dreamy."

"Dreamy?" Landon teased, giving a genuine chuckle and an eye roll that turned to a wince. The ache in his ribs reminded him of the bruising there and the laugh became a non-committal grunt as he swallowed the pain.

"Yeah, that's what we decided was the best way to describe him. He looks like Paul Walker. So 'dreamy' absolutely fits him. Now do what the doctor said and open up," she ordered, advancing on him with two small paper cups.

"What is it?" Landon moved his head as far away from the offering as he could, which turned out to be nothing more than a few inches. He strained to see what she was trying to get him to take.

"Does it matter? The doctor prescribed it. Now stop being difficult. Open up." She tipped the paper cup to his lips. Clearly, she was made of tough stuff with the way she rolled her eyes at his most fierce look. She stared him down. He finally gave, swallowing the two pills dry. She wasn't having any of that either, she tipped the second cup with water to his lips. "There's no reason to choke to death trying to prove your alpha status."

"Why's he here?" he asked when Holly wiped his chin.

"Don't know, but that's what everyone's asking. I heard he got special permission and he's been here a few weeks, maybe a month. Totally keeps to himself much to the entire nursing staff's regret," she said. The puzzle of Robert Adams grew more complex. "We've become a fashion show in fatigues around here."

He'd sure bet Dr. Adams got that reaction everywhere he went. All those blond, sunny good looks. The first time Landon had ever seen him, he'd sucked in his already tight belly and puffed out his chest even as he'd done something as somber as stand guard over Vice President Avery Adams's state funeral.

The doctor definitely fit in the "dreamy" category. For

Landon, there was something more appealing about Dr. Adams than just looks, but there was no denying the doctor had hit the motherlode in the gene pool. "What's the rumor... why's he here?"

"The speculation is that he's planning to run for office and getting military time under his belt, but I don't think so. Usually people like that don't come to places like this. He could volunteer at any VA hospital in the states." She gave a noncommittal shrug. "He jogs around the hospital in the middle of the night. Usually about three in the morning we can see him out there, then he spends twelve to fourteen hours working. I don't know when he sleeps, but we all love to watch him when he runs. He's seriously sexy."

Landon nodded. The mental image playing in his head of the doctor jogging in those little running shorts and a tight-fitting T-shirt stole his breath. He'd be all hot and sweaty... Damn.

"You should sleep good with what I just gave you." She gave him a wink. He sure as hell hoped it was good enough to keep him from tenting the sheets while dreaming of the gorgeous doc. "I'll be back later. I need to get Dr. Dreamy's signature before shift change."

Landon watched her leave as a very weird feeling washed over him. Why did he feel so territorial all of a sudden? He tried to shrug it off. What the hell did he care if Holly had the hots for Dr. Adams? He had zero claim on anyone in the Adams family. It didn't matter how Avery Adams had inspired Landon on his life's journey—that had been done from afar and was completely one-sided, personal only to him.

As his eyelids grew heavy, Landon remembered those fine lines of worry he'd seen on Dr. Adams's face. He'd also noticed the hollowness lurking in the depths of those baby blues. The smile he'd offered hadn't reached his eyes. Sadness floated around the man. If he could help Dr. Adams, he needed to try. Landon's brain wasn't quite fuzzy enough to agree with his heart, and it mocked him immediately. What in the world did his redneck ass have to offer such an accomplished man?

Chapter 2

With each pounding strike against the pavement, Robert's anxiety slipped away. Who knew jogging in the middle of the night could be so freeing? He stared into the distance, listening to the rhythm of his steps as the lights of the hospital grew brighter with every stride. At this point in his run, his body flew on autopilot, permitting his mind to wander.

He'd always been too serious—reserved and analytical. At least, that was what he'd been accused of while growing up. He supposed he got those traits from his daddy—Kane—which, oddly enough, was the reason he'd allowed himself to delve into the spiritual side of life.

To be so much like his daddy, yet share none of his DNA, made him curious. But accepting something he couldn't see, touch, or study, went against all his training and had proved a hard pill to swallow. He'd held a beating heart in his hand, and in that moment, he'd been the only thing that stood between his patient's life and their death.

Yet, there had to be more to life than just the exactness of science. A metaphysical something that required him to suspend his incessant need for facts. That wasn't an easy concept for him, but the thought of something more helped him process all this heavy weight holding him down, suffocating the very life from him.

Surely there had to be more to life. More for his fathers. Something bigger than all of this. He had to cling to the hope, or he would most certainly drown in all his confusion. Therein lay his quandary. He didn't know what to believe or where to find the truth. His whole heart wanted him to believe in something his intellect told him couldn't exist.

Life moved so fast, so aggressively and harshly that he had become lost somewhere in the turbulence, searching for a life preserver. At least he was practicing medicine again. Robert's mind drifted to the feathers. Who would have ever thought his path back to medicine would come by way of a hospital in Germany? Robert slowed his steps, thinking about his dad—Avery—and his last words to him. They weren't anything close to the last words he'd shared with his sister, Autumn, who was a carbon copy of their father. His dad had used the tone that always made Robert listen, a voice that echoed through his head even now.

"I'm proud of you, Robert, and I couldn't have asked for a better son. You're so much like your daddy, so serious all the time. Relax, be open for what life has to offer. Don't lose yourself in the science of things. It's okay to chase feathers in the wind, son. But remember... It's not enough to have the feathers. You must dare to fly."

Feathers… It was silly how he clung to such a simple notion. Robert slowed to a walk and wiped his brow with his shirt sleeve. Hope, self-preservation, and one of his father's favorite quotes by Cass Van Krah were the reason he was here in Germany in the first place.

A little over a month ago, he had met Autumn at their childhood home in Stillwater, Minnesota. It had taken him months to even agree to return. There was so much work ahead of them to finalize the estate. Except Robert never really understood why he needed to be present. His sister was an attorney and the executrix. It made sense to him that she'd just handle it all. She was efficient and fair. Besides, Robert didn't care about the inheritance. Autumn could have it all. He was lost in this deep sense of betrayal and he carried so much guilt for going against Autumn at the end of their daddy's life. He should have listened. Instead, he'd let his sick father dictate his own care, allowing him to stay in his home even when he was so clearly declining a little more every single day.

Shit, he'd blown it when it mattered the most. He'd all but killed his father by not insisting on professional medical care sooner. He was a surgeon. Medicine was his life. How had he let this happen?

Stop. Nothing good would come from rehashing all of this again. *Believe in the possibility, it's your only hope. Believe in destiny and fate and a connection so deep one couldn't live without the other. Believe that the two people who showed you what extraordinary love truly meant were now together in the heavens.*

Believe your fathers were truly each one's other halves and were only complete when together. Accept the end was predetermined.

But he wasn't certain he believed it—any of it. His innate logic wanted to ruin the only thing that offered him comfort and hope.

"It could be true," he whispered against the sadness building in his heart, assuring himself the blurry vision was more from perspiration and humidity than tears forming in his eyes. He used the bottom of his T-shirt to wipe away the sweat on his brow as he looked around to see how far he'd run. It was hard to tell from the layout of the building.

Robert let out a deep sigh. Man, he missed his dad's middle of the night conversations. He could use one right now. Just him and his dad and the quiet of the early morning hour. Avery had a way of explaining and engaging Robert, pulling him from his tunnel vision. Would his dad be proud of him for being in Germany? Avery always believed in humanity and giving back to the world that had given him so much.

"God, this sucks so bad," he hissed, staring up at the twinkling stars. A soft breeze blew across the open greenspace area, rustling the leaves on the trees and cooling his heated skin. He had to trust there was a reason for everything that happened. There was some sort of master plan in all of this.

It just seemed like he was grasping for excuses to help justify his actions.

Frustrated with himself, Robert looked around the building and headed for the closest unlocked set of doors to enter the hospital.

Landon listened to the almost deafening silence surrounding him. The utter quiet seemed out of place especially since he was in a hospital. There was no staff talking, no sign of human existence beyond his own. He'd heard rumors that the hospital was going to be rebuilt—they were too busy and the facility too small—so where were all the hurt soldiers he'd been hearing about?

Maybe the zombie apocalypse had happened. Kind of reminded him of the scene where Rick Grimes woke in the hospital and all hell began. Maybe he was the lone survivor of the massacre of Landstuhl Regional Medical Center.

Nah, that didn't make sense for many reasons, but the primary one was his door was wide open. He'd have been massacred too, no doubt about it. If he just had his cell phone, he could prank call the guys in his squadron and wake their asses up, make them keep him company.

"You okay?"

Landon jerked his head toward the doorway. The voice startled him from his thoughts. *Holy hell.* And now he knew what Dr. Adams looked like in a tight-fitting T-shirt and running shorts. Yeah, he understood why the nursing staff spent so much time watching this man run. The visual treat likely explained the floor going silent a few minutes ago. The noises of hustle and bustle were filling the halls again as he took in the other distraction that had commandeered his thoughts this evening. The man was absolutely and most certainly *dreamy*. Sweat ringed the thin light blue T-shirt and highlighted the lean, muscular body just beneath.

The doctor lifted his arm, doing a small stretch as he stepped inside the room. The action caused the shirt to ride high across his waist and expose his firm abdominals. Landon lowered his eyes and swallowed hard when his gaze landed on the low-slung navy running shorts hugging Dr. Adams's slim hips. The silky material clung to his body like a glove, and he could almost make out the lines of a really nice cock underneath the fabric. He shouldn't gawk, but fuck, Dr. Adams was mouthwateringly hot.

Shit, now he'd have to bribe Holly to help him get near the window on the other side of the room just to watch Dr. Adams run past in the middle of the night. All those firm muscles in full stride would be breathtaking.

"Yeah, fine," he croaked, finally getting his words out as he dropped his head back on the pillow. Landon slid his free hand under the thin blanket to cover his dick just in case it managed to plump even with all the medication they insisted he needed for pain. He stared at the ceiling and cleared his throat before trying again. "Never been much of a sleeper."

"Me either. Bored?" He heard more than saw Dr. Adams move farther inside the room.

"Yeah." What a serious understatement.

"I know it's torture to keep you guys confined like this." The doctor stopped beside his bed. Landon gathered the courage to steal another glance. Dr. Adams's casually muttered words didn't fit the conflicted look on his face as he lifted an arm and used his sleeve to wipe at his forehead. "I've got some time. Want some company?"

Oh hell, now Landon was as conflicted as Dr. Adams looked. Landon had to admit, he was intimidated as hell and that sure didn't happen to him very often. "I don't wanna keep you."

"You're not. Want some coffee? I smell a fresh pot

somewhere."

"Coffee'd be great." Just the mention of a hot cup had him perking up. God, he hoped it was better than the lukewarm stuff that came on his breakfast tray.

"Hang tight."

Landon had to halt the urge to check his breath. If it was bad, there was nothing he could do about it anyway. Instead, he ran a hand through his close cropped, dirty dark hair, feeling it standing every which way. Why did he have to look his worst?

"I brought it black. You look like a no-frills coffee drinker."

"What's that mean?" he asked and immediately started searching for the bed controls to lift his head. He couldn't do anything about his appearance but he sure as hell didn't have to look helpless in front of the doctor.

Dr. Adams caught him off guard again when he smiled a small smile and placed both cups on the rolling tray positioned by his bed. "I didn't mean anything. You look like a guy that drinks his coffee black. Do you?"

"I do," he admitted grudgingly as if that were a bad thing and he couldn't quite figure out why.

"Then I was right. And besides, not one person in this hospital seems to use creamer. I'm a creamer kind of guy. I like my soy lattes. I miss my lattes," he explained, walking around the bed to Landon's other side.

Yep, that was exactly how Landon saw the man—a fancy latte coffee drinker. "It's a ways for a Starbucks. I never thought anyone would be willing to pay five bucks for a cup of coffee."

"You sound like my dad, but I'm pretty sure Starbucks is the investment I'll be most proud of in twenty years." Dr. Adams found the control that had somehow slipped underneath the torture device keeping his arm locked in place. "Let me lift you."

With a strength that surprised Landon, the doctor lifted him from the back while working the bed's remote buttons. He felt little to no pain as he rose to an almost sitting position. Dr.

Adams expertly stuffed pillows under Landon's arm, keeping it comfortably at the desired range he'd been instructed to stay within.

"You know what you're doing," Landon said, watching the doctor work.

"I've spent most of my adult life in medicine. I've learned a thing or two." Dr. Adams gave a soft chuckle at what he must have considered a tease as he went for a chair in the corner and scraped it across the tiled floor, bringing it closer to Landon's bed. "Last night, I got the impression you knew who I was."

"I do. I recognized you." Landon nodded his confirmation as Dr. Adams came back to his side, lifting Landon's coffee cup to his lips. Landon sipped at the piping hot brew, loving everything about the scalding coffee. His sudden nervousness eased at the kind gesture of helping him drink. It was as thoughtful as he'd expected the man to be and a much-needed break in the monotony of his boredom.

"I think I can manage with this hand," Landon said, wiggling the fingers of his good hand.

Dr. Adams looked at his uninjured hand and seemed surprised it was even there then chuckled again before handing him the Styrofoam cup. "I suspect you can."

Landon had needed this whole exchange. He felt human again as an odd normalcy settled between them. Since Landon had read all three of Avery Adams's autobiographies, he knew Robert Adams was a world-renowned heart surgeon, but in the brief few interactions they'd shared, Landon could attest to his genuinely kind manner. There was something very appealing and inspiring with the way Dr. Adams considered others, putting them first before himself.

Dr. Adams took his cup and settled in his seat, blowing to cool the hot coffee. "How did you end up here?" he asked, before taking a drink and screwing his face up in revulsion at the harsh bitter taste.

Landon smiled his first genuine grin since he had arrived.

"This is why I have to have creamer and lots of sweetener."

"At least it's hot," Landon said, taking another drink.

"Completely agree. So, how'd you end up here?" Dr. Adams asked again, putting his cup on the tray as he sat back, crossing his arms over his chest. The move drew Landon's attention to the nice sized bicep flexing with the doctor's change of position.

"Me being an idiot," Landon answered honestly and took another drink before returning the question, "What brings you to Germany?"

The casualness and ease that had developed between them surprisingly held against such an invasive inquiry. Dr. Adams gave a smile of his own, something that took his handsomeness to the next level. Landon grinned bolder as if he were commiserating over something he had no clue about. "I could say the same—me being an idiot."

"Why's that?" Landon asked instead of saying his first thought, which was how much he doubted the doctor could ever qualify as anything other than spectacular.

"I left everything I know to come halfway around the world based on a sign." A full-on grin broke across Dr. Adams's face, making Landon amend his original thought. This smile made the man gorgeous, and something about the response paired with all those handsome features kept Landon's suddenly good mood intact. "Bet it makes you doubt my medical ability. I don't blame you."

Since that was literally the exact opposite of what Landon thought, he left that right there. He'd come back there in a minute. "What kind of sign are you following?"

Maybe the doctor hadn't expected that kind of a question because the man's grin faltered and his brow furrowed. Dr. Adams continued to hold Landon's direct stare, looking speculatively as he reached for the Styrofoam cup again. Since the coffee was awful, Landon decided the move was for liquid courage. Dr. Adams's took a longer drink this time, holding the cup in his hand as he again crossed his arm over his chest. He didn't answer

Landon's question. Instead, he gave a total non-answer.

"That was a different response than I expected."

"Why's that?" Landon tried for casual as he took his own sip of the strong brew.

"I'm not sure why except I'm new to the idea of believing in signs. It's been hard because my personality needs to see the proof of things. Were you able to read anymore?" he asked, nodding to the book on the tray, changing the subject—a subject he clearly was uncomfortable with.

Movement at his door caught Landon's attention as Dr. Adams pushed away from the chair to reach for the paperback on the tray. There were two female med techs—one being Holly— hovering in the hall, peering through the doorway. They were in stealth mode, peeking around the edge of the doorframe. They pointed at Dr. Adams as smiles broke out on their faces right before giving him an encouraging thumbs up.

Thank goodness for his olive complexion. Landon would have turned ten shades of red for how dumb they were being.

"I could read to you. I've wanted to read this." Dr. Adams's offer caught him off guard, making him forget all about Holly and her friend.

"I don't wanna put you out," Landon replied immediately only because his southern manners kicked in, but he instantly liked the idea.

The doctor looked over the book, both front and back, before he flipped through the pages. "You aren't. Most of the time I don't really feel needed around here. I just come in early because I've got nothing else to do."

"I feel like I'm the only patient on this ward. It's so quiet," he said, watching as Dr. Adams ran a hand down the seam of the paperback on the first page of the prologue.

"Not the only one, but close." Dr. Adams looked up at him with his gentle smile back in place. "Can I start from the beginning?"

"Yeah, I struggled with the pages so bad I got pissed off. Who knows what I read?"

The doctor nodded before looking down again. He cleared his voice and began to read. "Prologue, *'We should start back,' Gared urged…*"

Oh yeah, the doc's reading voice was the shit. Landon placed his half empty cup on the tray and settled back on the bed. For the next two hours, his room was filled with the deep cultured sound of Dr. Adams's sexy voice enticing him with the intricately woven story. Landon couldn't even be bothered by the fact Holly and her friend found a reason to walk past his room about every ten minutes, peering inside to watch what they were doing. By the end of chapter four Landon was completely relaxed. The usual chaos running through his head was gone. He lay there staring at Dr. Adams as the hypnotic cadence of his voice came to an end and didn't continue.

"It's excellent. Just like my dad said."

"Yeah. So much better without the frustration on trying to turn the pages. Thank you," Landon offered, truly grateful for the help and companionship.

"I bet. Do you have a bookmark or do you want me to dog-ear the page?" For the first time since Dr. Adams had looked down at the book, his bright blue eyes lifted to Landon. The sweaty guy who had entered the room was now dry and looked appealingly rumpled. His blond hair had a natural wave, and Landon's fingers itched to run through the silky strands. Dr. Adams was handsome…and kind, and Landon couldn't help his gentle smile of appreciation.

"It's in the back of the book. My uncle sent it to me. Said he saw it sitting on the book and it caught his attention."

Dr. Adams thumbed through the pages until he found the thin metal bookmark.

"He believes in signs and that's why he sent me this particular book. The whole reacting to signs thing from earlier… I've watched my uncle do it for years. People think it's weird, but he's right more often than not."

Dr. Adams lifted the bookmark from the book. Light reflected off the thin metal feather. The doctor's eyes brightened as he studied the intricate design. "A feather, huh? I don't think it's weird at all. I'm trying hard to readjust my thought processes. I'm trying to go with it."

Landon gave a humorless laugh at the silliness, not believing for a second there was truth in Dr. Adams's words. The way he studied the feather, the look of doubt creasing his brow, the purse of his lips all stated the true direction of the doctor's thoughts. One thing Landon knew for sure: Robert Adams was a gentleman, nice enough to sit with Landon for hours reading. Of course, he wouldn't verbally disagree, but Landon didn't have those same innate manners.

"My uncle believes they're a spiritual guide. He's a librarian in the town we live in. He lived with my parents when I was a child, so I grew up listening to him talk about all the mystical and spiritual signs we dismiss every day. When I was younger, I thought everybody believed the things he said. It wasn't until I was in high school that I found out people thought he belonged in the looney bin. Got in plenty of fistfights over that one." Landon remembered more than one fight he'd had defending his uncle's honor. It wasn't as gallant as it sounded. Back then, he'd have gone to blows with the devil himself for just giving him the side-eye, all in an effort to prove his manhood.

"You ready for your medication?" Holly's voice interrupted the moment as she stood in the doorway. Landon narrowed his eyes at her full makeup and expertly fixed hair. When she finally came strolling farther inside the room, you'd have thought she belonged on an armed-forces fashion runway.

"I'll leave you to it," Dr. Adams said, getting to his feet, seemingly ignoring Holly completely. "If you're up for more bad reading, I can swing by this evening."

"That'd be great, but I don't want you to feel obligated." Maybe his manners were a little more intact than he thought. Landon absolutely wanted to hear more, and he definitely wanted the doctor's company. This had been the best few hours he'd spent in a very long time.

"I don't feel obligated. I'll see you later."

Landon got an absently given over the shoulder nod and Dr. Adams was gone from his room.

"He's been in here for almost three hours. His voice is amazing." Holly gushed. What made no sense was the calming of the commotion always beating against his brain. His inner badass, the part about him that continually churned with chaos and needed an outlet, the same part that had been responsible for this hospital stay, had settled down around Dr. Adams.

"You're difficult. Open up." The small pill cup rattled in front of his face, drawing his attention back to the here and now. Landon opened his mouth without questioning every medication she held out for him. Maybe whatever he was taking would knock him out so he could stop the flow of questions starting to race through his head.

Chapter 3

"Two questions. Are you interested in some company and have you had dinner?" Dr. Adams asked, coming through the door of Landon's room carrying a tray of covered dishes.

The man was a welcome sight. The sour mood plaguing Landon immediately dissolved. His bad attitude had developed from being forced to sit in this damn bed, feeling very much out of place, trapped with nothing to do. Landon was bored off his ass. Shockingly, his already terrible day had been made worse by the horrible tasteless meal they'd tried to serve him for dinner.

Whatever look he had on his face caused Dr. Adams to lift his brows and flash that sexy motherfucking grin, instantly having a sedative effect on Landon which made him lower his brow and consider such a visceral reaction.

"What's bothering you more? The food or the being tied to the bed?"

Landon used his good hand to shift his current dinner tray to the side, wanting more than anything to dramatically send it flying across the room in a show of his disgust and frustration. Good thing he'd matured over the last few years because there was damn sure a time in his life he would have done that very thing.

"Equal irritants."

"I figured as much." Dr. Adams pushed the tray he'd brought in front of Landon while, at the same time, efficiently removing the one the hospital had given him. "There's reasons why they're giving you certain foods, but I think we can do better. Here, how's this?" The doctor lifted the lid on the two plates he'd brought. One looked delicious. The other looked okay for healthy food—a large salad and a big serving of sliced fruit. In his heart, he knew that one was his. "I also read through your file. You're stuck in a room by yourself because you've been a bit of a rabble-rouser while here. Know anything about that?"

There couldn't have been a more perfect diversion for his thoughts. "You offering me food to get the inside track?" His grin broadened when Dr. Adams lifted his brows at such a cocky answer and reached for the salad and fruit plate. His heart soared that the Salisbury steak plate had been left for him. "Hey, thanks for this. I really am going stir crazy."

"You're welcome. I cut the meat into bite size pieces before I came in. You're going to have to drink the juice so I don't get into too much trouble." He saw the small container of dark brown liquid and didn't need to read the packaging to know for sure it was prune juice, understanding better what it was for.

He crinkled his nose and reached for the silverware, pushing the cup to the edge of the tray. "I took care of that today, Doc."

"I didn't see it in your chart," Dr. Adams said, taking a big bite of the almost dry salad. In no world could Landon see that tasting good. He picked up his fork, scooping up a bite of the steak and mashed potatoes before the doctor changed his mind and tried to share his food.

"Doesn't mean it didn't happen," he replied, taking his first bite. Salt had to be the most underrated seasoning on the planet. Man, it tasted good. After swallowing, he reached for his glass of water, giving a nod toward the food. "Thanks for this."

"You've already thanked me," Dr. Adams said, crossing one

leg over the other as he concentrated on his bowl, moving the vegetables around to create the perfect bite.

"You eat any meat?" Landon asked. When Dr. Adams looked up, he pointed to the meatless salad before taking another hearty bite of his own food.

"Not usually. I'm not a hundred percent plant-based but close. Heart disease runs in my family."

Landon gave the doctor a small nod before he took another bite, chewing it as the remnants of his bad mood dissipated.

"I thought I was flying under the radar here. You burst my bubble when you knew who I was."

Yeah, right. The idea of Robert Adams not being recognized tickled Landon, and he rolled his eyes for good measure, again reaching for his glass of water. "I hate to be the one to break it to you, but I suspect every person in this hospital knows who you are."

Dr. Adams looked up from the salad, confused, stopping with a bite midway to his mouth and shook his head. "No, I don't think so."

"They absolutely know who you are." Landon left no room for argument, stopping just short of telling the sexy doctor how all the single women and even a few of the men had tried to catch the guy's attention. The doctor seemed truly unaware of all the subtle flirting going on around him. In fact, he acted somewhat dejected as he continued eating. "Why's it a bad thing they know you?"

"It's not," Dr. Adams answered, running a paper napkin over his mouth.

"Not convincing. Everybody's trying to figure out why you're here. Rumor has it you're running for office and want military credentials under your belt," Landon explained before again filling his mouth just about as full as he could. He couldn't seem to get enough of the food or the conversation. It was hard to balance the two without talking with a mouth full of food.

"What? I'm not running for public office. That's my sister's deal, not mine at all," Dr. Adams stated, seeming somewhat annoyed when he stabbed a small tomato with his fork and brought it to his mouth.

"Why's it not yours?"

"I'm too single-minded. Things have always been cut and dry with me," Dr. Adams replied, taking another bite.

"Then if what you say is true—being here based on a sign—it must be really treading on some seriously new ground for you."

Dr. Adams stopped chewing and lifted a single brow at him. In some circles, the pointed stare might be considered intimidating, but not for Landon. His Italian father was a red hot, fire-breathing dragon about eighty-five percent of the time. Dr. Adams's look only made Landon chuckle while reaching for his napkin.

"Didn't mean to tread into territory you didn't want to discuss. Sorry if I stepped over whatever line you have, but you have to admit, leaving everything behind to come here is kind of drastic."

"What's your story then?" Dr. Adams asked, maybe a little defensive if Landon read his tone correctly. He couldn't help the laugh that innocently bubbled up from his chest again. Like Landon had any of those funky lines that shouldn't be crossed or secrets that wouldn't be told. His whole life was an open book—literally in the public record.

"I grew up on the south side of Houston, Texas. My dad's full-blooded Italian, born in Italy. My mom's from Texas. We were raised middle class. I have an older sister who's a badass with two badass kids. I was a badass; it's why I joined the military. And before you say anything, I was in the wrong place at the wrong time which is kind of the story of my whole life." He pointed to his bandaged arm as if to prove his theory before he continued, "But I didn't have anything to do with what went down." Landon tossed out his own indignant attitude over his troubled teen years. He'd been leaving Kelly's, a local restaurant, walking out to his car when he spotted a couple of buddies. The police blazed into the parking lot, lights flashing, sirens blaring. Landon had gotten himself in just enough trouble in the past that no one really believed the truth of his lack of involvement in the drug deal going down. "I've been enlisted since I graduated high school."

"Hmm. So a career man." Dr. Adams nodded, not saying one word about Landon's admission. He dug back into his salad again, eating with gusto, taking several bites. Landon couldn't detect any judgment or condemnation about what he'd confessed, which was weird. Most people thought it was their responsibility to police others. The holier than thou do-gooders always looked down on men like Landon. "Why did you choose the Air Force?"

Landon had respected Dr. Adams, but now he was beginning to really like who he was as a man.

"My uncle told me they get the steak where the rest of the branches get the hamburger. Few things beat a nice thick juicy steak in my book," he answered honestly before putting another bite in his mouth. It had truly been that simple of a decision.

"Okay, that's funny even if I felt my arteries clog from just the mention of red meat. I understand the Air Force isn't easy to get into."

"That's what they kept telling me. They kept pushing me away until I scored in the ninetieth percentile on the ASVAB." His chest swelled with the accomplishment, still proud to this day of his test score on the Armed Services Vocational Aptitude Battery. He'd gotten major bragging rights that he used when needed.

"So, what do you do?" Dr. Adams asked, lifting his fork in the air, prompting Landon to say more while he ate.

"I work intel." What a simple word for something so complex. Dr. Adams furrowed his brow again. This time, Landon could see the unasked questions forming.

In the end, he didn't ask any of them and just said, "I have a feeling you're more complicated than you let on."

"If that's a nice way to say you don't see me as a fit in the Air Force, I'll admit, it's been a struggle." Landon couldn't help the genuine laugh that rumbled in his chest. He'd done well, but he had left a trail of frustrated superiors beating their heads against walls. "It's my nature to go against authority, but I sure don't like to be looked down on. I got my bachelor's degree last fall. I made Tech Sergeant. That's how all of this happened with my arm. I was celebrating to the extreme."

"Hmm." There was silence between them as they regarded one another, and from the look, Dr. Adams was still trying to figure him out. Landon took another bite, bigger than he probably should have, just to give himself a little longer to gather his thoughts.

"Since I'm putting it all out there, I should probably say, I've read all your father's books. I have a signed copy of *The Man I Am*. I waited in line for seven hours for that signature." Landon picked up his glass of water, stopping short of taking a drink. "My fucking phone lost battery and I didn't get a picture." He confessed that with all the irritation of the moment coming back in a whoosh of frustration. The drink of water didn't help wash away the bad taste that memory caused.

"Really?" Dr. Adams seemed oblivious to Landon's agitation and stopped eating, the fork dropping into the almost finished bowl of salad. He looked and sounded totally shocked.

"I did. I give your father credit for making me pull my shit together," he stated with all sincerity. He used his fork to push the meat around his plate as memory after memory of his struggles as a youth played out in his head. After a moment's pause, he took the last bite, wishing like crazy there was more left of the meal.

"You're blowing smoke up my ass," Dr. Adams finally said, reaching for his fork, clearly dismissing the comment as he dug back into his salad.

"No, I'm seriously not. I was acting out, bad. I should be in prison right now—I was headed there. I didn't understand what was going on with me. I was confused and felt so alone. I couldn't accept myself. I was angry and scared as shit. My uncle gave me your dad's first book. It changed my life. I'm gay and your father made me see it was okay. I wasn't alone anymore. I give him all the credit for everything turning out okay with me," he replied honestly, scrubbing the napkin over his whiskered face before tossing it on the empty plate.

This time, Dr. Adams sat back in his seat. Landon felt the intensity in the doctor's stare as he watched him, the salad in his lap seemingly forgotten. "It's not the first time I've heard something along those lines, but I'm surprised to hear it here. So, you know I'm gay?"

"Yeah. I wondered how you felt about him writing about you." For the second time since Dr. Adams had arrived, Landon felt a kinship with the man, if for nothing more than the reverent respect Landon had placed on the entire Adams family. The Adams men were gay, but that didn't define them. It was a side note to their extraordinary lives, a lesson Landon had really needed to learn. "Your childhood was anything but the norm, but from what I read, you seemed really well adjusted and happy."

"As hard as it is to believe, I lived a very normal life. I grew up probably more sheltered than most kids, but that was out of necessity. They kept us—me and my sister—in a little bubble, safe and secure away from the negativity. I grew up in a home filled with love and respect for each other. My daddy, Kane—he was very protective of us. He gave up everything important to him to become a buffer between us and the hatred aimed at my family. Autumn and I knew some people weren't happy with two men raising children, but it never really touched me personally. I just never understood why it mattered. I was maybe twenty-two when my dad's first book was released. Of course, he asked before he wrote about me, and I agreed to him discussing my journey because there was literally no drama to my coming out. When the book released, that's the day I understood how influential my father truly was."

Dr. Adams put the almost empty salad bowl on the tray and picked up his glass of water, taking several long drinks. Landon didn't know what it was, but the mood had shifted in the room. He sensed underlying pain or sadness in the doctor. Something deep and unresolved. It covered him like a weighted blanket.

"I had just started medical school when the book dropped, and reporters tracked me down. I still had secret service on me, and I was so confused. I had always been boring for the agents to guard. No one had ever wanted to talk to me before. Even then, the conversation was more about the in-vitro conception that interested the media the most, not my sexuality or being raised by two fathers. They wanted information on something that meant nothing to me."

"What was it like being raised by two men? I've wondered, if my father had been like your dad, would it have been easier for me? I don't think I would have struggled so hard with getting good with myself if I had someone like your dad around," Landon said humbly, saying anything that might keep Dr. Adams talking.

When Landon admitted he'd read Avery's book, he hadn't been completely honest. He'd read and re-read all three of Avery Adams's books. He had studied those books like textbooks. He could quote lines that had stuck with him through the years. Avery Adams showed him a very different and achievable side of life. A life he dreamed of having for himself someday.

"I was raised with lots of parental guidance and balance. We spent every Sunday in a progressive church environment. It was something my daddy— Does that confuse you? My dad is Avery, my daddy is Kane." When Landon nodded, Dr. Adams continued. "He wanted us to have a spiritual… No, that's not quite right. He wanted us to have a religious understanding of the world. Autumn and I went to an Episcopal school and church. I didn't know until that first book came out how much my daddy struggled with being gay or how hard my dad had to push for their relationship. I'm sorry to say, even then, it didn't hold a lot of interest for me. They were just my parents, nothing really special at all. I was never rebellious with them or anything like that." Dr. Adams grinned, staring past Landon at something unseen. He shook his head at whatever memory came to mind. "I did like to best my sister any chance I got. That caused lots of lectures about the importance of not overpowering people, putting others first before yourself, and the importance of personal growth." Dr. Adams's grin grew as his eyes focused back on Landon. "My parents made it too easy. The four of us were just a unit. Does that make sense?"

"Yeah, I guess." Even though he didn't fully understand. His family was close, but they all could go from zero to ten on the anger scale in seconds flat and did it often. "I did the exact opposite of what my parents wanted me to do. I borrowed their car without telling them for the first time when I was fourteen then fifteen and again at sixteen." He shrugged when he caught the doctor's smile, again surprised at the complete lack of judgment from his confession. "I was a bad kid."

That caused a bit of laughter as they stared at one another, settling into a comfortable silence. Landon watched Dr. Adams as he crossed his arms over his chest, leaning back comfortably in the seat. His leg followed, one crossing over the other. Landon couldn't help it. Dr. Adams oozed a natural, maybe even instinctual, sophistication. He was a classy guy, something Landon had wished for in his life, but had never been able to achieve.

"It seemed to work out for you." Dr. Adams's grin broadened as his eyes slid down the length of Landon's battered body. "All things considered."

"You've got jokes." Landon chuckled, enjoying the easiness between them. "My parents are proud of me now, but I carried guilt for a good long time. My father still struggles with my sexuality. It's hard on him, but he tries. That's all I can ask for."

"Yeah, guilt can rip you to pieces and sometimes those pieces never quite fit back together again, no matter how hard you try to twist and turn them." Dr. Adams gave a resigned sigh as he reached for the paperback on the tray. "So, are you ready for me to read?"

Landon didn't like hearing the rawness in the doctor's tone. The words were packed full of emotion; the earlier smile had vanished as Dr. Adams scrubbed his hand down the length of his face. The friendliness they had shared vanished. Walls seemed to drop between them or maybe the walls were dropping to protect Dr. Adams from the world. Either way, it wasn't good. Landon watched the doctor open the book. He couldn't decide if he should bring up his role as honor guard in Avery Adams's funeral. In the end, he decided against it. Something told him he needed to tread lightly.

The soft, even snores had Robert looking up from the book to find Landon sound asleep. He looked around the room, spotted the clock on the wall, surprised to see it was almost nine at night. He moved the feather bookmark back two pages, not a hundred percent sure when Landon had fallen asleep.

He stared at the thin metal bookmark before sliding his fingers up the feather's shaft. He wasn't sure what happened today to solidify his certainty of signs, but without a doubt, there was meaning to this feather. Not only this one but all the others that kept materializing in the strangest places since he'd found the one floating across the top of a LRMC brochure—the whole reason he was even in this hospital to begin with. Robert pulled the small feather from his pocket that he had found at his feet seconds before he entered Landon's room for the first time last night. When had he gotten to the point of keeping them like some long-lost treasure?

He conceded that there was no question he felt better inside these four walls than he had in a long time. He didn't know Landon any more than anyone else in this hospital—hell, in the whole country for that matter—but Landon had a settling way about him, countering Robert's newfound negativity and giving him a much-needed breather.

"You're being weird," he muttered to himself as his eyes were drawn back to the sleeping man.

Robert closed the book, crossed one leg over the other, and reached for the glass of water he'd been sipping to help keep his voice from growing hoarse. He couldn't force his gaze away from Landon. *Gay*. He didn't know why he was surprised, but he had been. In another place and time, he suspected he'd be all over those dark good looks. Landon looked Mediterranean, dark hair, dark eyes, olive complexion, and built like a brickhouse—all of it just Robert's type.

Who the hell was he kidding? Landon wouldn't be interested in a train wreck like him. Landon had a different meaning to his life, and Robert marveled at Landon's strength of character. It amazed Robert to meet people who came from adversity and changed their course in life. He knew nothing of overcoming the odds to achieve. His life had been handed to him on a silver platter. His dad would have truly liked Landon.

Robert had had a real conversation with Landon tonight, something he rarely ever did, and he was better for it now. He had reminisced over his life, opened up in a way he certainly hadn't done since his fathers' deaths. He took another drink from the almost empty water glass and continued to stare openly at Landon.

Landon had asked him direct questions, but never pressured him to answer. Where Autumn was a natural at evading questions, Robert wasn't. He remembered one summer, sitting on the back porch of his Minnesota childhood home waiting on a reporter from a magazine to arrive to interview the entire family. His dad drilled him and his sister with pre-questions. Every single time Robert answered honestly, much to his father's growing frustration. In the end, his dad encouraged him to just play mute. That had pretty much become his strategy on life since then.

Robert looked down at his lap, a silly smile playing on his lips as he remembered Avery calling to Kane, telling him there was no question Robert was his son. Maybe his dad would have been proud of him tonight for his evasiveness. More than anything, he wished his father was there with him to hear all the glowing praise Landon had given him.

Instead of going down that dark rabbit hole again, Robert stood, moving closer to Landon's bedside. He carefully adjusted the pillows, giving his patient's bandaged arm more support. Landon moved, those long, thick dark eyelashes fluttered open. A crooked grin spread across his full lips as those sleepy eyes focused on him. "I fell asleep."

"It's late. We knocked out five more chapters."

"Your voice is amazing; I could listen to you all night. It's a really good story," Landon mumbled, turning his head away. He fell back asleep in seconds. Robert smiled under Landon's approval as he reached for the overhead light, darkening the room before leaving. He closed the door softly behind him. He was tired too. Maybe he'd finally get a full night's sleep tonight.

Chapter 4

Four days later

Robert walked the long corridor of the hospital, and for the first time in his medical career, he abandoned his single-minded focus and paid attention to the stares burning holes straight through him. Per Landon's refusal to believe anything else, the looks were based on interest. Not just interest, but how had Landon phrased it last night? Robert's cheeks instantly flushed at the audacity of Landon's chosen words: They all wanted a go at him.

How utterly absurd.

Robert had decided those looks were more in line with wondering how in the world he and Landon had built such an unlikely rapport. There was no denying the staff regarded Landon as difficult. Robert saw the patient differently. He saw a smart, clever man who didn't like to work in the confines of status quo—in that, Robert completely agreed. Robert easily recognized the hot-blooded temper. He had grown up with his granddaddy Paulie barking at everyone and everything. The only exceptions to his grandfather's ire were him and Autumn.

Landon's fast-paced intellect challenged Robert to keep up when he discussed…well, everything. Robert respected the challenge, saw himself very much like Landon. He just kept his feelings in his head where Landon's came tumbling out his mouth. Robert would have never achieved what he had if he had just accepted instruction as he'd been taught.

Regardless of how the staff described his and Landon's time together, the sergeant was becoming his friend. More importantly, Landon seemed to be the therapy source he had been searching for. Landon had a way of opening Robert, slowly helping him see something more than the depression and guilt that had taken over his life. Of course, he understood he had a long way to go to get himself back—if that was even achievable. But the start of something significant built inside him and every bit of him clung to the hope of healing his soul. He was sleeping again, smiling more often, and enjoying the hell out of reading *A Game of Thrones*. Such a simple form of entertainment that he looked forward to every single evening.

Robert rounded the corner into Landon's room. He must have been waiting for his arrival, Landon spoke the second he saw Robert. "Look, Doc, I'm not saying you have to bring me dinner every night— Oh hell, yes, I am…" His words trailed off when two physical therapy aides followed right behind Robert inside the room. Skepticism instantly invaded Landon's expression. "I did my therapy today. Why're they back?"

Robert couldn't help his laugh; one he absolutely shouldn't have let slip free. Landon's PT was minimal, but still incredibly difficult for his bruised body and most likely painful with his arm still locked in place with the immobilizer brace. His tough, take charge patient had likened the physical therapy to medieval torture and had been scheduled for another round today.

"Don't worry. It's not what you think. They're not here to torture you. The weather's cooled down. It's beautiful outside. I thought we'd do something different. I got approval to take you out, if you follow all my rules." Robert tossed a smug look Landon's way and cocked his brow in a clear message that he was now the boss. He reached over to pick up the paperback, waving it like a dangling carrot at Landon.

"No way," Landon gasped, disbelieving.

"I did." He nodded. Landon's excitement made him proud of his decision.

"Badass." Landon extended his fist for a fist bump, one Robert happily obliged. It took a few minutes to load Landon in a wheelchair thanks to his battered body, and the aides helped get him outside. Robert grabbed the bag he'd left at the nurses' station that held their dinner. The hospital cafeteria had been a little chaotic for some reason today, and he hadn't wanted to waste one single second of daylight waiting in the long line for the hot entrée. He'd gone with sandwiches, something easy to eat outside.

Robert stepped ahead of Landon, opening the doors wide for the wheelchair to fit through. He watched the smile spread and wonderment fill Landon's eyes as the evening sun bathed his olive skin in rich light. One hundred percent, he'd done the right thing.

"If I had my choice, I'd spend my life outside," Landon said, closing his eyes and lifting his chin toward the sun.

"Yeah?" Robert asked, pointing to the aides, then heading for the table closest to them.

"Oh yeah. Even in the hot, muggy summers of Houston, I spent all my time outside. My dad put a tent in the backyard, and I'd sleep out there on the weekends."

Robert nodded his appreciation to the staff before opening the bag containing his and Landon's dinner.

"We'd have campouts too in our backyard when I was a kid." Robert unwrapped Landon's sandwich, a roast beef hoagie, placing it on his lap for easy reach. "We weren't really a camping family though. My granddaddy Paulie insisted Autumn and I become one with nature. He'd take us out exploring all the time. He had a tool shop in the back of his house. He showed us how to use a buzz saw once; my fathers had a fit over that."

"He owned the pizza place in Alabama, right?"

Robert stopped pulling the rest of the food from the bag and stared at Landon. These bits of knowledge, intimate details of his life were growing in frequency, proving what Landon had confessed several times now—that he'd paid close attention to his father's writings.

"What?" Landon's tone said he didn't give a shit if he had come off as a creeper. His only real interest lay in the sandwich he took a big bite from.

"You really paid attention to what you read."

"I told you I have mad respect for your old man," Landon said, after swallowing the bite and nodding toward one of the ice-cold water bottles, jarring Robert into action again.

"I know. So do I." He opened the bottle, placing it within Landon's reach on the edge of the table then opened a bag of chips, setting them in his lap next to the sandwich.

"I wish he would've run for president. He would've won," Landon stated emphatically.

"Hmm, maybe." His father had given a lot of himself to try and make a difference in the world. Sometimes Robert had sensed his daddy's loneliness when his husband was on the road campaigning all across the country. Even then, Robert hadn't paid much attention to everything both his fathers gave for Avery to fulfill his mission of giving back to a country he saw as the greatest in the world.

"What?" Landon asked, making a show of swallowing a big bite down while reaching for the water bottle. Robert made sure he could reach it before opening his vegetable sandwich.

"You're the first person to make me see my family differently. I'm not sure why," he explained.

"I told you, because I'm a stalker." Landon chuckled at the term he'd given himself last night then nodded to the sandwich in Robert's hand. "If you aren't gonna eat that…"

"Get your eyes off my food. You still have half of yours left, and besides, it's all vegetables. Your body wouldn't understand how to react to such a healthy alternative," he said playfully, knowing Landon was pushing him to eat, certainly not wanting his food.

"You're wasting daylight and I got a bad feeling about that House Targaryen prince. That was a shitty place to stop last night."

"I'm pretty sure that's your fault. You keep falling asleep on me," Robert shot back. He took a bite of his sandwich, reaching for the book, loving the freeness of the unguarded conversation. Outside of Autumn, he wasn't sure he'd ever had this kind of banter with anyone.

"Quit placin' blame and start reading," Landon said gruffly. Robert nodded his understanding while taking another bite of his sandwich and opening the book. He was all too happy to oblige.

Out of the corner of his eye, Robert caught Landon's side grin. He'd already long established the sergeant was a handsome guy. As much as they shared personal information, he'd never heard Landon mention if he had a special someone. Robert took a bite and reached for his water bottle, unscrewing the cap. Of course, Landon would be taken. He was smart, fun to be around, good looking, and in the military. Someone would have reeled him in a long time ago. Maybe he'd found the kind of love like his fathers had. Maybe it was even the reason Landon spoke with such certainty over that kind of a connection. If so, he was happy for him.

Clearing his throat, Robert began to read.

"Your voice is getting raspy," Landon said, feeling some guilt for keeping the doc outside reading for so long. Dr. Adams lifted his head, closed his eyes, and rolled his shoulders.

"It's a good book. We'll be finished soon. I need to find the second in the series," Dr. Adams said, closing the book, one finger holding his place. "It's late. I didn't realize how late. You haven't had your medication. Are you tired?"

"I'm not ready to go back inside." Landon laid his head back, staring up at the dark sky, wishing they weren't sitting in the light so he could see the stars sure to be twinkling. After a minute more of silence, he slightly cocked his head toward the doctor and gave him the side-eye. "Doc, you could just walk away and leave me outside. I won't tell a soul." The cool gentle breeze that had blown from the north picked up its gust as if it agreed with Landon's need to stay there a little longer.

"You might not talk, but I'm sure there are cameras all over the place." This time, Dr. Adams moved the bookmark to act as placeholder, signaling an end to tonight's session. Man, he didn't like that one bit. He had grown to really look forward to their evenings. The doc had made this whole stay bearable, and that was before he had taken their time together to the next level by bringing him outside. "Tomorrow they're expecting rain."

"The weather's bipolar here. More so than any place I've been stationed." Surprisingly, Landon found himself with a hard decision. He could lose himself looking up at the night's sky, but the man beside him held more of a draw, causing Landon to roll his head in Dr. Adams's direction and just stare, memorizing the alluring face.

"Have you been around the world?" the doctor asked, seeming willing to stay out a bit longer. He was a selfish bastard not to let the man take him to his room and go on with his night.

"Not as much as I'd like. Bet you traveled a lot." Yep, selfish bastard, talking about traveling was a long sort of conversation. It could go on for hours, and he secretly hope it did.

"Not as much as I'd like."

Hope crashed and burned right before him. So much for getting the doctor talking. Luckily, the silence between them was comfortable as he stared at Dr. Adams who looked out into the night.

"You never answered me on why you're here," Landon prompted, not a hundred percent sure where the question had even come from.

"I did," Dr. Adams answered, his tone causing Landon to take a closer look. Dr. Adams lowered his head, staring down into his lap. "I told you a sign brought me here." Something had suddenly changed; his voice held a hint of desperation. Instinct more than anything else told Landon it was time to press for the truth.

"Let me ask you a different way." Landon forced himself to sit up to face Dr. Adams when he said, "What're you running from that brings you halfway across the world?"

"You think you know me?" The words and tone said something different than the playfulness dancing in Dr. Adams's eyes as he lifted a single brow.

Yeah, in another place and time, that look would have been sexy as hell. Now though, wasn't that time. "No, I don't know you, not at all. I don't even know people like you, so I don't know how to guess. It's why I have to ask."

"What does 'people like me' mean?" Dr. Adams asked, the fun tone vanished as his eyes narrowed and his brow dropped into a hard V. The intensity coming off the man kind of impressed Landon who lifted his good hand in a peace offering.

"Don't get defensive. I meant sophisticated, if that's the right word?"

Dr. Adams did another one of his sudden visual mood shifts and started laughing. Shit, this wasn't working out well for Landon at all. The man had a wonderful laugh, even if it was directed at him, and his dick took notice, plumping underneath his hospital gown.

"You mean stuffy," Dr. Adams corrected, his face filled with amusement as he gave Landon a racy teasing look.

"You're messing with me on purpose, and I can't really tell if you're joking, so let me tell you something I haven't said because I didn't know if I should. When you're contemplating your signs and their meaning to your life and whether you should open yourself to understanding this world is bigger than you thought, you need to know I stood as the honor guard on duty the night you stayed with your father while he sat by your dad's casket."

The air stood completely still. The confession caused Landon's heart to drum steadily in his chest as he stared at the utter shock filling Dr. Adams's face. He waited through the range of emotion until disbelief hit, and he narrowed his eyes, shifting toward Landon for a closer look. "That was you?"

He clearly didn't believe him.

"I volunteered to stay all night with you both." Landon scrunched his face into his serious I'm-a-badass-sergeant expression then put a hand to his brow partially covering his face like the brim of his wheel cap would do. Recognition instantly filled those blue eyes.

"I tried to find you to thank you. Did you get my email?" Dr. Adams asked, sitting back in astonishment, like Landon had given the best possible gift. He seemed sincerely appreciative, not in the least bit angry that Landon hadn't mentioned this before now.

"I did. The email was forwarded to me by my CO, but I didn't do it for a thank-you. I'm not kidding when I say your father was a great man. I moved heaven and earth to get there. I owed Vice President Adams my respect to watch over him as an honor guard, but when I watched his husband, in person with my own eyes, grieve like he did, I realized true love was possible for guys like me." Landon didn't waver in speaking his truth, damn the consequences of confessing his belief in something so filled with romance and lacking in any solid reason.

"Do you have someone in your life?" Dr. Adams asked, shifting closer, leaning toward Landon. "I decided I thought you had to have."

"No, I don't. Not yet, but I'll be open to it when it happens. I didn't grow up around gay men. I had no idea what was going on with me. I keep saying that to you, but I struggled mightily. I couldn't accept it. I contemplated suicide many times, even came close to following through a couple of times. I was disgusted and thought I was broken… I didn't have to worry about my family being hard on me; I was doing it to myself. I lived a destructive, nightmare of a life, then I read your father's books and he gave me hope, but for a different reason than I've said."

Landon took a deep breath, not really questioning why he was laying out the locked away secrets of his life, and the fairytales he believed in. "The true meaning to Vice President Adams's life was his husband. I felt their connection in every word the man wrote. Then, when I stood watch with you and your father overnight, seeing him sit for hours holding onto the casket, not wanting to let his husband go—I saw the strength of their love, and the depth of their bond, with my own eyes. The next morning, I left as a different man. Even in death, the love between those two men couldn't be denied. Your parents helped me realize everyone deserves a love that powerful."

Landon had so much emotion driving his words that he could feel the tears welling in his eyes and forced himself to shut his mouth, to stop the insane information dump he was giving, and swallowed the lump threatening to clog his throat.

Landon wasn't the only one emotional. Dr. Adams's eyes were red and tear-filled. He bent, lowering his head as he dug his finger and thumb into his eyes, not saying a single word to what Landon had just confessed.

"Let me be there for you like you've been here for me. Tell me why you're really here. I know you're hurting over your fathers' deaths…" Landon started, trying to help in any way he could. Dr. Adams sat up, and they stared at one another until the doctor dropped his gaze to his lap. His face scrunched in intense pain. His skilled hands were moving over each other. Not necessarily wringing, but probably as close to it as this fine man ever got.

"You're my patient," Dr. Adams started, lifting his head to look at Landon, definitely shying away from him.

"Stop the bullshit, Doc. Just say what's on your mind. You're safe with me, and no one can hear us out here," he encouraged.

Dr. Adams's body shuddered as his head hung, his tone sounding shamed. "I'm responsible."

"Responsible? For what?" Landon's mind raced, trying to understand. The deep pain was evident in the rawness of the doctor's voice. It showed physically when his body seemed to crumple in front of him like the man was shouldering the weight of the world.

"I did it." Dr. Adams scrubbed a hand down the length of his face. "I let my father die. I save strangers' lives for a living, but I let my father wither away to nothing when I had the power to help him."

Landon was so confused. He grappled with the little bit he knew about Avery Adams's death. "I thought he had heart disease. He lived twenty years longer than his father or grandfather…"

"No, not him. My daddy—Kane. He was in my care when he died. Autumn had wanted him in the hospital weeks before. She and I had a huge fight a couple of days before he died, but I gave into my daddy's wishes. I stayed with him at his home. I was so arrogant. I thought I'd be able to handle the situation. He needed care, more care than I could provide at home. I should've forced him to see a psychologist months before he died. I knew he'd given up. He missed my dad so much." There was deep anguish and pain in those blue eyes. Landon had no choice but to reach out and take the man's shaking hand in his. He gave a gentle squeeze for reassurance. "Why did I so blatantly disregard his health? Even when I finally got him to agree to go to the hospital, he talked me into stopping by the cemetery. Why would I have ever allowed something like that to happen?"

"Doc, listen to me," Landon said, hurting for this man's immense pain. "There was nothing that was gonna keep Kane Adams alive. I saw it the night I stood watch. Your father died the day his husband died. His body lasted longer than I thought it would. He didn't want to live without your dad. His purpose and reason was gone the day Vice President Adams died."

There was a helplessness on the doctor's face as he clutched Landon's hand and lifted his eyes, searching Landon's face. "I've lived an intellectual life. I believe in science. These decisions I've made make no sense to me. I know better than to believe in the mystical, but I can't let go of all this guilt." Tears gathered and spilled down the doctor's cheeks, breaking Landon's heart in two. "I let my parents down and I can't get past it."

Landon racked his brain, desperately trying to find the right words to help this fine man's unbearable grief. "I promise you didn't let them down. It was always going to end for them just like it did. I know in my heart you made the last months of your father's life better. You need to understand that and let it be enough."

"How do you know with such certainty how their end would be?" Dr. Adams held his hand as tightly as if Landon was a life-preserver in a deep dark turbulent ocean.

That was a harder question. Landon searched for some answer he thought Dr. Adams could accept. "Because it was in Vice President Adams's words. It's all there. He loved and was proud of you and your sister—very proud. He loved his family, but he saw his husband as his soul mate, and he didn't mince words in making that clear to the world. Your father was his reason to live. They weren't going to live without each other. I wouldn't hesitate to bet my money on Vice President Adams being proud of how well you took care of your father to the very end, until they could be together again."

Dr. Adams just shook his head, instantly denying his explanation. With his free hand, he wiped at the tears sliding down his cheek. "I can't get there."

"You've got to. I promise you they're together. That should be enough. To hang on to the idea that you could have saved your father, that your actions could have stopped the inevitable, means everything Vice President Adams said in his books wasn't true. It means they weren't connected souls," Landon said, his head and his heart vehemently holding on to that truth.

"What if it's not true?"

Landon's brow dropped and his eyes narrowed. Dr. Adams was a hardheaded thing. "You can't think that way, Doc, because you're wrong. I know it. I keep telling you I saw the truth that night." A strong breeze blew across them in the otherwise still night, sending a small smattering of leaves stirring between them. Dr. Adams let go of his hand, reaching for the napkins on the table, stopping them before they blew away. He used one to wipe his eyes. Those vibrant blue orbs still brimmed with tears as he spoke.

"I chose cardiology to help make a difference in my family's legacy. Now I can't see myself ever performing surgery again. Something's turned off inside me." Dr. Adams let out a sigh and reached for his water bottle, draining the last little bit. "I'm sorry I dumped all this out on you. I know there's no way for you to know, but I don't do this. I think I've talked to you more this week than I've talked to anyone in my life."

"I'm honored," Landon said simply, making Dr. Adams smile.

"I doubt that. Before I came here, I was stalling on finalizing my parents' estate. I didn't want to deal with any of it. I was remembering Dad's last words to me. He said, 'It's not enough to have the feathers. You must dare to fly.' Within seconds of the thought, a fluffy white feather blew across my desk and landed on a brochure for this hospital. There was no reason for any sort of feather to be in my house. I know it sounds crazy, but that's how I got here. I even had to pull strings to get approval to come. I'm trying as hard as I can to see life from a different perspective." Dr. Adams took a deep, cleansing shuddering breath while Landon held his tongue, hoping to hear more. "We should get you inside."

Landon surely didn't qualify as any sort of a counselor, so he reluctantly let the doctor change the subject only because he didn't know how to keep him talking. "I'm still volunteering to be left out here for the night."

"We're late for your medication. They'll be looking for you soon."

"Buzz kill," he teased, watching Dr. Adams quickly grab their things before taking them to the closest trash bin. When he came back to Landon, Dr. Adams took the seat again, silently staring at him for a good long second before speaking.

"Thank you for this tonight. Thank you for everything you've done. I don't know how to ever repay you, but you've helped me." Dr. Adams placed his hand on Landon's arm, giving a gentle squeeze then lingered there. He liked this doctor touching him far too much, but more importantly, he wanted the doctor eased from the heavy burden he carried. Humor seemed the best possible way.

"Doc, I've told you how. Leave me out here." Landon got the smile he wanted, that sexy grin was back as Dr. Adams placed the book in Landon's lap and shoved to his feet, going around to the back of his chair. He started pushing Landon toward the door.

"Then let's just leave it at a verbal thank-you for now so I can keep my job." The intimacy of the moment passed as an aide met them at the back door, helping him inside.

Chapter 5

Robert did what he had done almost every morning for the past month: opened his eyes wide and listened to the noises around him. The energy felt odd. It was lighter in the room than normal, and he lifted his left arm to look at the time. Seven-oh-three in the morning. He had slept in by about four hours, and he felt good. The much-needed calm held, and he dropped his arm back to the bed, closing his eyes again. He inhaled deeply and stretched his long body in the soft sheets. A smile ghosted his lips. That was new too.

Such a simple act of waking late would normally cause him great anxiety as he wondered what he'd missed and how in the world he'd catch up his day, but now it made him grin like a Cheshire cat. He could feel the constrictive bonds that had held him in a constant state of anxiety relaxing their grip. *Landon.* Images of the man filled his thoughts. Robert had been right to fight to come to Germany. He had needed Landon to convince him to rethink the possibilities of forever. Today, although really too early for such an assumption, he didn't sense the heavy burden of oppression or dread that always greeted him when he woke. Robert did a full body assessment, grinning broader when his initial thoughts held.

Now, he had to make sure he harnessed whatever this was. *Landon.* His mind wandered again to the dark-haired sergeant. The guy was handsome as sin. He'd always been attracted to dark and devilish-looking men. And he stopped his wayward thoughts right there. He wasn't sure he should let his mind go roaming freely—it wasn't yet on the short list of approved activities to keep himself on this side of depression. This calm was too precious and fragile. He needed to focus on a full recovery before he let too much back into his life.

He looked around at the cold white walls as if seeing his small room for the first time. He'd never thought about it until now, but it was empty. Not that there wasn't furniture there. It had been a quiet place for him to hide in his grief. There were two beds, one that he'd never used before. There were also two locker style pieces of furniture, two desks, and two chairs. He hadn't used those either. The room lacked character and bordered on sterile. He'd never been a messy person, but this was ridiculously tidy even for him.

Maybe the room was a metaphor for the last nine months— *don't think about that either.*

Maybe a good old-fashion cry with a commiserating friend was what he had needed the most. His smile gentled as he rose, purposefully leaving the bed unmade as he reached for his cell phone. He had a personal friend for the first time in a long time. Of course, he had work acquaintances—lots of those—but when the workday ended, they all went their separate ways. He considered Landon's friendship an entirely different entity.

From the first moment he'd looked into the sergeant's dark eyes, he'd felt the draw pulling them together. The man had showed him kindness and listened without judgment. Landon's understanding of his family and the carefully placed words had methodically stripped back layers of the protective walls Robert had been hiding behind to help cope with this tremendous guilt. Robert had always known his fathers had something special, but the sergeant had shown him the truth. His fathers were two halves of a whole. Soul mates were real, and Robert had lived his life with two men who were ultimately one.

There was no way he could change what he had or hadn't done. Whether or not his daddy's life was always going to end the way it had didn't change the fact he could have done things differently. He'd have to live with that knowledge for the rest of his life, but Landon had offered him solace in the understanding that wherever his parents were, they were together. Robert needed to pick himself up and honor their extraordinary legacy in every step he took for the rest of his life. And he would. What a heady thought and tremendous redirection of his life.

Robert sat in the chair instead of on the edge of the bed just to use something inside this room besides the bed—to give it purpose. He rolled his eyes at that. Maybe he was taking all this meaning of life a little far, but whatever.

He stared down at the phone screen and his stomach dipped when he realized there were eighty-eight unread text messages. The sheer volume seemed a little daunting, so he chose his sister's text messages first. Forty-three of the eighty-eight messages were from her. He scanned the list of messages, not really reading them, knowing if something had gone wrong, she would have made sure he knew.

The last text message she sent was in capital letters, showing her irritation. *"I'VE NEVER GONE 26 DAYS WITHOUT SPEAKING TO YOU. There was a time I would have appreciated that, not today though. PLEASE MESSAGE ME BACK, BRATBERT."*

He grinned at the nickname she'd given him when they were children, trying to decide if he should make it twenty-seven days just to get further under her skin. As a teenager, he thought his towering height and strength automatically made him superior to his sister. He'd go out of his way to beat her at every task that required muscles or height. He'd purposefully go into the kitchen pantry and place everything he could out of her reach and then practiced becoming a master at opening jars—pickles, mayonnaise, jelly—all just to be better than her. She'd get so frustrated with him when he'd pluck the object out of her hands and open it with just a pop. He loved that memory. Those were the only arguments he ever heard from his fathers. His daddy would get on to him for overpowering Autumn. His dad seemed to understand what was going on with him and tell Kane it was part of growing up.

Under the weight of this newfound consciousness, Robert decided he shouldn't make her worry any longer and typed the message he'd picked up his phone to send.

"I need a favor." He pushed send, staring down at the screen. Maybe he should have started with a "hello, sis…"

Less than fifteen seconds passed before Autumn responded.

"It's one o'clock in the morning and you want to chat?"

Hmm. He hadn't considered the time difference.

"I knew you'd be up." Which of course he hadn't.

"I don't know why I worry about you. What favor?" Autumn shot back. He couldn't deny their twin bond, which allowed him to practically hear Autumn's aggravation—frustration, sarcasm, and all—through her words.

"I need you to send me some sort of reading pad. Something that has audio and earphones, good earphones that cover the ear. I don't know the buying options here in Germany, so maybe load all George RR Martin's books and whatever books complement his genre. Also, load all Dad's books on there, but it's got to have audio, even if the books aren't on audio. Make sense?"

Maybe as much as a minute passed before she answered.

"What? Robert that's asking a lot. I've got a lot going on. When do you need this by?"

Since he was asking the world, he might as well dump more pressure on her.

"Tomorrow? Can you overnight it today to arrive tomorrow? For sure by the next day. I'll be heading home then."

He could practically hear her screech as her thumbs furiously typed if the three little dots were anything to go by.

"What! No, I can't. Call Dad's assistant. She'll do it. I really do have too much going on."

The time difference made reaching out to his father's office a difficult task. In seven hours, he'd be knee deep in patients and forget to make the call which was the whole reason he'd enlisted Autumn in the first place. *"Can you call her in the morning for me? I've got to go to work."*

"This isn't as easy as you think. It's asking too much. Why do you need it?"

Yeah, there was another glaring reminder of what a self-absorbed ass he had become. Technically, this information was where he should have started this text message exchange.

"I found the honor guard who stayed with Daddy and me that night at the funeral. Remember? I want to gift all this to him. He's a reader. We've been reading together. I was hoping to give it to him personally, from the both of us, before I leave day after tomorrow."

He pushed send and waited, startling when his phone rang in his hand. Robert shoved back in the chair and smiled as he answered as if he didn't know who called. "Hello?"

"You found him? Are you sure it's him?" she asked, her voice raspy and thick, clearly she'd been sleeping so he'd forgive the dumb question.

"Of course, it's him. Who would even know about his generosity and why would they lie?"

"What did he say? Did he get our thank-you message?"

Robert nodded to the empty room before she finished asking the question. "He did. He read Dad's books, and it helped him overcome a situation in his life. That's why he did what he did. He did it out of respect," Robert explained. The words filling his heart with admiration.

"Is there a chance he's gay?" Her voice sounded excited and wide awake now as she shifted gears on him.

"Is who gay?" a male voice in the background said. Autumn had been going out with Cameron Connors for about a year now and seemed happy with him. Cam had been his work colleague and friend for years before he and Autumn ever got together. He was a good guy and clearly the relationship had progressed if he was there with her in the middle of the night in Minnesota, not DC.

"The honor guard that was at my dad's funeral happens to be in Germany with Robert, and he's read Dad's books. That was why he stayed overnight with Daddy and Robert that night at the capital." Autumn succinctly filled Cam in before turning the conversation back to him. "I bet he's nice looking, Robert."

He shrugged that one off. Landon was very nice looking—he'd give her that, but he was so much more. Robert valued his friendship and wanted to repay him for his kindness. "He's been hurt, and he can't do much of anything else, so he reads. I want to give him a gift he'll use. I also want to get his rehab care transferred to the States so he'll need a US device, if that's even a requirement. Can you make it happen for me before I leave here?"

"Yeah, I'll figure it out and text you later." Autumn's words made him smile. He could always count on his sister to move mountains.

"Thank you. How's Nonnie?" he asked, wondering about their aging grandmother, Kennedy Adams.

"She's unstoppable. She's in her nineties and her memory is better than mine. She told me to send you her love and remind you her birthday is in a few weeks, and she expects a call." His grandmother was a feisty one. He needed his Nonnie to stay in his life for as long as he could have her. "I miss you, Robert. I'm glad you needed me. Your voice is lighter. You sound happy. I'm glad this trip was good for you."

"I am lighter. It's new and fragile, so I'm hanging up before you ruin it." He laughed at her quick intake of breath, knowing she was preparing to blast him for her error in caring about his wellbeing. "Thank you for looking into the e-reader. I'll be back home in a few days. I thought I'd come straight to Minnesota. I'm ready to finalize the estate, so get ready."

He quickly hung up before deciding to put off his second call to Senator David Burch. He should at least wait until morning on the east coast to ask for another monumental favor of the government. Robert wanted Landon moved to the States for his final rehab. It seemed the best option, somewhere where his reputation of being a difficult patient didn't precede him. Honestly, it shouldn't be that big of a favor to grant his request, at least not compared to whatever David might have had to promise to get Robert to LRMC in the first place.

These were things he could do for Landon. He appreciated the man so much. With that thought, Robert shrugged and made the call now.

"Do you know what time it is?"

"Uncle David, I'm sorry to wake you, but I need a favor."

"You used your favors when I had to promise the world to get you to Germany, son." The gruffness and surly attitude were all a cover. David was a teddy bear down deep, and Robert grinned, knowing right then that he'd get his way.

Chapter 6

Twenty-four hours later

Every single fiber of Robert's body rejected each keystroke of medical charting. The more he worked, the murkier the waters became regarding his decision to return to medicine when he went home. And going home was happening. He had about twenty-four hours until his flight departed. That knowledge was the only thing making this charting doable and probably the most likely reason he'd been assigned this horrible task. On the bright side, once he finished this large stack on his desk, he'd never have to deal with LRMC's tedious, outdated reporting system again.

"Dr. Adams?" Robert looked up to see the aide extending a large overnight mail packet. At the same time his cell phone, lying on the desk, began to vibrate.

"Thanks." He took the package and lifted his phone. Autumn's named appeared on the screen. With a swipe of the thumb, he answered, "Hello?"

"Did you get it?" she asked.

The timing of her call was so on point that Robert lifted his eyes and looked around the room to see if there was a camera on him. "How could you know?"

"Know what?" Autumn didn't give him time to respond before she added, "I received an alert that the package arrived about ten minutes ago. Is that what my articulate brother is trying to ask me?"

The shit-giving never stopped. "Hang on."

He placed the phone on the desk, letting Autumn wait as he opened the package. He found a rumpled decorative bag with all the colorful tissues sticking out the top and an envelope with his name scribbled on the front. He opened the card and a five-hundred-dollar Amazon gift card dropped to the floor. He slowly bent to retrieve the gift card as he read Autumn's neatly written instructions.

I had them wrapped because it just seemed nicer. It's an Amazon e-reader and the headphones you requested. He'll have to set this up under his account, so I've sent enough money for him to buy whatever he wants to read. This will also cover audio books. I've also included a thank-you note from me. Let me know what else I can do.

Love you, brother,

A.

His dad always signed everything with an A. Autumn was so much like their father in so many ways.

The phone rattled against the desk, drawing Robert's attention back to the cell and a text message from Autumn.

"You know I hate when you do that. I'm not sure if we lost connection or you stopped talking to me. I'm sitting here waiting and waiting AND WAITING for your answer and you leave me hanging."

Another text message popped up on the screen before he could finish the first one.

"Robert, augh! Answer me."

He gave a sinister little laugh. He should answer. She had handled all this for him, but having Autumn irritated with him never grew old. He checked the time and grabbed the new goodies. Maybe Landon was back inside his room.

"Hey, Doc, I got surprised with orders today. Know anything about that?" Landon asked, when he spotted Dr. Adams in the hallway just outside his hospital room. He allowed the physical therapist to help him back into bed and adjust his pillows before he leaned back. Like normal, nothing else mattered when the doctor strolled the rest of the way into the room, a big grin sliding easily across his face. Dr. Adams's shift in mood since their heart to heart the other night seemed to have a domino effect by easing Landon's heart too.

"Orders? I might know a little something," Dr. Adams answered, nodding at the physical therapist as he left the room.

"You know, now that I'm getting all this special treatment, they're calling me a kiss ass." The grin spreading across Landon's face matched Dr. Adams's and hopefully spoke volumes over the hard-ass tone he'd used when saying those words.

"And what does that matter?" Dr. Adams crossed his arms over the package at his chest.

"Not a damn thing. Thanks for pulling those strings." He winked and extended his fist for a fist bump. One easily complied with.

"It's not a problem." Dr. Adams straddled the small stool and rolled closer to the bed.

"You live in DC, right?" Landon asked.

"I have a townhome in the Georgetown area. It's really nice there. You need a place to stay after you're released from the hospital?" The offer completely caught Landon off guard.

Only if you're going to be there.

The words were so clear in his head he prayed he hadn't let them slip out on accident. The desire accompanying the thought was such a startling and overwhelming emotion Landon paused, tamping down his racing heart at the sudden yearning that stirred in his belly. Oh shit, had the doctor noticed his reaction? Landon wasn't sure, but the best way to cover his possible mistake was to tease the man.

"Already askin' me to move in with you, Doc?" Landon asked cockily.

"No, I'm not that smooth." The doctor immediately shook his head, chuckling at such an absurd suggestion. Landon enjoyed the instant blush staining the doctor's cheeks. "Actually, I'm not going home. I have to go to Minnesota and take care of a few things. You would have the whole place to yourself, which you should consider yourself lucky that I won't be around to bother you. I imagine I'd be a horrible roommate. I like my space to be orderly and I don't like wild parties." Dr. Adams's grin grew into the most beautiful smile he'd ever seen. "My place will be empty for as long as you need it."

Lost to Dr. Adams's handsome good looks, he almost missed that the man had truly just offered him his home to stay in while in DC. What a seriously thoughtful guy.

"What if I have wild parties?" Landon asked, sticking with the theme of teasing. It was so much easier than trying to sort out what in the hell was happening to him right then. Dr. Adams let out a big sigh, making Landon wonder exactly where the doctor's generosity ended.

"Well, if you must, then please keep the bands in the house not in the yard," Dr. Adams quipped. "It's a quiet neighborhood.

The HOA will have a problem with it. You'll most likely get a noise violation fine but do what you must. Party on." The old school *Wayne's World* reference kept the smiles on both their faces.

"I'll think about it. The offer, not the parties." Having a place to lay his head when he got back to the states was something to consider. Light from the overhead fluorescents caught the shiny paper sticking out the top of the bundle pressed against Dr. Adams's chest, drawing Landon's attention there. "What's that?"

"I wanted you to have something to help you continue to read the series. I had my sister track something down for you." Dr. Adams held out the package. When Landon didn't readily take it, the doctor removed a gift sack from the large mailer and began pulling the tissue paper from the top like a kid on Christmas morning.

"You didn't have to get me anything," Landon said, politely rejecting the gift, but loving how Dr. Adams couldn't wait to show him what was inside. He almost felt guilty for saying those words when he caught the flash of uncertainty in the doc's gaze when he looked up from ripping the paper from the gift.

"I wanted to do this," Dr. Adams said plainly as if that settled it.

"Is this because of what I told you about the honor guard?" He didn't mean to come across so bluntly. He was shit at receiving gifts; he just hadn't confided in Dr. Adams for any other reason than to show his respect and admiration to a man who encouraged him to set life's bar higher.

"No, not at all. I had this planned before you told me. It's more of a thank-you from me. Talking to you was better than therapy. I've got a ways to go, but I'm on my new path where I need to be. This new revelation is all because of you." Dr. Adams's smile slid easily across his face. The man looked rested, the dark circles under his eyes were gone. He seemed genuinely happier.

"I can't see how," he replied honestly.

"Well, it's still true, so look at this. It's an e-reader and headphones." Dr. Adams kept talking as he dumped the contents of the package on the side of his bed. "There's an audio option on here so you can listen to the rest of the series and whatever you want until you get yourself better situated. She also threw in a converter. Good call on her part."

"That's too much. I can't accept this." Landon shook his head. They'd removed the immobilizer this morning, and even though the brace on his arm was still cumbersome, he'd have a much easier time reading now. He stared down at all the different components of the gift. Dr. Adams shouldn't have done this. Landon had enjoyed the time they'd spent together. Nothing was owed to him as far as he was concerned. "Doc, I appreciate—"

"I wanted to have the books loaded before I gave it to you, but apparently you need to add your account information so my sister sent you a gift card with a note from her," Dr. Adams continued to explain, not thwarted by Landon's objection.

"This is too much," he repeated, raising his voice this time to be heard by the hardheaded doctor.

"I'm not taking no for an answer. I thought we could charge it, and when I come tonight, I'll help you set it up." Dr. Adams's grin grew, and Landon was convinced it was his own scowl that had prompted the twinkle in the other man's eyes as he opened the e-reader's box. Landon tried to pick his words. Outside of his family, no one gave him gifts, and including his family, no one ever spent this much money on him. "I'll take that silence to mean 'you're a smart guy, Dr. Adams. Great plan.'"

Dr. Adams rose, looking around for a plug. He opened another box which held an adapter and plugged it in. "Dude, I didn't do anything but show my respect. I don't deserve this."

"Just take it. I want you to have it. Here's the note from my sister," Dr. Adams said, still completely ignoring his wishes. "I've got to run. I'm tying up all my loose ends before I head out. I'll see you tonight. I think we can set this up and finish the book before I go."

Landon watched Dr. Adams pivot and leave the room. What

the hell just happened? Landon looked down at the envelope then looked over at the e-reader. Without knowing anything about the shiny black pad, he was certain it was one of the fancy ones, all new and sleek. It was as if the device had a life of its own, the battery light lit up in the middle of the screen, garnering all his attention. Those things were expensive and easy to break. All the courage he'd had to build in order to deal with Dr. Adams in the first place slipped several notches. Apparently, he didn't like getting gifts from the Adams family. It made him insecure and uncertain, and he lowered his brow, staring at the pretty penmanship of his name scribbled on the outside of the envelope.

As if the envelope held a secret mission and a self-destructing recording, Landon slowly opened the flap and pulled out the card.

Dear Landon,

My heart is filled with gratitude to you for the way you honored our father, and I wanted to thank you for your service. I also believe that you're the reason for the change I noticed in my brother. I know it's your influence on him that has made the difference.

I'm sorry to hear of your injuries. I wish you a speedy and complete recovery. I'm happy Robert had this time with you. You managed to do more for him than any of us could. I'll have to give you a hug in person someday. Please take care and know I owe you so much.

Wishing you the best,

Autumn

A sigh slipped free as he read the words again. He kept a tight grip on the card before dropping his fist to the mattress as he stared up at the dingy tiles—a ceiling he'd stared at for so long he knew each blemish by heart. Why was every member of the Adams family so incredibly kind?

Why did he feel like crying? Emotion squeezed his chest, making it hard to get a full breath.

Why did he want to save this note as one of his most cherished items until the day he died?

This wasn't supposed to go like this. He owed the Adams family, not the other way around. Now Dr. Adams was buying him expensive gifts and offering his place for Landon to live. Then Autumn Adams wrote him a personal note that seemed heartfelt and sincere.

He was the one trying to pay back a kindness. Now, all lines were blurred. No matter how many lectures he gave himself, he was developing real feelings for Robert Adams. Big feelings. Like more than just someday hoping to find a guy like the doctor, kind of feelings. Now, he wanted the doctor. The thought had his heart racing and his internal anxiety spiking for even admitting to himself such a confusing truth.

Oh. My. God. When the fuck had that even happened?

As if Dr. Adams would ever want a guy like him.

He rolled his eyes at the idea he'd be a fit partner for someone like Robert Adams. Pain sliced across his heart, stealing his breath.

No! Landon steeled his spine. He absolutely wasn't doing this. All of these super emotional feelings were just an infatuation bubbling up because the doctor had shown him some much-needed kindness. That was exactly what it had to be. Dr. Adams could have his pick of men. He could see him with someone with equal parts intelligence and sophistication.

"Time for your medication." Holly startled the shit out of him as she strolled into his room.

"I don't want it," he said irritably. "It makes me tired."

"Omigod, Landon, you're always so difficult. Do I need to go get Dr. Adams? He'll make you take this medication."

Landon's head jerked toward Holly who held a small cup with his pills inside and a paper cup with water. Seeing the doc right now was the very last thing he wanted to do.

"For fuck's sake, don't do that." His abrupt anger had her

rearing back in surprise.

"What happened? I thought you two were friends."

"And I thought you and I were too," he snapped back harshly, liking the anger so much better than all that confusing emotional bullshit. What was he doing fighting sleep? Anything was better than realizing he'd never be good enough for the man he'd been crushing on. Landon reached for the pills, popping them in his mouth and swallowing them dry.

"You're not making sense." Holly rolled her eyes and left without making him drink the water.

He was alone again inside the room, and he stared at all the walls before he dropped his head back on the bed.

Nothing changed, dick-weed. Calm your ass down. He's going one way; you're going another. All he's done is set a standard. That's it. That. Is. It.

Right. He eyed the tablet charging in the corner before he closed his eyes and willed himself to go to sleep.

Chapter 7

"Fuck, Doc. You look like a million bucks." Landon stared at the doctor's reflection in the wall of mirrors in front of him. He dropped the weight in his hand and pushed back on his bench as Dr. Adams joined him in the physical therapy workout room.

"You're at it early," Dr. Adams said, setting an expensive looking leather duffle bag on the bench beside him.

"Couldn't sleep." Which was a big fucking understatement. Robert Adams had fucked with his head in a major way, making him restless as hell until this very moment when a peace settled over his heart, calming his ass down.

"You're heading out?" Landon could only stare at the doctor who had lost that hollow expression over the last few days. He looked vibrant and whole, ready to move forward with his life again. For some reason, realizing that helped Landon's heart more than any of his own self-lectures over the last however many hours. This was the man he remembered from the funeral. Strong, supportive, and poised. Landon hadn't come up with a solid game plan on how to control his attraction, but he needed to figure it out. The doc's friendship was important to him.

Landon scanned the entire length of Dr. Adams's body,

which didn't help tamp down all this carnal need coursing through him. He was gorgeous, dressed to the nines from head to toe, and he smelled good too. He did literally look like he was worth a million dollars. Which he absolutely was—another reason Landon should get a hold of his runaway libido. He slid his gaze down the perfect frame, tight waist, slender hips, and thick thighs. His attraction blurring lines and his feelings surging deeper as he admired the man.

"What? Do I have a stain?" Robert looked down at his chest then his slacks before comically lifting a foot. For Landon, this one moment helped break the spell he'd been under and tucked his rampant thoughts back in place. Landon was an average guy. Robert was the top one percent.

"No, you just clean up really well."

That brought the grin Landon was partial to seeing to Dr. Adams's face. "Thanks. I've been in scrubs or my jogging gear the whole time I've been here. It feels odd to be back in real clothes again. I brought you my house key. I've notified the neighborhood security that you're staying at my place. I have housekeeping three days a week. I've sent them emails that you'll be in residence."

"I don't wanna put you out." Staying in the doc's home had dominated their conversation all last night. It felt like an imposition, and he couldn't let it go no matter how many times Dr. Adams assured him differently.

"Stop. It's truly no problem. I've also given you my cell number and email. Contact me with whatever you need." He offered up a padded envelope. "Stay as long as you want."

Landon had to force himself to reach out and take the package. He was a stubborn guy, hardheaded as hell, but somehow Dr. Adams beat him in the tenacity department. "Thanks, I can't tell you how much this is going to help."

"As I've said many times, it's no problem."

He and the doctor stared at one another. Over the course of the past week, they had spent a significant amount of time together.

He couldn't remember a single time that words had failed either of them. Landon didn't want their time to end. Logically, the odds of seeing the doctor again were highly in his favor, but he still didn't want the man to walk away.

Dr. Adams broke Landon's inner turmoil when he cocked an eyebrow and said, "You do what your doctors say to do. They generally know what's best."

Those blue eyes bore into his, but the teasing made Landon swallow the words forming in his throat. Now wasn't the time to gush out all this appreciation he had. The way Dr. Adams looked at him had him dropping his gaze. This was all too much. Instead of risking giving away his feelings—feelings he didn't truly understand—he studied the name scribbled in an elegant yet efficient penmanship on the front of the envelope. The style fit the man perfectly.

"I'll try my best," he finally muttered, a promise he was determined to keep.

Robert chuckled to himself while staring down at the bent dark head. The one thing he and Landon had never been was awkward. Yet, here they were struggling to say goodbye. Maybe that was it. He didn't want to say goodbye, which was the sole reason he'd given Landon every bit of his contact information, including Autumn's email and personal cell phone number. He'd found someone to help him find a way to shoulder his burden, and he would always be grateful. No question…he wanted to keep Landon in his life.

Maybe that was why a strange feeling crept through him. It was like he was leaving his best friend. Robert drew in a deep breath. If he didn't get a move on, he'd miss his car. He reached for his bag's strap and slung it over his shoulder then extended his hand to Landon. The sergeant instantly looked up, taking his hand in a firm grip. "Thank you for everything."

"Doc, that's what I should be saying to you." The genuineness of Landon's tone caused Robert's smile to grow and dissipated any unease that had developed. Landon's character was so solid.

"Then I feel better about dominating your free time. I'm heading out. Call me if you need anything." It still took a few extra seconds to release Landon's hand. When he did, he took a step backward, his gaze remaining fixed on the man.

"I will." Landon lifted the envelope as Robert took another step or two backward before forcing himself to turn away.

He had said his goodbyes to the staff during his last shift, but he nodded to the few he saw on his way out. He caught the same curious stares. They were always there whether he was with Landon or not. But he let that go and headed toward the door of the rehab center.

In the doorway, he turned back. Landon was still staring after him. He lifted a hand in a wave, already missing Landon, and he hadn't even left yet. They had become friends, and he appreciated that friendship more than Landon would ever fully know. He turned away and headed toward his waiting car. He was going home.

Chapter 8

August 2014

One month later

Robert sat, quietly listening to the DC attorney who spoke by live video feed, answering his sister's question regarding the final division and terms of their late fathers' vast estate. When Autumn had ushered him into the small conference room, she had taken the seat to his left, closest to the door. His Nonnie, Kennedy Adams, had quickly claimed the chair to his right. He suspected he'd ended up in the middle so his sister and grandmother could block any potential escape routes. Both women were worried about him, and he couldn't blame them. They had every right to be, considering his track record, but he was working through his issues and didn't plan to exit until everything was wrapped up and he could move on with his life.

The family's Minnesota law offices still looked the same as he'd remembered, classically decorated with tranquil colors and rich woods. A laptop placed in the middle of the conference room table separated his family from the attorneys on the other side of the screen. It wasn't any surprise that his sister and his grandmother had come prepared, both women were amazing. Autumn was a force in her field of law, and his Nonnie hadn't lost her business edge, not by a long shot.

A lot had happened in his absence, and for the most part, his role in the proceedings was to nod appropriately when Autumn directed and sign his name where she tapped her highly polished, pointy fingernail—those perfectly manicured claws were new for her too. Where Robert had become a pathetic mess after his fathers' deaths, Autumn had gone in a completely different direction. She was a boss in the workforce, and from what he'd witnessed today, a quick study in probate law, efficiently cutting through all the red tape to finalize their fathers' estate as quickly as possible.

"Finally, we have the contract with the Presidential Library Agency to turn the Stillwater home into a memorial library and museum for Vice President Adams," a second voice piped in, drawing Robert's full attention. He swung his gaze from the laptop toward his sister.

Autumn immediately looked at Robert, turning her body fully in his direction to get a good look at him as she asked, "Are you sure you're good with this?"

Just as quickly as she turned, he gave a single nod then looked over at his grandmother for her acknowledgement. The National Archive Administration had approached Autumn about the possibility of turning their childhood home into a national library to commemorate his father's life. Since neither he nor Autumn wanted to sell the home—or live there—it seemed a good option.

With everything decided, Robert had agreed to be the family liaison to head the archive committee, making sure the estate was preserved as authentically as possible. This allowed the family to continue to own the property, collect the rents from the archive administration, and provide a place of remembrance for the world to see. A vice president being honored with a library wasn't something regularly done, but their father had worked tirelessly as a champion for human rights and equality for all. He'd made their country a better place to live. This would publicly document his efforts and achievements.

"Sign here and here." Autumn tapped her deep red fingernail on the contract in front of him. He scrawled his name on the documents. One signature allowed for the rezoning of their carved-out piece of land and the other guaranteed the hefty monthly rental fee for years to come.

"All right, I think we're done," Autumn announced, running a finger down the long list of to-do tasks she'd worked on throughout the meeting.

"You all have done an excellent job," said the representative from the archive administration who sat with their DC attorneys. "It's been a pleasure to work with the both of you. Robert, thank you for chairing the oversight committee. I think we have a great draw on our hands. I'll be in touch to start the ball rolling."

"It was all her," Robert stated, indicating his sister and not allowing any of the kudos to come his way. Autumn was the brains behind this whole deal and deserved all the credit.

He scooted back in his chair. Autumn lifted her eyes from the pages in her hands, tracking his movement as he bent, offering a hand to help his grandmother up. "That's not true. You came back, ready to work."

"I think this calls for a celebratory dinner," Kennedy Adams announced loudly, getting to her feet. She brushed his hand away, refusing any aid. Their grandmother was as stubborn as she was loving. Her feisty attitude would never change. "I think having a meal at La Bella Luna would be a good memory now."

"Nonnie, I don't think so," Autumn started then hesitated. Her uncertain gaze darted to Robert and her brow crinkled with worry.

"I'm good, Autumn. I think I'd like to go. I haven't been there in ages." He held up his hand to halt her protest. He wanted to do this; he missed the food that he'd heard stayed true to the original recipes his granddaddy Paulie and his daddy had created all those years ago. She narrowed her eyes as if to say she didn't believe him, so he ignored her. "I'll call Rodney to see if we can get a reservation. Will Cam be there?"

"No, he's flying back to DC this afternoon." As if just remembering the other attendees, Autumn turned back to the laptop screen. "Thank you, Anna. Bob, I'll get these contracts overnighted to you today."

After a round of goodbyes, the screen darkened. Once alone, Autumn sank back in her seat in what could only be utter exhaustion. "Oh, my goodness, I can't believe we did it. It's really done."

"Avery would be proud of the library and the decision to keep the house," Kennedy said, shrugging on her sweater.

"I was surprised the rezoning wasn't a bigger deal," Robert added, picking up his grandmother's purse and waiting to walk Kennedy out.

"We own the entire edge of the property all the way to the main road. The city'll do well with the tax dollars something like this brings with it. I didn't see it as a problem," Autumn said, sitting forward enough to gather her paperwork. "I'm glad they'll handle everything; we don't have to do anything but oversee the committee. Robert, are you sure you're up to heading this project?"

"Autumn, I'm fine. Stop bringing it up every thirty seconds," he said, with a little more bite than necessary.

"You both did great. I'm proud of you two. You didn't even need me here."

Robert kept pace alongside his grandmother, smiling as her stern voice reminded him of the simple way she had at gaining both his and Autumn's attention no matter their age or life experiences.

"It was easier with you here, Nonnie," he added, winking at Autumn who sat there grinning after them. "I can take you home."

"My driver's waiting."

Robert stopped close to the door, letting her walk out before him, and she patted him on the chest as she passed by.

"Walk me outside?"

"Of course." Robert extended an arm, nothing overtly obvious but he wanted to help steady her steps. He'd learned that particular lesson the hard way. If his grandmother ever thought he purposefully offered aid, she would refuse the help every time. He must have been coy enough, because she took hold of his arm in a loving gesture as she walked toward the foyer of the office space.

When he pushed open the front doors of his dad's—now Autumn's—law firm, his grandmother slowed her already unhurried pace until she came to a stop in the middle of the doorway. She had shrunk a few inches over the years and had to crane her neck to look him in the eye, stopping him from doing anything more than holding the opened door. "You seem better."

He glanced down at her caring and concerned face. This was the same look he'd gotten over and over since his return to Minnesota from Germany a month ago. His actions over the last ten or so months must have seriously scared people. He didn't like that he'd caused his family so much concern while they had grieved themselves.

Remorse had become Robert's most constant companion, replacing the hollowness of depression. He had so much to make up to his family.

"What's just happened, son?"

He immediately masked his expression, but it was too late, her keen gaze saw right through his moment of reality and she wouldn't budge until he told her the truth.

"Nonnie, you know me so well. Come sit on the bench."

He pointed to the metal benches on either side of the walkway leading up to the building. They sat beneath the shade of the stately old oaks. She nodded and went that direction. Once settled, she asked again, "Why did you look so lost just a moment ago?"

He sat beside her, taking in the blooming landscape around

them to gather his thoughts. He loved summer in Minneapolis—if he had to pick a favorite time of year, this would be top of his list. She reached out, clasping his hand.

"I'm doing better, Nonnie. Much better. Now though, I'm carrying around some guilt and regret for everything I put you and Autumn through." The confession was as much as he'd ever admitted aloud to his grandmother about the pain and grief he had suffered. This keen-eyed woman seemed to understand his grief and need for distance, but she worried over him too.

"I suspect that's natural. You have to know all we want for you is to get back to being yourself."

"I'm not sure I'll ever be that man again. Life has changed me." That was putting it mildly. The rebuilding of his inner self had turned into a complete overhaul of who he was as a man. He wanted a different life than before.

"Will you be returning to medicine?" she asked, her bright blue eyes locked onto his. His dad had had identical eyes, so full of expression. Robert and Autumn had inherited the same blue eyes from their grandmother.

"How do you always know just the right questions to ask?" he inquired with a chuckle. His grandmother always stayed one step ahead of him. Nothing ever slipped that woman's attention.

"Dear, I've buried a beloved husband and two cherished sons. I know a thing or two about grief." She patted their joined hands. "I lost a piece of my heart each and every time, but through the grief, I also realized I had been blessed beyond measure by ever having them in my life to begin with. If I hadn't had them, I wouldn't have you. The time I shared with them shaped me, and they're still a part of me. Each time, I changed inside. I'm certain that's what you're going through, too." Her hand tightened around his.

He nodded, sensing her pain. There wasn't anything he could say to change his actions over the last year, no matter how hard he wished it were so. He lifted his eyes to the black sedan pulling to the front of the drive. His grandmother's driver, Mr. Kinkaid got out and rounded the hood of the car. He stayed several feet away to respect their privacy but stood ready for when needed.

"Everything that I thought was important doesn't seem to matter now. Every goal I set for myself has shifted. I'm looking for something different for my future. I've put out some feelers with a general practice group I know. I might like to try the emergency room, maybe the fast pace will appeal to me, but also maybe not. Medicine seems an obligation now. My drive— No, my passion for it is no longer there…Who knows what I'll do? I've got a new outlook on a few things. I have some ideas."

"As long as it's for the right reasons, I'll support your decisions. I know you well enough to know you aren't rash."

"I don't know what the right reasons are, but I think I went at medicine too hard. It was all consuming. I lost a lot of my life—a lot of time I can't get back," he said, staring down at their joined hands, taking comfort in the warmth she tried to give. "When I look back over my adult life, it's all a blur. I can't help feeling like I've missed the important parts."

"Burnout is real, honey. Your whole family's extremely proud of you. I know Avery was…and Kane. They both worried about you taking on so much. Did they tell you?"

He shook his head. They had most likely tried, but he was lost to his world.

Instead of continuing down this rabbit hole, he let go of her hand and patted her thigh. "He's waiting." He nodded toward her driver. "You should go."

Though his grandmother was the most aware person he knew, she seemed surprised to see Mr. Kinkaid there. The sternness was back in her tone when she raised her voice to say, "I didn't call for you."

"Nonnie, he's good at his job," Robert said, intervening on behalf of the man who had been employed by his Nonnie for all of Robert's life. He took her elbow, trying to help her rise to her feet.

She let out a sigh and did finally let him help her up. "I don't like to be rushed. He knows that."

"He's just standing there at the ready," Robert said, taking slow steps toward her waiting car. "I like that he looks out for you. I'm glad he's traveling with you now. You need someone you trust with you."

Kennedy gave Robert a hard-edged side-eye. She was so damned independent that he was certain he was about to be called out for implying she needed help, but his grandmother surprised him when she said, "Sophia called this morning. She thinks you're romantically interested in the young man from the honor guard…"

A loud bark of laughter burst from his chest, startling her to a stop. He nudged Kennedy forward, taking bigger steps toward the waiting driver who had edged closer to open the back door. Robert motioned the man to take her arm. "No, no, no, we're not having this conversation. Come get in the car."

She halted him, clasping his arm with surprising strength, not letting him go as her steps slowed to an almost stop. "Why? I want to know if you have someone in your life. I want you to be happy. You need to find yourself a nice young man, settle down, and think about a family of your own. Courting a military man sounds very romantic. I've always loved a man in uniform." A dreamy look flitted over her face before her expression changed to one of indicating she expected a reply. The tips of his ears heated under her assessing stare. She didn't budge and neither did he.

Why did every member of his family have to be so frustratingly single-minded and hardheaded? Sophia was his biological mother and had been in his and Autumn's life since their birth. They had a healthy relationship based on the circumstances of his birth. She never considered herself their mother in the traditional sense; neither had he or Autumn. She was more like a proud aunt who had gallantly picked up the pieces after his fathers' deaths. He loved his extended family, even when he had to remind himself of the love in times like this.

"I promise you I don't have anyone significant in my life. I haven't spoken to Landon in a month. There's nothing there between us. He's just a real good guy who was there for me when I needed him." Robert undid his grandmother's hold and handed her off to Mr. Kinkaid then took the four steps toward the open back door of the car.

"Then why does Sophia think something's there?" She did walk his way as her brow lowered, assessing him again. "I think there's something you're not telling me."

Robert rolled his eyes. How he had wound up in this conversation on this particular day, when the focus should be on breathing a sigh of relief that everything with his fathers' estate had been settled was beyond him. Even more than that, he didn't want to talk about Landon.

It had been a solid month with Landon occupying his thoughts both day and night, and the only bit of communication he'd received was a short quick-witted email saying Landon had arrived at his "badass" townhome. When Robert had received that email, he'd been so excited — too excited. He'd planned his response carefully, writing and rewriting each word, but he'd never received another response again from his sergeant.

Not receiving a reply had been a hard pill to swallow. He'd checked and double checked, dozens of times to make sure he'd given Landon all his correct contact information. If the guy was interested, he would have replied or texted or called or something by now. The rejection sucked and had certainly messed with his head, but he didn't want to give his family something else to worry about. Not necessarily on their behalf, but on his—they were suffocating in their caregiving.

"I'll see you tonight for dinner." Robert lifted a hand in a wave and walked away, reaching for the key fob inside his pants pocket.

He sure hoped Thomas, Sophia's husband, would be at dinner this evening. He'd help Robert navigate any of the matchmaking or harping they may have planned for him, and just like that, his mind filled with Landon again. The mental image of Landon's dark eyes and that sexy crooked grin hijacked his thoughts. It was enough to make his dick take notice, like it wasn't always eager to stand up at the thought of Landon. What the fuck was wrong with him?

Robert dropped down in the front seat of his brand-new Audi R8 Coupe that he'd splurged on as a rejection gift for himself and started the V-10 engine on a roar. As satisfying as the rumble was, what he needed more between his thighs was a hard, masculine body. It had been far too long since he'd had sex. But when he had gone out with the purpose of scratching that itch and found some willing partner, Robert could only see Landon every time he closed his eyes. That sexy stare, eyes dark as smoke, fringed with those long black lashes. Nobody held his interest. His dick only wanted to slide between Landon's full, wet lips.

"Move on, Robert. That's not in the cards for you," he muttered out loud, hoping it would finally sink in and stick. Instead of getting lost in the fantasy, he backed out of his parking spot. Robert decided to buy a place nearby as Minnesota was home. He had appointments to keep, no time for thoughts of Landon to derail this newfound motivation.

Landon stared at his reflection in the floor to ceiling mirrors lining the physical therapy clinic at Walter Reed as he executed a wrist curl with the weighted bar in his hand. Thankfully, his body was mending faster than he thought possible, faster than he could remember ever hearing anyone say. He wasn't sure why he was different, but he'd take it, be appreciative for it so he could get himself back to normal as fast as possible.

"Good job," Donnie, his physical therapist, said, watching his form as he performed the exercise exactly the way he'd been instructed.

"I got a little ways to go," he said, looking at his casted left arm. In the best-case scenario, it was going to be a struggle to get back the functionality he'd had before his accident, but if determination had anything to do with healing, he'd get there. Besides, based on his new Master Sergeant, he didn't need his left arm to be a hundred percent to get off his bullshit light duty job they'd assigned him at Joint Base Andrews.

Donnie chuckled at him. "I think the motivation's coming from this place. Nobody ever wants to stick around for long."

Donnie had hit the nail on the head. Landon had volunteered to help with some administrative duties in the understaffed PT clinic until he was placed back on regular duty. What he got stuck with was managing deliveries, schedules, and the cleaning crews.

Landon's gaze met Donnie's. Whatever Donnie read of Landon's menacing stare had him barking out a laugh, so loud everyone in the large room turned their way. "I bet you won't be climbing up any more abandoned towers."

"You heard about that?" Landon shot Donnie a hard stare in the mirror and his brow gave a critical arch.

"Yeah, we all did. Heard about your little talking to, too." Donnie waggled both brows and a grin split his lips as he let that secret slip.

"Yeah, that's a real ha, ha," he said dryly.

His letter of reprimand hadn't bothered him in the least. His Master Sergeant was a realist and hadn't given him too much shit for being stupid in public. Instead, he'd handed Landon a pen and said, "Sign the reprimand." Then told him two things: stay out of trouble for the foreseeable future and volunteer his time somewhere worthy in order to prove to the Air Force that he deserved to be there.

Since that had been Landon's plan, and currently what he was doing, he'd decided they probably saw eye to eye on things in life. Now all he had to do was get through the next six days, then he'd be back on regular duty, and at the end of being everyone's bitch inside this clinic.

"You'll shake us free soon." The therapist focused back on the clipboard in his hands as Landon dropped the weight.

He was overdoing the workout; he could feel his body's

exhaustion in the way his muscles quivered when he pushed them. He should go enter the stack of purchase orders waiting on him. He'd let three days collect because he hated data entry so much. No one ever had to worry about him straying off course again. Maturity had finally won out.

Chapter 9

"Granddaddy Paulie's birthday's tomorrow. I think we should go to the cemetery together," Robert said, ripping off a piece of the fresh baked Italian bread—a recipe Paulie had mastered years ago—before dipping it into the flavored olive oil La Bella Luna served; another old family recipe he had always loved. He took care to get a good helping of the freshly cracked pepper on his perfectly portioned bite before executing a quick toss in his mouth, hoping no oil dripped on the front on his dress shirt.

Man, he missed eating at La Bella Luna. They served the very best ingredients, freshly prepared just the way he liked. It didn't matter that the dinner dishes had been cleared and dessert was coming, bread this good should never go to waste.

Robert reached for the linen napkin in his lap, looking up to see every eye at the six-seat table focused on him. He didn't even have to ask why. His entire family was still treating him with kid gloves, constantly walking on eggshells around him. As far as he was concerned that needed to stop right now.

"Guys, seriously. Let. It. Go. I'm better," he said, giving each person at the table a pointed stare. His date for the evening, his grandmother, who was also the boldest of the group, looked at him with defiant disbelief. Sophia and Thomas looked cautious.

Autumn had a gleam in her eye and a sassy cock to her brow. Rodney, a longtime friend of the family and the owner of La Bella Luna for the last twenty years, sat in as Autumn's dinner partner. He, at least, looked semi-neutral. Robert decided to go with humor to prove his point and lifted a finger to his twin. "Except you, you need to be overly nice to me for as long as I can get it."

"Too late," she said, grinning broadly. "It's been a hard ten months for me. Being nice to you goes against my moral code."

"You two, don't start," Kennedy reprimanded like she always did. "I'm leaving tomorrow. Have I told you?"

"No, are you going home to New York?" Autumn asked.

"No, dear, I've decided to spend some time at the Cape. I've started painting." Kennedy's announcement effectively took every eye off Robert and landing, instead, on his grandmother. "I seem to do a better job near the turbulent tranquility of the Atlantic."

"Painting?" Robert asked, not ever remembering a time in his grandmother's life where she had ever mentioned the desire to be artsy.

"I don't remember you saying anything about painting," Autumn added, narrowing her eyes, clearly sharing his confusion over this turn of events.

"Dears, you don't know everything about me. I bought some pieces from a young artist a friend of mine suggested. He's so talented. I told him I'd always wanted to learn, and he offered to teach me. I went to Dallas over a few weekends. Now, we work by live video," she explained.

Thomas reached over, tapping the bottom of Robert's jaw, reminding him to close his gaping mouth.

"That's exciting, Kennedy," Sophia said.

"He's very nice looking," Kennedy said, turning to Robert as if she had just conjured a plan in her head. "He's gay, too. You might know him."

With all the ricocheting topic changes, Robert forced his lips together to keep from grinning. Whenever his grandmother met another gay man, she either thought they had to know one another, or she immediately tried to hook him up.

"He's so kind to spend his time teaching an old lady to paint."

"I want to see what you've been working on," Autumn said.

"Oh, honey, I'm not ready to show anyone," she said, shaking her head. "I'm not a natural, but this young man's working out my kinks."

"Nonnie, you're amazing," Robert said, finishing off the last bite of the bread, knowing he'd be taking a closer look at the artist in the very near future. "Tell us what's going on with you, Autumn. You said you had news."

His sister took a hearty gulp of the ice water. Reality sank in before she ever said a word. She hadn't had anything more than water to drink this entire evening even though the wine flowed freely with the rest of them. Autumn loved her wine, always had. Robert sat back in his seat, a little bowled over at the prospect of what this might mean. His gaze held hers. He smiled a small smile. Her shoulders squared. At the same time, the waiter came forward, placing slices of his father's signature tiramisu dessert on the table.

She didn't wait for the waiter to leave before blurting, "I'm pregnant."

"Autumn!" With spoon in hand, Sophia jumped up to wrap both arms around her, which led to a round of congratulatory hugs from all of them.

"There's more—a lot more. Sit, eat your desserts, I'll be quick." With the genuine happiness of the family, it was hard to think in terms of a lot more news. "Cam and I have decided to marry. Not a big ceremony, something quick at the courthouse—"

"Absolutely not. I agree with small and intimate, but not dingy," Kennedy said, her first bite of tiramisu halted in midair. Since that was her favorite of all the handmade desserts, Robert knew she meant business.

"Nonnie, we don't have a lot of time. We're moving permanently to Minnesota. I'm making Minneapolis my home office and leaving the DC office to Sebastian."

Robert nodded, surprised. Autumn loved the hustle and bustle of DC. She never showed much interest in moving back to their childhood home. The DC law firm had started as a partnership between Autumn and their father shortly after she finished law school. Sebastian had been with them from the beginning, so he could more than handle running the office, but that didn't change the fact that Robert was just stunned.

"There's one last thing. I've decided to run for Dad's former senate seat." This time the smile on her face was as genuine and sure as he'd ever seen. The same burst of enthusiasm had the members of the table standing again. Robert stayed back, watching his family make a big deal about her choices. He couldn't be prouder of Autumn. She was made for the political world. His father had been grooming her since she was a little girl. She'd do great. He was more than certain she would make a difference in this world, just as his father had before her.

"Oh, there's more," she said as they all took their seats again.

"Oh, honey, I'm not sure I can take more," his grandmother said, the spoon back in her hand.

"This is the easy part. Well, easy for you, harder on me. Cam and I would like to have a large family." Her face flushed with what he could only see as happiness, and she lifted her glass of ice water, taking a long drink.

"Oh, honey," Kennedy said. The wonderment in Autumn's expression seemed to hold Kennedy spellbound. "You'll be an excellent mother."

"Autumn, these are big changes," Sophia said.

"I wanted to wait until we were all together to tell everyone." Possibly the relief of venting her secrets had Autumn lifting her spoon and taking a hearty bite of the dessert. The bliss of the taste had her looking at Robert, giving him a wink he interpreted to mean their daddy had been on his A-game when he'd created that recipe.

"When's your due date?" Thomas asked.

"You're not going to believe this, but it's December seventh. Dad's birthday." She beamed as if she couldn't have planned it better. "I'll need help finding an OBGYN around here," she said to Sophia, which was right up her alley as a gynecologist.

"Absolutely. I know someone perfect; I'll get us in next week," she nodded happily, fitting herself into Autumn's good news.

"What does Cam think about all this?" Robert asked. He'd known Cam for many years. He would have never paired his lively sister with the quiet, focused physician, but clearly opposites attracted. They were perfect together.

"He doesn't say a lot." That got a round of laughter as a huge understatement. "But he's excited and on board with everything. I've tried really hard not to bulldoze all this over him." That got another round of laughter because Autumn was a force when she wanted something. Good thing Cam seemed ready to strap in for the ride.

"What about his DC practice?" Robert asked.

"He's sold his half. That's why he went back suddenly," she explained with a wave of her fork as she dug in for another bite.

"One month from now, everyone mark your calendars. We'll have a wedding on the balcony of my summer home," Kennedy announced, placing her spoon on the small plate, lifting a hand to the waiter to clear her dishes. "It'll be a lovely affair with the view of the Atlantic as the backdrop. I wanted your father to marry there. The St. Croix is stunning, but nothing compares to the Atlantic."

"Nonnie, don't go to the trouble," Autumn started.

"Of course, I'll go to the trouble." She turned toward Robert at the same moment the waiter tried to sneak between them to clear her plate, causing his grandmother to give an irritated huff and shoo him away. "Call my driver, dear. There's much to be done."

Autumn rolled her eyes, sitting back in her seat. "Nonnie." She looked hard at her grandmother who was standing, ignoring her wishes completely while pointing down to her purse, silently instructing Robert to hand it to her.

"However this plays out, we'll make sure we're free. My vote is a summer trip to the Cape sounds amazing," Sophia said, placing her napkin on the table beside her plate, turning to Thomas. "Are you ready?"

"Whenever you are," her husband replied.

"Just let her do it," Robert urged Autumn when she looked like she was digging in her heels, preparing her protest.

"I'm thinking an afternoon wedding…"

Autumn's protest didn't matter. Kennedy was already in preparation mode. Robert rose to walk her out when Sophia stopped him.

"We'll follow her out." Sophia looked over at Rodney who was getting to his feet too. "Put this on our tab?"

"Tonight's on me," Rodney said, gathering some of the remaining dishes off the table. "I needed the Adamses back home. It's been a great night."

"Thank you, Rodney. I always liked you," Kennedy said, turning away from the table, and with slow, sure steps, she started for the front doors, leaving them all behind.

"I got her," Rodney said, putting the dishes back on the table. "Mrs. Adams, hold on." He was once a young, twenty-something bartender who had been with La Bella Luna since the beginning. Rodney had to be in his mid-sixties by now. His steps were a little slower getting to Kennedy, but he extended an arm, which she took, and they walked toward the front doors.

"Honey, we're so happy for you. I love this new direction." Sophia hugged Autumn tightly. "I'll be in touch. I'm glad we did this tonight." Sophia's attention turned to Robert. She stepped around Autumn, giving him a quick, loving hug then rearing back, keeping him in the circle of her arms. "Now it's your turn to find someone. What about that airman you were reading to?"

"Why do you even know about that?" Robert asked, throwing a hand and an accusatory expression Autumn's direction. Sophia shot him a sheepish glance and let him go. "We're family. She should tell me these things. I understand you two aren't talking right now. My advice to you is to just take a chance. See what's there. Life's too short and you're certainly not getting any younger."

Both his hands went to his heart. Her arrow couldn't have taken better aim. "Oh Lord, now I'm *old*? You're doing wonders for my ego." That got the desired laughter and earned him a kiss on his cheek before he and Autumn were left at the table alone. Autumn wasted no time reaching for his untouched dessert then plopping down in Kennedy's abandoned chair.

"Sit with me," she said, motioning with her fork then digging into her second piece of tiramisu before her bottom fully settled into the seat. "I've started craving this. It's so good. I ordered several slices last week. I'm going to gain a million pounds."

"Well, don't do that," Robert teased, reaching for his glass of melted ice water. "Keep it under forty pounds. I should say less, but you only live once."

"Right? That's what I say." She took another heaping bite, rolling her eyes as if heaven had actually landed in her mouth. "You know, I told Cam I wanted lots of children because I want them to have a big family. I don't ever want my children to feel as lonely as we feel right now—or I feel, I don't want to put feelings on you that you might not have."

Like normal, they were so in sync with one another. She nailed how the world had gotten much smaller since their parents had died. Robert put the glass down and reached out, patting her thigh. "I'm sorry I haven't been around more."

"It's not that." She held the full fork midair. "I realized I took us for granted. We were a really great family. They gave us so much love and everything felt complete. I loved our life. I miss my family; I miss it all so much. It's not been the same since Granddaddy Paulie left, but we were young, and Daddy tried hard to make sure our lives were full. I don't want what I feel right now for my children or yours if you have any."

"I don't see children in my future. Hell, I can't even find anyone who wants to go out with me," Robert said with a huff, sitting back in the seat, crossing one leg over the other.

"You can find a date anytime you want one." She again moved the fork back and forth to her mouth. He wished what she said was true. "I wanted you to bring that airman home with you. He looked so…" She dreamily looked away as the fork paused again halfway to her mouth. "Dreamy. He looked dreamy, like the pictures of the soldiers in the movie *Grease*. Remember them? He has that strong jaw and full lips."

"When did you see him?" he asked, knowing there'd not been a single time he'd shared anything more than Landon's name with her.

"A guy helps my brother out of the worst funk I've ever seen, of course I'm going to search for him," she said in a tone indicating he might be the dumbest person on the planet. Even with his need to keep Landon to himself, tucked away in that private place where no one could mess with the memory, he decided Autumn had a point. If the tables were turned, he'd want to thank the person who helped Autumn.

"Yeah, he's nice looking," he grudgingly admitted, intentionally understating the beauty that was Landon. In fact, the man might be the most gorgeous guy he'd ever seen.

"Better than that." Autumn sat back, taking a deep breath. She looked down at the almost empty plate before pushing it away as if it no longer held power over her and turned her full attention to Robert. "So why didn't you make a move?"

"I wasn't thinking about that at the time." Which was a very honest answer. How could he hit on the very man to whom he had cried? A man with intimate knowledge of exactly how weak he'd been. He absently rubbed at the twinge of pain that scraped across his heart.

"Are you thinking about him now?" she asked, lifting an eyebrow.

"No… I don't know. Yeah, I guess. Doesn't matter though. He's not interested," Robert said, grabbing his fork then reaching for the dessert plate, taking the bite Autumn left behind. Landon stressed him out, totally pushed him to dysfunctional eating.

"Why do you say that?"

"He has all my contact information and has made zero moves, which is outlined in the first chapter of the he's-not-into-you playbook. I've thought back over the time we shared; he never gave me the interested vibe. He was just kind when I needed it the most." Again, another very honest answer on a subject he didn't want to talk about.

"So, you're thinking about him." She looked thoughtful before she asked, "How's he doing with his rehab?"

"I hear really well. He should be released to full duty soon, get back to his life," Robert explained. Robert had continued to pull strings after Landon had arrived back in the States. He'd gotten him the best care money and connections could provide. From the latest reports, it seemed to be working well for Landon.

"You're checking up on him?" Her brows lifted in question and a slight smirk curled the corners of her lips. Of course, she'd be leading him, trying to get him to whatever point she wanted to make. She did things like that all the time, making him say way more than he was comfortable confessing.

"Autumn, just stop. That ship's sailed. Focus on this wedding you're apparently having." Luckily, for him, that instantly changed the subject.

"Ugh, Nonnie's so frustrating. How can I get her to understand the word *no*?"

He laughed straight out loud. How many times had they had this very discussion over the course of their lives? The problem, Autumn and his grandmother were cut from the same cloth. Neither of them would ever back down. "You can't. Besides, she needs this diversion. Just go with it."

"So, what're you doing now?" Autumn asked, then let out a nice long yawn. "Unemployment seems to suit you. Is medicine still out of the question?"

"Most likely, at least for now," he said, lifting a hand to gain the waiter's attention as he reached for his wallet. The waiter came to the table, and Robert handed him his credit card.

"Sir, the meal's on us tonight." The waiter lifted two hands as he stepped away, refusing his credit card. "Your family's legendary here. Paulie's picture still hangs proudly over the kitchen. He looks ready to yell at any given moment."

"Oh, I'd love to see that," Robert said, his grin broadening, remembering his rough and ready grandfather. Paulie had been that way with everyone except him and Autumn. His deep, thick accent always soothed as he spoke to him and his sister.

"Me too," Autumn said as if they had been given an invitation.

"I'm sure Rodney won't mind. Come this way."

Autumn grabbed her purse as they followed the waiter, a route they had taken thousands of times over their lives. Time had modernized the decor, but pockets of memories still assailed him. The time he and Autumn had snuck their first sips of liquor behind the bar at his dad's fiftieth birthday party. The time he and Autumn played waiter to an empty dining room—that had always been Robert's dream job as a small child. When he grew up, he either wanted to become a chef like his father and grandfather or wait tables in this very restaurant. That dream ended when Robert fumbled a tray filled with empty dishes right outside the kitchen door.

Paulie had given him strict instructions not to play with anything breakable. He hadn't listened. The dishes crashed to the floor, and Paulie started yelling from deep inside the kitchen. He came barreling through the swinging door and stopped short when he saw Robert there with big tears welling in his eyes. Paulie's face softened even as his daddy's face held a pointed anger as he came into the dining room right behind Paulie.

His grandfather scooted him away, taking him off toward the back, far away from the trouble he deserved to be in. Paulie told him that night he should start another dream and stick with the sciences where he excelled in school. Maybe that was his first inclination of a career in medicine. Paulie had also taught him to cook, not dashing all his hopes for the future.

Autumn reached for him as they started through that same swinging door. He almost didn't take her hand, so tired of all the attention his down feelings had created, but he realized, this one wasn't for him. Her red-rimmed eyes looked back at him and held his for a moment. Clearly, she was reliving her special memories just as he was. He took her hand, letting his thumb brush across hers as they stepped inside a kitchen that instantly jolted him back in time.

The hustle and bustle of the busy staff felt and sounded the same. The frantic scurry to achieve the perfect dish each and every time was still first and foremost at La Bella Luna. Nothing had really changed, even the feeling of pressing tightly against the wall to try and stay out of everyone's way as they rushed about. The excitement he felt every time he entered this kitchen still held true today.

"Take a look around," Rodney said, moving past them into the kitchen.

The voice in this kitchen wasn't booming or gruff like Paulie's had been, but it was assertive, robust, and young. A woman, who commanded the kitchen with a mix of English and Italian.

"Look up." They lifted their eyes to see a picture of Paulie, his spoon raised, his white toque, his chef's hat, crumpled in his fist at his hip, his face masked with that scowl that made the smallish man seem ten feet tall. Robert immediately laughed. He remembered the look well. What a mood-lifter. Autumn's grin followed.

"I miss him," she said, though her voice broke and her smile faltered slightly.

"I do too." Robert lifted his phone and snapped a picture of the photograph hanging on the wall.

"Wanna go to the back?" Autumn asked hesitantly, not budging an inch in that direction.

"Nah, I've seen enough," Robert said, unsure of what it would be like to see the back-office part of the restaurant. To see their nursery turned playroom turned small library for after-school homework. A lot of their young lives had been nurtured within the old walls of this loving family restaurant.

"Me too. Let's get out of here," she said, leading the way out of the kitchen. At the front doors of the restaurant, she grabbed his arm, stopping him from fully stepping into the parking lot. "Robert, I want you to get in touch with Landon for me."

"Stop. Please. Sailing ship," he reminded. She looked ready to argue, and he placed two fingers on her lips, then kissed her on the cheek. "Go home. Goodnight."

Robert turned on his heel, heading to the parking space up front where he and Autumn had parked side by side. At the driver's side door, he looked over to watch her get inside her car. If only he thought calling Landon would change things. He lifted a hand and gave her a smile. She returned the wave.

"Call him!" she shouted before closing her door. Of course she'd have the last word.

Chapter 10

Just as Landon had done every single time he entered Robert's townhome over the last month, he tossed the keys on the tray by the front door and stared at the super tidy, richly decorated living room and kitchen. Hardwood floors polished to a high shine made the room glow. The contrast of the dark wood floors and white marble accents made the place look like a picture on the cover of one of those fancy home magazines.

That same first awestruck moment of realizing he was staying in such a gorgeous place still crept up on him and left him overwhelmed. Men like Robert Adams were few and far between, and he was honestly very grateful for the help.

The open floorplan had a spacious gourmet style kitchen with a long granite-topped island separating the two rooms, making the downstairs the exact right setup for entertaining. This place was perfect and fit the doc to a T.

As homey and comfortable as the place looked, it didn't seem as if anyone had ever lived there. That had really gotten to Landon. He spent lots of time figuring out how Robert's barely lived in townhome felt like an old cozy blanket that he'd love to curl up in. Especially with furniture that looked fresh from a delivery carton and a kitchen full of pots and pans pristine enough they'd likely never been used for any real cooking. The refrigerator had nothing more inside than a bottle of amino acids and a package of coffee beans.

Maybe the warmth came from the pictures. The walls and tables held personal knick-knacks and frames with images that allowed for small glimpses into the doctor's life. Pictures of his fathers and grandparents—Landon recognized the people from Avery Adams's books. There were shots of his sister and who he guessed might be their biological mother.

Interestingly enough, the pictures that he kept coming back to were the shots of Dr. Adams with other men. One looked like a college-aged Robert surrounded by teammates. Landon couldn't identify the sport, but they'd won big by the size of the trophy. Another was of an older Robert, maybe mid-twenties, on a fishing boat the size of a small yacht. Three fishermen wore big prideful smiles, one being Robert. All held a large catch of the day. There was no way to know which of them had actually caught the giant fish.

Another picture that captured his attention had to be a love interest. It was a snapshot of Robert and another man, both dressed in tuxedos. In all the pictures, Robert's natural handsomeness shone through, but in this one, in clothes that looked made for his body, he looked spectacular. Robert was truly gorgeous in every way. The expression on his face, the unguarded look and bright smile—yeah, that one did it for Landon. He had snapped a picture of the photograph, just to make sure he always knew exactly how Robert looked in the one shot.

Just like Landon had done every day since he'd moved in, he bypassed the living room and went upstairs to the spare bedroom. He pretty much lived in that room and spent all his time there. As much as the house needed people, he wasn't the one to do that.

The first day he had arrived, the housekeeper who answered the door already knew his name—that had been surreal. But he'd taken it in stride. He'd gone out and explored his surroundings, excited to discover he was in walking distance of everything. That was a nice bonus, and from what he could tell, the neighborhood was a mix of young and old with different ethnicities. They all seemed to live in harmony in their fashionable walking shorts and knit tops.

But the number one thing on Landon's ever-growing what-the-fuck list was the Cadillac CTS-V Coupe sitting in the garage. The key fob had arrived by courier on the same evening he had arrived at the townhome. He almost couldn't believe his eyes when he read the note, written in Robert's efficient handwriting, letting him know he was welcome to use the car. Landon had dropped the note on the counter and rushed to the garage. After having an internalized shit fit over the vehicle, all he could do was shut the garage door and never dare open it again. No matter how badly he wanted to accept the offer, there was no way he could repay all the kindness he'd already been given. He sure as hell couldn't pay the damages if he wrecked the expensive loaner.

Behind the closed door of his guest bedroom, Landon immediately snagged the remote control off the nightstand and turned on the television. The background noise helped absorb the loneliness he'd experienced lately. He didn't bother to check the channel or adjust the volume from whatever he had watched this morning.

After stripping to his T-shirt and underwear, he picked up his laptop and dropped down on the bed. Another habit he needed to break was how he checked his personal email at least fifteen times a day. There was a message from his dad, which was actually from his mom. Quickly doing the math, he calculated the time difference between Texas and Germany. He hadn't told his family about his accident or that he was back in the United States yet. He didn't want them to worry, and he didn't want to have to explain how he ended up in this condition. Outside of a straight-up lie, he just couldn't stand to hear the disappointment that they'd have in him for fucking something up again.

Landon rubbed his sternum and groaned because not telling them caused him guilt. What the hell? He was too young to be having all this guilt. Landon scanned his inbox for Robert's name, bypassed all the incoming mail from other people. He frowned, his brows descending into a hard V as he once again felt the sting of disappointment.

Robert confused him. Hell, his own feelings confused him. For fuck's sake the man starred in his dreams every single night. He wasn't sure he actually went a solid minute throughout the day that he wasn't thinking about Robert in some way.

Somehow, Landon and Autumn had struck up a friendship. They had exchanged several emails over the last month. He would be forever thankful for her kindness too. She was friendly and open and talked about her brother freely. She even sent a photo of Robert sleeping in the reclining chair at her apartment. He liked Autumn. She was sweet and funny, very intelligent, and for some reason, determined not to lose track of him. In contrast, her brother had gone radio silent.

It shouldn't bother him, but it did. He shut the lid and tossed the computer on the bed, staring at the wall in front of him. It was the only wall in the place that didn't have a picture on it.

"Get a grip," he said to himself and pushed off the bed. He was driving himself insane. There was a whole world waiting outside of these walls. He needed to shower and go find a date. Hell, he had his phone. He could swipe right. He'd need to go someplace else to have sex, though. Bringing anyone back to this room wouldn't feel right. Robert probably wouldn't care, but Landon did.

Maybe he'd drive that fancy Cadillac. That thing alone was sure to get him laid. He smirked to himself as he headed to the shower. As if he'd actually let himself do any of that.

Robert tossed his keys on the desk in his hotel suite, his chest still heaving from the workout he'd just had. As much as he'd wanted to lighten up on his diet, sneak in some bad choices here and there, he sucked at cheating. His punishment for the less than four bites of one of the best rib eye steaks he'd ever had was two extra miles on the treadmill. He'd logged six miles tonight. Funny, the amount of help jogging provided for his depression equaled how much he didn't want to do it anymore.

Being a creature of habit, Robert took a seat at the desk and opened his laptop. He lifted his arm, wiping the sweat with his shirt sleeve before opening his email program. He scanned his inbox and his heart sank: mostly junk mail, nothing worth opening. Robert rocked back in the chair and stared at the screen. Disappointment creeped through him.

"Move on."

That was good advice. Yet he didn't budge from his seat.

"You need a life."

Again, a solid nine out of ten on the scale of good advice, and he still didn't move.

"If you're not going to do either of those, then go take a shower. You stink," he said, lifting his eyes to the mirror on the wall behind the laptop.

He spun the chair around and got to his feet. A shower was exactly what he needed. Maybe he could wash all these confusing thoughts away. He had started for the bedroom when he stopped and turned back to the laptop. What if he reached out? Literally every person in his life wanted him to be with Landon. Of course, they didn't know anything about the man other than his generous act of volunteering to guard his father's casket overnight, well past the responsibility of his shift as honor guard.

Robert needed some friends with testosterone. All these females were suffocating him with all their in-depth analyzing of everything about him.

Landon had been his friend. He hoped they could be again. Robert went for the laptop only to force himself to pivot away again. "He's obviously not into you. Don't beg."

Screw it. He wasn't above begging. Maybe they could turn into friends with benefits. At least, he'd get to let off steam. Besides, he needed to go to DC to meet with the library committee and start putting his life back together. Robert sat in front his laptop and opened a new message. After a long heavy exhale, he began typing.

Chapter 11

Landon flexed in the mirror, a big silly grin spread on his lips before he busted out into a full laugh. He shook his head. His body looked deformed. He'd worked out hard to get back on his feet, but the result was a body that could be a before and after picture all in one. His physical therapist had made such a big deal out of giving the bone of his still casted arm time to heal that he'd been careful not to overuse that arm. Based on his reflection, he had followed the advice a little too well. Now, he just looked ridiculous. The arm without the break had a bicep bulge made for a fitness magazine. Above the cast on the other was almost as scrawny as a pre-Captain America Steve Rogers. He could only imagine how the muscles had atrophied under the cast. Once he had finally shed the cast, he'd have his work cut out for him.

A ding from his computer drew his gaze as if he could see the computer through the bathroom wall. At the soft sound, hope and anticipation nagged at him until he turned around, drawing the haphazardly tied towel off his waist.

His connection to his laptop drew him forward as his heart thumped faster, vibrating against his ribs. Landon tilted his head to the side as he approached. The lowered lid to the laptop should have put the computer in sleep mode. He grabbed the device and dropped down onto the edge of the bed. When he lifted the top, the normal security entry code didn't initiate. Instead, Robert Adams's name flashed in his inbox.

Drawing his lip between his teeth, his nerves threatened to choke him. Landon sank his teeth into the flesh, hoping the move would inhibit his excitement. Landon might say he had wished the email there with all the thinking he'd been doing about Robert, but he'd been wishing for thirty damn days.

Landon gripped the laptop carefully, as if he were handling precious fine china, and scooted back to the headboard. His heart rate sped up as he touched the screen to open the message.

Landon,

I'll be back in DC in a few days. Are you free for dinner?
Robert

Landon only thought his heart had been beating fast before he read the words. Now, it stampeded like he'd come in first in an Iron Man Triathlon and the excitement had released an endorphin overload in his brain. He took a deep breath then read the email again. What did it mean? Asking him to dinner… Like a date? Why would Robert ask him on….*shit.*

Not a date. It was probably a polite way to give an eviction notice, a way to gently let him know he had overstayed his welcome.

Crap. His chin hit his chest in shame. With two simple sentences, his emotions had run the gamut, from one extreme to the next. He should get whatever it was he had hoped to happen between the two of them out of his head. Of course he had overstayed. Robert had offered his home for a short stay not a permanent move in.

"Dammit!" He hadn't found a place to live because he fucking liked being among Robert's things. Even though Robert wasn't physically in the house with him, the connection to the doctor remained strong. Was he fucking crazy? He seriously needed to get on with his life. This wasn't healthy behavior. Even the damn feather coincidences Robert had mentioned screwed with Landon's head. Several times he'd walked into this house to find a feather haphazardly placed between the front door and the guest bedroom. The first time it happened, he'd shrugged it off even though he couldn't figure out where the feather had come from, but he hadn't given it much thought until it happened more than once.

Landon dropped his head back until it hit the headboard where he wanted to bang it over and over to knock some sense into all his weird actions and continuous lusting. He knew how this would work. Dinner would be a place for Robert to ease into a polite conversation as to Landon's exit plans.

The pain in his heart made him frantic. He'd known this day was coming, but he hadn't known it would feel so final.

If he didn't answer, would that give him a few extra days?

"Fuck no!" he growled. He should reply to this email and say he'd be out of here tomorrow. He nodded to affirm his thought, but both his head and his heart played a part in his refusal to say those words to Robert.

Be honest. Tell him you have feelings. Tell him you want a date, not an eviction.

In the end, his and Robert's vastly different places in life held him at a distance. Begging wasn't his thing, and he made his fingers move to type those words. The sooner he did this, the sooner he could get on with his life.

I can be out of here tomorrow, if that's what you need.

Sadness and a deep sense of loss overtook him as he pushed send. What the hell had he thought would happen here? *Think toward the future, Landon. You need a new game plan.* His heart hurt, and it made it hard to think straight.

Okay, so he could get a hotel room for a couple of days until he figured shit out. The ding of a message in the inbox drew his eyes down to the screen. If he didn't open the email, maybe his heart wouldn't shatter into a million pieces when Robert thanked him for moving out.

Did this make him one of those weird squatters who parked themselves in someone's home while they were gone?

Wait, was he a squatter or a stalker?

Shit. Landon again touched the screen to open the message. All the self-doubt and self-reprimand didn't matter. His heart was in his throat as he read each word.

There's no reason for you to leave. Stay as long as you like. I've booked a room downtown within walking distance to several meetings I have planned—it's easier access for me. If you're not free Monday evening, then perhaps Tuesday or Wednesday? Let me know your schedule.

What? Robert had booked a room when he owned this place, his home, that happened to be a few miles from anywhere in downtown DC? What was up with that? Was it believable to book a hotel room to be closer to planned meetings?

Landon didn't know what to make of it. The doctor was very health conscious, seemed environmentally aware, and the traffic was a motherfucker to deal with. Still, was it worth staying in a hotel instead of his own home?

Landon started to ask that very question, going as far as typing the words, but stopped himself from pushing send. The doctor was a direct guy. If Robert wanted him to leave, he'd say it. Right?

Maybe.

Maybe not.

This newfound insecurity was a fucking killer, and he didn't know what to say in reply.

As he warred with himself, another email message came through.

If you're busy, it's fine. We can have dinner another time.

Clearly his hesitancy was being interpreted as though he were putting him off. He didn't want that. No matter what their relationship, Landon wanted to spend time with the doc. He just wasn't sure what was happening here.

Fingers flying as quickly as he could type, he replied.

It's not that. Whatever night you want to have dinner is fine by me. Where I'm getting stuck, I mean, what I don't understand is why you're staying in a hotel when you have a perfectly good unused bedroom here. If it's because I'm here, I can leave. No harm, no foul—I promise.

He waited maybe two minutes. Two minutes that crawled by and left him feeling anxious and uncertain before a new email popped into his inbox.

Honestly, I didn't want to assume or crowd you. I gave you the townhome for as long as you need, however long that is—no rush. I'll look forward to Monday night. There's a steakhouse close to you. I believe it's the Bourbon Steak House. How does that sound?

There was so much in those six sentences that Landon decided to tackle the last one first.

What would you eat if we went to the steakhouse?

He had never voluntarily turned away a steak dinner. Even

more telling was that he'd never in his life put anyone before himself—not one time. It wasn't in his nature.

What the fuck was going on with him? He pushed away the little voice in his head that whispered Robert's name as the answer to his question.

Impatiently he clicked the refresh button to see Robert's new reply.

Then maybe we could go down to Farmers Fishers Bakers. My friends say they have good steaks, and I can find something to eat there very easily. Washington Harbor is within walking distance of the townhome. The area's fun for locals and tourists.

Clearly his dick had as much control as a horny teen as it hardened the moment Robert had asked if he were up to it. Yeah, he was definitely *up* to it. Landon rested his back against the headboard, his eyes remaining fixed on the screen. He was very close to giddy inside, his belly fluttering with anticipation, and all he did was stare at the screen trying to find something appropriate yet clever to say.

Landon didn't want them to be awkward when they met again after all this time, so he decided to turn the conversation a different direction.

You never asked how my PT's going. I'm pretty much a phenom to my therapist. Might be the fastest recovery they've seen for my injuries.

He pushed send and reread his message. He'd tried for cheeky but instead sounded arrogant. That was dumb… He wished he could call the message back.

I've been keeping tabs. I know your progress. It is impressive.

Robert had a way of saying a whole lot in a few simple words. The man had been keeping tabs on him? All the chaos Landon had been experiencing instantly settled. All the uncertainty and unrequited desire just vanished. Keeping tabs had to be a good sign. Right?

Stalking me, Doc?

He typed that back with a smile on his face.

Absolutely. I wanted you to have as good a shot as you could get. I understand you're doing very well, far better than expected.

Happiness swelled at Robert's praise. Proud that he had kicked ass in his PT, but Robert Adams didn't know him well enough to know he didn't let anything stand in his way.

What happened to privacy laws? He pushed send and immediately typed a new message. *I'm kidding. ;) I appreciate the concern.*

Ha! I have a controlling side to my personality. If I've crossed any lines, I apologize.

Robert replied right as Landon sent his second message, prompting Landon to ease his concerns again.

You didn't at all. I really appreciate what you've done.

And he did, very much. Even right now, Dr. Adams had a way of easing his natural state of anxiety.

What time should I meet you for dinner?

He waited, his fingers drumming on the edge of the laptop, willing the reply to be there a little faster.

How about six? We can meet out front of Farmers Fishers Bakers. There's lots to see. It's right off the Potomac. You may have already been there. Like I said, it's a few blocks from the townhome, but close enough to walk.

He had and nodded.

Six o'clock Monday.

He stared at the screen waiting for the final confirmation.

Great. I'll see you then. Message me if anything changes. We can always reschedule.

Yeah right, he'd risk going AWOL not to miss this dinner. His heart was happy. Sincerely happy.

I'll be there. See you then.

Landon closed the screen and placed the small laptop on the bed beside him, grinning at the television mounted to the wall. His spiraling downward mood had lifted in an instant. They were back to being friendly, and this road might lead them to a solid friendship. He wasn't in the doctor's league and never would be, but he had a thing for the man—a big hard thing, based on the erection sticking up, begging for his attention.

"Stop overthinking," he told himself. The cast restraining

his arm was turning into a big pain in the ass. He'd have to go short-sleeved. He needed clothes and a haircut. He needed a professional shave, maybe a tan, his olive skin was looking pale from being indoors so much. He'd figure it out.

Chapter 12

After three hours spent inside the men's department at Barney's and countless number of complete outfit changes, Robert stared at himself in the full-length mirror. He squinted at his reflection. Full-on critical mode had taken over as he assessed every single inch of the tight-fitting slacks and knit top the saleswoman insisted accented his body structure. He scanned all the way down to the casual loafers she'd chosen.

"I'm not in tune to the current trends. Are you sure this isn't too casual?"

"You look incredibly handsome. It's the perfect style for you," his personal shopper and longtime friend, Krista, said from directly behind him.

"And you can take in the seam through here?" He ran a finger down the side of the shirt. He didn't necessarily want the shirt to fit like a glove, because he wanted to move comfortably. He wished he could talk to the tailor himself. No, he wished he would have thought of the possibility of their date sooner, then he could have better prepared.

Robert lifted his gaze to the mirror again. He guessed this was as good as he could get and finally nodded his approval.

He had scheduled a hair appointment, deciding on some subtle highlights to help bring the summer blond out in his hair, and he needed a full manscape. He'd gone without any real grooming since his father had died. His heart twisted, but he stopped the thought right there. Not today. No negativity today. It was hard because whatever this was with Landon, it had him confused and all mixed up. He wished he could talk to his parents about his feelings. He'd always trusted their advice. What he wouldn't give to have had more time. Damn, he missed them.

Robert tugged his lip between his teeth, worrying the soft flesh. Maybe he should go back to the light blue Hawaiian shirt style. It implied easygoing, and he wanted Landon to see that side of him.

He scanned the clothes again. About halfway down, something caught his attention. A small, almost unnoticeable, feather danced as if suspended in air by unseen hands before slowly floating gracefully down to the floor. Robert bent, picking it up. If there had been any lingering doubt about his clothing choice, it ended in that moment. He shook his head at the absurdity, but it didn't change the outcome. He was doing the right thing, and this was the outfit his parents wanted him to wear. Maybe. It was hard to know if he was going crazy or if he should keep following what he could only explain as his designated sign.

"Robert, is this a go? The tailor's waiting."

The words pulled him from his thoughts. He went back into his dressing room. "We got our yes. I'll hand them over the door."

He carefully laid the feather on the blue jeans he'd worn into the store. He was collecting the feathers he had found, saving them. If anyone found out, they'd think he had lost his mind, but for some reason, it gave him comfort to believe in such a simple notion.

"Great. You'll look great for your date."

He pulled the shirt over his head, handing it over the door. "I didn't tell you I was going on a date."

"You've been my client for almost ten years, and you've

never been this picky. It has to be a date," she called out.

He chuckled under his breath. Yep, she knew him. He wasn't going to confirm or deny her observation and began unbuttoning his pants.

"Hey, have you seen any birds in here?" He had to know. All these weird coincidences had to have an explanation.

"No. Why?" Her tone sounded confused and maybe a little on the *you-so-crazy* side.

"I was just wondering," he said, kicking off his shoes.

"About birds?" she questioned. That time there was a distinct insinuation of crazy.

He really didn't feel like explaining. How could he? He'd come off as either sad or deranged, making her tone dead-on correct. "Never mind. It's crazy, and I'm going to be late to my appointment." He tossed the slacks over the door. He'd lost some weight and was between sizes, so he needed them taken in.

"I'm taking these downstairs. Leave the rest in the dressing room. I'll get them when I get back. I'll have your alterations ready by five."

"Thanks, Krista." Five o'clock was cutting it close, traffic could be a nightmare, but he didn't try to rush her. It was almost one o'clock now, and he had hours of grooming ahead of him. "Throw in a bottle of Clive Christian."

"Got it. Now get going. You're late for your appointment."

He quickly put on his jeans and sweatshirt, carefully tucking the feather in his back pocket. Glancing at his watch, he breathed a sigh of relief that the spa was just upstairs.

The lengths Landon went through to get the afternoon and evening off from his *volunteer position* were insane. He had to promise to continue volunteering at the PT clinic at least one day a week for the next month after he was released to full duty.

He'd been perfectly—sort of perfectly—okay with that. What concerned him was the tattoo parlor/barber shop the guys in PT had referred him to. Apparently, the chick that owned this place was a veteran and gave the best care to current and retired military. That was the good part. The worry came when the hard as nails female with a buzz cut of her own rounded the corner with what had to be seventy percent of her body covered in tattoos.

He narrowed his eyes behind his sunglasses. Maybe he should have given this idea more thought. To get all spruced up might have been better accomplished by going to one of those hair salons full of women, at least they would be up on the latest trends.

"You Landon?" Her raspy, harsh voice matched her exterior.

"I am," he answered, pushing down all the doubt encouraging him to bolt.

"I'm Lottie. Come on back." She jerked her head to the side, indicating the direction, and headed that way.

Landon followed, the blaring music growing louder the farther they went inside the shop. The place looked like any other tattoo parlor he'd been in, dark with lots of art and photographs on the walls. They passed several small rooms, each with a busy tattoo artist hard at work.

"What's in the bag?"

Landon had forgotten he was holding the clothes he'd purchased—blue jeans and a button-front shirt. He'd also picked up a package of socks and splurged on a pair of shoes. "New clothes."

"Want me to take 'em to the office?" They walked into an open room with four barber chairs—only one was empty. Other guys seemed to just be hanging around. When he crossed the threshold, the doorway seemed to dampen some of the hard rock music blaring from the shop speakers. The music and the '50's barber style set-up and décor made for an odd combination.

"Yeah, thanks." He handed the bag to Lottie and started for

the only free chair without being told.

"He's gettin' the works," she announced loudly to the barber who would be doing his cut.

"Got it." No other words were exchanged. There seemed to be an innate understanding of exactly what he wanted. Once the black cape snapped around his neck, he stayed in that chair for the next hour. The barber worked efficiently, doing a good job, all the while shooting the shit with all the men hanging around. It didn't take long for Landon to settle in and just enjoy the environment.

With the towel wrapped around the edge of his freshly shaved face, Landon closed his eyes and listened to the conversations going on around him. There was something about men in a barber shop and their tall tales, each one trying to one-up the other.

"I'm just going to clean up the eyebrows. Keep the shape natural," the barber said, right there in his face.

"Sure," he replied, his eyes still closed.

"And do his nose." The eye not currently being shaped popped open at the unnerving announcement. The owner stood over him, giving a critical assessment.

"Nose?" he asked to make sure he'd heard correctly.

"Nobody wants to see what's going on in there," Lottie said with such distaste he had to resist the urge to lift a hand, wanting to feel what she found so offensive.

"I've never had a problem with nose hair," Landon said, sounding lame even to himself. Didn't nose hairs protect or something?

"That you can see."

Well, hell. Self-doubt flooded him. He didn't want Robert to discover a stray nose hair. But he also wasn't sure he wanted to do whatever cleaning nose hair might entail. The conviction in her voice didn't leave him much room for argument. This was her job. She knew best. Right?

"Okay. I guess." He did want to look as nice as possible for Robert. His stomach did a flip as he thought about the other man.

Should he shave his chest? Maybe he should shave and clean up his junk…

You're such a dumbass. He's not gonna see or care about your junk. It's just dinner. But he can see the hangers out your nose.

A stick with warm liquid assaulted his nose. "What the fuck is that?" Man, he wished he wasn't lying back in the chair or he could see what was going on.

"Stop talking, and breathe through your mouth," the barber instructed.

"Give it time to harden," the shop owner said from his other side. Were they double teaming him? Another stick was inserted in the other nostril. Immediately Landon regretted this decision as his mouth popped open to breathe. He should have just passed on the service. What in the world had he been thinking saying yes to waxing the inside of his nose?

A finger poked the outside of his nose. "It's ready."

"One at a time or both together?" the barber asked. Why was the barber asking him? Wasn't this something they did all the time? He panted as his heart thumped out of his chest. He wasn't afraid of anything, not ever, until right at that moment. His fingers dug into the arms of the chair and his whole body tensed. Why had he agreed to do something so stupid?

"We gotta get it out. I'm calling it. Let's do together. Ready?" Lottie said.

"No, I'm not ready. Give me a minute," Landon said, his eyes screwed tightly shut.

"I wasn't talking to you. On the count of three. One, two, three." They yanked in unison and Landon lost his mind. The pain was sharp and excruciating. He bounded forward, dislodging the now cooling towel from his face as he tried to leap from the chair in its extended setting.

"Motherfucker!" He hissed and awkwardly stumbled, getting a good look at the whole room as a booming round of laughter filled the space. He saw red as the intensity of the pain immediately ebbed, and he marked each motherfucker in the room just in case he ever wanted to get even.

"You did that on purpose." Exactly what a six-year-old might say, and the laughter of the room proved his point.

"Calm down, sugar. We do it to all newbies," she said, tossing her waxed filled Q-tip— that had given new meaning to the words hard limit—in the trash.

"It's an initiation," the barber said, whacking him on the back, clearly misreading the depth of his anger.

"Fucking initiation to what?" he asked, going toward the mirror, hoping they had left some skin behind in their not-so-hilarious joke. "That shit hurt."

The barber held up his instrument of torture and dried wax. "But you needed it."

Maybe, once he calmed down, he might see it that way, but his nose felt raw as shit. Then he eyed the stick and his fingers went to his nose again. If he had all that up in there… Did they get it all? He couldn't be seen out like that. Robert was sure to look his normal hot self. Landon took a closer look, checking out their handiwork. The laughter grew, and he honestly didn't know why, but he didn't care either. Looking his best just got way more serious.

Chapter 13

"Drop me off right here." The driver made an illegal stop, blocking the lane. Horns sounded immediately, drivers irritated even though traffic had been at a slow crawl anyway. Robert slid from the backseat and quickly took the curb up to the sidewalk, combing the crowded walkway right outside Washington Harbor. He didn't see Landon.

The place was too big. Maybe it hadn't been the best idea to agree to meet out front. The entire area was packed with tourists and locals alike, all enjoying the summer evening. He searched over the perimeter again, slower this time, scanning everyone and everywhere. Still no Landon. Robert checked the time on his watch. *6:03* His gut told him Landon was a prompt guy. With his heart steadily thumping against his ribs, he decided to check the foyer of the restaurant, and started that direction when he heard the distant sound of a voice that seemed embedded on his heart.

"Doc!"

Robert turned, and the butterflies in his stomach took flight when he caught sight of Landon standing with a group of people on the other side of the street, waiting to cross. Robert lifted a hand, schooling his features as his body absorbed the visceral reaction he had to the beautiful, smiling man. He could no longer doubt his connection with Landon; his body hummed at the sight of the sergeant striding toward him with that long, self-assured gait. Enthralled, or maybe captivated would be a better way to describe the moment of realization and his decision to fully surrender to the draw of this intriguing, handsome man.

Slow down. He tried hard to tamp down the overwhelming desire strumming through his body. It wasn't working. His gaze never drifted from Landon as the gorgeous guy returned the wave. Robert strolled toward the intersection on instinct, just needing to be near Landon a little sooner.

All the same feelings from Germany were there, rushing over him, further inciting the butterflies already fluttering excitedly in his stomach. The connection they shared hadn't faded; it had only grown. Landon's smile widened, and in that moment, Robert knew he wanted to spend the rest of his life making Landon smile in just that same way. All he had to do was convince Landon to let him try.

"It's good to see you, Doc." Landon's dark eyes held his, and damn if that sexy crooked grin didn't melt the few lingering icy remnants of his heart.

Robert went in for a hug, something full body, because all he wanted to do in the world was to grab this man and never let go, but Landon stuck out a hand for a handshake at the same moment. Robert didn't even care that he'd managed to make their first few moments together awkward. He just needed to touch Landon.

Recovering quickly, Robert redirected his hand and clasped Landon's while following through with the embrace. He closed his eyes and breathed Landon's unique scent into his soul.

Trying to conceal the fact he'd almost come on too strong, he reminded himself there was a rule to dating. Robert patted Landon's shoulder and pulled away, still clasping the man's warm hand. "You look great. Really good. I'm glad to see it." Less than a foot separated him from Landon's lips, which drew him like a bear to honey. But he forced himself to try for some semblance of casual.

"I still got a couple of weeks to go on my arm, but otherwise,

I'm good." Landon lifted his casted arm, giving a small wave.

"Great. I heard you were an exemplary patient, going above and beyond in your treatment and attitude. I suspected you were seeing good results."

Landon's smile was contagious, and Robert grinned, hoping it didn't come off as goofy. Landon stood almost the same height; Robert was just a little taller but only by maybe an inch. He finally let go of Landon's hand, balling his fingers into his palm to keep from reaching out and touching him again. All he wanted to do was wrap this stunning man in his arms and hold him forever.

Slow down, he lectured himself, watching Landon's lips move. He needed to listen. *Focus, Adams.* "…quick walk like you said." Landon's thumb hooked over his shoulder in the direction of his townhome.

He hadn't heard most of what Landon had said because he'd been lost in those lips, he hoped he filled in the blanks well enough. "I like the area. I've got a buddy that's the general manager at Farmers. I walk down here quite a bit."

Landon tucked his hand inside the front pocket of those form-fitting blue jeans, and Robert let his gaze follow the move. His blunt nails bit into the heel of his palm as he balled his fist tighter, fighting the urge to hold Landon's hand in his, where it belonged.

"I've got reservations. We should probably go inside," he said. He made himself move, cocking his head toward the eatery. They walked side by side toward the front doors. "I requested my favorite spot, but we can eat outside if you prefer. It's very casual—plastic chairs—but you can see the river," he offered, glancing at Landon from the side of his eye because he couldn't take his eyes off the man.

"Good. I was worried I was underdressed after seeing you," Landon said, opening the door to the restaurant. That comment almost had Robert stopping in his tracks as he walked into the entryway at Landon's invitation. Robert glanced down at his own clothing.

"I aimed for casual…" he said, trying to understand why

Landon thought they were dressed any different.

"You look like a million bucks all the time. It's you, not the clothes," Landon said, chuckling at something Robert had evidently missed.

Tugging his sunglasses off, he narrowed his eyes, scanning Landon's face. Money had never been a topic between them, and Robert didn't want it to be one now. He was raised very normally and continued to live a reasonable life as an adult. Just as he tucked his sunglasses into his collar and opened his mouth to object, Landon placed a hand on his bicep, and ushered him farther inside the restaurant.

"Go inside, Doc. I meant it as a compliment." Landon's touch and the potential of a compliment had him letting it go for now. His gut told him there was more to that exchange than Landon was letting on, but he was needy enough to let it ride for now.

Holy. Fucking. Hell. Robert moved in front of him, heading to the hostess stand, and Landon's inner teenage boy jumped into high gear. His gaze traveled straight to Robert's perfectly round ass. What the scrubs and running gear hid so well was on full display right in front of him in those tailored slacks. His body heated and his mouth watered as he studied the spectacular curve to Robert's ass. His hands itched to feel the firm globes pressing against his palms. The man was incredible, and what-the-fuck-ever, Robert was chic as shit. Casual? Landon scoffed. Not one fucking morsel of Dr. Robert Adams could be considered casual.

And Landon was apparently cursing a lot. He needed to make sure that stayed in his head.

Thankfully, he had worn his shirt untucked tonight. From the time he'd watched Robert leave the car to when he'd finally gathered enough brain cells to call out to the man, his dick had gone from a level zero to a straight-up hard-as-stone ten, straining against his zipper. How he'd ever kept his dick down in Germany was a testament to the pain he'd been in. Robert Adams was the poster boy for every carnal thought or wet dream he'd ever rubbed out. The guy just did it for him in every single way.

"Hey, Robert." The hostess's greeting drew Landon's gaze up to the woman behind the counter, but she couldn't keep his attention off more important views as he lowered his eyes again. "I haven't seen you around in forever."

"Yeah, it's been a while," Robert said good-naturedly. "We have a reservation for two."

Landon glanced up again, and Robert smiled at him. A flush rushed his cheeks and he quickly averted his gaze.

"We've got your table ready. Follow me."

He trailed behind the two of them, forcing himself to survey the packed restaurant instead of Robert's ass. He'd never heard of Farmers, but it seemed down-to-earth, in a trendy sort of way. When they stopped, she directed them to a booth close to the bar and kitchen doors, not the primo spot he thought they'd have. It didn't matter where they sat; he enjoyed being there with the doctor. He scrambled into the seat when Robert extended his hand for him to sit first.

"I'll tell Lee you're here," the hostess said, handing Landon then Robert a menu.

"Don't bother him. I'll call him later," Robert replied in that polite way he had. Landon supposed it was a gentleman's way, keeping his eyes on the person he spoke to, making sure everyone around him was comfortable and settled before he took care of himself.

Landon understood this wasn't a date, but his eyes narrowed on Robert's upturned face as he wondered who this Lee was to Robert and what it might mean that Robert picked this place for their dinner.

"He'll want to know. He's been asking if anyone's heard from you. I'll get your drinks. What would you like?" she asked.

"What would you like?" Those brilliant blue eyes returned to where Landon wanted them to be, back on him. Robert's full lips curled into a warm smile.

Instantly, his mind lost focus, and he couldn't think of one single drink. He rested against the back of the booth as his brain misfired, struggling to come back online. What did he want to drink?

A fucking shot of Patrón. Then another. Then another. Followed by something whiskey related. His nerves were shot. He should have had one before he'd ever left the house.

"Are you drinking tonight?" he finally asked.

"Maybe, is it safe with your arm?" Robert questioned then nodded to his cast resting on the table. Though it wasn't a full cast, it still ran from wrist to forearm. He'd gotten used to the thing. Kept him from banging his arm around.

"Advil, only every once in a while. I'll take a Bud Light," Landon said and forced his gaze away before drool ran down his chin.

"I'll have the same." Robert flashed him that mind-dazing smile.

When the hostess left, Landon looked down at the menu, Robert's penetrating gaze proving to be too much. "What're you getting?"

"I really like the Spaghetti Squash Pomodoro," Robert replied.

Landon scanned the menu; he was having a hard time deciding, because he missed one word out of every three he read, thinking about how overwhelmed he was. "Hmmm."

Robert chuckled at him, and Landon stilled his heart before lifting his eyes. "I know that sound. I hear the New York strip and enchiladas are excellent. Lee's a master chef, amazing. Very much like my father in the way he cares for the food he's making."

Because he didn't want to hear about Lee, Landon's claws came out and he verbally swiped at the chef's ability. "Can't be as good as the enchiladas from South Texas."

Guilt sat on him like a wet blanket. What the fuck was wrong with him? Jealousy was an ass move. He wanted to take back the words. "That was—"

Robert playfully lifted his hands in a gesture of surrender. "I have no point of reference so I can't say, but my friends like them. Also, the pork ribs are good. I have eaten those but have no real frame of reference compared to Texas where I hear food has some serious flavor."

"I might just have to try the enchiladas. I don't think it's right to eat meat in front of you," Landon said then lowered his gaze back to the meatless options. "I like enchiladas, but I'm not sure I'm in the mood for Mexican."

That caused a bark of laughter, very clearly pointed directly at him. "You didn't have a problem eating meat in front of me in Germany. Besides, I don't care what you eat. You know my family's history. When you're working on diseased hearts and see the cause of so many..." A giant grin broke out across Robert's face. "I'm teasing you. Seriously, please order what you want. I don't miss meat."

"Here you go. Are you ready to order?" the woman asked, placing both beers on the table.

"Have you had enough time?" Robert asked, giving an encouraging head nod toward the menu.

He hesitated, but finally gave. "Yeah, how about the all-American burger with no cheese and fries."

"How do you want it cooked?" she asked, without writing anything down.

"Let's do medium..." He looked at Robert who slightly lifted his brows. "Or medium-well. Maybe change the French fries to coleslaw." Healthier, right? He didn't really question why he wanted to make Robert more comfortable. Maybe he should have gone with the squash deal in the meatless section. What the hell was spaghetti squash anyway?

He was in over his head with this man sitting across from him. The only refined man in his life was his uncle, and he wasn't nearly as well put together as Robert. Landon reached for his beer and tipped the bottle back, taking several gulps for nothing more than liquid courage.

Robert sounded so poised as he ordered then handed over their menus and stared straight at him. The waitress left, and they were alone again. He pushed down the urge to squirm under Robert's intense gaze. Their silence was deafening and awkward as hell. He didn't know what to say.

"Did you listen to anymore of George R.R. Martin?" Robert asked.

"That was too nice of a gift. I shouldn't have accepted it," he said, shaking his head. He had used the hell out of the e-reader, but he hadn't touched the gift card, feeling like he should give it to someone who needed it.

"That doesn't answer the question." The lilt in Robert's voice implied he was teasing.

"I told your sister it was too much. You shouldn't have. I told her you were too hardheaded to accept *no*," Landon continued to explain.

"You've talked to my sister?" Maybe the first sign of real emotion he saw on Robert's face. His eyebrow shot up and his head tilted to the side.

"Yeah. She messages me about once a week."

Robert's body language changed as he shifted positions.

"She's amazing. You two are very much alike." Landon felt like he was suddenly under the microscope, he just wasn't sure why.

"You've been talking to Autumn?" Robert asked again as if Landon hadn't answered that very question seconds ago.

"Yeah." Silence descended between them again. Landon lifted the beer bottle and took a couple more gulps. He wasn't normally tongue-tied. He'd been told a time or two that he was charming, but none of that mattered now. Robert made him insecure as hell, and he wasn't sure why he let it bother him this much. "She messages me every Sunday evening—well, the last four Sundays in a row—pretty much like clockwork. It starts a conversation that lasts a few days."

"What does she say?" Robert asked, his expression becoming hard to read. The doctor's upper lip kicked up in the corner as he reached for his cell phone in his back pocket.

"She just talks. She checks in. Is that bad?" he asked.

"No, of course not. You aren't talking to me, like you talk to her, but it's fine. She's very encouraging where you're concerned. I'm glad she's getting to know you. You'll like her." Robert's thumbs moved quickly over the keypad on his phone. Landon raised up slightly, leaning over the table, trying to see what Robert was typing, but the angle wasn't right, and he kept the phone hidden from his sight. "Did you tell her we were having dinner?"

"I did." He ran a hand down the shirt he wore. "She suggested this shirt. Found it at H&M and had 'em hold it for me. What do you think? She a good personal shopper?"

The phone lowered as Robert's eyes held his. "I think you look handsome." His smile brightened and something inviting flashed in those light eyes, but it was gone just as quick as Landon had noticed it.

He quickly fought off the effect the look had on his body and kept his eyes on Robert's. "Thank you."

Robert smiled before glancing at the phone in his hands, his thumbs moving in quick synchronization until he pressed the side of the phone and put it in his back pocket. "Autumn and I talked about you a few days ago. I told her I hadn't heard from you, and she never said she'd been in contact with you. That's a sister for you."

"I feel like I'm navigating a mine field here."

Robert laughed and extended his bottle for a tap with Landon's. He offered his up, but didn't really participate in the tap, unsure what was even going on.

"She messaged me. I didn't initiate the conversation with

her…"

Robert took a drink, a much smaller sip than Landon's, and lifted a hand. "I want you two to become friends. She's important to me, but I'm pretty sure she set me up. We were talking about you, and I hadn't heard back from you. She encouraged me to reach out anyway. She was certain I should. I didn't know if you wanted to see me or at least explore the friendship I thought we shared."

"No, I thought… I, yes, we were friends at Landstuhl—are friends." Shit, he wasn't even making sense to himself. Being called out about his radio silence took him by surprise. Guilt washed over him, and he wasn't sure why. To distract himself, he lifted his near empty beer bottle toward the waitress who nodded her understanding. "I don't know. I just didn't want to bother you. You've done so much for me. I'll never be able to repay you. I can't help feeling like it's all one-sided."

"Explain to me why you believe this is one-sided," Robert said, his eyes turning icy with intensity as he waited for a reply. An older man stepped up to the table. Big, burly, and luckily for Landon the man held two plates of hot food, saving him from answering Robert's question. Going down that path would end in an argument, again.

"Boy, where you been? I've been worried about you!" The man was apparently the chef if his uniform told the story. Boisterous and possibly Cajun from the sound of the thick accent.

The chef got a good look at Landon, placing his plate on the table in front of him while Robert took his plate from the outstretched hand.

"Why doesn't anyone ever try to contact me?" Robert's good mood and teasing words seemed to take some of the huff out of the chef's attitude. "I've been to Germany then Minnesota. I met Landon…in Germany." Robert's hand extended across the table toward him. "Landon, this is Lee, general manager, head chef, good friend, father of a godchild of mine. He lets me in here in the middle of the night to cook when I need an escape."

"And I've missed you showing up like you do. I'll let you

eat, but we're talking before you leave," Lee said, pointing at Robert then giving Landon a nod.

"Sounds great. This looks delicious." Robert dug in.

He didn't know what he had been expecting this evening, but it certainly hadn't been this friendly, down-to-earth gentleman who everyone in Landstuhl had deemed unapproachable. Robert was brilliant, an amazing listener, and easy to talk to. Not deserving of the reputation he'd been given at that German hospital. Landon just decided to go with it. He was happy the doctor seemed back to his normal self. Landon lifted the burger and took a big bite. The savory flavors exploded across his tongue. It was delicious. He took another bite, Robert chuckling at his groan of satisfaction.

"I told you the food was good."

The smile on Landon's face made Robert's body grow warm all over. He almost felt drunk. The happy kind. He was on cloud nine. They'd both been drinking, but not a lot, just enough to relax. He had set out for them to have fun and had accomplished it—with the help of the restaurant. He and Landon ended up moving to the bar, where they tested drinks created by the lead bartender, sampled desserts Lee brought out especially for them, and just had a really good time. At least Robert had, and judging from the smile directed at him, Landon had enjoyed the evening too.

"Wanna walk along the harbor?" He took the chance and asked Landon, hoping to keep the man with him a little longer. Time had flown by, and he wasn't ready to call it a night just yet. Reaching out, Robert pushed the door open for Landon, encouraging him through.

Landon's lips turned up into a smirk as he tipped his head for Robert to go first while reaching around him to hold the door. Landon was so close that Robert felt the heat of his body and got distracted by his alluring scent.

"You first, Doc." Landon's voice was a little thick and rough. The implications in that sexy growl curled around Robert's balls.

Did that mean *yes*? Robert was feeling the effects of the alcohol they'd drunk, maybe he should ask again to be sure they were on the same page.

"The harbor?"

"Sure," Landon said eagerly, but then withdrew, tucking his fingers into the front pockets of his blue jeans as he stepped away. Those moves sent mixed signals; one second Robert could swear Landon was flirting with him, and the next, he felt as if Landon couldn't get away quick enough. When the sergeant forgot and let his guard down, he was hilarious, genuine, and charming, but when Robert felt comfortable enough to test the waters and try to hold the man's hand or show Landon he was interested in more, Landon did things that sent a different message. Like tucking his fingers in his pockets or crossing his arms over his chest, making Robert rethink his approach. "It's a nice night."

"Yes, it's perfect. I'm so glad the weather cooperated. Let's go this way." Robert dropped his hand to the small of Landon's back, guiding him down the partially lit walkway right along the river, farther away from the noisy crowd. The soft sounds of the night blanketed the hustle and bustle they left behind. The lights of the nearby restaurants and streetlights reflected off the water and the moon cast dark shadows along the bank. A soft breeze blew across his skin, reminding him of all the nights he'd spent searching for answers along this path. At that time, he'd never imagined he could feel this happy again.

"I had a nice time tonight." Landon's words brought a grin to his lips.

"Me too. Best night in a long time." Robert was hyperaware of everything Landon. He knew the second Landon's hand dropped to his side. If Robert didn't do or say something, he would absolutely regret it. His nerves spiked. The butterflies took flight again inside his stomach. Overthinking the situation wasn't helping. His heart told him it was now or never. He didn't allow himself time to back out before he caught Landon's hand in his, something he'd wanted to do all night.

The moment he slid his hand around Landon's, the man

jerked away like he'd been burned and stepped away. "What're you doing?"

The shock on Landon's face stunned Robert and held him frozen in embarrassment as his world tilted and his heart dropped to his stomach. He'd messed up and now he felt stupid. How could he have misread the signs? He'd been so eager to discover everything about Landon, but he hadn't taken into consideration the real possibility that Landon might not feel the same. He'd confused their chemistry as something otherworldly. Based on the scorn in Landon's eyes and the rapid rise and fall of the man's chest, Robert had read their connection wrong.

"I'm sorry. I thought— I was trying to hold your hand. I… Did I mess up?"

"Why would you hold my hand?" He heard accusation and outrage. Oh man, this wasn't good.

"Isn't that what people do on dates?" he said simply, his heart breaking in two.

"I'm on a date with you?" Landon took another small step backward as if he'd been caught off guard by Robert's words.

"Aren't we? We just spent the last five hours having dinner and drinks. I had a wonderful time. I enjoyed spending the evening with you. Yes. I believe we were on a date. I don't…"

Landon must have found what he'd said amusing. He laughed a mocking chuckle and shook his head as he spoke. "No, Doc. There's no fairytale in which you date someone like me." Landon spun around as though he were searching for an escape route.

That was the last thing Robert wanted. He gripped Landon's elbow, stopping the sudden retreat. "Wait, please don't walk away. Explain what you mean."

The hot-blooded man reared around on him, taking several steps into Robert, almost throwing him off balance, not with his body but with the words that came out of his mouth. "I'm not sure what you want from me, Doc. What do I have to offer someone like you? Do you just wanna fuck?"

Landon was magnificent in all his indignation. Absolutely,

he wanted to fuck Landon into the mattress, but first, he had to remove whatever social stigma or economic class hierarchy Landon was trying to place between them.

"Right now, I just want to hold your hand and walk along the harbor. I see couples do it all the time. I want that with you. I don't expect anything more."

Landon studied him, searching his face with uncertain eyes as if Robert's words hadn't been truthful. Landon started to turn away then looked back at him again. Robert was serious—dead serious. But he could tell Landon struggled to understand exactly how serious he'd been. Robert stepped forward and the man backed away again. They repeated that move once more, until Landon lifted a hand to keep Robert at a distance.

"What're you saying?"

Feeling completely undone, Robert's heart demanded he do whatever it took to halt the sudden derailment of this magical night. They'd had a great evening together. Better than he'd dreamed. The connection they'd shared in Germany was right back, drawing him like a moth to a flame. All he wanted to do was get closer to Landon.

Take a breath, be patient, and don't get frantic.

He slowly drew in a breath, allowing the fresh air to fill his lungs, and forced himself to calm down.

"I need you to answer the question, Doc."

"I want this to be our first date, and I'm asking for more dates with you. I want to get to know you now that we're both healthier and located on the same side of the world. I feel a connection with you that I can no longer ignore. I felt drawn to you in Germany. The second I stepped into your room everything in my life shifted. I don't want just a friendship with you. I'm asking for more." He lifted a hand toward the restaurant, reminding Landon about the wonderful time they'd shared less than five minutes ago. "We get along very well together. You're all I've thought about for the last month. I can't get you out of my head."

Robert's words trailed off as energy charged the air. He

could almost hear the transfer of negative to positive the moment Landon grasped the meaning in his words. Their connection snapped back into place. There was no mistaking what he felt. Their attraction was a tangible, physical force. An amatory current raising the hair on the back of his neck, sending tingles down his arms. Landon shook his head as if trying to clear the haze of the recent revelation.

It was a lot to digest, but Robert would be a fool if he let Landon walk away without fighting for him. Landon was his future. Those dark eyes locked onto his, passion swirling in their depths, but the uncertainty that blanketed the sergeant's brow had Robert's breath trapped in his throat. What if Landon rejected him? Pain lanced his heart as it hammered frantically against his ribs.

Landon's hand curled into a fist, grabbing the front of Robert's shirt. Robert was wrenched forward, completely caught off guard as Landon's open mouth forcefully met his lips. Emotions arced wildly before their bodies ever connected. Landon's tongue thrust forward, demanding and eager. His casted arm locked around Robert's waist, holding him in place.

In a whiplash of emotion, Robert's head finally caught up and his heart sang its praise. Landon's mouth was as greedy and sweet as Robert had dreamed it would be. He surrendered to the passionate kiss, melting against Landon's hard body, kissing him with total abandon. Every single one of his senses flared to life as he palmed Landon's face and sucked the sergeant's tongue deeper inside his mouth, so hungry for more.

Robert took the kiss to next level when Landon tried to break free. He wasn't having any of that and slid his hands down Landon's sides, tightening his arms around the man's waist, determined to keep him right there. There was no denying the chemistry they shared or the passion that ignited in his belly as the kiss slowed. Landon drew back to look at him, his dark eyes still full of desire.

"I'm sorry. I shouldn't have done that." Landon's shallow breaths puffed across his heated skin. "I've been dreaming about kissing you." The pad of Landon's thumb stroked sweet desire with each caress across his cheek. "I couldn't stop myself."

"I'm glad you didn't," Robert replied, refusing to move away from Landon, their lips so close all he had to do was lean forward to taste their sweetness again. He was addicted, one taste was all it took.

An unseasonably cool breeze whipped around them, sending a welcome chill along his overheated skin. Landon shivered and pressed into him. Robert took advantage of the moment and bent his head again to take Landon's mouth in a softer sampling of his lips. This time the kiss was slower, and for Robert, it was a claiming. A way to show Landon exactly where he belonged—right there with Robert.

The moment didn't last as long as he'd wanted. The sounds of the busy harbor penetrated his lustful haze, and he reluctantly pulled away to give Landon his space. "That was amazing, better than I thought it would be."

"Not for me. I knew it would be that great." Landon's words came out in a sweet whisper.

"Let's walk." Robert encouraged him, gaining only a minuscule amount of space when he pulled away, but Landon wasn't about to let Robert get too far from him. His lips still tingled from Robert's kiss, and his head spun from the wonder of it all.

"Let's go back to your place," he countered. His voice sounded husky and needy, a true reflection of what Robert did to him. The doctor adjusted his hips, rubbing the thickness trapped behind those slacks against his equally hard cock. Oh, yeah, from what he could tell, Robert liked his idea a lot. "I didn't know you were interested in anything other than a friendship with me."

"I'm very interested," Robert said and stepped back as blue

eyes bored into his. "I want to do this right, Landon. At least explore what this is between us."

Landon reached for Robert's hand, almost giddy inside; he hadn't had to make that move himself. It seemed important, something to help solidify the flood of emotions.

"All right. Let's do this right." Landon slid his hands down Robert's back and over his firm ass. "I've wanted you since you showed up in my hospital room wearing those damn running shorts." Oh, how he'd wanted the man. Landon ground against Robert. The hardness pressing into him sent another wave of intense desire racing through his already overheated system. "Your ass captures a lot of my attention." He squeezed the sexy globes. "It's so perfect." Landon leaned in, nipped Robert's earlobe. "And at some point, I'm gonna be balls deep inside you, Doc." That was a promise he intended to keep.

"What're you waiting for?" Robert's words spurred him on. If they weren't in a public area, he'd already be lost in the man. Robert made him so fucking hot that he wasn't positive he could actually wait until they were home to have Robert's naked body pressed against his. He grabbed Robert's hand in his and tugged him forward.

They weren't making it very far, very fast. Every twenty or so feet, either Landon or Robert had to stop to kiss the other. Keeping his hands off Robert proved much harder than he'd thought possible.

Yeah, nothing had changed with the way his brain kept pointing out that he didn't have money or anything to offer such a fine man. Robert would wise up before too long, but Landon pushed those heavy thoughts away as Robert's hand moved to the small of his back then around his waist to draw him back against the doctor's perfect body. Refusing to let himself question what was happening, Landon worked to keep self-doubt at a distance and allowed himself to get lost in the moment.

The distance between the streetlights had increased the closer they got to Robert's house, and the darkness worked to their advantage, hiding them from any bystanders as the kisses turned incendiary. He could no more help his hands roaming Robert's body than he could help taking the kiss to the next level. Everything about Robert drew him in—the spicy scent of his cologne, the scruff of his five o'clock shadow scraping along his palms. He was already addicted to Robert's touch as the doctor's skilled hands pushed under the hem of his button-down. His body was on fire, consumed with need that only Robert Adams could relieve.

"I can't wait to get you naked." If they didn't get somewhere quick, Landon was going to lose it.

Robert's lips pressed to his one last time before he grabbed Landon's hand and towed him down the neighborhood street.

At the base of the front porch steps, Robert leaned into him, plastering himself against Landon. As Landon started to take the invitation of those perfectly formed lips, Robert held up his hand as he drew back and stared directly into his eyes. "I want to do this right, Landon. I don't want to mess it up. If it's too much or you feel we're going too fast, I want to know. Even if that means I need to leave for the night, then I will."

Yeah, right. In what world did Robert believe Landon would ever let him go? He used a bit of force to tug Robert more fully against his chest. "You aren't going anywhere, Doc."

"Good. I was hoping you'd say that, and call me Robert," he said, holding Landon's stare.

"Robert," he whispered, earning the kiss he'd been trying to get for the last several seconds.

Robert pulled away to enter a code into a keypad Landon hadn't known was even there. A buzzing sound penetrated the hushed night, lasting only a fraction of a second before he heard the lock disengage and Robert brushed past him to push it open.

"That's cool as shit," he whispered. "Beats digging for a key."

"Yeah. Comes in handy," Robert said with a wink, drawing Landon against him for a heated kiss before pushing him through the front door.

Chapter 15

Landon wheeled around to face him the instant the door shut. Their lips met again, this time behind closed doors. Landon's hand roamed his chest before sliding up to capture his jaw, controlling the kiss.

Dazed by the intensity flaring along his spine, Robert submitted, allowing Landon to set the pace. If Landon kept kissing him like this, his mouth would be tender in the morning, hopefully his ass would be too. Robert reached to unbutton Landon's shirt, eager to get him naked. Landon's hand drifted from his face and joined in tugging at their clothing, his actions almost frantic. Robert was desperate to feel Landon's skin against his.

Their eyes locked as he pushed the shirt from Landon's shoulders and ran his palms over all that warm naked flesh. The man tempted him. He gazed into Landon's eyes and let his fingers roam. Even with the cast on his forearm, he felt strong and solid. Robert brushed his thumb across Landon's nipple, which hardened at his touch. He lowered his head to lick across the responsive bud, eager to feel it against his tongue. He lifted his gaze to see Landon's dark eyes following his movements.

He dropped his gaze to Landon's chest as his heart jumped

to his throat, keeping his words trapped. The tattoo just above Landon's heart held him spellbound. A single feather with the words 'Dare to Fly' inked in elegant script across his pec. The words… He couldn't believe it. His heart dropped back into place but raced faster. How oddly perfect. Ever so lightly, he traced the feather tattoo with his thumb.

"Dare to fly," he whispered as he glanced up at Landon, those dark eyes watching him intently when he bent to place a kiss on the tattoo. "When?"

"About ten years ago. I saw it and had it inked that day." Landon had to know the tattoo only added to the connection Robert already shared with the man.

Too many emotions swirled in his head as he rose, eager to claim Landon's mouth again. Robert forced his tongue deep as he tightened his embrace. Landon moaned and pressed his hips forward, grinding their hard cocks together. Reaching between their bodies, he undid Landon's jeans to give himself enough room to slip his hand down the back of the man's pants and grip his firm ass, forcing their bodies closer together.

He worked his fingers between Landon's ass cheeks and squeezed. Oh, heavenly father, he was going to come from all the rutting and dry humping. Not only his body but his feelings were inflamed with need.

"Upstairs." He nudged Landon toward the stairs, attempting to get them to the bedroom as quickly as possible. Landon caught on, not wasting any time toeing off his shoes and heading up in front of him.

Landon's pert backside remained perfectly within his grasp. With every step, Landon's pants slid farther down his slim hips and the top of his underwear peeked out invitingly. The deep blue of the band highlighted the olive skin of Landon's muscular back and delectable ass. So sexy and too damn irresistible. His fingers itched to touch all that flesh.

They'd only made it halfway up before the last of his willpower fled. Robert grabbed the belt loops on Landon's pants and drew him back down a step. "So damn tempting I don't think

I can wait."

"Then don't." Landon turned, slamming his mouth down on Robert's. He opened, welcoming the kiss as Landon shifted into him. Landon's fingers raked across his scalp then tightened roughly in his hair at the back of his head, forcing their kiss to deepen. A delicious twinge of pain edged with urgency fueled the kiss, making his dick harder than stone.

Robert reached down and unbuttoned his own pants, slid the zipper open, quickly working the material down his hips before pushing his underwear below his balls. Landon's hands dropped from his head to grip his ass. He liked the man's hands on him.

"Want to feel this in me," Robert growled as he palmed Landon's thick cock through his clothes. Landon's breath hitched as Robert gave a firm squeeze to emphasize his request. Those sexy hips flexed in response, and he pounced, pinning the irresistible man against the wall of his stairwell as he feasted on his mouth.

Fire and lust rushed through his veins as their tongues danced and twisted in unison. The press of Landon's firm body felt so damn good against his. Greedy little noises escaped Landon as he returned the kiss with heated enthusiasm.

He pushed at Landon's pants, shoving the material and those sexy blue briefs down his muscular thighs. Landon's cock sprang free, and Robert dropped to his knees right there on the stairs, eager to taste the man as he undressed him.

Drawing back far enough to appreciate the whole picture, he took in the beauty of a fully naked and aroused Landon. The light-colored cast stood in contrast to the richness of Landon's skin tone. The man was built—not overly muscular, but Robert could tell he spent a lot of time in the gym, working on his body. Landon's thick erection jutted proudly from a dark thatch of neatly trimmed hair. Plump and veiny, the man's cock twitched under his gaze, and he couldn't wait to feel it push into him. He helped Landon with his socks and sat back admiring the man once again.

"Gorgeous," he praised, running his hands up the back of

Landon's legs, the fine hairs tickling his palms. His fingers skimmed possessively over the man's ass as he leaned in and nuzzled Landon's groin. "Just one taste," he promised, pressing his lips to the warm skin.

Landon shuddered as Robert took him in his fist. What a heady feeling, knowing he held that much power over Landon just made his desire shoot up tenfold.

Dragging his tongue across the flared head, he lapped at the leaking tip and moaned at the salty taste. The smell of their arousal wrapped around him and his hole clenched at the thought of that thick head pushing deep into him. Landon's hand came to rest on his hair as he took Landon's length into his mouth and bobbed his head.

"Robert." The needy, reverent tone made his stomach flutter. Lifting his eyes to Landon, he gazed at his sergeant as he swallowed him over and over again. Landon's legs shook, but Robert continued to work Landon's cock with his fist and his mouth. His own dick throbbed at the sight of Landon watching him, his kiss-swollen lips parted, his eyes burning with desire.

"Let's go to your room." Landon gently, but forcibly pushed Robert's head back and urged him to his feet. "I want your ass," he murmured, sending a shiver of lust down Robert's spine.

He crawled up Landon's body, losing his shoes and ridding himself of the rest of his clothing, which didn't take long. He pressed his lips to Landon's while wrapping an arm around his waist. He walked them up the remaining stairs then the few steps to his bedroom.

The kiss deepened with Landon fumbling with the doorknob and shoving open his door. They fell on the bed in a controlled rush, both panting and trembling. Careful of Landon's arm, he situated them as the kiss continued. Landon's mouth, so sweet and intoxicating, drew him in with every swipe of his tongue. Robert hadn't ever been this needy, but he wanted Landon in him in the worst way.

Robert broke from Landon's hold long enough to roll over to the nightstand and open the drawer. "I think we're going to need these." He kept a full bottle of lube and a new box of condoms in there, not that he'd needed them a lot in the past, but he was sure thankful they were there tonight. After gathering the supplies, he dropped them on the bed within easy reach and scooted back to Landon.

"Prepared…I like it." Landon's warm palm slid up and down Robert's shaft, and he closed his eyes, enjoying the touch he'd dreamed of—that strong hand stroking him as Landon's lips began the sensual exploration of his body.

Liquid pleasure ran up his spine as Landon took him to the back of his throat.

The suction on his dick had his toes curling, and he slowly thrust his hips up into Landon's mouth, losing himself in the welcoming heat. Landon pulled off him. "Want to make you come."

He spread his legs wantonly. He wanted to come too. Landon grabbed the lube, a click of the lid followed, then slick fingers rubbed over his hole, making him antsy with need.

"Yes, please." He lifted his hips as Landon breached him with a finger and started to play. The instant pleasure had Robert dropping his head to the mattress.

Landon winked at him and lowered his head. That wicked tongue circled his cock, and he almost cried out when he hit the back of Landon's throat and the man swallowed. He buried his fingers in Landon's hair. Damn, it felt so good to have Landon's mouth on him. He squirmed, wanting more as Landon prepared him. Two well-lubed fingers circled his hole, teasing and pressing in and out until Robert thought he'd die if Landon didn't fuck him. His body trembled, and he spread his legs wider, wanting his lover's fingers deeper.

"Please, Landon, fuck me." Desperation filled him as he released his lover's head.

The fingers in his ass disappeared, and he immediately missed the feeling as Landon got into position, quickly rolling on a condom. Landon fit perfectly into the cradle of his body. Robert drew his legs higher toward his chest.

The heat of Landon's cock pressed against his hole, taunting him, made him tilt his hips in an attempt to hurry the man along. Sweat broke out across his brow, the anticipation too much for him to handle.

A groan escaped Robert's lips at the first bite of pain when Landon's thick head pushed into him. The burn was a sweet relief as Landon sank into him inch by delicious inch. Landon's cast brushed against his skin as their bodies became one.

"Oh God…you feel so good." His throat was raw with passion as he moved his hips, allowing himself to adjust to Landon's size. Closing his eyes, he reveled in the feel of his lover's thick cock stretching him. So full. Landon was perfect in every way.

"Fuck, Robert. You're so damn tight. You feel amazing." Landon rolled his hips, and Robert groaned at the pleasure as his lover slowly moved in and out of him in the most carnal way.

They fit as if they'd been together forever. Landon's lips brushed against his in a sweet but hungry kiss. Landon had him panting and begging for more. Slow yet thorough, his lover's cock dragged over his prostate with every flex of his hips.

Landon sped his movements, and every thrust made Robert greedy for more. "Harder. Fuck me harder."

Landon sat up on his knees and tugged Robert's thighs over his. The man's thrusts were more powerful in this position, bringing him closer and closer to the point of no return. He smoothed his hands up Landon's stomach, feeling the muscles working under his palm as he filled him, bringing every nerve ending in his channel to life.

Robert stroked himself as Landon fucked him. Nothing could compare to the way Landon made him feel. Liquid fire ran down his spine as his body exploded from the inside out. Their gazes locked as Landon changed his position, gripping Robert's hips tighter, and pressed deep into him, fucking him so hard that the sound of their bodies coming together echoed through the room.

He couldn't stop the freight train of a release that barreled down on him. He slammed his eyes shut, overwhelmed at the power and connection of it all. Waves of pleasure sent nerve-searing vibrations along his body and bowled him over.

"Landon, *yessss*. Don't stop." His hot release landed on his chest and stomach. His ass clenched around Landon as he struggled to catch his breath.

"*Fuckkk, Robert*… I'm—" Landon thrust into him one last time then dropped down to kiss him. Landon's movements froze as their bodies seized together. Their tongues curled and prodded as they panted into each other's mouths.

Landon's weight kept him from floating away as he struggled to calm his racing heart.

"Damn, Doc. You wore me out." Landon pushed to his hands, favoring his casted arm as he smiled down at him with that crooked grin that made his insides all goofy.

"Back to Doc, huh?" Robert chuckled and slid his hands up Landon's ass. "I'm so blissed out right now that it sounds sexy. How's the arm?"

"You're definitely sexy, and it's fine—forget about it most of the time." Landon leaned down and kissed him long and hard.

Robert's mind went blank, and he melted into the kiss.

Chapter 16

Robert stared down at the sleeping man beside him, his heart overwhelmed with all the emotions running through him. Dark hair and beautiful full lips, the man stole his logic with every kiss. Even though Landon's eyes were closed, the thought of their intensity pierced Robert's soul, the memory branded on him forever. Being with Landon had been magical; they shared an unexplainable connection that upended all reason. He usually didn't sleep much, but tonight, he'd slept for hours with Landon curled around him.

From the moment he'd spotted Landon crossing the street until right this minute, the night had been enchanting. More than anything, Robert wanted Landon not only in his bed, but in his life. He wanted a relationship, something meaningful and long-term. He wanted to lose himself in Landon and have Landon lose himself in him. Yes, this was all new to him and fast, but after last night, there was no doubt Landon was meant to be his.

He lifted his hand, carefully brushing a small wisp of hair off Landon's forehead, taking a full inventory of Landon's face, hoping to commit every gorgeous detail to memory. "Doc, I can feel you staring at me. Why aren't you sleeping?"

"I'm not much of a sleeper." Robert smiled when Landon's

eyes opened and immediately found his.

"Do I need to leave your room so you can sleep?" Landon asked softly.

Those words made his heart drum frantically. He never wanted the man to leave. Landon belonged in his bed. It was like Landon to give him an out, though, showing how considerate he was. Robert wanted to give that back tenfold.

"Not at all. I like knowing you're in my bed." Robert grinned. He was so out of practice at this kind of thing and hoped his flirting was obvious.

"Do I need to be awake because you're awake, because I seriously need some rest. You stressed me the fuck out, trying to get ready for our non-date date. And then you kept me up until all hours of the night…" Landon couldn't finish the sentence from the involuntary jaw-cracking yawn tearing free.

Robert laughed at the honesty of Landon's refreshing remarks. There was no coy game-playing. Landon had been open and upfront so far as he could tell. At least he'd always know exactly where he stood with his man. "I'll let you sleep, but I'm going to get up for a while. Are you good with that?"

"I feel like this is a trick question or a test of some sort. Should I get up too?" Landon asked, his sentence ending with him lifting his head, trying to rise.

"No." Robert pressed a hand on Landon's chest, keeping him down. "You go back to sleep. We've only been asleep a couple of hours. I'm going to clean myself up." As he spoke, he untangled himself from the warmth of Landon's body and tucked the blankets back around the alluring man then kissed his lips. "You're tempting as sin and gorgeous in my bed."

"You too, Doc," Landon mumbled with a sleepy smile.

"Call me Robert. I like hearing you say it."

"Got it…"

Robert waited, watching Landon, who had closed his eyes. Maybe as much as a minute passed before Landon opened one eye, looking straight at him.

"What?" A big grin parted Landon's lips, causing the skin at the corner of his eyes to crinkle as he finally gave in and said, "Robert."

Robert's heart sped at the sexy growl in Landon's voice. He loved when the sergeant called him Doc, but that title of doctor seemed to act as some sort of a status marker for Landon in whatever social class limitations he perceived to be between them.

"Wake me up if I sleep too long," Landon added while turning to his side and burrowing under the blankets.

Robert wanted to crawl under those covers and make out with Landon until they both were mad with need. The thought was enticing and tempting just like the man, but in the end, Robert rolled away, pushing to his feet from the other side of his California king. They had plenty of time for sex. Landon should sleep now for all the energy he'd be expending soon enough.

Robert went for his bathroom, taking a quick shower and dressing as silently as possible. When he walked back into the bedroom, Landon was still on his side, sleeping soundly with the blanket drawn up to his chin. He lingered at the foot of the bed, lost in thought as he took in Landon's sleeping form. Any distance he'd managed to keep between Landon and his raging feelings had vanished. His heart fully and completely connected as he stared down at the man. Landon was beautiful, inside and out, and a caring, giving lover—things Robert had instinctively known since day one.

He stepped away, not wanting to wake Landon, and quietly padded across the carpet with his tennis shoes in hand. After quietly shutting the door, Robert took the stairs down to the first floor. He stood at the landing looking over the house before dropping down to put on his running shoes. The twinge in his ass made him smile as he shifted his position. The place looked as it had when he'd left. Nothing was out of place, except the clothes on the stairway where they'd shed them last night—the main reason for his extremely good mood this morning.

The nagging voice in his head quickly drowned any happy memories from last night, questioning why it didn't look like anyone had been in the house since he'd left months ago. He bypassed the living room, going straight for the kitchen. Not a thing was out of place in there either. He opened the dishwasher. Empty. Then he went for the refrigerator—only the few things he'd left were inside. Robert checked the pantry. It was bare, and there was no trash in the trash can either. Had Landon even been staying there?

Curiosity had him jogging back up the stairs. He headed the opposite direction from his bedroom and pushed open the guest room door. The room was as tidy as every other part of the house, but there were footprints in the freshly vacuumed carpet and faint traces of Landon's delicious cologne. So, he had been in the townhome, but wasn't utilizing the space. *Hmmm.*

He'd have to ask about that later. He wanted Landon comfortable here. It was four thirty in the morning, and for the first time in a long time, he felt like cooking. The mere thought gave him the certain knowledge that he was leaving his funky mood behind. Robert liked to prepare meals, and those bursts of cooking and baking usually came when he was happy and content in his life. He'd have to make a grocery store run. He went back down the stairs toward the garage, wondering what Landon might like to eat the most.

The minute he pushed open the garage door, he realized his car hadn't been moved. Robert scowled. He'd have to ask about that later too. Unhooking his bike from the wall mount, he ticked off a grocery list in his head. He could buy things for breakfast now and place a bigger order to be delivered later.

Robert shut the garage door and took off, the wonderful ache in his ass a sweet reminder of his extraordinary night as the crisp morning air filled his lungs. He was back, happy and complete, all because of the man who was currently lying in his bed; he gave him something to aspire to.

He'd fallen for Landon, fast. Considering the possibility that he was falling in love, or hell, was already in love, both excited him and confused him at the same time. But now he finally understood what his dad had meant when talking about his father. Avery had known from first sight that Kane was his. Robert might have been slower on the uptake. He'd been too lost to see Landon clearly while in Germany, but last night, from the second he'd watched Landon cross the street to him, he'd felt it. He'd known. The grin on his face broadened. Surely Landon had to be feeling this way too. Man, he felt amazing.

Landon opened his eyes and blinked once, staring at the bright spots dancing on the wall across the room. The partially drawn window shade let in the small amount of light that held his attention. There wasn't that moment of uncertainty on where he'd spent the night. Landon knew exactly where he was and whose bed he was in. Thinking about Robert made him smile as he rolled to his back and stretched out his legs.

The wonderful memories of the night before rushed back. Happiness jolted him, shooting straight through his body. His dick filled at the vivid images flashing in his head—the way the length of Robert's body seared his back as they'd slept, the feeling comfortable and grounding and fucking hot. It had been so long since he allowed himself to let go and trust another person. He couldn't recall ever feeling this safe and this right with any man.

Landon didn't even have the after-sex regrets that always plagued him as soon as he'd gotten off. Usually the condom hadn't hit the trash can before he'd have his pants zipped and be searching for the door. But this… This was exactly what he wanted. It felt right to be in this bed, in this man's room. Robert Adams had a hold on him. Everything would have been perfect had the doctor stayed in bed with him this morning.

But Robert wasn't in the room. Landon realized that about the same time he smelled something fantastic and enticing in the air. It wasn't just the smell of bacon that filled the room and made his stomach growl. A variety of scents melded together, creating a unique and delicious aroma, overloading his senses.

Landon pushed up on his elbow to check the time on the nightstand. *Shit.* He'd slept in this morning, not that he had much to do other than to sit in the PT center and make sure he was there for anyone needing anything done, but it was already seven forty-five. He was supposed to be at the facility by eight. He kicked off the covers and jumped out of bed, scanning the floor for his blue jeans to get his cell phone from the pocket.

Flashes of memory from the entryway and stairs flooded his brain—Robert pinning him to the wall, teasing him with deliberate drugging kisses. Those brief moments seared into his soul. He'd never been so needy and taken with another man. They had abandoned their clothes, in various places as they'd made their way to the bedroom. Surprisingly, he spotted his jeans draped over a chair along with his dress shirt. His shoes were neatly placed right underneath.

He shouldn't be too surprised; thoughtful consideration fit the doctor's personality to a T. Landon walked barefooted across the room, going straight for his cell phone in his back pants pocket. Standing in the room naked, he sent a text to the rehab facility, letting them know he'd be a couple of hours late. His stomach grumbled as the smells grew stronger. He gathered his clothes and headed to his room to take a quick shower.

Even with the aggravation of the cast, Landon made record time showering and dressing. He didn't go for his ABUs. Instead, he wore a pair of jeans and an Air Force T-shirt, tugging it over his head while taking the stairs down two at a time. He heard music playing quietly in the kitchen and the homey sound of dishes being washed in the sink.

Maybe it wasn't Robert in there after all. Could be a housekeeper. That thought slowed his steps. Disappointment lanced his heart. Maybe Robert had left earlier and gone back to wherever he was staying… He scrubbed a hand down his face. He was an idiot. He wasn't thinking clearly. His heart was making decisions, which meant his brain wasn't thinking logically. He needed to find a new place to stay. Robert was back in DC, so of course he'd want his place back.

Landon pivoted on his heel to head back upstairs, his decision made. A male voice stopped him mid-step. His heart sped as he listened to Robert Adams quietly singing along with Shinedown's "Breaking Inside."

He lingered at the base of the stairs and listened to the sexy doctor singing the all too real words to the popular tune. He too loved that song. His earlier freak-out had taken a backseat to his sudden eagerness to see Robert singing in person. Landon headed for the kitchen.

He rounded the corner to find Robert elbow-deep in sudsy water. It looked like he was washing his last dish. Several pans lined the cooktop and held a variety of what looked and smelled like a smorgasbord of delicious breakfast dishes warming on the stove. There was so much food and no one else around, at least he didn't think anyone was around. The normalcy of the whole scene struck him. Well, except for the amount of food and the doctor washing dishes.

The sight of the rich, highly educated man actually doing dishes after cooking a meal—correction, enough food for his squadron—made his heart do stupid things. Domesticity was something he'd never have thought Robert Adams did so easily. In fact, the doctor looked amazing, and just for a split second, he let himself get lost in the image.

"Good morning," he finally said. The dish in Robert's hand dropped back into the water, causing the suds to bubble over the side of the sink as he reached for a hand towel. Robert dried his hands as he moved toward Landon. The intensity in the doctor's eyes held him still as their gazes connected and that deep want spread selfishly through him. He wasn't sure he'd even blinked as the domesticated doctor stepped into his personal space and crowded him.

Landon closed his eyes seconds before their lips touched. Robert gave him a sweet good-morning kiss before attempting to pull away. Landon wasn't near done, so he cupped the back of Robert's head, holding him in place, and pressed into the kiss. Robert hesitated, putting a hand on his chest, keeping a little distance between them.

"I've been sampling our breakfast."

"Mmm…" He nipped at Robert's lips and said, "And you taste amazing."

He locked his casted arm around Robert's waist and drew the suddenly shy man back to him, certain he'd never get enough of moments like these. He deepened the kiss, and Robert finally gave in, surrendering to him. Landon was growing to really like that move. No one had ever made him feel so wanted. He slid his tongue over Robert's lips and made himself break from the kiss before their breakfast could grow cold.

"It smells great," he managed, tilting his head toward the stovetop.

"I'm a little rusty, and I got carried away. I'm just really happy this morning," Robert replied with a sexy, sheepish grin.

Landon shifted, keeping Robert close as he glanced over at the breakfast selections.

"Looks like you made enough to feed an army. What all do we have?"

Robert moved with him, staying close as he explained.

"Let's see. This is a recipe my father made while we were still eating meat. It's an Italian bread with brie, prosciutto, eggs, tomatoes, and topped with a secret-recipe olive oil blend. It was my dad's favorite. Over here I made something we would eat every time we traveled to Australia. It has a zucchini base. It's delicious, and I made some for you with the different cheeses. Then I remembered a crostini, pear, and honey snack I used to love. I made that too. I got carried away." Robert reached for the oven door and pulled out a stack of photo-worthy pancakes. "I kept waiting for you to wake so I made lemon-blueberry buttermilk pancakes. And started a pot of spaghetti sauce for later. The dough for pasta is doing its thing in the refrigerator."

"Wow…I…thank you. How long did I sleep?" he asked,

giving Robert his best grin before reaching for the prosciutto, egg, and cheese deal for a small finger sampling. He popped the bite in his mouth, the savory flavors flowed over his taste buds. His eyes rolled at the aromatic blend of ingredients. So good.

"Not long at all."

"You cook like this all the time?" Landon asked, breaking from Robert's hold to reach for one of two plates sitting nearby. He wasted no time in carefully picking at a hot piece of bacon lying on a paper towel.

"I used to. When I had time off. I spent an extraordinary amount of time at the hospital," Robert explained, anchoring a hip on the counter, watching as Landon gathered something from each of the selections.

"You know I'm part Italian, right? My dad cooks. He thinks it's a skill that comes with birth, but nothing like this."

"I hoped you liked Italian food. I grew up at La Bella Luna. That's where I learned the ropes. Right after we moved to DC, when my dad was working long hours, I wasn't really acclimating well to the change. I missed my Minnesota home and family. My daddy would spend hours in the kitchen with me, occupying my mind. I always connected closest with him—I've told you all that. He taught me everything he knew. Now, after all this time, I understand I wasn't the only one struggling with all the changes. I think it helped him with everything he gave up in Minnesota when we moved." Robert was silent, staring down at the table when Landon looked back over his shoulder. "Whatever the reason, it's a de-stressor for me."

"You can de-stress for me anytime." His tease got the desired effect when he heard Robert chuckle. Landon loaded his plate full, throwing two pancakes on top. He wasn't a huge eater, but every bit of this food looked better than anything he'd ever eaten in his entire life, and he wasn't going to let a little thing like appetite get in his way of enjoying every bite.

He was looking for where to sit when he saw the place settings Robert made in the center island. He set his plate in the spot before heading for the coffee pot and pouring himself a cup.

"I made that fresh about thirty minutes ago."

"Doc, you outdid yourself." He claimed his seat, taking a sip of the hot coffee before looking at Robert. Penetrating blue eyes caught his as two deep lines formed in the area just above the bridge of Robert's nose.

He couldn't help but grin; an intense Robert Adams would be a formidable opponent.

"What?" he asked as if he didn't already know.

"Please call me Robert. Colleagues and patients call me Doc."

Landon's grin broadened. He couldn't hold off the chuckle that rose from his chest any more than he could help breathing. He only gave in, not drawing out the teasing a little while longer, because his food and his coffee were getting cold.

"Robert, thank you for breakfast. You have serious kitchen skills."

That instantly appeased Robert, who went back to preparing his plate.

A few minutes passed and neither had spoken, something that rarely happened when they were together. It wasn't awkward—maybe because he was busy stuffing his face as fast as he could with the spread in front of him.

"Mmm. This is delicious."

"I'm glad you like it," Robert said, his eyes brightened by the smile on his face as he took his seat next to Landon. "What're your plans today? I was thinking if you didn't have to work, I have a friend with a boat…"

"Can't," he said, swallowing his bite. Disappointment nagged him as he explained. "I made a commitment to the PT clinic. I texted them that I'd be late, but I gotta go soon."

Robert took a napkin Landon hadn't noticed in Robert's lap and wiped his mouth. The doctor's table manners were so much better than his own. He reached for the napkin still on the tabletop. Robert's appropriately sized bites contrasted with

Landon's shovel-the-food-in technique too. He gave himself a break on that one. Robert was used to the tasty fare. Landon wasn't at all.

"How long do you work today?"

"Usually until about five thirty," he replied, wiping a napkin over his mouth. "What d'you got going on today?"

"Not much." Robert gave a non-committal shrug.

"How does that feel?" he asked, watching for any signs of the sadness he'd noticed haunting the man in Germany.

Robert took a bite of his food, swallowed, and took a drink from the glass of water nearby. "Weird."

"I bet." Landon nodded. He wasn't a medical professional on any level, but he didn't pick up anything other than the good-natured man he'd been reacquainted with yesterday. Robert shifted in his chair, turning toward him, this time bringing the coffee cup with him.

"You haven't used much of the place. The car doesn't look like it's been moved. How have you been getting to your appointments and rehab?" Robert asked, the weight of his warm hand came to rest on top of Landon's. Robert curled strong, skilled fingers around his hand as if testing the hold. Probably the only thing that would slow his primary goal of cleaning his plate before he grew too full.

In more of an instinctual move, definitely nothing planned, Landon lifted Robert's fingers to his mouth, kissing his knuckles. The intimacy of being seated so close to Robert, who seemed to want him near, somehow erased all the reasons he shouldn't be there. There was no denying, in many aspects, he and Robert seemed to fit together like pieces to a puzzle. This moment, like so many others, felt right and calmed his soul. He relaxed around Robert, remembered to just breathe and take life as it came. It was all so foreign to him.

"It didn't feel right driving that car, Doc…"

Robert's brow rose instantly, making Landon laugh as he tossed his napkin on the table. The man was too enticing and captured all Landon's attention.

"I mean, Robert. You've done too much. I can't drive that car. What if I wrecked it?"

"I have insurance. And it doesn't look like you even stayed in the house. Have you been here the whole time?"

"Yeah, after that first few days in the hospital." He looked down at their joined hands. Landon had both his covering Robert's now. Content to stay sitting right there for however long he could. He turned Robert's hand over, letting the pad of his thumb slide across the doc's lightly calloused palm. His nerves flared briefly, allowing Robert's touch and their natural connection to soothe him enough to answer honestly. "I'm used to making my own way. I'm a prideful guy. I don't expect or want handouts. So, it's weird being in this situation, taking you up on your offer, but it felt weirder not to accept your generosity. When I get to the clinic, I'll get my housing situated. It's not a thing. I appreciate what you've done for me."

"Don't go," Robert said, placing his coffee cup on the counter in front of him. His grip on Landon's hand tightened and he tugged him forward, close enough that Robert's lips captured his in a sweet, chaste kiss.

"I can't stay here and let you stay in a hotel. It's just not right," Landon said, trying to rear back.

"I could stay here too," Robert said, his voice wispy and soft as he caressed Landon's cheek with his palm then cupped his neck, keeping him close, forcing Landon to have this conversation eye to eye.

"Live togeth—" Landon started, but Robert cut him off.

"I'm not trying to make it weird. I just have the room and enjoy your company. Stay for a week, and we'll talk again in seven days. I like the thought of you here more than I probably should at this point in our relation— Just stay."

Landon stayed silent, hopefully masking his facial features from the freaking the fuck out he had tumbling around on the inside. Could Robert feel him trembling?

"I wasn't trying to put you on the spot. Look, you can stay in your room. I'll stay in mine. It doesn't look like you used much of the house anyway. Just stay. If it's too much or doesn't work out, then you can call for a place to live." Robert sounded so reasonable while painting a picture Landon's heart yearned for more than anything ever before. This was dangerous ground, for both his soul and his heart. How deep would he be when Robert realized his mistake?

"I don't know…" He needed space and tried to pull his hand free. Robert wasn't having any of that. Robert's lips pressed against his again. They were so fucking sweet. Landon's heart flip-flopped as he had no choice but to return the kiss. He had to be crazy to even consider the arrangement. He'd never be able to keep his hands off the man.

"Give it a week. Give us the time we need to find out what this is." Robert's ocean-blue gaze held him in place. Could Robert hear his heart banging against his chest? His defenses were practically nonexistent. This man was too much. Robert Adams was everything Landon had always wanted but never imagined he could have.

He needed to find perspective in a huge way. "Let's play it day by day."

"I'll take what I can get, but I'm sticking to a week." The corner of Robert's mouth kicked up in a satisfied smile. Robert was off the stool, taking his plate to the sink before the words sank in. Landon didn't fucking know what had just happened or what to think. He was still trying to come to terms with what he'd just agreed too. But watching Robert at the sink made him feel all warm and fuzzy inside, especially knowing the man enjoyed his company. He also loved knowing he'd made Robert happy with his decision. He wanted Robert happy forever.

Landon rose, going to the sink. "Let me do this. You cooked."

Robert bumped his hip, nudging him away from the sink. "Your cast can't get wet. I got it. How have you been getting to the rehab center?"

"Public transportation, sometimes Uber, then I rented a

car, because it just seemed easier," he said, understanding the complications of the cast, but not ready to give up on helping with the cleanup.

"Where's the rental? It's not in the drive."

"I parked on the road just in case you needed your car."

Robert pressed a kiss to Landon's lips as if it was the most natural thing in the world to do.

"Thank you for thinking of me. I have to go get my things from the hotel and stop by the store, but I'll be home the rest of the day. Come back when you can." Robert cocked his head toward the kitchen door, encouraging him that way. Landon let his hand travel the curve of Robert's ass, giving him a gentle squeeze before he left the kitchen. Everything felt so in sync, so together.

Chapter 17

One week later

Waking with Landon in his bed was the sweetest way to start the day. Robert stretched his legs, curling his toes. Mornings like this were already on his list of favorites. Well…more like afternoons like this. It was past noon. Landon's day off had been dubbed a lazy day, a day they slept late and usually stayed in.

"Good morning, handsome," Robert whispered, pressing his lips against his sleeping beauty's warm skin. He loved the way Landon smelled, all warm and happy, like forever and sunshine. Sunshine, exactly what Landon was to his life. His lover didn't stir. "I mean, afternoon, Mr. Russo," he said, kissing and mouthing along the back of Landon's neck. He skimmed his fingers lightly over the goose bumps springing up along his lover's tan skin.

"Grab my dick, Doc," Landon mumbled sleepily.

Jesus, he loved when his man got bossy first thing upon waking. He chuckled at Landon's greeting. He'd never thought about all the perks of having Landon move in with him when he'd suggested it, but damn, he was sure enjoying the rewards.

Robert snuggled closer, sliding his hard-on along Landon's

perfect ass as he reached around, wrapping his fingers around his sergeant's hard shaft. Landon's hips moved, and Robert pumped his fist over his lover's erection. The hard as steel length felt like velvet against his palm.

"This right here..." he said and nipped Landon's ear as he squeezed his cock. "You're so hard for me. I'm gonna ride your ass until you scream my name." Robert stroked Landon a little rougher. Landon turned his head, capturing his mouth in a hungry kiss. Robert let Landon take control. He'd always submit to Landon. He smiled into the kiss and sucked Landon's tongue into his mouth.

He rocked against Landon and used his leg to nudge Landon's thick thigh forward. "I want to make you come," he said before releasing his lover and rubbing his palms over Landon's firm ass.

"Me too, hence the 'grab my dick' request, Doc," Landon replied flatly.

"A request?" He licked the shell of Landon's ear. "I do believe you ordered me, Sergeant. He gave his lover a rough tug just to rile him up. "You're testy when you wake. Did you know that?" he asked, laughing as he reached behind him for the supplies left on the nightstand from their late-night festivities. He quickly rolled the condom down his erection and opened the bottle of lube, coating his fingers then his dick with a few gratifying strokes.

Landon glanced impatiently over his shoulder, those dark, needy eyes...damn. The desire blazing there burned a hole straight through Robert. Such a beautifully intense shade of dark umber, at times almost changing to black when he was aroused or angry.

"I'm not. And I thought you were gonna get me off. You promised," Landon demanded in that sassy tone that got Robert all hot and impatient. Had he promised? He couldn't remember, especially when Landon arched his back and deliberately rubbed his naked ass against him again. He was learning Landon was quite the tease. He drizzled more lube on his fingers and rubbed the slick liquid around with his thumb then slid his fingers down

Landon's crack.

"So, I promised…" The moan he got from Landon when he pressed against his lover's hole made him smile. If they had more time, he'd have his tongue all in Landon's ass. Teasing Landon was so gratifying.

Last night he'd found out just how long he could torture Landon with his tongue and fingers before he begged incoherently and promised Robert all sorts of things in exchange for completion. The thought made his dick jerk at the perfection of that moment. Landon had taken him hard and fast when he'd finished teasing the man and let him free.

"You were so hard last night," he whispered against Landon's ear. He slid his fingers around that tempting pucker, making sure to work as much lube into Landon as he could. Loving the noises coming from him, he kept massaging Landon's opening, teasing and touching him.

"Let me in, Landon." He pushed two fingers past the resistant ring of muscle. The heat enveloped his digits. Landon wiggled his ass against him.

He caught Landon's hips and spread him open. Lining up his cock, Robert pushed into his lover's body, groaning as all that tightness gripped and swallowed him with searing intensity.

"Damn, so hot. You feel so good. Gonna bury myself deep in you, Landon," Robert promised as his body sank into Landon. He held himself back from thrusting too quickly, giving Landon time to adjust to the intrusion. The pleasure gripping his shaft made it almost impossible to keep still, driving his need higher.

"Now, fuck me like you mean it, Doc." The impassioned command in Landon's deep drawl was unmistakable and sent liquid fire down Robert's spine and flames licking at his balls as he flexed his hips.

He rolled into his lover and thrust as deeply as he could, over and over again, driving into Landon as he mouthed the back of his neck, sucking color to his skin. Landon turned his head for a kiss, and Robert obliged. The kiss became a frenzy of lips and tongues, going from smoldering to incendiary in no time. Landon brought out a different side in Robert, a hunger only this man could sate.

"Hold on," he said and pulled out of his lover. Placing a palm against Landon's shoulder, he encouraged him over and pressed him to his back. Robert ran his hand over Landon's stomach and gripped his erect cock. He sat up higher, giving Landon's hard length a good stroke before lowering his head. He kissed the tattoo on Landon's chest. He loved the scrolled letters, so much meaning in those words.

He shifted on the bed so he could lick around Landon's leaking slit to sample the moisture gathered there. This man had been sent to him from above. He swallowed Landon's cock, the salty flesh sliding over his tongue. As he bobbed his head, Landon's moans grew louder. His throat tightened around the soft head, and Landon tugged at his hair. He pulled off to mouth Landon's balls, licking and sucking them into his mouth as his lover writhed beneath him.

With Landon's dick between his lips, he curled his tongue around the head one last time before kissing the leaking tip. Robert kicked the covers to the end of the bed and crawled completely between Landon's spread thighs for better access. He slid his palms over Landon's body then positioned his cock as he pushed his leg back to his chest and sank into all that searing, gripping warmth for the second time this afternoon.

"Damn, you feel good. I'm addicted to you, Landon," Robert said as he forced himself to stop moving and stared down into those heavily hooded eyes the color of night. *Damn.* Landon's lips twitched in a small smirk.

"Then we're both addicts. Finish me..." He thrust his hips into Landon faster and harder, every time those sexy sounds escaped his lips. Every nerve in Robert's body ignited as his thighs quivered from the exertion of holding his orgasm at bay.

Robert moved in and out of Landon, held spellbound and so desperately close to the edge. He couldn't look away, didn't want to look away. With every thrust, every roll of his hips, he was lost, letting the desire swirling in the depths of his gaze hypnotize him, saturate him. Landon's lips parted on heavy pants.

"Oh, God… God, don't stop. So good. Gonna come."

Robert dropped his chest to Landon's and thrust harder, determined to make Landon his—to watch his name form on those lips as he came deep in Landon's ass.

He rolled his hips into Landon's quivering body, making his thrust slower and more deliberate. He wasn't finished with Landon. He wanted to hear him lose his mind. Robert pushed up on his forearms to allow himself better control.

He lifted his chest and bent his head to mouth Landon's nipple, licking across the hard tip. He flattened his tongue and dragged it over Landon's collarbone and up his neck before taking his mouth in a brutal kiss, all while driving in and out of Landon's tight ass. Landon clung to him, his strong arms holding him tightly. He fed on Landon's kiss, stroking his lover with a firm fist, working his cock as their bodies connected. Robert soared closer to bliss. The hard body beneath him urging him further and further away from his control.

"You're squeezing me so good…can't hol… *Lanndon*…" His voice cracked on his lover's name as he shoved his hips forward and filled the condom deep in Landon's clenching ass. His orgasm went on forever as he curled Landon into him, grinding against his lover. His cock twitched one last time, and he gasped from the pleasure. He couldn't take his eyes off Landon's face, not wanting to miss when Landon followed him over the sharp edge of completion. His lover was close. Landon's eyes locked onto his, and he watched, helpless to move, as Landon came apart beneath him. Landon's dick jerked in his palm and hot come hit his stomach.

He lowered himself, careful to keep his cock deep inside his man and kissed Landon just to sample his sweet lips as he tried to catch his breath. Landon's heartbeat mirrored the rat-ta-tat of his own excitement.

"My legs are jelly." He chuckled against Landon's ear. Happiness and contentment surged through him as Landon's lips found his once again.

"You're hot as sin," Landon gasped breathlessly as Robert rolled to his back next to him. He was still riding on the afterglow of his orgasm and could barely move. His body was heavy with satisfaction. They had slept till noon only because they hadn't gone to bed before seven this morning. Landon could stay right there and drift back to sleep in total bliss. He lazily watched Robert bound from the bed. Like he'd done several times over the last few days, Landon wondered how the man had such an endless abundance of energy. Maybe it was those damned vegetables. He might have to add more of them to his diet if he planned to keep up with the guy. And as the days had passed, Landon found he seriously wanted to keep up with the energetic Robert Adams. He planned to do that very thing after a fifteen-minute catnap.

"Stay out of my shower or we'll be late," Robert teased him. He knew damn well Landon liked to follow wherever he led, especially the shower.

They'd spent a lot of time in Robert's shower. Landon curled on his side and pulled the covers over his chest. He'd just been fucked into a coma, and there he was thinking about Robert all soapy and wet.

"Late for what?" he asked, trying to divert his attention from imagining Robert's mouth on him. Dropping his arms over his eyes, he let out a long breath. Man, he could use some sleep. He wished Robert would just come back to bed and cuddle up next to him.

"The concert," Robert called out.

His eyes remained closed as his breathing slowed. He tried to remember anything at all about a concert. With the funky haze in his brain, it took longer to process that Robert hadn't shut the bathroom door. Landon considered that a blatant invitation.

He heard the shower door click into place, and his dick plumped as if it had been called to duty. The need to feel Robert's lips wrapped around him, forced him to roll from the bed. His cock was already filling. Robert would suck him off then wash him from head to toe while Landon reveled in the glory of back to back orgasms.

He'd found his perfect lover. When he and Robert were together, the world slipped away, and they became one. Nothing but Robert mattered, and at times, he couldn't get close enough to him. Being with Robert renewed him while chasing away his anxiety and calming his mind in ways he hadn't known were possible.

Landon stumbled as he made a beeline to the bathroom. He stepped through the open door to see Robert's naked body through the glass, standing under the hot, steaming spray. He stared at Landon as if he'd been waiting there just for him. The smirk and open invitation tugged at his heartstrings, pulling him with some unseen magnetic force, helpless to do anything more than take the steps separating them. When he entered the shower, Robert ducked his head under the spray of water, filling his mouth. Robert squirted the water on his chest, teasing him.

"It took you long enough."

"At some point, you're gonna have to let me get some sleep," Landon quipped, wrapping his newly cast-free arm around Robert, stepping thigh to chest against the man.

"In the words of Arya Stark, 'Not today'." Robert encircled him with both arms, pulling him closer against his hot, wet body. This was when the internal doubt eased the most, when Robert held him almost possessively. That striking, expressive face reflected all the longing Landon held so deep inside his heart.

"It's a good thing you're so sexy. If you're nice, I'll let that sassy comment slide."

Robert laughed at his hard-edged tone, changing their positions abruptly. He spun Landon under the warm spray as he dropped to his knees in front of him. Robert lifted his eyes, the intensity swirling behind the blue gaze took Landon's breath, and he lowered his hand to cup the back of the fine doctor's head.

"I learned from the best." Robert expertly gripped his shaft, giving a toe-curling stroke before lowering his mouth and sucking Landon to the root. Warm, wet pleasure engulfed him, and his eyes rolled to the back of his head. His breath hitched in his chest as his lover's mouth nearly made his knees buckle. Robert's mouth was indeed magical. Landon closed his eyes and let the magic take him under.

Chapter 18

"Linkin Park was excellent."

Robert had to agree. They were his favorite band of all time. When he turned to say those very words, he discovered a distracted Landon with his focus elsewhere. Following Landon's gaze made him grin. His guy stared openly, almost lustfully, at a long row of food vendor booths lining the sidewalk outside the concert venue. Robert read the signs of each space, ticking off the different varieties of foods. The entire line of selections looked fried, super processed, or filled with sugar, exactly the kinds of food Landon loved to eat.

"They've always been a favorite of mine," Robert said about the band, now almost as distracted as Landon as he started to head the opposite direction toward the bright flashing colors of the carnival rides, maybe a hundred and fifty feet away. Surely, Landon couldn't be hungry after the huge meal they'd shared before the concert.

"Have you met 'em?" Landon asked, his fingers closing around Robert's elbow to stop him in his tracks. That was all it took for Robert to clasp the extended hand, entwining their fingers together. Since he always itched to touch Landon, the hand hold was the lure he needed to step back toward Landon, whose gaze bounced between Robert and the beckoning food vendors.

"I did meet them. It was the summer before my sophomore year of college. They played in a small venue in Minneapolis. My parents bribed us home with the tickets. We went backstage and met the band. There was lots of smoking and partying going on, if I remember correctly," he said with a smile, remembering how self-conscious his daddy had been in that kind of an environment.

"Rich kid," Landon muttered teasingly, giving his best Italian *pfft* then nodding toward the sausage on a stick street truck. Landon started toward the truck, turning back to him after a couple of steps and then walking backward. When their arms stretched as far as they could, Landon gave a quick, forceful tug to get him moving. Of course, he had no choice but to follow. A playful Landon was a sexy guy. He was beginning to understand he'd follow this man anywhere he led.

"I think it's more like the benefits of having a father who was vice president. He could get us into a lot of things. He also opened our eyes to some of the most extreme poverty I've ever seen in my life at the places he had us volunteer our time. They made me see the whole world for its good and its bad," Robert said, trailing after him. Landon corrected his stride, turning back in the direction of the truck, giving Robert another nice view.

Landon had a natural strut to his gait, his ass swinging with every step he took. Landon let go of his hand when he reached the counter and placed his order. Robert caught up, pulling his wallet free from his walking shorts.

"You know that's a heart attack on a stick."

"Is that your expert opinion?" Landon asked, grinning as he barely spared Robert a glance. His whole attention was on the man shoving a stick inside the long Italian sausage.

"Yeah. Pretty much everyone's expert opinion." Robert slid a ten-dollar bill across the ledge to the cashier as Landon reached for his wallet, thumbing through his cash. Robert stepped back, giving Landon access to the small row of condiments on the side of the truck. "Keep the change."

"No, wait. I'm paying," Landon said, the sausage forgotten as Landon swiped a finger through the air, instructing the cashier to give Robert back his money. "I'm paying. Not him."

Robert tucked his wallet back inside his pocket and stepped farther away. He brought forward his hard, unyielding stare, something he inherited from his dad and shook his head, getting a deer-in-the-headlights look back in return.

Now, both sets of eyes stared at him, but Landon's had shifted to angry. For as well as he and Landon had gotten along over the last several days, money was becoming a budding problem between them. More than anything, Robert didn't want that to be the case. Last night, while waiting for Landon to return home from his shift at the base, he gave himself lectures, trying to gain perspective regarding all these intensely possessive, caveman urges that kept welling inside him regarding Landon. One he refused to shake off was his need to be the one to provide for Landon. He liked paying Landon's way. He liked it more than he ever thought possible, and he wasn't nearly ready to stop. Actually, he never wanted to stop. He wanted to spoil Landon. Give him a life he deserved…

"I don't even want this now." Landon's words took Robert from his thoughts of a long-term, loving committed relationship. This was what Robert kept doing over and over again—getting ahead of himself. He was so focused on Landon that anytime he let his thoughts go, it ended with them walking down the aisle. With extreme effort, Robert reined in his wayward thoughts and tucked his hands inside his short's pockets.

"I doubt that," he quipped when Landon started toward him. Robert ventured a glance in Landon's direction. Landon looked pissed, his gaze darting anywhere except for Robert's direction. The fact that the man still walked side by side with him was a win in his favor, so he figured he'd just keep the rest of his comments to himself for now. When Landon finally took a big bite of the mustard-coated sausage, he hoped that meant they were done with the argument.

Silence held between them for maybe as long as the next

twenty steps. Robert pretended not to notice the irritation evident in Landon's heavier than normal steps.

"Have I messed up the evening?" he finally asked. They had traveled along the outskirts of the carnival, not immersing themselves in the crowd. Robert stared up at the colorful Ferris wheel in the distance, watching his hopes of riding the ride with Landon fade with every second of silence that passed between them.

"I have money. You don't need to keep paying for everything. I can pay," Landon blurted out, coming to a sudden stop, causing the people behind him to walk around to avoid bumping into him. Robert was slower to stop. When he did, he scanned their surroundings, wondering how many eyes were focused on Landon. There were several, and by default, they were now looking at him since all Landon's irritation was aimed straight his way.

"Of course, you can," he said calmly, maybe too reasonably with the fire that sparked in Landon's gaze. "Do you want to go home?"

"You mean to your home?" Landon gave an exaggerated eye roll before turning and heading toward the trash can. He tossed the partially eaten sausage toward the can when he was still several feet from the container. It easily flew inside before Landon flipped back around again. He seemed surprised at the distance between them and stomped straight toward Robert. "Doc, I appreciate everything you've done for me…"

"Don't call me that." Robert steeled his spine as his own anger surfaced. God, it was such a foreign feeling, harboring all this possession inside him.

"That's what you are."

Robert's heart drummed in his chest as he entered a standoff with Landon. His guy was determined to argue. So be it. Robert would accommodate him, just not out here for the world to see.

"That's right. That's what I am, but that's not *who* I am, at least not to you. Not anymore." Robert took the phone from his pocket, pulled up the Uber app and searched for the closest vehicle to them. As much as he wanted to pretend he was an everyday kind of guy, he couldn't do this—have an argument—for the whole world to see. "Can we talk at—" He stopped himself from saying 'home' and bit out, "In private?"

"I'll get the Uber," Landon said, pulling out his cell phone.

"It's already done." Without saying anything more, Robert started for the blue Acura as shown on the app. He was at the car with verification and addresses exchanged and pulling open the back door before he ever looked over his shoulder. Landon hadn't moved a muscle except to stand there glaring at him with his hands on his waist. Robert ignored him as he lowered himself down into the seat, but left the door open for Landon. He glanced toward the driver. "We may argue in front of you."

"Nothing new. It happens about every third trip," the driver said, unfazed.

"Really?"

The driver stayed quiet as Landon entered the vehicle, making Robert scramble to the other side of the seat. In all his cavalier attitude, he hadn't actually been entirely sure if Landon would follow. He breathed a small sigh of relief even as Landon stayed hugging the door. It had to mean this quarrel wasn't going to end in a deal-breaker. Right?

Robert stared down at the phone in his hand, thinking about the possibility of a breakup. His natural defense mechanisms kicked in. If this was some sort of breakup, he had to be ready to fight against that end. His always steady hands trembled, and he glanced over at Landon again. His guy sat there, fuming, with his leg bouncing. How had such a simple act of paying for a heart-disease-on-a-stick caused this much tension between them?

Luckily, the ride home didn't take long, and Landon had waited to say whatever he planned. Before Robert could finish the transaction and give his thanks, Landon slammed the car door shut. Robert was slower to leave the vehicle, fighting off the dread building inside as he trailed behind his sergeant. This time, watching Landon's ass swing didn't hold quite the same draw.

Landon opened the front door and walked over the threshold before pivoting around and standing in the entry. Those strong hands curled in fists at his waist. He took a step or two backward as Robert entered the doorway.

"What's happened? I thought we had a nice evening." Maybe playing dumb wasn't Robert's strong suit with the way Landon gave one of his expertly executed exaggerated eye rolls and threw his hands in the air.

"I'm so fucking unsure with you. I'm going with it. I swear to God I am, but damn, you're so much." Okay, those words were completely unexpected. Robert moved around Landon standing in the entry, for nothing more than to close the front door and get them out of the entryway.

Since he wasn't entirely sure whether those words were meant as a compliment or not, Robert decided he was now navigating potential landmines that might blow up in his face. Honesty was the best course of action. "In the best possible way, that's the way I feel about you, and I'm trying my best to go with it as well. I'm treading new territory, but I like us and what we're doing."

"And what are we doing?" Again, the aggressive tone confused him with the simple question asked. When he didn't readily answer, Landon sighed and threw his hands in the air again, pivoting around toward the stairs. Robert watched him go, filled with a desperation he couldn't quite understand. The deep draw connecting them pulled him forward to chase after Landon.

"Please don't walk away. I'm not sure what happened tonight," Robert said, forcing himself to stop at the base of the stairs. Landon climbed up them only to retreat back down in his direction again.

"What're we doing, *Doc*?" Landon came right for him, getting so close Robert took a step back. Fire lit his soul. Landon couldn't have done a better job of drawing him into this one-sided argument had he tried.

"Don't call me *Doc*. That's what you do when you want to put distance between us." The intensity of Landon's stare bore straight through him as he continued speaking. "What do you want me to say? I've told you I'm into you. Do you want to say more? Because I'm prepared to if that's what you're wanting me to do here."

"No! Absolutely don't say anything more than that." Landon ran his fingers over his close-cropped hair. "Where are the fucking voices in my head when I need them the most? Ugh." He paced away from Robert into the living room, keeping his head cocked toward Robert, his eyes glued on him until he pivoted around walking past him the opposite direction. "I can't help feeling like I'm trash compared to you, and I'm not trash. You're making me feel— No, I'm making me feel less than I've ever felt before in my life. I hate all the uncertainty."

The words weighed heavily on Robert's heart as he stared, unbelieving, trying to absorb all the meaning in those unguarded words. He stood there transfixed by Landon, whose chest heaved, his olive complexion now pink with anger. Robert was bowled over with the love he had for this man.

Landon brought out a side of him he'd never known was there. He made him feel to the depths of his being. All the happiness of budding love, all the worry that he might not be enough to keep this magnificent man, but also the understanding and calm associated with knowing you found your one. Yeah, Robert got it, but more than anything, he wanted a chance to prove Landon was his other half. They shared equal halves of the same soul.

A breath escaped his chest as he realized his soul mate stood across from him. It was real—the spiritual connection that pushed him to Germany in the first place. Robert's gaze immediately cut to the almost full crystal vase of feathers he'd collected. The most prominent being the fluffy one he'd found first that had guided him on a journey to meet Landon. He moved his focus back to Landon and took a small step forward, hoping beyond anything measurable that the same overload of emotions fueled Landon's uncertainty. Their feelings were just too strong to fully navigate.

Robert's worries faded as he gave a silent prayer to please guide him in a direction that ensured he and Landon remained together for the rest of their lives.

"You're not trash, but we'll come back to that one. What makes you uncertain?" Robert asked, trying his best to follow all Landon's disjointed thoughts.

"I'm living with a man I've only really known a week." Landon lifted a finger, silencing Robert's immediate rebuke of the actual time they had known one another. "Don't say I have my own bedroom, because I've been in yours every day since you got back."

"We're both happy with you being there," Robert countered, stepping closer because he wanted to be touching Landon, take him into his arms, tell them both they would figure out their way. This didn't have to be so scary or unsure. "What's got you so upset tonight? I haven't been letting you sleep enough—you're right about that, and it's selfish of me."

"That's not it. You're filling my head with too much fantasy. I don't live this kind of life. My feet are solidly on the ground. I know what this world's about. I was taught to pay my own way, and I make enough money that I could live a pretty good life on my own." Landon's chest swelled in front of Robert in all his proud-man syndrome. "I need some definitive lines drawn between us. I gotta know what's up with us, with where I'm laying my head each night and how I'm paying for that bed."

"Okay." But it wasn't okay, and Robert wasn't a liar, even when it might be the best thing to end this weirdly twisting and turning conversation. "My bills are minimal, but I guess we could look at you contributing to the house if that makes this argument between us end."

There was deafening silence between them again for several long seconds. Robert wasn't certain Landon was willing to hear him out. Landon's stance physically eased, but it was something in the way his face remained passive that let Robert know the invisible barrier separating them still held.

"I should've paid for my sausage tonight."

Robert tried for a small smile. "Have you calmed down enough to talk about those definitive lines?"

Landon couldn't help closing the distance between them anymore than he could help breathing. The tight control he'd held on his red-hot temper had slipped. His new fucked-up state of mind, the one he'd developed from the first second his lips had touched Robert's, had been racked with epic mood swings. Robert did this to him, made him desperate and needy. He didn't like it one bit. Now that all his extreme frustration had subsided, all he wanted was to have Robert in his arms, comforting him, telling him they were going to be okay.

He caught Robert around the waist and drew him close as he reached for Robert's arms, urging him to reciprocate and wrap those strong, sure arms around his body. The beautiful moment came when Robert complied, holding him tightly. For every minute of the last week, Landon had been sick with worry that he'd do something to mess this up between them.

Thankfully, his outburst hadn't scared Robert away. Landon pressed his face into the crook of Robert's neck. "I'm sorry."

"There's no need for apologies. I like buying things for you, Landon. I wasn't trying to imply anything other than my new and clearly deep-seated need to take care of you," Robert said as Landon pressed his lips against the warm skin of Robert's exposed neck.

Landon stayed close with his head buried, trying to make Robert understand his feelings of inadequacy. "I don't need to be taken care of. I don't want you to take care of me…" He stopped himself just short of adding that he wanted to be the one caring for Robert. Him trying to take care of a man like Robert Adams— hell, he was setting himself up for disaster.

"But I want to. I wish you would let me," Robert continued in a plea. "I want a lot of things with you. I'm ready to define the lines. There's so much I want to say but haven't. Landon, you have to know that what we have is real. I feel it to my core. This last week has been one of the best of my life. I know I should let you sleep more, and I try. I just want to be with you every second of every day." Robert pressed his lips against his ear before his handsome lover's cheek came to rest against the side of Landon's head.

"Robert, you're killing me." Landon forced his head back to look Robert straight in the eyes. "You make it so hard to keep perspective."

"It's becoming increasingly difficult for me too. So, I say, we don't try to keep perspective. We just go with the moment and don't get upset when I do something like pay for our food. I have an uncontrollable need to take care of you…and of us. It's new for me. I don't fully understand it, but it's real, and you're important to me."

Whatever this was with Robert was important to Landon too. Robert's fingers lightly covered Landon's mouth, stopping him from speaking those words.

"Just give it to me. Let's say in a few months, if you haven't gotten sick of me and bolted, then we'll talk money arrangements." Robert's fingertips stayed against his lips, a clear indicator he wasn't finished speaking. "Now, tell me what I've done to make you feel less than."

That was the comic relief Landon needed. He was torn between leaving the embrace and pulling Robert closer to him as he laughed right in his face. He hated the feelings plaguing him, the glaring insecurities holding him back. "You're like a rare diamond, and I'm a five-dollar piece of cut glass. You know that. We're on the opposite ends of the spectrum."

"I don't see us that way at all." Robert stepped out of his hold—to Landon's regret—and pressed a strong palm against Landon's chest, keeping him in place. "Not even a little bit." Robert shook his head, that intense blue gaze locking with his. "Landon, I'm all in. I'm just waiting for you to catch up."

Those heart-seizing words were so matter-of-factly stated that Landon had to play them over in his head to make sure he'd heard them correctly. Robert stepped away from him as he spoke. Landon didn't follow as the words momentarily glued his feet to the floor.

"Take whatever time you need. Throw whatever fit you must. Play it however you need to, but I'll be working hard to make sure I'm the only man you ever want for the rest of your life. So, if I pay for a sausage, now you know my reason."

When Robert disappeared into the kitchen, Landon followed. Then watched as Robert opened the refrigerator and took out a water bottle.

"I don't want… You're going to wake up one day and see me differently."

"I'm certain I see you clearly, Landon. I know who you are, and I feel this is real." Robert came to him, unscrewing the top of the water bottle and handing it to Landon, giving him the first drink. Robert's actions proved his words—he always put Landon first. Landon took a long drink as Robert finished. "I missed you like crazy after I left Germany. You're all I've thought about. I think I see you very clearly, maybe better than you see yourself."

Landon handed the half empty bottle to Robert who gulped the rest of it down. Of course, he didn't agree, but he'd take what Robert seemed so willing to give and appreciate the time they had together.

"Then we'll reconvene this conversation in a month." Surely no longer than a month would go by before Robert realized he'd made a mistake and none of this would even matter anymore, except for the lifelong pain Landon would have to endure from losing such a tremendous and fine man. A man he wanted more than anything to be worthy of. His heart was breaking, but he smiled at Robert anyway.

"If that's what you need," Robert said indulgently, a wicked grin tugging at the corners of his mouth.

Landon shook his head as if that might clear the painful tumble his heart just took. Robert's unspoken suggestion was clear. Landon moved enough to entwine their fingers. Nothing else needed to be said about this tonight, and if he could find a way to hold his tongue, they wouldn't ever have to speak of it again.

"Now that we've had our first fight, I think a bout of makeup sex is in order."

Landon was on board. He committed to doing anything he could for Robert. He'd make as many memories as possible. Landon pivoted on his heels and pulled Robert along with him up the stairs, eager to get on with the makeup part.

Chapter 19

Another week later

"I think I'm gaining weight." Landon sighed, patting his belly as he left the kitchen, going in the direction of the living room.

"I've never really cooked for anyone before. I might be going overboard, but I'm glad you like it," Robert said, hand drying the last dish, watching Landon walk the length of the living room toward the television. Four days ago, they had started watching HBO's *Game of Thrones* in lieu of going out. It didn't matter that it was already past midnight. The night was young for someone who worked second shift and for Robert who was still happily unemployed.

Robert placed the clean plate inside its cabinet and tossed the hand towel on the counter. It had been two solid weeks since his and Landon's first real date, and they were already so in sync with one another. Robert spent an extraordinary amount of time preparing their meals, cooking gourmet dishes every night while waiting for Landon to arrive home from base.

Since Landon worked three to eleven, when he got home, they had dinner together, many nights under the soft glow of candlelight. Robert had a big need to romance Landon, and apparently, he had a newfound knack for creating ambience. He strode past the carefully placed fresh flowers—arrangements he'd started purchasing since meeting Landon. He fiddled until he found the perfect position for each lamp shade to add just enough light to the room to see Landon's pouty lips when he needed a kiss, but not enough to do something like work a puzzle. He had even lit small candles and strategically placed them around the open living room. His beloved feathers—the one's he'd carefully collected since that first one landed on his desk, sending him to Germany—were in a vase positioned in the center of the coffee table, a reminder of a force bigger than either of them that had led him to Landon and now connected the two of them.

Okay, yeah, when he thought of it like that, it did seem a bit much, but his heart was full, his mind happy, and his new direction in life solidifying.

Some things had changed for Robert. Since he'd prepared their food, Landon insisted on doing the dishes. Washing dishes was Robert's least favorite household chore, but helped Landon, just to be close to the man until they made their way to the living room to relax. They stayed huddled there until the wee morning hours. Most of their time was spent snuggling together and making out like teenagers until it was time to go upstairs.

"It's hard to believe you don't have any formal training," Landon added distractedly as he aimed the remote toward the television and clicked it on.

"About that," Robert said offhandedly, turning off the lights to the kitchen, walking toward Landon who went for the wine bottle chilling at the wet bar—another one of those preparation deals that Robert seemed to love doing. His guy expertly opened the bottle and poured two glasses while Robert took a seat in the middle of the sofa.

Landon's dark gaze came back to him. "About what?"

"I can't decide if I've lost my mind or if I'm a man who's now on a different course in his life," he confessed, taking the glass Landon offered before taking the seat right beside him.

"I told you a week ago, and I'm pretty sure every day since, you've absolutely lost your mind. I watched a television show once where the person was doing things out of character. It turned out he had a brain tumor. I was thinking dating me might mean you have a brain tumor," Landon said cheekily, waggling his brows as he took a drink from his wineglass then bent forward to place it on the coffee table. His guy moved in closer as Robert turned, angling his body in such a way he could better see Landon's face. Robert draped his arm across the back of the sofa and around Landon's shoulders.

"You're silly, but after you hear what I was thinking, you might decide I should have my brain scanned."

Landon didn't move from his spot, lips puckered so Robert obliged the request, kissing him. He was just such an alluring man and being so close… Robert kissed him again. He couldn't control his compulsions.

"I have an appointment with a student advisor at the Art Institute tomorrow. I think I'm interested in their culinary program."

"Really?" Landon asked excitedly, rearing back to get a better look at Robert's face. "What about medicine?"

"I can't find any interest in going back," Robert confessed. He slid his hand through Landon's short hair. He lifted the glass, taking another long drink as he watched Landon's face go through a range of emotions, starting at passive and ending in utterly perplexed. Landon gripped his thigh and gently squeezed. A move Robert took as support. He appreciated that since he hadn't told another living soul about this possible life redirection.

"Medicine was my world—my whole life—but to add it back in my life would mean it would become all-consuming again. I don't want that. I want to live. I've enjoyed spending the day open to whatever direction life leads. Most days are spent at the market, going through all the fresh produce, finding just the right ingredients. I get why my daddy loved it so much. I enjoy cooking. It's a labor of love for me. I thought taking classes might help me understand the whys of what he and my grandfather taught me. They were both exceptional in the kitchen."

"Hmm." The strong hand at his thigh squeezed again. "When would classes begin?"

"I'm not sure. I'll know more tomorrow. I'm not even sure I'll commit. We'll see," Robert said, loving the connection they shared, of telling truths for the sole reason of needing and respecting the other's opinion.

"That's good then, if it's what makes you happy. I think you're talented enough to go to one of those top schools like your dad did in Italy," Landon said. The words couldn't have been kinder had Landon reached out and caressed Robert's heart. Robert leaned in again, pulling Landon's head toward him to help encourage another kiss. This time he kept Landon right there to let the lip play linger a little longer. Landon was so accepting of him, giving him the highest praise he'd ever known. He did it all the time.

"Even if I could get into one of those schools, I wouldn't want to leave. I don't know if you know this, but I've met someone I'm interested in, and he's tied to this area. I think I'll stick around."

Landon did what he always did when Robert said things like that. He smiled, averted his gaze, and tightened his hold on Robert's leg. "I have some news." Landon's voice grew quiet, maybe a little husky. Such a sexy sound. The butterflies in Robert's tummy that seemed always ready to flutter took flight. Now Robert was smiling.

"What's your news?" Robert asked, running his hand through Landon's hair again. He loved the way the short strands felt against his fingers.

"I'm not sure how you'll feel about this. Actually, I'm pretty sure you'll be against it, but it's better for me…" Landon trailed off, giving Robert a side look as if assessing him while he took another drink. He tried hard to pull off passive at such a declaration. "I decided on a motorcycle today. It'll make the drive to and from the base much faster."

"I didn't know you were a motorcycle guy. It makes sense.

You've just never said anything." Robert wouldn't even try to pretend he hadn't seen the worst possible outcomes of motorcycle rides, but he could say the same thing with so many parts of daily life. He also understood the draw and kind of settled with the idea of riding so freely. "You gonna take me riding?"

Landon cocked his head toward Robert, studying him closely with a skeptical gaze. "You always surprise me. Of course, I'll take you riding. My boyfriend needs to be on the back of my bike."

"Your boyfriend, huh?" Robert asked, his heart leaping excitedly, instantly loving those unguarded words.

Landon must have liked claiming him as much as Robert liked hearing it, because he took the wineglass from his hand and set it on the coffee table beside his. Then he slid an arm around Robert's back and pushed him against the soft cushion. He melted at the look in his lover's eyes. Landon caressed his cheek, angling his face as the tempting man descended. Seconds before their lips touched, Landon whispered, "You're so fucking handsome, my God."

Landon slanted his mouth over Robert's, his tongue tracing the path it instinctively knew. Robert opened for him as they came together hot and heavy. Their kisses were wet and hungry, tongues swirling as he probed the depths of Robert's sweet mouth. He slid his hand over the hard bulge of Robert's cock, itching to feel the warm flesh against his palm. Robert clawed at him as he massaged his lover through his clothes. They both gasped for air as he released the top button of Robert's jeans, nibbling at Robert's lips and licking into his mouth. He couldn't wait to be inside his lover.

An odd digital ring broke the haze of the fevered kiss. Robert stopped skimming his hands over Landon's stomach muscles, and

Landon almost whimpered at the loss of the other man's caress. The ring sounded again, and Landon lifted his head from the lock he had on Robert's neck. They both looked in the direction of the sound. Robert's laptop came to life and his grandmother's name and picture appeared on the screen.

Landon immediately jumped up as if they'd been caught in the act and went for the computer. Through the hours of their conversations, and even longer, as he'd read Vice President Adams's memoirs, he knew Kennedy Adams was older, and he panicked when her name appeared at such a late hour.

"I'll get it." He grabbed the computer and brought it back to Robert, who answered without hesitation.

"Nonnie?"

Landon took the seat next to Robert, without getting into Kennedy's view. He ran his fingers through his hair, making sure he was put together then angled his head against the back of the sofa to see for himself that she was okay.

"Can you see me, Robert?" Kennedy asked, a perplexed expression on her face as she looked at the screen.

"I can. Are you all right?" he asked as Kennedy moved in and out of the camera's range. He must have seen enough to know everything was good because Robert smiled, his gaze never leaving the screen.

"I can see him. How do I know if he can see me?" she asked someone off-screen.

"Right here, Mrs. Adams." A younger woman came into the camera's view and tapped on the screen's lower corner. Mrs. Adams looked down, and her worried gaze lightened when she lifted her head and stared at the camera.

"This is called Skype," Mrs. Adams explained as if Robert wouldn't already understand the program. That caused Robert to chuckle, and Landon's grin split ear to ear. "I can video call you now. It's not that hard to work."

"I can see that, Nonnie. What's going on that you're up so late?" Robert asked, sitting up straighter on the sofa, angling the laptop better in his lap.

"We're up planning Autumn's wedding. Lauren here's helping me, and I haven't heard from you since I left Minnesota. I've changed the plans. We'll have the wedding on my downstairs terrace. It's such a lovely time of year. I've decided it's best for you to give Autumn away. She's arguing with me, saying she wants to give herself away, but we're not having that. I've got the local bed and breakfast willing to house Cameron's family. You and Autumn will of course stay with me." Robert grinned as Kennedy gave all the random details of a wedding Landon had heard about in passing, from both Robert and Autumn. He wasn't a hundred percent certain when the nuptials were planned, but he could see, whatever age Kennedy had on her, it hadn't dulled her mind. She was sharp as a tack.

"I'll do whatever you two decide." Good answer, not committing to either side. Landon nodded his approval.

"Son, you'll tell her you're walking her down the aisle. She's impossible to deal with when she gets something stuck in her mind." Mrs. Adams shook her head in frustrated disgust.

"Okay, I'll make the suggestion next time I talk to her." Again, Robert answered by giving himself wiggle room, and it made Landon laugh; probably not the first time Robert had been placed in this situation, but Mrs. Adams seemed appeased and nodded.

"Autumn wants me to go heavy on the flowers to help represent your fathers. I like that idea, plus they're so easy to decorate with. I think we're doing a variety of flowers, but probably not the calla lily. That flower seems depressing to me."

Robert laughed, causing Landon to take a closer look for whatever he'd missed. "And Autumn wants them, right? So, I'm supposed to say they're depressing?"

Kennedy scowled at Robert. "You were always too smart for your own good."

With a happy grin, Robert's gaze landed on him. "The women of my family are a force. You'll learn soon enough to navigate them."

"I can see they are," Landon whispered quietly as if Robert's looking and talking to him might not have been noticed.

"Are you with someone?" Mrs. Adams tilted her head as if she could see past the range of the camera to where Landon sat. His nerves shifted into overdrive at her words. "Is that why your hair's all messed up?" That question made Landon's face heat in embarrassment as Robert brought both hands to his head, straightening the mess when Mrs. Adams just laughed. "I was teasing. Is he the soldier?"

"Yes, it's him. Nonnie meet Landon. Landon this is Kennedy Adams—you know, my grandmother."

Landon shook his head until Robert moved the laptop and the full screen landed on him.

"My goodness, he is handsome, Robert. You've done *very* well," Kennedy said, making Robert laugh again. A sudden blush of embarrassment colored Robert's cheeks and warmed Landon's heart.

"Thank you, Nonnie. I think he's very handsome too." Robert reached over for Landon who refused to hold hands in front of Mrs. Adams. He sat woodenly next to Robert, keeping several inches of space between them.

He didn't know why he was doing it, and that didn't matter in the least. He just knew Robert had to respect the boundaries, especially in front of Kennedy Adams.

"Have you invited him to the wedding? You have an unused plus one," Mrs. Adams said, her voice becoming softer as she stared straight at Landon.

"I've mentioned it. He's shy and is intimidated to meet the family. Although, I'm finding he talks to Autumn as much as he talks to me," Robert answered, calling Landon out in front of his grandmother.

"That's not true," Landon whispered, trying hard to keep his face neutral. He also didn't let himself dwell on the fact that his whisper had probably been loud enough to be heard on the mic, making him seem as clueless to Skype as Mrs. Adams.

"Nonsense. Of course, he's coming. He'll stay here with you." She seemed to be directing Lauren in committing Landon to the wedding party. "I suppose with such a late hour in committing him, you two won't mind sharing a room."

"No, ma'am. That's fine. I don't want to put you out," Landon answered quickly. Within two seconds, he realized he'd just agreed to share a bedroom with Robert at his grandmother's home. His face instantly warmed with regret.

"Please put us in the same room, Nonnie. It'll make it easier than having to sneak around your house trying to find him." Robert elbowed him in the stomach as if that was a shared joke between the both of them. The minute this session ended, he would be making it clear there was no sharing anything, including a room in Mrs. Adams's house.

"You know, with your fathers— When Avery first met Kane, it was the only time Avery was ever silent with me. Our long distance bills each month were astronomically high, then he went quiet. I should have known you'd be like your father. So, I'm guessing this is already serious?" she asked, looking as if she knew the answer.

"It is, Nonnie, but you're embarrassing him," Robert replied, lifting the pad of his thumb to smooth over Landon's heated cheeks.

"Oh, son, don't be embarrassed. Avery had proposed to Kane after just a week of dating, and I had only heard of the man hours before. I suspect the Adams men just know. I can't see why Robert would be different. Have you proposed to him, Robert?" She looked at Robert expectantly.

Landon's heart suddenly stuttered so violently he had to look down to see if it had fallen from his chest.

Robert busted out with a hearty laugh, straightening the computer in his lap, glancing over with a smile aimed directly at Landon. "I haven't, Nonnie."

"It's just a matter of time." She angled her head again, trying to see Landon, and thankfully, Robert didn't accommodate her movements. "Landon, you come to the wedding. You two come early if you can. I want to get to know you, and if I wait for Robert to bring you, I might die of old age first."

When Landon didn't have to look at her, and he had the second to calm down, he decided she was purposefully goading him. She definitely had a sense of humor. Since her comment was directed to him, and he didn't know how to respond, he gave his standard, "Yes, ma'am."

"Look at those fine manners. He looks Italian. Paulie would like that, Robert," Kennedy's voice grew softer.

"Yes, I agree. He'd like him." Robert nodded his confirmation to Landon who seemed to be mute with how quiet he'd grown.

"On a serious note, Landon. You've helped put a smile back on our Robert's face. We all appreciate what you've done. I look forward to meeting you in person, young man. Robert, call Autumn for me."

"I will. I love you."

"I love you too. Now how do I turn this off?" she asked. Her assistant came back into view. She smiled at Robert and lifted a hand before the screen went blank. Robert closed the lid and placed the laptop on the coffee table before sitting back and casually taking Landon's hand in his. This time he didn't fight the hold.

"So, you're going with me to the wedding?"

"If you want me to. I gotta make sure I can get the time off, but if you'd rather me not, I can use the lack of time off as my excuse not to go."

"I want you to. I've just been putting on the brakes to all this emotion to help build time for us, keep from coming on too strong." Robert lifted Landon's hand to his lips. "I'm pretty sure I'm failing miserably, but I'm trying."

"Yeah, if this is putting on the brakes, I can't imagine what you'd be doing otherwise," Landon answered honestly.

"Yeah, that's why the brakes are needed. You look freaked out." Robert scanned his face, caution in his gaze.

"When I read your father proposed so quickly, I thought that was his way of speeding up the story," Landon confessed.

Robert grinned at him and reached for the remote. "You ready to watch *Game of Thrones*?"

"So, it really was in the first couple of weeks of meeting your dad?" Landon asked, curious for some reason, wanting to know the truth.

Robert pushed the power button on the television, and the screen again flashed on. "I wasn't there, but it's the story I heard. I think it was like ten days. They didn't head down the aisle for a year, but my dad moved to Minnesota to run for the senate and then met my daddy. Things had to be sorted quickly."

"You aren't running for office, are you?" Landon asked, knowing one hundred percent, if he didn't fit in Robert's current world, he certainly wouldn't fit in a political world.

Robert fiddled with the remote, pointing it at the screen as he barked out another laugh. "Zero plans for anything political. I'm a people pleaser. I don't have the temperament."

"Good. Don't." It seemed enough for right now. Landon reached for one of the new sofa pillows and started to lie across the seats, trying to redirect his thoughts. Robert obliged him, scooting over to the end of the oversized couch as the HBO app came up. Normally, having his head in Robert's lap would lead to them both getting a blow job, but he didn't see that happening tonight. He was, in fact, completely freaked out. What would he have done if Robert had asked him to marry him like that?

He'd marry him.

That answer was so loud it echoed in his head. In fact, the words were so loud, he looked up to see if he'd blurted them. Robert looked down in question, and Landon shook his head, turning back to face the television.

Fuck. Now, he was wondering why Robert hadn't asked him to marry him. If all the men on the Adams side of the family declared their forever devotion at warp speed, why hadn't Robert?

"You're getting agitated," Robert said, running his fingers through Landon's hair as the show began.

"Because I'm a fucking idiot," Landon muttered, and Robert laughed again.

"You're anything but." Robert increased the volume.

Landon decided to ignore himself and adjusted his body, getting more comfortable. After a second more, he settled his head back on the pillow only to be poked in the cheek. He lifted to see a gray feather edging out of the pillow's casing. Of course. Only because Robert seemed to be keeping every feather they found, he tossed it on the coffee table close to the others and focused on Ned Starks's face.

"No more kisses then?"

"Not right now," he said gruffly. Robert's good nature held. He heard the low rumble of a chuckle before Robert reached over and tickled his side. It helped the anxiety. He wrapped an arm around Robert's legs and watched the episode.

Chapter 20

Robert darted across the street at the light, checking the time on his wristwatch as he stepped up on the curb. He was fifteen minutes late to meet Autumn for lunch. It wasn't necessarily the concern of holding Autumn up for lunch that worried him, but the cooling vegetable burger she had agreed to pick up before meeting him in the nearby park. He was starving. Luckily for him, he spotted Autumn taking a seat on the edge of a fountain under the large oak trees that surrounded the area. Robert strolled with purposeful strides past the crowded food vendors, straight toward her.

"You're late," she said, shoving her sunglasses on top of her head, the glasses keeping her long blond hair off her face. Instead of teasing her, he said the next thing that came to mind.

"Pregnancy agrees with you."

Her skin seemed to glow with her sun-kissed complexion and bright eyes. Even her hair seemed full, silky, and thick. He loved seeing his twin looking so vibrant and healthy. Happiness radiated from her.

Autumn took offense to his assessment, rolling her eyes and ducking her head. "Cam told you to say that, didn't he?" she accused and resumed unpacking the sack of burgers.

"I haven't talked to him since I left Minnesota." Robert sat on the empty place beside her. She stopped moving the food to the space between them and eyed him closer, clearly trying to see if she believed him.

"Tell me what I'm missing," he said and counted three burgers and two large French fries between them where he had only ordered a single vegetable burger and nothing more. "Is Cam coming?"

"No, Robert, he's not," she said as if he were adding salt to a wound he knew nothing about. "I'm five months pregnant and starving all of the time. I literally can't stop eating. My bigger clothes aren't fitting. Now, my pregnancy clothes aren't fitting. I don't have a craving for one thing. I have a craving for all things." Her distress matched the gravity of the tone she used and caused him to give an almost silent chuckle. The glare he received proved she'd heard his humor and wasn't impressed.

"I'm not sure exactly when cravings truly begins—" He began to explain the ins and outs of pregnancy when she cut him off, snapping at him while sorting the burgers.

"Stop. You aren't helping."

"Okay, then I'll tell you the truth," he started and paused until she looked over at him, placing his burger and napkin on his lap. "I didn't notice that you'd gained weight. You look beautiful and happy. It's all anyone can see."

She softened all those prickly edges and looked genuinely relieved. "That's a real good step in the right direction."

As his reward, she opened the drink carrier and handed him his beloved favorite guava juice blend.

"Thank you." Robert unwrapped his braised mushroom burger—his absolute favorite meal out—and gave an "*mmm*" as he ate a nice-sized bite. "My God, it's good. They never disappoint."

"I know, right? I'm just about finished transitioning my files. I'm afraid I won't be back in DC for a while. What am I going to do without those pop-up restaurant stands?" she asked then took her first bite, having the same look of euphoria that he was certain he'd had. That was the one thing about living in this area for most of their lives, she and Robert had eaten everywhere, trying everything, leaving very little in DC untasted, and Brazen Burger, a small vendor stand in FreshFarm Market, was at the top of their list.

When he didn't answer, because he didn't pause in inhaling his burger, Autumn filled him in between bites. "Brazen's going to open a brick and mortar location. The funding's been approved."

"No way, really?" he asked after taking a drink. They needed to. He just hoped it was still reasonably close to where he lived.

"Yeah, Suzi told me today. Also, they started on the construction for the library. That happened fast." She side-eyed him, and he nodded, because he knew about the library. He'd found out early on that he wasn't truly needed to oversee the library staff. They had their ideas, believed in keeping the integrity of the home, and knew what they were doing. "Tell me about today. Why were you at the Art Institute?"

"Well, I'm not a hundred percent sure of anything except I'm sure that school's not for me." The weather was fantastic this time of year. Summers were the very best part of living in DC. Robert lifted his face to the sun, letting it warm his skin.

"I'm guessing this is for the culinary classes. Landon says you're cooking all the time again. So, I agree, that school's not for you," she said as if she had any part in the decision. He shot her a look and lifted his brow. Autumn only laughed. "What? I agree. I bet the reason is that you're not the young chicken you once were."

As much as he hated to admit it, she was right on. He nodded and lifted a finger to pause the conversation right there, quickly chewing his bite then swallowing so he could talk. "I'm going to pretend you didn't just call me old, because you're right, it's entirely too artsy and a little on the younger side for me. I called *The National Culinary Review*, left a message for their new associate editor. Daddy used to write articles for them, remember?" When Autumn nodded, he continued. "Maybe they can offer me some training locally."

"Look at the school Daddy went to in Italy," she suggested and dug into her food with gusto.

"I don't want to leave DC, not yet. Plus, it's only a hobby for me, not a career path. I'm just enjoying it right now."

"Then what's your career path?" she asked, her mouth full, but that didn't slow her down.

"Hey, get off me. I said you were pretty. That should've been enough to give me a break. Besides, Nonnie skyped me in the middle of the night last night." He got the desired reaction— Autumn's head whipped around, the bite nearing her mouth completely forgotten.

"What?" she exclaimed.

"Right? That was pretty much my thought until I found out the reason for the call. She wants me to walk you down the aisle, and she doesn't want calla lilies. She considers them a funeral flower," Robert explained, laying out the arguments as he knew them.

"That's absurd. I love calla lilies. Those were Daddy's favorite, especially when all the colorful ones started coming out. They were always his first choice whenever he had to choose, and Daddy was the most sophisticated, polished man I've ever known. The calla lilies are staying." She left no room for an argument, just as he'd suspected.

"I thought you might say that," he said then took the last bite of the burger.

"Am I unreasonable?" she asked in a tone that answered her own question.

He chewed then reached for his drink, taking a long gulp, biding his time. His sister was something else, so strong and certain. He loved her like only another twin could understand, but she did come with challenges. Much like Autumn knew how to work him, he knew how to work her too.

"You're frustrating me, Robert."

"No, I'm thinking."

"No, you're making me angry."

Yeah, okay, he was doing that too. On purpose. He grinned as he said, "I would like the honor of standing in and walking you down whatever aisle Nonnie has created. I truly like that idea. We aren't as alone as it sometimes feels. We have each other, and I'd like to be there by your side when you take this next step in life."

"That's all you had to say." Autumn nodded once and turned back to the French fries.

"So, let's negotiate this with Nonnie. What else are you two butting heads over?" Robert asked, tucking his trash inside the bag before crossing one leg over the other. He tilted his face toward the warm sun and closed his eyes.

"If the weather holds, I would like to have the wedding along the back edge of the property, not on the terrace. You know the spot where the ocean meets the corner of the property? She's very against it, says the winds are too unpredictable there, but I don't care. I think the problem is more that the land is harder for her to navigate. I wouldn't be opposed to having everyone watch from decorated golf carts. She'd never have to get out of her cart. She's the one making this an elegant affair. She's hired a quartet, Robert. Me? A quartet…seriously?" Yep, he'd unwittingly opened a flood gate. Autumn had worked herself up so much that the food she claimed to crave was left untouched. "We should have just eloped."

"How many people are invited?"

"You, Landon, Sophia, Tom, and Cam's mom and dad, his two brothers, one has a wife," she said, counting off with her fingers.

"Christine and Nicole?" Robert asked. Both were Sophia's daughters and technically their half-sisters.

"Christine's in India teaching English. She's met a man and getting married there, I think. Nicole is touring Europe with her band."

He nodded at that one. Nicole was an anthropologist who'd dropped everything to sing in a techno-folk band. "How's that going?"

"Apparently they're all the rage in Europe. I like the music," she said with a nod.

"Have I heard it?" he asked, trying to remember.

"How would I know that except you were in a really bad place, so I doubt it. I was thinking about you being an extra on the *Walking Dead* with how zombie-like you were." The immediate silly grin, and the way she let that sit between them for maybe as long fifteen seconds, showed how proud she was of her joke. "Too soon?"

"No, but you aren't funny," Robert added dryly, knowing her words were too close to the truth.

"How's Landon?" she asked in that same happy tone.

"I'm not sure I've ever truly confronted you about your matchmaking," he said, though he'd called her out from the beginning, but all by text.

"Now, hang on. I did that for you. I just didn't want to lose him before you opened your eyes to what you were missing. So, I technically wasn't matchmaking. I was keeping him close. I don't think he would have stayed in your house and been there like he was if I hadn't built that relationship with him. He seems resistant to taking anything from anyone."

Robert gave an almost silent grunt at that one. "That's an understatement."

"Is he going to fit, Robert? You're very complicated and run in high circles," she asked seriously, and it was a valid question. He'd walked away from his world, done everything he could think of, and Landon was still so uncomfortable at times.

"He's already struggling with it all, and we've barely left my house. We'll both have to compromise when we need to." That thought gave him a bit of worry and anxiety, so he left that right there and thought about the positives between them. "He fits me very well—the real me or maybe the me I'm just getting to know.

I feel different when I'm around him, and I like that person. He makes me happy. I'm crazy about him."

"I can tell. I knew you would be." She looked very proud of herself, and just like that, the food was back to being the main focus.

"Autumn, if things work out like I hope they do, he's going to be with us for a long time," Robert confessed as she continued eating.

"I know. I knew after the first time he and I spoke. You have such passion in you. I'm surprised you haven't pulled a Dad move and tied him down yet." She took a bite and chewed while eyeing him. When he stayed silent, her eyes grew big. She put the napkin to her lips, covering her full mouth as she spoke. "Have you considered putting a ring on it?"

Robert dug inside his pocket, pulling out a small ring box he'd been hiding. He opened the lid and showed her the ring he planned on giving Landon. "I picked it up on the way here." He'd seen it in a window some time ago and known it would be perfect. He had called the jeweler and had them hold it for him.

Maybe it wasn't the best idea to pull it out in such a public place. Autumn made a show of hiding the box from any potential prying eyes while still getting a good look herself. "It's titanium? Isn't that dangerous?"

"Maybe, but this one's made to slide off. I like the strength of the metal." Robert lifted one finger and touched the ring. "It reflects the unbreakable bond I feel with Landon."

Wonderment lit her excited gaze. "When are you going to give it to him?"

"Not for a while," he said, though those were some of the hardest words he might have ever said. "I'm so ready. He's not at all. He's the kind of person who needs to be absolutely comfortable before he acts. He's also the kind of guy who can be challenged, and he'll act." He snapped the lid closed and pushed the ring box back in his pocket. "I prefer the first option for something this important."

"I agree." Her tone was soft and gentle, which didn't really fit Autumn. Tears welled in her eyes as she stared sweetly at him. Her hands came together to rest close to her heart. "Robert, you needed this. You were growing so cold and distant even before Dad died. You were doing great things, incredible I'm sure, but we were losing you. I feel like you're back, and I'm so happy."

She reached out, wrapping him in an awkwardly tight hug. He couldn't even pretend to be offended with her assessment of his life. He agreed with her completely.

"Now, you know why I'm undecided about my professional future." A small shift in the breeze happened, so small it may not have even been noticed by Autumn, but Robert was learning to pay attention to the small things he used to take for granted every day. He looked around, and sure enough, he spotted what he'd suspected he'd find. He pried himself from Autumn's hold and bent to pick up the feather at his feet. His heart burst with completeness.

"What just happened?"

Robert tucked the feather in his pocket, hesitant to share with Autumn. "Nothing."

"It's beautiful, but why are you keeping a feather?"

He wouldn't look at her, not yet, and instead reached for his trash and hers. "Nothing I feel like discussing right now." He wished he could share, but he didn't want to worry her or have her call him crazy, depending on how she processed the news.

"Then when?" she asked, staring up at him.

"Probably never. I love you. Go finish closing your office and get back home to Minnesota," he said, taking her hand and pulling her to her feet.

"I miss you. Minnesota isn't the same without you," she said, her arm wrapped around his waist.

"I doubt that. Let me know if you hear any warning bells from Landon. He's really set in his ways. I don't want him to bolt based on uncertainty." Robert leaned in for a side hug and kissed the top of her head.

"I'm glad he's making you work for it. I was tired of watching man after man throw themselves at you and you completely ignoring them," she said, pushing her sunglasses over her eyes.

"There's never been a single instance of men throwing themselves at me. You're ridiculous. Want me to walk you back to your office?" he offered.

"No, I'm grabbing a cab. I've got to stop by Nordstrom before I go back. Wear black to the wedding. I'll get you a necktie that matches my dress. That's another issue. Nonnie wants me to wear white. I have a beautiful cream-colored Zac Posen picked out." She walked several steps backward, heading toward the curb. "You know, maybe you should call Helene. She's become a partner at Buon Appetito and is back in the area. I think she could offer up some private kitchen tutorials—whatever that's called. Think about it."

That wasn't a half bad idea. Helene had the same stern way about her as Paulie. He would absolutely learn a thing or two from her. He lifted a hand goodbye and called out, "Take care of my niece."

"Nephew!" Like an expert, she lifted her hand and a cab stopped immediately. She had serious talent at hailing a cab.

The sales manager pointed to the line on the bottom of the page for his last signature before the sleek black Kawasaki Ninja was officially his. Landon scribbled his name then looked over the page before pushing the small bundle of paperwork toward the man who had painstakingly haggled the very last possible penny from Landon.

The key fob was placed in front of him on the table. "It's been a pleasure doing business with you."

Landon clasped the manager's extended hand while pushing out of the chair then reached for the key fob. Finally, he had something that was his—that he was paying for with his own money—and it felt damn good. "It's right out front?"

"Yeah, I'll walk you out."

Landon grabbed his new helmet and trailed out with his eyes fixed on the black and chrome beauty just feet away. He nodded at the sales rep who pushed the door open for him.

"You familiar with the bike?"

"Yeah. I got it. Thanks," he said, not slowing his stride. He couldn't wait to get out on the road. Seconds before he stepped up to the bike, he stopped short, digging his phone out of his pocket. With one hand, he snapped a picture of the motorcycle then repositioned the phone, putting himself and the helmet in the shot with the bike in the background. His grin was as big as he'd ever seen, but that wasn't unusual these days.

Landon straddled the bike, put the helmet on the fuel tank and took a second to send Robert the picture of his new beauty. Before he was able to shove the phone away, it vibrated. The excitement over his new bike came second to the possibility that Robert had messaged him back so quickly. He palmed the phone again seeing a picture of Robert pointing to his head. Another picture came through with a thumbs up.

Landon chuckled, prepared to tease Robert when he caught a shadow approaching out of his peripheral vision. He didn't look over right away and quickly typed a reassuring message to Robert, promising to wear his helmet.

"Landon Russo?" He looked over to see a man in standard construction work clothing—dusty T-shirt and jeans, equally dusty work boots. The guy was about his age and kind of looked familiar...

"Yeah?" He took a closer look. Since he'd first arrived at Andrews, he'd kept his head down and worked like a dog, trying to build the respect of his squadron and his Master Sergeant. He hadn't really met a lot of other people.

"Don't remember me? I'm Mark Peters." He shoved his hand forward and Landon automatically clasped it in greeting, still unable to place the guy. "We went to high school together."

"Yeah?" His eyes had to have bugged out of his head. Landon had grown up with Lance, meaning they had gone from kindergarten all the way through graduation together. Mark had always been on the shorter side and skinny as a rail. Not anymore. Although he wasn't super tall, he was built like a Mack truck. "What the hell happened to you?"

The easygoing smile transformed the guy's face into exactly the young man he had known most of his life. "Late puberty. I heard you were in the military."

"Yeah. Air Force, stationed at Andrews. What're you doing here?"

"I'm a contractor, me and Branson. 'Member him? We were always hanging out together back then." He waited for Landon to nod. Landon obliged, but didn't remember anyone with the first or last name Branson. "We were hired as part of the renovation team for the pentagon. Been around here about three years now. It's a good gig." Mark tucked his hands in his front pockets as he nodded at the bike. "Brand new?"

"Just this second. Speaking of which, I'm gonna be late. Give me your number and we can catch up," Landon said, exiting out of Robert's message and going to the contact portion of his cell phone. He typed quickly, adding Lance's name then extended the phone for Mark to add his number.

"Me and my lady have a place in Clinton. Branson lives next door. It's small, but good enough. You should come have some supper with us sometime," Mark said as he typed.

"I'm on second shift, but yeah, that could work." The obstacles immediately presented themselves. His gaze slid down Lance's work attire and stopped at his boots, and he instantly disliked himself for doing so. He wasn't the kind of guy to judge anyone, for any reason, but it didn't change the facts. Mark was as blue collar as they came.

Oddly, Landon's usual shields no longer dropped into place, keeping him at a distance, making him wonder if Branson or anyone from his past knew he was gay. Instead he thought about how Robert might fit into the mix. He took the phone and tucked it away. "I'll text you."

"I'll tell Branson you said hello." Mark stepped back a couple of steps, that same easygoing smile stayed in place. "Seriously, let me know when you can have dinner. We need to catch up."

Landon nodded and put his helmet on. He couldn't see that happening anywhere in the near future. He spent all his free time with Robert, and the refined, cultured man probably hadn't ever sat on a lawn chair at a backyard barbeque. With a push of a button, Landon started the engine, letting it rumble, loving the vibration surging between his thighs. He couldn't wait to get his handsome doctor on his new bike. Landon revved the engine for good measure, then he lifted a hand to Mark before starting out of the parking lot.

Chapter 21

Two weeks later

Landon edged his bike inside the garage next to Robert's Cadillac before engaging the kickstand. He lifted his leg over the bike and pulled off his helmet. He admired his sleek black and chrome Ninja next to the black sports car. As far as he was concerned, they looked good side by side. One might be substantially cheaper than the other, but they suited one another just like the two men who owned the vehicles.

He admitted he was growing comfortable playing house with Robert. His first thoughts were no longer of his military career nor were they of the partying that had always occurred in his free time. They were of Robert, always of Robert. He placed the helmet on the seat and started for the backdoor, absently hitting the garage door button as he climbed the two small steps to the door.

A crash inside the house had him looking up at the closed door as he reached for the doorknob. A string of curse words followed, all in Robert's husky voice, but they didn't fit the most patient man he'd ever known. Then he heard another voice, much softer, and pulled his phone free to look at the time. It was half past eleven—half an hour until midnight. What could Robert possibly be doing?

Landon pulled open the door and the most delicious smell assaulted him. His mouth watered and his stomach let out a pitiful growl. The chaos that greeted him only added to his confusion. The house was a mess. Disaster area didn't cover the enormity of destruction. Empty boxes and Styrofoam had been discarded randomly and littered the counters and the floor. Dishes filled the table. Some appeared new and unused, and others were filled with cooling baked goods. There were plates of pastries, meats, and various vegetables, some burned and some not, but they all looked as if they had been sitting there awhile.

He stuck his head inside the kitchen to see a short brunette standing next to Robert. She'd been spared from whatever had exploded in the kitchen, her khakis, white short-sleeved shirt, and apron all clean and well-kept. Robert, on the other hand, was filthy from his loafers to his T-shirt, including the apron he wore. Puffs of something saucy splattered his face, and his hair was an absolute mess.

"He should be home soon. This needs to be finished," Robert said, his whole concentration resting on the stockpot on the new stove he had purchased earlier in the week and had installed yesterday.

"Concentrate on this, Robert. Don't rush it, and don't lose your attention. Timing is key with most things. It's why the others failed today. You need to find the patience of the surgeon you are." Her voice was wise with instruction and had a thick French accent.

"I think this is overly complicated. It seems like it could be made easier," Robert said, his brow knitted as he stared at whatever he stirred.

"Of course, coq au vin can be made simpler, but then it wouldn't have this taste."

Landon stood in the opening of the kitchen, watching her dip then lift a spoon to Robert's mouth. He took the taste, his hand steadily stirring, and he looked relieved, moving the pot off the burner.

"Do you see the difference between cutting corners and preparing the dish as it was intended?"

"It's very good." Robert's gaze suddenly shifted to Landon. "I didn't hear you come in."

"When I offered to do the dishes, I'm not sure it covered all this," he said teasingly, lifting his hands wide enough to encompass the multiple rooms of mess. Any tension he had sensed in Robert eased as the always relaxed and composed man glanced around, maybe for the first time, to see the disaster zone around him.

"We've been in here since right after you left. I think I've finally gotten something right. Come taste," Robert said and reached for a clean utensil from the open drawer beside the oven. Robert dipped the spoon inside the pot and lifted it. "Come on. It's good."

Landon stepped into the circle of the two and opened his mouth, eager to taste the dish Robert worked so hard to master. When the spices and perfect flavor combination hit his tongue, he closed his eyes to savor the divine taste. He opened to see two expectant stares waiting on his review. He didn't have to pretend at the greatness of the concoction. His eyes grew wide as he chewed the bite down. "That's incredible. What is it?"

"Coq au vin or translated to rooster in wine. You must be the mysterious Landon he keeps referring to." She lifted her hand to shake Landon's. Her clasp was warm and friendly and lasted a second or two longer than normal. "I'm Helene Hermes."

"Landon Russo." She had a way about her that he instantly liked. "It's delicious. Are you eating rooster?" he asked Robert and leaned over to grab a new spoon for another bite when Robert must have mistaken his advancement for a kiss. There was no hesitation. Robert kissed him as if there was no one else in the room. His heart fluttered at the bold gesture. Now the delicious meal was runner-up to the man staring at him with a twinkle in his eyes.

"No, but I've had little tastes here and there. We've been at it all day. I wanted to make you something special, but I'm not sure there's much edible out there," he explained, cocking his head toward the table full of food.

"Nonsense." Helene had the same forceful tone his Master Sergeant always used. "You have the talent I suspected. No son of Kane Adams would lack talent. We just need to hone your skill." Helene stepped back and untied her apron. "Starting tomorrow, we'll begin breaking you of your bad habits with better control of the basics like keeping the precious ingredients inside the cookware, not on you," she teased, eyeing Robert's complete state of utter destruction. Robert looked down at himself before giving Landon his charming grin again.

"She gives a compliment then takes it away. We made homemade egg noodles—" Robert said to Landon before Helene cut him off.

"Not my choice for such a dish as coq au vin," she said with a *tsk,* and Robert interrupted her as she did him.

"I thought you"—Robert lifted a hand, his palm running down the length of Landon's arm—"would like the noodles with your Italian upbringing, and you're who we were cooking for. Which was technically today's lesson: know your audience." Robert got an arched brow and another *tsk, tsk* from Helene who went for the edge of the counter where her purse sat. "Let me walk her out, and I'll be back."

The camaraderie between Helene and Robert showed they had known and appreciated one another for years. Of course, his dick noticed Robert's playful yet take-charge tone, along with his sweet teasing and gentle caresses as he looked over the kitchen and thought about Robert's confession. This whole state of disarray was with the sole intention of pleasing him. Oh man, he was so fucked. Robert made him feel cared for, special, and wanted. Landon reached for some discarded packaging to help clean only to find the trashcan completely full. Shrugging, he started there first.

"You don't have to do that," Robert said when Landon came

in from taking the trash to the bin in the garage.

"I can tell you had a good day," he said, really liking the image greeting him. Robert folded his apron with the underside out to keep the mess on the inside and off the table where he set the bundle. He pulled his T-shirt over his head. Robert was the only guy he knew who actually wore a white undershirt under his T-shirts. Then he brought that over his head too. Oh, goodie. Landon's dick hardened, watching the ripple of those defined stomach muscles the shirt had been hiding.

"I did. I'm a mess. Cooking properly is much harder than I thought it would be." Robert's eager lips came for his again as he started to pass by. Landon kept telling himself he should eat the food prepared before showing Robert exactly how he felt about having this man slaving away for him all day, on food Robert himself wouldn't even enjoy. It was those endearing things that wove around his heart.

Overwhelmed with the urge to hold the man against him, he watched as Robert worked his belt free, letting the pants slide to his feet. Robert gave a happy laugh before saying, "I shouldn't track this mess into the rest of the house." His eyes were filled with excitement as he explained, "I'm not sure I've ever been this messy before in my life. Maybe there's something I could do, like tucking my elbows against my sides, that will alleviate all the rest of this mess from getting anywhere else." Robert was happy. Landon felt it radiating from him as he stepped out of his pants and stood there in nothing but his red striped briefs.

Landon's heart swelled with Robert's delight, proving what he already knew: Robert's happiness was his happiness. All the defenses he'd kept dragging up against Robert had slipped away. He loved him. Loved every side of him. The acknowledgement sent a shockwave through his body. Then peace settled over Landon. All the anxiety and confusion melted away as he allowed himself to admit the truth.

"I hope you like this dinner. I learned the hard way today that any skill I have is elementary and very limited to my father's style of cooking. Today was the trial, but I think Helene and I will be meeting a few times a week. She told me that I could have a culinary future if I want it. I did have talent."

"Of course, you do," Landon said, proud of himself for still being able to listen as the world rocked then settled under his feet with his insights. "You're very talented."

"It's tremendous praise from both of you. Go change. I'll start pulling this together. I had William Sonoma on speed dial today. They delivered all day long. I think we'll be renovating the entire kitchen." Robert started to walk away from him, but Landon locked an arm around his waist.

"You're talented in so many ways." He watched the moment of surprise light Robert's extraordinary face before understanding set in. Landon swept his hand inside the waistband of Robert's underwear, pushing them down.

"What's gotten into you?" Robert asked, his eyes dropping to Landon's lips. Landon took the moment to admire the naked man at his leisure.

"Hopefully you," he muttered and turned Robert, the table stopping any chance of retreat as he dropped to his knees.

He opened his mouth and sucked Robert to his root. His nose pressed into the blond hair at the base of the sexiest cock he'd ever known. He breathed in the intoxicating scent, inhaling the heated arousal. His dick jerked in his pants, leaking against the now uncomfortably tight material. His need to make Robert orgasm overruled any common sense or etiquette he'd learned about blow jobs in the kitchen area. Landon managed to pop the button on his own pants and slide the zipper down. He shoved the material far enough to free his aching cock.

Landon wrapped his palm around his shaft and gave himself a hard tug, needing some sort of relief. This was what Robert did to him, kept him in a state of ready arousal. He licked the underside of Robert's balls, brushing his lips over the soft skin as he fucked into to his own fist, guiding Robert's cock back to his lips with his other.

Robert's sticky hands moved from Landon's shoulders to

his head and began to guide him. Loosening his jaw, Landon let Robert's velvety arousal slide deeper, the firm flesh hitting the back of his throat as he bobbed his head and shuffled closer. He ran his palm up the back of his lover's thigh, swallowing around the cock filling his throat. He pulled off his lover, stroking him roughly with his free hand before mouthing him again. Robert was holding back, he could tell. His movements measured and tense.

Landon dipped his head, taking more than he should, causing him to gag. He lifted his eyes and watched the pleasure bloom on Robert's face. The salty flesh moved over his tongue in measured thrusts. He gripped the base of his lover's cock, curling his tongue around the tip before licking into the slit, sampling more of his man.

He used his hand and hollowed his cheeks, encouraging Robert to fuck his mouth.

Fingernails scraped against his scalp as Robert's fingers tightened in his close-cropped hair, and his hips moved more freely, picking up speed.

Landon took himself in hand, stroking faster with each bob of his head. He was close to coming, and from the way Robert's sac had drawn up against his body, Landon could tell his man was close too. Robert's hips snapped in rhythm, his low moan reverberating in Landon's balls.

Robert's thick length battered his throat as he pumped desperately into his fist. The heavy feel of his lover's cock against his tongue excited him, making him work even harder for Robert's release.

"Gonna come, Lan." Robert panted as he fucked into his mouth. Landon opened his throat and let him take what he needed. "Oh, fu…com…"

Robert bucked wildly above him. Landon's dick twitched in his hand as the first bit of come surged across his tongue. He didn't waste any time and greedily swallowed Robert's salty essence. His own release hit, his stomach muscles contracted so hard it almost bowed him over. His eyes slammed shut, and he milked his shaft, riding out his pleasure with Robert's cock still in his mouth.

He managed to lick Robert clean as they both calmed, basking in the afterglow, their panting breaths the only sound in the house. Landon kissed the tip of Robert's softening penis then grabbed the shirt Robert had discarded earlier and ran it across his fingers before wiping up his mess on the floor.

Robert pulled him to his feet and crushed him against a solid chest. Robert's lips found his for a quick kiss. "You're amazing."

The last of his lover's taste vanished from his tongue. He tucked himself back inside his pants, but Robert didn't bother to cover up. He just stood there, naked and smiling. Landon smiled back, appreciative of the gorgeous view.

"I think you're amazing. Look at all this food." He didn't bother to zip his pants before he grabbed a fork, hijacking a casserole dish closest to him, and dug in. He pressed a kiss to Robert's cheek and chewed the food in his mouth. "I'm starving."

"I think that's a pretty good thing. We have lots of food," Robert said, reaching for his dirty clothes.

Italian flavors flooded his taste buds. The recipe was the best he'd had, even cold nothing could touch it. "Oh my God, Robert, this is delicious." He loaded up his fork with another big bite and took an empty seat at the table, while Robert watched his every move. "It's a good thing we have all this food. I'm gonna need my strength, Doc. The blow job was just an appetizer."

Chapter 22

Autumn's wedding

Their driver, Mr. Kinkaid, stopped in front of Kennedy Adams's Cape Cod estate, and Robert smiled at Landon, who couldn't seem to drag his attention away from the view out the side window. "Oh my God, one person lives here?"

"No, I think there's about ten people if I remember correctly," Robert said, opening his side door as Mr. Kinkaid went to the hatch for their luggage.

"I'm not dressed right," Landon mumbled. Robert barely caught the words as he'd already exited the car and started for the back of the small SUV. He pivoted around and stuck his head back inside.

"You look perfect. I told you that. Please get out of the car, Landon." Of course, Landon didn't do as he'd asked. His guy was nervous. Landon turned back toward Robert. That weird uncertainty that he hadn't seen for a few weeks was back on Landon's face.

"I don't think this was the right thing to wear." He patted down the front of his shirt as if to emphasize his point.

"You made me pick your clothes out. We're dressed the same. If I'm dressed appropriately, why wouldn't you be dressed appropriately?" Robert could feel his own nerves starting to unravel and lifted his head to take a deep, centering breath before peering back inside the vehicle once again. "Babe, get out of the car."

Robert shut his door with more force than necessary and rounded the rear of the vehicle. Mr. Kinkaid closed the hatch with their carry-on bags at his feet and garment bag in his hand.

"It's a lot to take in." Robert tried to explain Landon's reluctance and received a courtesy nod in return.

"I'll get these to the house," Mr. Kincaid said.

"I've got them. You should go pick up Autumn. We would've been happy to wait so you didn't have to make two trips," Robert said, reaching for the garment bag. Landon finally opened his door, ending their conversation as Robert turned enough to watch him exit the vehicle. His lover stood motionless, staring up at the multi-story, sprawling mansion overlooking the Atlantic Ocean. Robert grabbed both his and Landon's cases and hoisted them over his shoulder.

"Let me take them, sir." Mr. Kincaid reached for the bags Robert had balanced over his shoulder.

"No, once he breaks out of this trance, he'll want to carry his own bags. He's a hardheaded one," Robert said, waving the man to head around the vehicle.

"Hardheaded, you say? Seems like a perfect fit, sir."

Robert froze in place, momentarily shocked at Mr. Kincaid's comment—it was so rare that any of Kennedy's long-term staff showed their personalities. Mr. Kincaid didn't stick around for Robert's reply, going straight for the driver's side as Robert headed for Landon.

"You're making me regret bringing you to the front of the house," he teased Landon who remained motionless, standing like a statue in front of the walkway. Robert shook his head and walked toward the front door.

"I'm intimidated as hell," Landon said from behind him several moments later, showing he had followed Robert up the front sidewalk. At the front doors, Robert glanced back at the anxious man. Landon nervously ran his palms down his button-down and exhaled a slow, steady breath.

"Stop freaking. You'll make yourself upset. Nothing's changed."

Landon's eyes flashed at him as he looked Robert up and down then reached for both bags hanging on his shoulder. "Everything's changed—again." The *again* was laced with accusation, and the flash of anger was Landon's way of dealing with the uncertainty of his thoughts. Robert ignored both and opened the front door.

"Welcome to my grandmother's home."

Kennedy was already coming toward them from the back of the house.

"Nonnie." He smiled as he called out her name.

He diverted from his plan to usher Landon in before him and stepped over the threshold, tossing his garment bag over a side chair and heading straight for his grandmother. Every time he saw her, she looked a little older. This time was no different, but she was strong and self-assured, her slow steps never faltering as she came toward him.

She allowed the hug but kept her head angled. Someone else had the bulk of her attention. Robert glanced over his shoulder too to see if Landon had followed him inside or if he still hovered on the front steps. Robert drew in a breath, marveling at the sight of Landon backlit by the bright sunlight emphasizing all his dark features. Landon's chest expanded as he took a steadying breath. His hands came together as if trying to stop the fidgeting, and his eyes sparkled as he stared at Nonnie. He looked the epitome of respect as he waited for Robert to finish the hug. Landon was as gorgeous as Robert had ever seen him.

"You must be Landon." There was kindness and warmth in his grandmother's tone as she released Robert and stepped toward the door.

"Yes, ma'am." His handsome sergeant came forward, and his grandmother extended both arms and took Landon in a hug.

"I'm Kennedy Adams, but you can call me Nonnie."

Landon seemed in straight-up reverence mode. The tension eased, and he seemed lighter than he had in hours.

"You have a beautiful home." His rich, southern accent sounded cultured and self-confident.

"Oh, it's ostentatious. Avery and I inherited it when my husband died. It's too much, but I love the view and access to the Atlantic, so I stay. How was your flight?" she asked, taking both of Landon's hands in hers.

"It was good, ma'am."

"None of that *ma'am* business, makes me feel old. Why don't you show him to your room, Robert? Take a look around then join me on the patio. Autumn and her young man should be here by then. I'm dealing with the final details of the wedding. The wedding planner's in the living room." She looked to the room she'd just come from.

"Absolutely," Robert agreed.

"I wanted to greet you properly, Landon. I'm so pleased you're here." She let go of his hands and patted his arm. She started her slow but sure steps back toward the living room. When she rounded the corner, Robert gathered the garment bag, and Landon picked up the two bags he'd set down to greet Kennedy.

"Good job," Robert whispered, nodding toward the stairs.

"I was nervous." Landon's mood brightened as the tension disappeared. He started toward the stairs, stopping at the first step to encourage Robert to lead the way.

"I know, but you need to trust me, you have no reason to be nervous here." He made his way slowly up the grand staircase while keeping his attention on Landon. "I want to show you around a bit. By 'meet her on the patio,' she means we have about forty-five minutes for you to get your bearings. The layout is a little complicated. The house was built by my great-grandfather and the additions seemed architecturally designed by kindergartners."

Landon nodded and looked around. Robert suspected he marked the territory to help find his way back, making Robert have to turn away to hide his smile, but thankfully, Landon followed him up the stairs and didn't head right back out the door.

Landon sat ramrod straight in his seat, hoping he didn't appear awkward or uncomfortable. His legs were slightly apart, his right palm rested on his thigh. In his other hand, he gripped the edge of his linen napkin, worrying the fabric underneath the tablecloth. Nervousness rolled over him in constant waves. Robert's palm caressed along his thigh. The thin material of his slacks did little to diffuse the heat burning a trail from his knee to his thigh with every caress. His body was all too aware of Robert's charismatic charm and how the man tried to ease him.

Dinner had been served in the comfort of Mrs. Adams's personal dining room. The table seated six where the five of them sat together and ate then had coffee and a delicious dessert, a custard-filled something with a crunchy sugary top. He'd forgotten the name, but he'd loved the rich creamy concoction. The meal had been intimate, friendly, and everyone strived to make him feel welcome. Maybe more welcome than he had ever felt anywhere before. Kennedy Adams, Autumn, and her soon to be husband, Cam Connors, were just like Robert—very personable and down to earth.

Landon couldn't shake the anxiety tugging at his happiness. When he and Robert were alone at Robert's place, he'd been able to ignore the glaring contrasts. Here, within these walls, all the reverence and respect he'd formed for Vice President Adams seemed open and on display. On the wall were pictures of the Adams family throughout the years. They had dined with world leaders, fought for human rights, given their lives for the betterment of mankind, and here he was being wined and dined by these extraordinary people. Being surrounded by such grandeur paled in comparison to being surrounded by such genuineness.

"So, Landon, Robert tells me you're shy. I wasn't sure I believed him until now."

Landon nodded at the statement and looked over at Robert who had pushed his seat slightly backward to extend his long legs, those bright blue eyes focused right on him, awaiting his reply. His heart did the slipping in his throat thing and his breath caught in his lungs. That look in Robert's eyes got him every time. Landon glanced at Autumn who seemed interested in his answer as well.

"Maybe. I get quiet sometimes," he said. A warm flush rushed up his neck and his cheeks as everyone looked his way. Did Robert really think he was shy?

"I can see that," Mrs. Adams said with an easy smile. She had very kind eyes and he felt her honesty. "I don't want to make you uncomfortable, but I want you to know what a debt our family owes you."

Oh yeah, Landon didn't like those words at all and immediately started shaking his head. Nobody owed him anything. It wasn't like that.

"Lauren, bring the box," Mrs. Adams said, ignoring his reluctance.

"Landon, you showed our family a great kindness at my son's funeral, and I'm certain Kane would echo my sentiments if he were here. In his place, we'd like to give you something that meant the world to Avery." The assistant set in front of him a wooden box no bigger than a CD case, and maybe three inches thicker.

"Oh no, ma'am. It was my honor." He stopped, instinctively knowing Robert tried to derail his denial when he lifted his hand and pressed a kiss to his knuckles. Robert released his hold and nodded toward the box.

"Open it."

Landon stared at the polished wood, torn with emotions. He lifted his hands, trying to do what Robert asked, but not wanting to accept this gift. He hadn't requested the detail for any other reason than to show his respect. Landon looked around the table for help, but all he saw were three sets of loving blue eyes trained on him. The tips of his ears burned, and he diverted his attention, meeting Cam's sympathy filled gaze, maybe commiserating in his misery.

After a second of pushing down his nerves, he finished reaching for the box and lifted the lid. He couldn't believe it. No way. A medal with a five-pointed white star, with red and gold trim, and a silver eagle that sat on a blue ribbon edged with white. The Medal of Freedom, he knew instantly what it was and immediately shook his head. The tight rein he had on his tongue loosened. "I can't accept this. It's too much. The thank-you was enough."

"You will accept it on behalf of our family," the matriarch of the Adams family said with all authority, leaving no room for further argument. "And I've had enough for today. Autumn, you and Cameron are going to go for drinks with his family—is that what you were telling me?"

"We are, then I'll be back and…" Autumn looked at Cam and pushed out her lip in a pout. "He'll be staying with them."

The moment surrounding Landon's gift was over before he realized it. They were on to other things, just like that. Even with his brain on overload, he had to give them credit for how smoothly they'd glossed over his protest. Kennedy Adams had spoken from her heart and infiltrated his with her graciousness. But more than that, she had also saved him the awkwardness of accepting such a cherished gift. Landon couldn't seem to close the lid on the small wooden box. He didn't want to cover it. Not only was it stunning, but the medal and its meaning were too significant to hide.

His emotions grew stronger the longer he admired the piece. He'd never be able to express the pride filling his heart at the kind gesture.

"Robert, you entertain Landon for me," he heard Kennedy say, drawing his attention back to the room and his gaze back to her. She smiled at him and laid her napkin on the table before scooting out of her seat with the help of the server.

"Yes, ma'am. We're taking the golf cart out to tour the property," Robert explained, his palm going back to Landon's thigh.

"Excellent. I'll see you all for breakfast. Autumn, I've got your glamour team coming at ten," Kennedy stated with a mischievous grin that twinkled in her eyes.

"Nonnie, how do you know about glamour teams?" Autumn asked, laughing at Kennedy's choice of words.

"I watch the Kardashians, dear."

Robert jumped up. Landon rose too when Kennedy passed by. She did very much as she had when he'd first arrived and extended her arm, this time for a side hug. "I don't want you nervous around us, Landon."

"Thank you for everything. About the medal… I don't think I can accept something so valuable. It needs to stay in the family," he said, reaching for the small chest to hand back to her.

"Nonsense, dear. I'm certain it will be in the family. I'm happy Robert found you." She ignored him and his outstretched hand, turning away, heading toward the door.

Autumn came around the table to hug Kennedy right before she got to the door.

"You all stay as long as you want."

Landon said nothing more. Robert's hand came to his back, caressing down his spine, keeping him grounded. "You know I can't accept this," he said when he glanced up and caught Robert's eyes on the medal. As much as being here made him want to be part of this family, chances were high he'd never have that, especially since he woke up every day afraid this would be the day that Robert wised up.

"I thought you would say that. Our reasoning, mostly my

grandmother's suggestion, but it's still true for us all, is that you stood watch over the heart and cornerstone of our family, my father. He would have given you this medal if he could," Robert explained, his hand gliding up Landon's back before his sincere gaze held Landon's, beseeching him to understand.

"It's too much," Landon said again. "The e-reader you gave me was too much. This was earned by your father, and I'm not so sure I'm the—"

"I'm positive you are," Robert rushed to say as he smiled brightly at him.

"Sir?" The moment fled as Robert turned to face the person who'd spoken.

"Thank you. You can leave it there," Robert replied, and Landon looked up to see a thick blanket and a wicker basket one of the household staff had placed on the table. "Come on. Let's tour the grounds before it gets dark. You can leave it here. They'll get it up to our room."

"Where's Autumn?" Landon asked, carefully laying the box on the table.

"They left. They said goodbye, but you must have been caught up in the moment and tuned them out." Robert had his elbow now, turning him from the table and the gift.

"This is too much," Landon said again, looking back at the table.

Robert just chuckled at him and applied more pressure to his arm. "I'm starting to see some possible obsessive-compulsive tendencies. Put it out of your mind. We'll talk about that later."

Chapter 23

The salty breeze ruffled Landon's hair as Robert parked the golf cart along the outer edge of the property. Nothing but a ledge of rocks and a four-foot drop stood between them and the Atlantic Ocean. He loved this part of the property, always had. This small grassy knoll was the only thing between the water and the thick patch of trees on the ten or so acres they had traveled to get there. Landon was quiet, his gaze transfixed somewhere past the horizon as the wind guided the water to gently lap against its rocky bank.

The sun was just beginning to lower toward the west. They had a couple of hours at most before dark. Robert kept the golf cart running, pulling back from the magnificent view to give them a large unobstructed area to sit on the grass and enjoy the scenery. He always wished he had more time here.

This had been his place to come and contemplate his career path, to devise a plan of action when he'd struggled to balance his studies and then his residency. The last time he'd sat here, he'd been in a dark place. The world had seemed hopeless, his future uncertain as he pleaded for guidance from the universe. To be here again, to have found Landon and have him by his side filled Robert with happiness.

"I love it here," Robert said, bringing the golf cart to a stop.

"I can see why." Landon's smile matched his.

"This was the other place my granddaddy Paulie took us camping." Robert parked the cart and left the keys in the ignition. He went to the backseat and checked the basket strapped there. "We'd come out here in the fall and play in the leaves. Autumn would get them snagged in her hair. She'd cry while they had to brush it all out. I once tried to show her that brushing her hair was better than being pinched. I got in some trouble for my reasoning."

Landon came around the cart. With his hands tucked in his pockets, he stared down at his feet as he walked. He had on his new walking shorts and a short sleeve button-down. He looked like a J.Crew model straight off the pages of a magazine. The wind played with that short, dark silky hair, giving him a rugged windblown look. Robert extended his hand. Landon glanced up and didn't hesitate to take it. Their instant connection radiated through Robert every time they touched.

"You're being quiet. Tell me what's wrong," Robert said as Landon walked out in front of him, stopping at the cliff's edge.

"It's incredible here. The ocean's very calming to be so dangerous."

"I know. I've always been drawn to water," Robert said and wound both arms around Landon, encircling his firm body before pressing himself fully against Landon's back. The water wasn't the draw it had once been—it came second to the man in his arms—and Robert lowered his head to Landon's shoulder. "Tell me what's bothering you."

Landon gave no hesitation when he answered. "I'm afraid I'll embarrass you or your family when people start digging into my past," Landon said quietly, his eyes downcast and chin tucked to his chest. "I'm in over my head with you. I can pretend it's all okay when we're alone together in your house, when it's just me and you, but coming here…"

"You could never embarrass me, Landon," Robert answered

honestly, turning Landon in his arms. "Not ever."

"That's not true and it freaks me out. One wrong move and you might wake up and see what you've done," Landon said, his indignation shining through in his tone. Robert respected the honor and integrity Landon brought to everything he did, but it did make for a war of wills sometimes, and that was okay, he was up for it.

"Wake up and realize I'm with you?" he asked.

"Yeah. And I'm waiting for that day. I'm trying to keep perspective, but you make it so fucking hard." Landon tried to turn back toward the ocean, and the struggle was real to keep him facing Robert so he could look into his eyes.

"You want to stay with me?" he asked.

"Yes, of course. You know that." He lost the battle and got Landon's back again.

"I hoped. You haven't actually said that's what you wanted." Robert had long past decided he and Landon were worth fighting for, and that was exactly what he intended to do. There was no way he was going to let Landon's reservations slice away at their forever. "Stop putting all this between us. I'm crazy about you. Are you crazy about me?"

"You know I am, and I can't accept the gift… And you know I can't," Landon said decisively over his shoulder. Robert didn't want to spend their precious alone time together rehashing it all again.

"I want to show you something. Follow me." Robert took his hand, glad when Landon relented and followed without another argument. He led him to the grouping of stately trees. Trees so tall they towered over the property like guardians. Dense foliage acted as a barrier, blocking them from view of any boats that might pass along this part of the coastline. The only part of the property kept in its natural state.

"All the Adamses who have lived here have treated this particular piece of the property as sacred ground. The history goes like this…" He scanned the area until he found the tree he was looking for and went there. "My great-grandfather bought the property while in office. He missed Minnesota, but my great-grandmother mourned her home. Back then, it wasn't considered such an easy jaunt just to fly home so freely. This was as close as he could get to bringing Minnesota to her. The first night he brought her here, he carved this into the tree. He made her a promise: if she would trust him, he would build her a house on the property and together they would make this their home."

Robert ran his fingers over a faint heart that had been knifed into the tree many years ago. Initials carved inside. "My grandfather proposed to my Nonnie right under this tree and she accepted." He stepped to the next tree in the row where a second carving was etched into the bark then moved to a third tree. "The first time my dad brought my daddy here, he lovingly carved their initials. My daddy was like you—hesitant." Robert felt the rough bark beneath the pad of his finger. "I believe this happened after they were married." Robert's heart grew full as he outlined his fathers' etched heart on the old oak tree like he had done many times in his life. The wounds the memories used to open had dissipated, only their love filling his heart as he stared at the sweet declaration that remained of his parents.

"What's this?" Landon let go of his hand, moving to a tree diagonally opposite from his fathers' tree. Robert chuckled, following Landon the few feet, remembering Autumn had met the man of her dreams when she was twenty-two years old. She proclaimed that tree as hers and carved their love there. There were now three hearts on the tree, the biggest being hers and Cam's.

"Autumn's love history carved for the ages."

Landon's fingers lightly traveled down Autumn's etched hearts.

"Do you have a tree?" Landon asked.

"No, I've never brought anyone here before. You're my first," Robert confessed, watching Landon weaving between the trunks.

"Which tree would be yours?" Landon asked, stepping to another large tree, feeling the wood with his hands. Robert had never seen anyone but Paulie do something like that before.

"I don't know." Feet from Robert, Landon stopped in front of a larger oak then rounded it before coming back to the spot next to where Robert stood.

"What about this one?" Landon pulled a small knife from the pocket of his shorts. Robert's heart swelled as he began to understand Landon's intention. Landon stared at the other hearts before digging into the tree. He worked at defining their initials for a good fifteen minutes before he set to making a heart encasing their initials. Robert came in behind Landon, laying a hand on his back so not to startle him as he worked. He trailed both palms down the flexing muscles and slid them around Landon's waist. With a loose hold, he watched Landon work until the knife stopped.

"It looks good, right?" Landon asked, staring at the tree.

"It's perfect," Robert answered honestly against Landon's ear. Everything about this moment was perfect.

"It is." Landon bent the blade into the knife and pocketed it. He brought his hands to Robert's where they still circled his waist. "I don't know what's going to happen between us, but I wanted you to always remember your first."

"Me too. It's why I showed you. You're my first, and if I get my way, you'll be my last, Landon." There was silence again, and Robert pressed his lips to Landon's neck and breathed the man in, letting that fresh masculine scent fill his soul. Landon was his last, the man who owned his heart and would forever. He didn't let himself overthink as he lifted his lips to Landon's ear and said what he had wanted to say so many weeks ago, "I love you. I don't want anyone else's initials on our tree. Just yours and mine." He pressed his lips to the warm pulse in Landon's neck, opening his mouth over the tender flesh. "I want forever with you, Landon." Robert felt his lover's heartbeat accelerate against his lips.

Landon stiffened, not in the good way. There was a second of hesitation before Landon relaxed fully back into him. "I love you, too."

"Say it again." Robert wanted to hear those quietly muttered words said again and again.

Landon turned his head slightly, their breath mingling as Landon repeated the words. "I love you. I suspect I've been in love with you since Germany."

Robert tightened his embrace, crushing Landon even closer to him. If he'd only known. "When I left Germany, I couldn't stop thinking about you. You were in every thought I had, every day. I was disappointed when I thought you friend-zoned me. I wanted you. I knew from the minute I saw you crossing the street to me on our first date, right then, I knew I loved you."

"Let me turn around, Robert," Landon said, but Robert found he couldn't let go of the tight hold he had on Landon.

"I don't think I'm going to like what you're going to say," Robert said. He felt Landon maybe overthinking his response and he didn't want to entertain any negativity, not right now.

"It doesn't change reality." Landon pried Robert's hands apart and turned, encasing Robert's face between strong palms, keeping him from leaning forward and kissing the protest from Landon's beautiful lips. "We're too different, and I can't see how we're meant to be. I don't belong in your world. I'm not comfortable there, and you're gonna resent being tied to mine."

Landon couldn't have been more wrong, and Robert had to tell him. Landon pressed a thumb to his lips, stopping him from speaking. "I love you. I know I'll love you until the day I… no, even longer than that. I'll love you forever. I want this to be everything you want it to be. I'll follow where you lead, but I'm being careful…" Landon shifted nervously against him, sighing deeply before continuing. "If it doesn't work out, it'll end in heartache for both of us. At least for me it will. If we were smart, we'd cut and run now before this gets too far out of our control."

Robert didn't want to cut and run. He pushed through Landon's hold, crushing the man to him as he took his mouth in a claiming kiss. He was never leaving Landon, and by God, he'd never let Landon leave him. In a dance of tongue and teeth, he devoured Landon, taking every nip and suck into his soul. Slowly

Landon relaxed, becoming pliant in his arms.

Seconds later, Robert yanked his mouth free. He needed air. Landon's lips found his neck as his lover's hands tugged at his polo. "I want you."

"I want you too. Make love to me out here under the trees and the stars with the waves crashing against the rocks. I've dreamed of us that way." Robert brought a hand to Landon's chest, holding Landon in place as he started for the blanket and basket he had secretly hidden the supplies in. "I brought condoms and lube."

"You thought of everything." Landon smirked and manhandled him back into a kiss, continuing to tug at his clothes. "I just want you naked right now." When Landon's hard dick pressed into his, Robert abandoned his plans of grabbing the supplies and just kissed Landon back with everything he had. He licked across Landon's lips before deepening the kiss. He held Landon pinned against the trunk of their tree, the tree that held their initials for all eternity.

Landon broke the kiss and nibbled a path along his jaw. "I'll bottom," Landon growled in his ear as he cupped Robert's cock through his shorts and massaged, making Robert grind his hips from the pleasure. Landon was such a tease. Robert wanted inside Landon so badly he couldn't think as it was. "And you use that sexy voice to ear fuck me with all those love words." Oh, if Landon didn't stop talking like that and playing with his dick, he was going to come right there before they ever got started.

"Okay," Robert panted. His brain cells scrambled. At this point, he'd be just as willing to drop to his knees and suck Landon off right here. The hand on his crotch slowed, the pending orgasm eased, and Robert opened his eyes to a grinning Landon.

"You agreed."

"That I did," he said and nipped Landon's ear.

Robert's love had come through in every touch, every kiss, every soul searing glance. In the way he'd carefully placed the basket within reach, then spread the blanket in the perfect spot beneath their tree. They'd managed to kick off their shoes before tumbling to the blanket to make out. It would always be their tree. A hundred-year-old oak with massive branches that now had their initials carved deeply into its bark, the intimate gesture meant to solidify their commitment. Landon still hadn't come back down from the thrill of it all, and he didn't want to.

The sinking sun in the western sky colored the evening with brilliant shades of reds, purples, and golds. But that perfection couldn't compare to the man he held in his arms. This moment would be etched forever in his memory. The beauty surrounding him. The look in his lover's eyes. Everything he'd been afraid of had been chased away with the sincerity in Robert's gaze. He should know, he'd drowned in their depths.

He lost himself in the feel of Robert's hands as they moved over his body, almost reverently. Robert undid his shorts between hurried kisses. Waves crashed against the rocky cliff, and the wind rustled the leaves above them, urging on his frantic need.

Robert's tongue slid across Landon's lips then slowly dipped inside when he opened for more. Robert mapped Landon's chest and stomach, and that wicked tongue danced over his in a sweet and tender exploration. The wind kicked up, sending a salty gust of water-cooled air ruffling Robert's blond hair. Landon ran his fingers through the silky strands and tilted his head to draw a breath of fresh air into his lungs.

"Want you." Robert latched on to his neck and…*fuck*. Robert was so damn intense, and sexy as hell. Those lips moved over his jaw, and he stole them back for his at the first opportunity, letting Robert seduce him with hungry kisses. Landon searched for the button on Robert's shorts in a panic to rid him of the clothing. His moves were clumsy and awkward, frantic to feel Robert's naked skin on his.

"Babe…"

"Let me." Landon almost protested when Robert gripped his

wrist to release his hold and wiggled out of the khaki-colored material then flashed that sexy ass smile that had Landon almost coming. "You're killing me here."

"Just trying to help you out. The quicker I get out of my clothes"—Robert pulled the shirt over his head and tossed it to the side—"the quicker I can get you out of yours." Those big blue eyes twinkled with mischief. The moment so endearing and sweet it sent a rush of emotions through his veins and wrapped his heart in a blanket of happiness.

Robert was romancing him, and he was falling…had fallen.

Head.

Over.

Heels.

Landon finished pushing his own shorts and underwear down. His hard cock slapped against his belly as he kicked out of them and he ripped his shirt over his head.

"I'm yours," he said and let his gaze slide down to Robert's erect cock. His own cock twitched at the sight.

Robert kissed the tattoo on his chest and sat up on his knees. Landon knew the fascination the tattoo held for Robert. The smile on Robert's face as he stared down at him let him know he was in trouble about two seconds before he was flipped to his stomach.

"Yes. You are."

Robert's strong hands pulled his hips high into the air, then his lover locked him in place, nudging his thighs apart with his knees. Those cruel lips traveled over his spine and the swell of his butt as he balanced on his forearms. Robert smoothed a heavy palm over his ass cheek, his fingers sinking into his flesh to spread him, exposing his most intimate place. A warm tongue slid over his hole, electrifying his body. Robert always knew exactly what he needed.

"Robert," he sighed and melted back into the pleasure of Robert's mouth.

His attention was zeroed in on Robert's tongue as it slid over his balls then penetrated him over and over again while those long slender fingers moved in him in all the right ways. Felt so good that his thighs shook with anticipation.

"Want you in me." He didn't care if he sounded desperate. He was way past that.

Robert pulled away from his body, bit his ass cheek, dragging kisses over his bare skin before reaching for the wicker basket next to the blanket. Landon glanced over his shoulder to watch as his lover quickly produced the supplies.

Robert tore open the condom package then rolled the latex down his cock. He used the lube to slick his fingers. The brush of Robert's hair on Landon's thighs made his ass clench in anticipation when Robert moved in behind him. He circled Landon's opening then two slick fingers breached him. He pushed back against the digits pumping in and out of him. Just as he'd considered begging, Robert withdrew his fingers and teased his entrance with the cock he craved.

Robert pushed into him from behind, stealing his breath as his body stretched, opening to accommodate his lover. Damn, Robert filled him so damn full, the delicious burn making him pant through the sweet pain of being taken in this way. He used his hand to stroke himself as his body squeezed around the welcome intrusion.

"Fuck me now."

Robert flexed his hips, pushing into him, and stars danced behind Landon's eyes. His lover did it again, and he tilted his ass, chasing the growing pleasure. He let go of his dick and pushed up on his hands, raising his chest off the blanket, unashamed of how needy he'd become as he took his man deeper.

Robert pounded into him then slowed, driving him mad with the variation. Hard and fast. Deep and demanding. His lover gripped him so tightly, controlling his hips.

He turned to watch Robert over his shoulder. Robert changed his angle. Landon slammed his eyes shut and quickly squeezed his shaft to keep from coming. That move had him biting his lip to conceal his moan.

"*Fuuckk…*"

"Love that filthy mouth…" Robert skimmed his lips up his spine before ending at the base of his neck. "So perfect for me."

His lover kept doing things to him that left him defenseless, stealing what was left of his heart with every word mumbled against his skin.

"I love you, Landon." Robert lifted Landon's head and their eyes locked. Landon's heart pounded against his ribs, heat rushed up his cheeks, and the butterflies took flight in his belly. Robert wouldn't let him look away. He saw every bit of love reflected at him, bowling him over with the truth in Robert's words. He loved hearing those words. He'd craved those very words.

Landon couldn't speak as Robert pulled out and maneuvered him to his back and sank into him again, watching him from above as he moved carnally inside him. Their bodies fit so tightly together they became one and he never wanted it to end.

Robert rolled his hips so slowly, dragging along every nerve ending in his channel, pushing him toward the edge. His heart so full of joy it might burst. He loved Robert. He would never deny that fact. He loved everything about the man. Landon's ass clenched, squeezing Robert's dick, making his lover moan.

"Yes, baby." Robert rolled into him faster and faster, picking up speed. The delicious friction in his ass made his toes curl and his dick weep. He was caught in the most splendid agony. His body coiled with need so tightly he might explode.

"You're mine." Robert moved in him, hitting him in just the right spot, stealing his control with every thrust. Robert tightened a warm hand around his dick as those blue eyes bore straight to his soul. Stroking him in time with his thrusts, Robert demanded his submission.

"I love you, too," he gasped.

"Stroke yourself for me," Robert hissed.

Landon's hips sped to meet his lover's thrusts as he worked

his cock like he'd been instructed. His lungs burned from the exertion of chasing his release. He let go of his dick as the orgasm crawled up his spine and spots danced in his vision before he shattered into a million pieces. He couldn't utter a sound; his body was caught in a never-ending wave of pleasure as his hot come hit his chest and stomach in heated spurts.

Robert's movements went wild, faltering as he thrust into him one last time, going so deep Landon's body clamped down as his lover brushed that spot inside him and spasms overtook him once again, forcing the last of his seed onto his belly. Robert's gaze remained locked with his.

"Landon." Robert cried out his name on a shudder, his lover's whole body quivering as he succumbed to his release. Robert's dick jerked in Landon's ass as he pulled Robert's mouth to his. Landon was totally wrung dry, and couldn't catch his breath. As Robert's full weight settled on him, Landon hooked his legs around his breathless lover to hold him there. Their bodies were slick with sweat from their exertions. Neither one said anything. They both just lay there not moving as their heartbeats kept time. Robert's lips pressed against his neck. Landon kissed the top of Robert's hair and lowered his legs. Robert's softening cock slipped from his body.

"That was…"

Robert pushed up on his hands, chuckling, his hair all messy from Landon's fingers. His eyes were still hooded from sex, and their intensity nearly claimed Landon's soul. Looking down on Landon, Robert hesitated then attacked… "I love you…I love you…" Robert kept repeating the phrase as he peppered his face with kisses. "I love you, Landon."

"And I love you." He laughed and caught Robert's mouth in a sweet kiss. The cool breeze chilled his damp skin as Robert kissed him back.

Chapter 24

"I was concerned about the wind. I was wrong," Kennedy said as Landon approached her side of the golf cart and extended an arm for Robert's Nonnie to take.

He'd been placed in charge of the precious cargo; it was his job to make sure Kennedy Adams made it to the ceremony in one piece and that meant helping her off the golf cart and navigating the uneven ground until she made it to her seat in the first row. He took his job as seriously as he'd ever taken anything, not taking his eyes off Kennedy's feet until he was sure she was on the temporary walkway added to help her bypass any unseen ruts or holes in the ground.

"It's the perfect day for such a wedding."

"Yes, ma'am, it is," he said, keeping a tight hold of her arm. He wished he could just carry her to her seat.

"What did I tell you about the *ma'am*?" She stopped moving, scolding him with a look while swatting at the hand that held her in his grip. Kennedy was so in control, so independent, most likely stubborn as she could be. He wasn't certain she actually needed him there with her. Much like he felt around her grandson and granddaughter, it was hard to be anything but comfortable around her.

"I'm afraid you're going to have to endure the sentiment for a bit longer. I can't bring myself to say anything different to you." He answered her honestly and urged her to walk again, taking her to the first seat in the first row of the bride's side.

"You're a cheeky thing, aren't you?" she whispered, her tone approving. Once she was fully seated, he took the seat he'd been instructed to, leaving a place between them for Robert.

"I believe that's a nice way to put it." He gave her a playful wink and the music began playing. They both turned as Cam's brother and mother walked down the aisle before the best man took his place next to the groom at the floral arch where a priest stood. Next came Autumn's maid of honor, a longtime friend from their early days of college. Then came Autumn and Robert in a golf cart. This one, though, made its way more slowly over the rolling lawn.

Robert rode in the passenger seat, Autumn in the back. Flowers decorated the exterior of the cart—her own personal carriage. When they arrived, Robert exited the cart and went to the back to help Autumn off. The "Bridal Chorus" started, and Landon stood, extending a hand to help Kennedy stand as everyone joined in. With his head angled, he could see unobstructed as Robert and his sister approached. Everything faded for Landon as he stood transfixed over the pair. With each step down the aisle, Robert drew closer to him and Landon's heart burst with pride. He wanted to live with that man forever. He wanted to love Robert Adams and be loved in return. He wanted this—the wedding, the happiness, the hope of tomorrow and all the tomorrows that followed.

Their eyes met. Robert stared at him as if he had somehow read his mind. A slight breeze ruffled Robert's hair. That one stray piece that Landon was beginning to see as unruly fell across Robert's forehead. They stared at one another until Robert passed by. The moment had Landon's heart drumming in his ears. He looked down at his trembling hands. Luckily, Kennedy took his arm, pulling him from the trance. She seemed to somehow know his struggle.

With the gentle pat she gave to his arm, she said, "Help me sit, dear."

He did, taking the seat next to her until Robert made his way over. Landon slid to his designated place, his hand following the length of Robert's arm until he could intertwine their fingers, getting an unexpected side-eye from Robert at his eagerness before Robert could manage to fully take his seat. Landon ignored the look. Robert now added life-preserver to the long list of growing reasons Landon needed to keep the man close.

Hours later, Kennedy's "young and fresh" string quartet had turned into a pretty good acoustic cover band with the help of Cam's brother, who played his guitar. Dinner had been served, drinks flowed plentifully, and the cake was nothing but crumbs. As for the family, including the bride and groom, they'd chosen to spend the evening together, taking the reception into the night, enjoying each other's company.

For Robert, he'd lost his suit jacket and tie hours ago. He'd eagerly rolled up his sleeves to help the kitchen staff earlier but had pretty much been consumed with Landon the entire night. And he'd probably had too much to drink. That seemed okay too. He tipped the cocktail glass to his lips for good measure. Robert loved his family, and he loved his man. His smile hadn't faded all day, and unlike just a few months ago, he hadn't had to force it at all.

"So, you were saying you're training to be a chef?" Sophia asked, her eyebrows scrunched in confusion. Since she'd had as many drinks as Robert, she had a harder time schooling her facial features. It seemed saying it out loud hadn't helped her process the one-eighty about-face Robert's life had taken.

"I guess so. Yes." Robert tipped the cocktail glass to his lips again, taking a much longer drink this time, and Sophia mirrored his actions.

"What do your sister and grandmother say?" she asked, stopping the pretense of casual and turning more fully toward him.

"They're supportive." He guessed and nodded for good measure, although he hadn't really asked their opinions.

"What does Landon think about it?" Apparently, Sophia asked all the hard-hitting questions.

"He believes I have a brain tumor," he answered, hiding his smile with the next sip he took. Sophia laughed straight out loud.

"Have you had that theory tested?" she asked, happily.

"I haven't. I decided if I'm dying, then I'm dying a happy man." He reached over, clinking his almost empty glass with Sophia's as the current song came to an end. "I have to go steal my date back. I'm tired of being sidelined."

Robert placed his glass on a side table and went directly for Autumn and Landon while the band took requests.

"Go find your new husband." Robert stepped in between Autumn and Landon, taking him in his arms at the start of a slow sexy song. He nearly moaned out loud as Landon moved his hips in time with the tune. His man had moves.

"You're sexy when you dance," Robert muttered, swaying to the music.

"You're tipsy," Landon laughed, giving him the same grin.

"Maybe just happy."

When the song changed to "A Thousand Years" by Christina Perri, Robert pulled Landon in closer. He loved this song.

"I'll have to remember you're a happy drunk," Landon said, his body flush against Robert's who laughed at him, pressing a kiss to Landon's lips. Landon moved with him, swaying slightly, keeping Robert close much like he wanted.

"What you need to remember is *you* make me happy," Robert whispered in Landon's ear, closing his eyes, letting himself get lost in the movements of their bodies. He breathed Landon in. *Intoxicating…* All that happiness and sunshine moving effortlessly in his arms. He brushed his cheek against Landon's hair as they swayed and moved to the song playing in the background.

The words of the song rang true. He'd died every day waiting for the man he held in his arms. He lowered his mouth to Landon's ear, whispering, "I have loved you for a thousand years." He sang the words to Landon as they floated across the dance floor. The warm glow of the lights filled the room with romance. The candle flames even danced to the music. The romance of this perfect night radiated through him as they held each other close. Yes, without a doubt…he'd love Landon for a thousand more.

Dare to fly.

His sway faltered at the words so unmistakably spoken in his ear. He looked over his shoulder to see who had said them, but there was no one there. He'd heard them stated plain as day and looked the other direction. Landon put a miniscule amount of space between them with a questioning expression on his face. Their fluid steps faltered.

"Did you hear that?"

"Hear what?" Landon glanced over his shoulder, searching.

Robert kept his gaze fixed on Landon and repeated the words. "Dare to fly." Joy bubbled in his heart.

Now Robert's heart was leading him. The utter certainty flowing around them was palpable. Everything slowed as Landon's gaze landed back on his, searing his love to his soul.

Forever… Nothing less than forever.

The music and noise of the party faded away. Robert's thoughts strayed to his childhood where he'd witnessed the love his fathers had shared, more certain now in his belief that they were together somewhere in their forever.

He would promise Landon forever.

Nothing but love and total certainty in his decision, Robert released Landon who was slower at letting him go. He dug in his slacks pocket, finding the loose ring, and took a deep steadying breath. Chasing feathers had led him to Landon, but the man's genuine selflessness and beautiful spirit had captured his heart and made him fall in love.

"What's going on?" Landon asked.

Robert dropped to a knee in the middle of the makeshift dance floor. Landon looked momentarily confused before he caught on and then his expression morphed into complete shock. Robert extended his hand up to Landon, the ring he'd carried for weeks between his thumb and forefinger, and said simply, "Marry me."

The only sounds had been from the faint music of the band, and even those halted. Landon's expressive face went through a range of emotions before he took a small step backward.

"What are you doing? We just met." When he finally spoke, Landon's voice sounded unsure, but the desire that flashed in his eyes and stayed there told Robert all he needed to know.

Robert's focus never wavered nor did his resolve. "Marry me, Landon."

"We can't marry, Robert." He could see Landon's mind racing as sadness and insecurity laced his dark eyes. His gut told him those were the issues of their union, not the legality.

"Last night you said you'll love me forever. You'll follow where I lead. Marry me, Landon. One year from now, marry me." Robert rose, keeping the ring extended, but taking a step into Landon. He wasn't going to let Landon bring up any more excuses. "Forget the uncertainty. Forget the obstacles. We'll tackle any that arise together. Be mine. You said forever. I want our forever."

Landon's breath hitched, and Robert lifted his lover's chin, forcing Landon to look him in the eyes. Those black orbs were filled with so much emotion that he couldn't help the caress of his thumb across Landon's cheek. One maybe two heartbeats passed before Landon's face softened, and his sergeant's strong hand came up, molding around Robert's, grounding him. Landon took the ring and kissed Robert's lips.

"In a year."

The room erupted in a chorus of cheers. Robert paid attention to none of it and wrapped his arms around Landon, holding him close. Landon's face went to the crook of his shoulder and he spoke low, only loud enough for Robert to hear.

"If you ever think we've made a mistake and you want out—"

"I'm not going to let you finish, because I'm not strong enough to offer that in return. I'm afraid I wouldn't survive losing you."

The arms around him tightened, lifting Robert slightly off his feet. He smiled, kissing the side of Landon's head. He was so in love with this man.

Chapter 25

One month later

"Are you sure you want to do this?" Landon asked Robert, juggling their luggage as he pivoted around on the sidewalk leading to the front porch of his parents' Houston, Texas, home. His nervous energy vibrated wildly inside him, not knowing how Robert would feel about him after this trip. In all his years, Landon had never brought anyone home before, let alone the accomplished son of a vice president. It was a lot to dump on his family at one time.

Shit. Needing an outlet to expel his pent-up anxiety, Landon had hauled all their bags out from the trunk of the Uber they'd taken from the airport. From the backseat, as he finalized the payment, Robert glanced over at him and smiled with the car door pushed open.

Every day over the last month, Robert had persistently tried to convince Landon that their coupling was fated. He repeated over and over how he saw their future and stated emphatically how they were meant to be together. Per Robert, their souls were destined and intertwined regardless of their differences. And maybe, while they were alone together in DC, Landon had to agree because they sure got along really well together. But he couldn't seem to stop the dread or worry of his parents meeting the sophisticated Dr. Robert Adams.

"Stop, babe," Robert said, somewhat distracted as he stepped out of the vehicle. His gaze focused only on Landon as he tucked his cell phone in his back pocket then began immediately ensuring his crisp dress shirt was still tucked neatly into his slacks. Like always, Robert looked like he should be stepping off the front cover of some *look-at-me-I'm-so-perfect* magazine.

Landon's leg started bouncing as the car pulled away from the curb. He wanted so badly for Robert and his family to work out, but it was hard to see how that could ever be. Robert came to stand directly in front of him, reaching for one of the over the shoulder bags as his eyes narrowed on Landon's face. "You need to calm down. Do I need to explain to you the heightened risk factors of anxiety on your cardiovascular system?" His blond brow arched in question.

"You aren't funny. This whole deal's already scaring me, and we haven't knocked on the door yet," he said, exasperated. Why were they even here? They should be easing his family into this whirlwind relationship, introducing Robert to them in baby steps like he had planned to do. Instead, they'd taken a private jet in a fast, twenty-four-hour turnaround trip so Robert could meet his mom. The same mom Landon had only told he was dating Robert a week or two ago. When had he lost such complete control of his life?

"Stop being a snob, Landon. That's another thing we need to work on. Do we need counseling before we even make it down the aisle?" Robert asked, giving Landon that sexy smirk he liked far too much while hitting the real issue right on the head. Landon was flat overcome with the weight of the class structure differences between Robert, him, and his family.

"Again, you're not funny. You need to leave the jokes to me." Landon took a deep breath, letting Robert's magic ease some of his anxiety. Robert had never given him a reason to feel insecure, not ever. Still, his heart raced in his chest.

"Then be funny, not anxious." Robert pointed to the large window in front of his parents' small older brick home. There were six heads peering out, watching them as they stood outside.

Of course they were.

Landon had done everything possible to give himself a different life, and he had built a very disciplined and respectable one. Then hurricane Robert blew through, dropping him into a fairytale that happened to also be filled with embarrassingly awkward moments, like this one.

Landon rolled his eyes and turned back to Robert. "See? They're already embarrassing me."

"My grandmother was waiting for you to arrive, Landon," Robert reminded as if it was perfectly normal for an adult man to have his family staring through the living room window in anticipation of his arrival.

"Not by the door," Landon shot back as Robert passed by him, heading toward the front door.

"Only because she's slow and couldn't get there fast enough." He watched Robert lift a hand, waving to his family, that knock 'em dead smile easily sliding into place.

"Remember, my father's not as accepting as yours," Landon said under his breath.

"Warned like fifty times now. But they raised you, so they have something good going for 'em. Come on."

The front door flew open, and the group from the window looked as if they had moved in unison to the doorway. Like always, his sweet mother was the first to step out. Her face full of sheer joy as she looked back and forth between Landon and Robert. She wore a navy blue dress that complemented her complexion. She'd left her long dark hair in silky waves. A welcoming smile lit her face as she took Robert in an immediate hug.

"I'm Karen."

Robert's genuine happiness curved his lips as he bent to

accept the hug. His uncle came walking out the door next, patting Robert's shoulder while coming toward Landon. When his uncle reached for one of the bags, he saw a commiserating look in his eyes before he was enveloped in a tight hug.

"You look great."

Landon took the intended comfort from the compliment and the hug and let out a shaky sigh.

"I'm nervous," he admitted. His uncle Michael reared back and stared at him.

"What? You're always so self-assured. Too sure. Cocky, even. What's happened?" The genuine concern on his uncle's face somehow helped ease his heart.

"I'm just trying to hang on to him," Landon confessed, tilting his head past his uncle toward Robert, to see his sister Lori, and his niece and nephew, Presley and Parker, being introduced to Robert. "I think he's going through PTSD."

The joke fell short. His uncle looked confused as he turned back to Robert, lost at why Landon would say such a thing. Maybe it was for the best that his uncle didn't understand Landon's worry. He loved his family and didn't want to contribute to any hurt feelings, and he was throwing shade all over them. "Why PTSD?"

"You'll see." He didn't say more, nodding toward Robert, and started that way.

"Uncle Lan," Parker said, extending a fist for a knuckle bump. He fist-bumped the kid who wasn't necessarily a child any longer. Parker had grown several inches since the last time he'd seen him, his fifteenth birthday was a few months away. Presley came in for a sweet side hug. Her sixteenth birthday had happened the day he left Germany for DC. Usually, these two held all his attention, because again, he had to remind himself, he did love his family, but instead, he watched his father amble through the front door.

"The air conditioner's on. Why're we doing this out here?" His father's hard-edged tone didn't go unnoticed.

"Honey, meet Robert. Robert, this is Antonio," his mother said as if his father's comment had actually been something kind and inviting.

His father came out past the threshold a step or two, his voice loud and gruff as he offered his hand to Robert. "Call me Tony. I hear you're Paulie's grandson." Those words had Landon narrowing his eyes, glancing between his boyfriend and his father. When had that information exchange happened? His family must have searched the internet on Robert before they arrived. His stomach roiled again, the sensation turning into a constant companion in his life. Why had he never considered the idea they may have googled Robert? What else had they learned?

"Yes, sir, I am." Robert grinned, completely at ease with all the attention and gruffness hitting him at once.

"He's a legend where I come from. I hear he taught you his secrets?" His father looked and acted like Robert may have been privy to highly classified information and proud that he had discovered the knowledge as he crossed his arms over his chest. That same chest swelled with speculation.

"Pop…" Landon started, trying to stop wherever this was headed.

"He did, sir. I'm not half the chef he was, but I've recently been working to fine tune my skill in the kitchen. It's coming back to me."

His dad reached out, circling Robert's shoulders. "Then you come with me. I'll show you what good tastes like." He tugged Robert forward into the house without even acknowledging Landon's return home for the first time in two years.

"Pop, let him get acclimated…" Landon called out. He had mentally prepared for Robert to hear every ailment his family could come up with, but he'd never considered his father trying to one-up Paulie in the kitchen.

"Pop, Pop. What is there, a parakeet around here?" His father threw the words back over his shoulder, looking at Landon with a giant grin on his face like he'd told the funniest joke in the world. Then he did something Landon had never seen before, he winked. "Get in the house. I'm not air conditioning the whole neighborhood."

His father and Robert were gone, Robert only casting a playful smile over his shoulder as they turned away from the entrance and out of sight.

"He's been cooking all day," his mother said, reaching up for Landon, giving him a hug and a kiss.

"He's been planning this since he found out who you were bringing home," Lori added, hip-bumping him before moving past them into the house.

"He's been talking to his mom and her friends, getting a good recipe for dinner. It's been sweet," his mother said, a smile lighting her face.

Landon gave a humorless laugh at his father ever being considered sweet and followed the rest of his family inside, still analyzing what that wink from his father had meant. Landon cocked his head toward the kitchen, listening to his father bragging about the fresh ingredients he'd used to make his gravy from scratch.

"Honey, go put your stuff in your bedroom. You two are staying in there tonight. Parker and your uncle are sleeping on the pullout sofa."

He immediately shook his head, knowing firsthand how uncomfortable the old sofa sleeper was. "We planned to get a hotel room. It's already reserved."

"No, sir," she said, instantly looking hurt and offended. "You two are staying here. We never get to see you anymore, and it's only for one night."

"Mom..." He started to protest again, but Robert's voice stopped him.

"We can stay here, babe. Let your uncle and nephew have the hotel room tonight," Robert suggested, sticking his head around the kitchen door. "It's the closest Hilton to here. I reserved a small suite with room service. I believe there's an indoor and outdoor swimming pool. It's all on us. Enjoy yourselves."

"Badass," Parker said, doing an all-air fist pump before reaching for his cell phone and leaving the living room in a rush.

"Mom, I wanna go," Presley said in a distinct whine, never lifting her head from her cell phone.

"Parker, what did we say about the language while Landon and Robert are here?" his mother scolded, but Landon knew Parker didn't care in the least. He and Parker were too much alike. He didn't even have to look to know Parker was already inviting all his friends to the Hilton for whatever impromptu party he planned. "Get your luggage in your room, son. I'm going to talk with Robert. It's so exciting, you bringing your first friend home." She hugged him again and started toward the kitchen. He saw the bag Robert had been holding lying on his father's La-Z-Boy and grabbed it.

"Let me take it. You go with them," his uncle suggested.

"I need to go wrangle Parker before all of Houston's invited to the hotel," Lori said, heading off after her son.

"Mom, I wanna go," Presley said again, right on her heels.

"Lori, you all take the hotel. I'll take your room tonight," his uncle said, following them down the hall. Landon didn't say another word. He'd let them decide. It was better not to leave Robert alone with his parents for too long.

"What an incredible meal. I was sorry to see Robert walking in the door and immediately drawn into the kitchen, but my goodness, you two created delicious goodness," Karen said, dabbing the napkin to her lips, sitting back in her chair in the dining room, her dinner plate almost empty.

"We always eat meat. I'm surprised how much I enjoyed the vegan dishes, Robert. You have a true talent," Uncle Michael said, taking another bite of the panzanella.

"I didn't do much. It was all Tony," Robert said, placing his fork at the edge of his finished dinner plate, not wanting to mess up the clean linen tablecloth. "It's rare to see a carnivore so willing to try meatless options."

Landon abruptly stood with his empty plate in hand and reached to take Robert's. The move was part of their normal routine. Landon always insisted on cleaning after Robert prepared their meals. Robert just wasn't certain their routine should hold tonight. He wanted Landon to spend time with his family. After hours together, he could see they were all so connected with one another. Robert took hold of his plate and reached for Landon's, but Landon held on tight as Robert started to stand.

"Let me. You stay."

"No way," Landon said. The struggle of the dirty plates became real until Robert shifted his gaze toward the family who had gone utterly silent, gaping at the two of them. Robert's engrained sense of manners kicked in, and he let go, giving Landon the win. When Landon noticed their shell-shocked expressions, he barked out a loud laugh. "It's not that big a deal."

"I've never seen it before," Karen exclaimed as if Landon had suddenly grown two heads.

"I'm pretty sure I second that," Michael said, pushing back in his seat, finding humor in the whole scene.

"Thanks, Uncle Michael. You're supposed to be on my side." Landon reached across the table for his father's plate. "You done?"

"Yeah, I guess."

Landon took his dumbfounded father's plate then went for his mother's. His uncle readily lifted his to Landon, having no problem with Landon taking his dirty dishes.

"Are you planning on washing those?" Karen asked, still seemingly unsure what she was seeing. Robert couldn't help his own quiet chuckle at their reaction. Apparently the helpful, generous man he'd grown to love beyond anything reasonable wasn't necessarily that same man his family had always known.

"I will later, if that's all right. I thought it would be easier to talk without the dirty dishes in front of us," Landon explained.

The suggestion Landon would indeed clean the dishes, he just wanted to wait until they finished talking, had them all speechless. The perfect comic relief Robert needed to grow comfortable again. He took his seat, pushing backward, and reached for his wineglass. Landon started around the table, stopping beside Robert's chair.

"I'll bring more wine."

"Thank you."

Landon's loving gaze slid over his face. His mister was happy, which made Robert happy. Landon winked as if he'd read Robert's thoughts and started for the kitchen.

"You've been good for him," Karen said when Landon disappeared around the corner into the kitchen.

"I can still hear every word you say," Landon called out in a fake irritability.

"He's been good for me," Robert replied, taking a long swallow of his wine to help hide his humor.

"How did you two meet?" Karen asked as her cell phone started vibrating on the table. She lifted it then turned it for the table to see. The phone showed a picture of Lori, Presley, and Parker playing in the hotel's swimming pool.

"They're having fun. That's wonderful," Robert said, reaching for the cell phone. He tapped a finger on the screen as it began to darken to get a better look at Lori. She was beautiful. She and Landon looked so much alike. "They're great kids."

"That's debatable," Tony said, giving one of his regular gruff grumbles. "Until your car's gone at two o'clock in the morning."

Karen slapped her husband's arm. "You hush. They don't want to hear all that right now, and it only happened once."

"Once with each one of my kids and grandkids." Tony gave a *pfft*, rolling his eyes as he called out, "Landon, have you told

Robert about the time you took our car for a joy ride?" Tony reached for the almost empty bottle of wine and topped off his glass to the brim, the memory seeming to need some fortitude to get through.

"Maybe," Landon yelled back, completely unfazed by such a topic. Three pair of expectant gazes turned toward Robert to find the answer.

"I'm not sure," Robert said, mentally ticking off the different topics Landon had broached about his youth. Honestly, Landon had readily admitted he'd been a lot to handle. "He told me he had a sordid past."

Tony burst out with a loud bark of a laugh, and Karen again instantly scolded him. "We're not rehashing all this tonight, Tony. Robert, how did you two meet?" Karen asked again, redirecting the conversation.

Robert paused to see if Tony had anything left to say before he answered. Met with silence, Robert began. "We were at the military hospital in Germany together," he stated as Landon came back into the room with a new, uncorked bottle of wine. "I had taken a temporary position there and met Landon a day or two after his surgery. We read together every evening and—"

"You had surgery?" his father barked in a shocked bellow, this time startling Robert with the unexpected outburst.

"Oh shit, I forgot…" Landon had started to pour a refresher in Robert's glass when he paused and looked down at him. "I hadn't told them about that."

"You didn't warn me," Robert said as their panicked gazes collided. "I wouldn't have—"

"You forgot you had surgery?" The volume of his father's voice increased by a full octave. Robert swore the table vibrated under the force.

"Listen to me!" Landon demanded, his voice strong and loud.

The wine bottle was forgotten, discarded on the table as Landon turned to face off with his now standing father. His mister grew ten feet tall, his chest swelling as he prepared for a war of words.

"It wasn't that big a deal. I broke my arm." He flung his arm out for them to see he was fine. "See? You didn't have to worry." Landon then threw out his hands like a true Italian, giving his words meaning. "And good thing it happened because that's where I met him." Landon's thumb hooked over his shoulder toward Robert as if it wasn't a given that Landon had been talking about him.

Tony looked ready to blast Landon further. Robert cleared his throat, trying for the best words to help defuse this sudden burst of anger. "Not met exactly. We reconnected there. I should have started a little further back. He and I first met when Landon generously aided my family during my father's state funeral," Robert explained and reached over, taking Landon's hand in his, urging him down to his seat. Landon threaded their fingers together as he sat, doing a full body turn toward Robert. His mister's face turned ten shades of red, pausing Robert's explanation.

What had happened to cause embarrassment?

Holding his hand?

Another first for his family, no doubt. It was so automatic for Robert that he hadn't thought twice.

His heart melted, knowing Landon hadn't chosen to reject his touch. "In Germany, we started reading *A Game of Thrones* together. I believe Michael sent the book to Landon at some point. Landon struggled reading with one hand, and I had always wanted to read the series. The book brought us together."

"Why're you keeping secrets?" Tony asked as if Robert hadn't spoken. His hand tightened around Landon's. As much as Robert loved Landon might be as much as he was growing to love his family. They were hilariously wonderful, Tony intent in finding his answers while scolding Landon with his tone.

"Pop, it wasn't intentional—" Landon started only to have Tony cut him off.

"Sure, it was." The blustery, animated man turned serious, maybe even hurt by everything Landon had neglected to tell them. "We're your family. Why're we just finding out about all this? You've been back in the States for months. You got hurt and you got a friend and we don't know?"

Tony reminded Robert of his granddaddy Paulie. He'd been a forceful man. On nothing more than a gut reaction, Robert decided to side with Landon's family on this matter. He and Landon had been so in sync that it was time to put aside whatever fears and insecurities Landon had about how well they would all fit together.

"Yeah. Why, Landon?" The swing of Landon's head made the air shift in the room. His mister had a *what-the-fuck* look on his face to which Robert winked and swiped a thumb over Landon's thumb, hoping to show his teasing.

"Honestly…" Landon gave a deep exhale and rose enough to push his chair backward, closer to Robert's. "I've been a little overwhelmed." Landon cocked his head toward Robert, his funny nature returning. "This one looks like he's a gentleman— *pfft*. He's a lot to deal with." Then Landon tossed the imaginary gauntlet toward his uncle. "Besides, I did tell Uncle Michael."

"You knew?" Karen said accusingly. "And you didn't tell us?"

"Thanks for throwing me under the bus," his uncle said in hopefully faux outrage. "I kept all your secrets. I didn't even tell them you two planned to be married." Michael's hand slowly came to his mouth, showing he'd absolutely meant that slip of the tongue.

"Oh, my fucking God." Landon gasped and jumped to his feet at the same time his father did. "You did not just say that." Both father's and son's faces flushed with the news. Karen, though, garnered all of Robert's attention. Instant tears filled her eyes as she rose from her seat and came straight to him as the other men began to argue.

"I'd hoped that's where this was headed."

Robert stood as she closed in on him, taking him into her arms, pure happiness in her tone.

"Hush, Landon, and get over here." She reached out, drawing a still arguing Landon into the hug with them. "I wanted this to be the reason you brought Robert home to us. You two seem to share a great love."

The awkward angle had her releasing Robert to take Landon more fully into her loving embrace. She held him tightly, pulling him down by the neck to get a better hold. Landon's eyes lifted to Robert's as he bent to give her better access.

"Mom, I didn't mean to keep secrets. It's all happening fast, and I'm trying to hang on. I love him so much."

"I know you do. And nothing else matters now. You're getting married. I wanted this for you." She pulled away, wrapping an arm around Robert, still holding Landon by the waist. "Are you going to have children?"

"Well, how's that gonna work, Karen?" his father asked as if that was the dumbest question on the planet. He had come around the table from the other side with his hand outstretched to Robert, eagerly pumping his hand in a congratulatory way. Their immediate acceptance had to mean the world to Landon, which again, filled Robert with unbelievable joy.

"I believe we eventually want children, right?" Robert asked. Landon gave a single nod, which might have been the easiest answer he'd ever gotten from the man. "And it'll work pretty much in the same way I came into the world," Robert continued, watching Landon get wrapped into his father's arms. "It worked out well for me."

"That's right. I read that in your father's book. Michael gave it to me to read." Tony beamed with pride and took a step back, letting Michael into the huddle they'd formed in this small section of the dining room. Michael gripped Landon's shoulder, giving him a tight squeeze. His excitement was a little subdued since the three of them skyped regularly, and he'd been told weeks ago.

The connection Robert and Landon shared had Robert so in tune with Landon that he felt the moment when everything settled into place for his guy. He watched Landon initiate another hug with his father who held him tight in return. Whatever happened in the past had clearly been left there.

"I'm proud of you, son." There may have been a quiver in both men's bodies; clearly tears were being fought by the tone of Tony's voice. Robert reached out, circling Karen's shoulder, and she wrapped an arm around his back, hugging Robert as they watched their two men connect.

Chapter 26

From what Robert had learned on the tour of the house, the bedroom where he currently stood used to be Landon's and those were the first layers of memories secured to the walls. Pictures of Landon playing youth sports were next to dated posters, one being a *Grand Theft Auto* poster. Robert smiled as he wondered whether that might have been a foreshadowing to all the auto theft from the youths of this household. There was also a picture of Landon and a very pretty young lady with delicate features and long blond hair, dressed formally, possibly at a prom.

Michael also had had some influence on these walls. A pretty hand painted landscape hung there—Robert didn't recognize the artist's name—along with pictures of destinations. Snapshots taken in real time, some with Landon in his service dress uniform. Landon looked young, proud, and very, very handsome. Robert lifted his cell phone to take a picture of that photo to store for later.

The more updated décor had to be all Parker. Graphic video game posters were haphazardly thumbtacked over other memories and pictures, causing Robert to pry off an edge of one to see what was underneath.

"Remember, you said you wanted to do this."

Robert looked over his shoulder to see Landon in pajama pants and an Air Force T-shirt, shutting the bedroom door behind him.

"I like getting a peek into your life," he said, sweeping a hand over the wall, stopping at the picture of Landon and his female date. "Where is she now?"

"That's Heather. She's married, has some kids, works somewhere. I heard her husband was arrested for burglary, spending time in the pen," Landon said, turning on the nightstand lamp then going back to turn off the overhead light. "Back then, I hadn't accepted the me you see now. I signed up for the Air Force the day after that picture. I think she thought we were to be married."

"Really?" Robert left the wall of memories, drawn to the real version of Landon. Over the last couple of hours, Robert had watched Landon flourish under the acceptance of his family. His guy's shoulders were a little straighter, his expansive chest a little fuller. Robert saw Landon's anxiety flee, and in return, he got his cocky, fun guy back. It had been wonderful to witness. Robert went right for him, his hands needing to touch Landon with the same need his body had to breathe.

"Pretty much. At least the best I remember. I've always had a thing for blonds." Landon seemed just as eager to have Robert near, snaking an arm around his waist, pulling him snugly against his body. "Thank you for today. You're always such a gentleman. I'm working on trying to be one myself. They all really like you."

"I like them too, and you're my perfect gentlemen," Robert said quietly, knowing all three of the bedrooms were at this end of the house and everyone had gone to bed at the same time. "I like you in pajamas."

"I like you out of your pjs," Landon said with a pronounced Texas twang. Landon puckered his lips, his intentions clear. Robert narrowed his eyes. After a moment of speculation, he allowed the kiss, but purposefully kept it light, pulling from Landon's arms after the smallest brush of tongue.

"Your parents are right across the hall," he whispered,

shaking his head. "You'll get me excited, and I can't rub one off with your parents across the hall."

"That wasn't my plan at all. More a full-fledged fuck. Boyhood fantasies," Landon whispered loudly as he furrowed his brow and watched Robert circle to the other side of the bed. Landon didn't follow, which meant his words were more a tease than an actual plan Robert would have to truly fight off.

Robert chuckled as he placed his cell phone on the nightstand and pulled down the bedspread on his side of the bed. "That's absolutely not going to happen tonight. Change of subject. Your dad worked hard on his spaghetti sauce. I'm impressed."

Landon mimicked his moves, climbing in bed beside him. "Remember, I've tasted my father's cooking. Believe me, he's never cooked like that before. I think you had a hand in that sauce."

Robert grinned. He and Tony had worked together in the kitchen for a couple of hours. Most of Robert's time in this house so far had gone from the kitchen to the dining room. Landon reached for the lamp, plunging them into darkness. Robert scooted closer to Landon, stretching out along his side. They usually slept nearly on top of one another, but not tonight. This was as close as it got.

"I don't think the mattress has changed since I left."

"I'm good." Robert tucked his hands together under the pillow to keep from reaching out and touching Landon. Of course, they had been together long enough that they no longer had to have sex every single day, but Robert really enjoyed their cuddle time. He might even go so far as to say that he and Landon were expert cuddlers, already mastering each other's needs. Robert regularly stayed in bed well past the time he woke just to hold Landon who claimed to sleep better in his arms.

"Is your e-reader in reach?" Landon asked, caressing his index finger across Robert's bottom lip. As much as Robert wanted to take care of Landon, Landon seemed just as determined to care for Robert. Since he only needed a few hours rest, Landon had made sure to pack his e-reader and charger for Robert to have something to occupy his time in the middle of the night.

"It is." He barely moved his lips to keep Landon's finger touching him.

"No reading *A Storm of Swords* without me." Landon cupped his cheek, and Robert smiled, knowing he'd never tell Landon that he had in fact sneaked and read the entire series since they had reconnected. He couldn't help it; the books were just too addicting.

"I love you, Landon," Robert whispered by way of an answer.

"That's not confirmation on not reading ahead," Landon whispered, eyeing him closely.

"I promise not to read *A Storm of Swords* when I wake in the morning." His hand went to his heart, giving his oath. "Now, tell me you love me and everything's right with us."

"I do and it is. I just want to be enough for you."

Robert moved to press his lips to Landon's in a chaste kiss. Landon snaked an arm around him, holding him there. His guy was strong, keeping him right there in his face as he tugged his pillow over, giving Robert his share with no more than three inches of space separating them. Landon inched closer. He craved Landon. The desire in his gaze drew Robert closer until Landon's rock-hard cock jutted against his hip. They couldn't, not here. It could ruin all the ground they'd made tonight.

Robert shifted away, one of them had to be strong, but Landon locked an arm around him. His own dick jerked at the manhandling move. The heat of Landon's body enveloped him. Suddenly, Robert was on his back with Landon's thicker body pinning him to the mattress, his lips pressed heavily against Robert's ear.

"Shh, Doc. The bed squeaks. Don't move. Don't make a sound. These walls are paper thin."

"Landon, not a good idea," he hissed. Truth be told, his dick was completely on board and leaking in his pajamas. Landon's moist tongue traced the shell of his ear before darting inside. Fuck, he loved that move, and his body warmed, his dick straining as he locked his arms around Landon's upper back.

"It's gonna happen. So be quiet," he said with an intentional puff of breath caressing Robert's wet ear. A shiver crawled along his skin as a flood of desire shot down his spine. Landon used the moment to slip from his hold and tug Robert's pajama pants lower with expert skill. Then Landon was between his legs, swallowing him whole in three seconds flat.

God, he loved Landon's mouth. Robert's eyes slid back in his head as Landon mouthed him, driving him to the edge of sanity with every lazy lick of his tongue. Robert couldn't speak, his voice silenced by the rush of desire flowing under his skin. He scrambled to grab Landon's head to push him away, but instead, he tightened his grip and held him while he thrust his hips into all that wet heat.

Landon swallowed around him, and he had to bite his tongue to keep from moaning his lover's name out loud. Landon knew exactly what he liked and didn't waste any time working him to a frenzy. The guilt he had about being in Landon's parents' house had flown right out the window the second his lover's throat constricted around him so perfectly.

He fought to remain quiet. He wasn't sure how much longer he could contain the orgasm vibrating up and down his spine in the most delicious way. Landon moved a hand over his balls before cupping and rolling his tender sac in his rough palm. The pleasure from his touch sent hot flames licking hungrily up his spine. He was so close. Closer and closer. With every bob of Landon's head, the orgasm grew stronger and harder to fight. "Oh, God…baby."

The first waves of searing pleasure rushed up from his spine and rolled through him, hijacking his muscles. Robert held his breath, his body quivering uncontrollably as he gave into Landon's wicked assault and spilled his seed down his lover's throat.

Chapter 27

Robert looked down at his wristwatch. If nothing more than based on the cost per hour of renting a private jet, they should be on their way to the executive airport by now. Lifting the glass of spiked punch Landon's mother had made, Robert took a long drink, looking around the standing room only living room. Landon's extended family and neighborhood friends had all collected to see him before he left again to go off and explore the world.

The way the people gathered around Landon, the excitement in seeing him and hearing his stories, showed exactly the high respect they held for him. Landon's dad had the same swell of chest that Landon carried, clearly very proud of his son. For Robert, it was wonderful to see and maybe showed another side to Landon he hadn't necessarily understood before. Landon had some deep-seated insecurities that were clearly all self-inflicted, because this community and family loved their son. They truly couldn't be any prouder.

And the clock still ticked.

Robert scolded himself. He needed to stop being cheap, and let Landon have his time. If they left in the next two hours, they would easily be home in enough time for Landon to make it to the base for his shift. Robert's controlling mother-hen nature was getting the best of him. He looked around the living room then through the large sliding glass door into the backyard to see Landon's Uncle Michael sitting alone on the patio.

Robert turned toward Landon. Like normal, they were so connected. Landon lifted his head and their gazes locked. Robert inclined his head toward the patio where Michael sat. Landon didn't give an immediate nod. Instead, he craned his neck to better understand Robert's message. Once he'd spotted Michael, Landon nodded before turning back to the conversation.

Robert slid open the back door, stepping outside, loving the feel of the warm sun and instant quiet once the door shut behind him. A sweet fragrance filled the air. He wasn't certain if it was jasmine or honeysuckle, but the scent surrounded him with contentment. In all his recent self-discovery, Robert found he really lived a quiet life. He'd always cherished his alone time. The way Michael's gaze settled on him, a small smile touching his lips, but no greeting, he assumed Michael must be enjoying the peace and quiet too.

"Will I bother you if I sit out here?" Robert asked, coming to the edge of the table.

"No, please do." Michael's leg extended, pushing out the patio chair next to him, inviting him over. "There's a lot going on inside there." Michael's thumb hooked over his shoulder, indicating the commotion inside the house.

"Seems they missed him," Robert said, taking the seat, placing his near empty glass on the table.

"We do. Not that he sees it that way. Landon told me about the feathers. I saw you pick one up this morning."

Robert hadn't realized he had and his hand went to his slacks pocket, a place he normally gathered his treasures, feeling the outline of the feather there. Michael's soul-searching gaze held sincere curiosity and a little understanding. The calm that seemed to surround Michael seeped into Robert for the first time—maybe because Robert had finally let his guard down. Whatever the reason, it was almost eerie and tranquil at the same time.

Robert held Michael's stare. It seemed somehow disrespectful to turn away. *Patience.* The word reverberated through his head. Landon held great respect for his uncle. Right now, in this moment, Robert could see why. Sitting there with Michael in this way, they were back to the unspoken knowledge. The knowing without being told. The realm of belief Robert still struggled mightily to believe in.

"What do you want to ask me?"

"How do you know I want to ask you anything?" Robert countered. Michael smiled an indulgent grin, saying nothing more.

The connection between them became unsteady. Robert tensed and decided to stop playing games. With knowledge came understanding. That thought caused him to lean in closer to Michael.

"I'm trying to open myself to the possibility of something more than our conscience being the driving force for our decisions. I still wouldn't call it divine intervention. I don't know what it is. I've come a long way, but it's hard. I've always needed proof. Now I find myself questioning what exactly proof is. On one hand, without the expansion of belief, I might not have ever opened myself enough to see Landon." Instant sadness squeezed Robert's heart. The idea he may not have ever opened himself up to Landon caused such enormous pain that Robert crossed his arms over his chest to keep his heart from shattering.

"What just happened?" Michael asked, his head tilted to the side as if he could see into Robert's soul.

"I..." Robert had to mentally force himself to move out from under the scary, sorrowful emotions. "I love your nephew with every fiber of my being. The fear of never fully seeing him makes me afraid of my actions in the future. I'm following signs. Really just one, based on something my father said to me in the minutes before surgery. I'm making many other changes to my life— my entire life—but I'm struggling with the process of letting it naturally unfold. I try to find scientific explanations for things that have no bases in science or sanity for that matter. Does that make sense to you?"

"It does," Michael said with an encouraging nod. "What're you trying to understand?"

"The balance of my head with my heart. But it seems my head keeps getting in the way of my heart." They both chuckled at his basic way of describing such a complex problem. "My heart's winning. I want to keep it that way. I just don't understand why, and until I understand, I keep reverting back to my old ways."

"Robert, the only exactness I can give you is the understanding that metaphysics is a branch of philosophy that deals with the first principles of things, including abstract concepts such as being, knowing, substance, cause, identity, time, and space—"

Robert stopped Michael, lifting an apologetic hand for the interruption. "Abstract with no basis in reality," Robert countered, placing his elbows on the edge of the table, clasping his hands together. Every bit of his concentration focused on Michael, appreciative of his willingness to participate in this thread of conversation.

Michael shook his head in such a way that Robert knew he flat wasn't getting it. "Let me say it like this, in a way that may help you reprogram your resistance. What's happening to you is based in science. A transcending of what's physical and natural. It's the truth of existence—all existence. Mindset is everything with the metaphysical. Landon's gone as far down this path as he's willing to intellectually go. You may have too, and that's all right, because look what you've found by opening yourself to more."

"I guess I see," Robert said, straining his brain to understand Michael's words.

Michael laughed at him, reaching out a hand to clasp Robert's joined hands. "You'll get there. And sometimes it's enough to believe there's more. It allows the possibility in, like with Landon."

Those words nailed Robert's growing thought process to a tee. He didn't understand, and that was okay because the evidence of the possibility had given him his life back. "You're a librarian. Landon gives you credit for his success; he's told me you're the rock of this family."

"Don't think less of Tony. He's tried. His personality is just so big and always ready to invest in the next big thing. He struggles to keep his jobs. My sister is a kind woman. She cleans houses. We all work together to make ends meet," Michael explained, painting a picture Landon hadn't necessarily explained to him. "Landon also helps. He sends money home. He's also claimed responsibility for Presley's and Parker's school clothes and supplies and their extracurricular activities. He provides a lot of their Christmas and birthday gifts…" Whatever look Robert held had Michael breaking from the topic, saying, "You look surprised. He didn't tell you?"

"No, he hasn't." Robert shook his head and crossed his arms. What a kind deed. Robert had enough money to live ten lifetimes and something as generous as that might not have occurred to him to do.

"Landon's a good man, solid and full of personality. He's also complicated. On one hand, he's self-assured and determined. On the other, he's insecure as hell. I see him like that with you," Michael said.

"I don't know what to do to stop it?"

"Time."

Robert nodded. He'd hoped as much. All he wanted in the world was to give Landon all the time he needed, making confidence in their relationship seem achievable.

"I pushed hard for this relationship with Landon. I didn't know how to manage all these feelings. I went gangbusters with him. I didn't want to lose him—maybe I was insecure too or maybe I took the meaning of my father's words and the feathers that ended up in my path too closely to heart. Something in here"— Robert pointed to his heart before he continued—"tells me that's not what happened. I love Landon with more…intensity than I've ever loved anyone or anything before. I know we're meant to be together. My world immediately locked into place with Landon.

My father talked openly about soul mates. I understand him now. I just don't know how I know. It seems my only purpose in life is to live as authentically as I can with Landon by my side."

"I suspect he feels the same, which is the reason for the insecurity," Michael added, looking very much at peace with what Robert had just confessed.

"I've never said all this out loud before, but I thought by pushing to come here this weekend that he and I could have all the formality out of the way and start living our life."

"Good plan. And, Robert, your words are safe with me." The patio door sliding open drew both their gazes that direction. Landon peered out, glancing over the backyard until he found Robert.

"I don't want to rush you, but we should go." Landon eased his large frame more fully out the doorway, his keen stare probably picking up the seriousness of their conversation. "Everything good?"

Michael got to his feet first, stepping out of the way. "We were having a good talk. I'm glad you made time to come home."

"Me too," Landon said, his unsure gaze remaining on Robert.

"Stop worrying," Michael said, patting Landon's shoulder as he stepped closer to the doorway. "Robert's a good man, as handsome on the inside as he is on the outside."

Michael gave Landon the perfect diversion. Humor immediately danced across Landon's face. "He's like *GQ* Ken. His sister looks like *Vogue* Barbie. There's almost too much pretty in their family."

Robert laughed straight out loud at that comparison. A couple of weeks ago, Landon had come home with a Ken doll wearing a suit. He insisted the doll looked like Robert. Robert had scoffed at the idea, but the compliment sure stuck with him long enough to show Landon exactly how appreciative he was.

"If I'm Ken, you're Max Steele. I had the action figure, and I remember very clearly that I thought he was hot as hell." Any lingering worry fled. Landon must have liked the comparison, because he stepped straight into Robert, caressing a palm down his back before taking his mouth in a playful kiss. Robert loved the easy display of affection in front of Michael and anyone looking through the window.

"I'll keep you safe from harm," Landon said, laughing against his lips.

"Come on, you love birds. My teeth are hurting from all the sugary sweetness," Michael said, leaving the sliding door open behind him.

Chapter 28

December 2014

"Autumn, you can do this. Concentrate on breathing, not the pain. Look at me. Breathe." Robert immediately began the Lamaze breathing technique. He tucked his body close to hers, holding tightly to her hand, ill-prepared to be her birthing coach.

"Shut up, Robert. Where's Cam?" She bit out between panted breaths.

Exactly. Where the fuck is Cam?

"He's coming." The perfect storm of a somewhat early in the season snowstorm along with Autumn's hardheadedness in arguing that her contractions were nothing more than false labor had them preparing to have a baby within fifteen minutes of arriving at The Mother Baby Center in Minneapolis. She might have had this baby in her office had Robert not thrown caution to the wind and boarded a flight to Minneapolis after talking with Autumn that morning. A call where he had insisted Autumn go straight to the hospital, but his well-deserved *I-told-you-so* would come later…and often.

"I hear we're having a baby." Autumn's doctor came through

the hospital room door, trying for a light, calming presence but falling short with the intensity of his tone.

"Right now, Doctor," the nurse said, confirming Robert's suspicions. Robert heard nothing more as Autumn bore down, her face turning beet red as a sound came from her throat that mixed a screaming moan with a string of curse words. He wasn't sure he'd ever heard anything like it before.

Robert lifted his brows as a hand clamped down on his shoulder. Relief flooding him when he turned. Cam had arrived. Robert stepped aside to let her husband and actual birthing coach take over. Within minutes, both Autumn and the baby were crying loudly. Her newborn baby daughter going straight to her chest, cuddled skin to skin with her mama.

Robert did something he'd never done before after any medical procedure, he lifted his cell phone and snapped a picture of Autumn in the seconds after her baby had been born. Cam and their daughter, Kylie—if her name hadn't changed—were also in the shot. His sister would want this moment captured as their little family grew by one.

It was all so emotional. His heart nearly burst with pride as he angled his head to better see his new niece. Her small and tiny body had a healthy set of lungs, seemingly having her mother's spirit. Kylie may have been the most beautiful baby he'd ever seen in all his life. Everything inside him solidified his need to have children of his own one day.

"Come see her, Robert."

He changed his focus from the baby to see Autumn's adoring gaze staring at him. Unspoken love and devotion passed between them as he stepped closer, not wanting to get in the way of Cam's and Autumn's bonding family moment, but helpless to do more than move toward them.

Minutes later, a nurse came forward, carefully taking the baby from Autumn. "Dr. Connors, come with me, sir."

All the initial baby assessments were performed inside the room, keeping Kylie with them always. Even with Autumn less than twenty feet away, when the baby and Cam stepped away, Autumn's questioning gaze, filled with so much emotion, cut straight to Robert's heart.

"Go with them. Make sure everything's done right." His sister's voice was full of concern.

He opened his mouth to say this was Cam's time with his daughter. That Cam was a top-rated general practice physician, and he'd know far better than Robert, but the intensity of Autumn's worry had him giving her a nod, hoping to give her some peace.

He stayed a respectable distance back, watching the medical staff do their jobs. Robert couldn't believe how emotional the birth had been for him. He wasn't sure being in the operating room when his father had died had affected him this much. Everything inside him wanted to love and protect their little baby girl with everything he had. Robert's eyes filled with tears, and he reached for his phone again to video Kylie as she let out another loud cry. He knew it was too soon to tell, but all the preliminary signs were there. He'd place money on this baby having her mother's personality.

Cam turned away from Kylie for only the briefest of seconds to tell Autumn, "She's six pounds, two ounces." He turned back to the table as they measured her. Then he said, "Nineteen inches."

As the initial assessment came to an end, Robert focused on his phone. He sent Landon the video he'd just captured then pocketed his phone. Cam motioned for him to again join them by the bed. Autumn looked exhausted, but more lovely than he'd ever seen her. He could also say the same thing about Cam who stuck out his hand to shake Robert's.

"Thank you. I should have insisted she come to the hospital earlier. I don't know what I was thinking."

"There's no appreciation necessary. She's stubborn," he said, moving around to the other side of the bed.

"I can't argue. I'm too tired," Autumn said, never looking up from the baby in her arms. "Do you want to hold her?"

"I do. Is her name still Kylie?" His hands itched to touch the baby. Robert carefully picked Kylie up, gently cradling her in his arms. She was tiny, swollen, and completely held his heart.

"Yes, Kylie's our final choice," Cam said.

He couldn't take his eyes off the small bundle in his arms or hide his grin when he said, "I was thinking Roberta, named after her favorite uncle."

Based on the groans, he got the desired result of his joke and lifted a hand, caressing the pad of his thumb over her tiny forehead. The well of emotion built so fast that he had to swallow the lump in his throat as he thought about his fathers, knowing the pride they would hold in their granddaughter. They had always wanted grandchildren to spoil. He'd do his best to fill in for them—that was a promise.

"Fuck, it's cold out here." Landon might seriously have to reconsider the whole motorcycle thing. He'd been cavalier when Robert offered up his sports car for Landon to drive tonight, on one of the coldest nights of the season so far. There weren't leathers warm enough to guard against this kind of biting cold.

Landon dropped the kickstand in place, pulled off his helmet, and scanned the numbers on the townhomes. It was late, past eleven thirty on a school night, but he could hear classic rock music thumping from a unit in the row as he peeled off his leather gloves. That had to be Mark Peters's place. He bet the neighbors loved living next to them.

For the first time in his life, he reconsidered accepting his buddy's invitation to party. Since he'd seen him at the dealership, Mark had been relentless in trying to get them together. Based on what he was seeing and hearing now, he'd made the right decision to assume Robert wouldn't fit whatever get together Mark had planned. Besides he'd never really been out to his hometown friends, but the news of his family visit with Robert had gone neighborhood-viral, spreading like wildfire through the small circle of friends in Southeast Houston. He guessed Mark had probably heard the news too. Maybe?

The crazy overthinking had returned. Landon noticed it earlier in the day but chose to ignore it like he used to do and hadn't let himself overanalyze how quiet his head had been since arriving back home from his parents' house all those months ago. In an effort to continue to ignore his self-doubt, Landon cocked his head, gave an internal shrug while squaring his shoulders as he started for the apartment.

Robert's presence in his life had settled him except apparently when he wasn't home. And since his calm seemed contingent on Robert's physical body being near him, it might be a day or two before he settled down again. This time, though, he didn't doubt Robert returning to him—that was a point in favor of his confidence. Landon barely got his knuckles to the metal door when it opened, and Mark's giant, easygoing grin spread wide.

"'Bout fuckin' time you came."

The faint smell of pot hit him as soon as the door had opened.

He should go.

What a puss he'd become. It was just a little pot.

Peer-pressuring himself… How lame was that? "It's late. I can't stay long."

"Come on in. I'm glad you came by. Hey, guess who's here," Mark called out as Landon stepped inside the entryway. Mark's wife Jessica, also an old classmate, came around the corner, stumbling a bit as she walked forward, not stopping as she got closer. Her glassy eyes and bright smile came within inches of his face as she wrapped herself around him in her drunken excitement. Clearly, nothing had changed here. Landon was instantly taken straight back to high school.

"You look great," she cooed in his ear.

"Jessica, let him in so I can shut the door," Mark said, irritably.

"Heather's gonna be shocked as shit that I saw you."

As Landon moved aside to shut the door, a flash of a camera blinded him.

"You really do look great, Landon. Better than in high school, and you were the cutest boy in the school back then." She twirled around and left them standing there, focused on her phone as she walked away.

"She's trashed, ignore her. Come get a beer, man. Branson's in here, and I got some buddies for you to meet." Mark took off down the small hall leading into the apartment. The needling in the back of his mind kept up a steady anthem, urging him to leave, but old habits won out. He nodded once and moved forward. He'd have a beer then take off.

Two hours later, Landon was in deep conversation, shooting the shit about everyone and everything that had ever happened in his hometown since he'd left all those years ago. The loud, thumping classic rock and roll music had softened. The pot hadn't really been an issue since they'd let him bow out without giving him too much shit about his new outlook. Truthfully, as the night wore on, Landon had remembered he'd spent quite a bit of time with Mark and Branson in their youth. He was having a pretty good time strolling down memory lane.

Jessica's phone seemed an extension of her body. The time of night gave her no pause in texting or calling people. The loud, annoying alert sounded again.

"God damn, I'm fuckin' sick of that phone," Mark blurted.

Landon lifted his brows at the sudden burst of anger but couldn't deny the message echoed Landon's exact feelings. Jessica didn't seem fazed in the least, maybe even pleased she'd gotten that reaction from Mark as she stared disbelievingly at Landon.

"Omigod, you're marrying a doctor?" she asked, surprised. For the first time since he'd arrived, the conversation turned from reminiscing about the past into the world around them in present day. "What the hell, Landon? You've been here for hours. Why am I hearing that from Heather?" She looked as if he'd been caught with his hand in the cookie jar.

Landon grinned at her outrage, probably fueled by her wish to spread the word herself. He reached for his second beer of the night, tipping back the warm liquid, drawing out the suspense. "Well, a retired one, I guess."

"Dude, you got yourself a rich cougar?" Branson said, his extended good job hand-slap was immediate.

"Sweet," Mark said, reaching across for the hand slap sequence they had shared in high school.

Luckily, before Landon had to explain the *'cougar'* was in fact a young man, Landon's phone vibrated, drawing his attention to the device stuck inside his pocket. With a tap to the screen, he saw Robert calling from WhatsApp.

"I gotta take this. I'll be back." Landon stood, looking around the apartment for somewhere private. With the front door closer than the back porch, he started that direction.

"Hello," he said.

"Are you asleep?" Robert's face appeared on the screen as he shut the door behind him. The cold winds had turned blistering, instantly finalizing the decision he'd been playing around with all day. Tomorrow morning, he'd be a proud new owner of a pickup truck.

"No, not yet," he replied with a full body shiver. "How are things going there?"

"Good. I'm still at the hospital because I don't want to leave," Robert answered with a yawn.

"You missing it?" Landon asked, voicing another concern plaguing Landon all day as he shivered. Would Robert be in that hospital environment and want to jump back into the medical game, finally realizing everything he'd so easily given up.

"Oh, hell no." Robert vehemently shook his head. "I'm just in love. You got someone bidding for part of my heart."

Landon's grin grew as he opened the door and reached inside

for his jacket, quickly shrugging it on.

"Are you outside?" Robert looked past Landon, seeing his surroundings. "Where are you?"

"I stopped by a buddy's house on my way home," Landon said, trying to zip his jacket with one hand.

"Someone from the base?" Robert asked, still looking at everything but Landon, trying to see where he might be.

"Some people I went to high school with. I got your pictures earlier. She's a beautiful baby. How's Autumn?"

Robert's tired face contorted, which had Landon furrowing his brow while going over the sentence he'd just asked, wondering what might be confusing about his question. Silence held between them as Robert's face went from confused, to angry, to hurt in less than ten seconds flat.

"What?"

"You have friends from high school there and I didn't know? Shouldn't that be something I know?"

Shit. Landon's heart plummeted as the hurt in Robert's words sank in. He should have kept this to himself.

"It's not like that, Robert. They're just people I used to know. You and I haven't been apart since our first date. I didn't really want to go home alone. I miss you already." Landon tried to explain his decision to come there tonight and hopefully pacify Robert enough to lose the hurt on his face.

"I don't necessarily believe that answer, but I miss you like crazy too. I wish you were here with me."

"Me too." Landon smiled a small smile, hoping they were somehow changing the subject without further dissecting his reasoning. "How's Autumn?"

"She's good. She did amazing. We almost didn't make it to the hospital."

"You were afraid you wouldn't make it."

Robert had called it this way when life stopped this morning, pushing him to Minnesota based on nothing more than a hunch.

"Yeah, she kept thinking her contractions were false labor. She talked Cam into believing it too. He walked in as Autumn started to push." Robert brought his hands to his eyes, digging in as he fought another yawn.

If Landon were a good guy, he'd offer to say goodnight, let Robert get some needed rest, but instead he asked, "Can I see the baby?"

"Yeah, we have to be quiet. Autumn and Cam are asleep in the room. I'll take you in to see Kylie then step out into the hall again before we speak."

Landon nodded, and Robert quietly opened the hospital room door, careful of the noise. The darkened room turned into a blur as Robert adjusted the phone. Seconds later, a tightly bundled baby appeared on the screen. He'd never been around many children, never really his thing, but he had to agree with Robert that she looked pretty damn perfect to him. This tiny baby had already done so much in helping to heal her family, so of course she'd be perfect. Robert's hand lowered into the crib, running down the length of the sleeping baby's back, and she moved into his touch. Landon instantly connected to her, because he did the exact same thing with Robert. When Robert touched him, he moved closer, needing more from the man.

Robert's face reappeared on the screen, his finger going to his lips until the light of the bright hallway shown. Robert's deep fatigue became more pronounced.

"You look exhausted," he said, concerned.

"I am. I'll head out now. I just wanted you to see her in real time," Robert said, moving down the hall.

"I wanted to too. How far away is your hotel?" he asked, not remembering ever seeing Robert looking so tired before.

"I have a place downtown. It's not far, a few miles away." Robert kept him on the phone as he went down the hall, his voice lowering. "So, what's up with these friends, Landon? Why do I feel like it's a class thing that makes you not mention them to me?" Robert fucking did that shit all the damn time. Hit the nail right on the head like he lived inside Landon's brain.

"Babe, you know I've settled that down."

Robert scrubbed a hand heavily across his face. "Are you sure of that?"

Landon grinned at his mister, seeing that maybe all cylinders weren't firing like they should in Robert's head for how easily he seemed to be giving in again. This time Landon told the full truth. "Maybe not a hundred percent sure, but I'm trying. I love you. I'm not sure it's wise for you to drive."

"I love you, too. But I'm not diverting the conversation. Since we're having an uncomfortable talk, let me just add that I want children with you. Not a lot, not like Autumn wants, but two would be nice, maybe three. Four makes an even number." Robert narrowed his eyes for a second then shook his head. "Maybe as many as Autumn wants then."

Landon's heart did a little flip in his chest. Since the mention of children at his parents' house months ago, he and Robert hadn't discussed anything more. Honestly, Landon hadn't ever wanted to have children, but Robert made him believe in fairytales. He envisioned one day that he and Robert would be living a happily ever after, and for some reason, that included a couple of blond cherub babies.

"I could be into that," Landon whispered huskily under the weight of such an agreement. "Not now, but maybe when its closer to retirement."

"And when is that again?" Robert asked.

"Twenty nineteen," he said, already counting his time down.

"What? That's too long to wait. I'll be close to forty." Robert pushed through the main doors of the hospital, stepping out into the night, snow flurries danced around in the background as Robert shrugged on a coat Landon hadn't noticed before now. "But it gives us time alone first, but if you have to change orders, we'll just go with you." Robert slowed, looking around the covered drive.

"We'll see," Landon said. "First, we gotta make it down the

aisle. I'm still not convinced you won't wise up before then." Landon's ass hit the wall of the apartment. He grew tired and colder, but content to stay there talking to Robert for as long as he could.

Robert motioned with his hand, drawing a taxi forward. Then he stepped forward and gave a shiver as the crisp wind blew across his hair. He quickly spouted out his address to the driver. When he returned his full attention to the phone, he spoke as if he hadn't missed a beat.

"You keep wearing that sexy leather jacket, and you'll have me good and locked down. I like looking at you a lot." Robert's eyelids lowered as he closed himself inside the taxi. Landon wanted to pretend it was lust reflected back at him, but most likely it was exhaustion.

"I'm getting a truck tomorrow. I'm caving on the I'm-a-badass-I-can-drive-in-the-cold theory," Landon confessed.

"I told you to take my car," Robert countered, that sexy look replaced with one designed to show Landon what a dumbass he'd been.

"I'm never driving a car that costs more than I make in two years, Robert. Not gonna happen." Words he'd repeated over and over for the last five months.

"You know, after we're married what's mine is yours. You'll be a rich man." The waggle of Robert's eyebrows coerced a smile from Landon.

"Are you trying to talk me out of marrying you?" he quipped.

Robert's laugh was genuine. "I love you. Be safe going home. Text me when you get there."

"I'm heading out now," he said, pushing himself off the wall.

"Invite your friends over, Landon. You don't have to feel like you need to sneak around." Robert was like a dog with a bone. He never, ever left well enough alone.

"That's not gonna happen just like you don't invite your friends over. Our worlds don't mesh near as well as you want to believe."

"That's not true…" Robert perked up, ready to argue his point.

"I'll text you. Say bye," he said, lifting a finger to end the video call.

"Not until we settle this," Robert said urgently.

"It'll never be settled. I'm hanging up. I'll be home in about twenty minutes, freezing my ass off. I'm hanging up. I love you." Another first of the night between them, Landon actually ended the call. There was a time when he wouldn't have. Besides, he was truly freezing his ass off. Landon scurried to the apartment door, ducking inside to say goodnight.

Chapter 29

July 2015

From the second he and Landon had stepped off the airplane yesterday afternoon to this very moment, Robert questioned the tradition he'd required they follow on their wedding day. Even now, as Robert took the first step off his golf cart, automatically bringing his hands up to button his suit coat jacket, he doubted the wisdom of the no-seeing-one-another-on-the-wedding-day rule. As much as he'd wanted everything perfect for his and Landon's special day, it had been months since he'd spent this much time without Landon by his side—eight months to be exact. The memory of Kylie's birth, the last time he'd spent a night away from Landon, helped tamp down Robert's anxiousness, focusing him back into the moment. It was his wedding day and his sweet little niece was tucked tightly in her mother's arms and all their guests were looking his way.

Marriage equality pushed him and Landon to move up their wedding day. At Landon's suggestion, they were having their nuptials under their tree in the small grove at his grandmother's Cape Cod home. The one Landon had expertly carved their initials into almost a year ago. His gracious Nonnie seemed on board and happy to accommodate all of Landon's requests.

What Robert hadn't known and wasn't prepared for were the mind-blowing, intricately designed decorations Kennedy had added to help glamorize their simple wedding ceremony. His grandmother, a skilled wedding planner even in her advanced age, had outdone herself.

Kennedy had stunningly created a romantic ambience with carefully placed walkways, leading into a freshly trimmed landscape roomy enough to accommodate all their immediate family. The meticulously chosen flowers coordinated perfectly with the theme. His daddy would have certainly given his stamp of approval at such whimsical, intricate displays. Swags of lush greenery and blooming flowers hung from the canopy of tree branches above with hundreds of white feathers woven throughout the floral mix. The simple addition of the white, fluffy feathers meant everything to Robert. His family respected him enough to accept the value he had placed on such a simple notion. The same flower, greenery, feather choices were artfully arranged in large urns strategically placed close to a floral arch showcasing the heart Landon had etched into their special tree.

The spiritual connection Robert held to such a lovely display had to mean his fathers were there with them today, celebrating the best moment of his life with him.

As Robert came forward, he smiled lovingly at his sister and niece, his gaze lingering there for a few seconds before his focus drifted to the new, welcome faces of Landon's family who would soon become his family too. He started down the path, careful to stay within the lines of the hundreds and hundreds of rose petals and small feathers scattered over the walkway.

As he walked under the beautiful canopy, he spotted their families standing together, gathered around twelve white folding chairs facing the middle of the small space.

Parker, Landon's nephew, broke the imaginary line holding their families in place. Clearly, he didn't care about disturbing the path of rose pedals as he cut a beeline, straight to Robert.

"Uncle Robert."

Robert slowed as his brows shot up. He'd never been called uncle before.

"Whatever you're about to do, don't," Tony's voice boomed to his grandson in that passionate Italian way. Just the comic relief Robert needed to ease his nerves. He fought the curl of his lips as he kept his gaze on Parker.

Parker didn't appear to have heard the instruction as excitement danced in his eyes. "You're loaded. I mean you look like you bank, but shit."

"Parker…" his grandmother warned, most likely about the language.

"Sorry." Parker barely cast a glance over his shoulder before his awestruck gaze landed on Robert once again. "I'm gonna change my birthday gift list. I think I need a car."

"Me too."

Robert looked past Parker to his sister, Presley. She took a seat in one of the chairs seemingly ignoring everything with her head bent, her thumbs working on her cell phone screen.

"Get over here, Parker," Tony barked, true irritability reverberated in his tone. This time his grandson seemed to listen but not before nodding at Robert and lifting a fist for a bump. He obliged the bump, hoping it wasn't some sort of a teenage commitment where he had agreed to buy vehicles for these two.

Sophia and Thomas stood by Autumn and Cam. They were standing close enough to Landon's family that they already seemed one big happy family. He was sure that was Autumn's doing. He appreciated her effort, especially after the shell shock Landon's family had gone through when first seeing his grandmother's estate yesterday evening.

Another difference between his and Autumn's weddings were the sleeping arrangements. Last night, after a family dinner, Robert was escorted to a local hotel along with Autumn, Kylie and Cam. His sister had been given strict instruction to keep Robert from his Nonnie's home, where Landon and his family spent the night.

The Russos were given full access to the property—the swimming pool, sauna, tennis and basketball courts, and all the golf carts to make the jaunt to the oceanside a bit easier. Based on the steady stream of pictures Landon sent, his family seemed to be having a grand time playing all over the estate.

Again, Robert knew he'd never be able to repay his grandmother for making sure Landon's family was comfortable and happy with their stay. From what he understood, although he and Landon were leaving for Minnesota following a quick lunch after the wedding ceremony, the entire Russo family planned to stay a couple of extra days to spend more time with his grandmother and tour the area—the Cape being somewhere Landon's mother had always wanted to visit.

Robert went for Kylie instead of taking his place close to the arch. He lifted the baby from Autumn's hold as he spoke to Landon's family. "I heard you guys had a fun evening last night." His cell phone vibrated in his suit coat pocket. He had no idea how the Russo family responded, because all his attention diverted to his cell. He reached for the phone, careful not to disrupt a busy Kylie slapping at the pocket square in his suit jacket. Normally, he'd ignore his phone, but this handheld device was his only lifeline to Landon, and the possibility of Landon's internal jitters getting the best of him had Robert anxiously checking his messages.

"It's not too late to back out." Landon's text read, then a second text message came through. *"You know, I've been waiting for the day you suddenly wake up and realize what you're doing. It's okay if it's now."*

Robert's heart drummed in his chest as he read the concern in Landon's words. He had no doubt that Landon loved him. Every single day, his mister made sure he knew exactly how cherished he was, yet his lovely Landon still tried to give him an out. He shook his head and smiled at the words on the screen. Robert could feel his cheeks warming. Someone must have noticed because Kylie's weight lifted from his arms. His whole focus remained on the phone in his hand.

"*Quit trying to quit me,*" he typed and pushed send. His phone vibrated seconds later.

"*Really? Quoting Brokeback at a time like this?*" He could almost hear Landon's testy, teasing tone as he read the words. God, he loved that man.

"*Are you nervous? Do I need to come get you and bring you out here myself?*" Robert asked and took a step toward the golf cart, ready to do that very thing.

"*We're on our way. The pastor was late, but here now. Your grandmother is making me call her Nonnie or I get in trouble.*"

That had Robert stopping his movement back to the golf cart, his grin stretching from ear to ear when the next text came through.

"*She wants everyone sitting and you standing close to the arch. She's directed me to tell you to get there. She suspects you're talking with the family. Something about you've always had a problem minding...*"

His grin dimmed a bit as he slid his phone inside his jacket breast pocket, reluctantly heading the direction his Nonnie had insisted on, instead of waiting at the entrance, an idea he'd just come up with, hoping to catch a glimpse of Landon when he drove up with his grandmother and the pastor.

"I've been told to ask everyone to please take their seats," he said distractedly over his shoulder.

"He's not normally like this," Autumn whispered loud enough to make sure he heard. "He used to have nerves of steel. Right, Cam?" Autumn spoke a little louder this time, but Robert continued to ignore her. He kept his attention glued to the entrance as the golf cart's front two wheels came into view.

"He did. Nothing rattled him." Cam, who was usually quiet, said in agreement, proving they were having loads of fun at his expense.

A photographer rounded the corner first, camera in hand.

Then the pastor took his spot next to Robert before instructing those still standing, "Please take a seat."

Robert skimmed the length of his suit coat before he fisted his hands, refusing to give into the nervous energy racing through him. He straightened his jacket, shifting his weight to his left leg as he waited patiently. Through the cluster of trees, a soft gentle breeze caused the ribbons adorning the flower garlands to dance while cooling his sweat-dampened skin.

Robert buzzed with excitement, making his skin flush. He wasn't sweating because of the heat. In fact, the day had turned out nicer than forecasted. No humidity, which was a blessing, especially in the summer. The sun even played its part, hiding every now and then behind the few puffy white clouds floating lazily across the endless blue sky.

The perfect day in his opinion—his and Landon's perfect day to be exact.

He dropped his arms to his side and took a deep steadying breath as his grandmother then Landon came into view. The sight of the two caused his heart to melt. The anticipation he'd carried in his body loosened its grip and his muscles relaxed as he watched his soldier carefully offering his arm to support Kennedy's walk into the ceremony.

Robert's heart swelled with pride and overflowed with love. Not only was his future husband devastatingly handsome, he was loyal and compassionate, sweet and kind. The epitome of gallant. Robert's cock plumped. Super sexy too. Landon kept his focus trained on making sure his Nonnie stayed sure-footed until she took her seat.

"Thank you, dear. You go be with Robert now." Her voice carried, giving everyone a laugh as Landon's cheeks darkened with color. The blush unleashed a swift but excited flutter of butterflies in his stomach. *He's mine. Landon is my forever.*

Landon, the very definition of tall, dark, and handsome, had decided to go formal with his Air Force mess dress uniform. His soldier was certain to have turned a few heads wearing that uniform. When his future husband finally looked up, the deep concentration faded. His dark eyes quickly scanned the intimate area, no doubt taking everything in. But when Landon's gaze locked on his, their souls embraced, and all Robert saw was the same wonderment reflected at him that he'd felt all day.

Robert's attention remained focused on Landon, who visibly swallowed and misstepped, his feet giving a slight stumble. Robert got it. His heart still tripped in his chest when he thought of how the course of their lives had played out to bring them together. And even now as he gazed into those dark orbs, he saw happiness between them. He saw a loving partner who would remain by his side forever. They would travel, have children, and grow old together. He vowed to himself he'd be Landon's everything, and he saw that same commitment in Landon's eyes.

Their gazes broke only long enough for Landon to bend and scoop a tiny feather just feet from Robert. Landon's loving gaze found his once again as he extended the treasure, offering Robert the feather. "Save that with the others."

He took the soft feather from Landon, unable to hide the smile at such a thoughtful act, and deposited the feather inside his suit coat pocket while grasping Landon's hand with his other.

"Thank you, love," he whispered. He'd never doubt he'd been given a special gift with a second chance at life. From the first feather that floated across his desk, to the feather now resting in his pocket, he'd felt his fathers' gentle nudges.

Absolutely, he had a little help from above. Probably more than he deserved.

The fact that he'd managed to keep Landon interested in him this long had to prove miracles did exist. Happier than he'd ever been in his life, Robert couldn't hold back the joy of the moment and gave Landon the smile he knew his lover liked the most. Landon returned the smile and completely stole Robert's breath with his sincerity. Happy tears filled his eyes. He had to fight hard to keep his composure, the overwhelming love and devotion hard to contain. Robert lifted Landon's hand to his lips and kissed his knuckles.

Landon had lectured himself to be chill. When he'd arrived at the ceremony, if Robert hadn't bailed on him, then he had planned to acknowledge his mother, shake his father's hand then walk, cool, calm, and collected, toward his future husband. *Pfft,* as if that would have ever happened. Like every day for the past year, Robert had such a way of detouring his plans. Nothing in the whole wide world compared to the man standing in front of him. The beautiful inside and out Dr. Robert Adams captured Landon body and soul, making him unable to do anything more than go straight to Robert's side.

"You're stunning," Robert whispered, tears brimming in his blue eyes.

"You keep saying that." Landon ducked his head but kept his gaze fixed on Robert. If Robert started with the waterworks, Landon would be screwed and, undoubtedly, follow suit.

Robert caressed his palm with a thumb. "Are you nervous?"

"Having second thoughts?" Landon shot back, an exchange they had had many times over the last week.

"Absolutely not. Not ever." Robert's words held strength, and the tears cleared as he nodded his affirmation.

"Me neither." He said those words with such force and certainty that laughter from their families reminded him they weren't alone. Like normal, Robert wrecked Landon's concentration. He'd momentarily forgotten they had an audience. He glanced toward the pastor who smiled indulgently. "We're ready."

"Good." The pastor slid a finger over the pad in his hand as Landon squared his shoulders, standing to his full height, and turned back to Robert. Robert's bright smile made his confidence bloom. Everything right in his world was staring back at him.

Chapter 30

After pushing the top floor button on the elevator board, Robert turned back to his new husband who stood with his butt against the back wall, looking disgruntled as hell. For their plane ride to Minnesota, Landon had allowed Robert to pick his travel attire. Robert had chosen black jeans that clung to Landon's body in all the right places, a tight-fitting sheer dark T-shirt, black boots, and a black leather jacket. Landon looked gorgeous in his dark good looks.

Robert found he had a new attitude—his lighthearted teasing was all because their signatures sat side by side at the bottom of their wedding license. He should investigate becoming a paid negotiator, because somehow, he'd managed to talk his husband into marrying him. Now Landon was obligated to legally stand by Robert's side no matter the pursed lips and narrowed brows staring back at him right now.

"It's our wedding day. Stop trying to count every penny I've spent."

Landon arched an eyebrow as Robert slid between his parted thighs. Robert counted it a win when Landon placed both palms on Robert's hips, drawing him closer. He tilted his head back to look Robert in his eyes, a move Robert loved. Even with the frustration on Landon's face, Robert bent in to place a chaste kiss on those pouty, upturned lips.

"I like the sound of '*we're married,*' and '*you're my husband*'. Thank you for marrying me and making all my dreams come true," Robert said and leaned in again. This time, Landon rested a firm hand on his chest, keeping him at a distance.

At the same time, Landon said, "Why do I feel like this elevator is going to open into your apartment?"

"It's not an apartment," Robert countered, looking back over his shoulder as the doors slid apart to the entry of the penthouse Robert had purchased almost a year ago, right before he'd gone back to DC to woo Landon into his life. The lights were on, soft music played throughout the house, and even from inside the elevator, Robert could see one of the many floral arrangements he'd requested from the building's concierge. If they'd followed all his directions, there should be a light dinner warming in the oven with ice-filled buckets chilling champagne, wine, and Landon's choice of IPA.

"Come see," Robert said excitedly, taking Landon's hand and stepping out from between his parted legs. He tried to tug Landon with him as he stepped off, but Landon's superior strength kept him in place, their hand hold breaking apart instead. Robert stood about a foot from the open doors, putting his hands at his waist. "The elevator doesn't close and descend automatically. You can't escape."

Landon still didn't move.

"They can't bring our luggage up until I send the elevator back down."

Landon crossed his beefy arms, drawing a line in the sand. Robert just shook his head. He was starving. The brief lunch they had shared at his grandmother's house had held little interest for him with his husband sitting next to him. Now, at eight thirty in the evening, he was hungry and needed sustenance to help get him through the next several hours of the sexual quest he'd planned for their wedding night.

Reasonably sure Landon couldn't figure out how to work the elevator to leave, Robert headed for the kitchen. A trip he had only taken a few times when he had stayed there when Kylie had been born. After a couple of wrong turns, he found his way to the right room.

The property management hadn't skimped on his requests. The dinner looked enough to feed a party of eight. Robert took a few bites of the veggie fajitas before pouring himself a glass of wine and grabbing Landon a beer. He headed back to the elevator.

"It's my wedding night and my new husband won't leave the—" The sight of Landon off the elevator and shrugging out of his jacket froze Robert's words as he rounded the corner. Landon's enormous biceps flexed as he crossed his arms again. "That's a start, but you can see our place better if you come more fully inside."

"It's the whole floor?" Landon's dark brow lifted again.

"No. Just half. It's got an incredible view of downtown Minneapolis." Robert handed him the beer, and of course, he didn't readily accept it. "You can't be mad at me tonight. It's our wedding night."

"You've been hiding this from me." The tone of the grumble closely resembled the frustrating boom Tony might give his grandchildren.

"Not hiding, just omitting, so I'll go ahead and throw in the Audi R8 Coupe. Which was a purchase I made to make myself feel better because I thought you didn't want me." Robert left the beer bottle perched precariously on Landon's crossed arms before going to the elevator and sending it back downstairs to have their luggage brought up. "You know, you're a reverse snob. I think we're going to have to get you some therapy to help you get past your hang-ups."

"I haven't known you a full year—" Landon started his terrible line of thinking, and Robert came back to him, placing his finger over Landon's moving lips.

"I love you, but you have to get over it. I'll only ever marry once, so what's mine is yours. I refuse to have it any other way. You're technically a wealthy man whether you like it or not." Robert leaned in inches from Landon's lips and said, "Come show me what a bad boy I've been by keeping secrets. Make sure I know to never do it again."

Robert leaned back, drained his glass in a couple of long swallows, then started to pull his shirt over his head. A daring gleam twinkled in Landon's midnight eyes, and he knew he had him. Robert discarded the glass on the closest flat surface and tossed his shirt over Landon's head as he started for the bedroom. He kicked his jeans off as he went. When his underwear dropped to his feet, he heard Landon's heavy boots coming his way. Robert barely made it inside the bedroom door before Landon's strong arm locked around his waist, tugging him back against his solid bare chest.

"I love you, too," Landon whispered huskily. Robert grinned, turning his head as far back as he could. Landon had a thing about always returning the sentiment no matter what they were going through at the time. This last two minutes might have been the longest it had ever taken for Landon to say those words back to Robert. "You need to stop keeping secrets. They blindside me."

"I know, I've been bad. Punish me. Make sure I know who's the boss." He tilted his head a little farther back, trying to see Landon better to gauge his mood while grinding his ass against Landon's jean covered hard-on. He hoped he was edging Landon out of his funky mood, because more than anything, he wanted them to have a perfect night then many more just the same for the rest of their lives. "Unless you're not up to—"

The firm fist that gripped Robert's cock answered the challenge, leaving no doubt as to his ability or intent.

Landon worked the boots off his feet, not willing to let go of the cock searing his hand. "I'm plenty up to it." He couldn't stay mad at Robert for long, his sour mood never a match for the sexy man in his arms. "How about you fuck me tonight, Doc?" He gave Robert a playful stroke.

"My husband says all the sweetest things." Robert thrust his hips forward, driving his dick farther into his palm.

"I love you, Robert," he growled. Robert turned and Landon tightened his fist, making Robert groan.

"Mmm…feels good." Robert worked to free him of his belt and jeans as he backed Robert up against the bed. "See…the sweetest things." Robert trailed his lips over Landon's jaw and down his neck, raising goose bumps all over his body. "And I love you."

Robert slid his warm palms down his waist, Landon's cock twitching as those strong hands then shoved his jeans down his thighs. He kicked them to the side, the underwear too. His husband's smirk made him chuckle. He blushed at the giddiness bubbling inside him.

Heat spread along his front as their bodies pressed together. He pulled Robert even closer, clutching him to his chest.

Robert bent to take his mouth in a possessive kiss full of passion and hunger.

Landon returned the kiss as if he were possessed, claiming Robert as thoroughly as he'd been claimed.

Robert eased him down on the bed. As soon as his back hit the soft comforter, he scooted up to make room for Robert and spread his legs in an open invitation. He craved his husband, possessively mapping every inch of his heated body.

Robert forced his legs back, locking him in place as he manhandled him, trapping Landon against the mattress, holding him in place. He squirmed playfully against his lover's hold, but one swipe of Robert's tongue and that was fucking it. He almost bucked off the bed.

Robert wet his fingers then a familiar pressure stroked his entrance. God, that one touch had his ass clenching for more.

Robert teased his gland, then his tongue joined in and worked him into a frenzy. Robert knew exactly how to undo him.

All the sensations overloaded his senses, and he wiggled to get away. Robert just laughed, releasing him long enough to grab the lube. Robert coated his fingers then tossed the bottle back to the nightstand. Landon's body trembled with excitement, the anticipation building.

Robert turned back to him, zeroing in on his ass again. The pleasure swirled rapidly through him and coiled in his balls.

Landon grabbed his legs and opened himself, letting Robert pump in and out of him. Robert brushed over his prostate, again and again, making him quiver with his need for release.

"Just fuck me. I need to know this is real." Landon panted. Robert had him inside out with lust. He couldn't help but beg for more. He needed Robert inside him.

"Does this feel real?" Robert breached him fast and deep with three fingers. Landon's body convulsed around the sudden invasion. It wouldn't take much for him to come all over both of them right now.

"Ride me, baby." Robert pulled out with an invitation he couldn't refuse.

"With pleasure," he growled, scooting back and yanking Robert forward then flipping him. When his husband settled on his back in the middle of the bed, Landon quickly straddled him. "Yee-haw," he drawled, holding Robert down to pepper him with kisses.

"So sexy." Robert ran his fingertips up and down Landon's back before skimming along his sides.

"I'm too close. Gonna make me come if you don't quit with the teasing." Landon loved when Robert teased him, but right now, he needed his husband buried deep inside his body. He leaned across Robert to grab the lube. Of course, Robert had thought of more than lube. The bedside table held everything from breath mints to bottled water, all within easy reach. His lover's hands traveled over his ass and stomach then up to trace the tattoo on his chest before rolling his nipple between strong fingers…his chest concaved, the move sending a bolt of electricity straight to his balls. He clenched his ass cheeks together, straining to keep from coming. The stuff on the table could wait.

"You're not helping," Landon hissed as Robert wrapped his fingers around his aching cock. He tipped the bottle to drizzle the liquid over his own cock and Robert's fingers.

"I'd have to disagree." Robert's hard, slick stroke had him moaning and pressing his hips forward for more friction.

He forced himself away from his lover's grip long enough to coat Robert's length, getting him nice and slick before tossing the lube to the side. "You sure you want to do this?"

"More than ever," Robert said. Landon lifted, using the muscles in his thighs. Robert guided his bare cock to Landon's entrance. Landon eased back down.

"Fuck, yes…" Landon held Robert's gaze as he impaled himself slowly. The delicious sting of Robert stretching him always stole his breath. Robert arched his hips and strained beneath him as he worked himself down his lover's hard length. The sweet feeling of his body giving away to Robert's caused sweat to dampen his brow.

Landon bit his lip to try and hold in the moan when Robert was fully seated into his body. Their bodies were joined so tightly together he could feel Robert's heartbeat in his ass. The sound of their eager pants filled the room. Robert's palms seared the skin on his hips.

Lifting with his thighs, Landon slowly started to move, his body relaxing and eager for more. Damn, Robert felt so good inside him.

Landon closed his eyes, committed every touch, every word, every plea to memory as he canted his hips, frantic to have his husband deeper, closer, as he chased his orgasm.

Rough fingers grabbed his hips, Robert thrusting into him hard, a fast-building fire so hot it threatened to consume them both. He wanted to come, and he also wanted this feeling to last forever, caught in the sweetest torment.

When Robert curled a hand around him and stroked, he lost his battle and fell right over the edge. His release hit him hard, exploding from the inside out. His ass clamped down as pleasure overtook him, and he painted Robert's chest and neck with his come.

His lover's muscles froze, becoming tense as Robert's thick cock pulsed hot and deep inside him. Landon's muscles twitched in pleasure as Robert's liquid heat seared his channel.

"Fuck!" Landon dropped his chest against Robert's, gasping for air to fill his oxygen-deprived lungs. Robert seemed to be doing the same. He nuzzled Robert's damp neck, trying to catch his breath. Evidently, they were so hot when they'd spontaneously combusted that it had sucked all the oxygen from the overly large suite. He smiled at the thought. Robert pulled him closer, and he let him, excitement still buzzing through his body.

"I can feel you smiling," Robert whispered hoarsely.

"I was just thinking about how perfect we are together."

The sun warmed Robert's skin as he rolled from his chest to his back on the double recliner he shared with Landon at their private adult swimming pool in their building. His eyes were closed, the hot sun hopefully doing its job to tan his skin before they hit the beach in a few days. Landon lay next to him, close enough to have their sides touching. Landon found his hand and threaded their fingers together. "Do you need more sunscreen?"

Robert broke out in a giant grin, squeezing Landon's hand. "Enough with the pale jokes."

"It's not a joke. Skin that white fries like bacon. Best way to ruin a honeymoon is a sunburn."

Robert reached for his sunglasses on top of his head and dropped them over his eyes while lifting enough to look at his gorgeous guy.

"You've got a never-ending supply of pale jokes, don't you?"

Landon reclined back in his seat, eyes remaining closed, a lazy smile curling his lips as he said, "What was that you said last night? We're married now, you gotta accept me for who I am."

Robert barked out a laugh, nodding. "I like it better when I say it, not you."

His gaze traveled the length of Landon's body. He itched to explore Landon's defined stomach muscles. Landon's head tilted toward him, lips puckering, somehow knowing he needed a kiss. Over the last fifteen hours, they'd taken the wedding night rituals to heart. He'd been with Landon repeatedly, and based on the need running through him, that clearly wasn't enough.

"I love you," Landon whispered in that husky way he had that seemed to unintentionally reach out and caress his heart like a soothing balm.

"I love you, too." Robert leaned forward, kissing Landon's sweet lips.

"Robert. Seriously?" Autumn said. Her voice acting like a bucket of cold water tossed their way.

The moment with his new husband ruined by her screechy tone, like nails on a chalkboard. Robert hoped for no outward reaction, like his back tightening, so he could pull off indulgent when Landon jerked away, dislodging Robert as he quickly sat up. Robert was slower to turn, and when he did, he sprawled out on the recliner.

"I've been waiting in your apartment for a half hour."

Time had completely gotten away from him, and he was sorry about that, but he looked around Autumn in search of Kylie. Not a day had passed since her birth that he hadn't seen his niece. Yes, only through video, making this brief stop in Minnesota that much more special so he could spend time with her before they left for Fiji, their official honeymoon destination.

"Where's Kylie?"

"That's what you have to say? We agreed on one o'clock." She looked at the imaginary watch on her wrist with her index finger hitting the skin there. "It's one thirty. I'm on a schedule to feed Kylie, and you're wrecking it." The disgruntled attitude she gave him dissolved as she looked over at Landon with a warm, loving smile. "Your tan's really amazing. I wish I had your complexion. I'm jealous."

Landon was off the seat, grabbing his towel and the small

cooler of beer they had brought out while slipping on his sandals. Robert guessed they were done. Regret filled his heart. This afternoon and evening were filled with prearranged engagements. Their quiet time was done until they left tomorrow morning.

"Italian genes. My skin tone gets to a certain point then kind of stops tanning. I'm sorry we made you late. I wasn't watching the time." Landon and Autumn started for the doors, leaving him there. He was glad they had become fast friends. Autumn had been tearfully excited yesterday, calling Landon her brother—the brother she had chosen, not the one forced on her. But Robert had become massively territorial over Landon's attention, something made next-level worse after their wedding ceremony yesterday. His resentment of her interruption had him using force while grabbing his sunscreen, towel, and sandals before stalking after them barefoot.

When he saw them inside the elevator, chatting happily, the only thing that saved Autumn from getting a talking to about disrupting him on his honeymoon was Landon's hand holding the elevator doors. Robert had to remind himself the whole reason he was in Minnesota in the first place had to do with the effort Autumn had put into making sure Landon had access to all his assets. In Robert's grand scheme, he'd decided Autumn might be a better spokesperson to explain the wealth Robert had accumulated in his life.

"I'm polling with an eight percent lead. That seems positive. The man I'm running against is the incumbent, but he's had just enough controversy that they think I have a chance," Autumn said. Luckily the arm holding the door slid around Robert as if he were being claimed. He liked that move. It seemed automatic, and public displays hadn't always been easy for Landon.

Robert reached over, punching in the quick access code to his floor as Landon said, "We've been watching your debates. You're a natural up there. I'd vote for you. Can I vote for you if we claim a home base here? I can change my driver's license."

Landon looked sincere, his gaze going between Robert and Autumn, who just shook her head, grinned, and looked at Robert.

"I like him a lot. You got a good one."

"No argument there."

Landon looked a little lost at the compliment, because he'd been very genuine in his suggestion, which made Robert that much prouder. Luckily though, the doors slid open to his apartment, keeping Autumn from regaling them about voter laws.

"I'll go grab you a T-shirt. You and Autumn start." He looked pointedly at Autumn. "Don't linger over an explanation. Just get his signature where you need them. End with the name change. I'll be right back."

"You're talking like I'm not standing right here," Landon said gruffly, causing Autumn to laugh as she nodded at Robert.

"Landon, come this way. He's already signed his legal name change. He told me you two agreed to hyphenate your last names with Adams coming last, is that true?" Giving Landon a choice on the front end, with something already long agreed upon, was brilliant of his sister. Maybe he should just let her handle Landon. They were behind schedule, and he needed a shower. He chuckled as he abandoned his mister when he knew they were certain to argue over everything Landon learned in the next ten or fifteen minutes.

"It's a beautiful view. I bet you loved growing up here," Landon said, coming to a stop at the window in his fathers' bedroom at their childhood home in Stillwater. Robert came in behind him, placing both hands on Landon's waist as he stared out at a view he'd seen over and over again throughout all his life.

"It's different than before." Which was true about so many things. The Library Association had preserved large portions of the house in its original state. Only the living room and adjoining dining room had changed, now highlighting his dad's accomplishments throughout his life with a maze of moveable walls. A small souvenir shop had been placed in the office right off the main front doors. The part of the house that hadn't been open to tourists had been his and Autumn's childhood bedrooms. Those had been closed off, used now for storage. Robert had made that decision, feeling very much like having his private space memorialized bordered on a breach of privacy.

"Is it hard to be here?" Landon asked, leaning back against his chest, taking his hands and threading their fingers together before clutching them around his waist.

"No, not now. You're my magic healing balm." Robert leaned in, kissing Landon's shoulder. "Had things not happened exactly as they had, we may not be standing here today. What if I hadn't found you?"

Landon looked back at him with a certainty before he said, "I would've found you. You may not have seen me, but I would've seen you."

"You may not have wanted me. I was pretty self-absorbed." He brushed his mouth against those plump lips.

"I would've wanted you." Landon turned back to the window.

In the distance, the St. Croix could be seen. His dad had been so smart to angle the house just like this. He wondered how many times his fathers had stood in this window, watching the river churn. How much had Robert missed by taking this all for granted for so many years?

"From the second I heard your voice in Germany, I wanted more. Hell, I wanted more when I watched you care for your father at the funeral. You take care of everyone around you. I wanted to find a man just like you."

Robert smiled at Landon's sweet attempt at making sure he didn't grow too melancholy being there. A place Landon had asked to see, one Robert hadn't been back to since the same day turnaround trip he'd taken for the dedication and official opening.

"We've been married for over twenty hours. What's your assessment so far?"

"Honest?" Landon's chin hit his chest, pausing for a moment.

"I'm so in love with you I can't quite process it all." The confession was whispered in that sexy, husky tone Robert loved. Landon sounded vulnerable and unsure, reflecting Robert's exact feelings. He could hear people downstairs. Since the library had opened, it had been surprisingly busy, more so than anyone had anticipated. Their conversation had turned intimate, maybe too much so for prying ears, and Robert left Landon there, going to the bedroom door to shut and lock them inside the room.

"You have to know I feel that same way." Robert started back for Landon who had turned his way, leaning against the window's edge. "I say this cautiously, but I'm beginning to understand how my daddy died so quickly. I realize I had no say with how it was going to end for him." Robert motioned between the two of them, struggling to find the right words. "I can't imagine the depth of how this will grow between us over forty years if we're already here."

"I want more than forty years," Landon automatically said, the blurt maybe a surprise to him as his eyes widened at the revelation.

"Me too. I want forever." Robert had never been surer of anything in his life. Robert came within inches of Landon, standing before his husband who looked concerned.

"Do you think they'll repeal marriage for us?" Landon asked. "Our country has a history of doing shitty things like that."

"I don't know, but it won't change anything for us. That's a big reason for what Autumn took care of today. I want you cared for throughout your life."

Landon didn't say a word, he just took Robert's hand and turned back to the window, bringing Robert's arm around his waist again.

"I added you as my beneficiary. It's small, kind of embarrassing compared to some of the numbers I saw today, but it's yours."

Robert grinned at the back of Landon's head. Just knowing Landon had made sure he was taken care of in case anything happened filled him with a deep completeness.

He didn't want to dampen their conversation, and all this talk of possible death seemed a bit morbid, so he changed the subject, pulling away to look around the room. Robert went for the enormous king-size bed, running his fingers over the bedspread he remembered from his youth.

"So many items in the house were found saved in the attic. I remember this bedspread. I was young, like four or five. I remember hearing noises. Their door was shut, and I thought something was wrong. I tried to get inside the room, but the door was locked. I ran for Autumn. We listened outside the door, and Autumn swore something was terribly wrong. She banged on the door. We were crying…" He stopped talking, remembering their fear for their fathers. His daddy opened the door in his robe, his face all red. Robert hadn't thought of that memory in so long and wasn't sure he'd ever reconciled what they were doing inside this room until right that minute.

Landon came toward him, a big grin on his face. "I caught my dad checking out my mom's butt when I was about five. I'm pretty sure by second grade I figured it all out. My best friend's older brother taught us all about sex. I couldn't understand why anyone would ever do something like that. It seemed gross."

"I was pretty sheltered," Robert said, letting Landon walk right into him, that naughty smirk on his face. "I didn't have sex for the first time until I was in college."

"Top or bottom?"

"Top."

"Yeah, me too." Landon's grin enchanted him. "How have we not discussed our firsts in all this time?"

Maybe because he liked to pretend Landon hadn't known another man before him. Which of course sounded insane.

"Your size fits a big house like this." Robert ran his hands down Landon's muscular arms. A knock on the door interrupted his thoughts as he looked in that direction.

"Hang on," Robert called out, clasping Landon's hand, keeping him in place when he started for the door. "It means the world to me that you made me your beneficiary, that you want to give me access to your world. Thank you."

Landon looked uncomfortable, but resigned when he said, "I told Autumn I wanted to put my paycheck into the joint account you started. I send money home to my parents every month. If something happens to me, I'd need you to keep that going. I don't send much, but it helps them." Robert had already learned about Landon's generosity from his uncle then again when a notification popped up on his phone while Robert had been holding it, a text from his mother, thanking him for the money.

"Landon, keep your money..." The fierce look he got immediately had him changing the direction of his words. "Whatever you want to do. Send them more if it helps. We're in this together now."

Landon nodded, letting out a pent-up breath. The subject of money always weighed heavily on Landon, who left his hold and went toward the bedroom door. Right before his guy pulled it open, he tossed a cocky, teasing grin over his shoulder with a gleam in his eye making Robert know something was coming, he just didn't know what.

Landon yanked it open wide and hooked a thumb over his shoulder toward Robert. "He's Robert Adams, their son." Landon twirled a finger to indicate the house, and therefore, Avery and Kane's child. He saw excitement register on the eager faces where they stood just beyond the threshold. As the couple came forward, Landon stepped out, "I'm going to walk to the river's edge, then I'll meet you at the car."

No, he did not! Robert stood there, stunned, as more visitors came for him, introducing themselves. His engrained manners suppressed the desire to get Landon back...for now. He did allow himself to call out to Landon, though, with a, "Well played!" before he greeted the tourists.

Chapter 32

"It's been slow," Rodney said, taking the seat next to Robert at La Bella Luna. Robert glanced at his wristwatch, a sweet and thoughtful wedding present from Landon. Half past eight. Then he looked around the restaurant. It did seem pretty empty.

"It's Sunday night," he replied, returning his concentration to the sleeping bundle in his arms. Kylie was the most precious little thing. But she'd been a tiny Tasmanian devil for the entire length of their dinner, pounding on the table with her little hands, throwing her cookies and crackers to the ground repeatedly.

Kylie had been so disruptive that Autumn had tried to bail on their dinner maybe fifteen minutes after arriving, afraid Kylie would bother the other guests. Robert wasn't having any of that. He imagined his niece would slow her roll sooner or later. It took some time, but Kylie finally exhausted herself, crashing hard in his arms where she'd been for a good thirty minutes now. Her sweet warmth seeped into his heart. She was precious and soundly sleeping in his arms. He didn't think a pack of stampeding elephants would wake her.

"I'll finish cleaning up her mess when I can tear myself away from her. She's addictive. I miss her."

"We have a vacuum that'll clean this right up. I just don't want to wake her," Rodney said, looking over the table at Kylie.

"If the music doesn't wake her, I'm not sure anything could." Robert cut his gaze toward the new dance floor placed in the front corner of the restaurant where Landon currently danced with Autumn. His guy had the moves. Robert had already learned that lesson. They went dancing regularly when at home, but Autumn had been delighted to see she had a willing partner and had had Landon on the dance floor for a good fifteen minutes now.

"Tell me what's going on with you now. You're married. I like him. What else's going on? Are you ever going back to medicine?" Rodney asked, not sugar-coating his inquiry.

He'd been asked that same question a few times since arriving back in Minnesota. In DC, Robert's focus had been Landon, making sure he was enough to keep Landon with him and finding a way to bring them to this point. Now a bigger picture future seemed a little more accessible, and looking back, he could see how his actions over the last year and a half may have seemed erratic to other people.

He trailed a finger over one of Kylie's silky blonde curls before looking back at Rodney. Robert had changed so much; he couldn't really remember the man he used to be. His peers obviously thought he'd lost his mind. His family had been indulgent and supportive, but maybe not quite sure what had happened to him. That man, who was maybe twenty feet away, expertly spinning his sister around the dancefloor, had been his life support, accepting Robert however he came.

Landon believed in him and thought he could pull off a culinary career if he wanted one. He'd even encouraged Robert to try.

Maybe he had just made the decision.

Robert released a pent-up breath as he revealed the plans he'd been chewing on for a while now. "I'm retiring from medicine, at least for the foreseeable future, but I've been cooking, taking lessons. I think I'm... I mean we, Landon and I... I think we're going to start a pop-up lunch tent in DC."

Rodney's brows shot up in surprise. His mouth opened then closed again before he finally got out, "Like street food?"

"Something like that." Robert nodded, adjusting Kylie in his arms as she moved to a better position. "I've gotten pretty good at vegetarian cuisine. I've been making these tacos—Landon likes them spicy. They've drawn some interest from a buddy of mine who has access to a professional kitchen. He's a trained chef and a partner at a restaurant chain nearby. I think we're going to take him up on his offer to use his kitchen. We only started talking about this over the last couple of weeks." Robert stopped speaking, realizing the information dump he'd just laid on Rodney's shoulders, but he couldn't seem to contain his enthusiasm. "You got more than you counted on when asking that question, didn't you?"

"Maybe." Rodney grinned. "You've really made some changes to your life."

Robert nodded, unable to hold Rodney's gaze so he looked down at Kylie as he fought the edges of doubt trying to creep in. "I'm enjoying it all. I like my life now."

Rodney nodded his understanding, if not approval, sitting back in his seat. He could feel Rodney's fixed stare on him for several long seconds. "You're so much like Kane. Everything he did had to be in order, set a certain way before he could commit. Paulie pushed at him a lot in the beginning. Your father worked long hours like you did, every single day. He was the hardest working man I've ever known. I was barely nineteen years old and the military had disabled me. I was lost. I lived in New York and I heard about Paulie and what he was doing here. I came all this way, looking for a job and a life. Paulie and Kane took me in before I even had a chance to fill out the application. Kane taught me how to be a good man, a gentle man. He taught me it was a choice not a destiny. I see so much of him inside you. Now, Autumn… She takes after Avery, and I suspect that little one will too."

Robert smiled and nodded, still looking at Kylie. He'd heard these same references many times before. Nostalgia of times long gone seemed to keep Rodney's tongue going.

"I remember the day Avery walked inside this restaurant. We were in awe of such a celebrity being here. Your dad's only focus was on Kane. He swept your father off his feet then kept sweeping. He was a force, and that day, Kane's life picked up and moved to a new course. I believe he started actually living that day and was smart enough to never look back. I see that same change in you. He's good for you like Avery was good for Kane. You're not gonna miss what you've let go of."

Robert had never considered such a comparison, and for some reason, he agreed. Even though he knew nothing more about that time in his fathers' lives than the memories sporadically shared over Robert's life. Rodney nodded toward Landon, and Robert looked that way as the music came to an end. Landon caught his quick peek. Like normal, Landon had a way of picking up on Robert's emotional cues. His husband's smile turned quizzical as he encouraged Autumn back toward the table.

"But Avery left his mark on you, that's for sure. You're the spitting image of that man."

"Yeah. Always hear how much I look like him." He smiled at the thought of his dad. "I was hoping to show Landon around. It's part of the reason we started our honeymoon in Minnesota. He wanted to see where I grew up," Robert said, looking up as Landon touched his shoulder. The gentle caress moved across his shoulders until Robert could capture the hand in his and bring it to his lips. His gaze stayed on Landon's as his lips pressed against his knuckles.

"I'm running to the restroom," Autumn said. Robert nodded, turning his hand to fully grip Landon's. This moment right here, holding his precious niece in his arms with Landon by his side... Perfection.

"Of course, you know you have access to it all." Rodney's attention shifted to Landon. "Robert was just telling me your plans for street fare. Does that mean you're leaving the military?"

"No, sir. I've got four years until retirement. I'm sticking it out." Every time Landon spoke of his military career, his tone dripped with pride.

His mister was proud of his accomplishments. Robert was too, but if given a choice, he'd vote for Landon to quit or deny orders—however the Air Force did their thing. Robert was ready to take off with their new lives, but Landon dug in his heels, holding them in place.

"I work second shift. I can lend a hand every day, but Robert does all the heavy lifting. He keeps saying it's a *we* deal. It's not. It's a *he* deal."

Robert grinned, tightening his grip. "You do all the heavy lifting—literally. We did a test run last week. Landon's expert-level good at lugging things around. He had us setup in record time without breaking a sweat."

"Like that matters." Landon squeezed his hand, drawing Robert's gaze up to see Landon peering down at him, making his heart sputter. "He's happier here in Minnesota. He's different here. Less weight on his shoulders."

"They grew up here—right here in this restaurant. The Adamses are the first family of Minnesota. They're all our children," Rodney stated proudly, winking at Robert.

"All right, guys. It's almost nine o'clock. She's passed out, so I need to do the same," Autumn said, carefully taking the sleeping baby from his arms.

"I'll walk Autumn out then give you a tour. I'll be back." Robert got to his feet, kissing Landon on the way up before he grabbed the diaper bag and Autumn's purse, helping Autumn and Kylie out to the car.

Landon stood transfixed, committing every detail of this restaurant to memory. How Robert kept saying their honeymoon hadn't officially begun was in direct contrast to his views. For Landon, they had started the minute they'd stepped off the plane in Minnesota. To have such a tour of all the places Avery Adams had spoken of inside his books, and the tour guide to be his son, who also happened to be Landon's husband, just made everything more special.

From the picture of Paulie hanging on the wall in the kitchen to the place where Avery had dropped down on one knee and proposed to Kane—Landon was seeing where it all happened and mentally committed each place to memory.

"We had a nursery in this room." Robert pushed open the door. Stacks of boxes now filled the space. "We spent all day here when we were children. My fathers hired a caregiver, Patty, who would watch us all day in this tiny room. It seemed so big at the time."

"You didn't stay home?" Landon asked, sticking his head inside the room. The walls were still painted in primary colors, in patterns Paulie had chosen and painted.

"No, not after those first six months or so. In the beginning, they tried to take care of us themselves while running the restaurant and my dad's law firm, but they said we were a handful. We double teamed them, so we started coming here so my granddaddy could keep an eye on our nanny. My dad would come here after work and help out then we'd all go home together." Robert flipped on the light and pushed through the boxes. "Come in and shut the door."

Landon entered as Robert pushed along the back wall until he found what he was looking for. A door opened under his pressure. "We had a bathroom in here. I'd wondered what they'd done with it."

Landon followed Robert into the dark bathroom and flipped on the light. The bathroom was dated with its metallic blue wallpaper and gold marble sink.

"Through there was my dad's office." He pointed to a side door along the opposite wall. "One time Autumn flooded the place. She was mad at me and tried to flush one of my action figures." Robert bent at the sink, tapping the side boards until one popped open. He pulled out an old, three-quarter used bottle of lubricant and laughed. "They thought they were sly, hiding this in their secret place. I think we found their hiding place long before they realized it. Maybe they never knew." Robert reached for the toilet paper, carefully picking up a very outdated, cumbersome looking butt plug. "I couldn't imagine what this was used for when we found it. During my residency, I pulled something like this out of a man's ass in the ER."

"You did not."

Robert gave a devious grin. "Oh, I did. That was the longest rotation of my life. I've pulled many, many things out of men's asses." Robert placed the butt plug next to the lube before turning back to the cubby.

"No condoms?" Landon asked.

"No. I never found where they ever used them. It was awkward when we had the talk and they insisted I use a condom when they never had. My daddy had no experience with them at all," Robert explained.

"Well, we have condoms, but I don't want to use them ever again either. I love having no barriers from you," Landon said, meeting Robert's gaze in the mirror. "We have lube and I do want to use it." The suggestion seemed to take a second to marinate, but when Robert caught on, the gleam in his eyes said they were thinking the same thing.

Robert's look grew heated, his cheeks pinkening and his blue eyes lighting with mischief.

"We don't have long," Robert insisted and didn't waste time. He spun around, working to get their pants and underwear pushed out of the way while their mouths fused together in an instant lip lock. In seconds flat, heavy pants and urgent moans filled the small space. He pushed his lover's shirt from his shoulders, running his fingers over Robert's nipples, teasing the flat brown discs and rolling them as they pebbled.

His heart filled with joy and his body burned with searing intensity for the man standing in front of him. He wished he could take his time with his husband, but right then, he understood every second mattered.

Landon spun them around, changing their position so that his front was against Robert's back. Landon eased Robert's shoulders forward, watching his lover's reflection in the mirror as he ground his hard dick against Robert's gorgeous bare ass and shifted his weight forward.

"I want you so fucking bad," he whispered against the warm skin of Robert's neck, smiling at the shiver that ran down his lover's body beneath his. Landon grabbed a lube packet from his wallet, ignoring the one they'd found in the hiding place, and squeezed a good amount on his fingers. He tossed the rest of the unused packet on the countertop for later.

"Do you know what you do to me, Mr. Russo-Adams?" He growled into Robert's ear, lifting his chest to take in all the tempting flesh. His palms tingled as he smoothed his hand down Robert's long back and over the firm pale skin of his lover's ass. Robert groaned and tilted his ass higher.

He bent, spreading Robert's thighs, nipping at Robert's ass cheek as he lowered and dragged his tongue across his lover's hole. Fuck, what this man did to him. They only had a few minutes at most before their disappearance got suspicious, but he couldn't get enough of touching Robert, of tasting his mister. He bathed Robert with his tongue and adoring kisses, loving on him. Landon slid his fingers between his lover's cheeks and teased his hole.

He traced the opening with his thumb before dipping into the waiting heat. Robert tensed around him, and his dick jerked, weeping in response. The sweet memory of being lost in his man flooded him with excitement and desire. Robert pushed back, working himself on his digits. Robert's thighs quivered with each of his exertions.

God, he wanted to drown in all that sweet flesh. Landon worked his fingers in and out of Robert. He prodded and teased, pleas falling from his husband's lips as Landon explored his ass, intentionally curling his digits just to make his man squirm. Spending hours making Robert beg had become a favorite pastime, but he didn't have that kind of time right now.

After withdrawing his fingers, he reached for the remainder of the lube on the counter, coating his cock with more than enough, swiping the rest on Robert's ass just to make sure. Landon gripped his shaft and teased the man's hole, letting his dick slide up and down Robert's crack in the slippery lube.

"Babe, stop teasing m— Oohh." Robert's voice faded into a groan as Landon pushed forward. The head of his dick shoved past the lingering resistance and sank, inch by inch, into his lover's searing tightness. His heart pounded as he seated himself against Robert's firm ass, watching him in the mirror.

The feeling of being buried so deeply in Robert's body overwhelmed him in the most amazing way. Time no longer mattered. All the signs indicated this was going to be over before it ever fully got started. The sensations ran rampant. His nerve endings flared as he slowly started to move inside Robert.

The drag and pull of easing in and out of his husband bordered on the sweetest forms of torture. Their destinies collided. Their bodies joined, truly making them one. Nothing would ever be sweeter. Robert's body was made for him. They fit so perfectly together in every way.

"Fuck me harder." Robert's husky voice wavered even as he issued the command. Landon sped up. The friction of Robert's body accommodating his curled his toes and drove his hips with powerful thrusts.

Their slacks tangled at their ankles as he pushed into Robert's sweet ass over and over, the friction on his cock driving his hips greedily.

Fast and deep, he took his man like he'd begged him to do. His thrusts became more desperate the longer he tried to hold back his impending orgasm. Landon reached around, wrapping his fingers around Robert's rigid shaft. He stroked him with determination, Robert's quick breaths letting him know his man was just as gone as he was.

"Come for me," Landon commanded, his movement almost

frantic with his own need to feel Robert lose control.

"Fuck…yes…Landon." Robert gasped, his dick twitching in Landon's grip before covering his fingers with hot come. The smell of sex was so strong in the room that his head spun from the sweetness of it all. He dug the fingers of his other hand into Robert's hips and pushed so deep into that constricting heat that he saw stars.

He barely pulled out before his release erupted in tremors of pleasure that made his stomach muscles contract as he painted Robert's ass with thick streaks of come. He stroked Robert one more time, milking the last of his orgasm from his cock.

Landon collapsed over Robert's back, brushing his lips in a tender kiss against the skin of his neck. "I'll love you forever." A promise that would be so easily kept.

"Forever," Robert replied.

"Thank you for bringing me here," Landon said, nuzzling his face in the crook of Robert's neck.

"Thank you for asking to see my home. I didn't realize how much I missed it," Robert said on a yawn. "Now, I'm happily covered in come and completely worn out."

"Covered in come, yes, but I highly doubt you're worn out. Besides, this is just practice for the rest of the honeymoon." Landon forced himself to move, easing away from Robert. He reached for the drawer beside him, grabbing a hand towel for Robert and another one for himself, wetting them both once the water heated. "I'm excited for Fiji. You're spoiling me." He offered Robert the warm towel.

"Yeah, it's spoiling me more. I get to watch your hard body running on the beach. That's exciting," Robert said quickly cleaning himself.

"Let's go home, Romeo." Landon laughed as he straightened his clothing. He loved these stolen moments. And was excited for whatever his guy had in store for him in the years to come.

Chapter 33

November 2015

"Babe, we need another pan of the brazen tacos," Robert called over his shoulder, looking down the line of waiting customers ready to place their orders for his vegetarian and vegan lunch tacos. Pride swelled within him as he focused on counting the change for the current customer's order.

"Your sister gonna win tonight?"

Robert checked the guy out, making sure he wasn't supposed to know him before looking down again, quickly sorting through the coins. This was election day for the Minnesota senate seat. The one Autumn had campaigned hard for and left no room for anything other than a resounding victory.

Robert smiled and handed the customer his change, then rolled down the top of the brown paper bag next to him, holding it out as the guy pocketed the money. "I sure hope so. If you know anyone in Minnesota, encourage them to vote today."

"Will do. We need another Adams in politics."

Robert grinned at the guy's kind encouragement. Those words

had been echoed many times over during the last few weeks. Much like all politics today, the Minnesota senate race had turned ugly, a tactic Autumn had prepared well for. Her responses and courses of action had regularly made national news. His sister was smart. He would swear the Google search engine ran inside her brain. She had an arsenal of quick-witted facts and a vast knowledge of history, politics, and policy at the ready to sling at any given moment. The whole nation seemed riveted to this race while speculating on the broader picture of Autumn's political career.

"Thank you. I think so too." Robert tried for a warm smile then looked past the guy to the next customer.

"Next. Got two brazens and a corn," one of his staff called to him. Robert looked inside the bag to check the accuracy of the order before he rang the selection into the cash register.

"Give me a guava juice, please," the customer added, holding his phone under the scanner, ready to digitally transfer payment.

"Heard," Landon said loudly behind him.

The teenage boy living inside him caused Robert to spare a glance over his shoulder as his husband, the one who'd become the backbone and brawn of their little family owned business, bent over to retrieve the beverage. Robert's cock stirred. Old habits died hard, and he suspected this one might not ever go away; he'd always ogle his husband's butt, especially when it was displayed so sexily.

"Here you go." The juice bottle being thrust at him caught his attention as it danced at the end of Landon's fingertips. Robert had to resist the urge to pat that ass right next to the bottle.

Professionalism was a bitch. Robert took the juice, handed it directly to the customer, and waited for them to finish the payment. He looked over the next in line. There were two full sacks of tacos pressed together. The register beeped, indicating the sale went through, and Robert handed over the tacos.

"Thank you."

"Twelve total. Six of each," his lineman called.

"Heard." Robert thrived in such a fast-paced environment. He quickly entered those into the cash register, watching the time as he worked. Barely twelve thirty in the afternoon. At this rate, they wouldn't make it to one o'clock with their current inventory of tacos. He and Landon had started their street market taco stand two months ago today, and they'd already garnered enough business to sell out almost four hundred tacos during the average lunch rush.

"We're on the last pan of corn," Landon whispered in his ear. Goose bumps sprouted on his arms as he nodded and looked up to see two smiling faces. The momentary mental blip that was all Landon Russo-Adams's fault had him blinking at the unexpected sight of his past staring inquiringly at him. Two physicians he had worked with for years stood in front of him. He narrowed his eyes at the dawning of meaning behind those smug grins. These two were arrogant and ignorant, part of the reason doctors were thought to have a god complex. He'd never really liked either of them.

"Are these for you?" he asked, not waiting for any polite exchange to happen, nodding toward the two bags of tacos.

"Do you need drinks?" Landon asked, staying focused on moving the line as quickly as they could.

"Yeah," Williams said, seemingly answering both questions.

"Landon, this is Dr. Brown and Dr. Williams. We worked together in the past." Robert patted Landon's thick pec with the back of his hand. "This is my husband, Landon."

Both sets of eyes swung their full attention toward Landon. Landon stiffened, his hand automatically shifting to Robert's back in a protectionary move. Landon was intuitive. He'd picked up on the possible jeering in their smarmy grins. Landon nodded at both men, but said to Robert, "I got this. Step out and talk to them, so we don't hold up the line."

He didn't want to leave their lunch rush to catch up on anything from his previous life. At the expectant stares, he did finally step out of the tent, letting Landon hand over the tacos without accepting payment. They had done that same move a few times when old friends of the family had ventured out of the capital to come see what Robert was doing down there. His vegetarian tacos had created a buzz around the Hill. It seemed their small radius had expanded if the reputation of his tacos had made it to the hospital. His gaze lowered to the two bags. He wanted those tacos paid for. Brown and Williams made more than enough money to cover the tab.

Landon handed him another brown paper bag, most likely cans of juice. He took it, then saw Landon winking at him. The gesture caressed his heart and gave him the encouragement he needed to have this conversation.

"We weren't sure we believed the rumors," Williams spoke up.

"If the rumors are these tacos are delicious, then they're right," Robert said somewhat arrogantly, giving the men a practiced grin, daring either to contradict him.

"Yeah, that's it," Brown said with a humorless laugh. "The renowned Dr. Adams serving up tacos."

"And the marriage. You sure were quiet about that one," Williams added in a less than congratulatory tone. His gaze veered to Landon who seemed to be completely ignoring them. He doubted that was the case. Landon's insecurity about their relationship had faded, but this was the first time Robert's past had so blatantly caught up with them.

"Landon and I met in Germany last year. Landon's in the Air Force," Robert announced proudly. He was insanely in love with his new life, and even more crazy in love with his incredible husband who had stood by his side no matter what harebrained idea he came up with. Landon never doubted or judged him, unlike what he saw on these two men's faces. "It's our business. He keeps our operation going. I've got to get back to work. Let me ring up these tacos so you can be on your way and help spread the word for us."

Robert dismissed Landon's questioning gaze as he slid in before Landon could total the next customer's order. Some of the smugness wiped from their faces when Robert gave them their total with no discount.

"I'm going to stock the cooler." Landon caught his eye and did a quick assessment of his face. He must have been fine with what he saw, because he left, going back to the job he did so well, monitoring everything to keep their flow efficient.

While they used a credit card to pay, Robert grabbed a clean hand towel for a nearby spill, barely nodding at his colleagues as they finalized their transaction with a quick signature. "Thanks for stopping by."

Minutes later, with Brown and Williams out of ear shot, Landon leaned in behind him, whispering in his ear, "Nice friends, honey. Seriously, how were you friends with those guys?"

"Not sure, but now I have a bigger fear. I'm afraid I was just like them." Robert tilted his chin, looking back over his shoulder in Landon's direction, and whispered, "Thank God you saved me from such a fate." He got that broad sexy grin he loved, and this time when Landon turned away, Robert did run a hand over the enticing curve of his ass. They were still very much in honeymoon mode, but Landon considered his ass off limits in public, charmingly claiming he was too sensitive to Robert's touch. Robert got a deep groan from Landon, meaning his cock must have plumped.

Seeing those two assholes he used to work with hadn't bothered him. In fact, it shined a bright light on how happy he was—truly deeply content with his choices.

Landon visually lined up his shot, preparing to sink the eight ball and win the game. He walked around the table, pretending to contemplate the best angle. This evening, winning gave him a little more swagger than usual, and it was hard to hold back teasing his husband. He and Robert were on a date-night out at The Hill, an older local bar where politicians regularly hung out.

They didn't normally go to places like that, but they'd chosen a setting where the focus stayed on the national election coverage. No matter where they were inside this building, they could easily see the mounted monitors all displaying information about the big wins of the night.

Robert had gotten them there early, picked a small alcove with a pool table, and commandeered this area for the night. A Minneapolis/St. Paul television station with up to the minute coverage played in one corner, cable news in another, and Landon had systematically beaten Robert at pool for the last two hours, giving him bragging rights from now until eternity.

Finally, Landon found something he was better at than his sexy husband.

"You could give me a break," Robert mumbled from his casual perch on a barstool behind him. Landon laughed smugly, venturing a glance his husband's direction. He'd seen a new side of Robert tonight. His mister had a wicked gleam in his eye, rolling the pool cue between his palms, most likely waiting on his next turn to cheat.

"You won't learn if I just give you the win." He wanted to laugh but gave himself a mental high five for that comeback instead.

Robert only chuckled and shook his head. "I love you, husband."

"I love you and you're trying to distract me."

Robert chuckled again, proving Landon's point. Landon had drawn out his latest winning shot long enough and walked back around the table as if he'd finished strategizing. There was no strategy. It was the easiest shot of the night. The only drawback was that his back was to Robert, making it harder to see his reaction when he sank this last ball. Oh well, he couldn't have everything.

"We should shoot pool more often."

That got a bark of rousing laughter from the man behind him, bringing a smile to his lips as he leaned across the table, his concentration on positioning his pool cue. He reared back intending to take his shot with a quick thrust forward to add a little extra force, ensuring he got the sharp clack of the balls making contact before the ball slid into the pocket.

Seconds before he snapped his wrist to drive the cue forward, the tip of Robert's pool stick slid up the inside of his leg, straight to his balls. His dick jerked with excitement and his concentration faltered, which sent the ball barreling off course. He'd missed an easy shot and lost the game when the tip skidded across the felt, straight into one of Robert's balls, sending it rolling with enough power to knock it and two others into their holes. Landon watched it all happened in what felt like slow motion before turning to glare unbelievingly at Robert. His handsome but underhanded husband sat there, grinning like a Cheshire cat.

"I think it's my shot." Robert's smirk made him lift a brow as he watched the guy happily rise off the stool.

"That's cheating," Landon adamantly protested.

Robert came forward in what Landon could only describe as a gloating saunter to stand chest to chest with him. His husband looked rather pleased with himself before bending in for a quick press of the lips.

"Punish me later."

His cock jerked at the growl in Robert's voice. He seemed overly proud of himself as he stepped past Landon to take his shot. Robert Adams was one sexy motherfucker. He'd be more than happy to even the score tonight, and he was just about to voice his terms when the news anchor's voice caught both their attention.

Landon lunged for the small remote control sitting on the barstool Robert had just vacated. He increased the volume at the mention of Autumn's name. As predicted, she had a large enough margin to call the win. The opposing candidate had no choice but to concede.

Robert clapped, along with others throughout the bar. Where Robert was sedately excited, Landon was over the top, high fiving

Robert before letting out a rip-roaring whistle. His heart pounded in his chest from the rush of excitement. The pool cue carelessly tossed on top of the table as he reached for his cell phone. Landon had Autumn on speed dial, and he pressed the number like he'd done several times over the last few hours.

"Hey, brother number two, did you see?"

Landon put her on speaker as Robert came forward, tightly circling an arm around Landon's waist.

"We did. Congratulations," Robert said as their little alcove filled with well-wishers, all sending her their excited, congratulatory love.

"Thank you. I've got to go give my acceptance speech. I love you both. Call me later. Tell Nonnie I'll call her tomorrow morning," Autumn said before the call disconnected. As the crowd grew and pushed forward, Robert let him go to shake the hands of the bar's patrons. Robert eagerly introduced Landon who had never seen politics where affiliation became irrelevant. The Adamses were admired, and being back in politics seemed an exciting thing, at least to these people. Though, probably not for the man Autumn had defeated.

The bar grew silent, all eyes drawn to the screen as Autumn took the stage. There was a commanding air about her, regal and elegant, as she stood behind the podium. Autumn radiated the same peaceful inner strength Avery had possessed. Her words, like his, held the audience on both sides of the screen captive. Landon wasn't even there, and he knew her powerful speech owned that stately room packed to capacity, because she easily owned each and every patron in this bar. Landon's phone vibrated. He glanced down to see Kennedy Adams's name appear on his screen. A smile tugged at the corner of his lip.

He couldn't deny that he had truly been accepted into the Adams family. Kennedy was just on a different level. He had mad respect for her. He wanted to hand the phone to Robert, to have him take the call, but he was surrounded, everyone's gazes fixed on Autumn as she spoke. They all seemed to critique every word she said in a positive way. On the third ring, Landon drew in a deep breath and swiped a thumb over the screen.

"Hello," he answered, sticking a finger to his other ear as he headed off in search of a quieter section of the bar.

"Hello, dear, have I bothered you while you're working?"

"No, ma'am. I took the night off. We're at The Hill, watching the election results," he said, having heard Kennedy was a legend in this bar. A picture of her from many years ago, standing with her husband and his father, the former President Adams, hung above the bar in a prominent position. "Did you see the win?"

"Oh yes, very exciting. Have you spoken to her?" Nonnie asked.

"Yes, I hung up with her right before you called. She was taking the stage for her acceptance speech, so she asked us to make sure you knew and to tell you she'll call you in the morning," he said.

Kennedy gave one of her few laughs. "I knew she would win. Her opponent was dreadful. I'm so disappointed in politics today."

"Yes, ma'am," he said, because he always agreed with her, but he wasn't sure much could have been worse than Avery Adams's treatment during his first race and term for the vice presidency.

"You go celebrate. Tell Robert to call me tomorrow. I'm going to bed." A hand on his shoulder had him turning to Robert who gave him a questioning look.

"It's your Nonnie."

"I'm your Nonnie too, Landon," Kennedy scolded, all humor gone from her tone.

"Yes, ma'am," he said, causing Robert to smile that knowing grin. His husband knew how he felt around Kennedy. "She says for you to call her tomorrow."

"Will do. After lunch." Robert spoke loud enough for Kennedy to hear. Landon got a warmly voiced, *goodnight, dear* before the call disconnected.

"We should go. It's late. Four o'clock comes early," Robert

said, sliding his hand down Landon's back and hooking a finger into his belt loop.

Four in the morning represented the time he had to drag his ass out of bed and begin prepping for the lunch rush. A yawn tore free, not surprising, since he'd been burning the candle at both ends lately. Working the breakfast and lunch rush four days a week then reporting for duty right afterward was beginning to take its toll. He didn't know how Robert could get up an hour earlier than Landon every morning to exercise.

"I'll go settle the tab."

Landon took the second to text his parents, letting them know Autumn had won, before heading to meet Robert at the edge of the bar.

Chapter 34

March 2017

The garage door began to open as Robert ended the phone call. He looked at the time on his Alexa display screen, surprised it was already close to midnight. He and Landon had had their routine set for a while now, years in fact, but usually by this time at night, Robert was in full-on Jonesing mode. Every night he went through what he'd determined to be mini Landon withdrawals, caused from the nine long hours of not seeing his husband while he worked his shift at the base. Technically, that was the only amount of time Landon wasn't attached to his side. Yet, tonight, he had no recollection of the time or how long it had been since Landon had left earlier in the afternoon.

"Hey?" Landon questioned, coming through the garage door leading into their home. Robert sat at the dining room table in perfect view of the door. Still in a state of shock from the phone call, he watched as Landon's gaze raced across the living room then kitchen before landing back on him. His husband's brow furrowed into a hard V as he came closer. "I tried to call, but you didn't answer. Has something happened? Is it Nonnie? Is she okay?"

His news didn't reach a level as bad as something happening to his grandmother, but he was still unnerved, causing anxiety to swim in his gut. He stood to greet Landon like always and stopped short before reaching for Landon's lips to kiss him. Instead, Robert ran his hands down the front of his own T-shirt, rubbing away the sweat gathering on his palms. He was undeniably upset.

"Nonnie's fine. It's about my daddy."

"Kane?" Landon's confusion was clear on his face. Robert hadn't had time to process the information. His gaze connected again with those dark, questioning eyes. Landon brought his hands to Robert's waist. He was thankful for the support. The two of them were well past the honeymoon stage of their relationship, but they were both touchers, and being this close and not touching the other was a rare occurrence.

"Rodney called," he finally said and waited for a nod of recognition of Rodney's name, hoping Landon remembered the owner of La Bella Luna. When Landon's brow lifted, Robert finished his sentence. "He's decided to sell."

"La Bella Luna?" Landon asked in a clipped tone, showing he immediately understood the gravity of the situation.

"Yeah. I know Rodney's not family, but it feels like he is. It feels like La Bella Luna's still in our family," Robert explained, trying to put reasonable words behind all the chaos running through his head. "My father handpicked Rodney to continue the legacy of La Bella Luna."

"Why's he selling?"

"He says he's getting too old, and he can't pull the restaurant out of the slump it's in. He says sales are barely paying the bills. By the nature of the contract he signed with my father, he had to tell the family before he can move forward with a sale of the restaurant." Robert tried to condense the hours' long conversation he'd had with Rodney into a few short sentences.

"Does he have a buyer?" Landon asked, tossing his phone and keys on the table before pulling Robert's chair out a little farther. Landon encouraged him down before taking the seat adjacent to his.

Robert couldn't get past the feeling his daddy wouldn't like this one bit. "I understand Dishology approached Rodney. They're a restaurant chain. Thane Walker—I'm not sure if you've met him or not. He lives in Maryland, but he owns Dishology. I think you'll remember him best for being the owner of Reservations."

The mention of the exclusive gay club in California had Landon nodding his recognition as the club Landon wanted to visit once he retired from the Air Force. "Besides the restaurant leaving your family, is there any other complication with them being the buyer?"

"They'll have all my father's secret recipes. I'm sure that's the only reason they want to buy La Bella Luna in the first place." The crux of the situation became apparent as Robert said those dreaded words out loud. "Dishology'll own my father's life's work, and he won't get an ounce of credit."

Robert dropped his head to his palms. He couldn't help wondering if Autumn knew. Most likely not, since she hadn't called. She wouldn't like this one bit either. The weight of Landon's hand came to rest on his shoulder, giving a gentle, comforting squeeze.

"Can you stop the sale?" Landon's tone radiated concern. He had to understand what this would do to him. Since Landon had entered his life, he had been able to push all his grief aside, believing in the greater good and circle of life theories. At the idea of his father's legacy being sold to the highest bidder, he couldn't help but feel he'd let his fathers down again.

Stop the sale? How could he do such a thing? Robert looked up at Landon. "And what? Buy La Bella Luna myself? And do what with it?" His heartbeat picked up as he said the words.

"I don't know." Landon crossed his arms over his chest, eyes narrowed as if he were in deep thought, trying to find the solution. "If you buy it though, it stays in the family."

Robert pushed back in his seat. All right, he'd bite. Play this game of back and forth, maybe a solution would present itself. "Then it'll certainly run into the ground. My father tried to run the restaurant after we moved, but it's not that kind of place or atmosphere. It's different there. It's a restaurant that needs the owner inside the dining room, remembering the community, learning their habits, and serving to them. The owner needs to be in the kitchen, demanding excellence in every plate served. I can't do that from DC."

"What about the chef I met when we were there?" Landon asked as Robert started bouncing his leg. He hadn't wanted to be critical of Rodney's hire, but Robert had never warmed to the merits of Chef Pacino. She didn't have the precision to create a full masterpiece in every meal she served. Her plates lacked that something special, maybe appearance, maybe the hint of a unique blend. Robert had never taken the time to pinpoint the problem.

Instead of voicing his real opinion, he stuck to the small list he could bullet point about Pacino. "She doesn't have the people skills to run the front end and barely knows English. It would never work." Robert got to his feet, moving past Landon into the living room. His heart hurt at the prospect of La Bella Luna leaving their family. He'd wondered about the wisdom of adding the dance floor to an already crowded dining room. For Robert, it took away from the cozy feel of the restaurant. Maybe it had been Rodney's way of trying to bring in new customers.

His mind raced. Autumn was already spread too thin. She spent a lot of time going between DC and Minnesota. Cam didn't have the time or people skills to jump in and help.

"You know how to run a restaurant. You said you watched Paulie and your dad work. You could do it. I know you could," Landon said quietly behind him.

"Not from here…" Robert turned, stating his current thoughts. Landon cut him off, turning to pace away from him, walking the length of the living room.

"You could move there. I know you're only here because of me." Landon's words had his heart hammering in his chest. He couldn't imagine being without Landon.

"Could you quit and go with me at this point?" Had Landon meant he would go too? That didn't make sense with the fight Landon had put up over retiring with the military. To Robert, it was clear that Landon didn't need to work ever again. He owed Landon the world. Hell, his husband worked hard enough keeping their mobile restaurant going four days a week, but Landon had stayed firm about his career choice and the benefits they both would receive once he retired. They had a little more than two years to go before this assignment came to an end. Landon would retire, and they could be free of the constant hustle of the DC area, forever.

Finally, when Landon turned to face Robert, he saw something on Landon's face akin to the uncertainty weighing on his own heart. "We could make it work. With how successful you've been with the taco stand, it's the natural progression that you go to a brick and mortar location. La Bella Luna's perfect."

Desperation had his head automatically shaking as he moved into Landon. Those words weren't right. They caused confusion, and he gripped Landon's forearms, not wanting to let go. "I'm not leaving you, Landon. I don't even think I could. I'm staying right here with you."

Landon visibly swallowed before he said, "The list came out for Master Sergeant today. I was on it." Landon's voice held a solemn note as he muttered what should have been celebratory news.

"You did?" The whiplash sent his heart crashing a different direction. Robert's mood instantly changed. A giant genuine smile pulled at his cheeks. So many emotions ran through him, some trampling his heart, others filling it with hope and pride. Landon had worked hard for his promotion to Master Sergeant.

Robert slid his arms around Landon's waist, drawing him forward into a tight embrace. "I'm proud of you!"

Landon stiffened, not reacting to the praise Robert wanted to give. He loved this stubborn man. Landon never wanted any kind of praise for his accomplishments. Robert didn't care. His shy guy deserved the fuss. When he reared back for a kiss, he stopped short at the sober intensity in Landon's stone face.

"What?"

"They selected me to attend a special training course on a new system. I'll have to come back and train my squadron. I've gotta go to Oklahoma." The highs and lows of tonight were too much. Robert felt like he took a right hook to the gut. His brain blipped, and he stared at Landon as if he hadn't understood. How had this day gone so terribly wrong?

"Then I'll go with you. Isn't that how it works? A spouse follows?"

"Not with this. Even if we found a way for you to be nearby, you can't leave everything we've been working for," Landon said, shaking his head.

Robert's heart sank, his breath suddenly harder to draw into his lungs as he stepped away, needing room to think. He didn't want to believe it was really happening. "I can't manage our business without you. You keep everything running smoothly. We'll have to take a temporary break with the taco stand and start back when you return. So, I can go—" It seemed so reasonable. Why was Landon shaking his head again?

"You know it won't be the same. We can hire people to help while I'm gone. We'll have to anyway. I'll be moved to days, Monday through Friday, when I get back. I won't be available like I am now," Landon said, his thick arms crossed over his chest in that stubborn way he had.

Robert dropped his head between his shoulders, the heavy weight of the world weighing down on him. He had to remind himself that this wasn't about him. He had always known Landon could be relocated from DC at a moment's notice. He'd just thought he would follow along too. Their life had been going too smoothly, and now their course had changed in a matter of hours.

He took a deep breath. They loved each other, and they would figure it out. He could be brave. On a deep exhale, he asked, "How long will you be gone?"

"A minimum of six months."

What? "Okay." Now, he wanted to cry. What little bravery he thought he had vanished. The concerns of La Bella Luna didn't compare to the prospect of Landon leaving him. Robert tried to act untouched. He had to keep this in perspective, try to hold back the depression edging forward, praying it didn't win.

He started for the kitchen, not wanting to breakdown in front of Landon and ruin the excitement of his husband's accomplishment. Landon had achieved his goals, things important to him, so they were important to Robert. He pushed all the negative thoughts away. They needed to celebrate, not mourn.

"I didn't cook tonight, so let's order in. Or we could go out and celebrate with some drinks. Maybe dancing for a couple of hours."

"Robert." Landon clasped Robert by the wrist, stopping him before he could get too far away. He tried to school his features before turning and lifting his gaze to Landon's. "I'm saying this without thinking through it all… Buy La Bella Luna. Move to Minneapolis and modernize the place, bring your ideas and fresh approach to the restaurant and the menu. You have the talent to turn that restaurant around." Landon spoke in his firm level tone. The stubborn set of his jaw told Robert that Landon thought what he said had merit.

Reasonableness just wasn't anywhere on Robert's radar, and he shook his head.

The picture Landon's words created helped to alleviate some of the pain gripping his heart, but Landon owned him body and soul, and he couldn't willingly be away from his husband. The more the news closed in around him, the more unrelenting dread seeped in. As much as he liked to pretend he had gotten himself back, Robert knew the truth, healthy or not, his happiness was contingent on Landon. He couldn't do it. He didn't have it in him to leave Landon behind.

As Robert rejected Landon's suggestion, he could see Landon building on the idea, turning confident in his plan. "Listen to me, Robert. I want you to call Rodney back and tell him you'll buy La Bella Luna. We'll make it work. It'll make leaving you easier for me if you're in Minnesota. Revamp everything about La Bella Luna—remodel the interior, rework the menu, hire better staff. When I'm done with training and can take leave, we'll have a re-grand opening. By that time, I'll only have a year and a half left before retirement. We can go back and forth on the weekends—"

"Babe, I don't want to do any of this without you. I consider the taco stand *our* business. You're the driving force behind everything. You decided on every recipe we use. I can't do this without you," Robert explained, twisting his wrist free. He didn't like the divide Landon had placed between them, making their business only Robert's accomplishment. Landon knew they were a team.

"I'll be with you the whole way. We can talk all the time. I won't be restricted from technology. Call me, text, video call—whatever we need to do. I'll take leave. I can fly there even if it's only overnight. You can do this, Robert. I know you can. Bring La Bella Luna back in honor of your father and your grandfather. They taught you what to do. Now, go do it."

Robert had to say, as a motivational speaker, Landon had a talent.

"What about permission from the Air Force?" Robert hedged, his mind racing over the possibility.

"They'll give it to me. They had no problem with the taco stand," Landon said, efficiently cutting through the military's red tape.

Thinking made his head hurt. He didn't feel ready for any of this. Landon's brown gaze remained locked with his. Landon believed his words. He wasn't backing down. So much to take into consideration. Maybe the taco stand had been a precursor to prove he had what it took to run a restaurant.

"I can see you considering my idea. We don't want to live in DC after I retire. Minnesota's your home. You have deep roots there. It seems the best place for us."

"What about where your home is?" Robert asked, though Texas wasn't even on the long list of places Robert had ever considered living.

"My home's with you," Landon stated quietly, with full conviction, making Robert's heart melt and a smile to tug at the corners of his lips. He walked into Landon, laying his head on his shoulder. His husband accepted him there, wrapping him in his arms.

"I wanted us to travel after you retire. I've got all these plans to take you around the world—see Rome, visit the castles of Germany and Austria. Take a train across Europe. If we buy La Bella Luna, we'll be tied down again," Robert said quietly, knowing the lame excuse didn't hold much merit.

"We've got time. We're still young. Besides, since we're changing our life course, I need to say, I've been thinking about having those babies we've talked about."

Robert had moved to place his lips against Landon's neck, but pulled back at those words to stare disbelievingly at his husband.

"You never really say anything when I talk about children."

"You know, I keep thinking you'll wise up," Landon explained, a playful smile curving his lips. "I watch you with Kylie. You were born to be a father, and I like the idea of settling down. Roots are becoming more important to me. It'd be nice to have children growing up in a place with so much family history."

"You have thought about it," Robert said a little astounded, wanting Landon to expand on those thoughts.

"I think about it every day. I love us. When I found out I made Master, I went from a level ten excitement straight to a zero when they explained the training I had to do. I don't want to leave you or the taco stand. I do feel like we're a team. It'll make it easier on me if you have something you're working on that you're good at. Something that's building our future."

"I don't have your confidence," Robert confessed.

"That's okay. I have enough confidence in you for the both of us. I think you should call Rodney right now. Tell him you'll be the buyer. Don't overthink it." Landon left him there, starting for the dining room table where Robert had left his cell phone. "I bet he's hoping you'll want to buy it."

"I think I should call Autumn first," Robert hedged, so uncertain if he could pull it off.

"There's no need. Call him, Robert. Just do it. Keep La Bella Luna in our family." No doubt, Landon knew how to work him. He said all the right words. Robert didn't have Landon's vision, but he did see the merit in buying the restaurant and loved the life Landon had so plainly set out in front of him. Robert, nodded. It might be a reckless venture, but at least, come whatever may, he'd own his father's recipes.

After hedging a minute more, Robert said, "I'll call Rodney and ask him to hold off on talking to anyone else to give me time to talk to Autumn. I feel like she should have a say in this. I'm not sure why. I just do. Then we should probably go to Minnesota and take a look around…"

"Whatever you think as long as you buy the restaurant." Landon entered his phone's security code then extended it to Robert. "We'll just need to move fast; I leave for Oklahoma City next week. I suggest you tell Rodney you'll buy, then tell Autumn about the agreement in the morning. Her firm can draw up the contracts pretty quickly."

"Next week is like five days from now?" How could he live without Landon every day? He loved the life they shared. Landon was his world. What would he do?

Landon nodded toward the phone, encouraging him to take it, a pained look on his face as he said, "You're making it worse again. Make the call." Landon pressed his thumb to Rodney's contact information and handed over the phone, staying right there as he spoke to Rodney, nodding his encouragement when he offered to buy the restaurant.

Chapter 35

Five days later

Landon stared absently at the legal documents on top of the conference room table of the Adams DC law firm. He somewhat listened to the explanation and details, watching Robert sign his name when instructed. As he'd come to learn of Robert Adams, once things were set in motion, it was just going to be that way. A genetic trait he was certain came from Avery Adams. After Landon signed where instructed, he'd become a part owner of the legendary La Bella Luna restaurant—Robert's family's business.

He hadn't intended to be a real part owner, not on paper and legalized. Those were just words given to make Robert see the benefit of buying La Bella Luna. No amount of arguing could penetrate Robert's thick head and make him see anything other than this being a joint effort between them, a happily married couple. Landon had tried to explain that many marriages ended once the initial intensity fizzled, but his steadfast husband couldn't even comprehend the idea. To Robert, he and Landon were soul mates, two people who would absolutely be together forever.

Funny how intimidation worked. Landon had thought he

was done with being made to feel inferior after he had signed the paperwork granting him half of everything Robert owned. At the time, Robert explained his desire to have Landon comfortable with their life, and since his money was a trigger for Landon's insecurity, Robert had just given it to him. Even stranger, for some reason it had worked. Landon had understood Robert's line of thinking and explanation, and Landon had settled into their lives. Of course, he wouldn't touch any of Robert's cash. Landon lived his life on what he made. He contributed to their household by paying all their utilities with his income, but the act of giving Landon access to Robert's wealth had settled his nerves.

Now though, he'd gone full circle. He shouldn't ever be part owner in something that held such historical value to the Adams family. And damn the Air Force for moving so quickly to grant him permission. When had they ever moved that fast?

Instead of going down that downward spiraling headspace again, Landon concentrated on the dream he'd been having for the last several months. The one that had the word *children* tumbling out of his mouth the other night. In his dream, a blond-headed little boy stood by his side. He and the little guy were flying a remote-controlled airplane, and the boy's big blue eyes and bright smile beamed at Landon with excitement after he had properly executed a flying maneuver. The boy called Landon *Papa* when he excitedly asked him to make the plane do it again. His heart connected so strongly to the little boy that it felt more like a premonition than a dream, at least to his heart.

He hadn't shared his dream with Robert, probably one of the only secrets he'd kept from his husband, who'd also become his very best friend. Landon loved the little bubble they lived within, but their secluded world appeared to be coming to an end. Robert was going one direction, leaving for Minnesota at the end of this meeting. Landon planned to head out for Oklahoma shortly after. Maybe he should have left the Air Force years ago.

"Sign here, babe," Robert said and managed to wrangle his hand free from Landon's tight grip. Two sets of eyes focused questioning gazes Landon's direction.

"Sir, if you aren't comfortable—" the attorney started, looking unsure at Landon.

Both Autumn, who was on a video call, and Robert blurted out, "No, don't give him an out."

The brother/sister team provided the perfect comic relief. Landon chuckled and leaned forward, picking up the pen to scribble his name—his hyphenated last name, Landon Russo-Adams—alongside Robert's.

"Perfect, I'll get you copies."

"It's not necessary. Give mine to Robert." Landon got to his feet, assuming the meeting had come to an end. They had a driver waiting, needing to go straight to the airport. Time was an issue. Handshakes were given then Landon went to stand by the office door, while he waited on Robert to follow him out.

Robert pressed his hand to the small of Landon's back, guiding him to the elevator as if he didn't know the way. His husband did those possessive moves all the time. Heads turned as they made their way out of the office. No doubt stealing glances at Robert. When he wore his custom-made business suits, the fit and cut only drew attention to Robert's handsome features like a damn neon sign. The guy was so fucking GQ sexy.

Once inside the elevator, Landon tucked his hands inside his pants pockets. He fixated on Robert, memorizing everything about him. His heart clenched at how badly he already missed their lives. Robert gave an audible sigh of relief as he poked a finger in his knotted silk tie, loosening its tight hold. "I wish I had thought to bring a change of clothes for the plane."

Out of the whirlwind last few days of haggling out the details of buying La Bella Luna to managing the complaints of the sudden shutdown of the taco stand to closing their DC townhome, Robert's frustration remained on his clothing. This morning, he'd complained adamantly about having to wear the suit in the first place.

"Did I hear Autumn say you're canceling all reservations and closing the restaurant down already?" With everything going on, the details were beginning to blur.

"Yes. Remember, we agreed upon the final design details last night?" Robert pulled the silk tie free, reaching inside the collar to unbutton the small buttons at the top. "I woke you and showed you. You nodded; I felt like you were awake. It was the design we both liked from the beginning. We're using Layne Construction's remodel crew. They had a sudden cancellation, and I jumped on the opening."

Landon nodded, having no idea which interior design he'd agreed to. It didn't matter. Robert had hired the very best design company in the world. When money wasn't a worry, things moved quicker than Landon thought possible.

With those details hammered out, Robert could spend his energy working with Helene and Chef Pacino to modernize the recipes. Landon could see heads butting between Robert and Chef Pacino. Robert wanted the cleanest, healthiest foods available with a strong emphasis on both fresh and unique vegetables, something currently unimportant in the restaurant's serving patterns.

"You have no idea what I'm talking about," Robert stated at his silence, extending a hand to encourage Landon out of the elevator when the doors opened on the ground level.

"It's been a lot," he said over his shoulder, not trying to pretend he remembered.

"I'll send the design to your email. It's not too late to change some of the details, so look when you can." Robert went straight to the front doors of the high-rise building and out to their waiting town car just feet away. The unseasonably warm DC winter was coming to an end. A cold front had been forecasted to arrive right as Landon was scheduled to fly out.

Robert's rush and the chaos of trying to complete everything before they left had dulled the glaring fact that they were leaving one another. Understanding hit them both seconds after Robert climbed in behind Landon and shut his door. Robert's blue eyes bore into his as his husband reached for the button to lift the glass partition separating them from the driver.

"I miss you already."

Landon pushed himself to the center of the seat. He cupped Robert's neck to draw him forward. "You're coming to Oklahoma next weekend. It's not that far away. We can do this."

Robert's lips rested against his, kissing him softly before moving inches away. "Next weekend then every two weeks until you can get free and come see me. I'm not sure how well I'll handle this separation. You're the center of my world. I'll go crazy without you."

Landon laughed and tapped his temple with his finger. "I'm worried about the chaos coming back." His attempt at lifting their mood failed as Robert furrowed his brow and took Landon's hand in his.

"No matter what happens, you remember how much I love you. That's never going to change. I'll schedule everything around the times you can call. You remember I'm there waiting for you, building our life until you can join me." Robert's sorrowful tone and desperate edge shredded his heart and had Landon tightening his grip at his husband's neck.

"I wouldn't be doing this if I didn't have to."

"I know. I can be brave, waiting for my soldier to come home to me again." The sweet, overly dramatic words had Landon lifting Robert's hand to his lips.

He pressed a kiss on Robert's skin, feeling like he wanted to cry. He'd sounded so cavalier when he had suggested they could make this work, but his own despair made him edgy as hell.

"I never took us for granted. I knew this could happen… you're very important to me."

This time, Landon memorized Robert's hand in his, the pressure and weight imprinting on his soul. The swell of emotion building in Landon was reflected in Robert's eyes. Those blue eyes turned bluer as they filled with tears. He was losing the battle of keeping a stiff upper lip. Robert looked away, clearing his throat before he could speak.

"This will make us stronger…"

"We're already strong." Landon's faced looked pained. He certainly didn't expect Robert's response to be a laugh straight in his face before leaning in and pressing his lips to Landon's. This time his tongue slipped past his lips. Landon opened and kissed Robert with all the love and devotion he held inside his heart. The drive to the airport took no time, which was about the amount of time Robert had to get to his flight. Robert exited one way and Landon went the other. They reached the trunk along with the driver at the same time. The driver reached for Robert's two suitcases. Landon grabbed his winter coat and computer bag, handing them over as they walked toward the front doors of the airport. "Sir, I can't park here."

"Go. I love you. Call me when you get to the hotel," Robert said, leaning in to kiss Landon as an airline employee came forward to take his bags.

"Fuck, I don't want to do this." Landon felt like he was being ripped apart on the inside. He wanted to run away with Robert while they still had the chance, but he didn't. He stood there, fisting Robert's shirt to keep him as close as possible and kissed him again.

"Babe, go. You'll be late for your flight," Robert said, gallantly trying to step away. His fist in Robert's shirt tightened, drawing his husband in for one last hug. He needed to feel Robert's arms around him.

"You take care of yourself. You don't have me watching your back," Landon whispered in his ear.

"Same goes for you. I love you," Robert said, kissing him again, a hard press of lips before pulling away. "Go, you're making this too hard."

Landon nodded. "I love you, too."

Robert was right. He made this harder than it had to be. He forced himself to let go of Robert's shirt and walked backward to the waiting car, hearing airport security yelling at their driver to get the car moving. He had one foot inside the backseat as Robert looked back and lifted his hand. His life disappeared inside the airport. Landon dropped down inside the car, waving the driver to start moving. This felt wrong. He should be by Robert's side.

Chapter 36

Ten days later

Landon stared at the utter destruction of La Bella Luna's interior dining room as Robert used WhatsApp to catch him up on the progress in the restaurant. He narrowed his eyes at what could only be described as a renovation gone wild. Actually, it looked more like a bomb had detonated. Wires, insulation, and exposed bricks filled the screen. Robert seemed so proud of how quickly things had come together. Landon couldn't help but wonder how bad it must have been before.

"I feel like you can't fully see from this angle, but it's really coming along. They're doing drywall tomorrow then the magic begins." Robert's handsome face came back to the phone's view.

His mister looked tired from the long hours he'd put in, but happy and perhaps more content than Landon remembered ever seeing him. Maybe some of Robert's ghosts were finally being put to rest.

"We've been testing recipes all day. I have a lot to bring with me tomorrow. I need my taste-tester to see if we're heading in the right direction."

"Mmm." Landon's stomach rumbled. He missed Robert's home cooking. He'd taken all the good food for granted. It only took his first meal on base for Landon to understand he'd become a food snob. For his next meal, he'd gone to Bricktown for something considered gourmet. After that, he'd understood Robert's truly unmatched skill and talent in the kitchen. Landon wanted every bite of the new recipes Robert planned to bring tomorrow. He'd even requested freezer ready meals to help tide him over until their next visit. "I already know you're heading in the right direction."

"You're good for my ego." Robert stepped through the kitchen door, and Landon looked around, seeing the remodeling in the kitchen. That was new.

"What's going on in there?"

"Oh, I forgot to tell you. I approved an upgrade in here. We've moved to a test kitchen. I'm not changing a lot in here. Rodney updated the kitchen a couple of years ago, but it needs a better workflow. They've promised it won't extend the time for the remodel so don't worry." Robert headed toward the back offices. Landon caught a glimpse of Paulie's picture that had been covered with a piece of clear plastic, still hanging intact on the wall. Even when they had only decided to paint the kitchen, it seemed important to Robert that Paulie's picture stay exactly where it had always hung.

Landon had been on the phone to witness Robert's unyielding dominance with the contractor who argued the complications of keeping the picture hanging during a remodel. Robert hadn't budged. Moreover, he'd threatened legal action if anything happened to Paulie's picture as they worked. Robert's firm tone had wound Landon up so tightly that, while on lunch break, he had gone straight to his room to fuck his fist, making Robert talk him through his orgasm in just that same hard tone.

"How's training going?"

Complicated, Landon immediately thought. Since joining intelligence, Landon had managed to hold his own in most technical situations, maybe helping to inflate his ego a bit, but this training was difficult. Since he'd chosen to spend all his free time on the phone with Robert, he had fallen behind. They spent so much time together, both their cell phones drained of battery every night. They were kind of ridiculous in that way, and Landon needed to find a way to clock more quality study time.

"So, like normal," Robert said, misreading his silence. "No talking about the secrets of the United States Air Force, huh? How about talking about that dream you had?"

Landon rolled his eyes to disguise his embarrassment. Two nights ago, in a particularly loving phone call, Landon had confessed to Robert about the dream he'd had with the little boy who called him Papa. They had talked at length about every second of the dream. What the boy looked like, whether there were other children in the dream, what kind of remote-controlled plane had he used—just every minor detail until Landon had nothing left to describe but scenery. Robert became silent and reflective, insisting Landon had described the pond at his great-grandfather's northern Minnesota home. Landon finally had to concede that, if he had dreamed about a home he'd never been to or seen, then the dream could in fact be a premonition. That had been all Robert needed in order to run away with the idea.

"I'm struggling with a formula," Landon said teasingly as a diversionary tactic. "Maybe you could help…"

"Hold up. I also decided the playroom needed to be an actual playroom again. So, I'm thinking about going up with the restaurant. We own this building, so adding a second story isn't out of the question."

"What? Robert, that's way outside the plans." Building a second story would take months at the very least to accomplish.

"I don't care. You're free in two years. We can start the second phase of the remodel after the grand opening and go slower to not inconvenience the customers. It'll be great. We'll have storage and additional tables, maybe large enough to be a meeting place." Robert took a breath, staring off as he relayed his vision. "Maybe a small dance floor can be added up there. We'll see, but we need a place for our children. I grew up inside this building, and with you working here alongside with me—"

"We never talked about me working there," Landon interrupted, and Robert's eyes focused back on him.

"Of course, we have. You're handling the front end and the accounting. You have excellent organizational and leadership skills, and I know you're brilliant, so the accounting thing is a no-brainer."

Landon shook his head. Unless that conversation had been while Landon slept—which happened a lot with his mister—he was certain he'd never heard these details.

"What's that look you're giving me? You don't want to work here? We worked well together in the taco stand. Are you planning something else?"

"No, I'm not. We just didn't talk about it. I'm not sure I'd be a good front man. It seems like it's gonna be an awfully fancy place. I'm good at the heavy lifting," Landon said, thinking about all the pictures he'd ever seen of Kane Adams. He was a well-put-together man who wore suits fitted to his body. Even in the snapshots, Kane Adams had a refined grace Landon knew he could never pull off.

"You're a better fit than you think." The old office chair squeaked as Robert took a seat. A chair Robert swore had been in this room since before he'd been born. "We'll go over things to get you ready, but you'll do fine. We'll make a great team."

"You sound so certain," Landon said, looking at the time. This evening, they had already been on the phone for over an hour. Then tonight, after dinner, they would talk until Landon fell asleep. Dinner would be in his room with his study materials at hand. He had to get some study time in before Robert arrived tomorrow to spend the weekend. "I gotta go. I need to study. I love you. The place looks great. You should be proud."

"I love you too. I'll talk to you tonight," Robert said. They stared at one another. This lovesick thing had to end at some point, right? Landon still stalled before forcing himself to lift a hand to wave then end the call. He put the phone down next to the giant textbook. Looking at the time, he cracked the book open and logged into his laptop. He had a lot to learn in a short amount of time.

"I'm pretty sure I exited the plane less than thirty minutes ago." Robert did the quick math in his fuzzy brain and decided it may have been closer to forty minutes, but not much longer. "Since then, I've had my first orgasm, and you're halfway through the veggie lasagna. I think it's a record for us."

Robert lay sprawled diagonally across the mattress in the bedroom so he could watch Landon eat in the small dining area off the kitchen of the hotel's mini suite. He had his head resting on his hand and his slacks still pushed underneath his ass. He vaguely remembered having them shoved down in their rush to get Landon's mouth on him then stayed that way through the best fast-fuck of his life. His husband had acted like a depraved caveman, just barely coming short of knocking him over the head and dragging him through the door by his hair. That would have probably been the case had he not had the two suitcases and his laptop case.

"This is excellent." Landon was naked from the waist down, sitting at the small table with a fork and an eco-friendly takeout dish Robert had chosen for the restaurant's to-go orders. "So, you're still thinking about a meat and meatless option for every item on the menu?"

"Yeah, that's the plan. We've set the tentative menu. Now it's just figuring out how to make the taste exceptional. My daddy's traditional recipes are all there, upgraded to his last changes based on the instructions I found. He kept great notes. Helene's helping me find my edge with the meatless options. She's great to work with."

Landon lifted his gaze to stare at Robert, chewing silently.

His husband always had that same caring look when Robert spoke about something dear to him. He loved how Landon watched out for him, he couldn't remember anyone ever looking out for him so completely.

"I've worked hard to make the vegetarian dishes more unique. Those I brought are a mix between my ideas and my father's. I think I'm finding my own style."

"It's great. What else did you bring?" Landon asked, that same intensity now focused on the suitcase splayed open nearby. He stretched his leg out and used his toes to draw the case closer for inspection.

Robert reached for the towel, still too blissed out to really move. "Everything. You need to take notes on what you taste and your first thoughts. The smaller containers are for the freezer. We should get them put away. The dry ice won't hold much longer." Robert had taken Landon's complaints about the local food to heart and brought several freezer containers since the mini suite had a full-size refrigerator in the small kitchen.

"Are these the biodegradable containers," Landon asked, lifting several containers and taking the couple of steps to the freezer.

"Yeah… I'm also looking into straws made from agave." A knock on the door had Landon glancing that direction. He thrust the containers inside the freezer and slammed the door shut then dropped his hands to cover his junk. Robert had about the same reaction; the mattress squeaked as he scrambled to his feet.

"Who is it?" Landon called out.

"It's me. Open up." It was a guy's voice.

Landon mouthed a quick *oh shit* to Robert as he darted for the door, picking up the pants he'd stripped off when they'd entered the room.

"Hang on." Landon tugged the jeans up his legs and looked over his shoulder. Robert was already fully dressed, running his fingers through his hair, smoothing it in place. Robert had quickly dressed then rushed to straighten the bedding, frantically throwing the crumpled towel across the room in the general direction of the bathroom. Robert edged to the side, leaning around the wall enough to look in the bathroom mirror to make sure he looked in order. He didn't want to embarrass Landon, who with his short hair had a much easier time of pulling himself together.

"Do they know about me? Can I be here?" Should he stay hidden in the small bathroom? He decided against it and stepped into the small living room in the suite.

"This isn't church camp," Landon said, teasing him, and pulled open the door. Robert stood in the middle of the room and shoved his hands into his pockets. In all this time, Landon hadn't introduced him to anyone in his military world. He hadn't met any friends or work colleagues, but he hadn't pushed Landon either. He had wanted the introductions to happen naturally.

"Hey, come in." Landon high-fived the other man who was dressed in civilian clothes—dark jeans and a smoky gray Henley, casual but clearly military with his short hair and the general way he held himself. A petite brunette walked in with him. She was pretty, seemed a little shy, but definitely happy to be by her guy's side.

Landon stepped back, and Robert stayed rooted in his spot. Waiting. He gave a nod as the two came the rest of the way inside the room, their curious stares jumping between him and Landon. His heart leaped in his chest. He couldn't tell if they had been expecting him to be there.

Landon took the woman's hand. "You got here just in time. I thought Norris was gonna ditch class and go to the airport this morning to wait for you."

"I'm Shelly." She smiled at Landon then beamed back at her soldier, clearly happy with Landon's words.

"I'm Landon. This is Robert, my husband." He had to fight to keep his brows from rising at Landon's automatic endearment. He hadn't thought Landon spoke of him while around the other soldiers. He did step forward, feeling comfortable enough to stand by Landon's side. Robert shook Norris's extended hand. He assumed that was his last name.

"We're heading to Tapworks, you two coming?" Norris seemed to ask Robert as if it were a given plan.

"We haven't gotten that far," Landon said sheepishly, turning a questioning look his direction. Robert had nothing to say, not understanding what Tapworks was and if he should agree or not.

"Is that food in the suitcase?" Shelly asked, staring down at the various containers yet to be put away.

"Yeah, he spoils me." Landon smiled over at him. "Robert's a chef. He, or we I guess, just bought a restaurant. His family's restaurant," Landon explained and bent back to the case, gathering several containers to place in the freezer. "These are his recipes. He brought 'em for me to try."

"Lucky," Norris said, bending over the suitcase to draw one container up.

"Stop looking at my food, Norris," Landon quipped, snatching the container from his hand.

"Shelly brought me a cake. I'll share if you do."

Landon stayed quiet, eyeing Norris while gathering the rest of the dishes. "We'll talk, but slice for slice. You don't get a whole meal every time I get a piece of cake."

"You two are funny," Shelly said, shaking her head. "Are you guys coming with?"

Landon shut the refrigerator door before looking over his shoulder at Robert. "It's a bar with pool tables and darts. They serve grill type foods. Not a lot you would eat there, except they have an avocado wrap you might like," Landon explained.

"I could play some pool," Robert said, pleased that Landon had scoped out the menu on his behalf. Landon did those sweet things all the time. He loved his man and would enjoy a night out. It would be fun.

"Of course you could, because you cheat!" A moment of uncertainty passed across Norris's and Shelly's faces at Landon's sudden spurt of self-indignation. Robert burst out laughing, because he knew exactly where Landon's mind had gone.

"I don't cheat, per se," he tried to explain to the two sets of eyes trained on him.

"Yeah," Landon countered, giving him a look he interpreted to mean he should try telling another lie. "Get a table and give us fifteen minutes. He just got here."

"Sure thing," Norris said and ushered Shelly out the door.

Happy with this turn of events, Robert went for his suitcase. He needed to find something else to wear. Landon had been generous with the lube. It had to be all over his slacks.

"You sure you're really good with this?" Landon called out from the kitchen, putting the rest of the food away.

"Very. I've gotta clean up. I tried to stay facing them." He went for the bathroom and showered and dressed in record time.

Chapter 37

"You're the best-looking guy here," Landon whispered, running his palm up Robert's back and across his shoulder as he scooted past him for a turn at the dart board. "I'm glad you're here with me," Landon said a little louder.

"He's sweet-talking me because I'm winning." Robert hadn't allowed Landon's win-at-all-cost strategy to get inside his head. This wasn't the first or second time he'd played a game with his husband. All bets were off for Landon when it came to winning. Currently, Robert held the lead by a decent margin and that made his husband a little crazed. Landon was very competitive. Years now of the give and take of game playing told the truth. Landon didn't like the current score at all, no matter how relaxed he seemed.

"You're only winning because of those new-math skills you have," Landon quipped, making both Shelly and Norris softly chuckle, but Robert laughed straight out loud. The volume of his laugh was designed to startle Landon just as he took his shot, and it did. It also drew every eye in the bar toward him. Landon missed the dartboard completely. Before the dart even struck the wall, Landon cut his gaze to Robert, giving his most unapproving glare which Robert totally laughed off.

If truth be told, Robert was happy tonight. This trip had already been made better with the inclusion of Norris and his wife who sat with them at the small, round table. Norris played along in the battle of the dartboard. To be in Landon's world like this canceled another of Landon's relationship obstacles. It didn't matter that Robert had figured out Norris was a safe bet. Besides being Landon's study partner, Norris's little brother was gay, but the rest of the bar was filled with soldiers, and they had been nothing but personable and accepting.

"Got something to say about my math skills?" Robert asked as Landon came toward him. Norris scooted off his seat.

"You know, I'm an elementary school teacher. I think Robert's correct. He's winning," Shelly added for good measure. Landon gave one of his dramatic eye rolls, landing on the stool beside Robert before draining his bottle of beer. Robert reached across the table for a high five for Shelly's remarks.

"He's a doctor. You two would get along great with all your education."

Shelly, who'd had her fair share of drinks that evening, turned instantly serious, reaching for her cell phone in her back pocket.

"You're a medical doctor? Can I ask you a question?" She started going through her phone, quickly working the screen. Robert figured if she had a medical question it probably had to do with one of her children. Landon didn't seem to clue in until she turned her phone to Robert. There was a beautiful little girl with a rash covering her arm. "She's had this rash all week. No fever, but it won't go away. The nurse at our school said it was a heat rash, but it's January."

The twinkle in Landon's eyes was back as Robert took the phone to get a better look at the rash. Norris took his seat and Landon hopped off his. "I'll take your turn. You help that sweet little girl with her rash."

The kind tone in Landon's voice was designed to mock him in his current predicament. Robert knew it and had a comeback ready. When he started to say it, he saw Shelly's worried expression and held his tongue, using his fingers to widen the screen to take a better look. "Have you changed soaps recently?"

"Not at home," Shelly said.

"Maybe check her school or care facility. It presents as a contact dermatitis. It's hard to tell without seeing the patient, but I'd say it's something she's coming into contact with. That's not really my area of expertise, but I'd start there," he said, handing the phone back over the table.

"Thank you." She stared down at her daughter, running a finger over her screen. "What's your specialty?"

"I'm a retired cardiovascular surgeon."

Both Shelly and Norris sat back, just blinking at him until Norris snapped his fingers and pointed at Robert.

"That's where I knew you from. You were in Germany. Your father's the vice president. And your grandfather was president, right?" Norris asked like he'd solved some intricately woven mystery.

"My great-grandfather, but otherwise, yes, I was in Germany. It's where I met Landon." Where Norris was animated and excited with his discovery, Shelly just looked dumbstruck, silently staring at him. It could be she tried to place him, or she might have been formulating a question about someone's ailing heart.

"Landon was the honor guard at Vice President Adams's funeral," Norris said, knocking his wife in the arm as if she would remember something like that. Robert hadn't understood the length of Norris and Landon's relationship, and it caught him a bit off guard.

"That's right," Robert nodded.

"Have y'all been together since then?" Shelly asked, folding both arms on the table, leaning in, clearly wanting all the details. "Landon didn't even tell me he'd gotten married until we met up here."

"I think he's ashamed of me," Robert teased as his heart gave a small ache. It had truly never occurred to him that Landon might have kept quiet about their marriage. He had thought Landon led a life of separate compartments to help make his military career easier, never that he'd just not spoken of Robert.

Robert felt the gentle grip at his shoulder as Landon squeezed him, their competitive game seemingly forgotten. Landon must have heard his reply, because his hand stayed on Robert in a telling PDA.

"I've been wrapped up in him. I didn't tell a lot of people outside of my squadron. I'll admit I'm pretty whipped." The words eased Robert. He covered the hand on his shoulder. Honestly, he could probably say the same thing. It was hard to see outside of the life he'd carved out with Landon.

"Brinkley said you were dating someone with money. I'm guessing drinks are on you tonight." Norris popped his hand out for a fist bump, one neither Landon nor Robert reciprocated.

"*Har har*. I think drinks should be on the winner," Landon turned a pointed stare at Robert most likely waiting for him to change his tune about winning in the first place.

"What? I think the loser needs to pay," Robert quipped back. They both knew he would jump in and pay the bill before ever letting Landon slide the card across the counter. Robert snaked out an arm to pull Landon against his side. They'd had another relationship milestone, and it hadn't blown up in their face.

The shove Landon gave Robert sent an instant arch to his eyebrow. Landon laughed at the look. The challenge was set. Landon met the arch of the perfect blond brow with one of his own, his gaze dropping to his love's full bottom lip. So fucking tempting. Landon stalked forward until he met Robert, chest to chest, then pushed him into the brick wall outside of the entrance to their hotel.

Maybe they were out of the direct light of the hotel's main door. Perhaps they weren't necessarily seen by anyone in the hotel's lobby, but it didn't matter either. Landon had had a great time tonight. Now it was time to pay up, for Robert to show him exactly how good a time they were still going to have tonight. Promises had been made, and he intended to collect.

"I didn't embarrass you tonight in front of your solider friends," Robert quipped. Landon placed both hands on the wall, caging Robert there, pressing his chest in harder. As if Robert could ever embarrass him.

"You know that's not what they're called," Landon growled. Robert's cocky grin mesmerized him. That smile made his dick leak and his knees weak. He leaned in for a kiss. A fraction of an inch before he swept his tongue forward, Robert turned away, giving Landon nothing but cheek.

"Come upstairs and tell me what they're called."

Landon guided Robert's face back to him, and Robert turned fully the other way, giving Landon his other cheek.

"You lifted me off my feet at the airport. That was really hot."

Landon held Robert's face in his palms, hovering his lips close to Robert's. "You talk a lot. I'm pretty fucking possessive over you. I'm gonna hate you leaving me again."

Robert slid his hand up Landon's sides, over his pecs. "Tell me about it upstairs, away from prying eyes." Robert pressed his fingers under Landon's chin and angled his head in such a way that Landon had no choice but to look back over his shoulder to where he saw five guys watching them. When they caught his attention, they began all the kissy face bullshit that kindergarteners thought was fun, trying to have a great time at his expense.

He turned back to Robert who had a smirk on his face. "Solider friends of yours?"

"You think you're pretty cute, don't you?" he asked, teasing his sexy husband.

"I think you think I'm cute. Take me upstairs." Robert moved his palms back to Landon's chest. "I had a great time tonight."

"If I have my way, it's only going to get better." Landon

pushed back, taking Robert's hand in one hand and, with the other, shot the finger at the guys in the distance. That only increased the volume on the teasing. They had a code to follow, and they'd all just guaranteed he'd get them back.

348

Chapter 38

September 2017

Landon stood in the foyer of the newly renovated La Bella Luna with his iPad in hand. He'd finished his training and had a couple weeks of leave before he had to be back in DC. He concentrated on each profile Robert had loaded into the restaurant's new proprietary software, memorizing names to faces and the highlighted notes of each person attending their private pre-grand opening party tonight. Where Robert had done all the heavy lifting, remodeling the interior and revamping the menu, Landon had secretly started etiquette training in his very limited free time in Oklahoma City. He'd learned what he had feared to be true—he didn't have the innate sense of manners to even pretend to be refined. Emily Post now topped his reads each night before bed. If nothing else came from all the study time, at least he now knew what that small fork was really for.

"You look handsome," Robert said, edging past Landon to place a stack of electronic menus on the hostess stand. "I'm glad we splurged on a hand-made suit for you. It really brings out your build."

"Stop distracting me," Landon said and slid his finger over the screen to bring the next profile forward.

"Stop giving yourself anxiety." Robert pulled the iPad from Landon's hands and placed it in the top drawer of the hostess stand. "You know every bit of that information by heart. Now, go inspect your waitstaff." Robert motioned with his thumb to a row of waiters and waitresses standing perfectly straight in a line behind them.

"This isn't the military."

"No, but the same rules apply." Robert started their direction, and Landon trailed after him. "This will help you visually find things you might otherwise miss. Tonight's too important to miss anything."

Landon nodded and looked over each server. Robert supplied the uniforms—black pressed slacks, a freshly pressed white long-sleeve button-down, black belts, and polished black loafers. The men wore black ties clipped to their shirts, and the women wore a silk scarf pinned to their clothing. They were all well-groomed with any long hair pulled back off their faces—no messy buns allowed. They all smiled. Landon looked over at Robert and said, "What am I looking for?"

Robert clapped his hands once and broke out in a grin. "You all passed inspection; he's got a good eye. Good job!" High fives and fist bumps were given from the group that seemed friendly with one another. Robert had personally trained each one himself. "Remember, Landon's nervous. Keep an eye on him for me."

"I'm not nervous…" Landon started to argue, knowing that was his defensive side spiking, because he did in fact have some major anxiety, so he turned back to the group to say, "I don't want to embarrass y'all."

"You won't embarrass any of us," Sebie, Robert's right-hand man and team lead, declared with a confidence Landon didn't possess then turned to the waitstaff, taking over the instruction. "Get your trays. Remember, for tonight only the champagne flutes are in the back of the kitchen, not the bar. A person is dedicated to filling those trays and will have them ready to distribute. And

Chef Pacino's a little stressed in there. Get in and out. Don't linger." He dismissed the waitstaff handling the drinks and turned to the others still standing in line. "Each tray has an assortment of entree samples of the *new* menu items. Stay in your section and quietly name each plate, stress the fresh ingredients, but any other questions, refer to Robert or Landon." Landon immediately started shaking his head. "Okay, refer to Robert."

"Can I talk to you?" Robert asked, not waiting for Landon's answer. He took Landon by the arm and pulled him through the restaurant to the back office.

"We've got less than five minutes before the doors are unlocked. I need to be up front waiting," Landon said once they made it to the office, away from any prying ears. Robert used a key to unlock the door then pushed Landon over the threshold, crowding him into the small space.

"You have to calm down," Robert said, taking both of his hands, giving a gentle, firm squeeze.

"I can't," Landon shot back, exasperated. "I told you this wasn't for me. I'm just so out of my league."

"You can't know that. We're just getting started."

When Landon started to object again, to explain exactly how he knew his words were fact, Robert pressed his fingers to Landon's lips to stop him from speaking.

"You have to trust me, Landon. I would never put you in a situation that's over your head. La Bella Luna is our restaurant. Yours and mine. From the napkins to the menu selections to the uniforms we chose, you've played a part in pulling this restaurant together."

Landon edged past Robert, not that there was a lot of room to pace, but he attempted it. "That's not true, and I don't know that I can do this."

Robert let out a frustrated huff, his hard stare pinning Landon, stopping his movement. The look brought Landon's honest fear tumbling from his mouth.

"What happens if we fail?"

Robert looked at Landon as if he were insane and his greatest fear meant nothing to the big picture, making Landon blurt out the obvious result of failure.

"We'll lose La Bella Luna."

"That's right. We—me and you—lose the restaurant, not anyone else and nothing more." Robert came toward Landon, taking the steps to him. "We won't sell to the highest bidder like Rodney planned to do. La Bella Luna may have run its course, but now I own my daddy's recipes and at least we tried."

Landon stood there, processing Robert's explanation, not quite ready to let the fight go, even as he better understood Robert's perspective, knowing his husband was right. If they tanked at operating the restaurant, it wasn't anything close to being as bad as losing the rights to Kane Adams's signature recipes. As important as those were to Robert, Landon felt Robert would have paid anything just to secure those back into the family fold. Landon muscles softened as tension leaked out of him, then he rolled his eyes and looked up at the clock above the door. They had one minute before the front doors opened.

"You shouldn't have spent so much money on this suit."

Robert laughed. "I'll take that as a win in my favor."

"It's only a win because you cheat." Landon's grin grew as he formulated his argument as he went. "You bring up your father, and I want his recipes protected too. It's not a fair win, but I see your point." Landon bypassed Robert to open the door and start for the dining room. He was so distracted with his thoughts that the hand that reached down and patted his ass instantly woke his dick. He swung around, his gaze landing on Robert. What was the man thinking? They had a party to throw; he couldn't roam the restaurant with a hard-on. It was going to be a long night.

"Dear, help me to my chair," Kennedy said to Landon. She'd

been their surprise guest tonight, not letting Robert, Landon, or Autumn know she had planned to attend the party. It had been such a surprise when she walked through the front doors and made Robert's magical night turn epic. Reasonably, he understood the private party couldn't truly be a measure of the restaurant's success with its free food and alcohol, but he did concede they were off to a great start. The patrons attending tonight really seemed to enjoy some of the changes they had made to the menu and many reservations had been booked for the future.

The way Kennedy had commandeered Landon warmed Robert's heart. His husband was right on board with her plan too. Kennedy had hit her mid-nineties and needed an arm to hold on to every now and then. His grandmother seemed a bit vain in that she didn't want to appear weak—her words not his. Instead of the chauffer standing nearby, she'd replaced him with Landon. It had been the perfect diversion for his husband.

He had taken Kennedy around, and with that photographic memory of his, his husband had reintroduced her to the pillars of the community. Landon had the guests eating out of his hands, knowing all their stats and accomplishments. Kennedy had then helped ease Landon with her ability to engage in small talk.

Robert was pleased to see Landon relax and enjoy their hard work. His beautiful husband had captivated the crowd at the party. Robert had had many guests comment on Landon, wanting to know more about him. It made Robert proud. Landon had found his place inside the La Bella Luna world.

Kennedy took her seat at one of the booths lining the inside walls of the restaurant. All the other tables and chairs had been removed to allow for the large number of guests invited to mingle.

"You look tired, Nonnie. You should go home."

"I've decided to stay with you two tonight. It's too far a drive to Stillwater only to drive back here early in the morning and fly home," she explained, causing Landon to lift his gaze to Robert. Of course, she was always welcome to stay wherever she wanted of Robert's, but the slowly built plan of showing Landon exactly how proud he was of him for such a job well done this evening crashed and burned in a fiery blaze inside his head. Based on Landon's pained look, he'd had the same ideas.

After the briefest pause, Landon cleared his throat and nodded to Kennedy. "Probably the best idea."

Kennedy only chuckled, clearly understanding the meaning behind their long stare. "You two go finish saying your goodbyes to your guests. Send a waiter with a glass of champagne."

In that, she was right. Robert searched for a waiter, making eye contact, and nodded toward Kennedy then extended his hand to slip his arm around Landon as they started toward the last few guests still remaining in the main dining area even though the party had ended an hour ago.

"We did it and I didn't embarrass you," Landon whispered, giving Robert a gentle, relieved smile.

"I told you that you wouldn't. Most people prefer real people, and you pull off real really well," he teased and tightened the hold around his husband's waist.

"Watching you tonight, you were meant to run a restaurant. You kept everything going smoothly like you'd been doing it your whole life." The words were sweet and did their job to ease Robert's hidden insecurities.

"Thank you. I admit, I love it, but I'm exhausted." That had Landon looking over at him as if he'd never seen Robert before. He chuckled, grinning a silly grin.

"What is that you say? Tired? Robert Adams is tired?"

"I know, right? It's new for me too. All I want to do is go home and sleep, and I have to be here by six in the morning to begin prep." They had made it to the small group standing in the entryway. Autumn and Cam were there with three other couples, all friends and prominent local figures in the area. "We wanted to thank you all for coming tonight."

"We're so pleased to see what you've done with the place," Kelly, a local news anchor said. "I'll be back tomorrow for the grand opening with a news crew in tow. This is exciting for downtown Minneapolis. I'm not supposed to tell you, so you'll all have to stay quiet for me, but we had our food critic here tonight, and he was very pleased with the samples. He's a hard nut and made a comment that he hadn't had vegan taste so good."

Autumn beamed, and Robert nodded. "Thank you for sharing. Those particular items have been years in the making," Robert explained, his heart in his hand with appreciation. "Tomorrow, I believe our noon lunch reservations are full. Outside of the twelve to one timeframe, you have access to the whole place. We're adding a second story, but that work's being done overnight not to bother the guests." Robert racked his brain for any other talking points he should share, worried the construction vehicles parked out front might keep people from venturing in if they didn't understand their purpose. They had managed to complete the outside of the building, limiting the construction to the interior.

"He's worked hard. You should see the wine cellar. It's spectacular. He followed my father's lead, stocking with the rarest varieties available. Good thing I get a family discount," Autumn teased, reminding Robert not to get too serious.

She got the desired result as the group laughed then said their goodbyes with promises of returning soon. Even Autumn and Cam made their leave, waving goodbye to Kennedy and hugging them both. They were left alone in the foyer. The tension Robert had tried to hide all evening drained away as Landon locked the front doors behind them.

"What do we have to do now?" Landon asked, shrugging off his suitcoat.

"The kitchen closed down an hour ago. Pacino has that under control. Sebie's closing the front end for me. There're no receipts to total, so closing tonight won't be difficult. I should stay until everyone's done," Robert said, watching Landon roll each shirt sleeve up.

"Let me do that. You take Kennedy home," Landon offered, nodding Kennedy's way.

His grandmother waited patiently for them, and by patiently, that meant her head was resting on the back of the seat and her eyes were closed. Her age and the care she needed had Robert agreeing he should see her home.

"You go. I'll finish up here."

Landon shook his head at Robert's head shake. "You go rest for the morning. It's only seven hours away. You need to be sharp and ready for our first day open. I'll be along shortly, and you need to be asleep by the time I get home." Landon left no further room for discussion. He did, though, kiss him chastely on the lips, and as he drew back, he complimented him. "You did it. I'm super proud of you. I know your father is too. Now go."

Robert watched as Landon left him standing there. It wasn't within him to just leave like this, but he also loved watching Landon become an active part owner of the restaurant. If something wasn't done properly, he could make the change in the morning. He was worn out. The last six months of rebuilding this restaurant and traveling back and forth to Oklahoma had taken its toll, stressing him out more than multiple twenty-four hours rotations during his hospital days. He gave a single nod, affirming his decision to leave, and made his way to his grandmother. Mr. Kinkaid, her trusty chauffer who had been propped against the wall started her way too. This time he had a wheelchair, which Robert hadn't noticed him bring inside.

"She won't want to use it, but she's unsteady on her feet when she gets tired. She gets tired faster these days."

Robert nodded his understanding. He was so thankful he still had her in his life. And as he leaned in to wake her, he said a simple, selfish prayer to give him more time with his grandmother.

Chapter 39

Two weeks later

Soap bubbles covered Landon's gloved hands, which were currently submerged in a tub of hot sudsy water. His last assigned task in a long multitude of miscellaneous jobs had him cleaning the dishes Robert dirtied this morning while working the prep station for the lunch rush. Over the last couple of weeks of his leave, Landon had performed just about every job the restaurant required. He played host more times than he could count. He ran food, bused tables, and tended bar. He carried glass racks, plate racks, and case after case of anything heavy that anyone needed lifted or moved. He also became the sole janitorial service, cleaning the front end of the restaurant completely by himself for three nights in a row after Robert had a rare display of aggression and fired the cleaning company on the spot.

The restaurant appeared to run best while in a fast-paced state of controlled chaos. An environment Robert flourished in; one Chef Pacino hadn't appreciated at all. By Landon's estimation, she'd lasted longer than he thought she might before getting heated over Robert's perceived criticism of one of her so-called specialty dishes—her *Baccala alla Livornese*. In her frustration, she began yelling in Italian. Landon knew just enough to understand she compared Robert to the rodents running around the alleys of her hometown. Landon hadn't liked that at all, but when she sent a metal spatula flying at Robert's head, Landon had seen red and become the aggressor, firing her without a second thought.

Luckily, Helene had volunteered to be on the first flight back to Minnesota to help until Robert could find a replacement. Everything fell into place as if it were meant to be when the replacement came by way of his friend, Chef Lee from Farmers, Fishers, Bakers. Robert had offered Lee a huge salary and maybe threw in an arm and leg as incentive to get the chef to La Bella Luna. It had worked. Lee eagerly took the job and planned to arrive later this week after Landon returned to DC.

"We're gonna miss you around here," Sebie said as if reading his thoughts while dropping two bowls into the sudsy water.

"Hell, I need to go back to work to get a vacation," he quipped, finding some truth in those words. Besides, he didn't want to think about leaving. It made him miss Robert already.

"When're you coming back?" he asked, pausing there beside Landon.

"I'm not sure. I've been in training and have to be back to train my squadron. I'll come as soon as I can," he explained, looking over his shoulder to see Robert slowing the dicing, most likely tuning in to their conversation. Little had been said about Landon's departure tomorrow morning, but they both knew it was coming. The fear they shared that things might be different between them after such an extended time apart had been for naught. He and Robert had easily fallen back into their routines. Landon never tired of being with Robert, and it seemed Robert felt the same way. Their strong connection had persevered, maybe even strengthening. Now the pain of being apart would begin anew.

No, don't go there.

He had a year and a half before retirement. By then, La Bella Luna would be running smoother, and he and Robert could begin their life and their family.

Stick with those good thoughts.

"Air Force, right?"

Landon tuned back into Sebie and nodded, adding an absent, "Yup." He'd felt this internal shift for a while now. The last two weeks firming up all this change inside him. The Air Force had been such a source of pride for Landon. Now, he hated to admit that it had all fizzled out. He was counting the days to retirement. Everything he cherished stood just feet away from him. But more than that, even Autumn, Cam, and Kylie had become his family. He loved spending their free time with them, even babysitting Kylie on occasion.

As if on some cosmic cue, Landon turned back to Robert who stopped chopping and stared at him. He experienced a rush of sadness, not just his own.

"He'll be back in twelve days for two nights. We'll save all the heavy lifting until then," Robert said to Sebie, giving Landon a wink before turning back to his workstation.

"Guess that answered that," Sebie said with a knowing chuckle and left Landon to finish the dishes. Seconds later, Robert's hard body pressed against his, pushing him into the metal wash tub. His husband buried his handsome face in the crook of his neck, nuzzling the skin there.

"We've been so busy, I'm not sure I properly showed you how happy I am to be right here with you. Now you're leaving." Robert's warm breath tickled against his skin. Landon angled his head, giving Robert access to his neck, releasing the dish in his hand, letting it slide back into the hot water.

"You show me every day. Do I show you?" he whispered.

Robert pressed his lips against the sensitive skin underneath his ear as he spoke. "Every minute of every day."

"Good. You remember it while I'm gone." Regret clogged Landon's throat, and he looked down, working hard to swallow the sudden lump.

"I'll remember it forever. No need to worry about that." Robert locked his arms around him, hugging him tightly. Landon loved these unexpected, intimate moments. Closing his eyes, he was back to memorizing the feel of Robert's body pressed exactly like this against his body, holding on to the image to pull up during the lonely nights headed his way.

"Robert, the florist's on the phone. They're running late and won't be here until after eleven. They want to know if you still want them to come." The spell broke. Robert turned away, and Landon felt the instant disconnect of his body. It hurt to think about not waking up to this man every morning. This was going to be so much harder than he'd ever imagined.

"There's a big difference in flying private," Robert said, following Landon up the steps to board the small private jet he had rented for Landon's flight home this morning. Robert ducked his head, stepping inside. The pilot sat in the cockpit, preparing for the flight. He and Landon turned the opposite direction, heading into the main cabin.

"It's nice, but I should've flown commercial—"

Robert lifted a hand to Landon's lips, stopping him from saying the same words he'd already uttered several times over the last twelve hours when he had learned what Robert had done.

"I told you, if we're going to live separately, our travel must be done efficiently. This is an expense we'll have to budget for."

Landon tossed his bag on a leather chair and did a full turn, taking in everything about the cabin before twisting to stand face to face with Robert. Robert reached out, taking Landon's hands in his. He couldn't believe how badly his heart already ached. It made him vulnerable, and he blurted, "Maybe we should've bought the restaurant and held on to it until you retired."

"No second-guessing." Landon stepped into Robert, brushing

against his chest. "I'm gonna harp on this, so listen to me. You're not sleeping enough. I watched your diet. You're not near as strict as you used to be, and you're not exercising regularly. You have to do better. Your health's too important. You're living in a constant state of exhaustion." The words warmed Robert's heart, and he fought the smile but lost as it broke across his face, stopping Landon from saying more.

"You love me."

Landon's brow dropped into a hard V. He could see Landon trying to understand where Robert had misinterpreted his words. "I do and I want you to stick around. We're not getting any younger and heart disease runs in your family…" The look and tone told Robert more than the words. His mister wasn't playing, and this wasn't open for anything more than Robert's complete agreement.

"I know. When you get home, set me a schedule, and I'll follow it," he promised and released Landon's hands to cup his face with his palms. He softly caressed the skin under Landon's eyes with his thumb as he met the dark stare.

"I'm not sure I believe you."

"I give you my word. I've already been thinking about it. I'll make an appointment to get my labs done." He slid his hands over the width of Landon's shoulders then down his arms. He couldn't stop touching his love. "You can track my progress. When Lee arrives, I'll feel more comfortable leaving the restaurant. Maybe, we can work out together. Speaking of that, we'll have different schedules. I'll work nights and you'll work days."

"We'll figure it out. We always do."

"We do." And they would. Robert bent for a kiss; he couldn't help it. They had officially said their goodbyes on the tarmac. He hadn't intended to follow Landon inside the plane. He hadn't wanted to hear all the complaints Landon had about this particular expense. Robert just couldn't help it. He didn't want Landon to go, and an aggravated Landon was better than no Landon.

His lips touched Landon's again, and Landon opened for him.

Strong fingers gripped Robert's beltloops, tugging him closer. He loved the aggression in his husband's attention. He slipped his tongue forward, meeting Landon's halfway, melting into the kiss. His body heated quickly with the way Landon took his mouth, dominating the kiss. He could kiss Landon forever.

"Sirs, it's time," a female said behind him. She came closer, reaching for Landon's duffel bag to secure inside the luggage compartment to the side of them. Landon leaned his head back but didn't release his hold.

"I love you."

"I love you."

"You should go," Landon rasped against his ear then wrapped Robert in his arms in direct contrast to his instruction. "Go, because I miss you already, and I'm gonna cry."

Robert's eyes filled, making everything blurry as he tightened his hold. He squeezed his eyelids closed, trying to hold back the full-on cry threatening to spill over. He hugged Landon tight then released him. He had no choice but to look away. It hurt too badly to look at his life's desire standing there as he was forced to step away. He pivoted around, the pain in his heart too much to bear. He only looked back as he started to duck through the exit.

"I love you. You be safe," he mouthed.

One of Landon's tears slipped free, rolling down his cheek. More than anything, he wanted to wipe his husband's pain away. Instead, he did the grown-up thing and blew Landon a kiss then took the steps down to the tarmac.

Robert stood in the distance, watching the plane take off. He stayed until Landon was long gone. He was frantic inside, the ache holding his heart hostage. So many things could happen. He tried to push away the anxiety that kept his feet planted to the concrete. How did so many military families do this very thing every single day?

Brushing a tear from his cheek, Robert turned to leave, reaching for his sunglasses. As he pulled them from his collar, a small, white feather floated from their fold. He stooped to gather it in his hand, needing the sense of reassurance it instantly brought. The feathers were fewer and farther between lately, but this one spoke directly to his heart. He and Landon would get through this. They were strong and committed. The calm strength surrounding him grew into something tangible. Everything was going to be okay.

Chapter 40

October 2018

"Babe, where'd you go?" Robert called from the downstairs dining room. He looked around the first floor of their DC townhome, twisting around in his seat to see the kitchen then the living room. Landon had gone missing. He'd just been right there with Robert as he began to explain all the historical and romantic adventures he'd found for their long-awaited trip to Italy.

"Babe?" Robert called out a little louder.

"I'm in the bathroom." Landon opened the downstairs bathroom door no more than a slit. "Keep talking. I can hear you."

Robert looked down at all the printouts he'd brought with him on this trip home. Paper littered the entire top of the dining room table, except for the far corner where Landon's laptop sat. His husband had commandeered the space as his desk and sat there every night, on video with Robert and the restaurant, while working on the restaurant's accounting.

Landon's area looked super-efficient, only the laptop and a pen and pad of paper left out. Robert's trip plans took up the entirety of the rest of the tabletop. Maybe he'd overdone in his detailed planning of their retirement trip, but he quickly brushed the uncertainty off. Landon retired from the Air Force in seven and a half months and Robert had dreamed of the day they could travel the world together. Apparently, when dreams come true, they required lots of printed sheets of paper showing everything he wanted to do while they were away.

"I want you to see as I explain," he finally said.

"I'm good with whatever you decide." Those six words had grown to grate on his nerves, because Landon used them often. Robert mashed his lips together and furrowed his brow. If he could shoot laser beams with his eyes, he'd have singed Landon where he sat on the commode.

A gut feeling had Robert glancing over to Landon's edge of the table. His cell phone was nowhere to be seen. He narrowed his eyes and stood, going for the bathroom door, shoving it open with enough force to give a slight bang. Landon looked up, startled. Sure, he did in fact sit on the toilet, but he was fully clothed with his phone resting between his palms. His thumbs poised over the screen.

"Are you playing a game?" Robert asked in all his outrage.

"What? No." Landon immediately shook his head and sat back on the seat, his phone held protectively in his hand. "I'm on Reddit."

Hurt knifed through him. Robert had worked hard on their plans, and their itinerary needed to be decided so he could book tours and reserve hotel rooms for their stay. Anger rose like bile, because this trip meant something to Robert. He'd stayed up well past his scheduled time to sleep to pull this information together. He wanted Landon to have the trip of his lifetime to remember forever. All the sadness this last year had been hard on Robert. He'd hidden his loneliness, trying to stay positive and focused on their future, but it was a constant companion, there with him all the time.

"Stop looking like that," Landon said, getting to his feet. "I saw pieces of *Star Wars Solo* yesterday. I wanted to see what Reddit had to say about it."

Robert took a step back out of the small room, doing a quick shake of his head in shock. "We were supposed to watch that together."

"Babe…" Landon came toward him, tucking his phone in his back pocket as Robert continued to back away. "I maybe watched twenty minutes then turned it off so we could watch together. You know I really want to see it. We should watch it tonight."

Robert's ass hit the table and Landon stepped into him.

"Don't be mad." Landon shook his head, seemingly trying to guide Robert's thoughts. "I know you watched *Game of Thrones* without me. I turned on the app and saw the episodes were watched. I didn't get mad…"

"The only reason you'd see such a thing was because you tried to watch them without me too!" Robert accused. He did see the hypocrisy of his claim, but he wasn't willing to let go of his hurt feelings or this argument.

"I'm sorry. I did listen to you about all that." Landon swept a hand over the table. "You just take care of everything, and whatever you decide is great with me because you know best."

"You hurt my feelings," Robert started and tried to move out of the cage Landon held him in.

"No…" Landon stepped all the way into Robert, locking his arms around Robert's waist. "I was listening. Cinque Terre and Tuscany for a week and a half. Florence sounds amazing. Rome for an entire week. Then the rest of the time we're touring from the Amalfi Coast to Venice. I wanted to see Naples, definitely Pompei. See, I was paying attention."

Landon appeased him. Maybe more the glint in Landon's dark eyes or the possessive hold his strong arms had, but whatever the reason, Robert lifted his hands to those brawny biceps and caressed his way across Landon's defined pecs.

"You did listen."

"I did. I always listen to you."

Robert let Landon's little white lie slide by.

"It's been hard on me being away from you." He couldn't meet Landon's concerned gaze under the heavy weight of his confession. "I don't tell you because I don't want to add pressure to an already hard situation."

"We've done pretty good so far. Don't think about it. It'll be over soon. Tell me about Autumn." Good diversion. His pregnant sister was due to give birth any minute there in DC. Another reason Robert had chosen to spend the entire week there with her and his little niece, Kylie.

Autumn, in her firestorm of constant activity, had become the poster child of progress for the country. In today's social media world, he'd watched her regularly celebrated as well as crucified, all at the same time, even in the same thread. He couldn't stand any of it, but she seemed to thrive, flourishing in her growing popularity.

"I haven't checked in today. Let me text her." This time, when Robert tried to move, Landon let him go. He went for his cell phone. He'd only been home for about twelve hours. Like normal, all those hours were spent catching up with the love of his life. Neither had checked on the restaurant since he had arrived. Robert saw he hadn't missed a call then checked text messages to find a long list of unread messages. He opened Lee's first and quickly read the update.

"Chef tells us not to worry. I guess we haven't."

Landon's grunted response seemed to agree with him as he headed for his laptop. "You're right. I need to close the books from yesterday."

The next text answered Landon's concern. "Sebie says he closed QuickBooks last night, but you should check to make sure he did it right," Robert said. He honestly loved his team back in Minnesota. Each one of his managers had been an expensive hire. The cost had worried him in the beginning, but they'd all earned their pay in a big way, allowing Robert some needed free time.

"Babe, you're funny!" Robert said after reading the next message. "My workout app's getting me in trouble for not reaching my exercise goal. Did you program it to do that?"

"I did, last year. If you're just now seeing it, then you've been following your schedule."

"I told you I am." An unexpected name showed on the list, a text from Helene earlier this morning. They hadn't said more than hello in the last couple of months, and he'd never received a text from her before. He quickly opened and scanned the cryptic words instructing him to open the link she'd sent in email. His confusion turned to disbelief after reading the few paragraphs of the cover letter.

"She did it."

"Who did what?"

Robert's heart drummed in his chest as he read the exchange between Helene, *Buon Appetito* and Sony Productions. Robert lifted a hand, covering his mouth, afraid to look away from the phone in case it came with a self-destruct option.

"What?" Landon read the screen over Robert's shoulder until his husband reached around, taking the phone out of his hand, tapping the screen to keep it from power-saving mode. "Is this saying they want you to do video podcasts and cookbooks? Like multiple cookbooks?"

"Yeah. Back over a year ago, when you were in Oklahoma and Helene and I were working out the menu, we talked about the idea of doing what we were doing in YouTube series format. I added the idea of small, specialty cookbooks, because we liked what we were doing so much—you know, trying new things, some turning out great, others failing spectacularly. I thought it was just casual brainstorming. She never told me she was shopping the idea."

"Robert, they're offering you a million dollars," Landon said, his eyes going wide, his finger poking the front of his cell phone screen again.

"No way." Robert yanked the phone out of Landon's hand, having to reopen the attachment from all of Landon's poking at the screen. He quickly read until he made it to the offer. "Ohmigod, they want to buy exactly what Helene and I talked about, and they want to film inside the La Bella Luna kitchen."

"No fucking way!" Landon gave a solid whoop and wrapped his strong arms around Robert, heaving him a few inches off his feet. "I told you! You're a chef."

"I'm self-taught… I don't have the experience." The insecurities tumbled from his mouth at the idea of such a large cash payout along with the investment of time and money he'd have to make. Landon put him on his feet and reached up, grasping his face between his palms, drawing him in for a quick hard kiss.

"Stop the bullshit. You know you have a talent. Text her back and tell her you're in."

"We have to work out the logistics. I can't take anything else on that takes time away from you…"

Landon rolled his eyes and commandeered his phone. When Robert tried to reach for it, his husband gave him his back and quickly typed in the passcode. Helene's text message opened, and Landon typed as fast as his two thumbs could.

"What're you saying?"

Landon pushed send and handed him the phone to read for himself. His words were perfect, ones Robert wished he had chosen. "Helene, you sneaky thing. What an incredible opportunity. I'm in. Thank you for everything."

Helene's reply came through as he stared at the phone. Robert read it out loud, "Speaking as your friend, you've made such a name for yourself so quickly, we should probably shop this around. I feel sure we can get a better deal. Speaking as a partner and editor of *Buon Appetito*, I say we should sign this contract and get started right away. Come see me while you're home. We'll decide what's best."

Landon's grin grew broader and his fist came forward over the phone, a knuckle bump Robert willingly obliged. "It's a great compliment."

"It is," Robert agreed. It seemed, yet again, they were at another turning point. When did the turns get to be too much? Maybe the bigger picture did include putting this on hold until he and Landon were together again every day. "If we're going to try and have babies…"

"You aren't having the baby. Our lives still go on," Landon shot back, puffing out his chest and anchoring his hands at his waist, taking on his debate stance. "You need to do this. There's no question that you have to take this opportunity. Do it in memory of your father. I can't even understand your hesitation."

Robert exhaled in a rush and struggled to hold Landon's gaze as he said, "I can't take on anything more that draws me away from you. I need you, Landon. It's the same need that drew me to you from the beginning."

Landon's perfectly executed *you're stupid* expression remained trained on him as he spoke. "We spend as much time together now as we always did. It's just by video. I'll be there with you the whole way through. Anyway, we've only got a little over seven and a half months until I retire."

Robert nodded, knowing Landon spoke the truth. They had really committed to putting their relationship first and they had. They woke up together, fell asleep together, and talked as much as they possibly could. So, where did this insecurity come from?

"Besides, you're hot. The chicks and gay guys are gonna love you." Landon stood, resigned to what he felt was obvious. His guy kissed him again and slapped his ass as he started back to the table. "I should be the insecure one. I've gotta up my game to keep my man."

Since Robert couldn't seem to breathe without Landon with him, Landon should have no fear of any attention he garnered. "A million dollars, and she wants to shop it for more."

"Chump change for you, but for me, Daddy's gonna buy me something stupid expensive," Landon teased. Robert burst out laughing at the ridiculousness of those words. Nothing had changed between them regarding finances. Landon still lived off his income, even buying commercial flights himself to offset what he considered as Robert's waste. His husband was never going to allow Robert to buy him anything. "Listen to me, Daddy Warbucks. It feels like all this heartache of being apart has helped achieve a bigger goal. You've built something substantial, Robert. I'm proud of you."

"We built it—you and me. You pushed me and gave me the courage and confidence to try. You supported every inch of progress. You have such a way of knowing what works and what doesn't. We're a good team. I'm proud of us too."

Landon let him say the words without an exaggerated eye roll or some self-deprecating reply. *Shocking*.

The hush of the chaos in Landon's head allowed him to just enjoy the accomplishment. He didn't see how Robert kept giving him credit for anything, but he did love his life as much as he loved his man. So, he took his role in all this while thinking about the viewership of the web series. His handsome husband would have people tuning in just to watch him in action. Robert's easygoing attitude and the fun-loving way Robert had of laughing at his own mistakes mixed with all those engrained manners—yeah, grade A great video material, for sure.

Landon could see for himself that Robert had truly made his own name in the culinary world. Maybe his father had given Robert a leg up, but Robert had brought all media, from social to print, into La Bella Luna. Reservations were full months in advance. Celebrities stopped in to see what all the fuss was about then posted their praise online. Their upstairs dining/event room had parties reserving the space as far as a year out. Robert had created something special, and thanks to such a connected world, everyone got to see its success firsthand.

Landon just wished he'd thought of the idea.

"What about Autumn?" Landon asked, seeing the wheels in Robert's head still at work. Not sure if Robert plotted against or for the web series.

"Damn, I forgot to check again. I'm a horrible brother."

Now *that* he wasn't. Landon fought the smile as he sat down to check QuickBooks. Robert came toward him, taking the seat next to his—they did that, stayed glued to one another for the first twenty-four or so hours they were back together. He didn't know if Robert even noticed, but Landon had.

"Ask about Kylie coming over."

Their niece was three and a half years old and the light of Robert's world. When Robert and Kylie were in Minnesota together, at least once a week she had a sleepover. Sometimes those nights included him. Robert treated every interaction with Kylie as something special. They built castles in the living room, played games, and had tea parties with princesses and unicorns. Whatever Kylie wanted, they did, including ice cream sundaes for breakfast and a loop of the Disney movie *Frozen* playing constantly in the background as they covered their art in glitter.

"She'll spend a couple of nights here with us when Autumn goes into labor," Robert said, putting the phone on speaker mode. It didn't even ring before Autumn answered.

"I'm going in for a vote. What's up?" Autumn's harried tone had Robert shaking his head.

"We're checking on you," Robert answered quickly.

"Hi, Autumn," Landon added.

"As of this morning, I'm dilated to three. I've got to get these things done. Stay by your phone." Autumn disconnected the line.

Their silence lasted for several long seconds. He couldn't believe her tenacity. Landon's sister had been down for days before she finally had her second baby. "She's something else."

"Yes, she is. Just don't tell her. She'll get a big head."

Landon scanned Robert's face, looking for any worry. When Landon didn't see any, he went back to the task at hand, entering his security code to open his laptop. Maybe he and Robert could sneak in a quickie or two before the world required they leave the house.

Robert's bird chirping ringtone drew Landon's gaze to the

phone again.

When Robert said, "It's grand central station around here," Landon definitely agreed. Their morning had certainly gotten busy. "It's Sophia." He picked up his phone and pushed a button. "Hello."

Landon tried to refocus on QuickBooks, getting as far as opening the program before Robert's strong hand came to his thigh, squeezing.

"No kidding. That's fast." Robert started nodding happily at Landon, grinning broadly. "We have time right now. We're just waiting for Autumn to go into labor. Right, Landon?"

"For what?" he asked, having no idea how he should respond.

"Sorry, Sophia's found a potential egg donor for us. She's a first-year medical student at University of Minneapolis but lives local in Centerville, Virginia. She fits all your requirements that aren't necessarily mine." Of course, Robert got his little dig in. Landon wanted a blond-haired little boy—their little guy had been predetermined by something bigger than them. After they got him, Robert could have his way on finding donors closer to each other's looks. So, Landon gave a single nod to keep Robert talking. "Sophia's talked to her and she's available to meet. I say today since you're off and Autumn's holding her own."

Landon nodded again, because it seemed his standard answer for anything Robert-related, but finding a possible egg donor who matched all their requirements had happened awfully fast. Since he and Robert had first started seriously talking about having children and setting their timeframes to accomplish each step, Landon had had two requests.

One, Robert refrained from speaking doctor-speak. He wanted all conversations explained to him in layman's terms so he fully understood what they were doing.

Second, he didn't want to rush any part of this. He wanted to explore all their options before any decisions were made.

Landon had been surprised to learn that Sophia Richardson owned a fertility company in Minneapolis. She'd apparently spent her career helping couples achieve their family goals. His and Robert's initial conversation with her had only happened six days ago via video chat for him. How were they already meeting potential egg donors?

"He doesn't look well, but since this is all his idea, I'm going to wave that look off as nerves. Can you message me her information and I'll give her a call?"

His and Robert's gazes held. How had the tables turned so quickly, now Landon was filled with anxiety while Robert seemed cool, calm, and collected.

"Thanks, Sophia. I'll call you when I hear from Autumn." Robert ended the call while staring at Landon.

He used his super calm voice usually reserved for when Landon was ready to blow his stack about something Robert had purchased for him.

"Don't freak out. Just like you told me, we got this."

"I'm not freaked." Landon said that lie and rolled his eyes for good measure.

"Good. Go change. I'm starving. I'll see if she has time for lunch."

Landon nodded again, and shut the lid of the laptop, feeling very much like the wuss he was becoming.

Chapter 41

Landon sat back in the booth-style seating, trying to make more room for his bulky frame. Robert sat next to him, finishing off his plate of Pad Thai like a man who hadn't eaten in days. Maybe if they couldn't fit comfortably in a normal-size booth, Landon had hit the gym too hard. His clothes didn't fit him anymore either. He'd had to go a size bigger from all the lifting he'd been doing to kill time during Robert's absence.

Forgoing his meal, Landon lifted an arm to lay on the edge of the booth and across Robert's back. His mister looked over at him, those clear, blue eyes shining with love, and he moved in closer, flush against his side. The gesture of wanting to be nearer to him was sweet, and he tucked his arm around Robert's shoulder, keeping him right there. It helped ease his fear.

Before they ever got inside the building, while sitting in the vehicle, looking through the front windows of Ocha Thai Café, Landon saw that Stephanie met all his physical requirements of being their egg donor. She was tall, lean, blonde, and pretty in a classic kind of way, or maybe better said, in that Robert kind of way. Stephanie held herself with a poised grace that seemed natural, not forced, making her very comfortable to be around. After meeting her and going through his first round of questions—

the basics like who are you, why are you doing this, what's your nicotine usage, and what's your political affiliation—because that mattered in the Adams family—Landon had known they'd found their donor.

Robert though hadn't seemed to clue in on Landon's early decision. His mister inundated Stephanie with questions, going overboard on her and her family's medical history, their levels of education and again on their political affiliations.

When the questions ended, and they had maybe as long as a minute of silence, Stephanie dropped her hands to her lap and said, "If you guys chose me, I'll consider it an honor. Your schedule fits mine perfectly. Dr. Richardson told me you were looking for a fresh egg donation. I'm good with whatever you decide."

"You all done?" the waitress asked, reaching for his and Stephanie's plates.

"I am." Landon watched Stephanie turn a bright, friendly smile to the waitress. He really liked that maneuver, making sure everyone around her was respected and comfortable. Robert did that same thing all the time. Landon nodded, extending his plate.

"Did Sophia's firm talk to you about payment?" Robert asked and hurriedly added his last bite, encouraging the waitress to take his plate too.

"She did. You two are very generous. My family and I have worked hard to support me through medical school, your generosity will help. I'm willing to begin my clinical evaluations when I return to Minneapolis."

"So, money's your motivator in doing this?" Landon asked.

"No." She shook her head and looked down at her hands in her lap. "The truth is my older brother is gay. He's ten years older than me. His coming out happened when he was twelve years old and he didn't out himself. Times have changed and I understand they have, but his life hasn't been easy for him. It pleases me to give you two something like this. Especially now that I see it's you," she said, nodding at Robert. "It's my way of putting good out into the world."

"Thank you," Robert said, in his normally kind way. "What involvement do you want in our lives if we move forward?"

"I've thought about this quite a lot. I believe Dr. Richardson stayed in your life, is that correct?"

"She did and has. We always knew her and what she did for us, but my parents were my fathers." Robert seemed direct and clear in what he'd allow and not allow.

"I don't intend to stay in Minnesota after med school. I'd like to travel with a Doctors Without Borders type program, but I understand the value of staying in all your lives, at a distance. Is this the only pregnancy you plan?" she asked.

"No," Robert answered with certainty. "We'll have at least one more, most likely more."

"I'll let you decide my involvement. How's that?" Stephanie offered.

Robert seemed good with her answer, giving a firm nod. His hand came to Landon's thigh, giving a firm squeeze. "We need to talk more about it."

"Okay, well, it's been a pleasure to meet you. My brother's going to be excited I met you. Your father helped my brother," she added, explaining how she recognized Robert.

Robert was no longer dealing with all his guilt and depression. He seemed profoundly sincere when he said, "My father was a great man, one I aspire to be like every day. I hear things like what you've said quite a lot. What I can say, he helped me meet my husband and he guides my decisions to this day."

Robert's hand at his thigh gave another gentle squeeze. His loving gaze lifted to Landon. He couldn't help shifting the hand behind Robert's back to his head, moving his mister closer for a kiss on the lips.

Stephanie beamed at them then gathered her things and scooted out of her seat. "Thank you for driving all the way out here and thank you for lunch."

Robert pushed out of the booth, taking her hand in a shake. "Thank you for wanting to be a part of our journey. We need to talk, but we'll let you know either way." By the time Landon got to the edge of the booth seat, she lifted a hand to him and started out of the restaurant. Thankfully, Robert took Stephanie's seat across from him.

"So, what do you think?" Robert asked. The sparkle in his eyes and the way he leaned across the table were big indicators of his excitement.

"I like her. She fit every one of our requirements," he said honestly, finding no reason why he should say anything more. Between Robert and Stephanie, he could see a really great kid coming from the two.

"Me too," Robert nodded, steepling his fingers together.

"She's got a long way to go before we really know if she's truly a candidate, right? We need to check out her background and her mental soundness?" he asked, feeling like Sophia wouldn't have suggested her had she not already done those things.

"Yep, you've paid attention. I like her too."

"What happened to my lecture of not getting too excited and how we're not taking the first woman who steps up?" Landon reminded Robert with a playful tilt of his head.

"You don't agree that she seems perfect?" he asked as if there was no other choice. "Wait. For me, I'd still like to start with you."

Landon dropped his hand to the table in a hard whack, slicing through Robert's bullshit. "The vision. Remember the vision. We've been told what to do. You need to listen, featherman."

The bubble of laughter had Robert sitting back in his seat, teasing Landon. "At first, it was a dream, then a premonition. Now it's a vision and direction?" Robert's phone rang and he fished it out of his pocket. "It's Autumn."

Autumn's intense voice vibrated across the small, empty restaurant. Landon could hear every word clearly even though Robert hadn't put her on speaker.

"He's coming fast. Go get Kylie. She's at home with the nanny who leaves at *threee!*" She panted, and Robert did too, in unison with her. "Damnnn, this hurts."

"Keep breathing. You know what to do. Where are you?" Robert said firmly.

"I'm at the hospital. Where do you think I am!"

Landon raised his brows. He'd never done well with his sister shouting at him like that, but Robert stayed cool as he continued to ask the questions designed to care for his sister in the best possible way.

"Where's Cam?"

"He's asking terrible questions. You talk to him!" A rustling came through, and Landon had to lean across the table to hear the next line.

"Hello," Cam said, and Robert put him on speaker for Landon to hear.

"We're in Centerville. I'll go get Kylie and head your way. It'll be a couple of hours before we get there." Robert started edging out of the seat, and Landon followed, pulling his wallet free. He motioned for the waitress who nodded.

"This is gonna happen fast. I'll call you when he's born," Cam added.

"Let me know." Robert didn't argue with Landon paying for their lunch like he normally would. Instead, he dug for his keys as Landon went to cash out. "Meet me in the car."

Robert loved so completely. He was nervous and anxious, and Landon decided he should drive. Robert had a new nephew to fret about.

"Uncle Wobert!" Kylie squealed with excitement and jumped up, standing in the center of the leather barstool at the kitchen counter. She'd been in the middle of her snack when Robert and Landon entered the kitchen of Autumn's DC townhome. When he got within a few feet of her, she gave no warning before launching herself at him. He easily caught her, wrapping both his arms tightly around her. She did the same, hooking her little arms around his neck, and leaned in, touching her forehead to his. "I'm sick, Uncle Wobert."

He didn't move, not even an inch away from her, holding his precious niece close to him. "What have we talked about? You're supposed to tell me you're sick before you get in my face."

"Mama says it my sinusays." She leaned back and beamed proudly at him. "I've been using the handatizer like you said. The germs are all gone." As if his little bundle of energy had just seen Landon, she jerked her head his way, beaming while shoving the blonde wisps of hair out of her face. "Uncle Wobert misses you. I bet he's glad you're here."

"I'm glad I'm here too. Your mama's having a baby."

Kylie's face went through a range of emotions before she went utterly stiff in Robert's arms, indicating she wanted down. He obliged, placing her on her feet. She was off, tearing through the kitchen. Her sparkly shoes clomped on the hardwood floor as she ran through the house.

"She's been waiting for you to get here," her nanny, Lauren, said, taking his niece's half-eaten plate of crackers and apples to the sink.

"We were in Centerville when Autumn called. It couldn't have been fifteen minutes later that they called to say Avery had been born," Robert explained at the edge of the large center island. Landon took Kylie's vacated seat beside him.

"Avery, huh? They were on the fence on which of your father's names to start with," Lauren said. She'd been a godsend to the family. Lauren was young, in college for an early childhood degree, and eager to put all her training to the test with Kylie. They were perfect together.

"I think the deciding factor turned to age," Robert explained.

"He was the oldest out of my two fathers." The most perfect idea had Robert knocking Landon in the arm with his own excitement. "Maybe we can steal the name Kane out from underneath them."

"I'm ready Uncle Wobert." Kylie came back inside the kitchen with her jacket on, sequined unicorn backpack over her shoulders, and a baby-blue stuffed elephant in her arms. "Mama says to get my car seat out of the garage."

His efficient and sometimes sensible niece had him envisioning his sister to be just like Kylie at that age. His fathers had to have had their hands full with the two of them. No wonder his daddy wouldn't have any more children. Kylie had everything under control as she walked past Robert, taking Landon's hand and pulling him to his feet. "Bye, Lauren. I'm going to stay with Uncle Wobert and Uncle Lolo."

Robert had to mash his lips closed to keep from laughing. To Landon's horror, they had no idea how she'd created Lolo out of Landon, but it had somehow stuck. It looked like he'd be Uncle Lolo forever now. She guided Landon toward the garage door. It seemed she worked out the best options, getting her strong Uncle Lolo to pick up the car seat.

"Start the car so it's warm for her?" Landon said, over his shoulder.

He nodded, bending across the center island to see Landon taking the stuffed animal to hold as Kylie guided him through the kitchen. "You excited about your little brother?"

"Yes, but I'm the big sister. I'll always be bigger than him," she explained reasonably, causing Landon to laugh as he opened the door leading to the garage. When she brushed her hair away from her face, Landon looked over at him and winked.

"Bye, Lauren." Robert left the kitchen, heading straight out the front door to his waiting car.

He'd barely gotten the car warming when the garage door lifted. Landon came out, carrying the car seat in one arm, and Kylie and the stuffed animal in the other. She chatted endlessly to Landon. He sweetly nodded to whatever she said. By the time they got to the car, Kylie happily announced, "I get to sleep with you tonight, Uncle Wobert. Uncle Lolo said I could."

Robert lifted his brows to Landon, questioning that decision as he placed Kylie in the car first to get her out of the chilly October air then placed the car seat inside. "We can sleep in our clothes or on an air mattress next to the bed. It's reasonable since she'd be in a new place and she might be scared."

Robert's brow lifted a little higher, watching Landon try to figure out the buckles to the seat. "I always thought I'd be the one to spoil and you'd be the strict one."

Landon gave him a side smile. Letting Kylie take over, getting herself locked in, showing Landon how to work the car seat properly.

When she was strapped in, and he dropped down in the passenger seat, Landon said, "I've got a lot to learn."

"We'll figure it out," Robert said. "We always do."

"Let's go see my bwother." Kylie kicked her feet in her excitement as he backed out of the driveway.

Landon placed his forearm between his head and the headboard then repositioned his ass, staring at the television in his and Robert's bedroom. Robert lay on the other side of the king-size bed. He looked pretty comfortable with his head raised by several pillows and a bowl of popcorn balanced on his toned abs. He munched steadily, showing Landon his husband was well-acquainted with this position. Kylie lay between them, on her belly with her head closer to the foot of the bed. She had a smaller bowl of popcorn beside her and her gaze riveted to the television where *Frozen* played. She wore her Elsa sparkly blue gown and slippers, apparently the only thing packed inside her backpack, and her feet had a steady rhythm of kicking, one right after the other. This was the second time tonight he'd watched this animated movie.

"She likes it a lot," Landon whispered, bored out of his mind.

"You have no idea," Robert whispered, turning to show he wasn't quite so absorbed in the movie as he appeared. "I can recite the lines, sing all the songs, even do some pretty solid impersonations."

"Shh," Kylie said as if she might miss something special.

Landon cocked his head toward the door, urging Robert out. His mister nodded and shifted until he sat on the side of the bed. He placed a hand on Kylie's back.

"We're going to make more popcorn. Do you want some?"

She shook her head, her bowl still full.

"I think you're fighting sleep. It's well past your bedtime. You should try to go to sleep. We need to go see your brother again in the morning."

"Are you sleeping down there?" She pointed toward the ceiling, but he assumed she meant the twin-sized air mattress he'd inflated earlier. He suspected Robert planned to sleep in the guest bedroom tonight while he encouraged Landon to take the air mattress. They had a pending power struggle over that one.

"Yes. Now, go to sleep. I'm going for more popcorn." Robert took her bowl, stacking it on top of his then grabbed her drink. Landon was already at the door, watching their exchange. He had worried about the stairs with Kylie being new to their place, so he went to the store to find a moveable childproof gate to block it off. For Landon, it then became a death trap to navigate over it each time they needed to go down the stairs. It seemed so easy for an adult just to tumble over. Landon went first, hiking one leg over the gate then the other, glad he hadn't caught his junk on the metal frame this time like he had before, then trotted downstairs. Since Robert didn't yell out or roll down on top of him, he must have made it over the gate safely too.

"How can such a little girl be so much work?" Landon asked, grabbing one of Robert's IPAs from the refrigerator.

"They consume all your time." Robert went for the trashcan and stopped, lifting the still partially filled bowl to Landon. "Do you want some?"

"No, I'm done." Landon used a bottle opener to pop the cap, then took a long swig. Robert placed the empty bowls in the sink before going for Landon. His ass hit the counter as Robert slipped in between his parted legs. Robert wrapped his hand around Landon's holding the bottle, urging Landon to give him some.

"It's because I didn't set boundaries with her that she controls so much of my world. Our children will have a schedule to follow. Don't worry." Robert's explanation seemed more of an encouragement, as if Landon might be second-guessing his stance after tonight. He wasn't at all. His guy had such a nurturing side. He cared for everyone, anticipating and meeting every need. Landon couldn't wait to watch Robert father their children. He was born to be a family man.

"I've been thinking about Stephanie all day," Landon said and drained the rest of the bottle.

"Me too." Robert's lips pressed against his T-shirt covered pec.

"I held Autumn's little guy. It's the first time I've ever held a newborn like that before. I'm ready." He brought his hands to Robert's waist, sliding inside the waistband of his sweats. His skin was soft and warm, exactly what he craved when he reached down each ass cheek.

"I think we should look at anyone Sophia suggests, but I think Stephanie's the one. If everything holds together, she's exactly what I want in an egg donor."

"I liked her too. She seemed very balanced. I messaged Sophia to move forward with her. It'll take time, but we have time." Robert pressed against his body and tilted his head for a kiss. They had hoped for a little more time alone before Autumn went into labor. He could no more stop his hands from roaming Robert's warm skin than he could help breathing and pushed his palms under Robert's T-shirt.

"Good. Thank you," Landon said and kissed Robert, lingering over those fleshy lips. Man, he was glad Robert liked kissing, because he did too. After all these years, he could still get lost in Robert's lips.

"There's something else. I wasn't going to tell you for fear I was pushing you too fast, but Sophia's also found a potential surrogate."

Landon nodded again, the feeling of things happening quickly did give him a brief moment of anxiety, but with Kylie spending the day with them, Autumn giving him a new nephew, and his true belief things happened for a reason, Landon pushed away the negative worry.

"We'll need to talk to her. If she works, we'll have to reserve her time, but she's in Minneapolis, so there's that."

"Good. Then you can watch over her if she gets pregnant." Landon said the obvious positive. Robert wouldn't let anything happen to compromise the baby or the mother.

"You give me too much credit. I haven't practiced medicine in five years," Robert hedged, running his fingers up a trail to his shoulders then down again.

"You still got it. I like her living close to us, and I like knowing you're taking care of her. We can be more involved. I was reading about the bonding benefit for us if we go to doctor's appointments, especially the ultrasounds. It helps with the connecting…"

Robert's handsome face softened, and he nodded at Landon all doe-eyed, a slow smile spreading. "I'm glad you're researching and planning." Those perfectly formed lips puckered again. Landon kissed Robert, this time licking his way between his lips. "If we were alone, I'd show you how pleased I am, right here in the kitchen."

"Like that's anything new," Landon said with a distinct *pfft*. "I've been sucked off in about every inch of this house."

"Are you complaining?" Robert countered.

"Not at all."

Robert moved away, going for the refrigerator, pulling out a bottle of water, the small one with a straw for Kylie. "So, tell me about these sleeping arrangements. I spend twelve nights alone, and now we're in our home and I'm sleeping on an air mattress?"

"Or I can. She just feels more comfortable with you. I can take the guest room." Landon crossed his fingers, hoping Robert would bite in the direction he led.

"This wasn't what I'd planned," Robert said, leaning his hips against the counter beside him, crossing his arms over his chest. "She's fine sleeping in my guest room in Minneapolis."

Landon repeated the conversation she'd had with him while getting her car seat from the garage. "No." He shook his head just like Kylie had done to him. "She thinks of the guest room as her room in your house. She hasn't been here. She might get scared."

In the same simple tone, accentuating every word, Robert said, "I don't think that child's afraid of anything. Did Cam tell you she held a tarantula at zoo day with her school?"

Oh hell no. Landon shivered. Spiders were at the very bottom of his list of bugs he would ever deal with.

"She volunteered to hold it and named the damn thing. So next time, Kylie the fearless gets the guest room. I miss my man." Robert saved it with his last sentence. Even though he loved the little princess, Landon was already thinking of ways to get Kylie, the spider whisperer, back to her house. He missed his man too.

"You're being sweet."

"I'm being territorial." From upstairs, the credits to the movie began. "Let's go check on her then go make-out in the guest room." He clasped Landon's hand and started out of the kitchen. "I thought the gate was very thoughtful as long as I don't go headfirst over it myself."

"Yeah, I worried about that too. We'll leave the hall light on," he said, cocking his head to watch Robert's ass as they started up the steps.

Chapter 42

One month later

Robert, along with maybe ten others, all production staff and Helene, sat at a large round-top table in the upstairs event space of La Bella Luna where they had been since the early morning hours. The web series, *Cooking with Chefs*, began in the morning at six o'clock sharp to avoid interrupting or bothering the kitchen staff during their prep time. He'd made the decision to close during lunch hours on both Saturday and Sunday for filming. He worried about that decision, but it seemed best for right now. He had no way to measure what he'd gotten himself and the restaurant into.

The outside door opened, and Robert instinctively got to his feet, knowing Landon entered. "I'm sorry. I couldn't meet you at the airport."

"Am I interrupting?" Landon asked, his purposeful stride slowed as he came forward to meet Robert in the center of the room. "I can wait downstairs."

"No, we're done." He already felt like he'd let Landon down by not meeting him at the airport. No way would he have Landon leave.

These first moments together always tugged at his heart, putting his world right again, if only for the next couple of days. His hand came up, cupping Landon's neck, drawing him in for a soft, tender kiss that lingered a little longer than he'd intended. Something he'd do fifty times over the next couple of days to make up for the next twelve unbearable days when Landon left him again.

"I missed you."

The softening of Landon's face and the twinkle in his eyes spoke as loud as any words. Landon had missed him too. He gave Robert another peck and took his hand.

"We're far enough along that it's just getting redundant at this point. Let's be done for now," Helene said, drawing both his and Landon's attention to the table. There seemed to be a chorus of agreement and thanks from their production team. "We'll meet back here in the morning. The prep team has their marching orders."

"Remember the section I cleared in the walk-in cooler," Robert said. His hand tightened around Landon's when he felt him trying to move away.

Again, there was a chorus of comments, none really mattering. The entire team of people knew Landon, maybe by nothing more than nightly video chats, but his husband got fist bumps and pats on the back as they left. Helena though stopped to give Landon a hug.

"I'm glad you're here. Robert's nervous about tomorrow."

"I'm not nervous," Robert countered, completely lying, but feeling okay in the fib designed to build his confidence and spirit for the challenge ahead.

"I don't know why he's nervous. He's got his role down. He's the Laurel to your Hardy, right?" Landon said, giving his slapstick comedy comparison.

Where Helene laughed straight out loud, Robert gave him a hard side-eye, wondering how long he'd been holding that joke to say in front of both of them. "*Har har.* You had to go old school for that one."

"If I had more time, I could've done better," Landon teased, clearly proud of himself. "I'll never forget walking into Robert's always pristine townhome to find what looked like an explosion after Helene's first day with him. The destruction took days to clean."

He released Landon's hand and gave him a solid pat on the ass. "Don't tell our secrets. I'll lose street cred."

The round of laughter helped ease the uncertainty Robert had in this whole process. He really liked to control his surroundings. His philosophy had always been—throw enough time and money into things and the outcomes were predictable. Winning Landon over had placed a solid dent in his theory, but the rest of Robert's life ran smoothly under that mindset. Tomorrow though, he only had a minor say in how things happened. If this tanked, it could destroy all the progress he made in building La Bella Luna back to its original glory. He felt like such a fraud in this culinary world anyway…

"You're overthinking," Helene said, patting Robert's arm. He'd gone silent, lost in thought as the others left the room, and she saw right through him. The knowing look on Landon's face said he saw it too.

"You're right, and we have a surrogate to meet," Robert said instead of voicing all the self-disparaging thoughts he'd been thinking.

"I'll keep working on his self-confidence," Landon assured Helene as if those two were having a separate conversation right in front of him.

"He's going to see he had nothing to worry about," she said and started to turn away. "Be here at five in the morning. We'll do another run-through. You'll be ready."

Robert nodded, unreasonably relieved at the idea.

"We'll find our groove, and it'll be great."

When the door shut behind Helene, Landon came forward, taking him in his arms. "I missed you."

Any lingering doubts or thoughts outside of Landon vanished. He moved in, wrapping his arms around his husband. Landon was such a masculine man; his brawn increasing in size every time Robert saw him. He took in Landon's strong jaw, chiseled cheekbones, and smooth olive complexion. Landon was so beautiful, inside and out.

When Landon lifted his lips, a move Robert loved, he obliged with a kiss, sweeping his tongue deep into Landon's inviting mouth. More than anything, he wanted to be back in the penthouse, spending alone time with his husband. He breathed Landon in then once again claimed his sweet mouth.

The work/life balance Robert had created was designed with heavy work in mind to get him through the long, lonely times without Landon. Times that were getting longer and lonelier by the day. God, he missed this man. Their busy schedules now bled into their few spare hours of alone time. Between La Bella Luna's weekend rush and the web series, they had so little time to themselves. Now, what precious time did exist was being split to interview surrogates.

If they didn't leave now, they'd be late for their meeting with the third woman willing to help them have their children. Robert placed his palms on Landon's cheeks, holding him there as he dominated the moment, swiping his tongue deeply into Landon's mouth before pulling away. He watched Landon follow, wanting more as he ended the kiss, his husband's eyelids still closed.

"You're my world, Landon. I miss you so much."

"Then keep kissing me," Landon whispered, refusing to open his eyes. Robert grinned and forced himself away. Landon clutched at him to keep him there, grinding that heavy, thick cock into his.

He fought against his urge to give in to Landon's request. "We'll be late if we don't leave now. I should've picked you up and gone straight to meet her," he said and forced himself to pull away before his hard-on burst through his pants. He wanted nothing more than to get inside of Landon and lose himself in his husband's body, but time had slipped by on them. Robert went to the table, closing his portfolio and shoving it under his arm to free his hands to fix the hard-on in his slacks.

"After we're done, I want to go home so you can fuck me into the mattress," Landon growled in his deep sexy voice.

"We can't. I've got your suit here. We've got to come back and prepare for the mayor's election party. He's rented the whole place, remember?" A first for La Bella Luna. The press would be on hand, and the mayor planned to give his acceptance speech in this very room.

"Oh hell, I forgot." Landon dropped his hand to his tight jeans, pushing against his erection, trying to control the bulge Robert wished he had time to take care of himself. "Are we ready for everyone? Did I do everything you asked?"

Robert started for the door and Landon followed. Once outside, he locked the bolt and trotted down the stairwell.

"I believe you did. You always take care of everything. I never double check your work." When Landon didn't respond, it made Robert second-guess the decision, so he began asking questions. "You placed the food order—I saw the truck arriving earlier. No one's freaked out that they're missing something so that has to be right. Did you schedule the rental chairs and tables? The linens arrived earlier so I'm guessing you did. What about the flowers?"

"The mayor's team's handling the flowers," Landon said, stepping out under the porte cochere at the entrance of the restaurant. As if they had been called, the rental company's truck drove into the parking lot. They went for Robert's sports car, Landon dropping inside the passenger's side. "I believe the flowers are arriving at three."

"Good job," Robert said and pushed the button to start the car.

"I'd rather you show your appreciation by fucking me into the mattress tonight." Landon looked over at him with a sly look. "Like manhandling me until you get your way."

Robert dropped his sunglasses in place and put the gearshift in reverse, looking in the rearview mirror. "I think it'll probably be more like a blow job then fall asleep in each other's arms. They rented the restaurant until one in the morning. We have to be back here by four thirty. I've got to check the setup of our ingredients. I don't trust the production team like I had hoped."

"Robert, you're killing me," Landon groaned, his body slumping in the seat as his head rolled back and forth on the head rest. "I've been really planning on this…with you. I need you inside me."

"Sunday afternoon is all ours. It'll be our funday." Robert pulled the car into the traffic, dropping the sun visor down to block the sun shining right in his face. Landon didn't say anything more. Robert couldn't see how he could give in—not right now, no matter how badly he wanted to. Landon had insisted he do these things; this was part of it. Robert had told him it wouldn't be easy.

Even though Robert had every intention of making it up to his husband, he had to fight the urge to lean across the seat and kiss that pout right off Landon's handsome face.

Weird coincidences that often staggered Landon in his day to day life were in play right now. Scarlett, their third possible surrogate, sat across from them at a small table inside a coffee shop off the beaten path in Minnetonka, Minnesota. Landon had never ventured out this far, wasn't a hundred percent certain where they were, but it seemed reasonably close to Minneapolis and the hospital where Robert preferred to have their baby.

As with all their meetings, Landon stayed quiet and let Robert handle things. Instead of voicing his questions, he chose to watch and listen to her replies to Robert's inquiries. Both physically and mentally, she appeared ready to embark on this adventure with them. She was twenty-seven years old, worked in the health food industry, and sat on the board of the food bank. She had a six-year-old daughter and had been married seven years ago to her college sweetheart. Their pregnancy hadn't been planned. Neither was her husband's car accident over a year ago. They were swimming in healthcare debt. Since surrogacy was something she had always wanted to explore, now seemed the perfect time.

Yes, her history mattered, but Scarlett had sealed the deal with Landon the minute she took the seat across from them. His gaze fell to the inside of her wrist, where she had an intricately inked feather standing in stark contrast to her porcelain skin.

Since Scarlett sat across from them, Sophia had already screened and approved her. The feather tattoo tipped the scale in her favor. Apparently, Robert had thought so too. After the initial introductions, Robert asked questions as if it were inevitable that they'd work together.

"Do you have any other questions?" Robert asked Landon, the weight of his hand resting on Landon's thigh, drawing him back into the moment.

"Nothing more than I'd like to meet your family. It's not a rush, I think Sophia has met them, right?" Landon asked.

"If you're talking about Dr. Richardson, then yes. We've had home inspections, job references checked. They've interviewed my direct supervisor. They've talked to my daughter's school and some character references. Dr. Richardson is very thorough. She explained to me that you matter to her." She nodded as though saying if they mattered to Sophia, then they mattered to Scarlett too. That was another thing he liked: her positivity and willingness to help.

Robert did something Landon had never done in meeting any surrogate. "Sophia's my biological mother. She's been through all this personally. She takes such care with all their clients. I couldn't have asked for better than her and her firm."

"I did check you two out before I agreed to this meeting. I wondered if Dr. Richardson was involved in your birth," she asked.

"I, of course, don't remember that time." Robert gave a throaty chuckle and a playful squeeze to Landon's leg. "But my fathers would talk about the relationship they shared with Sophia throughout the pregnancy." Robert hooked a thumb between him and Landon. "We'd like to be involved, attend doctor appointments—"

"And all the ultrasounds. I think I want one or two of those 3D ultrasounds," Landon interrupted, seeing what the baby looked like fascinated him.

Robert nodded, giving him the where-had-that-come-from face. He got that same look a lot from Robert, and said, "Correct, we want to be very involved."

"I hope you'll be," she said. "If you select me, I'll take time off work and can be available anytime you want to check in."

"Great, let us talk and we'll be in touch. I think it's safe to say we should schedule time to meet your family." Robert looked at Landon for confirmation, and he nodded. "I'll also have our legal team reach out to you. Make sure we're all on the same page financially."

"Great. Thank you for considering me. I'm excited to work with you two." Scarlett gave them both an excited smile— Landon loved her genuineness—before she reached for her purse and jacket. They had some talking to do, but it sure appeared as if they'd found their surrogate.

When she handed over cash to pay her portion of the tab, Landon was sold right there. Literally everyone expected Robert to pay. Of course, his husband did so happily. Just like he refused Scarlett's money. Robert understood his good fortune, but it helped Landon's heart to see the effort she made to not take advantage.

Once Scarlett left, neither he nor Robert made a move to follow her out. They watched her through the front window all the way to her car. Landon broke the spell by saying, "I like her."

"Me too. The feather was a nice touch." Robert's casual demeanor showed none of the intensity of the stare pinning

Landon in his seat.

"You noticed that? I had to force myself not to tell her she was hired on the spot," Landon said with a chuckle.

"Me too. I think she's our woman." Robert reached for the tab and signaled the single waitress working the small area. "Let's meet her family next time you're here. Until then, I'll have Autumn's firm reach out to them. I'll get her an attorney too."

When the check and the credit card were handed to the waitress, Landon said another thing he'd been considering while trying to decide how good a father he'd actually be. "We're gonna be parents. It's a good thing I've settled down since I met you. I used to be pretty hot-headed. I think I'm close to ready to do this."

"Used to be?" Robert blurted pointedly, showing his serious doubt in Landon's words.

"You didn't know me before," he said and lifted his arm off the back of Robert's chair. Since the accusation in Robert's words didn't go unnoticed, Landon eased his hand up to mess that perfect model swoosh thing his hair did naturally. His husband didn't like that move one bit, never did. Within two seconds, Robert finger-combed his hair back in place as he ducked away to sit on Scarlett's side, knowing Landon would do it again. "At least I'll be a parent before I'm forty." Another teasing point. Robert turned forty next year. Landon wasn't far behind him, but like Kylie had schooled them, Robert was always going to be the oldest no matter what.

"Stop talking about being forty. You're such a killjoy." Robert rose from his seat, reaching for his jacket, looking disgruntled as hell. It made Landon insanely happy, and he promised himself only twenty-five more age digs before their big day. Robert's phone rang as he scribbled his name at the bottom of the tab. Landon reached for the cell, seeing Kennedy's name flash on the screen.

"It's your grandmother," he said, sliding the phone over.

"Answer for me." Robert stepped away, bringing both hands

to his hair again, quickly smoothing it into place. Only because they were this far into their relationship did Landon not roast Robert, teasing him for worrying so much about his hair.

"Hi, Nonnie," he answered, getting to his feet. "It's me, Landon."

"Honey, how did it go today? Did you like her?" Nonnie's age could be heard in her voice, her tone a little lower and softer, but her mind was still sharp as a tack. Her timing was so on point that he looked over his shoulder to see if she had a surveillance crew monitoring their activities.

"We just finished meeting her. How do you know these things?"

"It's a skill you'll learn once you have children." She laughed, a sinister sounding chuckle, making him believe he might someday have her skill. "What did you think?"

"I think we liked her. Right, Robert?"

Robert agreed then nodded them to the door.

"We want to meet her family, but we think she's the one unless something major happens."

"Good, I was afraid you were being too picky with the first two." Kennedy held nothing back. She spoke her mind a lot more freely these days. "Now, remember, I'm not coming there for Robert's television debut tomorrow." She insisted YouTube was television because it was on a screen. "You wish him good luck for me. I'm sending flowers. Put them in the kitchen somewhere so I can see them."

"Yes, ma'am," he said, following Robert out the door.

"You know I don't like *ma'am*. It makes me feel old."

Landon laughed at her serious scolding.

"You be safe going home on Sunday. Tell Robert to call me Monday morning and not to forget. I want to catch up."

She disconnected the call and he handed the phone to Robert once inside the car.

"I'm to put the flowers she's sending over in the camera's

range tomorrow. She's something else."

"You're just now seeing that?" Robert asked, looking at him as if he were crazy. Landon just shook his head and prayed he and his husband made it to her age.

Chapter 43

April 2019

Robert tucked his hands in his slacks pocket and leaned against the wall of one of Andrews Air Force Base's many event centers. He did his best attempt at being a wallflower, blending in with a sea of military uniforms. He'd opted for a Kiton gray two-piece suit for today, hoping to keep from standing out. Not that he would necessarily, but occasionally, in these types of military settings, his father's memory could hijack the event. He didn't want that to happen. This was Landon's day. His last big hoorah. Landon's retirement ceremony and luncheon.

From here, when he and his honey left this celebration, they would board a plane to Minnesota to begin their lives together again. His haggard heart didn't even know what to make of such a thought for fear of something presenting itself as an obstacle, keeping Robert just shy of all his dreams coming true.

Robert looked over to see Norris, Landon's friend, walking up to him. Robert extended a hand in greeting.

"Russo said he's on the next flight out," Norris said, thumbing over his shoulder to indicate Landon.

Norris was one of the few friends of Landon's who Robert had really gotten to know well. He had spent time with Norris on every one of his trips to Oklahoma then again when Norris received his change of service orders, sending him to Andrews. Out of a need to keep Landon from being too lonely, Robert had offered Norris their guest room until he found a place to stay. The deep friendship had grown from there. Robert and Landon had even extended an open invitation to Norris and his wife, Shelly, to visit them in Minnesota anytime they could. He really liked this man.

"He says his shit's already gone. Y'all didn't waste any time."

"No. You know how lovesick I can get." Robert had sent packers to move Landon's belongings from the house over two weeks ago. He was antsy as hell to have Landon in Minnesota, making his mister live out of a suitcase until today. Norris burst out a loud laugh at Robert's honesty, turning heads their way.

"I think that's more Russo. I'll never stop teasing him over video calling you every night for hours." Norris just shook his head and leaned back against the wall with Robert. "I've never seen anything like that before."

"Remember I was on the other end of that video call. I like Landon a whole lot." Robert knew he was stingy with the time he allowed anyone else to intrude on. He just loved his husband so much, and a long-distance relationship had been hard work. Harder than he'd ever realized. Luckily, none of their passion had faded or settled for him. He'd learned to compartmentalize his heartache every time he had to leave Landon. It meant all the desperate feelings of longing and need were still there and didn't stop until they were back together again, but he could work on them one at a time.

"You can tell. I'm heading out. I wanted to say *hi* and *bye*. We're gonna miss Russo around here."

Robert nodded. "Tell your wife I said hello," Robert added and reciprocated the friendly handshake again.

"She watches your YouTube channel. She wanted me to tell you that you're killing it. She leaves comments and subscribed.

She's making everyone she knows subscribe." Norris rolled his eyes, but Robert loved hearing every one of those words.

"I knew I liked her," Robert teased, a grin pulling at his cheeks. No matter what anyone said, Robert was no natural behind the cameras, but his editors were magic. He and Helene had come off as they had hoped to, friends who loved to cook together. Their subscribers had hit one hundred fifty thousand within the first week of the first video dropping and had grown steadily since then. "Please tell her *thank you*, and I'll send her the cookbook. *And* to keep up the good work. We appreciate her positive feedback."

"Will do. Tell Russo bye." Norris left, and Robert turned back toward the thinning crowd. Landon captured all his attention, strolling purposefully toward him. His husband looked so distinguished and striking in his service uniform. Everything but Landon faded into the background as his husband's cocky grin slid into place. Damn, he couldn't wait to peel that uniform off him.

"You're so fucking hot," Landon growled, still feet away. "You got a haircut. I like the angle of your swoosh. I can grow a swoosh now too." Landon walked straight into Robert's chest and shamelessly took his lips in front of anyone who happened to be looking their way.

Nothing had changed, outside of Norris, Robert hadn't ever become a part of Landon's military life. This had been one of the very few events he'd attended with Landon. When they were together like this, they usually refrained from any sort of PDA. Robert had resigned himself to that fact long ago, because he and Landon were kissers in normal situations. They touched and kissed all the time when home, making this kiss in this environment more significant than the thousands they had shared before in private. Moreover, the air around Landon seemed overall lighter, his mood brighter. The teasing attitude and pep in his step eased some of Robert's worry over the difficult transition some service members experienced when leaving the military.

"I meant what I said during my ceremony. Your being patient

with me and letting me finish this career when you so clearly had a much bigger plan really means everything to me."

Robert grinned. Happiness flooded him, sending him floating into sensory overload. The words along with the little puffs of breath from Landon warmed his soul.

"You ready?" Landon asked, his gaze refocusing on Robert's lips.

"I love you," Robert whispered.

"I love you. Let's go start our life together." Landon kept hold of his hand, drawing him to the door.

"Did you get your service medal? I want to get it framed."

"It's in my pocket." Landon's grip on his hand changed, switching Robert's hand to his other before stopping in the threshold. Landon's grin grew bigger as he stepped into the room and lifted his hand for one last salute. He received wild cheers, cat calls, and loud whistles in return. Landon turned away, stepping back toward Robert, wrapping an arm around his waist. They took long strides down the hall. "Let's go home."

Robert followed behind Landon, moving past him when he entered the kitchen of the Minneapolis home. "Now remind me why we needed to pay to have a four-and-a-half-year-old truck shipped here?"

"First of all, we didn't have to pay a dime; the military covered all the cost. Second, we just left your little swimmers behind to begin the fertilization process, and you're thinking about my truck?"

Robert seemed so indifferent to something Landon had incredible anxiety over. Robert reached for a coconut water then slapped his ass and left him standing in the center of the kitchen. "Speaking of leaving the guys behind, do I need to suck you off now to pay you back, or can you wait until we get home tonight? It sucked not being able to have sex on your retirement night. I'm sorry it worked out that way."

Since Landon hadn't had what he considered real sex in weeks and had only been in Minneapolis less than twelve hours, he assumed he'd at least get a quick blow or hand job, but Hurricane Robert had every one of their minutes scheduled before they left in forty-eight hours for their trip. A trip Robert had also planned in meticulous detail.

Landon preferred to stay home. He had a deep desire to find his way in his new life. He wanted to settle down, stop traveling so much, and plant his roots into Minnesota soil. Well, unless his new life was this life where literally every minute was timed to the exact moment. In that case, he may as well be in the military.

"I think you should've just sold it and bought something new here," Robert called out.

Landon narrowed his eyes, feeling the slow burn of irritation building. He followed after Robert, trailing through their penthouse. How the hell did he, a small-town boy from Texas, live in a penthouse? Instead of voicing the ridiculousness of him being so hoity-toity now, Landon tried to tamp down the frustration growing inside him. "That's something a rich kid would say. My truck's still in good condition," Landon replied, turning the corner into their bedroom. Robert had already made it through to the bathroom.

"You're a rich kid, remember? Daddy's got the sweet YouTube deal." Robert stepped back inside the bedroom, one of his many handmade suits on a hanger. A pressed dress shirt and matching silk tie in the other hand. He carefully placed them on the bed before untying the drawstring knot in his joggers. "You up for a quickie, rich boy?"

Landon let go of his pent-up breath, the tight muscles in his neck had him rolling his shoulders. He found he didn't want to act on Robert's offer which was weird. When had he ever turned down Robert?

Robert narrowed his gaze and slowed after the initial push

of his sweats down his legs as he tried to read Landon. "What's wrong?"

"You seem so unfazed about what we're doing with the egg donor and the surrogate. Like it's no big deal. They harvested her eggs and you just left your sperm. It's a big deal, Robert. We have three days for fertilization. Have you talked to the surrogate or her doctors? Is she ready?" Landon asked, saying a bunch of words that didn't speak to the true reason of his irritation.

"Of course, I talked to her, Landon. What's causing this uncertainty?" Robert asked, laying his sweats on the end of the bed, standing in his boxers, looking at Landon as if he had all the patience in the world to wait for his silly questions.

"I'm not uncertain. I just feel like we're rushing through everything right now when we probably shouldn't be." All right, that might be closer to his truth, but still not hitting the true cause of his anger.

"How do you figure? We've been waiting to begin all this. I wasn't the one who wanted to start this directly following your retirement. This is what you wanted." Robert grew silent, his head drawing back, blue eyes locked on his. Robert's face darkened as his brows lowered. "You do want this, right?"

"What's that supposed to mean?"

"You wanted me to take care of every detail. The egg donor looks like me. Norris moved in with you and you didn't make it back for the family visit. I've gone to every procedure, handled all the contracts. I've done it all, and you barely squeezed in time to spend more than a few days here over the last few months. Are you trying to tell me something?" Robert asked.

The last four months had kicked Landon's ass. Transitioning his position hadn't come easy and keeping up with his nightly responsibilities for La Bella Luna took so much of his time. Besides, he wasn't the one who'd offered Norris a place to stay, Robert had done that shit without even asking him. Landon was at a complete loss as to what Robert was implying, except he hadn't missed all the shade thrown his way in his mister's tone.

Landon's frustration boiled to full-on anger. If Robert could talk to him in a shitty tone, so could he. "What exactly are you asking me, Robert?"

"Are you planning to leave me?" It seemed neither of them expected that question. The pain on Robert's face instantly made Landon feel like a heel. "Because if you are, you're going to have a fight on your hands. This whole life is for you, for us. Everything I do every day is for you. I work myself into the ground—"

"Hush, Robert." He rushed to his husband, his hands lifted in surrender. "No, of course I'm not. I'm overwhelmed that's all."

Robert took a step back from him, and that twisted Landon's heart.

"Seriously, I had a moment of not understanding where I fit in. That's it. You have this life that's carefully planned. I didn't see where I fit in, that's all."

"Every single thing I've done is for you. For us. I'm busy, Landon. It's been hard managing it all without you. My schedule's full." Robert took a step backward again, and he still looked so hurt. "I took care of the in vitro because it's something you said you wanted. I've kept my schedule full to help you with your retirement. I worry how you'll cope with the military not at your back. You insisted on staying enlisted when all I wanted was for you to believe I could care for us, that I could make you happy. I've wondered if the Air Force mattered more than me—"

"Never more than you!" Landon shot back and broke through the invisible barrier holding him back.

"Stop, Landon." Robert's palm pushed against his chest. "I worry you'll miss the Air Force and your buddies and want to go back there. Transitions are hard on military men. I want you to see we have a good life waiting here for you. I'm fucking trying so hard to make you happy."

"I'm sorry." Landon shifted forward, pulling Robert's stiff body to his. "I guess I was shit at showing you how much you meant to me. You'll always be first in my life. You've been first since you walked into my hospital room in Germany and gave me a heart attack or at least I thought I must've had one. I appreciate what you've done. I was stupid and afraid. I felt like you had a whole life without me."

Robert's gaze mapped his face. He could almost see his words fighting for control in that handsome head. When Robert didn't immediately speak, Landon knew he had to do something to stop Robert's runaway doubt in him.

"I've been thinking about something I haven't said. I don't know if it's the right time or not, but I don't want our children's names to be hyphenated."

"Landon, it's not the right time." Robert tried to pull away, but he held on tight. "I knew it was hard for us to be apart, but I always thought we were solid. I don't want to have children if you're not my partner and my co-parent. This wasn't a path I'd choose by myself. I'm doing all this for you. I need to put a stop to everything if you're thinking of leaving me."

"Robert, please stop. I'm saying we all need to be Adams. I think it'll be easier for our children in the long run. I'll be an Adams too. Just don't tell my parents." The idea that he had caused Robert this much pain had him desperately seeking forgiveness with a kiss. He lifted his lips, knowing Robert wouldn't deny him.

"Landon…" Robert looked skeptical.

"Let it go," he said. "I'm an ass. You know I'm hotheaded. I get territorial about you. I like to occupy your time." He lifted on his toes to plant a kiss on Robert's lips. When Robert hedged, he slid his hand up over his husband's heart, letting his palms rest there. The frantic thump had slowed to a strong, steady beat. Landon tried for a bit of humor to help move them back in the right direction. He caressed Robert's cheek as he said, "Don't worry. You can make it up to me tonight."

"Make what up?" Robert asked, his tone outraged, but hopefully lighter.

"Saying I put the military first. I never have. I'll fuck that thought right out of you tonight if you can pencil in the time."

The *pfft* Robert gave made him smile. His husband had tossed the gauntlet with that grunted response. Fine, he looked forward to being fucked into the mattress as long as it was Robert doing the pounding.

Chapter 44

"You made time for me," Landon teased. "It's two o'clock in the morning."

Robert followed him inside their bedroom, shrugging off his suit coat, his tie already in the pocket, and draped it across a side chair. He watched Landon, his ass accentuated by his strut across the room, as he pulled the tails of his dress shirt free then worked the buttons undone.

"Hang on, babe," Robert called out as Landon headed toward the master bathroom, his own suit coat and tie dangling from his arm. "Stay in here."

Landon tossed a sexy smirk over his shoulder. Those tired eyes held a glint of excitement. Robert grinned, tugging the dress shirt off his body. They both tossed their stray clothing toward the chair, who knew if they'd succeeded in hitting their target. Robert circled Landon's waist with his arms. Landon stepped completely into Robert and slid both arms suggestively around his neck. They stared at one another. Those dark brown eyes were so alluring that Robert always lost himself in their depths. No more words were spoken. Robert stole his husband's mouth, determined to show Landon exactly how much they both needed this.

Robert traced Landon's lips with his tongue then pushed past the sweet flesh to delve inside his mouth. Landon's tongue met his and the heated kiss deepened. Robert pushed his hand between their bodies and worked quickly to unfasten his lover's slacks.

Landon broke from the kiss to gasp for breath as Robert slipped his hand inside his lover's underwear. The slacks hit the floor, the underwear followed, and Robert ran his thumb over the sticky head, curling his fingers around the thick shaft. A moan vibrated in Landon's chest as he pumped his fist over his husband's rigid cock. He couldn't help but grin when Landon thrust his hips, never missing a beat.

His body responded instantly to Landon's sounds and the sweet smell of his arousal. Landon had been feeling neglected. Robert had felt the same way. But this…this right now had been worth the wait.

"I know you're tired, and I know it's been hard. All of this…it's been a lot to deal with. I just want to make love to you tonight. I don't want any more distractions. Just me and you, Landon." Robert felt the shiver break out over Landon's body as he whispered the words against his love's ear.

Robert mouthed the soft skin along Landon's neck, nipping the warm flesh between each word. Landon responded by dropping his head back between his shoulders, giving full access by exposing his flesh.

Landon fumbled for Robert's buckle, working the belt free. He found his way inside his slacks and pushed them down his legs.

"I wore these just for you …" He spoke into Landon's hair, closing his eyes as he breathed in the intoxicating scent of his husband. Landon drew back to look at him and lifted a brow before grinning and trailing his fingers over the backside of the special underwear Robert had chosen to wear.

"Fuck, Robert. Had I known you were wearing assless underwear, I'd've tagged—"

Robert ran his tongue around the shell of Landon's ear then flicked the tip into the opening, drawing a deep moan, and halting Landon's words. He managed to undo a few buttons of Landon's shirt as his lips found Landon's again. He worked the tailored shirt over Landon's head. Their shoes were kicked off and undershirts stripped away.

Landon forced his tongue into Robert's mouth. They rutted against each other like teenagers on prom night. Even pressed head to toe against Landon, he still couldn't get enough. Landon cupped and molded Robert's hard cock on the outside of his jockstrap. As good as it felt, he hurt to have the man's hands on him. Finally, Landon pushed his palm inside, shoving the material down his legs. "Wear these tomorrow night."

"You approve?" Robert asked, closing his eyes at the wanton pleasure of pushing his cock through Landon's fist, canting his hips, chasing the pleasure Landon's hand provided.

"Oh yeah," Landon whispered. "I've missed you." His body vibrated with pent-up anticipation as the words settled into his heart.

"I've missed you. I love you."

"I never want to live away from you again. I want us to stay like this forever," Landon sweetly confessed, running his cheek and nose against the strands of Robert's hair.

Robert wholeheartedly agreed. Landon was his forever, his soul mate. He'd only made it through the last year and a half on the promise to himself that he'd never be without Landon again. He was so lost to the man in his arms that his knees were weak. Robert wasn't entirely certain if he was supporting himself or if it was Landon holding him upright.

"Me too."

Landon released the grip he had on his cock, sliding his palms up Robert's stomach and chest. Beautiful brown eyes locked onto his.

"I want you in me so bad," Landon whispered. Those tempting lips curled into a smile as Landon's big body pushed solidly against his.

"I think we can arrange that." Robert's legs hit the back of the bed, and he pulled Landon down on top of him, their lips met quick and hard. He ate at Landon's mouth, dominating and submitting simultaneously. Tongues and teeth clashed, dancing and devouring one another as he coaxed Landon forward, guiding them to the center of the bed.

Robert flipped his husband to his back and stared at the beautiful man beneath him. His world tilted on its axis. Robert ran his hand through Landon's short dark hair, gripping the back of his head and drawing them together. He attacked Landon's mouth again. Landon squirmed underneath him, driving him mad with the urgent thrust of his hips.

"Stop fucking with me," Landon demanded as he wrenched free from the kiss, arching his hips forward against Robert's rock-hard arousal. Robert chuckled as he stretched, reaching for the bottle of lube he'd placed on the nightstand. Landon's mouth never left his body, his lips and tongue laying claim to whatever part they could reach.

Landon reached for Robert as he sat back, situating himself between Landon's parted thighs. He just grinned down at his husband, ignoring his protest, and toyed with his dick, rubbing his thumb over the tip, spreading the moisture across the sexy flesh. Robert bent forward and placed a loving kiss on the broad head. He licked around the slit and moaned at the salty essence that coated his tongue. He stroked Landon, adding the little twist at the end that he knew drove his lover insane. Like he'd hoped, the effects were immediate. Landon's body arched, his feet digging into the mattress.

"That's it… Yes!" Landon cried out. Robert stilled his strokes and tightened his grip on the base of Landon's cock when he thought he might come.

Landon spread his legs wider, drawing them up and bending them at the knees giving him more access to his open body. Robert took advantage and used his free hand to cup Landon's balls, slowly rolling them in his palm before sliding his fingers over his lover's perineum, teasing his tight rim with the pad of his index finger.

"So beautiful. Want in here so bad, Landon." Robert's dick wept from his desire to push into that pink puckered flesh.

"Then fuck me, Robert."

"I thought you'd never ask." He let go of Landon's cock long enough to open the bottle of lubricant and coat his fingers. The time apart hadn't dampened his need for Landon.

"Want you deep in me." Landon's plea had him moving to push a finger into his husband as he watched the expression on his gorgeous face. He easily found his prostate and teased the fleshy bundle at the same moment he gripped Landon's cock, stroking him hard and fast.

He knew exactly what he was doing to Landon, and he loved that he could still make him crazy with need. Landon lifted his hips, groaning loudly. He worked his husband until he had three fingers sliding in and out of his heated channel with ease.

Robert kept a firm grip on Landon's cock as he sucked him down his throat, deep throating him in one dip of his head. Landon's hips bucked; his fingers tangled in Robert's hair, forcing him further down his rigid cock.

Landon gasped for air as that broad head hit the back of Robert's throat. He pumped his fingers in and out of his husband's ass, Landon's moans shooting straight to his balls as he continued to play.

"Now…" Landon growled, his hips punctuating the singular demand.

He broke free of his husband's desperate hold, taking a second to catch his breath. Landon always got him so worked up that he wasn't even sure he wouldn't come the second he sank into his love. The man was so damn sexy.

"I need to feel you, Robert," Landon cooed and frantically pulled him up his body. "I can't believe we're gonna be able to do this every day." The grin on Landon's face grew seconds before their mouths met and the insistence of Landon's tongue forced him to open. Landon probed deep into his mouth. Robert answered by kissing him with all the passion flowing through his veins.

He shoved back on his heels, coating his cock with lube, positioning himself against his husband's rim. His gaze locked onto Landon's as he pushed against the tight muscle resisting his advances. Landon moaned as Robert pushed into his welcoming heat.

Landon gasped at the burn as Robert slid into him with a forceful roll of his hips. The move nearly stole his sanity. Robert's thick cock stretched him perfectly, sizzling through every nerve ending in his channel. He relaxed his body and clung to his husband's shoulders, staring into his intense blue eyes.

Robert remained frozen above him. He was impatient, had waited too long. Landon wanted to feel every inch of the man he loved pounding him into the mattress just like he'd been promised. He rolled his hips, encouraging Robert to move.

It didn't take Robert long to catch on and slowly start to drag his cock along his passage. The fullness eased as his husband withdrew and returned as Robert pressed back in. The heated desire in his eyes warmed Landon's body in a flush from the bottom of his feet to the top of his head and all the hard parts in between.

When Robert started to withdraw, Landon's breath caught, and just when he thought Robert was going to break their contact, his husband sank back deep into to his body, forcing his breath out in a needy moan. His ass clutched around Robert's length.

Robert's hips caught their rhythm and reminded him with every thrust just who he belonged to. He lifted his hips higher, opening his body for his lover. The friction of their union made his dick leak like a faucet, dripping on his stomach. He lifted his hips to meet each one of Robert's torturous thrusts. Those intense blue eyes never left his as Robert's body owned him.

Robert leaned in, taking his mouth in a slow, demanding kiss. Tenderly and thoroughly Landon slid his tongue against Robert's.

That mouth, that fucking tongue, working him.

"You're so hot. You look so good with me fucking you." Robert growled, his blue eyes dark and heavily hooded. He lifted his head, watching as Robert worked his body over. Robert always knew what he needed. Nothing ever felt as right or as grounding as being with his husband. So perfectly whole and complete in Robert's arms.

"I love you so much, Robert." He sank his fingers into Robert's thick blond hair and pulled him down, capturing his mouth. Their tongues probing slow and deep. Robert's lazy kisses drugged him, his lover's sweet taste lingering on his lips as he drew back to gaze into those blue eyes. Emotions flooded him, overwhelming him. His dreams were now a reality because of this man. Everything had been put into place. They would hopefully be a family in the next year.

"I'll love you forever," Robert whispered into his mouth, picking up the lazy roll of his body until he pounded into Landon, sharp and thorough, making his body ignite like a fucking rocket set to take off. Landon tilted his hips, rocking back and forth, as Robert pistoned in and out of him, hitting his spot with practiced skill, driving him closer to the edge with each dip of his hips.

He writhed as Robert's weight shifted and his skilled hand pushed between their bodies and claimed his dick, stroking him in time with those powerful thrusts. Robert's grip tightened and his thumb spread the moisture leaking from his slit across the head of his cock, stopping only briefly to delve inside his slit, teasing. His eyes rolled back in his head and a moan escaped his lips. He really wanted to draw it out longer, fought hard to draw it out longer, his toes curled from the heated pleasure boiling in his balls. It wasn't going to happen.

"Gonna come." Waves of heated energy spiked in his spine. His heart drummed in his chest. His balls drew up tight against his body. Pleasure imploded to gather energy, incinerating him from the inside out, in the promise of an impending explosion of passion.

Intense heat shot down his spine, engulfing him, stealing the oxygen from the room and robbing him of his breath as his dick twitched in Robert's grip. His eyes slammed shut.

"I can't hold…" was all he managed before his ass contracted and sent him into speech-stealing, mind-blowing spasms.

"You're mine," Robert choked out in deep punishing grunts, intentionally pegging Landon's prostate and making the orgasm piggyback with another. Landon's body vibrated with toe-curling aftershocks. Robert plunged in one last time, then his whole body tensed. His ass continued to clench and constrict while his husband's dick twitched inside him, flooding his channel with liquid fire.

His body involuntarily shuddered at the amazing feeling of erotic rapture holding him hostage. His ass tightened around Robert one last time before Robert collapsed on top of him. Landon gasped for breath, his heart racing so fast it thundered in his ears. He pressed his lips to Robert's sweaty skin, willing his heart rate to slow. He was dizzy with pleasure, his body sated and heavy with contentment.

They lay there, totally blissed out, for several seconds. Robert's full weight kept him from floating away with all the endorphins drifting around in his body. Neither spoke. Landon loved these moments of just being with his husband, knowing at least for right now, they were one.

Robert's sweet lips brushed against his, and his husband's soft dick slipped out of him, drawing him from his thoughts. Their bodies were no longer connected physically, but their souls were and would be forever. He loved his man. He loved the life they shared and the future they were building. His heart filled with joy as he thought about the journey they were about to begin.

Chapter 45

Three weeks later

This shit was unbelievable! Robert loved him and clearly intended on spoiling him. How had he never recognized the greatness of being pampered? After spending ten days on the Mediterranean coast and touring the breathtaking Tuscany area where he wasn't sure anything could beat the beauty of Florence, they were now in Rome, and Landon's inner warrior couldn't be happier. Of course, his legs were sore from all the walking they had done, but he had found his promised land—if Rome could be such a thing. Landon had taken a thousand pictures already, marking every inch of the landscape they'd covered.

From the quaint hotel Robert had booked for them close to the Piazza Navona, to the Pantheon, Trevi Fountain, and all the steps up the Spanish Steps, he had lived in the moment, wanting to experience it all. The food, the smells, the sounds, and energy—it was so damn amazing just being there in the first place, let alone physically standing in the same spots he'd read about in history books. Today might have hit an all-time best day of his life, well except his wedding day and the day he met Robert. Today garnered the third spot as they toured the Colosseum and Roman Forum. What he wouldn't give to throw Robert over his shoulder and hop back in time to when the Roman Empire was at its prime.

Landon had assigned picture duty to Robert, and he had spent the entire tour filming their tour guide, Marcelo, from What a Life Tours, who had also been born in Houston, Texas. Ironically, his and Marcelo's parents knew one another as both were transplants from Italy. All Landon could say was that he wished he'd paid better attention to learning Italian. He could see himself living in this country someday.

"What're you thinking?" Robert asked quietly, passing him as they moved forward with the group. The crumbled white marble pillars of the once beautiful structures surrounded them like skeletons of the past, each with its own story to tell.

"I'm thinking I can't wait to watch this video tonight and see everything I missed."

Robert must have taken his words to mean a job well done on his part, because he kissed Landon's shoulder before he moved around him to walk as close as they could to the ancient Roman ruins. Robert looked over the map while Landon stood there soaking in the history, letting his soul fill with the idea of his ancestry on this very land thousands of years ago. Of course, he had no idea of the truth of what they did, but he wanted to believe he'd fulfilled his destiny, serving in the military even if it wasn't for this country.

"There's the Arco di Settimio Servero. It's made of marble, and I believe it commemorates the victory of something," Robert said the names of the locations with what sounded like perfect Italian as he pointed Landon in one direction. "Then there, I believe that's the Curia Julia, the senate house. I love how sea levels have affected the entrances over the years."

"You've never mentioned you speak Italian." He was impressed.

"You never asked," Robert replied smugly, giving him a wink.

"How fluent are you?" Landon had the camera now trained on Robert's retreating back and, of course, that gorgeous ass was framed perfectly in the shot.

Robert turned, looking over his shoulder and lifted two fingers, indicating a little. "*Poco*, very *poco* since I can't remember at all how to say a little bit in Italian."

"Hmmm," he said, cocking his brow as he thought about how he wanted Robert to mutter whatever Italian phrases when they played gladiator and naughty roman emperor tonight.

"Are you hungry?" Robert asked, coming to a stop and waiting for him to catch up.

"I could eat. I think I'm losing weight here." His waistband rode low on his hips and he'd had to tighten his belt buckle a notch. Robert walked at his side, heading to the main road.

"We can walk over and see the Theatre of Pompey, the place where Caesar was assassinated in the Curia. I believe there's something about a historic cat colony living there now too." Everything halted as Landon hurriedly started the video on his phone again.

"Say that again for the camera," he said, taking a step backward to get Robert in the shot. "This is the senate house, right?"

"The Curia Julia… Caesar was having this remodeled at the time of his demise. The senate had been meeting in the Theatre of Pompey. I can't remember how to pronounce Pompey correctly. Anyway, Caesar never got to see the end result. He was killed in the Curia at the Theatre of Pompey on March fifteenth, in forty-something BC." Robert stepped out of the frame to give him a minute to record all he could before they started the trek toward the spot where Caesar was killed.

"Thank you for today," Landon said, tucking his phone inside his pocket. Robert had laughed at him, but Landon had still taken all the tourist precautions suggested to him. He'd bought a few articles of clothing with hidden compartments that buttoned and zipped at odd angles to keep his passport and cash safe. He'd even bought shoes designed to help his arches while walking over the cobblestoned streets of Rome. The shoes were stiff and hurt his feet. The rest had been complete overkill.

Robert had insisted common sense tourism was all that was needed. He wore his most comfortable walking shoes. If something didn't change soon, Landon might need to do some shopping or lose some of this uncomfortable gear. Lost in thought, Landon walked straight into Robert's extended arm, which stopped Landon in his tracks.

"Take my picture." Robert quickly turned with his back facing the street and struck a pose. He automatically reached for his phone, blindly doing what his husband requested until he caught Robert's eyes darting wildly to the side. Finally, he figured it out and looked past Robert to the armed military man. He and Robert had both developed a fascination with the Italian Army men stationed randomly throughout the city. They generally came in pairs, wore green fatigues, and were armed with both pistols and Beretta automatic rifle. They were beefed up, tough as nails, and hot as hell. They had both started taking these men's pictures yesterday, capturing them to prove they were real.

"If we ever need money, you could come guard this city. You fit the look."

Landon grunted in response. He was fine wiping drool off his own lip, but he wasn't quite so excited about his husband's ogling. Robert saved himself though and got an A-plus for bringing him into the mix.

Reservations had turned out to be the best idea for their travels through Italy yet the hardest to come by. Robert had tried to thoroughly plan this trip, thinking of Landon's tastes, but he readily admitted, he'd never traveled on such a tight budget before. They were down in the trenches so to speak and he loved every minute. They were tourist by day and fun-loving partiers by night. They'd drunk their way through Cinque Terre, Tuscany, and now it seemed Rome would be no different.

He and Landon had really enjoyed the freedom they'd shared with one another in this extraordinary place. Back home, of course, Robert was out and proud, so was Landon for that matter, but they also picked their surroundings carefully. Here, especially in Rome, they may have found their forever home. He could totally see them retiring somewhere in this region. Especially after today. Landon had changed in front of Robert's eyes, taking in the Colosseum and Roman village as if he had absorbed them into his soul. Landon had connected to this place, making this trip perfect and right. Robert wasn't sure Landon could be happier.

They lived like the locals, staying planted in the restaurants for hours, taking in the atmosphere, eating the foods and drinking their wines. Another very telling thing was that Landon seemed to really enjoy his meat tartare. He ate whatever raw thing anyone put in front of him. Robert had even teased Landon, saying his heart might be blocked beyond repair. Secretly, Robert had scheduled himself a note to take a closer look at Landon's health when they returned home.

"Toast!" Landon declared with a slight slur to his words. Robert readily reached for his glass with only a swallow or two left. "To you, I love you."

Robert paused in clinking his glass with Landon's. "That's not a proper toast."

"The hell it isn't! Best retirement trip ever."

Robert agreed with that being closer to a toast and clanked their glasses together. The problem was that Landon's sly side was coming out. He'd repeatedly given some variation on that same toast, maybe even every night since they had arrived in Italy, and it always resulted in a free round of drinks.

"You're a mess," Robert whispered against Landon's lips.

A retort was coming when Landon's phone rang loudly. They both looked down at his cell phone on the table. Landon instantly grew serious.

"It's a Minnesota number." That had Robert pulling his cell phone from his pocket as Landon answered. "Hello?" Their gazes locked, and Landon's eyes widened to the size of saucers. "Can you give us a minute? It's loud in here. We need to step outside."

"It's Sophia. She's been trying to call you. Hurry and pay." Landon shot out of his seat like a bullet discharged from its chamber. He was zigzagging through the narrow walkways between the tables before Robert ever fully got to his feet. He quickly called over the waiter, asking for the tab. He followed the guy to the back where he laid cash on the bar.

As Robert started for the door, Landon pushed it open from the outside, making him jump back or take a hit in the face. Landon's irritation with him was clear on his face when he said, "Babe, what the hell?"

"What'd she say?" he asked, pushing past Landon in the small space between the doorframe and his big body.

"I don't know. I'm waiting for you. I'm nervous, Robert." Landon let the door shut behind them. He held the phone in his hand, hanging at his side. His breath came in short pants, like he was about to hyperventilate. Robert instantly prioritized.

"Give me the phone," he said, reaching for the cell, surprised at the anxiety spiking as he took the phone and put the call on speaker mode.

"Sophia?" he asked a little breathlessly, hoping she was still there. His gaze locked on Landon's, trying to determine where he was in the passing out process.

"Yes. Hi, is this Robert?" she asked. Her singsong happy voice showed she'd heard everything they'd said. "Are you having a good time?"

"Yeah, real good. Landon's here with me. You're on speaker." Robert reached out, taking Landon's hand in his. Landon squeezed Robert's tightly. The butterflies in his stomach stretched their wings a little more excitedly. His heartbeat picked up as he waited for her reply.

"Good. I don't want to bother you on your trip. I just want you to know— Wait, let me say it like this for Landon. We have a pregnancy. Congratulations."

Landon's eyes grew even bigger before he let out a full-lung whoop and reached forward lifting Robert off his feet. He readily wrapped his arms around Landon, hugging him tight as his feet dangled in the air. "We're gonna have a baby."

"Celebrate after this first trimester," Sophia encouraged.

"It's gonna last. I feel it," Landon whispered, kissing his neck, moving to his jaw to kiss him there before reaching for his lips and kissing him there as he put him back on his feet.

Robert lifted his eyes to the heavens, sending a quick prayer of thanks as Landon took the phone out of his hand. "Sophia, how's Scarlett? Is she doing okay?"

"I spoke with her tonight. She's doing great. She sends her love," Sophia said.

"Thank you, Sophia," Robert called out. He still couldn't believe it. Happiness filling every cell of his body. They were going to be fathers. The goodbyes were given as Landon wrapped one of those strong arms around his waist and tugged him closer.

"It happened so fast. I didn't think we would find out anything until we got home," Landon said with all the wonderment of new beginnings in his eyes. "She said pregnancy, so that means just one, right?"

"We'll know more after the first ultrasound," he explained, pulling Landon to him again. Robert had never let himself lose hope. Even on the dark crushing days of missing Landon so badly it hurt, he'd held on to the hopes and dreams of this moment. On the trip of their lives, standing in an alley in Rome, finding out they were in fact going to be fathers… Robert's heart was so full he couldn't contain it any longer and tightened his embrace.

"Do we call our families now?" Landon asked. Robert replied by taking Landon's lips with his, kissing him passionately.

The bells of a nearby church rang loudly as if announcing their news to the whole city of Rome. He slowly pulled back from the kiss. He hated the loss of Landon's sweet lips, but they needed to make their calls before time got away from them. "I need to call Autumn."

"I'll call my mom and dad."

He dialed Autumn and watched Landon as he put the phone to his ear. They smiled at one another, joy bubbling as he waited for Autumn to answer. When she did, he heard Avery's loud cry in the background before Autumn said hello.

"Robert, how early is too early for cutting teeth?" Autumn asked by way of a greeting.

"I'm not a pediatrician," he said for about the millionth time since Avery had come into the world. Her husband would know the answer before he would. "Call me later. I've got news."

"No, hang on. Cam! Take Avery. Robert's on the phone." He heard a rustling, something about Motrin and then silence. As it grew quieter on Autumn's end, he could hear Landon's excitement as he told his parents the news.

"Okay, what's up?" she asked. He didn't try to pretend he'd called for any other reason than he had.

"She's pregnant." When he said the words aloud, his eyes instantly filled with tears. He couldn't help it and didn't know where they came from. They were going to be parents. He and Landon were going to have a baby. His world bowled him over, and he had no choice but to feel the joy filling his soul with every breath he took. "I know we have a long way to go. I know anything can happen, but she's pregnant, and we're going to have a baby."

"Oh, Robert, that's wonderful. I'm so happy." Autumn's voice trembled, making him concentrate to hear her words. "I knew it was going to happen. I knew it. Our fathers weren't going to let you go without children."

"I feel like they had a hand in this too." Robert fought to stop crying, turning away from Landon as he wiped at his eyes. They stood in front of a little romantic restaurant in Italy, fresh flowers decorating the entrance on a quaint narrow street. This wasn't the time or place for Robert to give in to his unexpectedly scattered feelings.

"Remember the story of when they found out there were two of us. Daddy said you were protecting me. That's why you hid me for so long—you were protecting me from the world. It's the way I've always felt about you. You were my protector. You always looked out for all of us. When Daddy was lonely in DC, when we first moved there, you cooked with him. When Dad was stressed out and couldn't sleep, you'd take his calls and stay up all night, talking with him. You take care of everyone around you, even when we make it impossible for you to. You deserve to be happy, and I'm so glad you've found it. You're going to be an excellent father, and I know Dad and Daddy are celebrating this moment with you just like I am. I love you, brother."

Robert's happiness outweighed his struggle for composure as a rush of tears slid down his cheeks to drop to the cobblestones at his feet. The wind picked up, the breeze sliding through his hair and over his skin as if someone tried to comfort him. He had tried to be everything he could for the people around him. He recognized he'd had more failures than successes, but he had tried to help any way possible.

His heart burst with joy, opening the floodgates of love and wonderment for his beautiful life. Yes, Robert knew with certainty his fathers were there with him tonight. They had to be. Robert looked around the street, hoping to see a feather.

Landon's strong hand gripped his shoulder. "Mom wants to talk to you." When he turned to Landon, his husband's look of happiness morphed into one of grave concern. "What is it?"

"It's Autumn." Robert refocused on the call with Autumn, holding Landon's worried stare. "I love you, sis. Here's Landon." They exchanged phones but stayed within a foot of each other, hovering close. Landon's expressive face seemed focused on trying to understand what had happened to cause all his tears.

Robert had to focus and spoke quietly to all of Landon's family, accepting their congratulations. They were loving and kind like they had always been, making him marvel at the size and scope of the people who loved him and the ones he loved in return. When both calls ended, Landon traded their phones back, still cautiously taking in everything about him.

"Baby, what happened?" Landon didn't try to crowd him like he normally did when he tried to fix whatever problem Robert had. Instead, Landon gave him room, which spoke to the level of concern Landon must have.

"I don't know. I got really happy." Tears filled his eyes again. He had no control over them. They were tied to the overload of emotions charging through his system. Landon stepped forward, wrapping him in his arms, squeezing tightly. "I love the life we have. I guess I wouldn't let my hopes run wild. It's probably why I created such an unhealthy workload to keep me from overthinking and connecting…"

"I saw it. I tried to figure it out. You're always so certain, driving us forward. I couldn't understand." The rawness of the moment and of their confessions eased when Landon squeezed him tighter, and thankfully, allowed those explanations to be enough. Robert probably needed some sort of therapy or maybe he just needed to allow himself to breathe every once in a while. Let fate handle the rest.

Instead of saying any of that, he chose to stick with his happiness. "We're having a baby."

"I have a feeling it's twins," Landon whispered against his ear.

"It's my feeling too." He smiled at Landon's words but didn't allow himself to go there—having two babies with Landon might just cause his heart to cease beating right there on the spot.

"Thank you, Robert. I'm the happiest man alive. I've loved this trip." The *loved* part had him knowing exactly where Landon was headed next, and for some reason, Robert wholeheartedly agreed. "But I think we need to go home. I feel like we should be there right now and come back here during a summer vacation with our children." Landon pushed back as far as Robert would let him to look him in the face. "I don't like seeing you cry."

"Let's go home tomorrow." He pressed his lips to Landon's.

"After the morning Vatican tour," Landon said, making Robert smile. Landon had been looking forward to touring St. Peter's Basilica.

They were having a baby. A child, their child. An extension of him and Landon and the love and devotion they shared. Five years ago, Robert had lost everything and struggled to know his place in this world. He'd had to lose himself to find this love. Landon's lips spread into a sweet, genuine grin.

"Thank you for what you've given me so freely," Landon said.

"Thank you for what you've given me so freely." Robert finally let Landon go and immediately started looking for a cab. He lifted his hand and three sets of vehicle lights turned on. They hadn't been near as alone as Robert had thought. The car that got to them the fastest won the fare.

"You need to call Kennedy," Landon said. "It won't be good if she finds out from anyone other than us."

"You call her. She likes you better anyway," he quipped, going around the small vehicle and dropping down into the backseat. Something caught his eye. Robert reached to the floorboard, picking up a multicolored feather. He fought the tears and clutched the feather in his hand as Landon sat in the seat beside him, working his phone. His life was no longer his own and it felt damn good.

Chapter 46

January 2020

Snow fell heavily beyond the windows of the downtown high-rise, creating a beautiful backdrop to a cozy scene inside the large inviting living room. The glow from the marble faux fireplace cast shadows along the back wall. Heated air blew through hidden vents along the top and sides, adding warmth to the room. A soft instrumental played on the surround sound. Over the last nine months, he and Landon had worked hard to prepare for special family moments like this. The redecorated penthouse now had a comfortable, homey feel, which fit their growing family perfectly.

They had also had lots of help getting ready for their little bundles' arrival. The majority coming from Kennedy. She added the Amazon Alexa video displays to the living room and kitchen. A project she handled by herself, sending technicians to the house without asking his or Landon's permission. His nearing a century old grandmother had gone out of her way to learn to use the device so she could watch over the twins.

They'd only brought the babies home a little over a week ago, and Kennedy had already logged in many hours with her eyes glued to the screen, offering her advice on how he and Landon should care for them. Yesterday, she'd come up with the brilliant plan to send the devices to Landon's family. What seemed like a sweet gesture in the beginning was growing old, quickly.

"Robert, Kane's starting to fidget. It's about twelve minutes until his next feeding. He's going to be our eater," Kennedy said quietly, causing Robert to look over the center island in the kitchen to the two swaying baby swings slowly rocking the twins, Kane and Kennedy. Every time he looked at his babies, his heart gave a little squeeze. They were so small and special. Kennedy swore they looked just like him and Autumn at that age.

"Their bottles are almost ready." He spoke as quietly as Kennedy, checking the time at the wall of clocks they'd designed to keep up with their schedule. The blizzard-like conditions had forced him to close the restaurant for the evening. Since Landon had decided he should *not* be left alone with the babies just yet, he'd gone on his own the few blocks to La Bella Luna to manage the sudden decision to close. By Robert's estimation, he should be home by now.

"Have you heard from Landon? It's been almost three hours." Before too much worry could build, the front door buzzer alerted him that someone had entered. At the same time, the timer on the bottle warmer beeped.

"My God, it's cold out there," Landon said, emphasizing his statement with a shiver as he stepped from the foyer into the living room. He went straight to check on the babies, crossing his arms over his broad chest to stave off the cold. He stopped about a foot from the swings, peering over to check on each one. "I tried to make it home for the feeding. Did I miss it?"

"Perfect timing." Robert smiled, lifting the bottles, drawing Landon's eyes to him. "Nonnie, we're saying goodbye."

"Goodnight. Call me if anything happens that I should know about," Kennedy said in a firm but sweet tone.

"Bye, Nonnie," Landon whispered and went for the fireplace,

holding his hands out to warm. When the screen on the Echo Show went dark, Landon turned more fully to face him. "We need to put the brakes on that. My parents are getting all set up to call. They'll all be here twenty-four seven."

"I know. I feel the same way. Are you ready?" he asked, placing one bottle on Landon's rocking chair and the other by his.

Landon's gaze widened as he asked anxiously, "Can't you do it and let me watch you again, so I get it right? You're a doctor—"

"Babe, you can't be scared to hold your own baby. This is our bonding time. Come sit down."

Kane, just a little over five pounds, began to squirm in earnest. He loved bottle time and didn't like to stop eating for the burp. Kane made Landon the most nervous with all his kicking and stretching. The little guy was a very active baby.

Robert carefully picked up Kennedy. When he went to place her in Landon's arms, his mister rubbed his hands together, warming them as he took his seat. The exchange went normally with Landon extremely careful while taking her in his arms. Once Landon was comfortable with her there, he tucked the blanket around her and reached for the bottle.

Kane broke the sweet moment with his soft newborn-baby cry, which made Kennedy stir and Landon stiffen in his seat.

"Relax, Papa." He cupped Landon's shoulder, caressing a path to his jaw, making him look up at him. "If you're tense, then she'll be tense." A phrase he'd uttered every feeding since their babies had been born two weeks ago.

"I'm glad they're home," Landon said and rolled his shoulders. "They didn't have to stay in neonatal as long as I thought. You hired that nurse to come here with me during the day, right?"

Robert only nodded. Landon knew the answer to his question. He'd been there when they'd set her schedule to match Landon's. Landon claimed those times with the registered nurse were designed to be his tutorials, even though they'd taken all the birthing and parenting classes they could before Kane and

Kennedy's arrival. Robert hoped his protective papa bear learned to manage his nerves before the children got too much older.

"They're so beautiful, Robert." Landon carefully put the nipple in Kennedy's mouth then monitored each move Robert made with Kane until he sat in the rocking chair next to Landon. He quickly placed the nipple at Kane's moving lips. Kane aggressively took the bottle into his mouth and sucked the breastmilk down.

"He's funny how he does that. I bet he's gonna love food all his life," Landon said, still focused on every single move their babies made, so much tenderness in his dark eyes.

"I think so too." He placed the bib under Kane's chin to pick up any stray dribbles. Landon mimicked his move with Kennedy. Robert's heart was so full of love and blissful happiness as he drank in the moment. His father's words echoed softly in his head. He'd taken the chance—dared to fly—and now the *always* and *forever* he'd only dreamed of became complete with his family at his side.

He darkened the room by remote control. This had become his favorite time of the day. When his family settled in together like this—the sound of the chairs on the bare wood floor, rocking back and forth, along with the soft music filling the room. Nothing could ever be sweeter than sharing this with the love of his life. He watched Landon's profile in the gentle dance of the flames as the snow fell quietly just beyond the large glass window. Yes, he had been blessed beyond measure.

The End

NOTE FROM THE AUTHOR

Send a quick email to kindle@kindlealexander.com and let us know what you think of Forever. For more information on future works, sign up for our new release newsletter or come friend us on all the major social networking sites.

ABOUT
KINDLE ALEXANDER

Amazon international number one best selling and award-winning author Kindle Alexander is an innovative writer who writes contemporary male male romance and erotica. It's always a surprise to see what's coming next! Happily married with too many children and dogs, living in the suburbs of Dallas.

Usually I try for funny. Humor is an important part of my life – I love to laugh and it seems to be the thing I do in most situations – regardless of the situation, but jokes can be a tricky deal. I don't want to offend anyone and humor tends to offend. So instead, I'm going to tell you about Kindle.

I tragically lost my sixteen-year-old daughter to a drunk driver. She had just been at home, it was early in the night and I heard the accident happen. I'll never forget that moment. The sirens were immediate and something inside me just knew. I left my house, drove straight to the accident on nothing more than instinct. I got to be there when my little girl died – weirdly, I consider that a true gift from above. She didn't have to be alone.

That time in my life was terrible. It's everything you imagine times about a billion. I love that kid. I loved being her mother and I loved watching her grow into this incredibly beautiful person, both inside and out. She was such a gift to me. To have her ripped away so suddenly broke me.

Her name was Kindle. Honest to goodness – it was her name and she died a few weeks before Amazon announced their brand new ereader. She had no idea the Kindle was coming out and she would have finally gotten her name on something! Try finding a ruler with the name Kindle on it…Never happened.

Through the course of that crippling event I was lucky enough to know my writing partner. I would have never gotten through those dark days without her unwavering support and guidance. There wasn't a time she wasn't there for me. For the first time I used the hand offered. I know without question I wouldn't be here today without her. It takes a special person to stand beside someone at a time like that. I will love her forever. I could go on and on about both of them, but I won't and now you know a little more About Us.

Website
https://kindlealexander.com

New Release Email Sign Up
https://www.kindlealexander.com/contact-us/

Newsletter Sign Up
http://www.subscribepage.com/s8y4c3_copy

Amazon Author Page
http://amzn.to/2hKE4YA

Facebook Author Page
https://www.facebook.com/AuthorKindleAlexander/

Twitter
https://twitter.com/KindleAlexander

BookBub
https://www.bookbub.com/authors/kindle-alexander

BOOKS BY KINDLE ALEXANDER

If you enjoyed *Forever* then you won't want to miss Kindle Alexander's bestselling novels:

Reservations
Painted On My Heart
The Current Between Us
Closet Confession
Secret
Texas Pride

<u>Nice Guys Novels</u>
Double Full
Full Disclosure
Full Domain

<u>Tattoos and Ties</u>
Havoc
Order

<u>Better If Read Together</u>
The Current Between Us
Secret
Painted On My Heart

<u>Always & Forever</u>
Always
Forever

ALWAYS

*Winner, Book Execellence Award,
2020*

*Book of the Year 2014 Member
Choice Awards*

Goodreads MM Romance

Book of the Year 2014

Sinfully Sexy Book

*LGBT Book of the Year 2015 eLit
Awards*

Born to a prestigious political family, Avery Adams plays as hard as he works. The gorgeous, charismatic attorney is used to getting what he wants, even the frequent one-night stands that earn him his well-deserved playboy reputation. When some of the most prominent men in politics suggest he run for senate, Avery decides the time has come to follow in his grandfather's footsteps. With a strategy in place and the campaign wheels rolling, Avery is ready to jump on the legislative fast track, full steam ahead. But no amount of planning prepares him for the handsome, uptight restaurateur who might derail his political future.

Easy isn't even in the top thousand words to describe Kane Dalton's life after his father, a devout Southern Baptist minister, kicks him out of the family home for questioning his sexual orientation. Despite all the rotten tomatoes life throws his way, Kane makes something of himself. Between owning a thriving upscale Italian restaurant in the heart of downtown Minneapolis and managing his long-term boyfriend, his plate is full. He struggles to get past the teachings of his childhood to fully accept his sexuality and rid himself of the doubts brought on by his religious upbringing. The last thing he needs is the yummy, sophisticated, blond-haired distraction sitting at table thirty-four.

HAVOC
(Tattoos and Ties Duet Book 1)

Keyes Dixon's life is challenging enough as a full patch member of the Disciples of Havoc Motorcycle Club but being a gay biker leaves him traveling down one tough road. With an abusive past and his vow to the club cementing his future, he doesn't believe in love and steers clear of commitment. But a midnight ride leads to a chance meeting with a sexy distraction that has him going down quicker than a Harley on ice.

Cocky Assistant District Attorney Alec Pierce lives in the shadow of his politically connected family. A life of privilege doesn't equal a life of love, a fact made obvious at every family gathering. Driven yet lonely, Alec yields to his family's demands for his career path, hoping for the acceptance he craves. Until he meets a gorgeous biker who tips the scales in the favor of truth and he can no longer live a lie.

Can two men from completely different worlds…and sides of the law… find common ground, or will all their desires only wreak Havoc?

Tattoos and Ties Duet

PAINTED ON MY HEART

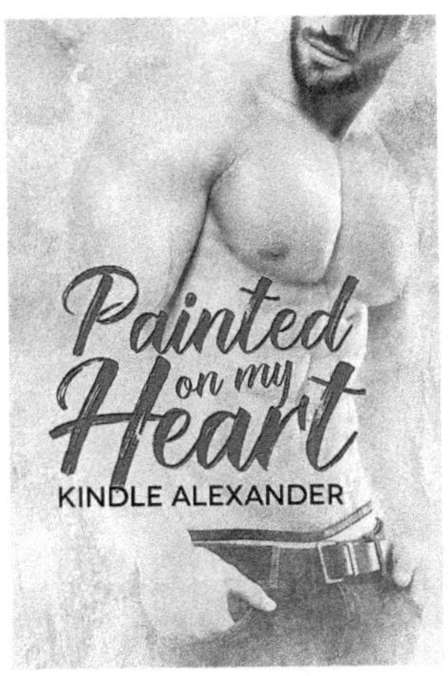

Winner of the 2017 eLit Award Romance category
Winner of the 2017 eLit Award LGBT Fiction category

Artist Kellus Hardin let love and loyalty cloud his past decisions, a mistake he definitely won't make again. Now, lost and alone, he's left to pick up the shattered pieces of his broken heart while facing the truth of his reality.

Arik Layne exudes power, confidence, and determination. But when an encounter with the guarded artist shakes him to the core and alters all his future goals, he finds more than just his heart on the line.

For Kellus, opening himself to love isn't an option.
All Arik wants is to make the artist his.
Can love create a masterpiece when it's painted on your heart?

FULL DISCLOSURE
(Nice Guys 2)

Book of the Year 2014 ~Sinfully Sexy Book

Deputy United States Marshal Mitch Knox apprehends fugitives for a living. His calm, cool, collected attitude and devastatingly handsome good looks earn him a well-deserved bad boy reputation, both in the field and out. While away on an assignment, he blows off some steam at a notorious Dallas nightclub. Solving the case that has plagued him for months takes a sudden backseat to finding out all there is to know about the gorgeous, shy blond sitting alone at the bar.

Texas State Trooper Cody Turner is moving up the ranks, well on his way to his dream of being a Texas Ranger. While on a two-week mandatory vacation, he plans to relax and help out on his family's farm. Mitch is the last distraction Cody needs, but the tatted up temptation that walks into the bar and steals his baseball cap is too hard to ignore.

As Mitch's case gains nationwide attention, how will he convince the sexy state trooper that giving him a chance won't jeopardize his life's plan...especially when the evil he's tracking brings the hate directly to his doorstep, threatening more than just their careers.

SECRET

Silver Award Book of the Year, 2015 elit Awards

Tristan Wilder, self-made millionaire and devastatingly handsome CEO of Wilder-Nation is on the verge of a very lucrative buyout. With tough negotiations ahead, he's armed with his acquisition pitch, ready to launch the deal of a lifetime. There's just one glitch. The last thing he expects is to fall for the hot business owner he's trying to sway.

Dylan Reeves, computer science engineer and founder of the very successful social media site, Secret, is faced with a life-altering decision. A devoted family man with three kids and a wife, Dylan has been living a secret for years. Fiercely loyal to his convictions, his boundaries blur after meeting the striking owner of the corporation interested in acquiring his company. For the first time in his life, reckless desire consumes him when the gorgeous computer mogul makes an offer he can't refuse.

WHAT READERS ARE SAYING ABOUT KINDLE ALEXANDER BOOKS…

Secret

"INSPIRING, HONEST, BRAVE, RELEVANT—A MUST READ!!!"
~ Natasha is a Book Junkie

"This is a powerful story and truly one of Kindle Alexander's best books."
~ Beyond the Valley of the Books

"Secret tells the story of men who are mature enough to value integrity over pleasure and know that loving each other means caring about the others priorities."
~Indie Bookshelf

Full Disclosure

"In the end… OMG the end… let's just say Mitch and Cody have their happy, one that touched my heart."
~Denise, Shh Mom's Reading

"I give this story five+ perfectly delivered stars."
~Toni FGMAMTC

"Mitch and Cody are perfect and so bloody hot, it made my IPAD melt."
~Jules Swoon Worthy

Double Full

"These two hunky men had me in tears, their love for one another is magical."
~Jennifer Robbins, Twinsie Talk Book Review

"Kindle Alexander sure can write a red hot sex scene like nobody else."
~Vickie Leaf, Book Freak

"Without a doubt one of the BEST m/m romances I have ever read."
~Mandie, Foxylutely Blog

Texas Pride

"I have a severe case of book hangover. Seriously readers – you need to read this book. Ten stars for me!"
~ Mandie, Foxylutely Blog

"Definitely a great read…I didn't want this sweet story to end."
~Christi Snow, Author

The Saga of Fidonhaal

Daughters of the East

Lucas Gant

M&B Global Solutions Inc.
Green Bay, Wisconsin (USA)

The Saga of Fidonhaal
Daughters of the East

ISBN: 978-1-942731-40-5

Published by M&B Global Solutions Inc.
Green Bay, Wisconsin (USA)

Dedication

To Mom and Dad
To family and friends
To the tale-weavers of past, present and future

A Prophecy's Time Draws Near

Onu has bestowed upon me yet another array of sights under the light of Yorun's lantern. As with all the visions that have been given unto me, I cannot say the certain day nor hour in which these things will come to pass. Perhaps, due to Onu's will of freedom, these might be only glimpses of a possibility and not a certainty. Nevertheless, I tell you now what I have seen that you might realize them should they indeed come to be.

A wounded heart will fall to hatred and madness, goaded on by both the darkness within and a servant of the Hateful Heart. In secrecy and falsehood will they conspire great horrors, all to serve a hate defying all reason and unlike any known before, which Raakaru will hold as another proof that his ancient call for freedom's end is just. The horrors will be unleashed on a day of life and love, tainting it with death and hatred, and they shall spread across Fidonhaal as the light of the sun, covering the world from east to west.

But in this terror's wake will follow the Daughters of the East. Three women of Enmayar will they be, and their victory will be brought on wings of fire. By these women and all who stand beside them shall the mad hate be combated, and on them and their alliance shall rest the hope of Fidonhaal. They will be known by the mark they bear upon their brows, for they shall be of the Elect, should they rise to the call, following in the footsteps of those who first moved our hearts to return to Onu. Thus shall they share in the fate of all others who will be of Onu's chosen in the days and ages to come.

The Daughters of the East, having risen with the sun, shall come to follow its course into the west, but not without first passing under the light of the Sapphire Star. Three men, out of faith and love, shall follow them out of the east, but shall then journey to the land under the Golden Star. By the joined deeds of these separate hearts shall Fidonhaal be united against the rising hatred. They shall then reunite upon the isle of our beginning, where they shall take fiery flight and return to the east, where the fate of Fidonhaal shall be decided.

Know this, dear Fidonhaal, that though the wounds dealt in this time may be deep, they might yet be healed, at least in good part, before the passing of all things mortal should the Daughters of the East rise to the call and triumph.

— Excerpt from the prophecies of the Elect, first spoken by Elukus Aganon, the blind seer and co-founder of the Temple of Onu, as is recorded in Beldsantu, *the holy book of Fidonhaal.*

Contents

Contents

PROLOGUE

An Introduction to the Fidons
and the World of Fidonhaal

The pages within this book tell a tale from a world other than our own, one that is home to a race of creatures that, while not of the human race, is bestowed with the blessings and burdens that make up what we tend to call "humanity." This world, which is named *Fidonhaal*, and its people, who are called the *Fidons*, have an extensive history of heroes, heroines, and great beings of holy and unholy powers, along with their many respective events and deeds. The tale told here is but one small part of that history.

The Fidons

The Fidons are the prominent, sentient beings that inhabit the world of Fidonhaal. If you were to encounter a Fidon with no prior knowledge of them, you most likely would describe the Fidon as a wolf bearing the form of a human. A Fidon possesses the basic facial structure of a wolf, as well as a tail and coat of fur that covers the body. The coat is not as dense as that of a wolf, necessitating heavier clothing in colder weather and sweat glands to compensate for higher temperatures. Alongside these canid features, the Fidon possesses an upright, bipedal anatomy that reflects much of our physiology. These similarities include hands that have fingers and thumbs like ours, though they have claws more akin to that of wolves than our fingernails. The Fidons also possess the general array of bodily differences between the sexes, and essentially the same patterns of physical and mental development in growing from newborn to adult.

In addition to our physical commonalities, the Fidons also have the capacity for speech and sentient thought, and overall engage in the same array of activities as humans do. They use tools and wear clothes in accord with both cultural inclinations and necessity. They live in houses and societal groups, and engage in the cultural pursuits of art, academics, economics, government, religion and spiritualty, and so on.

Regarding the Fidons' fur, there are four base colors: black, brown, grey, and white. Since the earliest times of the Fidons' known history (specifically since the generation known as the First Grandchildren), there have been those born of mixed lineages, who can in turn sport a virtually endless array of patterns with their inherited colors. A Fidon is described as being either a *Balon* (White One), a *Kason* (Brown One), a *Mavon* (Black One) or a *Zaron* (Grey One). Fidons with more than one fur color are described simply by listing their respective color names together, be it a mix of two, three, or all four colors. For example, a Fidon with both brown and grey fur would be described as having "Kason and Zaron heritage." The exact level of presence one fur color has over another in a mixed-heritage Fidon varies, and the order in which the colors are listed in a description is not necessarily an indicator of which color is most prominent in a given Fidon's appearance. Further details are subject to elaboration depending on the nature of the description, especially if a distinctive pattern or marking is present.

The word "Fidon" translates as "Faithful One." This name for the people of Fidonhaal reflects the ancient bond they have with the entity they call Onu, the Ultimate Creator of all Existence. Throughout the Fidons' turbulent history, the overwhelming majority of the people have struggled to keep a bond of faith with their Maker, as well as with one another, in an effort to resist the hate and evil that had been sown into their hearts long ago by the one they call Raakaru. This struggle plays into what the Fidons refer to as the Ultimate Conflict, which began in the days of the making of the universe and has carried on throughout the ages.

The World of Fidonhaal and the Ultimate Conflict

Fidonhaal, especially at the time of this tale, is the home of many people who possess a global culture that is both diverse and homogenous, as well as a common language. It is a world of heroes and heroines who have done their part for the world and the greater good throughout the ages.

It is a world of magic, where remarkable powers can be witnessed, and indeed worked by those of sufficient mental, spiritual and physical aptitudes. It is a world with an array of extraordinary, supernatural beasts and entities, benevolent and malevolent, that have existed for millennia alongside the Fidons, both within and beyond the world.

The history of Fidonhaal is long and heavily laden with good, evil, peace, and strife. All of the single causes behind any of these happenings are beyond counting. However, all of them, according to Fidon lore, are ultimately sourced from the First Conflict, the Ultimate Conflict, which originated in the time when all things were initially formed.

In the beginning, there was *Onu*, whose name simply means "The One." As he began to create and shape the universe, he also brought forth the angels, the first of his children, and revealed to them his work and told of his intentions. All of the angels marveled at the Great Design, and eagerly took the part that their Maker gifted them, except for the first of the angels. This one was named Lovaariinu, or The All-Keeper, who was given the lot of watching and guiding all his kin and those under their care, being second in might only to Onu.

At first, Lovaariinu took to his task gladly and in cooperation with his kin, but he soon grew discontent with Onu's permission of freedom and chance. Lovaariinu saw this as naught but chaos and potential for great harm and suffering. So Lovaariinu spoke to Onu, arguing his view. Onu, speaking his love and understanding of Lovaariinu and his concerns, explained that freedom was the most crucial part of his relationship with Creation, for no true love could be if it were not given freely from one to another. Onu told Lovaariinu that his design was to have both order and freedom in their due measures, woven together as the threads of a grand tapestry.

But Lovaariinu rejected this, insisting that Onu's allowance of such things was uncaring toward those beneath him. After further argument, Lovaariinu was then calmed for a time, and he grudgingly continued to oversee the making of the universe. But as time went on, the self-certainty of his own sense of righteousness twisted into spiteful arrogance, and what was once his relentless care for all beneath him became warped into the darkest of hatred and contempt. When Onu at last revealed to the angels a glimpse of his design of the Fidons and their purpose, and declared to them that these mortals were to share in the power of Onu and the angels and be guided by them, Lovaariinu rebelled against the design in a great rage. He then called back to his opposition of Onu's permission of freedom and happenstance, and declared that the possibility of his revolt was the first proof of the Maker's folly. Lovaariinu then left the hallowed domain of Onuhaal to devise his own realm and servants, declaring that if Onu would not see the folly of his own design and yield to the righteous wisdom of his firstborn, then he would bring all manner of pain and ruin to Creation until absolute order was brought to all things. He could not stand to see the mortals and those below him be free and able to have a part in the ultimate design that might go against his own intentions. Lovaariinu has since been called Raakaru, the Hateful Heart, by all but himself and those who blindly follow his will.

Since then, Raakaru and his servants have sought to bring destruction and ruin to the Fidons and their world, either by assaulting Fidonhaal directly or manipulating and, at times, outright possessing Fidons to inflict evil upon the world. The gravest of these incidents was the Era of Raakaru's Reign, when Raakaru, having seen that the Fidons had at last slipped completely away from their bond with Onu, conquered Fidonhaal utterly and cast the Fidons into a period of horrendous barbarism. This was also the time when demons, ill magic, and horrid monstrosities came into the world, from the first of the Curse Spawn to the first of the undead.

That age lasted a thousand years, and was only ended when penitent heroes and heroines throughout the world rallied the people against Raakaru and renewed the Fidons' bond with their Maker. Since that time, the Fidons have sought to rise from the darkness and return, as best they could, to the greatness of old, holding their connection with Onu as a matter of paramount importance. A significant manifestation of this effort is seen in the Temple of Fidonhaal and the Faithguard, the latter being a broad order of warriors trained for the defense of the Temple and the faithful at large. Another product of these efforts, one that is relatively more recent in the greater span of Fidonhaal's history, is the formation of the Four Nations, an alliance of four domains that now govern the whole of the world. Generally cooperative in nature, these four countries, forming from the consolidation of the smaller, feuding realms of the past, have striven to balance their own autonomy with the benefits of aiding one another in times of prosperity and trouble alike. From trade and aid with essential supplies to martial assistance in times of civil unrest, the Four Nations have, until times recent to that of this tale, been largely successful in furthering and maintaining one another's prosperity. With these happenings and more, this age of attempted penance has now spanned just over four millennia, and has yielded a great saga of strife, triumph, and tragedy.

The tale told in this book is but one little part of that saga.

Part One

The Queen of Enmayar

The Tides of Life

1
11/10/4012 G.M.

SHEEVA MIVINAAR awoke with a start, her grey fur soaked in sweat and her shoulders heaving as she gasped for breath. She had dreamed of the funeral again, the one of the south warden that had been held months ago in the summer. The first few times it had happened, the princess thought it was surely nothing more than her mind acting in sympathy to the Greystones. Now, however, she began to dread that the dreams were dark omens. The nightmare she just had, as far as she was concerned, all but confirmed that fear.

She stood before the body of Valor Greystone as he lay in the family garden, in sight of all the mourners before being laid in his tomb. Nikolas, son of the south warden and Sheeva's suitor, stood beside her. His mother, Halla, stood by her husband's body in silent and exhausted grief, her anguish spent in the days before. As the princess paid her final respects to the handsome Balon noble, all the world went quiet and the sun suddenly vanished behind a curtain of grey cloud. A lone beam of its light bore down upon Valor's face. A gust of soundless wind blew across the dead warden, stirring his long, white hair and the snowy fur of his face and folded hands, even moving his head to face Sheeva squarely in the eyes.

His eyes opened, and Sheeva stood frozen to the spot. Then his mouth opened, and chills rippled throughout her body as a cry of horror lodged in her throat.

"All is connected," the warden's voice echoed hollowly from his unmoving lips, "and all leads to all else to be."

Valor's right arm fell limply from his chest, and he rose with open hand outstretched to the petrified young princess. Sheeva pleaded for her legs to move, or to even give way, so long as she might escape the dead man's touch, but to no avail. She gaped in terror as the arm extended beyond its natural reach, continuing to approach despite Valor's otherwise still corpse. Her vision tunneled to focus on nothing but the hand reaching for her shoulder.

"Where will this lead you?" Valor's voice rasped. "And where will you lead what is to come?"

The hand clasped upon Sheeva's shoulder, and began to shake her.

Then, the Princess of Enmayar awoke.

She sat up with a cry of alarm, clutching her shoulder as the hand pulled away, and found herself staring into the eyes of her tutor, Xalu Vernifel. The risen sun poured its light in through the window, giving the grey fur of both princess and teacher a warm glow, and highlighting Lady Vernifel's worried face.

"Sheeva, my dear!" Xalu exclaimed. "What's all this?"

The princess pulled her blankets about her, trying to stop her shaking.

"It was Valor's funeral again," Sheeva explained, "but it was nothing like the dreams before."

Xalu hugged her pupil as she listened to the account of the nightmare, speaking to her as a second mother.

"That would have certainly scared me, too," she said. "But I think it could well be a good sign, if indeed there is any meaning to it."

"How so?" the princess asked, at a loss for how to view the bone-chilling vision in a positive light.

"That 'all things lead to what's to come' sounds like a herald for new opportunities in life," Xalu explained as she helped Sheeva out of bed. "I was coming in to tell you that your parents have wished for you to consider other possible suitors in light of ... well, how things have been these past few months."

The princess looked at her teacher uncomfortably. Both Sheeva and Xalu had the same brown eyes, and the two pairs were now looking intently into each other as Sheeva mulled over the thought.

"How could I just end things with Nikolas, even with how things have been lately? It's not like I can't understand why he's been the way he has, or Lady Halla, for that matter. Surely you can see it?"

"Of course, Sheeva. That's why we're only talking of *thinking* about others. After all, this sort of thing with just courting Nikolas this whole time, even though it's gone as well as it has until recently ... it's not exactly the usual course for most Fidons anyway. We'll be happy for you whether you married Nikolas or an innkeeper from Janrenar, or even if you didn't marry, though that would of course make for some complications in setting the course for the future, given your lot."

"I know," said Sheeva as she turned and went into her room's bath and toilet chamber, "but this is still a bit sudden, wouldn't you say?"

"I suppose so," Xalu called out softly into the bath chamber, "well, specifically for you, though we've discussed it over the past few weeks."

"We?"

"Your parents and I, and a few others."

"I don't suppose the 'others' were, or included, Nikolas or Halla?"

Lady Vernifel hesitated before speaking. "Not until last night."

Sheeva sighed heavily in weary resignation as she washed her face. Already on edge from her dream, the princess suddenly found herself feeling very agitated toward her parents and Xalu. Why keep her, Nikolas, and Halla in the dark for weeks over this? She and Nikolas had been friends since they were little, and as upsetting as Valor Greystone's death and the events surrounding it had been, she was finding it very difficult to see herself possibly ending up with someone else. An uncomfortable silence followed, and Sheeva feared her sigh may have sounded angrier than she initially thought. She quickly finished her washing and came back into the bedroom, where she found Xalu seated on the edge of her bed. The tutor looked at Sheeva, her dark, brown eyes laden with regret.

"We didn't mean to keep this from you as though you were a child, Sheeva," she said gently. "We just didn't want you to worry over it too much until we discussed a few things first. I'm sorry if you feel we didn't want to give you more of a say. Remember that this is just something we were hoping you'd consider."

"Very well," said Sheeva, "and I'm sorry if I sounded angry. It was just so unexpected."

"Of course, dear," Xalu said as the two held each other in another caring embrace.

"So, is there anyone in particular that I may want to consider?"

"Well, we thought that perhaps you might be interested in getting better acquainted with Allor Indovis, the boy you met at the funeral."

"The one from Nelahaal?"

"Yes, that's the one. His family helped in settling matters with the south famine and ... that bit of unrest. Your mother and father were very impressed by how they handled things, and have invited them to come and visit us for Sardonmay. The invitation was sent last night, and after that we told Halla and Nikolas."

"And how did they take it?" Sheeva asked, wincing as she did so.

"Not very well, I'm afraid. We've stressed that this isn't the end of the courtship, and they're still living here with us until further notice."

With this, Sheeva sighed with both relief at Nikolas's continued presence and a touch of resignation for the present circumstances. Her intent to keep the situation in mind and consider alternatives, however, was sincere nevertheless.

"Very well then, I guess we'll just have to see how this goes. Is there anything else, Xalu?"

"No, that's essentially it. Your mother and father may wish to talk with you about it themselves sometime today, maybe even at breakfast, but it should otherwise be another normal Fusmay. We'll have our lessons after breakfast, continuing with Sorrenar's unification and how the other three continents followed suit in the decades after."

"Alright. Thank you, Xalu. I'll be down once I'm dressed."

***

Breakfast that morning was uncomfortably quiet. Sheeva sat between her parents, Queen Talrah III and King Samuel, with Nikolas Greystone and his mother, Halla, now acting South Wardeness of Enmayar, across the table from them. Lady Xalu was seated alongside the Greystones, as was the castle's resident priest, Ranoth Windsbreath, and a few others who were visiting court that morning. Neither Nikolas nor Halla spoke a word to Sheeva, nor did they make any eye contact with her or her parents. The princess glanced at her parents from the corners of her eyes, hoping for one of them to break the silence, but not a word was spoken for the entire meal apart from the prayer at its beginning. Sheeva did notice, however, a few glances being exchanged between the king, queen, and Xalu, which were concluded by a series of satisfied, if weary, nods.

When breakfast finally ended, Sheeva and Nikolas followed Xalu to her study for the morning's lessons. The princess looked to her longtime friend, wanting there to be a word, a caring glance, anything to break the silence and give hope that, whatever came of the next few months, all would turn out well in the end. But Nikolas kept his eyes to his front. It wasn't until they reached the door to the study, as the tutor was opening the door and Sheeva began to turn her sight back to her front, that she caught a glimpse of any acknowledgement from the boy she had known for nine years, since she was five and he was eight.

The look she caught from the edge of her sight set the furs on her neck to rising. The south warden's death had led to anger from Halla and Nikolas, an anger inseparably entwined with grief. Then came disconnected silence and a lessening of cordiality to her and her parents. But those were understandable, given their loss and the feelings of injustice they must have felt, despite how things had played out overall.

But the glare that Sheeva caught in Nikolas's eyes showed that the news of another potential suitor had set his heart to utter loathing.

The princess thought of her nightmare. Where would all this lead her, and all else yet to come?

2

11/13/4012 G.M.

ALLOR INDOVIS strode into the study of his mother, Egrah, mayor of the town of Nelahaal. She was seated at her desk with her husband, Alphaar, seated beside her. Although Allor's father was not an official member of the public office, his counsel and support had always been valued by the mayor as that which came from her official advisors. He was constantly alongside her at council meetings and other such affairs as in general life.

Upon hearing his parents call to him, Allor's mind raced through all he could recall from the past several days, wondering what matter called for this talk, and its nature. Once he saw the looks on their faces, however, he knew this summons was a pleasant one. His mother beckoned him to sit in one of the chairs in front of her desk. She was holding a small, unrolled piece of ornate parchment in one hand while stroking the head of the heraldwing bird that delivered it with the other. Intrigued by what his involvement with the good tidings might be, Allor promptly sat in front of his mother's desk, his dark brown eyes turning from his mother to his father and back before Egrah finally spoke.

"We have word from the royal family in Genverdell," Mayor Indovis announced warmly, "an invitation to join them in celebrating Sardonmay."

Allor felt his eyes widen. It had been over three months since he had been to the town and estate of Oakhall, home of the Greystones, present south wardens of the country, to pay respects to the deceased warden, Valor. His family, like most others who were in civic service within Enmayar's south ward, had come to witness the funeral and give condolences. However, in light of the reasons for Valor's death and Egrah's handling of the crisis, which came to be applied to the entire ward, the Indovis family was regarded as esteemed guests and had spent a fair deal of time conversing with the royal Mivinaar family. Allor had heard the flow of praises that the queen and king poured onto his mother and father, and thought he may have caught wind of some meeting with them in the future. A few months then passed, however, and the events simply went into the back of his memory. To suddenly hear of an invitation for something so festive, and so soon, had taken him off-guard.

"W-well, will we be able to make the trip in time?" Allor finally sputtered after an embarrassing moment of silence spent looking at his parents' grinning faces.

"If we can leave soon and it all fares well, we could be in Genverdell with at least a week to spare," Alphaar calculated. "I know this is sudden, Allor, but this could lead our lives somewhere we've never expected."

"How so?" Allor asked. "It's just to celebrate winter and the New Year, no?"

"Not quite," Egrah said warmly as she handed the parchment to Allor from across the desk. "Here, see what else it says."

Allor took the letter and read through it, his eyes widening again, and more than before, as he reached the end.

"They think I could be a suitor for the princess?"

"Do you think you can't?" Egrah asked as she took back the letter.

"I-I just talked to her for maybe five minutes or so!"

"Sure," Alphaar said, "and if it turns out well, it turns out well. If it doesn't, it doesn't. It's too little and too soon to say either way, wouldn't you say?"

"Well, I guess, but ... it's just a lot."

"Of course, dear," said Egrah. "It's about the greatest bond two mortals can have. But don't let it trouble you now. It's a possibility, nothing more at the moment."

"How possible, though?"

The mayor of Nelahaal smiled at her son's question, then gestured to her husband and over the whole room of the mayor's office. Allor gave a small smile of acknowledgement. He knew what she meant; he'd heard the story before. His mother began her career by following her family's long-standing tradition in tailoring, but one day found in her the makings of a mayor, the office of which she had successfully held for as long as Allor was alive. Three years before that, she delivered some mended tunics to a woodcutter, and that woodcutter now sat beside her as husband and confidant.

Allor gave a shrug of nervous acceptance. "Well," he said, "if nothing else, I'll be able to say I celebrated Sardonmay with the leaders of Enmayar."

"Indeed," said Alphaar with a smile. "We still need to make some arrangements, of course. Whatever comes of this, your mother is still the mayor here, so we'll need to sort out how that will be handled in her absence, as well as let the school know you'll be gone for at least a couple of months. We'll let you know more when we get matters settled. In the meantime, let your friends know; depending on how things play out, it may be a while before you'll see them again."

"Alright," said Allor in a voice touched with renewed discomfort at the latter prospect, "I'll get on that now, if there isn't anything else."

"That's all for now," Egrah said as the three rose from their seats and shared an embrace. Just before Allor parted, however, a thought occurred to him for which he privately chided himself for not minding before.

"Wait," he said, "isn't the south warden's son still the princess's suitor?"

"He is one, and has been the only one until now," Egrah acknowledged, "but surely you know by now that that's quite unusual for anybody, especially the royal family."

"Well, yes," said Allor, "but I mean, it's been that way for a long time, right? I thought they've been close for years. Wouldn't the princess be fairly comfortable with him and less likely to be interested in someone else? And wasn't that encouraged between both families to begin with because they've been really good friends?"

Allor's mother lovingly patted his back as an uncomfortable silence lingered.

"The Mivinaars and Greystones have been great friends for several generations, actually, and hopefully they'll stay that way. But, well ..."

"Was it the food riot?"

Allor waited patiently as his mother drew a deep sigh. He didn't look, but he could feel his parents giving each other uncomfortable looks.

"That seems to be the short of it," Egrah said at last. "How much do you know about that, or have at least heard?"

"Not much, just that it had to do with that shortage during the summer because of the drought." Allor actually felt a light twinge in his stomach from the memory of those lighter months before continuing. "That, and the south warden got himself killed over it somehow. The shortage was a problem across the whole ward, wasn't it?"

"The whole country felt some of it," said Egrah, "but it was indeed worst here, though thankfully not too serious when all is considered. Fidonhaal has seen far worse."

"So why did the riot get so bad?"

"Because it could've gotten very bad if Valor Greystone kept to his initial plan. Do you know much of what's been going on in Kellmayar lately?"

"I'm afraid not," Allor admitted meekly.

"Don't worry about it," his mother assured him. "You're not tasked with being in politics, especially not to this extent. Not now, anyway. Besides, even I'm not the most informed. Simply put, Kellmayar has been having unexpected problems the past few years with their food and trade, and there has been unrest in some places. The other three nations have been trying to help by sending some food and soldiers to help keep order. The problem is that when the drought came over here, the queen and king called for a halt on sending food until further notice, but Warden Greystone continued to send rations on the quiet."

Allor was taken aback. "Why?"

"Because Kellmayar's east warden, a man named Ohdan Karvinthaal, has been a lifelong friend of his. Valor's mother and father were diplomats for that region when he was a child, and he and Ohdan grew up together. Kellmayar's east ward was also the one hurting the most from the country's recent troubles, and Warden Greystone wasn't going to let that go."

"I see."

"When word got out, a lot of people gathered at Oakhall, where the Greystones' house is, and called for him to step forward and explain things. The king and queen were very displeased as well, and sent him and the whole family out there, telling them not to return until matters were settled."

"And that's when you and Father left to go there, too?"

"Yes. Your father and I arrived on the day it all came to a head. I don't know what exactly happened, and I've heard many rumors over what exactly was said. Whatever happened, a heated argument began, and Warden Greystone, by nearly all accounts, said something to the effect of the people being unsupportive ingrates for not trusting in the alliances between the nations. I've heard that he twisted it to sound like they were calling for us all to go back to smaller domains, like when we were just beginning to rebuild after Raakaru's reign, or some other lunacy of the sort. Whatever it was that he said, several people in the crowd got riled up to the point of murder."

Allor's ears drooped as he digested the morbid turn of events, disturbed at both how quickly normal people could be so provoked and a crucial leader could speak to his people so contemptuously.

"So, what happened then?"

"Four people bolted through the crowd and stabbed him before anyone could react, right in front of Lady Greystone and their son. Your father and I didn't see it happen ourselves because of our spot in the crowd, but we heard it and then saw the aftermath. The warden may have spoken rashly, even foolishly, if I may say so ... but he didn't deserve *that*. He had been a fine leader of the ward for years, and I'm sure it wouldn't have come to that if there wasn't the personal factor of his connection with Warden Karvinthaal."

"I definitely didn't know about all of that," Allor said grimly. "I mean, maybe I did hear a little bit of something, but that was on top of a bunch of other rumors that I've been catching lately. I didn't know what to think because I didn't know what was true, if any of it."

Alphaar sighed in distaste. "Gossips," he remarked.

"It was very ugly all around," Egrah continued. "Lady Greystone demanded that the culprits be executed on the spot by the guard, and when they were detained for the queen and king to arrive, she wanted the authorities to sentence them without trial. I can only imagine her grief and anger, but such a course of action was obviously out of the question."

"I don't know if it's such a good idea for me to even consider being a suitor for the princess, then," said Allor worriedly. "Wouldn't that just be salt in the Greystones' wounds?"

"It could be," Egrah admitted, "but this whole ordeal has, obviously, already strained the two families' friendship. That was part of what we were discussing at the funeral, to be honest. The king and queen have begun to worry that the Greystones may not be the sound companions they originally thought. Now they're hoping to broaden the possibilities for their daughter in case the Greystones end up falling short of their standards."

"So they thought they'd start with looking at the family who helped calm things down?" Allor asked.

His mother gave a small, humble smile. "Yes." She then looked at her son, reading the frustration to grasp the situation, and growing suspicion and cynicism of the politics that was playing out on his face. She lifted Allor's chin, looking straight into his eyes with the firm gentleness of a mother's understanding.

"Believe me, Allor," she said, "I was not helping with that fiasco because I planned for you to have a chance to become the King of Enmayar. I've managed to lead this town for fifteen years, but I'm afraid I'm not nearly as far-sighted, or politically driven, as that. Nor, if I may risk sounding self-righteous, that conniving. Even if I was, I would never force you into a marriage with no love. I'm not going to lie and say that no Fidon has ever used marriage for politics. You've had your history lessons and know that isn't so. But those same lessons also show that very few were done without still trying to ensure some genuine affection in the bond."

Allor lowered his head. "I'm sorry. I didn't mean to think like that. It's just ... well, a lot to take in."

"Of course," Egrah said gently. "Don't worry about all that right now. Just go along and get ready. We'll talk and plan things out more later."

Allor kissed his mother and father, and went out of the study, down through the rest of the mayor's house, and out onto the main street of Nelahaal in the crisp evening air, looking for his friends so that he could tell them the news.

3

11/24/4012 G.M.

LERANNU STONEFAITH focused her sight and thought on the eagle feather, watching it sway about in the breeze that she had conjured. It had been two years since she began taking lessons at her town's chapter of the Mage Society, beginning her education in magic with learning its history and principles. Now, after two years of studying the mages of the past, incidents that had been debated between willful magic or divine intervention, and the lectures on ideal rejuvenation and the potential concerns of revitalizing tonics, Lerannu was finally casting her first spells. In the short span of an afternoon, the young Zaron pupil had gone from only flicking the feather about with the lightest gust to managing almost five seconds of continued suspension in a gentle, stable breeze.

Her enrollment began when she was ten, when she and her parents had found she could potentially work the elements with relative ease, though it was largely involuntary at first. Now, at age twelve, she was more in control than ever before, and the great joy she felt from her own strength, coupled with her connection to creation, welled within her heart.

Sudden fatigue, however, quickly dampened her elation. Watching the feather fall to the creaky wooden floor through blurring vision, Lerannu staggered back into the waiting arms of Ahvrom Salinoth, one of her tutors, as she pressed a hand to her aching head. Her other teacher, Dalle, who was also Ahvrom's wife, rushed to her side with a beaker of cool water, offering it to the young mage student.

"It's alright, Lera," Dalle assured her. "Getting the feel for your own mind and spirit is typically viewed as the biggest hurdle for a beginning mage. I'm afraid that's a part of magic for which even the most thorough lectures won't be able to prepare you."

With a slightly trembling hand, Lerannu took the cup of water and began sipping it gently. As she drank, Ahvrom made sure she was standing steadily before withdrawing his support.

"But you did very well all the same," Ahvrom remarked. "Most would still be struggling with all the main points, but you had hardly any trouble focusing on your targeted object and intended action."

The teacher then began to chuckle.

"The first time I tried this, I couldn't focus my mind on just guiding air into wind because I was distracted by the light of a candle. Long story short, I nearly burned the house down!"

Lerannu gazed up at the Mavon teacher incredulously, trying to determine if he was just trying to be funny and making up a story for her benefit. She could not imagine Ahvrom as ever having made such a mistake. The black-furred mage and his Balon-Zaron wife smiled at their pupil's disbelief, with Dalle going on to confirm her husband's account.

"It's true," she declared. "I watched him just before I took my turn at it. Our teacher thought about calling it a day then, but Nora, our other classmate, and I both convinced him not to." Dalle shook her head, breathing a laugh and a sigh. "We were all so excited to finally start practicing spells, and we didn't want to cut the day short when only Ahvrom had a chance to try. So then I went next, and my first attempt put all our schooling on hold for the rest of the week."

Lerannu turned wide-eyed to Dalle. "What happened? Surely it wasn't as bad as almost burning the house?"

"The candle fire could've been bad," Dalle admitted, "but our teacher was quick enough to stop it, so no real damage was done."

Dalle lifted the grey and white-streaked locks of hair draped over the right side of her face, revealing a deep scar above her brow. Lerannu's jaw dropped.

"The teacher didn't think to position himself behind me in case I drained myself from the spell," Dalle explained, "but that's exactly what happened. I tired myself out so badly and so fast that I fell almost as soon as I cast the spell. I turned a little as I was falling and slammed my head onto the teacher's desk before hitting the floor. I was out cold before I even hit the ground and was bleeding pretty badly. I didn't come around until after noon the following day."

Lerannu's eyes dropped from Dalle's scar to the water in her half-drained beaker, which was rippling tremulously as her nerves set her hands to quivering again. The young student quickly regained composure, however, as Ahvrom, placing a warm reassuring hand on her shoulder, finished the tale.

"Once Dalle recovered and we resumed our lessons, our teacher always arranged for either his brother or a friend to be present in the study so that someone would always be on hand to catch a student if they fainted. We kept this in mind when we took charge of this branch of the Society and have worked together ever since."

At this, the night-furred mage began to smile, his eyes moving from his student to his wife. "The two of us started here as colleagues, but it didn't take long before we got married ..."

"And have a wonderful daughter," Dalle gushed, "who's no doubt waiting for you now that it's well past noon. Lessons are done for today; just try not to tire yourself out with whatever outing you two have in mind. Have a good dinner and a good night's sleep; that's the best way to keep up your strength in magic, as with any other task. Have fun!"

"I will!" said Lerannu as she ran happily out the door. "Thank you, and see you tomorrow!"

Lerannu took a deep breath upon leaving the chapter house of the Mage Society, savoring the change of the air's scent from the sweet musk of books and candles to the crisp air of mid-autumn's later days. Glancing about the southern highway, which ran right through Bravagoth and served as her hometown's main road, she quickly spotted Kiiva, her teachers' daughter and best friend, playing absentmindedly with a fallen oak leaf while talking to their friend, Zalden. The two were under the massive oak that stood in the town square, which the highway enveloped as a river does to an isle in its midst. Lerannu ran up to the pair and greeted them, explaining her delay from her lessons' normal ending time. She excitedly told them of her new experience in manipulating wind.

Kiiva, though the child of two mages, was not of the inclination to dedicate herself to that particular discipline, instead showing a great interest in plants and the beginnings of a potential career to suit it. That said, Kiiva still had a fascination in the craft she saw her parents practice daily and was always eager to know of her friend's progress. After hearing Lerannu's account of the eagle feather, Kiiva could hardly contain her excitement. The flickering shadows of the oak's thinning top played across Kiiva's face of black, grey and white fur as she pleaded, eyes wide and bright, for her friend to show off her new skill.

"Oh please, Lera," she begged, using the nickname all Lerannu's friends and family used when not in formal circumstances, "I've been waiting to see you do something like this ever since you started! Ma and Da hardly ever tell me what you've done so far; they keep telling me to ask you about it."

"Because I'm not always ready to talk about it," Lerannu explained meekly, "and neither of them, nor me, wanted to bring attention to it until I felt like showing people. Not that it's exactly a thing that most mages go out of their way to show off, anyway."

Kiiva's pleading eyes, an asset that nearly always moved those who saw them to yield to her requests, continued to pierce Lerannu's resolve.

The young mage shrugged humbly. "It's just keeping a feather in the air, Kiiva. I haven't really been able to guide it anywhere, and I've only been able to keep it up for a few seconds."

Zalden, who had been listening quietly up to this point, spoke up. "That's more than anyone else in town can say, apart from Kiiva's parents."

"Maybe, but I really should rest up for tomorrow."

Kiiva, holding up the leaf in her hand, then played her bargaining abilities, which rounded out the three blessings she had that hinted at a promising career as a shrewd apothecary. "Oh, come on, Lera. Just one time, a few seconds, *please?* Just blow this leaf here a little and I won't bother you about it anymore unless you decide to show me. Please?"

Lerannu sighed in resignation, walking over to the oak to sit beneath it.

"Alright, fine, fine!" she said, both annoyed and amused at her friend's persistence. "But at least one of you needs to stand next to me in case I pass out or something, and I want to sit here and rest a few minutes before I start as well."

The young apprentice rested her head against the oak's trunk and closed her eyes. She began to follow the process of meditation while half-listening to Kiiva as she and Zalden began jogging down the road.

"Of course," Kiiva agreed. "We'll let anyone else who wants to see know about it while you rest. Just relax for a bit, and when we come back, just blow around the leaf I have for a few seconds if you can. After that, I promise I won't ask you to show us any more until you're ready. Okay?"

"Okay," Lerannu breathed as she shifted against the oak to get more comfortable. "Fifteen minutes or so should be enough."

"Alright!" Kiiva said as she and Zalden ran off into town. "We'll be back in a bit!"

Lerannu began to relax as her friends' footsteps quickly faded away. It wasn't until they were well out of earshot that Lerannu realized that Kiiva said she was going to let "anyone else who wants to see" know about the demonstration. The apprentice's eyes snapped open as anxiety rocked the beginnings of her meditation.

"They're going to bring the whole town here, and all those passing through, if they can!" she grumbled to herself, massaging her brow as her head began to ache in frustration. "What made Kiiva think that I was up for showing this to anyone other than her and Zalden?" She lifted her head, looking at the clear sky through the falling leaves and the dwindling number of those that still clung to the oak's branches.

"I don't know if I should be meditating or praying," she said with a rueful sigh.

The young pupil took a deep breath and tried to reason herself back into calmness. She was already feeling refreshed just from stepping outside, and a good few minutes of focused rest would surely be enough to restore her for one last little demonstration. After all, she knew that Kiiva was sincere in her bargain that it would only be this one time, and she would otherwise let Lerannu decide when she felt ready to show anything else. As frustrating as Lerannu found it to be so easily swayed by her, she had to admit that Kiiva always kept her word if she could. Lerannu began to relax again, having run her feelings and her plan for the rest of the day through her mind. Once this little show was over, she'd go straight home, rest until dinner, and retire to her room for the rest of the night. Then she would tend to tomorrow's lessons and practice.

Her confidence now well on the way to recovery, Lerannu returned her attention to the oak before she began her meditation again. It was almost the end of the year's penultimate month, and many of the great tree's darkening leaves were still holding on as Kyse's time of year began to yield increasingly to that of Sardoth's. Taking a minute to watch the leaves sway, the young mage saw a few of them finally release their grasp to blanket the acorns that lay around her. Lerannu rested her head back against the tree and began her meditation anew.

The young apprentice was pleasantly surprised at the sensations she had from her first experience in meditating as a recuperating mage. Dalle and Ahvrom had gone over the practice at great length over the past two years, and she had practiced it before, in some fashion or other, as part of her studies as well as in private. But this was the first time she had done this in an effort to regain her mental and spiritual strength for the act of spellcasting, and while the feelings themselves weren't entirely new, the heights they reached were. Within a minute or so of closing her eyes, Lerannu began to feel that she was both rooted in the earth and floating on the breeze. Her sight, from behind her eyelids, beheld a marvelously tranquil interplay of black and various shades of gold, which came from the descending sun and the oak leaves casting their shadows above her.

Then she heard a sound: someone was calling her name. It was a woman's voice that spoke: beautiful, gentle, friendly and oddly familiar. To Lerannu, the voice sounded as if it was echoing across the entire space between her place on Fidonhaal and the Eternal Realm of Onuhaal, for it felt at once both immediately present and unfathomably distant. For this reason, as well as the fact that the spell she was preparing to cast was one that drew from the winds, Lerannu at first thought she was hearing the voice of the angel Vente herself. Her tranquil reverie was shaken, but not broken, by the voice. With the ensuing rush of awe and apprehension, and her mind, heart and soul soaring, she placed all her focus on the angelic voice, which now felt very close.

Suddenly, a hand fell upon her shoulder. It was friendly and gentle, but heavy with the weight of the Mortal Realm. This shocked Lerannu from her serenity as though it were a strike to the face. The young mage's eyes snapped open and a great rush of air filled her lungs as she gasped deeply from being pulled from her meditation, as a diver would when surfacing at the utmost limit of their breath. Finally released from her reverie's grasp, she looked up and found herself laughing as she looked into the faces of Roniil Stonefaith, her father and mayor of Bravagoth, and Uriah Silverwind, the advisor of the town's treasury and a good friend of the family. It was Uriah who had called out to Lerannu in her trance. Roniil, his fur as grey as his daughter's, held out a hand to help her up. Uriah, a beautiful Fidon with the face and body of a porcelain-white Balon, and with long and flowing hair that was the jet-black of a Mavon, looked on as she questioned the young apprentice.

"Zalden and Kiiva are telling the whole town that you're going to keep a leaf on the wind for as long as you can. Is it true?"

"Yes, Uriah," Lerannu answered as she got to her feet with her father's help. She and Uriah had been on friendly terms for years. She had referred to Uriah by her first name, as opposed to "Lady Silverwind" or other such titles, for nearly as long as she had known the treasurer at her own request. "I just started to learn how to move wind a little," she continued, "but Kiiva convinced me to show her, as well as all the town, apparently."

The three shared a laugh as Uriah remarked on Kiiva's penchant for persuasion and attracting greater attention than what was at first expected. To Lerannu's self-frustration, however, she found herself beginning to get nervous again, and confessed it to her father and friend.

"She and Zalden are getting the whole town excited," she explained, "but I just don't know how it's going to go. It's not like I can really move it around, either; it's just been about keeping it in the air for a few seconds."

"That's more than I could do," Uriah said as she looked at Roniil. "What about you, Roniil? Any secret penchant for magic you've been keeping from us?"

The mayor laughed. "I wouldn't be able to do it for a second. Not of my own actual will, anyhow."

Roniil turned at the sound of an approaching crowd, then turned back to his daughter a few seconds later, beaming with pride.

"Looks like almost everyone's taking some time out of their afternoon to see what you can do! I see a number of travelers taking a few minutes to stop and see, too. Many folks love to see a mage if they can, Lera, but I bet they'll be especially interested in seeing a young one at the start of her path."

Lerannu looked on as the great gathering, led by Kiiva and Zalden, congregated in front of the square's oak. She recognized nearly everyone in Bravagoth, from the clergy of the local temple to the innkeeper and the blacksmith, who was Zalden's father. The array of traveling strangers that frequently passed through town by the south highway also comprised a good part of the crowd, including a woman from Sorrenar's eastern highlands and merchants obviously hailing all the way from Janrenar, given their robes and hairstyles. Having regained her strength from the meditation, Lerannu, while still nervous, began to feel a great sense of exhilaration at the sight of such a varied and intrigued audience. Kiiva interrupted her friend's observation of the crowd with a tap on the shoulder.

"Just about everyone in town has come to see you, Lera!"

"I know," Lerannu said with mostly mock annoyance. "That's a whole lot more people than I would've agreed to if I could've said anything, but you and Zalden ran off so fast I didn't have a chance."

Kiiva, noting that Lerannu's tone wasn't completely serious, nevertheless dropped her ears in discomfort. "I'm sorry, Lera. I just thought that ..."

"Don't worry about it," the apprentice said as she hugged her friend, any bother she might have still felt now fading completely away.

Kiiva smiled with relief. "So, do you think you'll be ready soon? Did the meditating work?"

"It did," Lerannu answered, "and I think I'll be ready in just a few more minutes. Thank you."

Zalden stepped in, pointing to his father the blacksmith and his mother, who worked as a general goods vendor. "My folks are here, too, and they're really excited to see this!" The young Zaron boy paused awkwardly before continuing, his slate-grey eyes showing a great effort to phrase his next words with tact. "I don't want to be pushy, Lera, but did I hear you say you'll be ready soon? Ma and Da would love to see this, but they can't stop their work for too long just yet, and a lot of these travelers can't wait around very long, either."

"Don't worry," Lerannu replied, "I'm pretty much ready, I just need to see if ..."

Lerannu's voice trailed off as she surveyed the crowd once more. There were the two priests from the temple in their beautifully simple robes, and the town's high priestess, who wore much the same aside from her brilliant bronze amulet. There was Zalden's father, in his smith's apron, his friendly green eyes peering through his sooty face, which was purely grey when clean. Beside him was his wife, also of fully Zaron heritage, well-groomed and dressed to charm the customers in her shop. There was the northern highland woman, fur white as snow from head to toe, and donning the kilt and marital nose ring of her culture. And there were the five merchants from the great south rainforest of Lidrovgla. Their fur, black and brilliant as obsidian in the late afternoon sun, along with their lush Mohawks and vibrant, sleeveless robes (with light cloaks draped over them for the chilly air), likely would have made them the center of the town's curiosity for the day if it weren't for Lerannu's impending demonstration.

There was only one person absent as far as Lerannu could tell, and that was the only one she cared about aside from those who already stood with her beneath the tree. Turning to her friends, who were now standing alongside her father and Uriah, Lerannu questioned them in a low voice.

"Where's Mama? Didn't you stop by town hall when you were telling everybody?"

Kiiva scanned the crowd intently as she answered. "Yes, that's where your dad and Uriah were when we told them. They were sitting right next to her and they were all talking with each other."

Roniil, having overheard the conversation, quickly verified Kiiva's response. "She's right. We were just about to finish for the day and told your friends that we would be along soon. Your mother said she'd only be a few minutes behind, because she needed to finish writing the day's record. Maybe something came up at the last minute. I think I heard the receptionist say something about Dr. Gahdos coming in just as I walked out the door."

With this thought, Roniil turned aside and spoke quietly to Uriah.

"Did she perhaps mention to you that she was going to do anything else?"

"No, I thought she was just about to wrap things up, too. Why do you ask?"

"Unless Gahdos had something really pressing to say, she might've just let other things take up her focus. Things that could easily wait until at least tomorrow."

The mayor's voice suddenly fell into a weary tone.

"She's been doing that quite a bit lately, come to think of it. I don't want to be against her commitment to managing things here, but she seems to have gotten more into that than other things lately. Like Lera and me."

"I had no idea, Ron. Is ... is everything alright?"

"It's just been a little difficult lately. Like last month ..."

Lerannu, hearing this conversation over the soft hum of the crowd, closed her eyes and tried to calmly tune them out and sort her feelings. While Bravagoth itself was not a very large town, its location on the south highway leading to multiple ports in the west and south wards of Enmayar made it a popular stop for travelers at all hours of day and night. This continuous flow of travelers brought an exceptional amount of traffic and commerce for a town of Bravagoth's size. Thus, the mayors of Bravagoth, practically since the town's founding, almost always had a good more to tend to than those of most other settlements of comparable sizes.

Lerannu's father had been mayor all her life, and her mother worked as the office scribe, presiding over the daily matters with her husband and writing the records. As a result, Lerannu had experienced a number of times when, for one reason or another, at least one of her parents wasn't present for one life milestone or another. She also observed times when the demands of both jobs placed strain upon her parents and their bond.

She had tried to become accustomed to it and usually prided herself as being, in her own mind at least, fairly understanding of her parents' situation, having been told by both on numerous occasions that they loved her and were proud of her. She went by the notion they were always with her in spirit as often as she could. Regardless, she couldn't help but feel particularly crestfallen at the thought of her mother not being able to see her demonstration.

Her ponderings were interrupted by her father's hand resting gently on her shoulder.

"Lera," Roniil whispered, "Uriah and I are going to see what's keeping your mother. We'll try to be quick, but we might not be able to bring her here in time. If we don't come back without her ... well, maybe we could–"

"I'll just show her later, if that's how it goes," Lerannu said calmly.

"But Lera, this is your first time–"

"I know, but it's not like this sort of thing hasn't happened before. Mama took me to my first day at the Society, and you weren't able to come, so maybe this will even it out a little, if she can't make it?"

Lerannu grinned faintly, hoping a little attempt at humor would lighten the mood. Roniil, however, looked at her with pained sea-green eyes, and her smiled swiftly wilted.

"We're really not trying to treat it like that, Lera," the mayor said quietly. "We'd both be there for you always, if we could."

"I ... I di–didn't mean–" Lerannu stammered, growing hot in the face and seeing her vision suddenly blur with tears that brimmed on the brink of falling. A few seconds passed as both daughter and father, each understanding the other, regained their composure.

"Just come back if you can, okay?" she asked.

"I promise."

With that, Roniil and Uriah swiftly made for the town hall. Lerannu let her eyes roam about the crowd once more as Kiiva and Zalden positioned themselves behind her in her father's stead.

Zalden spoke up. "Is everything okay?" he asked quietly.

"Yeah," said Lerannu in a mildly subdued tone. "They're just checking to see if Mama's going to be able to make it. If not, I'm still doing it."

"I'm sorry, Lera," said Kiiva guiltily. "I didn't think there would be any serious holdup with your parents' work at the time because of it getting close to evening. Like your Da said, they were just about to call it a day."

"It's okay," Lerannu said, now more evenly. "This wouldn't be the first time. And besides, I really want to do this now. Really."

"Going to try it one more time, eh?"

The three children wheeled around, finding themselves face to face with Ahvrom and Dalle. As Kiiva embraced her mother and father in turn, Dalle, who had spoken, looked at the crowd admiringly.

"You've got quite the audience together! Are you sure you're up for this, Lera? You shouldn't overwork yourself just because of some impatient friends."

Dalle gave Kiiva and Zalden a mild glare of disapproval, her prime focus placed on her daughter. Lerannu, seeing both shifting awkwardly under her gaze, quickly came to their rescue.

"I'm sure, Mrs. Salinoth. I rested a little before everyone arrived and I'm only doing it once. Then I'm calling it a day, I promise."

"Very well," said Dalle. "Minding your limits and figuring them out is important to learn, mage or no, and it pretty much always starts out as a matter of trial and error, anyway. I guess we'll see soon enough." The tutor observed Kiiva and Zalden's position behind her student. "Looks like you've already got your help in case you push too hard, but we'll be here, too."

"Thank you, but Papa and Uriah should be back any minute, hopefully Mama too, and they'll be with me for that. I'm worried it'll be too crowded here if you're with us, too."

Ahvrom, having been looking through the crowd during the conversation, pointed toward the back of the audience. "I see your father and Uriah, but not your mother. They look like they're trying to tell you to go ahead. They seem a bit worried about something, too. Do you see them?"

Lerannu followed her teacher's gesture, quickly catching her father and the treasurer in the throng. Her heart sank at Roniil's troubled face. She caught her father's nod, and closing her eyes and taking one last deep breath, whispered to Kiiva to get ready to throw the leaf. She then stepped forward to address the crowd.

"Thank you all so much for taking the time to come and see this. My friends were really excited to see what I learned today, and what started as me getting ready to show only them is now a chance to share it with all of you, whether you live here or are passing through."

Lerannu looked over to Kiiva, who confirmed that she was ready to toss the leaf when signaled, as the crowd politely acknowledged her introduction with encouraging applause.

"I only just learned to work with wind today," the young mage continued, "and only a little at that, but I'm happy to show you what I can do."

The crowd applauded encouragingly once more, and Lerannu, bracing her mind and body for the task, nodded to Kiiva to toss up the leaf. Just as her friend wound her arm back to throw, Lerannu became conscious of the sudden stillness in the air. It felt as if Vente herself wanted to make sure a stray breeze did not meddle with the apprentice's efforts. The sensation of stillness and silence came and went swiftly, and Lerannu found herself focusing completely on the leaf the instant it flew from Kiiva's hand.

Pressing her hands together at the sides, palms up, Lerannu kept her sight, mind, and soul fixed on the leaf, its former green now faded to an earthy orange by autumn's breath. She could feel the wind being channeled across her palms. She could see the leaf fluttering about, but staying afloat, by the steady breeze that she had called forth. A smile crept onto her face as she became aware, faintly, of the growing cheers of the onlookers. The moodiness she felt from her mother's absence and the unintended hurt she had caused her father melted away.

When her sight began to blur into tunnel vision, Lerannu didn't trouble herself with trying to sustain the spell a second longer. She simply let go of her focus with a blink of the eyes and a quick, deep breath. The crowd's applause was now booming, and Lerannu, her heart soaring high, promptly took a bow. She was caught off-guard by Zalden's sudden grasp upon her shoulders, followed by the gasp from the audience, until she realized that her bow must have seemed more like a swooning stagger. The apprentice laughed, explaining her gesture to the crowd, who then laughed alongside her.

"I am pretty tired now, though, so that'll be all today. Thank you all again so much for coming! Onu keep you all well!"

As the crowd applauded once more, Lerannu turned to her friends and teachers, surprised at their wide-eyed gaze. When she asked what the matter was, Dalle stepped forward, stooping slightly so she could speak to her student eye-to-eye.

"Nothing's wrong, Lera," the mage assured her, a smile of wonder spreading across her face. "Nothing at all. But you should know, you nearly doubled your time from this afternoon."

Lerannu felt as if her jaw was going to unhinge. "Are you joking?"

"Not at all," said Ahvrom. "You kept that leaf in the air for almost ten seconds that time. It's possible that things were just lined up in your favor, for lack of a better way of saying it, but very few students your age have been able to do that, especially on their first day. Honestly, five seconds is a bit above average to begin with, and you were managing that over the course of one afternoon. Lera, I believe you could really become a great mage."

"Really?"

"Of course! And you could go anywhere in the world, and there would be plenty of people who'd love to have you around. The Temple, kings and queens, everyday travelers ... anyone and everyone!"

Dalle, still crouching to Lerannu's eye level, placed a hand on her student's shoulder and patted it affectionately. "And I can tell you, with no doubt in my mind, that your mother is very proud of you. I hope you aren't thinking otherwise."

"No, it's not like that," Lerannu sighed. "This has happened before, I just—"

The mage pupil's words were cut short as the voice of Ban Gahdos, the head physician of the town and her father's advisor on health-related affairs, cut through the lingering applause of the crowd.

"Attention, everyone!" the doctor cried out. "I have received a message this afternoon reporting several outbreaks of Endallian Fever across Enmayar! Please remain calm and follow the guard and doctor that approach you. We are awaiting further news on the situation, and will keep you informed as we learn more of what's going on. Thank you for your cooperation!"

Silence reigned over the crowd at the mentioning of the dreaded disease, which was said to kill two of every ten infected despite the progress in medicine since its first recorded cases. Glancing worriedly at the faces around her, Lerannu saw her father and Uriah striding up to her through the crowd as it dispersed according to the doctor's instructions. Reaching his daughter, Roniil took her hand, bidding her to say farewell to her friends and teachers until a course of action was decided about the town's affairs during the alert. He led Lerannu up to Dr. Gahdos himself. Beside him was Sarah Stonefaith, Lerannu's mother. Seeing her daughter, Sarah pulled her to her side and hugged her tightly.

"I'm so sorry I couldn't see you with the leaf, Lera. I was just on my way out the door when Dr. Gahdos came back with the news."

"It's okay, Mama. What's going to happen?"

"We're not sure yet, but we'll probably need to keep people from coming into town for a while ... or leaving, for that matter."

"We'll have to wait and see, though," her father remarked, "because our choice, whatever it be, could risk either spreading the fever or holding back help, if not both."

Lerannu held tightly to her mother, whose sigh of exasperation filled her ears. With the crowd now dispersed into different groups to undergo medical inquiries, Lerannu followed her parents and Dr. Gahdos, who led them back to town hall for examinations.

4

12/5/4012 G.M.

OWEN LOVONHAAR left the infirmary of Genverdell's archtemple after hours of tending to the sick alongside his brothers and sisters of the faith. The constant racing from bed to bed heavily drained the tall and portly salpion, his spectacles frequently steaming up from the breaths that passed through his plague mask. He was glad for the prospect of sitting in his study for the afternoon. Sadly, while the day's remaining tasks of Fidonhaal's highest cleric weren't expected to be nearly as physically exerting, they nevertheless brought heaviness to the heart, being matters of loss and likely uncomfortable revelations.

There was the matter of accounting for the ones who had died that morning, which were thankfully few. There was also the matter of listening for any news on the progression of the fever, which, despite it not yet having been a fortnight since the epidemic began, was already being reported as the worst outbreak in living memory. Six days ago, the queen and king sent word to the other three nations declaring the entirety of Enmayar under quarantine, with all ports and the border in the Whitemanes closed until further notice. The capital, Genverdell, was itself under lock and key, permitting only those supplying medicine to enter. Every citizen donned a plague mask, casting a macabre air over all the day's tasks. Silent anxiety reigned over the great city of the two hills, broken only by the coughs of the sick and the mourning for the departed.

As troubling as these matters were, there was another issue that was prodding the salpion's heart more personally. It was what he needed to tell Ruth and Verdok in case the fever either claimed them or him before he would otherwise have the chance. Having entered his private rooms and seating himself at his desk, Owen turned to face the mirror that hung to his left and talked to himself as he usually did in these sorts of situations. It was his way of unwinding as well as preparing for what lay ahead.

"Four Breaths," he sighed wearily as he stared into the hazel eyes and jet-black fur that reflected back at him. "Today, I'm feeling twice my age."

The salpion smiled ruefully, taking a deep breath as he reached for the water on the table beside his desk.

"Sister Loru will be here any minute," he reminded himself as he poured. "We'll document the lost and inform the necessary people, same as the past five days, then it'll be time to talk to Verdok and Ruth."

Having drained his water glass, Owen opened a drawer in the desk, taking the dear memento he had kept safe for the past seven years in preparation of this day, though it had come quite sooner than expected. He held it lovingly in his hand during the duration of his talk with Sister Loru, absently turning it about in his palms as the temple mortician counted the dead and composed the notices with him.

***

When the task was finished for the day and Loru returned to the mortuary, the salpion sent for Sister Arza Pionaar to bring her daughter and Verdok Merchill in to see him. He closed his eyes, the heirloom now firmly clasped within both hands, and waited in silence, reflecting on the year when both children came into his life, and the gains and losses that came entwined with them. His eyes opened at the gentle creaking of the door, and Sister Arza, holding hands with both Ruth and Verdok, quietly entered the room. All three seated themselves on the sofa in front of him, with Arza having the middle seat and the children on either side of her. Owen looked affectionately at each in turn before finally speaking.

"I'm sure you two are wondering why you're here," the salpion said to the children. "As I'm sure you know, a lot of people have been getting sick these past few days, and many are dying."

Ruth and Verdok nodded in somber acknowledgement, their youthful eyes looking intently at their mentor from over their masks.

Owen took a deep breath, trying to maintain a level voice, before continuing. "Sister Arza and I have things to tell you both about your parents. We were meaning to wait a little longer before telling you; we felt it would perhaps be easier if you two were a bit older, but seeing how bad the fever is–"

Both of the children cut in, their eyes now filled with worry.

"Are you sick, Salpion?" they asked in unison.

"No, it's–"

The two then looked up to Arza.

"Sister Arza?" asked Verdok.

"Mama?" asked Ruth.

"We're both alright," Arza assured, hugging them as they clung to her in anxiety, "but we might not be before this is over, or ... or it might be one of you that gets sick. And in case it comes to the worst, we ..."

The sister had been fighting back tears with each word. Now she could go no further, and as she gently stroked the children's heads, let out one sob. Arza nodded to Owen to continue, and held Ruth and Verdok tightly to her sides in silence.

"We just feel that you both should know the full stories about your parents, and we don't want to risk not being able to tell you in case something happens to us or you, be it this fever or anything else. Are you two willing to listen? It is a bit hard to talk about, but it's important for you to know."

Ruth and Verdok exchanged glances with one another. In addition to the two of them being schooled together, along with the other children residing in the archtemple, the two were specially mentored by Owen himself as a father figure. Sister Arza, though only Ruth's mother in truth, was as a mother to Verdok as well. This led the two to becoming fast friends, and the looks they gave each other seemed to be simultaneous requests and promises of support for one another. Both then looked to Arza and Owen, finally nodding for the salpion to begin.

"Very well," he sighed as he concealed the memento in his hand. "I suppose we'll begin with you, Verdok, since you were born first."

The boy, his fur marbled brown and black, locked eyes with those of his mentor. They were very haunting eyes, of the deepest blue. His mother's were the same.

"You've already been told that your parents died shortly after you were born, but we haven't gone any further than that, have we?"

"No, Salpion," Verdok answered solemnly.

"Come now, both of you," Owen said gently as he looked to both children, "that's just for when we hold services and such. Please, call me Owen, or Father Owen, if you'd rather."

Verdok and Ruth nodded in reverent acknowledgement.

"Anyway, Verdok," the salpion continued, "you need to know that you weren't just sent here because you had nowhere else to go. We take in plenty of orphans with no other home, true, but as your friends and classmates can tell you, that is far from being the only case for the young here."

"Were Ma and Da priests here?" Verdok asked.

"No, but they were very good friends of mine, and many others in this temple. Your mother was a Mavon named Quenda, and she was a potter. Your father was a Kason named Zantor, and he was a stoneworker; usually doing things for buildings, from shaping the bricks to working decorations into the walls, but he liked to sculpt art as well. They came here at least once a week, seeking Onu with me and everyone else who came here, and helped us in trying to help those struggling with life in the city."

Owen paused to turn to Ruth, who was listening as attentively to the story as her friend.

"That included your mother, Ruth, but we'll get to that in a moment."

The young girl looked up to her mother in surprise, as did Verdok, until the salpion resumed his account.

"Your parents and I met each other when were all fourteen, Verdok. I had been a novice for a few years, and the two of them were simply going to the day's service with their parents."

Owen paused, furrowing his brow in thought. Then, after a moment of silence, he softly laughed, shrugged and continued.

"I can't for the life of me remember how exactly we met or what it was we talked about, but the three of us quickly became great friends. I watched them grow older and excel in their work, and saw them grow closer together as the days became years. I ministered their wedding as one of my first acts as the new salpion. A year later, I helped them bring you into the world."

Owen, blinking back the tears that blurred his vision, stood up, came over to Verdok, and drew him into a father-like embrace from Arza's side.

"Four moons passed, and then I had to see them die. They were taken by the very same fever that is running through our land right now."

The boy, who had been looking up into Owen's eyes, lowered his gaze to the floor as the two remained in their melancholy embrace. His ears, however, stayed erect, and the salpion knew that he was still listening intently, so he continued.

"Before they died, I went over their last wishes with them, what they wanted done with their home and businesses, where their families were so that they could be told what happened, all those sorts of things. Then we finally came to what to do with you."

Verdok's ears pricked up even further.

"When the fever was sweeping through Enmayar then, it was bad. Not as bad as it looks to be this time, but still bad. So, when it started, your parents worried about what to do with you if the worst happened. They were torn between having you either sent to Quanithe or raised here."

"Quanithe?" Verdok asked, still looking down at the floor. "Isn't that really far away?"

"It is a good way from here, yes. Both pairs of your grandparents, from your mother and father's sides, moved there shortly after the wedding, along with an uncle and aunt or two. Last I heard, they're running a vineyard together there and doing well, though I'm yet to hear any news about their health since this all started. They've known about you since you were born, and about you being here since you were placed in our care."

"So they decided to leave me here, then?"

"Not entirely. We agreed to raise you here at least until you were ten so you could have a good start in schooling. Then we'd have your family at Quanithe come here, and we'd talk about what to do from there. You'll be there, too, so you can tell us what you'd want, and we'll hopefully be able to settle it all out then."

Verdok lifted his eyes back up to his mentor once more. His eyes, though teary from learning more of his parents' passing, were also shining with a light of gratitude and respect that perhaps was there before, but not with the strength now seen.

"I'll be able to say what I'd want?" Verdok asked in awe.

"Of course, dear boy!" Owen said in surprise. "Why wouldn't you?"

"Well, it's just that I've heard from some of my friends, like Michael, that when grownups talk about things like this, the kids don't usually get to say anything about it."

"Michael wasn't exactly wrong, I must admit. But he was in a very tough, and different, situation from yours. Both of his parents wanted him, but it was clear that neither wanted to truly care for him. He wanted to still be with his mother, but she simply wasn't a good mother and he wouldn't have been safe with her. And his father, well, Michael's limp ..."

Owen cut himself short, shaking his head and looking back to Verdok, his eyes now marked by worry and sorrow for his friend.

"I'm sorry," he said with a chuckle of regret, "I'm just piling on more for you to worry about, and I'm trying to keep to the point for both you and Ruth. My point, Verdok, is that isn't the case here. I mean, I can't promise it'll go exactly as you'd want, but we intend to hear everyone's side of things."

Verdok hugged the salpion closer to him. "What if I want to stay here and be like Brother Jordan, or Sister Arza ... or you?"

Owen's eyes were now fully fixed on Verdok's. The deepness of blue that the boy's eyes held, coupled with the voice in which he asked the question, made the salpion feel as if he were about to drown in a sea of palpable hope.

"Then as I told your mother and father," Owen said, his voice on the verge of breaking after a moment of silent reflection, "you'll be welcome to stay, and ... and I'll love you as if you were my son."

Verdok finally broke his gaze from Owen's sight as he buried his face into the salpion's robes, weeping freely from the turbulent winds of grief and gratitude that raged within him. Owen, though silent, let his tears flow freely as well, looking affectionately at Ruth and Arza as they rose from their seat and joined him in consoling Verdok, Arza with a hand on his head, Ruth with one on his shoulder.

After a few minutes passed and Verdok had calmed down, Owen finally opened the hand in which he hid the keepsake and showed it to Verdok. It was a stone-carved amulet, fashioned from white marble that bore the crest of the Temple. The carvings that formed the design on the other-wise smooth marble disc were inlaid with jet, making it a beautiful piece that had both stark contrast with the jet on the marble and subtle variance within the marble itself, shifting from snow white to bright grey. A black strip of sturdy leather ran through the loop at the top of the amulet, shining almost as much as the jet inlays.

"This was your mother's," said Owen quietly. "Your father made it for her himself, and gave it to her when he asked her if she'd marry him. She wore it every day from then on, parting with it only when she gave it to me to keep for you. She said that she always meant for you to have it one day, though she wasn't able to give it to you herself. Here, it's yours now."

Verdok took the pendant from his mentor's hand. After looking at it in reverent silence a moment, he put it on, tying the leather thong about his neck. He then held it close to his heart, looking at his three friends with eyes of thankful comfort.

"It suits you very well, Verdok," said the salpion, with Ruth and Arza nodding in agreement as they returned to their seats and Verdok resumed his place beside Arza.

"Well, that about covers it for Verdok," Owen laughed lightly and sadly as he turned to Ruth and her mother. "Now we just need to talk about you, Ruth. I'd like to say that your story shouldn't be as hard to hear, but ... well, Sister Arza?"

"Ruth," the sister said as her daughter turned her full attention to her, "when Father Owen said Verdok's parents helped the Temple in helping the poor here in the city, he mentioned that once included me."

Arza then turned to Verdok, bringing Ruth closer to her side as she spoke.

"I met your mother and father about two months before you were born, Verdok. They were with Father Owen and some other priests and helpers when he came to what was my house at the time, and offered me a chance at a new life."

"Where did you live then?" Ruth asked.

Arza, turning her eyes back to her daughter, now pulled Verdok closer to her as well.

"On the southwest riverbank, in that little wooden house just across the second bridge."

Owen saw Ruth and Verdok wince, their ears twitching once at the strike of realization that came from Arza's revelation. Ruth and Verdok, having accompanied the sister and the salpion to that part of the city to help those who lived there, knew that Arza's past would be hard to swallow. For all of Fidonity's efforts over the past four millennia to rise back from the losses that came from the era of Raakaru's reign, and the progress that had indeed been made, the claws of poverty still dug deep wherever it was able to fix. Such was the case for the southwest bank district of Genverdell, the poorest area of the city, and consequently one of the poorest in all of Enmayar. With this reality being seemingly borne in mind as well as a seven-year-old child could manage, Ruth, after a few seconds of thinking over what her mother had just revealed, nodded for her to continue.

"Spring was just starting, and the city was beginning to return to its full life. It had been a bit of a tough winter and the Temple, which had done what it could to help us in the cold, was now able to do so in full force again. Sadly, for all their efforts, they still couldn't get to everyone at once and some were missed ... or they avoided help out of pride ... or shame. I was among those who didn't want the Temple to help me because I was ashamed of what I had done, what I felt I needed to in order to live."

"Did you steal, Mother?" Ruth asked, her little grey-furred ears twitching again as she braced for whatever blow the truth would deal to her.

"A few times, yes, but ..."

Arza's eyes were clamped shut, her face showing the struggle within to bring herself to confess her past to her daughter as well as hold back tears. Ruth, after trying to patiently wait for her mother to continue, finally spoke up, hoping it would prompt her to push on.

"What about Father? Was it something he did? Did he die, too? Did he do something wrong and died before he could do anything to make it better? Or is he still alive somewhere?"

"Ruth!" Arza gasped with a sudden sob. The girl, at first wilting in apparent fear of angering or hurting her mother, hugged her closely when Arza, tears brimming in her eyes, spread her arms wide to show that she wasn't angry at her daughter's barrage of questions. A moment later, Arza looked straight into Ruth's eyes, and confessed all.

"You could say that your father's deeds were a part of my shame, too, but it was because he took up on an offer I gave him: my body. I sold my body to him, and from that you came to be."

Ruth sat beside her mother, crestfallen. While she was yet to know or understand all that went on between man and woman, her schooling led her to understand enough to get the essential picture, especially for one her age. She had even met and helped a prostitute or two on her trips with the priests to the riverbank, so she had come to understand the situation even if only on a very elementary level. This included the understanding that some turned to such measures on an "as needed" basis, and potentially had a limited clientele, perhaps even comprised of only one person.

Knowledge of this notion was obvious as Ruth, her voice aching with hope, asked her mother if she at least knew who her father was. Sister Arza shook her head, and Ruth wilted into her mother's arms. There were no tears, nor outbursts, but Owen felt that the silence that followed was even more painful.

"For all I know," Arza said at length, "your father could be dead or alive, rich or poor, or anywhere in the world from this city to the southernmost reach of Janrenar. All I can tell you is that he was a full-bodied Zaron, same as me, since you'd have more than just grey in your fur if he wasn't."

The sister gently patted her daughter's back, looking briefly at Owen with eyes pained by the past, but also showing gratitude and friendship for the help he had given her that day. "Your father may have even been the man who visited me moments before Owen and Verdok's parents came."

Ruth lifted her head, her face a picture of shock at the thought that her mother had sinned in desperation mere moments before the arrival of the head of the Temple.

"Yes," Arza continued with a laugh of both glum confession and lighthearted thanks. She looked again to Owen.

"Father Owen saw me at my worst," she continued. "I was naked, my fur was matted, and I was crying. I was holding two silvers in one hand and feeling for you in my belly with the other. I didn't see Father Owen come in, I was so lost in thought. Then he spoke up, and when I noticed his Temple robes, I was so scared at first that he was going to shame me more with a sermon or drag me into the street to make me an example to people. Then he said that he didn't want to do that, and then I was afraid that he ... that he wanted to pay for my body, too."

Owen caught sight of the uncomfortable faces on both children, and was about to ask them if they had learned about how the men and women of the Temple could also fall to such vices as anyone else could. Arza beat him to the question, however, and the salpion nodded approvingly, both to the children for their education and understanding, and to Arza that she may resume her account.

"I almost gave up on both Fidonity and in what little trust I still had in Onu himself at that moment. But then he had Verdok's mother and a priestess bring in clean clothes and some water to wash with, and Verdok's father brought in some water for me to drink. After that, Father Owen gave me his hand and offered me a chance to begin life anew, and to give my baby a good home."

The sister had brought her daughter onto her lap, and the two held each other so closely that Owen could see only nursing as a closer physical bond between mother and child.

"So, I spent the rest of that day helping them in helping others along the bank. I helped those we came across, and even led Father Owen's company to some that I personally knew there. Some we fed and clothed, others we gave guidance, and still others did the same as me. We went back to the archtemple that evening, and I ate the best dinner I ever had."

Arza and Owen laughed at the shared memory of the newly inducted sister tucking into the food that night, a meal that might have been described as "generously modest" by most, for the simple bread and meat may as well have been a banquet for royalty to her. Arza quickly returned to her tale, however, and placed an arm about Verdok as she neared the end of her account.

"The kindness your parents showed me, Verdok, along with Father Owen, led me to having a healthy body, mind, and soul again. They showed me that my past was behind me, and that I was no longer a woman who carried a fatherless babe and sold herself to eat. I had become a sister of the Temple, a loving daughter of Onu, and a helper to Fidonity. No longer did people look at me with pity or disgust; I was instead greeted with smiles and blessings. And when your mother had you, Verdok, she showed me how to be a mother by showing me how she cared for you. I may owe Father Owen for leading his group to my house the day we met, but your mother and father played a very big part in helping me become a better person, too. They were my best friends along with Father Owen, and I was very sad when they died."

Verdok, leaning into Arza's shoulder, began to weep again. The sister joined him.

"They were so happy when you were born," she sobbed. "They loved you so much."

Arza then looked to Ruth once more as she told her story's end.

"I had you about a month later, just a few days after the news came that the fever was over. After that, I've worked with you and the other children, because I love to care for you and your friends. I admit, you and Verdok are special to me, because you are mine and he is the child of two of my greatest friends, but I've come to live for seeing children grow up happy and safe, and not fall into the troubles I had."

A moment of silence passed as the four reflected on the afternoon's revelations, the only sound being the gently muffled breaths of air passing through their masks.

Then Owen sniffed and got up. He drew back the curtains of the window behind his desk and peered down at the grounds below.

"Well, I'd say that about covers it. How about we join those in the garden for tea?" he proposed cheerfully.

5
12/6/4012 G.M.

SHEEVA sat in a chair on the balcony outside of Xalu's study, taking respite from the day's lessons and enjoying what sense of fresh air that she could. She looked somberly over the subdued city that spread below Genverdell's great eastern hill, on which the castle rested at its top. Normally at this point in the afternoon, she could see countless little dots of black, brown, grey, and white milling about like ants, and hear the sounds of the city, which reached the castle as a steady hum of activity. But now she could only pick out the odd individual specks of a Fidon, most likely either a doctor, cleric, or mortician, as they made their rounds up and down a street or district. She could hear naught but the late-autumn breeze.

It had been just under two weeks since the fever's outbreak began, according to what her mother and father had told her. The first reports went out on the twenty-first of the previous month and became widespread knowledge, along with the disease itself, within the following week. A few days after that, a letter came from the Indovis family stating they were presently in good health, but were being kept from further travel in a town halfway between their hometown of Nelahaal and the capital. Depending on how long the fever's course continued, it was likely they wouldn't be able to reach Genverdell in time to join them for Sardonmay. The princess did her best to hide her feelings when she heard the news. She was unsure if she was successful, despite her parents not making any remark toward whatever reaction she may have shown.

It wasn't as if she couldn't understand the reasons for the delay, of course. Endallian Fever rarely spread this widely nowadays, and the centuries since the first recorded diagnosis had yielded medicine that made it no longer a near guarantee of death. Nevertheless, the illness was not to be taken lightly, especially on the occasions when it did spread like this. Sheeva even remembered, to a point, the last time the fever had spread at an abnormally severe rate. It was seven years ago, when the princess herself was of seven years. Her parents, her tutor Lady Xalu, and the recently arrived Greystones had done their best to explain the disease and matters of death to her and Nikolas as best as they felt they could, considering the children's ages at the time. Sheeva certainly understood the severity of the situation now at fourteen, and was not holding anything against the Indovis family, least of all the boy Allor, for not braving through a plague-swept country just to celebrate the first day of winter and the New Year. After all, she barely knew them anyway; it wasn't the same as lifelong friends canceling a visit at the last minute.

But Nikolas and his mother, Halla, had become unbearable company since the invitation her parents had sent to the Indovis family. Being confined to the castle with them due to the fever had only made matters worse. Sheeva now sorely wished for new, hopefully more cheery company. She was at first reluctant to consider another suitor, given that her past seven years with Nikolas had been very good. But the distant glares, cold shoulders, and general envelopment of doom and gloom that the lad and his mother gave the princess and her family had soon driven Sheeva quite apart from her old friend. She was now beginning to feel a desperate need for a more optimistic companion, and she prayed that Allor, should they eventually meet, would deliver.

The princess adjusted the mask on her face, grimacing at the oppressive feeling around her muzzle. She hated the masks, how they felt and looked both now and the last time she had to wear them seven years ago. Her memory drifted back to that time as she reflected on when the Greystones first came to live at the castle. Everyone was so much happier then, it seemed, though perhaps Sheeva's present mood stilted her memories. She remembered Xalu waking her up that day, telling her they had arrived. The queen and king had been speaking so well of them up to that point, and had told their daughter they were all going to be great friends. And for years, they were. It started with the grand images each of the Greystones struck in the young princess's eyes, from Valor's tall and handsome northern bearing and Halla's composure of stately grace to Nik's combination of charm and awkwardness.

Nik.

Sheeva felt a sudden welling of sadness as she said the nickname again in her mind. She had said it interchangeably with his proper name, depending on the circumstances, throughout their friendship, but she couldn't recall a time she had said it since Warden Valor's death. The princess blinked back the tears that tried to flow, and swallowed the sob that so suddenly charged from her heart to her lips as she glanced back into the window of her tutor's study. Nikolas was there, apparently talking to Xalu, though the warps in the glass and the mask on his face made it hard to tell if he was presently speaking or listening.

He was so sweet when they had first met. He never changed all that much until four months ago. He was the embodiment of gentlemen's etiquette and had greeted her when they first met with all the charm that a prince from a storybook would have displayed. The sole detractor, debatably, was the light stutter he had at the time. In hindsight, however, Sheeva thought it may have made the introductions better. She was somewhat shy and humbled when she first saw him. His dazzling appearance featured a star-like mark on his face formed by the inheritance of his father's white fur set against his mother's grey. Indeed, she perhaps was even a little envious as well due to her plain grey fur, which came from her full Zaron heritage. Combine that with Nik being three years her senior and the truly majestic air that he and his family carried, and Sheeva, despite being the Princess of Enmayar, was honestly intimidated.

When she heard the odd stutter pass from Nik's lips, however, she felt immediately better. She did not laugh, nor make some jest. It was not a feeling of superiority in regards to speech, but of comfort in being reminded that all Fidons were mortals with weaknesses great and small. The young princess thought about how she would support her new friend, encouraging him not to hold back because of his speech impediment, and that he could perhaps overcome it in time. Indeed, he did overcome it a couple years later, and his voice, which was already endearing to hear, flowed freely from his lips. It soon grew into a handsome, full voice like that of his father.

In those early days, the two were having lunch following the morning's lessons alongside their mentor and parents. It was just when the fever was going through the land, and the diners were cautiously eating outside on the same balcony where Sheeva was presently brooding. All at the table spoke little and quietly between quick lifts of the plague masks and the ensuing bites of food and sips of drink, their spirits subdued by the same graveness of the situation that had returned in the present day. The last epidemic had occurred in the middle of autumn as well, and as they ate, a sudden gust of wind blew and chilled Sheeva to the bone. A convulsive shiver shot through the princess, and Nikolas, ever the young gentleman, tenderly wrapped an arm about her shoulders in an attempt to curb her embarrassment from the display.

"None of us expected that, m-my dear princess," said the young man, "and the air is certainly c-cold."

Sheeva, moved by another of her friend's acts of gallantry, remarked that the lunch wasn't a formal occasion and that he could simply call her Sheeva in such cases. The boy, with a voice marked by the realization of friendly familiarity, stammered excitedly, "An-and you c-can call me Ni-Nik."

Since that day, when not in formal situations, the two had almost always addressed one another by their nicknames. Their friendship had since grown to the point where, at least in Sheeva's mind, it was only a matter of time until they were married. She had looked forward to a time when they could call one another by their pet names with the same intimate tenderness as she had heard her mother and father do countless times. But then the drought happened last summer, and matters escalated so rapidly to a point that no one was expecting. Nikolas's father lay dead at the feet of an angry throng, who were then calmed just as swiftly by a humble mayor who was among the present officials. The princess tried to console her friend as they stood side by side at the south warden's bier, but her words were met with silence. Sheeva left it for grief and simply stood beside him in reverent silence. But as the days went by, and the king and queen discussed matters with the wardeness and her son, things clearly began to sour. What was first only the silence of mourning became laden with resentful glares that the princess caught mother and son giving to her parents, and then herself, from the corners of her eyes. The announcement of the impending arrival of the Indovis family, the mother of which was the mayor who managed to calm the riot, and the implications of an additional suitor for the princess through the mayor's son, heightened the tension. While Sheeva blamed that revelation for partly worsening the relationship between her family and Nik's, she was now eagerly awaiting the Indovis's arrival, as well as worrying for their well-being as the fever broke out during their travels to Genverdell. If it could lead to another happy companion, she was now ready to take one, even if it meant losing one from the past. She still hoped it could end well between her and Nikolas, if not in marriage, then at least in remaining as friends.

Sheeva had constantly debated with herself whether or not to say anything, fearing what could happen as far as politics in Enmayar, and perhaps even all of Fidonhaal, was concerned. Although so much of the various shifts and pains of the realms from the past had largely retired into the history books, the princess was still in the process of comprehending all of the current states of the country and world, and she knew enough to understand how this could lead to something ugly if handled poorly. Thus, the princess had resigned herself to silent observation and endurance for the present.

The light click of the balcony's door opening interrupted the princess's brooding. Sheeva turned to see Nikolas standing in the doorway, his sea-green eyes looking at her above his mask with a light she couldn't quite determine. She saw the dulled look of grief that still clung to him, as well as bitterness, but there seemed to be at least one other emotion. Was it love or friendly affection, still lingering in the depths of his heart despite the past turbulent months? Was it a desire to make peace, struggling to shine through the darkness of his other feelings? Hoping for the best, Sheeva decided to make it a point to call him by his pet name, whether he said anything or not.

"Lady Vernifel's ready to resume lessons," the grey-and-white lad said flatly after a few seconds of silence. "It's history now. We're continuing from how Karanor rallied most of Sorrenar against the Snoweyes's reign after his parents were slain in the previous battle."

"Thank you," said Sheeva. "I'll be ready in just a minute."

The princess held out her hand, beckoning for Nikolas to take it and stand beside her.

"Care to have one last minute of fresh air before we go back into the room of parchment and wax, Nik?" she said with a grin.

His eyes narrowed and became hard as flint, then turned away with the sharp closing of the door.

Sheeva's grin vanished, and the princess returned to the study with sad resignation.

6

12/7/4012 G.M.

LERANNU gently climbed out of her bedroom window, the muffled and wearied voices of her parents fading to silence as she sprinted over to the quarantined clinic. Only four days had passed since Kiiva began coughing while watching her friend practice magic with her parents. The need to rush her to the doctor abruptly ended the lesson, and Dalle and Ahvrom were by their daughter's side ever since. Lerannu constantly visited them, much to her parents' fears despite her wearing a mask and maintaining some distance from Kiiva in the sickroom.

On the fourth day of Kiiva's sickness, Lerannu returned home from visiting that afternoon and was greeted by her mother and father, and their civic advisors, all seated in the mayor's waiting room. They stated that she was not to visit Kiiva anymore until the fever had run its course. She asked why, pleading her case by noting her careful use of the plague mask and distanced contact with Kiiva. The young mage swiftly came to regret it. What began as a simple statement of facts, among them the plausibility that Kiiva could die from the fever, quickly fell into a heated matter of argument and blame. When news of the fever first arrived, Roniil, being the mayor of Bravagoth, argued for keeping the town open to travelers. The great southern highway ran right through the town, and closing off the town would delay the arrival of general matters of commerce, including the medicine and supplies needed for treating the fever. This would affect not only Bravagoth itself, but potentially all of Enmayar due to the highway's importance, especially in the south ward.

Sarah, Lerannu's mother, though not the official mayor, played a role in governing the town as well. She had argued for complete quarantine, with a curfew and the allowance of only those bringing medicine into the town; and even then, only after an extensive examination to ensure they weren't sick.

Roniil's decision, both being that of the actual mayor and the one with the majority support of the advisors, including Uriah the treasurer, ultimately became the course of the town. It was decreed on the grounds of the need for continued general trade, in addition to bringing supplies vital to combating the fever, and the belief that it would hinder those vital routes for Bravagoth and other places if part of the south highway was essentially turned into a barrier. The initial argument was heated, placing great strain on the relationship between Lerannu's mother and father, as well as between them and their daughter. Now it had flared up once more, this time to its worst pitch yet. Roniil and Sarah, with supporting advisors in tow, rapidly raised their voices and placed blame upon one another for the occurrence of the fever in Bravagoth.

Lerannu, tears welling in her eyes, realized it was her question that had provoked the argument. She fled to her room, unnoticed, and hid under her blankets, weeping into her pillow as the divide raged outside her door.

It was now the midnight hour, with all others having resigned from the argument but Sarah and Roniil. Even they were finally running out of passion, their voices now sounding of frustration rather than furious yelling. Lerannu, resolved to see Kiiva once more, left her room by the window and set out, the mask secure on her muzzle and determination in her tear-drained eyes. She strode toward Dr. Gahdos's house through a silent town, with the few travelers passing through on the highway quiet as ghosts, their masks adding to their spectral, macabre appearance. Her parents' bickering had completely faded into silence. As the town clinic came into sight under the waxing half-moon, Lerannu began to pick up sounds again, as if she was wandering a graveyard and approaching a haunted tomb. Muffled coughs and moans passed eerily into the night air along with words of comfort and assurance, some sounding more confident than others.

Lerannu stood at the door to the clinic, intent on slipping in quietly and unhindered, as every visit had been before. She began to turn the handle, halting her breath when it ceased to turn. Given Bravagoth's traffic of travelers, especially during times like this, the town's doctors tended to work all hours of the day in shifts. If Ban Gahdos himself was presently away or sleeping, there were surely at least two or three doctors still looking over the patients. Such had been the case for medicinal practice across all of Fidonhaal for the past several centuries, especially in major settlements. Those who knew Ban Gahdos knew him to be especially keen on the matter. As a consequence, the clinic's door was almost never locked, and the young mage feared what this may bode regarding the state of those within. A second of total silence followed, with Lerannu's hand still grasping the handle, and then the young mage knocked firmly on the door.

"I'm seeing Kiiva again, one way or another," she said aloud to herself, trying her best to summon and keep her resolve, no matter who or what tried to stop her.

She gazed upwards, preparing to look straight into the eyes of whichever doctor or nurse answered. She wavered for only a second when the door opened to reveal the head physician himself. Lerannu stood silently, looking fixedly into the doctor's brown eyes. A few more silent seconds passed, then Gahdos spoke, his voice touched with irritation, but by far more with concern.

"What are you doing here this late, Miss Stonefaith? Only family of the sick are permitted to stay the night here, and I recall quite clearly that you weren't to visit Kiiva again until the fever passes."

"And she might pass along with it," Lerannu stated with a level bluntness that nearly set the doctor's eyes to popping out of his head.

Ban bent his knees a little, getting to eye level with the mage pupil and examining her almost as if he wasn't sure it was really her. When the doctor saw Lerannu's dry, bloodshot eyes, he gasped, and his face and ears flared up in alarm. He quickly softened with sympathy as he began to piece together what the girl's state of mind must have been since the afternoon.

"Lerannu," the doctor said gently, taking off the mask of impersonal medical professionalism, "I'm sorry that it went so badly when you returned home from your last visit. Your mother and father don't want to keep you from seeing Kiiva, it's–"

"I know, I know," Lerannu said flatly, but understandingly. "They're just trying to keep me from getting sick."

"Well, Lerannu," the doctor continued, "the thing is ... they were scared of you getting sick, but told me that they'd still allow you to come. I don't know if you noticed, but I've only been here maybe half the time since this all started; the other half has seen me trying to keep up with the news and make sure everything was in order with your parents at town hall."

"I know," said Lerannu. "You were there just this afternoon. You were on Mama's side. You saw how it went."

Ban's voice, though still gentle, now became laden with exasperation.

"Because there are other ways for the rest of the country to get medicine around, including here in South Ward!" The doctor drew a deep breath before continuing. "I understand your father's thinking, but my concern, and that of your mother's, was to do everything we could to keep the fever *out* of Bravagoth, plain and simple. I fear that some people, particularly your father in this case–and I mean no disrespect–may be underestimating the fever nowadays. Yes, we have been able to fight it and prevent it far better than we ever could in times past, but even before this outbreak, there have been cases that haven't been as widespread, but very deadly. We have our medicines and all, but the fever is far from being as small a matter as the sniffles, if such a day were to ever come. This sickness could still, in theory, kill this entire town."

Lerannu's voice, shaped by resolve and frustration, became increasingly calloused.

"How many other things could kill this whole town, in theory? A demon summoned in secret? A long-sleeping golem buried deep beneath the town? A bunch of brigands, or violent rebels that start a revolt from out of the blue? Perhaps just a different sickness?"

"Please, Ler–"

"And what might happen, in theory, if *everyone* decided to completely close themselves away from one another in a time like this? Would people be able to get enough medicine? Could they transport and trade what was needed to get it, or make it?"

The doctor stood, hunched over, struggling to find the words to say, completely unprepared for Lerannu's tone and tenacity.

"We all argued for what we thought was best," Ban said resignedly, "from it being for all of Enmayar to it being for our own here, and in the case of what I was originally going to say ..." the doctor sighed deeply once more, staring levelly into Lerannu's eyes, "being out of worry for a family, one that is made of two good friends of mine, and their child."

Lerannu's eyes gently lowered to the floor as she took in Ban's words.

"Your mother and father would've probably let you keep visiting, anxious as it made them, at least for a while longer, but I'm the one who told them to keep you from coming back until the fever passed. So, whatever feelings you have about your parents' arguing, you might need to place at least some of that on me."

The young mage's eyes snapped back up to the doctor's, which then widened slightly before taking their turn to look at the floor. Lerannu, dreading to think of the glare she had just given him, took a deep breath to calm herself. Ban then stood up, his hand gently reaching for the door.

"You need to go back home now and get some sleep, Lera. I'll see if we can–"

Lerannu cut him off, having spent all the strength she had summoned and reserved in herself for this moment. All measure of level frankness and steadfastness had gone away, and the tears, which she thought had been completely exhausted by the evening's end, poured down her face as water from a broken dam.

"P-please let m-me see her," she sobbed weakly.

Dr. Gahdos stood on the threshold, silent and motionless. A moment later he took Lerannu's hand and led her to Kiiva's room, down a hallway that housed others stricken by Endallian Fever.

When the doctor opened the door, Lerannu was greeted by the sight of Dalle and Ahvrom, sitting hand-in-hand, looking on with weary, but persistent, hope at their sleeping daughter. The two mages started at the sound of the opening door, but quickly gave a tired, sad smile at the sight of Lerannu entering. It was a smile that the pupil could easily see on her teachers despite the masks on their faces. The young mage nodded respectfully to them, then promptly took the chair opposite them, shifting it quietly to the side of Kiiva's bed. This was the closest she had yet sat by her friend since she got sick, and Lerannu made sure her mask was securely set around her face before taking her hand. There she sat, joining her tutors' vigil, uttering only a quiet "thank you" to Ban Gahdos as he left to tend to his other patients, simply saying to call for him if they needed him.

In all the rest of her days within the Mortal Plane, Lerannu never knew for certain how long she sat there until Kiiva, taken by a fit of hoarse coughing, weakly opened her eyes and looked at her best friend's hand within hers. Lerannu then clasped both hands around Kiiva's, and listened intently to every word she rasped out, whether it was to Lerannu, Dalle, or Ahvrom. Kiiva looked at Lerannu intently, her reddened eyes moistened by fever or tears, or perhaps both. Kiiva whispered to her friend hoarsely.

"Dr. Gahdos, and Mama and Papa ... they told me you couldn't be here anymore ... that I wouldn't see you until I got better."

Lerannu squeezed her friend's hand, breathing deeply as she fought to keep her composure.

"Well, looks like the plan changed," she said with a sad chuckle.

Dalle, still holding fast to her husband's hand, leaned forward to speak.

"I'm glad to hear that you remembered earlier today, Kiiva," her mother remarked. "A lot of times, especially when it's at its worst, either the fever or the medicine can make people forget things a bit."

Dalle's voice then became sad again. "But I'm also sorry that we told you that; we were just worried about Lera getting sick, too."

"I know," Kiiva whimpered. "I'm not mad." The sick girl then gripped her friend's hands as strongly as she could. "But I'm glad you're here, Lera. Aren't you scared, though, that you might catch it from me or someone else here?"

"Not really," Lerannu said immediately, though doubt began to set in just as quickly. "Well, not as much as ... I'm–I'm scared anyway."

Ahvrom and Dalle, having risen from their seats, placed a hand each on Lerannu's shoulders. Ahvrom's voice, tired as it was, came soothingly through his mask.

"It's alright, Lera, we're all scared right now."

A silent moment passed before Ahvrom, his voice one of sudden realization and alarm, spoke once more.

"Lera, if you're here and we weren't expecting you, especially at this hour–by the Four Breaths, Lera, please tell me you got your parents' permission to be here!"

The young mage shook her head in silence, and looked into the alarmed eyes of her teachers before speaking, the tears beginning to return again as her mind flew back to that tortuous afternoon. Her efforts to explain herself fell quickly into sobbing, and the two mages embraced their student as Ahvrom spoke gently into her ear.

"Come now, Lera, we're not scolding you, but your mother and father would be worried sick if they found you missing!"

Lerannu shook her head fervently as she wailed. "They've been fighting over what should've been done about the fever for hours, ever since I went back from here last time! They were still yelling at each other when I left! They didn't even notice when I ran crying into my room, and I asked the question that started it all! It's all my fault!"

Ahvrom and Dalle kept Lerannu in their embrace, now beginning to rock gently as they tried to comfort her. Dalle began to gently stroke her student's soft grey hair.

"Lera, I'm so sorry that happened, but it's *not* your fault, do you understand?"

"She's right," said Ahvrom in turn. "Your mother and father have very demanding jobs as it is, and when things like this happen, it puts an awful lot more on their shoulders. They might not be able to keep themselves from getting upset sometimes. But these things pass, and once the fever's spell around here is over and things start getting back to normal, I'll bet whatever you'd like that they'll be much less upset."

Lerannu, having largely calmed down, sniffed and wiped her eyes across her sleeve as Dalle spoke again.

"Yes," she said, "and we'll be able to get back to our lessons. Next thing you know, you'll be lifting and throwing stones with wind and who knows what else!"

Lerannu smiled at the thought and looked back to Kiiva, who was giggling weakly.

"I hope this passes before winter's over, because whenever it snows, I want to see you blow a bunch of snow at Zalden for his snowball attack last year."

Everyone in the room began to laugh, both at the memory of the past winter's escapade and the prospect of future justice done through the sport of youths. Lerannu, pulling away from her tutor's embrace, returned to Kiiva's side and held her hand again.

"I'll make sure I'm able to do that by the time we get a good snow," the young mage said with a grin, "and maybe I'll even be able to stop his snowballs in the air and throw them back!"

The two girls were now giggling fitfully, both pairs of eyes seeing the other's joy return.

Then Kiiva coughed harshly, again and again, and the mask on her muzzle suddenly went from dry and white to soaked and red.

A second of deathly silence hung in the air as Lerannu, still grasping her friend's hand, stood frozen to the spot in horror. When the sounds came back, Lerannu became conscious of her friend's violently shaking hand along with the terrified cries of Dalle and Ahvrom. Dalle shoved Lerannu aside, gripping one of Kiiva's hands like a vise in one hand and cradling her head in the other.

"No, no Kiiva! Please stop shaking! Oh, Onu, please no! My baby! MY BABY!"

Lerannu heard rapid footsteps behind her and turned to see Dr. Gahdos, an assistant physician in tow, looking mournfully at the scene before turning his sight to her.

The doctor drew a deep breath. "You have to leave, Miss Stonefaith. *Now.*"

Lerannu stood trembling for a few seconds, then silently walked out of the room. The horrid sounds of deathly coughing and the scent of blood seemed to follow her, however, and the young mage began to run. She dashed down the hall, which now seemed endless, until she finally burst through the front door, screaming as she ran into a being of horror. It was a tall creature with no mouth, and another figure of the same sort stood by its side. The creature grasped her and lowered its face to hers, and it wasn't until the voice of her father reached her ears, passing softly through his mask, that she realized it was only her parents.

Lerannu looked from her father to her mother. Both of them seemed to be finally spent from their hours-long tirades against each other. She then buried her face into her father's robes, weeping inconsolably as her mother strode into the clinic, which was now filled with Dalle and Ahvrom's wails. Overcome by weariness and grief, Lerannu fell asleep in her father's embrace, waking the next dawn in her bed.

***

At the sun's zenith the following day, Lerannu stood alongside her parents, dull-faced and dry-eyed, as she watched Kiiva being lowered into the earth.

7

12/13/4012 G.M.

ALLOR woke with a start, his father's strong hand pressing firmly but gently onto his shoulder. It had been hard for him to sleep ever since the fever broke out on their way to Genverdell, with the plague masks being dreadfully uncomfortable in addition to the general worry of catching the disease. He became elated, then, when he saw that his father had his mask off. Upon closer inspection, Allor observed the mask wasn't completely off, but was hanging loosely about his chin. Alphaar explained to his son that all reports were now saying that the fever was beginning to die down, and that, while they still needed to keep their masks handy and wear them when in crowds until further notice, the town in which they were staying was now fully open to travelers again, thus enabling them to resume their ride to the capital.

Allor quickly got up to gather his things, stopping only to embrace his mother when she came into the room in which they had been staying since the fever started. The family and their small entourage from Nelahaal had a brisk, quiet breakfast in the inn's otherwise empty dining hall. The air about them and the town at large was relieved, yet still subdued. They then promptly packed up and left the town two hours before midday. A minute or two after riding out of the town's gate, Allor, following suit with his parents and companions, lowered his mask and breathed the late-autumn air deeply. His grey fur bristled, and he shivered lightly with a feeling of renewal as the cool morning air played at his skin and filled his lungs.

"So good to breathe freely again!" Egrah remarked as she reined in beside her son and patted his shoulder.

"Mm-hmm," Allor agreed, invigorated by the air, yet feeling the discomfort of unfamiliarity at the same time. They had, after all, spent more than two weeks essentially confined to the tavern and the family's room therein, and the memory of open space had somehow felt somewhat forgotten. Even the few times he did go out, his mask had kept him from being able to enjoy fresh air since the whole epidemic began. In addition to these mixed feelings, he was also preoccupied with worries of how things were faring back at Nelahaal. His mother, picking up on the boy's tone, asked if he was well. She commented that the ordeal had been hard on everyone, and she and her husband were proud of how Allor had handled the matter.

"Thank you," Allor said pensively. "It's just … I don't suppose you or Father had gotten any news from home yet?"

Egrah's ears lowered somberly. "Not yet. We hadn't been able to send any word, by heraldwing or courier, since we got stuck back there, apart from the letter to Genverdell. If it weren't for the fact that the message was for the queen and king, the mayor there wouldn't have let me send even that. I wasn't even able to send a letter today before leaving, to let them know that we were on the move again, because we all still need to keep our guard up. The mayor, understandably, wanted to keep his own bird handy just in case another emergency came up."

She patted Allor's back again, then began to guide her horse back toward her husband, who was conversing with one of the advisors accompanying them.

"I'll see if I can ask the queen and king to send a message or permit me to use one of their birds to send one myself once we get to Genverdell and settle in. We're all worried about how things went back home; don't think you're alone in that."

"Of course," Allor said with a nod. "Thank you."

Allor turned his eyes back to the road, glossing over those of the family retinue that rode before and behind him, when a breeze blew strongly from up the road. Allor shivered vigorously as the cold wind blew into his fur and through his cloak, and laughed as several in the party swore at the sudden bite of cold. The chill reminded him of the impending winter and new year, and after counting the days until then, and trying to figure the remaining distance to the capital, he called back to his mother and father once the brief gale passed.

"Is it still possible that we could be there in time for Sardonmay?"

Alphaar and Egrah smiled. "If we do, it'll be only by a few days at best, but it is possible, provided there aren't any other major problems."

The hope at the chance to still make it to Genverdell in time for the initial purpose of their invitation, combined with the beautiful day and fresh air, rose Allor's spirits high. He could see plainly that the rest of the party were of a like mind. They rode on at a determined pace, eager to see the capital's two great hills.

***

They were fairly worn out when they finally reached Genverdell. Twelve days of riding through increasingly colder weather for hours on end had definitely taxed some of the group's reserves of cheer, but never to the point where it matched the days cooped up in a quiet inn within a town paralyzed by a plague scare. As each day passed with no further incident or word of the fever, the members of the party as well as those they met on the road began to recover their spirits. All the highs and lows had faded from mind when the party rode up a hill and saw the capital in the distance. Its walls and buildings rendered a warm, golden grey in the early morning light.

"Should be able to get there by sundown if we can step up the pace a bit!" Alphaar said with renewed cheer amidst several praises to Onu called out breathlessly from others in the party. "Might even be able to get started on settling in the castle in time for supper!"

"And we made it with three days to spare, too!" the mayor of Nelahaal remarked as she kissed her husband. "Let's go!"

Alphaar's prediction proved largely accurate, as they reached the great east gate of Genverdell with the sun just beginning to touch the top of the capital's west hill and still having a ways to go before meeting the horizon. The gate was open, as was typically the case when no crisis was at hand, but Allor's parents needed to address the gatekeepers, given the nature of their visit's purpose. The sun was a thumb's breadth from touching the far-off western hills by the time the company was finally escorted to the castle. When they reached the main gate, they rested on benches in a small green area set aside for waiting visitors, their cloaks wrapped snugly about them. They were fairly winded by the hike up the great hill in conjunction with their hours-long ride. Allor sat between his mother and father, pulling his cloak tighter about him as his eyes roved absentmindedly over the evergreens and bare shrubs that stood in the garden. He began to think of his friends back in Nelahaal.

The great double doors to the castle opened, and Allor started at the sight of the royal family personally approaching to greet them.

8

12/25/4012 G.M.

SHEEVA was making the last adjustments to her gown and jewelry, with help from her mother and Lady Xalu, before joining the others at the castle's main door. Dinner had been postponed at the last moment as news of the Indovis family's arrival reached the palace, and the princess's appetite vanished at the combination of anticipation and anxiety regarding the new guests and her future suitor.

The men and women of the household rushed to their quarters, alone and in groups, to dress in their best to greet the arrivals personally at the gates. The king and queen had decided upon this manner of reception, as opposed to the usual greeting of guests in the throne room, in light of the risks the Indovises took on the road due to the outbreak, and the subsequent air of joyful relief that had filled the capital and the nation for the past twelve days.

The princess reflected on the day the news broke of the fever's apparent end. It began with cautious optimism, but the mood grew more secure with each passing day. One week later, it was completely official: the outbreak of Endallian Fever, which reports had pointed to having begun around the twenty-first of the previous month, had largely died out as abruptly as it started. It had been only a matter of essentially three weeks, but the brief outbreak was the worst in Enmayar since the one from seven years ago, and thus one of the worst in living memory.

Sheeva scanned the ladies' dressing room with the corners of her eyes, looking to see if Lady Greystone was perhaps with them, but had escaped her notice. Not to her surprise, the south wardeness was not with them, as she had rarely been ever since the Indovis family had been invited to Genverdell. Nikolas was not much better. The princess wondered if Halla and Nikolas would even be present at the greeting, and found herself beginning to feel an encroaching dread at the thoughts of what unpleasantries might arise from the whole affair. Relatively speaking, very few courtships and marriages, regardless of the societal stations of those involved, were imposed upon the prospective couple in a manner that one would likely deem absolute or forced, even in days long past. Sheeva knew this, as well as the reality that, regardless of the formerly great friendship between Mivinaar and Greystone, her case of being a princess with only one prospective suitor up to this point was not exactly common. But she also knew of those few cases in history where bad blood arose because of changes of heart or other reasons. She had reached the point where she no longer wondered if unpleasantries would follow, but rather feared how difficult they would become.

In an effort to take her mind off the matter, the princess gave one last look over her gown. It was a deep blue dress with embroidery and latticework done in the blue of the sky. It was one of her favorite dresses, and one that had been remade for her several times over as she grew. Sheeva also felt the color suited the impending season, when the nights were longest and the snows to come, when viewed from afar, would appear of the same blue as the gown's ornamentation. The only thing about it that she didn't fancy at this time of year was that it left much of her neck and shoulders exposed. Though she now wore a light cloak of matching blue, Sheeva felt that the chilly breezes would still be too much. She quickly rummaged through her armoire once more, looking to see if she had a scarf that might match. Not finding one, she selected a beautiful black scarf of fine wool and wrapped it snugly about her neck. Two gasps of admiration in the room, followed by footsteps racing about and wardrobes opening again, prompted the princess to wheel around in surprise.

Queen Talrah and Lady Xalu, having searched through their closets, pulled out black scarfs of a like to Sheeva's. The queen looked at her daughter affectionately, her eyes tinted with humility.

"Wonderful idea, Sheeva, to wear something like that in light of those lost to the fever. I should've thought of something like that myself and suggested it to your father and the others."

Sheeva was about to open her mouth to explain her simple reason for getting a scarf, but decided to let it go and appreciate the thought.

"Something that's there, but simple and not overbearing," the princess agreed.

The three women gave their attire one last look-over, then strode down the halls and stairways to the castle's front hall, where the others were gathering to await the announcement of the new arrivals.

***

A quarter of an hour passed, with the high windows of the main hall showing a sky of faint orange steadily being overtaken by the dark blue of night, when a guard peered through the great doors and signaled to the assembly that the Indovis family and their companions had arrived. King Samuel and Queen Talrah, each on one side of Sheeva, placed a hand on the princess's shoulder as the assembly ceased their small talk and turned to face the door. The guards opened the doors, and Sheeva, alongside her parents, led the castle's household out into the opening courtyard.

The three new arrivals were seated together on a stone bench, huddled against the bracing wind. The son, Allor, seemed to be the first to notice them approaching, his eyes widening slightly and ears pricking sharply as he patted both his parents to call attention to their approaching hosts.

The princess focused her sight on Allor, trying to recall what she could of him from the south warden's funeral. She remembered him being handsome and courteous enough, but didn't think much of it at the time, as she presumed she was set on Nikolas. Looking at him again, however, with the prospect of other suitors in mind in addition to the simple sight of a lad's face that bore a smile when looking at her, Sheeva found him startlingly sweet-looking and had to hold herself back from immediately greeting him directly. The princess gave a quick look at the approaching parents, both giving an eerie feeling of the past repeating in the way they presented themselves. Alphaar, the father, had a tall, handsome, and strong bearing that echoed of the late south warden. Egrah, the mother, seemed to have the same air of stately beauty and grace that Halla Greystone had when the princess first met her, and indeed bore even presently, despite being shaded by bitterness.

Sheeva then returned her gaze to Allor, and found herself beginning to feel the same feelings of charm that Nikolas had given her seven years before. Apart from the absences of the beautiful snow-white fur from Balon heritage and the faint touches of Sorrenar's styles of hair and dress from Valor's ancestors, Allor was looking to have very much the same sort of bearing as Nikolas had that bygone day.

The queen, king, and princess greeted each of the new guests in turn, quite informally, but in friendly fashion. Each guest thanked the royal hosts, with Allor giving an exceptionally gallant response.

"My undying thanks to you, your majesties, for the gracious invitation that you have offered us. I sincerely hope that we will come to know each other well." Allor took Sheeva's hand, holding it in the form of a gentleman's greeting as he looked her squarely in the eyes. "Especially you, dear princess."

Sheeva thanked him for his courtesy, feeling that the heat growing in her face could produce steam from the cold breeze that was brushing by. Accepting Allor's hand, she walked with him, his parents, and the rest of those gathered as they turned to go inside and begin dinner, the prospect of which was met with great enthusiasm by Alphaar.

Walking back, Sheeva nervously searched the gathering for Nikolas and Lady Halla, preparing herself for whatever icy glares they may direct at her, her parents, or their guests. But they were nowhere to be seen, and Sheeva began to wonder if they had gone so far as to slink off to return to their home at Oakhall, unwilling to stand on any sort of ceremony with their longtime friends any longer. She presumed the most likely case was they were simply sulking somewhere in the castle.

A crow flew above and cawed its ominous cry, prompting Sheeva to look up. Nikolas and his mother were staring intently at the procession from a balcony overlooking the entrance courtyard, their eyes seemingly locked onto the princess. In the bright light of the torches on the balcony, which had been lit to compensate for the evening's failing light, Sheeva could see the two in marvelous garments, ones that somehow looked quite familiar.

Sheeva, seeing their menacing stares amplified by the orange lights and stark shadows from the torches, was almost frozen to the spot by grim realization. Lady Halla's gown was the same that she wore when the princess first met her, and apart from being several sizes larger, Nikolas's doublet was the same he wore the day he and Sheeva first met.

The same was also the case for Sheeva's dress, aside from the black scarf.

9

12/28/4012 G.M.

ALLOR leaned on the stone wall of the balcony, his cloak wrapped about him as he looked up at the cloudy afternoon sky. He had been quite overwhelmed the first two days residing in Castle Genverdell. Despite not having left the castle or its grounds since he had arrived, he had barely talked to, or even seen, Sheeva or her parents. There was the one day of lessons he had with the princess and Nikolas Greystone, which was on the day following his arrival. It was the last day of studies for the week and the year. He sat in a room alongside the princess and Nikolas as they listened to Lady Xalu Vernifel, the castle's resident tutor. They had courses in literature, science, history, and government. Apart from that, there were the meals he had with his parents and the rest of the castle's household, but even then, the conversations were light and relatively far in between. Much of this could easily be noted as the consequence of everyone focusing on preparing for the festivities that were now ready to commence the coming evening. Even his parents were largely preoccupied with settling in, as well as the anxious anticipation of receiving word from Nelahaal.

Allor shared the latter concern greatly, desperate to hear of how his friends and all the others back home had fared over the past weeks, during and following the course of the epidemic. When his mother explained the matter to the queen and king, they promptly wrote a letter and sent it off with a heraldwing from their own aviary the night of their arrival, just after dinner. Though he knew it would likely take at least a few more days for news to come back, especially given the impending holiday, Allor found himself frequently spending his free time lingering about outside, on balconies, and the now mostly barren gardens, searching the skies for the returning message bird.

The presence of the Greystones did not lighten his anxieties. Neither Nikolas nor his mother, Halla, had given him any trouble, nor his parents as far as he knew. Nevertheless, he could sense the tension between the Greystones and the royal family, and dreaded the thought of eventually being dragged into the matter as well. He had hardly spoken to the south wardeness, but would catch her eyes scrutinizing him when no one else seemed to be looking. Apart from what little discussion Allor shared with the princess and Nikolas during the one lesson he had with them so far, he had not spoken to Sheeva's longtime suitor at all. Even then, Nikolas had barely expressed any interest in him, speaking very flatly and hardly even looking at him. There were occasions when Allor saw him at the end of a corridor, and he would have sworn that he was always looking at him the same critical way as his mother. But he always seemed to turn away whenever Allor's eyes caught sight of him. Whenever Allor tried to call him over, as politely as he could manage, Nikolas always turned away and went down another corridor as if he didn't hear him.

Wishing to clear his mind and focus on the New Year's festivities, Allor returned his attention to the bright grey sky from which the first snows were beginning to fall.

Allor started at the sound of the door behind him opening. He turned, hoping it to be either Sheeva or one of his parents, feeling that either would make for good company at the moment.

It was the castle's resident priest, whom Allor had seen at dinner and about the castle, but with whom he had not yet spoken personally. He was a lean, handsome, well-kept Zaron man, his grey fur shining cleanly, and his hair and beard cropped close and neat. His light blue eyes met Allor's with curious concern.

Allor nodded respectfully to him, uncertain of the conversation to come, but welcoming the prospect of some company.

"Good afternoon, servant of Onu. I'm afraid I haven't learned your name yet."

"It's no trouble," the priest said kindly. "My name is Ranoth. Ranoth Windsbreath. You're the new potential suitor for Princess Sheeva, correct? Allor's your name, no?"

"You have it right on both counts, Brother Windsbreath."

"Whatever are you doing out here in the cold like this?"

"Looking to see if the heraldwing that the queen and king sent might make it back today. I know it'll probably be another day or two at least, given the holiday, but ..."

"Oh, of course. You and your family are still waiting to hear from home since the fever first started."

The priest had by now come to stand beside Allor. He patted his shoulder in sympathy.

"It's never easy to wait for news like that, when you don't know how those you care about are faring. But while the spell that just passed was no light matter, it was thankfully short-lived, all things considered. I'm sure in a few days you'll get word and it will turn out alright when all is said and done."

Allor, grateful for the cleric's kind words, still felt worry gripping his heart. His throat tightened as he held back a sob brought on by a wave of fear for the worst scenario he could imagine. He could not shake the feeling despite his efforts and Ranoth's assurances. He looked the priest in the eyes.

"May I trouble you for a prayer for my home and friends, Brother Windsbreath?"

The priest's eyes glittered with compassion. "You can just call me Ranoth, dear child, or Brother Ranoth if you feel you must; everyone else does. And it's no trouble at all, Allor. It's a big part of my job, after all."

The two then sat on a stone bench that rested against the castle walls, and joined a hand with one another. The priest guided Allor in a prayer for news to arrive that was swift in coming as well as good, along with an appeal to Onu for the benediction of any in Nelahaal who may have perished, and their guidance and deliverance by the angel Morinaar.

When the prayer was finished, Allor thanked Ranoth, who then asked if anything else was the matter. Allor, his lightened mind now darkened again, though not as before, hesitantly told the priest of his experiences and feelings thus far in regards to the Greystones.

"It's only been a few days," Allor conceded, "and we're new arrivals, strangers, that may change the course of their lives from what they've had almost every reason to expect until now. And seeing how our arrival has ties to the loss of Lady Greystone's husband and Nikolas's father, I wouldn't be surprised if it was salt in their wounds."

"You have a very understanding heart, Allor," Ranoth said in a commending tone, "and I must say myself that I can understand, and even relate to, what the Greystones must be feeling."

"How so?" asked Allor.

"Well," said Ranoth with a sigh, "I was almost the salpion."

"Really?" Allor asked in awe.

"Indeed," the priest continued. "I was a great friend and student of the previous salpion, Helga Renlarv. My dedication to my Onu-given mission, alongside our great friendship, led her to take me under her wing and guide me toward being a candidate to be the next salpion. This went on for years, until I was twenty. Then one day, seemingly out of nowhere, the salpion took an interest in this other priest named Owen. After Salpion Helga reviewed his work, which, I will not hesitate to admit, was most commendable and very well verified by the accounts of others, she suddenly began to split her attention between Owen and me. He and I are the same age, and over the course of three years I watched Owen win over Helga more and more. I must confess I resented it. The day came when Helga, just weeks away from her deathbed, had gathered all the alpions of the world together and tasked them to vote between Owen and me. I had hoped that my years of learning the Temple's ways and my long-groomed ability to manage would ultimately ensure my place as salpion, but the alpions voted overwhelmingly in favor of Owen's renowned compassion and generosity."

The priest chuckled sadly, shaking his head before continuing.

"Such qualities are, or certainly should be, a must for the one who is going to act as Onu's highest of mortal servants, so I have no desire or intention to resent their reasoning in and of itself. But the man had nowhere near as much administrative experience as I had under Helga's instruction. I feared, and continue to fear, that his kindness may outweigh his sense of judgment as far as keeping order in the Temple and its locations, to the point of possibly endangering the Temple's stability. I worry he may trust too many others' judgements on things with which he isn't familiar; things that he would otherwise have a thorough knowledge and understanding of if he had the same experience as I had."

Ranoth was now beginning to shift uncomfortably on the bench, brows furrowing as he concluded his story.

"And I worry that he might be ... too generous too often. I feel like I'm resenting goodness itself when I say that, but I fear that if he dotes on or takes in every other beggar and whore he meets down at the riverside, he's going to find himself running out of room and food. And that's just one point of concern."

The priest shrugged after a few seconds of silence. "He does seem to be managing well enough, for now at least. Maybe Onu himself is keeping matters in check as a blessing for Owen's goodness, and it's not as if I know all that he's done or gone through since he took the seat after Helga's death. I admit I've rarely spoken with him since then, or even before, following his election by the alpions. I applied to be the court cleric here once the vote was cast and, with Helga's blessing and the Mivinaars' acceptance, I've since occupied myself with counseling the souls of those living here."

Ranoth looked at Allor, shrugging and smiling sadly.

"I guess I can still relate to the Greystones' feelings more than I'd care to admit. But all that being said, Allor, just because someone can be understood, that doesn't make them in the right. I'll try to see if I can't talk to Lady Greystone and Nikolas soon. It shouldn't come to something like what's been troubling you, and hopefully we can keep this from getting any more unpleasant than it's already been."

"You have my deepest thanks, Brother Ranoth."

"It's what I'm here for, Allor. You and your parents are welcome to talk to me anytime, day or night, same as all else here."

The two sat together in silence a few minutes longer, then Ranoth, wrapping himself snugly in his cloak, headed back to the door.

"Well, I've had enough of this cold for now, and I need to see to a few more things before we go to the archtemple this evening. I trust that you're mostly ready?"

"I am," said Allor, "but I suppose I've had my fill of the first snow as well, at least until we need to go through it to get to the service."

The priest smiled affectionately, opening the door and holding it for Allor.

"I'll see you and everyone else in a few hours, then."

"See you then, Brother Ranoth."

The two stepped into the corridor, going their separate ways as they went to prepare for the Sardonmay festivities.

10
12/28/4012 G.M.

SHEEVA walked out of the dressing room with her mother, Lady Xalu, and nearly every other lady of the court except for Halla Greystone. They headed to the great hall to meet with all those residing in the castle before leaving for the procession to the archtemple. Upon reaching the throng and wading through to the king, the princess searched the crowd for the Greystone and Indovis families. Nikolas and his mother, dressed in their best, were by the far-left wall, conversing, seemingly coolly, with some other men and women of court. Allor and his parents, all dressed in festively modest robes of warm brown with wine-red cloaks, were making their way through the gathering to greet the royal family.

Sheeva felt her face grow warm as she saw Allor walk beside his mother and father, transfixed by the princess's snow-white gown, white bear pelt cloak, and trimmings and jewelry of gold. She nearly burst into a fit of giggles as he nearly walked right into one of the royal advisors for not paying attention. She struggled to recompose herself as the three new guests reached her and her parents.

"My thanks once more for your majesties' invitation," Mayor Egrah said warmly to the royal family. "I fear we may be a touch underdressed, but–"

"Nonsense, Lady Egrah," said Queen Talrah. "You three look wonderful. Besides, should you stay with us for a while, we may look into setting you up with some new clothes."

"That sounds most pleasant, my queen. You have my thanks and the thanks of my family."

The mayor's husband and son said their thanks in turn, with Allor stepping up to the princess and her parents.

"My utmost thanks for the hospitality and opportunity that you have given my family and me. And I must speak my admiration for each of your clothes. Dear Queen, you glow as a great fire in the hearth to ward off winter's cold; my king, your robes are of the deepest winter's night; and dear Princess, your gown and gold make you look as a field blanketed in snow and touched by the dawn."

Sheeva saw the king and queen smile as she nodded appreciatively to Allor.

"I appreciate your compliments, dear Allor," she said, "and your robes make me eager for the feast this evening, for their colors make me think of the wine and meat to come."

The six laughed, with King Samuel patting his daughter's shoulder lovingly.

"Well put, Sheeva! And that feast will be ready once we return from the Temple's service! Everyone's ready now, so let's start the procession!"

The king and queen signaled to the procession's leading guard, who promptly called for all in the crowd to take their positions. The doors opened to a swiftly darkening evening sky.

***

The Mivinaars and their entourage, having made their way through the snow-dusted roads down the east hill, across the river, and up the west hill to the archtemple, waved all the while at the cheering crowds that lined either side of the procession. Having arrived at the great temple's front gates, the royal retinue was greeted by a great crowd led by Owen Lovonhaar, the Salpion of the Temple of Fidonhaal himself. The handsomely rotund holy man, black fur sparkling gold from the lights of the candles, torches and lanterns that flooded the last eve of autumn, came forth and greeted them with arms spread wide in blessing and welcome.

"Welcome, dear leaders of Enmayar and guests! May Onu keep you in good health and guide you to good judgement when your crowns weigh heavy!"

The massive congregation raised a great cheer, which then flowed down the roads and swiftly filled the entire city. Sheeva and her parents reciprocated the good wishes, bowing reverently to the salpion, with those behind them following suit.

"Our thanks to you, dear Salpion! May Onu keep you well, and may your light never be drowned by the darkness we still face!"

With another great cheer flooding the capital, the salpion, with a small group of attendants in tow, led the procession into the great cathedral of the archtemple's compound. All others who could fit within followed, and everyone else crowded within the grounds if they could, huddling around great braziers and preparing to have the salpion's words echoed to them by priests and priestesses that spread throughout the sea of people. Sheeva's eyes fell to either side of the salpion, where a child, around half her age, held aloft a great candle as a guiding light for the procession. Both children, while keeping well to their task overall, occasionally looked back at the royalty and their following guests, eyes glittering in the candlelight with an expression of awe that the princess found endearing. One of the children, a boy of fur marbled black and brown, had eyes that seemed to match the blue of the king's robes. The other child, a fully Zaron girl, had eyes of dazzling green. When they weren't facing straight on their course or looking back at the following throng, the two children would glance up at the salpion, whom Sheeva noticed give an assuring nod and smile each time they did so.

Once all who could sit in the cathedral were seated in the pews, the choir and orchestra, at a signal from a Zaron sister, struck up a joyous hymn to bid the passing year farewell and the coming year welcome. When the song had ended, following another signal from the grey-furred priestess, the choir and all others in the cathedral rose from their seats. The salpion, carrying the Beldsantu reverently in his hands, walked down the central aisle to the podium before the altar. Placing the holy book upon the stand and opening it, the leader of the Temple of Fidonhaal read to them from the account of the First Ancestors. He proceeded to a sermon on how each new year is as a new beginning, which all Fidons could relate with the First at the time of the Awakening, and the importance of new beginnings and the chances of redemption given to all of Fidonity.

The evening passed into night, and the salpion announced an invitation to all present to the feast that was to be held at the archtemple's banquet hall following the service's end. A great cheer filled the cathedral and temple grounds, and Sheeva, following her parents, led those of the procession who wished to rejoin the royal family for dinner back to Castle Genverdell. All others, of the procession or not, went their own ways to either attend the feast at the temple or partake in revelry elsewhere in the city.

***

The feast at the castle was splendid, with tables laden with prime meats, fish, bread, and drink, as well as a grand cake as the centerpiece. The attendees passed much of the remaining hours before midnight relishing the feast in scattered groups throughout the great hall, with Sheeva and her parents conversing extensively with Mayor Egrah, Alphaar, and Allor, since the Greystones had again seemed to vanish.

As the midnight hour drew near, however, Sheeva wrestled with what she sensed to be her better judgment. She yearned to give Nikolas another chance to continue their potential courtship. Roaming throughout the hall and combing her sight through the crowds, the princess caught sight of Lady Halla walking out from behind a pillar in the corner of the hall and turning to ascend the stairs toward some other place in the castle. Nikolas, also emerging from behind the pillar, proceeded to lean glumly against it as he turned a small glass of wine in his hands. The blue-green doublet he wore, studded with silver, matched his eyes, which gazed bitterly into his drink from the white-furred star that marked his face. The eyes snapped onto Sheeva and hardened as she drew near. The princess cleared her throat lightly and greeted him.

"A merry Sardonmay's Eve to you, dear Nikolas," she said with a gentle smile.

"What do you want, Sheeva?" Nikolas asked tiredly.

The smile disappeared, and the princess's ears drooped as her desires to resign and persevere battled within her heart.

"I ... I wanted to know if you'd wish to join me for the Midnight Dance."

"We've done that every new year since I came here, Sheeva," said Nikolas with an increasingly steely voice. "Have your new man dance with you, since you and your royal parents are so tired of me and Mother."

"Nik, it's not li–"

Sheeva's eyes widened and her fur stood on end from head to toe. Nikolas's eyes, narrowed to venomous slits and reflecting the candlelight, seemed to spark with the fires of Raakhaal. The princess tried to recoil from him as he suddenly leaned forward, but she stood petrified in sudden fright at the sudden turn of face.

"Don't," said Nikolas through clenched teeth. "Don't call me that ever again. Ever. Do you hear me?"

Before Sheeva could respond, Nikolas turned sharply on his heel and strode up the stairs after his mother.

After standing in shocked silence for a moment, the princess made her way back to her parents and their new guests. The trouble in her heart swiftly faded away as she saw Allor's face when she offered her hand.

"Dear Allor, would you care to join me for the Midnight Dance?" she asked with regal grace.

Trials and Loss, Growth and Learning

11
1/5/4013 G.M.

DONOVAN VELAVIS stood beside his father, Jonathan, looking at the pyre on which his mother and baby sister lay. The sun had risen to its peak, and the light of the early winter's clear noon cast a brilliant diamond sparkle onto the blankets of snow that covered the town of Therohl. The Balon boy, tired and numbed from the past two days of grieving, let his sight rove across the cloudless sky, the blue of which matched the young eyes that beheld it. He reflected on how it would soon be marred by the smoke of a funeral pyre. Distraught that he could bring himself to weep no more, he returned his gaze to his mother and sister.

Envah, Donovan's mother, lay in the chillingly beautiful peace of the dead. Her eyes, the same color as her son's, were now closed forever as the soul behind them had departed to Onuhaal two days ago. Sani, his sister, lay cradled in her mother's arms, as was the custom for funerals that mourned a mother and newborn that were lost to problems during birth.

Donovan thought back on the joy that his father and mother had shared in the past months, and the anticipation he himself had for the prospect of an addition to the family. There was an even greater amount of excitement the previous week, when all wondered if the baby would be born on Sardonmay. The babe ended up missing the new year's start by two days, but when the time came at last, happiness filled the house. Thus Donovan, pacing eagerly in the entry hall of the house and just outside its doors, was taken completely aback when his father, with a tear-streaked face of dread and grief, urged him to hurry inside to his mother. He ran to his mother's bedside, the doctor and priestess looking on sadly, as she tearfully cradled Sani's lifeless little body as she herself began to slip away. She implored Donovan to not resent his little sister, or her memory, for taking her mother with her when she had already flown to Onu's side. Donovan, sobbing, swore that he would never look on this memory with anger, as he watched the blood from his mother spreading steadily over the sheets on which she lay.

"Please, Mama," wept Donovan, "I want to ask just one thing before you go. Please, would you and Sani ask Onu to keep me and Papa strong and happy? I'll do what I can, but I don't think I have what it takes to go on by myself."

Donovan would hold faith all his days that the souls of his mother and sister heard his request and brought it to the Maker, for an answer never passed from Envah's lips before she passed from the world. Unable to brace against the sudden loss any longer, he collapsed to the floor, clinging to the bedside, crying freely as he yielded to grief. His father soon came in, sobbing his regret for not being strong enough to see his wife off in her last moments. He lifted up his son and embraced him as the priestess told him of Donovan's final request to his mother.

"May they ask Onu to bless you doubly, my boy," wept Jonathan, "for you did what I could not."

Now, Donovan's reflection was interrupted by a light gust of biting cold, which stirred the settled snow and lifted some into the winds. The lad had now seen eleven Sorrenarn winters, knowing his beloved land of the North to be renowned as the home of the coldest climes. But this was the coldest he had ever felt, and upsetting as the sensation was, he was nevertheless thankful for it, as it broke the dullness inside him and rekindled his heart and mind. He took his father's hand, and the two huddled closer to one another and the brazier by the pyre. Then the priestess, the same one who witnessed the deaths of Envah and Sani, called for the packed town square to be silent as she stepped forward and began the service.

***

When the priestess finished her prayer, sermon, and consolation to those left behind, she took up two torches, lit them from the brazier, and handed one each to Donovan and Jonathan before taking another for herself. The three then set the pyre alight, and once it was done, Donovan wrapped his heavy cloak around him and took additional shelter in his father's as the two resumed their embrace and gazed into the growing flames. Donovan let his memories of his mother, and the thoughts of the sister he didn't get to know, roam around his mind as the fire's glow began to place him into a sorrowful trance.

His reverie was soon shaken, and his ears sharply pricked up, by the sound of a stranger singing. He knew the voice to be of a man from the eastern highlands, and blinking away the bright lights of the pyre and dazzling snow, he soon found the singer, harp in hand, standing on the opposite side of the pyre. He sang the first pass of the chorus with only his voice, beginning to play his harp on the start of the first verse. Donovan had heard the dirge that the stranger was playing back when his grandfather died. It was a song written for surviving spouses and was played to console his grandmother. Now, drawn closely to his father, Donovan felt that despite not being the widower, he could feel at least a measure of both the pain and comfort that the song evoked in Jonathan.

I gaze upon your silent face,
Which now lies veiled in eternal grace.
I ache with yearning for your lips,
To once more feel the warmth of your kiss
And hear the voice that always set my heart alight.
Your eyes, through which I saw your soul,
And felt Onu's love, and thus felt whole,
Have been hollow and locked since your spirit took flight.
I gaze upon your silent face,
Which now lies veiled in eternal grace.
Your heart, which once raced beside mine,
Lies still and silent; silent as mine.
My heart is as one who has been robbed in the night.
I wishfully weep for your arms
To embrace me again, and thus warm
This cold soul, but to no avail, plead as I might.
I gaze upon your silent face,
Which now lies veiled in eternal grace.
But even though my grief is great,
My love endures, and I trust to wait
'Til the day when I too depart from Dodmorhaal.
Then, if by the grace of Onu,
My soul may be rejoined to you,
We'll relish our bond forever in Onuhaal.
I gaze upon your silent face,
Which now lies veiled in eternal grace.
The joy I trust that we shall have
Does heal my heart and soul as a salve,
And shall keep me 'til the day I heed Death's call.
On that day, I shall embrace you
Forevermore, before Onu,
And we'll share a love with Him that shall never fall.
I gaze upon your silent face,
Which now lies veiled in eternal grace.

When the song ended, Donovan looked up into his father's eyes, which bore continued grief, but also the first hints of a healing heart. The boy then looked over the crowd, seeing everywhere faces of empathy, sadness, and hope. Weeping couples clasped their arms about each other in a gently rocking embrace, parents held their children closely and spoke their love for them gently, and every man, woman, and child gave a deep nod to the bard in silent praise of his work.

The singer returned the gesture with an appreciative nod. The priestess, stepping forward once more, called for a time of silent prayer and the giving of condolences to the bereaved. The crowd carried out the task compassionately, each person in their turn, as the sun began its descent and the pyre's flames continued their work in rendering Envah and Sani's flesh into ashes.

***

Evening had come. The funerary fire had done its task, and the remains had been gathered into a joint urn. It now rested on a small adorned table that stood in the midst of the dining hall of the Three Widows Tavern, the largest such establishment in Therohl. The wake was now in full swing, and Donovan, doing his best to eat what he could alongside his father, was lost in memories when the highlander bard's voice broke out once more in song. Catering to the now more festive side of the event, the bard was singing from the great song of the reigning Mountainborn dynasty. Though having its measure of tragedy, it was overwhelmingly a song of bravery, action, great heroic battles, and for the people of Sorrenar, patriotic pride. The bard plucked and strummed his harp in an uplifting melody.

After Donovan and his father had eaten their fill, the two separated to speak to the guests at their own pace. Donovan, thinking of how the song he heard earlier had moved him in ways he had never felt before, made his way to the great hearth. There the bard sat, harp at his side, in respite of his singing. Making his way through the crowds, Donovan focused his sight on the singer. He was a grizzled, older man of Balon and Zaron heritage. His bicolored fur, which formed patches about his arms and split his face into an angled divide of white crown and grey chin, had lost some of its luster with age. His hair and beard grew freely, unbraided, as was typical for the highlanders of Sorrenar. He was, nevertheless, well-kempt and nicely dressed for a roaming performer. His kilt was patterned wine-red and silver-grey, and his nose ring, which was the highlanders' fashion of marking nuptial bonds, was only half a loop, set into the nose, which marked him as a widower.

As the boy approached him, the bard peered over the horn of mead from which he was taking a deep swig. He wiped his hand across his lips, only to lick the drops that caught in the fur. The guests that were gathered about him, upon seeing Donovan and recognizing him, bowed their heads in silence, an act that the bard didn't notice. He addressed Donovan in a friendly, if frank, manner.

"Guid eve t'ye, young lad. Are ye wantin' tae make a request? Ah'm afraid Ah'm nae yet done with singin' o' the Mountainborn, and that'un will likely take the rest o' the night. But if ye don't mind tae come back later, Ah still plan on bein' here fer at least—"

Donovan was about to explain himself when one of the listeners, who was seated beside the bard, leaned closely to the singer and whispered into his ear. Although the boy didn't know what was said exactly, he knew the essence of it, especially when he saw the bard's ears drop and bright brown eyes soften in sympathy and apology.

"Ah—Ah'm deeply sorry fer yore loss, dear laddie. Ah didn't realize who ye were. This is as much fer ye and yore Pa as 'tis fer yore Ma an' dear sis, so Ah'll sing ye whatever ye'd like; the Karamuses won't mind."

"Thank you for your offer, kind sir," said Donovan with an appreciative bow, "but my request is not for a song, but a lesson or two in how to do what you do, if I may ask for it."

The singer's ears pricked up and an eyebrow raised in surprise.

"Ah'm afraid that only one or two lessins is sorry-pore service, tae both ye an' tae the art itself. 'Tis nae a matter that can be mastered in a few hours, ye ken?"

"I suppose so, but I guess I don't know as much about being a bard as I should have before asking you. I've heard a few songs from other bards before, including what you sang at the pyre, but I never felt before, from song or music, what I felt when I heard you sing for us today. And I've heard much of the song of the Mountainborn before, but the way you've been telling it ... it's just amazing."

The bard smiled, clearly being one who was always glad to hear how he opened someone's mind, heart and soul to the blessed power of music and song. He looked around the tavern, and seeing that all but those nearest him looked sufficiently occupied with food, drink or conversation, he dismissed the ones seated around him. When they had parted, the bard moved two chairs closer to the fire and called for a refill of mead.

"Now," he said, "let me tell ye about bein' a bard, and then we'll see what ye think."

"Thank you, mister ... sir ... thank you, sir."

"The name's Jak, mah good lad. Jak Kelldren."

***

The two talked well into the night, hardly noticing the thinning crowds as Jak told Donovan of the Onu-given ability to write, sing, and play the words and notes that could stir or express any feeling known to Fidonity. The bard told of his career, which spanned thirty-five years and counting, and the sights he had seen and the people he had met.

"So ... I take it you're still on the road?" asked Donovan.

"Aye, laddie. Nae many bards make a guid enough livin' if they stay in one place fer too long, even the really guid'uns, unless they work fer the king an' queen, or some other Fidon o' higher station. Besides ..."

Jak's eyes focused on the tip of his muzzle, where the band of his nose ring hung incomplete.

"... Ah dinnae have anyone tae go home tae. Nae as long as Ah still roam this world."

"Don't some bards settle, at least for a while, to teach others on how to become the next ones? It would be a bit difficult to do that when always on the move, wouldn't it? I suppose some do it that way, but ..."

Jak looked at Donovan squarely in the eyes, his face seemingly one of both reluctant thinking and of intrigued longing.

"O'course there are those, but they can be sore pricey, since they gotta pay fer long-term housin' an' all."

"Have any ever lived with their students?"

Jak smiled gently.

"Aye, that's been done before."

The two suddenly became aware of the great quiet that had fallen over the tavern. Apart from those clearing the tables, and Jonathan and the priestess, who were talking quietly at the far end of the hall, the boy and the bard were the only ones left in the common. The two returned to their earnest discussion.

"Is there any way I might convince you to stay here and teach me to be a bard, at least for a little while?"

Jak's eyes drifted into his mead-horn, which he turned about in his hands as he wrestled out the various thoughts in his head.

"Can ye two afford tae feed an' provide a bed fer another man?"

"We ... we were planning to be a family of four," said Donovan softly. "It'll just be the three of us if you stay at our house, so having enough room and all that shouldn't be a problem."

"Are ye two *willin'* tae do that?"

"I am," said Donovan without hesitation. "Though, I can't say I know for sure about Papa."

The sound of approaching footsteps interrupted their conversation. The priestess, having finished her talk with Donovan's father, now approached Jak, a plump little pouch in hand.

"My utmost thanks to you, Mr. Kelldren, for a wonderful performance. You did *Eternal Grace* great justice, and every other song you played today, for that matter. Here's your payment."

Jak looked back at Donovan, decisiveness plain on his face.

"If it nae be too much trouble, guid Sister, there may be a change tae the arrangement. No problem on yer end, mind; Ah just need tae speak tae the widower first, if Ah may have a few moments."

"I ... of course, Mr. Kelldren."

Thanking the priestess, Jak gestured for Donovan to stay put, got up from his seat, and made his way over to Jonathan. The two spoke for several minutes, and Donovan could see from across the hall his father's face change from surprise and wonder to a smile of approval. Turning his head to face his son's eyes, Jonathan nodded. Jak shook hands with the widower and strode back to Donovan, beside whom the priestess was waiting patiently. Helping the boy out of his chair with one hand, the bard placed the pouch of coins back into the priestess's hands with the other.

"It would appear that Ah will nae be needin' this," he said to the surprised cleric.

"Thank you very much, Mr. Kelldren," said Donovan in quiet gratitude.

"Call me Jak, laddie. We'll see how this goes, Ah reckon. Might be nice tae nae keep roaming."

12
1/7/4013 G.M.

ALLOR wandered the castle gardens, which, though largely barren save for the scattered evergreens, had a somber beauty enhanced by the dusting of snow. He constantly checked the sky, anxious at the continued lack of news from Nelahaal, as he largely had every day since the Sardonmay celebration. Trying his hardest to stay calm, Allor took a seat on a bench that rested in a corner between a low wall and a statue, which kept him out of the wind. He closed his eyes and paced his breathing, trying to focus his thoughts on the encouraging words of Brother Ranoth from Sardonmay's Eve. He also tried to set his mind on the dance he shared with the princess that midnight and all the other small pleasantries he had experienced in the past few days.

A door bursting open and two voices arguing from the other side of the wall interrupted Allor's reflections. Though the wall that Allor was sitting against was tall enough to hide him, he pressed himself lower and drew himself further into the niche formed by the wall and sculpture. He pricked his ears intently, his whole body tensing as he recognized the disputing voices as belonging to Sheeva and Nikolas.

"It's final, Sheeva. Mother already told them last night. We'll be out by the end of the week. It's time we returned our focus to keeping the south ward in order; we don't want a repeat of last summer, and there's no point in lingering here when it's over between us."

"I keep telling you, Nik, it's not over if—"

"Stop calling me that!"

Allor's claws set into the stone of the statue as his mind battled between intervening and staying out of the matter at least for the moment, after which he could tell the queen and king. In the end, he decided to stay put.

"I'm ... I'm not going to throw the past seven years away just because Mother and Father have invited another to have a chance at my hand. You know the way things have been between us before your father died wasn't the norm, and that it wouldn't have been whether I was a princess or a farmer's daughter, or you a warden's son or a cobbler's."

"You seem to have taken a liking to Allor well enough, and quickly enough."

"Because you've had almost nothing to do with me for months!"

"Because you're just your mother and father's little harlot!"

Allor's mind was screaming for him to move, to confront Nikolas, but he felt petrified by the shock of the outburst. Furthermore, he also feared a potentially violent altercation, and not necessarily one that would be initiated by Nikolas.

"Ni-Nikolas ... wh-why would you—"

"They didn't tell you about inviting the Nelahaal mayor and her family in the first place, until after the fact, and they didn't bother to tell you about us leaving this morning when they had more than enough time to do so at breakfast. You know why? Because they don't want you to object to their plans. They keep you in the dark until there's no point in protesting, if you even would've thought to do so, and tell you that it's for the best or that it'll probably do you good, to make you feel better, if you seem bothered about it. Then you just take it all in stride, and do what they want. My father and mother had served yours faithfully for twenty years, and they cast us aside over one mistake, and one that took my father away from me, at that! They're using you, Sheeva, just whoring you off to whoever can pose the best political image. If something makes matters difficult with Allor's family, they'll look to swap suitors again, and again and again, as many times as they feel they have to and for as long as it's in their ability to do so, mark my words! And they'll do all they can to keep it to one suitor at a time, so that you don't have any other choice other than what they give you. It's happened in families before, Sheeva, whether they were royal or not, and you know it."

"B-but that's n-never been the way that was encouraged, not even in the first days after the Return!"

"Of course not, and especially not *solely* for politics or social-climbing. But it's that way for you, Sheeva, and you'd see it if you'd just open your eyes!"

A second of icy silence filled the winter air, then one set of footsteps stormed off down the snowy stone path and back to the door that led into the gardens. The door closed loudly. Allor, straining his ears, finally was driven to move by the sound of Sheeva's sobs. He walked quietly to the gazebo past the low wall where the princess sat, face buried in her hands. He called softly to her.

"Sheeva ..."

The princess, startled, looked at Allor, stumbling over her words as she simultaneously tried to invent a reason for her state and calm herself down.

"I-I'm sorry you have to see me like this, Allor. I ... I just had a-a hard talk with Mother and Father over what ... what'll be expected of me in a few years, and ... a-and, there was also this—"

Allor gently took hold of Sheeva's hand, standing close to her as he whispered confidentially.

"I was here when you two came over, Princess. I heard everything. We should tell your mother and father immediately; Nikolas and his mother have no—"

"No, Allor. I appreciate what you're trying to do, but if you heard all that, then you know they're leaving within the week. Aside from the whole fiasco last summer, the Greystones have managed to lead South Ward very well, and it'd just make everything more of a mess if we dragged this up. Just ... Just let it go."

Allor looked levelly into Sheeva's eyes. "Very well, Princess, if you feel that's best."

"You can just call me Sheeva, Allor."

"Very well, Sheeva."

The two stood together, hand-in-hand, for several moments in silence. Then Allor, suddenly growing conscious of Sheeva's steadily tightening grasp on his hand, spoke.

"Sheeva, I have no idea how things will go between us or between our families, and I know that other suitors will likely come your way regardless. And I see no point in acting like there isn't even the slightest trace of politics and whatnot when it comes to my family's interest in yours and yourself, but I swear by Onu, by his hand, mouth, heart and eye, and by the Four Breaths, that that is not all it is. It's not that way for me, not for my parents, and I'm certain not for yours, either. You and your family have been very welcoming, and it's been an honor and privilege to have met you at all."

Allor looked into Sheeva's eyes, admiring their bright hue in comparison to his own, which were quite dark. Suddenly, before Allor could react, the princess leaned into him and kissed him on the cheek. Allor, with a face that felt hot as a furnace, silently held onto Sheeva's hand as she continued to lean against him.

A little more time passed quietly, then the door that led into the garden opened. Lady Xalu Vernifel emerged, took a few steps outside, and then, noticing the boy and the princess together the way they were, had a warm smile spring from what at first seemed a melancholy face. Allor at first thought his impression of her countenance was a mistake, but upon seeing the smile quickly fade, he began to feel a creeping dread that he couldn't explain. Sheeva's tutor approached the young pair, and Sheeva put a little distance between her and Allor, letting go of his hand. Xalu reached the steps of the gazebo, looking squarely at Allor as she spoke.

"You and your parents have visitors, Mr. Allor. Visitors from Nelahaal. The queen, king, and your parents will be receiving them in the throne room soon, and they want you there with them."

"Thank you, Lady Vernifel," said Allor apprehensively.

"Sheeva," Xalu continued, turning to the princess, "if you would, please come with me to the study. We have some things to discuss."

Allor and Sheeva shared an anxious glance. Then, after giving one another a silent nod of respect and well-wishing, went their separate ways.

13
1/7/4013 G.M.

SHEEVA sat with Xalu in the study, discussing the matter of the Greystones' departure.

"I know all this, Lady Xalu. Nikolas and I spoke of it just a few moments ago. What I'd like to know is why we didn't discuss this at breakfast, or right afterwards."

"Your parents and I didn't want to needlessly trouble you over all this tiresome bickering. Lady Halla has been making things difficult for the king and queen, saying they've cast her and Nikolas aside in their time of mourning, and have thus thrown the past seven years away."

"And Nikolas has been doing the same to me."

"What?"

The princess, having tried to contend with the past months of spite in relative silence, now told nearly all to her teacher. She ended with the dispute in the garden, though she left a few choice parts untold.

"Oh, Sheeva," Xalu said wearily, pressing a hand to her brow, "why didn't you say something sooner?"

"Because I was still trying to hold onto the hope that they would get over their grief and still be open to keeping friendship with us," said Sheeva flatly. "I just thought, with enough time, maybe ..."

Lady Xalu huffed angrily. "She *said* that she wouldn't get her son involved in this mess, because we were still trying to talk things out."

"What's done is done," Sheeva said with tired resignation. "As brief as my acquaintance with Allor has been, he's proven to be very pleasant so far. I'd like to think that it could fare very well between us, if he and his family are still welcome to be with us. Even if one of them were to make a mistake sometime later. Even a grave one. Especially if I still had feelings for him."

Sheeva said the last three sentences in a very deliberate tone, eyes fixed to Xalu's, which widened as she began to speculate on the princess's implications.

"Sh-Sheeva ... we—your mother and father, me, all of us here ... we did not *drive* the Greystones away, and *certainly* not to end your relationship with Nikolas."

"But we did *seem* to shut them away, looking back. Don't you think? Perhaps we could've tried a *little* harder to be by their side in their time of loss?"

"What do you think we've been trying to do since this whole business started?" Xalu asked levelly. "Don't you think that at least some of this is on them? Any effort to reach out to someone is pointless if they themselves won't reach out as well. I can't imagine the grief they've felt, but I can't really sympathize with them either, when they've just kept pulling themselves further and further away, and especially since both of them have been causing trouble to you and your parents. Besides, their loss was something that Valor inflicted on his family by his own folly. How sorry for them can we, should we, really be?"

"Valor paid for his mistake with his life," Sheeva replied, "leaving behind two members of a family that had proven very capable of leading when that one grave blunder is set aside. Or am I mistaken? Were the Greystones actually terrible wardens these past twenty years, and I've somehow heard wrong this whole time?"

Lady Vernifel stared at Sheeva. The tutor was clearly quite uncomfortable with what the princess was seeming to suggest as far as the cynicism of politics was concerned. Sheeva's tone certainly didn't lighten the impression that she was making, and she knew it.

However, there was a slight hint of satisfaction in the tutor's eyes as well, as if she was pleasantly surprised by the princess's apparent rise in determination to express her thoughts. Sheeva had largely been a quiet young lady in regards to matters such as these up to this point.

"They've been very capable, Sheeva," the tutor said with an even tone, "and that's why we all agreed that Halla could take up her husband's office, despite the recent difficulties she's been giving us. And Nikolas, if he proved capable enough, could take that seat as well in due time."

Sheeva got up from her seat and made her way to the door leading out of the study.

"I hope things get better for them," Sheeva said as she took the ring of the door's handle in her palm, "despite all that's happened."

The princess, opening the door, stood in the doorway and looked back at her tutor. Xalu nodded, and Sheeva looked intently at her once again.

"I'm willing to try and humor other suitors besides Allor, Lady Xalu, but I'm not up for being kept in the dark about them until they're already invited, or if anything arises that changes the matter. If there's someone new they'd like me to consider, I'll consider them, but not before being more informed of them prior to an invitation being sent. And if there's a problem, I don't want to be the last person told about it. Not anymore."

Xalu nodded, ears lowered, and looked away, staring at her bookshelf.

"Very well, Princess. You'd best tell the queen and king yourself. They ought to hear this straight from you, not me or anyone else."

"I'll do that now, I think," said Sheeva calmly, "provided that they're done with going over matters with the Indovis family and the Nelahaal visitors."

Sheeva pushed the door fully open. Xalu's voice sounded sadly behind her.

"I'm sorry it turned out this way, Sheeva."

"I am, too."

"Nik was such a fine young man."

"That he was," said Sheeva, her heart stinging at hearing Nikolas's pet name again. "I loved him for some time. Now, though ..."

The princess sighed heavily, then left the study without another word.

***

Sheeva strode down the corridors, making her way to the throne room, when she passed by Allor's guest quarters. Seeing the boy from the corner of her eye as she passed the open doorway, the princess reversed her steps to peer in and thank him for his kindness in the garden. Her ears pricked up in worry as she saw him, seated at his small desk, slouching miserably with his head hanging mournfully and staring blankly at the floor. Sheeva quietly stood in the doorway, calling out softly as she clasped her hands together anxiously.

"Allor?"

His head snapped up, and Sheeva was taken aback by his drained, tear-streaked face. He stared briefly at her in silence, then, gesturing to Sheeva to sit by him if she wished, spoke lowly in a grief-wearied whisper as the princess came to his side.

"Seven ... seven people came in from Nelahaal ... from home. Dr. Kollus, one of the town's main doctors ... Rennah Whitemoon, one of Mother's advisors ... an orphaned boy named Martin ... a priest named Benlok ... twin sisters who were merchants, I didn't catch their names ... and a carpenter named Nathan. They came in ... and the reason that the heraldwing hadn't come back yet is because ... because there was no one in town ... that was ... alive ... when it got there. Those seven people ..."

Allor gave a choked sob before continuing. "They were all that were left of the whole town! That-that fever ... it ... it killed almost everyone I've ever known! All my friends at school, Jordan, Kahldiin, Zeera, Tavon the baker, Sasha the priestess ... all of them ... all of them ..."

Allor, unable to go on, slumped even further in his chair, weeping. Sheeva looked on in silence, numbed and petrified by the morbid revelation. When Allor calmed down again, he looked fixedly at the princess.

"So now, Mother's basically the mayor of a dead town. People might come around to settle again, once it's all been cleared up and enough time passes, but until then, we'd just be going to a mass grave if we go back. And even if things are settled in time, even if more quickly than expected, I just don't think I can bring myself to go back."

Sheeva took Allor's hand. "Then stay here, you and your parents both, and any of those others, if they've nowhere else to go, at least until they can figure something out."

Allor smiled sadly, gratitude and admiration shining in his teary, dark brown eyes.

Sheeva continued. "I won't forget the kindness you showed me today in the garden. Nikolas will be leaving soon, and I don't know how many other suitors may come along, or in turn, how things will fare between us when all is said and done. But I do know that I would like to get to know you better in the time to come. I would like it very much."

"Thank you, Prin–Sheeva. Thank you. I look forward to it, too. But, if I don't come off as rude, I'd just like to be alone for now."

"Of course, Allor," said Sheeva as she got up from her chair. "I'll see you later."

"I look forward to it," said Allor as he rested his head on the desk.

Sheeva left the room, and going down the corridor, passed the stairway that led directly to the throne room.

"I'll talk to Mother and Father in a minute," she said to herself. "I think it's time to start learning something new, or at least try and arrange for *when* I can start."

The princess then made her way to the door of the castle apothecary's chambers. She knocked gently. The healer came to the door a moment later, his eyebrows rising in concern on his thin, grey-furred face.

"Princess Sheeva! Is anything the matter?"

"I'm alright, Dr. Kamlof, but ... well, this may be a bit sudden, but I wonder if I might learn some things about herbalism and medicine from you."

Dr. Kamlof's turquoise eyes widened with surprise behind his spectacles, but his smile clearly indicated it was an enthused surprise.

"That's wonderful, Sheeva! I don't know if you know already, but there have been several kings and queens that studied medicine to some extent or another, or otherwise was a great patron of medicine, and have made no small contributions to the advancement of the field. Queen Kahnda-rah of Janrenar helped in developing a powerful, multipurpose antidote—"

"After she lost her husband to a poisoned chalice of wine," Sheeva finished to the herbalist's delight.

"Indeed! Indeed!" said Kamlof. "Speaking of motives for studying this craft, am I wrong to presume that you have one in particular? It's purely out of curiosity, mind; I've no objections if it's purely for the sake of knowledge, and I won't pry if you wish to be silent on it."

"It's quite alright, Dr. Kamlof. It's ... it's Allor."

"The new suitor?"

Sheeva nodded.

"What's the matter? Is he sick?"

Sheeva shook her head. "No. I trust you haven't yet heard? Were you not in the throne room this afternoon?"

"Indeed not, Princess. I've been in here nearly all day so far, taking stock of my supplies and making some batches for the chills and such in preparation for the rest of winter. What's happened? I see from your eyes that it isn't good."

Sheeva explained the near annihilation of Nelahaal, along with a light account of Allor's kindness in the garden earlier that day.

"How dreadful," said Kamlof sadly. "Well, I'd be only too happy to teach you whatever you'd like to know, especially given why you're wanting to study it. But I must say, even though I suppose it should go without saying, that there are plants in this place that are very dangerous if you aren't careful with them and don't respect them. I trust that you've obtained your parents' permission before coming here?"

"Not yet, Dr. Kamlof, and I wasn't meaning to start right away. I can see that you've been busy today and I have other matters I need to discuss with my parents soon. I just wanted to see if you were willing to take the time to teach me, and then I was going to mention that to Mother and Father along with the other affairs."

"Ah, I see. Well then, know that I'm only too happy to teach a princess the wonders of the plants that Onu has given us, and if indeed you do intend to try, then I'll look to hear from the king and queen about it soon. If they approve and if you're up for it, I'll be ready whenever you are."

"Thank you, Dr. Kamlof."

"Of course, Princess," said the healer with a smile as Sheeva turned to go to the throne room.

14
1/12/4013 G.M.

LERANNU stepped out of Dalle and Ahvrom's home, having finished her last day of lessons for the week. In the spreading pale gold of the winter's afternoon light, the young apprentice went to the great oak in the square. She sat under it, rested her back against it, and looked up at the branches. The oak still stood grandly, but was now bare to the last leaf and acorn, and its branches were lightly draped with snow. The young mage then closed her eyes as she thought back on the past two months that had passed since Kiiva died.

Only a week passed following Kiiva's death when Lerannu's lessons resumed, much to her surprised gratitude. She spent that prior week fearing that her teachers, unable to move on from their loss, might resign from their work, leaving their apprentice to either abandon her learning or try to continue it elsewhere. Those worries, in turn, birthed dividing thoughts within Lerannu, for she wanted to respect the feelings of her teachers and friends, but also feared that she herself would be utterly devoured by grief if she couldn't practice and advance her craft. As much as she wanted her pursuit of magic to be purely out of love and satisfaction in the practice, she now felt it would be as much a retreat and source of solace as anything else. Lerannu confessed these thoughts to Ahvrom and Dalle when she came back to them the first day of resuming lessons, and was relieved to hear that they not only understood, but even shared her feelings. The three then agreed to be there for each other, and to seek consolation together in the furthering of Lerannu's skill. They had since taken to each other nearly as that of a second family, and both were greatly pleased at the progress that Lerannu had made in the following weeks.

However, for all the comfort the three shared with each other, there was no denying that much of the spark that once filled the Salinoths' study had now dimmed. Lerannu, feeling what she believed to be the same sort of dampened passion, was inclined to trust and hope that time would eventually rekindle the mood. Despite her efforts, however, she couldn't help but fear the wounds may have simply cut too deep for her tutors to ever reach a state that might pass, at least to the unfamiliar, as normal. Ahvrom spoke kindly, but rarely, and Dalle always looked tired, as though some great, dark thought was ceaselessly scratching at the back of her mind. Furthermore, for the entire first weekend of each month since the lessons continued, the Salinoths would completely shut themselves away within their home, routinely mourning for their daughter.

Then there was the matter of home. Although just under two moons had passed since the outbreak had ended, Lerannu would still catch the occasional reignited dispute between her father and mother over the town's response to the fever. Despite Ahvrom's assurance to Lerannu on the night Kiiva died, matters had not seemed to get all that much better since the outbreak's passing. Admittedly, at least as far as she knew, they had not had an argument as heated as the one they had the night of her friend's death. But the young mage had since begun to pick up more and more on the tension, disagreement, and discontentment that seemed to have taken root between them. She began to wonder and worry if it might have started sometime even before the fever. Nevertheless, her father and mother still seemed to manage well enough together, as Bravagoth continued to rebound from the fever and fare well, thanks in no small part to Mayor Roniil's leadership and the input from his advisors, which of course included his wife.

When it came to her father's advisors, Lerannu had also come to grow a closer friendship with the town treasurer, Uriah. The treasurer frequently came to check on the young mage in private, asking how she was doing, as well as her father and mother. Lerannu always felt better after talking to Uriah, who constantly assured her that both her parents loved her very much, despite the recent difficulties.

Lerannu's ponderings came to a halt as she became aware of the sounds of nearing footsteps crunching through the light sheets of snow that covered the ground. She opened her eyes to see Zalden standing before her.

"Hi, Lera."

"Hi, Zalden."

Apart from the Sardonmay festival, Lerannu had spoken very little with Zalden and her other friends in the past two months. It was something that the mage pupil had been trying to get herself to rectify for some time, but she had tended to keep to the Salinoths, Uriah, or herself. Now that Zalden had actually approached her, Lerannu struggled for a moment to find what to say. She was grateful for the chance to catch up, but at a loss for how she wanted to start. Eventually, she decided that a simple, if obvious, remark would suffice.

"It's been a little while, huh?" Lerannu offered.

"Yeah, I guess so, but it's been a pretty unusual couple of months ... and a pretty hard couple, too."

"I still should've taken time to talk to you all."

"Don't worry about it. We get it. Well, I get it, anyway, and I trust everyone else does, too. We ... we all miss her."

Lerannu got up from her place under the oak and hugged her friend. She didn't weep; she had largely drained herself of tears by now, but she sighed deeply in appreciation of Zalden's words. After a moment in silent embrace, the young apprentice looked up to Zalden's face, ears pricking up and a thin smile growing at the sight of his light green eyes, which were widened slightly by surprise. She could sense that he was blushing under his grey-furred face. With her arms still around him, Lerannu put a little distance between them.

"Are you okay?" she asked.

"Y-yes," Zalden stammered.

"I'm ... I'm sorry," she giggled.

Zalden laughed, too. "It's alright ... I'm ... I liked it. It was just unexpected."

A light gust, chilling to the bone, blew past the two youths and pushed Lerannu's hair into her face along with a dusting of snow. As she prepared to blow the hair out of her eyes, her breath caught in her mouth as Zalden gently brushed it back and patted out the snow. Lerannu looked again into Zalden's eyes, and her face felt as hot as Branok's forge.

Now it was Zalden's turn to smile. "There," he said, "we both took each other by surprise."

Both held each other for another moment, the heat of their blushing faces immediately melting the odd snowflake that fell onto the fur of their faces. Then Zalden pulled gently away, chuckling.

"The reason I came over here," he said with a broad grin, "was to see if you'd like to play hide-and-seek in the wood with us, with snowball hunting thrown in."

The young mage grinned impishly. "I'd love to. I promised Kiiva that I'd get you back for the trick you pulled last year, and I've got magic to help me do it!"

Zalden's ears drooped in mock fear, and he spread his hands as one trying to defuse a fight.

"Actually," he said, "you really shouldn't join us. You might wear yourself out and not be able to do spells for a long time if you get too carried away. Shouldn't you get back to meditating or something?"

The two laughed as Lerannu playfully cuffed Zalden's ears, then jogged off to the edge of the nearby woods.

***

The wood that lay a couple miles from Bravagoth was too small for a cartographer to really bother with charting, unless the task was to draw up a local map. It was a very dense wood, however, and the modest covering of snow made it an ideal venue for hiding, seeking, and hunting one's friends with snowballs. The snow on the ground added further need for some wit when it came to dealing with the tracks. Lerannu and Zalden met up with three more of their friends, Maria, Lokov and Maywuthe, on a small dirt road at the edge of the wood.

Maywuthe, holding five straws of dry hay, called for a drawing to see who would start as the seeker. Lerannu drew the longest, and looked at her friends with a mischievous grin. Her gaze fixed particularly on Zalden, who clapped a hand to his brow in melodramatic dread. Leaning against a nearby tree that marked the beginning of the small forest, the mage pupil covered her eyes and counted out a minute, grinning as she heard four pairs of frantic, scurrying footsteps crunching through the snow and icy leaves.

When the minute was up, Lerannu looked from her spot, grinning at the chaotic scattering of footprints and tracks, true and false, that ran on the path and into the wood beyond. She decided to begin with a trail, any trail, and follow it until it ended or yielded a hider, or her own intuition prompted her otherwise. She then picked a set of tracks and followed them through the trees, scooping up a handful of snow and preparing her snowball on the go.

Lerannu followed the tracks for a good ten minutes, gliding swiftly between the trees and over the snow. Numerous other trails overlapped the one she followed, and she was certain that a few of them were a continuation of it, as she made several abrupt turns around and found herself seeing familiar spots of the woods. But the trail had yet to end, and nothing else prompted her to change course. She eventually came to a sudden, but fairly short drop, which she managed to avoid careening over just in time. The trail had suddenly stopped, and Lerannu set to looking around for any further hints of one of her friends. Just a small distance away from the trail she had pursued, Lerannu noticed another trail of footprints. Curious, she went over to take a look. The tracks did not match those of any of her friends. The footprints were the size of an adult's and, though still clear in the snow, had a dusting over them that put them at being at least a day or two old by the young mage's estimation. Seeing that the tracks went down to the bottom of the drop by a nearby sloping hill, Lerannu looked back at the trail she had followed and saw a new set of tracks that began with a deeper set of prints and a scattering of snow. Whoever made the first trail had made a wide jump away from it and began a new course that led away, back where Lerannu had come. Aware of the trick, Lerannu still felt an urge to investigate the strange footprints.

Following them down the sloping hill and to the foot of the short escarpment, Lerannu discovered the small mouth of a cave. She knew that her friend's trail went in another direction, and she saw no signs of other tracks going into the cave aside from the stranger's, but Lerannu felt compelled by curiosity to look into the cave. She couldn't help but feel a need to see what a grown person would be doing in the cave. Plus, it was too good of a potential hiding spot to just ignore, regardless of the likelihood that one of her friends would be there. Adding some more snow to her snowball, which had slightly melted in her palm, Lerannu crouched down and carefully edged her way into the cave, going slowly both for stealth and to take time to get used to the dark. Having made her way into the cave, her sight's acclimation, along with sunlight that managed to reach into the cave, revealed a figure hunched against the far wall of the subterranean chamber. It appeared to be a girl, hunched over in an attempt to hide. Grinning in smug triumph, Lerannu threw the snowball. It was a direct hit, striking right on the back of the figure's shoulder.

"Got you!" crowed Lerannu. "Come on out here, Mary! Or is it May? Whichever one you are, come on out and we'll split to get the other two!"

The young mage giggled happily, only for her laughter to lodge in her throat at the sound of chains clinking, and a raspy, guttural groan.

Lerannu stood, hunched over and petrified, as she gazed in horror at the fiery, glowing eyes that arose to meet her sight, and an outstretched hand, still shrouded in the gloom, that wavered closer and closer as the chained figure shambled quickly toward her. Lerannu knew the figure was that of an undead youth, a corpse reanimated by the demonic arts of necromancy. As much as her mind screamed within herself to flee, her fear, along with a horrid fascination, rooted her to the spot.

The cold, rotten flesh of the figure now became visible in the half-light of the cave, along with the dress it wore and the styling of its hair. The figure suddenly jolted as it reached the end of its chain, which snapped Lerannu out of her macabre trance. She looked once more at the figure, now that she could largely make it out in the diluted dark, and a horror gripped her heart with a coldness that surpassed any night of winter.

It was Kiiva.

Lerannu, finally breaking free of her terror, ran from the cave and bolted back the way she came, running as fast as her legs would carry her. She didn't have the breath to scream until she reached the path that ran through the wood, where she at last fell on quaking knees, threw back her head, and screamed a cry of horror and grief. A few minutes passed, and all four of her friends returned, running to the path to find their friend shaking and weeping.

***

The five young friends barged into the town hall, the startled faces of Lerannu's parents and their advisors all turning to them in the mix of candlelight and fading daylight. With ragged breath, Lerannu told them of what she had found. Her father and mother had the town guard called, along with the high priestess and a knight of the Faithguard, as the lot of them prepared to embark into the woods.

With the group assembled at the great oak, Lerannu looked at them and asked where Dalle and Ahvrom were.

"They should know, shouldn't they?" she asked. "Shouldn't we tell them? She is–was–their daughter."

Mayor Roniil looked at his daughter, glanced in the direction of the Salinoths' house, and nodded, gesturing for the company to follow him. As they approached the house, Lerannu felt a hand fall onto her shoulder. Looking up, she saw it was her mother.

"Let's hope that telling them doesn't end up doing more harm than good," said Sarah glumly.

Roniil, leading the crowd, knocked urgently on the door. A few seconds passed, and Ahvrom answered, asking what the matter was as he looked worriedly at the assembled armed guards. When Lerannu's father told him of what had happened, Ahvrom's face wilted from dread, and his voice, barely audible in the evening quiet, asked for details on the state of Kiiva's corpse. Upon hearing Lerannu tell of Kiiva being chained, the mage pleaded that the crowd wait until Dalle was present.

"I–I know that it's absurd to ask," he said waveringly amongst the stirring uproar within the company, "but Dalle isn't here right now. She's gone over to Redrock to see if there might be a potential student or two who might–"

Roniil put his hand on Ahvrom's shoulder, speaking gently, understandingly, but firmly.

"I'm so sorry, Ahvrom, but you know I can't let this sort of foulness linger any longer than can be helped. Kiiva's spirit isn't there anymore. That isn't really her, and her remains need to be returned to rest. Surely Dalle would understand that this needs to be done now? She wouldn't want us to let her daughter's body remain bound to something so foul, once we learned of it, would she?"

Ahvrom sighed, wearily and heavily, and brushed a tear away from his eye. "May I come with you? I want to be able to see her ... her remains, I mean ... be tended to with my own eyes, so I can tell Dalle for certain that–"

"Of course," said Roniil. "Come along; we're heading to her now."

***

Having reached the forest at dusk and painstakingly retracing the tracks that Lerannu had followed to the escarpment, the company looked over the edge and saw a faint light emanating from the cave's mouth. It cast a grim, flickering orange glow upon the snow that covered the forest floor. Lerannu, who had led the group alongside her mother and father, looked to the side where the tracks led down to the cave and saw a fresh set of the stranger's footprints. Pointing them out to Roniil, Lerannu watched as her father gestured to the company to keep as quiet as possible, for it was clear that someone, presumably the necromancer, was in the cave with Kiiva's possessed shell. Lerannu, her parents, and Ahvrom went toward the cave ahead of the company, with the Faithguard knight and two of the town guard accompanying them and guarding their front. The whole company began to approach the cave in a silence that was broken only by the crunching of snow and the faintest clinking of armor.

A pair of shadows, accompanied by the clamor of chains, emerged from the cave and spilled onto the ground before its mouth, and all the company froze still and silent. A figure, hooded in black, slunk out of the cave with a torch in one hand and the fettered, undead Kiiva by the other. Lerannu, consumed by grief for her friend's state, and utter anger and disgust toward the one who had befouled her remains, stepped forward and shouted in confrontation to the hooded stranger before anyone could stop her.

"You there! Stop! Who are you and why are you doing this?"

The figure froze at the shouting. There followed the steely hiss of unsheathing swords and the rush of guards beginning to close in. The figure's head turned hauntingly toward the crowd, though no one could yet see its face. Ahvrom came forward, his typically meek and mournful disposition now replaced by one of sheer wrath.

"Get away from her!" he demanded. "Surrender to the guard and step away from my daughter!"

The figure, noting that Kiiva's corpse was getting too close to itself, took several steps away from her as the company braced to take drastic measures. The figure then stopped, looked again at the crowd, and slowly lowered its hood.

A score of breaths were drawn in sharp gasps. Lerannu felt a numbness begin to overtake her mind and heart.

"She ... she's *our* daughter, Ahvrom," said Dalle brokenly as she shifted the chain in her hands. "I ... I just–"

"Why?" Ahvrom cried as his knees gave beneath him. "Why would you do this? You *know* that isn't her!"

"I know. I-I know..." Dalle wept. "I ... I just couldn't let her go yet!"

"I know," said Ahvrom in a voice that was torn between compassion and revulsion, "I haven't really been able to, either, but that's why we held to each other more. That's why we tried to focus more on teaching Lera. That's why we were looking to interview for more students from nearby. It was even your idea, and you–"

"It was a lie," Dalle confessed tearfully as she took a few more paces away from Kiiva's shuffling corpse. "I suggested it the night after she was buried, so that you would think that's what I've been doing when I'd leave for a while. I dug her up the following night and took her here. Then ... then every time I said I was going somewhere to look for more students, I was coming here. And there's been a few other times when I'd leave quietly at night–"

"Enough!" Ahvrom sobbed. "Enough, Dalle, please! You–you *know* how this will end ... don't you?"

"Yes."

"And you knew when you began, didn't you?"

"I knew it *might* have turned out this way, if I was found out. But I just needed a way to feel like I could let her go on my own–"

"You called a demon from Raakhaal and had it enter our daughter's corpse! Is that what you do to someone you love?"

Dalle lowered her head, weeping uncontrollably. Kiiva's remains, having lumbered within inches of Dalle, lunged at her. Dalle caught hold of the corpse, holding it back at arm's length. The two town guards and the Temple knight, swords drawn, closed in around Dalle and her undead daughter.

"Lady Salinoth," said the Faithguard as the three strode forward, "please, step away from the Lihmorlak, and we'll see to it that–"

"No!" Dalle cried, drawing a dagger from under her cloak. "Please, let me–"

Before Dalle got any further, one of the town guardsmen, panicking at the sudden appearance of the weapon, ran her through with his sword. Lerannu screamed. The other guard and the Temple knight cut down Kiiva's shell before realizing what had happened. Roniil, Sarah, and the town's high priestess ran forward, rebuking the guard and disputing angrily with each other over the handling of the incident. Lerannu looked over to Ahvrom and wept as she saw his face, which now seemed to age a score of years in only the same number of seconds.

As the shouts of her mother and father, and all the others gathered around the dead, raged about her, Lerannu lay flat upon the snowy ground, pleading Onu and Sardoth to have the winter's cold end her.

15

3/25/4013 G.M.

MIRA GREENHEART saddled up her horse, eager and nervous at going on her first hunt with her father, Virgaard. Having made sure that everything they needed was ready, the ten-year-old girl kissed her mother, Ann, and little brother, Isaak, goodbye before riding out. She rode a few trots out of the gate, then looked back at the village of Plen, her home in the great Santaru Forest. Her mother and brother were still standing together by the faded path that led past the main gate, waving their farewells alongside several other villagers who had stopped by to wish the two hunters luck.

"You two be careful!" Ann called out. "And don't risk being late over the hunt! We'll have a good Veronmay with or without fresh game, so don't go too far for this!"

"We won't!" answered Virgaard. "Though I've got a good feeling about this one. I got Mira here, and Onu willing, we'll be back in a day or two at most, hopefully with a good boar or stag!"

"Bye, Ma!" called Mira. "Bye, Isaak! I'll do my best!"

"I know you will!" her mother said.

Father and daughter rode steadily on until noon, conversing quietly over the techniques to employ for whatever beast that might end up as their quarry. They also went over what to do in the event of encountering a cursed creature, or a blessed one. At the sun's peak, the two reached a little clearing, a tiny island of nothing but grass in the vast ocean of trees, and stopped to rest a little as they fed their horses and themselves.

"You still feeling good and ready for all this?" asked Virgaard as he bit into a piece of dried venison.

"Yes, Da," Mira answered.

"Still all bright-eyed and bushy-tailed?"

"Yes, Da," she said with a grin.

"Not too nervous?"

"No, I don't think so. Not too much, anyway."

"It's alright if you are, especially for the first time. I know I was. I barely slept the night before my first hunt. Did you sleep alright?"

"Yeah. Maybe I had a little trouble at first, but I wasn't up all night."

"Good, good," Mira's father remarked as he made a brief inspection of the longbow, arrows, spear, and knife that each had packed onto their horse. "It's no fun hunting when you're really tired. Can be dangerous, too, depending on how things go."

Mira listened to her father as she ate a few pieces of dried meat and took a couple gulps from her waterskin.

"Is Santaru really that dangerous, Da? I've always felt safe here. I mean, I know there are plenty of normal animals that can hurt or kill you if you're not careful, but do many of those bad animals that Raakaru made live here?"

Virgaard looked levelly at his daughter as he fished out a piece of dried fruit from his bag, along with his canteen.

"Well, I'd certainly like to say that Santaru is far safer than not, especially these days. We've been hunting and fighting the Lakons for four thousand years now. They're still out there, of course, and I believe they'll be with us in some measure or other 'til the world ends. But many say their numbers are far fewer now than in days long ago, and I'm inclined to trust them. They definitely aren't gone, though, and it's always better to be safe than sorry when it comes to those creatures, especially out in a wilderness like here. Santaru certainly has its sacred places and havens, and the forest overall is good, I'm sure of it. But it's not totally free of those monsters; no place on Fidonhaal is except for Karzynhaal. And this forest covers hundreds and hundreds of miles, so who knows what exactly might be in any given cave here, or pool or stream?"

Virgaard then pointed randomly at a large tree at the edge of the clearing. "There could be nothing behind that tree over there," he continued, "or anything. A deer, perhaps, but then again, perhaps a Qualakar or some other monster. Who knows? Maybe even a—"

Virgaard and Mira froze stock-still at the movement that came from behind the very tree they were watching. With eyes wide, ears pricked, and nostrils flaring as they vied to determine what creature was moving through the trees, the two let out a breath of both relief and awe at the sight of what approached them.

An Arbonyn, one of the tree-folk, was walking gently toward them, gesturing peacefully that there was no need for alarm. When it reached Mira and her father, the Arbonyn bowed courteously. Father and daughter reciprocated as they admired its form. It was around two heads taller than Virgaard, who was quite tall for a Fidon at six-foot-eight. Its body had the appearance of yew bark, though the bark of the Arbonyns varied in hues and patterns similar to trees from all over the world. Its eyes glowed a haunting, but benevolent light of green-touched white. A great branch stemmed from its forehead like a horn, and its overall form seemed that of a man. After the greetings were complete and the tree-man had given the hunters a moment to look him over in silence, he spoke.

"Good day to you. Hunting, are you?"

"Indeed we are," said Virgaard politely. "Getting something good for Veronmay, if we can. Is there anything the matter with this place that we should not hunt or linger here?"

"No, no, not at all," replied the spawn of the angels Terranah and Stromarus. "No trouble have I seen here. Many deer just a little over that way, though. Very good to eat on spring's first day, I'd say."

"I'd say we're in agreement!" said Virgaard as he smiled at Mira's excited grin and shining eyes. "Mount up, Mira, and we'll see if we can't get a deer each. You have your bow and arrows where you can get to them easily?"

"Yes, Da!" said Mira as she turned to the Arbonyn. "Thank you so much ... do you have a name?"

A friendly smile creased the tree-man's wooden face.

"Rovnillath," he answered.

"You have our thanks, Rovnillath," said Virgaard as he mounted his horse. "Farewell!"

Mira and her father cantered swiftly back into the forest, toward the herd of deer and the promise of a fine and savory Veronmay feast.

16

4/17/4013 G.M.

RUTH PIONAAR walked out of the archtemple schoolhouse beside her mother, Arza, and friend, Verdok. Having finished their lessons for the day, the two children were accompanying the sister to join Salpion Owen and some others for tea in the main garden.

Ruth had been largely quiet and contemplative, especially for an eight-year-old, since the revelations of her parentage. Her past times of playing with the other children had now been largely replaced with questions of life and purpose that she levied at her mother, Father Owen, and some of the other clerics, to the extent she could think to ask for her age, as well as her own quiet brooding that she did whenever she could be alone. Her mood was not from shame of her origins, nor of disgust toward her mother, but out of the sheer gravity of the reveal and the somberness of the reason for the revelation to begin with. The death and gloom of the fever's outbreak, the severity of which had prompted her mother and Owen to bring it up when they did, had darkened the girl's mood significantly. It had driven her to try and sort out her life's purpose to the best of her capabilities, despite the fever's passing and her present youth.

The account of her friend Verdok's parents added further weight to Ruth's preoccupation. Despite the assurances of Father Owen and her mother that the two children had ample time to decide their paths, Ruth could not fully let it go. She noticed that Verdok had seemed to change in much the same way as herself, though she had yet to speak of it to him directly. Whenever he was free from study and chores, the Kason-Mavon boy was typically in the library, reading through books of poetry.

The young girl hoped the afternoon's respite would help her to think of other things. The tea and tidbits were always good, and the garden had just recently begun to stir from its winter slumber. Ruth focused her sight on the approaching gate that led directly to the prime garden, hoping that this afternoon would bring some lightness to her mind.

She was surprised, and a touch intimidated, when she saw Gothnaar Vyth, archgeneral of the Temple Faithguard, sitting beside Father Owen at the round stone table in the garden's center. Ruth had seen him numerous times before, along with other knights of the Temple, for they lived within the archtemple's compound alongside the clergy and other lay residents. However, though none she had met were abrasive or cold, she was daunted by their arms and armor, and had barely spoken to any of them. Now she, her mother, and Verdok where walking right toward the highest-ranking Faithguard in the world. Though Ruth figured, in hindsight, that the archgeneral and salpion would ideally be on at least agreeable terms, she hadn't realized they were good friends, as evidenced by how closely they sat together and how intently they were speaking to each other.

The grizzled but handsome Zaron man, in the unarmored white uniform of his office, looked up, halted his talk with Owen, and nodded with a smile at the three arrivals. Owen responded by turning in his seat to greet them as well.

"We've just more or less started," the salpion stated. "We've only had this cup, and barely even that. Archgeneral Vyth has been filling me in on some recent happenings that he's heard about from reports. We've been so caught up in that, we've barely had anything. Come, sit with us!"

The three joined Owen and Gothnaar, with Ruth sitting beside her mother and Verdok beside Owen, who put an arm about him and patted his shoulder as a father would do to his son.

"Did you two have a good day in school?" Owen asked.

"Yes, Father Owen," the two children answered in unison.

Ruth's eyes fell to the archgeneral as she continued. "I really liked today's history lesson. It was about how the Temple began, and what the first of the Faithguard did to help and protect the people back then."

"So you learned a bit about Konoth, I take it?" asked Gothnaar enthusiastically, "along with how he met Elukus and Sophia, and followed them around the world to protect them?"

"Mm-hmm!" Ruth hummed with a nod. "And how he started the Faithguard of the Temple, with the Konothian Knights being the first and oldest order."

"Indeed they are!" said Gothnaar.

Ruth, relieved to see that the archgeneral was approachable and realizing she was enjoying the conversation, looked at Gothnaar's wear to try to deduce his order, but saw no obvious indications.

"Are you one of them?" she asked. "I've seen you in armor and all before, but I didn't really look at it, you know?"

Gothnaar laughed. "That sounds like me lately, to see things and yet not *really* see them. Probably not good for the archgeneral to confess that," he added with a shrug directed at a grinning Owen.

"It can happen to anyone, especially when they're busy," the salpion said, "and you and I have had plenty to mind lately. We're also getting old, of course."

Gothnaar sputtered his sip of tea from laughter. "*Getting* old? I *am* old, Owen. And you might be getting *older*, but you're not old, yet."

"I sure do feel that way, though," said Owen with mock glumness.

"Then may Onu give you strength when you actually *are* old," the archgeneral jeered, "since you're only half my age as it is."

"I appreciate the prayer, Gothnaar," said Owen as he sipped more tea and reached for a small blackberry tart, "but I'll remind you that the young lady asked you a question."

"Indeed," Gothnaar said apologetically as he faced Ruth again. "No, young lady, I am not one of the Konothian order. I was trained in the Morganian technique: a shield with a mace instead of the Konothian axe. At a glance, it may not look to be much of a difference, but I assure you that it definitely is. The weight of the weapon is different, and the shields are also of a different shape and size; mine is larger than the Konothian-style buckler. That order was founded by Morgana Maygla, and she ... heh, well, that's another history lesson for you. Best not get me started on that right now or I'll be talking until way past dinner."

"Well, then," Ruth said with a smile, "I hope to hear about it soon."

"In the meantime," Gothnaar added, "if you'd like to see, and talk to, a Konothian Knight, there are plenty of them around the world, and certainly a good few here. One of them is someone I trust very much. Her name is Hanye, and she's coming in today to take charge of training those who have chosen to follow that particular order. You could talk to her if you're curious. She plans on spending most of her time here now, when not on a mission, and should be available whenever she isn't training and whatnot."

"She's already come in, by the way," Owen said. "She came in around noon and has been moving into her quarters since. I'd think that she'd be settled by now, or could use a break if she hasn't. Let me see ..."

The salpion looked about the garden for someone who appeared available to assist. Calling over a priest who was passing by, Owen asked him to go to Hanye's quarters and direct her to the garden if she was willing to join them. With the cleric promptly heading off to the Faithguard barracks, the five at the table began their afternoon repast in earnest. Several refills had been poured and a good handful of the pastries eaten before Ruth noticed the archgeneral looking fixedly at Verdok's neck, from which hung his mother's talisman.

"That's a beautiful Uqua pendant, dear lad," he said kindly.

Verdok, caught off guard by the compliment, held the amulet close to his heart while ensuring it was in a plainly visible position for the archgeneral. "Th-thank you," he stuttered. Verdok then nodded toward Gothnaar's pendant, which gleamed a gorgeous gold in the afternoon sun, same as Father Owen's. "Y-yours is, too."

"I'd agree overall," said Gothnaar. "Indeed, I've never seen a piece depicting the Four that I'd consider ugly. I'd like to think that isn't really possible. Shining metals and glittering gems express the unfathomable beauty of the Four and its ultimate meaning, and plain stone expresses its unending endurance. Even ones of wood and thread, in my eyes, tell of the Uqua's foundation for life and nature, and the intricacy and boundless craftsmanship of Onu himself. By his Four Breaths and Will was all ultimately wrought. The mark of the Four is a symbol that shouldn't be corruptible. Not that it's never been tainted, sadly; Fidonity has a remarkable talent for doing things like that, but …"

The archgeneral, having caught himself in his tangent, looked at those sitting with him and laughed before returning to his original point.

"All I meant to say, dear boy, was that I see a beauty in yours that I believe mine doesn't have. Salpion–Father Owen–told me about yours a while ago. The love and craftsmanship your father put into it, and the love your mother gave it when she passed it on to you, makes it very special and beautiful. Mine has a legacy, too, for many an archgeneral wore it before me, and I'd certainly like to think that the goldsmith who made it put plenty of passion and devotion into it. But it's still not the same as yours, nor would I really say it's better than yours for its history. I just thought I'd tell you, and I advise that you treasure it, whether you keep it for yourself all your days or pass it to another in time."

"I will, Archgeneral, sir," said Verdok appreciatively. "I don't think I've taken it off since Father Owen gave it to me. It means a lot to me, especially now."

The black and brown-furred boy looked over to Owen, sighing deeply.

"I've been thinking about all that you told me, back at the end of the year," he said, "but I still don't know what to do."

"Please, Verdok," said Owen with a pat on his shoulder, "don't worry yourself so much over it, especially now. There's still time to decide, and even then, it sometimes takes trying something before knowing if it's right for you. This won't happen until you're ten, and I'll be there to help you. So keep it in mind, but don't let it worry you all the time, alright?"

"Yes, Father Owen," said Verdok. "Thank you."

"And the same goes for you, too, Ruth," said Owen as he turned to face her. Ruth glanced up at her mother, seeing her nod comfortingly, as the salpion continued. "I know that what we told you two must've put a lot of weight on your mind, more than should be the case for anyone your age. We wouldn't have even done it then if it weren't for the fever being so bad at the time. Please, both of you, don't get so caught up in worrying about the future that you don't live at all in the present."

"Thank you, Father Owen," Ruth replied.

Verdok had just seconded his friend's response and the five were about to continue with their tea when a Fidon woman in shining armor entered the garden and caught Ruth's eye. She was a beautiful Kason woman, with her warm, brown fur glowing in the sun. Her eyes, which were the same deep blue as Verdok's, looked friendlily at the group as she approached. Her hair was done in a long, braided tail, which was draped across her right shoulder, and the buckler-shield of the Konothian order was strapped to her left arm, with the knight's hand-axe ready at her right hip. She seemed to be, at most, a little older than Ruth's mother Arza and Owen; an experienced Faithguard who was still in her prime. Noticing Ruth's intrigued gaze, Archgeneral Vyth looked over, saw the knight approaching, and pointed her out to Owen. The salpion turned to her and nodded with a smile.

"Good afternoon, Lady Commander Heartkeeper!" Owen said before gesturing at the remaining seats that encircled the table. "Have a seat and join us for tea, if you'd like. Has everything been moved to your rooms?"

"Almost, Salpion Lovonhaar," said Hanye, "but there's still the matter of getting it all arranged, and I've still to bathe and get my armor and uniform washed, if you'll pardon me on that."

"Please, Lady Hanye, that's no trouble at all. Have a rest and tell us how things have been. I'm very glad to hear you plan to focus on training the Konothian squires here for now, and this young lady here is interested to hear about you and your experience. She just learned about Konoth in school today."

Hanye turned to Ruth and smiled at the sight of the girl's attentive gaze.

"Always happy to hear of youths who find at least some of history interesting, especially when it comes to that of the Temple."

"Ruth's always been interested in history, actually," said Sister Arza, her daughter nodding in confirmation, "but she was especially attentive today. Verdok, too, actually."

"I liked the parts about Blind Elukus and his wife, Sophia," Verdok added.

"And I liked hearing about how Konoth wanted to help them after hearing them speak," Ruth explained, "and how he left his village to follow them with his wood-axe and a big pot lid."

"And that led to the founding of the Konothian Knights and the Faithguard as a whole," Hanye said, taking her axe and buckler into her hands, and showing them to the awestruck Ruth. "Our arms and fighting techniques are based on Konoth's style, from the day he began following the Temple's founders to the day he died as the first archgeneral. Since that day, my order, and those of my fellows in the defense of the Faith, have striven to protect the Temple, its servants, and all of Fidonity. Our history is full of both light and darkness, but still we stand, as is the case for the world itself."

"When—" asked Ruth, hesitatingly but eagerly, "when will you start training the squires? I know I'm still a bit too young, but I just wanted to see what it's like, in case ... well ..."

The knight commander looked at Arza and Owen, both of whom Ruth saw give a surprised but approving nod to her. Then, pouring herself some more tea and taking two pastries, she smiled and looked back at Ruth.

"That should be perfectly fine. I've still to finish moving in, though, and I also need to get reoriented with the archtemple and where everything is. I should be ready to train starting next week, on Onmay. I'll tell the salpion when I'm ready, and we'll be sure to have a spot ready for you to watch, along with anyone else who'd like to see."

"Thank you so much, Lady Hanye!" Ruth said gratefully.

"Yes, Lady Heartkeeper," said Owen, "thank you for accommodating young Ruth here, and all others interested. There are many youths here in our temple who are now nearing the age when they start wondering what they're to do in their life. Hopefully, being able to see you and the squires in action might help them come to some sort of decision, be it in direct service to the Temple or not."

The Faithguard lady nodded with a dutiful smile. Then, with all soon finishing their tea, she went on to tell of her handful of missions and experiences over the past several months, much to Ruth's fascination.

17

6/1/4013 G.M.

LERANNU put on her dress, looking out her window onto the view of Bravagoth in the late spring. It was early morning, earlier than the usual time she would get ready for school. Lerannu didn't sleep much the night before, but tired as she was, her desire to practice her magic had prompted her to try a little before the day started.

She hadn't been back to Ahvrom's since the week following the incident in the woods. As she lay miserably in the snow that night while her mother and father raged at one another, and the others present argued over the handling of the situation, Ahvrom and Uriah had picked up Lerannu and led her back home. Her parents still weren't home when she awoke the following morning, but upon leaving her room, she saw the mage and the treasurer in the entry reception hall of the house. They conversed quietly until Lerannu called out to them.

After a small breakfast, the two took her to the square. There, Dalle and Kiiva's remains were burned on a pyre and scattered to the winds in order to prevent them from being reanimated by any bond that may have lingered from Dalle's contract with the demon she had summoned. Many had gathered, whispering remarks that swung between pity and contempt, as Lerannu watched her best friend laid to rest a second time, along with one of her teachers. Ahvrom watched in grief-stricken silence. Uriah, hugging Lerannu and encouraging her to be strong, left the two of them alone as she went to stand beside Mayor Roniil, conversing with him about matters Lerannu couldn't catch over the prayers of the clerics. Taking Ahvrom's hand, to which the mage gave no response, Lerannu looked about the crowd for her mother. Sarah was nowhere to be found, and Lerannu's eyes brimmed with tears; not for Dalle and Kiiva, but for the downward spiral that had overtaken her mother and father's marriage.

A miserable week passed, during which Lerannu at one point found herself in an argument with her mother over how things went with Dalle and Kiiva. Lerannu agreed largely with what her father had said, that if Dalle had been approached more calmly and permitted to put down Kiiva herself (which she and her father both believed was what she was meaning to do instead of moving to attack the guard who killed her), then the mage would have submitted without further incident. And while necromancy was an abominable practice and a capital crime, as it entailed communication with demons and the desecration of a corpse that would invariably become violent, Lerannu and Roniil still felt sympathy for Dalle. Sarah, having nothing but contempt and disgust regarding the incident, opposed her daughter's comments and expressed great disdain for, as she described it, Lerannu siding with her erroneous father.

The argument escalated until at last the young mage had enough and stormed out of the house. As Lerannu stepped onto the street, her eyes fell onto Ahvrom's home. Hoping that she and her tutor could continue lessons as a means of coping with their respective troubles, she ran over to the mage's house. She knocked, and then knocked again, and Ahvrom answered several minutes later. Taken aback at the sight of Ahvrom's face, the young apprentice asked haltingly if there was any chance of continuing the lessons. The withered mage looked sadly at her.

"I ... I don't know, Lera. I don't know if I can do this anymore. Not after all this. I won't say never – not now, anyway – but ... not now. Not anytime soon. I'm sorry."

The matter was further burdened by her parents' reaction that following evening, when Lerannu expressed her desire to continue learning magic. While Roniil was still open to it, Sarah, still heated from the earlier argument, made it abundantly clear that she thoroughly opposed the notion. She spoke as though magic was an inherently corrupting force, and all attempts to persuade her to the contrary were met with heated refusals at worst and hurtful remarks of resignation at best.

"A terrible mother I must be," Sarah said at last, "for wanting to protect my child from a man who turned out to be living with a necromancer. Fine, Lerannu; I obviously can't change your mind, but if Ahvrom won't teach you anytime soon, then I don't see how you'll go about it apart from practicing in private. You're not going to go to some other town for it, and I will not stand to see you practice it myself, nor do I want to see you or hear of you doing anything with it in public. And until Ahvrom starts teaching again, when and *if* that ever be, it's normal schooling for you. Understand?"

Lerannu stared somberly at the floor. Both she and her father knew that there'd be no arguing the matter. "Yes, Mother."

Thus, the young mage attended a standard education for nearly four months after the incident in the woods. In her room, however, when alone or on the occasions when she had her father or Uriah as an audience, she practiced quietly with wind and water (earth was too messy and flame was obviously too risky to practice in the house for her current level of experience), and also absorbed what she could out of some books from the town library. Lerannu steadily refined her skill with growing encouragement from her father, Roniil, Uriah the treasurer, and her friend, Zalden, whom she now was seeing more often since they attended the same school. In time, she managed to transfer water from one bowl to another, and send a feather at least two laps around her bedroom.

Then her thirteenth birthday came, and Uriah gave her two small porcelain bowls from the Whitemanes with which she could practice transferring water. Zalden and Roniil gave her a parcel of feathers from the colorful, exotic birds of Janrenar's rainforest with which she could practice suspending multiple objects by the same body of wind. It had been a long time since she had treasured a set of gifts so deeply.

Now, in the early dawn, Lerannu got the porcelain bowls out and filled one from a water pitcher that she kept in her room. She placed them a few feet apart on a small table in a corner of her room. She had sent the water from one bowl to the other, in varying amounts and with several flourishes, for several minutes. The task began to become increasingly difficult, as she felt the pull of weariness in her head. Ideally, a mage should be well-rested and well-fed prior to engaging in magic. But, as Lerannu had learned, life doesn't always provide the ideal circumstances. In an effort to train herself to practice through fatigue and from simply not wanting to lie restlessly in bed, the young mage pushed on with a few more efforts. She didn't pause until she spilled half of the water she pulled out of the bowl and her head started to hurt. Massaging her brow and grabbing a rag, she mopped up the table and took deep, regular breaths until the headache subsided.

She was about to sit down and try a few more passes when a heavy, wooden crashing, followed by her mother's screams, caused her to bolt upright, knocking one of the bowls off the table and causing it to break into several large shards. Her father's voice, raised but carrying with it the effort to be calm, followed the commotion. Lerannu was petrified by her mother's outburst, fearing that her parents might be confronting a robber or other such intruder. After hearing the tone of Roniil's voice, however, she felt safe leaving the room and making her way to their location in the upstairs office. As she haltingly made her way from her room to the office's closed doors, she began to make out more and more of the conversation.

"Sarah," she heard her father say, "I-I'm so sorry. Uriah is, too. That's why—"

"You're not sorry!" Sarah shrieked. "You wouldn't have done this to me if you were going to be sorry!"

"I wouldn't have told you if I didn't regret it."

"And you wouldn't regret it if you didn't do it!"

Lerannu, having reached the door of the mayor's study, opened it quietly and her heart stopped at what she saw. The main table was on its side, the annals, parchments, and books that were on it now strewn about the floor. Her mother, bracing both hands against the mayor's desk, was quaking with fitful sobs. Her father, pressed against the upturned table, looked woefully at his wife. Walking slowly toward her, he placed a hand gently on her shoulder as he spoke.

"Sarah ... even after these past months, and all that's happened, I've still loved you, it's just—"

"Don't touch me!"

Sarah wheeled around suddenly and struck Roniil across the face with her claws. The strike was so forceful and unexpected that the mayor spun half-around and was knocked off his feet. He yelped in pain, of body and of heart, and placed a hand on his cheek. He gasped, and withdrawing his hand, he stared at the blood that covered it. His body began to shake, and he gasped several sobs before lifting his eyes from the floor. His gaze rose right into Lerannu's eyes as she stood horrified in the doorway. His breath and body abruptly froze.

"L-Lera—" he stammered tearfully. "I-I ... we—"

"Lerannu," Sarah said with dreadful numbness as her eyes pierced her daughter's, "get out of here. I don't care where you go. Just go somewhere in town until I come get you or send for you."

The young mage took a wary step into the study. "B-but w-what about Papa?"

"GO!"

Recoiling as if struck in the face herself, Lerannu scrambled away and ran down the stairs as her mother's screams began anew. As she bolted out of the house, she saw many people about the town and street, frozen in place, staring alarmingly at the town hall. Seeing Ahvrom standing at the door to his house just down the street, Lerannu began to quickly walk over to him, doing her utmost to lock her sight on him and not mind the people staring worriedly at her. She was in the middle of the road, nearing the mage's home, when she heard Uriah's voice.

"Lera!" the treasurer gasped. "Lera!"

Lerannu turned to her. The beautiful black-and-white woman's hair was tussled from her running, and her bright blue eyes were shining with sadness and shame. Before the young mage could say anything, the treasurer wrapped her arms around her and wept.

"I'm so sorry," she sobbed. "Please, Lera, whatever happens, don't hate your father or your mother. They both love you so much ... and I do, too. But if you must hate someone for all this, then hate me."

"What are you talking about?" Lerannu asked worriedly.

"Lera—" Uriah began.

"YOU!" Sarah screeched as she stormed out of the house and approached them. Terrified, Lerannu clung tightly to her friend as her mother roared wrathfully. "Get away from my daughter! Don't you dare touch her, you filthy rotten whore!"

Lerannu frantically broke away from Uriah and ran as fast as she could toward Ahvrom's home. Ahvrom stood there, having seen Lerannu coming and what was going on, and held the door open to let her in. As she hurried toward the house, she could hear more of the confrontation, especially given Sarah's overwhelming voice.

"Sarah," Uriah said, "please, did you at least hear what Ron had to say?"

The sound of a striking hand, immediately followed by a cry of anguish, cut the treasurer's question short.

"Don't call him that, you shitty little tart!"

"I-I ... we–"

"Tomorrow. The three of us. The courthouse. As soon as it opens. Do you hear me?"

"Ye-yes, Sarah, b-but–"

"But nothing! Be there or so help me, with Onu and all his host as my witnesses, I'll hunt you down and tear up so much more than your face!"

Lerannu, having reached the door to Ahvrom's home, stopped and looked back from the doorway. Without another word, Sarah wheeled around and stormed back into the town hall. Uriah, frozen to the spot, dropped her hand from her cheek, hung her head, and folded her arms across her chest in a miserable, self-loathing embrace. At last shuddering a wretched sigh, the treasurer went back to her home as those on the road looked on.

Lerannu then bolted past her former tutor and flung herself onto a sofa in the entrance hall, curling up into a ball and crying inconsolably. The Mavon mage poured a beaker of water, put it on the side table by the sofa, and took Lerannu into his arms, hugging her closely and speaking quietly.

"Lera, I'm so sorry this is happening. You've been dealing with far too much lately, and I can't think of any reason why this has all been happening to you."

"I just want it all to stop," Lerannu wept.

"I know it hurts, Lera, but one way or another it'll pass and life will go on."

"No, Ahvrom, I want it *all* to just stop! I can't stand it anymore!"

"Lera, please! Please, don't give up like that! There's so much more that Onu has for you in life."

"I don't want anymore, if it's just going to be more things like this. Besides, you just said you can't think of any reason for what's going on."

"That doesn't mean there isn't one, and things like these aren't all that life holds, you know that."

"But it's all I can feel ... all I can see."

"I know. I know."

"Why? Why would Onu let this happen?"

"Because Onu gave us freedom, and sadly we've abused that gift so many times. And many of the times we've done so, we've hurt others rather than ourselves."

"He shouldn't have given that to us, then. He should've known that it would come to this, and all the other horrible things that have happened in the world."

"Just as all the love that has come from it, and every grain of good that has been done as well. I know what you're feeling. I've felt it, too. I'm still battling with it now, in fact. I don't believe there's been a Fidon who hasn't, at one time or another. But the thought that Onu should've withheld freedom from us, that's what Lovaariinu believed as well, and that's how he became Raakaru."

"I–" Lerannu said, quivering as she tried to hold back the tears, "I'm just so ..."

"Let it all out, Lera. Don't hide it."

The girl buried her face into Ahvrom's shoulder and wept anew. When her tears were at last spent, Ahvrom pointed to the water he poured for her. She sipped from it as Ahvrom looked on.

"Have you been practicing magic at all?" he asked.

"Yes," she said. "I've never stopped, though it's been harder since ..."

"I can imagine," he said, "but I'm up for changing that, if you'd like to come back."

Lerannu embraced her teacher again. "Thank you," she sniffed.

"Have you made any progress since we left off, or has it largely been a matter of maintaining what you've learned so far?"

Lerannu then told Ahvrom of her progress, which was met with great delight from the mage.

"That's wonderful!" he said. "You really have a great aptitude for this!"

"I just wish that Kiiva could've seen it. And Dalle."

"Well ... they might still, in a way."

"Maybe, but you know what I mean."

"Of course."

***

Evening came, and the candles and torches were lit in the town. A weary knock on the door interrupted Ahvrom and Lerannu as they were finishing their dinner. Ahvrom got up to answer it.

It was Sarah, hair disheveled and eyes bloodshot. When she spoke, it was in a hoarse whisper that bristled the fur.

"Lera," she said wearily, "come home with me, please."

Lerannu looked at Ahvrom, who nodded solemnly as he assured her that he would talk to her mother about resuming lessons.

Mother and daughter walked together silently, with Sarah's hand limply holding her daughter's. When they entered town hall, Lerannu gasped inwardly at the state of her family's home in the glum candlelight. She saw scattered books and parchments, some whole, some battered, and some torn to pieces, along with some broken pottery and chairs knocked over. Her mother merely croaked "good night" before shuffling upstairs to her bedroom, leaving Lerannu in the front office. As the young mage began to head for her room, she saw the painted portrait of the family, which normally hung over the hearth of the front office, leaning against the wall on the floor. She sighed miserably when she saw that her father's face had been torn out, canvas and all, down to the back-paneling of the frame. She looked about, ears pricked in the hopes that Roniil was still there, but quickly shook her head, knowing that he wasn't.

She entered her room, closed the door, and got ready for bed. As she walked toward her wardrobe to change into her nightgown, she noticed the table in the corner, and froze and stared.

The porcelain bowls were gone, and she suddenly noticed that her window had been opened as well.

Lerannu peered out her window, looking to the ground below. The bowls lay shattered, lying as two little clusters of shining fragments of white and deep blue. Beside them lay the feather parcel, paper shredded, and feathers ripped and ruffled.

The young mage climbed out of the window quietly, as she did the night Kiiva died, and gathered the mess into a pile. After checking as best she could to make sure that she didn't miss a shard or feather, Lerannu clambered back into her room and pulled the casing off her pillow. She then climbed back out and gently swept the shards and feathers into the pillowcase, tied it about her neck as a sort of backpack, and climbed once more back into her room. She placed the fragments and feathers, pillowcase and all, in the bottom drawer of her armoire, and resumed her retirement for the night.

18

7/8/4013 G.M.

VERDOK MERCHILL sat between Father Owen and Sister Arza, thanking his friend, Ruth, eagerly for the cake she presented him for his ninth birthday. It was an appetizingly dense-looking cake, made with chocolate, and was so dark it was almost as black as Father Owen's fur. It was his favorite sort of cake, and adding to that the generous remainder of the Estonmay feast that was kept from a week ago, the young boy certainly didn't need to worry about sating his appetite. Neither did any of those who celebrated the occasion alongside him.

"Don't thank me too much," Ruth said with a laugh as she set the cake in front of him. "I helped stir the chocolate in when it was being made. That's basically it. Mama and Brother Trevor did the real baking."

"You still helped to make it, and you're the one who gave it to me," said Verdok. "So still, thank you. And thank you, too, Sister Arza and Brother Trevor."

Father Owen and the two clerics nodded happily as Ruth cut him a slice. Verdok then took a bite, ears flattening with pleasure as he savored it. Those gathered around tittered amusedly, with Verdok holding back his own laughter at the thought of how comical he must have looked until he finally swallowed a bite.

"This is great, everybody," he said. "Hurry and get a piece if you want it, because I'll have no trouble eating this all myself!"

The guests laughed as Ruth and Arza served the others before cutting themselves a piece.

When all had finished, Father Owen poured everyone at the table a cup of dark, sweet wine, including a small glass for Verdok and Ruth, and raised a toast to the boy's birthday. The salpion then gestured for Sister Arza to fetch something. She left the garden and returned a moment later with a sizable parcel. Placing it before Verdok, she returned to her seat beside him and her daughter, smiling as Verdok's face brightened at the exciting mystery of the gift.

At Owen's nod, Verdok opened the package and sat awestruck at what it held. There was a black-and-white leather journal, bearing the Uqua seal of the Temple, with the color pattern essentially matching that of Verdok's pendant. It was a large journal, not one of particularly easy portability, but with lots of large, blank pages for him to put down whatever he wished. Placing it on the table, Verdok was surprised to notice there was more in the bundle. Gently fishing it out, he was delighted to find another journal, one that could easily fit in his robe pocket or a satchel. The smaller journal was of the same design as the large one. Eyes shining with gratitude, he looked around the table at all present. All of them nodded to Father Owen and Sister Arza, who then pointed to Ruth. The fur on her cheeks took a slightly darker grey hue as the skin beneath blushed.

"I saw how much you've been reading the poetry books in the library lately, along with some of the history ones. I thought that maybe you'd like to write down your own thoughts, poems, your own history, whatever you'd like. The big one's for your desk, and the little one's for if something comes to you while you're out and about. I only *told* Mama and Father Owen about the idea, though. They're the ones who actually had all this made."

Verdok hugged his friend tightly. "Thank you," he said quietly. He then looked at Owen and Arza, both of whom had faces that showed plainly their melting hearts. "Thank you both, too."

"It's no trouble," Owen said with a pat on Verdok's shoulder. "The Temple's supply of quills and inks are yours, dear Verdok. Just come by and ask whenever you need refills or replacements, or if you'd like a certain color of ink, within reason."

***

That evening, Verdok looked intensely, yet distantly, at the large journal that now lay open on the desk in his little room. He didn't hear Father Owen come in, and started slightly when the salpion placed a hand on his shoulder.

"Already trying to write something?" Owen asked.

"Not yet," Verdok answered. "Well, sort of. I haven't gotten any fresh ink or a new quill yet, and I didn't want to use the stuff I already have here for it. They're too plain and half used up, and I just wanted to use a nice new pen and fresh ink for these. I suppose that's a bit silly."

"We all have our particulars," said Owen comfortingly. "I just came by to see how you were doing. I know you and Ruth have been thinking a lot about trying to sort out your thoughts and what you felt to be your calling since ... since Sister Arza and I told you both all those things during the fever. I was just worried that you might've been worrying too much about those sorts of things on your birthday. I saw that both of you seemed to lighten up a bit when you met Hanye and Archgeneral Vyth back in the spring, but Ruth seemed to get more out of that than you, seeing how she's watched so many training sessions after that. I've only seen you watch a little bit of one or two. And since next year you'll be ten, we were looking to talk with you and your family in Quanithe about what you want to do as you got older, but I didn't want you to worry about it now."

"It's alright, Father Owen," Verdok said, picking up the journal and hugging it closely. "I wasn't worried about it at all. I really had a good birthday. Thank you."

"I hope I didn't spoil it at the last minute by bringing all this up?"

"Not at all. I think that meeting with the Faithguards actually might've helped me about as much as it did Ruth, or at least more than you might've thought. I don't think I have what it takes to be a Faithguard myself, though. I don't want to hurt people."

"Well, no Faithguard, or any true warrior, should *want* to hurt people. I mean, there are those who have had such thoughts in their hearts, at least at times, but–"

"I-I didn't mean it like that, Father. I know that any good warrior shouldn't want to hurt people, but ... I just don't think I can do what they sometimes have to do. I want to help people and not fight. So, if I was going to be someone of the Temple, then ..."

"The life of a Faithguard is certainly not an easy one," Owen said understandingly. "But then again, neither is the priesthood."

"I guess that's true, too," said Verdok, "but ... thinking about how much I'd rather not be a Faith-guard has made me think how I would much rather be a priest. I suppose I should still consider my grandparents and the others, but I didn't really worry about all of that since I thought about being a priest."

"Why is that?"

"Because I've felt that my family's already here. For one thing, there's Mother and Father's ashes that I visit in your study, and then there's ... well, you. And Arza, Ruth, and everyone else here. So, yeah, I guess I shouldn't be completely decided, but ..."

Verdok, not sure of what else to say, shrugged and looked to Father Owen. He was startled by the brimming tears that shined in the salpion's eyes. Owen embraced Verdok as if he were his son, and without another word, the two went to the great dining hall together.

19

8/12/4013 G.M.

LERANNU sat beneath the great oak in the square, reading a book covering the histories of several prominent mages by the light of the summer afternoon sun. Having been back in the Mage Society for two months, she had now experienced some level of interaction with all four of the elements. She had just practiced with flame for the first time during the day's earlier lesson, that having been the last one for the week. It was very light practice, and highly cautious, entailing the flame of a single candle that was placed on a bare patch of dirt in Ahvrom's yard. Nevertheless, it was quite exhilarating. Ahvrom praised Lerannu immensely after she managed to make the little light shrink and grow, as well as mold its form like a tiny burning mass of clay on a potter's wheel. The veteran mage had since become the father figure in her life since Roniil was removed from office and left town.

"You really have an uncommonly strong grasp on this," the mage tutor said as the lesson ended.

Lerannu sat on a tree stump in the yard, taking deep, steady breaths. Ahvrom then handed her the book of historical mages. "If you keep it up, I believe you'll be in one of these someday."

"Thank you," said Lerannu as she brushed a hand across the tome's cover, silently enjoying its firm, grainy texture. "I'm not sure if that can really be said, though. Especially right now. I'm still having trouble with keeping my sense of strength going, as you can see. Four Breaths, my head's really starting to pound now."

Ahvrom knelt beside her, taking a small phial of sparkling clear-blue liquid from his satchel. Lerannu eyed it with simultaneous intrigue and timidity. Dalle and Ahvrom had told her before, at great length, of the Kamgenbew tonic and its properties, but it wasn't until now that the young mage had ever seen a sample of it in person. Realizing that Ahvrom was holding it out for her to take and drink, Lerannu promptly pulled the stopper and downed the elixir, bristling slightly at the odd, bittersweet taste, followed by a swift feeling of reinvigoration.

Ahvrom chuckled lightly. "It's a bit of an acquired taste, though I suppose I shouldn't encourage the concept of getting *too* used to it. I trust you remember what we covered about this?"

Lerannu nodded as she recited the summary of the tonic's qualities.

"The Kamgenbew elixir, when all is said and done, has the same essential effect as an exceptionally strong serving of coffee or tea. This similarity is strong enough to have prompted a number of mages to substitute such drinks in the tonic's stead, with varying degrees of success. However, these brews carry the same potential for diminishing returns, and the following sense of dependency, that results from overuse. Furthermore, these alternatives bear the additional drawback of not being as fast-acting as a Kamgenbew potion, which is near-immediate in its results. Furthermore, Kamgenbew yields a greater recovery of one's sense of energy with smaller doses when compared to coffee, tea, or other such brews. This enables a mage to carry many doses of the tonic on their person in the event of an emergency, or in drastic circumstances such as combat. Thus, the Kamgenbew elixir is overwhelmingly favored by the Mage Society, as with others who engage in potentially strenuous labor. But for all Fidons, mage or not, it is warned that excessive use tends to yield negative results. It is strongly advised that it be used in emergencies, or otherwise in moderation. Adequate rest, nourishment, and activities like meditation are ultimately the ideal course for recovering one's strength."

Ahvrom patted her shoulder. "Well done. And about all that business of you keeping your will and sense of energy in check, that is easily the hardest part of magic. I've had trouble with it, even recently, and there's eighty-year-old grandmasters who still struggle with it on occasion. That book there tells of several instances where that happened to very experienced mages, so don't think you're a lesser mage for that. Even the most experienced of us aren't always at our best, and you're still new to this, relatively speaking. You will get better at this in time, I promise. Anyway, that's it for today. Have a good weekend, Lera. Rest up, enjoy the Midsummer Moon Dance, and I'll see you next Onmay."

"Thank you, Ahvrom," said Lerannu as she left the yard and made her way to the oak in the square to read. "See you then."

Now, under the tree, the young apprentice had begun reading the book given to her. She was a good way into the accounts of Vikar Bluemoon, a founder of the Mage Society, when she became aware of someone standing nearby and looking at her. She looked up. It was Zalden.

"Hi, Lera," he said at length.

Lerannu promptly got up and hugged her friend closely. "Hi, Zal."

Zalden embraced Lerannu in turn. "So, are we still on for the dance on Setmay?"

"Of course we are! Why wouldn't we?"

"I just know that you've been busy lately, with the lessons and all, and didn't know if you wanted to stay focused on that. That, and ... well ... I'm still nervous about how your mother will react when we tell her at the dance–"

"I told you she didn't shred the feathers because of you. She did it because she knew that Father had a hand in giving them to me. I'm sure she'll be fine about it, especially once I tell her how much you've helped me along during these past months."

"I'd like to think so, too. It's just ... well, with what you two have been dealing with ..."

Lerannu pulled Zalden closer, resting her head on his shoulder as he patted her back.

"I'm sorry," said Zalden quietly.

"Don't be."

"If it's not too much for me to ask, do you know where they've gone? A lot of the town ... they seem to be thinking that they've gone off somewhere far away to get married, or at least live together."

"I don't know where they've gone, but they told me they weren't doing that, and I trust them. Well, I *want* to trust them, that is."

"You spoke to them before they left? When?"

"Right as they were leaving that evening. I heard from Mother's office that Father ended his stay at the inn, and that Uriah had sold off her house and things, and I looked all over town for them. I eventually saw them on the highway going northeast. I caught up with them at the gate, asking them why they didn't say goodbye to me. They said they would have if it wasn't for Mother, and I told them they could've tried to send someone, to tell me to meet them somewhere privately. Then Father started crying, and that got me going, too. We all just held each other a while, then I asked them why they did it. They said they didn't think they could explain it well enough for me, but Uriah said that she never meant for it to go as far as it did until it happened. I want to believe her, but ... I just don't know."

Lerannu sniffed heavily, picking up the faint scent of the blacksmith's furnace in Zalden's fur, before continuing.

"Anyway," she went on, "to answer your question, I asked them the same things then, and they said no. 'We're going to travel together for a while,' Father said, 'until we get to the capital. Then we'll go our separate ways.' Then I asked them where they were planning to go in the end. They looked at each other and said they didn't know, that all they knew was that they couldn't stand to be here anymore with all the talk that was going around and how Mother spoke of them."

"I see," said Zalden. "I feel I can guess, and tell me if I'm going too far, but how do you feel about all this? I mean, as far as how your mother has handled everything so far?"

Lerannu sighed. "I feel all mixed up. I mean, what Father and Uriah did was wrong, and Mother had the right to call for the divorce and for him to leave the house, but ... she was just so *hateful*. I want to say that I understand why she feels that way, maybe even to say that she's right to be that way, at least a little, but at the same time, just not like *that*, you know?"

"I know what you mean. How has she been since she took the mayor's office?"

"Better, I think, in many ways. She *was* a good candidate, with her experience in administration with Father, though I can't help but wonder how many chose her out of some sort of sympathy as well. But like I said, she's experienced, and I've heard no particular grievances against her yet, so I figure she's doing well as far as the town's concerned. I still feel that she's sad and angry a lot of the time. The other day—"

Lerannu, having turned her head absently in the direction of Ahvrom's home, was surprised to see the mage, with a face of wearied impatience, conversing with two knights of the town's Faith-guard and four of the regular guard. After a few words, Ahvrom moved aside, slumping down onto a chair on the front porch as the six guards entered the house.

Lerannu and Zalden went over to Ahvrom, perplexed at what just happened.

"Ahvrom," Lerannu asked worriedly, "what's going on?"

Ahvrom shrugged sadly, nodding toward the still-open door. "Every now and again," he explained, "a few from the Temple and the town guard come to check things here, to make sure that ... that I'm not trying anything like what Dalle did."

"What?" Lerannu asked in incredulous disgust. "How could the Temple think that just because—"

"It wasn't the Temple, Lera," Ahvrom said dejectedly.

"Who, then?"

Lerannu caught the mage's eyes, which fixed onto the distance behind her and to the side. She turned, and all seemed to suddenly stop still.

Lerannu's house, Bravagoth's town hall, was the focus of Ahvrom's wearily bitter gaze. On the front porch, looking intently in their direction, stood Mayor Sarah Stonefaith. Though her mother was far away and her face couldn't be clearly seen, Lerannu had the feeling that Sarah was not looking at the three in anger, but nevertheless felt an essence in the gaze that she found unsettling. Upset at the thought of her mother demonstrating such distrust toward a longtime friend of the family in the wake of the tragedy in the forest, Lerannu's heart began to pound in anxiety at another realization.

Sarah was staring directly at her, and even if she saw none of what had happened moments ago, Lerannu now realized that she was closely holding Zalden's hand. Zalden, catching on, looked at his friend nervously.

"Well," Lerannu said moodily, "we might as well go ahead and tell her."

20

9/28/4013 G.M.

DONOVAN sat beside his father, Jonathan, and the bard, Jak, eating the leg of a roast pheasant along with a baked apple, and drinking freshly pressed apple cider before the Kysonmay festival launched into full swing. Feeling both nervous and excited, Donovan looked at the vast crowds of people milling about the town as they partook of the food, games, and song. Food-laden tables had been brought into the square, and the doors of the taverns and numerous houses were open for the revelers to come and go as they pleased.

Though far from mastering an instrument or the art of song, Donovan had thrived under Jak Kelldren's instruction, and the bard's presence had greatly eased both Donovan and Jonathan's grief in the months that followed the funeral. Now, having practiced with the highlander for nearly nine months and observing his performances during all the major holy days and simple tavern nights that passed in that time, the Balon boy was going to accompany the skald in performing the opening songs of the feast.

As the first evening hour passed, all were eating fairly lightly as they waited for the festivities to truly commence. At long last, the mayor of Therohl entered the square, stood at the base of the statue of the legendary three widows, and called out with the ringing of the town's bells.

"Dear citizens of Therohl," he said, "and all those who have chosen to join us at summer's passing and autumn's return, let us now join our good kin of the Temple in prayer, that the feast of Kysonmay may begin in earnest!"

The square became flooded with cheers as the mayor melted back into the crowd, and the men and women of Therohl's temple took their positions. The leading clerics spread their arms and led the town in a prayer of thanksgiving.

"We thank you, Onu," said all in the square as they followed the clerics' words, "for a safe and bountiful summer, and strive to trust in you and your host in guiding and keeping us in the autumn to come, as with all the days and seasons to which we bear witness until the end of our days on Fidonhaal. We thank you, as always, for the offer of redemption you gave and continue to hold out to us since the days of the First Elect. We thank you for the continued love, will, and trust that you have placed within us, that by the bond we have sought to remake with you, we may bear goodness in this life and return to you in the next. We pray for those who have passed from this life since we last spoke to you, that their sins may be forgiven and their goodness be commended, and that they may be forevermore at your side. May they form and keep the link between you and us. In you we strive to trust."

After a brief pause, the clerics continued with a closing prayer for the seasons' changing.

"Estvii and Kyse, gracious servants of Onu and ladies of the angelic host, we thank you for the trust that you have continued to place both in Onu, your Maker, and in us, his mortal children and your mortal kin. Thank you for the keeping of your seasons, and thus your roles in our world and our lives. We bid now farewell to your season, good Estvii, and look with grateful hearts to the due return of summer. We now bid a joyous welcome to your returning time, good Kyse, and seek to relish its joys."

"Our love and thanks to you, Onu, and to the angels!" the clerics concluded enthusiastically, with the crowd happily echoing the prayer's end with equal passion.

"Let the feast of autumn's return begin!" the high priest decreed as thunderous cheers greeted his words.

A great bustling for another helping of food and drink ensued. Then, when the hum of the throngs had calmed down, Donovan, at Jak's signal, took up both his mandolin and the bard's harp, and joined him before the widows' statue. The old skald encouragingly tussled the boy's long white hair, which had been braided into one long tail. Donovan responded with a playful nudge into Jak's side, happy for his friend and mentor's efforts to break the tension building up inside him.

"Just ye breathe an' take it easy, Donny," Jak said kindly. "Just do it like we practiced. Ye'll do fine."

"Thank you, Jak," Donovan said softly, "for ... for everything."

"Och, Ah should be the one thankin' ye and yer pa. Ah ne'er really gave much thought tae teachin' a body the art before, an' Ah'm glad ye came tae me an' asked."

The singer gently ran a finger across the half-loop of his widower's nose ring. "All an' all, Ah'd say Ah've been happy as a bard, even in the later days, but it's guid tae be in a family o'sorts again."

"Jak," Donovan asked, "if it's not too much, what was her name?"

"Yoranye."

Donovan's ears pricked up in awe. "That name is beautiful."

"Aye, laddie, an' ye shoulda seen an' met the woman who owned it. Nae a lass in the world, in mah eyes an' heart, who could've fit the name any better. She was a wonder in every way. Ah wrote a song fer her when Ah proposed tae her. If ye an' Ah are still doin' this however far down the way, Ah'll teach it tae ye if ye'd like. Might be guid fer ye if ye ever meet the lass o'yer life, at least tae help ye come up with one o'yer own."

"I'd love to hear it, Jak, and to learn it."

"Very well, but fer now, we'd best get on with what we've got lined up, now, eh? Looks like near everyone's waitin' fer us!"

Donovan looked about, realizing that seemingly all eyes and ears in town were now directed at the bard and his protégé. Looking back to Jak, Donovan smiled, nodded, and took up his mandolin. He checked its tuning as Jak addressed the crowd. The bard thanked them for their ears and patience, and announced the performance of the traditional song of autumn's return. The two stood together, side by side, with instruments and voices ready. Then they began, with Jak's rich highland brogue and light harp notes in the lead and Donovan's young voice and the mandolin's deeper notes backing up the skald.

> *Good Lady Kyse has come 'round again,*
> *To herald the time of the year's ending gains!*
> *With the Basket of Bounty held in her arms,*
> *She blesses our lands, from forest to farm,*
> *By the power that Onu did give unto her*
> *In his sharing of love, which lives forever*
> *And was born alongside the birth of all things.*
> *Her kindness and beauty move all to sing,*
> *From the trees in the wind as they cast down their leaves*
> *To the beasts that make to roam elsewhere or sleep,*
> *And the birds that sing as they leave and take wing,*
> *We each to her and her Maker do sing!*
> *For good Lady Kyse has come 'round again,*
> *To herald the time of the year's ending gains!*
> *Welcome, dear Kyse, we welcome you again!*
> *We welcome the Bearer of the Basket again!*
> *We welcome the Wife of Vernid again!*
> *We welcome the Lady of Autumn again!*
> *Welcome, dear Kyse, welcome again!*

The crowd clapped and cheered, praised and whistled, and Donovan stood shaking in the euphoric release of music and song. He felt the pride of his father, who looked on happily from the table, and the pride of his friend and teacher, who patted him soundly on the back as he praised the boy's first public performance. He felt the divine appreciation of Onu and the angels, especially Kyse, feeling the crisp breeze on his cheek as a commendation for his efforts. With that feeling also came a sense of pride, love, and assurance from his mother and little sister, who he felt were watching and listening within the holy company from across the cosmic curtain in Onuhaal. Holding back a tear of both joy and sadness, the lad performed three more songs with the skald before retiring to dine and talk with his father for the rest of the night.

As he made his way back, he heard a good number of voices, warm and fluid from the generous helpings of beer, wine, and mead that were plentifully served, calling out for a song titled *What the Woodsman Saw One Autumn Day*. Not having heard of the song, an intrigued Donovan looked back at Jak, who was grinning and shrugging sheepishly at Jonathan. Donovan's father laughed, looked at his son, and called to the bard to carry on.

"It's your job, right, to sing what they want?"

"Ah can decline if Ah want, ye ken," Jak said with mock indignation.

"If you don't sing it, I'm sure plenty others will instead," Jonathan said laughing. "At least with you it'll be sung by a professional."

"Does Donny know much of … well, *that*, yet?"

"A little," Jonathan said with a grin. "Might as well give him a more thorough lesson now. Go on, Jak, do your thing!"

Jak gave a comical smile and salute to Jonathan, then nodded to Donovan as he checked again to make sure the harp was in proper tune. Donovan, puzzled, rejoined his father, who was trying to suppress his laughter as he took a drink of ale.

"What was that all about?"

"Just the song they want Jak to sing."

"Is something wrong with it?"

"No, not really. Well, it's a little hard to explain. Do you remember what your mother and I told you when we said that Sani was coming, how the two of us did our part in making her together?"

"Yes," said Donovan, ears pricking in intrigue rekindled by the memory. Jonathan giggled fitfully at the sight, which promptly sent the boy's white-furred cheeks to bearing a light pink undertone from blushing.

"The main thing to know," said Jonathan after regaining composure, "is that it's an Onu-blessed act, and is something that Fidons, ideally when married, do together for a number of reasons, mainly to bring forth new life if they can and wish, and to otherwise express their love for one another."

"Okay," said Donovan attentively.

"So, you know how the angels Kyse and Vernid are married to each other?"

"Uh-huh."

"Well, this song that Jak's about to sing is about a woodcutter who happened across Kyse and Vernid as he was making his way through the forest, and the two angels were ... doing *that* together when he stumbled across them."

"Is that bad?"

"Well, not in of itself. Most Fidons value some privacy when it comes to that, as it's a very special thing shared between two people, though some peoples have different mindsets, depending on the situation. As far as this particular story goes, it wasn't an intentional intrusion, it's just that ... it's *funny*, in a way."

"I'd have thought a song about that would be beautiful."

"Well, in a way, I suppose it is. At the end of the day, it *is* about a loving couple that can be seen as a model to inspire us when we seek for our mates. It's just that the *way* that the song is sung ..."

Jonathan laughed again, shrugging, and had his son sit close beside him as Jak began to play the song's first notes on the harp.

"It's a funny thing," Jonathan said, "how it can be so many things at once ... divinely beautiful here, hilarious there. Have a listen, Don. This isn't something I think can be truly explained in full in just one evening, let alone one song, but it's a start. I'd say you're at a suitable enough age. It's important for us all to know about it someday."

The father then began introducing his son to a more detailed course on that wondrously blessed aspect of life, that subject of such beauty, sincerity, humor, pain, and drama, as the bard played and the crowd laughed and cheered.

21

12/22/4015 G.M.

OWEN stood at his study's window, conversing with Okren and Alexis Merchill, Verdok's maternal grandparents from Quanithe. Being the parents of Quenda, both were Mavons, their fur being as black as the salpion's. The two had arrived the morning before, not yet known to Verdok, and the three had briefly discussed some points pertaining to Verdok's care before calling him in.

"If you two don't mind," the salpion added, "I will be discussing matters concerning a young girl who is under my care as well, with her and her mother. Her mother is a sister here, and the girl's fascination with the Faithguard will likely make her matters somewhat easier to sort out than Verdok's. The reason I wish to go over it with her alongside our conversation with Verdok, besides them both being under my care, is they've become close friends. We were talking about this day a little while ago, to try and prepare them, and they both asked me if they could be present at each other's discussion, and perhaps add something to them. I told them we'd discuss these things together, at least to a point."

"That's perfectly understandable, Salpion Lovonhaar," said Alexis. "Your respect and love for those in your care do you much credit as a servant of Onu."

A few moments of small talk passed, then the door creaked open with Sister Arza peering through. Owen looked to her and nodded. The sister, with her daughter and Verdok beside her, came in and sat with the Merchills. Ruth and Arza sat together, with Verdok sitting beside his grandparents. The boy looked at them, his face suggesting he had an idea of who they were, one that, if not precise, was probably close to the mark.

"Well," Owen said resolutely, "Verdok, Ruth, the two of you are now both ten years old. Depending on what you two decide, you will each begin the first steps of a new path in life in the coming months. Please, do not worry too much, for this is a time of learning and seeing what best fits you. Neither of you need to enlist in the Faithguard or priesthood, as there are a fine number of other ways by which you may live here and serve the Temple."

The portly Mavon salpion quickly took off his spectacles and polished them before focusing his gaze on Verdok and his grandparents.

"And that is, of course, *if* you should choose to stay here. Should you choose to leave in the coming months, know that our doors, be it of the archtemple here or wherever your local temple is, are open to all who seek us or wish to return. If you choose to stay and pursue a trade here, know that choosing one now or in the next few weeks will *not* bind you to it for life at this point in time. Not everyone figures out their path at first, and even if you are satisfied with your choice as far as the education and training goes, you may ultimately decide to use what you've learned in something outside the Temple. There is no trouble to this if that is the case, for one need not be of the Temple to serve Onu and Fidonity, and all you learn here should help you no matter where you go. However, if you stay and pursue an occupation here of either the priesthood or the Faithguard, there will come a day, when you have reached at least twenty years and are deemed sufficiently qualified for whichever of those two paths you have chosen, when you will take an oath if you choose to truly dedicate yourself to it. That is the *only* time where any bonding commitment is expected of you. Do you understand?"

"Yes, Father Owen," the two children said earnestly, with Verdok's deep blue eyes locked onto the salpion's.

"Very good," said Owen as he looked back to Ruth and Sister Arza. "Now, shall we begin with you, Ruth?"

"If you wish, Father Owen."

"Very well," the salpion said with a smile, as he had a very strong feeling that he knew what course Ruth was going to take, at least at the start. "So, you seem to have gotten on very well with Commander Hanye these past two years, as well as Archgeneral Gothnaar. It seems that, nine times of ten, if you aren't in school, playing, eating or sleeping, you're watching her training the Konothian squires. I take it that your interest in the Faithguard runs deeper than simply watching them, no?"

"Yes, Father Owen," said Ruth, smiling. "I don't know if it'll be right for me in the end, but I know I want to try. When I saw Hanye for the first time, I saw the kind of person I want to be when I grow up. Maybe I won't be like her in every way, maybe I won't even be one of the knights, but she ... she just gave me this feeling. It's hard to explain ..."

"I know it is," said Owen warmly, "because I've felt it, too, when I watched the priests and priestesses here when I was growing up. Then I eventually got to meet and talk with Helga Renlarv, the salpion before me, and I just felt the call, not necessarily to be salpion, but to definitely follow the priesthood. I then went on to speak with her more and more, and eventually got under her guidance with another priest, one Ranoth Windsbreath, who had been under her tutelage for years before I even spoke to her. A few years passed, and when Helga's time came near to die, she vouched for me, and all the alpions of Fidonhaal voted for me. I was very surprised to learn it was unanimous. Brother Ranoth was, and is, as far as I know, a very good man of the cloth, as worthy as I was, if not even more so, at least in certain ways."

"Where is he?" Ruth asked curiously. "Is he here? Have I ever met him before? I don't remember that name."

"No," Owen said, "he's not one of the archtemple anymore. He took up the position of Castle Genverdell's priest right after I was elected. You *might* have seen him on the occasions that the royal family have come here on holy days and the like. He's fully Zaron, and would've been wearing high cleric's robes whenever he came here."

"I don't think I've met him, then," said Ruth. "I definitely haven't talked to him before, and I don't think I've even noticed him when he would've been here."

"Me neither," Verdok added.

"Well," Owen remarked, "it's not like you two were looking for him. Like I said, he hasn't been here all that much since he left. I'm sure he's had his hands full as the private priest of the royal household. I wouldn't mind talking to him again sometime, though. He was a very agreeable person, if I remember right."

Owen shook his head to break out of his reminiscence.

"Anyway," he went on, "all that having been said, my point is that I understand your feeling completely, Ruth, and that you are perfectly welcome to try your hand at being a Faithguard. I'm sure Hanye will be delighted to hear of it, if you haven't already hinted at it to her. She's very fond of you."

"When do I start?" Ruth asked excitedly.

"A little later next month, once we've had some time to get back into the normal flow of things after Sardonmay."

Owen then grinned. "Can you stand to wait that long?"

"Yes, Father Owen!" said Ruth. "Thank you!"

Owen, still smiling, drew a deep breath and returned his attention to Verdok, Alexis, and Okren.

"Speaking of Sardonmay ... Verdok, these are your grandparents from your mother's side. They're the head of their household in Quanithe, where they live on a big, beautiful vineyard with the rest of their children as well as your father's side of the family. Nearly all of your uncles, aunts, and cousins from both sides live there, working to harvest grapes and make wine together."

"Hello," said Verdok with a respectful nod. The two grandparents watched the boy intently as Owen continued to inform him.

"We've kept in touch since your parents died and have discussed a little of our thoughts on how to take care of you over the years. But then, with what you told me back when you turned eight, I proposed this to them: that whoever could come over here when you were ten, and given the timing of our talks, would be invited to stay with us during Sardonmay and for a few weeks after. This will give you time to talk things over with them, and hopefully, when their visit is done, you'll have a much better idea of what it is that you want to do, even if still not absolute."

"Thank you, Father Owen," Verdok said solemnly.

Alexis, sitting nearest her grandson, patted him gently on the shoulder. Verdok looked up at her, and she, gasping sharply to repress a sob, pulled him close and hugged him tightly.

"Oh, Okren," she said tearfully, "look at his eyes."

Okren looked, then nodded, with ears flattening and eyes sparkling sadly.

"They're just like hers," he said softly.

The grandfather looked away for a moment, while Verdok looked on quietly from over Alexis's shoulder. He then sighed deeply, collected himself, and turned back to face his grandson again.

"We want to make this as clear as we can, Verdok," said Okren. "We would love for you to come home with us, but we will not make you leave here if you want to stay. We just want you to be happy and safe, and if you feel at home here, then this is a very good place to be. We can all come and visit you from time to time, including your father's side of the family. You can also come and visit us whenever you'd like. It is quite a trip, but we'll gladly make it to see you if you choose to stay here, and we'll do all we can to make visiting us worth the trip when and if you ever come our way. As the salpion—as Father Owen—said, we'll have time to talk all this out, so let's just try and take this one day at a time, shall we?"

"Yes, Grandfather," said Verdok, "of course."

"Well then," said Owen after a moment of silence, "dinner shall be ready soon, so how about we all go and wash, and then we'll meet up in the dining hall?"

"Sounds good to me," said Arza, taking her daughter's hand as they rose from their seats.

"W-wait," Verdok said suddenly. Owen looked inquiringly at him. The boy nodded toward the black marble urn on the small table in the corner. "Do ... do they know about that?" he asked quietly.

Owen nodded. The two grandparents looked quizzically at the salpion, then followed his eyes to the urn in the corner. Breathing deeply, Alexis and Okren took Verdok's hand, rose from their seats and walked over to their daughter's ashes. The three gazed upon it for a few seconds, then Okren spoke quietly to his grandson.

"Verdok, I forget ... your father is in there with her, right?"

"Yes, Grandfather."

"Oh, Okren," Alexis wept. "Wenda and Kiin ... they haven't visited for so long. They should've come with us ... they should be here to see ..."

"We'll remind them that they're here, as they've been ever since they left us," Okren whispered gently. "They'll be able to see them both, and Verdok, when they come to visit."

The salpion nodded to Arza and Ruth for them to leave with him, and the three left Verdok and his grandparents to pay their respects to Quenda and Zantor privately.

22
5/5/4016 G.M.

MIRA checked the saddle's fastenings on her horse and the provisions in the saddlebags while her mother and father, Ann and Virgaard Greenheart, bade her little brother, Isaak, farewell.

"We shouldn't be gone for much more than a week, like usual with these patrols," said Ann as she hugged her son. "Just mind Genna and Uld, okay? They've stood in for us before when we've both gone out, though last time we did that you were just a baby. I know you get along very well with Kahle, so listen to what they say if they ask you to do something, alright?"

"Yes, Ma," the nine-year-old said obediently, but sullenly.

Virgaard picked up Isaak and hugged him tightly. "In just a few more years," he said comfortingly, "you'll be old enough to go on your first patrol, and we'll both come with you then."

"I know," said Isaak, "but I'm going to miss you now."

"Sure," said Virgaard, "and we'll miss you. But we're going to do everything we can to be careful and be back soon."

Mira, seeing that all her things were ready, patted her horse and joined her family at the gates. She hugged her brother as the other villagers joining in the patrol rode out a little way before stopping to wait for their chieftains to lead them.

"Uld and Genna *are* really nice, though," she said, "so hopefully you'll feel like you're still with family. I know you haven't really seen Uld much when not working his forge, and he certainly is big and tough-looking, but he's nowhere near as mean as he looks. And Genna, I know she can seem a bit bossy if you've only seen her when she gives out medicine, but that's just her being a doctor. Well, that and I suppose it's also just her being a ma. Not yours, true, but you know how mas are."

Mira yipped and giggled as Ann playfully flicked her ear.

"And like Ma and Da said," she continued, "you're best friends with Kahle, and she's their daughter, so if nothing else makes you think they're nice, that should."

"Okay, okay," said Isaak, smiling. "Just come back soon, okay?"

"We will," Mira and her parents said in unison.

Mira and her parents left Isaak at Plen's gate once Uld, Genna, and Kahle Tillok arrived to take him in. They then mounted up and rode out to the head of the patrol. All present quickly checked their supplies one last time, then cantered swiftly into the green depths of Santaru.

***

Four days passed without incident, during which the patrollers conversed with each other over numerous things as they rode. One subject of particular intrigue for Mira, grim as it was, was a review and greater elaboration of the fell creatures they might encounter in the forest. Knowing the talk was for her benefit and that of the handful of other youths in the troop, the thirteen-year-old listened intently and asked what questions she could think of.

"So ... are there any in particular that are common here?"

"Well," Virgaard answered, "I'd believe, and hope, that none of them are 'common' here anymore. I doubt we'll ever be completely rid of them as long as Fidonhaal still stands, but we've been weeding them out for four thousand years. That said, any of them could potentially be found here, as is the case for anywhere other than Karzynhaal." Plen's patriarch laughed lightly. "I will say that since the forest isn't burning down, there shouldn't be many, if any, Bralaks in the neighborhood."

Mira nervously fiddled with the reins in her hands at the thought of the potential destruction that could be wrought by such creatures, composing herself when her horse fidgeted uncomfortably in response. "H-how do we deal with creatures like that, monsters made by Raakaru?"

"Well, it depends on a number of things," Virgaard explained. "It'll depend on what type of Lakon it is, how many there are, and what the surroundings are. Thankfully, while there's certainly more effective ways, like magic if one is versed in it, none of these creatures are immune to a well-placed arrow or blade. If it ever comes to you being against a Lakon, know that you *can* kill it; it's just a matter of knowing what's best against the creature given the situation. And of course, whether there's only one of them or more, there's always a strength in numbers when it comes to your side of the matter. That's why we're all in this troop together."

"I see," Mira said somberly.

"So listen, Mira," Virgaard said in a tone of both loving care and decisive authority as he pointed to the other first-timers, "and you lot as well. If we should encounter any sort of Cursed One out here, wait for one of us to see how things are, if possible. If it's something we think you can manage, we'll have you deal with it while we watch and help if needed. Or, at the very least, we'll have you close enough to watch how we handle those sorts of beasts. But if it looks to be too much, and if it can be helped, we're going to have you hang back with the bulk of the patrol and stay out of it until it's taken care of. We want to give you all experience in keeping Santaru as safe as possible, but we won't have you fighting an ogre or a big pack of Qualakars on you first patrol, alright?"

"Yes, Chief Virgaard," the youths said dutifully.

"Yes, Da," said Mira.

"Remember," Virgaard continued, "these sorts of creatures aren't like the other beasts of the world, which might turn violent to get food, or to protect themselves or their young, or anything like that. A wild beast might attack if provoked, and whether or not it was intended on your part, you may have to kill it to survive. But with Lakons, they were made ... twisted ... by Raakaru to destroy us and spite Onu. Your very existence, if they notice you, will set them into an awful, hateful bloodlust. For your own sake and that of your fellow Fidon, as well as all else good in this world, you *must* kill them if you can, or otherwise get someone who is skilled in the task, for they *will* kill you if they can. Hatred of us and all the rest of the world is what drives them, not the simple drives of life and nature that other creatures live by. Got that?"

"Yes, sir!" the youths shouted.

"Very good. Now, any other questions?"

A young lad, raising his hand, asked if they could have more thorough descriptions of the various Cursed Ones and their appearances, along with advice on tracking and dispatching them. The rest of that morning passed peacefully as Virgaard and Ann imparted their knowledge of the Lakons to the future keepers of Santaru and Plen, with several stressed reminders of why all the cursed beasts bore some resemblance, however twisted, to the Fidons. They descended from Fidons who were molded by Raakaru's foul craft into mockeries of their form and, for those also sharing the visages of certain other beasts, of the creatures with which they were conjoined.

***

It was just past noon when the company stopped for a light lunch and a brief rest. Mira, having eaten and obtained permission from her parents, went off to walk a little way about the forest within sight of the troop. As she passed a cluster of undergrowth, she heard a light grumbling that seemed to come from the ground. Pricking up her grey ears for a moment, she also caught the sound of irregular shuffling. She hesitated at first, worried at the thought of how irritated the company might be if she reported the noise and it ended up just being a badger or some other burrowing creature. She was still on edge from the morning's lecture and didn't want to give a false alarm and seem like a scared child. She wrestled with her self-consciousness only briefly, however, recalling her father's age-old maxim of it being better to be safe than sorry. She took a deep breath and went up to the patrol, where her father stood, and called him over.

"I think there's something over there," she said in a low voice as she pointed to the distant shrubbery. "It seemed to be in the undergrowth there, maybe even in the ground. I didn't really go over to get a good look, but I figured ..."

"Of course," Virgaard said understandingly. "Come with me. Let's see."

The chieftain then called for two of the other youths to follow them, along with a handful of adults, while the others held back, watching and ready just in case. As they reached the bushes, Virgaard pricked up his ears and listened carefully for a moment. His eyes widened, to Mira's alarm, and he took a few careful steps closer to the cluster of foliage. He signaled to his daughter to step in alongside him, and to those with him to have their weapons at the ready. The two then crept quietly into the undergrowth, rustling it as little as they could, until they found a small recess in the ground. Virgaard, gesturing for Mira to stay put, crept up to the little hole and peered down. He then turned his head to face his daughter, his face one of grim duty, and beckoned her to quietly come over to him and take a look as well. When Mira crept over and looked, she gasped, sharply but quietly, at the sight.

Three little creatures, like the cubs of bears or mountain lions, lay in a small pile, sleeping. However, unlike the young of such beasts, the short fur these creatures had was a splotchy, sickly looking pale brown, and the flesh was leathery and warty all over. Their heads, from ears to muzzle, bore a revolting resemblance to those of small Fidon children, and their tails, a touch shorter than that of a proportionate Fidon, resembled more of a rat's tail than a Fidon's for its lack of a sufficient fur coat. Mira looked morbidly at the sight, unable to speak. Her father leaned closely to her.

"I take it you know what these are, since we covered them this morning?" he whispered.

Mira nodded. The description she heard that morning left no mystery.

"They're Qualakars," she said quietly. "They're Qualakar young."

She turned to face her father. "I heard how all the Lakons reproduce and have young. It's in much the same way as all the other creatures of Fidonhaal ... like the bear and the deer, the fish and the birds ... like some of the Angelborn ... like us. I know what you said about how they were made and how they live to destroy us and the world. I understand that ... these little ones here, if they saw us, would want to kill us, same as if they were fully grown, but ... I just ..."

Virgaard gently patted his daughter's shoulder. "I know," he said softly. "It's hard to swallow."

"Maybe not as hard as the reason they're here, though." Mira whispered grimly. "We let them happen, long, long ago ..."

"Yes, that we did," Virgaard said solemnly.

"So, we'll need to ..."

"Yes."

Mira sighed deeply. "Okay, then ..."

Virgaard patted her shoulder again. "It's part of the bed we made."

Mira nodded, readying the spear she brought along as Virgaard, leaning out of the undergrowth, signaled for those following to join them. When all had gathered and observed the situation, two others stood beside Mira, spears readied alongside hers for a swift downward strike into the hole. They awaited Virgaard's signal.

The chieftain nodded. "Quick and quiet," he whispered, "then we'll all go over this area carefully and see if we can find out where–"

Virgaard, staring wide-eyed into the recess, froze in mid-sentence. Mira looked again into it, and felt her blood turn to ice.

One of the monstrous whelps was awake, staring at the petrified group with its shining eyes of black and red. The eyes shone with a light of hatred and contempt that Mira simply could not imagine a young creature being capable of having, regardless of what it was. And it was smiling. A heinous, fang-laden grin spread across its little face, one that clearly showed the atrocious delight that it felt at seeing the terror it invoked in the creatures that it, and its ancestors, were twisted into hating more than anything else in all of existence. It locked its stare onto Mira. The grin grew wider. Mira began to shake in horror. The smile was now abominably wide, seemingly unnatural. The creature shook a little. It was laughing. Silently, but it was laughing. Then it stopped, and, eyes piercing into Mira's, it wheezed slightly as it slowly drew in a deep breath.

Seeing the creature inhaling was what finally broke Virgaard's spell of stupefied terror.

"NOW!" he yelled. "IT'S GOING TO–"

The little Qualakar opened its fanged maw and let out an earsplitting scream. Mira and one of those beside her quailed at the sound as the third managed to slay one of the monster's siblings as it was just starting to wake. Mira dropped her spear in fright. The hunter beside her recovered from his shock and skewered the other Qualakar that had just awoken. The last one alive, the one that screamed, scurried out of the pit with shocking speed. Mira scrambled for her spear. She grabbed it. The young monster reached her and leapt onto her outstretched arm as she was picking up the spear. It set its fangs into her arm. Mira screamed. Virgaard drew his knife, grabbed the Qualakar by the waist to steady it, and plunged the blade into its skull. The monster's bite slackened, and in its last breath the horrid beast stared into Mira's eyes. It managed to grin again, and the hateful fire in its eyes slowly faded out. Virgaard unhinged the horror's jaws and pulled it from Mira's violently shaking arm, from which blood was trickling steadily. Mira couldn't stop crying, not from the pain of the bite, but from the horror of encountering a creature that, no matter how young, lived and died to carry out Raakaru's hatred of Onu's creation. Such evil seemed impossible to her until this moment. She also wept from shame, feeling that her wound was something she brought onto herself for hesitating out of fear. Her father wrapped his torn shirtsleeve around her arm and hugged her close.

"I-I'm sorry, Da!" she wailed brokenly. "I-I didn't kill it soon enough! Thi-this is m-my fault!"

"No, Mira, no!" Virgaard insisted as he patted her back and kissed her cheek. "We were all scared stiff, too!"

All the other patrollers concurred, gathering close and commending Mira for still trying to fight the monster as well as telling the group of her findings in the first place. Ann and a few others came crashing through the bushes, with Plen's matriarch crying out in alarm at the sight of her daughter's arm.

"It's alright, Ann," Virgaard said quickly. "She'll likely have scars, but we'll put something on it and she'll be fine." He then turned to Mira and kissed her. "That is the sort of evil we allowed to be made here long ago, Mira. Thousands of years have passed, but still we struggle with the evils within us that let such things come to be. Remember that, Mira, whether you're hunting down creatures like this or defending yourself from another Fidon who's fallen one way or another into the darkness."

Mira nodded fervently. "I will, Da. I will."

The ears of all gathered in the undergrowth shot up in alarm as they heard a distant, rapid thundering of large feet barreling closer and closer to them from behind. An unholy growling soon became audible as well. Then a horrid roar sounded just a short way off, where the remainder of the patrol was waiting. Many alarmed voices cried out, and a horse shrieked in terrorized agony. Bowstrings twanged. Blades pierced and cleaved. Silence fell.

Mira, her parents and the others with her, hurried out of the shrubbery. Mira, clutching her throbbing arm, looked in horrified awe.

The patrollers had gathered around a dead female Qualakar. It was about the same size as the dead, gutted horse that lay beside it, but with greater bulk in its chest and forearms than in its hindquarters, which still had the girth of a horse's middle.

"Well," said Virgaard at length, "I guess we won't need to look for the mother. Mira, go with your ma and get medicine on that bite, then we'll make the rest of our patrol go slow and steady. We need to do the best we can to try and figure out if there are any more out there. It'll take us a bit longer and there's a fair chance that we might not find much else, but it's better to be safe than sorry."

Mira took her mother's hand and went to the horse with the medicines in its packs as the company prepared to continue the patrol.

23

5/8/4016 G.M.

RUTH huffed heavily as she heaved the weight above her head one last time. She looked at Commander Hanye, who stood before her and the other boys and girls who were training to become Konothian Knights. Hanye, looking over the squires and locking eyes with Ruth, smiled and nodded, calling an end to the day's strength training. A chorus of relieved groans filled the training yard as the squires dropped their weights. Hanye stepped aside for them to drink from the opened water barrel.

"Very good, all of you," the commander remarked. "Ruth, I commend your drive to improve your strength, but try to pace out the rate at which you increase the weight. You won't be able to get stronger if you completely shred your muscles before they can rebuild, and I believe you're pushing too hard and too fast. It's not a contest, it's about steadily building yourself up as best as you can."

"Yes, Lady Commander," Ruth said dutifully.

"And Hektor," Hanye continued, calling out with a chuckle to a boy in the back of the group, "you ought to try to take a little of Lady Pionaar's drive so that the two of you might balance out each other's pacing. You've been working that same weight for the past month! You can lift it like it's nearly nothing now. That's great, but now's the time to raise it up a bit."

"Yes, Lady Commander," said Hektor.

"Very good," said Hanye. "Take fifteen minutes, then we'll wrap up the day with another round of sparring."

Ruth scooped her beaker into the cool water barrel and leaned against an elm in the yard. She'd been at the training for just under five months, and as hard as it was at times, the ten-year-old couldn't imagine her life without it, along with the support provided by those around her. She was also driven by the thought of being a protector of the Temple that took in her mother as she carried her in the womb, despite what she had resorted to previously in order to get by.

She loved putting on her heavy training gambeson each day after school, along with her padded coif and the light surcoat with the Temple's crest sewn onto it. She treasured the feeling she had when she held her practice buckler and axe, both of which were made of wood and padded with leather, but still invoked in her the sense of being a warrior charged with safeguarding the good of the world. It was a moment of immense excitement and pride when they were first presented to her. She loved the rush of the exercise, but was now struggling to adjust herself to lighten the weights and ease the pace, even if it needed to be but by a little. She valued the handful of times she had practiced horse riding and was eager for the day when she would ride one on a mission with her fellow knights. Lastly, she looked forward to the duo-combat practice sessions where, as Hanye said, both of those in a given pair would bring out each other's strengths and shortcomings.

Ruth, having taken a few gulps of water, was pondering what weight she should pick next time to try and better pace her exercise. Her mind soon wandered, and she began to wonder how Verdok was doing with his clerical education, which Father Owen and Brother Roth were conducting along with the other clerics tasked with educating the acolytes. Verdok had chosen in the end to stay at the archtemple and train to be a priest following his discussions with his grandparents, and the two friends frequently talked together about their progress. Each had continuously encouraged the other, and also had confided in each other that they no longer felt the uncertainty they previously had for their life purposes. They both felt the best they had since the day Owen told them of their troubled origins.

The young squire's ponderings began to be less about pacing her exercises and more about her friend, and how the two had fared thus far, when Commander Hanye called an end to the respite and assigned the lot into pairs. Ruth found herself facing Hektor. Catching Hanye's gaze, Ruth smiled and nodded, knowing the pairing this time was no coincidence. The two bowed to one another and took their sparring stances alongside the other squires at the commander's signal.

"This will be it for the day, until dinnertime," the commander announced. "Remember that you must do all you can to keep mindful of anything that can be accounted for in a combat situation. Do not overestimate, or underestimate, anything. I'll repeat that this is *especially* the case for the bucklers. Do not let its size make you feel under-protected. Remember that if you become a proper Konothian Faithguard, you will have strong plate and chain protecting your body as well, so the shield won't be all that you have to defend yourself. The buckler is there, however, to catch whatever your foe is swinging at you and deflect it. I understand that its size, and it being fastened to your wrist, might make it feel like you're sticking out your hand just to get it lopped off, but it *will* protect you, along with your gauntlets and pauldrons, if you use it right. But you won't learn how to do that if you don't trust it and test it. You need to get in there, up close and personal, and be it your axe or your shield, you need to use one to block and one to strike. Both work for either need, and you can even go beyond blocking if you can time it right and close in enough, as you can catch your opponent's swing before they finish it. That said, it's obviously not something you can hide behind from a volley of arrows or a massive warhammer. But if Konoth could travel the world with the Temple's founders and keep them safe with a wood-axe and a pot lid, then you all can certainly serve the Faithguard with proper axes and shields when they're made of steel. Is everyone ready?"

"Yes, Lady Commander!" all the squires said uniformly.

"On my call at three, then. One ..."

Ruth saw Hektor nod courteously. "Good luck, Lady Pionaar," he said.

"Two ..."

Ruth smiled and nodded in turn. "Good luck, Sir Blackstone," she replied.

"Three!"

The yard came alive with the clattering of padded wood on wood, and the thumping of wood on heavily padded cloth.

24

5/8/4016 G.M.

VERDOK closed his copy of the Beldsantu along with the other acolytes as Father Owen, High Priest Roth, and the other clerics called an end to the day's reading. The leaders excused the clerics-in-training to one of the smaller gardens for fifteen minutes of fresh air. After a brief chat with one of his fellow pupils, Verdok pulled out his journal to take notes on the blossoming trees and flowers, hoping to use them in composing a poem about the peak of spring. Eventually, he took note of the sun and realized it was a good touch higher than usual for the time of respite. He became aware of several of his classmates discussing something quietly, and putting his things back into his satchel, he pricked up his ears to listen.

"The reading definitely ended earlier than normal," a girl said. "Anyone know what's that about?"

"We must be getting into learning something else," said a boy, "like maybe a little about healing or some other bit of caretaking."

Verdok smiled in anticipation. As driven as he felt to further study the writings of the Temple, he was wondering when he and the other trainees were going to go over the famed actions of the clerics. He had become moved by Father Owen's example to himself, and to Ruth and her mother, to try and pursue the care and betterment of others.

"What about the fighting?" another boy asked.

Verdok's smile vanished, and his ears pricked up further. He went over to them, trying to recall the name of the boy who just spoke.

"Excuse me, er ... Yorbal, but did you just say something about fighting?"

"Yeah," said Yorbal, who turned to look at Verdok. Yorbal's face displayed a sense of surprise, which clearly told Verdok the look on his own. "What, you don't know about that part?" Yorbal asked.

Yorbal looked at his other two friends, both of whom looked about and shrugged inquisitively at him.

"You two don't know, either? Huh, I thought everyone knew."

"W–why would we need, or want, to learn to fight?" Verdok asked anxiously. "That's not our job. Our purpose is to heal, to guide, to teach ... not hurt."

"Well," said Yorbal, "okay, maybe I didn't say it the best way. I mean the 'self-defense techniques.' Sure, we're not *supposed* to fight, but even the ideal case for the Faithguard would be that they weren't needed. But they are, though they can't always be there for us, or anyone else. So, we need to learn how to protect ourselves just in case."

"I see ..." Verdok said worriedly, lightly wringing his hands.

As Verdok started to ponder this revelation, Owen, Roth the High Priest, and other participating clerics came into the garden, many of them carrying a rolled, woven mat under each arm.

"Alright, everyone," High Priest Roth called out as the clerics arranged the unrolled mats on the ground, "gather around and listen. Today's closing training may or may not come as a bit of a surprise to you, but it's important. Whatever one's path in life, be it in direct service to the Temple or not, our purpose is to live together in peace, striving to remake both the bonds between ourselves and between us and Onu. But alas, not all Fidons seek to follow that basic path, and even if all of us did, there are those of the Curse Spawn that remain on Fidonhaal from the era of our Fall. As such, a wise Fidon, regardless of occupation, would do well to learn some ways to defend themselves and those around them. We of the Temple, of course, have our orders of the Faithguard, but these protectors are not invulnerable, nor can they always be there for you. Thus, in times of danger, you must know how to protect yourself if no one else is able. And so that brings us here, to practice an array of unarmed and lightly armed styles of combat that have been developed by clerics and others throughout the ages. Know this, however, that what you learn here is to be employed outside these walls only in times of desperate need. Also, for any of you who worry or feel conflicted over being a Fidon of peace when you're tasked to have a knowledge of combat, know that all of these techniques have been refined with the intention of being as nonlethal as possible. Furthermore, it should be noted that one can also derive a curious sense of peace from the practice, for it is, in the eyes of many, a peculiar sort of art."

Verdok, still resistant to the prospect, struggled to push himself to accept the notion at least to some extent. He heard Roth still speaking, but as much as he tried to listen, his senses were too drawn within himself as he tried to sort out his thoughts. Then he felt a hand on his shoulder. Knowing it to be Father Owen, Verdok looked up to his mentor.

"Why didn't you tell me about this part?" he asked the salpion.

"Well," Owen said gently, "for one thing, while I won't say the whole world knows all about this side of us, it's hardly what I would call a secret, either. There are more than one or two books in the library on the matter, and I wondered whether or not you might've already learned a bit about it. If you had, I figured that you would've asked me questions about it, if you had any. It wasn't until recently that I began to wonder how, and if, I should say anything. That was because, for the other reason, I ... I didn't want you to shy away from this path just because of this part. I know who you are, Verdok; you're a good, gentle, loving young man. If all of Fidonhaal were as you are, then there would be no need for any of this, for these martial arts, for the Faithguards, for town guards, armies, or any weapons. Or, at worst, they would be needed only for the Lakons who still walk this earth. Remember what Brother Roth said, though, that we strive to be nonlethal and that this is only for the gravest of situations."

Owen patted the boy's shoulder again. "I'm sorry if I was wrong to not tell you," he said.

Verdok shook his head. "No, you weren't wrong, just ... I don't know." He then hugged the salpion. "And I'm not walking away from this, Father. I just need to sort this out with myself."

"I'm glad to hear that," Owen said kindly. "You know, practicing it might help you sort out your thoughts. Like Brother Roth said, there *is* an artful peace to be found in it."

"How, though?"

The salpion offered Verdok his hand. "Let's join everyone and you'll see."

Verdok walked with Owen to the other side of the garden, where all the mats were rolled out and arranged neatly in rows. A cleric and an acolyte stood on each, facing each other, as the high priest looked on. Owen led the boy to a vacant mat, and then looked to the high priest. Brother Roth looked at him with an expression of half-surprise, but then nodded. Roth called for the lessons to begin, and the garden's air became filled with whispered instructions and the rustling of robes as the teachers and pupils partook in various dances of self-defense.

25
9/24/4016 G.M.

ALLOR made his way down the castle corridor toward Sheeva's rooms, wanting to see if she was willing to walk with him in the garden before going to Lady Xalu's study. It was an important day for them, as their impending lessons would cover what was expected of them when the time came for them to lead Enmayar. Allor, having contended with his nervous anticipation all morning, hoped that a calming walk with his betrothed would help him, if not her as well.

They were both now eighteen, and though a couple of other suitors had come and gone, the amicability between them for the past four years had shown they were an overwhelmingly promising match. They were now preparing for the prospect of the wedding that would come in just a few more years, assuming all continued to fare well.

Such pleasant potential was a very welcome comfort that the princess and the mayor's son shared, as well as their families, in the years following the Greystones' departure. Nearly all in the castle felt strained by the Greystones' actions in the following years, with perhaps the most heavily affected being Sheeva, who, from Allor's point of view, frequently seemed to swing between joyous affection and crushing melancholy in boundless measures.

Despite South Wardeness Halla proving herself a capable leader of her ward, her agreement to refrain from dragging up the discord and tensions revolving around her husband's death, and the unhappy ending of Nikolas's relationship with the princess, was short-lived. She had implied to members of the court, as well as other civic leaders throughout the country, that the king and queen had proven either dishonest or overly presumptuous in their leadership of the land.

The tensions had come to a head earlier in the year, when she had called for the various leaders' opinions on the Mivinaars' leadership, asking if they felt a change was in order. She then announced that she would be on the ballot for founding a new royal line if enough concurred. The votes from South Ward and the rest of Enmayar were not enough to warrant an election. The results were, however, divergent enough to put King Samuel and Queen Talrah on edge as they scrambled to call in leader after leader, from warden to holder and even a few mayors, to determine and sort out their grievances. Ironically, in her bid to undermine the Mivinaars' reign, Halla Greystone, it so far seemed, had actually led them into garnering a heightened level of favor amongst the majority of Enmayar due to the fires she had tried to stoke.

Nevertheless, things were deteriorating badly between the previously friendly families, and a nation where one of its wardens was frequently troubling the monarchs was a matter that needed to be settled as soon as possible. Since the end of the votes, the queen and king had been frequently sending and receiving letters to and from the south wardeness, which grew increasingly heated as each response came back laden with spite. When Sheeva and Allor asked why Halla couldn't simply be removed from office, the king and queen, along with Lady Xalu, informed them that the monarchy wasn't as it was in the days before the Continental Unifications.

"We can't just outright depose her just because she's being difficult," Queen Talrah said before adding, "very, very Raakhaal-bound difficult" with a massaging of her brow. "If you remember your history, it should be pretty apparent that those who simply remove their foundational stones outright over disagreements, especially over pathetic ones like these, tend to cave in on themselves."

"Yes, Mother," Sheeva said wearily, "it's just …"

"I know, dear," the queen said consolingly. "We'll get this settled soon, somehow. You'll see. The Greystones *have* been good leaders, all things considered. It's just … if we could just settle this whole damned mess with Nikolas. I wonder sometimes what might've been if we had just introduced other suitors earlier on so they might've not thought it was an exclusive arrangement with them … but that should've gone without saying anyway."

The conversation largely ended there, as those discussing the matter simply drifted off into their own ponderings on what might have been.

In addition to the difficulties with the Greystones, there was also the matter of the warden from Kellmayar, Ohdan Karvinthaal, who had been Valor Greystone's friend in youth and in politics.

It was the controversy around aiding him in that time of famine that caused Valor's death, and Ohdan's region in Kellmayar remained troubled by a perplexing strike of famine and poverty to the present day. There was a disturbing level of tension amongst all of the Four Nations over the matter, but especially between Enmayar and Kellmayar. Word had spread over the years as to what had happened concerning Valor's efforts to help and what became of him, with not a few viewing the sudden introduction of other suitors to Sheeva as an addition of insult to injury. The Kellmayarn warden, in addition to losing a personal friend, was angry that Enmayar had since almost utterly left his region to its problems. Despite the support they had received from the other two nations, Kellmayar at large, and especially its east ward, was still struggling, and the educated opinion that Enmayar's contributions would drastically ease the burden was nearly unanimous.

Thus, when not trying to settle matters with Halla and the aftermath of her recent efforts to undermine them, the queen and king had been vying to arrange an agreement of trade and aid with Kellmayar, even proposing to visit the land personally if need be, to settle the difficulties there.

Now, however, with Kysonmay only a few days away, Allor was hoping to focus his mind on the coming festivities and his impending lessons. And he hoped to start with a pleasant morning walk in the autumn-touched garden with his fiancée and dearest friend. Reaching Sheeva's rooms, Allor was taken aback at what he saw as he came into the doorway.

Sheeva sat at her desk, head buried in her arms, which were folded across the desk. A blank parchment was in one hand, and an ink-stained, somewhat worn quill in the other. About the floor, near her chair, were a number of crumpled pieces of parchment. Though Sheeva wasn't weeping, Allor could tell that the princess was drained by sadness and exasperation. He knocked gently on the doorpost. The princess looked up, her eyes puffy from crying and clearly tired from her struggles at her desk. Allor rushed to her, embracing her and kissing her head gently.

"What's all this?" he asked.

The princess wearily handed him the letter that had been under her head on the desk. Allor looked it over, his anger growing hotter with every sentence he read. The letter was from Nikolas, and the contempt and spite that it held took Allor back to that winter's day in the garden, when Nikolas and Halla were about to leave and return to Oakhall. Allor finished reading it and slammed the parchment onto the desk. Huffing with rage, he still managed to keep his voice down.

"How many times do we have to tell him that he wasn't denied your hand outright, despite his father's stupidity? Sheeva ... this was bad enough the first time, in the garden. We should've told your mother and father what he said to you before they left."

"I know," Sheeva said, beginning to weep again. "I ... I just couldn't let him go like that. I know he and Halla have gone to lengths to cut off and bury all chances of keeping a friendship after all that happened. They felt insulted beyond amendment, and once they decided that, they just ... would not let it go. And it's only gotten worse, now ... so much worse. I'm so ... foolish."

Sheeva buried her head into her arms on the desk and began sobbing wretchedly.

"No," Allor said, holding her closely. "You're patient and loving, and willing to try to make peace. Many who were otherwise great leaders have lacked that quality, or struggled to keep it. Some still do, as Halla and that Kellmayarn warden, Ohdan, clearly show."

"No," Sheeva said tearfully. "I'm a fool. I've given them ... *him* ... far more chances ... beyond reason. Look ... look in there."

The princess pointed to a lower drawer in the desk, which had a key turned in the opened lock and was now slightly ajar. Allor pulled it open and peered inside. A sizeable stack of papers lay inside, which he pulled out and rifled through. Each was dated by Sheeva's hand, including those that clearly came from Nikolas. As he sorted through them, he saw that the first corresponding pairs of letters were dated only two months after the Greystones' departure. Each set of letters bellowed the fires of disgust and anger in his heart, with each one insulting the integrity and honor of the whole Mivinaar family. Sheeva's honor, however, was the most common target, with horrendous insinuations of the princess being but the political equivalent of a whore for her parents to auction off. At last, unable to bring himself to read any more, he tossed the pile onto the desk and looked at Sheeva, who was now sobbing silently.

"Sheeva ..."

"Oh, All!" the princess cried, bolting from her chair and holding her fiancé tight. "I don't know what to do! I still have a love for him from before, even after all of this. I just wish we could still get along ... an-and I *hate* him! I hate him so much!"

"Sheeva," said Allor, gently massaging her back as she wept into his shoulder. "This is far too much. Political pettiness and denied ambitions aside, this is simply too far. It's harassment ... abuse. It's unacceptable, and has been since the days of the smallest realms. There's no justifying this. We need to tell them. Now."

Wordlessly, the princess nodded and took Allor's hand. They walked past the three years of hateful and sorrowful letters on the desk, as well as the various books in the study, and the rows of plants, phials, and mortars from Dr. Kamlof's lessons as they left Sheeva's chambers on their way to the throne room.

Resolution at Oakhall

26
9/24/4016 G.M.

SHEEVA approached her parents with Allor at her side, and the young couple showed the queen and king the letters. The monarchs, utterly livid at what they read, began to draft a summons calling the Greystones to court for their cruelty toward the princess. Given how publicly known the problems between the Mivinaars and Greystones had become, however, Egrah and Alphaar proposed attempting to resolve the matter less dramatically than outright demanding their appearance at court. Word had spread across the world over the past several years regarding the tensions between the two families, and the other nations had been nervously eyeing Enmayar's leaders. The political tensions were exacerbated further when considering the connections to Kellmayar's difficulties pertaining to Warden Ohdan.

Queen Talrah and King Samuel agreed to their suggestion, and soon the two families jointly drafted a letter and had it flown to Oakhall. It announced their plan to visit the Greystones in the coming month in an attempt to resolve the matter face to face. The letter concluded with a warning to the Greystones against fleeing Oakhall, that doing so would prompt a call for their arrest.

The Indovis family would leave for Oakhall the next day, with the Mivinaars following a week later in case word reached them along the way that the Greystones were clearly unwilling to cooperate. If they were not even willing to talk, the Mivinaars would be able to turn back and regroup with Allor's family at Genverdell, and decide what to do next instead of making the entire trip in vain.

***

The following day, Allor and his parents, along with a handful of the royal guard, were saddled up at the gate and preparing to leave. Sheeva came to Allor and kissed him as he leaned over to her.

"Please be careful," she said softly in his ear. "I love you."

"I love you, too," Allor said calmly, "and I'll be careful; we all will. You be sure to do the same when you all leave, alright?"

"Of course."

As Allor sat upright in the saddle, Sheeva, her eyes still on him, caressed his knee, grinning as she saw his grey fur bristle and eyes widen with a surprised smile.

"I wish we were doing this just a few days later," she said regretfully. "Kysonmay won't be the same with you gone."

"I know," Allor sighed moodily. "I was really looking forward to it. I know how much you love to dance."

Sheeva laughed. "You like it just as much, if not more."

"I do. But, Onu willing, there'll be many more a Kysonmay to share together, as with all the other days, great and small."

They kissed again, then looked over to each of their parents, who were conversing quietly a little way past the gate. Allor's parents seemed just about to leave, and Sheeva, wanting to try to say one last thing before they parted, found herself at a loss. She looked back up to Allor, and his face hinted at the same sort of thoughts. A moment later he spoke, his face lighting up with a sudden thought.

"Are things still going well with your lessons with Dr. Kamlof?" he asked. "I haven't watched you much when you're in the study with him; I just don't have the aptitude for all that, but I've heard many praises from him about you being good and consistent in your studies."

"They are," Sheeva said with a smile. "Kamlof and I have been going over several different medicines lately, along with some antidotes and the poisons they counter."

"Anything on Endallian Fever?" Allor asked in a curious tone.

"I ... yes. We've gone over several treatments for that, as well as the history of how we've gone from it being nearly always fatal to it now being, usually, only two out of every ten or so."

Allor looked levelly at her. "It's baffling when you think about that, isn't it? You'd think it wouldn't be that much of a worry, or wipe out a whole town like Nelahaal in this day and age, with only a mortality rate like that. I guess *where* that twenty percent is lost can be scattered or concentrated."

Sheeva looked perplexedly at him. "I ... is there something ...?"

Allor leaned over and kissed Sheeva again. It was a deeper sort of kiss than Sheeva was used to, despite their being engaged. When he pulled away from her, the princess stared into his eyes, her face blushing, as Allor spoke softly with a loving smile.

"Kamlof told me you started studying all of that ... the day I learned that nearly everyone from back home had died from it. I didn't think you would've been moved to go to that length just because—"

"You showed me a great kindness earlier that day," said Sheeva, "so I just thought—"

"Allor!" Egrah and Alphaar called, "are you ready for this?"

"Yes!" Allor called back. He then turned back to Sheeva, caressing her cheek.

"We'll see you soon," he whispered lovingly, "and we'll settle this for good, one way or another. I love you."

"I love you, too."

Sheeva joined her mother and father in waving farewell at the gate. Allor trotted off to Egrah and Alphaar's side, riding alongside them down the east hill, and in time vanishing into the distance as they and their entourage rode out of Genverdell and onto the south highway.

***

Six days passed, and Sheeva found herself sitting in the castle's chapel the day before their departure, wringing her hands anxiously as she spoke to Ranoth Windsbreath. News of the flare-up of Endallian Fever, which now dotted areas of South Ward, had just come that morning on the very day before the royal household was set to travel to Oakhall. Despite the development, Sheeva and her parents had agreed they must deal with the Greystones as soon as possible. The castle had spent much of the day preparing to leave, and Sheeva, becoming overwhelmed by her fears for Allor, had made her way to the chapel to try and get some sort of assurance from the castle's priest.

"The news is that it's only in a few spots in the south, Princess," Ranoth said as levelly as he could, "and hardly anyone's died from it so far. You know how these things go. The fever isn't something that just vanishes when not ravaging a country or a region. It's always around; it just manages to flare up more than usual from time to time, and late autumn through early winter tends to be when such cases happen, *when* they happen."

"But this is early autumn, Brother Ranoth," Sheeva pointed out. "We just had Kysonmay three days ago, and if it's already happening this early—"

"That doesn't mean it'll get worse or spread more later on. We managed to contain this outbreak far better than the one from four years ago."

"But Oakhall's right in one of the areas ..."

Sheeva buried her face in her hands, trying her hardest to hold back the tears. Ranoth patted her shoulder comfortingly.

"You know they packed masks, just in case, right?"

"Yes, but that's no guarantee."

"True, but I've known them to be cautious, as we will be, too, when we leave tomorrow."

Sheeva nodded silently. Ranoth patted the princess's shoulder once more.

"Speaking of our leaving, you'd best go over your things again this evening and make sure you've got everything you need. I'm going to be doing that myself now, if there isn't anything else you wish to talk about."

Sheeva thought for a moment. "That's all for now, Brother Ranoth. Thank you."

"You're welcome, dear Princess," said Ranoth as he turned to leave the chapel. "If we all do our part, and be careful and sensible, and Onu willing, this will all be settled soon. Just stay calm and do your part, and trust to Onu for all that lies outside of that. Perhaps take a moment to pray, or at least reflect. Whatever you do, Sheeva, I'm sure it'll play out right in the end."

"I think I will," Sheeva said. "Thank you. I'll see you at dinner, I suppose?"

"Of course."

Ranoth exited the chapel, leaving the princess alone on the pew where she sat. She closed her eyes, praying silently for Allor's safety and health, and that of his family. As she prayed, her mind began to roam, and she found her thoughts of love for Allor and his family being replaced by her turmoil of emotions toward the Greystones. She had once loved them as much as she now loved the Indovis family, and now it had all fallen to pieces. She thought of the years of letters, the insults, the horrid, vulgar implications that Nikolas had thrown at her. She thought of how she was now torn between memories of love and her present hatred, and the chastisement she inflicted upon herself for being so foolish as to think that trying to keep contact would eventually make things alright.

The tears began to flow.

"Oh, Onu," she wept, "please, one way or another, let all this strife end. I should pray for peace, but I just want them to stop. I ... hate them. I *hate* them! I hate them both! Why did I ever bother with them, after all that happened after Allor came? I wouldn't–"

Sheeva froze at her own thoughts, then, after battling within herself to either hold it back or be honest to Onu, chose the latter course.

"I wouldn't weep for them if they died from the fever. I-I wouldn't cry if that ... that little *bastard's* rotten snow-white lips ended up blood-red. Calling me a harlot ... I don't want to think these things, Onu! I ... I just ..."

The princess inhaled deeply, embracing herself miserably as she continued to confess her thoughts.

"I just want it all to stop, and I'd not weep if they ended with it."

A voice came from behind her, suddenly, quietly; a voice that petrified Sheeva with horror. It was icy as a winter's midnight, yet heated as a furnace being worked in midsummer.

"There are no guarantees with Onu, dear Sheeva," the voice said in a cackling whisper. "His allowance of freedom enabled all those awful things that Nik and Halla have done to you and your family. Such has always been the case, for all the other horrors that have ever happened in Fidonhaal."

Sheeva held herself tighter, afraid to cry out, but driven to speak. She slowly turned around and saw it in the chapel's doorway. A shadow, black as night and eyes that glowed as lit coals. Fidon-like in form, yet somehow shapeless. A Raakon. A demon. A herald of Raakaru. Horrified that her conflicted prayer had drawn the abomination's attention, her words were broken by frightened stammering. The princess struggled to counter the demon's words as the shadow from Raakhaal shook with vile mirth at her state.

"Th-those evils w-were first sown by y-your master," she managed to say.

"Who did so to prove Onu wrong for permitting the possibility."

"S-stop it!" Sheeva quavered. "Onu's will was for freedom and order in their own measures. You ... you and your m-master had your chance to trust Onu and ... and now you–"

"Can prance about anywhere," the demon retorted coolly as it took several steps into the chapel, "even in this oh-so holy little room. Save your Temple doctrines, Princess; they will all come to nothing in the end."

Sheeva bolted from the pew, glaring at the demon. The princess's eyes were afire with both terror and indignation. Still shaking, she did her best to regain composure and stand up against it.

"And you can spare me the arrogance that Raakaru has hammered into you!"

"Do you *really* think that this whole Greystone problem will be settled by words? Given how both Nik and Halla have been to you and your family, I would think that your wish for their deaths ought to be fulfilled."

"I-I did not *wish* for them to die!"

"But you would not regret them dying, no? You just said–"

"N-no, I was just confessing to Onu–"

"And Onu will hold your thoughts in abhorrence and simply let things be, while Raakaru would try to set things to order and justice, especially for those who are faithful to him."

The demon glided steadily toward Sheeva, rooting the princess to the spot in terror. As the demon drew nearer, Sheeva noticed the shifting form began to take on a more feminine frame. When it reached her, it offered the form of a hand to her.

"I can see to it that Nikolas and Halla will pay," it said, "if you would just turn to either me or my master, for he–"

"NO!" Sheeva screamed, backing away. "GO! GET OUT!"

The contempt of the hideous smile that the now-female demon had on her face was palpable.

"Very well," she said levelly. "I shall leave. But we will be watching you. Think hard on all they have done to you, though, and simply call on me if you change your mind. I go by Raakmathna. Of course, given your own knowledge on certain things, you could always see to it yourself–"

"GO!"

The shadow dispersed instantly, and the princess slumped back into her seat, trembling and sweating.

A minute later, when she had largely managed to calm down, Sheeva got up and went to leave the chapel. Just as she reached the doors, Ranoth appeared, his face one of concern.

"Is everything alright, Princess?" the priest asked. "I thought I heard shouting."

Sheeva managed a light laugh. "Oh, that was just a couple of sneezes! I'm fine. Thanks for asking."

"Oh," Ranoth chuckled, only to suddenly look at her worriedly as he placed a hand on her head.

"That's all," Sheeva assured him, "nothing else is the matter. No fever or chills."

"Alright," Ranoth said cautiously. "Just make sure to check with Dr. Kamlof if you start to feel anything else."

"Of course."

***

The princess tossed and turned that night, her mind and soul torn over what happened in the chapel. She found herself thinking about her hatred of the Greystones, which grew with each thought and memory. Unable to sleep, Sheeva got up and quietly roamed the corridors aimlessly. She eventually found herself in front of the apothecary's door. Her sleep-deprived mind raced with uncounted memories and thoughts.

"Given your own knowledge on certain things ..." said Raakmathna.

"Make sure to check with Dr. Kamlof," said Ranoth.

Sheeva stared at the door, her mind blurring. A moment passed, and then, having fetched a candle from her room, the princess crept quietly back to Kamlof's quarters and slipped inside.

27

10/23/4016 G.M.

ALLOR rode into the town of Oakhall with his mother and father on either side. His drained energy and resolve had begun to rebound after the near month-long ride through the anxious South Ward. All three of them, with their accompanying guards, had their plague masks strapped to their muzzles as they passed through the town's gate. They trotted along the modestly populated streets and headed straight toward the Greystone estate.

The turbulence between tension and confidence had been hovering over Allor's family for nearly the entire trip. As worried as nearly everyone was that the outbreak would end up as a repeat of the one from four years ago, every update that they heard along the way told them that as persistent as the outbreak was, it wasn't nearly as widespread or deadly this time around. For this, Allor and his company were grateful, but knowing that their destination was one of the areas where the fever had been lingering, they were unable to completely shake off their fear.

Making their way toward the heart of the town, they soon reached Halla Greystone's home, a walled, stately compound atop a tall, gently sloping hill. The chief building of the estate was a large, beautiful house built from oak; the namesake structure of the entire town. Two guards and the household chamberlain greeted the company at the compound's gates. They looked nervously at the arrivals from the tops of their masks. After an uneasy exchange of greetings, a moment of silence passed over the gathering. Then, clearing his throat, the chamberlain addressed them.

"Wardeness Greystone ... she and her son await you, Sir and Lady Indovis, and young Sir Allor. However, given the present situation regarding the public health of the area, the wardeness was–"

"Surprised that the princess's *current* suitor would take the time, and dare to risk his health, to come all the way here over the royal tart's honor."

The chamberlain, eyes wide and ears wilted in discomfort, stopped his address short as Nikolas stepped through the gate behind him and cut into the conversation. Now twenty-one years old, the son of Halla and the late Valor cut a more dashing figure than he did when Allor last saw him. The star-shaped patch of white on his face was as distinguished and handsome as ever, and his sea-green eyes would have been immensely charming had they not been sparkling with animosity. Nikolas, having stepped to the chamberlain's side, set his sights on Allor as he continued.

"So, you left before celebrating Kysonmay with her?" he asked with mock pity. "How sad that you felt compelled to miss out just to defend her honor. How many others is she considering now? Do you know if she's seeing anyone else while you're here on—"

Allor, with bolstered resolve and shattered patience, refused to humor ceremony any further and bore his gaze into Nikolas's eyes. He was pleasantly surprised to see Nikolas's glare wilt a little as he raised his voice and spoke.

"Four Breaths, Nikolas, that is ENOUGH! Did you not even *read* the letter we sent? This is *far* past some sort of petty politicking; we're talking abuse of the mind and heart of the future queen of Enmayar, and continuous attempts to undermine the stability of the entire country! What part of that do you *not* understand? What do I have to do to put a stop to this? Do we have to do a duel, like in the old days?"

Nikolas rekindled the fire of his gaze a little as he composed his reply, though his eyes showed that other, less hostile feelings, were beginning to creep in ever so lightly.

"My father ... him dying like that, and you ... you just swooping in like a hawk ... after all that time I had with her, I *did* fall in love with her—"

"And then you fell right out," Allor said coldly. "And, if I may be so blunt, I don't even think I'm fully convinced that you ever truly felt for her."

"I ... I ..."

"You let it all fall to pieces just because another suitor came along. You know, as is the *normal* course for these things. You had plenty of chances, Nikolas, and if you're going to talk about parents using their children for politics, why don't *you* go and have a good, long talk with *your* mother? I may be just a mayor's son, but then again, that's just it. I'm the son of a mayor, a mayor of a town that has been nearly dead for almost four years, and the queen and king still offer my family and me the opportunity to live with them and court Sheeva. You, however, are the son of the south wardens. They offered your family a chance to bond with theirs, and if they were intent on having it done for some sort of gain, they would've held to it no matter what. Now, even though you've thrown your chance with Sheeva away, you're still set to be South Warden, if you prove yourself. That's just not enough for you, I take it? Or is that your mother talking? Yes, some other suitors have come and gone, but now it seems all but decided. We're engaged now. I'm going to be her husband in a few years, Nikolas, and if you must keep track of the politics, if I am deemed capable enough, I'll be her king, too. Enmayar's king. *Your* king, and I won't stand for—"

"That story sounds familiar," Nikolas interrupted flatly. "I don't know about you, but I hear in you the same sort of drive that I had when I was with her. I'm not sure if anyone can truly be innocent of such thoughts if they're given this sort of opportunity."

"But I won't look to make her life miserable if something changes all that. Even if it breaks my heart into a thousand pieces, I would never hurt her. *Never.* I don't know what you've been told by your parents, but my upbringing told me that isn't what you do to those you love."

"The only way you'd know if what you just said is true," Nikolas said quietly as he slumped against the heavy oaken doors of the manor's gate, "will be if you actually go through it yourself."

"Enough," Allor said with a level authority that sent Nikolas's ears shooting up in surprise. "Sheeva, the queen, the king, and many others will be along in a week or so, if all's gone as planned. We'll come back then. We'll stay in the inn in town. Nikolas, I *strongly* advise you to have a good talk with your mother in the meantime. We'll see each other again soon."

Allor then turned his horse around, seeing the approving gazes and nods from his parents as they all turned to ride back into town.

"You handled that quite well, overall," Alphaar commended him as they brought their horses into the inn's stables and dismounted. "I must confess I was a bit worried that you were going to punch him, if not worse, after what he said when he came out, as well as after seeing all those letters from earlier."

Allor sighed deeply. "I was afraid I would, too."

28

11/1/4016 G.M.

RUTH halted in the main gateway of the training yard as she saw Father Owen and Archgeneral Gothnaar enter from a side gate. The salpion and archgeneral called to Commander Hanye and the other squires as a company of Faithguard knights began to file in. The archgeneral began speaking to Hanye, and Owen, catching Ruth's attention, beckoned her to approach the gathering. After a few minutes of discussion with Hanye, the archgeneral began an announcement.

"Dear squires," he called out, "we have just received word from Castle Genverdell that a south ward town named Bravagoth has fallen under siege by necromantic powers. Reports imply that the powers of Raakhaal have reanimated the entire cemetery. The castle received this news from a message initially meant for the king and queen, but both of them, along with many from the castle, have been away the past month to discuss matters with the south wardeness. The message has been redirected to Oakhall, but the castle's steward thankfully informed us of the matter as well. Given the nature of this threat and with our duty being to protect Fidonity, I am sending out a company of Faithguard to ride for the town as fast as they can. There will be knights from several of the various orders in this mission; not all will be Konothian."

Gothnaar glanced across the yard, briefly looking at every trainee before continuing.

"But those in the company who are of your order have now come here to ask for any and all willing squires to come forth to accompany them. Please, now, think and decide for yourself what to do. None of you shall be forced to partake in this mission, as it will be a hard, long, and rushed ride for Bravagoth. And once you get there, as I'm sure you can imagine, the situation will be dangerous, much more so than we would ideally have for a squire's first outing into the field. There is no shame if you decide you aren't yet ready. However, this *will* give those who go an excellent source of experience and will be remembered by your fellows and superiors."

The archgeneral beckoned Hanye to his side, and he stepped back and gestured to the commander as he concluded his announcement.

"Commander Hanye shall be in charge of this mission and all involved, Konothian and otherwise. All knights of the Konothian order that seek squires for this mission will now come forth and speak with those who wish to go. If you are accepted, you are to immediately follow them to the armory to be properly kitted out and given rations. You will then join them in the stables, mount up, and ride out to Bravagoth. Time is of the essence, but please, do take a moment to think this over. Onu bless and keep you all, whatever you choose."

The archgeneral nodded to Hanye and Owen, and then turned and left as the Konothian Knights in the cavalcade stepped forward, earnestly looking over the pondering young trainees. A couple of the squires soon stepped forward, and the knights began to quietly ask them questions.

Ruth stood stock-still, her mind racing as she thought of what to do, when she suddenly noticed that Commander Hanye and Father Owen were looking directly at her. Her eyes locked onto theirs, and she viewed their gaze as being not of expectation, one way or the other, but of a curiosity that simultaneously spoke of hope and anxiety. Ruth thought of her mother, and how the Temple had cared for her and herself despite Arza's missteps in her past. She thought of her dear friend Verdok, who had also grown under the Temple's care, and of his own dedication to pursue the betterment of Fidonhaal. She thought of all the fellowship and support she had experienced since she began training with the Faithguard, and her friendship with Commander Hanye, which had grown beyond the mere respect of a pupil to her mentor. Looking at the small handful of squires who had now stepped forward, along with those who began to leave the yard and those still pondering their decision, Ruth at last stepped forward.

But she made her way over to Hanye and Owen rather than the other knights.

She drew a deep breath before speaking. "Do you need a squire, Commander Heartkeeper?" she asked with dutiful formality.

Both the commander and the salpion's eyes shone with loving worry and pride, their smiles telling which feeling was the stronger.

"I will," Hanye said solemnly. "Ruth, I am very confident in you, given where you are now as a squire, and I will be only too happy to take you as my squire on this mission. But remember what Archgeneral Vyth said: This is not being forced on you. The norm is for a squire to join a knight on a mission or patrol when they're fifteen at the youngest, and even then, a mission such as this is obviously not the sort of thing we'd usually assign to them. This emergency will no doubt provide a great opportunity for experience, but it's not something to jump into lightly."

"I know," said Ruth, "but with all that you've done, all of the Temple, that is ... I want to. I feel that I must, not from you, but in another way, you know?"

Hanye nodded understandingly. "I certainly do," she said with a hand on Ruth's shoulder. "Let's go to the armory, then, if you're ready."

Father Owen hugged Ruth and turned to the cleric's study quarters. "I'll let your mother know," he said. "She'll let you go, Ruth, I'm sure of it. I'll let Verdok know, too."

As Owen left the yard, Ruth, with a deep breath, followed Hanye and the other knights alongside their chosen squires to the armory.

***

Within the hour, Ruth was mounted on her horse and kitted out with real arms and armor, though still not to the extent of a fully fledged knight. She positioned herself alongside Hanye, who was just about to leave the archtemple grounds and ride south for Bravagoth. Sister Arza, tearfully worried as she was for her daughter, did not once voice any protest, and embraced Ruth as she leaned in her saddle.

"I'm so proud of you," she wept, "but you'll always be my baby girl, so please, *please* do everything you can to be careful."

"I will, Mother," said Ruth, her voice straining on the edge of tears. "I love you."

"And I love you."

As Ruth leaned in her saddle, she noticed Father Owen speaking to Verdok in earnest whispers. Verdok turned toward her, swallowing hard as he looked at her with shining eyes. The acolyte then strode purposefully toward her as Owen looked on, a very peculiar look playing across the salpion's features. Having reached her, Verdok stood briefly transfixed in silence, then spoke in a curious tone.

"Thank you, Ruth," he said, "for your courage in protecting the good of Fidonity. I wish I was brave enough to join the Faithguard so that I might've gone with you."

"Verdok ..." Ruth said, finding herself oddly at a loss for words as she found herself becoming completely engrossed in Verdok's deep blue eyes, "you ... you're protecting the good of Fidonhaal, too, just in a different way. If the priests and priestesses and their lessons could just get through to everyone, then maybe the Faithguard wouldn't even be needed. Well, apart from the monsters, I guess, but–"

A grand blow from a horn sounded, signaling the Faithguard to begin their ride and jolting Ruth from her odd state. She then looked intently at Verdok.

"And you're my friend," she said earnestly. "You'll be with me, in a way, as will Mother and Father Owen, and everyone else here."

Verdok breathed deeply, and in one swift motion, he took his mother's pendant off his neck and held it out to Ruth.

"Here," he said, "take this."

Ruth was speechless. Verdok held it out further, his eyes showing that he wouldn't take no for an answer. Ruth silently took it and put it on.

"By itself," Verdok said, "it might be a way of showing our faith, and of Onu's power and love. But there are other things it means to me as well, and I hope it will for you, too. It won't magically stop the undead itself, or anything like that, but–"

"Thank you," Ruth managed to say in an awestruck whisper. "I ... I appreciate it, and I will wear it with honor."

"And I'm honored that you wear it," said Allor, now shifting uncomfortably on his feet, his eyes dropping to the ground. "Go bravely, and Onu keep you."

"Onu keep you, too," Ruth said softly, catching her mother's smile along with that of Owen. She looked back to Hanye, who was grinning warmly, and then, feeling the heat spreading in her face, turned her sight straight ahead, only to see two Faithguards, a married couple riding the same horse, giving her the same look.

The blush burned red-hot in her as she and her commander rode out along with the rest of the troop. It wasn't until they were out of the city and riding swiftly in the autumn air that her face finally began to cool down.

29
11/3/4016 G.M.

SHEEVA and her parents, along with the royal retinue of guards and advisors, entered the courtyard of Oakhall's inn and dismounted at the stables in the autumn morning. Upon entering the inn's dining hall, the princess cast her eyes about the room of masked faces that rose to greet the royalty, and ran joyfully to Allor when she spotted him. The two embraced tightly as the king and queen went to converse with Alphaar and Egrah.

"I missed you so much," the princess whispered lovingly into her fiancé's ear. She then chuckled impishly, briefly appreciating the romantic sensations that she had stirred in him. His ears twitched gently as her words pierced them, and his fur bristled. She then went back to her sincerity. "I was so worried that you'd get sick."

"I missed you, too," Allor said warmly. He then began to massage and gently scratch the back of Sheeva's neck to reciprocate the feelings she kindled. Looking into Sheeva's eyes, his grin showed from under his mask as he saw that the desired effect had been achieved. "I'm glad to see that you're well, too. All news so far has shown this bout to not be nearly as bad as last time. Of course, there are the ones who *have* died, and all the same ..."

They turned their eyes toward the rest of the room, where all present were looking on intently as the two showed their affections. With a face burning from blushing, Sheeva held Allor's hand as they met with her mother and father, along with Egrah and Alphaar, to go over the plan for the upcoming talks with the Greystones.

"Egrah and Alphaar tell us that Nikolas seems to be open to changing his tune at long last," Queen Talrah said, "and that they've managed to talk Lady Halla down a bit as well, through Nikolas. This might actually turn out well after all."

The queen looked approvingly at Allor.

"They tell me you're the one to credit for getting through to him, and in turn his mother," she said. "Thank you, Allor. Whatever you did, I wish we had thought to do it sooner."

"Well," Allor said at length, "it may have come down to how this was affecting Sheeva that brought all this on. If we never learned of the letters ..."

Sheeva inwardly chastised herself again for not revealing the matter sooner. She then wordlessly leaned her head on Allor's shoulder and sighed heavily. Allor brushed his warm, grey cheek against her head, wrapping an arm about her and pulling her close as his words trailed off into silence. The king and queen, along with Allor's parents and the rest of the gathered company, looked on in warm silence at the sight the two made. A moment later, King Samuel spoke.

"What matters is that we're here now, and that there's even a chance this might actually be settled amicably." He nodded to all in the hall before continuing. "We'll have breakfast here, then go to them once we've finished."

***

Sheeva rode beside Allor as the two followed their parents and approached the gate of the Greystones' home. A masked guard on the wall spotted them and rushed down to the gate, calling for them to stay back. The queen raised her voice sternly, the muffling from her mask adding a touch of disturbing severity as she called back to the guard.

"We're all gathered now, sir," Talrah said bluntly. "We aren't going to stand for any sudden attempt to back out now!"

"It isn't that, my queen," the guard said worriedly, "it's that the chamberlain–"

"Don't worry, Kellgoth," a hoarse and muffled voice that sounded somewhat like Nikolas called from behind the closed gate. "We'll explain. Come along, Mother."

The doors opened, and the royal company froze in alarm at what they saw. Sheeva felt as if her heart had stopped.

Nikolas and his mother were leaning lightly against one another as two guards held the doors open. From over their masks, both of their eyes were bloodshot, and their fur was matted with sweat. Both had the shivers, but Wardeness Halla seemed to be especially affected. Nikolas, still propping himself against his mother, stepped forward slightly and nodded to the company. He then locked eyes with Sheeva. He stared at her silently for a moment, then spoke.

"Shee—Princess, hello."

"Hello, Nikolas," Sheeva said as levelly as she could manage.

"You ... you've grown into a beautiful young woman. No mask can hide that."

"Thank you. You've become a very handsome man. Even the fever can't change that."

"Thank you," Nikolas said with a rueful laugh and a short fit of coughing. "We believe that the chamberlain caught it a few days ago, and then spread it to us before we realized he had it. Almost everyone here has it. The town doesn't know yet, though, at least not as far as we're aware. We've been trying to keep it quiet until we could try and settle this. Mother and I ... we've talked a lot these past few days and—"

Nikolas fought through another fit of coughing, then continued.

"... and then, we both saw that this has just gotten far too out of hand. You tried to reason with us ... with me ... so did the king and queen, and Allor's parents. But it took all this and Allor's words, when he came here, to finally get through to us."

Halla was then taken by a nasty bit of coughing, followed by Nikolas again. Both held onto each other as their fits ran their course.

"We wanted to settle this proper," Nikolas continued, his voice increasingly taking on a morbid tone, "but given our states, we wanted to settle what should really matter before tending to the formalities. But regardless of that, and ... and just in case we end up not being able to ..."

Nikolas drew a deep, wheezy sigh.

"We just wanted to say that, Mother and I both ... we're sorry for all this trouble we've brought on ... to you, Madam and Sir Indovis, and you Allor ... to you, Queen Talrah and King Samuel, and to you, Princess Sheeva."

The south wardeness nodded at Sheeva and her company, and tried to say something, but all that came through the mask covering her grey face was a sickly croak.

"We're sorry," Nikolas repeated. "I'm sorry."

The princess gazed at her former friend and suitor, her mind and heart torn by all the thoughts, memories, and emotions within. She found herself at a loss for words and could only bring herself to nod. Dr. Kamlof, who was in the company, suddenly stepped forward.

"Do you have enough of the medicine needed for this?" he asked.

"No," said Nikolas with a shake of the head. "We used it up for the few who got sick in town a little while back. Once it all seemed under control, we sent what was left to Kannah, since it's both a port and one of the worst-hit places this time around. I guess we were foolish to do that, huh? We've sent for more, but who knows how long it'll be before it gets here. It's not as bad as last time, but the memory lingers and I'm sure no one is eager to travel much while this is still going on."

The doctor shook his head resolutely. "It wasn't foolish, Sir Greystone. You all had every reason to believe that the matter was settled here, and that you had the thought to deliver the rest to Kannah is commendable beyond words. I packed my stores of what's needed for this just in case the need arose. I'll see to it. I'll have it ready sometime tonight, but you may send your doctor to us to help, if you wish."

"Our own doctor is sick, too. The ones in town might be of help, though I worry you might be overcrowded if you bring too many others in."

"Maybe," Kamlof said after a moment's thinking. "Don't worry, though. It'll be fairly quick and easy to make. Have everyone who's sick lie down, and make sure they drink enough water. I'll have enough ready by nightfall. I'll also let the mayor know what's going on. How many of you are sick in there?"

"Fifteen live here," Nikolas stated, "and eleven are sick."

"I can brew up enough for that many, and some to spare if need be. Just give me until tonight, and I'll come in and help your doctor with giving the doses out."

"We can't ask you to risk your own health–"

"Those risks are part of my job, my good lad."

"I–"

"That's that."

Nikolas, looking at his mother and the doctor, nodded resignedly.

"Thank you," he said with a cough.

"Go now and rest."

"Yes, Dr. Kamlof."

Nikolas and his mother turned back toward their house as the guards closed the gate. The company then made their way back to the inn. Along the way, Dr. Kamlof turned to Sheeva.

"I won't have you risk getting sick by going into the house," he said, "but given your studies with me, especially the reason that you got started, would you care to assist me in making the medicine, Princess?"

Sheeva looked intently at her teacher and nodded solemnly.

"Very good," he said.

Sheeva set her eyes forward and caught in the corner of her sight Allor's gaze of commending admiration.

30
11/3/4016 G.M.

ALLOR leaned against a wooden pillar in the inn's common, watching Sheeva and Dr. Kamlof as they worked in a corner of the dining hall, which the doctor had cleared and cleaned for his emergency work. Allor's eyes kept turning to his fiancée. He was awestruck at the grace and compassion she showed as she worked to do her part in mending the health of someone who had tormented her for nearly the past four years.

"How bad does it look, Doctor?" Allor asked anxiously. "I've heard some basic things about the fever, but I can't say I truly know how it progresses or what symptoms mark exactly which stages of it."

The apothecary sighed lightly, and briefly paused in grinding several roots and leaves before speaking.

"I'll say what I told the mayor," he said. "Both the wardeness and her son have it pretty bad, but Lady Halla especially. As for the others, I can't say since I didn't see them, but they could very well be in more or less the same state. One of the chief difficulties in managing this fever is some people deteriorate far more quickly than others, so timing is always of the essence. Furthermore, even when the medicine is given, despite its vastly improved effectiveness, we still cannot say for sure if the patient will pull through until the fever has fully broken. We're getting better and better at handling it, but the reality is ... well ... situations like Nelahaal are still possible. Unlikely, but not impossible."

Allor caught Sheeva glancing back at him when Kamlof mentioned his lost hometown. As saddened as he was by the memory of that loss, he was gladdened by how it had moved his fiancée to reach for knowledge beyond politics. Allor simply gave a nod for the princess to keep her focus on making the medicine. Sheeva nodded in return, and resumed her task of boiling water and grinding a root.

"So, it's still no guarantee, Doctor?" Sheeva asked in a discomforting tone.

"I'm afraid not," Kamlof replied, "but compared to where we once were with this, there's far more hope now than not."

"Do you think we'll ever find a way to completely cure it, or at least make it so that dying from it would be highly unlikely, like how it is for a normal head cold or something of the sort?"

"We've been working our way toward that over the millennia," Kamlof said in an optimistically pondering tone, "and our progress has varied from case to case as far as what ailments we've tackled since the Return. Some diseases may always be a bigger concern than others, but, more and more, we seem to be getting the hang of it. I don't know what will end up being the case for Endallian Fever, but I have hope it'll get better in time, if not to the extent you put forth. I'd certainly love for that to be the case, though."

"I'm with you there," Allor said with a sorry smile.

"Me, too," Sheeva seconded with a somber voice.

When the doctor and the princess had finished brewing the medicine, Kamlof, grabbing a cloth-wrapped meal of bread, cheese and cold meat, and a waterskin, bid farewell to the company, who had since begun to take dinner.

"Well," he said dutifully, "I'm off to do what I can; give the Greystones their doses, then their doctor, and hopefully the two of us will be able to handle it overall from there. I should be back in the morning to report the matter. Otherwise, I'll send word. Goodnight."

Those in the room bade the doctor goodnight, good luck, and good health as he left. They then quietly returned to their dinner in the tavern.

***

It was around midnight. Allor lay on his cot in the room he was sharing with his parents and the queen, king, and Sheeva. He looked up into the sky from the window above him and gazed at the bright, hairline sliver of the newly waxing moon. He could not sleep. His mind raced maddeningly over everything, from all that had happened with the Greystones to the fever and all in between.

As he stared into the night, he suddenly pricked up his ears, thinking he had heard some distant sound. Training his ears for a moment, he became more and more sure that it was the sound of someone weeping. He looked about the room as best he could, trying to make out all the people sleeping in the room. He was sure that Sheeva wasn't there, and another moment of intent listening led Allor to be certain that it was the princess he was hearing, crying just outside the inn.

Allor quietly slipped out of his cot, crept to the window, and peered down as best he could without opening it. In the light of the town's lanterns, with the stars and the hairline moon, he saw Sheeva sitting in the inn's yard at a table for outdoor diners. Her hands were buried in her face and she was shaking miserably. Perplexed and pained at the sight, Allor quietly made his way out of the room and down the stairs, through the common, and out into the yard. Sheeva didn't hear or see him approach. He stood in front of her, a few feet from the table, and called to her softly.

"Sheeva?"

The weeping stopped as Sheeva's face darted from her hands. She stared into Allor's eyes. Her eyes, a beautiful bright brown, darkened by the night, were marked with alarm, dread, and seemingly some sort of shame or self-loathing. Allor joined her at the table, sitting across from her. He offered his hands, which she gratefully took into her own.

"What's all this?" he asked worriedly.

"Oh, Al," Sheeva said tearfully, "it's just ... this whole thing. We've come all this way to put this to an end, and thanks to you, it's looking to be a peaceful close to it all. Nothing overly dramatic ... no further problems."

Allor smiled gently and caressed Sheeva's hands, but the smile vanished and his fur bristled when the princess began to grip his hands like a vise. He called out, louder than he meant, in startled pain.

"Sh-Sheeva! What's—"

"I should be glad for this," Sheeva said brokenly, "but ... there's this part of me that doesn't want it to end peacefully, that doesn't want it to end just like that."

The princess looked into Allor's eyes, then pulled her hands away and buried her face into them again.

"I-I'm horrible!" she wailed wretchedly.

"Sheeva, no," Allor said, getting up to go to Sheeva's side and hold her. "I can only imagine how you feel. For all that he put you through to be burning for four years, only to end with a relatively simple 'I'm sorry.' I think I can at least understand that much. I don't think many of us could let something like that go so easily."

"It just hurt so much, Al. Every letter I sent to him with a hope that died more each time, and every letter I got back just broke my heart further. Why didn't I say anything sooner? Why was I too weak to speak up? All of this might have been avoided—"

"Sheeva, you were doing all you could to hold onto hope that there could still be something between you two, a hope that now might just prove true after all. Not everyone would be willing to do that. I don't believe you're weak; I think it took a very special sort of strength to do that."

"But I ... I'm afraid it's broken me."

"So have others throughout time. Devora Lothaar, Frelwin Springwind ... so many others have felt that sort of feeling, the fear that such pain, such hate, would break them in the end. Some were indeed broken, never to be mended. Others were broken for a time, but they eventually proved strong enough to survive and rise above it. Devora ... she forgave those who violated her, gave strength to her husband, Konoth, and helped in founding the Temple in the days following Raakaru's expulsion when the world was broken into the most pieces. Frelwin ... well, I suppose his tale isn't as peaceful or forgiving, so maybe his isn't the best example for now. But he, too, was weathered by darkness, even broken by it for a time. But he rose up and fought for freedom, and however fiercely he may have done so, he also proved to be a very loving man of family, friends, and peace, in the end."

"But if Nikolas was just going to apologize after talking to you and his mother, and so quickly afterwards, so ... so *easily*, in the end, why would he have gone to all that trouble in the first place?"

Allor shrugged humbly. "I don't know what to say, Sheeva, other than that's Fidonity for you, at times. Just hold on, Sheeva, and forgive. I know it's harder in ways, but it's better in the end."

Sheeva lowered her head in a moment of silence, then pulled Allor closely to her.

"I love you," she said sincerely, but wearily.

"I love you, too," Allor said gently.

Before Allor could say anything else, Sheeva, having pulled her plague mask down from her muzzle, lifted Allor's mask and kissed him deeply. The two held each other in silence for a time, and once Sheeva seemed fully calmed down, Allor led her carefully back to their room, where the princess once again kissed him before they crept back into their respective beds on opposite ends of the room.

***

Allor was woken gently by his mother, Egrah, as the others in the room began to rise and dress for the day ahead. Donning robes of modest stately elegance, Allor and Egrah led the rest of the company into the dining hall for breakfast, where they were surprised to see Dr. Kamlof already at a table. Three of the Greystone guards, who seemed unafflicted, were seated with him, along with a middle-aged woman with white and brown fur who was dressed as a gardener. All were staring at their untouched food, their faces frozen in morbid shock.

Dr. Kamlof eventually turned to face the entering company. Allor caught his face, and an icy dread began to fill him. The inn became as silent as a crypt. The doctor spoke quietly and numbly.

"Everyone ... except these four ... had it pretty bad when I came in, but I got Nikolas and Lady Halla their doses, then saw to the doctor. We rushed to give the medicine to the others, then patrolled the home to make sure everyone was okay."

Kamlof numbly drank from his cup before continuing.

"The doctor and I ... we were in the main hallway when we heard panicked cries in the guardhouse. By the time we got to them, one of the guards was already dead and another was in her death throes, mask all bloody. We gave the others a little more medicine and some water, and went to check on Halla and her son."

Kamlof sighed heavily.

"Halla was dead. Then, as we went to Nikolas to give him water, he coughed up a bunch of blood ... and that was it for him, too ... just like that."

Allor stared, focused in horrid awe at the doctor's words, aware of nothing else other than the sharp grip that Sheeva's hand had on his own. Kamlof slumped onto the table as he finished.

"By the sun's rising, all who had it were dead. Their doctor, their priestess, Nikolas's tutor, all but the three guards and the gardener here. They're ... all gone."

A Crisis in Bravagoth

31
11/4/4016 G.M.

SHEEVA stood petrified at the news, her hand gripping Allor's with near-crushing tightness. A moment passed, and then Sheeva, becoming conscious of her grip on her fiancé's hand, let go, only to then embrace him and weep quietly on his shoulder. The king and queen came to their side and embraced them, alongside Egrah and Alphaar, as the rest of the company silently made their way to tables in the common to sit and reflect on what they just heard. Dr. Kamlof rose and left the inn to inform the mayor. At last the princess, her tears subsiding, breathed deeply and looked to her mother and father.

"What are we going to do now?" she asked sorrowfully.

"Well," said the queen, "we'll need to call for an election to determine the founders of another south warden line, and soon. But, first things first. We need to lay them to rest."

"I can't believe that all those who had it are dead," Sheeva said with shocked numbness. "It's hard enough that the two of them are dead, when I just saw them yesterday. But eleven people ... in that house ... all of them."

"I know," Talrah said sadly. "I know." The queen turned to Allor, who still held Sheeva closely. "Allor? Are you alright?"

"As alright as I can be, I suppose," Allor said numbly. "It does make me think of Nelahaal ... of home, I suppose."

Allor lifted Sheeva's chin, his dark brown eyes shining intensely into hers.

"I cannot tell you how I feel, when I think of how the loss of my home to the fever moved you to study medicine ... even if only a little when compared to a dedicated physician. Besides that, your compassion shames me. Be strong in it, Sheeva, and don't let it be twisted by whatever pains you've had in life. And don't blame yourself. You tried to help them, you and Dr. Kamlof both."

The princess rested her head numbly on Allor's shoulder, wanting to cry, but unable.

King Samuel put a hand on both Sheeva and Allor's shoulders. "We'll sort this out later," he said consolingly, though he, too, was clearly numb with shock. "We shouldn't try to take this day on with an empty stomach."

All in the company were quietly having their breakfast when suddenly Dr. Kamlof burst into the tavern along with the mayor of Oakhall. Everyone looked up worriedly as the two raced up to the table where the queen and king sat. The mayor urgently handed them a parchment.

"This came from Genverdell," he announced, "having originally been sent from the town of Bravagoth on the south highway. The message is three days old. The Faithguard at the archtemple were informed as well, and have already sent out a company of knights."

"Thank you, sir," the queen replied with anxious courtesy. "I trust that Kamlof has explained–"

"Yes! Yes! There isn't time for you to see to that now!" the mayor said frightfully. "Read it!"

Sheeva watched her mother and father read the message, their faces growing more horrified as they neared the letter's end. The two leaders then bolted from the table, setting Sheeva and Allor to jolt in their seats.

"Everyone!" cried the queen. "Grab some food, take it with you, and be ready to ride as soon as you can! Guards! We must call on you to go beyond defending our own persons, as Bravagoth will need you! Let's go! LET'S GO!"

Everyone began to scramble, confused but dutiful, toward the horses, carriages, and wagons in the stable, taking positions for a frantic ride.

King Samuel turned to the mayor.

"Our thanks to you," he said, "but I must ask if we might take a portion of your guard. This sudden turn leaves us uncertain as to how many–"

"Of course, my king!" the mayor said. "How many?"

"Would a third be too many?"

"Take half."

"Thank you, sir. And send word that we call for soldiers from Genverdell as well!"

"Yes, my king!"

The mayor then ran off to call the garrison. With the queen already having rushed out the door, the king turned to his daughter and future son-in-law. Offering a hand to each, he helped the still-startled pair get up from the table and out the door.

"Some necromancer, or maybe more than one, has risen all the dead from the cemetery of the town of Bravagoth. Whoever's responsible must still be in the area, because the dead keep coming back if they have not been completely destroyed. That letter was calling for us to send help, any help. But since they obviously didn't know where we were … we simply need to go and see for ourselves."

As the three approached their horses and mounted up, the king continued, his voice clearly carrying fear and worry.

"Stay close to us and do what we say when we get there, both of you. We've no idea how exactly it will be when we get there, but there's no sugarcoating it: this is very dangerous. This isn't at all ideal, us going there ourselves, but we can't just go back and we can't just stay here, not with it being the way it is. We'll have to pay our respects to the Greystones after this is settled, but we need to go *now*, understand?"

"Y-yes, father," Sheeva stammered, with Allor simply nodding.

King Samuel, Sheeva, and Allor trotted swiftly to the town's west gate alongside Egrah and Alphaar, rejoining the queen and the rest of the company as half of Oakhall's guard joined them. With no further word other than repeated thanks between the monarchs and the mayor, the company rode off as fast as it could.

Sheeva, riding out of the gate with her parents and fiancé, looked back onto the town and distant estate of the late Nikolas and Halla. She caught sight of a tree that stood just beside the town gate, and what she saw beneath its branches made her blood run cold.

In the tree's shade stood the shadow of Raakmathna, her face twisted in a hideous, knowing grin.

32

11/8/4016 G.M.

LERANNU leaned against the desk that had been pushed against the front doors of town hall, exhausted from the week-long siege of the undead. Zalden was beside her, as was her mother, who had managed to send word to the capital of the sudden swarm of risen dead that now besieged the homes of Bravagoth. Their groans and screeches had filled the air, day and night, for the past seven days as they ceaselessly patrolled the streets and buildings they had overrun before the occupants could react.

The sixteen-year-old mage and those with her were lucky, for the three were having lunch in the front office of town hall. They had been discussing the potential future of Zalden's relationship with Lerannu when they heard screaming and shouting from outside. A quick look out the window was all that was needed to realize what was happening, seeing a skeleton dig its claws into a poor traveler's throat, and the three were quick in securing the building as best they could. Following that, Mayor Sarah dashed upstairs to her private study, took her heraldwing out of its cage, and wrote a message for Genverdell. She sent a request for soldiers from the capital, fearing whatever help that might come from nearby towns wouldn't be enough for the magnitude of the crisis. She then sent the heraldwing flying, and coming back down to her daughter and Zalden, stated that all they could do was hold out and wait for help.

The three had received no word as to the welfare of those outside Lerannu's home, and this, along with the unending moans from the rapidly shambling corpses and the anxious waiting for help, had set all three on the edge of despair. They had not been able to get any good sleep for a week. Lerannu constantly fretted over the unknown fate of Zalden's parents and her teacher, Ahvrom. Her mother and Zalden did their utmost to calm her, but they began to sound more distressed themselves as the week dragged on. She frequently held tightly to Zalden, whom she had now been officially courting for a year. Despite having had a tense relationship with her mother in the years following her father's departure, Lerannu now often looked at her with earnest trust. She resolved to try and become closer with her mother after this horror ended, if the two of them made it through.

After a week had passed, sleep deprivation took its toll on Lerannu. She had her worst bout of fear and anxiety yet, this time fully breaking down into weeping. Zalden held her closely, and Sarah, her typically hardened face and tone having softened with each passing day of the crisis, drew them both to her in a caring embrace.

"It's been a week, now," she said, sounding as though she were just as desperate to assure herself as she was her daughter and Zalden. "Help from Genverdell should be here soon ... anytime now."

"I just don't know how much more I can stand," Lerannu sobbed wearily. "I feel like my heart's going to give out soon if this keeps up. What if–"

Lerannu's words stopped short and her heart began to race when suddenly, almost as if on cue by Sarah's words, a horn sounded from just beyond the town's northeast gate, followed by a great thundering of many hooves. The three ran to the window, each sighing in exhausted relief at the scene that began to play out before them.

A large company of Faithguards, followed by a collection of guards from several towns and even what appeared to be several members of the royal guard, rode into Bravagoth from the south highway and began charging through the roads that branched from it. Several of the reanimated corpses were cut down as one of the rescuers galloped by, while others were trampled to pieces beneath the charging horses. Other knights and guards, having made a round or two of the area, had now dismounted and begun to comb Bravagoth on foot, their weapons at the ready. They wasted no time in cutting down and dismembering any undead they encountered.

A pair of Faithguards, Konothian Knights, dismounted in front of town hall and immediately became the subject of fascinated focus for the three barricaded within. One of them was a middle-aged woman of Kason heritage, her warm brown fur glowing in the early afternoon light. She was clearly the senior of the two, and judging from her armor and the color of her surcoat, may have been the leader of the mission itself. The other, who must have been her squire, was a young Zaron girl, her age by Lerannu's guess being thirteen at the oldest. The girl looked about the town with her axe and buckler at the ready, her face bearing the clashing feelings of determined courage and undeniable fear. Lerannu guessed this was her first mission, and watched with bated breath as the two huddled briefly beside their horse and spoke to each other. The pair pointed at various spots of town they could see from where they stood, and then, readying their axes and little shields, began to steadily make their way down the road side by side.

The barricaded spectators jolted when a sudden cacophony of screeches sounded all around them from outside. The greater part of the noise felt to be coming from their right, and seeing the knight and her squire brace and look intently in the direction of the street that ran by town hall, the viewers gasped and held their breath as five corpses bolted toward the duo. The decaying horrors had gotten hold of some farm tools that they now used as weapons and charged the two Faithguards with their spades and scythes raised to strike. Lerannu, Sarah, and Zalden exhaled in awe as the two put down the five foes with ease. Even the squire, shaking as she was, was decisive in her strikes with the axe.

The three viewers screamed, however, when they saw three more corpses suddenly dash from the road at their left and onto the highway, charging the pair from behind. The two rescuers were so caught up in the battle before them that they had failed to see or hear the rapidly approaching fiends. Two of the undead wretches had pitchforks, ready to try and skewer the knights from behind, while the third had a wood-axe raised in both bony hands above its rotting head. Lerannu's mind raced, quickly recalling a spell that Ahvrom had just recently taught her.

The Arrow of Vente.

Yelling for Zalden and her mother to back away from the window, Lerannu stood stiff and straight, feet apart, and rapidly mimicked the drawing and aiming of a bow and arrow. Her mind filled with images of the Angel of Wind and her longbow as the currents of air, drawn from the room around her, rapidly filled her hands. She aimed her sight onto the three corpses, which were now nearly upon the knights. As her ears began to ring and her sight began to narrow into a tunnel, she gestured the release of an arrow. The body of air shot from her hands. The window shattered into a hundred pieces as the violent gust blasted through it. The arrow of wind flew out to the highway. The knight-commander turned and yelled just as the undead reached them. The squire rapidly spun around in response, and raised her axe and buckler frantically. The bolt of air hit its marks, tearing through the undead trio like a gale through fallen leaves.

The young mage, her head pounding and spinning, managed to see the knight and squire look directly at her through the shattered window as she began to slump onto her buckling knees. Zalden and Sarah helped Lerannu up as the two Faithguards made their way to the front porch of town hall. They approached the window and carefully climbed through into the reception room. The brown-furred commander nodded to Lerannu, whose lightly blurring sight was set on the squire, who stared at her with a solemn gaze of awe and thanks. Lerannu noticed that the girl had a very unique-looking Uqua pendant about her neck, one that seemed to be made of white marble and black jet.

"My undying thanks to you, young mage," said the commander chivalrously. "We may well not be speaking to you now if it weren't for your help."

"We should be thanking you, Lady Knight," said Lerannu, quivering from the exhaustion of a week's lack of sleep and the casting of such an intensive spell. "I dread to think of how we'd all be if you and your company were even a little longer in arriving."

Her mother and Zalden, each bearing her by a shoulder, concurred. The knight and squire then leaned out the window, looking about the town from the view they could capture and holding up their ears intently for several minutes. Finally, the commander turned back to the three.

"It appears that the town is well on its way to being secured," she stated, "if it hasn't been already. On top of that, given that you now have a window that can't be closed, and trying to block it might leave you vulnerable in the meantime if there's any stragglers about, I feel that I must strongly advise you to come with us. We're all to make our way to the square, by the oak, when things seem to be more or less secured, so that we can try to figure out what has happened and find out who or what is responsible." The knight then focused on Lerannu's mother. "This is the town hall and mayoral residence, is it not? Are you the mayor, or was this simply the nearest place for you take shelter when this all started?"

"I am the mayor," Sarah said with a nod. "The three of us were already in here when it started, thankfully. Blocking out the undead was relatively easy for us."

"All the more reason for you to come with us," said the knight. "We, the Faithguard and the queen and king, will want to hear whatever you know about the situation since the town is in your charge."

Sarah was taken aback. "Th-the queen and king are here?"

"We just met up with them this morning, just a little way from here. They were in Oakhall earlier, talking to the south wardeness over something or other, and didn't get the message you sent until it was redirected from Genverdell. The steward they left in charge received it and informed the archtemple in addition to rerouting your message. We rode as hard as we could and met up with the royal company just a short way from here, and then joined forces to help secure the town. We'll definitely need to speak with you, so it's just as well that you come with us."

Sarah looked at her daughter and Zalden, took each in hand, and nodded to the knight.

"Very well," she said. "We're right behind you."

The mayor's voice trailed off as she looked at her daughter, who swayed as she struggled to stay standing.

"You two wouldn't happen to have some Kamgenbew with you, in one of your packs or something? I know it's mostly used by mages, but sometimes other people–"

"Just grab some from my room," Lerannu cut in feebly as she pointed to the door behind her. "It'll be in the armoire by the bed, bottommost drawer ... under some clothes ... next to a pillowcase with ... things in it."

Lerannu, not turning her head, looked up to her mother from the corner of her eye and winced at the injured look she saw in her eyes. It was uncomfortable enough to admit that she had to secretly get a small supply of the energizing tonic and hide it. Her mother had constantly voiced her worries that she might become dependent on it if she got any. The young mage dreaded to think of what might happen if Sarah learned of the reclaimed feathers and bowl shards.

The grey-furred squire, at a nod from her mentor, hurried into Lerannu's room, returning quickly with a case of several vials.

"How many do you need?" she asked.

"Just one," Lerannu answered. "Thank you."

Having drained the dose of blue liquid, Lerannu quickly regained the ability to stand with slightly tremoring legs. She took her mother's hand and followed the two Faithguards outside with Zalden at her side.

They reached the oak in the square without further incident, and Lerannu looked in awe at the amassed army of Faithguard knights, guards of various towns and the royalty, and the surviving townspeople who had made their way to the square from their shelters. Zalden, giving Lerannu a quick kiss, ran to his mother and father, who were calling out to him from under the oak in tearful joy. The two Faithguards strode up to the king and queen and began to make their report. Lerannu embraced her mother lightly.

"I'm sorry I hid it from you," the young mage said tiredly. "It's just that—"

"You were right to," said Sarah calmly. "If there were more undead, we might have needed your magic again. And if you didn't have any of those tonics, or if those two didn't ..." Sarah sighed deeply. "Lera, I know it's been hard for you these past few years, and I could've done better about ... everything. Your father ... I could've handled that better, and I could've done better to support your studies, trust your teacher more. I—"

"Don't worry about it, Mother," Lerannu said, hugging her closely. "It's been a hard time for you, too."

The two looked on for a moment, then approached the king and queen when they beckoned them to come forward. The mayor, with the knight-commander and the king and queen, began discussing the incident, asking and answering questions in turn. Also in the conversing company was a young royalty member whom Lerannu presumed to be the princess, and a young Zaron man, who seemed to be her suitor. He stood by her side along with presumably his parents. Lerannu, seeing that none of the conversation concerned her, stepped back and looked on, taking note of who was among the crowd of surviving townsfolk.

Lerannu suddenly felt a small tap on her shoulder. She turned around to see it was the young Faithguard squire.

"Thank you, again," the trainee said with a bow. "I-I was pretty scared the whole time back there when we first came into town, but when Commander Hanye and I turned and saw those three right behind us, I thought that might've been it for us. I was really scared, then."

"You were very brave, though," Lerannu commended her, "and if it weren't for you two and your company, who knows how it might've gone here? So, thank you, too. What's your name, young knight?"

"Ruth."

Lerannu looked at the young squire, smiling as she saw her quietly beam with fulfilment. "Is this your first mission, Ruth? I didn't think they started taking squires along on things like this until they were a bit older than you, unless I guessed your age wrong."

"This is my first mission, my lady, and I'm eleven right now. You're right; I normally wouldn't have been here unless I was a bit older, but this whole thing came up so suddenly and a lot of knights were suddenly calling for squires. We were offered a chance to go. There are several other squires about as old as me here, too. Hanye–Commander Hanye–she was training us and took me along."

"I take it she's a good friend of yours and not just your teacher?"

"Yes, my lady."

"I can tell a similar story about my magic teacher. It's always good when a teacher can be a friend."

"Mm-hm!" the squire hummed with a vigorous nod of the head.

Lerannu heard a small clinking sound about the squire's neck as she nodded her agreement, and her eyes fell onto the amulet once again.

"That's a very beautiful Uqua pendant."

"Th-thank you," the squire said bashfully, suddenly staring at the ground.

"That's not a normal one from the Temple, is it? Or are they doing something different with them now?"

"No, it's ... it's my friend's. His mother had it before him, and his father made it for her. They gave it to my friend when ... when they died."

"It must mean a lot to him, then."

"Yes, it does."

Lerannu, at first moved by the initial story of the amulet, began to smile impishly. "So it must be very special for him to give it to you. A gentleman giving a token to his knight and lady, perhaps?"

The blush was visible beneath the girl's grey fur. She chuckled shyly. "That's what everyone keeps saying. I ... I don't know what to think; he's been like a brother to me, and he gave this to me right before we rode off to ..."

Ruth's voice trailed off and Lerannu saw that she was looking intently behind her. Lerannu looked back, a creeping sense of dread beginning to take hold as she saw Ahvrom's house and a shadow slinking by the window. She looked back to the squire.

"Excuse me," Ruth said quickly as she ran to those gathered at the oak, calling the commander's attention and pointing to the house. Lerannu saw her mother look in the direction the squire was pointing. Sarah's eyes widened and snapped alarmingly to her daughter's. Shaking, Lerannu's hands rose unbidden to her mouth as she fought back her sobs. The young mage watched with dread as the commander, with Ruth at her side, signaled her fellow knights to surround the home as she, Ruth, and two other knights approached the door, two to each side. With the four in position at the door, each nodding to one another, the commander suddenly pulled the door open.

"Oh, Onu," Lerannu prayed, "please let it not be that—"

The commander and the other three Faithguards pulled away from the door with a shout of alarm. A large ball of flame flew out from the doorway and, missing the knights, went right into the scurrying crowd gathered at the oak, crashing and exploding into the tree. Many screams followed, and a man and woman wailed.

Lerannu ran toward the crowd, catching sight of the blaze that burned at the foot of the oak. She froze in her tracks, mouth falling open but with only a scream of silence pouring out.

A charred figure lay against the tree, thrown to it by the force of the fireball's blast.

It wore Zalden's jacket.

Lerannu fainted, the effects of her tonic having vanished in an instant.

33

11/11/4016 G.M.

SHEEVA stood beside the king and queen, along with Allor and his parents, as all looked on at the execution of the necromancer who had terrorized the town of Bravagoth.

Once it was certain that all the undead had been put down, collected, and burned, and those killed by the undead had been accounted for, the trial was very swift, commencing the very evening of their arrival into town. The arrested necromancer, Ahvrom Salinoth, was rushed into the courthouse along with all others present. He confessed immediately and showed next to no remorse, apart from how it affected his pupil, Lerannu, who was also the daughter of the town's mayor. Sheeva and her parents oversaw the whole process alongside the mayor and the town judge.

When asked for a motive, Ahvrom stated that it was to make a point on the handling of necromancy, specifically calling back to an incident a few years ago when his wife had reanimated their daughter's corpse out of grief.

"What Dalle did was a grave sin against nature," he said, "but she meant no harm to anyone. Her motive for the crime, severe and vile as it was, was only that of a broken, grieving mother. She was willing to accept the punishment that was due, but she didn't deserve to be skewered like a wild animal."

"She drew a dagger, Ahvrom!" Mayor Sarah said exasperatingly. "She looked like she was going to attack! The guard panicked and defended himself!"

"She was going to put Kiiva down herself!" Ahvrom yelled. "She would've gone peacefully if she were just allowed to have that one little sense of being able to have things done on her terms, no matter how delusional it might have been! That was the whole reason she did it in the first place; she just couldn't let her go then! It didn't justify her actions, but—"

"How do you *know* she was only doing it for that," Sarah asked, "and that she would've gone peacefully if she could've seen to Kiiva herself? Did you know what she was doing all along?"

"No, Sarah," Ahvrom said with bitter weariness, "I didn't, as I've told you a hundred times."

"Then how can you know her intentions with absolute certainty? She made a pact with a *demon*, Ahvrom, a being whose sole purpose is to serve Raakaru's will by contributing to the destruction and enslavement of Fidonity by whatever means it can devise. She might not have meant anything else, and she might not have even been truly possessed, but that demon did have a hold on her, and wouldn't have let it end so easily if it could've done anything about it. That's how demons are, and there's no excuse for it in the end. When all is said and done, she did no differently than you have done, and what you've done doesn't make a point to exercise differing treatment for necromancers on some case-by-case basis. Not in my eyes, at any rate. If it were up to me, I'd have them put down on sight, no attempts at arrest or trial, because there's *no* form of this revolting craft that doesn't invoke the powers of Raakhaal. Only the Onu-blessed efforts of the most devout Fidons, the ashes or tears of a Phoenix, a drink from Vitahla's flask, or the sole divine will of Onu himself can truly bring the dead back to life. Any other means is befouled by the hands of demons and those who would collude with them. You *know* that, as did she."

Ahvrom shrugged numbly. His voice began to break. "I suppose it doesn't matter, anyway. I ... I guess I didn't have enough to keep me going, in the end. I tried ... I tried to find strength and solace in teaching your daughter ... but in the end, I guess it just wasn't enough for me."

The necromancer gazed about the crowded courthouse, eventually finding his apprentice who glared at him with eyes overflowing with both disgust and grief.

"Lera," said Ahvrom, "I'm so sorry it ended up this way. I lost Kiiva, then Dalle ... and then your mother just kept putting salt in my wounds. Every time that she had the guards come and search my house, just because of what happened ..."

A horrible, rattling sob passed the necromancer's lips that set Sheeva's fur to bristling. Taking a deep, heaving breath, Ahvrom bore his eyes into Lerannu's.

"I've lost everything. And if she wasn't going to trust me anyway—"

Two shoes flew from the crowd and struck the necromancer in the face.

"YOU BASTARD!" Ahvrom's apprentice screamed. "I trusted you! How long have you been planning all this?"

Ahvrom held a hand to his mouth, pressing onto his lip, which one of the shoes had managed to split. "About a year."

Lerannu began to cry inconsolably. "Y-you planned it for a year? All-all that t-time you taught me ... What was going through your mind while you were ..."

"It's all still true, Lera," Ahvrom said with a sad calmness. "Just ... just don't fall into what I have—"

"I-I won't, but it won't be because you said so," the young mage said, her voice torn between sadness and rage. "You-you killed Zalden! And so many others! For what? Were you meaning to go down fighting?!"

"Yes. Of course I was. It was meant to be another part of my point. Besides all—"

Before anyone could react, Lerannu bolted from the crowd and leapt onto the stand where Ahvrom stood. She began pummeling him, screaming like a banshee.

"To Raakhaal with your points, you monster! You were one of the few people who made my life better after Kiiva died and father left! Now you've taken almost all of that away! Mother is all I have, now! Just ... Just ..."

Having been pulled off the necromancer, the apprentice, her strength clearly fading, wheeled around and bolted out of the courthouse, wailing like the damned.

The trial ended shortly afterwards, with the execution set for three days after. All the while that Sheeva watched the trial, the princess saw, in both the necromancer and Lerannu, what she felt to be pain so close to what had driven her to her own darkness. The dreadful whispers in her mind and heart had been unending for the past ten days, and seeing what had happened in this town, she now vied more than ever to convince herself that she could overcome it. Or, at the very least, that she could avoid being utterly consumed by it as the necromancer had been.

"I will not be ruled by a demon," she thought as the trial concluded. "I did what I did on my own, not with the demon's help, and I will not let it control me. It's past, and now I will look to make my future, my country, and my world better. I have done evil, but that isn't all that I am."

"Try saying that to Onu, dear princess," said the sneering voice of Raakmathna.

Sheeva's heart began to pound, the blood in her veins racing ice-cold within her. She saw it, standing in the shadows in the back of the far side of the courtroom. "You can try to amend for it, but Onu will not have it. You may as well just go ahead and side with my master and me. You will be on the side that will *actually* set things to order in the end."

"I will not!" Sheeva screamed internally. "Begone!"

The shadow dispersed, but not without some parting words. "We *will* see each other again, Sheeva. You can be sure of that."

Now, with the time of the necromancer's execution at hand, the princess looked levelly at Ahvrom as he was brought into the town square. The fallen mage was effortlessly pressed down onto his knees and lowered to the chopping block that had been placed before the partially charred oak in the square.

"Ahvrom Salinoth," said the mayor as the executioner readied his sword, "are there any final words you wish to say?"

"None," the necromancer said numbly.

"Then prepare yourself, necromancer, for you will now be sent to face Onu and whatever he wills for you."

Sheeva stared at the necromancer. "I will not let myself become like this man," she vowed to herself and her Maker, her inner voice breaking with sorrow and dread with each passing word. "I will not let my pains rule me ... not again. It happened once, and I will *never* do it again. I swear it to you, Onu. From this day forth, I will do all I can to make Enmayar, nay, all of Fidonhaal, a better place as best I can. I'll continue to study medicine as best I can, and help those who study it in full. I'll help the poor, try to find a way to give them better prospects; such a task should not fall only to the Temple, after all. I'll do whatever I can think to try and make things better, and pray that I might amend for what I've done. I—"

The princess's inner ponderings and vows were interrupted by the deathly whistle of the executioner's blade, and the sickening thud of the necromancer's severed head hitting the ground.

"I will *not* go down the same sort of path as this man," Sheeva repeated. "Not again."

***

The royal company stayed in Bravagoth for the remainder of the week, the Faithguard having since departed to return to Genverdell, and the guards of Oakhall and other settlements they met along the way having left for their respective towns. On the following Setmay, the day they were planning to leave, Sheeva sat beside her mother and father as they talked with Mayor Stonefaith over afternoon tea. They offered their condolences for the town's tragedy, along with a few other things.

"We're sorry, and completely understand if this is a bad time to ask," said Queen Talrah gently, "but, we've spoken to many of the people here about the situation and your leadership in its aftermath, as well as your performance as mayor overall. It's been very positive from what we've heard. Would you consider being on the ballot as a founder for a new line of south wardens?"

Sheeva watched the mayor just barely manage to swallow her tea.

"Is it really that bad with Lady Greystone?" Sarah asked. "I heard rumors, and there was that stunt she pulled earlier with that election call, but—"

"We haven't yet told everyone of what has happened in Oakhall," King Samuel cut in. "We've been so caught up with what's happened here."

The queen, king, and princess each did their part in telling the mayor of the happenings in Oakhall. When they had finished, Sarah stared into her now-empty teacup somberly.

"Onu's Four Breaths," she said at length, "you all sure have been preoccupied with death and sadness these past couple of weeks." She looked at them, collected herself, and breathed deeply before returning to the original proposal. "I am honored that you would suggest for me to try for the title, and I'm open to it. When do I need to register?"

"We'll begin that at the start of the New Year," said the queen. "We still need to pay our respects to Halla and her son properly, and with Sardonmay being just around the corner, we'll have our hands full for a time. We'll have our advisors oversee the ward in the meantime."

"Thank you for the offer and your continued assistance," said the mayor. "If I end up becoming a wardeness, I hope I won't disappoint."

The four passed a few moments silently as they finished their tea. Then Sheeva, finding herself to be musing over the mayor's absent daughter, spoke up.

"Where is your daughter ... Lerannu, isn't it? Is she here?"

Sarah sighed sadly, nodding to the door behind the princess. "She's in there," she said softly. "I don't know what to do when it comes to her. I've been torn over her learning magic, especially from Ahvrom, ever since the incident with his wife and daughter, and I've tried to limit her practice and involvement of related things when outside the Mage Society. But ... her magic helped people during the attack. I wish I had acted differently ... supported her better. I intend to do so from now on, presuming that her spirit for the craft hasn't been completely broken."

The princess looked intently at the queen and king. "How long has it been since we've had a court mage on retainer?"

Talrah and Samuel's eyebrows raised in surprise, followed by approving smiles.

"It's been a good while," said the king, looking earnestly at Sarah. "If your daughter is willing to finish her training and get her credentials from the Society, we'd be happy to have her with us, whether you ended up being south wardeness or not. From what you told us and from what we saw, the poor girl needs something good to come her way, and we'll offer it if—"

The door behind Sheeva creaked open, and the four looked to see Lerannu standing in the doorway. She was withered by grief, but her eyes hinted at a spark rekindling within her.

"I'll do it, if you'll have me," she said tiredly, but with clear resolve. The young mage looked at her mother, exchanging nods with her before turning back to the king and queen. "But ... I'm not sure how I'll go about studying the last stretch of it, with Ahvrom and Dalle both gone now."

"We have a very good chapterhouse of the Society in the capital," the queen said encouragingly. "Perhaps you can come with us, you and your mother both, and celebrate Sardonmay with us in Genverdell? You'll be able to see what the Society's like over there while you're with us, and the two of you can stay with us and finish your education there if you'd like."

The mayor and her daughter looked intently at each other, and once again exchanged nods.

"We'll need to make arrangements," said Sarah, "and I fear we may have to miss Sardonmay with you for the time we'll need. I'll need to make sure my advisors know what needs to be done while I'm gone, and we'll ... need to see to the funerals. But yes, we'd be honored to take you up on your invitation. Thank you, your majesties."

The royal company soon prepared to depart, and began making their way back to Oakhall and then Genverdell.

34

12/12/4016 G.M.

ALLOR let out a sigh of relief as they reached the top of the hill and Genverdell came into clear view from the carriage's window. It had been a long ride covering the nine hundred miles back to the capital. The whole company displayed both weariness from the past month's events and rekindled anticipation of the festivities to come. They had made it with just over a fortnight to spare.

The royal company had stopped at Oakhall along the way. They had resolved to spend a full day at the town, which had been cleared of concerns over the fever shortly after they left for Bravagoth. They took their time in paying respects to the Greystones and to inform the town of the impending election for the future south warden or wardeness. When they reached the Greystones' family tomb, which had been resealed since the interment of Halla and Nikolas, the royal company gazed at it in long silence. Sheeva, who seemed the most distraught by the whole turn of events, as well as the incident in Bravagoth, stared numbly at the likenesses of Valor, Halla, and Nikolas, which had been hewn into the vault's doors by a sculptor. The image, though not yet finished, was detailed enough for the scene to be clear. It showed the family, hand-in-hand, as they were led aboard the ship bound for Onuhaal by the angels Morinaar and Vitahla.

The princess had been almost completely silent, at least from Allor's experience, ever since Dr. Kamlof told the company of the Greystones' deaths. The execution of the necromancer seemed to stamp Sheeva's face with the countenance of one lost in the depths of morbid fixation. Allor had frequently tried to construct something, anything, to say to her in consolation. Between the jarring urgency of the ride to Bravagoth and his own macabre ponderings, his mind had been overtaken to the point where any words felt utterly inadequate.

Now, with the journey's end in sight, along with the promise of impending festivities that rekindled a sense of joy despite the company's weariness, Allor resolved to say something, no matter how simple. He took the princess's hand as they rode together in the carriage and gently brushed his thumb across her palm.

"Well," he said with a heavy sigh, "this certainly didn't go as I had hoped."

Sheeva's eyes displayed a torrent of emotions and thoughts that Allor could not fully fathom. Tears began to flow from them, but her mouth formed a sad smile, and a soft laugh passed her lips.

"No," she said with a sound that was a cross between a laugh and a sob, "it certainly didn't."

Sheeva kissed Allor gently, fully, on the lips, and rested her head on his shoulder. Allor looked at his parents and the king and queen, who rode in the carriage with them. They were looking at the pair with smiles of hope, though their eyes also displayed other thoughts and worries, not the least of which, he figured, was what to do in the aftermath of the Greystones' deaths. Allor looked at each in turn, then, following a moment of silence, asked what was to be done next.

"Celebrate Sardonmay, of course," said the queen. "After that, we'll just have to take it a day at a time. We suggested to the mayor from Bravagoth, Sarah Stonefaith, that she become a candidate for south wardeness, and she said she would try for it. It's certainly a big leap for her, but the townspeople said very promising things about her and I'd like to think she could manage if she gained the title. There's also her daughter, who Sheeva suggested might be a mage for the court if she desired and finished her education. They might not make it in time to have Sardonmay with us, but we've invited them both to live with us, at least for a while, whatever ends up happening. Whoever ends up with the position of leading South Ward, things should begin to settle down again in the coming months. There is also the trouble in Kellmayar, and what has been pinned to us on the matter. We'll likely be trying to sort that out in the coming months as well, though I fear it may very well be a matter that takes some years instead of months. Samuel and I ... we don't know how this will all fare in the time to come, but we want to settle all we can before passing the reigns to you two."

"I see," said Allor, his mind becoming burdened very quickly.

"But don't trouble yourself with all that now," said Talrah, clearly reading Allor's face. "Rest up, both of you. After all this, I'd love to see the two of you dance this evening ... and be happy again."

Allor and Sheeva laughed lightly, then, resting their heads together, soon dozed off, not being roused until they reached the castle.

Achievement and Reflection

35
12/28/4016 G.M.

DONOVAN sat beside his father, Jonathan, and Jak. The three were having an intermission of food and drink by the great hearth in the crammed Three Widows Tavern, preparing for the special performance they had planned right before midnight.

Jonathan had been persuaded to take up the drum in the years following his and Donovan's decision to take the old highlander bard into their home. It allowed him to partake in his son's blossoming career with his mentor. The three had since grown as close as family, with both father and son now calling the bard "Uncle Jak." It was the eve of Sardonmay, and the traditional rites had been tended to hours ago. Midnight was near at hand, and the feasting was still going at full momentum. It had been that way since the start of the festivities, with everyone having rushed to the taverns immediately after the starting ceremony due to the exceptionally cold winds of winter's approach. Besides the merriment that abounded in the town's taverns, the cold alone had done a lot to keep the revelers from going out. It said a lot for how particularly cold the day was, especially for the natives of Sorrenar.

Donovan, chewing on a savory bite of roasted pork, was still grinning at the memory of the three entering the tavern ahead of the crowds, both to prepare for the coming performances and to hurry out of the cold once the ceremony had finished. Uncle Jak had barged past them and into the tavern, striding swiftly to the hearth and leaning toward the fire. His pelvis arched toward the fire as he grasped the mantle with both hands to steady himself. The innkeeper and servers all averted their eyes, trying their hardest to keep from grinning, and Donovan and his father struggled to keep from laughing at the sight.

"Hoi," the old bard said breathlessly, "that icy wind is far too much fer mah nethers! Ah hate tae think how those in the highlands are farin'!"

"You folks have only yourselves to blame," Donovan laughed as his father grabbed their instruments from the barkeep, who had held them for safekeeping from the weather. "You all are the ones who insist on wearing those kilts like that! Where's all that heat you folks are notorious for claiming to have down there? I thought that's the reason you give for the kilts in the first place! I suppose it must cool a bit with age ..."

Both father and son laughed uproariously as the grizzled old bard, having taken both hands off the mantle, tossed the fig in their direction with one hand while lightly lifting the front of his kilt toward the fire with the other. While his father rested the instruments in the seats they had reserved by the fire, Donovan quietly got a horn of warmed mead from the giggling barkeep and took it over to Uncle Jak. He held it out to the old bard as he sighed a stream of oaths from under his breath. The bard, turning his head to his apprentice and grinning, took the peace offering, had a draught, and tussled the lad's white, braided hair. Jonathan, having placed the instruments according to the seating arrangement, proceeded to grab a few platefuls of food, and flagons of mead and light cider. He put them on the small table in front of the three chairs.

"The crowds are starting to pour in now," said Jonathan, his statement instantly confirmed by the influx of droning voices, which swiftly grew from a small trickle to a rushing torrent. "Better have something before we start; it'll be a while before we'll get to have another go at the tables."

The three ate their early supper, the first of several more helpings that eventually came, and upon finishing, thanked the tavern's mass of patrons for their attendance and patience. The crowd responded with cheers and eager requests. The three played into the night, sharing in the merriment of the crowds, and when at last midnight drew near, they looked at one another and exchanged nods to confirm they were ready. Uncle Jak signaled to Jonathan, who beat his drum loudly and rapidly to gain the throng's attention.

"Thank ye all fer yer ears an' cheers, as always," the old bard said, with the crowd responding with applauds of revelry. "We near the true beginnin' o' winter now, an' tae celebrate the moment, the three o' us would like tae play fer ye a new song that our youngest here, young Mr. Donny-vin, wrote fer the occasion. This'll be his first time performin' it tae more than his daddy an' Ah. What ye say? Care tae listen?"

The tavern boomed with eager applause. Donovan looked to his father and the bard, then closed his eyes and drew a deep breath. He gently plucked the strings of Jak's harp, which the old bard had lent him for the occasion, to cue the beginning of the song. Jak strummed the mandolin, and Jonathan set the song's slow, steady beat with the drum. Donovan breathed deeply once more and began to sing the first chorus and lines of his first composed song. His father and Uncle Jak accompanied him on the following choruses.

> *The land falls asleep in winter's embrace,*
> *To rest until the return of spring's grace.*
> *So, come again, Sardoth, come again, friend,*
> *And watch the land as you usher the end*
> *Of autumn's hold, and the return of cold*
> *And thus partake in life's endless turnings.*
> *When you arrive, many things pass away,*
> *But other things come, and in their place stay*
> *Until their own turn comes to pass away.*
> *But none of these passings are forever,*
> *For in Onu's sight, full death comes never,*
> *And all things good dwell with him forever.*
> *The land falls asleep in winter's embrace,*
> *To rest until the return of spring's grace.*
> *So, come again, Sardoth, come again, friend,*
> *And watch the land as you usher the end*
> *Of autumn's hold, and the return of cold*
> *And thus partake in life's endless turnings.*
> *Your time, Sardoth, heralds many endings,*
> *But a time there is for everything,*
> *And ends always mark a new beginning.*
> *The losses I've had have turned into gains;*
> *I keep that to heart whenever in pain*
> *And trust what I've lost, I'll one day regain.*
> *The land falls asleep in winter's embrace,*
> *To rest until the return of spring's grace.*
> *So, come again, Sardoth, come again, friend,*
> *And watch the land as you usher the end*
> *Of autumn's hold, and the return of cold*
> *And thus partake in life's endless turnings.*

The crowd thundered with applause, and Donovan became filled with the same wholeness of the soul that he felt when he did his first public performance with Jak. He felt his father and the bard each place a hand on his shoulder, patting with equal fatherly affection.

"Well done, Don," said Jonathan softly, barely audible over the crowds. "I could feel the comings and goings of life ... both overall and ... personally ... very well. You certainly did what you set out to do."

"Aye, Donny," said Jak. "A braw debut fer yer first own-written song!"

The young bard hugged them both. "You both helped a lot, though," he said humbly.

"But you had the idea first," said Jonathan, "and if it weren't for that, we wouldn't have had anything to help you with."

"Thank you both, all the same."

"'Twas nae trouble, Donny. Ye've been doin' me proud ever since ye first talked me into startin' with ye."

"And you've done me very proud, too," said Jonathan. "I'm thankful every day that you thought to ask Jak to stay with us. Life has been very good with us together ... as much as I still miss them ..."

The three embraced each other once more. Then, after another quick bite and drink, they joined the crowds' cheers at the announcement of midnight's arrival and played more songs into the small hours of morning.

36
8/13/4017 G.M.

MIRA sat with her mother and father on the bench behind the chieftains' house, watching Isaak and Kahle practicing archery in the yard. They were planning to go hunting the next day, and with the trip being Isaak and Kahle's first, the two youngsters were keen to get in what practice they could. They chattered away as they aimed and shot their padded shafts at the targets, their conversations alternating between playful teasing and sincere advice.

"They've been getting on well, haven't they?" asked Ann.

"Mm-hm," Mira hummed in agreement as she ate a chunk of the sweet bread with forest berries that she and her parents were sharing. It was one of her father's favorite things for offsetting the earthy taste of Fallowroot tea, which he was presently drinking. "They've gotten on fine since they were little, but they definitely seem to have become better friends since the patrol."

Mention of the patrol from last year made Mira look down at her right arm. The memories of the pain and horror from the incident with the Qualakar cubs flashed across her mind, setting her arm to shaking briefly. She regained her composure quickly, though, and looking back to her parents, she saw that her brief fret didn't go unnoticed.

"It doesn't still hurt, does it?" Ann asked worriedly.

"No," Mira said with quick assurance, "it stopped hurting just a day or two after it happened. It's just the memory of it. Have there been any other reports of there being more of those ... *things* ... in the forest?"

"No, thankfully not, but that doesn't mean they couldn't still be out there somewhere. Of course, that in turn doesn't mean we aren't at all safe. We've hunted all those times afterward just fine, and we even saw the Arbonyn that you and Da met that one time."

"I know. It was just so ..."

"I know," Ann said softly as she kissed her daughter's cheek. The three sat in silence for a moment, after which Ann spoke up again. "Going back to a more pleasant topic," she said with a short laugh, "or at least, what I hope to be a more pleasant one ... have you gotten along with any of the boys here like Isaak and Kahle have?"

Mira and her father snorted in surprised laughter, knowing the specifics of Ann's question by her tone. "You think those two are getting on *that* well?" Mira asked. "Don't you think ten is a *little* too early to be thinking about that stuff?"

"Well, yes," Ann said steadily while Virgaard gently shook with silent mirth, "but ... I mean ... can't you see where I'm coming from?"

Mira watched the two young ones for a moment, observing Kahle's continued advice on aiming and Isaak's gentlemanly retrieval and returning of Kahle's arrows.

"Sure, I do," Mira said cheerfully. "You just surprised me with the thought is all."

"I mean, I know it's not certain just by *that*, but I like to think it could become that way!"

Mira and her parents laughed lightly, then Mira, after another moment's thought, answered her mother's question.

"I guess I haven't really thought about it much. I mean, it's not like I wouldn't want to look into it sometime sooner or later, but I'm not ... I'm not sure how to say it."

"I understand completely," Ann said. "I gave it hardly any thought until your father and I went hunting together with our parents one day. We knew each other basically our whole lives, but that was pretty much it until we started talking that day. We didn't fall in love overnight, of course, but, you know."

"Sure," Mira replied. She paused briefly, then followed up with her own question. "Is there anyone asking about me?"

"Oh no; I was just curious. Trust me, if anyone asked me, I'd tell you. And I'll trust you to tell *me* if any of them ask you directly?"

"Of course!"

"Good, because if any of these rowdy forest-rovers want a chance with you, they have to get on well with *me*, too ... and your Da, I guess."

Virgaard chuckled, which set Mira and Ann to laughing, too. He finished his dose of Fallowroot, then promptly rose from the bench and made toward the archery targets, the bow he had resting across his lap now in hand.

"Let's show these two young archers some tips from a few who have been around the woods a bit!" he said with a smile.

37

12/26/4017 G.M.

LERANNU stepped up to the podium where the headmaster of Genverdell's chapterhouse of the Mage Society stood waiting for her. The head mage smiled as he held Lerannu's accreditation papers in his hands and prepared to present them to her. Lerannu glanced about as the headmaster began to announce the newly certified mage's accomplishments. She saw her mother standing alongside the king, queen and princess, all of whom were smiling as she received her documents.

It had been just under a year since she and her mother had made the trip to Genverdell to live with the royal family. Once Sarah had made arrangements with her advisors to leave Bravagoth under their supervision, mother and daughter journeyed to Genverdell and resided with the Mivinaars at the castle. A good deal had changed in the short time between then and now. Her mother went onto the ballot for the south ward leadership election and ultimately won the vote. In the first few months of Sarah's leadership, she had proven to be highly competent.

Lerannu, having enrolled in the capital's chapterhouse almost immediately upon arrival, finished the remainder of her tutelage with high acclaim from her instructors. The only aspect of magic with which she still had any real struggles was managing her inner strength and energy in the wake of prolonged spellcasting; a difficulty that, as many had told her, was a continuing challenge for even some of the most experienced mages. In every other discipline, however, she excelled to the great wonder of her peers and teachers. Thus, with just less than a year of further training, her education was finished and she was now about to receive her certification at the age of eighteen, ranking her among the youngest mages to do so.

Lerannu was very proud of herself and grateful for the support the royal family had given both her and her mother during the past eleven months.

But it had still been a turbulent time for her, and as perfectly adequate as the capital's chapterhouse and its instructors were, it simply wasn't the same as it was back in Bravagoth. Even the presence of several classmates and the pleasantness of their conversations with her only went so far to quell the lingering sadness from the happenings of the previous year.

Nevertheless, Lerannu now did her utmost to focus on the joy of achievement at hand. Accepting her documentation from the headmaster and thanking those gathered for their congratulatory applause and support, the newly certified mage returned to her mother's side, embracing her as she thanked her and the royal household.

"It's been quite a year," she said with both a tear and a relieved laugh.

"That it has," Sarah said comfortingly as she patted her daughter's back. "That it has, indeed."

Lerannu then looked to the royal family, particularly at Sheeva. As supportive and welcoming as all at the castle had been, the princess had been especially kind and compassionate. When Lerannu had first moved into the castle, the princess was quick to visit her as she was unpacking her things. The conversations started light, and then Sheeva asked about Bravagoth and what had happened in the years prior to the incident of Ahvrom's necromancy. In time, Lerannu told all, from her friend Kiiva's death and her father's adultery to the death of Zalden in the wake of her tutor's vile magic. Her story was met with great sympathy from the princess. Sheeva, in turn, told her of the finer details regarding her relationship with the Greystones, and how turbulent it had been with them in the times prior to their tragic deaths from the fever. The young mage was moved deeply by the princess's troubles, as well as her compassion toward her fiancé and her motives for studying medicine alongside her impending duties as the future queen. It did not take long for the two to become good friends, and the friendship between them swiftly went on to bolster the relations between the new arrivals and the rest of the royal household.

Now, having embraced her mother, Lerannu made her way to Sheeva, hugging the princess in turn as she spoke to her and the royal family.

"I'll never be able to thank you all enough," she said. "As overwhelming as this year has been, you all have been there for me like family."

"We've been glad to have you both," King Samuel said kindly as Sheeva held Lerannu close. "You've been very welcome additions to our home, both as contributors to our leading of Enmayar and as good friends of our household. We look forward to sharing many more years with you and your mother."

Once the remainder of the accreditation ceremony had finished, the group stepped outside to make the trek up Genverdell's east hill and return to the castle. The young mage lovingly tucked the encased certificates under her arm to shelter them from the blustering, snow-flecked wind, and spent the walk conversing with her mother and the princess.

***

It was late in the afternoon, a little while before dinner. Lerannu, having retired to her room for the time being, stared reflectively at the papers that rested impressively in their case, which lay opened on her dresser to display the graduate's achievement. After a while of thinking on her journey as a mage, and all the highs and lows that had accompanied it, she decided to treat herself to a private celebration by going as far as she could with a little practice in her craft. She went to her armoire and took the clothes out of the bottom drawer, which carefully concealed the precious mementos from the three loved ones who were now gone from her life. She carefully took out the ruffled exotic feathers that her father and Zalden had given her, and placed them lovingly on top of her desk. She then took out the two porcelain bowls from Uriah, which she had since managed to glue back together and keep hidden from her mother. Filling one with water from a pitcher in her room, she placed them on opposite sides of her desk. Lastly, she took a small vial from her stash of Kamgenbew tonic, which, though she no longer tried to hide it, was in a top drawer of her desk.

Taking a few deep breaths, Lerannu then swallowed the dose of the energizing tonic and focused her sight on the feathers and water-filled bowl. In a matter of seconds, the mage felt a warmth begin to spread within her as her heart started to pump more rapidly. Her sight and mind focused with the keenness of a razor, and with another deep breath, she raised her right hand toward the feathers in front of her and her left toward the bowl with water.

A firm, steady gust of wind began to draw to her right hand like iron filings to a magnet. Twisting her palm upwards and directing her split focus to the feathers, she soon had them fluttering overhead in a circular dance. Maintaining part of her concentration on the feathers, she then lifted her left hand and cupped it as though she were holding a small ball. The water lifted out of the bowl in a shimmering, rippling sphere and followed her hand's guidance steadily across the desk and toward the empty bowl on the other side. Still vying to keep her energy and focus, Lerannu allowed herself a smile and small laugh of satisfaction. She could feel just the slightest fatigue beginning to set upon her, but she knew that, at the very least, she could keep the feathers suspended until she placed the water into the other bowl.

Then she heard a small voice call her name, one that was weighted with sorrow.

Her concentration broke and the feathers fell scattered about the floor as the water collapsed onto the desk with a splash. She turned her head to see her mother looking at her sadly in the doorway. Her heart began to race, fearing what her mother would do to the recovered mementos that she had trashed and thrown out in her betrayed rage three years ago.

Sarah stepped into the room and approached the desk, her footsteps met with no other sound than the pattering drip of the water that now flowed over the desk's edge. She looked at her daughter, and the feathers and bowls, in silence.

"Princess Sheeva," the south wardeness said at length, "and her fiancé request your presence in the throne room."

Lerannu's mind was briefly at a loss as to what the reason could be for her summons. Then she remembered all the times the royal family had spoken of offering her the position of court mage upon her certification.

"So soon?" Lerannu asked with a nervousness that came from more than one source. "And the princess and fiancé-prince? Wouldn't that be something for the queen and king to see to?"

"Normally, yes," Sarah said with a voice that had been deflated from joy to sorrow, "but they're having Sheeva and Allor do it as a little 'exercise' in leadership; something to give them practice for the duties to come."

"I see."

"Besides, Sheeva has been requesting to do it anyway, as she wanted to offer the position not just to you as a mage, but as a friend."

Lerannu nodded, then got up to grab a towel from her bath chamber. "I'll just mop this up real quick, and—"

"Go on over," said Sarah gently, her voice now beginning to regain a tone of tender warmth. "I'll take care of it."

Lerannu looked intently into her mother's eyes. There was no anger or spite. Only love, dampened by regret.

"It'll all be here when you get back," Sarah assured her daughter.

Lerannu nodded. "Alright. Thank you."

"I'm sorry," Sarah said, her voice straining on the edge of tears. "I'm ... so sorry ... for all of that, back when ..."

Sarah buried her face into her hands and wept. The mage embraced her tightly, and the two held each other in a moment of tearful silence. Finally pulling away, Sarah brushed the tears from Lerannu's eyes, and with a smile made her way to the bathroom to grab a towel for the desk.

"Go on," she said. "I'll be there in a minute."

Lerannu smiled, nodded, and made her way to the throne room, quickly composing herself as she prepared to receive the honor that her royal friend had in store for her.

The Journey to Zefiil

38
3/1/4018 G.M.

SHEEVA stood near the carriage in the main courtyard with Allor at her side. Having grown in deep companionship and trust with one another, they eagerly awaited their wedding, which was set to follow the resolution of the country's ties with Kellmayar.

Sarah Stonefaith had so far proven herself an immensely capable leader of the south ward in the time following the difficulties and ultimate tragedy of the Greystones. The politics of Enmayar, at least domestically, had at last returned to a cordial, overall stable state.

Sarah and Lerannu had taken quite well to court life, especially after Lerannu's appointment as the court mage. Sheeva, being only two years older than the mage, felt a special connection with her. The feeling was born out of admiration for her exceptional talent in magic and sympathy for her hardships. Lerannu confided her past in more detail to the princess following her initial arrival to the castle, and the two had since grown into a good friendship. Sheeva at last began to feel a growing sense of things changing for the better again. It was a feeling she had not felt with any great confidence since she and Allor had first gotten engaged.

There was, however, still the contention between Enmayar and Kellmayar, which in turn stirred a measure of anxiety with the nations of Sorrenar and Janrenar as they watched the developments apprehensively.

Following the deaths of the remaining Greystones, word eventually reached Ohdan Karvinthaal, the East Warden of Kellmayar and Valor Greystone's childhood friend. Ohdan's region continued to struggle with famine and a bad wave of poverty in the years following Valor's murder, despite the continued efforts of aid from Sorrenar and Janrenar. Ohdan had regularly joined the surviving Greystones in scathing the Mivinaars, claiming they had injured both their domestic leaders and foreign allies in the way they handled matters following Valor's death. The fact that the royal family had all but backed out of aiding Kellmayar following the connections drawn between Ohdan and the late south warden did not help calm the matter.

He was not long in hearing of Halla and Nikolas's death, as well as the apparent swiftness of Sarah's rise to the position of south wardeness. Ohdan, overwhelmed by grief at both the end of his friend's family and his region's continued plight, spiraled into a storm of hostility and spite. He began lashing out at his citizens with an alarming level of venom, and blamed nearly all of the troubles of Kellmayar's east ward (and Kellmayar at large) on Enmayar and its leaders. Ohdan insisted that the situation in his region would only ever truly improve if Enmayar resumed aiding Kellmayar with a higher volume of supplies, at least matching that of the other two nations, and that they were purposefully keeping the matter dire for some sort of leverage.

The last straw came the previous year when Ohdan began to accuse the Mivinaars of having somehow engineered the deaths of Halla and Nikolas, somehow exploiting their illnesses at the time and, one way or another, "helping them along to Morinaar's side" in order to give Halla's position to Lerannu's mother. Following these outbursts, along with Ohdan's increasing hostilities with those of his own country and region, Markol and Shannu Bluemoon, the king and queen of Kellmayar, called for the east warden to come to court to be interviewed. The leaders of the West also called out to their country for a vote to potentially remove him from his position. No word came from Ohdan's home of Tedhaal, and when the authorities arrived to investigate, they found the estate abandoned. The town's residents all swore ignorance of the former warden's plans or whereabouts. A new east warden line was then elected, and Ohdan's location and intentions had been unknown ever since.

With this abrupt shift in circumstances, Queen Talrah and King Samuel proceeded to arrange a meeting with the queen and king of Kellmayar, along with the new east warden, to try and at last come to a resolution for Enmayar's contributions to the West Nation's aid. They had agreed to meet in person in Kellmayar's capital city of Zefiil. Sheeva and Allor, being about to ascend to the throne following the negotiations, accompanied their parents to gain experience in diplomacy and global politics.

Now, on the first day of Yortri, following breakfast, a gathering of the royal household assembled in the courtyard with their company of guards to begin the long journey. Sarah and Lerannu, who were the prime members of the council assembled by the king and queen to manage affairs until their return, arrived with the rest of the council shortly after the departing company had gathered. Lerannu embraced Sheeva and Allor, and Sarah bade the company a fond farewell as Priest Ranoth Windsbreath led a brief prayer for the group's safe passage.

With all having gathered into their carriages and wagons, or otherwise on their horses, the company then rode steadily out from the castle's gates, from Genverdell's walls, and out into the crisply cold land that still lay in the last moon of winter.

***

Thirty days of steady travel passed without incident apart from the occasional greetings and well-wishes from passersby who realized that the convoy was that of the royal household. The last stretch of winter was, thankfully, not overbearing, with what snows that came the company's way being only a modest dusting at most. They had managed to keep a very consistent pace and even went beyond their usual allotment of eight hours' travel time on several occasions, being in good spirits in light of their sure progress, to go a little further and treat themselves to a night in an inn as a change from making camp.

It was now late into the second day of Yorqua, and the company was in great spirits from their recent celebration of Veronmay in a little village on the road, which ran along the edge of the vast Santaru Forest. They became ecstatic, then, when the king informed them that Greenharbor, the port where they would board an assigned ship to sail to Kellmayar, was just another day's ride from where they were.

"Too bad the evening's coming on now," said Sheeva wistfully. "I would've asked if everyone was up for another extended ride if we were just a little closer and had more daylight."

"I know what you mean," King Samuel said, patting his daughter's shoulder as those of the company within earshot agreed. "Just one more night camping by the road, and then we'll probably be looking at about two months on the ocean ..."

The king's voice trailed off, taking on a tone of surprised curiosity, as he saw and pointed out a lone, large, cozy-looking inn on the side of the road. It nestled into the edge of the forest, looked newly built, and was of surprising size, given its location.

"Well," said Samuel, intrigued, "perhaps our last night on land for the next two moons will be in an inn, after all. Let's stop and see how things are here."

A halt was called, and all stood waiting on the roadside as the king and queen, with Sheeva and Allor's family, approached the front door and examined the great sign hanging over it. The sign was written in ornate, yet very legible, lettering. A tiny, winged Fidonlike figure within a glowing, sky-blue sphere was depicted beneath the inn's name.

"The Glowing Wisp, eh?" Queen Talrah mused. "It certainly looks like a fine–"

The door suddenly opened, and a gorgeous woman with white fur all over, except for her long black hair, stood smiling in the doorway with an adorable baby in her arms. The woman's face was stunningly beautiful, despite what appeared to be a few scars on her left cheek, which were well-healed and mostly covered by her porcelain fur. Her eyes were bright blue, of the same hue as the wisp depicted on the sign. The baby, which looked at the newcomers with shining hazel eyes, had black, grey, and white fur patching his body.

"Welcome to The Glowing Wisp!" she said cheerfully. "My husband, Harvus, and I saw the lot of you coming down the road, and we and our staff are ready to see to your needs, presuming you'd like to stay."

"That we would," said the king gratefully. "We're just a little shy from where we're headed, and were planning to make camp on the road until we saw this here."

"That's what a lot of our guests say. I presume you're headed for Greenharbor?"

"Yes, madam. We'll be on a ship for Kellmayar sometime tomorrow. Diplomatic business."

~ 110 ~

"Diplomatic, huh? Sounds like you lot will definitely need a good rest before sailing for the next ..."

The innkeep's voice trailed off and her eyes grew slightly wider as she looked the company over and finally realized whom she was addressing.

"My king ... my queen ... I–"

"No need to fret over formalities, my good lady," said the king kindly. "It's like you said, we'd appreciate one more good rest on solid ground before we take on two months or so of sailing. Let's just be as any other travelers that have come into your fine establishment."

The lady smiled and nodded, and her baby cooed as he snuggled up against her while she resumed speaking.

"Well, we can see to it that you and your horses are well-rested and fed for the last stretch of your journey tomorrow! It will be a touch crowded, but it shouldn't be uncomfortable. If you like, you can follow my husband around the back to the stables and get your horses put up for the night. We'll have baths and food on the way for you all by the time you get back."

Queen Talrah laughed in admiration of the innkeep's service. "Thank you kindly, madam. We certainly look forward to staying the night."

***

After the company put the horses and wagons away in the stables, the lot of them soon found themselves set up in bedrooms with warm tubs, with those not able or wishing to wait happily finding a roomy, decent bathhouse down one of the corridors. Once all had washed, the company met up again in the common, where they were greeted with tables laden with fairly plain, but filling and tasty, food and drink. The innkeeper couple made their rounds of the tables, conversing with the diners here and there, as a handful of others waited on them.

Sheeva, who sat with her mother and father, along with Allor, Egrah and Alphaar, eventually managed to catch the lady innkeep's attention.

"Is everything alright, milady?" the woman asked, again holding her baby son, who watched all the goings-on in contented silence.

"Absolutely!" the princess replied after a sip of wine. "I just have a question or two, purely out of curiosity, if I wouldn't be keeping you by asking."

"Ask away!"

"This place hasn't been here long, has it?"

"No, milady; it's just under a year old, almost as old as little Evor here."

The innkeep gently petted her son's cheek, smiling beautifully as he squirmed lightly to snuggle more closely with her, while listening to Sheeva's continuation of her question.

"What prompted you to set up here, specifically? I mean, it's not inconceivable for an inn to be just a little way from a big settlement and still fare well, but one of this size? I'd think it'd be better suited for being in the city itself."

"Well, as I mentioned earlier," the lady said, nodding to Sheeva's father, "a lot of our guests are folks that just weren't *quite* able to reach Greenharbor before the day's end, and end up pleasantly surprised to find a good inn where they might've otherwise had to make camp on the roadside. A lot of folks come and go this way, too. Those leaving Greenharbor like to come here as well, since we're also only eight hours away from them at a good trot. I'd say you lot were lucky this evening; we might've actually been close to full if it were a different night, but I think most are still staying put after Veronmay. In addition to our volume of business, we managed to quickly find the sweet spot between quality and quantity in regards to our rooms, food, and everything else. We're still not on the same level as a big inn in the city in most ways, but we made just the right calls for a great inn at the edge of a forest, and with good rates, as well. We still have a fair way to go in paying off our starting debts, but if this keeps up, it'll only be a matter of time until they're covered."

Allor laughed in an impressed tone. "Were the two of you bankers or something before you decided to build an inn here? It sounds like you have an exceptional intuition when it comes to financial decisions."

The innkeeper grinned, kissing her baby's head before answering. "Not quite. My husband worked at an inn in Peargrove for several years. That's where I met him. As for me, I had experience in ... municipal finances before I came along."

The lady said the last sentence in an odd tone, one that, over the hum of the diners, sounded like it might have carried a touch of regret for some reason. She smiled again quickly, though, and continued. "But that wasn't the reason we built here. Our original plan was, in fact, to set up in Greenharbor. A while after we got married and saved up a bit, we went to Greenharbor to get a loan for setting up there. We were just a day away as the sun was nearly setting, same as you all, and made camp alongside the road with the caravan we had been accompanying. That night, at around midnight, Harvus and I saw a faint blue glow coming from the forest's edge. We, along with a few others, went to see what it was. Sure enough, it was a moonwisp, hovering around a small circle of stones where several trees and a bunch of wildflowers grew in clusters. It must've been a little place for some druids at one point; it might even still be, though we haven't yet met any around here. It's just a small walk out the back here, and we've seen the wisp appear a good several times around midnight. When we first saw it that night, Harvus and I decided to take it as a sign, as well as bearing in mind our experience of camping on the road when we were so close to our destination. When we reached Greenharbor, we managed to get our loan, and afterwards we got the deed to the land here, and the rest is history."

"So that moonwisp is the namesake of your inn?" Egrah asked.

"Indeed!"

"That's such a nice story," Sheeva remarked warmly. "Very romantic, I think."

"I think so, too," the innkeeper crooned.

"So ..." Allor said intriguingly, "does the wisp appear every night?"

"Not every night, and I haven't noticed any particular pattern, but it's happened often enough to where I'd say it *could* happen tonight, if you wanted to try and see it. You'll need to wait around midnight, though."

"I see," said Allor. "Thank you very much."

Sheeva caught the look Allor gave her from the corner of her eye. She gently took her fiancé's hand and brushed it gently with her thumb. Both knew where they planned to be at midnight.

39
4/3/4018 G.M.

ALLOR looked from the window at the bottom of the stairs, in awe at the blue glow that began to appear and spread in the distance. It was now midnight, and he could see, by the growing blue light, the silhouettes of the stones and trees that grew in the druidic garden. He was deeply moved by the scene of sacred benevolence. He soon heard Sheeva's footsteps at the landing above, and turning to her, he pointed eagerly out the window. The princess hurried as quietly as she could down the steps, aided by the small, but bright light of the waxing crescent moon. When she reached the window, she looked out and gasped in delight. They each took the hand of the other, quietly opened the back door, and jogged together into the deeper end of the forest's edge.

Upon reaching the wild garden, they passed the first stones of the circle and stood, hand in hand, gazing at the moonwisp that danced lightly in the air above the carved stone at the center of the arrangement. Its glow was now bright, and at the center of the globular form, a tiny Fidonlike form with wings could be just barely made out. Sheeva and Allor drew closer to the wisp until it was right in front of them. Entranced by the Angelborn creature's glow and the warm feeling of peace it emanated in the cold, early-spring night, the young couple-to-be soon found themselves embracing, rubbing their cheeks and muzzles together, and kissing softly into each other's ears.

"Al," Sheeva sighed into his ear, sending a great tingle down his spine, "I once couldn't imagine myself with anyone but Nikolas. Now, I can't see myself without you. I still feel ... lost ... over all that happened sometimes, but ..."

"I can only imagine how you must feel," Allor said, gently petting Sheeva's head. "I can't tell you if that will ever pass, but I *can* tell you that, as long as I am able, I'll be here for you. You can talk to me about anything, and if it hurts, I'll do all I can to ease your pain."

"I love you, Al. I can't wait for the wedding."

Allor's face began to grow warm, and his heartbeat began to quicken. "Me neither," he whispered into her ear, which he began to gently nibble. Sheeva gave a happy squeak in response, and the two, looking intently at each other, then abruptly, but gently, pulled away from each other.

The princess gave Allor a sultry smile, then, leaning against one of the circle's erect stones, locked eyes with him. She looked amazingly beautiful in the bright blue light, coupled by the lights of the moon and stars that peered from above the gaps in the gathering trees.

"If we were married now," she asked, "and we were right here, enjoying the same view and ... everything else ... what would you do?"

Allor's face was now burning, but he returned the princess's smile as he stood by the moonwisp, which stood on the central carved stone and seemed to be watching the couple with the utmost curiosity. He crossed his arms and stared into Sheeva's eyes contemplatively.

"Well now," he drawled suggestively, "where do I start?"

"I presume this wouldn't be best suited for our ears," Egrah's voice sounded with a laugh from behind them. "What do you think, honey? Talrah? Samuel?"

Allor spun around, eyes wide and face feeling as if it were about to burst into flames from embarrassment. He could hear Sheeva giggling in a way that expressed surprise, embarrassment, and great amusement. His mother and father, along with the queen and king, stood together at a large stone the two had passed on their way toward the wisp, looking on with endearment that was, naturally, mingled with some parental wariness.

"I-I," Allor sputtered, "W-we weren't going t–"

"I believe you," Egrah assured him, albeit smugly. "We saw you two put some space between you when things started to warm up a little too much."

Sheeva stepped forward, standing beside Allor once again. "Did we wake you all up?" she asked.

"Not at all," said the king. "We all wanted to see the wisp, too, if we could. We were going to wake you and invite you to come along, but we saw your beds empty and it was pretty obvious what you were up to."

Allor broke eye contact with the king bashfully, scratching the back of his head with one hand and taking Sheeva's proffered hand in the other.

"Well," said the queen, "we're all here, now. Let's enjoy the sight together."

The six then gazed about the forest garden, and upon the moonwisp, in a great sense of tranquility that filled their beings. The wisp hovered about the circle of the druid garden for about half an hour. Then, with what the group thought they saw was a friendly wave, it quietly faded away into the night.

Allor and the others then returned to their rooms, and he swiftly fell into a deep, peaceful sleep.

40

4/3/4018 G.M.

SHEEVA looked out from the carriage, awestruck by the evening view of Greenharbor as the company began to descend the hill toward its gates. Having left the Glowing Wisp early that morning, the company upped its pace to an even trot and reached its first major destination about an hour before sunset. The port city made for a fine, complex scene, being at once an imposing urban center and offering an enduringly pastoral view of the coast. The fiery light of the setting sun bathed the buildings in gold and orange, with deep shadows of blue. The ocean lay sparkling beyond the city and stretched beyond the horizon.

The company entered the city and made straight for the docks. They saw their appointed ship, a great vessel named *Seastrider*, sitting tall on the water. As they rode up to the ship and lined up before it, they were greeted by the entire crew, which was divided into three units based on shifts, as they all stepped off-deck to receive them. The royal company boarded the ship and was shown to their quarters and fed by the head captain, while the night crew set off as soon as all the company and their supplies were brought aboard. As Sheeva and her family were retiring to bed that night, the princess looked out from the deck and could just make out the dim twinkling glow of the city they had just left behind as its lights flickered on the horizon.

***

Thirty days passed fairly easily for the traveling company, though a touch of restlessness now seemed to be slowly seeping into them. They had managed to occupy themselves with talks over the impending discussions with the monarchs of Kellmayar, and recurring advice for the two future leaders of Enmayar from their parents and trusted companions. The crews were fairly sociable as well, when they could afford to chat a little, especially when they shared mealtimes. Now, in the late afternoon, Sheeva and Allor were teaming up against Lady Xalu in a game of chess. The royal tutor was a master of the game and had beaten both in turn earlier that morning, prompting the young couple-to-be to try and see if their two heads could best her one.

The three laughed at the ensuing stalemate, with Sheeva and Allor calling it at least an improvement from their earlier thorough defeats. Suddenly, Xalu, gasping and smiling, pointed up at the sky. The two turned to follow her hand, and their mouths parted in awe at the great red bird flying high in the distance.

"Mother! Father!" Sheeva called as Allor did the same for his parents. "Look! It's one of the Phoenixes!"

The monarchs and Allor's parents rushed to their sides. Dr. Kamlof and some others of the household, and the on-duty crew, came over as well. They all watched the large blot of scarlet fly about freely, their faces marked by spiritual pondering.

"... Then as Raakaru's emptied citadel crumbled to dust above Karzynhaal," Lady Xalu recited from the Beldsantu by memory, "Onu spoke to the surviving followers of the Elect with a great voice, telling them of their sacrifices.

'Do not despair,' said he, 'for they have redeemed themselves and have driven Raakaru from the world, freeing you all from his chains so that you might follow in their footsteps. I will now welcome them to my side, and they will live a new life eternal, as will you all if you hold to your trust in me and strive to return to the good you have lost. So that you and your descendants may remember this time, and my words of renewed life unending, I now bestow unto Fidonhaal two new kinds of sacred beasts.'

Then Onu brought into being the Phoenixes and the Blessed Great Serpents, and for each lot, he wrought but four. The Serpents, which traverse the land and the great waters, live a century at a time, then perish, leaving nothing but their hide, their bones, and the unbreakable egg that they lay into the earth at death, into which their souls pass to be reborn into a new body. The Phoenix, which flies as the greatest of the birds, lives too for a hundred years. Upon death, they burst into flames, leaving an unbreakable egg in their ashes. From this egg is the Phoenix reborn, bearing the same soul from before. Thus is the lot for both creatures until the end of Fidonhaal's days."

The princess reflected on the words, holding Allor's hand and standing close beside him. She gazed out onto the ocean and gasped at the grand stretch of green that lay on the horizon.

"That's Karzynhaal, isn't it?" she asked excitedly.

"That it is, Princess," answered the captain. "Many who sail the sort o' route we're takin' look for the Holy Isle to their east, or southeast, to make sure they're on course, whether it's from Enmayar to Kellmayar or the other way 'round. On top o' the good ol' feelin's that seein' the isle gives for the soul, it's also encouragin' for lettin' us know that Kellmayar is about a fortnight away, if the winds are favorable enough. Just a while more, now!"

Sheeva sighed, a bit wearied to hear that it could be another two weeks before treading land again, but happy to hear an experienced prediction at the remainder of the voyage. Looking at the distant isle of Fidonity's origin, which was now beginning to pass from view, the princess turned to her parents, nodding toward the verdant paradise.

"Do you think that ... after we've done our task in Kellmayar ... we might stop by there, even if just for a day, or even just an hour? I had thought of making a pilgrimage one day, but if we're going to be passing by again ..."

Queen Talrah smiled. "Of course; it'll do us all a lot of good."

"I've seen the paintings," the princess said to her mother wistfully, "heard the words of others, including yours, with you having been there twice already, but to see it myself, even just from the sea ..."

"It's simply beautiful, Sheeva, as much as anyone has ever said, and more," her mother said.

Sheeva then rested her head on Allor's shoulder, taking his offered kiss as they watched Karzynhaal slowly drift below the horizon.

41

5/20/4018 G.M.

ALLOR stepped off the *Seastrider* beside Sheeva while the others and their transportation were being steadily offloaded. The vast sands of the coast and the great Tedjahven Desert cradled the port city of Korashka in its embrace, creating a scene of near-blinding brightness in the late morning sun.

The captain's prediction on the remaining time of the voyage was nearly spot-on. A good wind graced the sails just past Karzynhaal and kept with the company the rest of the way, finishing the remainder of the journey in fifteen days past the Holy Isle. Relieved to have his feet on land again, Allor kissed his fiancée and held her close as they waited for the rest to disembark. They were taken by surprise when they saw a cluster of royal guards from Zefil riding swiftly toward them from the city's main road, with a young man's voice hailing the Enmayarn company.

"Greetings, Mivinaars!" said the young man as he emerged from the encirclement of guards. "I'm relieved that you've come at last. I trust that your journey was safe?"

"It was," Sheeva answered as her parents and Allor's came to join them. "Not a single trouble the whole way."

"Very good," said the young man with a courteous bow of the head. He was a Kason man, similar in age to Sheeva and Allor. His eyes were the same warm brown of his fur, and long, lightly curled hair spilled from his sky-blue turban onto his shoulders. He wore elegant robes with Kellmayar's royal crest upon them. Seeming to note Sheeva and Allor's close studying of him, the young man smiled and introduced himself.

"I am Dominik Bluemoon," he said with stately courtesy, "son of Queen Shannu and King Markol, and heir-prince of Kellmayar. My mother and father have been preparing me for the past few years to soon take their place, and have decided to include me in these upcoming discussions. As my first role in this endeavor, I have been sent to receive you here and accompany you on the road to Zefil."

"Well met, Prince Dominik," said Queen Talrah with a smile. She gestured to her daughter and future son-in-law. "This is my daughter, Princess Sheeva, and her fiancé Allor Indovis. Like you, they are soon to take our places on the throne, and we've had them accompany us on this affair to give them some experience in communicating with the other nations."

Dominik bowed reverently to Allor and Sheeva. "It is lovely to meet you, and a comfort to know that both of our nations' future leaders are meeting each other as ones new to the task. I was nervous to be involved with the matter, but knowing I'm not the only one preparing for the great task of stepping up to the throne is already easing my mind a little. May we succeed in coming to terms, and may our experiences here and now bode well for our future."

Once the company from Enmayar fully reassembled off the *Seastrider*, they merged with the prince's retinue, which guided them past the port guards, out of Korashka and onto the desert highway.

***

The company had ridden steadily for twelve days. The desert was dry and warm, but thankfully not in the full summer heat as it was now breaching into late autumn in that part of the world. This, along with ample water and rations, a broad highway headed straight for Zefil, and a highly regulated, intermittent pacing of riding and resting, enabled them to cover ground at a good pace without much worry of thirst or heat stroke.

Queen Talrah and King Samuel, with Sheeva, Allor, Egrah, Alphaar, and Lady Xalu, conversed with Prince Dominik much of the time. The discussions helped them prepare an idea for the impending negotiations as thoroughly as possible, particularly regarding the balance between a proposed increase in spice growing for export while not neglecting domestic food harvests, as well as the continued goodwill in supplying Kellmayar by Enmayar and the other two nations. Sheeva and Allor, having taken a liking to Dominik, often chatted together over whatever came to mind when the arduous details of heavier topics weren't being discussed.

Following another morning of tedious elaborations on the impending talks, the three future monarchs, having since retired to a carriage they shared together, found themselves talking of Sheeva and Allor's impending marriage. This led to Dominik recounting his endeavors of seeking a loving mate to help him in the heavy task of leading his country.

"I've had a few suitors," said the Kellmayarn prince, "but none of them just quite felt right, especially when it came to their will for political matters. We've arranged, my parents and I, to have my sister, Bendra, serve as queen with me until I find a suitable wife, so ... 'sufficient wherewithal for politics' is a must here, I'm afraid." The prince grinned ruefully and pointed at himself. "No inactive royal spouse for this one. It's a shame, too, because Bendra's very smart for a lot of these things; she'll even be helping a bit with the talks. But, Onu bless her, she has nearly no tolerance whatsoever for what complications may arise from one policy or another. I've still got some acclimation to do as well, but I know I feel better in it than she does. If she were happy to stay in the position, I wouldn't have to worry about finding a woman who's up for all this. But I stepped forward to take up the throne, and I can't stand to think of Bendra being stuck with all that, so the search goes on."

"I'm sure you'll find someone," said Sheeva kindly. "You *are* in a tough spot, given what you've said, but not an impossible one."

The prince sighed in frustration, looking at Sheeva and Allor with a mix of admiration and envy.

"Thank you, princess. I just wish it could've played out as smoothly as it did for you two."

"It wasn't exactly easy for us either," she said. "I mean, we've gotten on well since we met, but—"

Allor winced slightly at Sheeva's voice, which, though not sounding grossly offended, carried a note of pain.

Dominik moaned, berating himself and slapping a palm to his brow. "I am *so* sorry, dear princess. I had heard all about what happened between you and the Greystones a while back, when things were getting out of hand here in the east ward. I didn't mean to make light of all that mess, especially given how it ended. My deepest apologies."

"It's no trouble, good prince," Sheeva replied, her voice carrying a tone of forgiveness. "I understand what you were meaning. It does still hurt, the memories and all, and they just came up all of a sudden. I'm sorry if I came off as—"

A faint whistle cut the air, followed by a sickening thud of cloth and flesh being pierced. The three jolted, and looking out from their wagon, saw the guard at their right fall from her horse with an arrow in her neck as cries of alarm began to flow through the convoy.

42
6/4/4018 G.M.

SHEEVA clung to the edge of her seat as the carriage veered sharply to the left. Going by what she saw from her window, the convoy was attempting to take up a defensive ring formation. The princess's wagon turned too far inward, however, and its pace was now rapidly slowing. Another look out the carriage showed several of the convoy's drivers, along with a few more guards, being downed by more arrows. Sheeva, hearing two sharp thuds from the front of the carriage, quickly concluded that their driver had met the same fate.

The wagon had now stopped, and the three inside, after a second's hesitation, scrambled outside to try and regroup with everyone else. Sheeva, sitting nearest to the door on her left, opened it and ran, calling for Allor and Dominik to follow her, since the initial attack seemed to come from their right. The princess ran for a few seconds, then, not hearing either of Allor or Dominik's voices behind her, looked back frantically and saw that they were not with her. She saw Prince Dominik on the horse of the first guard they saw fall, charging at a full gallop down the road to Zefiil. She then saw Allor emerge from behind the wagon, wide-eyed and shouting after him. The princess did not hear what exactly Allor said, but as she saw Dominik charge past the swiftly enclosing attackers, with none of them seeming to break from their charge to pursue him, she was sure she had an idea of what Allor may have yelled.

"That coward!" she thought to herself. "No, that TRAITOR! He must have had this arranged! Why would–"

"SHEEVA!" Queen Talrah cried out frightfully, cutting into Sheeva's thoughts. "Allor! Dominik! Get over here with us! Under the cart! HURRY!"

The princess bolted to where her mother and father stood, hunched over and gesturing urgently to the large supply wagon that was to be their cover. She scrambled under the cart, with Allor having caught up with her and now at her side. The queen and king, with Egrah and Alphaar with them, got down with everyone else beneath the wagon.

"Where's Dominik?" Alphaar asked worriedly.

"He's left us to them!" Sheeva cried over the growing clamor of combat. "He rode right past whoever's attacking us, and not one of them even followed him! I think he set us up!"

"Sheeva, wait," Allor cut in frantically. "Dominik–"

An armored guard crashed to the sand in a crumpled heap right in front of the hiding group, cutting short Allor's words. Three Fidon men, all Kasons, approached and reached under the cart, dragging Sheeva, Allor, and the queen out into the open, clustering them together into the center of the broken ring of wagons.

***

Five horrific minutes passed as the large band of marauders ganged up on every guard in the company and slew them. They proceeded to drag all the unarmed travelers into the growing cluster of hostages. Sheeva looked over their captors in silent fright. She guessed they were all likely Kellmayarn natives, seeing how most of them were fully Kason and none didn't have at least some measure of brown fur on them.

The brigands made way for a tall and handsome Kason man, green-eyed and with lengthy, curly hair and beard. His clothes, though a bit grimy and travel-worn, were luxurious. As he began to speak, the princess could sense a tone of experienced leadership in his voice.

"Yes," said the man in a grave tone of approval as he glanced at the captives. "He was right, this is them."

He walked up to the hostages and looked all of them over. His eyes, when they met Sheeva's, narrowed menacingly and then darted between her and Allor. He pointed to them. Sheeva felt as if her heart would stop.

"Put those two over there," he said as he gestured to a spot across from the rest of the hostages.

The princess, heart pounding in her ears, could barely make out the leader's following inquiries, which he directed at one of his henchmen.

"Where's the prince?"

"He managed to flee down the road as we were starting to close in."

"Which way?" the leader asked harshly.

"Just kept going west on the highway, sir, same as they all were."

"Well then, go after him!" the lead brigand snapped. "We can't do this the way it needs to be done without that pompous brat here, too!"

"Y-yes, sir!" the bandit stuttered as he took a horse and galloped down the highway.

The leader of the marauders gestured to two of his henchmen, who approached Sheeva and Allor, pulled their heads back, and held daggers to their throats. Sheeva and Allor gasped in terror, and they saw the horrified eyes of their parents, who, with the rest of the convoy, cried out for them to stop.

"I won't have them killed," the leader said coldly, "if they'll do as I say."

"Why them?" King Samuel demanded. "My wife and I are the leaders of Enmayar."

"I know," said the man flatly.

"Then why force your demands on them? What's this all about?"

"It's about all that you and yours have put me through," the leader growled, "along with my friends and all my ward!"

Sheeva's ears shot up at the mention of a ward. She looked at Allor, who also clearly noted the detail, and saw the same alarmed realization dawning on the faces of those across from them. The brigand leader gestured to a group of his followers, who then took position behind the rest of the convoy and pressed blades to their throats.

"Ohdan–Warden Karvinthaal," King Samuel continued, addressing the marauder by his former title, "I–my wife and I can't relate to the level of troubles you and your citizens have experienced these past years, but if you just kept calm and stayed put, we would've come and tried to work things out with you, along with your king and queen! We wanted to work this out as much as you did!"

"I'm not convinced," Ohdan said coldly, "when you let my friend, Valor, get butchered for trying to help us!"

"We had a famine to deal with ourselves, Ohdan!" cried Talrah in exasperation. "We were going to reinstate our aid once we had things under control on our end. But then Valor kept sending things behind our back! He got caught, he angered those who came to confront him, and he got himself killed!"

"And then you turned your back on his grieving family and began to have other boys come in and have a go at your little princess to spite them!"

"Ohdan–"

"And then you go to visit them, saying you want to 'talk things over,' and the rest of my friend's family dies within a day of you arriving! What am I to make of *that?*"

"For the last time," cried Samuel, "they were sick when we arrived. We did what we could, but it was just too late; the fever was too far along, or it just wasn't meant to be. I can't tell you how or why exactly it happened, but we did *not* have them killed or otherwise withhold our help!"

"And now you come here, to work a deal with my king and queen, to make us use up more of our precious riverside farmland to grow more damned spices for your tables. You're then going to give us money for them, but with that money we're to buy the food we need from you and the other two nations, instead of you all just helping us survive until we're able to get enough of our own food growing again!"

"Ohdan," the queen replied desperately, "please, this is supposed to help *all* of us. That's what we've been trying to do the whole past millennium as the Four Nations: help each other while not making ourselves be in need, as best as can be managed. We weren't going to make East Ward, or anywhere else in Kellmayar, use up all their land just for spices; it was just meant to be a little more output for you all to sell until the poverty problem got more under control. That was the main intention we had for the money we were to pay; to go for better wages to help get you all out of this rut, not just to pay for the food we'd send. In fact, most of the food we're planning to send is meant to be either free of charge or at a very low price. We're not trying to get you in some sort of endless bind with us. We're all in this together, but one nation can't just throw everything it has at another just because they're having some troubles!"

Ohdan stared at the queen, silently, as she pleaded the case, then glared at the lined-up hostages as he paced past them a few times.

"I've spoken with enough politicians to know which ones are sincere and which are just trying to save their necks!" Ohdan roared. "You lot are the latter!"

The former east warden then turned to face Sheeva and Allor. "Now, you two, listen here–"

"Leave them out of this, Ohdan!" King Samuel yelled. "If you have demands, let Talrah and I hear them!"

Ohdan stared at the princess and her fiancé, his face a mask of grave, horrid resolve.

"I'll be dealing with them," he said, turning to the others from the convoy, "because they're going to understand that I won't be ignored any longer ... and because they'll be the new queen and king of Enmayar, now."

Facing the line of hostages, Ohdan nodded silently to his gang of brigands.

Sheeva's screams set her ears to ringing as the bandits slit the throats of all across from her. Her mother. Her father. Lady Egrah. Sir Alphaar. Lady Xalu. Dr. Kamlof. They, and all the others, stared wide-eyed at Sheeva and Allor as they all crumpled into heaps, gurgling their last breaths as their blood sprayed onto the sands.

43

6/4/4018 G.M.

ALLOR couldn't scream or cry out; his throat was so tightened by grief and horror. His ears rang as Sheeva screamed beside him, and his eyes blurred as he felt himself on the brink of losing consciousness. Mindlessly, he tilted his head up to look at Ohdan, who, turning around to face them, bore a face of hideous satisfaction. Allor felt his heart begin to pound rapidly, his terror and grief swiftly becoming replaced by utter hatred and wrath.

"Now," Ohdan said flatly, pointing to the murdered convoy, "unless you're keen to join them right now, listen to me. I will not—"

A sudden blast from a horn sounded from the west, and all present turned swiftly to the sound with ears pricked high. A massive rumbling of an army of hooves grew from the direction of the horn's call, and Allor could now see, both down the highway and from over the dunes to the northwest, a great company of mounted riders. Tears of relief poured from his eyes, and a sighing sob passed his lips as he realized who they were. A great cavalry patrol of the massive, wild-dwelling tribe of Trichynay had happened to be passing by a mere few minutes away. As the charge rapidly gained ground, Allor could make out Prince Dominik. He was on the bright white horse that he took from the slain guard. He pointed urgently toward the captives and captors as he spoke to several members of the tribe who were leading the cavalry. Allor had told the prince to flee and seek help, but did not expect it to be so fortunately soon in coming. It was a circumstance that Allor would credit to nothing less than the grace of Onu to the end of his days, even though it was too late for almost everyone in the company.

At the sight of the great cavalry, a number of Ohdan's crew began to turn to flee. Ohdan, grabbing Sheeva by the collar of her dress and dragging her in full sight of the incoming cavalcade, raised his scimitar over her head and ordered all his company to stand and fight. The Trichynay riders were almost upon them now, their blades and spears poised, and their bows and arrows drawn. Allor, driven by love for Sheeva and hateful wrath for Ohdan, bolted from where he knelt and charged into Ohdan before the marauder could react. With the brigand on the ground, Allor saw Sheeva run toward the corpses of the queen and king, still wailing ceaselessly, and ran after her. He came to her side, having only stopped to pick up a sword from a fallen guard. The Trichynay cavalry had now reached the convoy, with some having dismounted as they reached the wagons. The tribal warriors maneuvered about, on horseback and on foot, to surround and penetrate Ohdan's band. A number of the brigands had already been slain, and Allor, for an instant forgetting Ohdan, called out to Sheeva as she continued to wail and scream, cradling her parents' bodies in her arms.

"Sh-Sheeva," he called, choking on the words and barely getting them out, though the princess's cries and the great clamor of battle seemed to drown them out anyway. "We need to get away from here—"

Ohdan's sudden, enraged roar caused Allor to wheel around, raising his sword barely in time to block the heavy swing that the brigand dealt. The force, compounded by Allor's inexperience in swordsmanship, sent a sharp pain into his wrist as the muscles sprained. Allor yelped in pain and, stumbling to the ground, quickly crawled to Sheeva and placed himself between her and Ohdan. He used both hands to hold the sword, and raised it to as good of a defensive position as he knew. He braced for the next strike, and jolted as a blur passed Ohdan. The hand which held the brigand's sword dropped from his arm and onto the sand.

Ohdan screamed in pain and clutched his bloody stump of an arm. Allor, his wrath and defensive fear flooding him, leapt up from the ground and pounced upon Ohdan, knocking him down with a swift kick to the shin and punch to the stomach. Allor raised his sword overhead, with both hands on the hilt. Ohdan looked up into Allor's eyes, his face a picture of both terror and unparalleled disbelief that his end was to be at the hands of a young nobleman who was so green with the blade. The sight of the marauder's face and the sound of his plea sent a horrible laugh up Allor's throat and out from his lips. As the fighting raged around him and the marauder pleaded for mercy, Allor brought the blade down onto Ohdan with all his might, ignoring the shooting pains that ran through his right wrist. Then he brought it down again. And again. And again. Again. Again.

Suddenly, Allor became aware of the sudden quiet, punctuated by Sheeva's hoarse weeping and a young man crying out his name. Allor continued to swing the sword down onto Ohdan's corpse until at last he felt his hands being held back by a strong grasp. The pain from his wrist shot up his arm, and Allor, crying out, tried to turn his head to see who was restraining him. As he did so, his eyes came upon Prince Dominik, who stood nearby in horror as he stared at the carnage. Allor realized it was Dominik who had called out to him, and he followed the prince's gaze to the broken body that now lay at his feet. Allor's knees gave in and his stomach turned at the sight. Ohdan Karvinthaal, the former, renegade East Warden of Kellmayar, lay sprawled in the grassy sand. He was cloven into three pieces, four counting the severed hand, with the other strokes from Allor's blade having scored the body to the bone. As Allor knelt, quivering like jelly, he felt the hands restraining him release their grip, and he sensed that the one who held him back was now walking around him to face him. He saw two grey-furred shins approach.

"Why did you do that?" the stranger asked levelly. "I took his sword-hand; he wasn't in a state to be a threat anymore. We should've taken him to Zefiil for a trial so we could try to figure out what in the world he was thinking when he decided to ..."

Allor looked up. There stood before him a man, lean and muscular, who was fully Zaron as far as he could see. He had a close-kept beard and long hair that was tied back in a tail. His eyes were of the same blue-green as the ocean, and while they were filled with anger at first, they soon softened into sympathy as he took in the sight around him and looked into Allor's eyes. There were scars on his left cheek that seemed to suggest he had been clawed in a nasty fight with another Fidon some time ago. He wore the riding clothes of the Trichynay people, but his accent told Allor that he wasn't born into the tribe, and was most likely a native of somewhere in Enmayar. His voice also carried a certain weight to it, as one who had been versed in leading others for some time. A moment passed with the two staring into each other's eyes, then the Zaron rider, saying nothing else, offered his hand to pull Allor back onto his feet.

Prince Dominik approached Sheeva, bending over and offering his hand.

"Princess," he said numbly, "I am so–"

Sheeva jumped up from the dead king and queen, screeching like a demon. With a vicious, clawing strike, she lashed out at the prince, sending him to the ground in shock as she narrowly missed ripping his throat.

"YOU!" the princess screamed. "You set us up! You abandoned us! You were going to have us all killed! I'll–I'll–"

The grey-furred rider sprinted from Allor and held back Sheeva's arms. Allor tried to call to her, to explain Dominik's actions, but his throat was lodged shut with grief and self-disgust.

"Princess," said the Zaron, "I cannot express my sorrow for your loss, but that gives you no right to strike the prince. If you try to harm him again–"

"Shee-heeva!" Allor cried hoarsely, finally getting the words out from his lips again. His speech was muddled by grief at first, but quickly settled again. "I told Dominik to run for help. He would've probably taken at least a week to get help from Zefiil if he hadn't had the fortune to run into these people. Dominik had nothing to do with this."

The princess dropped to her knees, weeping again. "I can't ... I can't do this, Al," she said brokenly. "N-not now ..."

"Sheeva," Allor said as tears began to flow down his cheeks again, "if we don't go through with this now, then ..."

The rush of battle had now fully faded from Allor's heart, and his drive to be rational flowed out from him alongside his battle frenzy as he looked upon the dead and his beloved's tears. He began to weep, taking Sheeva into his arms, as the others present looked on sadly. Allor turned to Dominik, with Sheeva still weeping in his arms.

"We ... we can't do the negotiations. Not now. We're ... going home. We need to see to the dead and make sure our new positions are officially recognized. Then we'll try and see if we can't arrange another meeting."

Dominik looked sadly at the mournful pair, silent, and nodded understandingly.

"I'm sorry, Prince Dominik Bluemoon," Allor said with as much dignified formality as he could muster.

"I'm sorry, too," said the prince. Dominik turned to the riders of the Trichynay Tribe, focusing on the Zaron. "Might I ask your people to help the ... the Queen and King of Enmayar ... see to their dead? There are many who have fallen, and as you can see, they are—"

"Of course, my prince," said the Zaron rider obligingly.

New Times for Enmayar

44

7/5/4018 G.M.

LERANNU concentrated the air rushing from her palms as she used it to levitate the book back to its place on the shelf. As she meticulously turned the book into position and gently pushed it snugly between two other volumes, three children applauded cheerfully. Lerannu took a deep, steady breath, easily recovering from the light spell of weariness that tugged at her, and took a bow. The children's mother, who was from the temporary council, then entered the mage's study to collect them.

"Thank you for looking after them," she said, taking the younger two in hand as the eldest stood close to her side. "I'm sure this isn't part of what you had in mind as part of the council, but–"

"It's no trouble," Lerannu said earnestly. "I enjoy being with them, and you all have always kept me in the loop at the end of the day."

"I think you'd make a great tutor for Sheeva and Allor's children, if they offered the task and if you were up for it," the lady said in a kind, but curious tone. Lerannu turned to remark that the thought had already occurred to her, and grew perplexed at the woman's grim face.

"I have thought ... My lady, what's the matter?"

The woman stood silently for a second, then, turning with her children for the door, answered somberly from over her shoulder.

"You are requested in the council room as soon as you are able, Lady Lerannu. There is urgent news from Kellmayar."

The lady and her children left without another word, and Lerannu, briefly rooted to the spot by worry, strode briskly out of her study and down the halls until she reached the council room. When she arrived, she saw her mother and the castle priest, Ranoth, along with a few others, sitting somberly at the table. They all looked at her as she entered.

"What's all this?" Lerannu asked nervously. "Lady Goldcloud came by to pick up her children and she told me that ..."

Her mother wordlessly pushed a piece of parchment to the table's edge, her face one of fading shock and growing sadness. The young mage slowly approached the table, a creeping sense of dread growing within her with each step. She took the letter and began to read.

> *The words of the impending Queen and King of Enmayar, Sheeva Mivinaar and Allor Indovis, dated the twentieth day of the month of Yorrek, of the year four thousand and eighteen of the Era of Reunion:*
>
> *Our journey had fared without incident until we were on the highway west of Korashka, bound for Zefiil. About halfway along the road, the royal company was attacked by an army of brigands led by the former renegade East Warden of Kellmayar, Ohdan Karvinthaal. The marauders and their leader have been put down, but not before they managed to murder all in the company apart from the princess herself and her betrothed.*
>
> *In light of this tragedy and the worrisome political circumstances arising therefrom, the negotiations of trade and assistance between Enmayar and Kellmayar have been suspended until further notice. Talks will hopefully resume in due time, following Sheeva and Allor's coronation and their acclimation to their new position as the leaders of Enmayar, as well as following an investigation into the attack and related events. The heir-prince of Kellmayar, Dominik Bluemoon, who was with the company at the time of the attack, swears ignorance of the former east warden's plans and motives, and denies any involvement. King Markol and Queen Shannu make the same claim, and have promised a thorough investigation on their*

part in addition to cooperation with investigations conducted by the other three nations.

In light of these events and their consequences, Sheeva and Allor desire to settle the matters of seeing to the dead, accepting the throne, and holding their wedding as swiftly and efficiently as possible. It is thus requested that, on the day following the return of the princess and her betrothed, a funeral for the late Queen Talrah III and King Samuel, with all others slain on the journey, be held in the morning. This is to be followed immediately by the coronations of Sheeva and Allor at noon, and the newly crowned queen and king's wedding at eventide.

It is presently estimated that the princess and her betrothed will be at least three months from the date of this message in returning to Genverdell. It is earnestly implored that all necessary preparations be made within that time.

Signed, Princess Sheeva Mivinaar and Betrothed-Prince Allor Indovis.

Lerannu looked about the room, shocked and forlorn, at a loss for words.

"The salpion has been summoned to meet with us," said Sarah levelly. "He should be here anytime now to begin to go over the arrangements with us."

45

8/21/4018 G.M.

SHEEVA sat in the main cabin of the *Seastrider*, staring mournfully at the four water jugs resting on the table. They did not hold water. They held ashes and bones.

Sheeva had looked on beside her fiancé, weeping frequently and quietly, as the riders of the Trichynay Tribe reorganized the convoy's supply carts. Having packed all that was needed for the princess and her betrothed into one large wagon, along with a carriage for transport, the riders distributed the rest of the supplies among themselves. It was partly out of need, as they agreed to escort the grieving young couple back to Korashka and required additional rations, but was also a gesture of thanks on Allor's part, as a number of modest commodities and fineries were left to the tribe as well. The emptied carts and wagons were then disassembled and fashioned into makeshift pyres for the king and queen, along with all the others slain. The ashes of Queen Talrah, King Samuel, Lady Egrah, and Sir Alphaar were then placed carefully into emptied water jugs. The remains of the others, including Lady Xalu and Dr. Kamlof, were scattered to the winds. As Sheeva watched her friends and family turn to ash, she either wept on Allor's shoulder as he stood in numb silence or simply stared into the flames as they reached for the darkening desert sky.

Once the ashes were dispersed or gathered, the riders, led by Prince Dominik and the Zaron stranger, escorted the two back to Korashka. They traveled into the night, not stopping to rest until the next night in an effort to make up for the time lost to the improvised funeral. There were urgent matters to settle back in Enmayar, and the sooner Sheeva and Allor could return home, the better. It still took them a few days longer to cover the same distance back, however, being a trip of sixteen days instead of twelve. All the while, Sheeva, her mind still seized by grief, fear and anger, was afraid that Prince Dominik and the riders, whom she still suspected of having a hand in the attack, would eventually swarm the two of them and murder them. When they first stepped into the carriage after the burning of the dead, she spoke of this fear to Allor, who refuted it with a harsh exasperation that, though she knew was largely agitated by grief, nevertheless stung her heart.

"Sheeva," he said with a sharp tone of weariness, "I told you, Dominik fled for help. I pointed at that guard's horse and told him to ride out and look for help. If he didn't manage to escape, he may very well have ended up dead or might have found himself having to live with wrongs done for survival, as we might have as well, if things went differently. And the Trichynay people are a good, brave and dutiful lot; you know that. We're lucky they were only a few minutes away and that Dominik came across them."

"And you don't find that suspect?" Sheeva asked meekly.

"No," Allor snapped, "I find it fortunate and I'll strive to remember it, thank Onu, and pray he bless each and every one of these people to the end of my days. You saw Dominik when the fighting was over and how he reacted to learning that Ohdan led the attack. And when we told him that Ohdan mentioned something about a person apparently informing him of our arrival, he was distraught beyond belief, because he figured it meant that Ohdan had an informant somewhere in the government. He said he and his parents were going to investigate the matter and be open to inquiries from us and the other nations. Does that strike you as something a person would do if he were involved in something like this?"

"It could be an act," Sheeva said defensively. "All they have to do is—"

"ENOUGH!"

That was the last conversation they had until they reached Korashka. It was a long, silent ride of sixteen days in the carriage. Both left the carriage at times, walking outside beside the Trichynay riders so as not to be cooped up with one another the whole time.

Upon reaching the city, the two went to the port city's mayor, informing her of the incident and requesting the use of one of her heraldwings. Once they had written and sent the message, Allor and Sheeva immediately returned to the *Seastrider*, where the crew, being informed in the meantime by Dominik and the riders, greeted them in reverent silence. The two boarded the ship, along with their transport and remaining supplies, and set sail without delay, leaving the prince of Kellmayar and the wild-dwelling riders to go their separate ways.

They sailed for fifty-seven days, silently lost in grief and taking little comfort in one another.

They saw Karzynhaal as the ship passed by roughly two weeks after embarking. They did not make a stop at the Holy Isle on the return journey.

Now, on the evening of the twenty-first of Yorok, after hearing the captain announce that Greenharbor was expected to be at most a day away, the princess retired to the cabin, staring at the improvised urns. Such was the manner by which she had spent the majority of the trip.

She heard Allor come down with a plate of food and a jug of water, which he gently placed in front of her.

"Sheeva," Allor said softly, "you need to eat more. I've seen you hardly eat a thing this whole trip, and it's been showing for a while."

The princess sighed wearily and stared at her hands, which were resting on the table. They were indeed getting bony, but the princess simply couldn't bring herself to eat. Allor sat beside her and slowly began to take her into his arms. Sheeva, still hurting from the talk in the carriage, was grateful for the affection and did not object. She rested her head on Allor's shoulder, and he began to gently kiss her alternately on the neck, cheek, and ear.

"I'm sorry about how I spoke to you back on the road," he whispered softly. "I was hurting, but so were you. I could've at least tried to help you talk through your thoughts better. And I'm sorry that I've barely had a word with you since. I love you, Sheeva. I can't imagine my life without you."

"And I can't see mine without you," said the princess gently. "I don't hold your words or tone against you, Al. They hurt, but it was nothing compared to everything else that's happened."

Sheeva's voice began to strain as she tried to keep the tears from flowing.

"Al ... I feel that ... every time my heart has beaten since that day ..."

"That it hurts?"

Sheeva looked deeply into Allor's brown eyes and saw the same pain of the soul looking back into hers. Her heart began to lighten, and taking Allor's head in her hands, she kissed him deeply. No more words were needed, by one or the other, to express the pain that had ravaged them for over two months. A few minutes passed with the two in their relieving embrace, then Allor, at last gently pulling away, nodded to the food and drink he had brought her.

"You *do* need to eat, though," he said lovingly. "I understand if it feels empty when you eat or if it tastes like ashes, but—"

"I will, Al," said Sheeva. "Thank you ... but I'll eat it later. I'd like to stand on deck with you and watch the sunset, if you don't mind. Or the stars, if the sun has already passed."

Allor smiled and took Sheeva's hand. "I think the sunset is still a little way off," he said. "And if not, it's like you said, there's still the stars."

46
9/27/4018 G.M.

OWEN stood in the grand opening courtyard of the archtemple, his palms turned up in supplication as he looked upon the four earthenware jugs that the princess and her fiancé placed before him.

Princess Sheeva and her betrothed, Allor, had arrived early in the afternoon the previous day. A frantic wave of criers ran through the capital, and Owen, along with Sister Arza, Ruth, and Verdok, made their way to the city's west gate in the midst of nearly all of Genverdell. The salpion and his company, at last reaching the gate, stood alongside the royal council as the princess and her fiancé at last entered the city. He looked upon the young couple as they approached him and the council, and sympathy pulled at his heart until it ached. Wearied by grief and the months of travel, the future monarchs held each other as they entered the city. Genverdell's citizens, having heard the news following the message from Kellmayar, received their future leaders with the silence of the grave.

"Welcome home, Sheeva and Allor," said Owen softly. "Your council and I have seen to all the preparations that you requested. Please, go and rest. We shall commence tomorrow morn, as you stated."

"Thank you, Salpion," said the princess quietly as she looked at him and his entourage alongside the council. "Thank you all."

Without another word, the court mage, Lerannu, tearfully embraced the two before the royal household turned back to the castle. They silently walked the streets that led up the east hill, past silent, reverent legions of citizens.

Now, in the morning that followed, Owen held the funeral for the late king and queen, and that of Egrah and Alphaar Indovis, the parents of Sheeva's fiancé. The salpion, prompted by the princess, also prayed for the benediction of the souls of the others who were murdered on the road to Zefiil.

"We pray to you, Onu, that they have now come into your home and are in eternal peace. We pray also to you that all the children and loved ones of the dead be given strength in the days to come, with a further plea for Sheeva and Allor, who must now take on so suddenly the charge of their parents in the wake of tragedy. In you we strive to trust."

"In you we strive to trust," answered countless voices.

Sheeva and Allor looked on in silence as Ruth, Verdok, Arza, and High Priest Roth emptied the jugs into two proper urns, joining the remains of the queen with the king, and of Lady Egrah to Sir Alphaar.

***

Immediately following the funerals, Owen and his company trekked up to the east hill to witness the coronation. The masses creeped up the hill over the course of three hours like a steadily rising tide. In the entrance courtyard of Castle Genverdell, the Forty Advisors of Enmayar, with two of them having been selected for the honor, placed the crowns upon Sheeva and Allor's heads following their oaths of leadership. Owen then led the masses in a prayer of blessing. The crowds cheered, and with their applause still echoing across Genverdell, the citizens swiftly made their way either to their homes or the archtemple in preparation for the wedding.

***

The portly salpion finally huffed past the archtemple's main gate after another three hours of wading through the legions of people. Verdok, Ruth, and Arza asked if he was alright.

"I'll be fine," he stated with a cross between a pant and a chuckle. "We're in the last stretch now and the wedding's still a few hours away. I just need to wash and rest a little."

Evening came, and having rested easily, as nearly all the preparations were put into place a month ago, Owen made his way to the grand cathedral. Soon the seats were packed, and the Queen of Enmayar and her king entered and took their places. Verdok, High Priest Roth, and the castle priest, Ranoth Windsbreath, stood at Allor's side in place of his father and the late king. Ruth, Sister Arza, and Lerannu and Sarah Stonefaith stood at Sheeva's side in place of her mother and the late Lady Egrah. As the couple approached one another in their veiled robes of white and green, and Owen spoke the words of matrimony, the salpion was moved by the earnest affection that shone, clear as day, in the couple's eyes as they lifted each other's veils and stared at one another. He pronounced them wife and husband, with Allor taking the royal name. As he concluded the ceremony, Owen silently said a prayer to Onu for another young man and woman in the cathedral, who looked on beside the new queen and king.

"Onu, I know not what the future holds for Ruth and Verdok, but I feel, in my heart, that they may well end up together. If that ever comes to pass, I pray that they have the same deepness of love that I see in these two before me. In you I strive to trust."

The new king and queen kissed and turned to face the crowd. Those in the cathedral, along with all of Genverdell, thundered in applause.

***

Owen slumped into his chair in the study after the wedding, once the couple and nearly everyone else had gone to the archtemple's great dining hall for the banquet. He poured himself and Arza a glass of deep, sweet wine, with a tiny glass for Ruth and Verdok, as they privately toasted the young royalty.

"To Queen Sheeva and King Allor; may they take comfort in one another from their tragedy and keep each other strong in the years to come of their reign." The salpion then lifted his glass. "Hail to Sheeva and Allor!"

"Hail!" the other three called.

The four took their wine, relishing the warm sweetness on their tongues.

"I know this was an exceptional occasion," said Verdok, "but I'm surprised you didn't just save this for Kysonmay."

"Well," Owen said simply, "it's like you said, this was *not* a typical day. Besides, Kysonmay is still ..."

The salpion froze in thought, then slowly lifted his eyes from his glass and to the three seated across his desk. They laughed hysterically at the face he made as he realized that Autumn's Eve was the very next day.

Owen woefully rose from his seat. "You three can enjoy the banquet if you'd like. I'm going to bed. We'll throw something together in the morning."

47

9/27/4018 G.M.

ALLOR walked with Sheeva from the archtemple, escorted by guards down one hill and up the other and back into the castle. They felt their pace quicken with nearly every step, as each one led them closer to their chambers.

They sat in the archtemple's dining hall as the banquet began winding down. Sheeva put a hand on her husband's thigh, petting it gently and whispering intimately into his ear.

"We can go home now, if you'd like," she said.

Allor choked down his sip of wine, looking at his wife intently and smiling knowingly. He nodded.

Sheeva kissed him, then dug her muzzle into his ear to whisper something more.

"If you're not ready for ... for children ... I can brew some Fallowroot for you before we ... start. It'll take a few hours to set in, but it's no trouble if you're not ready. I just ... I just felt that, if you were alright with it, it would be nice if, after everything ... we might ..."

The queen sighed deeply.

"If you're not ready, just tell me."

Allor licked his wife's face and pulled her close. Burrowing his nose into her ear, he spoke plainly.

"I'm ready if you are."

The two rose from their table, and after a brief and rushed speech of thanks that generated warm congratulations and lightly rambunctious tittering from the banquet's guests, they summoned their guards and made their way back to the castle.

They were now alone, hand in hand, walking up the stairs and down the corridors together. They spoke to each other in heavy whispers, their words broken by kisses and intimate caresses with their free hands.

"Sheeva," Allor breathed into his wife's ear, "I know we've both been hurting since Kellmayar and we still haven't spoken all that much since, but the last night on the ship, when we looked at the sunset and stars ... I was sure we'd turn out alright in the end."

"Me too, Al," Sheeva crooned as Allor's free hand gently brushed up and down her back. "I still feel broken, in ways, but with you, I believe–"

Sheeva's words caught in her mouth as the two reached their bedchamber. Allor, opening the door for his wife and swiftly shutting it behind them, turned to the bed, where Sheeva was already slipping out of her wedding robes. Allor followed suit, and the two soon stood before one another, bare as they were born apart from their wedding bands. Allor's heart began to pound in his ears.

"By the Four," he gasped as his eyes roamed up and down the queen's body, as well as catching her eyes and seeing that they were doing the same to him. "Sheeva, you're ... just beautiful."

Allor saw Sheeva's legs give as she slumped down onto the bed.

"So are you," she said as she crawled to the bedside to make room for her husband. She sighed, giving Allor a smile that immediately made him lightheaded, and patted the space of mattress beside her.

Allor strode to the bedside and sat beside her, taking her in his arms and kissing her relentlessly.

"I swear to you, Sheeva," he said in the times when his lips briefly parted from hers, "I will do all I can to be always by your side. We have been given the task of leading the East, and I know not what struggles await us. But whatever lies in store for us, I will do all I can to be by your side, and to help you when the burdens feel too heavy. When all else fails, I'll keep you in my heart. I will never leave you or hurt you. I will share in your pain and your joy. Hide nothing from me, and I'll hide nothing from you."

"I won't," Sheeva swore. "I won't hide anything from you, and I'll be by your side, help you with your burdens, and keep you in my heart every day."

Allor kissed Sheeva deeply once more and cradled her head within his hands as she clasped her legs around his hips.

48
9/28/4018 G.M.

SHEEVA stirred as the golden light of dawn beamed through the window curtains and the early birds sang their small, but lovely chorus. She looked out from her bed at the balcony and, feeling an urge to stand outside and see the last sunrise of summer, gingerly disentangled herself from Allor's embrace. Finding that she did not seem to disturb him, Sheeva quietly stepped outside, not bothering with any gown or robe. She gazed at the spreading glow of day that was touching the verdant hills and fields in the distance, and breathed deeply the near-autumn air. She closed her eyes, trying to focus on finding inner peace that seemed just beyond her soul's reach.

Then, a horrid sigh pierced her ears and her heart felt gripped by ice. She spun around and saw the shadow of Raakmathna once again. It had been nearly two years since the queen had been troubled by the demon's appearance, back when she sat in Bravagoth's courtroom to observe the trial of the necromancer. She had hoped that would have been the final time. She was wrong, as a part of her, deep down, knew was to be the case, given the hate she had felt and the things she had done.

"Begone!" the queen whispered harshly. "I will not hear–"

"All your pain is because Onu allows it," Raakmathna said bluntly. "You know it is true."

"The same is true for my joy," Sheeva retorted, glancing back anxiously at Allor, who still lay in blissful slumber.

"You can have all order," said the demon, "and turn the world into one with only joy, no pain."

"Perhaps for me, but not for the rest of Fidonhaal."

"They will have it with you if they follow you."

A short, soul-chilling pause followed the demon's words. Raakmathna then added a further requisite.

"And if they are of the worthy breed, of course."

Sheeva began to construct another retort, but her tongue froze, her brow furrowed, and her ears shot up at the last remark. "What *are* you talking about?"

"Look at history, Sheeva," Raakmathna said sharply, "especially your own. Nikolas, Halla, that horrid mage who devastated your friend's town and killed her suitor, Ohdan Karvinthaal and all his murderous conspirators ... they were all either not Zarons at all, or filthy half-breeds, or ones who forsook their own kind and lay with those of other, lesser ilk."

Sheeva's eyes widened and her mind pounded as she struggled to comprehend the concept the demon was proposing. Fidonhaal had been marred by violent prejudices before, but typically they were only political in nature, being matters of loyalty to this noble or that monarch in the days when the lands were broken into smaller domains. Once, there had even been a horrible division made amongst Fidons on the basis of how to commune with Onu. But that, as was the case for the other incidents, had now largely taken residence in history and remained there. Never, in all her studies, did the queen hear mention of a concept presupposing one's character based only on the color of their fur.

Sheeva tried to build a response, but the sheer thought that was placed in her head overwhelmed her. At a loss for words, the queen simply shook her head.

Raakmathna simply scoffed at her. "If you are not convinced by your own experiences, dear queen, then look at history from the rest of the world."

"Does that include the history of my own country?" Sheeva sneered. "Because if you seriously expect me to believe that only–"

"Just think it over, Sheeva, long and hard. All you have learned may be lies, since what goes into those history books was written by those who had the freedom to lie. You were going to cite the account of the First Ancestors, were you not?"

Sheeva stood frozen to the spot, speechless with dread as the demon probed her mind.

"Ah yes," said Raakmathna contemptuously, "the old story that says you all began on Karzynhaal and lived together in peace, eventually embarking across the ocean to settle the lands, and always getting along and helping each other until my master fouled it all up. Why do you trust that story?"

"Because–"

"Because people who blindly trusted Onu, the one who *allowed* all my master's deeds to happen, told you so?"

"I–"

"And what about Prince Dominik and those Kason tribal nomads? Yes, they *said* they had nothing to do with Ohdan's ambush, but are you going to trust them just because of that? Will you *really* just go along with what they told you, as your dear, but naïve, husband has? Watch your every step, Sheeva, and your back at all times. They will *all* conspire against you, those who are unworthy and those who blindly follow the ... *presumed* words of Onu. I can help you, Sheeva. I can see into the hearts of all Fidons. I can tell you which ones to trust with the plans we will have to make, which ones to dispose of, and which ones are worthy to be by your side, but would not understand if you told them now."

Sheeva did not need to follow the demon's gaze. She knew that it was staring fixedly on Allor as he slumbered peacefully.

"I will not make any plans with you," Sheeva said. "I don't believe your words, and I don't need your aid even if I did."

"That *is* true, I suppose," said the demon casually. "I only suggested a basic line of action on how to deal with Nikolas and Halla."

Sheeva, losing the use of her legs, leaned numbly against the balcony's stone railing. Raakmathna's horridly fiery eyes, beaming from the shadowy, pitch-black form, pierced into the queen's soul. She wanted to scream, but the horror of the impending truth shut her throat tight. She could hardly even breathe.

Raakmathna, relishing in the dread she inflicted, concluded her point. "But you poisoned the medicine all on your own. You did it so easily, too. I was very impressed. You simply played it off as another ingredient you were putting in, and did it so deftly no one noticed or questioned you. And you were willing to kill nine others just to get at the two, for all the trouble that she played on your family, and all the agony *he* inflicted on you. That is, indeed, the mark of a true champion of order: the willingness to make any sacrifices that are needed to ensure that all goes as it should, without fearing the trappings that those fools who follow Onu try to place before you."

The demon then approached Sheeva, putting a shadowy hand to her chin and lifting her gaze directly into her eyes. The touch was unfathomably cold, and the demon's gaze bound her tongue. Tears of horror – horror of the demon and of her own darkness – began to flow silently from the queen's eyes.

"I know you have what it takes to set the world to order, dear queen," whispered the demon in a horrid tone of perverse affection. "And you are not afraid to dirty your own hands if need be; that is a bit of an uncommon trait for someone in your position, especially to the extent that you have demonstrated. And, if you want only my suggestions, then I will offer just that, but imagine the *power* you would have if you would just ... let me ... *in.*"

A gentle mumbling from inside the bedroom broke Sheeva's horrified trance. Her eyes peered past the open doorway, and she saw Allor beginning to stir. The queen raised her sight back to the demon, her eyes shining with resistance.

"Leave," she demanded quietly.

Raakmathna withdrew her hand and stepped back slowly as her shadowy form began to disperse. The sun was now rising above the distant hills, steadily brightening the sky.

"Think of the children that you will soon have," the demon said, nodding at Sheeva's belly, which the young queen embraced defensively. "Think of your friend Lerannu, and of course, your husband, Allor. Think of your mother, your father, your tutor, and all the others you lost in Kellmayar. Ask yourself ... what are you willing to do to protect those you love from sharing their fates?"

Sheeva stared at the shadow. "Leave."

"We'll talk again, and soon."

"*Leave.*"

The shadow had now faded, and Sheeva, turning back to the bedchamber, saw Allor awake, propped on an elbow, and looking at the queen with an admiring smile.

"Would you like me to join you out there?" he asked sultrily.

"If you'd like to," Sheeva said warmly, "but I was about to rejoin you here, if it's all the same to you."

Allor lifted the blankets for her, rising quickly and caressing her face when he noticed the tear streaks.

"Are you alright?" he asked worriedly. "What's wrong?"

"Nothing, Al," Sheeva said with a kiss. "I just can't believe we're finally together. And the morning is just so beautiful."

The two embraced and kissed each other in silence, making love one more time and eventually rising to prepare for the upcoming festivities of Kysonmay, and their first full day as the King and Queen of Enmayar.

49
12/28/4018 G.M.

ALLOR stood beside his wife and queen in the main courtyard of the castle. It was late in the afternoon of Sardonmay's Eve, and the young leaders of Enmayar were preparing for their customary procession through the city on their way to the archtemple.

The first three months of their reign had been good and prosperous, though still darkened by lingering worries regarding the country's relations with Kellmayar. While Sheeva and Allor continued to appeal for more time to tend to their own land's affairs before making another attempt at resolving matters with the West, Enmayar had been blessed with an exceptional autumn harvest. It had been stored, sold, and traded in its measures to produce a surprising surplus of wealth and goods. Naturally, this development did not go unnoticed by Kellmayar and the other two nations, and the pressure to send a share of the surplus to the West quickly increased. Sheeva and Allor, however, were reluctant to do so, as they still felt driven to focus on improving matters in Enmayar first, though they admitted they were not yet sure as to what would be the best use for their sudden bounty. Confessing this in their correspondence with the Nations, they did end up sending a little of the surplus to Kellmayar, though not enough to relieve the pressure to any real extent.

Aside from those difficulties, however, Allor and Sheeva's reign had fared well so far, and the two had proven to be very popular with the citizenry in the brief time they had led the land. Being true to their words on their wedding night, the King and Queen of Enmayar loved and supported each other, and confided with one another in nigh everything they did. Though Allor noticed a continuing distress hovering over Sheeva throughout their first months as leaders, the two were happy together, and the queen had told him more than once that his love was what did the most to keep her strong. The king said the same to his wife of what she did for him, and the two cherished a deep love that thankfully had been untainted by the trials of their lot.

Now, with all the royal household having gathered with the queen and king in the courtyard as the horses and carriages were led in, Allor gently pulled Sheeva close to him and nuzzled her ear. The queen giggled quietly, then brushed her face against his neck.

"I sure needed this," Sheeva said with an exhausted laugh.

"You and I both," Allor said as he kissed her cheek.

The last carriage and horses of the procession lined up outside the castle gates, waiting their turn to enter the courtyard and receive their passengers. The queen and king took each other's hand as they approached their carriage. They paused at the step of the carriage and looked back into the crowd of the household to see if Lerannu and her mother had made their way outside yet. The court mage and the south wardeness called out to them with a laugh, making their way through the merry gathering and joining them as they all stepped into the carriage.

"Sorry we took so long to get over here," Lerannu said with a grin. "You know how long Mother can take to dress when it's an occasion like this."

Sarah Stonefaith playfully flicked her daughter's ear. "And *you* were going through gowns right alongside me, young lady."

Allor and Sheeva laughed lightly and leaned their heads together as their carriage rode forward out of the courtyard and just past the castle gates, where it waited for more of the procession to collect their passengers and follow. The two young leaders and their friends soon found themselves speaking of Enmayar's future, though with hope undampened by the lingering difficulties.

"I know it's been a rough start for you two, to put it lightly," Sarah said kindly, "but I hope you've been taking the reports from the wards to heart. You've been doing very well for us here, and it hasn't gone unacknowledged by warden, holder, mayor, or citizen."

Allor and Sheeva nodded and thanked the wardeness for her words as the carriage rode out another short distance to further the growing procession.

"It might still be a bit of work before we can finally get matters settled with Kellmayar," Sarah went on, "but I believe our efforts here will ultimately help them and everyone else, too. We're all in this together, of course, but we can't help each other if we can't take enough care of ourselves."

"A frustrating truth," Lerannu said levelly as she looked intently at the king and queen. "I hope it doesn't spoil tonight's pleasantries, though."

Allor noted Sarah's uncomfortable realization following her daughter's words. Sheeva clearly noticed as well, as she and the king were quick to relieve the wardeness of any guilt she might have been feeling for touching on the more sensitive aspects of current affairs.

"It's quite alright," they said in unison. Allor looked at Sheeva, and the two laughed at their shared reaction before Sheeva went on to assure Sarah further.

"It is," said the queen, "and a notion that I agree with, besides. We still need some time to secure

Enmayar's future. Thankfully, as difficult as some of the relevant matters we've been trying to settle have been ..."

Allor looked puzzledly at his wife as she suddenly grasped his hand.

"I'm very happy to say that one matter regarding our land's future has been a very hopeful endeavor through and through ..."

Sheeva gently pressed Allor's hand to her middle.

"... and, if I may speak plainly, one that has been quite pleasant to see to, in more ways than one."

Allor looked blankly at his wife for an instant, and then the realization dawned on him, as it did with Sarah and Lerannu. Allor gasped out a laugh of wonder and joy, kissing Sheeva deeply as he tenderly caressed her belly. Lerannu and her mother cheered, and looked on as the king spoke to the queen.

"How far along?"

"Around two months," Sheeva said warmly with a grin. "It doesn't look like it happened *quite* on our first night together, but ... close enough, I'd say."

"It's all good to me, my love," Allor said as he embraced her.

As the procession continued to inch out of the courtyard, the king, queen, and their two friends conversed excitedly over the possibilities for the Mivinaar child, or children, to come.

***

The line of carriages and horses embarked from the castle and were well on their way through the city and toward the archtemple. The crowds that lined the way greeted the procession with cheers and good wishes for the holy day and the year to come. Allor held Sheeva's hand, waving to the throngs and relishing the merriment and hope that filled the city.

Out of the corner of his eye, Allor noticed a young boy in the light of the fading day and brightening torches. He appeared to be underfed and was garbed in threadbare clothes, but nevertheless stood amongst the revelers and waved at the procession with a smile on his grey-furred face. Though thinned by hunger, his smile seemed one of irrepressible hope. The lad held what appeared to be food tucked caringly under his arm. Allor sensed Sheeva's grip on his hand slightly tighten, and he knew that she also saw the poor youth.

"That's one thing I'd certainly like to try and help in reducing," the queen said sadly. "I know that Kellmayar is having a time of it, too, as do we all to some measure, but I can't help but feel the need to try and help the poor here in our land, at least for a while, before trying to send things that might not even help all that much across the ocean."

Lerannu and Sarah followed Sheeva's gaze, then returned their sight to the queen and king, acknowledging what they saw with a sad nod as the carriage passed the crowd.

"If we are indeed looking to see to our own country before investing in others," Sarah said somberly, "I'd think that ought to be as good a matter to try and see to as any."

"I just don't know what exactly we ought to do, though," said the queen in frustration. "Should we use however much of the surplus to go in and try to better the poorer areas here, and Enmayar at large? Should we just reserve a fund and try to come up with some way to allocate it to those people? I don't know if–"

Sheeva suddenly bolted upright from her seat in the carriage. Allor, similarly taken aback, bore his sight into the crowd until he saw the boy again just before he passed from view. A small band of other poor youths had swarmed him, pulling him and the food he held into the depths of the crowd. Allor sighed sadly and drew Sheeva close as she put a hand to her brow. Sheeva explained what she saw to the south wardeness and the mage, whose ears lowered grimly as they looked on at the royal couple.

"We can think of something," Allor assured his wife. "We just might need some time to sort out a plan. But if you're for trying something, I'm with you."

"As are we," said Sarah as Lerannu nodded in agreement. "In the meantime, let us not lose sight of the good we have now, and let us keep those struggling in our hearts and our prayers."

The royal holiday procession rode on to the archtemple, where Salpion Owen Lovonhaar gave a service of hope and thanksgiving. Allor, seated beside Sheeva, found himself flitting between inner prayers of thanks to Onu for his wife and future family, for wisdom to devise a way to help the impoverished of the country, and for strength for the poor, that they might persevere until a potential solution was reached. Following the service, the royal procession returned to the castle, where feasting and dancing awaited the household and its guests. The Midnight Dance of Sardonmay came and went, and Allor and Sheeva, with love and revelry in their hearts, retired to bed together not long after.

***

The next morning, Allor turned in his bed to find Sheeva absent. Mystified, he quickly rose and dressed, and stepped out of the bedroom and into the corridor.

"I trust that you know where the queen is?" he asked the two guards he found waiting near the door.

"Yes, my king," one of the guards said. "Queen Sheeva instructed us to inform you that she and two other guards have set out to visit the southwest riverbank district."

Allor looked at the guards in bafflement. "Whatever could have possessed her to go there of all places, on Winter's First Day and this early in the morning, without telling me herself? I would've been happy to accompany her."

"She said she didn't want to disturb you," the guard answered plainly. "She mentioned something about taking a more thorough look at the state of things there, for some effort or other that you've discussed to try and help the less fortunate, Onu bless her heart."

Allor smiled lightly. "Onu bless her heart, indeed. Were your directions only to stay here and inform me when I awoke?"

"No, my king. She told us to accompany you to the district and join her, if you were inclined to do so."

"Good. I just need a few moments and a little breakfast, and we'll be off."

***

The morning was well underway by the time Allor and the guards reached the southwest riverbank. The city was fairly quiet, as most were resting or partaking in light festivities in the wake of the previous day's revels. Upon reaching the poor neighborhood, the King of Enmayar and his escort were met with a silence that seemed to be of both merry resting and poverty's subduing nature. Allor's thoughts drifted back to the boy in the crowd, and he wondered of his whereabouts and state following the previous evening's incident.

The king and his guards were only a little while in wandering the district before finding Sheeva and her escort. The queen threw herself into her husband's arms, where he held and caressed her tenderly as they conversed.

"I would've happily joined you from the start, you know."

"I'm sorry, Al. I just couldn't sleep after what we saw last night. I felt that I just had to come here. You seemed to be sleeping just fine, though. I didn't want to spoil that for you."

"Nonsense. I'm with you, remember?"

"Of course."

They kissed, and Allor looked about the sorry shambles of wooden shacks and worn stone buildings.

"We certainly will have our work cut out for us," the king said reflectively, "whatever course we choose. Have any other ideas come to you since last night?"

"Actually, there is a thought," the queen said with a voice of cautious optimism. "I'm still not sure how exactly we'd start going about it yet, but given the lot of these people and our efforts to try and build a steady cooperation between all the Nations, I've started wondering if we could—"

The sounds of a scuffle and young voices shouting cut the queen's words short. Allor and Sheeva, beckoning their guards to accompany them, strode quickly down the street toward the source of the commotion. The king and queen, their guards at their sides, peered around a corner to see a sorrowful sight. Two young Fidons, a Mavon girl and a Balon-and-Zaron boy, were standing over the miserably quivering body of a young Zaron boy that lay hunched up in the street. Though Allor could not yet fully make out the victim's face, he felt an overwhelming sense that it was the very same lad from the previous evening.

"P-please, Genlov," the grey-furred boy moaned piteously, "you an' Fendra an' the others got what I had last night!"

"And now it's today," the white-and-grey boy named Genlov said flatly. "I woulda thought ya'd know by now that we all gotsa eat again. How many times we godda kick ya arse before ya learn that?"

Allor watched with a pained heart. Feeling Sheeva's hand begin to tighten around his, he looked to her and saw a face that was torrential with pity and a startlingly dark indignation. The king made to whisper something calming to his wife, but his attention was quickly pulled back to the scene before them.

"An' *I* needs to eat, too! If you all leave me to starve, then you can't get no more from me! It's been gettin' harder an' harder to snatch more of it, you know. An' last night's food was given to me from the Temple. Why couldn't you let me have that, at least?"

"Because we were 'ungry, ye lil' shite, that's why," said the Mavon girl contemptuously. "And we don't care how 'ard it is to get more. If ye need more, ye'll find a way to get more. We need to eat, too, and we don't care about any who aren't with us. If ye don't like it, then either starve or piss off from 'ere. There's plenny more of you scraps around 'ere; we'll just find another one."

The Zaron then sat up, looking pleadingly at the pair of young robbers.

"Then lemme join you all," he said resignedly. "If this is how it has to be, then—"

"We only give folks one chance, Tommy boy," Genlov said scornfully. "Ya said ya were better'n us and weren't gonna join. Now live with what ya've chosen, and *give us that bread!*"

Genlov and Fendra landed the boy with awful kicks, each to his middle. Tommy gasped out a wretched sob as the air was kicked out of him, and he fell back onto the street curled up into a ball. Sheeva and Allor, gasping in dismay, gestured to their guards to intervene. The four guards sprinted around the corner, calling the two young robbers out as they approached. Before they could reach them, however, Fendra and Genlov grabbed the bread loaf from Tommy and bolted down the street and out of sight at shocking speed. The guards turned to the queen and king, looking to see if they would be told to pursue further.

"Leave them," Sheeva said with a dark flatness as she and Allor sprinted over to the Zaron boy, who now lay crying in the street. Allor and Sheeva knelt beside the urchin, with the queen gently petting his back before taking him into her arms while the king and the guards looked on.

"Come now, my lad," Sheeva said in a voice that was now one of heart-melting kindness. "No need for more tears. Someone's here for you."

The boy sniffed and looked up at Sheeva and her company. One eye was swollen from a punch he must have received the night before, but both opened wide as he looked upon the queen and those with her.

"Y-you," he stammered, still weepy, "you're the q-queen aren't you? I-I s-saw you an' the king in the parade last n-night!"

"I am," Sheeva said softly. "And this man beside me is your king, Allor, and my beloved husband. I don't know if you would know much about what's been going on in the country lately ..."

The boy shook his head and sniffed. "C-can't say that I have, my queen."

"Well, to try and put it simply, we've been able to get a good bit of extra food and other nice things lately, and we've been trying to come up with ideas on how to put that to good use. We've been thinking of trying to help you, and people like you, somehow."

The urchin sniffed again, and slowly, cautiously, made to embrace the queen. "Th-that'd be quite nice, my queen."

"I can't say for certain how we would go about it," Sheeva went on, now looking into Allor's eyes as she continued to comfort the boy, "but I've been thinking that we might try to find a way to make sure that you were taken care of, while possibly helping all of Fidonhaal."

Allor's ears pricked up and he looked at Sheeva earnestly, intrigued by the prospect.

"We're trying to focus on taking care of ourselves for the time being," Sheeva said directly to her husband as she continued to comfort the boy, "but we're supposed to be cooperating with all the nations in trying to help keep each other well. What if ... what if we could start a reserve of people, soldiers when necessary, and some sort of civil workers otherwise, that belonged to all the nations? I'm sure we'd all still need to send some of our own soldiers to help each other at times, but what if there was an order that served all of Fidonhaal besides just the Temple and the like? Of course, they do a good job with what they have overall, but if there was perhaps an additional way ..."

Allor smiled, in awe of what he was hearing. "I don't quite know how we'd go about it at the moment," he said, "but I love what I'm hearing so far."

"We'll try and figure all that out later," Sheeva said as she turned her gaze back to the urchin, who had now calmed down and was listening intently to their conversation. "For now, let's get you and your family somewhere warm and safe. Where's your mother or father? Is there anyone with you?"

The lad hugged Sheeva tightly. "No. I'm ... alone."

Sheeva sighed deeply and stood up, helping the boy to his feet. "You're named Thomas, yes? Well, 'Tommy' by those you know, anyhow?"

"Yes," Tommy said, "but I think I like being called Thomas, now that you say it."

"Well, Thomas, we'll take you home with us and make sure you're taken care of until we sort out what to do next for you and those like you. Is there anything you need to get and bring with you?"

Thomas shook his head silently.

"Then let's go," the queen said with a proffered hand. "We'll have you stay with us for now. We'll enjoy Sardonmay together."

Thomas sniffed one more time, and taking Sheeva's hand in his, as well as Allor's with the other, the company began to make their way back to Castle Genverdell.

"Wait," Thomas said suddenly, bringing everyone to a halt. "I'm sure you can't have everyone here be in the castle with you now, but what about a few others, like ... well ... Genlov and Fendra?"

Allor glanced at Sheeva, at once uncomfortable yet understanding of the face he saw, which was hardened and conflicted.

"Perhaps at a later time, we'll see to them," the queen answered at length.

50
1/7/4019 G.M.

SHEEVA stood alone in the throne room in the middle of the night. She had quietly gotten out of bed and made her way through the corridors, assuring the occasional guard she encountered that all was fine and she simply couldn't sleep at the moment. She now stood at a long display table placed against the wall of the throne room, looking over the collection of artwork, finery, and weapons that had taken up residence in the castle over the centuries. The display looked at once majestic and eerie in the pale, silvery glow of the waxing half-moon, and when her eyes at last fell upon the blade she sought, her fur stood on end.

The long, lightly curved form of the sword and its sheath, which was a Mivinaar heirloom from three centuries past, was of the sort commonly wielded by the people of the Whitemanes. It was a gift to the first Mivinaar monarchs, specifically to Queen Uberra from her parents, as she left her home in the Whitemanes to move to Genverdell and reign beside her husband, Rahldor. It was a hauntingly beautiful blade, having been forged in the prized fashion that was first taught to the Fidons long ago by the angel Branok and the flamehearts. The queen gently took it off its stand and drew it halfway out of its scabbard, darkly mesmerized by the river-like shimmer of the steel, which glittered lethally in the moonlight softly spilling in from the windows.

"A fine means to defend yourself and all those you love, my friend," said the shadow at Sheeva's side, "should the need ever arise."

The queen had finally yielded to Raakmathna's sense. She had earlier wrestled with the words of the agent of Lovaariinu, initially seeing them as senseless despite the other side of her that insisted otherwise. It all finally got through to her, however, after seeing how the non-Zarons treated the poorest and most vulnerable of their grey-furred kin. The mercilessness with which Thomas's assailants beat and robbed him, and their utter disregard for his ultimate well-being, had set the queen's heart aflame with fury. It was enough that this trouble plagued the topmost levels of Fidonhaal's leadership, but seeing that such a heinous conspiracy against her people permeated all tiers of society finally brought her to see sense. Her mind suddenly felt so cleared, so focused. Something had to be done, and with the first ideas she had for the new order of soldiers, along with Raakmathna's guidance, the queen was sure that one day, all of Fidonhaal would be set to rights and follow a perfect form of order.

Sheeva lightly brushed her fingers along the length of the katana. "I should think so," the queen agreed. "Such fine craftsmanship, and ironically forged in a way first taught by an angel and his offspring in service to Onu. It's funny, how something that can be traced to the enemy might help me in usurping their foolish and chaotic ways."

"Indeed," Raakmathna concurred warmly, "but of course it will take a fine measure more than a mere blade, however well-made, to fully secure the world and all its true people from the fiends that mean to destroy us and perpetuate chaos. We need to begin building our own armies as soon as possible. It may be a little slow at first, but I assure you that if you pursue the ones that I tell you to seek, and repeat my words to them, we will be able to construct our forces and instruct them properly without fear of discovery by our enemies."

"I confess that I still struggle to see it playing out that well," Sheeva said at length.

"That is entirely understandable, my queen. I assure you, I can sense the pains and wrongs that dwell in all Fidons' hearts. I can tell you which of the righteous breed have been hurt the most by the others, what those wrongs were, and how to appeal to them to see the way things are, and what must be done about it. It is all just a matter of patience."

"Very well, my friend. I suppose we should start with Thomas?"

"Indeed, though we should refrain from unveiling everything to him for a while longer. Continue to care for him, and perhaps have your friend Lerannu give him a little schooling before we see to his true education. As far as bringing more people into our plans from the outset, there are two in this very castle who will certainly serve you well, once you appeal to them properly."

"I have a feeling that neither of them would be Al at this point."

"Indeed not, the poor man. His heart is kind and trusting, but alas to a fault. But do not fret, we will be able to get to him in due time. For now, however, he must remain ignorant of our true intentions. It is Ranoth and Wardeness Stonefaith of whom I speak."

Sheeva looked at her mighty ally with intrigue. "Is that so? What wrongs did they suffer to warrant such a willingness to join us, once they hear what they need to hear?"

"You know what they are, my friend. Ranoth was denied his right to the position of salpion to that lenient Mavon swine Owen, despite all the preparations he went through to be a good leader of the Temple. And Sarah was betrayed by her town's treasurer, a black-and-white harlot named Uriah."

"Of course," Sheeva said with a shake of her head, incredulous toward herself for not realizing the reasons on her own. "When should I try and speak with them?"

"As soon as possible. Tomorrow, if you can. Just devise some way to get into a private conversation with each. Do not try and converse with them both at once, though. Not at first."

"I understand."

"I will be with you, my friend. Whenever you manage to speak with them privately, I will guide you through what to say. Their eyes will be opened in due time, and then we will see about conversing with them together soon enough."

"Very well."

"If I might ask, do you have a name in mind for our order? Something that will grace the history books for eons to come once Fidonhaal has been set to rights?"

Sheeva thought for a moment, again gently touching the edge of the Whitemane-style sword. She smiled, and looked intently at Raakmathna.

"They'll be bringing and keeping order, and therefore peace, throughout all of Fidonhaal. Peacekeepers, I think … yes, the Peacekeepers of Fidonhaal."

"A wonderful name," said Lovaariinu's agent with a smile. "I shall not keep you any longer tonight, friend. Go on back to bed, to Al, and have a good sleep. We will continue this in the morning."

***

Sheeva relished her luck as she took tea with Wardeness Sarah the following afternoon. Allor was occupied with a visiting advisor, and Sheeva, telling her husband that she had something to go over with Sarah, was easily able to make her time with the wardeness private while not provoking suspicion.

"Is there anything the matter, my queen?" Sarah asked as she sipped her tea. "I haven't heard of any troubles in South Ward, but if something's suddenly come up–"

"No, friend," Sheeva assured her, "nothing like that. I just wanted to make sure that everything was alright with you, and perhaps Lera as well, if anything might be the matter."

Sarah glanced puzzledly at the queen as she reached for a scone. "We're doing fine, I'd say. You and Allor have been very good to us. I am honored to serve you as the wardeness of Enmayar's south ward, and I don't think I need to tell you how happy and grateful Lera is to be your court mage. She's taken quite well to tutoring Thomas so far, and has told me that she greatly looks forward to schooling your children when the time comes."

Taking a bite of the scone and sipping some more tea, Sarah looked intently at the queen. "Have I given you any reason to think that something was wrong? Has Lera told you anything that I don't know, or didn't realize?"

"Not at all. It's just ..."

"*You are doing just fine, Sheeva,*" the queen heard Raakmathna assure her within her mind. "*Just keep to what I have told you.*"

Sheeva looked to Sarah, who was looking at her with perplexed eyes.

"It's just that I can't help but think about what you two have been through, particularly with Lera's father."

Sarah's eyes fell to look dully at the teacup in her hands.

"I'm sorry if I'm reopening the wound," Sheeva went on. "I just keep thinking about how much Al has been there for me, and there's that little part of me, in the far back of my mind, that can't help but wonder if it could ever happen to me."

Sarah's eyes shot up, a simmering anger threatening to unleash. "Are you saying you suspect him of it now? If so, you must make absolutely certain before–"

"Oh no, Sarah, not at all. It's just ... to think of such a grievous trespass against such a blessed thing. If he ever did that, I don't know how I would be able to handle it. And you've been so strong through it ... you and Lera both."

Sarah's eyes began to shimmer with threatening tears. "I'm afraid you're giving me too much credit, my queen. Sure, I've been able to move on, to a point, and with time. But ... I'm not sure if much of it has been a matter of strength. I feel like it might be more out of numbness."

"*Apologize and console her, Sheeva,*" Raakmathna's whisper echoed.

Sheeva rose from her seat and came to Sarah's side, embracing her by the shoulders as the wardeness began to quietly weep.

"I'm so sorry. I just couldn't get it out my mind, and I just wondered if–"

"It's quite alright," Sarah sobbed as she hugged the queen in turn. "I ... I haven't really talked about it, all that much, to be honest. It hurts so much ... but I'm glad to talk about it to you."

***

The afternoon tea passed, with Sarah's accounts of Roniil's affair starting with sadness and regret before steadily giving way to anger. When teatime ended, Sarah was tremoring with rage until she realized her state and made to apologize.

"I'm so sorry that you're seeing me like this, my queen. I ... I've been holding back more than even I realized, it seems."

"It was a great wrong that he did to you, him and that Uriah both."

Sarah massaged her brow in silence for a moment, then looked to Sheeva. "Please, as a friend, I ask that you don't tell Lera about this talk. I'm sure that she still loves her father, and it's not fair for her to have to deal with something that's between Roniil and myself ... and Uriah."

Sheeva nodded understandingly. "Not a word from me. I promise."

Sarah rose from the table, sighing sorrowfully.

"I still feel like I have more to ... to get out of me, though."

"We can talk more about it at tea again, or any other time we can get some time just between us, if you'd like."

Sarah smiled, and came over to the queen and embraced her. "I think I would like that very much. Thank you. Thank you so much."

"Anytime," Sheeva said warmly as she patted the south wardeness' back.

***

The next day, Sheeva was able to speak privately with Ranoth Windsbreath in the castle chapel, passing it off as a confession that she wished to keep between her and the priest. Allor, having walked with her to the chapel doors, embraced and kissed her.

"I'll be in the throne room talking with Ivonos again," the king said warmly. "Take your time, and may your heart and soul be lightened."

"Thank you, Al. I'll try not to be too long."

"I love you."

"And I love you."

Allor turned and made his way to the throne room. Sheeva stared resolutely at the chapel's doors for an instant, then opened them and entered the sacred room. Ranoth, reading his copy of the Beldsantu, looked up at the sound of the opening doors, nodded, and then closed the book. He stepped down from the podium, bowing his head and looking at Sheeva with caring eyes.

"Welcome, Queen Sheeva. What can I do for you?"

"I fear that I am weighted down with a constant darkness, Brother Windsbreath," said Sheeva with a reverent bow. "I wish to confess the troubles in my heart."

"Of course, my queen. Much weighs on your shoulders as you strive to lead your people. Come and sit with me, and tell me what ails your soul."

The queen and the priest sat together on the steps leading up to the podium. Ranoth looked intently at Sheeva, who, guided by the resonating voice of the All-Keeper's servant, drew a deep, wearied breath before speaking.

"I have been struggling against an ever-mounting anger, Brother Windsbreath."

"Toward what is this anger directed, my queen?"

"Toward the Greystones, even though they've passed from this world. Toward Ohdan Karvin-thaal, even though he too can no longer harm another Fidon. Toward ... toward all those who had attempted to undermine the leadership of my parents ... and mine, what with all the effort that had been put into it, to try and ensure that I would be able to serve Enmayar well."

Ranoth sighed in deep, palpable sympathy. "I can only imagine what those pains, that those people had inflicted on you, have sown into your heart. But it is as you have noted, they have passed from Fidonhaal and across the Great Curtain. Whatever their deeds have warranted, it is ultimately in Onu's hands, as it is for all of creation."

"It's just ... I'm not perfect, I know this ..."

"No Fidon is, my queen."

"I know, but I've tried all I could ... and to think that the Greystones thought they could try and tear down all my parents' efforts, for Enmayar themselves and in their efforts to make me a capable successor just because ... of something so ultimately petty."

"Well, I wouldn't call love a petty thing, especially when I look at what is between you and King Allor."

Sheeva looked at Ranoth and smiled. "I suppose so, but for what it was at the time, it wasn't an absolute with Nikolas. That's the point for that time of courtship, is it not?"

"Perhaps, but let's not forget what had been happening in their lives when Allor first came to us."

"Fair enough, but ... I don't know. Sometimes I wonder if it actually would've been better if the Greystones, or anyone else, ended up being elected to replace us back when Halla called for the vote."

"What makes you think that, Sheeva? I can tell you with complete confidence that you've been leading our country very well, even this early into your time as queen."

"I hope you're right. I guess it's just one of those things, not being able to know with certainty what would've happened otherwise."

Sheeva looked to Ranoth, her eyes searching his.

"I don't know if it's really my place to ask, because I'm not sure if it's really right to compare the situations, but ..."

"But what, my queen?"

"What do you think about Salpion Lovonhaar? Does it ever darken your heart, that after all the time and effort you put into being a worthy successor to Salpion Helga, that he should just swoop in, so to say?"

Ranoth stared flatly into Sheeva's eyes.

"I'm sorry, Brother, I'm not even sure if I really know or understand the full story. I shouldn't have–"

"No," Ranoth said with a deep sigh. "It's alright. Yes, I have had times when my heart was darkened by envy and resentment toward Owen. And I suppose I've wondered at times if I really would've been a good salpion after all, or at least as good as he, given how I let the turn of events so darken my thoughts. It's not that I think Owen is a *bad* salpion, or even ... I don't know, I believe I've pegged it as irresponsibility in the past, but I suppose it may really be more a matter of differing priorities and approaches instead."

Ranoth again looked intently into the queen's eyes, the torrent of thoughts turning within him plain to see.

"But yes, I've been quite ... angry ... with how that played out. I did all I could to show my intentions of leading the Temple and all the world's Faith in earnest. I loved Salpion Helga like a mother. And Owen just sort of appeared under her wing one day, and things started to change. Owen isn't a bad man, but I really ..."

Ranoth went silent, then suddenly shook his head, laughing sadly as tears brimmed his eyes.

"What in Onu's name am I doing? This is your confession, and here I am ... my heart going where it shouldn't."

Sheeva gently patted Ranoth's back. "Perhaps we can both exchange confessions? I may not be one of the cloth, but–"

"The idea is that all Fidons are to listen to one another's troubles," Ranoth said with a small smile. "If you're willing, I'd be happy to listen to yours and tell you mine. I don't want to keep you from anything important with Allor and the advisors, though."

"I think we would both fare better today if we tended to this, Brother. Let's just talk a while."

***

An hour passed, and both queen and priest had given vent to their anger. Both had relayed their bitterness toward those who, wittingly or not, had undermined all they had worked to achieve. Both had even braved to voice the darkest doubt in their hearts, the fear that Onu may indeed not care of their plight and had actually abandoned Fidonity to heartless chaos long ago.

Ranoth shook his head. "Listen to me go on like this! I'm starting to think that Owen is indeed the one truly worthy of being salpion, as much as I don't want to admit it."

"We should be honest about what dwells in our heart, though, should we not? Isn't honesty and trust the most vital part to a loving bond, especially with Onu?"

"Yes, but ... Onu's Four Breaths, it's just ... so ugly ..."

"Maybe we both need to talk together again, sometime later? We can help each other, I think."

Ranoth looked to Sheeva and smiled. "I think I'd like that, Sheeva. I think I'd like that very much."

Sheeva smiled, nodded, and got up from the podium's step. "I suppose I really should be getting back to Al and the others for now, though. Always something else to settle, it seems."

"Indeed," Ranoth said with a smile. "Just be strong, my friend. You're doing your mother and father proud, I assure you. From this matter of combatting poverty that you've been trying to get started, to just listening to the troubles of a fellow Fidon no matter their lot, you've already proven yourself to be a more than worthy Queen of Enmayar."

"Thank you, Brother," Sheeva said warmly as she turned to make her way back to the throne room. "We'll talk again soon."

***

Five moons passed, and the land of Enmayar continued to prosper under the fledgling leadership of their young queen and king. Sheeva's time to give birth drew ever nearer, with her belly having now swelled heavily with the East's hopeful future leaders. She sensed that they were twins, and on confiding her intuition to Allor, she was greeted with a loving, hopeful eagerness.

"I hope you're right," he said, "and if so, depending on whether they're both boys, girls, or one each, we can name them after one of our parents, just as you said before."

Meanwhile, Thomas had been faring well in the castle, receiving education from Lerannu and light training from some of the castle guards while a proper establishment for the Peacekeeper order was still being drafted. The boy had been ceaselessly grateful and well-mannered to the queen and king, and showed great promise for the duty that soon would be bestowed upon him.

All had been going well throughout Enmayar, and the relationships that Sheeva had cultivated with Sarah and Ranoth had grown strong and deep in the months following their first conversations. Just as Lovaariinu's servant had told her, the wardeness and the priest had opened up more and more about the bitterness, resentment, and as time revealed, hatred that they bore toward those who so wronged them. Now, Raakmathna had told her, was the time to bring them together

~ 138 ~

and converse with them in the same room, so the plans for the Peacekeepers and the new era of Fidonhaal could truly begin.

Again having the good fortune to have a visiting advisor to occupy Allor, Sheeva truthfully told her husband that Sarah and Ranoth had become strongly interested in aiding with the development of the Peacekeeper order. She arranged to have afternoon tea with them and the three now sat together, lightly drinking their tea as each looked expectantly upon the others at the table.

"I know you two have carried some heavy burdens within yourselves for some time," Sheeva said to begin the meeting, "and I'm here to tell you that our Peacekeepers, guardians of Fidonhaal who will rise from the most downtrodden of our people, can help us deal out justice to those who wronged you."

Sarah and Ranoth looked inquiringly at the queen. Raakmathna was right, much to Sheeva's elation. If she had proposed this earlier, both would have refuted the plan and fled to tell all. Sheeva herself would have foolishly done as much at first, until the injustices committed toward all Zarons became clear. Now, however, with both having confessed the dark truth of their hatred, along with Ranoth's persistent lust to rule the Temple and Sarah's desire for nothing more than to see Uriah and Roniil pay for their treachery to her, they were all ears.

"As we have discussed together before, these wrongs we have suffered are not a coincidence. They are the result of all non-Zarons coordinating our demises, and they affect so many more than just the three of us here. That is what the Peacekeepers are intended to combat, provided we can succeed in the coming years to establish them and plan our attack."

"A fine idea, Sheeva," Sarah said with a calm nod, "but how can we possibly manage to coordinate all that would need to be done? We'd need to be able to set things up across all the world, and what needs to be done ... someone's bound to talk. And besides those who would obviously fight our plans, there are those of our pure kin who are ignorant of the truth and wouldn't join us in our time of need, at least not before it was too late. How could we possibly keep this secret from those who would undo all our efforts?"

"We seek those who have suffered as we have suffered, and tell them of what we mean to do," Sheeva said confidently. "With the right words and the right people, we *will* be able to do this."

"But surely that wouldn't be enough to guarantee complete silence toward those outside our plans," Ranoth said with a shake of the head. "If any slip was to be made, and one of our own was questioned by the enemy, how could we count on them to not give us away?"

"It's simple," Sheeva said as she nodded toward the back of the room. "We turn to a servant of true order to guide us, and to bind us to an oath of silence, which, if broken, will smite us on the spot."

Sarah and Ranoth followed Sheeva's gaze, and the two gasped and stared in awed silence at the shadow that stepped forth from the corner in which it had been silently standing.

"This is Raakmathna," Sheeva explained. "She showed me the horrible truth of the world following the troubles that the Greystones caused, and the murder of my mother and father. She helped me show you the truth of your pains, as well. And now, here we all are, at the precipice of the new and greatest era of Fidonhaal. We must follow her words, seek out those she tells us to find, and bind each and every one in our order to this oath of silence. It will begin with us, if you will join me. Or have I misjudged you two?"

A brief moment of utter silence filled the room. Then Ranoth and Sarah looked to the queen.

"Your judgement of us has not been misguided," Ranoth said with a determined nod that Sarah seconded. "We are with you to the bitter end, and will do all we can to aid you in bringing justice and order to all the world."

"Then come," Sheeva said as she joined a hand to each of her new, closest confidants in the building of Fidonhaal's future. "Let us be the first to take this oath."

51
7/17/4019 G.M.

ALLOR tenderly clasped the hand that tightly gripped his own. Sheeva, shaking as she drew deep, steady breaths, lay in her bed as the doctor and midwife helped her bring the young leaders' children into the world. Lerannu and Sarah stood beside the king, speaking encouragingly to both parents in turn as the births began. Ranoth was there as well, though staying a small distance away for the time being. Beside him was Owen Lovonhaar, the Salpion of the Temple himself, who out of friendship and tradition had been invited to lead the children's blessing.

Also present was young Thomas, the former urchin whom Sheeva had so lovingly taken in on Sardonmay. The boy had grown into a handsome, respectable lad in the months following that day. He had lived at the castle for the first few months, but now resided at the burgeoning training camp nearby that served the fledgling Peacekeeper order. He had been given leave to visit the ones who had helped him find a better life.

Though still a small initiative, the Peacekeeper order was now steadily beginning to grow with the commendation of the other three nations, who were impressed by Sheeva's intentions when the queen explained them. A good number of other orphans and destitute children had since been offered a place in the order, and though still far from meeting Sheeva's vision, things looked very promising.

All of that was now far from Allor's mind, however, as he held his wife's hand, along with his breath, in anticipation of the birth of their children. At last the first one came, for Sheeva's sense that she was carrying twins had proved to be correct. It was a girl, one of beautifully gentle grey fur and eyes that matched her father's, which were barely visible as they strived to open wide and see the world. The second followed less than a minute later, and aside from being a boy, he was nearly a mirror image of his sister. After being caringly washed and dried by the doctor and midwife, the two beautiful babes rested together at their mother's heart, their brief, anxious whimpering quickly changing to peaceful cooing as they snuggled together in the queen's embrace. Sheeva gently wept with joy, and Allor, with tears of elation streaming from his eyes, knelt closer to his wife's side and gently petted his daughter and son.

"They're so beautiful, Sheeva."

Sheeva gently leaned in her bed and kissed her husband. "They certainly are."

The doctor, parchment and quill in hand, asked the queen and king their children's names. Sheeva looked to Allor, who nodded warmly. They had decided on the names, whatever the exact outcome, months beforehand.

"Our daughter is Talrah, Talrah Mivinaar IV. Our son is Samuel, Samuel Mivinaar II."

Shortly after, Ranoth and the salpion stepped forward to bless the little princess and prince. The two servants of Onu gently brushed the babes' foreheads with a drop of blessed oil and holy water. Then Owen, gently taking them from Sheeva's embrace, cradled them in his arms as he led all in the room through the blessing. The salpion caringly placed them back into the queen's arms, and as he did, Allor glanced at him, only to be taken aback by the odd look that flashed across the holy man's face. In the instant that he saw it, Allor would've described it as a face of shocked fright, though he had no idea as to what would have caused such a reaction.

The king made to ask Owen what the matter was, but his attention quickly snapped back to his children as an adorable sputtering and blowing sound began to come from them. The droplets of blessed oil and water had slowly flowed down Talrah's face, streaming to the edge of her muzzle and finally dripping onto her mouth. The little princess was now trying to blow it out and away from her lips, giggling a little as she did so, and Samuel, though the oil and water had dripped onto his cheek and far from his mouth, had begun to imitate his sister. The room filled with laughter, and Allor, overwhelmed with happiness, instantly forgot the look on the salpion's face.

52
1/8/4023 G.M.

LERANNU sat in the dining hall, smiling as she watched Princess Talrah and Prince Samuel finish their breakfast. The twins had celebrated their third birthday the previous summer, and the new year's first week had just passed, along with its festivities. Today was the day, the children's first day of schooling, with Lerannu set to serve as their tutor. The mage looked to Sheeva and Allor, seeing plainly that they shared in her excitement for the milestone.

In the first years following Sheeva and Allor's coronation, Enmayar had continued to fare well, with the queen's proposed Peacekeeper order going especially well, gaining ever more awareness, approval, and support from the country and the other three nations. Thomas was now a promising young soldier in training. He alternated between serving stints as a castle guard and continuing his training and education at the encampment a short ride outside the city. He had become almost an older brother to the young prince and princess over the course of his visits.

As for Fidonhaal's situation at large and relations between the Four Nations, things were definitely trending optimistically. Despite the lingering tensions and uncertainties that remained between Enmayar and Kellmayar, it seemed that, given the premise of Queen Sheeva's intentions with the Peacekeepers, long-term relations between all the nations were on their way to an unmatched state of stability and cooperation. Lerannu knew only so much of what exactly was being arranged between the queen, her mother, and the castle priest, along with the steadily growing handful of prominent Fidons who had begun to join the cause. Oddly enough, King Allor also seemed to be only lightly involved with the Peacekeepers at present. However, given the promise that had consistently shown itself in the formative years of the order, the court mage was not inclined to dwell on the matter, and she now eagerly looked forward to her task of seeing to Samuel and Talrah's education.

The princess and the prince, having finished eating, looked to their parents and the mage.

"We going to school with Lady Lera now, Mama and Papa?" Samuel asked.

"That's right," Sheeva said warmly as she and Allor rose from the table, followed by their children and the mage. "Things are going to be a bit different now, but you're going to learn so many things with her!"

The queen and her husband knelt and hugged their children tightly. Sheeva lovingly stroked their heads as she spoke in a voice that was laden with effort to avoid becoming overly emotional.

"You two behave well for Lady Lera, alright?"

"Yes, Mama," said Talrah as her brother nodded along with her.

"When it's time for lunch, we'll all meet up together here and we can talk about all you two learned this morning, alright?"

"Mm-hm," the children hummed in unison as they hugged their mother and father one more time.

"We love you two," Allor said steadily. "You both have a good morning!"

"You, too!" Talrah said as she and Samuel each took one of Lerannu's hands.

Sheeva approached the mage and embraced her as well, as did Allor, before the leaders of Enmayar departed for the throne room. Lerannu then led the princess and prince by the hand to her study, talking eagerly of their first lesson as they walked down the corridor.

Part Two

The Bard and the Huntress

A Bard's Winding Path

53
4/15/4028 G.M.

DONOVAN sat in the cellar of his house, in the memorial nook, looking at the urns of those who had passed before him. Grandparents where there, as well as great-grandparents, an aunt and uncle or two, and a few cousins. He focused meditatively on two, however. They were the ones that jointly held the ashes of his mother and stillborn sister, and the one that now housed the remains of "Uncle" Jak Kelldren.

The old bard had died two years back on the second day of spring. The morning after the Veronmay Eve festivities, Uncle Jack approached Donovan, offering him something that the young man had keenly, but patiently, been waiting for since it was mentioned over ten years ago.

"Ah've been torn," said the old highlander, "tae either teach ye mah wife's song, or tae keep it in mah own heart, fer a long time. It's not that Ah dinnae *want* tae teach it tae ye ... it's just ..."

"I understand," said Donovan gently. "As much as I'd love to learn it, or even just hear it, I don't want to press you for it."

"An' Ah thank ye fer yer understanding Donny, but Ah feel a need tae pass it on. So, if yer nae too busy at the moment ..."

"I'd be honored."

Uncle Jak led Donovan into his room, and after rummaging through his things, at last pulled out some parchments full of musical notes and lyrics. Sifting through them, the old bard handed two of them to his protégé. Donovan read them, playing and singing the composition in his mind, and when he finished, he looked up to see his mentor, misty-eyed.

"I wish I could've met her," Donovan said softly.

"Me too, Donny. Ah did what Ah could tae put her into words, but ... Ah don't believe words alone could ever do her justice."

The two practiced and played the song together for several hours, concluding with a private performance for Jonathan once he came home and after the three had dinner. Jonathan praised the song to no end, saying that despite it being written specifically for Jak's wife, he could feel it speaking for all loving husbands in expressing the love and wonder in which they viewed their wives.

"I can envision Yoranye with every word," Jonathan said to the highlander, "but I think more of Envah."

"Well, then," Jak sniffed, "Ah'm glad tae have passed it on. Ah sang it tae her when Ah proposed, on our wedding night, each o' her birthdays and every anniversary ... so many times ... but only tae her. Ah think she'll be glad tae see that it's now out there fer others tae hear, presumin' ye spread it out tae the world, of course. At least a little, anyhow. Ah know Ah am."

"Of course, Uncle Jak," said Donovan dutifully.

In time, the three retired for the night, and as Donovan and Jak went for their rooms, the old bard took his pupil's hand and shook it heartily.

"It's been an honor an' a joy immeasurable, Donny," he said, "tae have had ye as a student in the eve o' mah days."

Donovan stared into his mentor's eyes, perplexed by the curious light that filled them.

"The feeling is shared by the student," he said at last.

They bid each other goodnight and went to bed.

Donovan found Jak the next morning, lying still and orderly in his bed, with a gentle smile of fulfillment fixed upon his lifeless face. The old bard, having left all his remaining possessions to Donovan and Jonathan, was then burned ceremoniously in Therohl's square. A paper found by Jak's bedside table stated he would be pleased to have his ashes housed in the home of his student, if he and his father wished. The remains of his wife, the note explained, had been scattered to the winds from the top of Mount Temeleth, and the old bard was content for his earthly remains to rest in the company of those who he considered family in the end, if they'd have him.

Donovan and his father kept his ashes gladly. The young bard, moved by all that his mentor had done for him and his stories of traveling and singing around the world, found a drive sprouting within him to do the same. He confided the urge to his father, and for the next two years, Donovan travelled and performed around the region as he prepared and saved for a grand trip. He aspired to perform in many a prestigious tavern if he could, and if possible, perhaps in the courts of royalty or the household of a warden or holder.

Two years had since passed, and it was now the day after the first fortnight of spring. Donovan, having taken one last look upon those who had passed before him, climbed up from the cellar, stepped out of the house, and approached Therohl's north gate. His horse and supplies were ready and waiting, along with his father and nearly all of the town, who had become his friends and admirers over the past fifteen years. He approached his father and embraced him.

"Good luck, my boy," Jonathan said with a tearful sigh. "Be careful, may Onu and his host keep you safe, and may you one day come back with many a story to tell."

"Onu willing," said Donovan, weathering through the ache in his heart, "I will, and I'll write to you whenever I can."

"I love you, Don."

"I love you, too."

Donovan turned to the others gathered at the gates.

"Thank you all so much for coming," he said, "and all the encouragement you've given me these years. And the coin, too, of course."

Laughter rippled through the crowd as Donovan mounted his horse. The bard waved to the gathering as he steered his horse forward.

"Take care, all of you!" he called as he set the horse to a brisk trot. "Onu willing, I'll be back in a few years!"

He rode along the northern road, bound for the great pass of the Whitemane Mountains, with plans to travel through it and perform across the nation of Enmayar.

54

4/24/4028 G.M.

MIRA tied the boar's legs to the pole, having slung the spear that had killed him across her back. Her father picked up one end of the pole, commenting on his daughter's skill.

"He didn't know what hit him! Well done!"

Mira smiled as she picked up the other end of the pole. "He's a big one, too; just the right size for Kahle's announcement."

The two began to carry their quarry back to Plen, having only ventured out a few hours' distance.

"This really is a fine boar," Virgaard said appreciatively after a few minutes of silent walking. "You've always had a knack for getting the good ones, whatever the beast. Thanks for coming along to help; I always love to hunt with you, but given the occasion ..."

"It's no chore to me, Da," said Mira warmly. "I love doing this, plain and simple. And like you said, given the occasion, I'm all the happier to do it."

The two took another good number of paces quietly under the green shadows of Santaru Forest before Mira spoke again.

"I feel this must have come up before," she said ponderously, "but in light of things, how was it for you when Ma told you that you were going to be a father?"

Virgaard breathed a deep, cheerful sigh. Several seconds passed before he answered.

"It was a joy beyond words and a shock beyond measure, even though we had thoroughly planned for the both of you. The second time was no less a wonder than the first." Virgaard then laughed lightly. "Be sure to get a good view of his face when she tells him, if you can. Because, speaking from experience, his face is going to be a priceless sight. I–"

Virgaard's words were cut short by a nearby rustling of leaves and undergrowth. Snapping their eyes in the direction of the sound, the two hunters grew warmhearted at the sight of their intermittent friend of the forest. Rovnillath's eyes glowed benevolently as the Arbonyn nodded courteously to them. They returned the gesture, and then carried on toward home as the tree-man resumed his endeavors in the forest.

***

A few hours of walking and banter passed, and Mira and her father came to the gates of Plen. Mira frequently checked the dirt streets for Isaak, hoping not to bump into him until they could drop off the boar with Xadon, the butcher. Once they handed over the boar, father and daughter gave one another a pat on the back for a job well done. They were just about to close the door to the butcher's cottage when they happened across Kahle and Isaak, who were just about to enter.

"There you two are!" Isaak said cheerfully. He then peered past his sister and father curiously, seeing the beast that Xadon was just beginning to work on. Mira and Virgaard held back their laughter at the abrupt jeopardization of their intended secrecy.

"You got a boar?" Isaak asked. "Ma told me you two were hunting, but that was after I asked nearly everyone else where you were, and even then, she said nothing of what you were hunting or how long you'd be."

"We didn't entirely know what we were going for ourselves," Mira admitted, "but it worked out quite well for us, as you can see."

"Indeed," Isaak remarked. "But what's the occasion? We seemed to have plenty stored up for the moment, but all the same, I would've loved to join in if I could."

Isaak followed his sister's eyes, turning to face his newlywed wife. Kahle, looking at Mira and Virgaard, shrugged and grinned. She then looked intently at her husband, and wordlessly petted her middle. Isaak looked perplexedly at her for a moment. Then realization dawned on him.

Virgaard was right. Isaak's face was a priceless sight.

The young expectant father, gasping with shock and delight, dropped to his knees and set to caressing and kissing his wife's belly.

"How far along are you? Do you know?"

"Around two months," Kahle said warmly and with a sultry grin. "I was going to tell you at the surprise feast we have set up for tomorrow, but no matter."

Isaak looked back at his sister and father, his face blushing beneath his grey fur. He and Kahle had married only two months back, and Isaak, getting back on his feet, bore the face of one bracing for quips about the couple having "not wasted time."

No jests were dealt, however. Not verbally, anyhow. The smirks were enough, and Isaak, still dark in the face and now wearing a sheepish grin, simply nodded to Virgaard and Mira.

"Thank you both for getting such a fine beast for the occasion," he said simply.

"It was no trouble," said Virgaard as he patted his son's back. "We'll have a nice dinner with everyone tomorrow night, and we'll go on our patrol the next day as we planned earlier. You two go on with whatever it was you were needing to see Xadon about. Whenever you get the time, meet with us back home to make sure we have everything planned out and ready for the patrol, alright? Your mother, sister, and I will finish planning out the feast in the meantime."

"Yes, Da. Thank you."

Mira and Virgaard left the expecting couple to their business and headed for the house of the chief family.

55
4/25/4028 G.M.

DONOVAN crawled out of his tent and had a quick breakfast before breaking camp in the early morning light. He had passed the first major fork of Sorrenar's major northeast highway, meaning to follow it on through its eastward curve and past the second main fork. This would take him to the world-famous Whitemane Mountains and its pass of the same name, which in turn led through a mountainous isthmus that joined Sorrenar with Enmayar.

The bard, for the beginning of both his globetrotting performances and his seeking of inspiration for songs of his own, wanted to see the pagodas and beautiful towns nestled along the mountain road as he made for Enmayar. He had also recalled that Frosthaven, an industrious mining town that was just a good day's ride from where he now was, had been attacked and damaged four months back by a golem that had been unearthed in the mines. While the golem was slain and no one was hurt in the incident, a good several buildings had been destroyed or severely damaged, including the town's temple. Repairs and rebuilding had been underway since, and Donovan, hoping for a good helping of inspiration, was intrigued to see the town in its recovery and hear firsthand accounts from the townsfolk. Seeing as the town was on the way to the Whitemanes and that it was reachable in a day if he rode a bit longer and at a good trot, Donovan quickly gathered his gear and mounted up.

He rode on for a little over an hour, relishing the cold and bracing wind as it caressed his face. As he topped the next hill, he gazed about the country with poetic admiration. His eyes lit up as he recognized the great way shrine that stood just another mile ahead. Moved by the sight, as well as a sense of gratitude for the safeness of the journey so far, he set his horse to a gallop. As he reached the shrine, Donovan brought his horse to a halt and dismounted for a brief respite of prayer and meditation. The bard looked admiringly at the carvings and sculptures of the roadside worship site. They were stylized, yet with a rich sense of detail that had weathered through the millennia. Way shrines of all sizes and designs dotted all the lands of Fidonhaal, but this one was among the most celebrated in Sorrenar as one of the largest and most elaborate ones around. Whereas most shrines were dedicated to Onu and one or two angels, or otherwise just Onu himself, this one depicted all of the angelic host. For the relative symmetry of the shrine's design, all of the angels except for the ones of Day and Night were grouped in their spousal pairs. A depiction of Onu's unfathomable form overlooked all the angels, enveloping the sculptures within the shrine.

At the center of the sacred assembly stood Vitahla and Morinaar, the Angels of Life and Death. They stood together, with Vitahla on the left and Morinaar on the right. Both were robed and hooded, and held hands while also carrying their shepherd's crooks and bearing their flasks on their hips. On either side of them stood one of the elemental couples, with Terranah and Stromarus to Vitahla's side, and Vente and Branok to Morinaar's. Terranah, the Angel of Earth, and Stromarus, the Angel of Water, stood together with their stunning figures of strength. Terranah held her great hammer, and her husband held his spear. Vente, the Angel of Wind, and Branok, the Angel of Fire, each bore their slender, muscular physiques. Vente held her longbow and Branok held his smith's hammer.

Past the elements stood the seasons, with Kyse and Vernid on the left, and Estvii and Sardoth on the right. Kyse, the Angel of Autumn, stood beautifully plump and buxom as she held her full harvest basket. Her husband Vernid, Angel of Spring, stood beside her as a lean and virile man with a harp. Estvii, Angel of Summer, stood slender and graceful as she held the scythe. Her husband Sardoth, Angel of Winter, held his great wood-axe as he stood heavy-framed and barrel-chested. At either end of the angelic assembly, levitating and peering over the heads of their brethren, were Maywa and Yorun, the Angels of Day and Night. Gazing lovingly across the rest of the host into each other's eyes, Maywa floated upon the left side and Yorun on the right. Maywa, petite in her short gown and warm in countenance, held her mirror. Yorun, slender and sincere in his robes and veil, held his lantern-bearing staff. Behind Vitahla and Morinaar's joined hands was the root of the design that represented Onu's form, which branched out over all the host and formed the backdrop and overall structure of the shrine. It was simple and intricate, ancient, and yet timelessly pristine.

Donovan stood before it for a time, then approached it and sat down, crossing his legs and resting his hands on his thighs. He alternated between looking at the iconography and closing his eyes in contemplation and prayer. His mind, heart, and soul reached out to his Maker and the angels. Gratitude, reflectiveness, and hope for the future filled him.

Then, he heard footsteps crunching through the light sheet of snow that still covered the area. It came to his left side from behind the shrine. It was followed by the fur-raising sound of a bowstring being slowly pulled taut.

The bard's eyes snapped open, and his head jerked in the direction of the sound. A few feet away stood a tall, heavy man. He was hooded and cloaked, with a cloth draped over his muzzle to further obscure his face. Only his green eyes and the white fur that surrounded them were visible, along with the white fur of his shins, which were exposed from beneath his kilt. The kilt, along with the muffled accent, pointed to the bandit being a native of the highlands, though there was no certain telling as to how far he'd come to set up this ambush at the shrine.

"Hoi there, laddie," said the highwayman with a menacing sneer. "If'n ye'd kindly rise up, nice an' slow, an' hand o'er yer horse an' gear, an' whatever ye've got in yer pockets an' purse, Ah'd be most grateful."

Donovan, hands raised, slowly got up from his meditative position, locking eyes with the bandit and sizing him up as he slowly neared his horse. The bard had a dagger sheathed along the back of his belt, which was hidden by his cloak. In addition to music and song, Uncle Jak had taught the young bard a few pointers on self-defense as a man who had roamed the roads for many a year. He took his horse's reins with his left hand, continuing to burn his gaze into the bandit's green eyes, and cocked his right arm ever so slightly as he inched toward the robber.

"You picked a fine spot for targets, good sir," said Donovan in bitter sarcasm.

"Nothin' like makin' use o' a place dedicated tae the One who allows our lives tae go tae shite," the bandit retorted, "even with all our efforts tae reconnect with him."

"Who is also the One who guides and inspires those who look to help those down on their luck," Donovan countered, now just a few paces from the bandit.

"Unless they're more inclined tae sit on their high horses an' scorn those who did wrong a time or two before, an' tell 'em tae get lost."

Donovan was now in arm's reach of the bandit. He sneered bitterly, slowly holding the reins out to the highwayman.

"No point trying to convince you to check with the Temple, I see, or a druid or whoever else that may be a convenient option for you."

"Nae, laddie; nae point indeed."

"So, I've just got one question to ask, if you'd indulge me, since I'm surrendering all but the clothes on my back to you."

"Aye?" the bandit replied with a mock tone of interest and the raising of an eyebrow.

Donovan did not wish to kill, if he could avoid it. His sense of honor, however, mingled evenly with his thorough contempt of the bandit, given his choice of locale to spring a robbery. As his temper began to rise during his discourse with the ruffian, the memory of a taunt that Jak had taught him years ago suddenly came to mind. Jak had whispered it to him one night, out of earshot from his father, following a less-than-pleasant incident with an out-of-towner at the tavern. As the young bard suppressed a shocked laugh in response to the phrase whispered in his ear, Jak said to "save it fer when ye have nae intention of makin' friends with whoever's being the arse," as it had gotten the old bard banned, when he was a young rover himself, from ever performing in one far-off Enmayarn town in the wake of the brawl it set off.

Not seeing himself sharing a drink with the bandit anytime soon, Donovan figured he might as well indulge his crass streak and crack the taunt then and there. Hopefully, he thought, when combined with the sudden drawing of his dagger once the bandit got close enough, it would be enough to convince the hooligan that he was not someone to be trifled with, and that he should be left alone. As the bandit reached for Donovan's reins, the bard sharply pulled them from his reach.

"Why don't you just run off and brown a tart's muzzle?"

The bandit's green eyes narrowed, and Donovan grinned triumphantly as he made to draw his dagger.

It wasn't there.

A hand suddenly grabbed the top of Donovan's head from behind, cruelly digging its claws into his scalp as it forced his head back. Donovan's own dagger then flashed before his eyes, which now felt as if they were about to pop from their sockets, before pressing coldly to his throat. His eyes snapped onto the first bandit, who was now roaring with laughter.

"HA! Aye, laddie, Ah just may do that, an' Ah might use the shite in yer britches fer the job!"

***

Within minutes, Donovan lay on the crisp, cold ground in only his tunic and hose, tied up and cursing himself for not considering that a bandit rarely works alone.

"You damn idiot," he said to himself. "If there's anything about this that should surprise you, it's that there's only two of them."

The two bandits, having taken all of Donovan's supplies and rearranging them on his stolen horse, were now debating something in low voices. Donovan pricked up his ears, straining to catch the words. Amongst the discussion, he picked up that the first bandit's name was Ethan and the second one was named Broviir.

"Surely, Broviir ... hunt us ... if we leave him ..."

"That ... probably freeze anyway, Ethan ..."

"... Spare him the trouble."

Donovan saw Broviir draw his stolen dagger, then walk steadily toward him. The bard's blood froze in his veins.

"So this is how it ends, apparently," said Donovan inwardly as he fearfully struggled to somehow try and regain his footing, which only prompted the highwayman to up his pace. "No! I won't just let them slit my throat like it's nothing! If I'm to die, it won't be without a fight!"

As the bandit reached him, dagger ready, Donovan managed to turn onto his back and send his bound feet flying straight into the robber's stones. Broviir dropped to his knees, spitting on Donovan and yelling a stream of curses. Ethan, setting his bow across his shoulder, approached to hold down the bard.

The bowman had just pressed his foot down onto Donovan's chest when a sharp whistle sounded just down the road. The bard and the two bandits turned their eyes to the sound, and saw two riders galloping toward them from up the northeast road. Ethan told Broviir to get up and stand his ground.

"There's only two o' them," said Ethan, "an' only one o' 'em looks armed an' armored. We can take 'em if we need tae. We just got tae be smart."

The two riders reached the way shrine as soon as Ethan finished speaking. The armed one, a Zaron woman who wore the armor and coat of a knight of the Faithguard, called out to them with an air of blunt authority.

"Release that traveler, sirs, and surrender your arms and come with us! We of the Temple will see that, should you cooperate, the justice dealt will be light and swift. Afterwards, we'll offer you both a chance at redemption and a better life, either with us or wherever you wish under our endorsement."

Ethan the bowman raised his hands in mock surrender, addressing the two with bitter sarcasm. "Och, praise be tae Onu! The great an' wonderful Temple has come tae save us at last, Brov! An' it only took 'em twenty-seven years o' mah life, an' mah little sister dyin' o' fever, tae get around tae it!"

The second rider, a heavy-set, middle-aged Mavon man who was clearly a priest, had his horse take three steps forward to address the highwaymen. Donovan noticed the Faithguard woman pull up beside him immediately, her Konothian axe and buckler at the ready, to do all she could to protect the cleric if things turned violent. The look on her face seemed to resemble that of a grown child vying to help and protect an aging father.

"I'm sorry that you've suffered so, sir," said the priest. "Alas, for all our efforts, none of the Temple can be everywhere at once. But now, I am here, as is my Faithguard companion, and we swear that if you'll come with us peacefully, we'll—"

"Ye may nae be able tae be everywhere at once," Ethan said, "but ye all are never failin' tae give your guards good an' shiny gear, or yourselves plenty tae eat, eh, Brother Porky?"

Donovan caught the look in the knight's eyes as she stared fixedly at the bandits. They were bright green, same as the bandit Ethan's. The knight did not make a single move in response to Ethan's retort and insult, but the look in her eyes made the bard's skin crawl, and set a dreadful shiver down his spine as he lay on the ground. The priest seemed to sense the protective fury of his guardian, and made to hold her back, only to see that she remained still. He then gave the knight a quick nod of approval, which Donovan wondered if either of the bandits, or even the knight herself, noticed.

"We work with the resources that the dear people of Fidonhaal give us," the priest said with perfect calmness, "so that, in times like these, we can give the troubled a chance at a better lot, and guard and feed them as long as they're in our care. But we need what we can get, too; our mission may be Onu-given, but we are not Onu ourselves, and thus are not invulnerable to harm nor impervious to hunger. I assure you, you'll both have enough to eat if you come with–"

"Broviir!" Ethan snapped in exasperation, "What in Raakhaal's blazes are ye DOING?"

Broviir, his dagger hand having dropped to his side, had taken a few hesitant steps toward the Temple duo.

"Ah-Ah ..." he stammered, "Ah think we've had enough o' this sort o' living. We'll at least have a chance–"

"If yer goin' tae slink any closer tae those two, it better be tae catch 'em off-guard!"

"Ethan–"

The bowman swiftly drew his bow and aimed it at his comrade. All the others present gasped.

"E-Ethan," Broviir pleaded fearfully, "we ... we can have a chance–"

"The only chance ye've got is if ye stick with me, understand?"

"Ah–"

"Ah can't believe ye got swayed by a few comfortin' words from a couple strangers o' the cloth," Ethan yelled angrily. "After all the shite the ones back home gave us!"

The black-furred priest raised a hand, along with his voice, but only to speak clearly.

"Are those people still there," he asked, "wherever it is you two come from? If so, give me their names and where they are. I'll have inquiries made on their conduct and–"

"Stop tryin' tae win us over, ye chubby chanter!" Ethan barked horribly as he spun in the priest's direction, bow still drawn, more tautly than before. The Faithguard knight's eyes narrowed dreadfully, and she tensed, axe and shield raised, to pounce in front of the priest if necessary. Ethan looked to Broviir, who stood staring dumbly at his companion in crime.

"What ye starin' at, Brov? Rush 'em!"

Ethan let the shaft fly, and Donovan felt his heart leap up his throat.

56
4/25/4028 G.M.

MIRA pulled off a roasted boar's rib as a platter of the meat was passed around. The villagers had gathered around the great fire pit at the center of Plen's village square, celebrating the impending announcement of Kahle and Isaak's expectancy. Mira sat with her parents, along with Isaak, and Kahle and her parents, Uld and Genna, as she waited eagerly for her sister-in-law and brother to break the news to the rest of Plen. Chewing the roast wild pig, savoring each bite, Mira tilted her head back and gazed at the pillar of smoke. It rose past the tops of the tall trees that nestled Plen in the great forest's bosom, and at last faded into the clear, early evening sky.

The festivities began late in the morning, with those free of any particular tasks coming and going at the square and the feast hall to peck at the first of the food and sip from the first of the kegs. Mira had wagered since then that a good many of the village had likely guessed the reason for the occasion, but none had inquired her outright. She didn't know if any had asked anyone else in her family, either, and she didn't want to risk the surprise by asking and potentially being overheard.

As she reflected on the day so far, still gazing at the ascending pillar of smoke, the treetops and the slowly darkening blue sky, Mira felt a tap on the back of her shoulder. Turning to her left, where Isaak and Kahle were sitting, she saw that it was her sister-in-law who had reached over behind Isaak's back to get her attention. Isaak had also noticed, and after a quick glance at Kahle, he turned smiling to his sister as he put his arm around his wife, who now leaned over to speak to Mira.

"Thank you both so much, you and Virgaard, for getting that boar. You've all done wonderfully with everything you've gotten together for this, but that boar has gone over very well."

"I'll say," said Mira, her mouth still full of rib meat. "This wasn't just for you two, you know."

Kahle and Isaak chuckled, and Mira just managed to swallow her bite before she choked from laughing herself.

"I just meant to say," Kahle said between laughs, "I know you and Virgaard love hunting anyway. I do, too, when I can get the chance, but–"

"It's no trouble," Mira answered her. "I should be thanking you for requesting us to try and find something to add to the table. I enjoyed the hunt, and if it weren't for us stopping by Xadon's place to get the boar ready, we wouldn't have bumped into you two and I wouldn't have been able to see Isaak's face."

Kahle and Mira laughed as Isaak rolled his eyes. "If you all had managed to keep it secret," he said, "then you would've seen it anyway, once she made the announcement here as planned."

"I suppose so," said Mira, "but there was something about the way it happened then that I think wouldn't have been if it went as planned. At any rate, I'm just wondering, have you two thought of names yet?"

"You'll hear with the rest," Kahle promised.

Without another word, the expecting couple waved across Mira to get Ann and Virgaard's attention. A quick exchange of nods passed between them, and Mira scooted closer to her father's side as Isaak and Kahle got up and stood in front of the fire to make their announcement.

"We thank you all for coming," said Kahle loud and clear, "and we just want to take a moment to let you all know that this lovely little feast was no mere bit of spontaneous merrymaking."

Plen's young apothecary took her husband's hand, and the two drew close together, striking a magnificently romantic image in the bright firelight that danced high behind them. Isaak looked about the village crowd as he followed up on his wife's words.

"Kahle and I are overjoyed to tell you all that we're expecting!" he said as he gently rubbed Kahle's belly. Congratulatory applause flowed around the fire pit, with Genna and Uld, as surprised as Isaak was the day before, jumping from their seats and embracing their daughter and son-in-law.

"We've already agreed on names," Kahle followed. "Nova if it's a girl, and Novon if it's a boy."

As the second wave of cheers washed over the gathering, Ann and Virgaard, followed by Mira, rose up and raised their tankards.

"Let's give the little tyke a toast and a song!" boomed Virgaard merrily.

When all had drained their cups, Plen's patriarch called for a singing of *Blessed Fruit*, which the whole village boomed out with all the fullness of heart that befitted a community where all cared for each other.

57

4/25/4028 G.M.

DONOVAN shut his eyes tight at the sound of the bowshot. An instant later, they snapped open at the sound of the arrow shattering as it struck metal.

The Faithguard knight had leapt off her horse and positioned herself in front of the priest, getting there in time to deflect the arrow with her buckler. With axe raised and a dreadful look of purpose in her eyes, she strode steadily toward Ethan while also eyeing Broviir, who had Donovan's dagger and his own short sword drawn, but was standing rigidly from intimidation. It was the bowman's threatening words that finally goaded Broviir to attack.

"Brov, get her now or ah'll see tae it that ah'm the only one tae walk away from this alive! Fight now or ah'll kill ye mahself before even botherin' with these two!"

Broviir gave a half-hearted battle cry, charging forward toward the knight with his sword held out tightly like a short spear and his dagger tilted to parry. Broviir's strategy immediately proved futile. The Faithguard swiftly sent the sword off-course with a strike from her buckler, and when the bandit tried desperately to fend her off with his dagger, she simply swung her axe into his now-exposed chest. Broviir cried out, seemingly more from regret than pain, as he went down with blood pulsing from his broken torso and spreading onto the snow.

In the time it took for this to happen, Ethan was barely able to pull another shaft from his quiver and nock it to his bowstring. The Faithguard resumed her advance, now starting to sprint, and the bowman shot at her in a panic. He only managed to hit her in a gap between the arm and breast-plate. Though the shaft stuck into her, it did little harm, as was clearly evident from the unhindered pace of the knight's charge.

Donovan saw Ethan throw down his bow and draw his own short sword as he frantically turned to the bard, who was still lying bound on the ground. Realizing that the bandit meant to grab him as a shield and hostage, Donovan squirmed about the snowy ground and wriggled like a landed fish as Ethan struggled to pull him up. The bowman had finally secured a firm grip of the bard's arm and hair braid, and was in the process of pulling him up, when the lady-knight bulled into him and sent both men to the ground. Donovan, hitting the ground face down, turned over just in time to see the final confrontation.

Ethan scrambled up, sword poised at first to block while also open to potentially skewer the knight in the head. The bandit soon found himself stuck in a completely defensive stance, vying desperately to parry the avalanche of axe swings that the knight dealt with no sign of letting up. At last, Donovan caught the light of final desperation in Ethan's eyes, and flinched with an upturned stomach as his attempt at a sudden stab at the Faithguard's neck was rewarded with the knight's axe cleaving halfway through his own. A flash of blood spattered upon the snow, and more spread rapidly as the bandit crumpled into a lifeless heap.

Donovan sighed deeply in both relief and morbid fascination. The knight, having hung her axe back into the strap on her hip, crouched over him and used her dagger to saw through the ropes that bound him.

"A thousand thanks, my good lady," the bard said with a proffered hand. "The name's Donovan. Donovan Velavis."

The knight, though still clearly somber from the bloodshed, smiled and shook the bard's hand. "Well met, Mr. Velavis. I am Ruth Pionaar, an officer of the Faithguard that is quartered at the Archtemple of Genverdell. My companion you may address as Brother Owen, and ..."

The two turned to see the black-furred priest crouching over the body of Broviir, and realized that the bandit, still rasping out breath, was talking to him. The priest patted the bandit's head comfortingly as he made his final confession. The two approached as the conversation was concluding.

"Ah-Ah'm sorry that Ah ended up this way. Ah believe ... Ethan did, too, though he'd never admit it if he had been ... rotten stubborn bastard."

"I'm sorry it ended this way, too," the priest said softly. "I can pray for you two, if you'd like, but it will ultimately be between you and Onu in the end."

"Ah know. A-Ah'd appreciate it all the same. An-and don't ... don't bother tryin' tae find our home. Just ... just bury us here."

"Very well, son of Onu."

Broviir coughed up some blood, rattled and gasped, then stared silently up into the sky as the light left his eyes. A tear silently rolled down his white-and-grey cheek, and the priest, with a deep sigh, brushed it away.

"Such a waste," he said sadly. He sensed Donovan and the knight approaching, and turned his head. He smiled sadly at the bard.

"Well, at least we were able to save you. Well, Ruth did, specifically."

"I'll never be able to repay you two," Donovan said solemnly. "I thank you both from the bottom of my heart, and pray that Onu bless and keep you both well to the end of your days."

"Are you in a hurry to be somewhere, dear sir?" asked the priest.

"Not particularly."

"Might you consider helping us lay these two poor souls to rest?"

58

4/26/4028 G.M.

MIRA rose from her bed and dressed for the patrol that was set to begin later in the morning. Putting on her hide trousers and jacket, and gathering her long grey hair into a tail, she ate breakfast with her mother and father and walked with them to Plen's main gate. Many of those who were coming along were already idling about, chatting with one another as they waited. They all came to attention, greeting their chiefs and nodding respectfully to them as they approached. Ann conducted the first roll call to confirm who else was yet to arrive. Her husband, Virgaard, passed the reins of the village over to Uld and Genna Tillok, tasking them with managing Plen in the chiefs' steads.

It soon became clear that Isaak had not yet arrived from Kahle's apothecary cottage, which was also the newlyweds' home. Ann, Virgaard, and Mira looked at one another with a speculative smirk, looking to see who would be up for intruding into their home and getting Isaak up from sleep, or any other activity that he may or may not have been up to at the time.

"I'll go see," said Mira with a slightly mischievous tone. She turned to head in the direction of Kahle and Isaak's hut, and felt her father's heavy hand fall onto her shoulder. She looked back to see him grinning.

"Don't make too big a deal out of it, whatever's going on in there. Alright?"

"I won't," she answered in the same tone as before.

Virgaard laughed lightly. "Just get him over here soon. This'll be a long trip anyway, but all the same, the sooner we head out, the sooner we come back."

Mira soon reached her brother's new home and, with ears pricked up, she listened for any telltale sounds that would help her to decide on how to tactfully approach. Mira crept quietly inside, and as she passed the stores of plants, tonics, and salves, she began to hear her brother and sister-in-law talking quietly, their speech frequently interrupted by kisses. Mira slowly and quietly peered through the curtain separating the medicine stores from the living quarters, bracing for the most revealing scenario she could imagine, and was fairly surprised to see Isaak kneeling by the bed fully dressed and geared up. Kahle, who wasn't expected to come along on this patrol anyway, was another matter. Fur and hair ruffled, and wearing nothing but her wedding ring and a sleepy smile, she lay snugly in bed with the blankets wrapped cozily about her as her husband slowly bade her farewell. Mira could see that Isaak was fully ready to go, and likely had been for some time. She guessed that some last-minute passion had arisen, and what was probably meant to be a simple kiss goodbye had quickly turned into what she saw now.

Kahle stared dreamily into Isaak's eyes, taking every kiss that he gave her and lying stretched out contentedly as her husband spoke. Isaak held his wife's head in one hand, gently caressing her ruffled hair. His other hand was lost among the folds of blanket, but Kahle's face and composure left no mystery as to its whereabouts or actions. Kahle's eyes began to roam lazily, eventually finding Mira through the curtain and widening slightly. The healer laughed quietly, then pulled Isaak close and kissed him deeply.

"I wish you were staying here this time," she said. "You'd be in no rush, and we could spend the whole day doing this ..."

"If I had known about the baby sooner," Isaak said softly, "I might've seen if I could've gotten someone else to go in my place. It'll be alright, Kah; you know we're always as careful as we can be. We should be back in a month or so at most, and then we can ... pick up where we left off."

"Sounds wonderful," Kahle moaned pleasurably as she stretched and turned over, drawing the covers up to her cheeks. "But you better get a move on; everyone's waiting at the gate for you, and your sister's been sent to get you."

Isaak began to stand up as he took in his wife's words. "What do you mean—" he began, before turning and seeing his sister, who now stood fully in the doorway, having just parted the curtain quietly. In the dark of the room, the blush under Isaak's grey fur made his face darken visibly, and Mira's giggles were soon joined with Kahle's. Isaak turned to his wife.

"How long has she been watching?" he asked her incredulously.

"I don't know!" Kahle laughed. "I just noticed her a minute ago!"

"I'd say it wasn't much longer than that," Mira said, holding back the laughter as Isaak shook his head in exasperation. He slung his pack across his back and kissed Kahle one last time. "I'm sorry to rend you two asunder, but Isaak's one of the last few we're still waiting for."

"I know, I know," said Kahle with mock irritation. "I'm sending him out now."

"Bye, Kah," said Isaak with one last ruffling of his wife's hair. "We'll be back as soon as we can manage."

"Be safe, all of you."

"Always are, as best we can."

"I love you."

"Love you, too."

Isaak followed Mira out of the house in silence, coming to walk beside her once they got onto Plen's main street. After a few strides in silence, Mira turned to say something to her brother, only to burst out laughing at the sight of Isaak quietly keeping pace with his sister and, with a straight face, holding up the fig right up to her face.

"I—" Mira gasped between fitful giggles, "I'm sorry th-that I had to butt in like that! We were—"

"You could've knocked," Isaak said with a voice that clearly showed that he wanted to be annoyed, but couldn't. "That, or you could've tried calling out."

"I didn't want to interrupt any more than I could help, you know."

Isaak started to laugh and the two made their way to the village stables, where Isaak mounted up and promptly made for the gate. Once all those planned to accompany the patrol were accounted for, they trotted out into the massive, blooming forest.

59
5/13/4028 G.M.

DONOVAN rode between Ruth the knight and Owen the priest on the southbound highway, coming into sight of the port city of Kolnothir. The journey had been a pleasant sixteen days from the way shrine. Once the two highwaymen had been laid to rest beside the shrine, the priest asked Donovan of his traveling plans, inviting him to accompany them to Enmayar if he wished.

"I was meaning to go to Enmayar, in fact," Donovan said, "though I was originally planning to enter through the Whitemanes. I'm a bard, you see, and I was looking to travel the world a bit for experience and inspiration."

"Well, the Whitemanes are certainly an inspiring sight," said Owen, "as well as the folk who live there. We'd love to have you with us, for the value of your company as well as our desire to see you safe as best we can, but don't let our offer compromise your plans if you're set to keep them."

The bard shrugged contentedly. "I can make for the Whitemanes later if I want to. I'm looking to travel at least a bit around all four nations over the next couple of years if I can, so I'm sure I'll get the chance eventually. I guess I might miss seeing Frosthaven's recovery from the golem, though."

The priest and the knight both grinned. Donovan looked at them quizzically.

"That's just where we were coming from earlier," Owen explained. "We journeyed from Genverdell to come here and help with the remaining tasks of rebuilding the town. The view there is also inspiring, and you might not wish to settle for anything less than seeing it for yourself or asking those who witnessed it firsthand. However, if you choose to ride with us, we can talk about that plenty and you may find that to be sufficient material for a song or two, should you look to compose one."

The bard smiled at the serendipity of the situation. Checking his gear one more time to make sure his dagger, bow, arrows, and all other supplies were in order, he looked at his rescuers and nodded.

"I can visit Frosthaven myself sometime later, as well," he said. "I doubt *that* experience is going to fade from the local memory anytime soon."

"I agree," Owen said with a smile.

The three then mounted up and rode south, with no other word passing between them for a good several miles. Then Donovan, recalling where Owen said he and Ruth hailed from, inquired further.

"You said you two came all the way from Genverdell?"

"Yes, sir, that we did."

"A bit of a long trip just to help a town, no? I mean, sure, the incident was no small matter, but it was only structural damage. It wasn't as if half the town perished or anything like that. I'm sure that perhaps with some money sent from the archtemple's coffers, they would've been more than able to rebuild without having one priest and one Faithguard being sent over from so far. They've got their own clerics to oversee those things, after all. Not to mention, I figured it would've been done from Sorrenar's archtemple instead of Enmayar's."

"You aren't wrong," the priest conceded, "and we definitely saw to it that they had the funding they needed, but the salpion wished to send some personal help from his residence at the Archtemple of Genverdell. He thought the journey would be good for everyone involved."

"Salpion Lovonhaar certainly has a considerate ..."

Donovan's words froze in his mouth. Once he mentioned the current salpion and his surname, he suddenly remembered that his first name was Owen, and that he was of full Mavon heritage. He turned to face the figurehead of all the Temple of Fidonhaal, eyes wide and mouth agape, as he scrambled his tongue trying to address the salpion properly.

"I-Y-Your Holiness, dear guide of—"

Owen smiled as he gently pressed a finger to his lips. "Hush, dear son of Onu," he said kindly. "There's no need for that, especially not here and now. I suppose you could say that I wanted to do a little traveling, too, though perhaps not as far and wide as you are looking to do. I wished to go and help them myself, and if I could break up the pace of living in the archtemple a bit while I was at it, then all the merrier. I didn't want to draw too much attention though, of course."

"Hence why you have only one knight accompanying you?"

"Indeed."

"Well then," Donovan said at length, still awestruck by the revelation of his new companions, "thank you both, again, for rescuing me." He then tilted his head back to face the heavens, the frosty clear vault above matching the hue of his own eyes. "And thank Onu for the timing."

"Hear, hear!" said Owen with a small laugh. "We had just finished our work in Frosthaven and were heading back to our ship docked at Kolnothir when we remembered the shrine that we passed on our way to town. We both fancied stopping by to pray and meditate a little, so we got up early and upped our pace to get there. That's when we saw you, and well, you know the rest."

They then rode on, stopping in the evenings to make camp or rent rooms, for the following sixteen days. The three spoke of the details of the incident at Frosthaven and the rebuilding of the town, the sorry fates of the bandits, and other matters of one another's lives along the way, soon becoming good friends.

Now, with the port of Kolnothir just down the road, the trio set to a gallop, looking forward to the scenic sailing that lay in store for them. Upon entering the bustling town, Owen and Ruth led Donovan to the docks, where they boarded a humble, but comfortable ship. The bard noted the vessel's name.

"*Vente's Kiss*, eh?" he said appreciatively. "I'll need to look over some material, because if there isn't a song with that title out there, there should be!"

60
5/15/4028 G.M.

MIRA rode beside her parents and brother as they continued the patrol with their companions that began just over a fortnight ago. The going had been good and calm so far, and the group hoped circumstances would stay that way so they might return home a bit earlier than expected. Even with Virgaard's insistence on thoroughness, the company's round through the great forest was going surprisingly swifter than initially planned, and their spirits seemed irrepressible.

Now, in the early afternoon, the patrollers conversed and sang as they passed food and drink around, being so encouraged by their progress that they didn't feel the desire to halt for lunch. Mira was talking with Isaak about his future child with Kahle, inquiring on their choices of names, when a sudden, heavy rustling of nearby shrubbery made all in the company fall silent. Mira quickly pulled her bow from the saddle and set an arrow to the string as the others drew either bow or blade in unison, bracing for whatever that was in the bushes to show itself.

They were all just as quick to lower their weapons as they heard a man call out to them. A lone man, with fur patched black and white, and dressed in a simple robe of green and brown, parted the undergrowth and stepped forward. He was clearly a Wild-Dweller of the forest, like Mira and her company, having much the same manner of dress as them, though his robe and ceremonial staff further marked him as a druid. There were few other villages in Santaru that were like Plen, however, and Mira guessed that this fellow was likely from a small nomadic clan of the forest instead of one of the settled sorts of Wild-Dwellers. The man looked at the company and seemed to smile admiringly at their numbers.

"Fine lot of you there are!" he laughed in a friendly tone. "Are you all roamers, too, or are you from one of the villages around here?"

"We come from Plen, sir druid," Ann said, smiling. "We've just been doing a patrol of Santaru, something we do from time to time, to see if there's any trouble of notice."

"Very considerate of you all," the stranger said approvingly. "My clan is nearby and heading in this direction; I set out to look ahead of them a little."

"Well," said Virgaard, "we've been riding through for just over two weeks, and so far we've had no trouble whatsoever. What about you and your clan? Have you all come across anything?"

The druid's smile faded. "I'm afraid so," he said grimly. He then parted the bushes from which he came, and pointed to tracks that led up to the growth from behind. They were relatively fresh and ran perpendicularly to the Plen patrollers' course. They were lost in the undergrowth and did not cross the company's path as far as they could see. Had it not been for their encounter with the druid, the patrollers might have very well missed them despite their thorough efforts. Mira rode over to the tracks, leaning in her saddle as she stared gravely at the prints in the soil.

"A Qualakar," she said worriedly. Her right arm tingled at the memory of the monster cub's fangs, and a shudder ran through her body as she looked to her mother, father, and brother.

"These prints aren't very old," she said anxiously, "a day or two at most. It seems like it made for all the undergrowth around here, and the tracks look to be largely lost in there. I'm afraid it might still be close by."

"How many sets of prints are there?" Ann asked.

"It looks like there's just one here, thankfully," said the stranger, with Mira nodding to her company in agreement. "I've tried to look for signs of a pack, as that would make more sense, but those are the only ones I've found. I suppose–"

Mira, who was looking at her family as she listened to the druid's words, noticed Isaak's eyes suddenly widen before she heard thundering steps and cracking branches coming from the undergrowth behind her. Isaak tried to call out in alarm, but the words lodged in his throat as he scrambled to draw his hunter's sword. Mira wheeled around and leapt away from the bushes, reaching her bow and quiver in the same movement, just as the rest of the company began to react.

The druid, as quick as he was to catch on, was the last to react. He managed to raise his staff defensively with one hand, unsheathe a dagger with the other, and turn in the direction of the charging Qualakar as it bulled through the foliage and pounced upon him. The force sent the druid's staff flying from his hand. All in the company were now scrambling to act as the druid frantically wrestled with the monster's forepaw, which had landed on and was now holding down his dagger-wielding arm. The druid's shoulder was bloodied during the Qualakar's initial attack, and the monster, becoming ravenous and hideously gleeful at the sight and smell of blood, opened its fanged, salivating maw as it made to devour the man.

Mira, in the few seconds that passed since the start of the mauling, now had her bow fixed on the Cursed One's eye. Quickly tensing to minimize the shaking in her arms, she let her arrow fly just as the monster was about to bury its fangs into the stranger's chest. The shaft buried into the Qualakar's eye down to the fletching, with the arrowhead piercing and protruding from the eye on the other side of the skull. The monster let out a ghastly howl, convulsing violently as Isaak rushed forward and drove his sword into its brain. The Qualakar slumped dead onto the stranger, who now struggled to escape being crushed by the foul beast's corpse. Mira joined her parents, brother, and several others as they lifted the dead monster off the druid. Breathing heavily and scrambling up on shaking legs, he thanked the patrollers ten times over before finally being calmed down.

"It's alright, sir," said Ann as she bandaged the man's shoulder. "It's done; that's one less Qualakar to trouble the world."

Virgaard, having fetched the druid's staff, handed it back to him and patted his shoulder, offering to lend him his horse as he spoke. "Can you lead us to your clan? That seemed to be the only one of those monsters in the area, but we don't know for sure and we'd like to work with your group, if it's not too much to ask, for the rest of our patrol. We'll offer time for you and yours to stay with us for a while if you'd like. After we all get back to our village, we could perhaps trade some things and just enjoy each other's company."

"That sounds like a plan," said the druid as he gratefully got into the saddle. "Follow me."

61

6/6/4028 G.M.

DONOVAN gazed at the eastern horizon as the shores of Enmayar and the port of Greenharbor came into view.

It had been an immensely pleasant voyage of twenty-one days from Kolnothir. The bard had spent the time in the company of Ruth and Owen, with all three becoming fast friends during their voyage across the Springwind Sea. Donovan learned of the Faithguard's past, including the tale of her mother and how she had changed from a poor prostitute into a sister of the Temple.

He also learned of her time in training for her knighthood in the Faithguard, including her time as the squire of one Commander Hanye, who led the training of all the Konothian knights at the archtemple. He learned of how her mentor's kindness and guidance moved her to quickly take up a squire of her own once she herself was knighted. She had taken under her wing a young boy named Orson Whitethorn, who was from a family that had moved into the archtemple a few years ago to get away from Genverdell's impoverished southwest riverbank neighborhood. The mentor and protégé quickly became great friends, with a relationship not unlike that of an elder sister and younger brother.

Donovan then learned of Ruth's fiancé, Verdok Merchill, who was the high priest of Genverdell's archtemple and was presently leading it in the salpion's stead. He learned the story behind the beautiful marble-and-jet Uqua pendant that Ruth wore around her neck, from its original wearer to the tale of how it was gifted to her.

From Owen, the bard learned of the salpion's career as the Temple's figurehead and additional details of Verdok, who was his protégé. Owen made it clear that in all ways except by blood, he regarded Verdok as a son.

The bard, in turn, told them of his childhood, the death of his mother and stillborn sister, and how he came to meet the man who would make him into a bard. He told them of Uncle Jak's passing, and elaborated on his dreams of seeing the world and performing abroad as their ship neared the port. Upon hearing further details of Donovan's aspirations, Owen and Ruth looked at each other with a smile.

"So," said Ruth, "apart from seeing as much of Fidonhaal as you can in the next few years, you have no hard-set plan or route?"

Donovan nodded. "That's pretty much the size of it."

"Might you be in Genverdell, or nearby, a little before spring the year after next?"

Donovan cocked his ears in interest. "I might, or I might be on the southernmost tip of Janrenar by then. Why do you ask? Looking for some entertainment for the wedding, presuming that's when it's being held?"

"We'd certainly welcome you to perform, and be more than happy to pay you," said Owen. "We've both heard you sing, and we're sure you'd be a delight for everyone there."

Donovan leaned against the deck railing, looking at the steadily nearing shore and port as he considered the offer. "A chance to perform at a wedding held at an archtemple, in the presence of the Salpion of Fidonhaal, and with the wedding itself being between two of the salpion's loving protégés ..."

"Many great bards can't say they've done that," said Ruth coaxingly.

"Indeed not," said the bard reflectively. He pondered quietly for a few moments, thinking of all the places he hoped to eventually see, and figured it to be more than feasible to manage most, if not all of his dream destinations within the time before the wedding.

"Even if I don't," he thought to himself, "I can always try for the ones I miss sometime later. It's not as if I never mean to travel again after this journey. Besides, promising pay aside, I like these two. They saved my life, for one thing, and I now count them as friends ..."

Donovan turned to face Owen and Ruth, and smiled. "I'd love to attend your wedding, Lady Pionaar, and would be honored to offer my services of music and song for such a blessed day."

The knight smiled. "Just be at Genverdell, at the archtemple, with at least a few days to spare before Veronmay's Eve that year. If you should arrive sooner, we'll be all the more able to make a good arrangement for you. Just come in with some time to spare, and we'll be sure to squeeze you in."

"Thank you," the bard said warmly. He thought quietly for a moment more, and then looked to his companions again. "I know you aren't privy to all the matters of state, but since we're discussing opportunities in Enmayar, and specifically Genverdell, would either of you perhaps know if the queen and king would be open to receive a visiting minstrel, or even have a position for a court bard?"

Owen and Ruth looked at each other, and both furrowed their brows in thought. It was not the reaction Donovan expected.

"Is ... is something the matter?"

The salpion came quietly to Donovan's side, leaning at the railing with him as he explained.

"The king, Allor, is as welcoming a soul as you'll ever meet, and in my opinion worthy of being considered an Exemplar of Patience and Understanding. Queen Sheeva, however ..."

Owen sighed deeply as he tilted his head to the early morning sky, seemingly beseeching Onu for guidance as he sought to explain Enmayar's queen with tact. Donovan looked on quizzically as Owen resumed.

"The queen," he continued, "is very defensive when it comes to dealing with strangers, and even with a number of those she has known for years. She is unbelievably loving, though, to her husband, children, and country, but whenever a stranger comes along, she can come off as frightfully protective at times. There have been exceptions, but I can't for the life of me figure out what her reasoning is. It's even happened with me on occasion, when—"

Donovan's jaw dropped. "How could she possibly have a problem with you?"

"Well, to be fair, it's not like the Temple is without error or the potential for sin. Despite our efforts, we who make up the Temple are but mere mortals, same as those not of the cloth."

"But you? After all you and Ruth have told me, I'd say you're bound to be an Exemplar of Kindness and Integrity ... an Exemplar of Salpions, frankly. Or have I completely misjudged you somehow?"

Owen's head bowed to the deck floor as he wrung his hands humbly.

"Your opinion of me is encouraging, though perhaps excessively so. All the same, the reality revealed by history shows that whatever specific anxieties the queen may have felt regarding me are not utterly baseless. I remember when she gave birth to her twins, Samuel and Talrah, and I blessed them and welcomed them into the world. I don't know if it was her having just become a mother or the fact they were named after her late mother and father, or simply because of all the troubles she had endured so far in her life, but when I took them into my arms ... I caught her gaze from the corner of my eye. I've never really trekked through a forest before, but I have a feeling that anyone who has, and has stumbled across a bear cub, has seen a similar face on the mother when they suddenly see her approaching."

Donovan whistled loudly in disbelief.

"After that," Owen continued, "while I don't believe I've ever been met with that look since, I'd see her when her family came to the archtemple on holy days, and I could just sense this ... immensely critical stare."

"You mentioned the queen having troubles in the past?" Donovan asked. "What were they, if I may ask? I've heard something about her parents being assassinated in Kellmayar, but I'm no statesman, and I heard what little I did nearly ten years ago, so my knowledge is likely both hazy and incomplete."

The salpion gave a relatively brief listing of what had since come to light of Sheeva's life, from the troubles and tragic conclusion of her involvement with the late Greystone family to the specifics of the terrible incident in Kellmayar. Hearing the details, Donovan shook his head, bewildered by the queen's tribulations.

"I suppose I can understand her frame of mind," the bard said, "if she suffered through all that."

"All of that being said, though," said Owen with a pat on Donovan's shoulder, "if you have any interest in trying for an audience, I believe you should go for it. I did not mean to make the matter seem impossible, only that it may be difficult, and to explain why. There is a chance, though, I'm sure. As I said before, the queen's protectiveness, I've no doubt, comes from her love. A surpassing model of motherly love, or that of a wife, I haven't met. As for her nation, and indeed all of Fidonity, her drive to make things better is, in my eyes, commendable beyond words. Did you know that she has studied medicine for around fifteen years?"

"I did not," said Donovan with heightened interest.

"The story behind that itself is touching. The king confided it to me once in private."

The salpion told the bard of the fate of King Allor's hometown and how the queen, so moved by her suitor and friend's loss, began to take private lessons from the castle apothecary.

"Her first teacher was among those murdered in Kellmayar," Owen concluded, "but she continued her studies on her own and with the physician who came afterwards, and is quite well-versed in herbalism and medicine, especially given that it is a path she walks alongside her station as queen. And besides all that, she's allocated some of the tax surpluses from the past several years to funding others' studies. As a matter of fact, not long before Ruth and I left for Frosthaven, the queen and king announced that Sheeva had made a tonic that was given to a child with Endallian Fever, which brought a shockingly swift recovery and ease of symptoms. The queen then made a few replicated samples and sent them, along with money and copies of her notes for its production, to the Endallia School of Medicine for them to test it further. If it proves successful ... well, we may have a queen to thank for the most effective treatment for the fever we've ever seen. The disease may become something that's almost more like the common cold, compared to how it's been before."

Donovan stared at the salpion, amazed at his words. Before the bard could comment, however, Owen launched into another account of the queen's philanthropy.

"Then there's her project of establishing the Peacekeepers. Have you heard anything about that back in Sorrenar?"

Donovan searched his memory for a moment. "I think I remember something about that. They're units of soldiers that are meant to be for all of Fidonhaal. Instead of being the military of just one country, they're meant to help keep peace and provide aid wherever they're called. Was that all Sheeva's idea, too?"

"Initially, yes," said Owen with clear admiration, "and I believe this came from her experience in Kellmayar and the root of her troubles with the Greystones. But after her first garrisons were deployed and she stated their intended purposes, the other three nations have accepted them with open arms. At the moment, only a small portion of the Peacekeepers hail from outside Enmayar, as the other nations are presently occupied with other matters. But what they've been able to afford to give in support, they have. I suppose it's a bit funny that, at present, what's meant to be of international benefit has been overwhelmingly from Enmayar, but that's just where it began and it will doubtless take time to grow."

"The queen certainly sounds like an exemplary Fidon," Donovan remarked, "just one who is fighting off a lot of pain, and may at times be overtaken by it."

"That's what I'm inclined to think as well," said the salpion, "especially given that nearly all the recruits have been youths who were either orphaned, or from destitute or troubled homes. I firmly believe in her love and goodness; she just has some very heavy burdens, Onu give her strength."

"Well," said Donovan, "if I try for an audience and the queen refuses me, I'll do all I can to not bear any hard feelings toward her, given all that you've said."

"Here's to hoping, though," said Owen encouragingly. "And remember, whether that plays out for you or not, there's our offer for the wedding."

"Of course," said the bard with a reverent nod to both Owen and Ruth.

The bard, knight and salpion stood together by the railing until noon, watching the shore and the port of Greenharbor draw closer as Donovan pondered what Owen had told him.

***

The three reached Greenharbor late in the afternoon, and after disembarking with their horses and gear, and bidding the crew of *Vente's Kiss* thanks and farewell, they made for an inn in the city to rest up for the remainder of the day. The following morning, Owen and Ruth told Donovan of their next destination: a lovely inn at the edge of the great Santaru Forest, which they could reach in a good day's ride if they left promptly and could ride briskly. They rode out from Greenharbor an hour past dawn, holding a brisk and steady trot as they scaled the rolling hills, and soon reached the road that ran along Santaru's edge.

They came to the inn, the Glowing Wisp, just as the sun was beginning to set. Donovan had spent much of the ride hearing Ruth and Owen's account of their previous stay there, when they were making the journey to Sorrenar. They told him of the impressive accommodations of the inn, given its location, and of its remarkable success since its building roughly ten years ago. They also told him of the story that the innkeepers gave for the reason they built there and, in turn, the inn's name. By the time they reached it, Donovan was thoroughly intrigued and eager to see the grand inn by the forest.

The trio approached the door and were greeted by the beautiful black-and-white furred hostess of whom Owen and Ruth spoke. Standing on either side of her were her two young sons, ready to do their part. The other innkeep, the hostess's husband, took their horses to the stables as the three were led to their rooms, where they washed and briefly rested before meeting up again for dinner.

The inn was doing good business that night, though not overcrowded, and between helpings of good food and drink, and bouts of friendly banter with their hosts and fellow guests, the three discussed their future plans of travel. Owen and Ruth did the bulk of the talking as Donovan half listened, absorbed in his reflections of the conversation with Owen the day before. The mixed description of the queen, along with the still-distant wedding and the bard's growing desire to resume roaming the world on his own, led him to ponder a whim to explore Santaru for a while.

At the end of the meal, his mind was made up.

***

The bard stood in the stone-encircled forest garden that lay just beyond the inn and into the start of the forest. It was midnight, and though the inn's namesake moonwisp did not look to be appearing that night, Donovan still felt a wondrous sense of serenity in the little haven of flowers, trees, and stones. He stared at the distant trees, reflecting on his decision, when suddenly Owen spoke to him from behind.

"Wanted to see if you could meet the wisp?"

"Mm-hmm," the bard answered simply.

The salpion approached Donovan and faced him directly. His hazel eyes pierced Donovan's from his spectacled, black-furred face, which shone with a haunting handsomeness in the waxing half-light of the moon.

"Looking to be going your own way again soon?" he asked knowingly.

Donovan nodded silently. A moment later, he explained his thoughts following the previous day's conversation, and his unexplainable urge to spend some time in the vast forest before him.

"It's a stunningly beautiful forest," the salpion said understandingly, "and you've had your plans to see the world all along, so by all means go and see. Ruth and I shall certainly miss your company for the rest of the trip, but we understand and wish you well."

"Thank you, Sal–Owen," said Donovan warmly. He shook Owen's hand. "If the course of life permits, I *do* have every intention of trying to pop in for Ruth's wedding, whatever else may happen. With a little less than two years to spend before then, I'm hoping to see a good bit of the world."

"And I'm sure you shall," said Owen. "And just so you know, while I myself haven't been in this forest, I was told by a visiting druid that, in addition to good-hearted clans of rovers, there are some permanent villages nestled throughout. One is a fair way north of here and a touch east, but the druid said that if you start straight north from here, from this very garden, and keep your eyes open, you'll soon see a trail marked by cairns. It's fairly easy to follow, once you find it. I don't recall the village's name, but the druid said that he's been there and that it's a good place. Perhaps if you go and spend some time there, you might be able to rest, think things over, and have a good idea of where to go from there."

"I think I might just do that," said the bard after a brief moment's thought. "Thank you, Owen, for the advice and everything that you and Ruth have done for me. I hope to see you again in the not-too-distant future."

"You're not going to leave right now, are you? Not going to sleep the rest of this night in a bed? You'll be sleeping in a tent on the ground for the next while, you know."

Donovan chuckled. "I suppose I'll do that, at least."

The salpion and the bard laughed, then turned back to the inn for a good night's sleep.

62

6/8/4028 G.M.

MIRA rode back into Plen with her patrol and the nomads who joined them following the incident with the Qualakar. The roaming clan, both out of gratitude for the patrol saving their druid and for their proposal of the joint canvassing of the forest, immediately obliged to accompany the Plen riders for the rest of the trek.

The patrol heightened the level of its thoroughness significantly following the sudden appearance of a Qualakar and the uncertainty of whether any others were nearby. Despite already being quite thorough prior to the incident, the worry of another possible attack drove the group to ride more slowly and often check the areas they crossed at least thrice over. The previous impression that the combing of Santaru would end a good touch ahead of schedule soon vanished. In the end, the patrol ended up actually lasting a little longer than was originally planned. Nevertheless, the rest of the patrol was calm and uneventful, a fact that stirred mixed feelings in the hearts of all involved. Nearly everyone agreed that more of the monsters had to be out there, despite the lack of tracks, fresh or otherwise, that seemed to suggest the contrary. The vastness of Santaru simply would not allow any reasonable Fidon to dismiss the likelihood that something was overlooked.

Everyone, from the native villagers to their nomadic guests, were glad to see the gates of Plen peer through the trees. Mira, chatting with her parents, jolted in her saddle as a rider charged past her. She quickly realized it was Isaak, and once she got a better look at the group that came to the gates to greet them, she saw Kahle standing at the forefront of the gathering. Mira laughed, as she saw clearly what drove her brother to dash to his wife, and in turn was herself awed by the figure that her sister-in-law struck. The village herbalist, though now only three moons into her pregnancy, nevertheless glowed with an unmistakable motherly light. The afternoon sun that managed to pierce the forest canopy, along with the beautiful smile that spread on her face as her husband galloped to meet her, lent a lovely maternal radiance that seemed to border on the angelic.

Isaak, having reached his wife, was saying something to her as he frantically made to dismount from his horse. His foot caught in the stirrup and he fell flat on his face onto the soft forest earth. Mira managed to keep silent for one second, then burst into laughter along with the rest of the company as Kahle, herself putting a hand to her mouth to keep from giggling, stooped to help her husband onto his feet. Isaak, laughing as much as the others, drew Kahle close and kissed her, petting her middle in the process.

All the others soon passed Plen's gate, and Virgaard and Ann gave a report of the patrol's events to the villagers gathered around them, as well as an explanation of the nomadic clan in their company. A good feast was quickly thrown together to celebrate the patrol's safe return.

63
6/8/4028 G.M.

DONOVAN rose with Owen and Ruth at dawn, quietly leaving their rooms and sitting at a table in the inn's dining room as they waited for breakfast. The bard told the knight of his plan to depart as they waited, and though Ruth was clearly saddened to hear that Donovan would not be accompanying them to Genverdell, she nodded understandingly and wished him the best. Following breakfast, the three bade the innkeepers thanks and farewell, and made for the stables. As Owen and Ruth mounted up and got back onto the highway at the forest's edge, Donovan made his way around the stables, past the garden, and into the vast sea of trees beyond.

"Goodbye and good luck, Mr. Velavis!" Ruth called over her shoulder. "I hope to see you at my wedding, and that you have a good story to tell of your travels by then!"

"Thank you, Lady Pionaar!" the bard called in response. "I have every intention to meet both those wishes, if I can! Thank you for saving my life, and for the great company you gave me on the road and at sea!"

"And we thank *you* for your company!" said Owen. "Farewell, and remember to follow the cairns!"

"I will! Thank you both again for everything! Goodbye!"

Thus did the three friends part ways after more than a month in each other's company. The Faithguard and the salpion made for home, and the bard from Sorrenar trotted briskly into the vast green of Santaru, ready to begin the next chapter of his adventures.

***

Donovan, when not scanning the ground around him for the next pile of stones, gazed in awe at the myriad of rich green that seemed to blanket all in the forest, from the deep shadows cast by the canopy to the glow of the sun's rays that filtered through it. He imagined the green light that filtered through was likely the same or near to that of the angelic glow of Terranah herself. He rode on with fair ease over the forested hills, through clearings, across streams, and passed ponds and pools of varying sizes, keeping track of the cairns that marked the way as he relished the sights and sounds of Santaru. He breathed deeply of the earthy air of the forest, which was full of the scents of flora and fauna. Though heavy, the air was not oppressive, and rather more of the closeness of a mother's embrace.

As evening neared, Donovan stopped at one of the cairns, hitched his horse to a nearby tree, and pitched his tent by the arrangement of rocks to rest for the night. He noted a cairn that lay just within view amongst the distant trees, and assured himself as best he could that he was on the right path and that it would be easy to continue the journey in the morning. He promptly went about feeding and watering his mount and himself. Since his rations were already cooked or dried, the bard made no fire for cooking or warmth, as the late-spring air and closeness of the forest was of more than sufficient comfort for a man used to months of snow and freezing winds.

After eating, Donovan simply sat on a fallen log and idly sang and played his harp as he gazed about the verdant sea that enveloped him. The sky and forest grew dark and he was just about to crawl into his tent for the night when he heard a rustling of leaves and twigs nearby. Not taking any chances, Donovan sprang to his packs, grabbed his bow and quiver, and set an arrow to the string in a matter of seconds. Picking up quickly on the direction of the sound, the bard drew back the bowstring and aimed it, calling out for the source to identify itself, if it could.

Donovan immediately lowered the bow and put his arrow back into its quiver when he saw the treelike figure approaching. It faced Donovan with the glowing eyes of an Arbonyn, and waved an arm in a gesture of calm, understanding greeting. It strode up to meet the bard in his camp. The horse, at first spooked by the disturbance, quickly calmed and walked to his bridle's end to stand as close as he could in the Angelborn's presence. Donovan nodded respectfully to the Arbonyn, which bore a masculine form and had a distinctive branch growing out from his forehead like the horn of some beast. The tree-man stood before Donovan, hauntingly majestic in the fading twilight that still passed through the leaves and branches above, and gestured once more in friendly greeting.

"Good evening to you," he said.

"Good evening, Angelborn of Terranah and Stromarus."

"Appreciated is your formality, but needless. Rovnillath am I named."

"Very well, Rovnillath; I bid you good evening. My name is Donovan."

The wooden face creaked softly as it smiled. Rovnillath then nodded toward Donovan's supplies, chiefly at the bow and arrow still in the bard's hands. "Hunting, are you?" he asked. "Or scouting for your clan? Or perhaps you are a visiting wanderer? Not many Fidons of only white fur have I seen here in my time."

"I'm a visitor," answered Donovan. "I'm a bard, and I've come all the way from Sorrenar, looking to travel the world and sing as I go. I'm also hoping to have some interesting adventures along the way, something that I might put into songs of my own."

"I heard your music from afar," Rovnillath said, "and that is what moved me to come and see who was playing. I was wondering if it was perhaps either a Fidon or a faun."

Donovan laughed lightly as he indulged his ego. "A fine thing it is for a bard to hear that his music should intrigue one of the Angelborn to the point that he wonders if it's being done by one of his kin."

Rovnillath chuckled a warm, wooden-hollow laugh. "I doubt that not. Play by the great rivers or ocean, and my siblings of the waters would come as well, I bet."

The bard smiled, then took the opportunity to gain an ancient native's advice and directions. "I'm presently making for one of the villages in the forest. I was told that a trail was marked by these cairns." He pointed to the stone pile by his tent. "I trust that I've been following the right path? There aren't other such paths that cross around here, are there? I've worried at times that I might have gotten confused and gone in circles."

"The right path you are on," said the Arbonyn with an assuring nod. "A few other villages in this forest do indeed mark their main paths this way, but only one there is here; the nearest other such path is many miles from here. Confused you cannot get with this one, if you keep following it as you have. Plen is the village's name. Good people live there. You can resupply there, and probably have good chance for your work while you stay. Most of this moon will the journey take, but keep following the stones, and you will get there surely. You may even arrive in time to celebrate summer's coming there."

"Thank you kindly, Rovnillath," said the bard gratefully. "I know not what you mean to do from here, but if you'd like, I'll happily play some songs for you before I retire for the night."

The tree-man smiled, and promptly sat beside Donovan as he reached for his harp. As the light of dusk faded, Rovnillath's eyes glowed more intensely, enabling the bard to better see the strings as he plucked and strummed.

***

Donovan rode on for nineteen days, grateful for the ease of following the cairns while still being able to take in the great beauty and tranquility of Santaru. He reflected on his first night in the forest constantly, and wondered, indeed hoped, that he might encounter more of the wondrous creatures of Fidonhaal on his trek. By the twenty-seventh of the month, however, he had encountered naught but the simple creatures of the wilds. Figuring that he must be close to Plen by now, the bard regretted not seeing any other Angelborn. However, noting the likelihood that beings other than ones good or simple also called the forest home, he kept gratitude in mind for not having run afoul of any monsters or more bandits. His thoughts were interrupted when he noticed a grand stag standing amongst the trees and foliage that lay just ahead.

64

6/27/4028 G.M.

MIRA and her father rode out into the forest, hoping to get a good little harvest from the forest's bounty of fauna to bolster the impending feast of Estonmay's Eve. The clan that joined them during the patrol was still living with the villagers, having announced their plan to depart shortly after the holy day, so Mira and Virgaard decided to make sure there would be enough good meat to go around.

With spears, bows, and hunting blades at the ready, father and daughter rode on quietly, keeping conversation hushed and minimal as they looked about intently for both game and danger. Though all in Plen sought to celebrate and enjoy the festivities, there was still much talk of the uncertainty regarding the presence of Qualakars in the forest. As much as Mira and Virgaard intended to enjoy the hunt, they could see in each other a sense of apprehension that slightly dampened their enthusiasm. Neither brought the matter up, not wishing to darken the mood further.

They rode half an hour in near silence, when suddenly Virgaard clicked his tongue to get Mira's attention. She looked to where her father pointed and gazed in awe at the great stag that stood in the distance. It was one of the largest deer that either had ever seen; his antlers were tall and branched out seven times on each. They were sure he alone would be enough to ensure a good feast with the rest of the food that had been prepared from Plen's stores. Virgaard leaned in his saddle toward Mira, whispering his plan to her.

"I think we should both try to put a shaft in him, given what a giant he is."

Mira nodded eagerly, and the two readied their bows and arrows as they slowly and quietly dismounted and crept into a better position. They hunkered down into a bit of undergrowth, having a perfect view of the stag. Nodding to one another that they were both ready, the two drew their bows in unison. The grand beast was as good as theirs.

Then the crack of a twig cut the air, and the deer, snapping its gaze at something beyond the distant trees, bolted the instant Mira and her father let their arrows fly. An instant of silence, broken only by the swiftly fading prancing of the stag, filled the air. The sound of the two arrows hitting something broke the quiet. One carried the solid, wooden sound of a tree trunk. The other echoed with the sound of something softer. A man's cry of alarm immediately followed, setting Virgaard to bolt upright and gasp as Mira, still crouching in the bushes, became petrified with dread.

"Who's there?" Virgaard shouted anxiously. "Are you hurt?"

"I'm fine," said a man's voice that was marked lightly with a foreign accent. A horse's hooves stepped nearer. Then, emerging from the undergrowth mere paces away from where the stag stood and the arrows flew, was a young man, more or less of an age with Mira. He rode forward on his mount with his hands spread in a gesture of peace. He was fully Balon by the looks of it, and as he approached, Mira saw his eyes, which were of the icy bright blue of a clear winter's sky. They took on an apologetic gaze as he grinned with embarrassment.

"I'm afraid I'm the cause for you two missing your mark," he explained. "I saw the stag, and was trying to move around him and not disturb him. I was hoping to just enjoy the sight of him. My horse stepped on a bit of branch, though, and that set him off. I'm terribly sorry."

"Better that than us hitting you by accident," Virgaard remarked simply. "We didn't hit you, right? One of the arrows sounded like it might've hit something soft, like a body."

"It just buried itself in the ground."

"I see," said Virgaard as he looked the stranger over briefly. "Well, I was going to ask if you were from around here, but I can see that you must be from Sorrenar, yes?"

"You're spot on," the man from the north replied. The stranger then dismounted and offered his hand to both Mira and her father. "My name is Donovan, Donovan Velavis, and I am indeed from Sorrenar. I'm a bard, having set out to travel and see the world. I'm currently looking for a village around here named Plen. Would you two be from there, by any chance?"

"We are indeed. We were hunting to add to our feast for Estonmay Eve."

Donovan shook his head apologetically. Virgaard and Mira smiled, with the chieftain of Plen patting the Sorrenarn's shoulder.

"We really should have enough, though," he assured the bard. "How about you mount up and follow us? Plen's just a short ride from here, and we can get better acquainted on the way."

"Sounds good to me," said Donovan as the three made for their horses.

***

"So what brings you out here, Mr. Velavis?" Mira inquired once the three had ridden silently for a few moments.

"To put it simply," said the bard, "my quest to begin my career in earnest and hopefully find inspiration for songs of my own. I wish to see the world, and share my own fashion of song and music to those I meet in my travels. That said, my decision to see your village, both as an experience and a means to resupply, comes from ... a friend's suggestion. I also met an Arbonyn on the way here, and he encouraged the thought further."

Mira and her father halted abruptly. "You came across an Arbonyn earlier?" she asked.

"Yes, Miss," said Donovan cheerfully. "On my first night spent in the forest, in fact."

Mira grinned as she noticed the bard's chest puff out slightly as he went on, unsure of whether or not he was doing so consciously.

"He came to my camp because he heard me playing the harp and was curious to see who it was, wondering if it was either a Fidon or a springling. We chatted a little, with him assuring me that I was on the right trail to get here, and then I played some songs for him before he went back into the forest and I turned in for the night."

"Quite a story," said Virgaard, meeting his daughter's eyes with the same grin she had, having noticed the bard's little indulgence of pride. "I'll bet it's a rare honor for a bard to play for one of the Angelborn, be it one of the tree-folk or any of the others."

"I said the same to him," said Donovan. The bard suddenly noticed the looks that his guides were giving each other and, realizing his own posture, quickly tempered himself with some humility. "I am glad he came to see me, though, and not just for all that. The directions I was given earlier *were* quite straightforward, but with all these trees and shrubs, and me being unfamiliar with the area, I was worried at times that I might've missed a cairn or gotten disoriented one way or another. But, thanks to Rovnillath, I became confident that—"

"You met Rovnillath?" Mira asked in amazement. "Pale-green glowing eyes, a branch growing from his forehead like a horn?"

"The one and only, I suppose. Why? Is he like the chief of all the tree-folk in this forest?"

"No, at least not as far as I know, but my father and I have met him a few times over the years. He's the only Arbonyn I've met so far, and is the only one that Da has talked to. Right, Da?"

"Yes," Virgaard confirmed. "I once saw one from a distance that had branches growing all around the top of its head like a high-pointed crown. I want to say that it looked to be of feminine form, but I was too far away to clearly see. It either had somewhere to be or just wasn't in the mood to talk, as it simply waved and kept strolling on by. Granted, they're usually quiet by nature, but compared to our experiences with Rovnillath, this one was much more aloof."

"Interesting," the bard remarked.

"Anyway," Mira said, getting back to the set of questions she had in mind, "might I ask what you can do? Apart from singing and playing a harp? I'm just curious to know, since we'll be happy to have you with us for a time and supply you for your departure, but we may call for you to help out with some things in exchange."

"I understand," said Donovan. "I won't claim to be a master hunter, but I've done it before and would love to help you get something if you'd have me along. I might even be able to make amends for my untimely arrival."

Mira chuckled. "And what about other things? Fletching arrows? Preparing bowstring? Weaving cloth? Anything like that?"

"I've waxed and tied my own bowstrings a few times, and I've seen a fletcher at work, but haven't tried my hand at it myself. I've never weaved, but I'll do what I can to learn it if that's what's needed of me. And if that's too much for me to try, I'll help those who know what they're doing however I can. The same goes for anything else I might be called upon to do or help with."

"Fair enough," Mira said approvingly. "We'll take all that one step at a time."

***

The trio reached Plen in the late afternoon, with many coming over to meet the exotic bard from the North. Mira and Virgaard introduced him to the rest of their family and most of the village, and everyone promptly focused on the last few preparations for the Estonmay Eve's feast the following day.

All gathered about the village square's fire pit for dinner once the preparations for the next day had been completed. A nice dinner of bread and stew made from preserved venison and mushrooms was served, along with various drink. As Mira filled a bowl and made to hand it to the newcomer, she suddenly pulled her hand back and grinned.

"Will you sing for your supper, Mr. Donovan Velavis, terrorizer of stags?"

The gathering, having heard the story of how Donovan came into Mira and Virgaard's company, tittered slightly, but also applauded encouragingly, intrigued to hear the singing and playing of a trained bard from a foreign land. Donovan smirked at Mira's request, and rummaging through his baggage, he soon produced a beautiful harp. Plucking and strumming a few notes, he nodded to where Isaak and Kahle sat together.

"Something for the expectant parents," he said warmly. He then played the opening notes of *Blessed Fruit*, the song the village had sung to Kahle and Isaak when they announced their impending child. The ears of all gathered pricked up as the bard began to sing.

> *A blessed seed was sown*
> *Upon a loving field,*
> *And now we see that a wondrous fruit*
> *Will be what the union yields.*
> *Great joy there was in the joining alone,*
> *When the hearts of the sower and soil*
> *Became entwined and beat as one*
> *And embarked on life and love's toil.*
> *But now their joy is greater,*
> *Now that the sapling has sprung,*
> *And the two await with swelling hearts*
> *For the beauty that is to come.*
> *The sapling soon will blossom*
> *A glorious little flower,*
> *From which will come the blessed fruit*
> *That springs from love's great power.*
> *The fruit will be as all before it,*
> *And yet be one of a kind;*
> *For all the comparisons one may make,*
> *The same elsewhere, one will never find.*
> *May Onu bless you, both field and sower,*
> *For your joining of love and life,*
> *And may one day the fruit you bear*
> *Yield fruit of its own in his sight.*

The bard from the North played the last notes quietly and looked about him with a face of warm satisfaction. All the village, and their nomadic guests, seemed entranced by his work. Their faces showed deep contemplation in regards to life and love. The spouses in the gathering huddled closer together, nuzzling each other's noses and whispering into each other's ears, which flicked gently in response to the breath that carried their words. Isaak and Kahle were the most passionate in their display of affection, pausing only to thank Donovan for the song.

"It's my pleasure," said Donovan. He then turned to face Mira. "Miss Greenheart," he said in a friendly jest of formality, "was my performance sufficient for my feed?"

Mira, moved as deeply as the others, sheepishly handed the bread and stew to the bard, after putting in an extra helping and serving it up on a plate big enough to hold it all.

"You certainly did, Mr. Velavis. I apologize if I was coming off as–"

"Oh, nonsense," said the bard with friendly assurance. "I was happy to play; it's my passion and my job, after all."

"Who taught you, if I may ask?"

"A rowdy old codger who was also a refined elderly gentleman. His name was Jak Kelldren."

"Well, you certainly learned how to stir up ... various moods. I wonder how much this village is going to grow after the next nine or ten moons pass."

Mira suppressed a giggle at the sight of the bard nearly spitting up his stew from laughing.

"Anyway," the huntress went on, "we moved your things to the dining longhouse just behind us, if you hadn't already been told. It's a bit crowded at the moment, with all our other visitors, but it should be roomier once they leave."

"That sounds just fine, Miss. Thank you kindly."

65
7/4/4028 G.M.

DONOVAN rode out of Plen in the morning beside the Greenhearts, accompanying the roaming clan for a little while as they resumed their nomadic ways in the embrace of Santaru. The clan had stayed three days following the return of summer, and having exchanged with Plen an array of items and tidings, the two groups now parted ways in a spirit of kinship, with Virgaard and Ann inviting them to visit anytime.

The druid of the roaming clan gave the village a brief, warm blessing as he departed, and led his company back into the great verdant depths. When at last the nomads had gone far enough into the forest, Donovan and the villagers turned back to Plen and reached the village just before noon. As the bard and his hosts passed through the gate, Mira turned to him and cheerfully remarked that supplying him would now be a simpler and swifter task, with the bulk of their guests having now departed.

"Sounds good to me," said Donovan, who, enamored as he was with Santaru's beauty and Plen's pastoral serenity, was eager at the prospect of soon being on his own way, too. "What shall I be helping with today? I trust that I made it clear that I'll try my best with whatever you have in mind, even if I'm inexperienced in it?"

"You did indeed," said Mira. "And thankfully, at least for now, it's looking to be things that at least brush with your other skills. My family and I, and some others, are looking to go hunting tomorrow, so we'll be going over the gear of all those coming along. We'll make sure the bowstrings are good and well-waxed, and that the blades and spears are in good shape. If anything is too off with the blades and spearheads, we'll have Uld, Kahle's father, have a look at them. And we'll have Gahren fletch some more arrows; he's the best fletcher we have, though we might need you to help with sorting the shafts and whatnot for him. Once that's done, we should be set for tomorrow's hunt, and, presuming you're up for it, you'll come along and help us get some game for both your rations and our own stores. If you'd rather do something else, there's plenty other things to be done here, for which even the most basic help will always be appreciated."

"I'm all for doing so if it comes to that," said Donovan, "but I certainly would like to experience hunting in this forest."

"Very well. Just come along with us and we'll get to work."

The bard followed Mira, her parents, and her brother into the yard that lay behind the chieftains' home. There lay bows, strings, wax, blades, and spears, as well as a good pile of shafts, arrowheads, feathers, and sturdy strands of sinew. Beside these materials, sitting on a tree stump, was the fletcher, Gahren, who had already gotten a little bundle of arrows underway. Donovan and Mira's family promptly joined him, taking seats on logs and stumps, and beginning the process of checking the hunters' equipment. The bard recounted his journey as they worked, including the revelation of having met and traveled with the salpion, to the amazement of the head family of Plen. Donovan also noticed the bite marks that scarred Mira's right arm. He asked the huntress how she got them and learned of her encounter with three Qualakar young that happened twelve years ago.

***

They finished as dinner drew near, having every bow, blade, and spear checked and put into fine condition, and with full quivers placed beside each pack of equipment. Donovan and the Greenhearts gathered their things, putting them by their beds for the morning, while the other villagers who planned to accompany them came to collect their gear as well.

They had dinner in the feast hall due to the village now being less crowded as well as the arrival of rain. Donovan conversed with the Greenhearts over his future plans of travel.

"I confess I haven't any real, hard-set plans for a destination at the moment," the bard said, "but I suppose, for the sake of giving an idea for what I'll need, I may as well make for Genverdell until I think things over. There will be plenty of places where I can resupply along the way, so I suppose I'm asking for about a month's rations, give or take. If that's too much, I'm sure I can hunt or gather some things in the forest if I need to, but–"

"We should be able to manage that fairly easily," said Ann. "With a few more hunts and other things that need doing, and with the same level of help you gave today, I'd say you should be set by sometime next week. Perhaps a week from today, even."

"That suits me fine," the bard said contentedly. "I'm glad to hear that my contribution today was satisfactory. I was a bit nervous, I'll admit."

"Every bit helps," said Mira, "and you were plenty quick to pick up on whatever you didn't already know."

The huntress passed a nicely decorated drinking horn to Donovan, who sipped from it and stared into the cup with wide-eyed appreciation as the drink graced his tongue. He could make out the unquestionable golden hue of mead in the firelight, along with the fiery sweetness on his tongue.

"Well, then," he remarked appreciatively, "I thought all my life that the best mead to be had in Fidonhaal came from Sorrenar, but it appears that I was mistaken."

The villagers chuckled at Donovan's reaction, with Mira grinning as the bard passed the horn back to her.

"Well, I won't say if this is the best in the *world*," she said, "but perhaps you're used to, doubtlessly well-crafted, but farmed-honey mead?"

Donovan looked about the gathering in admiration. "So this was made from wild honey, from the hives of Santaru, huh?"

"Mm-hmm!" Mira hummed warmly.

"Why didn't you break this out with the wanderers? I'm sure we'd have had quite a time then!"

"Because it's hard to come by, of course!" Mira laughed. "We wouldn't have had enough for all of them and us, even if we wanted to pass it all around!"

"I suppose that makes sense."

"But hey, do a good job with helping us out and sing some more nice songs, and maybe, *maybe*, we'll give you a flask of this for the road."

"You got a deal, Miss!" said Donovan as he ran back for his harp.

***

When Donovan awoke the next morning, he was pleased to hear that the rain, which lulled him to sleep as it drummed on the roof of the feast hall, had stopped in time for the beginning of the hunt. Several different birdsongs filled the air, and Donovan, rested and eager to experience hunting in such a vast and ancient forest alongside experienced and hospitable company, gathered his gear and stepped outside.

Across from the dining longhouse was the Greenhearts' home. Mira and her family, including Isaak, and a good handful of other men and women were gathered at the door, each on horseback. All looked ready, but none seemed restless or impatient. Donovan, waving and bidding them good morning, leisurely made for the village stables to fetch his horse and pack his equipment. He swiftly rejoined them at the chieftains' house and the company then trotted briskly into the forest, which glittered as an ocean of emeralds as the lingering raindrops caught the light of dawn that pierced the canopy.

***

The hunting party quietly rode and whispered amongst themselves for several hours, keeping their eyes peeled for game and tracks. Donovan noticed a movement from the corner of his eye. It was a great bull elk, larger than the stag he accidentally scared off when he first met Mira and her father. He hissed for silence, then pointed to the grand beast. The hunters gasped in awe, with Isaak complimenting Donovan's good eye. The bard, along with Mira and her father, quickly formed a line, drew their bows, and fired their shafts. In the same instant, a rustling of distant undergrowth set the elk on edge. It bolted off with a squeal, and the hunters set their heels into their horses, charging forward as Mira laughed.

"You seem to bring bad luck when you notice big game, Mr. Velavis," the huntress jested.

"Just you watch!" Donovan called with a laugh as he charged ahead of Mira and her brother. "I'll get him; I'll make up for that stag!"

The riders charged and Donovan led. He saw the elk dart between some trees, then get lost among more undergrowth. Clutching his bow, the bard rode through. A few strides in, his horse tripped and he flew out of the saddle. Hitting the ground, he looked up and saw the shredded body of the elk lying in front of him, and the Qualakar that loomed over it.

66
7/5/4028 G.M.

MIRA heard Donovan's cries of alarm before she saw anything, as she and her father, who led the hunting party behind the bard's charge, were still catching up to him. Then she heard the Qualakar's roar and her heart skipped a beat. Her mind flooded with memories of the Qualakar that charged into her patrol twelve years ago and the horrid noise it made. Memories also came unbidden of the bite from the monstrous cub that day, and a flash of pain, produced solely from memory, ran up her arm as she braced to combat the monster. Then, just as she and Virgaard were about to charge into the undergrowth, the bard's screams of pain and horror filled the air, and Mira's blood froze in her veins.

The huntress and her father breached through the foliage, ready to throw their spears as soon as the monster entered their sight. Mira felt time slow to a crawl as the Qualakar snapped its head up to face the two who had interrupted its meal and sport. The monster and the huntress locked eyes for a second, and Mira saw that the Qualakar's eyes were widened with glee from the vile ecstasy brought on by the smell and taste of blood, flesh, and fear. She then saw her father's spear take flight from the corner of her eye, and with time's flow returning to its normal pace, she promptly threw her own. Both spears found their marks, with Virgaard's piercing the Qualakar's skull and Mira's driving deep into the shoulder and the vital organs that lay behind it. The monster's mouth immediately unhinged, releasing what it held in its jaws, and with only a single spasm upon dropping to the ground, it lay dead beside its ravaged prey.

Mira's eyes then fell upon Donovan's body, which lay fidgeting and bloodied by the great scratches that carved across his back and the bite marks that dug into his shoulder. She tried to speak to the bard, but found that he was unconscious. She turned him over so he could be carried back to Plen on his back, only to recoil in horror as she found that in the mere seconds in which Donovan had been in the Qualakar's grasp, he had been scored and bitten across the chest as well as the back. He was now bleeding heavily on both sides. Mira gasped for help, having to find her voice to call out again for the rest of the hunters to hear. Her father quickly looked Donovan over and started to sort out what medical supplies he had in his pack. The rest of the party, already at a gallop, hastened further at Mira's call and soon gathered around the bard.

"It's very bad," said Virgaard as he, Mira, and two others began to put a tincture on the bard's wounds and carefully bandage him, despite the fitful spasms brought on by the medicine's sting. "He's got more than no chance, though; we just need to get him back home as soon as we can."

The group devised a stretcher and placed Donovan across the backs of two horses. They tethered the horses together and led them along as swiftly and gently as could be managed. Mira and her family followed the transport, constantly scanning the forest in fear of another Qualakar charging in.

Grim Hunting

67
7/9/4028 G.M.

DONOVAN awoke with a start, having heard a light creak and the heavy thud of wood on wood. He could hear a group of footsteps milling about nearby. Realizing that what he heard was a door opening and closing, the bard quickly took in his surroundings. He was in a bed in a small room, with a light curtain covering the doorway. He sniffed the air, picking up the earthy sweetness of many herbs and roots that seemed to be coming from the room beyond. He then became conscious of the bandages that ran across his back and chest, as well as his left shoulder.

His fur bristled as he shuddered at the memories flooding into his mind. He saw again the vile fangs of the Qualakar, and felt the agony of the claws burying into his flesh. He felt again something being put on his wounds, which burned like fire, followed by strips of cloth pressed on and wrapped about him. He had blurred memories of being carried from the forest, into a house, and placed upon a bed. Some sort of urgent discussion, planning, and at times emotional debate barely reached his ears. Other sights, sounds, and feelings began to walk across his waking mind, including bowls of soup and water being pressed to his lips, along with medicine. He remembered being turned over onto his stomach and back at varying times, and the feeling of fresh poultices and bandages being applied.

"This must be Kahle and Isaak's house," the bard mumbled to himself, "since she and her mother are the lead healers here."

Donovan's ears pricked up as he heard what he thought to be a gasp.

"I think he might be awake," said the voice he recognized as Kahle's. "Isaak, would you get that poultice started, please?"

"Of course, honey."

"Thank you," said Kahle as she and Mira suddenly appeared at the parted curtain, with Ann and Virgaard behind them and peering in.

"Oh, Onu bless your poor heart," Kahle said gently as she and Mira knelt by his side with more soup and water. "You seemed to be right on the edge a time or two, but there shouldn't need to be any more worry, now."

"How long was I out?"

"Around four days."

"Four Breaths," Donovan sighed in disbelief. "What did I miss?"

He saw Mira and Kahle's ears lower somberly as Virgaard entered the room, having heard the bard's question.

"We had a few scouts comb the area," the chieftain explained, "and based on the reports, it seems that, while there's always the chance for the odd straggler or two, the bulk of the recent incidents with these monsters is due to one pack. We believe it's sizable, but can be exterminated if we can determine their location and numbers. This needs to be dealt with at the source, and as soon as possible, and we'll need many in the company. But ... there's still things that need to be tended to here, not the least of which being your recovery. So, half of us are going to head out and not come back until we at least find where these Qualakars are holing up. If it can be managed with our company as is, we'll wipe them out then and there. But if we decide that we need more with us, we'll come back and gather a larger party. We aren't doing that until we've located their den, though. We talked long and hard over who would go and who would stay, and Isaak and I are going to head the company, while Ann, Mira, and Kahle, along with others, will stay here to make sure things stay well, for you and for everyone else staying here."

"I see," said Donovan in solemn understanding, after swallowing the spoonful of soup that Kahle held out to him. "When are you leaving?"

"Tomorrow at dawn," said Virgaard grimly. "I'm glad that I was able to see you wake up before I left. I was starting to worry that I wouldn't know your fate until I returned."

"My thanks, Chief Greenheart, to you, your family, and all your village, for all that you've done for me. If I could've recovered sooner, I would've insisted on joining you."

"And I would've gratefully had you in my company if you were fit for the task," Virgaard said with a somber smile. "But please, rest now and get well. If we can resolve this soon and you're on your feet again when we return, we'll be able to see you off with good confidence in your safety."

"Very well," Donovan sighed before taking a drink of water from Mira's proffered bowl. "I'll pray for the safe and swift success, and return, of you and the company."

"Thank you," said Virgaard as he turned to leave. "Is there anything I can do before I go?"

The bard put on his best face of mock pain and woe. "Might I perhaps have but a drop of that wild-honey mead?"

"Don't push it, mister," said Virgaard, Mira, and Kahle in unison, a coincidence that set all in the hut to laughing.

Donovan grinned and shrugged, wincing slightly at the pain that ran across his shoulder as he did so. "A little ale then, maybe? Just a little something more to go with the soup and medicine? What do you have?"

Virgaard smiled. "I visited a town on the road outside Santaru a little while back," he said, "and got me a nice little batch of whiskey from some folks there. Would a few pulls of that do for you?"

"Certainly!" said the bard with a smile. "Thank you, and Onu keep you and yours safe on your mission."

68
7/10/4028 G.M.

MIRA stood with Ann and Kahle at Plen's gates, seeing her father and brother off along with the rest of the extermination party. The five embraced together in the green, tree-dimmed light of dawn, as did all the others with their families and friends. Both those departing and those remaining bade each other to be careful, and assured the other they would do their best with the tasks that had fallen to them. Mira looked intently, her heart at once both warmed and stung, at her mother and father, and her brother and his wife. Both pairs, the newlywed and the long-bound, bade each other farewell with the bravest faces they could muster.

When at last the expedition party had trotted away, the three women went to Kahle's home to check on Donovan.

"I hope tending to Donovan is the most we need to worry about, as far as me being needed is concerned," said Kahle a little nervously as she entered the cottage with them. "With Mother and Father both going with the others, it'll basically be just me who will be taking care of anyone else who happens to get sick or hurt."

"We're all going to be there for you," Ann assured her daughter-in-law. "As you are for all of us. We all talked this out before."

"I know," Kahle sighed as they made their way to Donovan's room. "It's just–"

"Donovan!" Mira shouted with an exasperated laugh. "What are you doing?"

The bard, having gotten himself to sit upright on the edge of his bed, was trying to push himself up, wincing at the pain that went through his bitten shoulder as he tried to rise.

"I want to see your father and brother off," he explained through slightly gritted teeth. "I–"

Mira, Ann, and Kahle gently pressed Donovan back onto his bed.

"I'm afraid you've just missed them," said Ann, "and we would've insisted that you stay put anyway, as would my husband and Isaak, no doubt."

"Damn it," Donovan moaned softly under his breath. He slumped crestfallen back onto his pillow, his face the picture of frustration, worry, and regret. The look in his ice-blue eyes melted Mira's heart.

"Come now," the huntress assured him with a gentle stroke of his head, "you should just need a few more days' rest, and then we can get you back on your feet and get you back in shape. Right, Kahle?"

"Yes," assured the herbalist. "And we'll get back to seeing to your supplies, and you'll soon be able to continue your journey whenever you wish."

"Thank you," said the bard with moody, but sincere, gratitude. "I don't mean to leave until they come back, though; not just to hear if those monsters are cleared out, but to see them all one more time and give my thanks again."

"Very well," said Ann understandingly. "Your sense and your courtesy should be doing your family proud, from your father to your mother and sister's spirits."

Donovan looked kindly on the village matriarch, and her daughters of blood and law, and meekly made a request.

"May I have my harp at hand, please? When I can't get myself to sleep, playing around with it a little is better than just lying here."

"Of course," said Kahle. Mira, intending to grant the request regardless of the doctor's answer, left the cottage and brought all the bard's packs from the feast hall to his room, placing them by his bedside. She brought the harp out from the baggage and gave it to him. Donovan took it from her hands gratefully and promptly began playing various tunes as Mira and Kahle prepared his breakfast and his next dose of medicine (along with a drop of the whiskey that Virgaard gave to him).

Ann, enjoying a few of the tunes in silence as she stood by the bard, reluctantly left to oversee the rest of the men and women who had stayed to keep Plen in order. Mira and Kahle soon joined her once Donovan was fed and had settled down to rest. Though the harp was now sitting quietly by the bedside, the songs Donovan had played echoed in the huntress's mind and heart, and she suspected the same could be said for Ann and Kahle.

69
7/13/4028 G.M.

DONOVAN relished the fresh morning air of the forest as he stepped out of the herbalist's hut. He had been confined to bed for just over a week. Mira and Kahle stood beside him, having helped him out of bed in case his legs faltered. With breakfast for four in their hands, the three made their way to the spot behind the Greenhearts' house. They joined Plen's matriarch, seating themselves on the stumps and logs arranged about them, and began to check and maintain the remaining villagers' gear. They were doing this for future hunts, as well as making preparations in the event Virgaard's company returned and needed more hands to combat the Qualakar infestation. The four exchanged more stories from their lives while completing the day's tasks, and when evening came and dinner was served in the long hall, the bard again played and sang to the people of Plen. He was rewarded with much rejoicing that his recovery was going well.

***

Days passed, with all the remaining villagers anxiously awaiting the return of the monster-hunting company as they carried on with their lives as normally as they could. Each day, Donovan went about to help as best he could with whatever tasks there were to be done. He grew in familiarity with nearly all the villagers in the following weeks, especially with Ann, Kahle, and Mira. In addition to the growing exhilaration of his recovering body and strength, he was pleasantly surprised with his growing handiness in a range of chores, from patching clothes to tending to the numerous house-side gardens that supplemented the village's meat stores.

"If, in my travels, I ever end up in a situation where singing for my supper isn't enough," the bard once said with a laugh, "I'll hopefully be able to use what I've learned from you to make up the difference with some little jobs on the side."

It did seem that singing would suffice overall, however, as he was rewarded every night with a warm reception from his newfound friends as he sang at dinner.

***

A month and a day passed from when Donovan rose from his bed. Then, as the bard was conversing with Ann and Mira in their home at noon, a villager cried out the hunters' return. All the village rushed to receive them.

Their hearts halted at the sight they met. The faces of all the company were utterly drained of spirit. A good few of them bore a wound, with one man bearing a particularly nasty-looking one on his shoulder, covered as it was by a bandage. Isaak rode in the lead, his countenance dreadfully numb. Lying across the haunches of his horse was a body, covered by a blood-soaked stretch of canvas that had been ripped from a tent.

70

8/14/4028 G.M.

MIRA stared at the arriving company, rooted to the spot with Donovan beside her. Her mother approached Isaak as he sat numbly in the saddle, her body quaking with dread. She heard Kahle hurrying to the gate, crying for joy, only to gasp and fall silent as she saw the state of her husband and the other hunters. Ann made to lift the cloth that draped the corpse lying across Isaak's horse. Isaak took his mother's hand, shaking his head tearfully and whispering something that Mira couldn't hear. Ann, tears flowing down her face, forcefully pulled her hand out of her son's, tore away the cloth, and with one heartrending sob, dropped to her knees, weeping quietly as those who could see the body gasped at the sight.

Mira at last managed to walk forward, resolving past her dread to see the body. She sensed that Donovan was right behind her, and the two approached Isaak's horse as silence surrounded them. Mira looked upon the body, her fur bristling, her blood freezing, and her heart creeping up her throat as she did.

Her father's body, mangled and riddled bloody by a Qualakar's claws and teeth, lay headless across the back of the horse. Tied about Virgaard's middle was a length of rope, the end of which swung over the horse's side. Tied to the end of it was a makeshift sack made from more tent canvas, its bottom saturated with dried blood. Mira turned away, unable to look any further, and embraced her mother as they both wept.

"We ... we started by going north, toward Lake Aidna," Isaak said hollowly as he began his account of the expedition. "We saw only the odd track until we neared the lake, then we began seeing a number of tracks meeting and parting in various spots. The closer we got to the lake, the more we saw, so we kept going. When we reached the shore, there were tracks all over, old and fresh, so we were sure they were near. Going by the tracks, we went along the east shoreline, toward the rocks and cliffs that run along it. Then we saw ... an Arbonyn lying dead nearby. Its body was carved up and stripped of bark by those monsters' claws, and it was gnawed from head to toe; I couldn't tell if it was male or female. We went on further and saw another one. And then another. And ..."

Isaak halted briefly. Then, drawing a deep breath, he continued the harrowing tale.

"As we neared the cliffs, we began following a trail of dead tree-folk as much as we were following the trail of tracks. The tracks were now consistently coming from, and going toward, the same direction. As we reached the cliff and went along its base, which was crowded by a good line of trees and shrubs, we followed the tracks until we finally ran into one of those foul beasts. We killed it quickly, and then managed another one just as fast when it came running in response to the other's howls. After that, we heard a bunch of growls coming from, seemingly, the rock of the cliff itself. There was still a sizeable pack of them hiding somewhere, and they *knew* we were there."

Mira felt Kahle approach. She looked up to her from her embrace with Ann, and saw her staring at her husband through misty eyes. Isaak breathed a shaky, heavy sob, dismounted, and held his wife closely. He gave a small, brief smile as he petted Kahle's growing middle, then went on as he kept her close.

"We were all frozen to the spot for a moment, but then Father got us going, and following the growls, we found a cavemouth nestled among a cluster of trees and foliage. The beginnings of the cave jutted out a good stretch from the cliffside, and it had earth and grass covering its top, along with a huge, gorgeous oak and several other trees. As we neared it, we found more dead Arbonyns scattered about the entrance, and ... we realized what we had found."

Mira and her mother, tears still flowing down their cheeks, looked in stunned amazement at Isaak, as did all the villagers that had come to receive the returning party. Donovan, wide-eyed, stepped forward.

"Arborhaven Cave?" he asked incredulously. "You all found Arborhaven Cave, and it's been made into a Qualakar den?"

Mira's skin crawled as the realization arrived in the wake of the bard's words. The cave was a legendary, once world-renowned abode of druids and Arbonyns in many centuries past. Knowledge of its location had been lost for several hundred years after the deaths of the last resident druids. Its grandeur endured in song, as well as the knowledge that it did lie somewhere in Santaru Forest, but the precise location had long slipped from memory despite uncounted efforts to find it again. For reasons unknown, the Arbonyns seemed to wish to keep it a secret. The rediscovery of the site would have, under normal circumstances, been a joyous find for many. But with the horrid discovery of it having been found as a den for foul beasts of Raakaru's perversions, disgust and horror were the reigning emotions, along with grief for those slain, Arbonyn and Fidon alike.

"It is as you say," Isaak said grimly to Donovan. "Needless to say, Father was appalled and furious, and had no trouble riling us up to finish the monsters off, for all of Santaru's security and to avenge the profaning of such a place, and the cruel slaying of the tree-folk. We all took positions around the mouth of the cave, and began yelling and making a racket. Soon we heard a most dreadful roaring, and suddenly nine of those horrors came running out of the cave. We were ready and felled the first four within seconds. Then they started closing in on some of us and we needed to turn to the spear. Only Ulkon got hurt, with a nasty clawing on the shoulder, but nothing else. As we were patching him up, we listened and could only make out one remaining source of growling. Figuring that it must have been the alpha male, we had Ulkon and a few others stay outside while the rest of us ventured in to end it. We crept through the tunnels, almost tripping over a few more Arbonyn corpses, as well as a few ... bones of varying sorts ... until we found the haven's central room. And there we saw it, at the far end of the chamber. Its eyes sparked awfully in the faint light from outside as it stared right at us. We charged into the chamber as it screeched and howled, and it began to charge at us in turn. It was a horribly large animal and we had an awful fight. We ... we lost Helen ... and Tarnov, but we finished it. Or so we thought."

Isaak looked about him, then suddenly fixed his gaze straight ahead, though he seemed to be looking at nothing in particular.

"While a few went to carry Helen and Tarnov out, Father and I checked the Qualakar ... and saw that it was only a female. The alpha female, perhaps, but not the male. We heard a growl like thunder ... turned around ..."

Isaak began to shake, and Kahle sought desperately to comfort him as he began sobbing wretchedly. Mira and Ann quickly rose from where they were, and embraced the two as Isaak forced through the final moments of the tale.

"An-and ... we saw him ... I-I never saw or heard of s-such a Qualakar of-of the s-size that this one was. He ... he ... was as big as f-four ... four bears. And th-then he howled as some h-horror from Raakhaal, an-and we all turned to run out and get ... get everyone together to take him down. We all got out, but when I turned to make sure Father was behind me, I heard him shouting ... and then ... a ... a crunch ... and I s-saw that horrid beast ... j-just standing there ... with ... with Father's h-head in his jaws. We were all rooted to where we st-stood, but then Kellii fired an arrow and put out his eye. He dropped Father's head ... and charged full-on at her. She w-was clawed to pieces as we all shot and stabbed at him. After we stuck him enough, he t-turned and ran back into the cave, but not before he swiped at Aaron and clawed his f-face off, and broke his neck besides."

The village of Plen stood in horrid silence as they took in all that the chiefs' son had told them. After a moment, Isaak managed to compose himself and look to his mother.

"Where are ... the families, Mother? Helen's husband and their boy, and Tarnov's–"

"I'll tell them, Isaak. You've done enough telling it once."

"Thank you."

Isaak kissed his mother and sister, and last and most closely Kahle, as he gestured to the five bodies laid over the backs of the horses that bore them.

"If there's any comfort," he said in weary sadness, "it's that we were able to get ... them ... all home and not leave them to be fed upon. But ... we don't *know* if that abomination is still alive or not. I ... I feel in my heart that he still is, though, and just licking his wounds. Yes, after seeing him kill Aaron the way he did, after being stuck so many times ... I fear he still lives."

Isaak took a deep, steady breath.

"After ... after we put ... the dead ... to rest, we need to make sure that monster is dead. Qualakar packs tend to repopulate if they aren't completely rooted out."

A hushed whisper of dread ran over the gathering, as there were clearly none who wished to venture to the befouled haven and risk facing the horror that may still lurk within.

Then Mira heard footsteps approach, and looked to see Donovan standing before the huddled, grieving family.

"I will go with whoever else goes," the bard said with a voice of ironclad resolve.

"Donovan," Ann said, "I-I can't express how much I appreciate the gesture, but we just can't put you in danger like that. You're our guest, and one that we failed to keep safe, for that matter. We can't–"

"You couldn't possibly have known that a Qualakar was there. You didn't fail in my welfare, and you have seen to my recovery as well as any could ask of you. The kindness you've all shown me since the day I arrived is more than enough to bind me to help you end this, or confirm that it's over, any way I can."

"But," Mira began, "you're still hurt. We can't expect you to–"

Donovan wordlessly grabbed the bow and quiver from Isaak's saddlebag. He then stood in the middle of the village's gateway, and pointed to the large bell that hung over the doorway of the dining longhouse.

"I'll make it ring," he said simply.

Mira watched as the bard braced for the shot, wincing as she watched him grit his teeth at the pain in the shoulder of his bow-arm. He released the arrow, and there was an audible gasp from the gathering as the arrow missed the bell by only a few feet, burying itself into the wall beside it. Donovan drew another arrow, grunting irritably, and shot again. The second shaft buried itself in the ground just in front of the doorway. The bard cursed under his breath and reached for another arrow. Mira gently grabbed his arm, giving him a small smile and a light laugh.

"Those were close enough," she said. "You can't expect things to always go like they do in those songs of yours, you know."

Donovan laughed softly, and thanked her for her acceptance.

"Just don't wear that shoulder out before we get there," she said. "You won't do me, or anyone else who comes along, any good if you can't shoot at all."

Mira looked to her mother, who nodded in acceptance of her daughter's intentions.

"We'll set out tomorrow," she announced, turning to all present. "Come with us whoever will. We'll leave at first light."

***

Five pyres were arranged in the fire pit, and the dead were laid upon them with Virgaard at the arrangement's center. The full moon beamed silver through the treetops and onto the grieving village, and contrasted with the bright, golden glow of the funerary fires. As Plen grieved and took their evening meal, Mira and her family looked on as Donovan strode up to the pyres and, with a word of acknowledgement to those whom the slain left behind, strummed his harp and began to sing a dirge.

I gaze upon your silent face,
Which now lies veiled in eternal grace.
I ache with yearning for your lips,
To once more feel the warmth of your kiss
And hear the voice that always set my heart alight.
Your eyes, through which I saw your soul,
And felt Onu's love, and thus felt whole,
Have been hollow and locked since your spirit took flight.
I gaze upon your silent face,
Which now lies veiled in eternal grace.
Your heart, which once raced beside mine,
Lies still and silent; silent as mine.
My heart is as one who has been robbed in the night.
I wishfully weep for your arms
To embrace me again, and thus warm
This cold soul, but to no avail, plead as I might.
I gaze upon your silent face,
Which now lies veiled in eternal grace.
But even though my grief is great,
My love endures, and I trust to wait
'Til the day when I too depart from Dodmorhaal.
Then, if by the grace of Onu,
My soul may be rejoined unto you,
We'll relish our bond forever in Onuhaal.
I gaze upon your silent face,
Which now lies veiled in eternal grace.
The joy I trust that we shall have
Does heal my heart and soul as a salve,
And shall sustain me 'til the day I heed Death's call.
On that day, I shall embrace you
Forevermore, before Onu's view,
And we'll share a love with him that shall never fall.
I gaze upon your silent face,
Which now lies veiled in eternal grace.

Mira looked at her mother, whose eyes, though clearly still bearing grief, began to shine with consoled gratitude as she listened, as did the others gathered who lost one of those who had perished.

When the song ended, Mira rose to thank the bard, and was surprised to hear him announce his retirement for the night.

"I'm feeling pretty drained," he laughed ruefully, "and I've got a big journey starting tomorrow. I'm off to bed now. Goodnight, all."

The villagers bade the bard goodnight, and he left to go to his bed in Kahle and Isaak's home, which had come to replace his previous arrangement in the feast hall. Mira followed him from a distance, finally calling to him as he opened the door to the house. He looked to her, his white fur and winter-blue eyes sparkling brilliantly in the moon's light. Silent tears were flowing down his face.

"Thank you, Donovan Velavis," she said. "For ... everything. I'll see you tomorrow."

The bard briefly looked fixedly into the eyes of the huntress, nodded courteously, and then entered the hut, shutting the door quietly behind him.

71
8/15/4028 G.M.

DONOVAN opened his eyes as the faint light of day worked its way through the treetops and into the herbalist's home. He rose from bed, full of the vigor in body, mind, and soul that is brought on by resolve, and relished the absence of his previous pain and discomfort as he moved about. He grabbed his packs, with his bow, quiver, dagger, and a spear from the village in addition to a huntsman's blade. He left the house, bidding Isaak and Kahle farewell as the two sat at breakfast, and met Mira at the door. The bard and the huntress went to their horses, packed their supplies, and met with the others set for the journey who had gathered at the gate.

The people of Plen had discussed who was going to the profaned site of Arborhaven the previous day, agreeing that Isaak was still too hurt and distraught to accompany them and lead them to the precise location. Ulkon, who had been wounded in the shoulder from the previous expedition, willingly assumed the task of guide. Four others from the previous party were going as well, including Kahle's parents, Genna and Uld, and four others from the village. Among those were Quelva, the wife of the slain hunter, Tarnov. With the company now all gathered, the villagers saw them off with prayers of safety. Ann gave a silent, solemn nod to the party. As much as the chieftain wished to go, she had decided to stay and look after her son and the others affected by the losses of the previous company.

As they began to ride off, the bard was taken aback as Ann called to him. He and Mira stopped as she approached, and Ann took his hand.

"Onu bless you for your kindness, honor, and courage," the widow said softly. "May he guard you and your companions from harm and ensure your success."

"And Onu bless you for your hospitality, and that of those you lead," Donovan returned. "And may he give you strength and solace in the wake of your loss."

Breathing deeply, the bard rode off with his companions for the lake and cave, guided by Ulkon's lead.

***

A fortnight passed with very few words passing among the company. No songs were played or sung by Donovan, or anyone else, both from worry of possibly attracting danger as well as a simple lack of cheerful spirit in light of the task ahead. Nearly each night at camp, however, Donovan thought he saw Mira looking earnestly at him, as though needing, or wishing, to speak with him. Whenever he tried to casually approach her, however, she headed off to check the outskirts of the camp or tend to some chore. He eventually began to feel that his sensing of Mira's gaze must have simply been his imagination, or perhaps the dark and the firelight were playing tricks with his sight.

They reached Lake Aidna at the end of the month, with the waters sparkling bright gold and blue from the clear, sunny noon sky above. The bard found the sudden appearance of such an open space to be refreshing, and realized it had been essentially two months since he had last seen such an open view of the sky. As he neared the wooded cliffs of the lake's eastern shore, he was suddenly seized by a morbid anxiety, wondering if this view was to be the last one of its kind that he would see in his life.

***

They reached the cave in the middle of the afternoon, as indicated by Ulkon's growing apprehension. Shaking slightly in his saddle, the guide pointed at the cave mouth that peered through the trees and shrubs, and the decayed corpses of Arbonyns and Qualakars that still littered the ground about it. No tracks were seen that pointed to the massive alpha male having left the cave, meaning that it either lay dead or still lurked in the desecrated haven.

"This ... this is it," said Ulkon worriedly. He turned to Mira, who he was inclined to view as the leader of the party, since she was the daughter of the chieftains and a sensible Fidon besides. "Do we have a plan?"

Donovan watched as Mira stared intently at the cave's dark entrance. His ears involuntarily shot up as she faced him and locked eyes with him. Her dark brown eyes were piercingly earnest.

"How's your bow-arm?" she asked.

"F-fine," the bard stuttered. "Just fine. Why?"

"If you're up for it, here's my plan. You and I go into the cave. We see if we can find him, and if we do, we shoot arrows at the body if we can't tell whether he's alive or dead. If we hit him and get no response, we'll bring everyone in and stick him good and proper to make sure. If he's still alive ... well, we run out, and assuming he'll chase us, we get him out here in the open, and we all jump him."

Donovan looked into the huntress's eyes and breathed a heavy sigh of resolve. "I'm with you."

Mira looked to the others and pointed to several spots about the cave entrance. "Everyone take up positions around here, and ... then we'll do this."

Once all were organized, Donovan and Mira crept into the cave, side by side and with bows and arrows at the ready. They made their way through the earthen corridors, bracing for the sight of the massive Qualakar at any moment. They reached the central den, and after a moment of scanning the dim cavern, they saw the hulking form of the monster lying at the far end. They could not make out any sight or sound of it breathing from where they stood, and at Mira's signal, the two fired their shots at the vile beast. An instant's silence filled the air, followed by the grimly satisfying thuds of two shafts piercing flesh. More silence followed. Mira softly patted Donovan's back, and the bard smiled at her in the dim light.

"It's looking good," she said. "Let's just go back and bring the oth—"

A blood-chilling rustling cut the silence, followed by the heavy thuds of large clawed paws striking the ground as the body they supported rose up from its rest. Then a horrifyingly low rumble of a roar began to fill the chamber. The two saw the Qualakar's eyes find their own in the gloom, and the roar swiftly rose to an earsplitting howl of wrath. The bard and the huntress gasped a short breath of fright, then, as the hulking monster came charging at them, they wheeled around and ran as fast as they could. Donovan's heart pounded as he heard the thundering footfalls and heavy, ragged breathing coming ever closer. He dreaded the thought that, even should they reach the cave mouth, the monster would likely be upon them both before they could do anything more.

Just as they reached the exit, Donovan heard Mira scream out a desperate maneuver.

"DIVE TO THE SIDE! NOW!"

Both dived to the side nearest them the instant they passed the edges of the cave walls. The monster dove into the air ahead and was stuck with a spear in his side the instant he landed. Five arrows pierced him from varying angles. Donovan and Mira scrambled to their feet, bows drawn again, and loosed their arrows at the monster, who turned about as it made to retreat into the cave. Mira's shaft put out the Qualakar's remaining eye, and Donovan's arrow joined the others that seemed to sprout all over the horror's body. As the Cursed One flailed about blindly, Donovan and Mira drew their hunter's blades and charged into him, driving their blades deep into his side. They at last pierced into his chest and belly, and twisted their blades. They recoiled in disgust as the monster's insides began to spill out. With a final, bloodcurdling screech, the alpha male Qualakar slumped down onto the earth, kicked about him three times, then lay still in the full grasp of death.

The hunters were overwhelmed with the sense of victory. Though some horror of Raakaru likely still lurked in the depths of Santaru, there was no doubt the threat of the Qualakars had been drastically curbed, and that the forest was, overall, at peace once again. Some wept in relief, others laughed. All looked upon Donovan in puzzlement as he took his hunting blade and cleaved at the monster's neck. After a few moments of strenuous chopping and sawing, the Qualakar's head fell from the body. It rested on the ground, standing as high as the bard's waist. Donovan carried it to his horse, securing it carefully behind the saddle as the horse briefly stamped his hooves in dismay at his macabre new burden. The bard then looked at the company, his eyes soon settling on Mira.

"Something for your mother, and all the others, to see," he explained, "that they may know that the slain have been avenged. We will show them the head of ... Mortenovu, and the chieftain may do with it as she wishes."

The company applauded the gesture, with Mira laughing as she clapped. "Mortenovu?" she asked. "The Mountain of Death? Did you *really* just come up with that on the spot?"

Donovan shrugged with a smirk.

"I swear, you bards," she said with a laugh.

***

They returned to Plen on the thirteenth of Yorjiv, the eve just before the full moon, to the joyous welcome of all the village. They told of their adventure, and Ann, gratefully accepting the head of the monster, had it burned.

Departures and Returns

72
9/13/4028 G.M.

MIRA rose from the soft, grassy earth beneath the shade of the tree where she slept. She looked about for a moment, greatly puzzled, before she saw Donovan and the other nine who accompanied her on the journey to Arborhaven, as well as the survivors of the first party. Her mother was also there, and each stood about and looked at one another with bemusement.

"I ... I believe we're dreaming," she called out to them, "or at least I am."

The others glanced about again, then voiced agreement as they gathered together on the path that lay before them.

"What is all this, though," asked Isaak as he stood by his sister, "if we are indeed all sharing a dream? Where are we, if anywhere?"

"We're at the entrance to Arborhaven," said Donovan as he pointed toward the mouth of the cave that lay ahead. The cave was now clearly visible, unobscured by foliage, and with the path on which they stood leading to it clear as day. "I'm sure it's Arborhaven, but it's as if ... as if it's been rediscovered and reclaimed by some druids, or the Arbonyns, perhaps. It's as if it was a regularly visited pilgrimage site again, or something of the sort."

The group quietly approached the entrance, with one of them pointing out a glow of vibrant green and blue light that came from within the cave. With only a brief hesitation, they entered together and followed Mira, Isaak, and Donovan's lead. They passed through the tunnels, which now felt of the peaceful solidness of earth and not the gloom of a foul monster's den, and into the central chamber, which now had the feeling of a great, tranquil haven. It was here from which the lights of green and blue came, and upon seeing their sources, the jaws of all in the gathering dropped wide open.

Before them stood Terranah and Stromarus, the Angels of Earth and Water and the parents of the Arbonyns and the merfolk. They stood together, hand in hand, and looked on the company as ones who had expected their arrival. They each glowed as a jewel held to the sun, with Terranah's light as that of an emerald and Stromarus's as a sapphire. Smiling, they wordlessly beckoned the company forward. As they neared the holy couple, the dreamers looked about and saw the ghosts of two dozen Arbonyns looking at them reverently, along with the spirits of the Fidons who had been slain by Mortenovu. Mira could see those who were from the previous hunting company: Helen and Tarnov, Kellii and Aaron. There were also a few others that the huntress didn't recognize, and she presumed they were some unfortunate souls who happened across the monsters while wandering Santaru.

When she noticed her father, Mira froze in her steps, as did Isaak and Donovan. She made to run to him, to embrace him and tell him how much she loved and missed him, but Virgaard, smiling softly, shook his head and nodded to the angels. The company approached Terranah and Stromarus, and bowed reverently before them.

"Rise, good children of Onu and Fidonhaal," said Terranah in the voice of the hardest rock and the softest soil. "By Onu's leave, we wished to commend you for your courage in ridding Santaru of the growing scourge of the pack led by, as the dear bard here has named him, Mortenovu. We also wish to give what comfort we might, in light of the loss and pain you have suffered."

"You both honor me beyond my ability to describe, as well as my worthiness," said Mira humbly.

"Nonsense," said Stromarus, his voice flowing gently from his lips and bearing the echoes of the deepest waters. "Your courage and resolve were great, as were your motives to make Santaru safer and exact justice for those slain, who comprised of both your people and our children."

Mira and her companions looked around them, awestruck at the sight of her father, the other slain villagers, the few strangers, and a host of the tree-folk nodding to them in great reverence.

"We know not the full design or purposes of Onu," Terranah said, "nor do we see fully how all that has passed here will play to the ultimate good, but Onu has assured us that it is so, and will be so. As his loving children, born in the wake of the beginning, we have striven to trust him and his word in this, as we ever have in all things. We ask you, dear people of Fidonhaal, do you, will you, aim to do the same?"

Mira made to speak, but fell silent as her mother, stepping forward, spoke as though she had taken the words from her daughter's own mouth.

"Though the mysteries of the Eternal One may cause unfathomable disquiet in my heart, and though loss and sorrow at times accompany them, I say yes. In Onu and his word ... I too strive to trust."

"And I as well," said Mira and the others with her.

Stromarus and Terranah lifted their hands, and the lights that they cast flowed about them, filling the company's hearts with a healing warmth that removed all grief and pain from the losses and fears that had plagued them in the wake of the Qualakar scourge.

"Go forth, then, in peace," the angelic pair said warmly. "Take your time in bidding the departed farewell, then return to peaceful slumber when you leave this haven."

All the gathering then went to each who had perished to the vile monsters, bidding farewell and eternal peace to them. When Mira, Ann, Isaak, and Donovan approached Virgaard, the late patriarch of Plen embraced each in turn, holding them closely as tears flowed freely down their faces.

"Ann, my love," he said to his wife, "be strong and keep faith. We will walk among the groves of Onuhaal soon enough, but you still have your time here to live. Don't waste it in sadness."

"I won't, Vir," Ann sobbed as she held onto her husband and kissed him, "and I'll do all I can to do as you ask. Will you wait for me under one of the trees, when you get over there?"

"Of course."

Virgaard then held Mira, who silently stared into his eyes as he spoke.

"The same words I spoke to your mother, I say to you. Your courage and resolve will serve you well, wherever your path leads you. Keep walking it in trust of Onu, and you will one day join us again."

"Yes, Da. Goodbye."

The huntress and her mother looked on as Virgaard embraced Isaak, telling him to not blame himself for his father's death, and how proud he was to call him his son. When he approached Donovan, however, Mira, Ann, Isaak, and all the others in the cave looked on, intrigued and mystified by the chieftain's words and tone, which nearly matched that of when he spoke to Isaak. It was of the same man-to-man straightforwardness that a father would use in speaking to his son when imparting some of the key wisdom of life.

"I impart the same plea to you, Donovan, to carry on in courage, resolve, and faith. Wherever you go ... whatever you do ... know that I give you my most sincere blessing, and hope to also meet you again in Onuhaal."

Mira gazed in wonder at Donovan, whose face bore the most solemn acceptance and resolve.

"I thank you, Virgaard. I'm still not fully sure of some matters, but I am comforted by your words, whatever course I end up taking."

"Very good," said Virgaard. "May you all go in peace."

A moment passed with all the company relishing the tranquility of the closure provided and the divine comfort bestowed upon them. Then all quietly turned back and left the cave, slipping again into the peaceful dark of simple sleep.

***

Mira awoke with the light of morning having risen above the treetops that enveloped Plen. She looked about the home, not finding her mother, and upon stepping outside, saw not a soul going about the village. She then looked to the dining hall and saw smoke passing out from the roof's vents, though not a sound could be heard from within. She approached the longhouse and opened the door. All the village was gathered together, eating silently and looking at one another with knowing looks. They then noticed Mira in the doorway, and the huntress soon noticed all those in her dream, from her mother to the bard, staring at her with the deepest of looks.

There was now no doubt in her heart; she had shared the same dream with all those she saw in it, if not even the entire village. Having nothing to say, Mira simply filled a bowl with the stew that was on the fire, and sat with her mother, brother, and Donovan.

73
10/1/4028 G.M.

DONOVAN saddled up his horse, with all the provisions he would need to reach the ends of Santaru and a fair distance beyond packed in his bags. The bard took another two weeks to fully recover from the wounds he had suffered, as well as to celebrate Kysonmay's Eve with all in Plen. He had deepened more in friendship with the village residents and now made to leave with a reluctant, heavy heart. As he approached the gate and looked back to all who had come to see him off, he was surprised to see Mira stride up with a sizeable flask in her hand. The huntress lifted it up to the bard, who took it and pulled the stopper. He sniffed its contents and smiled at the sweetness of wild honey.

"Thought you'd like some for the road," said Mira, "since you rarely stopped going on about it with Da and the rest of us."

"I certainly appreciate having some for the trip. Thank you."

"Farewell, Mr. Velavis. I wish you safe travels and success in your journey."

"My thanks, Miss Greenheart. I wish you and your village safety evermore in this blessed forest, and happiness for all your days."

Donovan then bade all of Plen goodbye. Now fully confident in the markers of the path that led back to the highway at Santaru's edge, he rode swiftly into the verdant vastness beyond, which now included red, orange, yellow, and brown in its leaves as autumn began to take hold. His mind raced as he contemplated what may lie ahead.

***

Sixteen days passed of long, but easy riding. Seeing and following the cairns with ease and confidence, the bard spent his time reflecting on all that had happened since he left home. Each time he did so, he was bewildered to realize that it had all passed in only six moons. He rode and rested as the mood struck him, looking upon the forest and all its growing autumnal beauty under the lights of sun, moon, and stars.

On the sixteenth night, as Donovan ate a light dinner of dried bread and fruit, with water and a rationed gulp of the preciously sweet mead, he pricked his ears to the soft cracking of twigs and rustled leaves that sounded nearby. He turned to the sound, and smiled as he recognized the distinct form of the tree-man.

"Good evening, Rovnillath."

"Good eve to you, Donovan. Thank you."

"What—"

"For making our haven safe again, for me and my surviving kin. Told by our mother and father, were we. We had no idea. We were those who decided to mostly roam the forest instead of simply lingering about Arborhaven. Greatly saddened were we to hear of our siblings' deaths, and those of Virgaard and the others. But glad were we to hear that the good folk of Plen put it to rights. Happy was I, also, to hear that you were in their company, alongside Virgaard's daughter. Told we were of the dream that our mother and father bestowed on you and the others. Again, I and my brethren thank you."

"Well ... you're welcome. I'm just sorry that we were too late for your brothers and sisters."

"Yes, most of us that lived here have been lost. But by our devices will our numbers grow again."

"If I might ask, why haven't you told any of us where Arborhaven was? A number of us have tried to find it again in times past. Did the Fidons who lived there offend you or your kin somehow, and you simply wish to have the site as a haven for only your kind?"

"Not at all. We simply haven't met any who were seeking the haven in our time. All whom we have happened to meet over the years, not one ever asked of it. We figured they must not have been overly concerned."

"I see," said the bard as he fished out his harp from his packs. "Well, no matter. Hopefully someone will come along soon enough who *will* be seeking it, as I'm sure most of us would be happy to hear of the place again, and not just from songs. Speaking of songs, would you care for some music, good sir of the forest?"

Rovnillath smiled. "Certainly, but I wish to give you something in thanks first."

"I ... very well. What–"

Donovan's jaw dropped as the Arbonyn wordlessly grabbed his own left arm and, with only a few seconds of pulling and twisting, pulled it from his body at the shoulder and offered it to the bard. He saw the pulled limb already begin to regrow, and took the length of sacred wood in dumbstruck silence. Rovnillath, as nearly all of the tree-folk, were a good deal taller than the average Fidon, and his arm alone was as tall as the bard himself. A fortunate few people in Fidonhaal's history had befriended an Arbonyn or gained its favor by one means or another, and had been given a token of their goodwill in the form of a piece of their body. Rare and precious were such occurrences, and Donovan wondered if any had ever been given such a measure of Arbonyn wood before, as most known artifacts made from it were typically instruments, cups, or the handles of swords or other such things.

"Rovnillath ... words fail me."

"Whatever you choose to make of this gift, go and with my blessing take it. If I might offer a thought, however ..."

"I'm all ears."

"If split properly, two good longbows you could make. Well in the hand they should sit. Not that missing will be impossible, mind; that magical our wood is not. All the same, your aim will likely be quite true, as will that of ... whoever the one is you might gift the other bow to."

"Do you have someone in mind?"

"Her."

Donovan stared into the softly glowing eyes of the tree-man, whose arm had already grown back as if he had never pulled it off. The bard knew who he meant. He laughed, making no effort to hide his befuddled state.

"I ... I'm sure I'd be happy with her, if she'd have me. But ... I still want to see the world and ..."

"Perhaps that, too, will happen in time?"

"Maybe. But isn't it a bit quick for it to come to that point?"

"Compared to many others, perhaps. But yet there are those that were even quicker."

"I suppose so."

"But again, do as you will, with my thanks and blessings."

"I will. Thank you."

Placing the beautiful length of wood beside him, Donovan returned to his harp and entertained his Angelborn friend.

***

Donovan reached the highway the next day, early in the morning. As he stared at the expanse of sky, hills, fields, and roads that stretched out to the horizon before him, the bard sought to decide between the two desires that wrestled within his heart. He looked at all the world that lay ahead of him and thought of all those whom he might move, entertain, or inspire by his artful labors. He sighed deeply.

"Perhaps at a later time, dear Fidonhaal."

He then turned his horse around.

***

He reached Plen again at daybreak in as many days as it took to reach the highway, and trotted up to the house of the chief in the cool early morning. He dismounted, harp in hand and with Rovnillath's arm resting across the back of the saddle. He approached the door and knocked gently, but firmly.

A moment passed, then the door opened, with Ann standing in the doorway. She stared at him in surprise.

"Donovan? What in the world–"

~ 183 ~

"Good Madam Ann Greenheart, if it might be met with your blessing, I would like to request a chance to offer courtship to your daughter."

Ann stood in the doorway, surprise soon changing to a warm grin as she looked into the sincerity of the bard's eyes. She then called for her daughter, who came and stared dumbfounded at her returning friend. Donovan then gently plucked the strings of his harp.

"I haven't played this song to anyone before, other than my father and my teacher. I feel that it might be a good one for ... starting to tell you how I feel, or may come to feel, about you in time. I didn't write it, my teacher did, for his wife. But ... I think it might do."

Playing the beginning notes, Donovan began to sing the last song that Uncle Jak had taught him.

> *Yoranye, my love, named for peace of the night,*
> *You awe me with your fur, white as snow.*
> *Your eyes, deepest blue, glitter in the stars' light*
> *And shine full of love 'neath moon's glow.*
> *I've tossed and I've turned under Yorun's lantern*
> *When I've looked upon you in my dreams.*
> *I've called out to Onu, seeking to discern*
> *How such beauty and bless'd love could be.*
> *Though the myst'ry sets my mind ever racing,*
> *And my soul fears that it's undeserved,*
> *My thanks, to you and Onu, will be given, never waning,*
> *And I pray fills the heavens and the earth.*
> *Yoranye, my love, named for peace of the moon,*
> *You seize me with your voice, honey-sweet.*
> *Your lips, heart and flesh grant my soul a great boon,*
> *And by your blessed grace, I'm complete.*
> *I've tossed and I've turned under Yorun's lantern*
> *When I've looked upon you in my dreams.*
> *I've called out to Onu, seeking to discern*
> *How a woman like you came to me.*
> *Though the myst'ry sets my mind ever racing,*
> *And my soul fears that it's undeserved,*
> *My thanks, to you and Onu, will be given, never waning,*
> *And I pray fills the heavens and the earth.*

Donovan let the last notes play and echo into the dawn-lit forest. He looked into Mira's deep brown eyes, which seemed to delve as deeply into him as he sensed his eyes did into her. After a moment's silence, the bard grinned awkwardly and shrugged.

"I ... I've no doubt it's a lot to take in, but ... if you're at all—"

Mira stepped out the door, and looked him levelly in the eye.

"I'm pretty busy today."

"I underst—"

She suddenly put her hand on the back of his head, and pressed his lips to hers.

"So, if you're up for coming along and helping out, we can talk as we tend to things."

Donovan smiled, his face red-hot from the kiss and Mira's grin.

"Sounds good to me," he said. "What's on the day's list?"

"Mostly taking care of Novon while Kahle tends to her herbs and whoever needs them."

Donovan gasped in surprise. "Novon? So they had a boy?"

"Mm-hm. He was born just last week."

"Well, of course I'll help you and her however I can, what for all you two did for me. If you don't mind, though, I just need to stop by Uld's place real quick, or maybe Gahren. Who's the best here at making bows?"

"That would be Gahren; he's the master of woodworking, at least as far as anything related to archery goes. Why?"

The bard grinned and gestured to the long piece of Arbonyn wood. "No matter what happens between us, I'd like to have a bow made for you, and me, too, if possible."

"Oh, Donovan, let's just start with—"

Donovan smiled as Mira stared wide-eyed at the long, beautiful limb.

"Is that ..."

"Rovnillath sends his regards," said Donovan with a grin.

Part Three

A Wedding on Veronmay's Eve

Homecoming

74
7/10/4028 G.M.

OWEN and Ruth brought their horses to a stop as they reached the top of the hill. They looked on the grand, distant walls and buildings of Genverdell, which stood bathed in the glow of the afternoon, and sighed in glad unison at the sight of home. Owen followed Ruth's gaze to the far-off sight of the capital's great western hill. The knight of the Temple looked with eyes that shined longingly, and her hand strayed from her reins to her pendant of the Four, which she handled gently as she wordlessly stared into the distance.

The salpion smiled. "Well," he said, pulling Ruth from her dreamy gazing, "what are you doing just staring, dear child? Let's gallop on home; I'm sure he's aching to see you as much as you are to see him!"

Ruth smiled, and with each goading their mounts to a swift gallop, the two breezed down the road toward the city and archtemple they called home.

They arrived at the capital's west gate just as the evening began, reaching the archtemple soon after. Greeted merrily by the knights who guarded the archtemple's gate and the clerics he met in the courtyard, Owen asked that their return be kept as quiet as could be managed until dinner, when he and Ruth would be ready to announce themselves. They wished to bathe and rest briefly beforehand, with as little disturbance as possible.

However, before making for his rooms, Owen saw young Orson Whitethorn, Ruth's squire, standing with the others in the courtyard. He asked Orson to find Verdok and tell him to visit the salpion in his study. Owen embraced Ruth before they quietly parted for their quarters. He thanked the knight for her company, and her protection of both him and the bard they had befriended on the way back home.

"I do hope to see him at the wedding," said Ruth reflectively as she turned for the Faithguard barracks.

"Me, too," said Owen as he made for his living quarters, waving back to Ruth as he went. "See you at dinner."

75
7/10/4028 G.M.

VERDOK finished blessing the congregation of the evening worship alongside his assisting clerics. Having returned the remaining holy water to the basin, he addressed the gathering one last time before the final hymn.

"Go forth, children of Onu. Put all the will you can muster into each step you take on the path we all walk in our trust of him, and do what you can to help others do the same. Onu bless you."

"And Onu bless you," returned the congregation.

The last hymn was sung, and as the gathering dispersed, Verdok placed the high copy of the Beldsantu back into its repository. He looked nervously about at those who lingered in the cathedral, hoping that he might see either Father Owen or Ruth. The three of them had gone over the salpion's travel plans before Owen and Ruth had departed, and the planning put the time of their return to be any day now if all had gone well. Furthermore, he received a letter a month ago from the salpion, its sender address being from Greenharbor, stating they had safely made it back onto Enmayarn soil. But he had received no other word since, and it was this uncertainty regarding the safety of their latter days of travel that weighed on his heart.

As he closed the Beldsantu's repository, the high priest looked the room over once more and was surprised to see young Orson jogging down the aisle toward him. The squire of his fiancée came up to him, and with a bow informed him that the salpion wished to see him in his study. The news made Verdok's heart skip a beat. He smiled and patted Orson on the back, thanking him as he ran for Father Owen's quarters.

Verdok knocked on the door to the salpion's study, and his heart rejoiced to hear Owen's voice as he bade him to enter. He entered the study, greeting his mentor happily.

"Onu be praised for your safe and timely return! I kept telling myself that it would be silly to expect a letter every time you reached another town, but ever since the message from last month, I've worried about something happening in the last stretch!"

Verdok looked at the seats facing Owen's desk and felt his heart nearly stop when he saw no one else sitting there.

"F-Father Owen," he gasped, "Wh-where's Ruth?"

"Breathe, dear boy, for Onu's sake," said Owen with a laugh. "She's just washing and resting before dinner. Come now, fill me in on what's happened while I've been gone."

76

7/10/4028 G.M.

RUTH lay back in the barrack bath, calmly relishing the warm water and fragrant soap and oil. With eyes closed, the knight reflected on the eventful journey, wishing the best for the gentleman they had met along the way, as well as thinking of how Verdok was never off her mind the moment she and Father Owen left Genverdell.

Her eyes opened and fell to the pendant Verdok gave her all those years ago, which rested upon her breast as though it had always been a part of her. She could not recall the last time she had taken it off. She had treasured it beyond words from the day Verdok gave it in friendship, and could hardly bear to part with it for even a moment. The feeling of attachment to it only grew stronger as the years went by, and the friendship between her and Verdok, at first nearly that of siblings, changed and grew into something quite different. The leather thong that held the carved stone, once jet-black and smoothly shining, was now faded and rugged. It had borne the stone well for all those years, and the pendant's brilliance of white marble and black jet had endured.

Ruth took the carving in her hand and brushed its face with her thumb, and a wave of memories of Verdok ran through her mind. She rose from the bath, amulet in hand, and reached for the lever above the bath basin's drain, from which the water would flow out into the Sunrise River that flowed between Genverdell's great hills. She let the amulet fall gently from her hand as she made to pull the lever, as it was a hefty thing that required both hands to properly operate.

The amulet fell to her chest, and the worn, soaked strap of leather suddenly snapped in two. Ruth felt a strange, heightened sense of nakedness overcome her. She saw the pendant fall into the water, which was now swiftly flowing down the drain.

Gasping, she scrambled about in the water, successfully grabbing the stone as the leather that suspended it slipped from its loop and down the drain. Laughing with relief, she slumped onto the bath's floor, clasping the stone to her heart as she relived another bout of memories. Placing the stone onto a table beside the bath, she put on her robes. She then took the stone in hand and went to see Fendis Whitethorn, the father of her squire, a friend, and one of the resident smiths of the archtemple.

The Mavon man looked with merry surprise when he saw her for the first time in months.

"Welcome back, Ruth! When did you get here? Does Orson know you're back?"

"He does, and I've just been back an hour or so. I've been washing up and trying to rest a bit since."

Fendis laughed. "I'd probably be doing the same in your place. So what brings you here right now? Just coming to say you're back?"

"I was going to do all that at dinner with Father Owen, but something came up."

The knight then handed over the stone pendant. "Would it be too much trouble to make a chain for this?"

77
7/10/4028 G.M.

VERDOK and Father Owen went over the main affairs that had passed in the salpion's absence, ending their talk with a few readjustments to the plans of the wedding to come. It was now well into the evening, and the two high clerics, with grumbling stomachs, made for the dining hall for a belated dinner, still discussing the wedding plans as they went.

They entered the dining hall, which was now mostly empty, and saw Ruth sitting at a table beside her squire, Orson, with whom she was speaking happily over matters they could not yet hear. Verdok's heart began to race. Orson noticed the two of them approaching and pointed them out to his mentor. Ruth looked up to them, her eyes locking onto Verdok's. The high priest ran toward his fiancée as she rose up from the table, and embraced her tightly as she softly kissed him.

"I'm so glad you're back," he whispered.

"So am I," said Ruth. "Sorry that we just missed your birthday."

"Nothing to worry about. I've got the perfect gift right here, even if it's a little late."

Father Owen then joined the three at the table. Orson stayed, as he was close to all three of them, viewing them as extended family ever since they took him and his parents into the archtemple to get them out of the city's struggling riverside district.

"Sorry that Verdok and I were so late in getting here," said the salpion. "We got caught up in going over what's happened since we left for Frosthaven, and then we fell into talking about plans for the wedding. I should've saved that for later. Oh well, I guess I'll just pop about and say 'hi' to everyone some time or other tomorrow."

"I doubt you'll need to trouble yourself that much over it," said Ruth, "since everyone saw me here while I was waiting for you two to come in. Pretty much everyone knows we're both back by now, I'd say."

"I suppose so," said Owen with a laugh. "At any rate, since we're all together now, was there anything either of you wished to discuss for the wedding?"

"Were you two talking about anything in particular?" asked Ruth.

"We were just throwing around some ideas on entertainment," Verdok answered. "I was looking to ask about music at the feast. There are plenty of talented singers and musicians right here in Genverdell, but who knows what other talent lies outside the capital?"

"Funny you should say that," said Ruth with a smile. "Load up your plate and cup, love. Father Owen and I have a story for you."

Sitting down with a full plate, Verdok listened intently to his mentor and fiancée as they told of their encounter with the dashing bard from the North.

Plans of Love and Hate

78
6/11/4029 G.M.

SHEEVA walked with Allor and her twin children, Talrah IV and Samuel II, as the family made for Lerannu's study. The prince and princess, just a month shy of turning ten years old, were almost always eager to have their lessons with the court mage, whom they had come to regard practically as a second mother. They were the dearest ones in her eyes and in Allor's. The queen constantly looked over them whenever she could, and entrusted a select few to step in when she could not. There was, of course, her husband, along with Lerannu and her mother, Sarah, who was now a stewardess of the court in addition to being the south wardeness of Enmayar. The last of those she trusted was Ranoth Windsbreath, the castle chaplain.

While she trusted these four to watch over her children, it was only Sarah and Ranoth whom she trusted of all in the castle when it came to directly aiding her in all the measures that went into securing the definite safety of her children and family. Only they could be trusted with helping her organize the sensitive matters that would finally keep her family, her country, and the world at large forever safe from those who would seek to harm or destroy them. The other two, Allor and Lerannu, were simply too innocent and naïve to understand at the present time. They were good, but she simply couldn't trouble them with such things until the new era dawned and all could then be explained.

That day was drawing ever nearer, with the Peacekeepers having grown to strong numbers and finally preparing to take their positions across all of Fidonhaal. Indeed, the very first company to be deployed beyond Enmayar's borders was to be sent out that very morning. With the careful selections of other wronged Zarons, thanks to Raakmathna's flawless insight, they had been able to establish an ever-expanding order of warriors over the past decade, unhindered by any questions from the world. None suspected a thing, as the oath which Raakmathna placed upon all involved bound them to absolute secrecy, even if it required the occasional feigning of friendship with the parasites of the world.

It had progressed so well that, if all continued to proceed as anticipated, there was now a date decided for the beginning of Fidonhaal's new age: Veronmay's Eve the following year, the day on which a high wedding was to be held at the archtemple. It was a perfect time to begin the campaign for Fidonhaal's order, as not only did the return of spring perfectly symbolize the coming of the new era, but many would not be expecting what was to come during such a time of revelry.

In the meantime, it was another peaceful day of the children getting their education, and ensuring that Enmayar carried on as always until the time for change finally arrived. When the royal family had reached the mage's study, the queen and king embraced and kissed each child in turn.

"Have another good lesson," Sheeva said tenderly. "I love you!"

"Love you, Mother," said the prince and the princess. "Love you, Father! Will we see you at lunch?"

"That's the plan," said Allor, "if we can get things more or less settled in time."

"Hope everything goes well," said the children with another kiss before knocking on their teacher's door.

"So do we," said the king with a sigh of resolve.

Lerannu opened the door smiling, and the children happily went into the study with their tutor. Sheeva and Allor turned to head for the throne room, each with the other's arm wrapped about them. They kissed, and Sheeva felt her middle, as she had come to frequently do over the years, wanting desperately to conceive at least one more boy and one more girl if she could. The king and queen had hoped to have a son and daughter that would each bear the names of their parents, and it was Allor's parents who were yet to have their namesake grandchildren. Allor, noticing his wife's hand on her belly, put his hand into hers and kissed her comfortingly.

"There's still plenty of time."

"I know," said the queen softly.

They reached the double doors to the throne room, and taking one door each, the Queen and King of Enmayar opened them together and took their seats, ready to resume their negotiations with Kellmayar.

79
6/11/4029 G.M.

ALLOR sat beside his wife, practically on the edge of his seat. Their talks with the ambassadors from Kellmayar had lasted over a month and had been their overwhelming concern since the diplomats had arrived. Now, at long last, it had finally come together. The first resolution to one of the gravest concerns of their reign since its beginning was drawing nigh. The queen closed the ledger that had been given to her by Nathan, the head advisor of the granaries, and with a relieved sigh, looked to the Kellmayarn emissaries. Sheeva smiled and Allor's heart began to race with anticipation.

"The seasons have continued to be kind," the queen said gladly, "and we have enough food to spare for your east ward. Does the agreement on the spices and cotton still seem manageable?"

"Yes, dear Queen Sheeva," the head diplomat said with a voice of desperate hope that Allor could barely stand to hear. The brown-furred man gently wiped his sweat-laced fur with a handkerchief as he continued. "After that proposal was given, we sent the details to our king and queen, and the east warden, that very evening. The response came back the day before yesterday, just over a fortnight from when we sent it. We have more than enough for the trade, and they're all in agreement in regards to the terms."

Allor looked intently at Sheeva, who turned her eyes to him and smiled. It was a beautifully small and gentle smile, the sort that came from a longtime burden being finally lifted. She nodded. Allor held her hand, sighing ecstatically, as they faced the diplomats again.

"We have come to an agreement," they said in unison.

The head ambassador alternated between thanking them and Onu several times over. Two others from the company of envoys, a married couple who were natives of Kellmayar's east ward, embraced one another and wept in joyful relief. The others in the diplomatic party looked on, speechless as they faced the prospect of their home's twenty-year-long struggles ending, or at least significantly lessening, in the near future. Allor put his arm around his wife, who leaned close and kissed his cheek and licked his ear. The king's fur bristled, and he laughed quietly in reflex to the tickling sensation that ran through his spine. He kissed her in turn and whispered quietly into her ear.

"Are they ready?"

"Yes, Al; they've been ready for this since we first started the talks."

"Shall we call them in, then?"

Sheeva brushed her cheek against her husband's, humming in approval before facing the emissaries once more.

"May this herald an end to your land's troubles in the coming years, good sirs and ladies," she said. "As a token of our trust in your land's commitment to the agreement and a means to further aid you, we wish to send a company of very upstanding young Fidons to accompany you back to your home."

The ambassadors pricked up their ears in intrigue. "Who are they, dear queen?" asked the head envoy.

"I trust that you've heard of our Peacekeeper initiative?"

"Of course, Queen Sheeva. Your efforts have impressed and moved the world. All the other nations have been looking to follow your example, though they still seem to have some hurdles to clear on that path. As for us, well ..."

"Your difficulties have been made abundantly clear. That's why I offer, to you and your country, a company of our first recruits. They have had eight years' worth of thorough training and education in defensive combat and an array of crisis scenarios. They would be honored to begin serving Fidonhaal by ensuring your safe return home. After that, and if you'll accept their aid, they'll help Kellmayar start the founding of garrisons for the order. They've been instructed on the priorities and procedures of recruitment and training. They and their recruits will work to aid your nation in recovering from this sorry time of famine and poverty, and help keep civil order in the meantime."

The head ambassador looked to his colleagues. Seeing them nod unanimously, he smiled and nodded.

"We accept this generous offer most gratefully," he said. "A thousand thanks, dear Queen Sheeva, and to you, dear King Allor. May Onu bless you both and see that your reign is long, and may your line continue, shine, and flourish in the light of what you've done this day."

"My thanks, Mr. Rentenov," said Allor humbly, "but your blessings should be focused on Sheeva. The Peacekeepers were all her idea to begin with. I've just tried to help with organizing their supplies and care, and even then, I've not been nearly as helpful as Chaplain Ranoth and Stewardess Sarah."

Sheeva pulled herself closely to her husband's side, kissing him again as she embraced him.

"You've helped more than I could ever explain, Al," she said softly, "with this ... and with everything else."

Sheeva then called to Sarah Stonefaith, who had stood beside the ambassadors the duration of the negotiations. "Call them in," she said.

The stewardess went to one of the doors at the side of the throne room. Opening it, she called for the company to enter.

Twenty and five of the Peacekeepers strode uniformly into the room, standing at attention before the diplomats, who had turned around to greet them. They were such handsome youths, lads and lasses both, the oldest being twenty and the youngest sixteen. They stood in their splendid uniforms, armor covered with surcoats of a beautiful silver-grey dye, and made for a gallantly heroic image with their kits of sword, shield, and spear. They greeted the ambassadors with an enthusiastic voice of duty, and declared their intention to aid them and their nation as their first acts of service to all the world.

Allor looked at the company, recognizing a handful of them as he reflected on the progress of the Peacekeepers. Ten years following their adoption of the orphan Thomas, the King of Enmayar had watched the order grow from a handful of orphans and recruits from poor families into a large and strong order of promising young men and women. Thomas himself was now the captain of the castle's own resident company of the silver-clad guardians, and had come to watch over the prince and princess like an elder brother. Soon, countless people across the world would have stories similar to those of the defenders who came to them, having risen from troubled lives to become guardians of Fidonhaal. The deployment of the first global companies of Peacekeepers was nigh.

Allor looked on as the first graduates of the order prepared to embark on their mission. His vision blurred from the tears of happiness that brimmed within them, despite having known only a few of the Peacekeepers personally over the course of the decade-long endeavor. His joy, while also being for the poor and lost souls that now had a place in the world, focused mainly on the one who had begun the course. For all the pain and sorrow that she had suffered, Sheeva had risen above it. Where others would have succumbed to hatred or bitterness, she, despite some continuous struggles to trust others, had been moved by compassion to help heal the world and the troubles within it.

And the first of those troubles she was looking to settle was the strife between her country and Kellmayar, the land where she had suffered the worst of horrors.

80

6/11/4029 G.M.

SHEEVA walked alongside her husband with her hand in his. Having seen to the negotiations with Kellmayar and the remaining morning affairs, the queen and king sent the ambassadors and their Peacekeeper escort on their way to Kellmayar, and set out to have lunch with their children and Lerannu. Given the time and the wonderful late-spring day, Sheeva and Allor made for the gardens, confident they would find them there. They left the throne room and took the side door that led to the most direct corridor to the gardens. As they reached the door leading outside, Sheeva and Allor turned to the sound of Sarah Stonefaith's voice as the stewardess called out to them.

"My queen," she said, "a moment, if it please you?"

Seeing Ranoth Windsbreath beside her, Sheeva knew her request was to confirm that their meeting for the next day would take place as initially planned. She turned to Allor, who, already aware of the meeting and plans between him and her for the next day, nodded understandingly as he made to go on and join the children if they were outside. Before he left, Allor drew his wife close, gently brushed his muzzle against hers, and briefly held the medallion that the queen wore. It was a medal of thanks and achievement from the Medical Academy of Endallia, which the institution had given to the Kellmayarn diplomats to give to the queen on their behalf.

The academy, having received the queen's samples and formulae, had tested and replicated her findings. With only a few relatively minor alterations, the academy announced to the world that the newly developed medicine would reduce the dreaded disease to being nearly the likes of the common cold. At long last, the Endallian Fever was not an illness to be met with such heart-gripping fear. The ambassadors had presented the medal to Sheeva when they first arrived, before even beginning the negotiations on trade and assistance. They informed her of the academy's success, and then proceeded to say that Kellmayar, and Fidonhaal at large, would commend her for her contributions to the combating of the disease, even if the impending trade talks had failed to conclude as hoped.

Looking into Allor's eyes, Sheeva could feel her husband's elation at how well all had fared with Kellmayar, as well as the results of her aid to Endallia and her own work in medicine.

"I can't believe," said Allor gently, "that your decision to try your hand at medicine, which you did out of friendship with me, has gone this far."

"Neither can I, Al."

Allor kissed her, looking at the stewardess and the castle priest before doing so.

"Are you just making sure that tomorrow's discussions over the Peacekeepers are still on?"

"That's probably what it's about," said Sheeva. "Are you sure you'll be alright going over everything else yourself while I try to settle that?"

"Absolutely. We have the ledgers you looked over from earlier, so Nathan and I should be able to iron out from where we take the food for this trade, along with whoever else we need to notify. The Peacekeepers are your brainchild, love; you've clearly shown that you know what you're doing with them. Just let me know how it goes, and how I and anyone else here can help."

"Thank you. You go ahead and see if Sam and Tally are out. I won't be long."

Allor opened the door to the garden and immediately gave a light laugh as he pointed to the gazebo straight ahead. There the children and their tutor were sitting with salad, bread, and roast chicken on the table. The twins and their teacher waved, and Sheeva and Allor waved back to them before Allor went out and closed the door, leaving the queen alone with her chief planners for the campaign of a better Fidonhaal.

"The ambassadors are beginning their return home," Sarah informed the queen, "and their escort is with them, having vowed to execute your instructions, as has been given them, at their appointed time."

"Good," the queen said simply.

"And of course," said Ranoth, stepping forward, "the other recruits have continued their education and training. They'll be ready to move and follow your orders when the time comes at the wedding next Veronmay's Eve, and you call for the new era."

"Very well," said Sheeva contentedly. "We'll go over those things tomorrow. If there isn't anything else, though, it's been a long morning and I would like to be with my family now."

The priest and the stewardess bowed silently and returned to their tasks as the queen opened the door and embraced the sweet air that heralded summer's imminent return.

81
7/8/4029 G.M.

OWEN and Verdok packed the last sacks of freshly milled wheat into the archtemple's storeroom. Enmayar had been blessed with another great summer harvest, and the archtemple's allotted land had fared as well as any other. It had been a week's work milling the bountiful harvest so far, and many of the archtemple's residents, including the salpion and high priest themselves, had given much of what time they could spare outside their duties in helping with the milling and storing of the flour. Now the bulk of the current harvest was finished, and the two high clerics dusted the flour from their hands as they looked with satisfaction at the sack-laden shelves of the larder.

"Thanks for all the help," Owen huffed gratefully.

"Always glad to help. Is there anything else?"

"Now that you mention it, there actually is."

"What would that be?"

"Let's get out of here and rest in the garden, first," the salpion said with a laugh as he wiped his brow with a handkerchief. "We'll talk there once we get some water. Four Breaths, all this heat and flour has me parched."

***

Owen and his protégé sat on a bench in the gardens, gratefully emptying a water pitcher between them in the hot, early summer afternoon.

"So," said Verdok after his first drink, "what's the matter?"

Owen sighed as he put his cup aside. "It's Orson, actually. He seems to be troubled by something these past few days, according to what Ruth's told me. He's been a little off in his training, like his mind is elsewhere. Ruth's tried to talk to him, but he doesn't seem to be opening up to her very much. I tried to see if I might be able to get through to him, but I'm afraid I'm not doing very well, either."

"So you want to see if I might be able to get to the bottom of this?"

"If it isn't too much trouble."

"Of course it isn't."

"Even if it doesn't work, I figured it wouldn't hurt to try. The boy's like family to all of us, but like in a family, some things ..."

"Are easier to talk about with some members than others?"

"Exactly, and in the same way that Ruth's been like an older sister to him, you've been like a brother."

"Do you have any idea what the problem might be at all? Are Fendis and Morre alright as far as you know?"

"His parents' health and marriage are both fit as a fiddle as far as I can tell. But, come to think of it, given his age ..."

A soft smile spread across Verdok's face. "A girl, perhaps?"

"Perhaps," said Owen with a small grin and a shrug that jokingly implied that he would have never guessed that to be what was on the boy's mind. "But what do I know? I haven't had to discuss such matters with any young man, or woman, before in my life. Oh, no sir. Never."

The salpion and the high priest looked at each other, grinning at Owen's sarcasm and the memory of when the two spoke of those very matters when Verdok reached adolescence and confessed his growing feelings for Ruth.

Verdok, having poured one more cupful of water, drained it and set his cup aside.

"I'll see if I can't find him and talk to him now. It's just past three, so maybe he's resting out here somewhere."

"Very good. Thank you, Verdok."

"You're welcome, Father."

Verdok turned and ventured into the gardens, where clerics, knights, and lay residents were taking their afternoon leisure alone and in various-sized groups. Owen watched him go, and waited a moment before following him at a distance. He laughed to himself. The act had worked.

"Has he really forgotten what day it is?" he thought to himself. "He hasn't said a word about it all day, or even these past weeks, as far as I've noticed."

The salpion reached the part of the garden that was nearest the Faithguard training yard, where the surprise was set up. Having seen Verdok approach the forlorn young lad on the stone bench, sit beside him, and begin talking to him, Owen quietly took a place behind a nearby pillar. He grinned as he noticed Ruth, her mother Arza, and Orson's parents hiding nearby. Both Verdok's maternal and paternal grandparents, Alexis, Okren, Wenda and Kiin, were also in hiding, having earlier arrived in secret to surprise him with a visit that was planned to last until after the wedding next spring. Owen listened intently to the conversation between Verdok and the squire, eager to see how the boy's performance and the high priest's reactions would play out.

"Is it a girl?" he heard Verdok ask plainly.

Owen peered around the column, seeing Orson hang his black and white head in embarrassment and raise a hand to his face as if to hide tears. Verdok took the young man into both arms in a brother-like embrace.

"Orson, there's nothing to be ashamed of; it's a very important part of how Onu made us–"

"It's not that which bothers me," said Orson with an amazing ruse of emotional torment, "it's who she is."

"Who is it?"

"Ruth."

Verdok's face was a hopelessly hilarious mess of shock, empathy, and a struggle to find a way to tactfully discuss the matter with the boy.

"Orson ... you shouldn't torment yourself like this. Yes ... this is a bit ... difficult. But this sort of thing can, and does, happen from time to time. If we can talk this out frankly and respectfully, though, it'll turn out alright."

"It ... it just feels so cruel, Brother Verdok."

"I know it can hurt a lot, but you need to understand–"

"Why would she do this to me?"

"Orson ... I ... what do you mean? Ruth would never purposefully–"

Owen struggled with all his might to keep from laughing before the act's conclusion. Orson had pulled something out from his training gear, which had been arranged carefully in a pile to hide it from Verdok's notice. It was something covered by a cloth. Orson pulled the cloth away, revealing a sizeable chocolate cake in a covered glass dish.

"She *knows* I love chocolate cake as much as you do, and she left it here for me to watch until you got here! Do you have *any* idea how hard it was to keep from eating it all myself?"

Verdok sat in total silence, staring dumbfoundedly at his fiancée's squire as he held the cake out with a gleefully impish smile. Verdok then looked about with the most sheepish face the salpion had ever seen. He caught sight of Owen's head peering from behind the column and put a hand to his face incredulously while playfully ruffling Orson's hair with the other. All those hiding nearby came forth, loudly bidding Verdok a happy birthday.

Owen now laughed freely. "I can't believe you completely forgot about it!"

"Neither can I," Verdok chuckled. "Is there any wine handy? I could sure use a good cup of it right about now."

82
10/14/4029 G.M.

MIRA woke up to the sound of her husband's heartbeat, the same sound that had earlier lulled her to sleep. Opening her eyes and lifting her head from his chest, she briefly looked admiringly at him and his fur, which glowed brightly white in the light of the full moon that penetrated the treetops and through the window. She slowly, quietly disentangled herself from him and stepped outside behind the house to take in the night air. She walked to the edge of the back garden, propping herself against the fence that encircled it, and looked out into the depths of the forest, and the stars and moon that peered through the canopy above. Enjoying the cool air that breezed over her bare fur, she reflected on the wondrous changes that had come into her life.

She and Donovan had been married for the past four months. Following Donovan's return and Mira's acceptance of his courtship, the two had spent nearly every waking moment together for the remainder of that autumn and the following winter. They hunted together and helped one another in seeing to the welfare of Plen, and halfway through the last moon of winter, they at last agreed that they would marry. They told of their intentions to Chieftain Ann and all the village, and with Mira's family in their company, the two traveled by ship to Sorrenar, to Donovan's hometown of Therohl. When they arrived and told their tale to Jonathan, the bard's father and friends warmly welcomed Mira and her family, and the wedding was held in a week's time.

Mira had loved the experience of seeing some of Fidonhaal beyond the trees of Santaru, from sailing the ocean to gazing in wonder at the hills and mountains of the North, and feeling the cold and cool that stayed nearly all the year. She loved meeting the man who was now her father-in-law, having seen that he had played no small part in shaping the man to whom she was now bound. She loved the experience, strange and hectic as it was at times, of being in towns and cities during their travels, marveling at all the people and activity that went on all about her. And of course, the wedding, where she and Donovan vowed to be together before Onu and Fidonity, was the happiest and most exciting time she had yet had in her life.

Now, having been back home for the past two months, in a new cottage that the villagers had built for them while they were away, the huntress began to ponder her future.

As much as she had loved seeing the world, she was overjoyed to be back in Plen. And yet, as glad as she was to be back home, she felt a returning, and growing, desire to travel and see even more of the world.

She thought again of the sea, of the snowy hills and mountains, and wondered how marvelous she would find the lands and peoples of the West and the South, not to mention the places of Enmayar and Sorrenar that she still had not yet seen. She also greatly liked the thought of seeing Jonathan again, for he was overjoyed to meet her and was himself a great joy to be with.

Then there was the matter of Donovan's original plan, which, happy as he seemed to be by the turn of events, had indeed been halted by their bonding. Much of her heart was reluctant to leave Plen again, especially so soon after their return. But her sprouting wanderlust and desire to accompany her husband on seeing his dream through led her to think more and more of again stepping beyond the bosom of Santaru.

Her thoughts were interrupted by the gently padding footsteps that she heard behind her. Feeling Donovan's arms wrap about her waist, Mira leaned back against him, sighing softly as she snuggled up against his chest. They embraced silently, relishing the cool forest breeze as it caressed their bare bodies alongside their own hands. Donovan kissed her and whispered into her ear.

"Are you alright?"

"Just fine, Don," she said. "I was just thinking of our past travels and your dream to see the world."

She told him of her thoughts, and Donovan, sighing appreciatively, drew his wife closer. He set her to giggling as he nibbled her neck and gently raked her breasts with the claws of his thumbs. After a moment of this, he whispered to her again.

"I want nothing more than having you beside me on this path of life," he said. "It doesn't matter to me if this path is walked only here and in Santaru for the rest of my days, or across all of Fidonhaal. As long as I'm with you, I'm fulfilled. Don't feel like you must leave here to make me happy, and certainly not for overlong."

"But I *do* want to travel the world, with you, and see you do what you first set out to do."

"Are you sure about leaving home again so soon, though?"

"I ... yes. Like you said, if we're together, I can go anywhere and be content."

They kissed again in silence, then Donovan, combing his wife's hair with his fingers, offered an idea for a plan of travel.

"How about this: we start by going around Enmayar and see if you, if we, are comfortable being gone from here for a while. If not, or if we just want to revisit for a while, it'll be relatively easy to come back compared to crossing seas or far-off and unfamiliar lands. Depending on how you and I feel in time, we'll decide what to do from there."

"I'm all for it, Don. Do you have in mind any place you'd like to go for first?"

"As a matter of fact, I do. I thought we might start with a trip to Genverdell. I'd like to try my hand at entertaining the royal court, if I can, and besides that, there are my friends at the archtemple and the wedding that's planned for next Veronmay's Eve."

"Oh, right," Mira recalled from Donovan's account of his adventures before meeting her, "Ruth and her fiancé."

"I definitely would like to see them again, and meet Ruth's fiancé himself as well. And if I can, I'd like to attend their wedding, if not also be part of the entertainment. We can see how we feel, being away from here during that time, and decide what to do from there. What do you think?"

"I'm with you, and ready to go wherever you go."

"We'll let your mother know tomorrow and start getting things ready."

The newlyweds then returned to bed, walking in an embrace as they spoke of their hopes for what was to come.

83
10/15/4029 G.M.

SHEEVA sat in the autumn-kissed garden, having a private breakfast with Sarah and Ranoth. With the help of both the wardeness and the castle chaplain, along with all the other loyal Zarons who had come to join the queen's cause, the Peacekeeper initiative had, under Raakmathna's continued guidance, grown well beyond Sheeva's expectations and hopes. In its first decade, the order had been able to reach wronged, destitute, and lost Zarons from all across Enmayar, and was now beginning to grow across all the world, having been welcomed wherever they were sent and being trained by their commanders without suspicion.

In training, schooling, and housing sites across the country, the youths had grown under Sheeva's words and those of Raakmathna as they learned of the importance of their roles for a better Fidonhaal. Now, with recruitment beginning in the other three nations following Sheeva's gift of the first soldiers to Kellmayar, all was looking to be ready for Veronmay's Eve, when the new era of Fidonhaal was set to begin.

Such was the topic of the day's meeting. With Allor entrusted with fulfilling the Kellmayar agreement by consulting the advisors over supplies and communications, the queen was able to speak freely with her confidants. As good a man as Allor was, he was, as Raakmathna said, too innocent and naïve to understand the true designs for the Peacekeepers at present. He and all the others who were good, but ignorant, would be informed once the new age began. Having decided on the matters of continued financing and supplying of the order, the three turned to going over the plans for the coming Veronmay's Eve once more, making sure that nothing had changed.

"I've spoken with the salpion," said Ranoth, "and he's welcomed the company of Peacekeepers we have here in the castle to join us when we return to attend the reception. Once midnight has arrived and the new day begins, as you have said, they will begin securing the area by first seeing to the guests. The festivities will be well underway by then, and none will be expecting it. Resistance should be minimal. They'll await your heralding of the new age before commencing, apart from those who will be seeing to the Davinurs, of course."

"Good," Sheeva replied with a nod. "And speaking of them, I trust they've accepted our invitation?"

"Yes, my queen," answered Sarah as she handed over a letter. "This response came last night. East Warden Luthor and his family have sent back their thanks, and going by the stated date in the letter, they're set to depart from Quanithe tomorrow. With good travel, they'll arrive in time for the Sardonmay festivities and stay until after the Veronmay holiday and the wedding. Of course, they'll be seen to before the reception, as you've instructed."

Sheeva nodded approvingly. With Sarah as the south wardeness, and with the wardens of the north and west provinces being fully Zaron, the only major domestic obstacle for the moment was the east warden, his wife Bellu, and daughter Arte. The whole family was entirely Kason, of the same ilk as Ohdan Karvinthaal. The thought that such people could hold such a significant place in Enmayar's government had set Sheeva's blood to boiling on several occasions. However, for the long-term gain of her nation and the world at large, she had kept composure and feigned a growing friendship with them over the years. She had invited them to the capital for an extensive visit on the pretense of celebrating both the beginnings of winter and spring in their company. Of course, it was to keep them close at hand and easier to monitor. Removing them here would be far easier than trying to coordinate the assassinations in a major city that was nearly twenty-five hundred miles away.

"Any further news from any of our garrisons or other allies?"

"Two, my queen," said Sarah as she presented four more letters. "There are these, from Kellmayar and Sorrenar. They're all the sorts that you requested: the intelligence gathered by our Peacekeepers that are for our eyes only, and the praises from those benefiting from the order, for Allor and all the rest of the world to see."

Sheeva took the parchments and, having read them, entrusted the espionage reports to Sarah and pocketed the other two letters for Allor to read later.

"He'll be happy to see these, the poor, dear man," said the queen, pitying her husband's overly trusting heart. "Is there anything else?"

"I suppose just a thought that had occurred to us earlier," said Ranoth, "and that's the matter of the other Zarons, those who ... might not understand or accept our intentions even when explained. For example, what about this Ruth Pionaar? She's an experienced knight of the Faithguard; a fine asset for us if she can be persuaded. But her fiancé is Kason and Mavon, and the salpion, who's practically a father to her, is Mavon. Can we trust her to be able to come to our side if she knows what it will mean? And if she were to resist, given that you'll be in her presence when the new era begins, I fear for your safety if you'll be near a seasoned combatant like her, and that of however-many other Faithguard knights, for that matter."

"I've pondered this as well," said Sheeva. "Raakmathna has said that we are to terminate any Zarons who resist, even if it's from naïve ignorance, but we are to give all of them a chance to come to our side. I appreciate your concern, but I assure you, whatever happens, I'll be fine."

The queen then pulled the Mivinaars' heirloom katana, which neither advisor had yet noticed, from under the table. Both of them looked with grim assurance at the long, lightly curved form of the sword and its sheath as the queen drew it half out of the scabbard. All three seated at the table gazed on the blade in silence, darkly mesmerized by the sparkling, flowing bands of its steel.

"Very well," said the priest at last.

"We'll keep watch on how matters develop as Spring's Eve draws closer," assured the queen, looking to Sarah. "And when the new era dawns, you'll be my chief advisor for Fidonhaal's safety."

Sheeva turned to Ranoth, "And you, dear friend, will of course be the new salpion, and together we'll see to it that the world at last comes under the proper protection and peace that will come from the order that the All-Keeper will bring to us."

Winter Meetings

84
12/28/4029 G.M.

LERANNU frantically took cover behind one of the statues in the garden, looking around her as she tried to sense the direction from which the remaining members of Allor's team were approaching. With a snowball in hand, the mage peered around the statue. She saw Princess Talrah grinning devilishly at her from behind a low wall and just barely managed to dodge her snowball. Lerannu then saw Prince Samuel crouching behind a nearby fountain. Beside him was Arte Davinur, the daughter of the visiting East Warden Luthor and his wife Bellu, who had been invited by the queen and king to stay through winter and into the start of spring. Apart from Lerannu herself, Sam and Arte were the last "survivors" of her team.

The mage waved to catch their attention and gestured to the wall where Talrah still lurked. Lerannu nodded toward a distant pine tree, indicating her intention to reach it for her next point of cover. She sprinted through the crisp sheet of snow that lightly covered the gardens, managing to shelter behind the tree just as two snowballs whistled past her. Only two were left on Allor's team: the princess and the king himself. Noticing that one of the snowballs came from the same direction where Talrah was positioned, the mage now knew the general area where Allor was hiding.

Lerannu quickly glanced in the direction of Allor's attack, making sure the king was neither advancing toward her nor in any other direction that might grant an advantage against her or her teammates. She looked back and saw the princess lob a snowball at the east warden's daughter. Squeaking in alarm, the brown-furred young beauty threw her snowball in a panic, missing her mark. In the same instant, Prince Samuel leapt in front of Arte, taking his sister's snowball to the shoulder and then sprinting to the long bench where all of the "fallen" had taken seat. Arte quickly recovered from the princess's startling attack, and swiftly forming another frozen projectile, she successfully took out Talrah before the princess could attack again. Talrah hurried over to the bench, where all seated were now cheering and taunting with delight as the game became an enthralling battle of two against one.

Catching Arte's attention once more, Lerannu pointed at another, distant cluster of pines to her side where she suspected Allor to be hiding. The two crept from their hiding places, closing in on either side of the trees like the ends of a pincer. Lerannu reached the trees first, with Arte still slinking along another wall as she made to join the mage. Suddenly, Allor burst forth from the trees, throwing his snowball at Lerannu with all his might. Shouting in surprise, the mage raised her hands in front of her face, and a sharp gust of wind that issued from her hands broke apart the incoming snowball. The mage laughed at her defensive reflex, then giggled fitfully as Arte's snowball hit Allor in the tail.

"Well, that was hardly fair!" said the king with mock outcry as the others laughed and gathered around him and the mage.

"I'm sorry!" Lerannu giggled. "I swear that wasn't ... fully on purpose!"

The king started to laugh along with everyone else, and Arte, approaching Samuel, gave the prince a friendly hug and kiss on the cheek. The grey fur on Sam's face seemed to darken slightly as the skin beneath blushed, and Lerannu believed that if one were to dump some snow on him in that moment, it would have instantly turned to steam.

"Thank you for being such a gallant gentleman, my prince," said Arte with a tone of playful formality.

The players did all they could to not burst into laughter as Samuel tried to stammer out a reply. Fortunately, Queen Sheeva stepped into the garden at that moment, calling for all to get ready for the Sardonmay's Eve procession to the archtemple. With the queen and her two advisors having a few quick words with the king, Lerannu joined the others in making for their rooms and preparing for the festivities.

85
12/28/4029 G.M.

SHEEVA sat beside Allor in the carriage as the holiday procession rode to the archtemple. The two monarchs hailed and waved at the cheering crowds of revelers that lined the roads. Occasionally, they also called out to the carriages behind and before them in efforts to talk to the others in their household over the loudness of the throngs. As the procession drew nearer to its destination, Sheeva, her mind still pondering all that had been planned for the ever-nearing dawn of the new era, suddenly found herself looking at the carriage ahead. It was the one in which her children rode, along with Arte, the daughter of the visiting east warden, and Peacekeeper Captain Thomas, who had been personally assigned to accompany and guard the children.

The children of several other families visiting the castle were also riding with the princess and prince, all conversing happily as the parade made its way through the city. Arte, in particular, was speaking very animatedly to Sam and Talrah, but seemed especially interested in the prince. After several minutes of conversation, the warden's daughter gave the prince a kiss on the cheek, and proceeded to sidle closer to him in the seat. It was only a little closer, but it was far too close nevertheless.

The queen felt her blood growing hot, and her ears began to ring as her protective fury threatened to overcome her. She began to hear what felt to be two voices, though only one clearly came through.

"Calm yourself, Sheeva," said the assuring voice of Raakmathna. "It is as appalling to me as it is to you, but you must not undo all our planning. I know it is hard to watch, but you must stay calm. I promise you, that little Kason tart *will* pay dearly for trying to push herself onto your dear boy. She will not trouble your family for much longer, nor will her parents. Nor any of these ... other 'people' who think they can destroy your family and all the true people you've vowed to protect as queen. Look to your husband, my friend; he has something for you. Something that should help take your mind off of things."

Sheeva blinked. Pulling herself out of her locked gaze, she looked at the vibrant, berry-laden branch of holly that Allor was holding up to her.

"Some holly for a kiss, my love?" the king said sweetly.

Sheeva smiled, and taking the holly and placing it beside her, she kissed him deeply as they closely held one another. A few moments passed wordlessly between them as they rested their heads upon each other, with the clamor of merrymaking sounding all about them. At last Allor spoke tenderly into her ear.

"What a year, huh?"

"Mmm-hmm."

"It would seem that many things are finally coming together, though."

"I hope so, Al. I sorely hope so."

"I believe they will. With things finally beginning to settle between us and the West, and your Peacekeeper project and your contribution to medicine, it almost feels like a new era is coming for the world. I'm sure it won't be literally listed in the history books as such, but—"

Hearing her husband speak of an impending new age struck her with an overwhelming sense of joy and hope. Holding her husband tightly, the queen began to sob.

Allor took her face in his hands, looking worriedly into her eyes. "Sheeva," he said softly, "what's the matter? I saw you looking out into the distance just now, and you seemed so—"

"I'm sorry to worry you, Al," said Sheeva, laughing lightly through her tears. "It's just been such a hard road since we started leading Enmayar. With all that's been going on, I've worried if it would amount to anything in the end. But to hear you say that it's like a new time for Fidonhaal ... I'm just so happy to hear you say that."

Allor held her closer, gently nuzzling her neck as he went on to assure her.

"You've done so much for us, Sheeva, beyond the call of leading Enmayar. Onu alone knows all of what's gone into the way things have fared these past few years, but whatever's all behind it, you're a part of it, and you'll be looked up to for generations to come. Trust me."

Embracing her husband tightly, Sheeva sniffed and nodded.

"I do, Al," she said. "I do."

"Speaking of future generations," said the king as he maintained his embrace, "I was wondering what you thought about Arte, and how well she's been getting along with Tally and Sam. Especially Sam."

An icy grip of dread seized Sheeva's heart for a second. Then, remembering Raakmathna's assurance and keeping in mind the king's naivety, the queen breathed a deep sigh to recompose herself, masking it as a sigh that was made by one deep in thought.

"I'm not sure. They've just met a few days ago, after all."

"Of course. These things would take time, and they still might end up with someone else, but we'll never know until we let opportunities come along. They've certainly gotten off on the right foot, I'd say, and I'd like to think that there's a lot of potential for both their happiness and Enmayar's future, *if* things between them were to blossom into something more. Arte's a smart girl, from what Lerannu's told me."

"I've no doubt about that. I'm just so worried that, if we rush things too much, it might turn out like ..."

"I understand," said Allor with another kiss, "and it's not anything I'm trying to rush, either. Let's just enjoy the holiday, shall we?"

"That's what I've been hoping to do," said the queen. She then gently scratched the back of Allor's neck and made a proposition on a way the two might later enjoy the occasion in private.

"Perhaps the new year would be a good time to try again ..."

"Oh, I suppose so," said the king with a jesting roll of the eyes.

86
1/6/4030 G.M.

ALLOR sat on the throne at Sheeva's side. As much as he believed that he understood the queen's sharp rejection of the visitor's offer to entertain the court, he was nevertheless quite saddened by it. Not only did it hurt to see the young man crushed after all his travels, but it reminded the king of all that he and his wife had lost. The memories of such things were, no doubt, a big part of what made the queen think the way she did.

Sheeva already had much on her mind; Allor could tell that much just by her eyes when the two took their seats to begin seeing to the day's affairs. Judging from the letters she had shown him over the past few days, and the meetings with her, Sarah, and Ranoth that he had recently managed to attend, Allor wagered that Sheeva was still heavily preoccupied with the Peacekeepers and diplomacy matters with Kellmayar. Though both issues had been faring well, they were still very demanding and ongoing concerns. It was beginning to take a toll on the queen. She had displayed discomfort and apprehension to strangers a number of times before, but there was no doubt in the king's mind that the recent increase in strain from her primary endeavors had heightened Sheeva's irritability considerably and likely made her more disagreeable than she would have been otherwise.

The bard was a dashing young Balon man, seemingly only a few years younger than the king and queen themselves. He was a Sorrenarn native, of lean but sturdy build, with handsome white fur, long hair braided in a tail, and eyes that were a stunning ice blue. Upon being announced by Stewardess Sarah, the bard came in and introduced himself as Donovan Greenheart. He gave a brief account of his life and travels, and then expressed his hope to play in the court for a time. He offered to sing a segment of the epic ballad *Mountainborn*, clearly hoping to do credit to the essential song of his homeland and reigning dynasty. Needless to say, he was taken aback by the queen's response.

"You lot sure seem to take pride in celebrating rebellion and regicide. Do you truly think that such a song is fitting to play in a *royal* court, especially a foreign one?"

Allor's heart sank at her words, sensing a bout of horrid memories, summoned by the pain from the past, that were surely tearing through his wife's mind. The bard, with a face that managed to seem both crestfallen and resolute, struggled to form a reply.

"I-I ..." he stammered, "surely, my queen, I wouldn't need to explain that it's not about *celebrating* the killing of kings and queens, but the ending of a specific, tyrannous dynasty, and ultimately, the uniting of an entire continent. The events of the song paved the way for—"

"I've had my history lessons, *sir*," Sheeva snapped, "and I ask you now, what did the Snoweyes do exactly, apart from what they thought best for the leading of their country? And what did Karanor really care about? Some vengeance for his family? Whatever sense of injustice it was that his father hammered into his mind? Or maybe, at the end of the day, all he wanted was to take control over all of Sorrenar and begin a hold on the continent that has now lasted a thousand years? How 'evil' were the Snoweyes, really, or how 'good' were Karanor and his allies? Perhaps they were more or less as stated by the songs and the history books, but I wonder at times if those sources weren't perhaps written by those who more than a little partial."

Allor sat in silence, wanting desperately to say something, but torn by the thoughts within him. He had not heard Sheeva speak quite like this before, but he could sense a certain validity to her point. But even if neither side of the conflict was purely good nor evil, the accounts that ultimately condemned the Snoweyes were overwhelming, as were those which praised the first of the Karamus dynasty and their followers.

The bard was hopelessly dumbfounded. "I ... my queen, the part that I—"

"I am *not* your queen, bard, nor is my husband your king. *Your* queen and king are in Sorrenar, and I suggest that you go back there, if singing such a song to royalty is what you aspire to do. That song might suit *your* leaders, but I doubt it would be particularly pleasant for the ears of the other queens and kings of Fidonhaal, especially if they really took the time to think about its implications."

The bard's ears flattened pitifully in defeat. With a silent, reverent bow, the northern minstrel thanked Sheeva and Allor for their time, and quietly departed. Once the bard had left the room, Allor turned to talk to Sheeva, and found her burying her face in her hands, massaging what looked to be an agonizing headache. Placing a hand on her shoulder, the king spoke to his wife gently.

"I'll have some water brought in," he said simply. "I ... I need a little fresh air."

"Thank you, Al. I'm sorry you had to see that."

"Just breathe, my love. Let it go. Let's just take a few minutes before we get into anything else, alright?"

"Of course."

The two kissed, and Allor left the room, stopping a patrolling Peacekeeper to request water for Sheeva. He left the throne room by the door that would lead out into the gardens, making it seem as though he were heading that way. He then briskly made his way through the hallways until he reached the main entrance of the castle and came out into the courtyard. There he saw the bard, just about to walk out of the gate alongside a Zaron woman with whom he was conversing. Allor called out to them, looking intently at the Balon man as he made to speak.

"Sir Donovan," he said, "I cannot express how sorry I am for how sourly that went. I don't know if you know much about my wife's past, or my own, for that matter, but if I could just have a few moments to—"

"I've been told of your losses in Kellmayar," said the bard levelly, "and the tragedy involving her former suitor and friend. I've no doubt that such things would leave scars that might not ever fully heal, which might in turn lead her to think Onu-knows-what, of past and present, and of stranger and friend."

Allor nodded sadly. The bard, though his eyes still held hurt and bafflement at what had happened, gave a light smile.

"I've also heard of her contribution to medicine, and what, or I suppose I should say who, played a role in motivating her to study it. I've heard of her Peacekeepers, and my wife and I have met more than a few of them here and on the road. You'd be hard-pressed to find more upstanding Fidons anywhere."

The king smiled.

"I pray Onu bless you for the patience and support that you have doubtlessly shown her, King Allor," said the bard, "and that he give you strength for the hard times. I cannot imagine what it was like to share the same losses as her that day in Kellmayar, nor how hard it must be to keep strong when the memories come back. I was told of these things a while ago, and while I confess that I was still caught off-guard by how our meeting went, I don't hold it against her."

Allor breathed deeply and wiped a sleeve across his eyes. He then pulled a small pouch from his robes.

"Your understanding is immensely appreciated," he said as he opened the pouch and sorted through the coins inside. "All the same, I can't stand to let you leave empty-handed."

"I appreciate that, King Allor, but you needn't worry. My wife and I are going to the archtemple now to see if we can attend and perform at the Veronmay wedding. We're friends of, well, the bride. And the salpion."

Allor laughed in surprise, but still held his coin-bearing hand halfway out to the couple.

"I suppose you'll be taken care of, then," he said. "But are you sure you couldn't do with a little something extra for the road afterwards? There's no telling what sort of expenses might suddenly come up in your travels."

The bard looked at the handful of silver, then to his wife. Both shrugged with a light smile, and the northerner stepped up and plucked half of the offer from the king's hand.

"This should be plenty," he said kindly. "You have my thanks, King Allor."

"Go with Onu's blessings, Sir Donovan and ... madam?"

"Mira," said the Zaron woman with a smile.

"Go with Onu's blessing, Sir Donovan and Madam Mira. May you be in safe and good company during your stay at the archtemple, and wherever else you lay your head."

The couple departed, turning to walk down the snowy hill and to the archtemple. Allor watched them walk into the descending distance, then turned back to the throne room once they had passed from sight.

87
1/6/4030 G.M.

DONOVAN walked beside Mira, leaving the castle gates and beginning their descent of the east hill on their way to the archtemple. The bard walked along, lost in thought on the exchange with Queen Sheeva and the words of warning that Salpion Lovonhaar had given him from before, when at last his wife's words pulled him from his ponderings.

"So ... what exactly happened?"

Donovan recounted the ill-faring encounter, and how the queen perceived his choice of singing a part of *Mountainborn*, despite not having been able to tell her which part of it he meant to sing before the queen refused.

"Which part was it?" Mira asked.

"When Karanor and Saphi met, and how their friendship would go on to grow into love and thus become the foundation for the Karamus dynasty."

"I see."

"Now that I think of it," the bard added, "I remember what Salpion Owen told me of his experience with the queen back when he blessed the newborn prince and princess. He told me of the look she had given him, which he described as horrifically defensive, like a mother bear protecting her cubs. I feel that I was met with the same look ... even as I was just introducing myself."

"Are ... are you sure?"

"It's hard to explain. Maybe it was some misunderstanding, or I was thinking too much on Owen's words at the time, but ... something just didn't feel right. As you heard the king and I mention, and as Father Owen told me before, she had some very troublesome times in her past. Considering all that, she has done much to help not only her country, but Fidonhaal at large. It hurt, the way things went and the way I think she looked at me, but with everything considered, I think it should ultimately be forgiven."

"I'm sorry you came all this way only for that to happen, all the same."

"I am, too, but I know it'll fare far better at the archtemple. Let's keep going."

The bard and the huntress continued their walk to the archtemple, having reached the bottom of the east hill. Crossing the Sunrise River that flowed through the valley, they began ascending the west hill, talking now of far more pleasant things.

***

They reached the grand temple gates at just an hour past noon. They approached the posted Faithguard knights and greeted them, stating the intent of their visit and promptly being escorted to the salpion's office.

When they reached Father Owen's quarters, the knight who led them knocked upon the door. It was opened once permission to enter was granted. The bard peered in as the two men conversing at the desk turned to greet their visitors, then stepped in with Mira at his side.

"Greetings, child of Onu," said the one seated before the salpion, whose fur was a beautiful marble pattern of black and brown. "What—"

"Donovan!" Father Owen boomed merrily as he bolted from his chair and raced to greet the bard with a friendly, nearly-crushing embrace. "I'm so glad to see you've come in time to be in the wedding! Well, I presume that's why you're here, that is."

"You presume right, Father Owen," said Donovan happily.

The Kason-and-Mavon man who had been conversing with Owen rose from his seat and joined them, looking admiringly at the two newcomers.

"I presume you're the famous Donovan the Bard I've heard so much about, he who was greatly pleasant company to my mentor and fiancée two springs past?"

"The one and only," said the bard with a grin. He then offered his hand to the stranger. "And you must be Verdok. Father Owen and Ruth spoke much about you. Ruth especially."

Verdok smiled.

"And who, pray tell, is this enchanting, sturdy lady you have in your company?" asked Owen.

"This is Mira, my wife."

Owen's eyes and smile widened in surprise and intrigue.

"Verdok," asked the salpion, "would you kindly have some wine brought up? I sense a very interesting story coming."

88

1/6/4030 G.M.

RUTH hung up her training gear alongside Orson and the other trainees as the day's exercises came to an end. Commander Hanye, still overseeing the training of the young Konothian inductees with Ruth as her assistant, breathed heavily as she put up her practice axe and buckler before slumping down onto the nearby bench.

"I'm definitely getting older," she said with a tired laugh.

"And you still have what it takes," Ruth assured her. "You're still our mother when we're in this yard. I don't know one trainee who doesn't look to you as I do."

"Oh, don't worry. Onu willing, I'm not going anywhere anytime soon, apart from my room for a nap, anyhow."

Ruth and Orson embraced the older veteran before they parted ways. Hanye left for the barracks, while Ruth and her squire made for Father Owen's study to rehearse the ring-bearer's role of the wedding ceremony. As they approached the door to the salpion's chambers, the knight and her squire grew curious at the sound of two unfamiliar voices conversing with Owen and Verdok. Knocking and being granted entry, Ruth called out joyously to Donovan, having swiftly recognized the bard from the North. She rushed over to greet him and was further intrigued by the introduction to his wife, Mira.

"So how did you two get together?" she asked.

"We were just going over that, actually," said the bard. "Have a seat with us, and some wine. We'll get you caught up with what we've already said, and take it from there."

The knight and her squire listened intently to Donovan and Mira's tale. They then introduced themselves to Mira, and explained their initial reason for coming to the study. The salpion assured the newcomers that their places in entertaining at the wedding were cemented. All in the room observed the rehearsal of the ring ceremony, then left together for dinner.

89
1/14/4030 G.M.

MIRA sat at the front central table of the archtemple's dining hall beside her husband. It had been eight days since they had arrived and were welcomed and hired as entertainers for the wedding as well as for their entire stay. Now, having had a week to get settled in and meet the rest of the temple's residents, the huntress and her husband were enjoying their first "official" performances on the night of winter's first full moon. Having played a few songs already, the couple from Plen were preparing for the main event.

Mira felt Donovan's muzzle brush against her neck, her husband's cue to get ready for the next song. She also saw the eager nods from Owen, Ruth, and Verdok, all three of whom she had come to like very much, along with the others at table with them. The huntress took up the lute that Donovan had lent her and began strumming the opening chords her husband had taught her. They were quite simple notes at present, with her still being new to the instrument, but they still added to the harmony of the song to come. The diners' ears pricked up at the lute's sound, and a quiet clatter of many forks and knives being put aside rippled across the great chamber. Donovan, plucking a couple of notes on his harp, addressed the audience.

"And now," he said, "with the beautiful full moon peering through the windows above us, who would favor a performance of *Winter Moon?*"

The crowd cheered approvingly, and Mira and Donovan began.

The light Yorun keeps rests aloft in the sky,
In the midst of the stars that sparkle as snow.
Whilst our land sleeps, in Sardoth's hands lie,
The moon bathes all in its full-lighted glow.
Will you walk with me, my love, out into the night,
And dance and sing with me in the winter moon light?
A haven for us alone I've found tonight;
Good Yorun helped me with the guide of his light.
A quiet little grove of snow-laden trees
Awaits our arrival, where we'll love in ease.
The light Yorun keeps rests aloft in the sky,
In the midst of the stars that sparkle as snow.
Whilst our land sleeps, in Sardoth's hands lie,
The moon bathes all in its full-lighted glow.
Will you go with me, my love, out into the night,

> *And kiss and embrace me in the winter moon light?*
> *Though Sardoth's hold may at first seem too cold*
> *For us to love, we'll keep warm if we hold*
> *Close to each other, our hearts and all bare*
> *To you and to me, and we'll have not a care.*
> *The light Yorun keeps rests aloft in the sky,*
> *In the midst of the stars that sparkle as snow.*
> *Whilst our land sleeps, in Sardoth's hands lie,*
> *The moon bathes all in its full-lighted glow.*
> *Will you embrace me, my love, out here in the night,*
> *And kiss and love me under the winter moon light?*

As they strummed and plucked the last notes, the feast hall resounded with the diners' applause. Mira, looking at the audience around her, caught the intense, wordless gazes that Ruth and Verdok gave to one another, and felt her cheeks start to grow warm as her husband put an arm around her. Looking to Donovan, she nodded toward the engaged priest and knight. The bard laughed.

"Maybe they need to move the wedding forward," he said with a fiendish chuckle.

"Oh, shush," Mira said as she playfully brushed her husband's arm off her shoulder. "They can wait."

"I agree, but Onu's mercy, I can just imagine how it's going to go once they–"

"DON!" Mira giggled.

Donovan pulled her close and gave her the same look that Ruth and Verdok had given to one another. Mira now felt the blush in her face beginning to quickly spread all over her.

"Thank you for encouraging me to start my travels again," the bard said softly, "and for coming with me."

"I ... you're welcome, Don."

"What do you say we wrap things up soon and turn in? Unlike those two, we don't need to wait for anything."

The Wedding Nears

90
3/19/4030 G.M.

LERANNU had been going over the lore of Fidonhaal's making, and the events prior to it, with Princess Talrah, Prince Samuel, and Arte Davinur all morning. It was a subject they had visited before, but now discussed more deeply given the children's furthered maturation. Having gone over the initial account of creation and the first days of the First Ancestors, the mage ended the morning lesson with a question for her pupils.

"So, when it comes down to the main cause of our strife, especially for the times when it's hurt the most in our history, what do you three think it is? Think back on the past few history lessons we've had, as well as what we've gone over today."

The children took the question in for a silent moment, then Talrah raised her hand.

"Yes, Talrah?"

"Well ... it looks like it happens when someone tries to make everything the way that only *they* want it. Raakaru wanted absolute order in all things and wouldn't allow us to be free. Salpion Gwellah Benarbu tried to make everyone think the exact same way about Onu, and pray to him the same way as well. The Snoweye dynasty wanted to make everyone in Sorrenar not only take them as their leaders, but also make them all look the same and do a lot of things in the same way."

"That's a very good start," said Lerannu with a nod. "Trying to force your will and your will alone ultimately leads to much pain, loss, and evil. But, there's something really important to bear in mind about the reasons why the ones that you mentioned did what they did."

The princess digested her teacher's reply, looking to her brother and friend to see if they had anything else to add. With eyes suddenly alight with realization, Samuel raised his hand.

"Yes, Samuel?" Lerannu asked, eager to see how well the lessons might be starting to connect with her students.

"They all wanted to try to do something good with it, or at least what they thought to be good. At least at first. The Snoweyes wanted to make all the people of Sorrenar the same, because they wanted to put a stop to all the fighting between them. But to do so, they ended up fighting a lot of people themselves, and then tried to force those under their rule to live *completely* the way they told them to. Salpion Benarbu only wanted to bring everyone together in how we believed in Onu, because she thought that if we all believed in Onu the exact same way, and prayed the exact same way, then Raakaru would never be able to hurt us like he did before. But as she got more frustrated, more angry, because not everyone agreed, one of Raakaru's demons led her to think that all who didn't think like her had to be punished. What ended up happening was the Temple's worst days."

"Very good," said Lerannu. The mage then turned to the east warden's daughter, who had been quietly taking in all that the twins said thus far. "Arte, what do you think these points in history show us? And how is it connected to the tale of Raakaru?"

Arte, processing the discussion thus far and taking in the teacher's question, hummed nervously for a few seconds as she thought up her reply. Her discomfort quickly vanished once she constructed her response.

"I think they're supposed to show us that some very bad things have come from what were at first good ideas, or at least ideas that weren't completely bad by themselves. Raakaru was first known as Lovaariinu, the All-Keeper, and he didn't like Onu's giving of free will because he just wanted to set everything in complete order to try and keep everyone safe. He thought it would be for our own good, but he couldn't, or wouldn't understand that, as Onu had explained, the freedom of will was essential to his design. If we weren't free to think or do things, we couldn't truly love Onu, or anyone, or anything, else. But ... Raakaru was so sure that his way was right, and because of that, he became filled with hate and went on to do horrible things, and made us doubt and start the first evils, which have since grown."

"Very good, all three of you!" Lerannu commended her pupils. "Some of the worst evils have come from good intentions. They meant well. But when there is no acceptance of any freedom, of any other thoughts, or the possibility of them, and when one is so full of pride as to insist that their way is the only way, it can lead to horrible things in time. Know this, all three of you, that this lesson is extremely important for all of us to learn, but especially for leaders and those who are to become leaders."

Lerannu looked at the three children in turn. "Samuel and Talrah, if either or both of you take up your mother and father's throne, as is currently presumed, this lesson may very well be the most important one you'll ever have. This goes for you as well, Arte, if you should ever take charge of the east ward. Do you all understand?"

"Yes, Lady Lera," said the children sincerely.

"Very good," said the teacher as she got up and stretched. "That should do for the morning. How about we all have our lunch in the garden again?"

91
3/19/4030 G.M.

SHEEVA left the throne room, leaving the updated developments on the Kellmayar agreement for Allor to go over with the advisors as she went into the small council room where she, Sarah, and Ranoth met. The queen quietly slipped inside, closed and locked the door, and then turned to her two aides with eyes shining of anxious anticipation.

"All of our Peacekeeper companies and selected ambassadors are well in place now," said the south wardeness as she presented the bundles of parchments she was cradling in her arms. "Everything's here. This is Captain Amanda's reports on King Dominik, his new wife, Queen Fida, and all the others in Zefiil. Here's Captain Tolnu's details on King Salos and Queen Vita, and everyone else of import in Benhotha. And lastly, there's the reports on King Viktor and Queen Xenia, along with the rest of the Karamus family and the others in Norkoth. They've covered all that you've ordered for, as best as they've been able. What all these people do, when they do it, and their plans for the festivities. What potential points of defense and escape there are for our soldiers to try and cover in the castles and the capital cities overall. What we've been able to get so far on places of concern and interest elsewhere in the other countries. And, of course, there are the praises that our troops have been earning left and right for the king to see."

"Good," said Sheeva, sighing heavily with relief as she began to read and sort the papers. "And what has Captain Thomas had to say since we last spoke to him? Is he and all his company ready, and do they all understand what's to be done with the Davinurs, and at the archtemple?"

"Yes, my queen," said Ranoth with a nod. "He and all the others have said they understand what's being called for. As you instructed, given how well Thomas has gotten on with Allor and the children, he'll lead them back to the archtemple when it's time to appear at the reception, after the Davinurs have been seen to. Are ... are you absolutely sure that the king and the children shouldn't learn of any of this beforehand? I know we've gone over this before, but needless to say, we can't expect them to be completely unaffected by such sudden events."

"It's as I've said already," Sheeva said calmly, understandingly, but firmly. "They're good people, all of them, but they just wouldn't understand until we begin the new era in full. I'll explain it all to them myself, once things begin at the reception. Please, don't ... say ... a word."

"Of course, my queen," said the chaplain dutifully. "I didn't mean to–"

"I know, Ranoth; your concerns are entirely understandable."

Sheeva finished reading the papers. Passing the intelligence for the attacks back to Sarah, she kept hold of the positive reports from the other nations to show Allor. "Everything seems to be going as planned," she said at last. "Just a few more days ..."

The queen looked intently at the chaplain and stewardess, their eyes glowing with an agonizing hope for the new world to come.

"... And we'll bring in a new age. No more chances. No more uncertainties. No more division. No more harm permitted by an uncaring Maker. Just order, thanks to the All-Keeper, and only us and the worthy to inherit it. Only Zarons. No more Kason monsters to kill our families, or Mavons to ruin the homes and lives of our friends. No more Balons to sow discord in our lands. No more half-breeds to muddy and disrupt the waters that we seek to still. No more adulterers. No more abusers."

The queen looked gratefully at her two confidants.

"And you'll both be at my side, and the side of my family, to help ensure that order. Thank you ... both of you ... for all that you've given ..."

"We should be thanking you, my queen," said Sarah, "for trusting us to help you in bringing the world to order. We will not fail you now."

"I know."

The three quietly left the room. As Sheeva made her way back to the throne room, her trusted shadow walked up beside her.

"It *will* succeed, my friend," said Raakmathna. "Soon, the whole of Fidonhaal will be safe. For you, your husband, and your children ... those who are now and those who are yet to come."

Sheeva smiled lovingly as she gently petted her middle. She looked forward to telling Allor on Veronmay's Eve.

"And all the rest of the good, long-suffering people who have had to be wronged by the others, as was permitted by Onu's will."

"Is there anything else I need to do?"

"Apart from staying to the plan and waiting, no. Go on to Allor now, friend; he could certainly use your company now."

Sheeva nodded, and the servant of Lovaariinu faded again out of sight. The queen then entered the throne room, and seeing Allor wearily massaging his brow, sat beside him and embraced him.

"Hopefully that's all the details done for now," said the king wearily, "at least concerning Kellma-yar, anyhow. Onu's Four Breaths, I'm looking forward to Veronmay."

"So am I," said Sheeva as she kissed her husband.

92
3/27/4030 G.M.

RUTH walked beside Orson as they headed toward Father Owen's study to rehearse the ring-bearer part of the ceremony one last time. The knight's mind and heart raced with anticipation as she pondered the great change that was about to take place in her life. As they passed through the gardens, Ruth pulled herself from her thoughts and realized that her squire wasn't beside her. Turning around, she saw the boy, at the start of adolescence, gazing fixedly at a statue of Konoth and Devora Alpharon, the founder of the Faithguard and his wife.

The first guardian of the Temple was in a time of peace in this depiction, with his armor, shield, and axe nowhere to be seen. It was not a depiction of his combat prowess, but of the love he and his wife had shared. They simply held hands as they walked together, looking tenderly into one another's eyes and smiling. Ruth, looking at the statue and the captivated young viewer, walked up to him and placed her hands on his shoulders in a sister-like embrace.

"Is everything alright?" she asked.

"Yeah," said Orson reflectively. "I ... I just wonder how it'll all be after tomorrow. I've told myself that it shouldn't really change all that much, at least as far as I'm concerned. I'll still be your squire, and my family will still be here. Father Owen will still be here, like a father or grandfather to everyone here. And you and Brother Verdok ... you'll still be here, and we'll still be like family ... and you two will love each other more or less as you always have, right? And yet ..."

"I know what you mean," said Ruth comfortingly as she patted her apprentice's back. "I'm nervous, too. And you're not wrong; so much will still be the same, more or less. And yet nothing will ever truly be the same."

Ruth looked at Orson, who sighed deeply and looked ponderously at the statue's base.

"But don't worry," she said. "I'll tell you what I've been telling myself ever since Father Owen and my mother told it to me. No matter what exactly happens, now or in the years to come, we're all family here, and we'll always be together, in spirit if not always in body, if we keep as close as we do now."

"Thanks, Ruth."

The two hugged as brother and sister, then, having looked at the statue for a moment longer, resumed their walk toward Father Owen's study.

A Day of Life and Love

93
3/28/4030 G.M.

ALLOR stirred from sleep, opening his eyes to see the first glow of dawn peering over the distant hills visible from the balcony window. He drowsily felt about him, turning over when he realized the bed was empty apart from himself. Getting up and donning a light bed robe, the king quietly opened the bedchamber doors and peered into the hall just in time to see Sheeva, herself lightly dressed, step out of the small meeting room along with Priest Ranoth and Lady Sarah. The three spoke quietly another moment until Lady Sarah, noticing the king, nodded toward him to inform the queen of his presence. Sheeva turned, smiled, and waved a hand toward the bed behind the king.

"Just some last-minute things about today's plans for the wedding," she said warmly. "I'll be right back with you."

The king smiled back, turned around, and closed the door. Still in his robe, he lay back down in his spot on the bed as he watched the golden glow on the horizon spread further into the reaches of the deep blue above. It had been a wearying past year, as had the first months of the present one. But at long last, with the Kellmayarn negotiations having finally succeeded, along with the development of a new treatment for the Endallian Fever and the worldwide reception of the Peacekeepers, things seemed to be calming down. The king was now looking forward greatly to the Spring's Eve wedding and the impending holy day at large.

A little while passed, and Allor heard the door behind him open and close, followed by the gentle rustle of Sheeva's robes falling to the floor. The queen's warm, bare body pressed up against him, and he snuggled closer to her in turn.

"Is everything settled?" he asked.

"Mm-hm," Sheeva hummed into his ear in answer. Her reply sent a tingle down Allor's spine, prompting him to laugh gently as she reached around him and began toying with the sash that girded his robe.

"Lera is going to be entertaining the children for the morning," she went on. "She's set up a treasure hunt guided by riddles."

"Sounds like fun," Allor said contentedly, turning to face his wife once she undid the sash and opened his robes.

"They'll be busy all morning."

"I see."

94
3/28/4030 G.M.

LERANNU read the last of the riddle clues for the treasure hunt. It had been a lovely day, with she and the children playing the game in reference to the angel Vernid being a lover of play and riddles. The children and the mage had been playing all morning, and the youngsters had been finding and trading amongst themselves the festive trinkets they had collected.

One last prize I leave for you,
Before you part to make merry.
You'll find it hiding in sky's blue,
Upon an arm of ...

The mage laughed as Prince Samuel, with barely a second passing since the riddle was read, exclaimed the answer. The other children, having been in the flow of riddle solving all morning, came to the same conclusion an instant later.

"Cherry!" they said in near unison.

Lerannu and the children sprinted through the garden, coming to the small grove of cherry blossom trees that grew in one corner of the garden. The trees were just beginning to bloom, and the children were looking intently over the pink-laced branches for the final prize. The mage watched them keenly, looking to see if any might catch onto the other subtle clue that had been planned.

Sure enough, it was Samuel once again who realized first. Being puzzled by the riddle and lack of a noticeable prize in the trees' branches, the young prince began looking around for something he missed. His eyes fell onto the statue in the grove's center, which depicted Vernid himself, harp in hand, looking into the distance merrily as some of his springling children danced around him. The prince followed the direction of the statue's gaze and saw that it looked squarely at one tree in particular. Running over to it, Samuel eagerly paced about the tree, looking as hard as he could.

"I found it!" he said at last, pointing to the prize. It was a necklace of strung ceramic, with the necklace itself appearing as tender green leaves and the centerpiece as a cluster of bright, pink cherry blossoms. Once noticed, it stood out clearly as it dangled against the sky on the branch that held it. The prince leapt onto the tree and climbed as the others gathered and watched, and once he had retrieved the prize, he climbed down and presented it to Arte.

The young Kason beauty accepted it gleefully, praising Samuel for his gentlemanly courtesy. Lerannu watched them happily. The prince and his twin sister had gotten on very well with the visiting east warden and his family, and their friendship with Arte had grown well and strong in the three winter months they had studied and played together. They were, of course, still too young for any major commitment, and the queen herself was hesitant to make any particular encouragement for possible matches at present. Lerannu, though she understood the queen's reasons, nevertheless pondered speaking to Sheeva on Sam and Arte's friendship, suggesting it might well blossom further. Now, however, the mage stepped in as the children made last-minute trades of prizes, and called an end to the game.

"We'll all be going to the wedding in a few hours," she announced. "Lunch should be just about ready. We'll eat and dress, and then we'll all go with the queen and king to celebrate the wedding and Veronmay itself!"

The children voiced their eagerness for the lunch and festivities to come, and Lerannu walked with them back into the castle.

95

3/28/4030 G.M.

VERDOK stood behind the curtain that draped across the doorway on his side of the altar in the grand cathedral. With the thick curtain and his own white-and-green veil obscuring his sight, he could not yet see how crowded the house of worship was. The great waves of voices that responded to Father Owen's words and prayers, however, were more than enough to tell him that it was packed to bursting, as so many had come for the wedding and the Veronmay festivities in general.

As he listened to the salpion's prayers for the blessing of the union to come, Verdok's mind drifted to his thoughts on the day so far. It had all been preparation for this moment, and he had not been able to talk to Ruth, or see her, for even a moment before the ceremony. Ecstasy and anxiety raged within him, and he clasped his hands together, fervently pleading that Onu make the crawling passage of time go swifter.

His heart pounded within him, and he nearly jumped out of his fur when Kiin, his father's father, gently tapped his shoulder. Verdok looked to him and his other grandparents nervously.

"Get ready," Kiin said softly. "It's almost time."

Verdok struggled to keep his breathing steady as he listened keenly to Father Owen's closing words of prayer. Then the salpion lifted his hands, beckoning the bride and groom to approach. The groom and his grandparents matched the procession of Ruth and those in her company step for step as they entered from the curtained doorway opposite from each other. Ruth's mother, Arza, was there, as well as Commander Hanye Heartkeeper. They met at the central altar, and the bride and groom looked at one another as best as they could from beneath their veils. Father Owen stood between them and addressed the massive congregation.

"Dear children of Onu who have gathered this day, I now present to you Ruth Pionaar, a high knight of the Faithguard, and Verdok Merchill, the high priest of this archtemple, as they come before you to give themselves to one another and become as one in blessed matrimony. If there is anyone who has an objection to this union, let them speak now or else forever hold their peace."

A moment of total, tranquil silence passed, where Verdok and Ruth, veiled and robed in white and green, stared at each other, yearning to see their faces again. When no objections were voiced, Owen beseeched the congregation to bless the couple.

"Onu bless you, and give you joy and strength to your hearts," said the salpion and the worshippers, "that you may gladly and faithfully uphold your bond to one another."

A brief silence followed, one that was not in tradition, and Verdok, looking to Father Owen, could see that his mentor was hiding his face in the Beldsantu as he blinked back tears with a quivering smile. No word of puzzlement or curiosity came from the crowd regarding the delay, as the family-like bonds that the bride, groom, and salpion had shared over the years was common knowledge. At last Owen recomposed himself, took a deep, silent breath, and turned his head toward Ruth and those beside her.

"Ruth," he said, "and those who stand by you in this high hour, it has been declared, before Onu and Fidonity, that you will take the man named Verdok Merchill as your husband. Is this true?"

"It is true," said Ruth clearly, but gently, as her voice, too, wavered in emotion. Her mother and Faithguard mentor echoed the words in confirmation.

"Verdok," Owen continued, turning to the groom, "and those who stand by you in this high hour, it has been declared, before Onu and Fidonity, that you will take the woman named Ruth Pionaar as your wife. Is this true?"

"It is true," Verdok said, just managing to keep his voice level. Okren, Alexis, Wenda, and Kiin repeated their grandson's answer. Verdok looked back to them and saw their eyes. They all glittered like stars as they witnessed the fruit of their own late children's union being bound in love.

Father Owen then bade that the couple join their hands in mutual prayer and oath, clasping his hands over theirs. "Ruth," he said, "will you take Verdok, and Verdok alone, so that, through children, other pursuits, or both, the two of you may bear good fruit that is planted in faith and love?"

"I will," said Ruth.

"Verdok, will you take Ruth, and Ruth alone, so that, through children, other pursuits, or both, the two of you may bear good fruit that is planted in faith and love?"

"I will," said Verdok.

"It has been said," Owen continued as he looked to both of them in turn, "that it has been agreed between you that Verdok shall put aside his family name and be joined to Ruth's, thus becoming Verdok Pionaar. Such has been the common practice since the first official unions following the end of Raakaru's reign, but by no means is this the only way. Is it true, Ruth and Verdok, that the groom means to take the family name of the bride in this union?"

"It is true," Verdok and Ruth said in unison.

"Ruth and Verdok, will you share in your joys and sorrows, gains and losses, triumphs and trials? Will you do so in honesty and trust, so that you live your life not as two, but one, and perform and pursue goodness and greatness together for as long as you both live on Fidonhaal?"

"We will."

"Ruth and Verdok, will you, as one blessed flesh, strive with all your being to keep Onu with you and in all you do, so that all of Fidonhaal may see the goodness and greatness that arises from those who seek to embrace life as Onu intended for his children? Will you do this, so that all of Fidonhaal may seek to follow your example and that of all others like you?"

"We will."

Still holding the couple's hands together within his, Father Owen called out to the back of the central aisle.

"Will the one entrusted with the rings of union come forth?"

Through his veil, Verdok could just make out the white-furred half of Orson's body at the far end of the aisle. The young man strode, carefully yet majestically, down the aisle as he bore the golden bands upon a small, ornate cushion. Presenting them before the couple and the salpion, Orson bowed his head as Owen took a ring in each hand. The salpion then gave one ring to each mate, who in turn put it upon the finger of the other. After this, Father Owen joined the couple's hands within his own one last time before the ceremony's end.

"In the sight of Onu and all creation, I, Owen Lovonhaar, Salpion of the Temple of Onu, by the power vested in me as a servant of our Maker, pronounce this couple wife and husband. May their days together be many and blessed, and may Onu bless this union eternally, that it may continue beyond this life and endure forevermore in Onuhaal. In Onu, and in this newfound union, we strive to trust."

"In Onu," echoed the congregation, "and in this newfound union, we strive to trust."

Verdok then looked intently at his mentor, who smiled as he addressed the couple.

"You may lift your veils."

Verdok and Ruth took hold of one another's veil, and gently lifted them over their heads as they looked into each other's eyes for the first time as a married couple. Ruth's eyes, shining in the light from the windows and the candles, sparkled like emeralds held to the sun.

"Before we conclude this ceremony," the salpion announced, "the groom wishes to read something to the bride and to all others present."

Verdok reached into the folds of his robe, smiling as he saw Ruth look on curiously from the corner of his eye. He pulled out the small leather journal that Ruth had given him on his ninth birthday. He opened it and turned to the last pages. With a voice that he struggled to keep level, he began to read a poem he had written.

We met so many years ago,
In this great house of Onu,
The one whom I thank every day
For the moment I met you.
With ease we grew in friendship,
Both being in the Temple's care,
But it wasn't 'til we were older
That we learned why we were there.
At first, we were met with sorrow,
With uncertainty and pain.
But with the love that all had shown us,
Soon love between us came.
Then, one day, you rode away,
On a mission to save the troubled,
And seeing your courage and flowering beauty,
My awe towards you had doubled.
I gave to you a token
Of my love, and my father's and mother's,
And from that day on, our form of love
Grew beyond that akin to sisters and brothers.
So now, years past, I stand with you,
To join our hearts together.
May our bond be blessed by Onu,
And may it last forever.

Verdok looked up and saw Ruth's eyes looking fixedly into his own. Her gaze pierced into the deepest depths of his soul.

"I-I ..." he stuttered bashfully, "I'm sure it could still use some work, but I've tried for weeks–"

Ruth took his wrists, pulled him to her, and kissed him. The congregation thundered in applause.

"I love it," she said tearfully.

"I didn't say 'you may kiss' yet," said Owen.

The congregation roared with laughter, and the couple looked bashfully to the salpion. He grinned.

"You may kiss."

***

The cathedral was now empty apart from Verdok, Ruth, and Father Owen. The salpion had declared that the festivities, both for the wedding and the coming of spring, had commenced immediately after the union, and that a feast was set to be held all the day and through the night in the archtemple's dining hall. The congregation then left, with some having gone on to celebrate the holy day at other venues. Others left to go elsewhere, meaning to rejoin the archtemple's feast at a later time. Others made immediately for the feast hall.

"Well then," said Owen, looking at the newlyweds, "I suppose we ought to get on to the feast! Donovan and Mira will be ready to perform soon, along with the other minstrels and players, and I'm sure everyone will be waiting eagerly for you two to start the meal. Some have probably held off from even having breakfast for this!"

Verdok looked to Ruth, who nodded with a small, warm smile.

"Might you go on and commence the festivities on our behalf?" the groom asked, his face growing warmer with every word. "Ruth and I aren't very hungry at the moment, and we ..."

The salpion gave the two an uncharacteristically impish grin, which made Verdok blush hotter and Ruth stifle a surprised giggle.

"Shall I tell them that they may begin now?" Owen asked. "And that you send your regards and will join them in due time?"

"Yes," the two said in unison.

Father Owen looked at them in silence, his grin giving way to a sincere, father-like countenance. He then smiled and nodded, and turned for the door leading outside the cathedral.

"Good afternoon, Ruth and Verdok Pionaar."

The two now stood together alone. They took one another by the hand and walked out of the cathedral at an easy pace. As they drew ever nearer to Verdok's rooms, however, their steps began to quicken, and they soon found themselves kissing and caressing each other as they walked.

At last they reached Verdok's rooms and closed the door behind them. Verdok and Ruth took hold of one another's robes, undressing each other gently. They stepped back from one another to admire their bodies. Verdok looked shyly at Ruth's eyes first, and smiled when he saw plainly that she was pleased by what she saw. He gazed upon her in full and was awestruck. He had seen her train throughout the years and knew that she was strong. He had seen her at feasts and formal gatherings, and knew that she had all the poise of a fine lady. But now, seeing her in all her natural beauty, Verdok stood transfixed by all that now graced his sight. Her short hair, which he had always found attractive, perfectly suited the look of a warrior and complemented her firm muscles. Her eyes, green as the fresh grass of spring, shined gently with the light of a loving, gentle woman, and added to her soft curves. She was simply beautiful, beyond what Verdok could put into words; a glorious figure of might and grace.

At last approaching to embrace her, Verdok noticed a thin strand about her neck that glittered of metal. He looked at it closely and realized that it was a slender chain. His eyes fell upon the pendant that hung by it, and his sight began to blur with loving tears as memories of years gone by began to flood his mind. He returned his gaze into the depths of Ruth's eyes.

"I knew you still had it," he said with suppressed sobs of joy, "but I didn't expect you to be wearing it today."

"I don't remember the last time I didn't have it on," Ruth said with a soft laugh, "other than when I needed to get a chain made for it."

"What happened? Did the leather break or something?"

Ruth laughed. "It's a funny little story." She then lay down on the bed, and looking at her hus-

~ 217 ~

band, beckoned to him with a smile both enticing and loving. "Why don't you come over here and join me, and I'll tell you all about it?"

Verdok's mind, heart, and soul soared as he joined his wife, whose arms and legs parted to embrace him.

96
3/28/4030 G.M.

SHEEVA returned to the castle with her family, household, and guests after the wedding. It was now the middle of the afternoon, and all were returning to the castle for a brief rest before heading to the reception banquet. Such had been the tradition for royalty of all the nations for some time, when it came to weddings of such stature as that of the knight and the high priest. It was also tradition that if the royal family had any other guests in their company, the guests would be sent back to the festivities a while before the monarchs themselves returned with the rest of their household. There was thus no suspicion in having the Davinurs "escorted" before Sheeva and her family returned to the archtemple. They would be quietly wiped away and would not be able to stand in the way at the archtemple once all was to be unveiled. And none would think to look for them before they reached the reception. It would be there, once the queen had explained herself to her family and all the others who would be saved, that the spring of the new Fidonhaal would surely begin unopposed. Apart by those who were to be removed, of course, but with the Peacekeepers at her disposal and every true Fidon by her side, it would be only a brief trouble to resolve.

The queen could barely contain her anticipation of the revelations for the future that she would soon declare. At last, having seen Allor and the children go in for tea, she called over Lerannu, who sat beside her in the entrance courtyard.

"Is everything alright, Sheeva?" the mage asked.

"It's been a long decade, Lera, trying to do what can be done."

"You've done very well, my queen. Where others would have been broken by the troubles they had suffered, you've risen above them and given so many a chance for a better life. The Peacekeepers, and those who might have otherwise died from Endallian Fever ... even myself and Mother, with all that we were going through back then."

"You've been a great friend to me," the queen said gently.

"And you to me."

"I'll never be able to repay you for how well you've helped us raise Sam and Tally."

"I think that was my way of repaying *you* for what you've done for Mother and me. Besides, they're like my little brother and sister; I've always loved teaching them."

Sheeva smiled, then petted her middle. She looked intently at the mage. "Do you think you can handle going through it all again?"

Lerannu looked quizzically at her for an instant, then immediately covered her mouth to keep from crying out in delight. She hugged her queen and her friend closely, laughing with excitement.

"Of course! I'd love to! Have you told Allor yet, or Tally or Sam?"

"Not yet," said Sheeva with a smile, "but I mean to tonight, once we've all gathered at the feast."

"Oh, I can't wait!"

"Neither can I, but not a word yet."

"Of course!"

"Thank you, Lera. For everything."

"Of course, my queen. You're welcome."

The two friends then entered the castle to join the others for tea.

97

3/28/4030 G.M.

MIRA sat beside Donovan, who had been placed as the lead of all the other players and singers who had gathered to perform at the feast. The salpion had already announced that the new-lyweds, having bidden the festivities to commence, would join the guests later on. The first rounds of food and drink were already well underway, as were the first songs and pieces of music. Having played a part in a few songs that were the work of other minstrels, Mira looked quizzically at her husband as he suddenly rose and called for the attention of the fully packed dining hall.

"Dear guests," said Donovan, "I'd wager that, while love and our bonds with others may be pondered at any time, nothing stirs us to reflect on them in quite the same way a wedding does."

A booming wave of agreement resounded throughout the hall.

"Having lived here these past three months, I've witnessed firsthand Ruth and Verdok's love, and soon began to ponder the marriage that I myself have been blessed with."

The bard looked to his wife, and a curious smile formed on his lips. Mira's ears pricked up in curiosity.

"And so," the bard continued, "if it would please you all, I would like to treat you to the first performance of a song I've written over the past few months. It is the result of having watched, and being inspired by, the love and union of two good people that I count as friends, and the gratitude I have for the love of my life."

The crowd eagerly bade for the performance to proceed. Donovan, approaching Mira, offered both hands to her. With one, he took her lute and rested it against the side of their table. With the other, he led her to a seat beside Father Owen.

"This is for you, love," said Donovan warmly before turning to the masses. "Dear ladies and gentlemen, I present to you *The Bride from Santaru.*"

Mira's mouth fell open, and a warm blush filled her face as the song began. A gentle melody sounded from the gathered musicians, and Donovan, plucking his harp as gracefully as Vernid, played a gentle yet cheery tune as he began to sing.

O my bride from Santaru,
Most gracious woman of loving heart
That is as verdantly alive and fertile
As the blessed forest of your home,
You set my heart and soul to race with wonder
As to how such a woman could be,
And in undying thanks to Onu
For this blessing he has given me.
I deem that such a blessing
Will be utterly unmatched
Until the day that he might will
To welcome me back
Into the embrace
Of his eternal home.
O my bride from Santaru,
Most wondrous woman of grace and strength
That rivals the oaks and the alders and yews
And all other trees in your blessed home,
You set my heart and soul to swell with pride and honor,
That I should be the one to tread
Life's path by your side
As we journey to Onu
And pursue as close of a bliss
In this mortal world

To that which awaits us
In the undying realm beyond,
And make to give what good we can
Unto this world while it yet lasts.
O my bride from Santaru,
Most gentle woman of beauty and love
That is surpassed by none but that of the One
Who has blessed our union now and always,
You set my heart and soul to flood with thanks,
That all my life's journey has led me to you,
And that all the joys and pains we had whilst asunder
Will now guide us to share in the ones to come,
That we may never again laugh nor weep alone.
My thanks unending, to you and to Onu,
For the love of my life, the Bride from Santaru.

The song ended and the banquet hall thundered with applause. Mira, smiling and with her face glowing warmly, got up from her seat and stood before Donovan. The bard, looking up to her and grinning, shrugged half-modestly.

"I have to say that I feel like I'm in the same boat as Verdok was with his poem to Ruth," he said with a light laugh. "I feel that I managed to make it work with the tune I came up for it, but it still doesn't have the same sort of flow or rhyme as Uncle Jak had for his song to Yoranye, which I was trying to do for this. Like Verdok, I've been trying to piece this together for weeks, but I wanted to have something for you tonight, and it was either this or–"

She leaned over and kissed him. "I love it," she said.

Donovan smiled and returned the kiss. "All the same, I feel I may need to try and polish it up a bit sometime later."

98

3/28/4030 G.M.

ALLOR stirred from his rest, opening his eyes to see Talrah gently nudging his shoulder. Samuel and Lerannu were standing beside her, refreshed for the impending festivities. The king smiled and, playfully brushing his daughter's hand aside, sleepily rose from his chair in the family's private lounge. The waning light from the windows put the time at well into the evening.

"Time to head back?" asked the king.

"Just about," said Lerannu. "Sheeva said that the Davinurs have been sent on ahead of us a bit earlier, and that she herself needed to go over a few last-minute things with Mother and Ranoth. She said she'll be waiting in the throne room once she's done, and that we'll be told by Captain Thomas when she's ready. He and some more of his company will escort us back to the feast alongside some of our standard guard. Sheeva suggested that we go to the library and stay there for the time being. She already let Thomas know to look for us there once she's ready."

"Sounds good," he said. "I wish that Sheeva didn't trouble herself with any more today, though. Surely it could wait until tomorrow? Oh well, I guess it's better than if she didn't care at all."

Allor straightened out his doublet and walked with his children and longtime friend toward the library. They entered the reading room, each quickly finding a book they fancied, and were making to get comfortable when Samuel noticed something on the tabletop. Picking it up, he smiled.

"It's the flower-petal necklace I gave her earlier today," he said. "I'm going to go over to her room and put it on the table for her."

The prince strode briskly out of the library. Lerannu and Allor looked at each other, and smiles spread across their faces.

"Sam seems to have taken to her quite well, wouldn't you say?" asked the king.

"It certainly looks that way," said the mage. "I've been meaning to talk to Sheeva about that. It's still too early for anything serious, of course, but it's something to think about, no?"

"I agree," Allor said, "but it may take some time for her to warm up to the idea; you know how she is. Not that I can't understand why."

"Of course."

Talrah spoke up. "And what about me?" she asked in a joking tone of jealousy.

Allor and Lerannu chuckled. "Do you have anyone in mind?"

The princess shrugged. "I suppose not really, not right now anyway."

"I'm sure someone will catch your eye eventually." Lerannu said encouragingly.

A few minutes passed and a sudden rushing of footsteps outside the library startled the three readers. The door burst open, and the three bolted from their seats, shocked to see Samuel standing in the doorway. He was shaking uncontrollably, his face frozen in horror.

"Sam!" Allor exclaimed, running over to his son. "What in the world is—"

"Th-they're ... they're d-dead," the prince babbled wretchedly. Allor took his son into his arms, trying desperately to calm him. He saw that Sam held the ceramic flower necklace in a viselike grip in his hand. "THEY'RE ALL DEAD!" Sam wailed shrilly.

"Sam! Please, calm down! Breathe! Who's dead? What do you mean?"

"Ar-Arte, and h-her mother and father. They're n-not at the feast, they're in ... in their room. I-I th-thought that they m-might've been sleeping, b-but I touched Arte's hand and it was c-cold! So cold! Cold and st-stiff like a rock! They all were!"

Allor tried to speak, but the sudden grasp of dread that gripped his throat kept him from speaking. He made to comfort his son further, only to be taken by the prince's hand and led frantically out of the library and through the halls with Lerannu and Talrah right behind them. They reached the Davinurs' guest rooms, where the door was wide open, and went inside to find the east warden's family being lifted stiffly from their lounging chairs by several of the castle Peacekeepers. The young soldiers looked up at the four intruders, their faces an apparent mix of alarm and confusion. Lerannu and Talrah gasped, and Samuel buried his face into the mage's gown and wept. Allor stepped forward, looking intently at the young guardians of Fidonhaal.

"H-have you noticed anything about their bodies?" he asked. "Are there wounds? What in the name of—"

"I-I'm terribly sorry, my king," said the voice of a young man. Allor looked over and saw that it was Captain Thomas, the first of all the Peacekeepers. "I'm afraid you weren't supposed to be here, or anyone other than us."

Allor stared at the young man, dumbfounded. "What ... what do you mean, Captain?"

Thomas looked nervously at the king, and his eyes darted also to the mage and children behind him. "I ... I'm afraid I'm not at liberty to explain. Queen Sheeva explicitly stated that she was to explain everything to you at the wedding feast."

"What is she supposed to explain?" Allor asked frantically.

"Why the Davinurs needed to die," the captain said after a brief hesitation.

Allor felt his blood run cold. "Sheeva *ordered* this? How? Why?"

"To protect you, my king, and your children, and every other true Fidon of the world."

The king was instantly, and completely, overwhelmed by what he heard. "What, by Raakhaal's fires, is a *true* Fidon?" he asked shrilly.

"Zarons, my king. Pure-blooded Zarons, that is."

Allor stood, still as a stone, for one silent moment, unable to speak or move. He wanted so desperately to ask further questions, as he could not understand what would've possessed his wife to order such a heinous act, especially for such a mad concept. It was one that he had never heard of before in all his studies in history. He quickly realized that, given the Peacekeepers' sprouting presence across Fidonhaal, the world might soon be consumed by a mad war if Thomas was speaking the truth. He thought of all the people in the city and at the archtemple, feasting and reveling in celebration of the newlyweds and the coming of spring. Whatever had driven Sheeva to do this, so many of the people, according to what the young captain had just said, were not "true" Fidons. Shuddering with dread, the king slowly backed away, took each of his children by the hand, and spoke to them and Lerannu.

"We need to get out of here," he said in a low voice, "and get to the temple. We need to let everyone know, that we possibly can, about this."

Thomas made to approach the retreating four. "I understand that this is a shock," he said, "but you need to underst–"

"Stay back!" Allor growled with startling viciousness. "Don't come near us! Don't follow us, or I swear I'll claw your throat out! LET US GO!"

Thomas stared at them as they backed further away. The other Peacekeepers, lowering the bodies of Arte's family, put their hands onto their sword hilts, looking confusedly at their captain.

"Don't," said Thomas. "Let them go. For now, anyway. Someone go and fetch the queen. Tell her what's happened. We'll follow her orders from there."

Allor didn't wait to hear any more of the order. With his children desperately gripping their father's hands and trying not to trip as they ran, the king bolted down the corridors with Lerannu beside him and made his way down to the ground floor. The four then maneuvered through the castle halls and came out of the door leading into the gardens. There, they reached the wall that separated the garden from the path that led to the main road that descended the east hill. Not wanting to risk being accosted by guards who may be waiting at the garden's gate, Allor and Lerannu helped the children over the wall before clambering over it themselves. Allor then took Samuel's hand, and Lerannu took Talrah's, and the four ran down the road, racing down the hill and crying to all they passed that the queen had gone mad and that all should flee the city.

99

3/28/4030 G.M.

RUTH gazed up into Verdok's deep sapphire eyes, her hands running through his short hair and caressing his back. Her husband rested gently over her, tenderly holding her head in his hands and stroking her face. Having given themselves to one another, Ruth and Verdok had spent the rest of the afternoon this way, quietly reminiscing on their younger days.

Verdok kissed her for what felt to be the thousandth time, and as their eyes clasped onto one another once more, a thundering grumble sounded from his stomach. Verdok's ears flattened in embarrassment, and his eyes rolled in annoyance at the dampened romantic atmosphere as he pulled away from her for the first time in hours. Ruth giggled hysterically.

"Hungry, are we?" she asked once she managed to calm her laughter.

Verdok laughed sheepishly. "I have been since we were at the altar, but, well ..."

Ruth sat up and kissed him. "I know; it's been the same for me, but I'm definitely ready to eat now."

"At least *your* stomach was still patient enough to not spoil the mood."

Ruth began to giggle again, only to laugh all the louder, along with her husband, as her own stomach roared an instant later. She glanced at the dimming sunset light that shone through the window. "It's a good way into the evening, anyhow. I suppose we ought to rejoin our guests soon. Besides, the king and queen are likely to be back soon, if they aren't already."

"Fair enough," said Verdok. The two embraced one last time before getting out of bed, and Ruth saw a thin smile on her husband's lips. "As a priest," he said, "I must confess that I fear our bond is testing my faith."

"How so?"

"I'm having a hard time believing that Onuhaal will hold joy even greater than what I have now, as well as our bond being greater there than here."

Ruth smiled. She knew by his tone that much of this was him simply trying to be a flowery and jesting romantic. She also knew that he was more than a little sincere.

"I feel the same, but one day, when we've done our part in this world, we'll see for ourselves. Apart only from Onu, there's no one else I look more forward to spending eternity with than you.

Stand by me, and I'll stand by you, now and forever."

She held him close as a tear ran down her face. "I love you."

Verdok brushed the tear aside, blinking back his own. "I love you."

The couple wordlessly rose from bed, washed and dressed, and walked arm-in-arm to the banquet.

100
3/28/4030 G.M.

OWEN sat beside Mira and Donovan, listening to the song and music as he awaited Ruth and Verdok's return. As the bard and his wife finished leading the chorus and band in another song, they leaned toward the salpion and asked if the newlyweds had given any estimated time for their arrival to the banquet.

Owen shrugged with a laugh. "I cannot say when they'll be joining us," he said. "I'd think they'd be getting hungry soon, if they aren't yet. But they've been pining for this day a long time now, so your guess is as good as mine as to when they'll have–"

Donovan, having caught onto the growing sound of excitement that was spreading over the crowd, looked over to the main doors of the dining hall. He patted the salpion's shoulder and pointed toward the entrance. Owen looked over and smiled. As if on cue, the bride and groom had entered the hall, and already the guests were eagerly greeting them. Owen then raised his voice, calling for everyone's attention, and spoke as he made for his customary place at the high table.

"Dear guests! I am overjoyed to announce that the bride and groom have now graced us with their company! Please, greet them with your best wishes!"

The hall boomed with responses as the salpion beckoned Ruth and Verdok to sit beside him at the table. The two took a place on either side of him, and Owen, having poured them and himself some wine, called for a toast.

"Here's to the health of the new couple, and to all other bonds so blessed by Onu's grace!"

"Hear, hear!" the massive crowd roared as they drank.

Owen looked to Donovan and Mira, and nodded. The bard and his wife then called for a song of greeting and blessing for the newlyweds, and the first notes were sounding in the hall when the main doors burst open.

The hall became as silent as a tomb. All wheeled around to see who had arrived so abruptly, and gasped in apprehension as they saw the King of Enmayar, alongside his children and court mage, heaving for breath as he tried to cry out between sobs.

"E-everyone!" Allor cried. "You all need to leave, now! Leave this place! L-leave this city! Flee the country! Hide! Hide! The queen has gone mad, and she seeks to kill every Fidon who is not a full-blooded Zaron! R-run! RUN!"

101
3/28/4030 G.M.

ALLOR gasped and heaved for breath, sobbing wretchedly alongside his children and Lerannu as they ran into the center of the feast hall. The crowds stared fixedly at them, petrified by confused terror at the king's words. Salpion Lovonhaar rose from his seat between the bride and groom, and carefully approached the four panicked Fidons.

"Good King Allor," he said, "whatever is all this about? What do you mean about the queen?"

"I mean," Allor heaved, "that my wife ... has somehow let it enter her mind that all who are not fully grey of fur ... need to die, and the so-called 'Peacekeepers' are a part of it somehow! The queen has had East Warden Luthor Davinur murdered, along with his wife and daughter ... and the Peacekeepers in our castle stated that it was to protect the queen's family and all Zarons. They ... they said that Zarons are the only 'true' Fidons!"

The king heard the masses whisper incredulously to one another, as bewildered by the concept as he had been. The salpion looked deeply into the king's eyes, bearing the face of one who could simply not believe what was being said, yet knowing that there was no reason for the king to lie, outlandish as the claim seemed.

"Allor," he said as calmly as he could, "please, have a seat, you and the children, and the mage. Let's go over this slowly ..."

Allor saw Owen's eyes gaze worriedly past him, to something that was behind him. He turned, and his heart froze as he saw Sheeva standing in the open doorway, along with the stewardess and wardeness, Sarah, the castle priest, Ranoth, and a large company of young men and women armored in grey. The queen stepped inside, and the Peacekeepers entered the dining hall. A line of them barred each door leading out of the hall, and the others took positions throughout the chamber, grabbing guests by their clothes and herding them into groups. Those who appeared to be fully Zaron were held back from running to their friends and loved ones, who, not being of grey or fully grey fur, were separated into other groups encircled by Peacekeepers. The bride ran to the groom, who sat frozen in his seat in terror, and guarded him fiercely, her claws poised to strike and eyes glaring with protective, loving fury. Those who were making to approach Verdok backed away slowly at the sight. The salpion, with two Peacekeepers at his back, spread his hands peaceably and addressed the queen as levelly as he could manage.

"Dear Queen Sheeva, I'm afraid that your husband has told us of ... some most upsetting news, if he speaks the truth."

Sheeva stared venomously at the salpion. Allor looked at her, dread clawing at his heart as he saw her. She was dressed in a fine gown that covered a long dress of chainmail, which peered from the ends of her sleeves and the bottom of her dress. At her side, hanging from a sash that went around her waist, hung the Mivinaars' heirloom of a curved sword. The queen's hand rested firmly on the hilt, ready to draw it from the sheath in an instant. Her long hair was gathered into a tail, which peered from under the chain-lined, crown-like helm that she wore. Her eyes shined with an eager malice.

The king then burst into an incredulous fury.

"What is the meaning of all this, Sheeva? You had Luthor and his family murdered, and Thomas said you're meaning to kill everyone who isn't purely Zaron! Why? WHAT MADNESS IS THIS!"

The queen stepped forward, her eyes shifting from the salpion to her husband. The light in her eyes changed from a dreadful hatred to that of compassionate patience.

"Al," she said gently, "I'm so sorry that you had to stumble across the Davinurs like that. I suggested that you all stayed in the library for a re–"

"I DIDN'T STUMBLE ACROSS THEM, SAM DID! Your son went into their rooms to leave something for his friend, and found her and her family dead in their seats! What do you have to say to him?"

Sheeva looked at her son and daughter, who huddled tearfully around Lerannu as the mage looked on in utter disbelief. Allor saw his wife's eyes soften, and though she had clearly gone too far with her deeds, he hoped the queen would be moved to stand down before she did any more harm.

"They were meant to be disposed of quietly," she said with dreadful simplicity, in a tone that was clearly supposed to be comforting, "so there wouldn't be an additional difficulty here and now."

The children, rendered mute by the horror unfolding before them, wordlessly buried their faces into Lerannu's gown.

"They weren't a 'difficulty,' Sheeva!" Allor said, finally managing to bring his voice down from screaming. "They never were! They were perfectly good leaders of their ward, and I thought they were your friends!"

"I had to bring them here to remove them more easily. They were the only wardens who weren't Zaron, and–"

"That doesn't matter! Why would that matter?"

Sheeva's eyes still looked on with a sense of patience, and perhaps even a light of pity, as though he was simply not understanding something that should be making perfect sense. "Because they were Kason, Al. They're of the same people who butchered our families and friends, under the orders of the Kellmayarn monarchy, and I–"

"Kellmayar did *not* conspire against us, Sheeva! One man, one broken, angry man and his discontented followers did that! I thought you understood that!"

"You were deceived!" Sheeva said in exasperation. "They're liars, all of them, Kason, Mavon and Balon! They're all trying to supplant us, slowly but surely! That little Davinur *whore* was brought along with her parents to try and seduce Sam! They would've weakened us, little by little, and would've destroyed us in the end, if we didn't stop them first! So I had the Davinurs poisoned and–"

"Poisoned? When?"

"At tea. I made sure they took the right cups. I put it in myself."

"Sheeva!"

"It was a slow and quiet one. They would've felt tired, sat down to rest, and simply drifted away. It's more mercy than they would've shown us, and a far less painful poison than the one I gave to Nikolas and Halla."

Allor stood in disbelief and the guests in the hall were silent.

"You ... you *poisoned* Nikolas and Halla? But I thought you were helping Dr. Kamlof mix the medicine!"

"It was Xerzyn leaf. It brings almost the exact same death as that of one who dies from Endallian Fever."

"But you would've had to take that with you from the apothecary before you left to meet up with us in Oakhall! You prepared for it, but how? You couldn't have known that he and Halla were going to get sick!"

"No, but with the outbreak that was going on at the time, I figured it might have been believable that they were simply hit hard and suddenly by it. That they genuinely caught it only made the matter easier; no one questioned the cause of death."

"But they weren't the only ones there who ... Sheeva ... you murdered nearly their *entire* household, just to get to them? Why? Because of what Nikolas said to you in those letters? Sheeva–"

"You knew how cruel he was!" Sheeva said shrilly, tears brimming in her eyes. "And his mother was trying to undermine us! She kept trying to have everyone vote us off the throne! She would've torn down the entire foundation of our government and our progress, send us back to the days of the squabbling little kingdoms, all just out of spite!"

"But she was a Zaron, Sheeva!" Allor said suddenly, desperate to try and steer his wife away from her course, though she clearly had already gone too far. "Where does that fit into your idea of what makes a true Fidon?"

"She betrayed her kind, letting a Balon into her and bearing his son. Whether it was out of ignorance or for some twisted sort of bargain, I cannot say, but–"

"Sh-Sheeva ..." Allor said, trembling in horror, "you ... you can't be serious ..."

"It all began with Valor causing unrest in the south ward, did it not? He was in league with Kellmayar, with Ohdan, and was trying to starve our people! Make us too weak to defend ourselves! Then, when he was rightfully cut down and I was no longer a guaranteed pawn in their plans, they sought to make me out as a cheap harlot and undo all that my mother and father had worked for! And it's not just with the wardens and the monarchs, but even at the local level, and within the Temple, too!"

Allor stood dumbly, unable to respond, as Sarah and Ranoth stepped to either side of the queen. The king saw Sarah look to Lerannu, who stared incredulously at her as the mage realized that her mother was involved in this mad conspiracy.

"I can see that you don't understand, either," said Sarah calmly. "But think about it, Lera. There was that rotten whore Uriah, who broke our family in an effort to undermine the governance of our town. And then there were your teachers, who practiced necromancy in an effort to destroy us."

"Uriah and Father hurt us both," said Lerannu, "but not out of some conspiracy against Zarons. And Dalle, what she did was horribly wrong, but it was only because she was a broken, grieving mother. She just couldn't let Kiiva go. And Ahvrom ... he did worse, far worse. But it wasn't to enslave Zarons, Mother. It was to try and make a point on necromancy, and how not all who've used it meant to do any real harm, as wrong as it may still be regardless. Surely you can see that? It was all in the trial–"

"And they were lies," said Sarah with a horridly flat and unyielding stubbornness.

Lerannu stood utterly still and silent, her mouth wordlessly opening and closing as she tried to speak further.

Then Ranoth called out to the salpion, his voice heavy with bitterness.

"And you," he said, "you impressed my mentor and friend, and manipulated her into giving you the position that she had spent years preparing me for, with a whole bunch of acts that coddled the weak and hindered the rest of us. She was deceived by the comforting lies of Onu, who would leave everything in chaos. And you took the role of salpion as an agent to further the lies."

Allor looked to the salpion, who, with eyes shining of abysmal grief, looked calmly upon the three conspirators.

"And I suppose that all these revelations came to you from Raakaru himself?" he asked levelly.

"That's Lovaariinu to you, you lying snake," Sheeva snapped, "and it's by the help of his herald that we have finally come to see the lies and chaos that you uphold."

A sudden, horrible cold filled the room, and Allor, gaping in terror, saw a shadow materializing from thin air and striding to Sheeva's side. The guests screamed, Allor's blood ran cold, and Owen stood resolute before the demon and those who had fallen under its sway. Sheeva, Sarah, and Ranoth stood indomitably as well, and the Peacekeepers held their positions, expressionless as thralls that thoughtlessly awaited commands.

"My dear queen," said the salpion gently, his voice one of great sorrow and pity as he slowly approached Sheeva and her fellow conspirators, "Sheeva ..."

Allor's heart pounded unbearably within him. He could see Sheeva's eyes just barely showing a return of sanity, of a willingness to heed one who was not an agent of Raakhaal. Ranoth and Sarah, though not seemingly as receptive, nevertheless slinked away and interfered with neither the salpion nor the queen. Only the demon stood where it was, and even then, it looked as though it were struggling to maintain its sway.

"Poor daughter of Onu," Owen continued as he inched closer to Sheeva, his right arm now gently being outstretched, "you have suffered so much injury and loss in your time, and in your pain and doubt, a demon has sought to take you. It has driven you to grievous sin, and has filled your mind and heart with horrid lies and thoughts. We were made in love, and in love we are meant to live, but hate has gripped your heart in a most horrible form. But I can help you, child, as well as those who have fallen into darkness alongside you. Come to me, Sheeva Mivinaar, and listen only to my voice, and I will free you from the reins of Raakaru."

Sheeva stared fixedly into Owen's eyes, and the demon could now be seen clearly wrestling against the words that the salpion spoke. At last Owen reached her, and gently placed a hand on her shoulder. In a final effort to break the trance, the shadow from Raakhaal screeched and conjured a gust of wind that blew across all the hall. Sheeva blinked, and her eyes widened in fear and anger.

"DON'T TOUCH ME!" she screamed, frantically drawing her sword and flailing it in a broad arc before her.

The feast hall was as silent as the grave, and Allor's stomach twisted into an excruciating knot as the revolting sound of flesh slowly grating against flesh began to echo about the chamber. The salpion silently dropped to his knees, and as he fell forward, his head slid off his shoulders.

102

3/28/4030 G.M.

SHEEVA stood frozen, her arms locked in the position they had reached at the end of her strike. A horrid silence filled the room, and for an instant, the Queen of Enmayar felt a dreadful doubt touch her heart, one that reminded her of when she foolishly regretted poisoning the Greystones. She regained her conviction just as quickly, however, when she remembered all those like her who were wronged by the lesser and the mongrels. She turned to Raakmathna and her two trusted advisors, relieved to see on their faces the grim satisfaction toward the first of the justices to be served.

She then jolted to an earsplitting scream that sounded beside her, one of horror, grief, and wrath. Snapping her sight toward the scream's direction, Sheeva reeled in shock and frantically made to raise her sword in defense from the woman who charged at her. It was the bride, the Faithguard knight named Ruth Pionaar. The queen faltered, lowering her sword, and called out to the charging Zaron in an attempt to reason with her. Surely, if she could just explain the matter, the knight would not only understand, but swiftly join her side and aid her in doing what must be done.

"Lady Pionaar–" she managed to say before the bride was upon her.

Ruth leapt onto Sheeva, slamming her to the floor and wailing hysterically as she pummeled and clawed at her face. The queen screamed in agony and shock as Sarah and Ranoth, along with an older Kason woman of the Faithguard and even the groom himself, pulled the crazed bride off of her. Sheeva scrambled to her feet, aghast at the sensations of flowing blood, shredded fur and skin, and throbbing jaws and skull that overwhelmed her. Supported by Sarah and Ranoth, Sheeva looked to Ruth, who held tightly to her husband and the Kason knight as she glared with tears and hatred in her eyes.

Sheeva turned to Allor, who stood before the salpion's headless body with a face of immeasurable fury and sadness. She glanced behind him and saw Lerannu kneeling numbly upon the floor, with Samuel and Talrah whimpering frightfully as they clung to her. All others she could see through her bloody, swollen vision were frozen in their segregated groups, seeming to have been shocked into forgetting the Peacekeepers who corralled them.

Shrugging her advisors' hands from her shoulders and with a thankful nod to each, the Queen of Enmayar slowly approached her husband. Her heart was racing and her legs trembled as she anxiously neared him.

"Al," she said shakily, trying desperately to explain herself through her shock, as she knew he could not yet see the necessity of what had happened and what was to come. "My love, I know this is hard to understand, but–"

"WHAT HAVE YOU DONE?" Allor cried with violently quaking body and voice. "H-How? How could you do this?"

"This was for us!" Sheeva cried desperately. "For our children and our country! Everyone who isn't–"

"Twelve years," the king sobbed wretchedly, "twelve years bound to you, and I've been so blind …"

"You just don't understand–"

"There is nothing to understand of this insanity! Can't you see that the demon beside you wants to destroy us all? It's taken advantage of your past hurts and has led you down this path of madness!"

"Raakmathna serves the All-Keeper," said Sheeva steadfastly, "who has been fighting for order since the beginning–"

"Has madness gripped you so that you can't, or won't, recall all the times this sort of thing has happened before? And what about this 'Raakmathna?' Can you truly be so willingly blind? Hate is in her very name!"

"And those names with 'hate' in them, who pinned those names to these who wished for order? Themselves, or those who reject, indeed *hate*, the thought of order itself?"

"Sh-Sheeva," Allor said brokenly, having become wearied by his shouting, "you *know* why those names came to be."

"Yes, because they were condemned for wanting order, and wanting to eliminate the possibility for things like what Lerannu's teacher did to her, and what her father's advisor did to her family ... what Nikolas did to me ... to my family ... what Ohdan did ..."

Sheeva stared beseechingly into Allor's eyes, exasperated at his stubborn ignorance and dreading what may have to occur if he continued to reject her explanation.

"Al, you've been my friend, my most trusted friend, for eighteen years, my husband for twelve, and the father of my children for ten. All that time, you've shown me love, kindness, patience, and understanding unlike any I've ever known. Do you remember our first night together, what you said to me?"

"Every day," said the king tearfully, "as though it were yesterday."

"You've kept your word, as any good Fidon would, as far as I care. You've never hurt me, nor left me. You've shared in my pain and joy. If you ever hid anything from me, I won't hold it against you, for I've obviously withheld some things from you. But I did it because I knew you wouldn't understand at the time, and I didn't want to trouble you before–"

"You hid it from me, and the world, because you KNEW it was EVIL! What could conjure up such a thought as what you've nurtured, other than madness, hatred and evil, which has been fed further by a demon's words and selective memories of past wrongs by others?"

"Allor–"

"NO! NO MORE! The oath I gave that day, in private and before Onu and Fidonity, was to a woman I thought I had known since we were fourteen. But that poor girl died only a few years after I met her, and hate, lies, and murder have taken her place!"

Sheeva stared, baffled and heartbroken.

"Sh-Sheeva Mivinaar," Allor said wretchedly, his voice broken by the tears that choked him, "I-I renounce my bond with you, before all who stand present with us! I cast from me the Mivinaar name, and will not stand beside you ever again!"

Sheeva stood petrified, and utter emptiness consumed her. She felt a curious comfort envelop her, at the same time invigoratingly cool and calmingly warm. She turned her head and saw that Raakmathna was embracing her, as consolingly as a mother.

"Dear Sheeva," said Lovaariinu's servant, "I cannot believe this. I am afraid I have gravely misjudged your husband's character, and that of all these other Zarons here who I thought could be trusted. It seems that Ranoth and Sarah are still true, at least, as well as your Peacekeepers. Are they not?"

The queen looked to her advisors, who despite the creeping uncertainty that shone in their eyes, nodded and resolutely remained at her side. She then glanced around the feast hall and saw the assuring nods of every silver-clad soldier present.

"Good," said the agent of the All-Keeper. "Keep your word, and you will be rewarded beyond your highest hopes." She then returned to Sheeva.

"Perhaps," she said quizzically, "Allor and these others are not truly of the pure blood? Such taint, no matter how distant, would surely show itself in the end. But ... oh, no ... that would mean your children–"

"SILENCE, DEMON!" screamed the king. "BEGONE!"

"I do not answer to you," said Raakmathna, "you who would continue to permit chaos."

She then turned to Sheeva. "Dismiss me, if you would yield to them, my friend, and I will go. Command me, and I will stand by you, and we will set the world to rights. Or ... permit me to join with you, and you will have all my power, and we will bring even greater order to all of Fidonhaal!"

Sheeva stared into the shadow's glowing eyes for a silent, fleeting instant. She then took her friend's hand.

"I trust you," she said, "to gift me with your might."

"NO!" Allor screamed as hysterical uproar began to flood the banquet hall.

"Thank you, my dear friend," said Raakmathna tenderly. "I will not fail you."

Raakmathna then seized Sheeva by the top of her head, pulling it back forcefully. A horrid chill began to fill the queen, whose eyes darted about the hall, aghast at the faces of unfathomable horror that surrounded her. Sheeva made to protest, but her lips were frozen shut. Her flesh began to crawl as she felt a razor-thin incision begin to run down her belly. A hand, cold as ice and hot as fire, reached into her and began toying with her insides.

"You won't be needing these," said the demon with a horrid cackle.

Sheeva felt something pulled out from her, and her eyes widened in horror as she saw two helpless babes, still being formed, cast out from her womb and onto the cold stone floor. She looked upon those who would have been named Alphaar and Egrah, after the parents of the man she loved. She looked once more upon the horror-stricken masses, and was devoured by immeasurable regret and fear. The horrific sensation of the demon's essence now flooded into her from head to toe, accompanied by horns and spines that began to burst from her flesh. Her mouth, though now unhinged, was powerless to scream or to speak. Darkness began to cloud her eyes, and as she looked upon her husband one final time, her madness left her at the sight of his wretched face, soaked by tears and frozen into a hideous mask of horror.

She knew she had given in to her pain, her trauma, her anger, her darkness, and let an agent of Raakhaal corrupt her mind and heart, despite all the history and all the tales that should have warned her well away from such a path. She then knew that Raakmathna's machinations were only to spite Onu and creation, and were nothing to do with actually believing in what had been sown into her mind.

And she knew it was now too late; far too late. There was no going back now.

Allor's horrified countenance faded into the blackness that consumed Sheeva's sight.

Thus did the Queen of Enmayar perish, utterly steeped into the unfathomable horror and regret of the damned.

Part Four

The Flight to the North

Fleeing Genverdell

103
3/28/4030 G.M.

RUTH stared, paralyzed by horror alongside everyone in the hall as she witnessed the terrible possession and end of Queen Sheeva. In the queen's place now stood an abomination with eyes of fire, dreadful horns and spines, and a black, smoky mist that floated about her. The vile eyes darted about the room with impatience, then snapped onto the castle cleric and the stewardess, who gaped in awe and terror at the demon.

"Well, my friends," the demon screeched, "are you still with me, and will you take the rewards I grant you, or do you wish to join the others?"

Ranoth stood dumbly, simply nodding in agreement at Sarah's stuttered answer.

"I-I stand b-by you, my queen."

"I am not your Queen Sheeva, Lady Stonefaith," said the demon with a laugh as she beckoned the two conspirators to her side. "I am your *empress*, and my name is Raakmathna! All whom I have chosen, if you are still with me, declare it here and now, and you will be under my protection and that of Lovaariinu. Be silent, and you will meet the same fate as those I have marked for death!"

Ruth looked frantically about, and then she saw the face of each Peacekeeper in the hall. Her heart sank into cold despair, for each bore the face of one who, despite being appalled at what had happened, either saw it as necessary for the sake of order, or that it was now seemingly pointless to try and repent. Each raised their hand.

"We stand with you, Empress!"

"Very good!" Raakmathna cackled as she spread her arms regally. "Then what are you waiting for? Now is the dawn of a new era, and all your brothers and sisters around the world are now doing their part in the cleansing! Now is the spring of a new Fidonhaal! Let it begin!"

A blade was drawn and immediately followed by the sickening sounds of pierced flesh, a dying gasp of shock and agony, and the flowing of blood onto the floor. The series of sounds began to repeat in rapid succession. Screams and fighting erupted from the group of non-Zarons who were herded to one side of the room, as well as from the Zarons who made to intervene. At last, the paralyzing spell of terror had broken. Ruth frantically looked to Verdok and those around her, which included her mother, King Allor, his children, and the court mage.

"We can't stay here and fight them all as we are!" she shouted as they gathered to her. "We need to get to the armory, grab what we can, and get out of here!"

"But where will we go?" asked Arza as she took her daughter's hand.

"I don't know," Ruth sobbed desperately as she grabbed a candlestick from a nearby table, "but we can't be here!"

Some of those standing with Ruth also grabbed candlesticks or cutlery from the tables, while others simply braced to bull through any who tried to stop the group. As Ruth looked around, she saw Orson flailing a candlestick at the Peacekeepers who approached him, tears streaming down his face and screams of wrath tearing from his throat. The butchered bodies of his mother and father lay between the squire and those seeking to overpower him. Crying out to him, Ruth charged into the fray, smashing in the face of a Peacekeeper as she reached her protégé.

"They killed them!" Orson wailed furiously. "They're killing all of them!"

"Orson!" Ruth shouted as she clung to the boy's shoulder. "We have to go!"

"I can't just leave them!"

"You must! They didn't die just for you to follow right after them!"

Orson continued to fight, seemingly unheeding to her words, when he suddenly quailed at the sight of a bloody, limping Kason woman rushing from the crowd and striking down a Peacekeeper from behind.

"Hanye!" Ruth and Orson cried in unison.

The veteran Faithguard commander, shaking and wheezing as blood dripped from all over her, wielded a candlestick and table knife with terrible effectiveness. Two more Peacekeepers charged toward her and the company, and Hanye swiftly brained one of them while simultaneously putting out one of the other's eyes. The blinded one swiftly fell beside her comrade, convulsing horridly as her broken skull hit the floor. Hanye then grabbed Orson and put his hand into Ruth's.

"RUN!" she screamed hoarsely. "Get out of the city! Send for help! Get help from the other nations!"

"Come with us!" Ruth pleaded.

"Look at me!" Hanye yelled before coughing up blood. "I can't hold out much longer! Take Orson and go!"

"Commander–"

"GO!"

With a tearful nod, Ruth took Orson's hand and led those in her company as they ran to one of the side doors of the dining hall, weeping as she went. Others were crowding about the exit, fighting off the Peacekeepers who had pursued them, including the bard Donovan and his wife, Mira. Ruth called out to them, along with the others, as she knocked a young Peacekeeper lad off his feet and bludgeoned him. The crowd soon broke down the door, and apart from Donovan and Mira joining Ruth's company, all others scattered into the night, crying at the top of their lungs for all to flee the capital. The knight of the Temple, calling to those who still followed, then led the company through the hauntingly empty gardens and to the Faithguard armory.

104
3/28/4030 G.M.

LERANNU shut and barred the armory door, panting as she tried to catch her breath and fight through the fog of mindless terror that had devoured her senses since Sheeva perished and became possessed. All had become a nightmarish blur, and the mage had numbly followed the commands of the bride's voice as she and those with her fled the feast hall.

Now, being in a fortified location of relative safety, the mage's senses returned, and she became conscious of the hand she gripped with desperate, iron-like strength. It was Princess Talrah's. She let go and knelt down to her, speaking brokenly as she gently massaged the princess's hand.

"Tally, I'm so sorry. Are ... are you hurt?"

Talrah simply buried her face into her tutor's gown and sobbed. "M-Mother ..."

"I know ... I know. I can't believe it either."

Lerannu looked about, finally taking in the state of the company who had followed the bride and groom into the armory, as well as truly taking notice of who was in it. There was the bride, Ruth Pionaar, who was frantically trying to properly don the plate, chainmail, and surcoat of the Faithguard. Beside the bride was a young lad, the ring-bearer, whom Lerannu understood was also her squire. Both of them were now taking a Konothian axe and buckler each. Ruth's newlywed husband, Verdok, sat on a trunk of gear, his face buried in his hands as he wept inconsolably. A Zaron sister of the Temple, whom Lerannu believed she recognized from the ceremony to be the bride's mother, embraced herself shakily, looking at the grieving high priest while attempting to speak to him. The words seemed to be stuck in her throat, however.

Lerannu then noticed two strangers, a Balon man and another Zaron woman, who appeared from behind some shelves with two magnificent bows in hand, alongside a full quiver each and a sword on the hip. The two, having geared up, held each other closely, and Lerannu presumed the two were wife and husband.

The mage's eyes finally found Allor and Prince Samuel, who held each other and gently rocked back and forth as they sat on the floor, sobbing uncontrollably.

At last the sister of the Temple seemed to get through to Verdok, and the high priest, lifting his hands from his face, sobbed brokenly as he tried to reply.

"F-Father Owen ... and m-my grandparents ... all four of them ... I saw them ... if this has been planned to be all over the world ... then the rest of my family ..."

Verdok could go no further. Burying his face in his hands again, he began to weep quietly.

Lerannu held Talrah closely, looking on in silence as she desperately tried to piece together all that had happened. She eventually found the attempt to be fruitless, and looking about her, weakly attempted to clear her throat to address the company.

"What are we going to do now?" she asked tearfully. "Are we even ready, to do ... whatever it is we're going to do ... or try to do?"

All lifted their heads and looked to the mage. Ruth approached her, her squire at her side, and looked Lerannu squarely in the eyes.

"It's as Commander Hanye said: we need to send for help. Get word to the other nations and ask for their help to put a stop to this."

"Who's going to help us?" Lerannu sighed in exasperation, making a sound that was both a sob and a pitying laugh at their circumstances. "If Sheev–if that demon has planned for this to be happening all across the world right now, then there might be no one living who is in a position to help us. Besides, even if there were, if they were to learn of the ... '*reason*' ... behind all this, do you think anyone would help us? Enmayar has more Zarons than anywhere else. For all we know, all the other nations might think that every one of them is involved, including those in this room. You, me ... the king."

Ruth looked intently at the mage, her eyes sparking with a newfound worry that she had clearly not yet considered. The two then heard a deep, shaky sigh, and turning their sight they found King Allor, having risen to his feet, stepping forward as he addressed the company.

"If we are to sincerely attempt such a mission, then we must leave Enmayar, or find somewhere where we can send a heraldwing to the other nations. I fear I haven't the faintest idea where in Enmayar we could go that won't be occupied or watched, though. The Peacekeepers have had years to spread out over the country, and I doubt it would be wise to try and wander about hoping to find a settlement that wasn't under Sheeva's – Raakmathna's – control."

Lerannu looked about the room and saw all looking intently at the king as ones who were counting on his thoughts for a plan. Allor looked at the company, read their faces, and laughed desperately as he shrugged.

"I figure our best bet would be to try and reach the Whitemane Pass, and by that way enter Sorrenar, with Norkoth as our first prime destination. For all I know, the Peacekeepers may have total control there, or will by the time we reach it. But I certainly wouldn't hope to find an unoccupied port, or any other sort of town, here in Enmayar, so I don't know how else we might have a chance to get the word out. I ... I don't know what else to do ... unless we just fight and die, here and now."

Silence filled the room. Then the Zaron woman with the bow spoke up, checking her bowstring as she did.

"I know that I'll fight if I must, but not simply in resignation to death," she said resolutely. "Unless anyone else has another idea, I'm for the king's plan. If we are to make for the Whitemanes, though, I plead that we stop by my home along the way. It's in Santaru, so it wouldn't be in plain sight for those '*Peacekeepers*,' but I fear that if we don't warn my people, they'll eventually be found."

The Balon man stood beside his wife, looking at the company. "I ask we do the same for my home, if possible. It's near Norkoth, and if we could just see what's become of it, if anything, then I would owe this company greatly."

Everyone looked to the king again. Allor nodded to them, his face one of both understanding and sympathy for their worries, as well as a sort of resignation, as though he simply wasn't expecting the company to ultimately succeed anyway, and figured there was no harm to indulge the requests.

"Very well," Allor said plainly, "but what exactly shall be our route, if any have ideas on that?"

"Speed is vital for this, naturally," said the Balon man, "as much as can be done without completely exhausting ourselves or our mounts. Of course, the same is true for secrecy. I say we go on the roads whenever we can manage, and go cross-country when we must. Frankly, I wouldn't suggest any hard-set course, or timing for travel. I know that isn't assuring, but I feel this is something we'll just have to take and manage day by day."

Allor looked solemnly at the Faithguard knight. "It's just so risky," he said. "I don't know how many Peacekeepers we might encounter along the way, or where they'll be stationed or where they'll patrol, or how we'll manage to evade them if they spot and pursue us. I don't even know how we're going to get out of this damn city. It seems so hopeless as it is."

Lerannu stared at Allor, her sight blurring from the tears that surfaced. She blinked them back, and saw that all the others were looking at him in a similar way. The king drew his son close to his side, drawing a deep, resolute breath.

"But I'll take it over just staying here and resigning ourselves to that demon's plans."

Ruth turned again to the stores of the armory, returning quickly with a sword, a lengthy hauberk, and a well-padded gambeson.

"Then I implore you to arm yourself, my king," said the newlywed knight. Allor wordlessly nodded and took the gear offered him. The knight then looked to the others and gestured toward the armor that lined the walls and shelves. "If you can't, or won't, bear a weapon, then please, at least go over there and try to find some armor that will fit you, as well as some ration packs from the back storage. Also, especially those of you who aren't fully Zaron, be sure to cover yourself with a long coat or a cloak, and some gloves. And find either a full helm or a good-sized cowl. I've got an idea on how to get out of here. Be as quick as you can; we'll make for the Temple stables once everyone's ready."

A few minutes passed, and then all gathered at the armory's entrance, as geared up as they could manage. Quietly lifting the bar from the door, Ruth peered about the garden outside, then nodded for the company to follow her. She called for Allor and Mira to walk either side of her as fellow leaders of the party, given that they were not only armed, but also Zaron and thus had no need to hide their faces. The two nodded understandingly, and Allor, not wanting to have Samuel too close to the front of any fighting that might happen, had him go with Lerannu, who also kept Talrah to her side. The Balon man, whose name Lerannu since learned was Donovan, took up position in front of the mage and the children as a guard for them if any Peacekeepers managed to reach them. The bard had managed to find a large hood, and its shadow dulled and significantly darkened the brilliance of his snow-white fur.

With everyone now ready, the company stepped out of the armory and into the gardens.

They reached the stables, and Lerannu's heart sank as she saw four Peacekeepers standing guard. They easily noticed the company, who followed Ruth's lead as she continued to approach the grey-cloaked killers openly. Their eyes scrutinized them as they tried to assess the situation. Ruth raised a hand in greeting.

"No need for alarm," she said with a voice of eager duty as she pointed to her face to call attention to her grey fur. "Empress Raakmathna explained very clearly how necessary this all is. We are all Zarons of the Temple, and we've been tasked to serve the All-Keeper by seeing how matters are faring in the city and with a brief patrol about the surrounding land. These three young ones are our squires, and we're meaning to take them to one of the Peacekeeper camps for training. Might we have seven horses, or have you been given explicit orders to not let anyone be here? We'll understand if that's the case; we'll just ask the empress for clarif—"

"That won't be necessary," said one of the grey-armored lads with a smile and a calm wave of the hand. "We trust your word, sister, and all those in your company."

"Thank you," said the knight as she nodded to Allor and Mira. Lerannu caught the intent in the knight's eyes, and gasping distressfully for the prince and princess to look away, she pulled the children tightly to her side. She shut her own eyes, hearing the young Peacekeeper man's sudden cry of surprise, followed by the sound of weapons being drawn, a few seconds of the ringing of metal, and then four bodies falling in rapid succession.

Lerannu opened her eyes, feeling the children's bodies trembling against hers, and looked sadly on the four Peacekeepers who now lay dead or dying in the dirt. The company walked dejectedly past the fallen as they entered the stables. The mage glanced down at one of the bodies, that of the young man, who wheezed in agony as he watched each pass him by. She saw that the prince and princess were also looking at him.

"Don't look," Lerannu said in a sad whisper.

"My lady," Donovan said levelly, "I don't want to sound cold, but I fear that they're likely going to see more of this than you can help to shield from them, possibly even for this very night. If I may be blunt, I'd advise you to save your breath."

The mage said nothing and, leading the children into the stables, mounted up with Talrah in the saddle.

***

The company had ridden out of the archtemple's compound, with Talrah riding with Lerannu, Samuel with Allor, and Orson, Ruth's squire, riding in the saddle behind his mentor and wrapping his arms tightly around her. The others had their own mounts, and the company made its way toward Genverdell's north gate at as nonchalant of a canter as they could manage. The screams and sounds of fighting and slaughter that echoed across the city were unbearable to Lerannu, and she pondered miserably on how the company was leaving so many in the city to die for the sake of their mission.

They reached the north gate, which had been taken over by the Peacekeepers, and one of the grey-clad soldiers raised a hand to halt them. Ruth then played the same act as she did at the stables, apart from the surprise attack, for even the entire company, if armed and capable of fighting, would not have been able to take on the company of spearmen and archers that garrisoned the gate and adjacent walls. She politely requested for the gate to be opened, and the young lady in charge of the gate guard, saluting her, easily obliged. The company began to trot briskly by, with the first of them passing through the gate and out onto the wide road beyond.

Lerannu's heart leapt up her throat as she saw the black-and-white tail of Ruth's squire peer from underneath his cloak. It showed starkly in the light of the torches that glowed outside the gates. She heard Donovan gasp in despair as well. One of the guards posted just outside the gate drew his sword and yelled for the company to stop while others scrambled to either close the gates or seize the party. Lerannu and all the company charged frantically out of the gates. Ruth made her horse step aside on the road, striking down the guard who tried to seize Orson and yelling for the others to ride ahead, saying that she would cover their escape. Arrows and bolts began to fly from the walls, and the company charged down the highway as some of the Peacekeepers began to call for mounts. An arrow flew past Lerannu and the mage looked back, seeing Ruth and Orson riding right behind her and five Peacekeepers quickly mounting up in pursuit.

105
4/1/4030 G.M.

RAAKMATHNA stood in the midst of the archtemple's feast hall, looking at the salpion's headless body with satisfaction in the candle-lit, midnight-darkened room. She looked around the hall, appreciating the swath of corpses and pools of blood that were spread across the room. Most were Fidons who weren't Zarons, or at least not fully, though more than a few were of the Peacekeepers, and of those grey-furs who resisted.

It mattered not; the more death that could be inflicted upon these loathsome creatures so they might see their error in trusting the foolish, uncaring Onu, the better.

It was never about some preposterous concept of one's fur color designating their character, of course; she had simply observed the circumstances of the late queen's trauma, saw her intense hatred and instability, and just happening to notice that those who gravely wronged her weren't of full Zaron heritage, quickly pieced together an idea.

In truth, given that Fidonity had experienced all possible combinations of such heritages within the first few generations after their Awakening, Raakmathna didn't actually expect it to work, especially not to the extent that it had. The Fidons had fought and killed one another throughout the millennia since the days of Lovaariinu's reign, when the All-Keeper's point had been the most thoroughly proven. Their wars and murders had involved a myriad of prejudices wrought by differences and disagreements, but never before by something so superficial.

If only she, or one of her fellows, had thought to introduce the concept to one of these pathetic weaklings long ago, the Fidons might have already wrought their complete self-annihilation by now.

But it was no longer of any matter; the concept had now been brought about, and so far, the results had been splendid. Even if it didn't end up taking as deep a root as it might, in Enmayar or anywhere else, this incident alone would doubtlessly cast a great shadow of distrust on all the Fidons for a long time to come, if not forever. That being, of course, if they didn't completely destroy themselves over it soon.

All over a matter of outward appearance.

Lovaariinu would doubtlessly be pleased. The horrors of this, permissible by free will, would certainly prove once again the folly of Onu. Who knew? Perhaps this would be the one to break the foolish Maker's delusions, and at last drive him to surrender the will of all to the All-Keeper, as it should have been from the start, once Onu's carelessness and naivety had been revealed.

Raakmathna turned her gaze to the horror-stricken Zaron civilians who had cowered in their group under the Peacekeepers' guard. She strode up to them, relishing in their terror.

"If you wish to follow me to order and glory," she said, still meaning to push the plan as far as it could go and for as long as possible, "rise and stand beside the Peacekeepers."

Raakmathna narrowed her eyes as menacingly as she could. She enjoyed seeing the Zarons' eyes widen frightfully in response.

"And those who refuse to join the cause, you have twenty-four hours to flee and hide wherever you can, and then you will be hunted down like all the rest."

The herded grey ones quaked in silent terror. With all weeping, many resigned themselves to join the Peacekeepers, while others turned and ran. Raakmathna turned to the Peacekeepers and their new conscripts, approaching them as she prepared to address them. She paused as she saw a young officer enter the feast hall and approach. The officer gazed wide-eyed at the possessed shell of the queen, then hesitantly saluted, at a loss for what else to do.

"O-Officer Kysarba r-reporting from the company stationed at the north gate, my queen," she said in the voice of one trying to manage the terrors that she witnessed and partook in, having resigned herself to what had unfolded.

"Speak," said Raakmathna levelly, "and I am no longer Queen Sheeva, but Empress Raakmathna."

"A mounted company of ten escaped by the north gate, seven adults and three children. There were Zarons leading the company, armed and armored with equipment of the Faithguard. The leader of the party claimed to have been swiftly brought to reason in the wake of the cleansing's beginning, and that she and her followers had allied with you and were following orders to patrol a stretch of the country outside the city. The children, she said, were being taken to one of our training camps. We trusted her word, having had no reason to doubt a Zaron's word, and opened the gate. As they passed, we saw that the young one who rode with the leading lady had a tail that was divided into black and white fur. We tried to stop them and detain them, but they all charged past and even cut down one of our brothers. Five of our Peacekeepers have mounted up and are pursuing them, and others shot at them from the walls. One of my company insists that he got one of them with a shot, but it's yet to be confirmed, provided that the chance to do so comes to us. As I made my way to report to you, some of our other brothers and sisters told me that the bride and groom of the wedding had escaped the temple with some others, and we now presume that these are the very ones who have escaped the city. I'm sorry to have failed you by being so deceived."

"Do not worry about all that," said Raakmathna with an assuring nod. "If your riders manage to capture them or kill them, all the better. If not, someone else will. No matter where they go, our presence is there as well, or soon will be. They will not be in this world for much longer."

"Very well, my empress."

Raakmathna then turned to Sarah and Ranoth, who had remained fixedly beside her.

"Sarah Stonefaith, Stewardess and South Wardeness of Enmayar," she said, "The plans that our queen had revealed to you, I will continue if you are willing. Will you stand beside me as my archgeneral?"

Sarah stared silently, then her eyes darted about the hall, taking in all that had happened. Her eyes were those of both grim resignation and determination to rise high from the chaos that had been wrought.

"I will," she said steadily.

"My heart is greatly gladdened," said Raakmathna as she turned to the castle cleric. "Will you, Ranoth Windsbreath, rise and take the position of salpion, for which you so long had labored, only to be cheated by one of the parasites that plague the world, and use it to teach the worthy of the need for the All-Keeper's order?"

"I will," he said with a slight nod.

"My thanks," Raakmathna said calmly as she looked once more about the corpse-laden hall. "You both shall wait alongside me for further news from our operatives abroad, from which we shall determine our courses to come. In the meantime, send word to the smithies in the city. Tell them to begin work for the arms and armor of the growing ranks that serve the All-Keeper's order, those of the worthy breed and those ... repurposed."

Raakmathna then spread her arms, and letting the power within her flow about the city, raised her arms and looked satisfactorily at the swaths of rising dead that now stood to await her bidding.

"I would also like to have some of these people tested for aptitude in magic," she said as she turned again to the officer and waved a hand at the Zarons who still lived. "Those with sufficient talent, I would like them brought to me and some of my mages at hand for training. I have only been able to have a few who can work with the powers needed to maintain the more ... expendable portion of my armies ... at a time, and most of those I have already sent out into the world. Some more to help manage things here would be ideal."

106
4/1/4030 G.M.

ALLOR painfully gripped his reins, riding as hard as he could to evade the Peacekeepers who were now pursuing them. He pressed his arms as hard as he could upon his son's shoulders, bidding Samuel to lean lower toward the horse's neck and cover his head. He looked back frantically, seeing Donovan riding behind him and readying his bow to fire onto the five pursuers. Mira had taken up position alongside him and was making to do the same. Ruth, the knight, and her squire, Orson, were bringing up the rear. The two archers called out to the knight and squire, who ducked in strikingly perfect unison and veered slightly off the road as Donovan and Mira fired their shots.

One found its mark, striking the Peacekeeper in the chest with enough force to send him off his horse. The other narrowly missed its mark.

Allor looked ahead to see who was at the head of the group. Verdok was just ahead of him to his left, as was Ruth's mother. Lerannu was beside him to his right, with Talrah taking cover in the same manner as her brother. No one seemed to be taking point, as all were just following the road. The king wished to get everyone off the highway and try to lose the Peacekeepers across wild terrain, but he didn't trust the distances between those who were engaging the pursuers, along with their clear focus on combatting them, to be able to get their attention and give directions. He thus simply kept pace with the others, looking back again to see what was happening.

He turned just in time to see Donovan and Mira fire another two shafts. This time each of them took one pursuer out of the chase, with one clearly killing the target, having pierced his eye, and the other bringing down the horse of the other Peacekeeper. With only two pursuers left, Ruth and the squire eased back, letting one of the Peacekeepers charge up to her side. The grey-clad soldier tried to drive her sword into the pair and was met with a swift deflection by Ruth's buckler along with a horrid cleaving to the head. Allor heard Lerannu at his side, shouting out to Ruth and Orson to charge forward and rejoin the group, along with Donovan and Mira.

"I can take care of this last one!" she shouted over the thundering hooves that stormed around her. "Come on! Hurry!"

The three heard her and promptly bolted forward to regroup with the others. Allor looked on as he watched Lerannu fall back behind them. The mage looked intently at the ground ahead of the final Peacekeeper, gripping her hands like one holding a large hammer. Allor's mouth fell open in awe as the mage pantomimed the intense swinging of the hammer, drawing upon the power of earth and its mighty lady, and putting a sizeable hole into the road. The king winced at the sight of the Peacekeeper's mount clearly breaking a leg or two as it stumbled into the small pit, sending the rider flying through the air and crashing hard to the ground. The mage then rode up to Allor, visibly shaking in the saddle.

"Are you alright?" he called to her.

"Yes, my king."

"Do you have any tonic on you, or anything else like–"

"I'll manage for now, Allor; I'm not going to fall out of the saddle right now. I can wait until we get to somewhere we can hide."

"That'll likely be hours."

"I can make it."

Allor turned back to the rest of the group. Ruth had repositioned herself and her squire at the rear of the company, calling out that some woods lay a few hours out along the highway.

"I'm afraid that's likely going to be our best chance at finding a place to hide and rest for a while before we ride on," she said. "We can plan out our course more precisely there."

"Very well," Allor called back. "Let's go."

The company galloped on as the king glanced back one last time, seeing the distant lights of Genverdell disappear from view.

***

They rode on for three more hours, constantly looking around to see if any more pursuers were approaching. They were chased no further that night, however, and at last they came to the little wood that Ruth had mentioned. Looking behind them to make sure no one was following or watching them, they wearily trotted into the cover of the trees and made their way well into the wood. Allor looked about at his companions in flight.

"I suppose we should just rest a while and collect ourselves before making plans and moving on," said the king as he gestured toward some trees in the distance.

"If anyone wishes to speak to me, I'll be over there. But first, I'd like some time to speak privately with my children and Lady Lerannu."

"Very well," said Ruth understandingly. "I wouldn't mind doing the same with my husband and Orson."

Allor noticed Donovan and Mira looking wordlessly at each other. The two then looked to the king and nodded in agreement that some time alone or with those one held close seemed to be in order.

"Don and I will just make a few passes of the wood, make sure it's safe," said Mira.

The company then splintered off three ways, and Allor, riding over to the trees, patted his son's shoulder and kissed his head. The prince looked up to his father with teary eyes.

"Are we going to talk about Mother?" he asked weepily.

"Yes," said the king numbly, "and about any thoughts we might have as to what to do. We'll all get together and talk about it later, but for now I think we just need to–"

Allor and Samuel jolted in the saddle, and the king's heart sank painfully within him as a sudden howl of grief split the night air. It was Ruth, and her wailing was soon joined by that of her husband. Allor put an arm around his son, and looked to Lerannu and Talrah as they rode in beside him. He sighed and shook his head in sympathy.

"The salpion was like a father to them both," he said sadly to his children. "For him to die that way, I can't ... well, maybe I can, in a way ... I don't know. I ... Sheeva ..."

Grief at last gripped Allor's heart in full, more than it had when the company was preparing for their flight in the armory. Sobbing loudly, he buried his face in his hands and wept. Lerannu, having dismounted, reached up and grasped his arm. He looked to her, seeing Talrah holding her hand.

"Come down and be with both of them," the mage said simply.

Allor dismounted and took his children in hand. They walked up to a nearby yew, and sitting down against the trunk, they held each other and wept for a time.

"Mother," Talrah said brokenly, "we were going to have more brothers and sisters, if she ... if that evil thing ..."

"Yes," Allor said, a new and horrible grief coming over him as he remembered the sight of the two helpless babes being torn from his wife's womb and cast onto the floor by the demon. "You would've had two more siblings, maybe another brother and sister each, if your mother hadn't let herself ... if the demon hadn't gotten to her."

"They're gone now though," Samuel said numbly. "And ... and Mother, too?"

"Yes."

The three sat together, their tears now spent, and eventually looked to Lerannu, who stood quietly watching over them. After a while, Allor rose and helped his children back onto their feet.

"I'm going to see how Lady Ruth and her husband are doing," he told them. "Stay with Lady Lera and get some rest. I'll be back soon."

"Yes, Father."

Allor walked back to where the company separated, and seeing Ruth and Verdok sobbing in an embrace, he went to them to give his condolences for their loss of the salpion. As he approached, he took the scene in further and his heart crawled up his throat in dreadful realization.

Whatever grief that the knight and her husband still had for the salpion, it was doubtlessly not his death that had set them to wail so suddenly and so loudly, but that of the boy, Orson.

Ruth's haversack, which had been strapped to her back as the company escaped the city, was now slung over the saddle. The squire lay over it, pinned to it by the crossbow bolt that had pierced his throat. Verdok and Ruth looked up from their embrace, and Ruth tearfully recounted what she figured to have happened.

"It must have been one of the shots from the walls as we ran out the gates," she sobbed. "He's been dead this whole time! W-why didn't I think to put him in front of me like you did for your son? I failed him! I failed him and his parents! How could I have been so foolish not to think to guard him better?"

The knight began weeping anew, and her husband held her tightly as he tried to console her.

"You were overwhelmed with all that had happened," Verdok said tearfully. "We all were. We were all in a panic. It wasn't because you didn't care or weren't thinking at all."

"He's right," Allor said as comfortingly as he could. "I honestly couldn't tell you if putting my son in front of me was something I consciously thought out, nor would I just assume that for Lady Lerannu, with how she had my daughter in the saddle. You mustn't blame yourself."

Ruth, still sobbing, simply nodded as she resumed her embrace with Verdok. "Th-thank you, my king."

"Just call me Allor, if it please you, my lady," said Allor somberly.

The Daughters of the East

107

4/1/4030 G.M.

MIRA quietly crept past the trees alongside Donovan. Both had their bows and an arrow at the ready, and were intently scanning the woods around them for any possible threats. They figured the present likelihood of any significant danger was low, especially regarding the Peacekeepers. But not knowing for certain and simply desiring to not idle around as they spoke to each other, they were determined to canvass as much of the wood as they could manage. The two had heard Ruth and Verdok's mournful cries and had gone a little way in silence before speaking to one another.

"I'm almost inclined to say I can relate," said Mira softly, "what with Father and all, but ..."
Donovan nodded in sad agreement.

"Perhaps we'll talk to them about it when we get back," he said, "along with what we're going to do next. Not to mention, what about the king and his children? To see his wife ... their mother ... and the babes ..."

Mira wordlessly went up to him and gently brushed her face against his. They looked silently at each other, their eyes being as accustomed as they could to the dark, new-moon night, where only the stars, as many as there were, lit the sky and the earth beneath it. With neither needing to state their plan to the other, having already done the same many times over during their times hunting together in Santaru, Donovan and Mira split up, keeping just within each other's sight, and began to comb the woods. Mira's gaze pierced into the dark, looking for the presence of tracks and other signs of Fidon or beast that might indicate a peril to their respite. She and her husband crept along in silence for a little while. The huntress became half-aware of a light glowing in the distance, which had been steadily growing brighter as they continued through the wood. Figuring that the company had fled Genverdell at around midnight and that they had ridden for several hours before reaching the wood, Mira at first thought it was the growing light of dawn.

She had just begun to fully notice it, and realized the colors of the light were varied beyond those of the rising sun. In addition, she was facing west instead of east, and she noticed the light was coming from within the woods itself when Donovan quickly crept over to her.

"Do you see that light?" he asked.

"Yes," she said, explaining her initial thoughts. The two stood still for a few moments, looking intently at the shimmering, colorful light.

"I suppose we should have a look," Mira said at last.

They quietly went together through the forest, drawing ever closer to the light, which grew more dazzling and colorful with each step toward it. They at last reached a thick patch of undergrowth, beyond which was clearly the source of the light. Having made their way through the foliage and to the edge before the light, Mira and Donovan looked to one another. They agreed that whatever lay ahead likely was not dangerous, despite them not yet knowing for certain. Keeping their bows in hand, they put their shafts back into their quivers and quietly parted the branches and leaves of the undergrowth to peer ahead.

Mira's heart stopped and she heard Donovan gasp.

Twelve glowing faces stared right into their eyes, standing in the little clearing beyond as though they had been patiently awaiting their arrival and were expecting them to approach from that very spot. The colors that emanated from their forms played across the trees and foliage like the reflection of the sun on water, glowing as the hues of sunlit gems and sparkling silver and gold. Their eyes shone with solemn benevolence. They were the angels, all the host of the lords and ladies that served Onu. Mira and Donovan were rooted to the spot, utterly frozen by the indescribable majesty of those who stood before them.

After a moment of silence, with their bodies shining like silver and sunlit diamonds, Morinaar and Vitahla, hand-in-hand and holding their crooks, gently strode over to the bard and the huntress. The Angels of Death and Life gave the couple a gentle, melancholy smile, and nodded back toward the way they had come.

"Might we ask that you two go to your companions and bring them here?" asked Morinaar. "We desire to speak with you all."

"Y-yes, dear Morinaar," Mira said as she took her husband's hand and began to turn around.

"Thank you kindly, dear Mira and Donovan Greenheart," said the unfathomably beautiful voice of the Lady of Life. "We await your return."

108
4/1/4030 G.M.

RUTH and Verdok, having cleaned the wound on Orson's neck as best they could, now rested the boy's body against a tall oak, pondering what to do next. The dead squire's face, a clean split of black and white, was no longer covered by helm or coif. His handsome young face shown faintly in the starlight that reached through from the trees above, and his eyes, still open, looked silently up to the heavens. Ruth's mother, along with King Allor, his children, and the mage, Lerannu, stood beside the knight and her husband, looking on in silence.

"We haven't a spade to dig a grave," Ruth said mournfully as she knelt beside Orson and at last closed his eyes, "and we shouldn't risk discovery from a pyre's smoke. Then again, we don't really have what we need for that either."

Ruth went to her mother and held her close. "But I can't just leave him ..."

"I know," said Arza quietly, "but I don't know what else we can—"

The company started at the sounds of cracking twigs and shrubbery, and veered around to see Mira and Donovan, their eyes wide as saucers, emerging from the darkness.

"The angels!" Mira panted as she and her husband pointed back toward the way they came. "All of them! They're waiting for us to speak with them!"

The company stared at the huntress and the bard, completely taken aback by their words. The two soon regained their breath and took in the scene before them, looking incredulously at Orson's corpse.

"W-what?" Donovan asked in sorrowful disbelief. "What happened to him?"

Ruth recounted Orson's fate, to which Mira and Donovan both responded by insisting that Ruth was not to blame herself for what had happened. The knight simply nodded, though her heart was still gripped by guilt.

"But," said Ruth, trying to change the subject, "what was this about the angels? We ... we *did* hear you right, did we not?"

"Yes!" Mira said, "They're waiting to speak with all of us in the woods."

The huntress looked once more upon Orson's body, then to Ruth, Verdok and Arza. "I ... I hate to pull you away from this, my friends, but ..."

"Of course," Ruth said simply. "If Onu's host is calling for us, we ought to heed them."

***

The company soon saw the brilliant light glowing beyond the undergrowth, and with bated breath they followed Donovan and Mira past the foliage and into the clearing. Ruth stared in silent awe alongside her husband and mother, and the rest of the company, as she looked upon the majesty of the angels. All twelve of the angelic host looked upon them with expectant gazes, and gestured toward Vernid and Kyse, the angels of Spring and Autumn. The heavenly couple were seated upon a rock in the clearing. Vernid, famous as being typically the most joyful and playful of the angels, looked at the company in quiet sorrow in response to the horrors that were unleashed on the eve leading to the first day of his season. His wife, holding his hands lovingly, shared in his sorrow, for the south side of the world, having held the night in honor of her season, had doubtlessly experienced similar atrocities at the hands of the Peacekeepers stationed there.

The company approached them, and Vernid and Kyse arose, standing tall and majestic alongside their brethren. Ruth and her companions bowed reverently to them, to which the angels responded with a benevolent nod.

"We have come to this wood, on this night, to speak with you," said Vernid levelly, "for in the wake of the horrors that have been unleashed, hope yet lies in this company, but especially in Lerannu, Mira, and Ruth."

Ruth looked intently at the Angel of Spring, then looked quizzically to the huntress and the mage. "How so?" the knight asked.

"This is the time of a long-standing prophecy's fulfillment," Vernid explained, "that being the one for the Daughters of the East."

Ruth's breath caught in her throat. The knight's memories went back to her days in the archtemple's school, and the numerous times she had heard the reading from the Beldsantu's compendium of prophecies during Temple services, as the angels recited the words of the prophet Elukus Aganon in a grand, tranquil chorus.

"A wounded heart will fall to hatred and madness, goaded on by both the darkness within and a servant of the Hateful Heart. In secrecy and falsehood will they conspire great horrors, all to serve a hate defying all reason and unlike any other known before, which Raakaru will hold as another proof that his ancient call for freedom's end is just. The horrors will be unleashed on a day of life and love, tainting it with death and hatred, and they shall spread across Fidonhaal as the light of the sun, covering the world from east to west.

"But in this terror's wake will follow the Daughters of the East. Three women of Enmayar will they be, and their victory will be brought on wings of fire. By these women and all who stand beside them shall the mad hate be combated, and on them and their alliance shall rest the hope of Fidonhaal. They will be known by the mark they bear upon their brows, for they shall be of the Elect, should they rise to the call, following in the footsteps of those who first moved our hearts to return to Onu. Thus shall they share in the fate of all others who will be of Onu's chosen in the days and ages to come.

"The Daughters of the East, having risen with the sun, shall come to follow its course into the west, but not without first passing under the light of the Sapphire Star. Three men, out of faith and love, shall follow them out of the east, but shall then journey to the land under the Golden Star. By the joined deeds of these separate hearts shall Fidonhaal be united against the rising hatred. They shall then reunite upon the isle of our beginning, where they shall take fiery flight and return to the east, where the fate of Fidonhaal shall be decided."

Ruth felt her knees begin to shake, and she could hardly breathe as the angels looked upon her and her companions. Vernid stepped forward and lifted his hands graciously as he addressed the company.

"You already have the beginnings of your course," he said gently, "and, I sense, the will to see it through. None here blame you for the doubts that nonetheless lurk within you. We do, however, hope that they will be greatly lessened with this revelation. But of course, the fulfillment of this prophecy depends on the Daughters of the East accepting their task. Onu bestowed upon you the freedom of will, and trusts in you as he asks you to trust in him. We ask you now: do you accept this task?"

Ruth dropped to her knees and bowed faithfully. "I accept this task, and in Onu I strive to trust."

Mira and Lerannu shakily, but resolutely, repeated the knight's words to the letter.

Vernid looked to the others in the company. "Though you are not to be given the Mark," he said comfortingly, "know that, as Elukus said himself, these three women, despite their blessing, cannot take on the entirety of their mission alone. Will you go beside them, in heart and spirit if not always in body, aid them when you can, and trust in them, and in Onu, when you cannot?"

"Yes," Verdok gasped tearfully, "and in Onu I strive to trust."

All the others, from Arza and Donovan to Allor and his children, answered the same.

Vernid stepped back in line with the rest of the angelic host, joining again his hand with Kyse's. "Then let it be," he said as he and all the angels prostrated themselves upon the ground.

A great mist of white, silver, and golden light suddenly swept into the clearing, enveloping all within it, mortal and angel alike, in its embrace. Within the mist, Ruth could hear the beating of the heart, and feel the breath from the mouth, the gaze of the eye, and the touch of the hand of Onu. Her heart pounded in her chest, her breath stuck fast, and she quaked in the indescribable sensations of body and soul that the embrace of The One bestowed onto her.

"I have heard your acceptance and your efforts to trust in me, Daughters of the East and those who follow them," said the voice of Onu, which sounded as a gentle whisper, yet bore within it a power beyond all else in creation. "In my trust to you, I bestow upon each of you your role against the darkness spreading from Raakmathna, the servant of Raakaru. Follow them as you can and will, and in the end, I say to you, you shall prove victorious."

Ruth gasped and closed her eyes, her body tensing and relaxing at the touch of Onu's hand upon her head. The gentle touch of a finger traced upon her forehead the pattern of the Mark of the Elect, the same as the Uqua sign of the Temple, accompanied with the heat of a fiery brand that nevertheless brought no pain. The hand then gently touched her cheek in the affectionate way of a loving father.

"Rise, Daughters of the East," said Onu.

The three women stood up, and looking to one another gaped in awe at the Mark of the Elect that now graced their brows. They looked to those in their company, who, looking up from the earth, stared in silent wonder. The mist of light began to dissipate, and as it dispersed, Onu's last words to the company echoed into the night.

"Go forth, my Elect, and those who follow you. Trust in the path that lies before you, and you will not fail."

Ruth and the others looked on as the mist departed, turning their sight once more to the angels. Morinaar and Vitahla stepped forward, and raising their hands, brought forth seven familiar souls. All gasped, and Ruth and Verdok began to weep as the faces of Verdok's four grandparents, Commander Hanye, Orson, and Father Owen approached the company. Owen's spirit stepped forward, looking affectionately upon the Daughters of the East and their companions.

"Your grief is, of course, understandable," he said. "But please do not weep for us. We are now in the company of Onu and the angels, and are not to be worried over. You lot, however, as with all others still treading the path of mortal life, are still here, and much now rests on your shoulders. Let not grief for us weigh you down any further than can be helped."

"Y-yes, Father Owen," Verdok and Ruth said shakily, with all the others in their company nodding silently with tearful eyes.

Orson then stepped forward, and Ruth, no longer able to keep her composure, ran to the boy's ghost and fell to her knees, weeping as she made to apologize for her failure to protect him. Orson gently raised a hand, shaking his head as he bade his mentor to rise.

"You did all that you could think to do in the moment, Lady Ruth," he said kindly. "Now you have to go and try to save so many more than just me, though many of them, too, will fall before the end. Trust in Onu, for all will come under his will in the end, and what comes after will be forever greater than anything that happens in this world. I go now to rejoin my mother and father, and when the day comes that we see each other again, you shall see me as I would've been if I had become a man, along with all the other joys that Onuhaal gives to those who hold to hope and faith."

Ruth sniffed, stood up, and looked at her squire for the final time in her mortal life. Orson stepped back in line with the other spirits, waving to her in farewell.

"Thank you for all you did for me," he said.

Ruth nodded, then returned to Verdok's embrace.

The spirits faded from sight, and Morinaar and Vitahla, lowering their hands, looked gently into Ruth and Verdok's eyes.

"Do not worry for the remains of Orson," said Morinaar comfortingly. "You will return to find that his dust has now been scattered to the winds, with all he wore placed neatly under the oak. Go now, Daughters of the East, and those who stand beside them, and rest until dawn. A long path lies ahead, but will be run and finished if taken in faith."

"My thanks, Lord Morinaar," said Ruth tearfully.

Suddenly, King Allor stepped forth. "Dear Lord of Death," he said in a voice struggling to stay level, "my ... my wife ... what she did, guided by the demon but otherwise of her own will, was horrible beyond words, and her final sin cost her both life and soul. But given her pain and the madness it sowed within her, might it not be pleaded that ..."

The king, unable to speak further, trembled pitifully and stared pleadingly into Morinaar's eyes. The Angel of Death placed a comforting hand on Allor's shoulder.

"I am ... afraid I have my doubts," he said compassionately, "but I am not the final judge. I wish I could tell you with certainty, one way or the other, but that is not in my power."

"I should have asked Onu directly when I had the chance," Allor said regretfully.

"Hold her in your prayers, if you will," said Morinaar, "but I pray that you do not let what good and love there was between you, however true, cloud your sight to what has happened and what is to come."

Allor sighed deeply, looked to each angel in turn, and nodded.

The angels then lifted their arms wide, and a graceful, restoring wind blew into the clearing, soothing the pains and weariness of body and heart that had burdened the company since their flight from Genverdell. Ruth closed her eyes, cherishing the sensation, and when she opened them, the angels were gone.

***

They returned to where Orson's body had been placed and saw that it was as Morinaar had described. With nothing else to do but rest, all of the company wished one another as good a sleep as could be had before the nearing dawn, and made off in varying directions for their desired measures of solitude and companionship in rest and contemplation. Ruth and Verdok, placing their bedrolls under the oak where Orson had rested, sat silently together in each other's arms.

"So, then," Verdok said at length, "it would seem that our quest has even more weight to it than we first thought."

Ruth laughed lightly, then sighed moodily as she reflected on the great commission that she and her newfound sisters in purpose had been given. "It would seem so."

"I'm with you, in any and every way that I can be."

"I know."

They kissed, and then leaned on one another in silence. Eventually, Ruth felt Verdok's body begin to shake, and presuming that grief had returned to his heart, she pulled away to brush aside his tears. He was laughing.

"Well," she said inquiringly, "what's this about?"

Verdok looked deeply into his wife's eyes, an endearing grin upon his lips.

"This was certainly not the wedding night I had in mind," he said with a chuckle.

Ruth pinned him to the tree, playfully swatting at his shoulder and tussling his hair as she, too, began to laugh.

"I feel the same," she said.

Chuckling quietly, the two rested together, hand-in-hand, as they made to prepare for the long journey ahead.

109

4/1/4030 G.M.

RAAKMATHNA stood beside Sarah and Ranoth in the growing morning light on the balcony that overlooked the castle's main courtyard. There, all the Zarons who had survived the night's pogrom and could be pressed into the yard had been herded in by a bolstered army made of the willing Peacekeepers, conscripts, and the horde of undead. All the other Zarons were pressed to stand as close to the courtyard's gates and walls as possible in order to hear the empress's decree.

"Zarons of Fidonhaal," Raakmathna announced, "the time for your submission to weakness and chaos is finally at an end! Now is the time for a Fidonhaal that houses only the worthy, those who will value and honor order!"

The courtyard and the city beyond were utterly silent.

"In order for this mission to be realized," the empress went on, "it is of the utmost importance that all traces of the lesser be wiped from the face of Fidonhaal. Not one spot of fur that is tainted by the colors of the Balon, the Kason, or the Mavon can be suffered to endure for the sake of our future. Henceforth, all citizens of the Zaron Empire are subject to examinations of body and heritage at the Peacekeepers' discretion. All who are certified as proper Zarons will then be examined for their skills and allotted roles for the service of their people. Refusal to comply with examinations or duties will be seen as a sign of impurity, and will therefore be punished by death. This punishment is also the lot for those who would harbor the impure in secrecy, and those abroad who, when contacted by the Peacekeepers, refuse to be escorted back to Enmayar for evaluation. Companies of Peacekeepers will be dispatched throughout all of Fidonhaal to state these articles to those beyond our capital's walls so that none may claim ignorance of them."

Raakmathna looked intently at all the Zarons not yet clad in the colors of the Peacekeepers, who wordlessly looked in resigned despair at the undead and the grey-clad soldiers who surrounded them.

"One final word," she said. "Those who fail or betray me and the Zaron Empire in life will serve in death."

The Zarons' eyes widened, and a few hushed gasps sounded from the masses as they looked again upon the lifeless eyes of the horde that penned them in on all sides.

"That is all," the empress concluded. "Long may the Zarons live in security and order!"

"Hail, Empress Raakmathna!" the Peacekeepers shouted resoundingly, followed by the whispering snarls of the undead thralls.

The rest of the Zarons looked about in miserable silence, which quickly ended when they were beset by the threatening points of weapons held by the empress's forces.

"H-hail, Empress Raakmathna!" the masses shouted in shaky voices.

The Journey to Plen

110
4/18/4030 G.M.

ALLOR rode alongside the Daughters of the East, this time with his daughter, Talrah, sharing the saddle, as the company followed the road that skirted the edge of Santaru Forest. They had ridden as hard as they could manage for eighteen days, having embarked on the first of the month after their rest in the wood where they spoke with Onu and the angels. They had avoided all the settlements they saw on the road and thankfully managed to avoid detection by the companies of patrolling Peacekeepers, even if at times narrowly. They had been able to stay on or near the roads far more often than the king had dared to hope, and otherwise went undeterred through the countryside without being pursued as they were on the night they fled the capital.

But they were at it for hours on end unless they had to stop and hide, and at times rode either from dawn to dusk or dusk to dawn. Rations were tight enough to begin with, and were soon even more desperate. The company had to turn to what vegetation could be had in the early springtime along with the occasional bit of game that they managed to hunt along the way.

Allor confided to Lerannu that if it were not for the revelation of the prophecy's connection to their quest, he, and perhaps all the company, might have lost all hope some time ago. As it was, all in the party had continued to journey onward with hope, if wearied hope, in light of the Elects' blessing and marks, and the roles that all the others had been allotted in their company. All had since shared the stories of their lives with one another, and were quick to grow in trusted companionship in their Onu-blessed task.

Now, having reached the edge of the great forest under Mira and Donovan's guidance, the company looked into the forest for a cairn or other familiar landmark to ease the party's navigation toward Plen. They had spent several days and nights along the road bordering the forest, debating regularly as to where would be the best place to enter the forest for as direct a route as possible. They knew they would soon reach the western coast, and the presumably Peacekeeper-occupied port of Greenharbor, if they did not turn into the forest soon. They stopped in their tracks to discuss whether or not to simply ride into the forest and trust to coming upon a familiar trail in time, along with the benefit of Mira's greater familiarity with Santaru than the rest of the company.

Suddenly Talrah, tugging at her father's arm, pointed to a pillar of smoke rising above the trees along the road's edge not far ahead. Ruth, Donovan, and Mira rode a little ahead, analyzing the smoke carefully.

"It looks like the burning has mostly stopped," said Donovan. "It looks too large for a camp, unless it's one with several fires, like what the Peacekeepers might use. I guess it could be from someone who doesn't know about what's happened, but I doubt it."

"So you'd bet that it's likely their handiwork, be it a camp or a place they've burned to the ground?" asked Ruth.

"Aye."

"But what would be out here, along the forest's border and only a little ways from a major port?" Mira asked curiously.

Allor started in his saddle from the memory that struck him. "An inn," he said abruptly, making all in the party turn their heads to him. "There's an inn nearby. Sheeva and I once ..."

"Of course!" Ruth and Donovan both said in recollection. The bard then looked to Mira.

"Do you remember the inn we stayed in on our way to and from our wedding?" he asked.

"I do now," Mira said in realization. "It was named after a wisp or something, right?"

"Yes," Allor said sadly as memories of days gone by, and of the journey that definitively unhinged his wife, began to return unbidden to his mind. "The Glowing Wisp, to be exact."

The company looked at the pillar of smoke in silence.

"Well," Mira said in a less than hopeful tone, "if that's what was there, I doubt it's there now."

"But even so," Donovan pointed out, "there is that marked trail that leads right to Plen just behind the inn ... or whatever might be left of it."

"True, but should we risk it? What if there's still Peacekeepers about?"

"Then we either fight them if we can or ride on into the forest. They might follow us, but presuming it would be only a patrol group at worst, I believe we could easily outmaneuver them, or otherwise devise a way to ambush them in the forest. Or, I suppose, we could just ride into the forest from here, and surely we would find the trail soon enough if we otherwise go in the same direction."

The party looked to one another, pondering what to do. At last Ruth spoke.

"If that smoke is the work of Peacekeepers," said the knight, "then I would doubt that they'll be lingering. Even if they were, I keep thinking about how we just left all those people in Genverdell. I know we had no chance at the time, but if we were to take a chance here ..."

All exchanged glances with one another, none seeming to outright oppose the idea, though also not fully inclined. Eventually, Allor realized that all were looking at him.

"What say you, my king?" Ruth asked.

Allor looked to the pillar of smoke, then back to the company. His eyes lingered on the brows of Ruth, Mira, and Lerannu. At last, the king simply shrugged and adjusted the sword set into his belt.

"I follow the Daughters of the East," he said calmly. "I will trust in their decision, and in their abilities and those of their companions."

The company voiced their agreement to the three Elect. And Mira, readying her bow and arrows, looked intently to the knight.

"I'm for it," she said.

"As am I," said Lerannu as she began to close her eyes and breathe steadily, trying to prepare for whatever spells she might need to cast.

The party then entered the very edge of the forest, and following the road's direction, they made their way toward the smoke.

Soon, they came to the smoldering ruins of the inn, and peered from the cover of the trees and bushes to examine the scene. The stables were still standing, though empty, and the horses had been gathered onto the road by the company of Peacekeepers that had commandeered them. Several corpses littered the grounds of the inn and the road. One was a woman of what appeared to be Kason and Zaron heritage sprawled alongside a Zaron man, and a girl who appeared no older than thirteen. The girl was also of brown and grey fur, and the company presumed they were a family.

Another man they saw dead, fully Mavon from what they could make out, and two Balon women. But there were four Fidons who were still alive, bound and lying on the road as the bulk of the Peacekeeper company awaited the return of a comrade who was scrutinizing the site for any hiding survivors. These captives appeared to be a family as well. There was a woman of mixed Balon and Mavon heritage, her face and body white as snow and her hair solid black. Beside her was a Zaron man, and alongside the adults there were two boys, seemingly in or nearing adolescence, with varying patterns of black, grey, and white fur. All four wore aprons over plain and practical clothes, apparel befitting ones who worked in an inn.

Allor turned to the company. "I remember that man and woman," he said. "They're the innkeepers, and those two boys must be theirs. I don't know why they're being kept alive, but if we want to save anyone we can here, we shouldn't wait. I can see seven Peacekeepers. Does anyone else see more?"

The party scanned the area as best they could. All agreed on seven.

Allor placed a hand on his daughter's shoulder. "Tally," he said gently, "I need you to stay with Sam and Sister Arza here in the trees. Don't come out until we say so, and if there turns out to be any other Peacekeepers out there, and they find you, call out to us as loudly as you can and run. Understand?"

"Yes, Father," Talrah said worriedly. Allor kissed her head, and nodded toward Samuel and Ruth's mother as they rode their horse further into the forest. Talrah quietly got down from the saddle and joined them. Allor then drew his sword and looked on as the others prepared for the fight. Donovan and Mira nocked arrows to their Arbonyn-wood bows. Ruth readied her axe and buckler.

Lerannu breathed deeply in preparation for whatever magic she would need to work. Verdok braced to employ his martial arts. When all were ready, they looked to Ruth and Allor, and nodded.

The king and the knight rode together, leading the rest of the fighting party out of the forest as they hollered a confrontation to the Peacekeepers. The grey-armored killers started at their call, readying their weapons as they scrutinized the company. The leader, a young man no older than twenty, stepped forward and pointed his spear at Allor.

"What business have you to meddle in our mission," he demanded, "and with parasites in your company?"

"I *was* your *king*," Allor barked menacingly, taking the officer aback, "before my wife fell into utter madness and became possessed by an agent of Raakhaal! I and those in my company will not stand for this vileness! If you value your lives, release those you have captured and run. Cast aside your arms and grey raiment, and take no further part in this evil!"

"You were indeed my king," said the officer as he recomposed himself, "but no more. The time of kings and queens has passed, and only an empress, and an emperor if one proves worthy of the title, will lead the world from now on. By order of Empress Raakmathna, Herald of Order, you have been declared an enemy of the people, as are those in your company, regardless of their heritage, for—"

"*Sir*," Allor said in a voice that sent a chill through his own bones, "unhand those people, surrender your arms and armor, and turn around. I will *not* say it again."

An instant of dreadful silence followed, then the officer, his confidence returning as his soldiers drew closer to him, planted his feet resolutely into the dirt of the road.

"We are not to release the prisoners, for they are high-priority targets of the empress. Her loyal servant and archgeneral, Sarah Stonefaith, has requested these four to be arrested and brought to Genverdell for justice dealt of her own devising. She was gravely wronged by—"

The officer's words were cut short by Allor's battle cry, which the king yelled as he pointed his sword at the Peacekeepers and charged forward. Ruth charged beside him, and as the Peacekeepers scrambled to get away, the king and the Faithguard charged into them and cut down two that were making for their horses. They turned around to charge again, but Allor's horse was cut down as he passed, and the king fell crashing to the ground. He scrambled to his feet just in time to dodge the thrust of a Peacekeeper's spear, and was about to strike back when two arrows pierced the grey soldier's heart. Ruth now stood beside him, and Verdok had dismounted and sprinted to aid them both.

Mira and Donovan had also dismounted, and were advancing toward the company for closer shots, as another Peacekeeper made to slash at Verdok. The high priest nimbly dodged the strike, and Ruth swiftly punished the soldier with a cleaving to his chest that crushed through his chain shirt, followed by a finishing stroke to the neck as he went down. Allor suddenly felt a stabbing pain in his thigh, and looked down to find a shaft buried in it. He looked up and saw the Peacekeeper who fired it. She had backed away from the fray and taken up her bow. Allor was just about to point her out to his companions when Donovan and Mira's shafts struck true once again, piercing the grey-clad archer's side and throat.

Only two of the Peacekeeper squad remained, the officer and a young woman. The female soldier swung her mace at Verdok, who swiftly ducked beneath the blow and dealt a sweeping kick to her feet, knocking her to the ground. Verdok then kicked the mace out of the soldier's reach, and pinned her down by pressing his foot firmly onto her chest, keeping her alive as the rest of the party turned their attention to the officer.

Allor yelled out to him. "It's just you who's left, sir," he growled through gritted teeth from the pain in his thigh. "What are you going to do now?"

The king had barely managed to finish his sentence before the officer roared and swung his blade, barely missing Allor's face. A small ball of focused wind suddenly flew into the officer's side, sending the sword flying into the grass on the roadside. The officer, trembling, raised his hands in surrender.

"Arza!" Allor heard Lerannu call out. "Sam! Tally! You can come out now, it's over!"

Allor heard the rustling of distant foliage as his children and the Temple sister approached to rejoin the company. His thigh was stinging horribly. His eyes fell again upon the slaughtered Fidons whose "crime against Fidonity and order" was not being of fully grey fur. He then turned his sight to the innkeepers and their children, still bound and terrified. His sight then clasped onto the face of the officer, who had overseen the cruelty executed at the site and ordered the deaths of those who doubtlessly had the same sort of face that he now bore. He thought of the demon, that being of utter evil, and the cruel manipulations it did to the woman he loved. Memories of another Fidon's cruel butchering of good people flooded his mind, along with the wrath he had felt when it happened.

Without a word, Allor grabbed the officer by the shoulder, pulled him forward, and drove his sword into the grey-coat's chest with all his might. The armor's plating buckled where the sword pierced. The officer gasped in terror and agony. Allor drove the sword in again. The chainmail under the plate snapped and the officer painfully begged the king to stop. The sword was now wedged into the armor, just piercing the skin. Allor drove the blade upwards and pulled the officer down onto it with one final, horrid force. The officer screamed. Lerannu screamed. Samuel screamed. Talrah screamed. Gasps of shock passed from the lips of those around him. Blood began to flow out of the armor and onto the hilt of the blade and the hand that held it. Allor threw the officer down and looked upon him, his eyes afire with wrath as the soldier sobbed and coughed up blood.

"ALLOR!" Lerannu cried. "What's wrong with you?! I disarmed him! He surrendered!"

"The people he killed here weren't armed at all," Allor said hollowly. The king then knelt beside the officer, staring into his eyes with piercing contempt. "How is it," he asked bitterly, "to throw away your life in the name of such senseless hatred?"

The officer stared back into Allor's eyes, his face the picture of agony and remorse. The grey-cloaked murderer let out a single, sob-choked gasp, rattled wretchedly, and lay still and silent. A lone tear flowed down his cheek.

Allor stood, rooted to the spot and shaking violently, as distant, nightmarish memories of Ohdan's pleas for mercy going unheeded began to flood his mind. He remembered how he himself laughed in the brigand's face as he begged. He remembered how he butchered him. He was a raging monster. He was still a raging monster.

He felt Lerannu's gentle touch upon his shoulders.

"Al-Allor," said the mage worriedly, "come over h—"

Allor bolted upright, sending Lerannu reeling in fright. He walked swiftly to the charred rubble of the inn, and seeing a burnt beam from the rafters lying nearby, he kicked it with all his might. The pain from the arrow still in his thigh shot up his body excruciatingly. The king fell to his knees, letting out a long and horrid howl of anger, pain, and sorrow.

111

4/18/4030 G.M.

LERANNU stared at the king as he buried his face within his hands. The mage felt the prince and princess clinging to her, shaking in fright from what they saw their father do. She looked to Sister Arza and saw her looking on somberly at the scene in front of them. She then heard a young woman weeping in fear and realized it was the one surviving Peacekeeper of the squad who lay pinned to the ground under Verdok's foot. The high priest promptly removed his foot from the young grey-clad soldier, and stepped back as the party let her rise onto her feet. Her tear-streaked face clearly showed that she had no further desire to fight. The Peacekeeper stood frozen in fear, waiting to see what the Elect and their companions were going to do next.

Allor's weeping ceased, and Lerannu looked to see him slowly get up, turn around, and approach the Peacekeeper with the gravest of faces. The king looked piercingly into the Peacekeeper's teary eyes.

"Will you leave your arms and armor, now," he asked in a voice of weary grief, "and leave?"

"Y-yes, s-sir," she sniffed. She then tossed aside her mace and dagger, and took off her chainmail coat and grey uniform. In her light pants and tunic, she looked one last time at the company and turned away, running and crying down the road to Greenharbor.

"My money's on her telling everything to every Peacekeeper at the port," Donovan said moodily.

"I wouldn't be surprised," said Ruth with a sigh as she walked over to the bound family and drew her dagger to cut the ropes that tied them. The Zaron man in the family spoke.

"A thousand thanks, my lady. I had begun to wonder if I was the only Zaron in Fidonhaal who hadn't fallen into this insanity."

"No, good sir," said the knight. "I assure you, there are far more who aren't in on this mad plot than those who are, but those grey-cloaked killers, and the demon who commands them, have doubtlessly overpowered the ones who would rise against them."

"So, this 'Empress Raakmathna' that I heard those grey-coats mention, is she the demon leading this horrid campaign? What about our queen?"

Ruth sighed sadly as she unbound the last of the family. "The demon has taken the queen's body; Sheeva Mivinaar is no more."

The family looked at the Faithguard in numb silence.

"We can explain things tonight," Ruth went on, "once we stop to rest."

Lerannu spoke up. "I think we should rest now, or at least soon, and for the rest of the day, with Allor wounded and all."

"You're right," said Ruth. "Let's get that arrow out of him and bandage it up, and just go a little way into the forest here. If the trail to Plen is as easy to find and follow from here as Donovan and Mira have said, we should be able to rest nearby until tomorrow before going on. Even if that Peacekeeper tells any others at Greenharbor about us, she still has to get there, and that would be a good day's trip even on horse, and then another day for a company to get back here. We should be well away by the time they would arrive."

Ruth and Verdok brought Allor with them behind the stables so they could remove the arrow and bandage the wound without making a scene in front of the rest of the company. Lerannu, meaning to go with them, took Samuel and Talrah's hand.

"Your father is hurt, and not just from that arrow," she said gently to them. "I know it was scary seeing him like that, but I'm sure he'd appreciate it if you were with him now. But if you don't want to—"

"I'll go to him," said Samuel, seconded by his sister, "but ..."

"But what?"

The prince leaned in closely. "That lady is looking at you very strangely," he whispered.

Lerannu glanced back to the innkeeper family, fully noticing the wife and mother of the family, and her appearance, for the first time. The mage froze in her tracks as memories of days long gone began racing through her mind. The woman had a beautiful face, with fur white as snow, crowned with long, flowing hair that was purely black. The divide between her white-furred body and black hair was perfectly clean, and her eyes were blue as the sky. Her face was almost angelically perfect, save for a few scars on her left cheek. The scars were of the sort that would form from a violent strike across the face by another Fidon if they had used their claws.

"Uriah ..." Lerannu said in an almost trancelike tone.

The innkeeper walked slowly to her, looking at her with eyes of fear and sorrow. Lerannu bade the children to go on to their father, and the two women stared at one another in silence. At last, Uriah spoke.

"You ... you aren't with your mother? You don't want to—"

"No," Lerannu said flatly. "I've moved on from that. At least, for the most part. And besides, there's no justifying this madness, nor of ... whatever it was that Sarah had in mind for you or your family."

"I'm so sorry," Uriah said as she began to weep. "Your father loved you and your mother so much, but as the years went by and the two of them began to be pulled apart by differences on how they felt Bravagoth should be managed, he just began to feel so alone at times ... and ..."

"I get the picture," the mage said, truly understanding the reason, yet bitter at the sudden reopening of the old wound. She looked at Uriah, weeping with her face in her hands, and saw her husband and sons looking on quietly. It was clear they already knew and had come to terms with the story quite some time ago. The mage nodded to them kindly. "If you know of any good place to hide from all this, go there and wait for news of any changes. My companions and I are set to do what we can to end this demon's campaign, and hopefully there will not be many more days to it. If you don't have a place to shelter, though, come with us, at least until we reach somewhere safe. Maybe

Ovistar would be a good place–"

Uriah suddenly wiped her eyes across her sleeve and knelt solemnly on one knee as a gesture of service.

"I will do whatever I can to aid the Elect and their company, however small a deed, if they will have me. I do this for the Elect, and for the world they're charged with defending, as well as to try and amend the wrong I have done to one of the Elect personally. If you will have me, then in your company I will go."

Lerannu looked at the rest of Uriah's family, who stared incredulously at the sudden realization of the brand on the mage's forehead. They then wordlessly took a knee and looked at her and those still in her company.

"And we will go with her," said Uriah's husband, "and aid her in aiding you."

The two boys echoed their father's words.

Lerannu took the hand of each in the family, helping them to their feet in turn.

"Let's go and see how Allor is doing," she said simply.

***

It was now midnight, and all the company had fallen asleep a short way into the forest. They had cleaned and bandaged Allor's wound. The arrow had not pierced too deeply thanks to the king's well-padded chausses. The first cairn that marked the trail to Plen was in sight, and the company took its greatest ease since its flight from Genverdell. They informed the innkeeper family, whose surname was Queniroth, of the happenings that had passed that fateful Veronmay Eve. The Queniroths, having learned of the Elect's commission and plans, resolved to accompany them, led primarily by Uriah's determination.

In the tree-filtered light of the waning moon, Lerannu abruptly stirred from her sleep and looked about. All in the company were resting quite well, with all the married couples sleeping calmly in their respective spouse's arms. Uriah and her husband, Harvus, lay peacefully together, and their boys, Evor and Ethos, slept quietly nearby. But then Lerannu noticed that Talrah and Samuel were sleeping alone. Their father had been resting between them when all had gone to sleep, but now the king was missing.

Lerannu quietly got out of her bedroll and looked about anxiously for any signs of the king. Seeing nothing, the mage resolved to sit and wait a while before panicking.

"He might just be relieving himself or something," she thought.

The minutes crept by as the silver-white of the moon shifted over the camp. The mage thought of Allor's wretched state after the battle, and then of the stories of people, high and low, who could not rebound from such events. She could bear to wait no longer. She rose and began to canvass the nearby trees and foliage as carefully as she could, with dread at the thought of finding him hanging from a bough or lying impaled on his sword beginning to fill her mind. As she searched worriedly, she eventually became aware of a blue light glowing in the distance. She neared it, and saw silhouetted against it the telltale pillars of stone that marked an ancient druid's garden. She could just make out the now-empty stables and charred remains of the Queniroths' inn in the distance beyond the garden.

When she finally reached the encirclement, she found Allor sitting on a rock, looking at the little moonwisp that flitted about the central stone. Lerannu recalled the times when Allor mentioned his stay at the Glowing Wisp with Sheeva on that ill-fated journey to Kellmayar. The sad gaze that the king gave to the wisp said it all. Lerannu quietly sat beside him, watching the wisp and taking in the comforting sensations that its glow gave to those who looked upon it.

"I guess you know what makes this spot so special to me ... and painful?" Allor asked quietly.

"Yes."

"Lera, I'm sorry that I ..."

"You were hurt and angry, and you did what you did. It's over."

"I thought the same, when I butchered Ohdan to pieces. I was horrified with myself. I thought I would never needlessly kill another like that, when they were disarmed and pleading for mercy. I told myself it was over then, but ..."

"It would seem that this is a time for pains of the past to revisit us," Lerannu said with a moody laugh, "or at least a couple of us."

"I suppose so," said Allor.

"We're in this together, Al. You and I, and all the others. I have my task to do alongside my sisters in fate, but you and everyone else are no less a part of it in the end. I'm with you."

"And I'm with you."

Lerannu then became aware of Allor's hand holding her own. She could not say who was the one to put their hand in the other's. She looked into Allor's eyes, smiling affectionately as she withdrew her hand.

"And," said the mage, "if we prove victorious and are still standing in the end, and life carries on as before, more or less, then perhaps I'll be with you then as well."

Allor smiled and nodded, and the two sat together silently for a while, watching the wisp as it flew and danced about the stones.

"I loved her so much, though," said Allor quietly as the wisp began to fade away, having had its fill of nocturnal frolicking.

"I know," said Lerannu gently.

The two wordlessly returned to camp, and Allor resumed his place between his children. Lerannu picked up her bedroll and placed it next to them, lying down and soon falling asleep.

112

4/19/4030 G.M.

RAAKMATHNA strode into the center of Genverdell's main square with Ranoth and Sarah on either side of her. It was early in the morning. Surrounding them were four stakes that had been erected and piled with kindling. Three stakes had a member of a Zaron family bound to them: a mother, father, and boy of ten years. Tethered to the fourth was the one that the family had foolishly tried to hide from the Peacekeepers: a woman of entirely grey fur but for thin bands of brown that marked her shoulders and legs. All four had been stripped to the fur, their heads bowed in pathetic resignation that only the blind sheep of Onu would practice. They had all wept and pleaded in the dungeon, but now were silent.

They wouldn't be for long.

The square and the adjacent roads, streets, and alleys were overflowing with people. They were all kept in place under pain of death at the hands of the Peacekeepers and throngs of undead that stood and patrolled among them. Surprisingly, Raakmathna could see that a few of the Zarons were genuinely eager to see the proceedings, not counting those whose minds were nurtured under the tutelage of the Peacekeepers. There must have been others she had overlooked, those who had also borne grievances for which they were happy to adopt the thoughts that she had awakened. The rest stood about in fearful misery, looking on silently, as they felt either powerless to act or that it would be in vain to revolt.

Raakmathna looked to Ranoth and nodded to the Salpion of Lovaariinu to pass the sentence. The figurehead of the Temple of Order stepped forward and looked upon each of the condemned.

"You have been condemned to death," Ranoth said to the Kason-Zaron woman, "for the wrongs of your ancestors and all your Kason kin. These crimes have been known to include conspiracy against a peaceful effort for diplomacy by a foreign power, and regicide, as evidenced in the attacks on the Mivinaar dynasty as they were traveling through Kellmayar. In continuation of your kind's deceptive ways, you guiled your way into the protection of a Zaron family, who now follow you to death for their folly. Do you have any final words?"

The woman said nothing, and Ranoth then turned to the Zaron family.

"You have been condemned to death as punishment for your foolish treason against the Zaron Empire. Rather than immediately surrender this tainted Fidon to the authorities, you refused to acknowledge the wrongs committed by such people and let yourselves be swayed to hide her. Our empress, Raakmathna, has already declared that such would be the fate of any Fidon, even those of the righteous race, who hide the unworthy. May your deaths be a lesson to all present that our empress does not make idle threats!"

A mumble came from one of the condemned. Ranoth looked about angrily.

"What was that?" he demanded.

It was the Zaron man who had spoken. "That demon is not my empress!" he shouted. "And *you* are not my salpion! May Raakaru take the lot of you when justice finally comes to you, and may he subject you to agony that is a thousandfold more than ours!"

All who were bound to the stakes, though silent, raised their heads and stared at Ranoth, Sarah, and Raakmathna with eyes alight with defiant scorn. Ranoth turned to his empress, who beckoned him to return to her side. Once he did, Raakmathna simply waved her hand across each stake, and they immediately burst into flame. The four condemned rent the air with their screams and curses, which soon ceased into deathly silence. The empress waved her hand across the charred wood and ashes, and the flames swiftly died out. She then raised her hands and gazed upon the blackened, reanimated bones and charred flesh that shambled up to her. The burnt corpses' empty eye sockets where now alight with the fire of her commanding will. She turned her sight to a Peacekeeper captain standing off to one side of the square, who promptly stood before her and saluted.

"Lead these to the armory," she said.

"Yes, my empress."

***

Raakmathna now sat upon her throne and inquired her archgeneral of any further news from their forces abroad. Three days ago, the empress had received word that none of the other national capitals had been fully captured and cleansed during the Veronmay Eve attacks. While a fine measure of damage had been dealt, all of the Peacekeepers who were not slain within their assigned city were driven out, prompting them to besiege the capitals.

Having bolstered their numbers with the corpses that their accompanying necromancers had reanimated, the Peacekeepers were now trying to formulate other plans for breaching the capitals and finishing what they had started. Raakmathna, though satisfied with the damaging legacy from all that had happened thus far, was nonetheless intent on pushing it as far as could be done. Thus, she was waiting intently either for plans devised by her forces and their following request for approval or a simple request for reinforcements, which she was more than happy to oblige if it would progress the campaign.

"Has further word come from any of the forces, Archgeneral?" she asked Sarah.

"None yet," she answered, "though I can't say when to expect it. Aside from the varying times for a Shanlof to fly from one place to Genverdell, there's no telling how long it will take for our forces to either form a plan and request approval, or otherwise request more troops. For all I know, the setbacks on all three fronts have already been overcome, and the next thing we'll hear is of all the capitals falling to us."

"Very well," said Raakmathna patiently. "Just have someone looking for incoming messages day and night, and inform me as soon as you receive any further word."

"Of course, my empress."

"Very good. And rest assured that your service will be rewarded with the vengeance you seek. Any time now, we will hear of the capture of the strumpet who broke your home, and she and her family will be delivered to you to await whatever manner of justice you deem fit for them."

"Thank you, my empress."

Raakmathna nodded in dismissal, and the archgeneral saluted and departed.

113

4/23/4030 G.M.

MIRA finished her breakfast with the company. Once all had packed their supplies and mounted up, the huntress and her husband again took the lead as they continued their journey to Plen. Judging from the tranquility they had seen in their past five days of riding, it appeared that Santaru had not yet been violated by the grey-coats' presence, at least not in any deeply invasive way, and Mira was confident that her home had not been razed by them. Nevertheless, her heart was greatly worried for her family and people, and she was moody at the thought of returning to them with such grave tidings when the occasion should have been one of happy reunion. Donovan interrupted her flow of thought.

"Are you alright, love?" the bard asked.

"Yes," she answered. "I'm sorry, I was just lost in thought. Were you saying something to me?"

"Just asking if you had noticed how Lerannu and the king have been getting on. She was a friend of Allor's family for years, a teacher for their children, so I figured they were close, but–"

"I have noticed that. The circumstances are certainly not typical, considering what happened to the queen, but if we make it through all this, I hope that–"

"If?" Donovan asked concernedly.

Mira looked into her husband's ice-blue eyes, which looked lovingly into hers, wordlessly imploring that she would say what was on her mind. The huntress sighed, then turned her head about as she marked the next cairn that lay ahead on the trail before speaking.

"Do you believe we can do this, Don?" she asked quietly. "I know we've been given Onu's blessing, but this hatred that's taken hold of the world ... it isn't quite like anything that's happened before. I would think the closest thing to it would be what happened during the Inquisitions, since it brought a hatred and distrust into the world unlike anything before that time as well."

"And that has passed in time, too, has it not?" Donovan remarked. "Even a wound dealt to the world such as that can mend in time."

"Yes, at least overall, but ..."

Mira and Donovan slowly came to a halt. Mira could sense the rest of the party stop, and not approach them, as if they could tell that the bard and huntress were wanting what privacy they could have at the moment. Mira looked to the forest floor, well-cloaked in leaves and twigs that had weathered winter, as she resumed confiding.

"It's still not quite the same, and I just don't know if the world can overcome this, with the damage done by a hatred so ravenous and unbridled, once Raakmathna and her minions are dealt with. I'm worried this wound might end up even deeper than that of the Inquisitions, somehow, even if we succeed. And I'm afraid I have my doubts if we can even succeed with this mission as it is."

Donovan leaned over to her in the saddle and gently caressed her cheek. His eyes bore soulfully into hers as he assured her.

"It *can* be done," he said with gentle resolve. "Onu would not have bestowed the Mark to you, or anyone, if it was impossible to defeat this. I am sure of it. You, and Ruth and Lerannu, are the first Elect to be seen in Fidonhaal in centuries. I cannot grasp the designs or will of Onu in full; no one can. But I've no doubt that those he chooses for his Elect will succeed. They've never failed before."

Mira's eyes began to blur with tears as she continued to gaze into her husband's eyes. "Not every one of them survived their quest to the end, though, nor those who followed and aided them."

Donovan tenderly brushed away her tears. "You're right," he said, "and that may well be the fate of some in our company. Maybe you. Maybe me. Maybe all of us in the end. But if the mission is ultimately accomplished, will it not be worth it, for us and all of Fidonhaal?"

Mira smiled and nodded. "It's just so hard sometimes, to keep faith, even when ..."

"I know. It's funny how that goes. In a maddening way, that is. Just know that I believe in you, not only as your husband, but as a follower of the Elect. I believe in Ruth and Lerannu, and all the rest of us who follow you and your Elect sisters."

"Th-thank you," Mira said with a gentle sob.

"It's no trouble, love," said Donovan with a gentle, assuring laugh. "You're welcome."

"I'm sorry."

"There's nothing to apologize for. It's happened to the strongest of us before, and is a part of the path of faith."

Mira kissed Donovan, then sniffling and drying her eyes, turned smiling to the rest of the company.

"Sorry for the holdup!" she called cheerily. "If everyone's still good to keep going, let's try and put in a good ride today. If we cover enough ground, we'll be just a few more days before reaching Plen!"

The company followed the huntress and bard in good spirits, riding on well past dusk.

***

The company had finished their dinner, such as it was, and were resting together by the small fire they had made. They were talking together over a little of everything, from ideas for future courses of action to bits from their life stories. Suddenly, Evor, the eldest of Uriah's two sons, jumped up and called alarmingly to a distant rustling in the forest. All scrambled up, their weapons at the ready, as they called out to the source of the noise to show itself, if it could comprehend them.

"Is Donovan and Mira among those I hear?" inquired a friendly, wooden voice.

Mira and Donovan lowered their bows in unison, laughing in relief as they turned to assure their companions that all was well. A minute passed, and the company was soon greeting a tall, handsome Arbonyn with a branch protruding from his forehead like a horn.

Mira stepped forward and shook Rovnillath's hand. "It seems that Onu wishes for you to meet Don and I as much as possible," she said with a grin.

"Maybe so," said the tree-man. "Glad I am to see you again, but apprehensive seems you and your company. Is there something amiss?"

The party told the Arbonyn of the happenings since the ill-fated celebration of Veronmay's Eve. Rovnillath frowned greatly by the tale's end, and shook his head sorrowfully at the tidings.

"Most troubling this is," he said, "and not eager am I to tell this to my kin. But let me give one comfort to you, that safe is Plen from these soldiers of hatred. Still would I advise that you stay to your plan to have them follow you in your flight, to that citadel in the Whitemanes, if no further."

"We figured as much," said the huntress, "and indeed, such has been our plan so far, but your words are appreciated all the same. Take care."

"And you as well," said Rovnillath with a bow.

Before the tree-man turned away, however, Mira, remembering her bow, retrieved it from her gear and showed it to him.

"And thank you for the limb," she said with a smile. "It made for wonderful wedding gifts for the both of us."

Rovnillath looked at the bow admiringly, his wooden face creaking lightly into a satisfied smile. He nodded warmly at it and at Donovan's bow, which the bard presented alongside his wife's.

"Very glad am I," Rovnillath said as he departed, "that they have served you well. Farewell."

114

4/26/4030 G.M.

DONOVAN sighed heavily with relief as he and the company came in sight of Plen, which reluctantly revealed itself in the darkening light of the forest evening. It had been raining since noon, and the chill of early spring, heightened by the descending sun, had been wearing on the Elect and their companions. Smoke rose from the chimneys of the village feast hall, telling the party that all in the village were taking dinner. With no further word, the company galloped into the village and came to the dining hall's doors. All dismounted as Mira knocked soundly upon them. Ann was the one who answered. She started with joyful surprise at seeing her returning daughter and son-in-law, and turned back to call to the dining villagers.

"Mira and Don are back!" she said happily, with the feast hall booming with cheers in response. Ann then turned back to the bard and the huntress, opening the door and gesturing for them and their companions to come in.

"You're all soaked, you poor things! Come on in, we've plenty to eat! Isaak has been on a roll with hunting since you've been gone, and there's venison and boar aplenty to go around! I am quite eager to hear about your friends there. How many of you all are there? I'm sure we'll have enough; I just want to ..."

Ann, finally getting a good look at her daughter by the light of the hall's grand fire pit, suddenly went silent. Her eyes widened at the sight of the Mark on her daughter's brow. She then looked the whole company over, staring in awe as she noted Ruth and Lerannu also bearing the Brand of the Elect.

"Mira ..?" she asked in a small voice. "Wh-what's all this?"

"We've come to tell you," said Mira calmly as she led the party into the hall and pointed out places for them to sit. All the village gaped at them in reverent silence. Ann soon came to them, handing a horn of the village's wild honey mead to each of the Elect and their adult followers as they ate from the plates on the tables. When they had finished eating, the company told the villagers of their flight from Genverdell and the happenings that had followed, as well as their plans to evacuate the village and have the people escorted to the Whitemane citadel of Ovistar. When all had been told, Ann looked to Mira and Donovan.

"I agree that we should take precautions and take shelter somewhere safe," she said, "and Ovistar sounds as good a place as any, but what of the other villages here, and the free-roamers? Surely we won't be leaving them to this demon's evil?"

Donovan glanced at Mira, who looked understandingly at her mother, but with a face of somber resolve. "If we're to try and help them," she said, "then we should send out a few small groups, have them find who they can, and tell them what's happened. Then they can lead them to Ovistar, or somewhere else. But my Elect sisters and me, and those with us, we cannot stay here and wait, and I can't stand to just leave you all here to wait for them. Our mission relies on as much speed as we can manage. We cannot stay long."

"I understand," said Ann somberly. "Very well, I'll have some folks go out, if they're willing, to try and get word to whoever they can, and have them regroup with us at Ovistar. But what about you all staying here tonight? Surely that can be done; you all look like you sorely need a good rest under a roof."

Mira looked at her companions, laughing in agreement at their imploring faces.

"We'll risk a night's stay here ... and perhaps one day after, for everyone here to make sure they have what they need for the journey."

The company then relished their first good meal and rest since their flight began, and rested well the following day.

From Plen to Norkoth

115
4/28/4030 G.M.

RAAKMATHNA read the messages from the forces at Zefiil, Norkoth, and Benhotha that had flown in earlier that morning. The Peacekeepers at Zefiil, at a loss for devising a plan with their current numbers, had sent a request for reinforcements from Enmayar to aid them in breaching the walled and river-spanning city. The forces stationed at Norkoth and Benhotha, while remaining in a stalemate, were still looking to see if they could manage with their present soldiers.

The empress was quick in deciding what to do. She turned to Sarah Stonefaith, who had handed her the messages.

"Would you care to lead some of our forces directly in the field?"

Sarah saluted dutifully. "Gladly, my empress."

"In just over a month's time, on the first of Yorrek, I want you to lead all the Peacekeepers and undead that are gathered here in that time to Kellmayar, to Zefiil, and help our army there break the siege and take the capital. You are to march from here to the port of Okrenar. I would send you to Kannah, but that is our central shipbuilding site at present, and trying to embark from there with an army the size we are planning to send would doubtless hinder the armada's progression. Once you have reached Okrenar, sail for Vahnon's Landing and follow the highway southwest from there to the capital. Wait for a heraldwing that I will send to you. I will send it early in Yorok, as you should be at least in Kellmayar by then, and should it reach Zefiil before you, it will wait until you arrive."

"Begging your pardon, my empress, but how so?"

"I will be sure to have control of it," Raakmathna said plainly. "Once you have reached Zefiil and the Shanlof has reached you, you will receive your orders ... and some of my power. Execute the orders immediately upon receiving them, and you will be able to take Zefiil. Once you have succeeded, send word and hold the city until I send further orders."

"As you command, my empress."

"Very good. You are dismissed for the present."

Raakmathna then turned to Ranoth, who stood attentively beside her. "Will we begin the sermons for order soon, along with how only the Zarons are capable and worthy of it?"

"I'm ready to give them whenever you're ready to begin, my empress."

"Good. Let us go and call the city to the Archtemple of Lovaariinu then, and begin."

116
5/6/4030 G.M.

ALLOR rode at the head of the train of riders, which now included the villagers of Plen since they had all left for the Whitemanes seven days ago. Lerannu and the other two Elect rode beside him, as did Samuel and Talrah, and the Queniroths. The mage and royal children were taking care of Novon Tillok, Mira's baby nephew, as the huntress and her family conversed with the king and the Elect. It was now late in the afternoon, and the start of the great pass that ran through the mountainous isthmus, and the road that ran by it, was visible through gaps in the trees. As they exited the edge of Santaru and came onto the road, the company trotted with ease down the road of the pass, and soon saw the first settlement of the people who lived there. All seemed peaceful from what they could see.

Suddenly, a gong sounded an alarm from behind the town's walls, and faint shouting could be heard over the lingering metallic echo. The king and his companions called for the company to halt, and looked on apprehensively as a small company of mounted riders rode out of the gates and galloped toward them. They were not Peacekeepers, as they neither had the grey surcoats nor were all of fully Zaron stock. Their charge toward the company, however, despite slowing as they drew near, certainly gave no impression of a friendly greeting. At last the riders came up to Allor and the Elect, their katanas drawn and at the ready, as the leader trotted a few paces forth. Unlike his fellow guards, who wore kabuto helmets both masked and unmasked, the officer's grey-and-white face was plain to see, and the high-set tail in which his hair was tied blew freely in the strong wind that was blowing through the pass. He looked with scrutinizing eyes at the head of the company, puzzling over the others who followed them, and looked intently at Lerannu, who was holding Novon.

"What are you doing with that baby, madam?" he demanded. "What are you lot doing with all these non-Zarons? Are you not affiliated with the grey-coats?"

Allor gaped at the officer, angered at the tone with which he addressed Lerannu and mortified as he fully realized just how deep a wound Raakmathna's campaign had dealt to Fidonity. As he tried to speak, Mira called her brother and her sister-in-law over to explain. Kahle gently took her baby from Lerannu, and Isaak, alongside his sister, spoke on behalf of the company.

"None of the Zarons here are in league with the grey-cloaks," said Isaak. "These here are opposed to what Queen Sheeva had engineered under a demon's guidance, and have made to either flee from it or fight it. Can you not see the Mark of the Elect on my sister's brow, as well as on the heads of these other two women here?"

The officer's ears shot up, and his eyes widened as he took in the sight of the three blessed brands.

"They have been chosen by Onu as the prophesized Daughters of the East," Isaak went on, "and have begun their journey to inform the world and gain the support of the other nations to put an end to this terror."

"And what of any Zarons who live in that town there?" Mira chimed in before the officer could speak again. "Do you suspect them all to have had a hand in this madness, too?"

The officer's ears then flattened, and he drew a deep sigh as he began to explain.

"No, madam," said the officer, in a hurt but understanding tone. "We don't suspect the Zarons who've lived here all their lives of having anything to do with this. But what about those from outside the Whitemanes? Two days after Veronmay, we at Ovistar received word from Norkoth that Sheeva's grey soldiers had attacked people within the city and the castle itself, all because their targets weren't completely grey-furred. While they failed to kill King Viktor or Queen Xenia, or every non-Zaron in the city besides, before being driven out, they still killed many and have since laid siege to the capital. Besides that, folks that have since fled to seek shelter here have reported small bands of these grey-coats riding about and raiding whatever towns and villages they come across. Plenty of those fleeing to the pass, and to the border citadel, have been full Zarons and, once questioned and admitted, they have given us no cause to suspect them. It's not because they're Zarons, but–"

"Questioned?" Allor asked with pricked ears. "You question the Zarons before letting them in? What if there were grey-coats right on their heels?"

The officer stared at him, baffled on how to reply. "Do I truly need to explain why we took precautions?" he asked in exasperation. "It's just been a matter of briefly detaining those who were Zarons and questioning them. None of those who have come to us, as far as I know, have been reported as being denied entry, and are being guarded along with all the other refugees in Ovistar and other towns along the pass. It's as I said, we aren't immediately assuming that all Zarons are in on this insanity, but–"

"Have you approached each of them as you've approached us? In a cavalcade, weapons drawn, and after sounding the gong as if you were being invaded?"

"No, *sir*," said the officer, eyes narrowing irritably. "The gong was struck on the initiative of the lookout, who saw a large train of riders coming up the pass. She called out that a lot of folks were coming up the road, and since this whole mess first started in Enmayar, and since a month has passed for the grey-cloak forces to spread out, who wouldn't think that it was potentially them?"

"So assume the worst, and come out as if you were making to cut us down, is that it?" Allor asked. Despite his understanding of the guards' reasoning, the king was rapidly losing his patience due to the officer's tone. "Also, why would you ask about what a Zaron was doing with a baby who wasn't Zaron, or at least not fully so? Do you think the grey-cloaks are the sort who would carry them around? More likely they'd stomp their little heads in as soon as they found them and—"

"THAT'S ENOUGH, BOTH OF YOU!" Ruth thundered as she trotted forth. Allor and the officer nearly jumped out of their saddles, and their horses stamped tensely in place for a moment before calming down. Ruth glared at them both, then softened her eyes as she addressed the officer.

"I believe we can all understand your reasons for caution, sir," she said levelly, "but I trust that you wouldn't doubt the word of one marked by Onu himself."

"No, madam," the officer said quietly, "and I apologize for letting the conversation turn sour."

"No harm has been done," said the Faithguard calmly. "That said, we need to try and get to Norkoth as soon as we can, and then move on to Kellmayar and Janrenar. We need to try and tell all the other leaders of what's happened, and explain how this isn't a coordinated attack from Enmayar itself, nor from some conspiracy engineered by all Zarons, but the work of a demon who managed to manipulate and possess Queen Sheeva."

The officer looked at Ruth with wide-eyed alarm. "Sheeva ... was possessed?"

Ruth nodded grimly. "Right before my very eyes, and the eyes of her husband."

The knight then nodded toward Allor. The officer, realizing what Ruth meant, and in turn who he had spoken with so heatedly, at last sheathed his katana, prompting his guards to follow suit.

"I ... I'm so sorry, King Allor," he stammered, "for both your loss and for my ... my tone."

Allor nodded somberly. "You had no way of knowing," he said, "and you were just trying to do your job."

The officer reached a hand out to the king, and the two shook hands in respectful greeting.

"I am Zirnoth Goldmoon," he said. "I'm an officer of the Ovistar guard and was sent here to help the towns on this side of the border keep a lookout for grey-coats, should any come from this direction, and otherwise oversee the taking in of refugees who have been coming from this way."

"Well met," said Allor. "If we could rest this evening in town, we'll fill you in on what's happened and be on our way in the morning."

"I would very much like to know what has happened," said Zirnoth, "and I would furthermore be honored if I might accompany you to Ovistar and to the end of the pass. It's not a difficult road itself, but if there were any unforeseen difficulties or, Onu forbid, some grey-coats that have managed to make their way in and start wreaking havoc, I would like to offer my sword, and those of the ones under my charge, to your service."

Allor looked at Ruth, who nodded agreeably.

"Very well," he said. "You have my thanks."

The Elect, the king, and all those who followed them made their way into the town ahead, where they rested and told Zirnoth and all who would listen of the fate of Sheeva and the rise of Raakmathna. Zirnoth had a message sent ahead of the company, informing all the towns along the way of the coming of the Elect. He rode alongside his guards at the head of the company the following morning.

117

5/15/4030 G.M.

RAAKMATHNA looked over the new message from the forces at Benhotha, the capital of Janrenar. The Peacekeepers besieging that city were now doing the same as those at Zefiil, calling for reinforcements from Enmayar. Only the ones at Norkoth were still trying to make do with their present numbers. The empress wondered with amusement if and when the Norkoth forces would request additional aid. It mattered not to her, of course; with original Peacekeepers, the coerced conscripts, and the undead, there was always enough to send here or there.

Raakmathna read the message aloud to Sarah, who had been preparing for her mission to Kellmayar and Zefiil since the day it had been assigned to her. Just less than a fortnight remained before the archgeneral was to depart from Genverdell, and already there were plenty of fighters, of one sort or another, who had arrived and now stood under her charge. More were bound to come before the first of Yorrek, so while Raakmathna still intended to continue adding to the archgeneral's forces, the empress was now setting to make the fulfillment of the new request her leading priority.

"Do you wish for me to be in charge of the new army that is to be formed for Janrenar, my empress, as opposed to the forces bound for Kellmayar?"

"No," Raakmathna said calmly. "I have plenty of others who are sufficient for the task; those at Kellmayar requested first, so they get first pickings."

Sarah nodded with a proud smile. "I am honored to be deemed by my empress as being among her highest champions."

"But of course. Why would I appoint you as my archgeneral if I did not think otherwise?"

"Fair enough, my empress. Is there anything else that you need of me at present?"

"No, Archgeneral Stonefaith. You are dismissed."

Sarah made to leave, but abruptly turned around with a reverent bow as she spoke to the empress again.

"I beg your pardon, my empress," she said, "but I haven't heard any word as to the capture of that harlot, Uriah. Might it be that you have received word of the matter in my absence?"

"I have indeed," said Raakmathna. "Alas, she and her family somehow evaded capture when some of our soldiers raided her inn. They are still searching for her and will notify us as soon as she and her family have been captured. I will send word to you personally, if she is not delivered before your departure, and will furthermore ensure that she and her family are kept alive until your return. If she is brought in while you are gone, I will send for your return as soon as your mission is accomplished. I promise."

This was not the full account of things, of course. Raakmathna had gotten word on the twenty-fifth of the previous month, shortly before the request from the forces at Zefiil, that had detailed the account of what happened at the inn from a deserter who had since been executed. It was sent from Greenharbor, and it told of how the capture of the Queniroths was foiled by a band of Fidons that matched the description of the small company that had escaped from Genverdell during the Veronmay's Eve pogrom. The company's whereabouts were unknown, as only the deserter had survived the encounter with them and knew not where they went. All that the empress knew of them was that Lerannu, Sarah's daughter, was in that company, and that she and two others, the Faithguard bride and some other Zaron woman, had been branded by Onu as being among the Elect. Sarah had disowned her daughter during the pogrom, so it was not the fact that Lerannu was involved which prompted Raakmathna to withhold the full story. Nor was she worried about the Elect, for even if they ultimately succeeded in expelling her from Fidonhaal, Raakmathna was content enough with all that had already been done.

Her concern came from whether or not Sarah would abandon her mission to hunt down Uriah herself, if she had learned that none had since been sent to pursue her. The empress had other plans than to go out of her way to sate Sarah's hatred of the adulteress, which, helpful as it had been to bring her into her plans, could now hold back the potential of the campaign if the archgeneral were to suddenly place higher priority on her own vendetta than Raakmathna's plans.

This was bigger than getting back on a woman who had some part in breaking another's family;

this was for the vindication of the All-Keeper and the ending of Onu's folly.

"Of course, my empress," said Sarah with dutiful trust. "I do not doubt your word, and I will see to the mission you have given me."

"Very good," said Raakmathna as she prepared to write up another order for more soldiers to answer the call from the Benhotha forces. "We will speak again soon."

118
5/15/4030 G.M.

DONOVAN rode beside Mira as Zirnoth Goldmoon guided the party to Ovistar, the city that marked the border between Enmayar and Sorrenar. It was early morning, and after nine days of steady riding, with grand mountains towering over them on either side, the great border citadel had at last come into view.

The going had been easy and pleasant, all in all, with Zirnoth's company and that of his guards being a far cry from what their first encounter might have foreboded under other circumstances. Though the journey likely would have been fine without them, their thorough knowledge of the pass and all the settlements that spanned it enabled them to make good distance each day, being encouraged to ride on a little further with the promise of a roof and hot food in the town or village that lay just a few more hours away. Zirnoth, having since learned the full account of the company's quest, was as sound a companion and ally as any could ask for. With his message having flown well ahead of the company to all settlements in the pass, the Elect and their companions had been in higher spirits than ever since their flight from Genverdell. They were well-received in each town they entered, and felt confident in the shelter of the mountains and friendly company.

Now they drew nearer to Ovistar's majestic Enmayarn Wall, which spanned the entire gap of the pass and featured three grand pagodas that stood equally distant from one another. Zirnoth hailed the watchers on the battlements and in the towers, and several gongs sounded lightly in response. Unlike the cries of alarm that followed the gong during the company's first encounter with Zirnoth, this time a celebratory announcement of the Elect's arrival echoed throughout the city and the pass, which was then followed by an awed silence. The gates opened, and the Elect and their companions steadily rode into the citadel, being greeted with reverent nods by the masses that lined the road leading to the keep of the Whitemane Warden.

The warden's keep lay directly on the border, with one half of the fortress resting in Enmayar and the other in Sorrenar. The keep, made of grey stone from the mountains and crowned with pagodas, had its roofs tiled with the glazed blue of lapis lazuli. A straight line of ornately carved stones ran across the center of the keep's top, signifying the borderline between the East and the North. It was here where all Fidons who made to cross into one country or the other by land presented their passes and declared their business in times of peace. Now, however, the keep was serving as a base of operations for the security of both the native residents and the influx of refugees who had come into the pass to escape the cruelty of Raakmathna and her grey-cloaks.

They were greeted by the warden, one Lendoth Kamstro, who brought them into his office to speak of what had happened and what was planned for the future of the quest. The warden shook his head grimly upon hearing of all that had happened. Donovan, sitting beside Mira and the others of the main company, looked on as he watched the warden and the king speak.

"I would send a Shanlof to Norkoth so we might devise some way to secretly get you into the capital. But I've received no further word from Norkoth, be it updates from the city itself or replies to the messages I've tried sending before you all came. I fear the heraldwings have likely been shot down or captured some way or other. As much as I would want to inform them of your coming, I'd hate for the enemy to get the word instead."

"Your wish to help us is greatly appreciated, Warden Kamstro," said Allor, "but it is as you say, our secrecy is important for the mission of the Elect for as long as we can hold it. We had been discussing the matter for some time, how we are to try and enter Norkoth, and we were wondering if there were any sewer drains that might be far enough away from the capital that might be outside the perimeters of the siege. You wouldn't know of any, would you?"

The warden smiled slightly, though his eyes still didn't hold much hope. "It's certainly possible, I would think, given there are ones that empty out from the rugged hills by Mount Norkoth and into the Silverarm. But I can't tell you how far the grey-cloaks' siege camp goes, and if there are any outlets that lie outside their range, they may still have some soldiers keeping a watch on them."

"Are there any other ways that you can think of, Warden?" asked Allor respectfully.

"None, King Allor," said the warden regretfully.

"Then it's a chance we must take."

"So it would seem," said Lendoth. "Please, if any of you have anything more to say, then stay here and talk with me. Otherwise, I offer you beds for the night here in the keep. Evening has begun, and I'll wager that you won't have as good a rest as you will here until you reach Norkoth, Onu willing."

The warden then opened one of the drawers of his desk and produced a fine spyglass.

"Take this," he said as he handed it to Allor. "I hope it will serve you well."

"Thank you, Warden Kamstro," said Allor as he took the spyglass and looked to his companions. Donovan, rising from his chair, looked to Ruth, Lerannu, and Mira, who each nodded to him as they remained seated. Allor seemed to still have things to say, and Verdok seemed intent on staying by his wife's side. Donovan then looked to Mira, and shrugged with a laugh.

"I'm afraid I can't think of anything to add," said the bard, "but I'll feel odd to be the only one to leave. I'm sorry that I've just been sitting here quietly for the most part."

Mira stood up and kissed him. "Don't worry about it. Stay or go."

Donovan sighed. "I think I'll take in the view. I've been wanting to get a good look of the White-manes for some time now."

Mira smiled. "I'll try to join you before it gets too dark."

They kissed again, and Donovan quietly left the room. He stepped out onto a balcony on the Sorrenarn side of the keep, and looked out over the homes and other buildings that stretched out to the west wall beyond. He saw many people milling about below, natives and refugees alike, and reflected moodily on the journey so far. In particular, his mind went to the talk he had with Mira back when they were still making their way to Plen. As much as he felt that he was indeed keeping faith in the Elect and the rest of the company, and despite the relative rise in everyone's spirits since they entered the Whitemanes, Donovan had found himself suddenly feeling a weight on his heart.

He didn't know if it was due to his lack of input in the talks with the warden and feeling like he wasn't giving enough help to the company in their quest, or if it was simply a sudden wave of weariness that had taken hold of him. He began to realize that his mind had long been burdened by his uncertainty of the fate of his hometown and father. He prayed that if the people of Therohl weren't in Ovistar, then they were in some other place that could hold out against the grey-cloaks.

He heard a door open and close, and turned to see Mira approach. She embraced him, rubbing her muzzle under his chin and leaning on his shoulder.

"That's a lot of people down there," she commented quietly.

"Mm-hmm."

"Is everything all right?"

Donovan told Mira of his thoughts, to which the huntress responded with a gentle lick on the cheek.

"You could've done nothing other than tell us that you believed we could make it through all this," she said warmly, "and as far as I care, that would've been more than enough to ask for."

Donovan smiled and put an arm around her, and the two quietly looked on at the people below.

"I think about how much I was looking forward to seeing the Whitemanes," the bard said a moment later, "back when I first left home."

"Well, you've had a good look so far, no? And there's more to come before we pass through."

"Indeed."

"What do you think of it, then?"

"It's beautiful, as much as what I've hoped for, and more."

"But?"

"But I certainly wasn't thinking that I would be visiting them as I am now, with three Elect in my company and with a demon-possessed queen trying to kill every Fidon who isn't solely grey-furred."

Mira laughed and squeezed her arm around him tightly. "You and me both, and I'm sure everyone else who has come here lately."

***

The rest of the company rejoined Mira and Donovan not long after, and the warden led them to a restaurant in the Sorrenarn side of the citadel for dinner. As they sat down on the mats that surrounded their table, a Balon man came over to serve them.

"Welcome, Elect and company, and Warden Kamstro. What can I ... *Don?*"

Donovan's heart nearly stopped as he realized it was Jonathan speaking. He looked up into his father's eyes and rose up, crying and laughing, as he hugged him tightly.

"I was so worried of what might have happened back home," said the bard. "Is everyone from Therohl here?"

"Most of us, yes," answered Jonathan, "though some have taken up in other places in the pass. Thankfully, as far as I can tell, most of us managed to get out of there fast once we heard of what happened in Norkoth. We were blessed to have heard the news before the grey-cloaks came."

"And now you're serving up food in the meantime, while some heroes and heroines embark on a quest for the ages?"

"Someone has to, and I couldn't stand to just sit about doing nothing while waiting for word as to whether or not those grey-coats had been dealt with."

"Maybe you ought to stay here even when everything's been settled. You look quite dashing in that serving kimono. Just saying."

"Shush, boy."

Donovan looked to the Elect and the rest of the company as they stifled their laughter.

"Well, I guess there's no need to stop by Therohl, then!" he said with a teary laugh. "Let's just ride on to Norkoth."

"We still might end up passing by it, if nothing else," said Ruth, "given its place along the way. But whether we do or not, and whatever state we might find it in, we can at least take comfort in having learned that there wasn't a total slaughter."

All at the table raised their glasses, with Jonathan indulging as well. They then told Donovan's father of all that had happened. Despite the heavy task of recounting yet again the horrors that had passed, Donovan and his companions spent their happiest evening since the ill-fated wedding, and looked with renewed hope at the quest that was still to be done.

When they made to retire to the warden's keep, Jonathan took his son and daughter-in-law aside.

"I'm so glad you're both safe," he said as he tearfully embraced them. "I've worried about the two of you since that rider fleeing Norkoth rode through home and warned us of what was happening."

"Well, I'm not sure if you can say we're really safe," said Donovan. "We're not going to be in the pass forever, and we have to ride out and face these grey-cloaks and their commanding demon sooner or later. We ... we might not ..."

"I know," Jonathan said as he tried to put on a brave face. "But if nothing else, I'm glad to have been able to see you two at least one more time in this life. Go with my love, son."

"Yes, Father."

"And Mira," said Jonathan, looking with intense reverence at the huntress and the Mark on her brow, "go with my love, as the father of your husband, and with my faith in you as a part of Onu's hand. I pray for your victory. Please pass the word on to your Elect sisters."

"Of course, Jonathan. Take care. Perhaps one day, not too far from now, we'll see each other again ... one way or another."

Jonathan, his face threatening to crumble, simply nodded silently. He gave Mira and Donovan a fatherly kiss on the cheek and strode briskly back into the restaurant. The bard and the huntress returned to their companions, drawing up the strength within them for what lay ahead.

119

6/1/4030 G.M.

RAAKMATHNA stood on the castle balcony, watching Archgeneral Stonefaith's army of Peacekeepers and undead ride and march steadily out of Genverdell, southward-bound for the port of Okrenar. In her hand was another message from the forces at Norkoth, which stated they were still set on trying to take the capital of the North with their present numbers.

As the empress watched the river of grey-clad soldiers flow out of the city below, she took notice of those coming in to answer the call that had been sent from the forces besieging Benhotha. They would be leaving later in the month, bound for the same port and then making the long voyage to the port of Humilaar, which was at the mouth of the great Vitari River. They were then to disembark and follow the river to Janrenar's capital, where they hopefully would be able to overwhelm the city.

Some past reports from the Peacekeepers stationed there, based on information gathered from captured enemy scouts, also mentioned there were some areas in the city that were serving as places of detainment for its Zaron population. The reports went on to suggest that some of them may have been sympathizers to the cause beforehand, or could now be swayed with relative ease, given the overt display of suspicion that the Janrenarn government had put into effect. Raakmathna had been ecstatic at the news, seeing that the effects of the initial pogroms had already set a rift among the Fidons, despite not having gone completely as planned.

The empress looked on the coming and going of the soldiers below, and the citizens who were meekly yielding the way for their passing. Everyone was in their place. Everything was in order.

120

6/9/4030 G.M.

MIRA rode alongside her sisters of the Elect and the rest of the company, which had been reduced to a far more manageable size. They had departed from Ovistar on the sixteenth of the previous month, having rested well from their travels in the brief respite that the border citadel had granted them. They were led to the end of the pass not only by Officer Goldmoon and his guards, but Warden Kamstro himself as well. All of Plen, including Mira's mother, had opted to stay behind.

"You cannot afford to be burdened by our presence," Ann told her daughter, "what with the frequent worrying for our safety that would weigh on you as we trotted along behind you."

"That's a burden I'd be willing to bear," Mira replied. "But I understand."

As they embraced one another before Mira had saddled up, the huntress saw Lerannu speaking to Uriah Queniroth and her family from over Ann's shoulder. The mage seemed to be pleading with them, and as Mira tuned her ears to the conversation, she heard that it was so.

"I've told you there's no oath that I, or Ruth, or Mira, or anyone else in our company have forced on you. I know you want to make up for what happened back home, but I can't let you risk your life for it. And your family says they won't let you go alone with us, either. I can't put them at risk as well. Please, stay here until it's all settled."

"I owe you and your company my life, and that of my husband and my boys," said Uriah resolutely. "And the kindness you've shown us, in spite of what I did to you and your family, has increased the debt. I *am* going with you."

Lerannu looked pleadingly at the rest of the family. Uriah's husband, Harvus, drawing their sons close, spoke to the mage with calm finality.

"We talked it out yesterday while you all were discussing matters with the warden. She's going with you and we're going with her. None of us will hold you or any other in the company responsible for our fate should any or all of us perish before the journey's end. Do what you must for the good of all of Fidonhaal, and do not make our safety your prime concern. We will accompany you and aid you in whatever way we can, if we can, as long as we can still put one foot in front of the other."

The mage sighed resignedly, and mounted up and made for the gate without another word. Princess Talrah was in the saddle with her, and Prince Samuel rode with his father, for Allor had stated that as much as he had initially wished to entrust his children into the citadel's care, he decided that taking them to Norkoth would be better.

"I would trust that King Viktor and Queen Xenia would have more on hand to take care of them," the king had reasoned to the warden. "And given the suspicions that would understandably be directed toward the husband of Sheeva, I feel that it could be a gesture of good faith if, well ..."

"I understand," said the warden with a sad sigh, "but woeful indeed is our state if you feel that such a measure would be needed or advisable."

The company rode on through the remainder of the pass in much the same manner as before, and like the first half of the trip, the second took nine days. When they had reached the end of the pass and the vastness of the North opened to them, the cool wind brushed into them past the fur, and the company looked about in a moment of silent awe. Verdok broke the reverie, speaking through a fit of chattering teeth.

"W-well, th-thank Onu that at least our f-flight has n-not t-taken pl-lace in w-winter," he said to the amusement of all his companions.

Warden Kamstro and Officer Goldmoon then bade the party farewell and prayed that the guidance and protection of Onu be with them. The party gave their thanks and promptly set out into the rugged country beyond.

They rode on intrepidly for another twelve days, weathering the late-spring chill of the North. It was not so cold that they could not survive with the clothes and gear they had on hand, but the conditions certainly left much to be desired in regards to comfort. They had been exposed to it the entire course of their journey in the North thus far, as they feared fire would reveal themselves to unseen grey-cloaks. Fortunately, the party's return to a small size, and the generous rations the people of the Whitemanes had given them on their way out of the pass, made their weariness of the cold their only concern aside from being found by the grey-coats. They managed both on and off the roads as needed, much as had been done during their passage through Enmayar. They had passed a number of settlements that, consistent with what they were told in the Whitemanes, had been raided and razed by the demonic empress's soldiers.

"Should we still end up passing by Therohl," said Donovan grimly after seeing columns of smoke rising from a distant village, "I certainly don't expect a pleasant sight. I will have to console myself in having heard from Father himself that most there had been warned and were able to flee."

As the party rode nearer to Norkoth, they indeed came across the remains of Therohl. And though they knew that nearly all had taken shelter in the Whitemanes, the ravaged walls and homes were still a heavy sight to behold. All stopped in their tracks, looking over the scene ahead of them in silence. Donovan, having ridden beside his wife, looked to her with his sad, bright blue eyes, and then to the rest of the party.

"We need not investigate, since we know where most of them went," he said as levelly as he could. "But since the road runs through it anyway and since there doesn't seem to be anyone else around ..."

"Let's go on," Mira said.

They rode through the town, glancing at the shattered windows and charred timber that lined either side of the street. They came at last to the town square and all the company halted, looking sadly on the sight ahead. The famed statue of the Three Widows, who long ago had put an end to the terror of a warlord who had raided Therohl and killed their husbands, now lay in pieces in the center of the square. For all that the three women had done for the town, and for all their tale had told of the value of family, strength, and the ponderings of justice and vengeance, their legacy was deemed unworthy of preservation by the grey-coats. All because the Widows had not been solely grey of fur. After a moment's silence, Mira looked to her husband, who had turned his gaze down the road toward the capital.

"Thank you for humoring me," he said to his companions. "Let's just get on."

121

6/22/4030 G.M.

RAAKMATHNA stood over the south gate of Genverdell, surrounded by a handful of her Peacekeepers and with Salpion Windsbreath at her side, as she watched the reinforcements bound for Janrenar leave the capital. Soldiers clad in grey, determined on erasing those who would undermine the Zarons' safety and prosperity, rode ahead of the vast train of undead. The corpses, in varying states of wholeness, either lumbered tirelessly forward or rode on horses that obeyed the wordless commands of their riders out of sheer terror.

Satisfied with the embarking of the army, the empress turned to Ranoth, who was looking to her expectantly.

"Is all well with you, Salpion?"

"Yes, my empress," said Ranoth as he produced a parchment from his pocket. "I was simply meaning to carry out my role as your informant in Archgeneral Stonefaith's absence."

"Very well. What news is there?"

"Just another update on the situation in Norkoth," said the salpion as he handed the message to her. "They're still trying to see if anything can be done to take the city with their current numbers, but they have said that, should no further progress be gained soon, they will likely request more troops in the near future."

"There should not be any trouble on that account, should it come to that. As long as Norkoth falls to us in the end, that is all that should be of concern."

"As you say, my empress."

Raakmathna turned away from the ramparts of the south gate. "Well," she said, "everything seems to be going as intended here. I think a good sermon for the campaign would benefit those still here, should they be starting to doubt. Are you up for it, Salpion?"

"Of course, my empress," said Ranoth with a bow, "you need but say the word."

"Very well. Let us call the people to the Temple."

122

6/22/4030 G.M.

ALLOR and the company of the Elect had ridden on from what was left of Therohl for thirteen days, thankful for the warmth that had begun to touch the land as summer drew nigh. It seemed that the roving bands of grey-cloaks, if indeed they were still riding about the country, had gone far out from where the party's path had led them, as they were blessed with no incidents during the ride.

Now, however, as they reached the top of a hill and saw the mountain of Norkoth and its name-sake city ahead of them in the high noon sun, Allor felt his heart stop with dread. Nearly all optimism that had grown since their time in the Whitemanes left him in that moment. Turning his gaze to his companions, he saw that all had felt the same blow to their spirits. Even the Elect, as much as they managed to keep a composed face, were clearly disheartened at the size of the camp that lay beyond the Silverarm River and stretched to the capital's walls. An army of grey-clad soldiers was milling about the camp, which was comprised of a mass of silver and grey tents. The king looked to the company, a desperate attempt at resolved courage on his face.

"Well," he said, "I suppose we'd best start looking for a sewer outlet somewhere around here. Four Breaths, there's just so many of them ..."

"Just how many did Sheeva and that demon manage to bring into their scheme?" Lerannu asked

Allor incredulously. "I know there are still more than a few have-nots in the world, but are there really so many, Zaron or not, who would be swayed but such a mad concept?"

"I don't know," the king said distressfully. "I can't believe the numbers I'm seeing here, either. And to think that there are still more of them elsewhere ..."

Donovan and Mira, dismounting, took their bows and quivers, and turned to the company.

"We're going to see what exactly is going on there, if we can," said Mira as she checked the spy-glass that Warden Kamstro had given them. "Whatever we do in Norkoth, should we even manage to get in, we ought to know what we're dealing with. I, too, have a hard time believing these are all poor orphan Zarons who have fallen into the grey-coats' service of their own will. Wait here."

"Please, be careful," Allor said tensely as they slunk down the hill and toward the camp.

***

An agonizing hour of waiting passed, with the company having fallen back to the other side of the hill to avoid detection. Footsteps sounded on the crisp grass ahead of them, and the company, tensing, quickly sighed with relief as the bard and huntress returned.

Then they saw their faces, and their tension immediately resurged.

"What is it?" asked Ruth breathlessly.

"There are more grey-coats than I would've ever thought could be," Mira answered the knight. "But given how the original recruits were all trained years ago when they would've been young, I can tell that not all in uniform were among the first trained. Many of them are around the age of the first troops, as they looked to be about as old as you or Verdok, but otherwise, an awful lot of them seemed to be several years younger. There are also ones a good deal older than the rest, and from what I could tell from the glass, not all of them seemed willing. I guess there were some in this world that were happy to be a part of something like this from the start, once the chance presented itself. Others, I suspect, are captives that the grey-coats have forced into service. But that's not all that the camp is made of."

"What do you mean?" asked Verdok worriedly.

"For every grey-coat in that camp," Donovan said with a chillingly hollow voice, "there must be around nine undead, and a lot of them are armed and armored more or less like the living ones."

The party fell completely silent, and Allor felt his blood freeze in his veins.

"But how could there be so many, even of them?" the king asked in a small voice.

The bard and the huntress looked gravely at the company. "They're reanimated corpses of those slain by the grey-cloaks," said Donovan. "They have necromancers in their army. We both saw a soldier or two who appeared more versed in magic than in martial combat, waving around a staff instead of a sword or spear. They must be the ones."

Another moment of silence passed as the company took in the revelation. Finally, Uriah gestured to the high, rugged hills that lay ahead of them on their side of the river.

"Well, we obviously can't fight our way into the city," she said, "though I thought that was always a given. We're to see if any sewer lines empty out here, right?"

The innkeeper and her family looked with quiet expectance at the company, and then turned for the hills after no word was spoken. Drawing a deep breath, the king and his son rode after them, followed by the others.

Within another hour, they had reached the hills, and after some canvassing of the nooks and crannies in the stone and earth, soon found a flow of water that spilled into the Silverarm and led to a large stone pipeline. The way was unguarded, contrary to Warden Kamstro's fears. Allor felt his flickering hope begin to rekindle, and he could see his companions felt the same.

"Looks like we'll just have to brave the muck, now ... and the smell," said the king with a light grimace.

Fortunately, the party soon found that the muck wouldn't be too much of a problem, as they found walkways on either side of the pipes. They split into two groups, each taking a torch from their supplies. Allor and Lerannu took one side of the pipe with Samuel and Talrah, accompanied by Uriah and her family, while Ruth, Verdok, Donovan, and Mira took the other.

They walked on steadily, calm in spite of the unpleasant atmosphere, knowing that while it would doubtlessly take a while, they were bound to reach the pipelines that stemmed from under Norkoth soon enough. At last they saw another pipe running perpendicular to the one they were in. Allor looked about the walls for a ladder that would lead to a cover.

"Should we go for the first exit we find?" he asked. "I couldn't tell you where any of the exits would lead out. Are there any that would lead right outside the walls and into the grey-cloaks' camp?"

"If it's like in Genverdell," said Lerannu, "then the first ring of them would be outside the walls. I couldn't tell you how it is here, so I'd say we should go at least a little further, just for good measure."

The party went with the mage's advice and soon reached the next intersection of pipe. All on both sides began to look for ladders on the walls. Allor heard an unpleasant-sounding thud, the kind one would hear if they kicked someone on the ground. A second later, there was a gasp of fright, followed by several others.

Allor looked down. There at Lerannu's feet was the decayed body of a man. From what they could make of him, the man wore a plain, dark blue gambeson and dark grey padded pants, and his gear included a hand axe, a bow and quiver, and a satchel. What remained of his shoulder and chest seemed to carry heavy, cleaving wounds as would have been dealt by an axe. Allor looked ahead, and just a few feet from the body was a ladder leading up out of the sewer.

"Are there grey-cloaks that patrol *within* the sewers?" Allor heard Verdok say in a hushed voice. "Have we just been lucky to have not been discovered here yet?"

"I don't know," said Mira quietly, "but if there is, we better get to that ladder over there and ... Lerannu, what are you doing?"

Allor looked and saw the mage crouched over the body and rummaging through the satchel. She pulled out a parchment and read it in the torchlight.

"This was a messenger," she said as she pocketed the parchment, "who was sent to get out of the city and try to get the word out about what happened here on Veronmay's Eve. He was tasked with trying to send for help wherever he could get to, even to Kellmayar or Janrenar, since they couldn't send a bird out of Norkoth itself. Someone must have been waiting for—"

All of the party fell deathly silent as they heard a raspy, threatening grunt, followed by the quick splashing of feet. Those on the opposite side of Allor and Lerannu frantically made to cross over to them, with Ruth leading the effort with her axe and buckler raised. Allor saw Lerannu lift up her torch, and the king and mage screamed as a rotting grey-cloaked corpse came dashing at them from the darkness. The undead had an axe raised over its head, and was charging straight for Lerannu. Allor and Lerannu stood petrified by terror.

Allor felt someone brush past him. It was Uriah, who placed herself in front of Lerannu with a short blade drawn. The innkeeper made to drive the blade into the oncoming abomination's skull, but didn't see the axe. The rush of air from the axe's swing almost put out Allor's torch, and in its frantically flickering light, the king looked on in horror as the undead grey-coat's axe cleaved into Uriah's head. Harvus and his sons screamed. Ruth bulled into the corpse's side, slamming it against the wall of the pipeline, and made short work of it with two swift strikes from her own axe.

A second of horrid silence fell upon the company, followed by the weeping of Harvus, Evor, and Ethos, who took up Uriah's lifeless body as they urged the company onto the ladder ahead.

"We don't hold you to this," said Harvus tearfully. "We need to get up that ladder, if we can—"

Allor's blood ran cold as he heard more splashes, accompanied by raspy growls, echoing in the distance.

"Harvus," Ruth cried out, "we'll have to leave her here for now!"

Weeping wretchedly, Harvus and his sons lowered Uriah's body onto the walkway as they ran for the ladder alongside the rest of the group. Without thinking, Allor clambered up the ladder first, followed by the others, and pushed the manhole cover up with all his might. He looked about for an instant, and sighed gratefully as he saw they were indeed within Norkoth. He shoved the cover aside and called for the others to hurry as he made to climb out.

"STOP RIGHT THERE!" a voice bellowed harshly.

Allor narrowly avoided being run through the throat by the spear of a guard as its tip struck the edge of the manhole.

Part Five

A Great Alliance

Meeting the Mountainborn

123
6/22/4030 G.M.

LERANNU started at the guard's shouts, which pulled her from the well of grief into which she had so suddenly fallen at Uriah's death. She saw the tip of a spear pointing squarely at Allor's throat and could hear the king frantically trying to explain himself.

The distant, rapid splashing of the undead in the sewers, however, was what caught the mage's ears the most. It was swiftly growing louder, closer, as were the groans and hideous snarls that accompanied them.

"I-I understand why this is suspicious, b-but I swear I'm King Allor, and I've come with the—"

"We're going to be swarmed by corpses if you don't let us up there!" Lerannu interrupted with a desperate scream. "Please, just let us in!"

Lerannu heard the guard stammer in surprise. "There's undead in the—come on, then! All of you! Hurry!"

The mage was the last out of the sewer, scrambling frightfully up the ladder as she heard the steps of a snarling corpse sounding on the stones just a few feet away. As she pulled herself up out of the manhole, she turned around just in time to see a bony head rise from the hole, only to be swiftly impaled by the guard's spear as another guardsman frantically shoved the cover back in place.

As those in the company paused to collect themselves, the guard spoke.

"So," said the white-furred man as he addressed Allor, "you say you are the King of Enmayar."

"I am, and I have in my company my children and other companions who have set out to put a stop to the madness that my wife had concocted under the manipulation of a demon."

Allor turned toward the party and pointed to Lerannu, Mira, and Ruth. The leading guardsman began to ask another question, but before he could make out a proper word, Allor continued his explanation.

"The chief of these companions ... are the long-foretold Daughters of the East."

The head guard and the others in his squad gaped silently at the sight of the sacred brand that graced the three women's foreheads. After a brief silence, the head guard sighed incredulously and looked the company over.

"So a demon has goaded the Queen of Enmayar into this horrid campaign, waging war upon all who aren't fully grey of fur, and the king has somehow managed to be utterly ignorant of these plots."

"I understand, sir, that it's hard to believe, but I swear—"

"I believe you; Onu would not grace the holy brand upon the companions of a liar. But ... these are *the* Daughters of the East?"

"Yes," said Ruth, stepping forward beside Allor. "We fled Genverdell on Veronmay's Eve and took shelter in a glen for the night. There the angels gathered, along with Onu himself, and revealed to us our destinies in this terrible time. We have come here to explain what has happened, to your people and your queen and king, and request aid in the war that's to be waged against Raakmathna and the grey-coats. We mean also to go to the leaders of Kellmayar and Janrenar, if we can, and do the same there."

The head guard nodded. "Very well, Daughter of the East. I'll have word sent to the castle immediately. Please, wait here."

He turned to send someone up to the castle, then paused. He looked back to Allor.

"Raakmathna?" he inquired with a morbid tone. "Such a dreadful name. But what of the queen? Is she not in league with the demon and otherwise in command of her so-called Peacekeepers?"

Allor's ears dropped sadly. "She was, for a time ... but she's just a shell for that Raakhaal-spawn now."

The guard's face stiffened in pity and revulsion. "I ... I am sorry."

"As am I."

The guard then departed, leaving the company in the presence of the other guards. Lerannu, suddenly remembering the dead messenger found near the sewer's ladder, addressed the squad as they stood about the company in silence.

"I don't know if you knew this already, but just beyond the ladder we climbed, we found a dead man who carried orders to send out warning and requests for help wherever he could reach."

One of the guards sighed, her ears drooping depressingly.

"That explains why we haven't heard sod-all from anyone this whole damn time," the guard said dully as she leaned wearily on her spear. "He didn't even make it out of the sewers and has been rotting there since the start of spring. Brendon ... poor soul. The king and queen need to know this as well."

"I can tell them," said the mage as she showed the guards the parchment she recovered from the corpse. "As for the body, I don't know if you would want to risk it at present, but if you want to recover it, it's not far from the ladder. Maybe you could send a squad down there and get him out. There's also a woman who was in our company ... and ... she ..."

Lerannu was struck with a renewed wave of grief for Uriah. Unable to go on, she sank to her knees and wept. Harvus and his sons knelt beside her and embraced her.

"We don't blame you," said Harvus. "She gave her life to protect you, and you are a Daughter of the East. You bear the greater role, and she did her part to protect you."

"But I didn't forgive her enough ... not for ..."

"You didn't do whatever unholy acts that your mother had in mind, and you took us all under your protection and that of your companions. It's clear that you forgave her."

"I just wish I could've spoken with her more ... more properly, I mean."

"It was enough."

Lerannu and Harvus, along with his two boys, held one another quietly for a time before the mage pleaded with them.

"Please, you three, stay here and be safe when we leave for whatever lies ahead. I know you promised to go with her in aiding us however you could, but you'll aid us by staying safe."

"Very well," said Harvus with a deep sigh that sounded of both resignation and relief. "Thank you."

Lerannu looked up to the rest of her companions and the guards through tear-blurred eyes. They all somberly looked on in silence.

"I'll let Captain Windon know," said the guard as she absentmindedly shifted her spear from one hand to the other. "We'll recover the bodies soon."

The squad captain returned a short time later, and after being informed of the dead in the sewers, he bade King Allor, the Daughters of the East, and the rest of the company to follow him.

***

A grueling hour of traversing the inclined roads of the mountain-city ensued. Once the company entered the castle gates and were led by the guard to some benches in the courtyard, they all slumped down and breathed heavily, massaging their legs and feet. Lerannu, still contending with her sadness at Uriah's death, was further irritated by the physical strain and glanced moodily at Ruth when she heard the Faithguard let out a small laugh.

"I thought I'd be fairly experienced in walking uphill," said the knight, not noticing the mage's look, "with all my comings and goings in Genverdell. But a mountain is quite a different matter, it would seem."

The company laughed lightly. Lerannu wanted to laugh with them, but couldn't find it in herself to do so. The captain, chuckling with the rest, stepped up to the party and explained the planned course of the evening.

"Your rooms should be ready in just a few minutes. Some of the royal guard will lead you through the side door over there, by the gardens. The rooms will be right there, and ... well, given the state of your clothes, we wouldn't want you tracking much throughout the castle."

"Of course," said Allor with a laugh as he fanned the smell of his clothes away from himself.

"Queen Xenia and King Viktor are giving you until after dinner to wash, eat, and rest. They'll send for you when they're ready, and you'll be led to the throne room from there."

"Very well," said Verdok as he took Ruth's hand. "Thank you, Captain Windon."

The captain nodded and then departed without another word. A few minutes later, four guards in royal uniforms emerged from the main doors of the castle. Lerannu and the rest of the company rose from their seats, and following the guards, went through the garden and entered the castle. They went just a short distance down the corridor before the four guards turned and gestured to the doors that lined the hall.

"These are all of the ambassador guest rooms," said one of the guards, specifically addressing King Allor and the Daughters of the East.

"My children and I will take one," said Allor, "and ... Lera?"

Lerannu sorely wished for Allor's company, and that of the prince and princess, but felt that she was in too poor a state to be with them at present. "I'll just take my own room for now."

"Very well," said the guard as Lerannu lowered her head and stared quietly at the floor. She saw Allor and the children looking intently at her from the corner of her eye, and simply drew a deep sigh and closed her eyes.

The others took their rooms. Ruth and Verdok took one together, as did Mira and Donovan, and Harvus and his sons. After a few moments, servants came in with food, drink, and bathwater to suit the occupants of each chamber.

When her room was ready, Lerannu entered and immediately went to the bath. Casting her soiled robes aside, she sunk into the warm water and washed, desperately trying to ease her grief for Uriah. Alas, all her effort to not overthink of the penitent woman and mother of two only led the mage's mind to dwell on her all the more. She thought of the years gone by, when Uriah was one of her dearest friends, especially in the wake of the loss of Kiiva. She thought of the pain Uriah dealt her and her mother, when her adultery with her father was revealed, and how, as upset with her as she had been at the time, she still hated to see her go.

She began to think also of her father, and how she hadn't heard a single word from him since he left Bravagoth all those years ago. She wondered if he was still alive, and if there was ever a chance of finding him. She thought of her own mother and the horrid, hateful powers with which she had aligned herself, knowing where it would ultimately lead her. She thought of how she and Uriah had not managed to fully talk out what had happened properly, and how Uriah had now left behind her own family to carry on without her. Lerannu began to weep.

She tearfully finished her bath, and draining the water and drying herself, put on a simple, clean robe that was laid out for her on the bed. She sat down at the meal-laden table and tried to eat. She managed a bite of roasted venison, which almost lodged in her grief-tightened throat, and a cup of mead. She sat there in silence for a time, then, feeling the room start to whirl gently around her, got up and slumped down wearily onto the bed.

***

Lerannu stirred as she heard a gentle knock at her door. Her head was throbbing and her stomach was painfully hollow. She got up and brushed her robes, then opened the door. Allor and the children stood outside, with the rest of the company and their escort behind them.

"The king and queen are ready for us," he said, his eyes quickly saddening as he took in the mage's state. "Do you need a few more minutes?"

"No," Lerannu said softly. "This shouldn't be delayed any further."

The king gently offered a hand to her, which the mage took gratefully, but silently. The company followed their escort and soon stepped into the grand throne room of the legendary Karamus dynasty.

124

6/22/4030 G.M.

ALLOR entered the throne room with his children and companions. It was a vast and marvel-ous chamber of stone, with majestic tapestries and paintings lining the walls. The fabled arms and armor of heroes from the Karamus line were on display throughout the room. Allor, the Elect, and their companions followed the escort past the wondrous art and relics, and approached the grand, joint throne of the Queen and King of Sorrenar.

On either side of the throne stood three of the six royal children, along with whomever of their own families they had at present. Three daughters, three sons. Each of them stood at least a good head taller than the average Fidon, be they man or woman, and the youngest of them seemed to be at least twenty years old. Allor looked them over as he drew near the throne with his company, admiring the majesty that each of them possessed with their snow-white fur, handsome long hair, and sincere gazes.

He then noticed one of them, the youngest of the princesses, looking at the company with grief-dulled eyes of grey. She was clad all in black. Allor observed the long, stone table that stood before the throne as he and his companions were led around it to face the royal family. On the table stood two beautiful porcelain urns. The larger of the two featured the dashing likeness of a Balon and Kason man painted on it. The other, a far smaller one, had the portrait of a smiling baby with brown-speckled white fur. Allor's heart felt as if it were pierced by an arrow, and he silently berated himself for his ignorance of Sheeva's plans and state of mind, for he felt partly to blame for the horror that had clearly transpired in the castle on Veronmay's Eve.

Beside the widowed princess stood a man with a scar that ran across the left side of his face. Though it was somewhat obscured by his lengthy hair, Allor could tell that it ran in a jagged line from the top of his head to the base of his jaw, marring the beautiful snowy fur that otherwise graced his face. If it weren't for the urns and the mourning gown, Allor would have thought that he was the princess's husband. A better look clearly marked him as a prince, one of her brothers, and going by their apparent similarity in age and physicality, her twin. The prince's wife and son were beside him, the picture of a strongly bound family, but the prince himself stood closest to his sister, holding her hand comfortingly as the entire Karamus family looked solemnly upon the company of the Daughters of the East.

Allor, being the King of Enmayar, stood directly before the throne alongside the Elect to address Queen Xenia and King Viktor. As the company introduced themselves, all the royal family of the North gave an awed glance at the three marked women, and in that brief silence, Allor at last looked intently to the king and queen themselves. They both bore the looks of an epic hero or heroine, as was the case for nearly all who were born from the line since its founding by Karanor, including the children of the present generation. They were both tall, though it was Viktor who came to that height by the Karamus blood. Both wore their hair in a long, graceful braid, and the king's beard, though not particularly long, had several plaits arrayed symmetrically across his chin. They had eyes of the deepest blue, the same blue of Verdok's eyes. Both were roughly twenty years older than Allor, being at around fifty years. They carried their age, and what few wrinkles they had, with the grace of the mountains.

King Viktor, his hand in his wife's, spoke to the company in his strong, but gentle voice.

"I bid you welcome, Daughters of the East and King Allor, along with those in your company. I was told of your basic intentions by the guard, and the essence of your quest is known thanks to the prophecy, though it does not necessarily detail the specifics. Might I ask what exactly happened on Veronmay's Eve, and what you mean to do in response?"

Allor recounted the horrors that transpired in Genverdell and its archtemple on the night before spring's return, along with the branding of Ruth, Mira, and Lerannu. He then told of their journey up to their entering of Norkoth, and ended with their intentions for the quest's future.

"We must reach Kellmayar and Janrenar," said Allor, "specifically their capitals, and inform their leaders as we have just informed you, if we can. We then must enlist the aid of their armies to get to Raakmathna and put an end to her and her grey-cloaked army of mind-broken murderers. As we seek to request the aid of the armies of the other two nations, so we now ask of you."

"And our aid we would gladly give you," said Viktor, "if this accursed siege upon our city could be broken and we could ensure that the rest of our land was sufficiently secured."

"Do you have any ideas in that regard?" Ruth asked the two monarchs.

The queen and king nodded. "We have been trying to form a plan to clear these grey-coats out since they first attacked," said Xenia, "though many of our ideas entailed waiting for help from other nations. We were told this evening that you found our messenger dead in the sewer. We sent him down there the day after the attacks to try and sneak out past the grey-coats and send word anywhere he could, but it seems he wasn't even able to get away from the city proper before being cut down."

The Queen of Sorrenar breathed a light sigh, gently squeezed her husband's hand, and rested her head on his shoulder before continuing.

"Thankfully, we eventually took another approach. Though we didn't know of his fate until now, we assumed the worst and decided to risk the old trick of sending out a few messages with Shanlofs disguised as crows. Thankfully it worked, and we eventually got word from Kellmayar and Janrenar, but their leaders have told us they too are besieged and unable to send aid, so support from them is presently out of the question. But there is some help we have managed to get, and there is one idea, risky as it is, that might be our only option. Given the arrival of the Elect and their urgent need to reach the West and the South, there may be more hope for it than would otherwise be."

"What would it be?" asked Allor.

"To put it shortly, a cavalry charge out of the city and through the grey-cloaks' camp," said Viktor.

Allor's ears dropped as he took in the desperate plan. He looked intently at the northern king, who nodded toward a set of doors to the company's right.

"Those are the council chambers," said Viktor. "Tomorrow, we will discuss the specifics of the plan with you and some of our advisors. The rest of the day, we shall rest and prepare, and then carry out our plan the following day ... or die trying. That is, of course, provided that no one has an alternative to propose between now and then."

The company was silent apart from a collective sigh of determination. Allor looked squarely at both the queen and king, and nodded reverently.

"So be it," he said. "Thank you."

The king and queen nodded to their assembled descendants, who then departed from the room. Viktor and Xenia looked to the company once more, rising from their throne as they spoke.

"My deepest condolences for what happened to your wife, King Allor," said Viktor, "for her fate, and for all the pain and twisting of her mind that led her to it."

"My thanks, King Viktor. Alas, I was a foolish man who blindly trusted—"

"You loved her and believed in her," said Xenia, "and she gave you no reason to doubt her. Do not berate yourself for having a loving and hopeful heart, that which should be within all of us. Direct your contempt toward the forces that drove her to deceive, those which have raged since before our beginning."

Allor strove to take the northern queen's words to heart. Not knowing what else to say, he simply drew a deep breath, bowed his head, and closed his eyes. He listened quietly as the two monarchs addressed the rest of the company.

"Our hearts," Allor heard King Viktor say, "anxious as they remain, have been greatly lifted by your coming, Daughters of the East, as well as the coming of those who walk beside you on your journey. Much has been placed upon your shoulders, but that which has been commissioned by Onu is not a thing that has ever been utterly defeated, whatever trials and losses that come to pass. Keep heart, and know that we of the Karamus line will do all we can ... even if it ultimately means our end."

"You have our thanks," said Ruth, "and know that we will do all we can to keep you and all others from sacrificing more than need be, and to be worthy of your trust."

Allor quietly seconded the Faithguard's words, along with the others in the company. The King of Enmayar then opened his eyes and watched Xenia and Viktor depart from the throne room as they bade the company goodnight. The companions looked silently at one another, with all but Allor, his children, and Lerannu soon departing quietly to their beds. When the four were alone, Allor approached the mage and gently took her hand.

"Do you wish to be alone?"

"No ... but ..."

"I'm here for you, and Sam and Tally, too."

Lerannu embraced him, and Samuel and Talrah joined them, silently taking comfort in one another. A moment later, Allor proposed a walk about the castle, at least wherever they would be permitted. The four then exited the throne room, taking a corridor to their left. They walked together for a time and conversed over the events of the past few hours. Eventually, Lerannu spoke softly to Allor.

"I just can't let her go," she said.

"Is anyone demanding that of you?" asked Allor. "It just happened a few hours ago. How could anyone expect you to let it go just like that?"

"I *need* to, Al. I wasn't able to fully talk things out with her, and it's clouding my mind and draining my heart. I'm a mage; focus is paramount in what I do, especially at a time like this. I can't be burdened by this now, not when all of Fidonhaal needs me, along with Mira and Ruth."

"Lera ..."

The four of them stopped as they reached an open door, where a guard stood in somber silence. The guard glanced at them and, realizing who they were, turned his head and called to the people in the room behind him.

"King Allor is here, your majesties," he said, "along with his children and one of the Elect."

Allor peered into the room from over the guard's shoulder. Viktor and Xenia were there, embracing who he recognized as the widowed princess and her scarred twin brother. Viktor's eyes locked with Allor's, and the northern king nodded.

"Let them enter, if they wish."

The guard stepped aside and nodded respectfully. Allor looked to Lerannu and the children, who told him they would follow his lead. Figuring that he may as well accept the permission, he walked in with Lerannu and the children behind him. A look over the room revealed it to be a bed chamber, with its décor indicating it was one for a member of the royal family. As Allor approached the monarchs and their two present children, he passed by the large, tidy bed. One of the pillows had a portrait of a man resting on it, the likeness of which matched the man depicted on the urn in the throne room. Allor looked past the bed and saw the cradle that stood beside it. Wordlessly, he approached it and looked at the little painting of the baby that rested in it. Tears began to creep into his vision.

He then heard Samuel gasp morbidly, followed immediately by a sob from Talrah. Blinking back the brimming tears, he saw them turn away and bury their faces in Lerannu's robes. Allor placed a hand on both his children, meaning to console them, when Samuel pointed back to the cradle.

"Di-did you see the blanket, Father?" the prince asked brokenly.

Allor peered back into the cradle and saw the blanket under the portrait. His blood froze, and his stomach turned at the dark red stain and small, jagged holes that were now plain to see. He turned his sight to the royal family and looked straight into the grey eyes of the widowed princess. The widow's twin brother then stepped forward, and Allor looked to him as the northern prince spoke.

"We were all celebrating Veronmay's Eve," he said quietly, "as we always had. We had the Peacekeepers in our company, as Sheeva had given them to us as a gesture toward a more unified Fidonhaal, and we trusted them with our lives as we did our own guards. Then we heard a horn sound somewhere in the city below, and then a great, violent clamor. We heard screams in the castle and saw what those grey-coats were doing. I fought my way here, but I was too late. My sister was here, trying to fight them off, even though Venkar and Jakob were ... already gone."

The prince tilted his head and brushed aside his hair, giving Allor a full look at the scar that ran down his face.

"I stepped in and one of them gave me this. We managed to drive them out of the castle and the city, but we've been trapped here ever since, wondering how we could put an end to this."

The prince put a hand on Allor's shoulder. "And now here you are, in the company of the Elect. Know that we don't hold you in blame for your wife's deceptions, and we pray that Onu guard you and all your companions."

"Thank you," said Allor as levelly as he could. "Might I ask your name? I think I remember the names of the present Karamus children, but I'm afraid I've forgotten the faces they belong to."

"I am Zarnyr," said the prince humbly, "and my twin sister is Alessia."

Allor approached Alessia, gently taking her hands into his. "Dear Princess, words cannot express my sorrow for your loss and the regret I have for my ignorance of the machinations that bereaved you. Know that my companions and I will do all in our power to see to it that the evil behind your grief is stopped, even if it cost my life."

Princess Alessia nodded silently and embraced Allor in thanks. The widow then spoke to him in a small, shaky whisper.

"Thank you, King Allor. In return for your efforts, I would be honored if you would trust me with seeing to the safety of your children."

Allor looked to Viktor, Xenia, and Zarnyr. Their eyes were wide, and tears were beginning to brim them. Zarnyr approached Alessia, who, having pulled away from Allor, now embraced her brother, whose gaze pierced Allor's soul with the warmth of rekindled hope.

"That's the first time she's spoken since ..."

Prince Zarnyr sobbed and held his sister closely.

"Thank you, King Allor."

Allor sighed heavily and nodded to the royal family as he turned to leave with Lerannu and the children.

"Our thanks again for your aid," he said. "I suppose we will retire for the night, now."

Once they left and began to make their way back to their rooms, Samuel spoke quietly to his father.

"So I guess Tally and I are going to have to stay here when you all leave?"

Allor drew a deep breath, forcing his voice to pass from his tightened throat as levelly as he could manage.

"We'll talk about that later."

125

6/23/4030 G.M.

RUTH woke to the sound of rain pattering against the windows of her room. She propped herself up slightly and put an arm around Verdok, looking out of the windows and into the dreary grey sky that lay over the castle and city. Her husband still slept soundly beside her, his muzzle resting intimately against her neck, and his warm, steady breaths brushed across her fur like a gentle summer breeze in a field. The knight lay quietly as she was, pondering all that had happened since the company's flight from Genverdell as the cool rain lightly continued to fall.

In time, a gentle knock sounded on the door. Ruth, feeling Verdok's ears flutter against her as he stirred, gently pulled the blanket a little further over them as she bade the person who knocked to enter. Verdok sat up alongside his wife, and the two watched the attendant as she came in, her sincere and dutiful face gently touched with a sly smirk as she observed the couple's state. Ruth snorted good-naturedly at the servant as Verdok drew her closer to him.

"Well," she said, "have you been sent to tell us something, or were you simply interested in seeing how we look together?"

"I beg your pardon, Lady and Sir Pionaar," the attendant said sheepishly. "Queen Xenia and King Viktor have sent me to tell you and the others that the council meeting will soon begin. Breakfast will be brought in while the lot of you discuss what's to be done."

"Thank you, my lady. We'll be joining them soon."

"Very well," the attendant said as she looked at the couple once more, her playful smirk vanishing as she looked sincerely at them. "Thank you, both of you ... all of you, for coming."

Ruth nodded silently and rose out of bed once the servant left. She dressed alongside Verdok in stately robes that the Karamus family had lent them, as their own clothes and equipment had been entrusted to the castle's launderers and smiths. Having dressed, the two took one another's hand and left for the council chambers.

***

King Viktor and Queen Xenia, along with a handful of advisors and who appeared to be the eldest Karamus prince and princess, were seated at the grand stone table. Three maps were laid out on the table: one of Norkoth and the surrounding lands, one of the continent of Sorrenar, and one of the entirety of Fidonhaal. Another table, one of oak, had been brought in and placed by the door. On it lay an array of food and drink from which the queen and king bade the company fill their plates and cups as they discussed the strategy for the breaking of the siege. Ruth and her companions, their breakfasts in hand, took seats at the table and listened to Viktor and Xenia explain the plan. The northern queen began by pointing to the map of the capital and surrounding countryside, moving around representations of various parties as she spoke.

"As we said earlier, our plan is to enact a cavalry charge out of Norkoth and through the siege camp. We mean to execute it at the sun's zenith. We must be swift in our charge once the signaling horns are blown so the grey-cloaks don't have time to fortify their camp any more than they already have, or otherwise mount up too many of their own to counter our riders."

"You know," said Ruth, looking intently at the maps as she digested Xenia's words, "for all the things to worry about with this, I don't think I ever fully realized that the grey-coats don't seem to have much, if anything, in the way of real siege equipment. Or am I wrong? I would've thought that if they did, the city would've been even worse off by the time we got here, if not already captured."

"You have surmised correctly," said Xenia, a small, thankful smile appearing on her lips. "They've had virtually nothing like that in their camp, and it would seem that both sides figure it wouldn't be worth the trouble for them at present. We would try to attack, or at least hinder them as they were building such things if they did it in the camp, as we'd be able to clearly see them working on it if they did it there. We've been watching them like a hawk this whole time, so we'd likely notice if any large number of them left to try and construct them off-site. And even if we didn't notice them leaving, we'd surely notice them returning from a good distance with devices like that. In short, they wouldn't have much of the element of surprise if they tried that now. As much as this is taking out of us, they're not appearing to be doing much better, truth be told. That's certainly one bit of fortune that we've been graced with in all this."

"I wonder why they didn't have many, if any, towers or catapults handy," Allor said, his brow furrowed in thought as he looked over the maps.

"I guess Sheeva—or Raakmathna, rather, was counting on us being caught off-guard and done away with during the initial attacks," said King Viktor. "After all, secrecy and deception were a vital part of the plan, and as much of a task as it was to try and get enough soldiers spread across the world without raising suspicion, I suppose trying to construct and store enough siege devices was deemed too risky, or perhaps simply too difficult, of a venture to attempt. Or perhaps it was simply overconfidence? Maybe the demon was so sure the first attacks would have been enough to wipe us all out, or at least break our spirits to resist? Either way, my guess is that the demon and its soldiers were counting on being able to sufficiently crush us, one way or another, on Veronmay's Eve and then strengthen themselves with the supplies that they would have doubtlessly helped themselves to when we were defeated."

"I see," said Allor. "Well, thankfully, as devastating as their actions have been, it seems they underestimated the strength, or perhaps fortune, of the capitals. Well, apart from Genverdell. Hopefully, that'll prove to be a great advantage for us going forward."

"Indeed." said Xenia. "But all of that being said, going back to the details of our charge, we will have archers covering us from the walls and a company of infantry following us out. Our crow-masked heraldwings have managed to secure us a fine number of additional fighters from outside the capital. Some are proper soldiers, while others are militia bands that gathered in the wake of the massacres. They've come to form no small number of supporters and have managed to get close to here, waiting for further word from us. Up until now, however, we were unsure of what to do with them."

"Thankfully," said Viktor, placing a handful of small parchments next to the maps, "they've been able to stay out of the grey-cloaks' notice, being in small bands that have hidden in the hills and mountains nearby up until now. Going by these messages that we received overnight, that remains the case. We'll send word to them today, if we can, and they should be in position in time to help us tomorrow with a pincer movement."

Queen Xenia looked intently at the company.

~ 280 ~

"When the horns blow," she said, "we will lead you and a company of supporting riders out of the city, and cut our way through the camp as needed. The cavalry is *not* to go out of their way to combat the grey-coats themselves, however. The archers, the infantry behind us, and the support from outside the city will be tasked with the direct battle itself. The cavalry is also not to stop for *anything*. If anyone falls, no matter who it is, the company *must* keep going for the greater good of the Elect's quest."

Ruth's eyes darted around the table, looking at the faces of those seated and seeing their countenances spanning from grim resolve to dread. She took Verdok's hand, beginning her efforts to steel herself for the worst that might happen the next day. She felt her husband gently brush his thumb across her hand and relished the comforting touch.

Xenia, seeing the reactions of those gathered at the table, sighed quietly and rose to pour herself some more tea, nodding to her husband to continue with explaining the plans.

"If—" the northern king began, his voice at first strikingly small for a man of such imposing form. Viktor stopped himself short, looking around the table as all eyes fixed upon him, and his ears lowered as he saw the growing fears that were setting into the faces of all present. Ruth herself felt a cold, spreading fear within her. She thought of her failure in protecting Orson and all the others in Genverdell that she had to leave to die in her flight. For a moment, she doubted that she, or her sisters in destiny, could ultimately succeed. The grey sky outside the window, and the chilly rain that now poured heavily from it, did nothing to help the mood.

Ruth felt King Viktor's gaze and looked squarely into his eyes. They were of the same blue as Verdok's, and she saw in them the same sort of beauty despite the doubt that filled them. She then saw them flit from her face to that of Mira and Lerannu. Viktor closed his eyes, drew a deep breath, and when he opened them again, the uncertainty that was meandering within Ruth's heart immediately faded. The Sorrenarn king's eyes were now alight with a fire of resolve that would no doubt have made Karanor proud of his descendant.

"*When*," Viktor said as he began anew, pointing out the planned course of the company on the map of Sorrenar. "*When* we make our way through the grey-coats' camp, we are to take the southern highway and make all possible haste for the port of Benevor. That port is the only one from which we have received word that has declared itself to be free of the grey-coats' control. They thankfully managed to wipe out the ones who were present on Veronmay's Eve with minimal losses, and have managed to keep any roving companies of them out. We'll send word to them today, and if all holds, we should arrive there and have two fully crewed ships ready."

Viktor looked intently about the whole company before continuing.

"Given that you mean to go to both Kellmayar and Janrenar for aid and that time is of the essence, it would seem clear in my mind that this company is meaning to split in order to cover both routes as close to simultaneously as possible. Or have I misunderstood your intentions?"

Ruth looked at her companions, who appeared as ones who had half-forgotten or even failed to fully realize the necessity for this part of the plan. Knowing that she herself had been of the same mindset, she sighed and answered the king. "It is as you say, King Viktor, though I do not know which way I would mean to take at present. I suppose that could be discussed on the road, unless it must be settled now for some reason."

"I suppose it could be discussed later," the king said thoughtfully as he directed the company's attention to the map of the world. "Whatever the case, if you look here, the places we think would be best for you to head toward are—"

"If ... if we are concerned with following the prophecy," said a woman's small voice, "then I know who should be going to Kellmayar, and to Janrenar."

The council turned in their seats, surprised to see Princess Alessia standing in the doorway.

Queen Xenia approached her daughter, embracing her and leading her to the seat beside Viktor. "If this concerns the course of the Elect, and if it's told in the prophecy, we should listen," she said plainly.

"I ... I had a dream," said the princess, having made to compose herself as well as she could after being in silent grief for nearly three moons. "The spirit of Elukus approached me and pointed out where he states the necessary courses for the Elect and their companions. He then bade me to point it out to you, saying that it's fairly straightforward, but with all that's been on your minds, you may have very well forgotten, or simply hadn't fully realized it yet."

Silence filled the room. Then Ruth, with a quiet, deep breath, asked the princess to point out the details of the course that needed to be taken.

"It's what is told in the latter part of the prophecy," she said, beginning to recite the part in question. "The Daughters of the East, having risen with the sun, shall come to follow its course into the west, but not without first passing under the light of the Sapphire Star."

"The North Star," said Verdok as he drank some tea. "Of course. That makes perfect sense, and it's where we are right now."

Alessia nodded solemnly and continued. "Three men, out of faith and love, shall follow them out of the east, but shall then journey to the land under the Golden Star."

Ruth grasped the significance of the reference to the South Star. Her heart began to ache.

"By the joined deeds of these separate hearts shall Fidonhaal be united against the rising hatred," Alessia concluded. "They shall then reunite upon the isle of our beginning, where they shall take fiery flight and return to the east, where the fate of Fidonhaal shall be decided."

Ruth's heart grew heavy as the princess finished reciting the lines from the prophecy. It did not seem to be particularly cryptic at all, now that she was hearing it again, and she berated herself for not pondering the words more in the times that would have afforded her the opportunity to reflect on them. She looked at Verdok, his deep sapphire eyes looking sadly into hers. As the knight looked about the table, she saw the same countenance on all her companions, with the pain in Lerannu's eyes being exceptionally sharp as the mage looked to Allor.

King Viktor and Queen Xenia looked at the company in silence, seemingly waiting for a reply from them before saying anything further. At last, Ruth composed herself, took Verdok's hand, and holding it tightly, spoke for the company.

"So be it," she said levelly. "All three of the Elect are bound for Kellmayar. The three men in our company will journey to Janrenar."

Verdok and all the company sighed, their voices ones of worry and sorrow, but ultimately of resolve, however reluctant. King Viktor then returned the company's attention to the map of Fidonhaal.

"Now that we've settled on who's going where, here's what we suggest based on what few messages we've managed to get from Kellmayar and Janrenar. The Daughters of the East, once they leave Benevor, shall make for the port of Vahnon's Landing. That port, last we've been told, has been free from the grey-coats this whole time. They were fortunate enough to not have been considered a priority target, and once they finally received word from Zefiil, they've since held the port secure. We'll send word to them and they should be ready for you when you arrive. From there, ride south for Zefiil."

The king and queen stared at the map in brief silence, at last breathing a joint sigh as the king continued.

"I wish I could give you some sort of information or plan for getting into the city, as they've been besieged much like we've been, but Zefiil's layout is obviously not the same as here. I'm not familiar with their particular infrastructure, or other such things, to give any solid advice. I'm afraid you may need to ask some locals about it or otherwise try to come up with a plan of your own once you reach the city. I am sorry."

"There's no need to apologize," said Mira. "It's supposed to be up to us in the end anyway, is it not?"

"I suppose, but if I'm to be among your allies, I, and all my family and our nation, owe it to you to do everything we can to help you put an end to this horror."

"What about the ones bound for Janrenar?" Ruth asked, trying to keep the council from feeling inadequate in their aid. "Is there a port there that has had the same good fortune as Vahnon's Landing?"

"Thankfully, yes," said Viktor. "Humilaar, unlike Vahnon's Landing, was a priority target, being at the mouth of the Vitari River, but last I heard it managed to withstand falling into the grey-coats' grasp. I don't know if you would want to sail up the river much, since I can't say where there might be grey-coats waiting in ambush. Even if you managed to make it all the way to Benhotha without incident, I don't think you'd be able to help very much by staying on your ship. We've also been told that Janrenarn forces have secured the south bank of the Vitari, but I'm not sure if you should stay on the river or disembark onto the highway along the bank. Like with the course of the Daughters of the East, we do not have much more information to advise further action beyond suggesting where to land, and the basic route to the capital from there."

"We'll find a way," Donovan said with grim simplicity, "or die trying."

"Then I suppose that's that," said Xenia as she grasped Viktor's hand. "The rendezvous point, which I would think to be a fairly sensible location even if the prophecy didn't address it, has nonetheless been foreseen by Elukus. Should Sorrenar succeed in ridding itself of these grey-cloaks, we shall do all we can to muster as many troops as possible and have them sail for Karzynhaal. Should we reach it before you all do, we'll do what we can to keep the isle and the surrounding waters secure. Once we've gathered all we can ..."

"We'll make our way back to Genverdell," said Ruth plainly, "and finish this demon's war against Fidonity."

A brief silence fell, and then Viktor and Xenia, rising from their seats, bowed respectfully to the Elect and their companions.

"We'll go and send the word," said the northern queen, "and see to everything being arranged for tomorrow and the days to come. Please, rest up while you can, and settle whatever needs to be settled."

"Thank you, dear Mountainborn," said Ruth reverently.

The queen and king departed from the room, and Princess Alessia, quietly rising from her chair, approached Allor.

"Might we discuss things with your children, King Allor, along with the widower and two boys who came with your companions?"

A sharp pain raced through Ruth's heart at the sight of Allor's face. The King of Enmayar, looking to Lerannu and taking her hand, rose up and followed Alessia out of the room.

***

Ruth and Verdok stood on the balcony outside the council chamber alongside Mira and Donovan. It had been several hours since the meeting had ended. The rain had stopped and the sky, though still laden with many grey clouds, was now open enough for some sunlight to pass through. The four of them had spent the past few hours reflecting on the happy times they had together prior to the horrors that befell them on Veronmay's Eve.

Their conversation faded as they saw Allor and Lerannu, with Prince Samuel and Princess Talrah beside them, talking with Princess Alessia, Prince Zarnyr, and Harvus, Evor and Ethos in the garden below them. They could not hear them, but were sure of the subject of their discussion.

Eventually, Talrah and Samuel embraced both Allor and Lerannu, their sobs just reaching the balcony above. At last the nine of them walked back into the castle together, and the four who watched them from above turned around to do the same.

126

6/23/4030 G.M.

ALLOR lay awake in bed as Talrah and Samuel lay snugly beside him. He had spoken with Alessia and Zarnyr, along with Harvus and his two sons, in regards to their caring for his son and daughter. Tearful as Samuel and Talrah were, they had understood the necessity for them to remain in Norkoth. The king and his children had sought to take as much comfort in one another as they could, as it was possibly the last night they'd be together on Fidonhaal. The children were sound asleep, but Allor, kept awake by the dreadful silence of the besieged city and the worries for the day to come, lay wearily between his children. His eyes alternated between staring at the ceiling and the lightly moonlit window to his side.

He thought back on the journey thus far and began to brood over the state of Lerannu. With her troubles regarding Uriah and her now-bereft family still clearly weighing on her mind, coupled with the pain she shared with Allor in leaving the children behind, Allor was greatly worried for her spirits. The mage had already been bearing a heavy weight within her despite being one of the Elect, and the king could only imagine the overwhelming burden that the mission ahead was adding to Lerannu's heart.

Allor started slightly at the sudden, quiet creaking of the bedroom door. His heart leapt and began to race as Lerannu's head peered through the door. The mage, seeing Talrah and Samuel sleeping on either side of him, lowered her ears and spoke quietly to Allor.

"I'm sorry to disturb you three. I thought maybe Sam and Tally would be in their own beds, and ..."

Lerannu sighed and looked piercingly into Allor's eyes. "Could we talk?"

Allor nodded, gently rising from the bed and taking care not to disturb Samuel and Talrah. He walked quietly to the door and leaned against the wall, bowing his head closely to Lerannu's as the two whispered to one another.

"I can't stop thinking about Uriah," the mage said miserably. "I know she said that she was willing to guard us with her life. She even mentioned me in particular, as an effort to atone for what she did with Father. I know that Harvus and his boys don't blame me, or any of us, for what happened; they've told me as much again and again. But ... I never got to properly discuss everything with her, even for all the days we had on the road. Then again, maybe I didn't want to. I thought I had let it go, but ..."

"Lera," Allor said as he tenderly lifted Lerannu's chin with his hand, gazing deeply into her brown eyes. "A pain dealt like that, and by someone you took as a friend, is not an easy thing to forget, no matter how much one may sincerely mean to let it go."

"Maybe so, but I should've talked it out with her, all of it, or at least as much as we could've helped to discuss along the way. I should've started the conversation as soon as we met again. I should've known there was a chance that something like this would happen."

"You must trust in her spirit now. Trust that she understands. In time, there will come a day when you might speak to her as much as you need. But that day is not here yet. For now, you, me, all of us ..."

Allor suddenly let out a quiet chuckle. Seeing Lerannu's puzzled look, the king drew her close and kissed her cheek.

"We have a world to save, and a prophecy to fulfill. For now, we must take up the roles of all the heroes and heroines that came before us, and set an example for those who are to follow us in the days long after we've passed from this world."

Lerannu smiled and returned the kiss. "Very well," she said, "but all the same, there's no guarantee as to who will be left still living in this world when all of this is said and done, even if Raakmathna is ultimately defeated. I don't want to leave anything else unresolved if I can help it."

"What else is there to settle?"

"Remember what we said in the forest garden, behind the burned inn?"

Allor's heart now raced even faster. He gently nuzzled Lerannu's neck, relishing her scent.

"I do," he whispered.

"I've thought about it, and if you feel the same, I would like to consider ... revising the specifics of our agreement, as far as not being ... together ... before our journey's end. But given that Sam and Tally are here, I don't want to ..."

"The beds are separated by a screen," Allor said quietly, "and they're both sound asleep. We can use one of the other beds here. We just need to be quiet."

The king and the mage quietly made for one of the beds on the other side of the room, gently kissing and caressing each other as they walked. They reached the bed and quietly began to undress one another as they whispered to each other.

"I love you, Al, and I want to be there for you, and Sam and Tally, always. But if we are to part in the near future, and if we don't all get through this–"

"Never mind that, Lera. Know that I take your word, here and now, as surely as if it were before the altar. Whatever awaits us in the coming days, I will do all I can ..."

Allor's heart grew quiet, and the words he spoke to Sheeva their first night together came back to his lips.

"I will do all I can to be by your side, and to help you when the burdens feel too heavy. When we must part ways, I'll keep you in my heart. I will never leave you or hurt you. I will share in your pain and your joy. Hide nothing from me, and I'll hide nothing from you."

Lerannu looked up into his eyes again. The two looked quietly at one another, their faces gently lit by the moon's thinning silver light.

"As you have said to me," Lerannu said softly, "so I say to you."

"I do not doubt it," Allor said quietly. "But ... I can't do this. Not now. I'm so sorry if—"

"No," said Lerannu, her voice completely calm and gentle. "I understand. Did you say something like that to Sheeva, once?"

"Yes," said Allor as he told Lerannu of the promise he made on his wedding night with Sheeva.

"I know she's gone," said the king as he donned his robes, "and not just gone, but to the way of the demons. But I just can't bring myself to do this while her body is still ... acting in the world. I know it's foolish, but—"

"It isn't," Lerannu said simply.

"When I see you, I see her in so many ways."

Lerannu, having also put her robes back on, quietly kissed him on the neck.

"At first," Allor continued, "I agreed to our plan out of respect for you. But now, I truly feel that this is what's best. For all of us."

Allor took Lerannu's hands in his, kissing them and holding them gently as he went on.

"Know that I have renounced my bond with her and now pledge my body, my heart, and my soul to you from this moment hence, to the deepest extent that may be pledged between two mortals. With this, I place my trust in you and in Onu's will and judgement, that should either of us perish before our quest's end, we will be reunited in Onu's home. Should we survive the journey and triumph, we can then settle things properly and live the rest of our lives together. In this agreement I place my faith. What say you, my love?"

Lerannu, her eyes shining tearfully in the thin moonlight, kissed Allor one more time before rising from the bed and making her way to the door.

"I, too, place my faith in our agreement, my love. Should the plans that have been laid for tomorrow fare as intended, we will journey together a little longer. Then we shall part, but one day come together again, in this life or the next."

Allor nodded, then quietly made his way back to his bed, where Talrah and Samuel still slept soundly. As he carefully resettled between his children, he looked to Lerannu, who quietly stood in the doorway.

"Goodnight, Allor," said the mage softly. "Thank you."

Lerannu closed the door, and Allor, his heart and mind now calmed, quickly drifted off at last into a peaceful slumber.

The Battle of Norkoth

127

6/24/4030 G.M.

MIRA and Donovan immediately awoke to the sound of knocking on their door. They asked for the one outside to wait a moment, and quickly throwing on their pants and undershirts, they took seats at the small table by the door.

"Come in," Mira called out.

Mira was stunned to see Queen Xenia and King Viktor themselves enter, both wearing grimly beautiful armor of plate and chain. Viktor, carefully maneuvering through the doorway, held a claymore that was as tall as Mira in one hand, resting it on his massive shoulder. Xenia, having a shorter blade sheathed at her hip, carried a long spear, on which she leaned casually as she and her husband looked intently at the huntress and the bard.

"The time is nigh," said Xenia plainly. "Your sisters in fate, along with the rest of your companions, are preparing as we speak. A quick breakfast will be brought in soon, after which you are to meet with us and your party in the throne room. From there, we'll ride out to the gates ... and then it will begin."

Mira was still taken aback by the king and queen's arms and armor. She glanced over to Donovan, whose small smile and shining blue eyes glowed with a patriotic pride.

"M-my thanks, Queen Xenia and King Viktor," Mira stuttered in awe as she returned her sight to the monarchs, "but I must confess that when you told us you would lead us and a company of riders out of Norkoth, I didn't think you meant ... well, *you* yourselves."

Xenia and Viktor smiled.

"When Sorrenar suffered evil and strife in times past," said Viktor dutifully, "those of the Mountainborn line took up arms to fight alongside their citizens for the sake of the nation they served. What would we say of ourselves now, if we did not do the same when all of Fidonhaal lies in peril, and the Elect came both to and for our aid?"

Mira was speechless at the northern king's words of resolve, and the legend-worthy visage that he and his wife struck. At a loss for words, she simply nodded gratefully.

"Th-thank you, your majesties," she managed to say at last.

"Thank *you*, Daughter of the East," said Viktor. "You, your sisters of destiny, and all others who have followed you on your path."

The queen and king turned away and departed without another word, and Mira and Donovan began preparing for the battle and journey to come as they waited for their breakfast.

***

Within the hour, Mira and Donovan were fully dressed, armed, armored, and fed. The clothes and gear with which they arrived had been returned cleaned and well-repaired, and provided alongside additional supplies courtesy of the castle stores. The huntress and the bard came into the throne room, joining Ruth, Lerannu, Allor, and the others, as a final farewell was bid to those staying behind. Allor and Lerannu embraced Talrah and Samuel one final time, entrusting them to the widowed princess, her twin brother, and the surviving members of the Queniroth family.

Queen Xenia and King Viktor, having clearly laid out the positions each of their children were to take in their absence, strongly embraced and kissed each of them, along with their spouses and children. Prince Rensard and Princess Viktoria, the eldest of the present heirs, bowed their heads reverently to their parents as they committed them to their stations as regents until their return, with the added task of bearing the crown in full if their parents didn't return alive. Viktor and Xenia then turned to the Elect and their companions.

"Follow us, if you please, Daughters of the East," they said in unison.

They were led first to the stables, where each took a mount that was seemingly as armored as its rider, if not more so. They were joined by a long train of soldiers, who divided themselves up within the long cavalry line, placing Mira and her companions in the middle. They then rode down from the castle, trotting past the many grand buildings of stone that wound their way about the city's namesake mountain, and came at last to the great stone walls that guarded Norkoth from the horde of grey-coats and undead that stood just outside. It was noon, and the sun shined brightly upon Norkoth from its seat in the clear blue sky.

Mira looked about apprehensively. She saw throngs of archers with bows and marksmen with crossbows all along the walls, crouched in cover so as not to give away their position or numbers. A few ballistae could also be seen lining the walls. She saw all about her men and women, armed and armored, on horse and on foot, who were preparing to follow the charging cavalry out to continue the battle after they had ridden off for Benevor. She also saw the civilians, men, women and children, young and old. They were pressed against the walls of the city and the sides of the roads, gazing upon the cavalry for which they stepped aside. Many more looked onto the procession from doorways and windows. Many of their hands were clasped in prayer.

"With Onu as my witness," Mira said quietly, essentially to herself despite meaning it for all those around her, "I will do all I can to fulfill my role in the defense of you all."

"As will I," Donovan's voice said quietly beside her.

Mira looked at her husband with a gentle smile, relishing another look into his sky-blue eyes.

She saw Donovan's eyes suddenly dart their gaze ahead of her. The bard breathed a sharp breath. Mira turned quickly in the saddle, and saw Xenia and Viktor at the head of the column. Each pumped a fist into the air, and suddenly a great chorus of horns sounded.

128

6/24/4030 G.M.

DONOVAN felt the fur on his neck rise and his heart start to pound. He looked up as the column of riders before him readied their horses as the great gates of Norkoth began to swing open. All the archers and marksmen bolted up from their places behind the wall, firing a great volley into the camp that lay beyond. The first great bolts from the few ballistae along the walls were also fired upon the grey-clad camp. The cavalry was now charging swiftly, and Donovan, his heart pounding in rhythm to the many hooves around him, gripped his reigns tightly as he set all his efforts on keeping up with the charging company.

They were now outside the gate, and carnage fell all around him. Arrows, bolts, blades, and more encircled the bard and his companions, along with the faces of soldiers. They were soldiers of Norkoth. They were soldiers of Sorrenar, who were now charging from the surrounding hills and mountains from which they had hidden, pouring into the battlefield as water overflowing from the top of a bucket. And they were the soldiers of Raakmathna's so-called Peacekeepers. The faces of all the soldiers around him were of those alive, dead, and undead. Some of the eyes that passed him by were alight with the fire of battle. Others were stricken with horror, agony, or both. Others were as blank as stone.

Suddenly, Donovan felt a horrid grip upon his ankle. Looking down, he saw an undead soldier, a skeletal wretch with only a few scraps of flesh and fur still clinging to it, digging its boney claws into his ankle and leg. Crying out in anger, fear, and revulsion, the bard yanked his short sword from its sheath and lopped off the undead's head. As he made to return his sight to his guiding riders, he saw a soldier fall from his horse, pulled down by another undead, and his heart and stomach turned at the corpse's shrieks and the soldier's screams.

A grey-coat soldier leapt up onto the side of Donovan's saddle, punching him in the face and nearly knocking him off. The bard grabbed the soldier by the neck and made to kick him away, but hesitated when he saw that the soldier was a lad who looked no older than eighteen. That instant of grim observation was nearly Donovan's death, for as he hesitated, the soldier drew a dagger and nearly plunged it into his neck in the same motion. An arrow suddenly soared into the boy's neck and sent him flying off the horse and into the carnage on the ground.

Donovan looked around frantically, wondering if he could find the shooter and determine if the shot was indeed meant for the grey-cloak or for himself. He saw Mira just a few riders behind him, her bow drawn and eyes looking fixedly into his.

The bard made to call out thanks to his wife, but seeing the tears pouring from her eyes and thinking of the weight of what she just did, he simply turned his attention to the riders that led the way before him.

129
6/24/4030 G.M.

LERANNU rode beside Allor in the cavalry column's midst, and looked ahead to see the rapidly nearing western edge of the grey-coats' siege camp. She had seen soldiers fight and fall all about her, the ringing of steel and cries of battle and death sounding constantly in her ears. Now, with the end to the nightmarish onslaught within reach, the mage charged on with the company past the last of the grey-coats and rapidly forded across a shallow path in the Silverarm River.

Despite the words of Xenia and Viktor to keep riding, Lerannu came to a halt as she watched the remainder of the cavalcade make its way through the camp and across the river. A great many of the grey-coats had begun to break off from the battle and pursue the cavalry on foot and horse-back. They followed the company with alarming speed. The grey-coat heading the pursuit appeared to be one of the mages that Donovan and Mira had reported seeing back when they first reached Norkoth. He held a grim staff, which he pointed toward the fleeing cavalry.

Suddenly, a small stream of flame issued from the grey mage's staff, swiftly reaching and consuming one of the soldiers at the tail end of the Norkoth column. Lerannu, seeing this, looked to the waters of the river. She waited for the last of her company to cross, then focused her sight on the river. With both hands, she drew up two spear-like shafts of water from its flowing course. Envisioning as best she could the might of the angel Stromarus, Lerannu hurled the spears of water into the pursuing grey-coats. The flowing spears crashed into the soldiers, and the torrential force of their flight knocked many of the grey-coats to the ground, mangling more than a few of their bodies. The grey-cloaked necromancer, being in the lead of his squad, took the worst of it. His staff flew from his hand and into the river, and his body crumpled into a splashing heap. It did not seem likely that he would get up again unless one of his fellows in the foul arts reanimated him.

Lerannu reeled in the saddle, nearly overcome by the weariness that suddenly engulfed her, and did not notice the grey-coat that managed to evade the spell. The soldier had rushed across the river, her mace raised high above her head, and screamed with the wrath of battle as she bolted right for Lerannu.

130
6/24/4030 G.M.

VERDOK was riding on with the rest of the cavalcade when he heard the mighty rising and splashing of the magically channeled water of the river. Looking back, he saw Lerannu wavering in the saddle from her exertion, and the straggler grey-coat that now came charging at her with her mace, ready to strike.

The priest cried out in alarm and charged back toward Lerannu in an attempt to grab her from her horse and carry her to safety. A tall, armored woman with a spear suddenly galloped past him. It was Queen Xenia, who with a mighty throw buried her spear into the grey-cloaked soldier's chest. An arrow then flew from across the river and buried itself into the queen's shoulder. With a cry of pain, she rode up to Lerannu, grabbed her reins, and led her back into the cavalcade as the mage began to collect herself, rummaging in her satchel for a tonic to drink. Verdok followed after them, calling out to the northern queen.

"Queen Xenia! Let me see your wound!"

"Not now!" she called back. "It's not that bad; it can wait until we stop for the night. Come on, everyone! Let's move! It's up to those remaining behind us to finish this battle!"

***

The company and its escort rode hard through the remaining daylight and into the night, stopping at last and making camp in a grove of pines a short way off the south road. Verdok was finally able to take full count of the company, and he sighed a deep breath of relief when he saw that none of the Elect or their closest companions had fallen in the ride. Ruth dismounted and embraced Verdok closely. She then sat down against a tree and began to wipe the blood from her axe, the sight of which sent Verdok's heart into the pit of his stomach. The priest looked away, and saw Xenia approach with the arrow still lodged in her shoulder.

"Come along now, Sir Verdok," said the queen. "Help me with this, please."

Verdok silently followed her to the edge of the camp, where King Viktor stood waiting. One of the soldiers in the cavalcade brought pliers, bandages, and a poultice, with which Verdok swiftly went to work as he steadily pulled the arrow out of the queen's shoulder. The armor had done its job well overall, having prevented the arrow from piercing bone or artery. Soon, with just a few growls of pain, a good dressing of the herbal compound, and a wrapping of bandage, the queen had been tended to as best as the situation could permit. Xenia thanked him, and rising up to stand beside Viktor, she called all the cavalcade together.

"Well, that's the first part of the plan done. Tonight, we'll rest here and begin our way to Benevor at first light. Rest well, everyone; it's looking to be a fortnight in getting there, and there's no telling what might pass along the way."

Verdok rejoined Ruth in the tent that was set up for them, and the two lay quietly side by side until they at last fell asleep.

131
7/4/4030 G.M.

RAAKMATHNA stood before the Zaron man shackled to the chair in his cell within the guardhouse jail. The fool had not heeded the empress's words regarding the punishment that awaited those who tried to secretly harbor non-Zarons. The Peacekeepers had found him out, though those he had hidden were long gone, and now the empress had come to interrogate the traitor personally.

"Why would you throw your security away, sir?" she asked in a weary tone. "My efforts to bring order fell into your favor. All you had to do was–"

"Your sense of 'order' is tyranny, as is that of your master," the grey-furred man said contemptuously. "My soul, imperfect as it may be, I have entrusted to Onu."

"You mean the one who has allowed all that I am doing to happen, including what is now befalling you?"

"Aye, demon, as well as the one who allows the good within us to rise against it."

"Enough, traitor," said the empress as she waved a hand over the prisoner, who suddenly threw his head back and strained against his bonds in agony. "Your fate has been sealed, but tell me where you sent those vermin, and I will grant you a quick death."

The prisoner spat squarely into Raakmathna's face. "RAAKHAAL TAKE YOU!" he yelled at the top of his lungs, "and may your master send you into the deepest pits of agony when you ultimately fail him!"

Raakmathna contemptuously raised her hand, her fingers set to snap. "Even if I do not fully realize my master's desires," she said, "I will have hardly failed him. These days, no doubt, will echo down the hall of time for many centuries, if not millennia. The distrust now sown among you, over something so simple, is not one that will be easily uprooted, I wager."

The prisoner twitched violently in the chair, his eyes bulging from his head in anguish and wrath.

"And besides," said the empress calmly, "who are you to say that I will fail? I am still standing ... and you are not."

Raakmathna snapped her fingers. The spark of flame she had set within the prisoner had been slowly consuming him from within, and now went off in a fiery explosion. Hot blood and scraps of the traitor's body spattered the room, coating the empress's face and gown. Raakmathna silently exited the cell, relishing the silent terror of the guards posted at the door, and nodded toward the cell.

"That traitor was not even worthy to serve me in death," she said plainly. "Have the cell cleaned, and burn whatever remains you scrape up."

"Y-yes, my empress," said the guards in small, fear-numbed voices.

The empress walked back up the eastern hill to the castle, savoring the submissive horror on the face of every Fidon that she passed as they stared at the gore that covered her. Once she reached the main doors, she addressed the gaping guards stationed there.

"Find Salpion Windsbreath and inform him that I require his presence in the council chamber. I will be having a bath in the meantime."

"Yes, my empress," the guard said as she opened the door for the queen and gestured to another guard to seek out Ranoth.

Raakmathna made her way to the royal bed and bath chamber, coming to a halt as she entered. In the dimness of the evening-lit room, the empress sensed there were people hiding in the shadows.

"Show yourself," she demanded levelly.

Three Fidons bolted from the shadows, clothed in dark robes and veils, and darted toward the empress with crescent-shaped daggers drawn. Raakmathna screeched shrilly, more out of agitation than alarm, and then swiftly flung a fireball at the head of one of the assassins. It only grazed the side of the head, setting the cheek aflame. The veiled figure cried out in pain, but managed to beat away the fire before it could reach the face. The assassin then tore off her burning veil to reveal a Zaron woman.

The other two closed in, and one managed to bury a curved dagger into Raakmathna's side. The empress roared in pain and wrath, and gripped the culprit by the head, digging her fiery claws into the veil and the face beneath. A young woman's voice squealed in agony and terror, followed by the raging bellow of a man, who was the third assassin. Raakmathna swiftly kicked at the man's groin with an armor-toed shoe, and was rewarded with a wrathful howl as the assassin bulled into her and knocked her off her feet. Her grasp on the young assassin was loosed, though only by the force of her fall ripping her claws from the face, as was evident by the fabric, fur, and skin that clung to them. The man and the older woman now had the empress pinned down, with both pairs of their daggers raised high in their hands to begin the dozen or more stabbings they doubtlessly meant to inflict upon her.

Then came many rapid footsteps from down the hall, and soon there were a group of Fidons that had barged into the chamber to aid the empress. A staff came crashing down upon the heads of the man and woman. As they cried out in pain, stunned for only an instant, the spears of two guards ran through their skulls. Another guard ran over to the young one, who lay curled up in pain, and swiftly ran her though.

The one who wielded the staff stepped over the bodies, approached the empress, and offered his hand to help her up. It was Ranoth. Raakmathna looked at the salpion with surprised approval.

"Well done, Salpion Windsbreath. Very, very well done indeed."

"I couldn't stand by and let my empress be slain when there's still so much to be done to set the world to order, could I?"

"I would think not, but I must confess my surprise that you would go so far as to fight for me like that."

"I have sworn my loyalty to you, my empress."

"Indeed you have, and I now see that your words were not lightly spoken."

Raakmathna turned to the dead assassins, looking them over in the light of the guards' torches. They were dressed in garb inspired by the visage of the Angel of Night, and their daggers were shaped in the likeness of the crescent moon.

"Yorunian Nightblades," the empress said contemptuously. "It is not every day one comes across *those* slinking cowards."

"Indeed not, my empress."

"Ranoth," said the empress as she lifted her hands and reanimated the slain assassins, gesturing for them to depart for the armory as they shambled to their feet, "I have already given you much to tend to."

"I hope that I have proven worthy of the tasks you've given me, my empress."

"Oh, you have done more than enough to show that you are worthy. So much so, in fact, that I would like to offer you some of my own power directly ... and appoint you not only as my salpion, but to reign beside me as emperor."

Ranoth's eyes shined widely in the flickering torchlight. "I-I ... I'm at a loss for words, my empress. If you truly judge me to be worthy, I will gladly take up the task. What must I do?"

"Surely you know," said the empress sultrily. She looked to the guards who accompanied Ranoth. They stared apprehensively at her and the salpion, knowing full well what sort of ritual was to come. She waved them away in dismissal, and once they departed, Raakmathna closed and locked the door. She then undressed and cast about her body a warm, alluring glow.

"I was just about to take a bath," she said seductively, "before those bothersome thugs tried to murder me. I must say, I am quite rattled from it all. Would you care to keep me company, Ranoth? Make sure there are no more assassins? Maybe help me wash off this filth? We can discuss your ascension as emperor in the meantime."

Ranoth swallowed. "As you wish, my empress," he said as he disrobed and followed her into the bath.

"There ... there is a message I should inform you of, my empress," he continued, "before we ... get too invested in other subjects. It's about the forces that have laid siege to Benhotha. There's been a sudden and great spike in guerilla-style attacks from people in the surrounding forests. Our troops there have abruptly begun to take more losses than they had before."

"The reinforcements are on their way," the empress said casually as she drew the hot water into the tub. "They will just have to hold out for them. If worst comes to worst, we will renew our campaign against them in due time. Come now, Ranoth. Do not trouble yourself with that now. Join me."

Joined Hearts
and Sundered Paths

132
7/13/4030 G.M.

MIRA sighed, both in relief and sadness, as the sea and port city of Benevor appeared on the horizon, kissed with the golden light of the rising sun. The company had ridden as long and hard as they could manage over the past seventeen days, traveling over road and country as needed, and had finally come within view of their journey's next step. They had thankfully encountered nothing worse than a small patrol of grey-cloaks, which the cavalry easily ran down and dispersed. They otherwise rode on mostly in somber silence, passing ravaged towns and slaughtered travelers as they traversed the hauntingly quiet and rugged landscapes of Sorrenar.

The company stopped briefly, looking over the great sea and sprawling port that lay on the horizon below them from the great hill they had just topped.

"Well, there it is," said Queen Xenia, wincing ever so slightly as she shrugged in the saddle and felt a lingering twinge in her shoulder. "And I believe I can even see your ships from here as well. The *Frostwind* and the *Alessia*. Both of them should be all ready to go once we get there. No smoke from the port, no scent of death or burning bodies, no besieging grey-coats. Things are looking well, so far."

"Then let's get on it, if we may," said Mira plainly, and the company set off down the hill and on toward the walled port that lay beyond.

They arrived shortly before noon and were greeted at the walls by mounds of earth that lay on either side of the highway. Improvised banners were planted in each mound. They were made from the uniforms of grey-cloaks, cut at the seams to create the crude likeness of a pennant and then tied to the tops of poles. Mira looked at the mounds sadly, knowing what lay beneath, and the grim purpose for them and their markers. She looked to Donovan, riding beside her as always, and saw him making the same grim observation.

The mayor of Benevor, who had been informed of the party's approach by the guards on the wall, peered over the ramparts and hailed them gladly, waving a parchment in the air as he addressed King Viktor and Queen Xenia.

"A great day for us all, my queen and my king!" the mayor crowed. "You have arrived here, alive and well, with the Daughters of the East by your side! Onu's Elect can now begin the next steps of their quest without delay, and the both of you can now hear that the battle at Norkoth ended in our victory soon after your departure! The report is that not one grey-coat, living or undead, was left standing!"

"I am glad indeed to hear it," called Viktor with a loud, relieved sigh. "What price did our victory demand, though?"

"The letter states that the last count stands at around six hundred of ours lost, and many more wounded and recovering for the call of duty that lies ahead. As for your own family, all are safe and sound."

The mayor leaned over the ramparts, waving to Allor to get his attention.

"That goes for your children as well, King Allor, and the family that has been helping Alessia and Zarnyr take care of them."

"Thank you, mayor," said Allor levelly. "Whatever lies ahead for my companions and I, at least I can depart with this comfort."

Mira looked to Allor and saw that his face showed both relief and persistent apprehension. Beside him rode Lerannu, whose eyes shone painfully as she looked upon the man she would soon be leaving as they went their separate ways for the prophecy's fulfillment.

The mayor leaned back and called to those who kept the gate, bidding them to open it without delay. The company rode through and kept to the main thoroughfare that led directly to the docks. Mira and all the company looked on quietly at the throngs of people who, having heard the news of the Daughters of the East, gathered in the streets and cheered them on as they passed by. The huntress nodded humbly to the crowds, still grappling with the weight of her commission from Onu and the angels. Looking to Ruth and Lerannu as the procession continued toward the harbor, she eventually caught their eyes and saw plainly that they were of a similar mind, not only of the continued awe toward their purpose, but of the sadness to part ways with those they loved.

They soon reached the docks, and Mira looked in utter amazement at the size and crews of the *Frostwind* and *Alessia*. Remembering the ship she had taken to Sorrenar to marry Donovan and how massive she had thought that vessel was, the huntress laughed at the thought she had then that no ship could have surpassed it. The entire crews of both vessels greeted the company, expressing their honor in serving the Elect and their companions. Mira looked to Xenia and Viktor, who bowed to them in the saddle as they began to turn away.

"Here is where we part ways, for the time being," said the northern queen. "We shall rest here briefly, and send word to Norkoth and everywhere else we can in Sorrenar, to clear the way for us to aid you, along with a message for this ... Empress Raakmathna. Onu willing, we will meet again on the shores of Karzynhaal. May Onu and his host guard you, and give you what strength you need to endure whatever you face, from battle ... to separation."

Mira sighed sadly and dismounted, embracing Donovan tightly as Viktor and Xenia turned and rode away without another word. Looking over her husband's shoulder, she saw Ruth, Verdok, Lerannu, and Allor doing the same. All had put on a brave face, but Mira knew by what was in her own heart that their impending separation tore painfully within them. She kissed Donovan, possibly for the last time on Fidonhaal.

"Please be careful," she whispered, just barely keeping the tears from flowing.

"You, too," the bard sniffed as he nuzzled her neck before sneaking one last playful lick into her ear. Mira squeaked with ticklish laughter, swatting Donovan on the shoulder as they both laughed. Recomposing themselves, they looked into each other's eyes one last time, and breathing deeply, they parted for their ships without another word.

Mira boarded the *Frostwind* with Ruth and Lerannu, and leaning on the deck railing, the three Daughters of the East watched Allor, Donovan, and Verdok board the *Alessia*. The bells on the ships rang out, and the crews unfurled the sails and lifted the anchors. They were soon out of the harbor, and the three women stared back into the eyes of the men, not budging from their places until the ship passed over the horizon.

133

7/15/4030 G.M.

RAAKMATHNA sat on her throne, reading the message that the captain of the Janrenar-bound reinforcements had sent from Okrenar two days prior. The forces were now sailing for the Janrenarn port of Humilaar. From there, they were set to embark along the Vitari River for the city of Benhotha, and hopefully overcome the capital at long last.

The empress showed the parchment to her consort, the newly coronated Emperor Ranoth.

"It is as I mentioned to you earlier, dear Emperor and Salpion. The forces besieging Benhotha will get their reinforcements in due time. They need only endure a little longer. Maybe a month or so at most. They all have their orders laid out before them. It is just a matter of waiting."

"Oh, I have not been troubled by that anymore," said Ranoth, his eyes glowing with the dark, fiery light of a warlock. "That worry vanished with your words then and there, as did any other uncertainties, once you so graciously granted me a share of your might. I'm so sorry if you had been worried that I still had misgivings after all you did for me."

"Oh, I had no doubt that you were committed overall, but I thought you still might have been concerned in regards to taking Janrenar."

"Even if the forces presently there and the reinforcements to come were to fail this time, Benhotha and Janrenar, and all of Fidonhaal, will come under our order one day. We have the means to rebuild our armies ... one way or another. They do not."

"Indeed, my dear. I am glad that you see now that it is only a matter of time. Let another millennium pass, if it must. We can still stand together and triumph over the chaos that Onu permits."

"Of course, my dear," said Ranoth confidently as he rose from the throne, offering his hand to Raakmathna. "If there isn't anything else that needs doing here, what do you say we go out for a walk? Maybe to the guardhouse? Perhaps there are some newly caught vermin that we can watch being crushed, if not see to ourselves?"

"That sounds like a fine idea," the empress said merrily as she took Ranoth's hand.

***

The prisoners of the day were caught in a most amusing story of the hysteria that Raakmathna had managed to sow among the foolish Fidons. They were yet another set of traitors, this time a mother and daughter, who had attacked some Peacekeepers in retaliation for the killing of the family's husband and father. The family, having worked as bakers before the cleansing on Veronmay's Eve, had been coerced into preparing rations for the Peacekeepers. The previous day, the husband had exited the bakery to dispose of some refuse, and some nearby Peacekeepers, seeing white on his otherwise grey fur, charged at him and slew him without a second thought. The baker's wife and daughter, seeing what had happened, cried out that the white on his fur was from the flour in the bakery. They attacked the soldiers in a fury, managing to kill one of them before being arrested and bound. They were now shackled to the wall of their cell, which Raakmathna and Ranoth entered in the company of two guards. The prisoners lifted their heads, their eyes boring into the empress and emperor with utter hatred and contempt, though it seemed as much directed within their own hearts as it was toward their captors.

"Onu forgive us, if he will," said the mother bitterly, "though we do not deserve it. We should have defied you at once, even if it meant our immediate deaths. We should have known that you were meaning to kill us all in the end, Zaron or not. We sold our souls just to stay a little longer in this wretched life, which you'll still take from us when it suits you, and would end in time besides."

"No, dear sister," said Raakmathna with feigned sincerity and sympathy. "It was a most tragic mistake. Your husband, your family, have served us well. Your grief and your rage are entirely understandable, but for order's sake, it is far better to be safe than sorry."

"So you aren't sorry for what you have done," said the woman, "as we all knew while nevertheless surrendering to your evil, whether out of fear or some deluded thought that you somehow truly cared for us."

"Dear sister, you misunderst–"

The woman and her daughter spat upon the empress in unison. Raakmathna nonchalantly wiped a hand across her gown.

"I give you one last chance to let go of this tragedy and continue to serve the empire. Stay strong, and one day you *will* reap the benefits of–"

"NO," said the mother and daughter together in complete finality.

Raakmathna shrugged. "So be it, you shall serve me all the same."

"Never," said the daughter. "You can only–"

Any further words of defiance were silenced by the spears that ran through both mother and daughter. They slumped from the wall dead, hanging from their chains, as Raakmathna looked to Ranoth with a smile.

"Care to try your newfound power, my dear friend?"

"Gladly," said Ranoth as he and the empress raised their hands and reanimated the dead traitors.

***

Thirteen days passed. Raakmathna, having received another message, read it to Ranoth.

To Raakmathna, the Empress of Madness:
We write this message to you in the event that you were wondering at the lack of further news from your grey-cloaked butchers at Norkoth. Know that they have been utterly wiped out, and that those remaining in Sorrenar are facing the same fate should any of our people cross paths with them and not be met with their immediate surrender. We of Sorrenar will no longer cower in fear of you or your deluded army of murderers, for we have been graced by a visit from members of the Elect; the long-foreseen Daughters of the East. We of Sorrenar rise and stand beside them, as will, by Onu's grace, all of Fidonhaal in due time. Come for us if you dare, or cower in your palace. Whatever passes in the end, we will not submit to your terror, and we will fight you to the last.
Xenia and Viktor Karamus, Queen and King of Sorrenar.

Raakmathna ripped the letter to pieces, not in anger, but in calm disdain.

"It is as you said, my dear," she said to Ranoth, whose glowing eyes showed no hint of worry. "We can always rebuild our forces with the power we have, a power that even the Elect do not possess." The empress chuckled spitefully before continuing. "Or rather, a power they would not employ for the sake of some sense of honor, that which resigns them to the uncaring chaos that Onu allows."

"Of course," Ranoth said calmly, "but I must ask, purely out of curiosity, if you have a plan in response to this development? The Elect have all been foreseen by the longstanding prophecies, and are not to be lightly dismissed."

"Indeed not, but rest assured that I do have ideas, my dear. For now, we will see if we cannot still manage to take Zefiil and Benhotha, and if successful, the rest of Kellmayar and Janrenar in time. If these Daughters of the East do indeed manage to break our forces and rally the rest of the world against us, they still have to break past our armada and then make it here. The number of our ships has been growing steadily since our crusade began, and by the time they try to make their way here, *if* they even make it that far, they will have a fine time trying to touch the shoreline. And then ... well, I will show you what I have in mind, should they manage to make it onto land."

"If such comes to pass, I await to bear witness to your genius."

"I am sure you will be quite impressed, dear Ranoth."

The empress and her consort took one another's hand, staying seated on their thrones as their officers entered to report the happenings of the day. Raakmathna looked on calmly.

"If these prophesized 'saviors' do indeed manage to best me in the end," she thought to herself, "I will *not* make it easy for them."

134

7/28/4030 G.M.

RUTH stepped up from below deck and walked anxiously about in the early morning sun. The *Frostwind* had sailed from Benevor a fortnight ago, and with the recent crossing of the equator, the captain told them they would soon reach the port of Vahnon's Landing. The air was still warm and dry as they neared the largely arid continent, but was nevertheless milder than when the Elect's ship crossed the equator, as it was now winter in the south half of the world. The knight finally paused in her anxious pacing, taking a deep breath of the mild sea air and remembering Verdok's remark of being grateful that the quest had not begun in winter.

She smiled, sighing wistfully, and pondered how glad he would likely be that it was presently winter in Kellmayar and Janrenar, as Verdok would doubtlessly want the hot and humid clime of Janrenar to be as tempered as possible. He was so amusingly fussy when it came to temperature

~ 295 ~

and humidity, always being the most consistently comfortable back home in autumn and spring. She looked absentmindedly into the waters of the ocean that surrounded the ship, thinking of how much she missed him, and prayed that he and the others bound for the South were safe.

She felt a hand on her shoulder and turned to see Mira. The captain was also behind her.

"Had enough o' the sea, Lady Ruth?" the captain asked lightheartedly.

"Perhaps a little," said the Faithguard with a light smile, "but I'd sail around the world a hundred times over as long as I knew that Verdok was alright."

"I understand all too well, m'lady. I'd like to think I'd say the same for my wife."

Ruth glanced at Mira, seeing the huntress nod in understanding.

"We were just meaning to tell you," said Mira, "that the port, or at least the coast, should be appearing on the horizon soon. We were going to tell Lera about it, too, and hoped to watch it appear on the horizon together."

The huntress drew a deep breath, clasping her hands together worriedly.

"The next step in our journey is ... well, just on the horizon, so to speak."

"We can do it," Ruth said as she gave the huntress a friendly embrace. "I know not what will happen before the end, but know that as long as I draw breath, my axe and my shield are both yours and Lera's."

"And I say the same to you and Lady Stonefaith," said Mira resolutely, "in regards to my bow."

Mira and the captain turned back for the rooms below deck to speak to Lerannu, and Ruth returned her sight to the sea, propping herself against the deck's railing as she continued to contemplate her journey and that of her companions, both with her and those bound for the South. Within a few minutes, the captain, Mira, and Lerannu were beside her, all watching the horizon for the appearance of the coast and the port.

Then it appeared, rising up from the waves, and the whole crew began to cheer in anticipation for the next part of the Elect's quest, confident in their abilities due to the words of the prophecy.

"HOI!" cried the woman in the crow's nest in dreadful alarm. "We need to land elsewhere! There's a whole fleet of ships docked at the port, an' they're all with grey sails!"

The cheers abruptly went silent. Ruth set her eyes into a hard gaze toward the distant port as she saw that the lookout spoke truly. She sighed wearily, doing all she could to hold to the hope of the prophecy and the Mark on her brow.

"Have you any thoughts on where we should try to land, Captain?" asked the knight.

"Aye, m'lady," he said. "There's a good stretch o' coast that runs south o' the port. The highway you'll be lookin' to take runs nearly right along the shoreline. If we can keep out o' the grey-coats' sight an' land somewhere along there, we should be able to drop you there an', hopefully, be able to stay at the shore an' await your return, or at least word from you on where to meet you."

"Sounds as good a plan to fall back on as any," said Mira.

The captain called out his orders to the crew, which quickly veered the ship to a more southerly course and out of sight of the shore.

"I guess the port ended up being a high priority target after all," said Lerannu in quiet frustration.

"Maybe," said Ruth, "but then again, maybe something has changed their plans, as they've changed ours."

***

They sailed the rest of the day and the following night with bated breath, dreading the possibility of looking back and seeing grey sails tailing them. Fortunately, it seemed they had evaded the grey-cloaks' notice, and they sailed with steady caution on a southward course until the following morn.

The sun had risen and the sky had turned to its full blue when the *Frostwind* turned sharply to the west again, set on a straightforward path toward the shore and the highway that lay just beyond it. Soon the shoreline appeared on the horizon again. The Daughters of the East prepared themselves to disembark, along with a handful of the ship's crew who were set to accompany them through the arid savannah and desert to the capital city of Zefil, where their next great challenge awaited.

Once the Elect and their fellows had gathered their supplies and gear, they stood along the railing beside the captain, watching the steadily approaching shoreline in quiet anticipation. Suddenly, at the sun's height, as the sights of the shore and highway became clearer, the lookout called once more from the crow's nest.

"There's an awful lot o' people on the road, Captain, an' it looks like quite a battle is goin' between them! I can make out an army o' grey-coats on one side, an' a swarm o' folks on the other!

It looks like a large company o' grey-coats has happened across a cavalcade o' the Trichynay folks!"

Hearing mention of the great tribe set Ruth to turn to the captain.

"We need to get to shore as fast as we can," she said. "We need to help them if we can, and otherwise try to speak to them. I don't know what they may or may not know of this whole mess, but if we can speak with them, we might have a far greater company to aid us at Zefiil than we would've otherwise."

The captain nodded understandingly. "So be it," he said as he turned and barked for the oars crew to double its speed and for the sails to be kept in the best position possible for the wind. Soon, the ship began to swiftly carve through the waters, and Ruth and her sisters in destiny, along with their companions from the crew, scrambled into the longboat that had been prepared for them. They watched the battle anxiously as it steadily drew nearer. The captain at last called out that they were as close as they could get to the shore, and the ship joltingly turned to put its portside to the coast.

Ruth looked to Mira and Lerannu, who looked tensely at her in turn. Without another word, Ruth took a deep breath, braced herself in the longboat, and prepared her mind for the battle carnage to come as the boat descended rapidly into the sea.

The crew in their company rowed strenuously the instant they hit the water.

135

8/1/4030 G.M.

LERANNU frantically rummaged through her satchel as the longboat skimmed through the water and neared the sandy shore. Finding one of the little flasks of the Kamgenbew tonic that had been supplied to her back at Benevor, the mage quickly swallowed the dose in preparation for the grueling combat to come. The company sprang out of the boat the instant its bottom scraped the shore. As she ran with Ruth and Mira, along with their accompanying fighters from the ship's crew, Lerannu grimly took in the sight of the chaotic dance of blood and death that unfolded before her. Mounted riders from both sides were galloping in circles around those on foot, charging into and disengaging from the clashing hordes in cycles. Arms and armor swirled about in the mass of combatants.

Lerannu saw Mira stop abruptly, and looking back saw the huntress begin to take careful shots into the battle, aiming for the grey-cloaks as the mage and the knight charged onward. Soon the battle was before them, and the cavalry of both armies were galloping past them in their charges and retreats.

"Hold back, Lera!" Ruth called out as she continued to charge into the mass of grey-cloaks. "Do what you can from there!"

The Faithguard, her axe and buckler ready, crashed into a grey-clad soldier, cleaving into his shoulder and chest with relative ease as the links of mail that covered him buckled and snapped under her force. Another grey-coat confronted her, only to fall to the joint efforts of Ruth's buckler striking him in the face and one of the tribespeople running him through the neck with a scimitar. The tribe warrior raised his blade at Ruth, and Lerannu's heart nearly leapt up her throat. Ruth lowered her axe and raised her shield, calling out to the fighter just as he was about to bring down his blade. The warrior halted, his face the picture of confusion, and was abruptly skewered by another grey-coat's spear. Lerannu saw nearby tribe warriors cry out in anger at the knight, only to falter in their accusations as they saw Ruth immediately turn to the spear-wielding soldier and chop her spear in two. Ruth did the same to the soldier's exposed face in the following stroke, and then turned back to the tribe fighters. The knight extended her buckler-holding hand to them as they pulled her to their side of the battle. Ruth turned to face the enemy head-on, and the surrounding Trichynay warriors called out to their fellows that the Faithguard knight was on their side.

Lerannu looked frantically about, seeing the fighters from the *Frostwind* crew here and there in the chaos. They seemed to be more or less holding their own, though she could not account for them all at a glance. The mage looked back, and saw Mira and the few other sailors who were attacking with bowshots start to advance toward the battle in an effort to bolster their precision. One of the grey-coats on horseback began to gallop toward them, and was swiftly downed by a volley from the huntress and those with her.

The mage then saw a face amongst the battling masses. The grey-furred face of a man who was fighting alongside the Trichynay warriors. The man appeared a little past middle-aged, had a close-kept beard, and long hair tied back in a tail. Oddly enough, for a grown man living in the great tribe, he had neither the earrings of a virgin man nor those of a married one that were customary for all adults in the tribe. There were scars on his left cheek, scars that seemed to be of the sort that would come from the strike of another Fidon's hand if the claws were purposefully used. They were similar to the scars on Uriah's face.

Lerannu could just barely make out the man's sea-green eyes. They were perplexingly familiar. Lerannu shook her head as she refocused herself on the battle. She looked back to the army of grey-coats just in time to see two of the soldiers running toward her with their weapons raised. The mage swung her arms upward in a panic, setting a blast of wind to kick up the grassy sand at her feet into her attackers' eyes. As they reeled back, an arrow found one of them, burying itself into the soldier's back. Lerannu braced herself for the Arrow of Vente spell. She let the bolt of wind fly, and flinched grimly as she saw the other soldier crumple into a shredded heap from the force she had channeled. The arrow of wind bolted through the soldier and carried on into the horde of grey-coats, where a number of agonized screams rang out as the wind struck them before at last dissipating in their midst.

Then the mage's heart froze as she saw another face, this time in the mass of grey-cloaks. The face from before was oddly familiar, but no certain memories had yet come to her. The face she now saw was that of her mother, who was staring directly at her as she sent another handful of soldiers after her. Sarah's face was consumed by a battle frenzy, and her eyes narrowed at her daughter as she shouted orders that, inaudible to Lerannu, were clearly being issued to the rest of the army in the manner of a general. The mage looked to the soldiers charging toward her and repeated the spell she had just cast. The soldiers fell swiftly, but now Lerannu could feel her energy draining. She looked despairingly at her mother as she ordered another, larger squad to go after her.

With tears of grief and anger threatening to pour from her eyes, Lerannu began to walk briskly toward the grey-coats. She positioned her arms and clenched her fists as if she were wielding a great warhammer. Breathing deeply, she swung her arms over her head and pantomimed striking the ground, screaming a battle cry of sorrow and rage. The Hammer of Terranah struck the sandy earth, and the ground shook amongst the warring hordes. Trichynay warrior and grey-coated soldier alike staggered in shock. Lerannu, her head starting to pound, braced herself in the stance of an archer and loosed one more arrow of wind into the grey-armored horde, her sight honed in on her hateful mother. The shaft of air cut brutally into the army, but faded just short of the general, who, just barely staying on her feet, promptly sounded a horn of retreat. In a desperate charge, the grey-clad mass of mounted riders, pulling what comrades they could reach into the saddle with them, bolted through the Trichynay warriors. Though there were those who were trampled under the sudden retreat, most of the tribe managed to avoid the grey-cloak cavalry and began pursuing them, bellowing the tribe's name triumphantly. Their pursuit was brought to a halt when another horn sounded. The tribe froze in their tracks as a woman's voice boomed amongst them.

"Everyone hold! We need to regroup with the rest of the tribe before we try to take them on again! We were just barely matched for them as it was!"

"Yes, Chief Ranye!" the tribe warriors boomed in reply.

"Now," the woman named Ranye called out, loudly but more levelly, "who should I be thanking for the magic?"

"Some people came over from that ship over yonder, Chief!" answered one of the soldiers. "One of them must be a mage!"

The loud, continuing voices, along with her distress from her magical exertions and the sight of her mother amongst the grey-coats, set Lerannu to reel and sway on her feet. Her head ached horribly and her vision was starkly tunneled. The mage fitfully tried to fish another vial of tonic from her bag. A gauntleted hand gently grasped hers, and another one steadied her by the shoulder. Lerannu looked up to see Ruth looking into her eyes, both thankfully and worriedly, as the knight gently reached into the mage's pouch and handed her another flask. Lerannu nodded thankfully and put the flask to her lips.

She sputtered and coughed with a start as an arrow flew and bounced off the Faithguard's breast-plate, snapping in two from the force of the ricochet. Ruth shouted and raised her buckler, putting herself in front of Lerannu.

"Fendoth, you dolt!" Lerannu heard the one named Ranye yell. "That was the one who came in and started helping us! So is the one right next to her! Didn't you hear the people around you say that they were on our side?"

"I-I thought—"

"Just put that bow up and keep quiet!"

By now, Mira and the surviving members of the ship's crew had rushed to Ruth and Lerannu's side. The huntress waved to the tribe, pointing at her forehead.

"We are not with the grey-cloaks!" she called out. "We have come to help Kellmayar, and all of Fidonhaal, to put an end to this madness! We have been marked by Onu as the Daughters of the East!"

A massive wave of awed whispers washed over Lerannu, who stood shakily as she leaned onto Ruth for support. The mage then saw a woman riding through the mass of warriors, who reverently parted to clear the way for her. At last she reached the mage and her companions, looking them over with wide eyes. Through her hazy vision, Lerannu saw that she appeared to be largely Kason, though she was fairly sure there were white spots on her in places, not unlike the markings of a young deer. Her short-sleeved hide jacket glittered from the studs that were set into it. The riding lady carried herself as a firm, caring leader. Her ears were pierced by large, oval-like holes lined with the sparkling brass earrings that were set into them, marking her as a mated and married woman by the customs of the great tribe. The woman looked over her shoulder and called back into the mass of warriors.

"Did you think that Onu-branded folks are the sort that would work with those grey-armored murderers, Fendoth?"

"M-my apologies, Chief Ranye, but they were armed a-and armored Zarons, and—"

"They weren't wearing all grey!"

"N-no, but—"

"But nothing. What about Dendra over there? Or Kaldor? Are they not Zaron, too?"

"B-but we know them—"

"So we assume the worst of strangers of a certain fur color? I thought you would have learned from this whole mess that that's not the answer, even though we never needed such a lesson until now."

"Chief Ranye, the grey-coats—"

"*Enough!*"

Ranye turned to the Daughters and their companions, breathing deeply before speaking to them.

"My utmost apologies for that, dear Daughter of the East. My warriors ... they're still a bit riled up from the battle. I am Ranye Onoraan. Are you hurt, dear friend?"

"I'm fine, Chief Ranye," said Ruth calmly as she brushed the small dent that the arrow put in her armor. "My friend here, however, has expended a lot of her strength to aid you, and I feel that she needs more than just a little tonic now."

"We will gladly have her come with us and rest," said Ranye with a smile. "I'm not sure if I'd want to think of how things might have gone if you lot hadn't come along, especially your mage friend. Were you seeking us, by any chance?"

"Not particularly," Ruth said as she briefly explained the reason for their ship landing on the shoreline behind them. "We are certainly glad to have happened upon you, however. If your tribe would be willing, we could use your strength to aid us in saving Zefiil from their siege."

Ranye nodded grimly. "We've been working on a plan to liberate Zefiil for the past three months, ever since we first heard of what had happened. We were hoping to act out our plan soon, but if that army we just fought was heading over to reinforce the siege, then I'm not quite sure if our plan will work. But we can talk that out later. Whatever comes to pass, I assure you that we of the Trichynay will gladly aid you."

"You have our thanks, Chief Ranye."

The chief then called back to her fighters from over her shoulder. "Roniil! Could you grab a few horses for our new friends here, and some water for the mage?"

"Aye, Ranye."

Lerannu's vision tunneled even more strongly, and her ears started to ring as a name, and a voice, from the past reached her ears. Quaking violently against Ruth's shoulder, the mage slowly lifted her head as she watched another warrior ride forth with three horses in tow. She recognized the face she had seen earlier in the battle. The rider approached them, holding three sets of reins and a generous waterskin, and offered them to the Daughters of the East.

"My thanks to you all," he said, "along with that of all my tribe. If you would care to follow us back to our camp, we would be–"

"P-Papa?" Lerannu heard herself ask in a small voice.

The rider looked to Lerannu, and the last sight that the mage saw before falling into darkness was the face of a man who had seen a ghost.

136
8/2/4030 G.M.

RAAKMATHNA looked over the message she had written one last time before rolling it up and binding it to the heraldwing's leg.

> *Archgeneral Stonefaith:*
>
> *With a month and ten days having passed since you set sail from Okrenar, I have judged that if your travels have not experienced any significant delays, you should soon be reaching Zefiil. I have sent this Shanlof on the second of Yorok, and hope that the time between its arrival to Zefiil and yours will be brief, if at all existent.*
>
> *Your orders are as follows, and are to be immediately executed upon reception: Take hold of the Shanlof that brings you this message, place your lips upon its beak, and breathe deeply. I have imparted a portion of my power onto the bird, and it will pass into you when you perform the prescribed act. You will then have within you a measure of my power and knowledge, and will be able to carry out with ease the remainder of your orders.*
>
> *Channel the newfound might within you and bring down the walls of Zefiil with fire. Tear down the walls and command your army to charge in. Wash over the city in a tide of blood. Strike down any and all who stand in your way. Storm the palace, kill the king, the queen, and all others within. Claim the city, and from there send word of your victory. Stay there and await further word in regards to the next step in our conquering of the West.*
>
> *The victory of order is nigh.*
>
> *Your empress, Raakmathna, has spoken.*

Satisfied, the empress carefully rolled and folded the parchment, and then bound it to the messenger bird's leg. Then, gently grasping it in both hands, she brought the bird to her lips and channeled her strength into her breath. The bird fidgeted distressfully in her grasp, but then froze in submission as Raakmathna's breath filled its lungs. The Shanlof's eyes soon glowed a dark, fiery red, and a small cloud of black mist began to envelope it.

Raakmathna closed her eyes, training a portion of her mind onto the bird, and uttering the name of the capital of Kellmayar, approached the open window and let the bird fly.

137
8/2/4030 G.M.

ALLOR looked somberly at the distant green paradise of Karzynhaal, which lay just on the horizon as the *Alessia* sailed by. The king looked squarely into the face of the past, pondering all that he could think of as to what could have happened differently. Such had been what he had largely done for the past seventeen days of the voyage, but seeing the Isle of Origin drove his heart deeper into the well of his regret and uncertainty.

"Such a wonderful sight, is it not?" asked the voice of Verdok.

Allor turned to see Donovan and Verdok standing behind him. Though he knew the unity they shared in their purpose stood firm, Allor had spoken relatively little to either the bard or the priest. His loss of Sheeva, along with the separation from his children and Lerannu, had sent the king into a deeply grim mood, which now ached more intensely than ever at the sight of Karzynhaal. Having wallowed in sorrow's depths enough, Allor breathed a heavy sigh as his companions joined him at the railing.

"The place of our beginnings," the priest went on, "and the site of more than a few great moments in our history. Heroes and heroines, incarnations of the Elect and otherwise, have tread its soil throughout the ages as they went about their journeys. If fate be kind, we and our loved ones will be added to that legacy soon enough."

"It certainly has marked the turning point of many lives," said Allor somberly, "from the hero of legend to the simple pilgrim. I haven't heard one Fidon say they were worse off for visiting it. We sailed by it together, Sheeva and I, and all our families, when we went to negotiate in Kellmayar. We were looking forward to stopping by there once we finished our business and made our way back home. Then Sheeva and I lost everyone on the road to Zefiil, and both grief and imminent duty drove us to pass by the Holy Isle as we returned home. Even then, Sheeva spoke of others being out to get her and the both of us. I just thought it was shock and grief, and that it would pass."

A shaky sob drew itself out of Allor as he braced against the railing.

"Do you think this all could've been avoided, or lessened in any way, if we stopped at Karzynhaal and spent even a little time in its consoling embrace?"

The king tightly shut his eyes, trying his best to fight off the tears. Verdok came to him and hugged him, patting his back as he spoke.

"I'm not one to say, Allor. Maybe, maybe not. After all, this was something long foreseen, albeit somewhat hazily through the sight of a prophet from long ago. These are the sorts of times that leave us all wondering; the hows, the whys, the what-ifs. All I can say now is that it has started, and cannot be stopped now until it is finished. I just ... I don't know. But you can't blame yourself. You mustn't."

"But I should've known," Allor wept. "I look back on it and it's all as clear as day now."

"Such tends to be the way when one learns they've been deceived."

"All the children she helped, all the struggling families ... I don't think I ever saw a single one that wasn't solely of Zaron stock, at least as far as I could've told at the time, and I never gave it a thought."

"Why would you have noticed," asked Donovan, "or had otherwise thought to say anything about it? We all bleed the same blood in the end, and carry within us the same struggles as we strive to reunite and commune with our Maker. It was, and still is, simply one of our fur colors. What would that have been to any of us until this mad concept was unleashed from the depths of Raakhaal?"

"It just should've seemed odd to me, at the very least."

"We've distrusted and killed each other over all sorts of pitiful things," said Verdok. "For this land, for that land. For this leader, for that leader. For this cause, for that cause. For this thing, for that thing. For power, for wealth. For freedom, for order. Even for the way we thought should be taken in order to 'properly' commune with Onu. That one should be, and perhaps still is, when all is said and done, the single worst division we have ever suffered at one another's hands and the goading of Raakaru. But to think that we could fall to something so simple as our fur ..."

The priest gave a grim chuckle and shrugged his shoulders as he continued to ponder Fidonity's sorry state.

"What'll we stir up next? A war between all men and women?"

Allor sharply pulled away from Verdok's friendly arms, watching the priest's ears flatten meekly under his gaze.

"It's probably just a matter of time," said the king darkly, "at the rate we're letting ourselves go, despite all that history has taught us."

Verdok stuttered in a regretful voice. "I-I'm sorry, Allor. I w-was just trying—"

"It was a poor jest," Allor said flatly as he turned away and went below deck.

***

Allor sat on the edge of his bed, staring wordlessly at the floor in the dimness of the sleeping quarters. The members of the crew who were set to work later were sleeping soundly, and the soft thuds and patters of the crew on deck sounded constantly overhead in an oddly soothing, if irregular, rhythm.

The king did not know for sure how long he sat there in grim solitude before Donovan peered in from the doorway. Allor looked up from the floor, looking sadly into the bard's bright blue eyes.

"Surely, Allor, you don't think he was trying to—"

"No. I don't. But is it so hard to imagine something like that actually coming to pass, now? After all, it's not as if there haven't already been some awful things to pass between men and women as it is."

"But we know that those were the acts of individuals. We haven't laid those things entirely at the feet of only one sex or the other."

"Not yet."

Donovan stood wordlessly in the doorway, his eyes bearing an immense sadness.

"Men and women," the bard said quietly, "we've worked together, side by side, since we first laid eyes on one another. Onu knows there have been troubles at times, but I have a hard time seeing us falling that low."

"We've blamed whole groups of other people before," said the king, "just not on something so ... basic. But then again, we fought over our basic bond with Onu before, and now it's come to this. We've been tearing ourselves apart over things more and more, things that shouldn't—"

"My friend," the bard cut in with a voice both gentle and firm, "every day, it's up to each and every one of us as to how, and if, we will judge others. Some will fall into the trap of laying blame on groups, others will at least try to curb such thoughts and look to the individual. Some will be hateful and bitter in their judgement, others will not. And it will change from day to day. But none of us will stand a chance if we let ourselves fall to this state, where we see ourselves as nothing but ever worsening. If we resign ourselves to thinking thus, so it truly will become in time."

The bard approached Allor, offering his hand.

"Will you hold to the hope that we can get better, the hope that has driven us to rise above the ruin wrought by Raakaru's reign?"

Allor drew a deep breath, then took his companion's hand.

"I will try, as best as I can bear to try."

"That's all we can do in the end."

Allor and Donovan went back onto the deck. It was now late in the afternoon, and though the light was beginning to slowly dim, the great green of Karzynhaal still stood on the horizon, though it was clearly soon to pass from sight. They approached Verdok, who stood at the railing as he quietly gazed at the Holy Isle. He turned to them as they approached and bowed his head somberly as he spoke to Allor.

"I'm sorry beyond words, my friend. I should've known that—"

"There's no need to apologize," Allor said as he embraced the priest. "These are the sort of times that place very strange thoughts within us."

"Indeed," Verdok said with a small laugh as the three companions stayed by the railing.

"If anything, I should be the one to apologize."

"Not at all. You have plenty of causes for a heavy heart right now."

They silently watched the Blessed Isle until it passed below the horizon, then promptly began talking of their hopes for the days to come.

An Alliance
with the Trichynay

138
8/2/4030 G.M.

MIRA rode alongside Ruth, Chief Ranye, and the warrior Roniil, who had his daughter, Lerannu, resting against him in the saddle. The mage was deeply unconscious, seemingly dead to the world apart from her light, steady breathing.

The Daughters of the East had set off for the great camp of the Trichynay in the company of the tribal riders they had met in the battle on the road. They had agreed with the crew members of the *Frostwind* that they ought to return to the ship and sail to the port of Korashka. Chief Ranye explained that she had received word from other scouts that the port was secured from grey-cloak control, and provided it would remain so, would be as good a place as any for the Elect to rendezvous after resolving the siege on Zefiil, if they did indeed succeed. The sailors then returned to the ship, and as the mass of riders set out for the great encampment, they looked back and saw the ship as it began to sail on further south.

The riders went on at a steady pace, making camp at nightfall and rising with the following sun. It was now well into the second afternoon of their journey to the camp, and the Daughters of the East had spent much of their time conversing with those in their immediate company. Each party learned more of the assaults of the grey-coats, on the eve of Veronmay (or Kysonmay from the perspective of those in Kellmayar and Janrenar) and afterwards. Mira and Ruth told the tribe's chieftain of their journey so far, and Roniil, listening to the account alongside Ranye, was greatly saddened to hear of what had become of both his former wife and his one-time accomplice in adultery. What grief he had for them, however, seemed to pale in comparison to his sorrow for how it had now come to affect his daughter. Ranye, in the meantime, told them of how the tribe first learned of the grey-coats a fair time after the first attacks. They had heard of the incidents after coming across survivors fleeing their homes, and had since been gathering their people in an effort to wipe out those surrounding Zefiil.

"We should be setting out for the capital soon, truth be told," the chieftain said with somber resolve. "I have wondered as to whether or not our efforts will succeed, but though its absolute outcome is still uncertain, I must say that my spirit is greatly lifted at your timely arrival."

"I will do all I can to prove your hopes well-founded," said Ruth.

"As will I," said Mira, "and I assure you that Lera will say the same, once she's recovered from her recent shocks and grievances."

The huntress looked to Roniil, her heart pained by the sight of him holding onto his daughter's swaying body, constantly working to keep her upright in the saddle. His face was one of immeasurable regret. He wordlessly looked at the Elect and the chieftain, and petted Lerannu's head with sad, fatherly affection.

"I wonder how much my actions have affected her," he said quietly. "Has she been slow to love, or would either of you know anything about that?"

"From what I've heard from her and King Allor," Mira answered, "she has been a very loving person, to his children, his wife ... and to him, now more than ever."

The huntress caught the faintest trace of a smile forming within Roniil's sorrowful countenance as he continued to hold his daughter.

"Good," he said quietly, "though I can only imagine how ... complicated ... the feelings between them must be, what with what's happened to Allor's wife and what I've done to Lera."

Roniil looked contemplatively at the Elect, then at his chieftain.

"You know," he said, "I was there when Allor and Sheeva's company was attacked by that rogue east warden, Ohdan. I saw Allor chopping Ohdan to pieces, and was the one to finally stay his hand. I saw what happened to their parents and friends, and the state of Sheeva as she looked on their bodies. Horrible. I can't imagine what twisted thoughts bore into Sheeva's mind in that time, but to see where it took her in the end ..."

"As dark as it may be for me to say," said Ruth, her eyes lost in pondering her thoughts, "I feel I can understand that more so than what happened to ... well, your former wife. I'm sure a lot of it was worsened by Sheeva's and Raakmathna's manipulations, but I fear that she might have been quite hateful enough to begin with, given what happened between you two."

Roniil sighed heavily.

"I'm sorry," Ruth said quickly. "I'm nosing into things that aren't for me to say."

"No," said Roniil, "It's alright. Sarah and I ... our bond had weakened over the years since I was elected mayor. The demands of the job were more than I had expected."

"Roniil," Ranye said gently, "you don't need to tell us this. There's only one here who ought to know—"

"I've held it within me for long enough, and Lera doesn't seem able to hear about it right now. I can talk to her about it whenever she wakes up, but I don't want it completely trapped inside me anymore."

Mira and the others rode on, listening intently as Roniil said his piece.

"It was after Lera lost her best friend to Endallian Fever."

"Kiiva?" Mira asked. "Lera told us a little about her during our travels. Really sad thing for anyone to go through, but especially for a young one, when someone her age passes from the world like that."

"Did she tell you of what happened after she died?"

"No, I don't believe so."

Mira listened, alongside Ruth, Ranye, and all those who could hear, to the horrible story of Kiiva's mother, how she resorted to necromancy out of grief and the abrupt end that befell her. After that, Roniil returned to the account of his infidelity.

"Sarah and I had an argument the following evening, over how Dalle's situation was handled. It went horribly, and I walked out of the house after I couldn't stand any more. I was walking along and I bumped into Uriah. She was coming back with things from the market, and when I told her of what had happened, she invited me into her home for dinner and to talk. As Onu is my witness, that's all we meant to do. But she spoke so understandingly, and she agreed with how I felt about the incident. She spoke like Sarah did when we first met, and we just ..."

Roniil sighed once more, shaking his head depressingly.

"We were both surprised when it went in that direction, and yet we didn't stop. At first, we tried to just keep it quiet, since it didn't look like anyone suspected anything. But for all our problems, I just couldn't let Sarah stay in the dark, even if it meant the end for us. So, I told her, and what happened happened. Sarah divorced me and cast me out of the family, and I took back my name before marriage, Tern. Uriah and I traveled together a little while, but it soon became clear that it just wouldn't have gone over well in the long run. She went off and, going by what you told me, eventually had a proper family of her own and ran a good inn."

Roniil was silent for a moment. Mira turned her eyes from the guiding riders ahead of her and looked to Lerannu's father. She saw the woeful face of a man reflecting on the lowest time in his life.

"I ... had nothing to keep me in, or from, anywhere, so I just wandered about a while, and eventually found myself at Greenharbor. I found myself at the docks, went up to a ship, and asked where they were headed. They told me they were set for Kellmayar, and I asked if I could buy passage. They let me on, and after getting off at Vahnon's Landing, I just wandered around some more. I've thought back on how I was then, and sometimes I'm not sure whether or not I was meaning to die in the desert or the grasslands. If there was some part of me that wanted to, or figured that I might as well have, it didn't win out. I was walking along the road, on foot and alone, with miles and miles between me and the next settlement. Some Trichynay riders were going about their travels and asked me about my business. I gave a brief account of what had happened, and once I told them that I didn't have any place where I felt I belonged, they offered me a place amongst them. I've been with them ever since."

Roniil's voice began to break.

"Where would we be now, me, Sarah, and Lera, if I hadn't thrown it all away for one night with her? If I had just stayed ... If I had only spoken calmly ... If only I told her that I felt us drifting apart. Sarah was so compassionate and patient, though you wouldn't know that now. From what you told me about Uriah and her family, when they were captured at their inn, I don't think Sarah would be supporting all this if I hadn't broken my vow to her, especially with a woman who wasn't fully Zaron."

"Maybe not," Ruth said understandingly. "But I don't see how that would've changed the outcome for Sheeva, and the overall state of things now. Even if things went differently between you and your wife, Sheeva's heart still would've been darkened by the pains that came to her, from what happened with the Greystones to when her parents were murdered here. Who knows what tragedy might have still befallen you and your family? What's done is done, my friend. You did trespass against Sarah, but that wasn't something that should've driven her to ... this."

"Aye," Mira agreed. "Sarah exercised her right as the offended one and chose to no longer have you by her side. But that should've been the most that it came to, and it should've stayed between you, her, and Onu."

"Don't forget the child that was born to the both of us," Roniil said tearfully. He at last burst into tears, and held his daughter closely in his arms. "L-Lera! My sweet little girl! I'm s-so sorry!"

Mira rode up to him, putting a hand on his shoulder. "She's going to be alright, Roniil. She just needs a good bit of food and proper sleep. Once we've made it to the camp, she should soon recover, if she hasn't already. Once she's gotten back on her feet, you can tell her everything. She loves you. She told us as much when she mentioned these things as we traveled. Whatever hurts she may have borne from what happened, she hasn't completely closed her heart to you."

Roniil began to try recomposing himself. After a moment of sniffing and deep, steady breaths, he looked to the huntress and nodded.

"If you say so," he said quietly. "Thank you."

***

They rode on for another seven days, the grassy sands of the coast steadily giving way to the Great North Savannah as they journeyed further southwest. Lerannu, though not showing any signs of worsening, had not fully awoken the entire ride, neither in the saddle nor during their nightly rests. The company kept on, and at last, as the sun neared the western horizon on the ninth of Yorok, they were met with a wondrous sight.

As far as the eye could see, tents and portable shelters of numerous shapes and sizes covered the grassy fields and low hills that stretched out to the horizon. Innumerable Fidons of all sorts, though predominantly Kason, were going about the grounds of the great encampment, their movements between the camp's structures like the branching of many flowing streams. Mira and Ruth looked to Ranye and Roniil, who sat grinning in their saddles at the awe on their faces.

"The Great Tribe of Trichynay welcomes you, good Daughters of the East," said Ranye with a warm formality. "If you can bear a little while longer, I'd like to bring you to our high shaman and have you speak briefly with him. Then we'll see that you're all fed and rested. We'll discuss things more fully in the morning."

Immediately following Ranye's words, Mira heard a loud gurgle. She looked over to the source of the noise, realizing it came from Ruth, and nearly fell off her horse from laughter as the knight let out a loud moan of hunger.

"Ugh!" the knight groaned in half-jest. "Make it quick, please."

Laughter began to ripple across the company as they entered the great camp.

139
8/9/4030 G.M.

RUTH rode with Mira, Ranye, and Roniil, who still kept Lerannu up in the saddle. As the company passed each tent and shelter, portions of the cavalcade broke off in varying directions, going about their own affairs now that they were back home. The Faithguard looked about, her preoccupations for her stomach and the state of Lerannu being lightened by the heartwarming sights of reuniting families and friends. She then heard a light gasp of surprise, and turned to see Mira looking at her.

"Look over there!" the huntress said in awe as she pointed to something further ahead.

Ruth looked, and smiled admiringly as she saw what could only be the Trichynay's great tabernacle. Having read of it in a number of books, and seeing its depiction in paintings and drawings, the knight was familiar with the massive tent's description and knew immediately what it was. She was still awestruck to see it in person, nevertheless, and her eyes stayed on the majestic array of blue, green, and white canvas as she listened to Mira.

"I had heard a little about the great tent in a few stories, and I know a little about the tribe's culture overall just from the story of the Three Sisters, but I must admit I still don't know very much. Especially not as much as I'd like to now, given our circumstances."

"I may have a slight advantage over you," Ruth said modestly, "but I'm far from a learned scholar on the matter myself. Once we get some time to ourselves, I'd be happy to let you know what I know, but I wager we'll both be getting a better education on the matter in the next few days."

"Any questions, just ask us," Ranye said over her shoulder. "Roniil knew a fair bit when he came to us, but there was still plenty for him to learn."

The cavalcade had completely dispersed, and the sun was kissing the western horizon when the Daughters of the East, Ranye, and Roniil reached the tabernacle. Ranye dismounted and tethered her horse to a post by the entrance, gesturing to Ruth and Mira to do the same. Ruth hitched her horse and looked back to see Roniil still in the saddle, holding Lerannu's unconscious body upright.

"Unless you still have need of me, Ranye, I'd like to go on and find a place for Lera to rest."

"By all means," Ranye said with a nod. "I'm just taking these two in to have a brief word with Xavier, and they'll be free to eat and rest after that. The real talking is going to be for tomorrow and whenever Lerannu wakes up, if she hasn't already done so by then."

Roniil nodded, his face both somber and grateful. "Thank you, High Chief."

Ruth whirled her sight back to Ranye, taken aback by the reveal of her full, true title. She saw the high chief wave farewell, and heard Roniil's horse turn and ride away behind her. Ranye then looked at the Daughters of the East, a small grin forming as she saw their faces.

"*High* Chief, eh?" the Faithguard said, intrigued. "I knew your people had one, and ones beneath him or her to help lead the tribe, since there's so many of you and you're seldom all together at once. But I have to say, I didn't hear your full title before and figured you were one of the other chiefs."

"Eh," Ranye said with a shrug, "I go by it when formality calls for it, or whenever someone chooses to address me that way, but I otherwise prefer to just go by 'Chief' at the most."

The high chief's grin began to grow a little broader. "The same goes for my husband," she said as she nodded toward the entrance to the tabernacle. "Xavier prefers to just be addressed as 'Shaman' at the most, whenever people can think to address him so."

Ruth looked intently at Ranye, smiling and with a raised brow.

"This is getting more interesting by the minute," she said. "Any other intriguing revelations? Do both of you have a lineage from the Three Sisters that can be clearly traced, or something along those lines, as well?"

Ranye laughed. "No, neither of us have that, at least not in any really clear way. But Xavier ... well, just come in and have a word with him."

The high chief parted the canvas of the great tent's entrance, reverently gesturing Ruth and Mira to enter before her. The knight and the huntress passed through, and sighed in awe at the dim, but warm light that gently bathed the vast interior of the tabernacle's worship space. Beautiful rugs and cushions were arranged in circles on the canvas floor, forming ring after ring that grew smaller and more tightly knit as they neared the center. At the center was a cushion, upon which was seated a man of an age with Ranye, being somewhere in his middle years.

Clearly, this was Xavier, High Chief Ranye's husband and the high shaman of the Trichynay people.

In the soft candlelight, Ruth could see that his eyes were closed as though in meditation or prayer. But there seemed to be a slight glow about the shaman's eyes, as though they were just barely open and catching the light of the candles. The knight saw a smile begin to grow on the high shaman's face. Without opening his eyes, he lifted his head and directly faced her, Mira, and Ranye.

"My joy is great, and doubled," he said in a strongly clear, but gentle voice. "My dear wife returns from her perilous journey and brings with her the Daughters of the East, who have come to aid us in fighting the mad hatred that has threatened to devour Fidonhaal."

Ruth felt her mouth fall slightly ajar, and her eyes darted to Mira to see that the high shaman's words had the same effect on the huntress.

"I'll greet you properly in a moment, if you don't mind," said Xavier as he gingerly raised himself from his seat with the aid of his ceremonial staff. "I haven't seen my wife in over a moon, and though I have sensed her continued safety the whole while, I have missed her greatly."

"Of course, H–Shaman Xavier," said Ruth, remembering what Ranye said of her husband's preference in being addressed. "Mira and I are ..."

Ruth's words stopped outright and her mouth fell fully open as the high shaman opened his eyes. They were indeed closed before, and the faint light she had seen about his eyelids were coming from Xavier's eyes themselves. The tabernacle suddenly brightened, as if several more candles were lit all at once, and the knight stared in awe at the glowing pools of gold and silver light that shimmered within the shaman's eyes.

Xavier was an Ecclesian, one of very few Fidons so blessed by Onu and graced with magic that their eyes forever glowed with sacred light. As her mind processed this revelation, another surprise showed itself in the form of Xavier's careful steps toward them, with one hand lightly raised before him and his ceremonial staff feeling the ground about him.

He was blind.

The knight stepped back in awe, standing beside Mira as both silently watched Xavier and Ranye's reunion. Ranye stepped forward and pulled her husband close, embracing and kissing him deeply for a moment before speaking.

"Eternal thanks to Onu that I'm with you again."

"Couldn't have said it better myself," Xavier said softly.

"How's Layna?"

"Perfectly fine, apart from being as eager to see you again as I've been."

"I'll find her once we're done here. Has she been handling things alright?"

"She's her mother's daughter; knows how to lead and encourage. She's done just fine in helping things along while you've been gone."

"And how about Garthon?" Ranye asked in a curious tone of both warmth and some sense of protectiveness.

"He's in as much love with her as he's ever been, at the very least. Whichever one of them finally makes the first move, I sense that it'll be very soon ... perhaps a bit sooner than even they'd expect."

"Then we need to see if we can't get them to pace it out a bit longer. I just want to see things be tended to properly."

"He's a good boy, Ran."

"I know."

"He loves her."

"I know."

"She loves him."

Ranye gently sighed, resting her head on Xavier's shoulder.

Ruth looked awkwardly at Mira, then gently cleared her throat.

"Would you care for us to step outside, or even wait until tomorrow? You two certainly seem like you need to talk some things over."

The high shaman laughed. "Stay, please, Ruth and Mira."

Xavier gently pulled away from his wife and steadily made his way over to the knight and huntress. As he stood before them, his sightless eyes nevertheless seeming to gaze at them with quiet approval, Ruth observed his appearance more thoroughly.

The high shaman was, as far as Ruth could see, a fully Kason-blooded man. He was dressed in a patterned robe of blue, green, and white cloth, matching the colors of the tabernacle's canvas walls. He stood fairly tall, about as tall as Verdok, and majestically upright, though his face had a slightly weary look about it. Some wrinkles had set about his eyes, marking him indeed as a seer who was particularly frequented, and at times wearied, by Yorun's tidings. The knight was not at all surprised at that point to hear him say her name before she could introduce herself. Xavier took one of Ruth and Mira's hands within his, staring intently at each in turn.

"I bid you two, and your wearied sister in destiny, welcome. I am Xavier Onoraan, Shaman of the Trichynay people."

"Well met," said Ruth reverently as she gently firmed her grasp within the high shaman's hand, "and my utmost thanks for the welcome reception and hospitality from you and your people."

"I will keep this brief," said the shaman, "as I sense that both of you are hungry and tired from your day's journey. I don't intend to speak too much of matters until Lerannu has recovered. Thankfully, I believe that should be the case come tomorrow, but nevertheless, I do wish to speak with you now, if only a little."

"Of course," Ruth and Mira said with a nod.

"You all have already had some heart-wearying times on this journey's course, I feel. I cannot see all that was, or is, or may be to come, especially not with perfect clarity, but I will say that there will be more of such times to come, for you and for those far away."

Ruth and Mira nodded in silent, somber understanding.

"But know this," Xavier went on, "that I have sensed your ultimate victory, which had been foretold nearly four thousand years ago by another man who, though blind, was given blessed light by which to see in another way. I cannot say what exactly will happen, who may or may not fall, or whatever joys or pains that are still to pass before the end. But I can see in my mind that this horrid demon *will* soon be cast out of this world, and that her hour of reckoning will be heralded by the Phoenix you will fly to confront her."

Ruth gaped at the mentioning of the Phoenix.

"W-what do you–"

"... and their victory will be brought on wings of fire," said the high shaman warmly.

Ruth, overwhelmed with awe at the premonition and revelation of another fragment of the prophecy, simply laughed, being at a loss for words.

Xavier gently patted Ruth and Mira on their shoulders. "That's all for now," he said. "I just wanted to assure you that your mission can, nay, will be accomplished in due time. I cannot say the full cost of the victory to come, nor will I try and quiet any and all of your worries. Your worries come out of love, and you know as well as I that times such as these, even when won by the good, have seldom been set to rights without any loss or sorrow. But know that this darkness *will* be ended one day, and one day soon. So, please, go and restore yourselves. Eat. Rest. Sometime tomorrow, if I have sensed rightly, Lerannu shall awaken, and we can all gather together and speak of our courses properly."

"Very well," Ruth said, her heart lightened by the high shaman's words. "Thank you, Shaman Xavier."

The knight's stomach roared loudly once again, and both the seer and Mira grinned.

"I would definitely advise eating soon. It would be a horrible thing indeed, if the prophecy were to be failed because of an empty stomach."

Laughing, the knight and the huntress reverently bowed to the high shaman, and the two turned and left the tabernacle, walking together as they sniffed out the location of various great-smelling foods.

140

8/10/4030 G.M.

LERANNU slowly opened her eyes. She was in a tent, lit with the canvas-filtered light of the bright morning. She slowly sat up, taking in the steady hum of activity that sounded all around the outside of the tent. She massaged her forehead as she tried to piece together where she was and what memories she could draw up from the depths of her mind.

She remembered landing at the Kellmayarn shore, and the battle between an army of grey-coats and Wild-Dweller riders. She remembered the other riders were those of the Great Trichynay Tribe. She remembered seeing her mother in the army of the grey-coats, directing them to attack her own daughter with the poise of the army's leader. She remembered aiding the great tribe with her magic. She remembered being greatly wearied by it.

She remembered another face. She remembered her father, and then falling into darkness.

Lerannu lifted her head from her hands, looking around the tent more carefully. She soon recognized, from her readings of books for her own education and that of Allor's children, an array of things that indicated her being in a Trichynay encampment. The mage looked to the side of her cushion-laden bed and noticed a pitcher of water and a bowl of soup. Still hazy from her ordeal and sudden awakening, and feeling famished, she began to eat and drink.

As she neared finishing her soup, she heard the gentle rustle of canvas at the entrance of the tent. She looked up, and her heart skipped a beat as she saw her father staring back at her. She saw Roniil's lips tremble and his eyes begin to shine tearfully as he struggled to stay composed.

"Good ... good morning, Lera."

Lerannu stared in brief silence. "Good morning, Father," she said at length.

Roniil breathed a deep, shaky sigh, then quietly approached his daughter and sat beside her.

"I was just about to come in and help you eat. I'm glad to see you're up. The high shaman believed you would be up by sometime this morning. I had no real reason to doubt him, but it's hard sometimes to keep faith when loved ones are involved."

"Sure," Lerannu said as levelly as she could, finishing her soup and taking another drink of water. "Wait," she said reflectively, "the high shaman? Has the great tribe's lead cleric happened across us in his travels, or are we in their main gathering?"

"We are indeed in the great camp."

"How far away are we from the battle by the road?"

"Around six hundred miles."

Lerannu was taken aback. "H-how ... how long was I ..."

"Nine days, basically. We got here yesterday evening."

The mage sighed incredulously, taking another drink of water and silently looking at her father as he gently put an arm around her.

"We've been waiting for you to wake up," he said lightly. "Your sisters in destiny, they're both alive and well, and are set to speak with both the high chief and high shaman soon. The great tribe has been building up a plan to help break the siege of Zefiil for months, and with your arrival, we believe more and more in the chance of victory. We wish to discuss it with you and your companions in case any of you have something to add."

Lerannu took another sip of water. "Very well. I'll try to be ready soon."

"Take your time. And ... after the plan is discussed, do you think we might ... discuss some things in private?"

Lerannu nodded.

"Thank you," he said gently as he rose from the bedside. "I'll wait outside the tent. Once you're ready, I'll lead you to the great tent."

***

The mage finished her breakfast, and having taken a little more time to recompose and change into another set of clothes, she stepped out of the tent and winced slightly at the bright sun. She glanced about in awe at the vastness of the camp and the many tribespeople milling about, only to avert her gaze awkwardly as she began to notice many of the people staring awestruck at the brand on her brow. She looked over and saw Roniil sitting at a little table set beneath an awning that branched out from the tent, and called to him as she approached.

"I'm ready," she said.

"Very well, let's go."

They made their way through the camp and soon reached the tabernacle, which Lerannu quickly recognized by its sheer size. Roniil parted the entrance open for her, and the mage passed wordlessly through. She entered the congregation space with Roniil behind her, and was glad to see Mira and Ruth seated on cushions and conversing with four other Fidons. The huntress and the knight looked over, having heard her come in, and jumped up to greet her. The three embraced in camaraderie, with Ruth and Mira briefly telling Lerannu of the past days' travel and their arrival at the great camp.

"Are you okay?" Mira asked her. "Shaman Xavier sensed that you would be awake today, but if you don't feel fully like yourself yet, maybe we can—"

"I'm alright," Lerannu said calmly. "We need to be carrying on with our mission soon, anyhow. Let's hear what the high chief and shaman have to say, and get ready to ..."

Lerannu finally took notice of the high chief, high shaman, and the two other Fidons who were seated before her. She faintly recognized the high chief as the woman with the fawn-like markings. To the left of the high chief were a young man and woman. The tribal lass, also having mostly brown fur punctuated by a few patches of white, looked very much like the high chief, and Lerannu presumed she was her daughter. The man beside the young woman was of an age with her. He, too, was mostly brown of fur, but several large patches of luscious black fur spotted his body, much of which was visible from his opened vest of studded animal hide. The young man held the young woman's hand in a strong, affectionate grasp, and the glances that passed between them left no mystery in regards to their relationship.

But the one who captured the mage's awe the most was the high shaman, whose eyes glowed brightly with holy light. He looked directly into Lerannu's eyes, smiled, and then, looking to the other Daughters of the East and Roniil in turn, gestured for them to sit with him and the others. The high chief and shaman introduced themselves to the mage as she took her seat, along with their daughter, Layna, and her betrothed, Garthon. Lerannu looked intently at each of those around her in a brief silence, then nodded.

"Well, let's talk of what we're meaning to do."

"Of course, good Daughter of the East," said Ranye. "First, we are meaning to spend two more days here, waiting for more of our roaming people to answer our call and join us. This should also give you some much-needed time to rest and prepare for the ride and the battle to come."

"Can we afford two more days?" Lerannu asked apprehensively. "I understand the reason, but time is just so precious here."

"Indeed," said Xavier understandingly, "but I assure you that we can afford the time. I can't see it completely, but I feel within my very bones that we *need* to gather everyone we possibly can before setting out. A little more time we can afford, but leaving now, even with all the forces we've gathered so far, is something I fear we'll deeply regret. People have been coming by the hundreds for the past several days, and that's on top of all who have come in the past months. We won't have all our people here, but at the rate they've been coming in, we should have enough in two days' time, and may or may not have some others join along the way."

"Very well," said the mage with a nod. "What then?"

"We've had some scouts look ahead, and we've since got a direct route set for Zefil. By our estimate, we should be able to reach the capital in no more than a week's time. When we near the capital, we'll have another few scouts look ahead while we take cover behind the dunes and ridges nearby. Based on what the scouts can tell us, we'll settle the specific details for our strategy from there, but essentially, we'll probably be looking to press the grey-cloaks against Zefil's walls, enabling the people inside the city to attack them from the other side. Caught between two sides of attack, we should be able to end the siege with our combined strength ..."

The high shaman drifted off in his speech, furrowing his brow as he seemed to become lost in thought. Lerannu and the others looked at him intently. A moment later, Ranye gently took her husband's hand and kissed his cheek. Xavier blinked and chuckled lightly.

"My apologies. For all I can sense, there's so much more that I cannot, at least not clearly. There's something ... else that I can't quite work out. But whatever it is, if it's further trouble, I do sense that it *can* be overcome."

Xavier shrugged, then kissed Ranye. "I suppose we'll see what it is in due time, as with all else in life."

"At any rate," Ruth inquired, "provided that we successfully liberate Zefiil, what, if anything, do you have in mind after that? We came here from Sorrenar, having allied with King Viktor and Queen Xenia, and we've agreed to meet with them at Karzynhaal, along with forces from here and hopefully from Janrenar. From there, we would set out for Enmayar and try to put an end to this horror. Can you sense anything that leads you to believe we should change anything in that regard?"

"At present, not at all, Lady Pionaar. So far, based on what I've been told and have sensed, the only thing that has needed to change from the original plan was where you landed on Kellmayar and where you are to go to return to your ship. You have been told about Korashka being secured from these grey-cloaks, yes?"

"Yes," the Faithguard said with a nod.

"Very good. In that case, provided nothing changes our course, be it by immediate circumstance or by some portent I am given, we should make for that port and sail to Karzynhaal. From there, as you have said, we will wait for this great alliance to gather together, and once all are ready, we'll embark for Enmayar to end this demon's atrocities ... whatever the price."

Lerannu swallowed worriedly and drew a deep breath. Xavier looked compassionately to her.

"But whatever exactly happens ... whoever falls ... know that Fidonhaal will be victorious in the end. It has long been foreseen, and I can tell you that you will have a great ally alongside you, besides the masses of Fidons who will gather to your cause."

"The Phoenix?" Mira asked with a hopeful smile. Lerannu started, and looked in wonder at her fellow Elect. She then looked back to the high shaman, whose smile and eyes glowed with a wonderful hope and confidence.

"Indeed," he said. "It is in the words of Elukus that your victory 'will be brought on wings of fire.' I may not be able to discern all that is to come, but I can say that the one thing I'm more sure of than anything else about all this, apart from the ultimate victory itself, is that the ancient prophet spoke of a Phoenix. I have seen him in my dreams, dwelling on the Sacred Isle, where the three of you shall meet him. In my dreams I have also spoken with him, and I can tell you that he patiently, dutifully, awaits the nearing day that you meet him. I can even tell you his name: Mercilaar."

A fleeting wave of utter silence washed over those seated in the tabernacle. Xavier, smiling warmly, went on.

"Once we've finished our part of the mission here and get to Karzynhaal, we'll meet with Mercilaar and await the arrival of the allies from Janrenar, and your loved ones, of course."

Lerannu's ears lowered wistfully as she was reminded of Allor and the others. She glanced at Ruth and Mira, and saw that Xavier's words had the same effect on them as well.

"From there, with our strength, we'll brave whatever is to be braved, by sea or land or air, and Onu willing, we will reach the East and journey toward the battle that will decide the course of the world."

Another brief silence fell over the meeting.

"Any questions, or thoughts?" Ranye asked patiently.

Lerannu looked to her Elect sisters and Roniil, each as silent as the next. The mage then looked to the high chief and her family, and bowed her head respectfully.

"It seems that much of what has already been planned, by the prophecy or our own devising, is clear enough at present and not overly lacking, at least in regards to what we can judge for the time being. If I have any thoughts, I'll be sure to run them by you."

"And I as well," said Mira and Ruth in turn.

"Of course," Xavier said with a nod, "and should I experience any further ... developments, I'll send for you right away. If there's nothing else to say at present, allow my wife and I to reaffirm that we extend all the hospitality of our people to you. Rest. Recover your strength for the journey to come. Go and meet as many of your newfound comrades as you wish. Reflect. Speak with us later if you want. Know that on the day after next, the last day before we set out for Zefiil, we will gather together and lend our founders' weapons to those deemed fit for them, should they accept them for the quest ahead. This will also include the touching of the arm of Brazofiil. You need not partake if you don't wish to, but our people would be honored beyond words, and just as inspired, if you at least made an appearance."

"I will join in the custom," Lerannu said swiftly, recalling with awe the tale of the Trichynay Sisters, and the millennia-enduring custom that the great tribe practiced to revere their legacy in times of trouble and import. "Whatever exactly comes of it, I feel that it might do me as much good as it will you and your people."

Mira and Ruth added their agreement with a nod, and Xavier gently rose from his cushion, smiling as he dismissed them.

"I look forward to seeing it," he said. "Well, in the sense that I can, anyhow. Go in peace, Daughters of the East. We will speak together again in time."

Lerannu, Ruth, and Mira nodded to Xavier and his family, and rose from their seats and departed from the tabernacle alongside Roniil. The mage glanced back curiously and saw that the high shaman and chief were looking with affectionate directness at their daughter and future son-in-law. The mage exited the great tent as the last of the four to leave, and saw Ruth and Mira looking at her with sisterly care.

"Are you sure you're alright?" Ruth asked. "You were out for almost ten days."

"I believe so. Thank you."

"If you're hungry, we can get some food over there," the knight said, pointing to a large tent a short walk from the tabernacle. "Or if you're feeling tired again, you can go back to our tent."

"Thanks, but I'm quite sure I'm over my shock. If you don't mind, I have some things to discuss with my father, and I'd prefer it just be the two of us."

"Of course," said the knight with a nod. "We'll be in the dining tent. Well, *I* will be, anyway. I don't know about Mira, but I'm starving."

"I feel I could eat a little, too," said Mira, an odd grin growing on her face. "But even if I didn't, I want to see how the bachelors act *this* time."

"Oh, for Onu's sake," said Ruth with exasperation, only to start laughing alongside the huntress, to the amused intrigue of Lerannu. Mira went on to explain.

"When we arrived here last night, and after having a few words with Xavier, Ruth's stomach was growling like you wouldn't believe. We found a dining tent with a lot of good food laid out. Ruth grabbed a bunch of ribs, a big mug of beer, and half a loaf of bread ... *for starters*. I sat with her, eating my fill along with her, though mine wasn't half as much as hers, and I suddenly began to notice that a lot of people in the tent were looking at her with a funny sort of admiration. I pointed it out to Ruth, and she nearly spewed beer out her nose before she explained the significance of all these people's ear piercings. Nearly everyone seemed to be appreciating the show that Ruth was putting on as she ate away, but the most captivated ones, shall we say, were all bachelors according to the earrings. Apparently, a lot of Trichynay men appreciate a lady with an appetite."

Mira barely kept herself comprehensible from her struggle to not burst into complete laughter.

"Then Ruth showed them all her wedding ring ..."

The huntress finally gave in to a loud fit of laughter, with Ruth quietly chuckling with a hand across her face.

"And ... and they were just so dismayed! So many faces, probably at least fifty or so, just immediately went from an intrigued, saucy smile to total disappointment! Their ears drooped and ... oh, you should've seen it."

Lerannu smiled, then felt her smile fade as she saw the ones on Ruth and Mira disappear.

"I mean, you couldn't help it ... I just meant—"

Lerannu shook her head. "Don't worry about it."

The huntress and the knight gave a small smile, then nodded to Lerannu and her father before turning for the dining tent.

"We'll be over there for a while," said Ruth. "If you two finish talking before we leave, feel free to join us. Otherwise, we'll see each other out and about here eventually. We'll be continuing our journey soon enough."

"Of course," Lerannu said as they left. She then looked to her father.

"I suppose we may as well go back to the tent for this," she said levelly.

Roniil nodded silently, and the two returned to the Elect's tent to say what needed saying.

"I've said much of this to your companions already as we were making our way here," said Roniil. "Hopefully it'll be easier to say the second time around."

A Desperate Landing

141

8/11/4030 G.M.

VERDOK sat meditating below deck with Allor, Donovan, and several members of the *Alessia's* crew. They had sailed another nine days, and with the captain's maps and long-accrued knowledge of the seas, along with the guiding golden light of the South Star, the company knew they would soon approach the coast of Janrenar.

The three men, and the ship's crew at large, grew anxious as the next part of the journey drew ever nearer, along with whatever perils that would follow. The priest had begun to meditate at least once a day, and it did not take long for his companions to join him. Though they could never fully shake their worries of what was to come, they left each period of prayer and meditation with a bond of respect and comradeship that grew ever stronger. Verdok was thankful that he was able to help the company in that regard, if nothing else.

The high priest was just nearing the end of the meditation when a thundering of many stomping feet sounded above them. Verdok and his fellows scrambled to their feet with tensely erect ears.

"Grey sails on the horizon behind us!" Verdok could hear the lookout's muffled voice cry out through the floor of the deck above. "They got the same good wind we have, an' oars like us, too!"

Verdok and everyone with him ran up to the deck, looking north and sighing a collective breath of dread at the darkly silver sails visible in the light of the late morning sun.

"Dammit," the captain swore under a distraught sigh. "We're so close to Janrenar, I can feel it! We won't be able to get to Humilaar like we planned, but if we could just get to the coast, we could at least jump ship an' make a run for it ... maybe lose 'em in the forest."

The captain turned to Verdok, Allor, and Donovan, locking eyes with the priest as she thought things through.

"We can't fight 'em all off; there's nearly a score o' 'em. But if we're as near to the coast as I hope we are ..."

The captain shuddered as she sighed in desperation, lifting her tear-brimmed eyes to the heavens in a silent plea to Onu that clawed sorely at Verdok's heart.

"We might be able to fend 'em off long enough to reach the shore," she said after a brief silence, having returned her sight to Verdok and his companions. "But we need to be ready."

The captain turned to some sailors, who were standing to attention beside Verdok, Donovan, and Allor.

"Get the pitch, an' what oil you can find," she said in a low, determined voice, "an' get everyone awake. Have them all get armed up, an' have 'em rotate their stations so we stay on the move while they get their gear. Make sure that all the oars an' everythin' else is manned, too. We can *not* stop for anything!"

"Aye, Captain!" the two sailors said with a quick nod as they rushed below deck.

Verdok looked to the captain, who looked grimly at each of the three men in turn.

"Whatever arms an' gear you've brought with you, get 'em now. If we're able to pull this off, we can't afford any delays when it's time to abandon ship."

Verdok nodded grimly. "Understood, Captain."

The priest strode briskly to the stairway that went below deck to gather his things. Once he reached the bottom of the stairs, he halted and, leaning against the wall, closed his eyes.

"Onu," he said softly, shuddering with fear of what was to come, "you who made us in love and from the desire to share in your work, please guard us from those who serve the hatred that stands poised to devour the world, that we may end this encroaching darkness as your prophet foretold long ago. By your hand, and by those of all your angels, with Vente and Stromarus as the first in my mind, may the winds keep us swift and the waters not hinder us, that we may reach the shore of Janrenar and continue our role in the mission you have given us and our loved ones. In you I strive to trust."

He swallowed back tears as he made his prayer, and started as he felt a hand on his shoulder. His eyes snapped open, and he looked up to see Allor staring solemnly into his soul.

"In you I strive to trust," the king said softly.

"In you I strive to trust," Donovan echoed with a nod from behind Allor.

Verdok breathed a calming breath, resuming his stride alongside his fellows.

"Thank you, Allor," he said softly.

"I should be thanking you, for that and for all the times you guided us in trying to keep up our spirits."

"I'm sorry for earlier, back when—"

"Have you been worrying about that this whole time? For over a week?"

"Well, I just—"

"I thought I made it clear that there was nothing to forgive."

Verdok said nothing further, but nodded as the three reached the trunks at their beds and began to gather their equipment for the impending battle and flight.

142

8/11/4030 G.M.

ALLOR rushed back above deck with Donovan and Verdok, armed and armored with his sword and the heavy coat of chain he wore under his clothes. His brothers in arms were as ready as they could be, with Donovan already having an arrow nocked to his longbow, and Verdok, though not armed, standing ready to aid in the coming battle however he could. The king looked around him and saw many sailors armed, armored, and rushing for positions. He looked at the base of the crow's nest and saw several barrels placed around it.

"That's the pitch I had those two bring up," said the captain, following Allor's gaze, "an' the oil. We also have some folks goin' through our trash crates, findin' whatever glass bottles an' other such things that are still in one piece."

Allor's ears lowered grimly. "Fire bottles?"

"Aye. We need to be ready to do whatever we have to if we're to try an' make it ashore. If they get to us before we can land ..."

The captain sighed anxiously.

"Just be ready for the worst."

***

The fleet was inching ever closer, and as the day passed into the early afternoon, Allor could begin making out many of the individual Fidons aboard the nearest grey-sailed vessels. All were donning the heinous grey jacket over their armor, and were standing to attention in positions all across their respective ship. The king stood beside Verdok and Donovan at the railing alongside the captain and many others of the crew, watching the steadily nearing enemy with silent dread.

As Allor watched the leading vessel draw horridly closer, he heard a hurried set of footsteps rushing from the direction of the crow's nest and making their way to the captain. Allor's heart began to beat with a small hope as he heard the hushed news that the lookout imparted to the captain.

"Janrenar's shores lie dead ahead, Captain. If we can tough it out, we can land near the shore an' make a run for the forest in a couple hours at most."

"Good," said the captain, her voice touched by hope. "Let's make sure we do."

A few minutes later, the leading ship of the grey-cloak fleet, having matched *Alessia's* pace, now sailed alongside her. The officer in charge, a young woman no older than Ruth or Verdok, stepped forward and called out in a strong, authoritative voice.

"Halt, in the name of Empress Raakmathna, the Champion of Order!"

Allor began to try and form a response, but the captain beat him to it.

"*Order*, eh? That's what they call murderin' Onu-knows-how-many Fidons for the ... 'crime' o' not having the right fur color? The correct outward appearance? To be fair, I'm just a simple sailor; I had some schoolin', but not as much as plenty o' others, so I suppose I might've misunderstood what 'order' meant when I learned it, but I would've sworn that order didn't involve massacrin' people left an' right, especially for a 'reason' such as what you lot have gotten yourselves so worked up over. Didn't your ma or pa, or a cleric, or anyone else ever tell you that it's what's in a Fidon that matters?"

"I have heard those lessons. They're the sort that are blindly repeated by those who serve Onu, the one who would permit us to fall into chaos, and by you lot of leeches who stand to gain from it."

"LEECHES?" the captain boomed irately. "Can you not see that this sort o' thinkin' is the work o' Raakaru? The Hateful Heart? The one who has vowed to ruin us because he couldn't stand to allow any freedom?"

Allor jolted at the captain's fury, but was quick to find himself sharing her rage as he looked on at the sinisterly smirking grey-coat captain.

"Onu's Four Breaths!" the *Alessia's* captain bellowed after heaving a great sigh of exasperation. "What's the point o' tellin' all the stories over an' over again when people just keep thinkin' that they're above their lessons, or that it's somehow different this time?"

"We keep rejecting them because we keep realizing that they're actually holding us back!" the grey-cloak captain snapped back.

Allor heard a deathly, wavering whistle on the wind, and saw a small axe fly across the gap of space between the *Alessia* and the grey-coat ship. It flew just shy of the hateful captain, who jolted wide-eyed at the swiftness of the attack, and buried itself into the chain-covered shoulder of the soldier right behind her. The young man dropped backwards, hollering in agony, as the captain of the *Alessia* bellowed out orders.

"I've had enough o' this! Everyone, loose arrows at will!"

The first arrows and bolts began to fly from both ships, and Allor, not having any means of attack from a distance, dropped behind the wall of the deck to take cover alongside Verdok, who was at his right. The priest braced against the railing, clearly struggling to stay composed.

"We can do this, brother," Allor said as gently as he could while still being audible over the sudden surge of battle clamor.

Verdok nodded. "Onu forgive me and give me strength; I have always yearned to never resort to killing. But now it might be ..."

The tip of a crossbow bolt suddenly sprouted through the railing between Allor and Verdok's faces. The two looked wide-eyed at one another, and started as a sailor came dashing over to them with glass bottles tied with lit cloths in his hands. He frantically handed one to each of them.

"For Fidonhaal, my friends," the sailor said grimly as he quickly ran over to supply the fire bombs to other comrades. The king and the priest looked morbidly at the pitch-and-oil filled bottles, along with its slowly burning wick of cloth, before turning their eyes back to one another.

Allor sighed, looking at the other sailors around him who now held a bottle in their hands. Some had already let theirs fly, their actions soon met with cries of alarm and some screams. Others seemed to be trying to carefully assess the target before them, and had yet to throw their improvised weapon. He looked back to Verdok.

"We're in it now, brother. There's nothing for us just sitting hunched over like this."

Verdok nodded, and the two of them rose from cover. Allor noticed Donovan fling his fire bottle at the ship, then immediately resume shooting his bow. A few other sailors were letting either their fire bombs, or their arrows or bolts, fly. A few others, armed only with swords or axes at the moment, cautiously positioned themselves across the deck in case the grey-coats attempted to board. The king and the priest gave each other one last passing glance, and nodded to one another as they looked about for a good target.

After a brief survey of the damage already dealt to the enemy vessel, Allor observed that the main way to the lower deck was still open, and saw some grey-coats running in and out of the entrance. The king, gauging the distance and necessary trajectory as best as he could, drew a deep breath, focused on the doorway, and threw the volatile bottle with all his might. It missed the entrance by a fair mark, instead crashing squarely onto the wood of the main mast. Struck with a grim satisfaction despite missing his intended target, Allor then saw three fire bottles flying toward the grey-coat ship in unison from his right.

One of them fell short of hitting the deck, but hit the vessel squarely in the side. The bottle exploded, and the clinging flames began to steadily burn into the hull. The second one shattered directly in the center of the deck.

The captain of the grey-coats was dashing about the deck with her soldiers, shouting orders for her company to return fire and try to ram the *Alessia* out of desperation. She turned her eyes quickly toward her enemies to give them a passing, scornful sneer.

That was when the third fire bottle struck her directly in the face, shattering and exploding into a horridly bright ball of searing flame. A bloodcurdling shriek erupted from the captain's immolating lips, and after a few horrifying seconds of flailing about in agony, her screams abruptly stopped and she dropped to the floor of the deck.

Allor gasped in both revulsion and morbid awe as he called out to Verdok.

"Verdok! Brother! Are you still with us? Were any of those—"

The king looked to where Verdok had stood beside him and saw that he wasn't there. With a heart gripped with dread, he cast his eyes downward to see if the priest had been hit.

Allor sighed in relief to find that Verdok's body, dead or alive, was not lying stricken on the deck, but his worry quickly returned when he looked about and could not find a trace of him.

143

8/11/4030 G.M.

DONOVAN fired the last arrow from his own quiver, missing his mark by just a hair out of shock from seeing the horridly fiery death of the grey-cloak captain. Quickly regaining his senses, he cast his sight about to see if there were any more arrows he could use. Seeing several loaded quivers lying atop a nearby crate, the bard sprinted toward the cache and the archers nearby, waving to them and calling out a request for some of their arrows. They answered with a nod and friendly salute before turning back to their grim task.

He grabbed a fully stocked quiver, and as he made to sling it across his back, his grip tightened sharply in reaction to the sudden, awful pain that penetrated his shoulder. The bard gasped and dropped to his knees, his head swimming as he realized he had been shot. With a shaking hand, he gingerly felt behind him to confirm the shaft had lodged itself in the meat of his shoulder. Thankfully, he could tell that the padding of his gambeson and the shirt beneath had kept the arrow from going too deeply, but he didn't trust himself to be able to extract the shaft properly. He was in the process of crawling for cover and about to call out for help over the battle's cacophony when a sailor rushed over and helped him to his feet.

"Come over here," the sailor said. "I noticed the priest running over to the bow."

The two shambled hurriedly past a group of sailors. Some were firing arrows. Some were preparing more fire bottles. The captain called out that enough had been dealt to the leading vessel, and the remainder was to be kept for the ships now rushing to envelope the *Alessia*. A few sailors checked themselves and their fellows for injuries, or braced behind cover for the possibility of a boarding. Others were frantically doing all they could to keep at their post in ensuring the ship's continued course for the shore of the South, which the bard, glancing up, could see inching ever closer at a maddeningly slow but sure pace.

The bard and the sailor reached the bow, and turning into a space between some crates for cover, they were taken aback at the sight of Verdok sitting hunched over on the floor, shaking and wailing wretchedly as he rocked back and forth. Donovan's heart pained in sympathy, sensing that the battle had proved too much for the peaceful, kindly cleric. Wincing from the pain in his shoulder, he gently hunched over and took the priest's hands.

"Verdok!" he called loudly over the commotion, but with as compassionate a voice as he could manage. "Brother! Don't burden yourself anymore with the matter of fighting!"

Verdok's face lifted up and stared horridly into Donovan's eyes. The bard, shaking off the dreadful chill that ran through him, turned to the side and pointed to the shaft in his shoulder.

"Be a healer! Help me get this out! Please!"

"I-if there's a-anyone I should h-heal f-first, it sh-should be her! B-but I can't! I CAN'T!"

"Her? Who's her?"

"The c-captain!"

Donovan bolted upright and ran to get a view of the deck, his heart gripped with dread at the thought that the captain had fallen and what might happen if the crew noticed. The captain was still standing, alive with the dreadful rush of battle, barking out orders and preparing to fight off the ships that were quickly gaining on the company. The bard ran back, kneeling once more and placing a hand consolingly on Verdok's shoulder.

"The captain's fine, Verdok. You must've–"

"N-Nooo! The g-gr-grey-coat!"

"What?" Donovan asked incredulously, until it occurred to him that the priest must have been speaking out of a sense of seeking to love all and give them a chance at redemption. Grimacing at the pain in his shoulder, the bard leaned further in and embraced Verdok sympathetically.

"I can't imagine how hard it must be for you to see all this, and I want to call for mercy whenever possible, too. But these people–"

"You d-don't understand!" Verdok wailed horribly into Donovan's ears, setting them to ring. "I did it! I threw the one that hit her! Sh-she looked so m-much like Ruth! An-and I threw it at her f-face! And she screamed and screamed and screamed! I can't ... I can't!"

Donovan's stomach churned horribly as he finally understood the full extent of the priest's agony. He looked to the sailor who helped him get to the bow. His eyes were both sorrowful and frustrated. The bard leaned closely to the priest, whispering into his ear with brother-like compassion.

"I'm so sorry that it played out that way, my friend. Please ... help me with this arrow, and I'll stay here with you. You don't need to do any more fighting for now. Just stay here and heal the wounded, if you can. Can you do that?"

Verdok held the bard closely, beginning to breathe deep, shaky breaths as he vied to compose himself.

"How can he heal them if he can't get himself to move about on deck?" the sailor asked in a voice torn between compassion and irritation.

"Someone will need to bring them, or guide them here," said Donovan as he lifted his eyes to look squarely into the sailor's. "That, or they'll just have to see if anyone else can help them."

The sailor sighed heavily and made to speak again, but Verdok's shaky voice interrupted.

"I-I ... I can go about the deck. Just p-please, don't hand me anything that isn't for healing."

"Of course," said the bard calmly.

The priest slowly rose up from the floor of the bow, and handing Donovan a thick cloth to bite down upon, he carefully pulled the arrow from his shoulder. Donovan let out one long, painful growl, then sighed with relief as the entire arrow clattered to the floor. He then took off his gambeson and shirt, and felt the quick sting and soothing relief of the poultice Verdok had taken from his bags, followed by the soft, sturdy linen bandage that he wrapped around his shoulder and back. Donovan stood up and put his shirt and jacket back on, thanking Verdok as they and the sailor returned to the deck.

"Let's set up over there," the bard said as he pointed to a stack of crates near the center of the deck. "We'll be in cover, and we won't be as far from one side or the other as if we stayed at the bow."

"Al-alright," said Verdok as he clutched his bags of supplies tightly.

"I'll be right beside you."

"Th-thank you."

***

In a curious, warped sense of time, where a second felt like an hour and an hour a second, Donovan watched the enemy fleet attempt to maneuver around and entrap the *Alessia*, only to be kept at bay with volleys of arrows, bolts, and fire bottles. Agonizing screams of burning men and women regularly pierced the air, and in response, Donovan would drop behind the crates to see if Verdok was still in a relatively functional state. The first several times, including when he was healing one of the sailors, Verdok would tremor violently for a few seconds, but would continue his tasks. By the eighth or ninth time, he no longer shook, but the bard could see a dreadful dullness filling the priest's deep blue eyes.

He continued to fight, having explained to Allor what had happened as the king briefly rejoined them behind the crates. At the sight of the fire bomb in Allor's hand, Donovan looked fully into the king's eyes and bade him to either find another position, take up a bow or crossbow, or else try to help Verdok with tending to the wounded. The king turned away, threw the fire bottle at one of the two ships attempting to ram the *Alessia* from either side, and then swiftly returned to help the priest.

At last, Donovan heard the cries of the lookout announcing they were mere moments away from being able to abandon ship and make for the shore. The bard looked up and saw the sun lowering with the light of the late afternoon. He turned his gaze south and his heart began to pound furiously as the vibrant green forest of Janrenar lay just ahead, a mere few yards from the nearing sandy shoreline.

Then his heart nearly stopped as he heard a shattering of glass upon the *Alessia's* deck, followed by the rushing roar of erupting flame. He turned and saw that the nearest grey-coat ships had now begun to adopt the same tactic as the *Alessia's* crew. A sticky, steadily spreading puddle of fire appeared near the stern, and there was a great clamor of sailors running to get away.

"Hold out just a little longer!" the captain bellowed as she noticed the eyes of the crew begin to look anxiously at the railing and the water below. The captain rushed over to Donovan, Verdok, and Allor.

"You three," she panted, "take these ropes an' tie 'em to the railing over there. Stay there an' keep your head down until I call to jump."

"We can still help you until then," said Allor.

"No," the captain said with a shake of her head. "Your fates are tied in with those o' the Daughters o' the East. You *must* jump as soon as you're able, an' try an' get to shore an' take cover in the forest. From there, we—"

Another fire bottle from the grey-cloaks shattered onto the deck, followed by a horrid scream. Donovan saw Verdok begin to quake again, and followed the priest's gaze to see a burning sailor directly in his line of sight.

"Get over there, NOW!" the captain yelled as she tossed the ropes to Donovan and Allor before running back to her crew. Donovan took Verdok by the hand and, passing him to Allor, took up the ropes and made for the part of the railing to which the captain had directed them. Donovan began tying the ropes to the railing, listening to Allor speak as calmly as he could to the priest.

"We can do this, Brother Verdok. Once we get somewhere safe, we can talk about all this and—"

Another fire bomb shattered onto the deck. A few seconds later, a massive jolt ran through the ship followed by the panicking sound of splintering wood. Donovan looked back and saw that one of the grey-coat ships had at last managed to ram the *Alessia's* stern. He had just enough time to register what had happened when he heard the captain shout.

"NOW! EVERYONE! ABANDON SHIP!"

144

8/11/4030 G.M.

VERDOK was still struggling to stop his shaking when the captain called for the crew to jump ship. He felt Donovan assertively place a rope into his hands, and heard him yell for him to climb it down the ship. Silent and trembling, he complied. He haltingly rappelled down the side of the *Alessia*, watching members of the crew either jumping outright into the water or clambering down ropes like his, passing the longboats they were unable to prepare during the frantic battle. He looked down and saw that Allor and Donovan were already in the water and had started to swim the remaining distance to the shoreline.

Not wanting to fall too far behind his companions, Verdok was trying to resolve to let go of the rope when a second jarring impact sent him plummeting into the water. It came from the same ship that had rammed them only a minute earlier, and was followed by an even more resounding crack from the *Alessia's* breaking hull. The force sent Verdok's rope flying outwards, and with the priest having lost his grip, he splashed into the water a mere few feet from Donovan and Allor. Quickly rising to the surface and gasping for breath, both from fretful sobbing and the abrupt fall into the sea, Verdok swam as fast as he could to stay with his friends.

They soon reached the shallows and began wading frantically toward dry land. An arrow whistled out of the forest beyond the shore and passed over Allor's head by a hair's breadth. The king shouted in alarm and raised his hands in a nonviolent gesture. Donovan followed suit, as did Verdok. Still wading forward, the three men were soon stricken with awe as a swarm of arrows and bolts issued from the forest line and over their heads. The shafts flew high and rained down on the grey-coat ships that had maneuvered behind the fleeing crew in an effort to provide their soldiers with easy targets.

Within another minute, the trio had reached the dry sands of the Janrenarn coast. Verdok was the first to reach shore. Looking back, he was disheartened to see Donovan limping up from the shallows with another arrow having found its way to him, this time in the right leg. Thankfully, Allor was unhurt and helped the bard along. Before Verdok could turn back to help them, two robed and hooded figures, staves in hand, ran past him from the forest and rushed them along.

The priest felt a small comfort grace his heart. Though Verdok still had what he needed to tend to the bard's new wound, seeing a couple from the order of the Vibonmor Shepherds was a relieving sight. The priest caught the sight of one of the robed figures, who gestured for the group to follow them into the forest line. Verdok was taken aback at the sheer number of women and men lining the road that lay just past the shore-lining trees. Each of them had either a bow or a crossbow, and ranged in age from adolescence to near-elderly. Before Verdok could take in the scene further, however, the Shepherd called out to him again.

"What is the purpose of your company's arrival?" he asked.

Still recovering from his experiences on the ship, as well as being somewhat rattled by the sudden question, Verdok started with a stutter, but soon found himself regaining composure.

"W-we come from S-Sorrenar, to give what aid we can in ending the grey-coats' besiegement of Benhotha, and to request your aid in return. We're here to confirm, to you and your leaders, that this madness is not the will of the Enmayarn leaders, but of a demon that has manipulated and possessed the queen. We were originally meaning to sail to the mouth of the Vitari, and then follow it to the capital, but, well ..."

The priest gestured to the fleet of grey sails and the burning *Alessia.* The robed man looked the scene over, nodded somberly, and returned his attention to Verdok.

"Did you originally hail from Sorrenar? Your accent doesn't quite match what I usually hear from there."

"I am not. Only those who sailed us here, and my wounded Balon companion there, are natives of the North. I come from Enmayar, along with ... with the king."

The Shepherd's eyes widened. He turned to his partner, who had removed the arrow from Donovan's leg and was in the middle of wrapping it. Both of them looked intently at Allor, who nodded as he tried to catch his breath.

"It is as he says," the King of the East said plainly. "My wife became ensnared by the guiles of a demon, who has since come to possess her now-lifeless body. Sheeva had been building up this plan for years, but it was ultimately this Raakmathna who actually devised and executed it. My companions here witnessed it firsthand, as well as our loved ones, who are journeying to Kellmayar with the same purpose as ours."

A few seconds of silence passed, and the Shepherd healing Donovan turned her attention back to her work, speaking in a gentle voice barely audible over the sounds of the flying arrows.

"My deepest condolences, King Allor."

"Yes," said the other Shepherd with a sad nod. "You mentioned other companions in Kellma-yar?"

"Yes," the king confirmed. "They have been given their mission by Onu himself. They are the long-foreseen Daughters of the East."

The Shepherd healing Donovan just finished her work in time to snap her widened eyes up to Allor. She looked to the other Shepherd, a small laugh passing her lips.

"This day is getting more interesting by the minute," she said.

"You can say that again," the robed man said as he approached Allor with an outstretched hand. "Your arrival is one befitting companions of the Elect, I'll give you that. I am Varnu Shaal, a Shepherd of the order of Life and Death."

"Well met," Allor replied as he shook Varnu's hand.

"And I am Kenora," said the female Shepherd as she rose and helped Donovan back to his feet, "Varnu's partner in the order, as well as his wife."

Verdok and Donovan introduced themselves, and Allor asked the two Shepherds about the massive wall of archers.

"About two moons ago," Kenora explained, "King Salos and Queen Vita issued a desperate decree across all of Janrenar that was not under the grey-coats' control. Nearly everyone of fifteen years and older has been conscripted to aid the country, with many of them now making patrols across all the roads to bring down any grey-coats they encounter. My husband and I were in the capital at the time, and we ended up going with the company you see here. They've been specifically positioned to have as much of a view of the coast as possible, and another large company has been set along the southern bank of the Vitari. We just happened to be helping the militia here at the time you all came along."

"I see," said the king. "I'm sorry that this horror has driven your country to such desperate measures, but I'm glad you lot were around when we came."

"Likewise," said Varnu.

"At any rate," Allor went on, "as you can see, we have many others with us from the ship. They have been instructed by the King and Queen of Sorrenar to aid you however they can. We must get to Benhotha as soon as possible. Do you know if anyone here has horses to spare?"

"We do," said Varnu, "and we should be able to have some of these folks here come along to aid you on the ride. We'll wait a little for your companions from the ship, and then we'll ride out."

"A thousand thanks, my friend."

Varnu called over one of the archers and told him to pass word along the line to have what horses that could be spared brought to them. The three men sat together under a large palm tree, watching arrows fly toward the nearing grey sails while they waited for the next stage of their quest to begin.

The Battle of Zefiil

145

8/12/4030 G.M.

MIRA walked among the many tents of the Trichynay camp, awed and warmed to the heart at the spirit of the great encampment. It was intriguingly exotic and yet felt so much like Plen. The Trichynay people clearly embodied much of the Fidon ideal, perhaps more so than those in many other places, despite a few distinctive cultural matters that were a bit foreign to her.

The huntress and her companions had been resting and preparing for the impending ride to Zefiil for the past two days following the conversation with Shaman Xavier, as well as acquainting themselves with their newfound comrades throughout the great camp. They conversed with any who approached them, especially when they were in one of the camp's dining tents, telling the tribespeople of their lives and the journey they had undergone thus far. They spoke more with Xavier and Ranye, along with their daughter, Layna, and her betrothed, Garthon, and were quick to befriend them beyond the initial bond of duty to their respective roles in the quest. The great tribe was full of women and men, young and old, who were sincere, good, honorable folk who doubtlessly did their founders proud. They were as cooperative as a massive family despite the many lineages that had come into the tribe's fold since its inception. Mira doubted there was a single one among them who would not trust any of their kin or fellows with their lives.

The huntress and her sisters in fate had gotten a prime example of the tribe's internal trust and respect two days ago, shortly after discussing their essential plan with the Trichynay leaders.

After the group had discussed plans for the journey and battle to come, Mira and Ruth went to eat while Lerannu and her father privately spoke their fill of the past and laid it to rest. The mage then rejoined the knight and the huntress in the dining tent, and once she and her father had eaten, Roniil offered to guide them through the camp and show them the various sights and qualities of the Trichynay. The three of them agreed readily, and were soon going through several of the encampment's tents, meeting and briefly conversing with those within.

They soon approached a small, silent tent, which Roniil explained was the personal abode of one Zongar Highsun, an esteemed champion of the tribe who had just recently arrived to join their journey to Zefiil. Roniil explained that prior to the Elect's arrival, this news was the greatest boon to the camp's morale. Lerannu's father began listing off some of the warrior's accomplishments as the group drew near the tent, and upon parting the canvas at the entrance, Mira and the others started slightly (and blushed strongly) at the sight of the warrior and his wife quietly relishing the carnal aspect of their bond together. Mira's face grew even hotter when the couple continued their intimacy with ease, even as they acknowledged the company's presence. The champion tilted his head slightly, looking past his wife's hips, and greeted the company with a nod that showed no discomfort or annoyance toward the intrusion whatsoever.

"Hail, Sir Tern," the warrior said to Roniil in a deep, friendly voice. "Am I needed somewhere? If I might just have another moment—"

"No, that won't be necessary, Sir Highsun," said Roniil with a mostly level voice, just barely tinged with the tone of an awkward chuckle. "You and Karla have journeyed far to join us for the troubles to come, and we weren't meaning to disrupt your repose. I was only meaning to introduce you and Karla to these three, who will be vital in the battle to come, but that can—"

The champion and his wife looked to the huntress, knight, and mage, and after a few seconds' glance, they paused in their union and gazed in awe at the sacred marks on the Daughters' brows. Mira's face felt as though it were about to burst into flame as the couple promptly rose from their bed and approached them with no hesitation, despite Roniil's attempt to tell them it was presently unnecessary. Standing before them as bare as the day they were born apart from their earrings, the warrior and his wife, still wrapping an arm about each other in a light embrace, nodded reverently to them.

"We heard that the Daughters of the East had come into our midst," Zongar said solemnly. "I was looking to seek them out soon, and speak with them if I could. I did not expect them to come to me."

"I was simply showing them around," Roniil said plainly, "and thought it would be good for them to meet one of the more accomplished of their newfound allies."

"I am honored beyond words to meet you, Daughters of the East," said the great warrior with another nod. The hulking Kason champion was a tower of muscle, marked here and there with a scar dealt by some monster or villain, and had a well-kept beard and hair that ran past his shoulders. He looked, at the oldest, a handful of years older than Lerannu or Allor, perhaps just starting to near the brink of his middle years. If he were a Balon, or at least showed some heritage thereof, he might have posed as an indirect descendant of the Karamus line, and Mira would have believed it. "I feel that your guide is overselling me, however. I have slain a few foul beasts, and battled a foe or two–"

"A huge nest of harpies when he was a lad," Roniil cut in with a smile, "and with only his father and a few others with him. He also helped his father and a couple others kill a troll in the Karzolex Mountains, with Karla helping as well if I recall. Then he and his father slew a vampire sometime after that, though sadly only Zongar survived that encounter. Then he led a battle against a necromancer. A good number of folks helped him with that one, sure, including Karla, but he dealt the killing blow to the villain himself."

"Those pale in comparison to the evil we face now and the lot that these three are to fulfill," said Zongar with a nod to Mira and her Elect sisters.

"I suppose so, but knowing of your experiences is more than a little assuring," Roniil said with a shrug. "At any rate," he said as he gestured to each of the Daughters in turn, "these are indeed the Daughters of the East. This is Ruth Pionaar, a knight of the Faithguard; Mira Greenheart, an archer and huntress from the Forest of Santaru; and Lerannu Stonefaith, a mage from the royal court of Enmayar ... and my daughter."

Zongar briefly left his wife's side and stepped closer to Lerannu, whose grey fur seemed to take a notably darker shade from the intense blush that flamed beneath it. Mira kept trying to avert her eyes from the tall and handsome figure, but then noticed the champion's wife Karla smiling smugly at the sight of the three Elect women glimpsing at her husband's form. The huntress realized that Karla was also quietly admiring his body while still being attentive to the conversation at hand. The huntress quietly looked on, alternating her sight between the warrior's sincere eyes and grand physique.

"Your father has told me a fair bit about you, dear Lerannu," the warrior said gently as his wife stepped forward and resumed embracing him. "We had the pleasure of each other's company in times past as we journeyed across the land. I understand that you carry more than a little weight in your heart in regards to the past, but know that in light of the lot that Onu has bestowed upon you, I have faith in you and your sisters in destiny, that you will overcome whatever evils that have arisen in these grim days."

"Y-your words are v-very kind, Sir Highsun," the mage stuttered bashfully. "I will do all I can to prove worthy of your confidence in us."

Roniil, suppressing a light laugh, cleared his throat.

"At any rate, I'm sure that we'll have time to talk later," he said as he nodded to Zongar and Karla. "We didn't mean to interrupt your shared repose. We can speak of all these things a little later, perhaps at dinner."

"It wasn't any trouble," said the champion as he and his wife returned to their bed, as well as their previous position together. "But that sounds good to me all the same. I look forward to it."

The four quietly left the tent. Mira looked at Ruth, who was trying to keep from giggling, and then at Lerannu and Roniil, who were grinning awkwardly at each other.

"I've known that the Trichynay's community environment has led them to be quite ... relaxed," the mage said as she scratched her head bashfully, "as far as most of them are concerned when it comes to ... some things that most of us would prefer a bit more privacy for. I don't think the books I read quite gave the full account of it, though. Or, maybe they did and it's just another matter to see it firsthand."

"Same here," Ruth said, still stifling laughter as the four of them continued their tour of the great camp.

Mira laughed, relieved that her cheeks were finally starting to cool down. "I'm afraid I don't know that much about these people at all," she said to the mage, "especially when compared to you or Ruth. I learned the details about the earrings when Ruth told me yesterday, and I've known the basic story of the tribe's founding Three Sisters since I was little, but that's about it."

Roniil laughed. "Well, now you know some more about them. I confess that even after all these years, I still feel a little awkward at times when something like that happens. And it's a fairly common occurrence, I might add. But know that this tribe is perhaps one of the most tightly knit peoples in all of Fidonhaal. They have a very deep respect for one another, and as Lera pointed out, their environment doesn't afford the same level of privacy you'd find, and probably expect, in most other places anyway. It's pretty rare to find what I'd call a shy Trichynay man or woman. Of course, they don't typically just waltz about camp flaunting everything needlessly, nor do they typically go out of their way to look for such a view. But they don't tend to get upset if one happens across them in such a state. And they typically don't object if there is a little bit of an audience, or if they linger a little in their observation."

"Oh?" said Mira with a giggle. The situation was not much unlike what happened from time to time back in Plen, and had even happened with her and Donovan a time or two. But she never had a couple carry on in their intimacy right in front of her, only to stop and get right out of bed to speak with her face-to-face without so much as keeping their blanket wrapped about them.

"Appreciation of the body's beauty is a value that's present everywhere, of course," Roniil went on, "but obviously, not many other places have people who are quite as ... easygoing in the approach or expression of it as you see here. Most of us would say that there *is* a range of times and places for such things, but the list of such circumstances usually isn't as generous as it is here. The people here admire one another's bodies, to whatever extent they might chance to view them–"

"Especially when it's a muscular lady putting away ribs like there's no tomorrow, even when she's fully clothed," Mira cut in with a laugh.

"Oh shush," Ruth smiled with a roll of the eyes.

"But she isn't wrong," Roniil said with a grin. "Clothed or bare, their respect for one another and their less private environment has led them to be very free in admiring one another's forms, and the married ones don't get jealous when their spouse is viewed thus by their fellows."

"But it *is* a matter of just looking, and not touching, right?" the huntress asked. "Especially for the married ones, at least? I can get the more lenient stance on viewing and all, especially in a place like this, but the sacredness of that bond, I still can't imagine that being lost on them."

"Absolutely," Roniil said with a chuckle. "They might not be shy at looking or being seen, but the bond of marriage is deeply revered here, same as with Fidonity at large."

Roniil stopped walking, promptly pausing the tour.

"Come to think of it, I'd say it could be argued that it's regarded and honored here even more so on average than much of the rest of the world ..."

Roniil's voice faded to silence. He looked somberly at his daughter, who silently nodded as if to implore her father to let go of his past offense. A faint smile returned to his lips, and he continued.

"After all, they all go around with one set of earrings or the other once they reach adulthood, announcing whether they're taken or available, and all of the tribe respects either status accordingly, but both allow for viewing the body. If they're available and in a situation where they're being viewed, they treat it as if they're ... casting the line out, let's say. If they're taken, and their intimacy as a couple or their individual body is noticed by others, it's a way of celebrating their bond, with the viewers looking on as a sort of congratulatory gesture to the person or couple."

"I see," said Mira amusedly.

"It's a fair bit different from most other places in Fidonhaal," Roniil said, "that's for sure. At any rate, enough just standing around. If we're going to talk, let's keep walking while we're at it. There are lots more people for you to meet and places to see here, assuming you're still up for it, that is."

"Of course," Mira said gladly, echoed by Ruth and Lerannu.

"Alright, then," said Roniil as he looked briefly about before pointing the way to their next destination. "Let's make our way toward the reliquary. Xavier mentioned the ceremony we're planning to have with the ancient weapons and arm bones, but whether you partook in it yourselves or not,

I think you'll enjoy looking at them all the same."

They went on to see the tent that housed the sacred artifacts of the Trichynay, along with other wonderful sights.

It was now the twelfth of Yorok, two days after their tour of the encampment. Mira had been meandering about on her own, having become mostly familiar with the camp's layout. She had heard the announcement from Xavier and Ranye that morning, telling all the tribe of the ceremony with the relics that was to be done that evening, and was now simply walking about, appreciating her last day of rest before the trying times that lay ahead.

She passed by a large tent. It was filled with many voices, mostly men, along with the warmly earthy scent of Fallowroot tea. The huntress paused in her wandering, and remembering the days when she and her mother would sit and talk with her father as he drank his seed-quieting brew, she was suddenly very intrigued to see how the tribe socialized around the drink. Mira entered the tent, deeply breathing in the tea's scent as she peered around inside.

She noticed Ruth and Lerannu sitting together, with Layna, the daughter of the high chief and shaman, speaking enthusiastically to them alongside her fiancé, Garthon. Garthon was sipping a cup of the tea as he chatted with the three women, alongside several other men sitting at the same table. Mira strode over to the table to join her fellow Elect.

"Lera and I were wondering where you went off to," Ruth said as she took a drink of water.

"I've just been going here and there," the huntress explained, "and then I stumbled across here and was curious to see what it was like inside. What are we all talking about so excitedly, if I may ask?"

"We were just discussing the ceremony tonight. Lera and I were curious about the specifics, and we didn't want to accidentally do something improper if we could help it."

"Garthon and I were assuring them that any misstep out of ignorance would be understood and readily pardoned," said Layna, "but all the same, since they wanted to learn about it, we were just going over things with them. If you'd like, we can run back through things real quick; we haven't gone too far in yet."

"I would be grateful to know as well," Mira said as she poured herself a cup of water. "Thank you."

146

8/12/4030 G.M.

RUTH sat beside Lerannu and Mira in the biggest dining tent of the encampment, with High Chief Ranye and High Shaman Xavier by their side. The eve before the ride to Zefiil had come. The tent was packed to bursting, and all of the tribespeople who could not get inside were sitting on carpets that had been laid out around the outside of the tent. It was an amazing scene of community, like a vast family preparing for a fateful journey together.

The meal was splendid, with many savory meats, sweet fruits, hearty breads, and good drink. When the people had eaten their fill, Xavier rose from his cushion and raised his hands high and wide. The great tribe fell utterly silent, and Xavier's voice, though immensely calm and gentle, seemed to flood the entire camp and reach each and every person as though he were speaking to them face to face.

"Sisters and brothers, daughters and sons of Trichynay, on the morrow, at first light, we begin our journey to Zefiil. There, we shall confront the foul army of mad hatred and death that has laid siege to the city, and fight and die as need be for our fellow Kellmayarns, and indeed, all of Fidonhaal. Though the shadow we face is vast and grave, we have been blessed with the company of the Daughters of the East, whose coming had long been foreseen by the Blind Seer Elukus. With this, and the sights that I myself have been given, I say to you that we shall prove victorious against this evil in the end. But alas, I cannot say with certainty the exact events to come, nor their costs."

Ruth looked about and saw nearly every head in the tent bow in deep contemplation of the doom that might befall them. The knight drew a deep, silent breath as she joined them in pondering what was to come.

"So, on this eve," Xavier went on, "I will enact the longstanding custom that we have practiced in such troubled times and invite all to accompany me to the reliquary, that all may touch Brazofiil's arm, and perhaps draw some measure of strength from it. I also request that the following people stand with me after the bones have been touched: Lerannu Stonefaith of the Elect; her father, Roniil Tern; our honored champion, Zongar Highsun; my wife, Ranye Onoraan; my daughter, Layna Onoraan; and my soon-to-be son-in-law, Garthon Benstro. I have seen that they will do well to bear one of the arms of our founders."

A strong, but quiet hum of awe flooded the tent and spilled into the air outside. Ruth and Mira looked with intrigue at Lerannu. They did not know for certain, but from what they saw when they toured the reliquary and their knowledge of the story of the tribe's founding sisters, both were quite sure of which item Lerannu was to be offered.

***

They left the dining tent and gathered around the outside of the reliquary. Ruth stood alongside her sisters of fate, as well as the high chief and shaman. She looked all about her, amazed beyond words at the sea of people that stretched beyond her sight in the darkening glow of the setting sun. A pair of tribal clerics who worked beneath Xavier strode through the masses, bearing between them the ornately carved case that held the bones of the arm of Brazofiil. When the two relic-bearing clerics reached the high shaman, they kneeled reverently and opened the case, revealing a large, long form wrapped caringly in linen. Xavier approached the case, lifted the wrapped form, and unwound the linen. The high shaman then presented to the people a long arm of great, strong bones that glinted hauntingly in the last golden rays of the sun, and the flickering torchlight that swiftly replaced them. Ruth saw the arm in its wrappings earlier when Roniil showed the reliquary to the Elect, but now she was seeing the bones themselves for the first time. She marveled at how, just like the weapons she saw in the same tent, they had been so well-preserved for nearly four thousand years.

"Behold the bones of the arm of Brazofiil," Xavier called out loudly as he lifted the great arm over his head, "the Champion of Trichynay, and the husband of the sister, Lovrena. In the final battle against the tyrant-mage Landoth, Brazofiil felled many foes before his right arm was severed by Xegon Magendaar, a villain of stature equal to his own. In memory of his heroism and that of his wife, his wife's kin, and his friends, we have kept these bones in reverence and touched them in troubled times in the hopes that we might draw a little strength from them, in one sense or another."

Xavier's glowing eyes flitted all around him. Though he was blind in the traditional sense, Ruth felt that he could see each man, woman, and child more truly than anyone else present.

"All are welcome to approach the bones and touch them, whether you are set to ride tomorrow or not. In battle or in caring for our young and old, there is always a need for strength, if not of body, then of heart."

Xavier turned to those standing around him, offering the arm to be touched by those who wished to do so. Ruth watched Ranye, Layna, and Garthon place a hand on it, their eyes closed and their breasts swelling as they each drew a deep, ponderous breath. Ruth looked on as the arm was then offered to Zongar and Roniil, who acted in the same manner, and then Lerannu and Mira before it was at last offered to her. Following their example, the knight gently placed a hand on the bones, closed her eyes, and took a deep breath. Though there was still a part of her mind that kept viewing the custom as a bit macabre, she was surprised to feel a comforting warmth and smoothness as she touched the bones, rather than the dry grittiness she was bracing for. She opened her eyes, nodded to Xavier, and looked on as the high shaman turned once more to the legion of tribespeople, again lifting the bones of the legendary warrior's arm high overhead.

"Come, any who wish, and feel the echo of strength from the times of our founding."

***

The waxing moon, a mere two nights away from its fullest light, had begun to pass its zenith in the starry sky once all who made to touch the bones had done so. All the people of Trichynay stood expectantly, intently watching those standing with Xavier as they waited to see who was going to be offered which armament of the Three Sisters and their husbands. Before beckoning for the relics to be brought forth, the high shaman turned to Ruth and Mira, leaning toward them and speaking privately.

"Had I not known the story of your own bow, Lady Mira, and if my visions had not said otherwise, I would have offered the bow of Abye to you."

Mira smiled and nodded. "I appreciate the thought, my friend, and the bow is clearly very fine. But my heart is bound within my husband's gift, and I couldn't bear to think of replacing it with another, even if only for a while."

Xavier smiled, nodded, and then turned to Ruth.

"Lady Ruth, I had pondered offering you the hammer and shield of Aaron, if you were open to the offer, though I wasn't sure just how dedicated you were to your order's axe and buckler. I know they're not the exact same thing, and that to a warrior so dedicated to a certain way of battle, trying to change one's arms is like trying to change ... well, their *arms*."

Ruth grinned and shook her head at Xavier's jest, to which the high shaman, looking at the knight as though he could clearly see her, smiled and shrugged in response.

"I appreciate the thought all the same," Ruth said warmly.

"But that is not why I shall entrust the hammer and shield to another in this gathering. I have seen that another awaits to lend his arms and armor to you."

Ruth's ears pricked up in intrigue.

Xavier smiled. "He awaits you on Karzynhaal, at his tomb. The founder of your order."

Ruth's eyes widened, as did those of Mira and Lerannu.

"I ... I trust you sense that his spirit is willing to lend them? I couldn't bear to just dig them up and—"

"He has told me."

Ruth and her fellow Elect gazed in awe at the high shaman, ever wondering what all he knew, and why Onu and Yorun had willed to impart it to him of all other people. The Faithguard knight simply nodded her head in reverent anticipation.

"My thanks to you for telling me of this future blessing," she said. "If I am to survive the coming battle at Zefiil and make the journey to Karzynhaal, I will not look to keep the Exemplar Warrior waiting any longer than I can help."

Xavier nodded and beckoned the relic bearers to approach. Each of them opened their ornate caskets, displaying the great armaments of the founders of the great tribe. Xavier lifted each item overhead in turn, announcing them to the gathered people before presenting them to their chosen bearer. The high shaman first turned to his wife and gave her the bow of the sister, Abye. Ranye took the beautiful bow and gently ran her fingers down the string, looking on as she watched her husband continue his task.

The hammer and shield of the husband, Aaron, went to Xavier's daughter, Layna, and the great sword of the husband, Ovtiir, to her fiancé, Garthon. Both took their given relics with bowed heads, then looked longingly into one another's eyes before looking to Xavier. The high shaman said nothing, but nodded to them with glowing, earnest eyes.

Then Xavier called forth Zongar and Roniil, and everyone apart from Xavier murmured and looked on in a measure of surprise when the mighty champion was given the twin swords of the sister, Korrah, and Roniil the great battleaxe of Brazofiil himself. Ruth watched the two, who did not question the arms they were given despite the clear bit of surprise that was in their eyes. The knight began to grin as she saw their surprise soon shift to an amused confidence as Zongar, putting space between him and all the others, lightly swung the two blades and flexed his large arms as he tested their feel within his hands. The champion grinned, pleased with how they felt, as did Roniil with the great axe, which he was able to hoist and swing without much trouble despite his frame not being as mighty as Zongar's or Brazofiil's.

At last, Xavier called forth Lerannu to lend her the last remaining relic: the staff of the sister, Lovrena. It was a beautiful staff, its acacia wood having been lovingly polished and well-kept by generation upon generation, and a large, gorgeously fiery jasper stone set into the headpiece.

"Lady Lerannu," said Xavier, "I understand that you don't often use staves yourself."

"I don't, but I always did like the one I had as a token of office back home. It was just more for show than anything else, personally."

"You need not borrow it if you don't wish to."

"But I do, and will gladly take it, if you are indeed offering me this honor."

"I am."

Ruth watched the mage take the ancient staff in both hands, handling it with a smile as she appreciated the smoothness and sturdiness of the wood and stone. Lerannu looked back to the high shaman and nodded, and Xavier's eyes seemed to glow even more brightly for an instant as he turned to address the people one final time.

"All is done now," he said. "All who have sought to draw from the strength of Brazofiil have touched his arm, and the champions who were revealed in my dreams have taken unto them the relics of our founders. A long day's journey awaits us at dawn. Go now, my friends and kin, and rest. May Onu, the angels, and our ancestors all give us strength for the times to come."

"In him, and them, we strive to trust," said the thousand voices surrounding him in gentle reverence.

147

8/13/4030 G.M.

LERANNU opened her eyes to the sound of many horns blowing. The great tribe's call for its people and allies to rise and begin preparing for the journey had sounded. The mage had slept quite well, much to her pleasant surprise given the daunting mission that was now beginning and the hours for sleep being short due to the long ceremony the previous night. Sitting upright in her bed for a moment, Lerannu gently massaged her brow, reflecting on the relic ceremony and pondering the troubles that, though not yet fully known, were doubtlessly coming.

"Everything all right, Lera?" the mage heard Ruth ask gently from the other side of the tent.

Lerannu looked up and saw the knight and Mira quietly dressing and gathering their equipment. Both had paused in their preparations, looking concernedly at their Elect sister.

"I'm fine," she said, "I was just thinking about ... everything."

Ruth and Mira nodded, and continued their preparations. Lerannu got up and dressed, then milled about the tent as she gathered her gear and belongings. She packed the rations and riding equipment the tribe had given her, and donned over her robes the armor of hide and cloth padding that had also been given to her. The mage checked her satchel and belt of small flasks of Kamgenbew tonic. There were still several from what was given to her in Benevor, but her supply had since been added to significantly, courtesy of the tribe's stores. Confident in her supply, Lerannu at last took up the staff from the reliquary, which she had placed caringly on a large cushion beside her bed the night before. She ran her palms across the shining wood of the staff and contemplatively felt the large jasper orb that was set into its head, enjoying its feel as it went from cool to warm from its time in her hand.

She heard Mira and Ruth behind her, along with the gentle rustling of the canvas at the tent's entrance. The mage looked from her staff to her Elect sisters, who were looking confidently at her as they waited for her to join them. She smiled, and with the staff of Lovrena in her hand, and all her other things packed either onto her person or beneath her arms, she walked out of the tent with them and made for the great tabernacle.

They reached the massive tent and were greeted with reverent cheers by the warriors who had gathered there. The Elect greeted them with thanks, and when they noticed that Xavier and Ranye were not yet among them, Lerannu asked the gathering riders of their whereabouts.

"I believe they're still in the tabernacle," said a warrior as he waved a hand at the great tent behind him. "I'm not sure what exactly–"

As if on cue, or perhaps in response to the thundering cheers a moment before, the high chief and high shaman stepped out of the tent. The gathering warriors began to enthusiastically greet their leaders, but their cheers quickly faded into an awkward silence as two others exited the tent after Ranye and Xavier. Behind them came Layna, the leaders' daughter, with her fiancé, Garthon, at her side. The two stood beside Xavier and Ranye, their hands in one another's as they looked intently at the gathering legion.

The young couple's ears were bandaged, telling all who knew of the tribe's customs that they had undergone the alteration in their piercings that marked them as no longer being virgins. Lerannu understood from her prior knowledge and her exposure to the tribe's ways that the slightly awkward atmosphere that hung over those gathered was due to the mild breach of etiquette that had transpired.

Perhaps out of the uncertainty of who would remain after the battle to come, the young betrotheds had surrendered to passion and sealed their bond prior to the traditional practices. Lerannu judged confidently from her brief time with Garthon and Layna that they were an excellent match, and was sure that this break from standard practice was no severe trespass, judging from what she had observed of the Trichynay customs and general attitudes. That said, she could also tell that their action was indeed a touch out of the norm, given what she was told of the people's sense of duty and honor, as well as the simple air of awkwardness she could feel around her as the gathering riders shifted about and looked to their leaders to say something.

The young couple, with eyes that bore only the lightest touch of regret for their impulsiveness, looked on in quiet confidence, clearly at peace with whatever the outcome was of their discussion with Layna's parents. Xavier's glowing eyes flitted all about him, his face one that seemed to have had no surprise or discomfort toward the turn of events whatsoever. Ranye's face was ultimately one of contentment. Lerannu had surmised from her time in the high chief's company that she cared deeply for the ways of her people, being a goodhearted traditionalist through and through. She could see in Ranye's eyes that she still wished they had waited for the ceremony, as well as the simple clash of joy and sorrow that now dwelt within her heart, that being of a mother who knew that her child's life was now forever changed.

Nevertheless, Lerannu saw plainly that Ranye trusted in their bond, and the high chief gazed upon her son-in-law with obvious trust and respect. Xavier stepped forward, lifted his hands, and spoke in his grand, yet gentle voice.

"Dear friends and kin, when all who are set to journey have gathered, we shall mount up and ride without delay. We will not stop for anything beyond what is absolutely necessary, and carry on until sunset."

The gathering riders hummed in acknowledgment of their high shaman's words.

"Then," Xavier went on, a gentle smile playing across his lips, "we shall make camp ... and hold a wedding for Layna and Garthon Onoraan, whose love for one another, I assure you, is as Onu-blessed and bound in honor as any other bond I have been blessed to oversee in my life."

The congregation cheered the new pair, congratulating them for embarking together on a new path in their lives.

"This ceremony," Xavier continued, his light smile growing into a benevolently smug grin, "is also planned to be extended to any others who may wish to affirm their bonds, regardless of whether or not the ... usual course ... has been taken."

Lerannu looked around and felt a small grin starting to form on her lips as she saw several "virgin-eared" couples silently flit their eyes toward one another before joining hands.

"We shall begin our ride soon," the high shaman concluded.

The gathering riders began to quietly converse, and Lerannu was just turning to speak to Ruth and Mira. Suddenly many gasps of awe sounded around her. From the corner of her eye, Lerannu sensed a bright light glowing from the direction of the tabernacle. She turned back to look at its entrance and bore witness to a sight that she would cherish in her memory for as long as she lived.

With bowed heads, Layna and Garthon stood before Xavier, who had placed a hand upon each of their foreheads. From the high shaman's fingers flowed streams of blessed light, which reached the ears of the impending newlyweds and bathed them in a sacred glow. The light flowed through the piercings, caressing the ears from tip to base, and at last dissipated into the brightening light of the morning. Xavier looked to Ranye, who had stood beside him with her hands clasped to her lips as she strove to stay composed, and wordlessly nodded to her. With tears of wonder and joy streaming down her face, Ranye approached her daughter and son-in-law, and gently removed their bandages. The piercings had completely healed, seeming as though they had been there since their wearers' births.

Complete silence filled the gathering for an instant, followed immediately by a roaring cheer.

Lerannu stared in awe for a moment, rooted to the spot in wonder, until she realized that Xavier was swaying wearily from his marvelous act. The high shaman waved away Layna and Garthon's concerned approach, simply taking Ranye's hand and leaning gently on her shoulder. Lerannu looked to Mira and Ruth, who stared utterly dumbstruck by what they had seen, and then approached Xavier with a flask of Kamgenbew that she had fished out of her pack. Xavier lifted his head from his wife's shoulder, his glowing, sightless eyes staring directly into Lerannu's, and smiled.

Lerannu tried to express her awe for his deed, but words simply failed her. She was filled with wonder by the healing itself, which was no small task for even an Ecclesian, and moved beyond words at the compassion that the high shaman so deeply expressed in the act. At a loss for words, the mage simply offered Xavier the flask of tonic, which he accepted gratefully and drank, quickly standing on his own again as he embraced his family.

Lerannu returned to the side of her sisters in fate, looking on silently as more riders arrived and learned of what had happened as they prepared for the journey to Zefiil.

The gathered warriors lingered around the tabernacle, checking their supplies, eating a light breakfast from their rations, and quietly chatting about what had happened. When the time came to depart for Zefiil, the great tribe's horns blew solemnly, the high chief and shaman rallied all to them, and the army of riders made for the camp's stables and corrals. All promptly mounted up and began to ride south and west with no further words apart from the farewells that passed between them and those left to tend to the great camp.

***

The first day's ride passed without incident apart from the dry, though thankfully milder, heat of the West's winter that beat down on them all the day, and the fatiguing nature of the daylong ride itself. Lerannu spent much of her time riding beside her father, the two of them speaking of their lives over the past seventeen years, as well as conversing with her Elect sisters. Xavier and Ranye, along with Layna and Garthon, also kept company with her on the hot, sunny day.

When the sun had kissed the horizon and the sky was a mesmerizing cascade of red and violet, Ranye signaled to the horn blower beside her, who promptly sounded the call for the riders to halt and make camp for the night. Lerannu dismounted and stretched gratefully alongside Mira and Ruth as she looked about and saw a number of riders already beginning to unpack whatever components of tents they were carrying. Within minutes, several tents were already set up in their entirety, and Lerannu saw Xavier staring with his blind, glowing eyes at the throngs of riders that milled about him. The high shaman at last called out a name, in response to which a nearby rider halted and pricked up her ears as she looked intently at him. Xavier beckoned her to him, and quietly said something to her. The rider smiled, and turning back to the masses, she called out several names as she took her pack off her back and began to rummage through it. Xavier turned back to Lerannu, Mira, and Ruth, smiling as he seemingly sensed their curiosity.

"I was just asking them to set up my tent and things," he said warmly, "so I can tend to the ceremony before supper."

Lerannu smiled. "Can I help at all?"

"If you wish; they'll certainly appreciate it."

The mage and her sisters in fate jogged off to where the riders were assembling the smaller traveling tent of the high shaman, all three of them grateful for something to do besides sitting in the saddle.

***

The sun passed below the horizon, and the stars and nearly full moon began to cast their marvelous lights on the grassy savannah as the impromptu wedding for Layna and Garthon commenced. Several other couples joined them in the ceremony, taking their vows after the leading pair. All the legion of riders looked on silently, booming into cheers only when each pair had finished their oaths before Onu and Fidonity. At the ceremony's end, Lerannu watched as the high shaman presented to his daughter and son-in-law, along with all the other newlyweds, their respective new earrings that marked the wondrous change in their lives. They were all fashioned from shining brass, which shimmered in an almost mystical manner as it glinted in the light of the moon and stars.

The mage looked on, endeared by the earnest love that each spouse showed to the other as they caringly set the jewelry into one another's ears. She found herself thinking of Allor as the cheers sounded loudly in the night and the improvised banquet of rations began.

148
8/14/4030 G.M.

DONOVAN rode alongside Verdok and Allor through the vast and dense Forest of Eternal Green, led by the Shepherds Kenora and Varnu, and guarded on either side by people of the gathered Janrenarn army and militias. The riding had been rough and relentless, with halts only called when the utter darkness of night swallowed the green light of the rainforest, and the bard was still sore from his wounds, mending as they were.

Verdok, still rattled by his dread and guilt from the battle between the ships, had hardly spoken any further word beyond those he spoke to Kenora and Varnu when they first met. The high priest had watched numbly as the great line of archers continued to fire onto the encroaching grey-cloak ships. Once the remaining ships drew close enough, and more and more of the grey-cloaks were disembarking as they made to charge into the archer line, the two Vibonmor Shepherds told the three men to prepare to ride south. Quickly gathering a sizeable company of warriors, the lot of them hastily rode off in an attempt to reach the capital before the remaining grey-coat reinforcements did.

Allor was also largely silent, though it seemed to Donovan it was more out of a sort of silent, contemplative confidence than of any trouble in his heart. The bard had heard him speaking with Varnu and Kenora at night, telling them of the journey he and the rest of the company had managed so far, and his voice was one of devoted resolve. The king's confidence seemed to falter only when he spoke of Lerannu, whom both Donovan and Verdok knew he loved, and even then, Allor's spirit seemed only a little dampened.

Now, after three days of hard riding, the bard and his companions were approaching an ever-widening flood of light as the canopy above them became sparser by the minute. As they neared the edge of the forest, Donovan could clearly see the waters of the great Vitari River ahead. The riders galloped past the last of the vast green trees and saw before them the mighty river flowing on its westerly course, its southern shore a good mile away from the spot where the company emerged from the forest. Donovan looked intently at the other side, seeing another line of soldiers and militia staring at them as they blew a horn. A soldier near Kenora and Varnu blew his horn in reply, and the soldiers on the south bank became at ease. The bard looked to the two Shepherds, both of whom had turned to face him and his companions. Varnu sighed deeply, sounding of both great relief and weariness.

"The south bank of the Vitari has been secure from these grey-cloaks for nearly the whole time since this mess started," the Shepherd explained. "Once we get over there, we should be able to ride along the riverside road, or at least close to it, thanks to all the people we have guarding it from here to the capital. Normally we would take a bridge, but ..."

Varnu looked glumly at the three men, who wordlessly checked their gear as they prepared to cross the river. Their horses stepped into the steady current with only a touch of reluctance, and the riders were soon bobbing across the river in small groups spaced apart by several yards.

Donovan and his companions, being in the leading group, were only a short way across when they heard the others behind them cry out in alarm and start rushing into the water. The shouts of the pursuing grey-coats could be heard in the distance, growing louder by the minute. The bard and his companions groaned in unison, and pressed on their horses' flanks to try to get them to swim faster. Whinnying anxiously, their mounts complied and began to churn the water more vigorously in their efforts to cross the river more quickly.

Then the arrows began to fly from behind them. The bard felt one fly over his head, and looking back frantically saw that the grey-coats who had managed to evade the archers on the coast had all gathered at the Vitari's north bank. They were firing arrows and bolts at those who had barely entered the water, as well as taking aim at those beyond. Donovan looked back to the south bank, where he could just make out the Janrenarn soldiers urging them on.

The group was getting further away from the grey-coats, though shafts were still flying past them. Donovan looked back to see what had happened in the seconds since he had last looked and was dismayed at the sight of many Janrenarns floating lifelessly down the Vitari, pierced by many arrows, while the few who had managed to get further away vied desperately to keep increasing their distance. Sighing with morbid frustration, the bard returned his sight to that which lay straight ahead, having resolved to focus on his own part in the mission as much as he could.

A deathly whistle cut through the air, and Donovan shrieked in agony as a shooting pain ran through his right leg once again, just a few inches above where he had been previously shot. Groaning in rage and pain, he looked down and saw another grey-fletched shaft sticking out of his thigh. He looked to his companions, who viewed him in dismay. Verdok slowed his horse to try and assist him. The priest grabbed the reins of the bard's horse silently, pulling it closer to himself, and looked as though he were trying to speak before Donovan let out a cry of bone-chilling dread.

The bard had taken another look at his leg, watching the blood seep through the thigh of his trousers and into the water. As he watched the blood disperse into the river, he saw a finned, tentacled form swiftly emerging from the murky depths below. His heart froze. Then another one appeared from the depths. And another.

Strolaks. The Cursed Ones of the waters.

Soon, the horse beneath the bard screamed in terror and agony, and Donovan flew into a horrid delirium as he felt a finned and scaled hand reach from the river and sink its claws into the flesh around the arrow. The vile creature proceeded to dig its grip deeper into the skin as it tried to pull him under. Verdok frantically struck the finned hand away from the wound, and Donovan, briefly unhinged by the macabre sensation of the burrowing claws, lulled his head back and stared in morbid awe at the distant corpses of the arrow-riddled southerners. A few were being pulled under by grasping tentacles and scaly hands, and the water was turning redder by the second.

Donovan felt a sharp tug at the neck of his shirt, and was snapped out of his delirium as he saw Verdok frightfully pull him away from his dying horse while fending off the persistent monster. He could hear Allor, Varnu, and Kenora shouting as well, but could not clearly make out their words. Taking the priest's hand and clambering onto the back of his saddle as his own horse sunk, neighing horridly below the red water, the bard began to laugh in shock from the experience. He spoke into Verdok's ear, shaking violently.

"He-heh-heh-heh ... the little shit was digging into my leg, Br-Brother Verdok!"

"I know," Donovan barely heard the priest say in a small, shaky voice. "I know. I got you, now."

"Thank you," Donovan gasped, clinging desperately to Verdok's back as the horse continued to swim frantically across the river.

A moment passed, and they were drawing ever nearer to the south bank. Verdok managed to staunch the bleeding, and continued fearfully looking out for another attacking Strolak. Thankfully, the water-fiends had since left them alone, likely drawn away by the easier meal that awaited them along the river's northern side. The arrows had stopped flying, or at least no longer reached them. Donovan leered his head back to look behind him, and he saw that the grey-cloaks had indeed stopped firing. They were now riding off along the riverside road, heading east, doubtlessly to join with their fellows trying to capture Benhotha. Sighing wearily, the bard slumped against Verdok's back, holding on tightly as memories of his life began to race across his mind.

Suddenly, the bard felt Verdok shift in the saddle, and he looked up to see the priest turn around with hands outstretched to him. Donovan took them and the priest helped him onto dry ground. They had made it.

Verdok guided him to a nearby tree and had him sit beneath it. The priest and the two Shepherds looked him over and began to treat and bandage the wounds of arrow and claw. Donovan watched briefly, then abruptly lifted his sight to the river as he heard the nearby splashing of several more people coming ashore. Numerous Janrenarn soldiers and militia had now made it across, their eyes either wide with horror, fiery with anger, or dull with grief.

Donovan felt a friendly pat on his shoulder. It was Varnu.

"That should take care of it soon, with some rest and not too much strenuous work put on it," the healer said. "Thankfully, we can ease our pace and still make good time to the capital. We're out of range from them now, and all land south of the Vitari has been secured for at least a month, as far as I know. We'll rest here a little and then get back to riding. Donovan?"

The bard looked intently at the Shepherd, his last bout of delirium finally fading. "Yes, friend Varnu?"

"Do you think you can bare to ride until nightfall, once we've rested here for an hour or so? We won't need to go as hard as we have the past three days, and we'll still get to Benhotha soon enough."

Donovan nodded and began to slowly rise up, wincing slightly at the lingering pain in his thigh. "Yes, I should be able to manage that."

"Good," said the Shepherd as he gently pressed down on the bard's shoulder, indicating for him to stay seated and rest against the tree. "Just stay here and relax. We'll continue our journey soon."

All gathered along the bank turned their gaze back to the river. The Strolaks had had their fill of flesh, blood and sport, and the waters, with the unclaimed corpses still floating along, became calm once again.

For a moment.

A wave of saddened sighs passed from the company as the waters about the corpses began to bubble and redden.

"Thank Onu," said Kenora grimly, "that, at the very least, piranhas don't team up *with* the Strolaks. That would've been a real disaster."

"Of course they don't work together," said Verdok flatly. "One creature is simply fulfilling its role as Onu intended and allowed, harsh as it may seem in the moment, and potentially dangerous to the careless as it may indeed be. The other was wrought by, and serves, the greatest evil in existence, living to torment us and spite all the good in creation."

149
8/18/4030 G.M.

RUTH and her Elect sisters looked with grim awe from their view on a distant dune at the grand city of Zefiil, and the great army of grey-cloaks that besieged it on both banks of the Stromarus River. The Daughters of the East and their Trichynay allies had ridden with steady urgency for six days since leaving the great camp. The journey had fortunately fared with no incidents, apart from passing a razed town that had been in the path of Sarah Stonefaith's army of reinforcements.

Now that the deciding moment of battle was nigh, the whole tribal army looked on in silence as they awaited word from their leaders. They took cover behind several large sand dunes and rocky outcrops overlooking the capital and the Stromarus River from the northwest. Already the tribe's army had been split, with the company in which the Elect were riding being set to assault the grey-cloaks on the west side of the siege. The other half had crept across a ford in the river that was well out of the grey-coats' sight, and was now awaiting the signal to attack from the east. A scout from the eastern division had just reached the west side, informing them that they were in place.

The Faithguard knight, looking through a spyglass, saw the majestic golden sandstone of the capital's walls and buildings, with their ornately pointed domes and flat roofs afire in the light of the high noon sun. The Stromarus River, which ran through the center of the city, sparkled brilliantly. Guards and archers lined the walls, patrolling and looking intently upon the sea of grey-shirted soldiers, living and undead, who stared back at them from below. The capital's great gates stood firmly shut and barred, despite the visible damage inflicted during past attempts to breach them.

After a moment of observing the scene, Ruth passed the spyglass to Mira as she looked to her other companions. Ranye and Xavier were near her, as well as Layna, Garthon, and Roniil. The high shaman was looking straight ahead, his glowing eyes squinted and his brow furrowed in apparent puzzlement. The high chief held her husband's hand, her eyes ones of wonder and worry.

"You seemed to be caught up in pondering something quite a bit yesterday," Ranye said gently to Xavier. "I was tempted to ask about it, but you really seemed drawn in. Is it the same thing now?"

"Yes," her husband said with a nod. He then lightly massaged his brow and began to utter his thoughts aloud. "Wings of fire ... here ... a great flame borne on wings ... wings of fire ..."

Ruth's ears shot up, and looking back to her sisters in destiny, she saw that they were both looking intently at the high shaman.

"Wings of fire?" Mira asked in a tone both excited and puzzled as she passed the spyglass to Lerannu. "Is the Phoenix you spoke of coming? Did you ask him to come help us here in your dreams?"

"No," Xavier said in a worrisome tone. "We wouldn't want to risk him being slain, or severely injured, before making the journey to Enmayar. I'm sure that Mercilaar is still waiting for us on Karzynhaal. Something ... isn't quite right."

"What should we do?" Ruth asked as calmly as she could manage.

Xavier took a deep breath, then looked at the knight and her sister Elect with a face of total resolve. "We carry on with what we have planned," he said, "unless something forces our course to change, be it these other 'wings of fire' or anything else."

Ruth and her companions nodded, and continued to look on at the distant siege ahead. Ranye, having called Roniil and several other scouts to her side, directed them to go ahead and get a closer look at the enemy camp. Roniil grabbed his gear, went to Lerannu, and gave her a fatherly kiss on the cheek.

"I love you, Lera."

"I love you, Father," the mage said in a slightly trembling voice.

"Whatever happens, know that I've never stopped thinking of you, and that I'm amazed and happy beyond all words to have you as my daughter, whether you were chosen by Onu to combat this evil or not."

The adopted tribesman looked to Ruth and Mira, nodding to them as well.

"And I am glad to know that you are companions of my daughter, as Fidons and sisters in her destiny. May Onu keep you."

"And may Onu keep you," Ruth responded, echoed by Mira and a teary-eyed Lerannu.

Roniil then adjusted his armor, grasped the great axe of Brazofiil, and made his way in swift stealth down the dune with his fellow scouts. As the scouts dismounted and strode out in a crouch to survey the area, Ruth, Mira, and Lerannu drew their horses closer to Xavier and Ranye. The two high leaders of the Trichynay people looked ahead with determined eyes, breathing slowly and deeply. They tightly held one another's hands, having reached across the space between their horses. The knight trotted up beside them, and the two turned their eyes to her.

"Thank you both," she said softly, "and all your people for the help you have given us. Whatever comes to pass here, know that I have felt many things since my marking as an Elect, but in your company, I have felt immense honor and hope. I will do all I can to fulfill my role for the sake of you and all your people, as well as for all of Fidonhaal."

"Hear, hear," the huntress and the mage said in quiet unison.

Xavier and Ranye smiled, and the high shaman was about to speak when Ruth suddenly noticed a lone bird flying above them. It looked like a heraldwing, but in the fleeting glimpse, there appeared to be something not quite right with it. The knight called it out to her companions in a low voice, and they all watched as the bird flew directly toward the grey-cloaks' encampment along the north-west riverbank. Lerannu, still holding the spyglass, lifted it back to her eye as she tried to follow the bird's flight.

"Can you feel whether or not if that bird is what you were sensing, Xavier?" the mage asked as she carefully looked about the siege camp.

"I feel that ... yes ... I think that was it. But I don't see how ..."

"We should've shot it," Ranye said irritably.

"I don't know," Ruth said understandingly. "Hit or miss, we might have given ourselves away if we tried."

Ranye nodded, but still sighed in frustration. Ruth looked to Mira, and saw that the huntress was of a like mind to the high chief.

Lerannu's voice sounded from behind the knight. "I just hope that we can still ..."

A dreadful gasp came from the mage's lips, followed by a sob. Ruth looked to her friend and saw her hands shaking as she held the spyglass.

"What is it?"

"It's Mother," Lerannu said in a small, sad voice.

Ruth rode up to the mage and placed a comforting hand on her shoulder. "What's she doing?"

Lerannu sighed as she returned her sight to the lens of the spyglass. "She's reading a message.

The bird we saw is on her shoulder ... it must be the message that it brought her. She's talking to a soldier ... maybe an officer ... it looks like it's really urgent. Maybe ... what ... what in Onu's name is she *doing?* No ... NO!"

"What is it?" Ruth asked urgently, her fur standing on edge at the mage's sudden shrill cry. The knight glanced about her, and saw all the tribespeople around her gripping their reins and weapons tightly with bated breath in response, fearing their position had been compromised. Lerannu began to sob, and she passed the spyglass to Ruth as she wept. The knight began looking frantically for the general, asking Lerannu pleadingly where to find her.

"Center of th-the camp," she said miserably, "b-by the big tent w-with the banner."

Ruth soon found the general. She gasped, and her fur bristled at the sight. Sarah Stonefaith stood stiffly in the midst of the soldiers beginning to rally to her, her mouth widely open and her head tilted sharply back as smoky black tendrils flew into her mouth from the now lifeless body of the bird that lay at her feet. The vile power filled the general, and her eyes began to glow red. Sarah then turned to face the city, her sight seemingly focused on one of the gates.

Ruth lowered the spyglass from her eyes and looked to Xavier and Ranye. "Call the scouts back and get everyone ready to charge," she said urgently. "I don't know what's going on, but I don't think we'll have the time to—"

A loud, dreadful boom suddenly reached the riders' ears, as if a great bolt of lightning had just stricken the ground ahead of them. Ruth snapped her sight back to Zefiil's walls and gasped as she saw a great pillar of fire erupting upon the western wall of the city. Great pieces of stone flew from the column of flame, leaving a massive gap in the wall. Many shouts arose from the grey-coats' camp, and the knight could see that all the soldiers were now charging for the breach. Tossing the spyglass into her pack, Ruth quickly strapped her buckler to her wrist and drew the hand-axe from her hip.

"If we're going to try to save even one soul in Zefiil," she said with grim resolve, "we need to go in there *now.*"

She looked to Ranye and Xavier, who, wide-eyed and slightly trembling, nodded to a nearby warrior, who promptly took up his horn and blew a loud call that was soon joined by others throughout the Trichynay army. Ruth looked to her Elect sisters and saw that Mira already had an arrow nocked to her bowstring and Lerannu was anxiously downing a vial of tonic as she gripped her loaned staff tightly. The Faithguard knight reared her horse and, looking back to her allies, pointed at Zefiil's walls with the head of her axe.

"CHARGE!"

150
8/18/4030 G.M.

LERANNU gripped her reins tightly as she felt a surge of alertness from her dose of tonic and the sudden anxiety of the charge. Her horse galloped urgently alongside those of her Elect sisters and other newfound friends and comrades, charging ever closer to the great hole in the sandstone wall through which the grey-clad soldiers were flooding into the city. The mage looked about as she charged, and saw in the distance across the river the rest of the great tribe charging from the east. She could not see her father anywhere, with him having just left to scout the area, and fear for him quickly gripped her heart.

Lerannu and her companions had now nearly reached the gap in the west wall, and looking up she saw archers and guards of the city shouting thankfully down to them as they fired arrows and bolts onto the grey-coats spilling into the capital. The horses clambered over the rubble and the dead. Ranye, readying the relic-bow that had been lent to her, released a shaft at some distant grey-cloak and shouted to the Elect over the great clamor of battle.

"We need to make our way onto the main west road! That'll lead straight to the three roundabouts that span the river at the city's center, and from there we can get to the palace! We need to do all we can to make sure that the palace and those inside don't get overrun!"

Lerannu, along with Mira, Ruth, and the rest of Ranye's company rode through several streets and alleys, downing numerous grey-clad soldiers as they made their way to the west road. The mage saw Ruth dealing gruesome wrath upon the grey-coats unfortunate enough to meet her, and the arrows dealt by Mira and Ranye as the two archers rode side by side found plenty of marks. Lerannu, positioning herself just behind the lead, found herself riding next to Xavier. Riding behind his wife, he stared straight ahead as if lost in thought, utterly unfazed by the surrounding carnage. The mage cast immensely strong blasts of wind that sent sandstone rubble flying into nearby clusters of grey-coats, which sent screams and groans into the air around her. A few times, she simply sent a gale to knock some soldiers off their feet, leaving them to the warriors who rode behind her as she and her companions continued to focus on reaching the palace.

At last they reached a road far wider than any they had yet encountered, and the mage looked to her left and saw a clear view of the palace in the distance. Before her lay a four-way intersection that was coupled with a roundabout, which stood along the edge of the western bank of the Stromarus. Its eastward path led directly to the palace's roundabout. Tall, ornately carved obelisks stood at the ends of each bridge that connected the roadways. The riders turned sharply to the east and began to gallop at full speed toward the palace. With a great deal more space now available to her, the mage positioned herself a little further away from the rest and, seeing many grey-cloaks running onto the road, began drawing power from the heat of the sun and the hot air to cast spells of fire. A few whips of flame lashed out from her hands to great effect, and pantomiming the strike of a smith's hammer, she also managed an effective casting of the Hammer of Branok, which sent a fiery shockwave into the midst of a large enemy company with devastating results.

Lerannu was starting to feel drained as the company reached the bridge leading to the first roundabout. Quickly fishing out another Kamgenbew flask, she drained it in one gulp and drew a deep breath as she braced to cast more spells. They were halfway across the bridge when a deafening boom flooded the mage's ears. A great fiery blast sent her flying forward from the saddle, and in the instant that she could see behind her while in midair, she saw another great pillar of fire erupting from where she and her companions were riding, utterly destroying that part of the bridge. Lerannu's heart stopped in her chest, and as she slammed onto the stone street, she began to shake terribly as she feared the worst for her sisters in fate and the rest of her comrades. Rooted to the spot, she stared with dread at the smoking rubble that now took the place of the spot on the bridge where she and her companions had just been.

Then an arrow flew past her, snapping her out of her fear and pushing her into action. Running across the remainder of the first bridge and taking cover behind one of the obelisks at its end, Lerannu downed another phial of tonic as she prepared to brave the city alone. She had to make it to the palace, and defend it and rally its residents to her aid if she could. The prophecy depended on it, and if indeed she was now the only remaining Daughter of the East, she could not falter.

Feeling fully reinvigorated, she peered past the obelisk and saw numerous grey-cloaks dashing across the north bridge of the roundabout. Several had stopped along the way to fire arrows at her and at those on the other side of the ruined bridge behind her. Drawing from the power of wind and the strength within herself, she cast several Arrows of Vente at the foe, the force of the air shredding gruesomely through several of the grey soldiers and shambling corpses. Lerannu dashed around the roundabout and over the second bridge, panting raggedly as she reached the palace's roundabout. Gasping for air, she shouted up to the royal residence at the top of her lungs.

Three arrows flew at her from the palace towers, just barely missing her. The mage frantically raised her hands, shaking her head in a desperate attempt to convey that she was not among the grey-coats. Thankfully, no more arrows came, and the mage began to sprint madly toward the gate that led into the palace courtyard, hoping desperately that there would be a guard or someone who could admit her inside so she could speak to the leaders of Kellmayar.

As she neared the walls of the palace courtyard, an unbearably searing heat ran across her back. Lerannu fell to the ground with a scream of pain and panic, pulling off her hide armor and the top of her robes, which were now engulfed in flames. Throwing them away from her, she looked up and felt the blood freeze in her veins.

Her mother was staring right into her eyes, sneering horrifically as she slowly advanced toward her. Sarah Stonefaith turned her head back only long enough to order the soldiers nearby to advance upon the palace, then turned her attention back to her daughter. Her sword was in her hand. With eyes glowing red, the grey-cloaked general slowly raised her blade overhead as she closed in for the kill.

Lerannu tried desperately to get up, but the burns on her back were far too painful to enable her to rise. She pushed herself across the ground with her feet, tears of grief and utter terror pouring from her eyes.

"M-mother," she said in a voice so small that she doubted Sarah heard her over the battle, even if she had cared to heed, "p-please ... you're not fully possessed ... w-we can help you–"

Sarah now stood towering over her daughter, her sword raised to finish her.

"Now, enemy of order," she said with a voice that echoed horridly with the voice of a demon, "you shall pay the traitor's price."

Lerannu could just hear the faint sound of rapidly approaching footsteps. They seemed to be coming from ahead of her, behind the back of Sarah. A loud shout of exertion and anger sounded from behind the warlock general, followed by the heart-stopping, stomach-turning sound of cracking skull, splitting brain, and gushing blood.

Sarah stood stock-still for an instant, her mouth hanging grotesquely open and her eyes bulging horribly as they stared at Lerannu. The red glow behind them faded and the general fell forward with a revolting thud. Blood fountained from her split and shattered skull, quickly covering the ground around her. A great battle axe was lodged into her head.

It was the axe of Brazofiil.

Lerannu looked up. Her father stood before her, looming over the corpse of her mother. With tears of relief, Roniil stepped over the body and offered his daughter a hand to help her up. Lerannu tilted her head and stared numbly into his eyes. She wanted to speak. She wanted to take her father's hand. But she couldn't. Nor could she hear anything around her apart from a maddening ringing. She screamed at herself to speak, to act, to do anything. Nothing. Giving up, she stared helplessly at her father.

She saw Roniil's relieved eyes turn to ones of worry. At last he looked back upon the corpse of the general. He frantically crouched over the corpse and lifted the cloven head. His fur bristled, and he turned back to his daughter, tears of horror and sorrow flowing freely. He knelt and embraced his daughter, lifting her into his arms, and gently carried her to a sheltered nook in the outer side of the palace walls. There, father and daughter sat in what safety they could find in the carnage around them, and Roniil, holding his daughter tightly, rocked back and forth while gently stroking her head, shaking violently from his weeping.

151

8/18/4030 G.M.

RUTH ran past the palace alongside a battered company of fighters, among them being Mira, Ranye, and Xavier. They were set to aid the warriors battling on the east side of the river before trying to directly defend the palace. Having cut down the grey-cloaks who were charging for the palace and seeing no others making their way into the area, the party agreed to help the warriors at the east wall deal with the grey-coats before trying to approach the nation's leaders. The knight's heart worried for the well-being of Lerannu, fearing the worst as she had seen no sign of her since the explosion on the bridge. Nevertheless, keeping the greater good of the mission in the forefront of her heart, she ran on toward the east wall of Zefiil, where the major remainder of the battle seemed to be.

The knight had been in a steadily wearying state of pain since she lifted herself up from the stone-brick pathway that had been broken by the pillar of fire. She was still bleeding lightly from a cut in her scalp, and it stung nastily at being touched. She was battered, bruised, and nicked from head to toe, and it appeared at a glance that the same could be said for all the others in her company.

However, all in her party still seemed to be in one piece apart from the unfortunate few who were crushed to death by debris from the broken bridge. Most of the company had lost their horses in the explosion, forcing them to run as fast as they could to the fray, hobbling on and cutting down the odd handful of grey-coats they encountered along the way.

When they finally reached the eastern wall, they could hear the great clamor just outside, with the sounds rising from it already seeming to suggest a probable victory on the part of the city's defenses and their welcome tribal allies. Nevertheless, with many of the warriors that had charged from the west having made their way across the city, Ruth proposed to Ranye and Xavier that they should try to reach the guards on the wall and have them open the gates. The two tribal leaders agreed, and happening upon a guard in the streets nearby, they convinced her to go into one of the gate towers and have her fellows send the order to open all the gates across the wall. Soon, the gates opened, and Ruth and her party charged out of the city and into the backs of the grey-cloaks who had been pressed against the wall. The knight, though still in pain, cleaved her way through the desperately aggressive remainder of the grey-coat army, with Mira and the rest downing others all around her. Arrows and bolts flew down from the walls, impaling the sand and the fallen like a grisly field of short reeds. Clanging steel and cries of wrath, terror, agony, and death flooded the Faithguard's ears.

Then, in the lowered light of early evening, all suddenly fell quiet. Ruth gasped as she noticed the change, and looked about her on aching, shaky legs as she saw no grey-clad soldier, of formerly living flesh or vile reanimation, left standing. A long second of grim silence passed, followed by the swelling cry of triumph from the great tribe and the guards of Zefiil. Ruth began to sob in elation, and finding Mira beside her, embraced her friend and sister in fate tightly to her. Both groaned in pain from their pressed bruises and cuts, and then laughed as they realized each other's battered state. They looked about them, and saw Ranye and Xavier still standing alongside their daughter and their son-in-law. They were as battered and beaten as the Elect, but still standing.

Zongar Highsun also emerged from the cheering masses of warriors, all of whom gasped and fell silent at the sight of the mighty champion as he limped toward Ranye and Xavier. Both of the swords of Korrah were sheathed at either hip, and his right arm was wrapped lovingly around his wife, Karla. His left limb, however, had been severed just below the elbow, and was bandaged loosely by a torn scrap of shirt. Karla walked beside him, her arm around him and her shirt clearly being the one that provided the improvised bandage. Her eyes, though clearly touched with sadness, ultimately shined of loving pride and relief. Zongar looked upon the high chief and high shaman, a resigned grin upon his lips.

"I may not have been meant to bear Brazofiil's axe," Zongar said with a flat chuckle, "but it would seem that I was to bear a similar fate."

Xavier and Ranye stepped forward, with the high shaman taking Zongar into a father-like embrace.

"I cannot thank you enough, Sir Highsun, nor can any of us, for your courage and sacrifice. Give me a few moments to catch my breath, and I'll see if I can't help hasten that wound's mending. Do either of you have the hand, by any chance? I could try to restore the whole arm if—"

"I was fighting on one of the bridges when it happened, High Shaman. When my foe struck off my hand, it fell into the river."

Xavier's eyes gazed sadly into Zongar's. The champion, however, smiled and patted the high shaman's back.

"It's alright, High Shaman. I'm alive, and I can still do my part for our people and the Daughters of the East."

"Indeed," Xavier said with a small smile. "All the same, I would like to heal what I can."

Zongar's ears flattened as he bowed his head in reverent anticipation. "My thanks, High Shaman. In the meantime, however ..."

The champion turned to look upon all his fellow warriors. He drew one of the twin blades at his side, and nodded to his wife to take the other. The two raised their swords to the sky, standing in a triumphant embrace. It was a sight for the ages, a scene fit to be preserved by the brush of a master painter.

"We are victorious!" Zongar shouted triumphantly. "That is enough for me!"

All the tribe raised their weapons high, shouting out in booming ecstasy their cries of victory, of thanks and commendation toward Zongar, and of praise and trust in the Daughters of the East and the One who had sent them.

152
8/18/4030 G.M.

MIRA and Ruth, alongside the leaders and champion of the Trichynay, turned back to the east wall and began to pass the gates on their way to the palace. The guards cheered and thanked them from the walls and on the streets, as did the many people of the city, coming out of their homes as news spread regarding the defeat of the grey-cloaks and the end of the siege. The huntress both basked in and wondered at the many praises and thanks that were showered upon her and her companions. She silently said a prayer of thanks to Onu as she and her party limped down the road toward the palace. With the calming of her battle-flooded mind, she suddenly realized that Lerannu was not with them as they neared the palace, and she whispered her realization to Ruth over the roaring cheers of the city.

"I know," Ruth said worriedly. "I hope she survived the fire on the bridge, but I haven't seen her since then. If she has fallen, we can only ..."

The palace residents, from the queen and king to all their surviving household and advisors, stood outside the palace walls, looking with great gratitude upon the approaching warriors. Before them, however, stood a weeping Roniil, who carried the limp body of his daughter over his shoulder as he stood before the leaders of Kellmayar. Mira and Ruth ran to them, fearing the worst.

"Is Lera—" Mira began, her voice choked by tears before she could say any more.

"Sh-she's alive," Roniil sobbed, "b-but she's not fit to talk right now."

"Why?" Ruth asked gently, but pressingly. "What happened?"

Breathing shakily, Roniil pointed to a form on the road a short distance behind him. Mira saw the body of a Fidon, an armored woman, lying face-down on the sandstone road near the palace. A great battle axe protruded from what remained of the dead one's skull, and a wide pool of blood had spread from it. The huntress heard Ruth gasp, and looking to the knight, she saw Ruth with a hand over her mouth and great sadness in her eyes. The knight looked to Mira, and she explained the sight to her in a whisper.

"That's what's left of the general of the grey-cloaks here ... Sarah Stonefaith."

It all came together in Mira's mind, and the huntress looked sadly into Roniil's eyes as he gave his account of the sad event.

"I was going ahead quietly when the wall was breached and the horns sounded. Seeing that the plan had changed, I and the other scouts ran for the gap along with you all. I tried to catch up with you, but I was just a little too far behind. Then I saw the bridge get broken by fire, and I noticed Lera on the other side. I made to get to her, but Sarah reached her first. I didn't know it was her, though. I figured she was just another grey-coat and I just ... I just ..."

Roniil buried his face into his daughter's shoulder, weeping wretchedly.

"I s-split her mother's head r-right in front of her!"

Mira and Ruth approached Roniil and Lerannu, embracing them both as they each tried to console Lerannu's father.

"You saved her, Mr. Tern," Mira said gently as she looked into Lerannu's dulled eyes, which looked about and seemed to acknowledge her and Ruth, though the mage still didn't say anything. "She knows it, and she loves you."

"It-it's just that I've wronged her so much ... and her mother, too ... and now ..."

"It's done, Roniil," Ruth said calmly. "We just need to give her time. We'll see what we can do later, but now we need to speak to the king and queen. Take Lera somewhere that's as quiet as you can find. We'll find you later and take it from there."

Roniil nodded and carried his daughter away, down the road and eventually passing out of view. Mira and Ruth turned their attention back to the king and queen, and those standing with them, who gazed at them with sad eyes and grateful smiles. The king stepped forward, bowing slightly as he addressed the huntress and the knight.

"Our undying thanks, Daughters of the East. Your companion, Roniil, has briefly told us of who you are and why you've come. As sorrowful as I am for him and his daughter's present state, I am overjoyed that our ever-trustworthy friends in the great tribe have come to our deliverance, and that three elected by Onu himself have joined them in their journey to explain the madness that has gripped the world."

The king's ears lowered and the thankful smile faded.

"I am also grieved that Queen Sheeva is behind all this. I was there when she and Allor lost their families. It was horrible, but to think that it would lead her to this ..."

"I'm afraid it isn't just her that was the source of this horror," Mira said as she stepped forward. "As darkened as her heart may have turned, we ultimately have the goading of a demon to thank for what has come to pass."

The king's eyes widened. "A demon?"

"Yes, King ...?"

"Dominik, my lady," said the king as he heartily took and kissed Mira's hand along with Ruth's. "Dominik Bluemoon, with my wife, Fida, and all my household, at your service."

King Dominik breathed a deep, saddened sigh.

"I have risen to lead Kellmayar alongside my wife in a time of great loss and strife, following the murders of my mother and father at the hands of those grey-clad butchers on Kysonmay's Eve. We have spent a long time not knowing the full account of the reasons for these attacks, and had feared the worst, that the whole of Enmayar, or perhaps all outsiders born of solely Zaron blood, where somehow in on the whole affair. Dreadful as this all is, I am glad to know that at the very least, this horror isn't the aim of an entire nation, or of all who bear only one certain color of fur."

"Indeed," said Ruth. "My companions and I would like to speak with you on what's happened, here and elsewhere. My sister Elect and I saw firsthand the death and possession of Queen Sheeva, and the rise of the demonic Empress Raakmathna. We wish to tell you of what has passed, and then ask of what aid we might be able to gain from you so we might put an end to this vileness."

Dominik looked to his wife, who took her husband's hand as the two of them vowed solemnly.

"You have every soldier and ally that we can possibly afford to spare," said Dominik plainly. "I can assure you of that, regardless of what you reveal to us. We will do everything in our power to aid the Daughters of the East, that they may fulfill the prophecy given to them."

"Our thanks in advance," said Ruth, "but if it please you, I ask that we may join you and your household in your home, that we may tell you all we can of what has passed and what we've come to plan, so that you might have a better feel for what you can and cannot spare, and when. There is much to say, and if I may be frank, I would greatly appreciate a seat indoors during our talks."

"Of course," said the king with a small grin.

With grateful cheering still sounding across the city, the huntress and the knight followed King Dominik and Queen Fida into the palace, where they began to tell them of their journey, their trials, and the plan to combat the demon Raakmathna.

153

8/19/4030 G.M.

RAAKMATHNA sat upon the throne placed in the main square of Genverdell, surrounded by living and undead guards, and with her emperor by her side. It was noon, and more fools who had rebelled against her law were now standing slumped and charred before her, bound to the stakes on which they were burned. The masses surrounding the square, submissive to the empress's will, stared in terror-numbed silence.

The empress was about to speak when a great, sudden feeling of reinvigoration filled her. Images of a broken sandstone wall and a split skull flashed across her mind, as well as that of three Zaron women with the accursed mark of Onu on their brows.

The archgeneral had fallen, of that Raakmathna was certain. She did not yet know for sure if the campaign against Kellmayar had failed, but she had a strong feeling that it had. It didn't ultimately matter, but she still wished to do all she could for the All-Keeper. Her mind began to race as she tried to formulate a plan for when, and if, the so-called Daughters of the East did indeed manage to return and confront her.

She looked around at the meek weaklings who had bowed to her and at last knew their place. She looked intently at the burned dead, and with a wave of her hand she set them to fidgeting restlessly at their stakes. The empress nodded to the executioner, who promptly unbound the undead, and gestured to another Peacekeeper to take them to the armory. She leaned toward her emperor, whispering softly into the warlock's ear.

"I regret to tell you that our dear friend Sarah has fallen in battle to those damnable Elect of whom we have been hearing from time to time. I fear that our efforts in Kellmayar have been halted until further notice, and that the same could very well be for our soldiers in Janrenar if things continue as they seem to be faring."

"Whatever you want of me," said Ranoth, "I will do it for you, for the order you and the All-Keeper have given us. Wherever you would have me go—"

"I wish for you to stay by my side," Raakmathna said soothingly. "If they indeed manage to halt our efforts in all the other nations, we shall stay here and wait to make a stand against them. We have our walls and our Peacekeepers, and we will call all those who can reach us if we suspect they have stopped our campaigns and are coming for us."

"So be it, my empress."

"We also have more means than those who seek to oppose us, as we always have. We shall wait a little longer for word from the West and the South. If we receive no word in the near future, or if it is only threats from our enemies who foolishly think we will be so easily cast down, we will need to be ready to take ... drastic measures."

"What is it you have in mind, my empress?"

Raakmathna leaned closer to her warlock consort, and whispered her plan into his ear.

The Battle of Benhotha

154
8/20/4030 G.M.

VERDOK halted his horse alongside his companions and escort as they reached a small bend along the south bank. The high priest, having been mostly silent since the battle on the sea, sighed in wonderment at the sudden sight of Benhotha, the great city on a massive stone bridge that spanned the Vitari from bank to bank. The fine stone buildings that spanned the bridge stood proudly in the early morning light. These included several ziggurats of various sizes, their tops peering from above the great bridge's walls.

They had ridden at a steady pace for the past six days, easily resting and going forward as needed thanks to the security of the south riverbank. Warriors and archers patrolling the paths lined the road the whole way, ready to take down any grey-cloak that appeared within range or attempted to cross the river.

Donovan's wounds, though still sore, were well on the mend by now, and the bard seemed to be in good spirits overall given his ordeal. Verdok still struggled with his state of mind as the vision of the burning, screaming grey-coat captain persisted in the front of his memory. He had done all he could to drive it away, telling himself that the soldier was mad and senseless from the hatred that had been hammered into her, a hatred that she willingly accepted despite all the lessons of history and legend that told Fidonity otherwise. But it was to no avail.

The priest berated himself for his weakness, recalling all the times when he trained in the clergy's martial arts as a youth. Back then, he was uncomfortable even when learning nonlethal means to deal with foes. He reflected on those memories with shame, resigning himself as doomed to weakness in a time when the world needed him to be willing to act against the evil in whatever way necessary.

Verdok further surmised that the company at large was in far higher spirits than he despite the large camp of grey-canvased tents that stood on the northern bank, reaching almost to the gates of the capital's north wall itself. It was clear that despite the grey-cloak threat still being very real, there was only so much effectiveness to their besieging of Janrenar's capital. The grey-coats had failed to cover both sides of the city, and the perpetual bounty of the rainforest on the secured side of Benhotha ensured the capital wouldn't starve anytime soon. The two Vibonmor Shepherds, Varnu and Kenora, had continued to lead the company, and the couple looked to the three men as they spoke.

"Here we are, friends," said Kenora in relief. "Your allies await you."

They rode up to the south gate, pausing only as Varnu and Kenora spoke calmly to the guards stationed at either side of the gates, who spoke as ones familiar with them. The two Shepherds briefly told them of their companions and their mission, and of the Elect across the sea who shared in it. The guards, looking at the three men with a reverent nod, called up to the guards on the wall to open the gate. Verdok soon found himself trotting steadily down the main thoroughfare with his friends and allies, on a straight course for the grand palace ziggurat that stood in the center of the city. The high priest looked around him, seeing many of the people going about what seemed to be normal affairs. There were a number of supplies and goods being checked in at the gates as he and the company entered, and though there was certainly an air of anxiety hanging over the city, people were still buying and selling in the shops and market, and were conversing with one another as soldiers kept a vigilant watch on the river and banks nearby. In short, it was nowhere near as grim and troublesome as it was back in Norkoth, nor as desperate, though there was still clear and present danger on the other side of the great river.

Verdok was about to comment on this when the company rode past a sizeable street that branched from the thoroughfare. He noticed makeshift barriers running across it. A small company of guards was standing alongside the barriers, looking intently at the city beyond their barricade. He could just see a cluster of seemingly temporary structures beyond the blockade before the scene passed out of his view. As they passed another, smaller street that ran from the central road, he saw another blockade. His curiosity piqued, he gently tapped the flanks of his horse and trotted up to the two Shepherds. Clearing his throat and drawing a deep breath as he made to earnestly speak for what felt like the first time in days, he leaned toward them in the saddle. Noticing his approach, the two Shepherds pricked up their ears to listen.

"What's going on over there?" Verdok asked as he pointed to another guarded barrier that appeared down the next street.

Kenora and Varnu's ears drooped moodily, and the two glanced at each other before Varnu replied.

"I suppose I should've mentioned this earlier," the Shepherd said quietly, but still clearly enough to be heard by those behind him over the hum of urban activity. "When Queen and King Avesson issued the nationwide call to arms, they also called for all full-bodied Zarons to be kept under surveillance in a designated portion of the city, and for other such arrangements to be made across the country where possible. We haven't known the full–"

"*I beg your pardon?*" Allor's voice rang out sharply behind Verdok, sending a cringe of discomfort running down his spine and setting his fur to bristle. The priest looked back and quietly inhaled through his teeth at the sight of Allor's incredulous, outraged face. The company came to a halt, with the escort that accompanied them looking away uncomfortably from the King of Enmayar, who stared with wide, fiery, and unbelieving eyes at the two Shepherds. Verdok also began to observe the looks of the passersby, including patrolling guards and soldiers, and realized that nearly all of them seemed tense and uncertain upon seeing Allor, as if he wasn't supposed to be wandering about. When the people took in the rest of those in his company, however, they warily returned to their own affairs. Verdok looked back to Varnu, who raised his hands pleadingly as he sought to explain the situation.

"I can only imagine how that seems to you, given what you know of all this, but I was just about to say that we haven't known the full story of who was or wasn't behind all this. We didn't get an explanation from the grey-coats, obviously, as they were simply butchering people left and right, and screaming about the purity of the Zaron people and how all the world was to be theirs. We were worried that maybe all Zarons in the world were somehow in on the whole thing, so the king and queen decreed that all cities, towns, and villages were to confine their fully Zaron citizens under watch until further notice, and to watch those who were children or kin of the interned, even if they themselves were not solely Zaron."

"The evil sown by this demon has certainly taken strong root already," Allor said in a low, dreadful tone.

"Not if you explain what's happened to the king and queen," Varnu said in a tone that indicated that he was desperately trying to both calm Allor and remain calm himself as he took in the king's words. "It was a precaution, that's all. Surely that's not so hard to understand?"

A heavy silence fell over the company, meddled only by the modest hum of the bustle surrounding them.

"No," Allor said grimly. "It isn't. But I fear how this sort of thing will seem to our eyes in future days."

"Just tell them what's happened," Varnu said as he attempted to calm himself as much as Allor. "I'm sure they'll stop once you explain that it's only a portion of them that are involved in this. At the very least, I'd think that they'd begin lessening the severity of the confinement, or something, however small at first, to convey good faith."

"I still can't believe you'd assume that an entire lot of people–"

"We acted on what we knew, and what we didn't know. Please, let's get to the palace. We can began discussing it with the queen and king there."

Allor drew a deep, heavy sigh, and urging his horse onward, the company continued to steadily ride down the main road toward the towering ziggurat ahead.

The morning was nearing noon when they reached the palace. Varnu and Kenora had an exchange with the guards stationed there that was not unlike the one they had when they first entered the city. Verdok, Allor, and Donovan were greeted with the same essential response as before, and after a few moments of waiting outside the palace gates, they were admitted through the courtyard and into the first hallway of the royal residence.

155
8/20/4030 G.M.

ALLOR sat with Donovan and Verdok in the entrance corridor of the Benhotha Palace on an ornately carved bench of stone. Majestically stylized carvings, as well as vibrant murals and tapestries, covered the fine stone of the walls around them. The King of Enmayar looked at them in silence. He heard nothing from the bard or the priest, if indeed they were even conversing. He himself was lost in thought over the depressing revelation of how the madness of the grey-cloaks had led to such severe suspicion toward all those in Janrenar who were fully grey-furred. He was still silently fuming over the Zarons' internment, despite understanding the reasons for it, and kept reminding himself of the explanation Varnu and Kenora had given for the king and queen's edict. He was determined to mention the matter when he and his fellows were finally granted audience.

Allor was not sure how much time had passed, but he suddenly pulled out of his moody contemplations when a man wearing a Mohawk and a fine, vibrant robe strode up to them and announced that the queen and king would receive them. The King of the East rose from the bench and stepped aside to let Verdok and Donovan follow the chamberlain ahead of him. The priest and the bard gestured for Allor to lead the way after the steward.

"You're representing all of Enmayar," said Verdok plainly, "and indeed all Zarons. Well, those who weren't, and aren't, followers of Sheeva and Raakmathna's aims. You should be leading our side of the conversations, don't you think?"

Allor sighed, nodded, and then stepped forward to follow the steward, with Donovan and Verdok following right behind.

The joint throne of Queen Vita and King Salos was a fine sight, sculpted out of the central pillar at the far end of the throne room and surrounded by more vibrant décor and brightly robed Fidons. The monarchs of the South, both handsomely full-figured and regally adorned, sat together and looked intently upon Allor and his friends as they approached. Allor reached the throne and nodded his head reverently. The King of Enmayar paused in his morose ponderings, then began to address Salos and Vita.

"My thanks for receiving us, Queen Vita and King Salos," Allor began, "and my utmost sympathies for all the losses and troubles that have plagued your country in the past months."

King Salos nodded in acknowledgment. "Your sympathy is appreciated, dear friend and ally, but if I may, I would like to hear what you have to say of all this, as we have been unable to fully know, and certainly do not understand, the ... 'reason' for all this. We received the letter that Queen Xenia and King Viktor sent to Humilaar a while ago; those guarding the port sent it to us after they read it. So, we have learned some things, such as how the Daughters of the East have come at long last, but I fear we still have only so much information upon which we might properly act."

"I can, at best, only imagine what strife and fear you and your people have suffered in these horrible times," Allor said softly, "and that is despite all that I have experienced firsthand of this madness alongside my companions."

Allor went on to explain the source behind the senseless violence enacted by the grey-cloaks and the demonic Empress Raakmathna, who now dwelt within the shell of his late wife.

***

The sun was well on its way to the west horizon, and its light beamed brilliantly through the western windows of the throne room. It bathed the room in a marvelous golden light as Allor concluded his account of the events in Genverdell and the journey with his companions up to the present. King Salos and Queen Vita held hands as they listened, and their ears and eyes lowered in sorrow as they learned of all that had transpired. Nevertheless, they also bore a radiance of lively hope as they learned more of the Daughters of the East.

"My condolences for your loss, King Allor," said Queen Vita, "and my sympathies to all of you for your trials and sorrows. The letter from Sorrenar did touch on a number of the things that you and your companions have said, but not as thoroughly as you have, so there's several things we'll soon be needing to settle."

Allor lifted his head and looked intently at the King and Queen of Janrenar.

"Such as the cordoning away of all Zarons in the country from their families and communities?" he asked in a voice that, though low, sounded throughout the throne room.

King Salos and Queen Vita's ears flattened somberly, and all the royal family and household that were in the room began to shift uncomfortably about where they sat or stood.

"I must say," said Allor after a moment of painful silence, "that while I obviously haven't seen how every place in the world has been trying to deal with this madness, I haven't heard or seen of one case where all Zarons in an area were detained simply because of their fur. Granted, we *were* met with suspicion a few times, but we were still able to explain ourselves without too much trouble, and we never saw any other place in our travels where they did as you have done. Did the letter from Sorrenar say *anything* as to how not every Zaron in the world was in on some plot against Fidonity?"

Queen Vita sighed. "A little, but we weren't sure–"

"That King Viktor and Queen Xenia could be trusted?"

Vita and Salos both looked irritably at the King of Enmayar. "We didn't know how to separate those who weren't involved from those who were serving the grey-cloaks in secret. Not all of the ones who attacked were in uniform; some had been swayed into the grey-coats' way of thinking sometime after they began coming in from Enmayar."

"Have you been investigating them, and letting those go who showed no signs of involvement?"

"With all that's been going on?" asked Salos incredulously.

"Are a few handfuls of inquirers truly too much to spare? Especially when you've been able to hold off the siege so well since driving the grey-coats out of the city itself?"

"King Allor, any of them could have lied, and no matter how well we've been holding them back, we've been too occupied with the enemy at the gates to–"

Allor was just about to cut the words of the southern king short, his exasperation at the situation boiling up to anger. His lips were stilled, however, when a young woman in the room, standing near the throne, spoke up in a gentle, pleading voice. She bore a likeness to the queen and king that only one of their children could possess.

"Please, both of you, let it go."

Allor, Salos, and Vita looked to the young woman, a stunning beauty of shining black fur and eyes the same deep blue as Verdok's. With hands clasped together and her eyes darting to each of her parents and Allor, she stepped forward and spoke with a voice that, disciplined and level as it was, carried great emotion underneath.

"What's done is done," she said plainly, "and the best we can now do is end this decree with an apology. It might not settle all matters relating to this terrible time, but we'll just have to trust that it *can* be amended and forgiven, at least in time ..."

The princess looked to her parents, her eyes shining with brimming tears as her voice began to break. "Please, *please* let Aaron come back to me. We understood your reasoning at first, but with the letter, and now all that King Allor has told us, this needs to end now. Not just for Aaron and me, but for all of us."

"Quanda," Queen Vita said gently, "we can't just end it right now. There *is* still the possibility that there are ones serving the grey-coats hiding among the rest."

Princess Quanda wordlessly stared into her mother's eyes. Queen Vita sighed as she continued addressing her daughter.

"We'll begin releasing them tomorrow, but not without investigating each one before release. We'll send out word first thing in the morning, and then–"

"You didn't dare to even trust your own son-in-law?" Allor asked flatly, unable to contain his contempt any longer.

Salos's eyes flared and narrowed dreadfully as he threw his hands up in a fit of exasperated anger. "IS IT REALLY SO HARD TO UNDERST–"

"Father! King Allor! PLEASE!" Princess Quanda cried. "I can let it go, I *will* let it go, and I know that Aaron will, too. We understood then and we do even now, and we won't hold it against you. Everyone else, they can understand and forgive it, too, and I believe they will, in time if not right away. But something being understandable doesn't make it right. We have to let them go and trust them to help us, for the sake of Fidonhaal and all who come after us. When the history of this horror has been written, and one can read of it sometime in the future, they should be able to see what was done by *all* involved, and see that even the wronged might have acted wrongly, too. Confining them all at first might have been understandable, but now, with both the letter and the words of Allor and his companions, it should be clear to us that this has been going too far."

King Salos sighed heavily, leaning back against the throne and massaging his brow for a moment as his wife sat beside him, looking intently at her daughter and Allor's company.

"We're going to have a company of guards come in," he said with a voice struggling to be level, "and we'll have them question everyone in the cordoned area that they can from now until noon tomorrow. At noon, we'll have them all released, those who have been questioned and judged to be trustworthy. And whoever the guards haven't managed to investigate by then ... we'll let them go, nonetheless, and place the future in Onu's hand."

Salos lowered his hand from his brow and looked intently at his daughter.

"Can you at least let us do that?"

Quanda nodded. "Yes, Father."

Salos rose from the throne and spread his arms wide toward his daughter, who ran to him and embraced him. The two sobbed quietly as they spoke.

"I'm so sorry for all this, little flower."

"I know you and Mother were just doing the best you could think to do," the princess said tearfully. "Trust them, trust us. All of us."

"It's just so hard to trust at times. It's been that way for so long, for so many, as it is ... but with all that's happened now ..."

"It'll be alright in the end."

"I keep trying to tell myself that. I keep trying to believe it."

As the King of the South and his daughter held each other, Queen Vita rose quietly from the throne and approached Allor and his companions.

"We'll have rooms ready for you shortly," she said quietly, "and once Salos and I have written and sent out our message to question and then release all Zarons, we'll have dinner ready. Come noontide tomorrow, we'll go to the internment quarter and release everyone there."

"So be it," said Allor with a calm nod, "but, if I may ask, what are we to do with those still laying siege to Benhotha? We came to explain what had happened as well as to ask for your aid, but we mean to see this siege ended before we call for your help in Enmayar."

"I think we can start discussing that at dinner, if it's alright by you. We can then talk it through more thoroughly tomorrow, before and after we release the Zarons."

"I hope we can act on the plan, whatever it be, soon, both for the sake of ending your trouble here as well as for getting to Enmayar and ending the root of this vileness as soon as possible."

"We all want the siege to end. We had thoughts on several strategies, but we didn't know what we were to do from there, since we didn't know the full extent of who was responsible for what's happened. But now, thanks to what you've told us, I feel we can assemble something fairly soon ... a few days from now, at most. And if we do indeed succeed, you will have Janrenar at your side, and that of your Elect companions, in whatever is to come after."

"Thank you, dear queen."

The queen called for the steward to see to the company's rooms before turning to join in her husband and daughter's embrace. The steward approached Allor and his companions and led them out of the throne room toward the guest chambers.

156
8/21/4030 G.M.

DONOVAN rose from his bed and sat along the bedside as he mulled over the planning and discussions for the battle to come, which had begun over dinner the previous night. After a brief time of reflection, the bard looked about his room and appreciated the brightening golden glow of the early morning sun spilling in from the window. He got up, grimacing slightly at the soreness in his thigh, and examined the well-mending wound. After applying a little ointment and a new bandage, he dressed in his freshly laundered clothes and left the room to see if there was any breakfast ready.

He went into the dining hall, where they had conversed and planned with the Queen and King of the South, and was surprised to find Allor and Verdok already seated with Vita and Salos, alongside their advisors and family. A bountiful breakfast was spread across the table, yet untouched, and all eyes turned to Donovan as he entered.

"I didn't keep you all waiting, did I?" the bard asked with a small, awkward laugh. "I didn't miss an agreed time to meet and speak again?"

"We have been waiting for you," said Allor kindly, "but not for long. You didn't forget or fail to hear anything as far as when breakfast was set to be had. Vita said herself that this is actually still a bit early for their normal routine, but it looks like most of us had been kept up by our thoughts. I began to just wander about and look at the art around the castle a few hours ago, and soon bumped into Salos and Vita. They told me they couldn't stay asleep, what with all we're set to do, and we just began to talk as we walked together. Then Verdok came along and Princess Quanda, and soon we just figured we might as well go ahead and have something to eat."

Donovan nodded and sat beside Allor and Verdok. The palace's resident cleric placed a blessing upon the meal, and they began to eat. Silence reigned for a fair while until at last Salos spoke up.

"With what we now know of the extent of this attack on Fidonity, we're confident that what we decided to do last night will be sufficient. We've already sent out the troops that are set to cross the Vitari further down, along with some aid from those who were patrolling the south bank. They should be in position around the grey-cloaks' camp by tomorrow morning. Once they're ready, they'll sound their horns and charge into the camp from all sides. We'll then open the north gate and send the cavalry we'll have stationed there into them, so they'll have nowhere to run. After that, we'll have some soldiers canvass the area, and once things appear to be in relative order, we'll prepare you and your company to make for Humilaar with all due haste. Vita and I will stay here for a time, and will send word ahead to Humilaar to have a secure ship ready for you when you arrive. In the meantime, we'll be calling out for soldiers to aid you and the Daughters of the East, and once we have gathered all those we can, we will join you at Karzynhaal as soon as we are able."

Donovan looked to Allor, who nodded satisfactorily as he chewed on a bite of smoked ham glazed with honey. "Sounds like as good a plan as any. And about the interned Zarons ..?"

"We're set to release them all at noon, apart from any who are still deemed suspicious by what inquiries are managed before then, as we said before."

Allor nodded again and ate a handful of pomegranate seeds before responding. "Thank you, for that and for everything else."

Vita sipped her blended drink of coffee, cocoa, and honey before adding to her husband's words. "Furthermore, we are releasing them from any obligation to aid us in the battle. If everything goes as planned, we should be able to manage with the forces we have anyway."

Donovan looked curiously at Allor as he leaned in his seat to look more fully at Queen Vita. "Are you releasing them from fighting, or forbidding them to aid you because you still don't want them to be armed in the city?"

The bard was just about to cut in and stress the queen's specific words to Allor, but he jolted in his seat and dropped his fork as Salos responded to Allor's question before he could. The southern king's voice was not a booming one of anger, but it was raised and carried a chillingly clear tone of indignation.

"We are *releasing* them, King Allor. *Releasing.* It's our attempt at making amends for how we've confined them for the past five months. We're offering them the opportunity to leave the capital upon release, if they wish, and we're intending to have them escorted out of the south gate before anyone else, if we can, in the event that our strategy should fail. If any of them wish to stay or to fight, they are welcome to do so, but we will not hold them to it as our attempt at penance."

Donovan looked at Allor, who bowed his head and stared silently at his plate with ears wilted by shame.

"I am sorry, Salos ... Vita ... It's just that–"

"Please, Allor," said Vita softly, "we understand. Just let it go. Trust us. We *all* need to trust each other if we are to have any chance of overcoming this evil."

Allor nodded silently and continued his meal.

***

When breakfast was finished, Donovan stepped outside the palace and walked in the gardens alongside Salos, Vita, and his fellows in fate. They were speaking quietly about the Daughters of the East. It was a subject that, to Donovan, seemed to lead both Allor and Verdok into a deeper melancholy, something the both of them had been grappling with in their own measure. Verdok had remained largely quiet since he killed the grey-cloak with the fire bottle on the ship, and Allor seemed to have been quite dampened in light of the cycle of suspicion he had fallen into from the sight of Benhotha's internment quarter.

"Here's to the hope that, if they have not yet succeeded in their mission in Kellmayar, they will soon," said Donovan as he tried to lift his friends' spirits. "Lerannu is a wise mage, Allor, and a fine woman overall. I'm sure that should we all come through this, she will make you very happy, and Sam and Tally, too. And Verdok, I don't know if there's anyone else I'd entrust Mira's safety to more than Ruth. I saw her fight splendidly the very first time I ever met her. And with her strength, Mira's sharp eyes, and Lera's magic, along with everything else about them, I'm sure it's just a matter of time before–"

Donovan's words were interrupted by the arrival of Kenora and Varnu Shaal, the two Vibonmor Shepherds, as they returned from their inquiries around the capital. They entered the garden with a guard accompanying them on either side. They hailed Vita and Salos as they approached, and began to make their report.

"The remnants of the grey-coat reinforcements, those that came in the wake of our three friends, have all arrived at their siege-camp, your majesties," Varnu announced plainly. "The watchers at the north gate have confirmed it."

"Are their numbers too great to carry on with our plan?" Salos asked worriedly. "Should we call them back?"

"I don't think so, my king," said Kenora. "It certainly has grown larger, but I still don't believe it has a good chance of ultimately overcoming what we've set up. We should still be able to surround and charge in on them from essentially all sides, unless they want to try and swim."

"Very well," Salos said with moderate relief. "Thank you both."

Varnu stepped forward. "It will also be noon shortly, my king. Is the plan still to–"

"Yes, my friend. Yes."

Varnu simply nodded, and he and his wife made to turn back and go elsewhere. Salos implored the couple to join the company in the garden for the time being, as well as for when they made for the internment quarter.

***

The sun was high. Donovan, thankful that it was winter on this end of the world, nevertheless opened his shirt to relieve himself of what his native Sorrenarn inclinations led him to feel as a less-than-comfortable warmth. He walked alongside Allor and Verdok, accompanied by guards and all the royal household, as they made their way to the cordoned area of the capital. The guards stationed at the barriers stood expectantly at attention, nodding their heads and parting from the street as the procession passed.

The Zaron citizens, having heard of the decree the night before as they were each being investigated, murmured anxiously and restlessly as they all made to approach Vita and Salos to hear their words. Their appearances, while a touch wearied by worry and oppressive confinement, were thankfully not those of wretchedly treated prisoners. The guards adopted a tensely defensive stance as the crowds stepped closer, though thankfully not to the point of drawing their arms or pointing them at the crowd. The mass of Zarons halted where they were, quieting down as Salos and Vita

~ 347 ~

stepped forward, hand in hand, and addressed them.

"We have learned of the source of the horror that assailed us on the eve of our Autumn's Day, dear people of Benhotha and Janrenar," said Vita loudly, but calmly. "We have found that this was not an effort on the part of all full-blooded Zarons, but of a relatively small, militant force of people who have been driven into their hateful state by Queen Sheeva of Enmayar, who in turn was manipulated by a demon from Raakhaal."

The mass of Zarons gasped, and Donovan saw many eyes look about their fellows in shock and dread at the news.

"Furthermore," Salos said, picking up where his wife ended, "we have been told that this demon, a horrid spirit named Raakmathna, has since possessed the late Queen of Enmayar, driving forward this heinous campaign in an effort to spite Onu and all creation. We have learned of these things from both a message sent from Queen Xenia and King Viktor of Sorrenar, as well as from the mouths of these three men who stand beside us. The leading representative of these three is this Zaron man, who is not only a Zaron like yourselves, but none other than King Allor of Enmayar himself, who witnessed the horrible fate of his wife firsthand."

The mobs murmured grimly at the news.

"However," Vita continued, "despite the graveness of these tidings, we now understand that our confined segregation of you all, out of fear and suspicion, was too severe and rash of a decision. Thus, unless any have been detained by reason of deepened suspicion from the inquiries made since the previous evening, all of you are released from this confining quarter immediately."

The Zarons sighed, then cheered with relief.

"We can never apologize enough for what we did out of fear, anger, and uncertainty," said Salos. "But we wish to inform you of this before you depart to wherever you will: We will make to break the siege of our city on the morrow, and though we will welcome any and every one of you who wishes to aid us, we will not hold any of you to do so, given what we have done."

The many voices in the mass of Zarons were ones of confusion and uncertainty.

"In addition, we offer you immediate passage out of the south gate to seek shelter elsewhere from the grey-cloaks, if you wish to take the chance to leave. If you choose to stay, and should our battle fail, we will–"

"I will stand with you, my king and my queen," said a handsome Zaron man as he stepped forward, "my family-in-law." The man was dressed in fine and vibrant robes of the court, and his hair was styled in the Mohawk that was customary to the people in that region of Janrenar.

"Aaron!" Princess Quanda sobbed joyfully as she bolted from the procession and leapt into her husband's arms. The two embraced and kissed tenderly, moving all who witnessed them, and Salos and Vita approached them as the king spoke to his son-in-law.

"Aaron," he said in a voice trying not to break, "I'm so sorry for all this, and my apologies go out to all those we confined here, but for my own son-in-law, who has done nothing but make my daughter happy–"

"We were under attack," said Aaron calmly, "in the name of such a senseless hate, by soldiers we had taken into our homes as Peacekeepers given to us in goodwill by someone we trusted. You had no way of knowing whom to trust."

"We still should've tried some other way–"

"It's done," Aaron called out in a voice loud, clear, but forgiving, "and in the past. Now, I am with you."

He then turned around to face the crowds of Zarons. "Who else will stand with Queen Vita and King Salos, and all of Benhotha and Janrenar?"

The vast cheers of support that boomed across the masses lifted Donovan's heart greatly. Aaron turned to Salos and Vita, smiling.

"We're Fidons first," the people declared. "Janrenarns second. Zarons third."

"Our thanks to you," said Salos happily, "to all of you. There is one more thing that you all need to know, something that, whether you stay with us or depart to seek safety elsewhere, will hopefully give you some hope and courage for whatever's to come. As we speak, three companions of these men who stand with us are working to gain the aid of Kellmayar against this demonic campaign, and have already gained the support of Sorrenar. They are not only warriors and bearers of the truth behind this rising madness, but are of the Elect, specifically the long-foreseen Daughters of the East."

The crowds gasped and murmured in awe.

"Know that we are not alone in this war for Fidonhaal," Vita called out comfortingly, "that Onu and his host have not left us to fall into utter destruction at the hands of these grey-clad butchers. Stay or go as you will, and know that the days of the demon behind these evils are numbered!"

The masses boomed a thundering cry of resolve. Donovan looked to Allor, who was speaking to Verdok. The high priest seemed reluctant, but Allor put his hand on his shoulder in an assuring way, saying something that the bard couldn't hear over the cheers. Verdok nodded, leaned toward the ears of Vita and Salos, and spoke to them. The two monarchs nodded solemnly and called out to the crowds once more.

"Whatever your decision," Vita announced, "if it please you, our companion, Verdok Merchill, High Priest of the Archtemple in Genverdell, would like to offer a prayer of reconciliation for the trouble that has sprung between us from the violence of the grey-cloaks."

The crowds gave a loud hum of approval, and Verdok, drawing a deep breath, raised his hands and prayed, seemingly back to his normal self for the first time in days as he led the people in communing with Onu.

"Onu, our Maker and dearest friend, we come together to ask you for your forgiveness for whatever wrongs we may have committed against one another out of the fear that this terrible time of violence and hatred has stirred within our hearts. We pray that you forgive our misdeeds, and we pray that you give greater strength and kindness to our hearts, that we ourselves may forgive them as well. We pray that you and your love will bring us closer together, that we may trust one another to overcome this horrible hatred and restore Fidonhaal to a time of peace and love. In you we strive to trust."

"In you we strive to trust," said Donovan, with Allor and every other soul around him joining in echoing the high priest's words.

157

8/22/4030 G.M.

VERDOK climbed the stairs that lined the wall comprising the north gate of Benhotha. Donovan and Allor stood alongside him, as well as Varnu and Kenora. In addition to the two Vibonmor Shepherds, a company of guards and soldiers lined the top of the gate and the adjacent walls, with blades and spears at their sides, and bows and crossbows at the ready.

The high priest and his friends had awoken early that morning, having requested arousal in time to join the battle. After a silent breakfast and a final exchange of farewells between them and their royal hosts, they had made their way straight for the north gate. Both official soldiers and citizen militia bustled about the three men as all made for their positions for the impending battle.

Verdok looked about, his mind at last coming to terms with what had happened on the ships and making peace with it in the wake of the prayer in which he had led the people following the ending of Janrenar's internment of Zarons. The prayer, and witnessing both parties involved in the internment forgiving and helping one another, had done much to lighten his heart. Though still wrestling with the horrible sight of the burning grey-coat and painfully missing Ruth more and more with each passing day, Verdok was now in the best spirits he had been in for nearly a fortnight.

"You seem to be a fair bit better, friend," Donovan said as he stood beside the priest, his Arbonyn-wood longbow at the ready with a shaft already nocked to the string.

"I agree," said Allor. "I trust yesterday helped?"

Verdok nodded as he looked at the grey-cloak camp on the north bank of the Vitari. "I do feel better, thank you. And yes, the way things played out yesterday certainly helped. A lot. Thank you for pushing me to lead the prayer, Allor. Thank you both, for not just leaving me to ... wallow."

"Why would we?" the bard asked plainly.

"Our mission can't be jeopardized by me just falling apart like that," Verdok said flatly. "If things had turned out differently, we might've not made it this far because I fell to pieces on the ship. While you, or anyone else, tried to pull me out of my hysteria, you could've been killed, or others could've died, ones who needed us, or–"

"An aversion to violence is not a sin," Allor said calmly. "It is how every Fidon should be toward their fellow."

"But it isn't that way," Verdok said glumly. "And alas, those who wish for the world to be anything close to that must be able, and willing, to fight for it."

A few seconds passed, silent but for the sighs that Donovan and Allor breathed as they tried to give a response. Verdok, tears suddenly brimming in his eyes, suddenly chuckled moodily.

"We've just completely shat our own beds with all this; what we've done to ourselves and the world. We started to fight, and then we've had to keep fighting to stop fighting. It's been this way for thousands of years, and I can't see it ever fully healing for as long as the world stands."

Allor and Donovan, along with several nearby soldiers, had been trying to keep their faces straight after the first words of the priest's sagely observation. Finally beginning to laugh, the bard slackened his bowstring, put his arrow back in the quiver, and put a brotherly arm around Verdok.

"Well said," the dashing northerner commended the priest, "though I can't imagine how Father Owen, or any number of your other fellows, would respond to hearing your opening line. It would certainly be a catching opener for a sermon."

Verdok began to laugh more heartily as well. "Oh, come now, there's always been a few rascals in the Temple with good hearts but foul mouths. We had one back in Genverdell, a Brother Korlaar, who was a sailor for most of his life before coming to the archtemple."

"Onu's Four Breaths," Allor said with a laugh and a shake of his head, "I can't imagine how that went! How did he even convince the clergy to let him in?"

"With a confession of the odd smuggling job he did back in the day. And a donation of everything he had on him, which he directed specifically for tending to orphans, regardless of whether they were in the full care of the Temple or not. He was an orphan himself and had slipped through the cracks, if you will."

"Aye," Donovan said with a grin, "That's certainly something. Did he ever host a sermon or anything like that?"

"Once," said Verdok, the tears in his eyes now being only of laughter, "and it actually started off wonderfully. But when it came to describing the evil of Raakaru, he was quite passionate in his phrasing. While none would likely say his words were untrue, let's just say that the delivery–"

The loud clanking of the north gate opening at a frantic pace cut off the priest's words. Verdok and all those around him tensed, looking about worriedly as the horns of those surrounding the grey-cloaks were yet to be sounded. Verdok looked back and saw that the city's cavalcade was not yet fully in position. They were scrambling frantically to mount up and charge. He looked back and saw a great mass of grey-coats charging, on horse and foot, toward the gates. Donovan and many of the soldiers on the wall began firing arrows desperately into the advancing troops. The soldiers who were meant to enclose the grey-coats, having lost the advantage, blared their horns desperately as they began to charge in from the dense trees and toward the advancing enemy as best they could.

"Who raised the Onu-damned gate before the horn?" Verdok heard an officer bellow wrathfully amongst the soldiers. The priest, not being versed in sword or bow, called out anxiously to the officer.

"I-I'll go and see what happened, sir!"

"Thank you. And beat the shite out of whoever it was on my behalf."

Verdok was already down the stairs and barging into the door of the gatehouse beneath the north wall. He stared in dumb, furious silence at the two Zarons who, garbed in the uniform of Benhotha's guard, were still turning the gears as they looked up at him. The priest's fur bristled, and his heart and skull began to pound with wrath. Without a word, he bolted toward them, felled the first of the two with one punch to the head as he tried to draw his sword, and grabbed the other by the collar of his shirt, lifting him off the ground and pummeling him as he exited the gatehouse.

"YOU BASTARD!" he screamed as he continued to pound his fist into the Zaron's face. "We trusted you! You idiot! Think of how this–"

In his blind fury, Verdok had not stopped to think of how far along either the charging grey-coats or the Benhotha cavalcade would likely be in regards to their position at the gate. He walked right into the clashing fray of the city's soldiers and the grey-clads. A rushing horse knocked Verdok to the ground and plowed into the Zaron that the priest was beating, carrying him away under-hoof. The force of the impact threw Verdok hard onto the stone roadway. He hit his head, and stars filled his vision, which then quickly plummeted into darkness and silence.

***

Verdok's head ached horrendously. The pounding in his skull filled his ears and set them to ringing. Something heavy was on top of him. His eyes slowly opened. A dead grey-cloak was sprawled on top of him. He shoved the corpse away, sat upright, and looked around. Bodies lay all around him, city guard, soldier, citizen and grey-cloak alike. He massaged his head. The ringing stopped and the pounding eased. He shakily got up, realizing that the city was fairly quiet. Verdok's heart at first leapt up to his throat, but then he realized it wasn't utterly silent and that the sounds present were not ones of battle. A fairly steady hum seemed to be sounding a way down the road, and Verdok, at a loss in figuring out what had happened, began to make his way toward the steady murmuring.

He passed a few streets when a guard called out to him. The priest turned, relieved to see that it was a guard of the city and not a grey-clad one.

"I take it we won," Verdok asked, "or at least didn't lose?"

"You guess right, sir," said the guard. "We were able to win the day despite those few Zaron shits that raised the gate before all was ready. Turns out that a couple of the ones in the internment quarter were indeed grey-cloaks, and they managed to persuade some of the others to their cause, saying that the internment was proof that all non-Zarons were out to get them, or something of that ilk. They got them all to play along with the appearance of making peace and vowing to help everyone, but once they were able to sneak into the gatehouse, they made to do us all in by opening the way for the rest of the grey-coats. The city is executing them now."

"Them?" Verdok asked in dread. "What do you mean by *them*? You don't mean all the Zarons here, do you?"

"No sir, not at all. The ones responsible, once they saw that they still lost the battle, either fell on their swords or confessed readily; those we managed to stop from ending themselves, anyhow. Justice is set to be swift. Everyone else is fine. Well, those who haven't already fallen, of course."

"What of King Allor? Or the Sorrenarn named Donovan?"

"Wait, you're Verdok, aren't you?"

"Yes, sir. I tried to stop the ones who were opening the gate, but I got caught in the middle of the battle and lost consciousness."

"They've been looking for you. They've joined Queen Vita and King Salos in overseeing the executions, and were then going to look for you some more before leaving for Humilaar."

"Thank you, sir. Where are they?"

"In front of the palace. Follow me, I'll get you there fast."

Verdok and the guard reached the front of the palace shortly. As they drew near, the humming of voices went completely silent, and as the priest rounded a corner, he saw the beheading of the first condemned conspirator. Averting his eyes, he followed the guard to where Queen Vita and King Salos stood, grimly overseeing the administration of capital justice. Verdok raised his eyes as he approached them, and saw Donovan waving to him and pointing him out to Allor. The King of Enmayar looked to him and breathed a sigh of immense relief. The three men embraced as brothers, and Verdok, thanking the guard as he returned to his patrol, asked his friends for the details of what had happened.

"I feel there isn't much more to it than what the guard told you," said Donovan. "Despite the attempt to sabotage the whole thing, we still managed to come out on top. Some soldiers are canvassing the area outside the city, and once they judge it to be secure, and once this ... business is settled, we'll have a rest and some food, and then we'll be on our way to Humilaar with an escort."

"Very well," said Verdok grimly as he steeled himself to observe the remaining executions.

Reunion on Karzynhaal

158
9/2/4030 G.M.

LERANNU sat in the saddle with her father, as silent as she had been for the near fortnight since the battle of Zefiil. She had screamed at herself constantly to speak, to do anything since the death of her mother, but all she could manage after a day's rest following the battle was to walk numbly about and do the most basic of things. She could eat, though there was no thought for it or relishing of it. She could drink, but no matter what it was, it may as well have been simply water. She could sleep, but not truly rest. She wordlessly kept close to her father as they traveled with the others to the port city of Korashka. It was all she could think to do to show him that she loved him, and didn't hold what happened to Sarah against him.

Ruth and Mira tried to get through to her, their efforts worthy of memorializing them as Exemplars of Compassion and Patience, but it was as yet to no avail. Soon, after reading the mage's eyes, they stopped and left things to run their course, settling for standing by her and Roniil until she came through. In the meantime, the mage was trapped within her own mind, which was flooded with the soul-shaking reflections on how the most personal of injuries could lead one to either enact, or otherwise partake in, the most far-reaching of horrors.

They departed from Zefiil on the twentieth of Yorok after resting the remainder of the day once the battle had been won, as well as all the following day, in the recovering capital of the West. They left with a good number of Trichynay warriors, along with Xavier, Ranye, and their newlywed daughter and son-in-law. A company of soldiers stationed in the capital were also sent along as the first lot of allies to depart for Karzynhaal. King Dominik and Queen Fida sent out calls across the country within hours of the victory at Zefiil, and assured the Elect that they would be sending more allies in the near future once the news had spread and more ships and ports were confirmed secured from any remaining grey-cloak forces.

Accepting this arrangement, the company had ridden on at a steady pace for eleven days without incident. Now, with the spreading glow of the rising sun stretching ever higher above the horizon, the port of Korashka and the ocean beyond appeared just within sight. The riders halted briefly, both to take some water and to gaze contemplatively at the view. The sight was a window to the next step of the mission, which was so close, in a sense, to the final one. It was a view that stirred both anxiety and hope in Lerannu's heart, and a glance about her companions assured her that she was not alone in such thoughts. Ranye and Xavier rode their horses a few trots ahead of the company, both looking quietly together at the city and the ocean beyond. The blind seer breathed the air deeply and raised a hand into the caressing, mild breeze that had both the desert and the sea woven into it.

"Soon we will sail the seas," the high shaman said cheerfully, "and come to the isle of our beginning."

He turned his head to face the Elect, who were now right behind him. His glowing eyes fixed upon the three women as though he weren't blind at all.

"Well, let's finish with our helping of water and get to it. We shouldn't be keeping the Phoenix waiting any longer than necessary now, should we?"

At the mention of the Phoenix, Lerannu gasped as she felt her tongue finally loosen. She struggled for a second to mouth the words, and then shakily spoke to the high shaman.

"Y-you said his na-name was M-Mercilaar, r-right?"

The ears of all about her shot up in surprise, followed by several sobs of joy, particularly from Roniil. Ruth and Mira sighed with relief, and they shed a tear or two between them. Xavier rode up to the mage and her father, smiling gently.

"You recall correctly, my friend. I am glad beyond words to hear you again."

"An-and I'm as g-glad to s-speak again."

Roniil embraced and kissed his daughter, tears pouring from his eyes as freely as a river. "Lera, I'm so sorry for everything. If I hadn't betrayed your mother, if I just held out and talked to her, none of this would have ever happened."

"N-none of it, Papa?" Lerannu asked as she turned her head to see her father in the saddle behind her, speaking as calmly and consolingly as she could through her stammer.

Roniil sniffed, looking earnestly into his daughter's eyes.

"Maybe Mama wouldn't have been involved," the mage said reflectively, "but all that had driven Queen Sheeva to her hatred would still be in play. Who knows what would've happened then? Maybe it would've been better, maybe not. What happened happened, from what happened at home to what happened in Zefiil. We're in this together now, you, me, my sisters in this fate, and all the rest of Fidonhaal who will rise with us against this damn demon."

Lerannu shifted in the saddle, putting an arm around her father in as close of an embrace as she could manage from her position in front of him. Her voice began to steady.

"Thank you for saving me from her, Papa. There's no telling for certain what will come to pass for us before this mission's end, but if it weren't for you, I wouldn't be able to help Ruth or Mira anymore, save by the will of Onu alone."

Roniil and Lerannu hugged each other quietly. A moment passed, then the mage began to climb gingerly down from the saddle.

"I think I can ride on my own again now. Is there a free horse around here anywhere?"

A tribal rider soon arrived, leading a horse toward her that was free apart from a few supplies set in the saddlebags. The mage thanked the rider and mounted up, and the company continued its ride toward Korashka. Xavier called out to Lerannu as they cantered along.

"Any idea what it was about me mentioning Mercilaar that got you to speak, friend?"

"Not particularly. Maybe it rekindled some hope when the Phoenix was mentioned again, or maybe I just really wanted to make sure I remembered his name, and my desire for that somehow outweighed whatever was holding me back."

Lerannu shrugged. "Maybe there was some sort of magic in the word," she said with a little laugh.

Xavier grinned. "I can think of more far-fetched things."

"I'm somewhat surprised you didn't already know, or at least have a hunch."

Xavier's grin grew a bit wider. "Haven't I already said that I'm truly not privy to *everything*, milady?"

"You just made such a good first impression is all."

The high shaman was now grinning very broadly. "It *is* a gift, I'll say that, and one that I am truly thankful for despite the peculiars that have come with it. I do what I can with what Onu has given me, and as sincerely as I can when all is said and done. That said, I must confess that I do also enjoy ... a little bit of theatrics. When appropriate, of course. Or at least not *inappropriate*, like when we first met."

Lerannu smiled. She looked over to Ruth and Mira, and saw them grinning too. A thin smile was on Ranye's lips as she leaned in her saddle and gently nudged her husband as they rode.

"Then I don't suppose you have much else on Mercilaar at the moment," Lerannu asked, "apart from his name and that he's waiting for us on Karzynhaal?"

"I believe we should be looking for him near the tree."

The mage chuckled lightly. "That helps narrow the search," she said good-naturedly as she thought of all the trees that blanketed the Isle of Origin.

Xavier laughed. "*The* tree, milady; *the* tree."

Lerannu felt a wave of awe come over her. "Oh," she said plainly, "I see."

"Apart from that, I haven't seen much more." The high shaman then winked at the mage. "If anything comes up, you'll be the first I tell."

Now in far higher spirits, Lerannu and the company began to gallop toward Korashka. There they were greeted with cheers as the people of the city accompanied them to the docks and helped them board the docked *Frostwind*, which had thankfully made the journey safely from where the Elect had disembarked from her, and was now fully set to sail with all haste.

159
9/4/4030 G.M.

ALLOR rode into the port of Humilaar alongside Donovan, Verdok, the two Vibonmor Shepherds, and the escort of Benhothan soldiers. The city opened the gates readily for them, and the mayor and a small company of guards led them to the docks. A modest ship named *Greenfin* sat on the water, fully crewed and ready for a swift voyage to Karzynhaal. Other ships of various sizes were being inspected, maintained, and supplied, presumably for the soldiers that were to arrive soon after the men's departure.

Allor thanked the mayor and the others for their efforts and prayed that Onu bless and guard them. He and the others swiftly boarded the *Greenfin* and soon were sailing steadily out of the harbor that formed at the mouth of the Vitari River. Allor looked down at the gently lapping waters, eventually becoming aware of Verdok standing beside him. The King of Enmayar looked to him, seeing that the high priest was staring into the water the same way as he was, a look of deep, moody reflection set into his face.

Verdok had told him and Donovan of what had happened to him during the battle of Benhotha. The king and the bard had been relieved beyond words to see that their companion had emerged alive and mostly well from the crowd in the capital, but were saddened to hear of his experience during the battle. Though clearly not as shaken as he had been by what happened during the battle on the sea, Verdok was still plainly hurting from the incident in the gatehouse. He had again gone mostly silent during the days they traveled to Humilaar, and though he spoke kindly and hopefully when he spoke at all, there was a numbed side to his voice.

Allor put an arm around his friend. "Do you want to talk?"

Verdok shrugged. "Somewhat, but I don't think there's really anything to say about my thoughts that I didn't say right before the battle."

Allor nodded and the priest sighed longingly.

"I suppose all I have left to say is that I've been praying that Ruth has made it," Verdok went on, "and that I can see her again, at least one more time before the last steps of our journey are made. I mean, I hope they're all okay, of course, but–"

"I understand."

A small, shaky sob passed Verdok's lips. "After all this hate and fighting, I just really need some of her love again."

Allor nodded once more, and the two silently turned their heads to gaze out at the wide-open seas that lay before them. The heart of the King of Enmayar, after hearing Verdok's desperate hope for his wife, flooded with thoughts of Lerannu. He silently joined the priest's pleas for the welfare of the Daughters of the East, though he also confessed inwardly that Lerannu was the one who first sprang to mind.

160
9/14/4030 G.M.

MIRA stared in awe at the beauty of Karzynhaal as the longboat carrying her and her Elect sisters was rowed steadily toward the Sacred Island. The Daughters of the East had sailed twelve days after embarking from Korashka, with no encounters with any grey-sailed vessels. The huntress and her companions were sure that the grey-cloak threat, though still existent, had experienced a drastic setback. When Karzynhaal appeared on the horizon, the company's hopes lifted further with the sight of several plain-sailed ships, bearing the blue flag of Sorrenar, anchored offshore of the Holy Isle. The North had come through and already sent a number of reinforcements to await the Elect's arrival. Despite the ever-growing presence of assuring sights, however, Mira still wrestled with the uncertainty of what exactly was still to come.

The huntress's lingering worries, however, were dispelled for the time by the marvelous beauty of the trees and flowers that came into view as her boat neared the isle. The flora canvassed the land in marvelous greens and nearly every other color. Every inch closer to Karzynhaal felt like a step closer to the most complete bliss that could ever be reached within the Realm of Mortals. It was the serenity in which the First Ancestors lived as they had the closest, simplest, truest bonds with Onu. Mira felt closer to the long-past ancestors, and the handful of heroes and heroines who were given the honor of being buried beneath Karzynhaal's soil. She felt closer to Onu, to the angels, and all the other wondrous creatures that joined the first Fidons as they began their part in the saga of Fidonhaal and all creation.

Xavier, who was riding in the same longboat as her and the Elect, looked levelly at Mira, Ruth, and Lerannu with his sightless, yet deeply insightful eyes. He breathed deeply and smiled as he held High Chief Ranye's hand. He was feeling the bliss of Karzynhaal, too, and probably even more deeply than Mira.

"It's wonderful, isn't it?" he asked. "The feeling of closeness to the beginning, and to divinity. One can seek and find a bit of it just about anywhere, if one's heart is set. But here ... it's like no-where else."

"Aye," said Ruth, to which Mira and Lerannu simply nodded in agreement, at a loss for anything else to add. "There's certainly nothing else quite like it."

The high shaman turned his glowing gaze directly at the Faithguard. "There are still a few things that can certainly *add* to the feeling, though," he said with a knowing smile.

Ruth laughed lightly. To Mira, the knight's face appeared to be of one resigning to play along with the shaman's previously confessed enjoyment of playing the cryptic seer. "Might I ask what those are?" asked the Faithguard.

"There are a couple such things that I can see waiting for you. I think I'll keep quiet about one of them, but I don't suppose you'd consider seeing and conversing with an Exemplar's spirit to be something that would add to your blessed experience?"

Ruth's smile, though now no longer playful, was still on her lips, being now one of sincerity. "Aye, my friend. That would certainly add to the feeling."

"I trust you remember what I mentioned to you before, milady? Regarding Konoth?"

"Of course."

Mira, listening intently to the conversation between the high shaman and the Faithguard knight, jolted in surprise as she felt the bottom of the longboat suddenly shift onto the shore of Karzyn-haal. She looked away from Xavier's gaze and took in the blessed beauty of the isle of Fidonity's or-igin. The golden sands of the shore, the flowers of countless colors, and the dazzling green of the leaves of plant and tree overwhelmed her in the early light of morning. It put the beauty of Santaru to shame. The huntress looked back to the high shaman, who nodded to her and her Elect sisters as he carefully got out of the boat with the aid of Ranye's loving hand. She then climbed out of the boat alongside Ruth and Lerannu, stepping onto the warm sands as she continued to relish the view.

"If you wish to accompany us to the Heartroot Tree, Lady Pionaar," Xavier said warmly, "and meet Mercilaar first, that is perfectly fine. Sir Konoth will wait, and all the joys that await you on this isle will still come to you in time. However, I feel that if you were to go ahead and make your way to him now, you might enjoy a ... more poetic course of events."

Mira saw Ruth's smile shift back to one of playful interest, while still seeming to carry a serious weight to it.

"Very well," said the knight. "I've always liked it when moments like that play out in the stories. I guess I might as well take one if I can get it."

Xavier nodded with a smile, and stepped further along the shore with his wife's hand in his. Mira looked at the two, moved by how they both stepped together and gazed in wonder at the beauty around them. Xavier could clearly feel the wonder more deeply than anyone else despite his lack of worldly sight. He began to tremble and tears began to well in his eyes, though his smile never faded. A moment passed as Mira took in all the wonder and beauty, then Xavier called out to her and her Elect sisters.

"Well, as much as I'd love to just stand right here, I suppose we should be getting a move on. Lady Greenheart, Lady Stonefaith, if you are ready, we can start making our way to the Heartroot."

Mira and Lerannu, and all the others that were coming ashore, began to gather around the high shaman and his wife. Xavier, his blind, glowing eyes gazing piercingly at Ruth, nodded toward the knight as she checked her things before embarking on a separate journey.

"See you in a few days, milady," he said.

"See you soon," the knight said as she turned and walked eastward.

The high shaman called out to a large company of his tribe as they came ashore, bidding them to spread across the coast to help the Sorrenarns who were stationed as lookouts keep watch for any more arriving allies or foes. He also asked for them to inform the company from Janrenar of the Elect's destination on the Blessed Isle, should they land wherever they were stationed. The tribespeople gathered their things and went in various directions as they made to set up camp across the coasts of Karzynhaal alongside the soldiers of the North.

***

A few minutes passed in relative silence before Mira stepped up to walk alongside Xavier.

"What's this 'more poetic course of events' that's in store for Ruth, if I may ask?" she inquired.

The high shaman smiled. "If I sensed things right, and I do my part, she'll be given the arms and armor of her patron Exemplar *and* be reunited with her husband at nearly the same time."

Mira's heart nearly stopped, and glancing to her side at Lerannu, she saw that the mage was having the same reaction. "D-do you know if the others–"

"They're alive and well," Xavier said calmly. "Well, apart from a few hurts that each are bearing, of one sort or another."

"One sort or another?" asked Lerannu worriedly.

"A few of the body, a few of the mind, a few of the soul. I feel that the greatest of their hurts, however, are those of being apart from you. They'll each recover in time, and you being beside them will be of great help. I wasn't going to tell Lady Pionaar what to do, of course, but I am glad that she went the way she did. I'm sure her husband would've been fine to meet up with her later, but I think the way it's looking to go will be better for both of them."

Mira sobbed joyfully, her vision beginning to blur from tears. Xavier gently patted her shoulder.

"Of course, you three haven't had it easy either, and I'm sure all of you are keen to see each other again."

Mira nodded. "I've been trying my hardest to accept that we might not ever see each other again, on Fidonhaal, anyway. But there certainly were those days when it tore at my heart."

"It's simply the way of such bonds, milady. Breathe easy; you'll see him soon. Now, let's try to make some ground. I'm as eager to meet the Phoenix as you are."

They stepped up their pace a bit and briskly strode along for another few silent moments. Then Mira heard Lerannu call out to Xavier from behind her.

"How will Verdok catch up with Ruth, though? Is he already somewhere else on the island? And even if he was, how would he know to look for her at Konoth's grave, and how would he reach her while she's still there?"

"Onu has told me that he will soon grace me with a chance to let Mr. Pionaar know about all that," Xavier said with a grin. "As far as him catching up with her, I believe that a few of Vente's children will be along to help him when the time comes."

Mira and Lerannu looked at each other, inspired and amused by the prospects of what awaited their sister of destiny and her husband.

"I must confess that I'm a little jealous," said Mira. "It sounds like they'll have quite the story to tell their kids someday."

Lerannu laughed. "Glad I'm not the only one thinking that."

Xavier looked back at them as he continued to walk beside Ranye. "We shall each get our own sorts of those stories, my friends."

***

The company journeyed to the heart of the Isle of Beginning, arriving at the great Heartroot Tree in just under a week's time. There they were met with two sights that set the heart and soul to soaring. There was the great tree Karzynu, under which the earthly remains of the first Awakened Fidons rested. Perched upon one of its great boughs was a grand bird, its feathers a dazzling array of fiery crimson and gold.

"Greetings, Daughters of the East," said the Phoenix with a gallant nod of his head, "and Xavier Onoraan, companion in my recent dreams. I am Mercilaar, a continuation of the Phoenixes wrought by Onu on the day of Raakaru's exorcism from the world. I have been eagerly awaiting your arrival."

Mira stood silently with her companions. All of them stood rooted where they were, overcome by awe.

"How about we converse as we await those yet to join us?" asked the Phoenix cordially.

161
9/17/4030 G.M.

VERDOK tossed and turned in his sleep, struggling to make sense of the vision before him. A stranger, a man dressed in a blue, green and white patterned robe, materialized from the darkness of dreams. The stranger's eyes glowed with the holy, haunting light of an Ecclesian's eyes. His lips bore a soft, friendly smile.

"Greetings, Verdok Pionaar."

The high priest stared intently at the stranger. He felt himself ask the stranger his identity, but did not hear his own voice in the asking, nor feel his lips move to form the words.

"I am Xavier, High Shaman of the Trichynay peoples," said the stranger with a bow. "My tribe has allied with the Daughters of the East, and together, we have liberated the Kellmayarn capital of Zefiil from the grey-clad murderers who sought to conquer it. We have since journeyed to Karzynhaal, and await your arrival and that of all our other allies."

Verdok's heart leapt with joy, though his uncertainty for Ruth's well-being suddenly came to the front of his mind. Still not truly speaking, he felt himself ask the stranger about her.

"She is fine," said the Ecclesian, "as are all three of the Elect. Indeed, that is why I have come to speak to you at this time. The loved ones of Allor and Donovan are presently in my company, and we are making our way to the Heartroot Tree, where we will meet another ally, a Phoenix named Mercilaar."

Verdok's eyebrows raised in surprised delight.

"Ruth, however, has temporarily parted from us to seek out the grave of her order's patron. She is to be offered the Warrior Exemplar's arms and armor. You do know the general location of Konoth and Devora's graves, I trust?"

Verdok's head did not nod, and yet he felt that he did so in spirit.

"Good. If you wanted to simply wait for her at the Heartroot, you can, but I can sense that your heart would likely prefer to see her again as soon as possible."

Verdok felt his soul nod again, desperately. No tears were in his eyes, but he felt there would've been if he were truly speaking to the stranger in the flesh. The stranger raised a hand and pantomimed resting it upon a person's shoulder. Verdok felt a consoling touch on his right shoulder.

"Your heart has ached for her, as has Allor's heart for Lerannu, and Donovan's for Mira. You will all be together soon. When you land, make for the grave of Konoth. You'll find some help along the way, and your fellows will be directed to Karzynu in the meantime. The two of you can join us later, once your hearts have been reunited."

Verdok nodded inwardly. The stranger began to drift back into the dark as he waved friendlily.

"Go to her. We'll soon meet in person."

Verdok pulled himself out of his slumber as there came uplifting cries from the deck above that Karzynhaal was in sight.

***

Verdok stood at the railing of the *Greenfin* alongside Allor and Donovan. The bard and the king listened gladly as the priest recounted his strange, but uplifting vision. The three men spent the remainder of the time before reaching the island leaning silently at the railing, their tails flitting anxiously about as they eagerly awaited to see their loved ones again.

When the *Greenfin* dropped anchor near the shore, the three got into a longboat and were rowed to the coast. Greeting them there were a handful of Sorrenarn soldiers, and several men and women, mostly Kason or of predominantly Kason heritage, who wore sturdy hide clothing and bore the telltale earrings of the Trichynay people.

"Our high shaman instructed us to look out for your arrival, dear companions of the Elect," said a tribeswoman. "We are to tell you that the huntress and the mage have journeyed to the Heartroot–"

"And that the knight has gone to speak to the founder of her order?" asked Verdok with a smile.

The tribeswoman looked at Verdok with a light look of surprise, though a second of thinking led her to smile as she guessed how he already knew.

"I suppose you're acquainted with the high shaman, at least in spirit if not in person?"

"Indeed."

The lookout company offered to lead the three to the Heartroot Tree. Donovan and Allor looked at Verdok with a quiet smile.

"I'll be coming along later," the priest said to the lookouts. "For now, I'm going to my wife."

The company parted from Verdok as they began to make their way to the heart of Karzynhaal, and the priest, on his own, took stock of where they had landed and soon deduced the general direction to Konoth's grave.

***

Verdok jogged resolutely onward for a day and a night, hardly stopping but for the briefest rest and the occasional picking of Karzynhaal's ever-bountiful fruit. He drank from a waterskin that had been supplied to him from the ship and refilled it from the many pure streams. He was otherwise sustained by naught but his love and longing to see Ruth's face again.

He carried on until the afternoon of the second day, at last starting to grow weary and slowing to a longer stop than he had taken before. Still resolute, he breathed raggedly and slumped against a tree, tilting his head back to gaze into the sky and branches above.

There he saw two of the Lofons, the winged ones, looking at the priest with large, friendly eyes from the branches overhead. Still panting for breath, he smiled and waved to them in greeting.

"Hail, dear children of Vente and Branok. I have been making my way toward the resting place of Konoth, the first of the Faithguard. Would you by chance know its exact spot? I'm sure I'm going in the right direction ... generally speaking, but as far as getting the exact spot, I'd appreciate any help I can get."

The two Lofons smiled. "Are you looking for the lady? A grey one dressed in the way of a guardian of the Faith? Eyes of emeralds? A black and white sign of the Four about her neck?"

"Y-yes!" Verdok cried in elation, still regaining his breath. "Yes! When did you see her?"

"Yesterday, about three hours past the sun's peak," said one of the winged people. "We heard her talking to herself about a man named Verdok. I presume you are he?"

"Yes! Do you know if the grave is close?"

"You are quite close."

"Thank you so much! Please, just point the direction and I'll leave you two to your–"

"Rest a little, friend, please. It wouldn't be fitting to meet her again so out of breath."

"I can't stop now! I just need to–"

"We can carry you. The flight will be far quicker, anyway."

Verdok stared incredulously at the two, laughing with awe and gratitude. "A fine part of the journey this is! Thank you, blessed ones. You do your mother and father proud!"

The priest then slumped fully against the trunk of the tree, gulped a hearty helping of water, and closed his eyes.

***

The sun, though still up, was sinking steadily toward the horizon, bathing all in Verdok's sight with a brilliant, deepening gold. He stood up, greatly refreshed by the rest despite its brevity, and looked up the tree to see if his newfound friends were still above him. They had shifted to the next tree over, and nodded warmly to the priest as he found them.

"Are you ready, Sir Verdok?"

"I am."

The two majestic creatures spread their wings, and swooping down together, they carefully picked up Verdok using their large, strong talons, with one taking hold of the priest's arms while the other took him by the ankles. Verdok trembled thrillingly as he was lifted high into the air and soared through the warm breeze, feeling truly blessed by the honor and privilege to be so aided by ones of the Angelborn. A brief, exhilarating flight passed, and the two Lofons soon gingerly lowered themselves and their passenger to the ground. Verdok looked about quizzically, not seeing Ruth nor the graves of Konoth and Devora.

"Just ahead that way," nodded one of the Lofons with a smile. "We thought you might like to surprise her. Goodbye, and may you and your companions fare well in your quest."

Verdok nodded and grinned. "Thank you," he said as he waved to them in farewell. He turned in the direction indicated by the Lofons, with the wind beneath their wings breezing behind him, and quietly crept along toward the hallowed site and the woman he loved.

162

9/19/4030 G.M.

RUTH had journeyed six days at a steady pace since the morning she and her companions had landed on Karzynhaal. She knew of the basic whereabouts of Konoth's tomb from the various directions and descriptions given in the Beldsantu, and in several pilgrims' journals. She followed the rising sun in the morning and kept going east into the night. She would then follow the stars that made up the handle of the constellation of Konoth's Axe. She rested when she tired, though such occurrences were few, brief, and far in between, and ate and drank from Karzynhaal's bounty as she needed. She walked along, conversing aloud to herself as she reflected on the journey she had taken since that sorrowful night on Veronmay's Eve, as well as her thoughts for Verdok.

At last, as the sun lowered well behind her, she came upon a clearing and sighed in awe at the sight of two monuments, still standing strong despite the near four thousand years since they were erected. She approached them slowly, silently expressing as much reverence as she could, until she at last stood before the graves of the first Faithguard and his wife. Ruth quietly got onto her knees and bowed her head, breathing and praying in silent meditation as she waited to hear the voice of Konoth.

She was not long in waiting, as she soon heard the warm, haunting echo of a man's majestic voice speak before her.

"Greetings, Ruth Pionaar, Guardian of the Faith and Daughter of the East. I understand that you come at the advice of a great seer, that you might be lent the arms and armor by which I protected the faithful in the days after Raakaru's banishment."

Ruth shut her eyes and prostrated herself upon the earth before the graves. "Yes, Sir Konoth Alpharon, First of the Faithguard and Exemplar of the Righteous Warrior. I strive to keep faith in the quest and purpose of me and my sisters in fate, which was foreseen by none other than he who you guarded in the days following the end of Raakaru's reign. I know not if I am absolutely fated to take up your arms to aid me in my quest ..."

"You need not, Lady Pionaar, but I have seen your resolve from beyond the Great Curtain, and with Onu's leave, I have awaited your arrival to grant you this boon as a gesture of blessing unto you, that your faith may be strengthened even further."

"My undying thanks, to you and to Onu, for this immeasurable honor."

"Please, Lady Pionaar, open your eyes."

Ruth opened her eyes and looked up to the monument, awed beyond words at the ethereal beauty of Konoth and Devora, standing together before their graves as they looked benevolently upon her. The two spirits floated gracefully to the monument of Konoth, and raising their hands they gently parted the earth and lifted from the ground the stone casket that housed the first Faithguard's remains. They lifted the coffin's top and beckoned Ruth to step forward. The knight approached the casket and looked inside, gazing ponderingly upon what remained of the brittle, dusty bones that lay within. The skeleton donned a beautifully sewn tabard and sparkling chainmail, which had a few segments of the earliest sort of plate fixed onto it in select spots. Sturdy leather boots, polished to a shine and fixed with steel on the toes, heel, and shins, were on the skeleton's feet. An ornate helm cradled what was left of Konoth's skull, and clasped within his gauntleted hands were a finely forged axe and buckler. All that the skeleton wore seemed hardly touched by the passing of the millennia, resting upon the crumbling bones in nigh-pristine condition. Ruth supposed this must be the work of some blessed magic, either preserving the articles all this time or repairing them now that they were being called to serve their purpose once more. She could not say for certain, nor did she care in the end, as it was a marvel regardless.

Ruth looked to Konoth and Devora, who nodded warmly in unison, and she began to reach for the axe and buckler, meaning to remove them first and then proceed to take the armor. She paused, looking with admiration on the craftsmanship of the early fashion in which the first equipment of the Faithguard was made, but feeling an unexplainable reluctance hanging over her. At first, she thought it was simply out of reverence. Even though the ancient knight had clearly given her his blessing, she couldn't help but feel a little off at the prospect of taking from the dead, even if she returned the items in due time. She also had a mild anxiety regarding the possibility of damaging the bones of the Exemplar in the process of removing the arms and armor.

However, after another moment's thought, she realized that she had begun to think of what Konoth had truly donned and wielded in the first days of his journey to protect Elukus and Sophia, and how she wished to see them, even if they were not hers to borrow. She turned to Konoth, smiling softly.

"I ..." she then started to laugh. "I don't suppose that you would've bothered to keep what you had before being officially knighted by the Temple. Why would you? By all accounts, these were what served you better in the end, and–"

Konoth silenced her with a friendly wave of his hand. He was smiling broadly. He nodded to his wife and they again raised their hands, lifting out from the coffin the stone slab upon which rested the Warrior Exemplar's bones. Setting it aside, Konoth gestured once more to the casket. Ruth looked in, placing a hand to her mouth in anticipation, and peered inside. Tears of wonder welled in her eyes, and as she wiped them away, she gazed in amazement at the simple gear that began Konoth's faithful and martial career. The heavy chainmail, covered by a long, draping jacket of sturdy hide, shone brilliantly within the coffin alongside boots and gloved bracers of hard leather. Alongside the crude, yet majestic armor were the woodcutter's axe and the large pot lid, the arms that the first Faithguard grabbed as he hurried to follow and protect the Blind Prophet and his wife on their journey to preach across Fidonhaal.

Ruth looked to Konoth. "Was this some sort of test? Am I supposed to take one or the other?"

Konoth laughed merrily. "No, milady. Either are yours to bear for the remainder of this quest. Take some from each set if you wish."

Ruth smiled. "One of them will be enough."

She carefully lifted the original articles of Konoth from the stone casket, starting with the axe and lid, which she rested caringly against the outside of the coffin. She then reverently bundled the armor in her arms. Her hands began to shake.

"I-I ... I can't believe I'm actually holding these," she sobbed in awe.

"Take them, Lady Ruth, and go with our blessing. Rise and fight for the faith, for all of Fidonhaal, against the foul darkness that now threatens it. Avenge your salpion, your father in all but blood, along with all others who have been cruelly slain by this vile hatred, and see that peace is restored to the world."

"I will, Sir Konoth. I will do this, or die in the effort. Thank you."

Konoth and Devora lifted their arms, reassembling the casket and covering it with earth as if it had never been disturbed. They each raised a hand in a gesture of benediction, and faded gently from sight.

Ruth stood in silence, rooted to the spot in wonder at what had happened. She then became aware of the steadily fading sunlight, and gently placing her newly gained gear aside, she quickly undressed in order to don it. Her mind raced in reflection of all that had just transpired, which then blurred with countless memories of the past and her wonderings of what lay ahead. She thought she heard a movement beside her, but feared nothing, as no creature would harm her on the Sacred

Isle. Once she was down to the shirt and pants that she wore under her armor, she turned to reach for the ancient armor of hide and chain.

It wasn't there.

Ruth gasped in worry and confusion, wondering for a split second if she placed the items elsewhere absentmindedly. She spun around, looking frantically, only to freeze in her steps and smile, tears of joy beginning to flow down her cheeks.

Verdok was before her, on one knee, holding up the armor, axe, and pot lid in a grand gesture of presentation.

"Might I assist my lady in donning her armor?" he asked with endearingly comical formality.

Ruth tried to laugh, but found herself breathless. At a loss for words, she took the ancient articles from her husband's hands, gently tossed them aside, and pulled Verdok close. They kissed deeply, silently, for one fleeting moment, after which Ruth started to tug playfully at the belt around Verdok's robes.

Xavier was right: there were a few things that added greatly to the feeling of wholeness that Karzynhaal bestowed upon those who visited it.

Part Six

The Battle of Genverdell

From Karzynhaal to Genverdell

163
9/20/4030 G.M.

RAAKMATHNA walked beside Emperor-Salpion Ranoth as they made their way to the herald-wing aviary and message room. A month and a day had passed since she felt the return of the power that she had lent to Sarah Stonefaith, thus alerting the empress of her archgeneral's death. After discussing her plans with Ranoth and her top officers of the Peacekeepers, it was agreed that if no word had been received by this morning, then the plans to enact a drastic defense of Genverdell would commence without delay.

They entered the aviary. It was empty but for one bird, which Raakmathna meant to send out to call all forces in Enmayar to rally at the capital. They then looked into the nook where the messages were received and read. There were no papers on the desk. The only other thing that was in the whole room was Captain Thomas, he who had at first led the watch on Queen Sheeva's household. He now stood as one of the chief officers of the Peacekeepers who maintained order in Genverdell and the surrounding region. His resolve for the cause of order was only now appearing to be challenged, for he now looked at the empress and her consort with eyes of dread.

Raakmathna approached him with Ranoth by her side. "Any news from Kellmayar, Captain Thomas?"

The young captain shook his head with eyes full of inner turmoil. "No ... no, my empress. No word from our forces, or the enemy's, as has been the case for over a moon."

"And from Janrenar?"

"No word from them as well. I fear you are right to suspect that our efforts have been gravely hindered at present, and with what you have told us of these 'Daughters of the East,' it would seem that they have set back our campaigns significantly, and will likely be making to come and confront us directly in the near future. That said, I cannot say for certain if that is the case, nor when to expect them."

"Which is why we must resort to what we have been discussing the whole of this past month. Immediately."

Captain Thomas lowered his head, his hands shaking as he wrung them together and attempted to steel himself for what was to come. "I ... I know it's for us ... all of us ... and the order that shall protect us ... but ... *everyone*? Everyone who isn't already among our numbers?"

"Yes. *Everyone.*"

Thomas sighed shakily, his eyes lifting to gaze into those of the empress. The young man's eyes were full of doubt. Raakmathna narrowed her eyes. She then saw horror, followed by the deepest, though still resigned and obedient, regret. The empress was deeply disappointed in the captain, seeing plainly that he now only stayed in his place out of resignation rather than true devotion. However, she also sensed he would indeed still follow through. It was enough, as far as it concerned her. And if not, she could simply assure his unquestioning obedience another way.

"Well," the empress said sharply, "do not just stand there gaping, Thomas. Call the other officers and their companies, and begin without delay."

Thomas, trembling where he stood, bowed numbly. "Yes ... my empress."

Raakmathna then went to the writing desk, beginning to write her orders to recall all Peacekeepers in Enmayar, while Ranoth opened the cage of the heraldwing that was set to carry it. The emperor-salpion gently held the Shanlof in his hand, standing attentively beside his empress as she wrote.

***

A new day dawned. Raakmathna and Ranoth stood on the balcony overlooking Genverdell. The morning was inconceivably silent after the previous day's unending cacophony, which ensued promptly following the empress's order. After an hour of looking upon the capital below, the two heard footsteps approaching. They turned to see Captain Thomas, though the lad seemed to have nearly aged by two score of years overnight. He nodded to them, his head slumping forward as he began to tremble and fold his arms tightly about himself. Despite the drowning silence that enveloped all, the captain's voice was barely audible.

"Th-the stakes for the barricades are be-being ... cut and fashioned as we s-speak, my empress. Th-they'll be ready when everything else is."

"Very good," Raakmathna said plainly, eyeing the captain with disdain for his change in fervor for the cause, which had endured so strongly since the beginning only to shatter utterly within twenty-four hours. "What about the mounds for the barricades? Are they being dug?"

"Th-they're beginning that as w-we ... as we speak, my empress."

"Excellent. Go and oversee the barricade preparations outside the southern walls. I would like that area to be the first that is fully ready if possible, in case we do not have enough time to completely ready everything before—"

"M-my empress ... I-I can't—"

"What sort of champion for order are you, Captain Thomas," the empress snapped harshly, "to fight so boldly and relentlessly for your people and the security of all things for so long, only to crumble at the hour you're needed most?"

A horrid howl suddenly poured from the captain's lips as he dropped to his knees.

"P-please, Em-empress!" Thomas bawled wretchedly, "I've f-followed you all this time without question, b-but w-what's n-now been done—"

"THOMAS!" Raakmathna barked pitilessly, silencing the broken officer's babbling. "I have no patience for turncoats now. Join your fellow Peacekeepers ... or the others. But willing or unwilling, you *will* continue to serve the All-Keeper and his cause for order. Zaron, Mavon, Kason, Balon, all damn four of them, and whatever combination of them that you care to imagine, *it does not matter*. It *never* mattered. It is all to show Onu the foolishness of his allowance for chaos, which he has always insisted on calling "freedom," and has always claimed to have permitted out of love for you pathetic creatures. And if Onu will not bow to reason, then we will see to it that you lot *will.*"

Silence enveloped all once more, broken only by the ragged breathing of Thomas, who could no longer even raise his voice enough to weep.

"Go to the south barricade trenches," the empress said flatly as she and Ranoth turned their sight back to the city below the castle, "and join your fellow warriors of order. Or ... stay where you are, and I will ... reassign you to join the others. Those are your choices. You have ten seconds. Take one or the other. *Now.*"

Five seconds passed, and Raakmathna heard the rattling of a dagger's sheath as the blade was drawn out of it by a trembling hand. The empress did not turn to look. She knew she had no need.

"Onu," Thomas's voice rasped out in a nearly silent whimper, "show me no mercy. I deserve not a drop."

The sound of ripping flesh echoed from behind the empress, immediately followed by the spattering of a torrent of blood upon the stone floor and a wretched gurgle. Another second passed, and the heavy thud of a falling body, along with the clanging of armor on stone, sounded loudly behind her.

Raakmathna and Ranoth turned, looking contemptibly upon the twitching body of Thomas as it fidgeted in a rapidly spreading pool of blood that fountained from his throat. Seconds passed and the captain lay still, his bloody dagger still gripped tightly in his hand.

"The fool," Raakmathna sighed wearily as she raised the captain's body with upraised hands. The captain's eyes were now lifeless and free of doubt or regret. Fully obedient.

"Come with us, Captain Thomas," said the empress as she put an arm around Ranoth's waist. "We have much to do today, and we would greatly appreciate your escort."

The following days were spent meticulously combing the city of Genverdell, the arms of Raak-mathna and Ranoth raised for nearly every waking second.

164
9/25/4030 G.M.

VERDOK walked at a steady pace beside Ruth, as the two had done for the past six days since their reunion. They stayed near the tombs of Konoth and Devora for their first night together in two moons, having slept together under a great tree that stood just a little way from the hallowed site. They awoke late the following morning, letting themselves indulge in the complete tranquility of Karzynhaal before finally bringing themselves to depart and make their way to the Heartroot Tree, where the rest of their companions now surely awaited them.

They walked long, but easy hours before resting each night, and passed the time telling one another of all that had happened on their journeys. By the time the sun had reached its peak on their sixth day of walking, Ruth had learned of Donovan's injuries, the battle of Benhotha, and Verdok's inner anguish at the times he had killed. Verdok, in turn, now knew of Lerannu's turbulent reunion and experiences with her father and mother, the battle of Zefiil, and the great aid that the Elect had received from the Trichynay and their leaders, Ranye and Xavier. They comforted one another's heart of whatever had troubled them since they had parted. Now, together and having learned that their missions had thus far proved fruitful, they were eager to rejoin their companions and meet their new allies.

"An Ecclesian," Verdok said in quiet awe as he reflected on what Ruth had told him about High Shaman Xavier. "An honest-to-Onu Ecclesian. Surely, we are blessed indeed to have one in our company. How many do you think are in all of Fidonhaal right now?"

Ruth shrugged and smiled. "Maybe *just* enough to count on both hands? Maybe?"

Verdok smiled. "That's probably a fair guess. Maybe even 'generous' is the more appropriate word. I'm looking forward to meeting him. Well, meeting him in person, that is."

The high priest sighed in wonder and gently put an arm about his wife.

"We truly are living a legend."

Ruth wordlessly drew herself closer to her husband, brushing her cheek against his neck.

"It was amazing beyond words just to see the three of you being marked by the Elect's Brand before my very eyes. Add to that the aid of the great tribe, an alliance of nations, the help of a couple from a renowned order, an Ecclesian and seer to assist us, and now us making our way to see and speak with a Phoenix. For all the sorrow and trouble we've weathered, I do feel that we've been truly blessed."

Verdok had no sooner finished speaking when he and Ruth looked up and saw Karzynu standing in view, lightly obscured by the trees that stood before it. They gasped and stared transfixed at the shimmering and multicolored bark of the massive tree, and soon saw a great shadow resting over the boughs above. The Phoenix was waiting, as were, no doubt, their companions. Looking to one another and taking each other's hand, Verdok and Ruth sprinted together across the short remaining distance to the hallowed tree, eager and hopeful for what was to come.

Karzynu, the Heartroot, stood with colossal majesty at the heart of the Sacred Isle, its glittering bark a myriad of the four colors of the Fidons' fur. Its leaves, of the brightest and liveliest green, abounded upon and cascaded from its branches. Passing the last of the trees and entering the open space that Karzynu occupied, Verdok and Ruth halted in their tracks and gazed in brief silence at the sight. Their eyes then drifted to a far-reaching branch to their left and widened at the great, fiery-hued bird that rested upon it, looking down at something below.

Ruth and Verdok followed the Phoenix's gaze, and were gladdened at the sight of their companions and allies resting there, conversing with Mercilaar and one another. Calling out to their friends, the priest and the knight ran together to rejoin them, to the warm and cheerful welcome of all. The six friends embraced one another, and then Ruth and Verdok, looking up to the Phoenix, found themselves at a loss for words, contenting themselves to simply nod their heads respectfully to the great bird.

"Mercilaar," the two acknowledged simply as they continued to gaze up at him.

The Phoenix nodded in return. "You must be Lady Ruth and Sir Verdok Pionaar. Your companions have been telling me about you and themselves while we waited for you to join us. I have also learned a fair measure of the world's plight thanks to the talks I've briefly shared with Sir Xavier for the past several months."

Mercilaar bowed his head and spread his wings in a gesture of reverence and respect.

"It is a wondrous honor," said the bird to Verdok and Ruth, "to be blessed with the opportunity to both meet and aid the Elect, their companions and their allies. I have been discussing the plan of things with your friends, and given that and the ancient words of Elukus, I am confident not only in our victory when all has passed, but that we will be able to make for the last battle soon. Sorrenarn ships have patrolled the waters around Karzynhaal for over a month, and with the arrival of you and your companions, and going by what they've told me, it should not be long before we see a fine gathering of vessels from the West and the South joining us."

Mercilaar glanced about the company gathered below.

"Thus, if it please you all, I propose that we make for the northern shore and send word to all incoming ships to gather there. Apart from a few vessels to keep watch around the isle and inform the other ships coming to join us, we should be ready to embark almost immediately once we have gathered all who will come to us. I will fly ahead to make sure that all remains well, and will await your arrival. Soon, Onu willing, we shall begin the last part of this journey."

The six companions, and those in their company, looked briefly at one another to see if any of them had something to add or some reason to propose another course of action. All nodded toward Ruth and Verdok in agreement, and the knight and the priest gazed back up to the crimson bird of fire.

"Very well," said Ruth. "We'll begin making our way to the north shore soon. Many thanks in advance for your aid and companionship, Sir Mercilaar."

The ends of Mercilaar's mouth, visible from the sides of his large beak, turned upwards in a kindly smile. The Phoenix nodded once more, and amidst gasps of awe from all in the company, he flapped his wings, leapt off the branch of the Heartroot, and swiftly rose in the air, nimbly navigating the branches of Karzynu and the neighboring trees as he soared northward.

165

9/25/4030 G.M.

LERANNU and her companions looked on as Mercilaar flew out of sight. The mage's heart had steadily grown stronger and more resolved for what lay ahead since she overcame her catatonic state from before. That said, the sight of their newfound, mystical ally departing ahead of them was easily the most uplifting event she had yet experienced over the course of the mission, as well as one of the most wondrous in all her life. Once the great bird of red and gold had passed from view, Lerannu looked to those who had gathered under Karzynu with her. She took the hands of her father and King Allor, and pulled them to either side of her as she made to walk northward.

"Well, it's looking to probably be another six-day walk, give or take," she said with a growing sense of cheer. "We'll have plenty of time to chat along the way, as well as while we wait for everyone else coming to help us. Shall we go on?"

The party agreed by simply following her, apparently feeling no need to voice it. They walked together for a while in silence, simply marveling at the Holy Isle's beauty. Lerannu gently let go of her father's hand and leaned closely to Allor, wrapping her arm around him and resting her head on his shoulder. The mage glanced at her father as she leaned on Allor, and glimpsed him looking at the pair with a quiet smile. Back when the company was passing time beneath Karzynu as they waited for Ruth and Verdok, Lerannu and Allor had told each other of what had happened on their journeys since they parted ways at Benevor. Though they still did not go beyond what they agreed upon back in Norkoth, both did much to comfort and strengthen one another for the journey's approaching end, and Roniil, having learned of the promising bond between them, had readily voiced his happiness for them.

That night, Lerannu awoke to the sound of a quiet conversation on the other side of the party's little camp. The mage quietly got up and caringly made her way toward the voices. It was Roniil and Allor, conversing beneath a large, sheltering tree.

"I know I've already said it," Roniil said kindly, "but just know that, whatever comes to pass, you have my blessing. In so many ways, it seems absurd to be dwelling on such things right now, with all that's been happening. But with what the two of you have told me, and with what I've seen her endure, I'm just happy to know there are still things that make her smile."

Roniil's voice, having grown increasingly emotional as he spoke, now broke into a quiet sob.

"Sh-she ... she's just been through so much ... and I was there for her for only a little of it."

"She still loves you," Allor said comfortingly.

"I know. And I've always loved her ... but I failed her, and her mother."

"It's done. It was done a long time ago. We all err, but neither one misstep nor a thousand are themselves enough to kill the good we might still do, nor the love between us and Onu."

Allor embraced Roniil, patting his back kindly. "I would be glad to count you as a father, if by Onu's grace she and I are able to bind ourselves together."

"And I would be glad to count you as a son."

Lerannu almost made to approach and speak to them, but after a moment's reflection, she quietly turned away and crept back to her bedroll, leaving her father and her love to continue the conversation as one man to another.

***

The company reached the northern shore of Karzynhaal six days later on the third day of Yorpar, passing through the remaining trees and stepping into clear view of the shore and ocean about an hour before noon. They looked on with heightened spirits at the many ships anchored offshore. The sigils on their sails hailed from all three of the allied nations, though most of those presently gathered were still those from Sorrenar, as the West and the South were still working to gather and send their forces. As the company looked on, a large shadow swept over them, and they looked up to see Mercilaar passing above. A mighty, fur-raising call sounded from the Phoenix's beak, and the great crimson bird swiftly landed on the shore in front of Lerannu and her companions. The Phoenix bowed honorably, and then addressed them.

"I have looked over each direction of the seas. Many more vessels are coming, but from what I understand of all that's happened, we will need to wait a while still before we've gathered enough forces to us."

"How much longer?" Lerannu asked apprehensively as she stepped forward.

Mercilaar looked into her eyes, his own bearing both patience and worry. "Unless we are explicitly informed beforehand that we have all who have been sent, I'd say until the end of this month."

The mage and her companions drew a heavy breath in unison. Lerannu dreaded to think of what horrors might still pass within that span of time, even if such things would now be mostly confined to Enmayar. That said, she also understood that Raakmathna and her forces were not to be met underprepared. She looked at her friends and her sisters in destiny, and saw plainly on their faces that they were of similar mind. Lerannu looked to Mercilaar and nodded.

"Very well," she said. "Thank you for looking ahead for us, Mercilaar."

Lerannu turned to her companions and returned to Allor's side, embracing him.

"I suppose there's not much else for it, other than to wait. Apart from any words we might have with our allies."

"Aye," said Ruth. "There's plenty to discuss with them. Would you happen to know if there's anyone in particular with whom we ought to begin talking strategy, Mercilaar?"

The Phoenix smiled, then pointed with a wing to a grand ship anchored close to shore just a short walk away. "Queen Xenia and King Viktor of Sorrenar are aboard that vessel and have been eagerly waiting for you. My call as I flew over you was to announce your arrival. I imagine they would greatly desire to speak with you as soon as possible."

"Thank you, Mercilaar," said Allor. "We'll speak again soon, I hope?"

"Of course," Mercilaar assured him as he stretched his wings. "I'll simply make another pass around the seas and see how things are looking. I'll let you know of any particulars when I return."

The company began to make their way to the royal warship of Sorrenar as Mercilaar began to flap his wings. As she walked past him, Lerannu thought she caught from the corner of her eye a friendly, knowing grin and wink from the Phoenix, seemingly directed at someone behind her. The mage glanced back and saw High Shaman Xavier's glowing eyes focused directly at the great bird, a small smile on his lips. Smiling and shaking her head at the eccentricities shared by Xavier and the Phoenix, Lerannu continued walking alongside her companions, trusting that whatever the bird and the shaman knew would be revealed in due time.

They soon reached the shore near the ship, where longboats were neatly beached, and were greeted by several high officers of the North's army. One of them bowed and beckoned to the company to follow him, gesturing to a large tent pitched near the shore.

"King Viktor and Queen Xenia are in there," he explained, "going over messages from the patrolling ships to make sure everything is in order. They'll want to speak to you immediately and–"

"FATHER!" cried two young voices in unison.

Lerannu's eyes darted toward the direction of the voices, which came from the entrance to the northern king and queen's tent. The mage's heart leapt at the sight of Samuel and Talrah as they bolted from the tent and leapt into Allor's arms. The King of Enmayar, having started to weep the instant his children came into view, embraced and kissed them while the rest of the company looked on. Lerannu glanced back at Xavier, seeing him smiling warmly as he held Ranye's hand. The mage was about to ask the high shaman if this was what the exchanged smile between him and Mercilaar was about, when suddenly Allor spoke to his children.

"I'm so glad to see you two again, but ... but why would Viktor and Xenia bring you along with them? For all they knew, they could've gotten caught up in a battle on the sea or something. You should've been kept back in Norkoth, for your own good–"

"That's what Viktor and Xenia did, Father," said Talrah quietly. "Well, what they meant to do."

Allor stared levelly at his daughter and son, with his lips forming a curious smile only thinly masked with disapproval. "I see. And how, pray tell, did you manage to go against that? I hope you didn't cause some awful scene in the castle over it?"

"Not at all, King Allor," said Queen Xenia as she and King Viktor approached. "One could not have raised finer, more mannered and mature children than yours. They've gotten on wonderfully with our family while we were riding with you to Benevor, and when we got back and told them of how things went, they took it very well, all things considered. They made no fuss whatsoever when we departed."

The northern king and queen looked at Samuel and Talrah with sly smiles.

"They just quietly dressed up in plain clothes and managed to sneak into one of our supply wagons. I don't know how they managed to go unnoticed for the entire trip. I'm convinced they managed to persuade a little help from a few in our company to keep things quiet, though they haven't yet revealed to us how they did it. By the time we found them out, we were halfway across the sea to Karzynhaal, so there was no point to protest or turn around."

Sam and Tally shifted on their feet, their eyes looking at the ground with only a touch of discomfort. Allor laughed, shaking his head incredulously as he embraced his children even closer.

"We were first found out by Fargon, Queen Xenia, on the road about a week or so out of Norkoth."

Xenia and Viktor looked with a raised eyebrow and a smug smile at the officer who was leading the Elect's company. He looked back at them with a resigned, sheepish face.

"Is that so?" Xenia asked. "Well, I suppose that explains a lot. For all his gruffness, he's always been a big softie."

"I'm sorry, my queen and king," the officer mumbled as a lightly pink hue began to show under the white of his fur. "I should've said something, but—"

"No harm was done, Fargon," Viktor said plainly. "It looks like this may have been for the better, anyway."

Allor nodded and held his children close. After a few moments, Talrah and Samuel came and hugged Lerannu, and warmly greeted each of the others of the original company as well as their newfound allies. Naturally, they were most intrigued by Xavier.

"What do you say we go and talk in the tent," the high shaman suggested, "or perhaps the ship, if there'd be more room for us to speak there? Going by Mercilaar's word, we've got a fine little stretch of time to talk things over, and we've got plenty to talk about."

Agreeing, the company went into the tent and began discussing the courses of action for the final journey and battles to come.

166
10/28/4030 G.M.

MIRA opened her eyes, stirring from sleep at Donovan's touch. It was the last morning of Yorpar. The allies of the Elect and their companions had spent the month slowly but steadily gathering in greater number along the northern coast of Karzynhaal. They had spent the days and weeks discussing possible strategies, as well as what further news they were able to glean from the world. When they were not doing that, the company and their allies often reached out to one another, whatever their familiarity, seeking and giving advice and encouraging words for what was to come. Mira often prayed that their numbers, and what knowledge they had of the situation, would be enough to overcome it. She saw plainly that she was not alone in doing so.

Two days ago, they were met with what they were told were the last of the ships and soldiers that would be sent from Kellmayar for the time being, having been informed personally by King Dominik and Queen Fida. The same had been the case for Sorrenar's aid three days before that. Now, waking and rising as Donovan helped her up, Mira dressed and stepped out of her tent, seeing a large group of sails with the Janrenar insignia. They were sitting a short way apart from the rest of the assembled armada. The huntress held her husband closely, looking over the vast assembly of ships as she rested her head on his shoulder.

"I guess this is the last of what Janrenar has sent us?" she asked, both encouraged by the sight of the many ships and anxious for the impending conflict.

"Queen Vita and King Salos came with that fleet," said Donovan, "and they said there were a few more making their way here, but otherwise, yes. Allor and the others told them they mean to sail tomorrow at first light, whether the last ones are with us by then or not. Vita and Salos said they're going to leave one ship here to wait for them if they're not with us when we leave, so they can let them know of our intended course and accompany them as they work to catch up."

"Have we decided on a final course? I remember a few spots being mentioned, but I don't think I ever heard whether we fully came to a decision yet."

"We did. I wasn't so sure if that had been settled either until I asked this morning. We decided to go with landing at Kannah and its bay. Greenharbor and its bay is of adequate size for us as well, but it would take a bit more time and maneuvering than it would with Kannah. Besides that, the way to Genverdell will be shorter and more direct than what we would've had if we took one of the other ways. We've waited long enough ... I'm afraid too long. We all agreed that any time we can save at this point, the better."

Donovan sighed and kissed Mira's neck.

"Of course, I also worry that we might doom things by trying to go faster."

"We can't get caught up in thinking like that. We might as well do nothing if that happens."

"Aye. That said, do you have anything to say about the planned course? I'm sure they'll still hear out any ideas if–"

"No," Mira said gently with a shake of her head. "All I'm concerned for now is finally moving on. It's time to end this ... whatever that ends up meaning."

Mira and Donovan continued to look on at the sail-laden horizon as they held each other close.

"All that said, I'll miss being here."

Donovan laughed and kissed her. "Me, too. When we finally put a stop to all this, what do you say we come back here and stay a little longer?"

"That sounds wonderful," Mira answered with a loving lick of her husband's ear.

***

By noon, Allor and all the other monarchs had finished discussing their plans for sailing to Kannah and their march to Genverdell. Mercilaar, as if on cue, descended from the air and landed on the shore before the Elect and their company. He nodded courteously to the group, his eyes alight with a fiery sense of purpose and duty.

"I see that Janrenar's leaders are now with us," the Phoenix said in a tone of high spirits. "Does that mean that all sent to aid us have indeed arrived within the time I speculated?"

"Almost," Allor said as he went on to explain the situation.

Hearing of the planned course and that all but a few remaining ships were now gathered, Mercilaar breathed a deep sigh of resolve as he heard that the plan to leave the next day was unchanged.

"Very good," he said as he turned to face the Daughters of the East. The Phoenix gazed intently at them, grinning.

Mira smiled. "What's with the smile, my friend?"

"I just figured it might be a good idea for you three to get at least a little acquainted with your primary means of transport for this part of the journey."

"Alright," said the huntress as she turned back to the gathered monarchs and officers. "And which ship would that be?"

Mira heard a gentle shifting of feathers behind her. She turned and saw Mercilaar offering the Elect a lowered wing. The huntress was speechless.

"You're not serious?" Ruth asked with an incredulous laugh.

"Their victory will be brought on wings of fire," Mercilaar recited alongside Xavier, who was standing right behind the Elect.

Mira, Lerannu, and Ruth looked briefly at one another without a word, their awe broken when Xavier moved aside and let his daughter, Layna, and her husband, Garthon, come forward. Between them and two other members of the great tribe, they carried a large, three-seated saddle. At the front of each seat was fixed a set of large handles, and six footholds were fixed onto the saddle's bottom. A large cloth was sewn under the bottom to make the saddle more comfortable for Mercilaar's back. As the tribespeople approached the Phoenix, he gently spread his wings and lowered his body. The saddle was soon strapped securely onto the great bird's back, and thanking the tribespeople as they stepped away, he returned his gaze to the Daughters of the East, looking at them expectantly.

Wordlessly, the three women approached the Phoenix and carefully climbed onto his back, sitting securely and comfortably on the uniquely devised saddle. Ruth sat in the front, Mira in the middle, and Lerannu in the back. The three looked to Xavier and those with him as the high shaman spoke.

"Mercilaar and I talked about it the first night we spent on the shore here. We've had people

~ 372 ~

working on it very carefully since then; it should be good to go."

"I'll say!" said Mira approvingly as she gently shifted about in her seat. "What about you, Sir Mercilaar? Are we too heavy?"

"Not at all," said the Phoenix warmly.

"What about my armor," asked Ruth, "or my axe or shield? None of its weight or shape is prodding at you through the cloth or anything, is it?"

"Everything's fine to me," Mercilaar assured the Faithguard knight. "You three should only need to worry about holding on tight. As we're sailing along, I can lower myself into the waters and you can board any ship you need to if you wish to discuss anything with someone on board, or simply wish to take a rest from flight. Once we reach Genverdell ..."

The Phoenix gazed out to the northern horizon, past the army of sails and into the blue sky beyond.

"Once we reach Genverdell, I'll be able to take you straight to the castle, presuming that's where we'll find that horrid empress. If she isn't there, we'll fly over the city until we find her, or even over all the East, all the world if need be, until we find her."

"Very well," Ruth said as she patted Mercilaar's back. "A thousand thanks for your help."

Mira and Lerannu echoed the knight's thanks, and followed it with thanks to Xavier and the tribespeople who fashioned the saddle for them.

"Shall we see how well this works?" asked the Phoenix.

"Yes!" Mira answered in near-childlike glee. "I'm ready when you are!"

"As am I," said Ruth.

"Me, too!" said Lerannu.

Mercilaar gently drew himself up to his full height, and after flapping his large wings a few times, he began to jog down the tideline, steadily gaining speed, and lifted off from the ground.

Mira gripped her handles with knuckle-straining tightness, her heart racing and her mind swimming with exhilarated wonder at the sensation of flying above the ocean. She, along with Ruth and Lerannu, were soon laughing and cheering as they raced above the gathered ships. The sailors on board cheered uproariously at the awe-inspiring sight of the Daughters of the East riding on the back of one of the great birds of flame.

***

Mira awoke the next morning, the first day of Yorparon, a few moments before first light. She turned over in her bedroll to look silently at Donovan in the last few moments of quiet they had before the journey to Enmayar commenced. The bard slowly opened his eyes, looked at his wife, and smiled.

"Did you sleep alright?" he asked.

"Just fine," she answered. "You?"

"Same. I just wondered if what's coming kept you up or anything."

"No. I was worried that might happen when I first settled in, too, but it turned out alright."

"Good."

"I guess you helped me ease my mind a bit," Mira said with a grin. "Like always."

Donovan breathed a light chuckle. "You did the same for me. Like always."

Mira snuggled up against Donovan, and the two tilted their heads toward the faint eastern glow they could just make out through the tent's canvas.

"Any minute now," Donovan said with a sigh.

"Mmm-hm."

"You three were an amazing sight yesterday, riding Mercilaar. Seeing you three above us and watching over us, it'll do wonders for the troops. And for me."

"Glad to hear. It was amazing to fly, but I'm not exactly looking forward to it as we get closer to Enmayar."

"I know, but you have all of us at your back. You, Ruth, Lera ... you've been graced with a destiny that has been given and blessed by Onu, and long expected. If we hold true to each other, we will not fail in the end. I promise."

Mira grinned and laughed lightly. "I wasn't meaning it like that."

Donovan looked quizzically at her.

"It's the next-to-last month of the year, honey. It's going to start getting cooler over there now. How do you think the wind's going to feel when we're flying however-high over you all?"

Donovan rolled his eyes and playfully nudged Mira's shoulder. The huntress giggled and tussled her husband's hair as she rolled over onto him and pinned him down.

Then the horns sounded from the ships.

Donovan petted her rump. "You'll be sure to descend from the heavens and visit us on the ships from time to time, won't you, dear guardian of Fidonhaal?"

"Of course."

"Tonight?" the bard asked sultrily.

"Mm-hmm."

They were on their feet, dressed, and making their way through the camp a moment later. Within minutes, they had joined Ruth and Lerannu, along with Verdok and Allor, as the men prepared to get into the longboat that would take them to their ship. Mira and Donovan looked on as they watched Allor and Lerannu embracing Princess Talrah and Prince Samuel.

"No stowing away this time, alright?" Allor asked with a tearful chuckle.

"Yes, Father," said Talrah.

"I hate to leave you two again, but it's for your own good. It was last time, too, but it's far more so this time."

"We know," Samuel said as he hugged his father.

"Be good to Layna and Garthon, alright? They're good friends of Lera and the others, and Xavier's left them in charge of the other people here that are staying to keep you safe."

"We will," the prince and princess said in unison.

Allor embraced his children one more time, then climbed into the longboat with Donovan and Verdok.

***

They sailed for eighteen days, the voyage beginning with the Daughters of the East mounting up onto Mercilaar's back. The three sisters in destiny, along with their companions and the monarchs of the three allied nations, each spoke encouragingly to all gathered around them. After this, the Phoenix called out a loud, gallant cry and raised his wings. A sudden gale blew over the Holy Isle's northern shore, and the armada, with both oars and sails in full action, easily glided toward the northeast, unhindered by the doldrums.

Mira, Ruth, and Lerannu flew for hours above the massive fleet, intermittently boarding one vessel or another to converse with their companions and allies as Mercilaar glided gracefully into the sea and came up to the ship's side. The three Elect rejoined Donovan, Verdok, and Allor aboard their warship each evening, not keen on trying to sleep in the saddle while in midair. They would mount up again the following morning. The armada appeared to be graced with a blessing from Onu and Vente, having had good, consistent winds each day of the voyage.

Then came the eighteenth of Yorparon. The first lookouts called out their sighting of land, which echoed across all the fleet and was met with high-spirited cheers.

The news was immediately followed by word of a vast armada of grey-sailed vessels, both proper warships and ships that had been commandeered and repurposed, that sat in the harbor of Kannah and the surrounding waters. This news was met with silence.

Mira and her sisters of fate, flying well above them at the time, saw the full scene before the entirety of the lookouts' news could fully reach all the ships. Mira sighed painfully when she heard the cheers, and the following deathly silence. She patted Ruth on the back, and the knight looked back at her in the saddle.

"I guess we should've thought it couldn't go *that* easy, huh?" she asked with a rueful smile.

The knight returned the grim smile. "I guess not." She turned and leaned toward Mercilaar's ears. "Any ideas, Sir Mercilaar?"

"Of course," said the Phoenix plainly, "and quite straightforward ones, if I do say so myself."

"Will they involve a bit of that fire breath of yours?"

"Indeed. And perhaps Lady Greenheart's arrows and Lady Stonefaith's magic, particularly from wind, to tear down their masts and such, if I might suggest it."

Ruth looked back to Mira and Lerannu, smiling confidently as she shifted in the saddle and raised her pot-lid shield to guard her front. "My axe won't be of much use up here, but I'll do my best to keep you two covered from any arrows those grey-coats might try to send our way."

Mira nodded as she readied her longbow. She glanced back to Lerannu, who was draining a small flask of reinvigorating tonic as she flexed her hands. The mage then readied her borrowed Trichynay staff and closed her eyes, breathing steadily as she prepared for her task.

"Are you sure you're up for it, Lera?" the huntress asked. "Taking out a mast ... I don't know how much that would take out of someone, but I'd imagine it would be a lot."

"I suppose so," Lerannu replied calmly, "but it can be done, and several times over, if one can stay focused enough. I feel I've got this, Mira. Thank you."

"Very well; you know yourself best."

Lerannu, her eyes still closed, grinned. "Besides, I've already taken a small precaution."

The mage pointed at the handles of her seat, where some rigging-rope had been tied about her waist and secured to the handles.

"The first night after we set sail, I thought it might be a good idea, so I asked around for some spare rope. I've been tying myself to the saddle each day just in case something happened. I can't say I was expecting it to be something like this, but there it is."

"I haven't even noticed," said Mira with a laugh.

"Just focus on noticing your targets when we get to those grey ships," Lerannu said as she patted the huntress's shoulder. "That's all we need from you right now."

Mira smiled, then turned to resolutely face the nearing grey armada as she set a shaft to her string. She and her sisters in destiny, along with all their companions and allies, may not have given much thought to the prospect of encountering an enemy armada, especially one of such size. But the grey-sailed fleet wasn't expecting to deal with a Phoenix.

Mercilaar raced through the air and reached the grey-cloak fleet in under a minute, leaving the allied fleet to catch up after he and the three women had dealt the first blows. Crowing a mighty war cry, the Phoenix drew a deep breath and let fly a great ball of flame upon a clustered group of grey-coat ships. The fire struck true, causing the stricken vessel to explode and begin sinking immediately as its splinters struck the ships around it and the crews on board. The fire that flew out from the explosion rained down upon the neighboring ships, making quick work of their sails and decks. Mercilaar cawed menacingly at the grey fleet, swiftly flying over them and focusing on another group of ships as arrows and bolts began to fly up at him and his mounted companions.

Ruth shifted in her saddle, holding up her large iron pot-lid in an effort to shield Mira and Lerannu to the best of her abilities. One shaft from a passing ship struck the shield and shattered to pieces, blocked from hitting the huntress just in time. As Mercilaar slowed his flight to focus on the targets ahead, Mira began to pick her own targets as she flew past other ships. Never having had the experience of firing from above on the back of a Phoenix, Mira was not at all surprised that more than a few of her shots strayed quite far from the mark. But she had fired at moving targets, and whilst on the move, many times before, and she was grimly satisfied to see that more than a few also struck true.

The Phoenix let fly another ball of fire, which inflicted devastation similar to the first, and was turning about to seek out another cluster of ships. It was then that Lerannu began to seek targets upon which to unleash the fury of wind. Mira was just about to fire at another grey-coat below when she started at the earsplitting crack that sounded behind her. Her grasp on the bowstring was loosed, and she missed her shot. The huntress turned to look back and saw one of the grey-sailed masts come crashing down upon the deck of its ship, as well as the grey-clad soldiers that had failed to get out of the way. Mira looked to see if the mage was still in fit condition, exchanging grim nods of acknowledgement and commendation when it was clear that she was still fully focused and energized. Another metallic echo sounded in front of Mira as Ruth blocked an enemy arrow, and she snapped her attention back to the targets below.

Mercilaar and his mounted companions made ten passes over the entirety of the silver-sailed fleet before their allies reached the fray. By then, at least a score and five of the grey-cloaks' warships had sunk, and a good ten were without their masts. Uncounted grey-coats, by arrows, splinters or falling masts and flames, had fallen. The first of the allied fleet began to pass through the devastated armada, firing arrows and bolts, throwing fire bottles, and even boarding a few of the enemy's vessels that still stood manned. As the naval battle began its final act, the Phoenix and his passengers turned back and descended into the sea, heading for the ship where Donovan and the others were staying. As Mercilaar splashed into the waves, he grunted irritably.

"Are you alright?" Mira heard Lerannu ask behind her.

"Yes, I'll be fine," the Phoenix said as he began to swim toward the ship, his face wincing with each paddling of his legs. "I got hit a few times underneath, but nowhere vital. The ocean is stinging quite sharply, however."

"You can go to shore once we get on board, if you'd like," said Mira as she patted the great bird's side. "We'll still be in the water for a while, and there's checking the port to see if it's clear or if it needs to be secured from the grey-coats. You can clear out a while and see to those wounds. No need to sit in the seawater."

"I appreciate the offer, Lady Greenheart, but I'll be alright."

Mercilaar swam up to the side of Donovan's ship, and Mira, Ruth, and Lerannu climbed off and came aboard as the Phoenix stayed beside the vessel. The huntress hugged her husband tightly, as did Ruth with Verdok and Lerannu with Allor. Donovan spoke softly into her ear.

"That was a sight for the ages, love."

The company looked on at the grim scene of impending victory, watching the rest of the fleet make their way through the grey armada and put down the remaining vessels and troops, setting each remaining ship alight as they finished clearing them.

It was just past dusk when they docked at the port in Kannah. The town was quiet as the grave.

167
11/18/4030 G.M.

RUTH and her companions cautiously stepped off their ship, weapons at the ready as they steadily made their way off the docks and into the town. Other ships had docked around them, and companies of the allied soldiers were joining the Elect and spreading out into Kannah as they made to confirm the area's security. Not another grey-cloak was to be found, and the streets were empty. Nothing, neither words nor attacks, came from the buildings as the allies combed the town, though they were yet to investigate them internally.

A nerve-racking hour slowly passed by, and the knight, her companions, and the leading officers of the investigating soldiers met up in the town square. One of them, from the Janrenarn forces, stepped forward and made his report.

"None of my company have seen a soul on the streets, nor have any of the other squads that we've checked with. We are preparing to investigate within the buildings."

"I'll go with you," the Faithguard knight said plainly as Mira and Lerannu came to her side with their weapons ready.

The southern officer nodded and called his soldiers together as Ruth kissed Verdok, who, wearied by the day's battle, had decided to stay at the square and rest with King Allor. Donovan, on the other hand, readied his bow and went to Mira's side. Once the company was ready, the officer directed them down a road and began pointing out buildings. He split the company into squads, directing them to take up positions at the entrances of the houses and buildings. When he and his personal squad, which included Donovan and the Elect, had taken positions around a large general goods shop, the officer looked about at his separated squads, signaled a countdown, and ordered them to enter the buildings.

Ruth took a defensive stance beside the soldier tasked with opening their assigned door. She swallowed anxiously as the soldier attempted to open the door normally. It was locked. Ruth looked up and down the surrounding street, seeing several squads enter their buildings effortlessly while others began to kick down the doors. A resounding crack of splintering wood and snapping metal brought her attention back to the door in front of her, and she and her companions carefully entered the shop as the soldier who broke open the door ushered them in.

The knight, with Lerannu and Mira on either side of her, carefully examined the seemingly empty room alongside the soldiers. As the trio neared the back of the room, Ruth tripped over a small package on the floor and veered sharply forward. Trying to halt her fall, she realized that she was going to go down as she half ran, half fell toward a large shelf that stood directly in front of her. She braced for impact, trusting the shelf and the wall to keep her from fully crashing to the floor.

She slammed against the shelf, and the knight gasped in surprise as she felt the shelf fall completely backwards, as though there was no wall where the shelf had stood. She flew through the doorway that the shelf had concealed. Screams and cries of alarm sounded all around her, and as she looked up, she saw a group of Zarons huddled in the back room as they looked at her fearfully. One of them, whom Ruth guessed to be the shopkeeper from her manner of dress, cautiously stepped forward and helped the knight onto her feet.

"W-what are you doing here?" she stammered worriedly. "You're not one of those Peacekeepers, I see, but are you with those who came in from the sea?"

Ruth was just about to explain when the woman and the others hiding in the room cried out in panic as several of the allied soldiers peered into the room. The soldiers tensed, seeming on the edge of attacking, but kept themselves in check and lowered their weapons when it became clear that the people hiding were civilians. When they realized that the soldiers weren't looking to harm them, the shopkeeper and the others stepped forward, looking anxiously at Ruth and the others.

"What were you doing here?" Ruth asked calmly. She looked at the shopkeeper with intense incredulity. "You all haven't been hiding in here since this whole madness started, have you?"

"N-no, milady. We went into hiding when we saw you all coming in from the sea and destroying that fleet."

"Why is that? We're here to help you all, to put a stop to this."

"W-we all panicked, milady. We didn't consider that there might have been Zarons amongst you all, at least not full-bodied ones."

Ruth laughed as she gently took the shopkeeper's hand and began to lead her and the others out into the front of the shop, where all the company could see them. It was a friendly laugh, though heavy with confusion. "Why would that be? Did you all think that you were the only Zarons who were against Raakmathna's actions?"

"N-no, milady. N-not at all ... but ... we didn't know if ..."

The shopkeeper and the other civilians were now in the front of the room, looking anxiously at the soldiers who stood all around them, their fur varying of all the four colors and in a myriad of patterns. Ruth's heart felt a sudden, stabbing pain as she began to realize the civilians' reasoning before the shopkeeper had finished explaining.

"We didn't know if ... if you all would have known, or understood," said the shopkeeper as she looked worriedly at the other soldiers.

The faces of the soldiers varied drastically from one to the other. Some were of pained offense, some were of outrage boiling just below the skin, and others seemed to be at least somewhat empathetic. Each of them looked at one another, however, and soon all looked at the shopkeeper with a saddened understanding. Ruth's ears flattened as she took in the depressing thought.

"I understand," she said sadly as she turned back to the shopkeeper. "In fact, as my companions and I were out getting help, there was a moment when something like that actually happened to me."

The Faithguard knight then told her and the others of the incident when she and her Elect sisters first encountered the Trichynay Tribe, where one of the tribesmen fired an arrow at her and Lerannu out of a quickly ingrained distrust toward all Zarons that he didn't know personally. The soldiers murmured as they began to recount similar incidents they had experienced, witnessed, or perpetrated, and Ruth put a gentle hand on the shopkeeper's shoulder.

"But everyone here now knows what's been going on," the knight assured her. "Before we could explain everything to them, there was indeed some suspicion that all Zarons were in on this horrid plot. But not anymore. All of us here have learned that this is just another attempt by evil to divide and destroy us, and now we are readying to stop it."

The shopkeeper nodded, her face awash with tears as she embraced Ruth and wept.

"W-we didn't want to have anything to do with this."

"We know."

"Th-they would have executed us if we didn't—"

"We know."

Ruth, Lerannu, and Mira, and all the rest of the company calmly led the shopkeeper and the others out onto the road, gathering them at the square. They passed by several other companies with civilians in tow, and it seemed that the experiences among them were not unlike what had just passed between Ruth's squad and those in the shop.

***

It was just past midnight, and the stars and the waning moon stood high overhead of the port and town as the people of Kannah listened to King Allor relay the tale of their journey. They gasped in awe at the revelation of the Daughters of the East, as well as the alliance between the North, West, and South that they and their companions had rallied together and the aid of Mercilaar. The Phoenix, having stayed by the Elect's ship until they had disembarked, had left the harbor and took to resting in the square alongside Verdok, Allor, and Xavier. The civilians, having fled to hide at the sight of Mercilaar's fiery devastation of the grey armada, looked anxiously at the great red bird when they entered the square. Now, however, many were approaching the Phoenix and thanking him. Allor ended his address with a simple statement and offer.

"We mean to rest here until dawn," the king said calmly, "and then begin our march to Genverdell to put this horror to an end. I can see plainly that you are not soldiers, and therefore place no demand for you to accompany us into the battle to come. Hide here or seek shelter elsewhere if you wish. However, if any of you should decide to join us, know that we will gratefully welcome every additional hand against this wretched demon. Do as you will; we will be on our way soon. Whatever you decide, take care, and I pray that Onu keep you well."

"And you as well, King Allor," said the townspeople solemnly.

A great hum of discussion then began to flood the crowds of civilians. Ruth, Mira, and Lerannu, along with Allor, Donovan, and Verdok, joined Xavier and Ranye as they conversed with Mercilaar. The Phoenix stood from his sitting position, stretching his large crimson wings as he made ready for flight.

"I'm going to make for Genverdell ahead of you," he said dutifully, "and see if I can't get any sense of how things are there. I don't mean to be long; I'll come back and rejoin you wherever you are on the march and let you know what I've seen."

"Very well, Sir Mercilaar," said Allor as he gave the Phoenix a friendly pat on his chest. "Go with Onu's blessing."

"And you as well, and all of you," he said with a caring look at all those around him.

The Phoenix then flapped his wings, asking everyone around him to clear a path. The great bird rose upon the wind, and began to fly north and east toward Genverdell. All present looked on in awed silence.

Ruth took Verdok's hand as she called back to her sister Elect and other companions. "If there isn't anything else that can't wait until dawn, I'm going to get what sleep I can. It's going to be a long day tomorrow."

***

Ruth and Verdok awoke to the horns that announced the arrival of dawn. An hour passed of preparation and the breaking of fasts, followed by a steady procession out of Kannah's gate. As the Elect and their allies made their way onto the road to Genverdell, Ruth saw Allor and Lerannu step aside and turn to face the gate, where a sizable group of townspeople were gathered.

Allor conversed briefly with the civilians, then called for all of the alliance to wait outside the town once they passed the gates. The allies of the Elect stood and watched, and Ruth's heart warmed greatly at the companies of townsfolk who stepped out of Kannah to follow the army. Compared to the alliance's total number, the new recruits amounted to only a few handfuls. Nevertheless, their joining showed clearly that Fidonity, however shaken by distrust from the horrors that had passed from Raakmathna's machinations, ultimately had remained unbroken.

Allor voiced his thanks to the volunteer citizen-soldiers, as well as some encouraging words to those who decided to remain in the town. The army marched on toward Genverdell as the new recruits conversed with the seasoned soldiers, trying to learn how to best work with the arms and armor they had taken from the town's garrison. Ruth, hearing an array of the citizen-soldiers' questions and comments, pulled her husband close as they continued down the road.

"When we make camp tonight," she told Verdok, "I'll try to see if I can help them."

Verdok kissed Ruth's cheek. "I'll be sure to bring some food over."

168
11/20/4030 G.M.

RAAKMATHNA stood on the ramparts along the south gate of Genverdell with Ranoth beside her. The two rulers of Enmayar were in full war regalia, such as they had been wearing for the past fortnight, and had been walking the walls of the capital since early morning. It was noon, and they stopped to look upon the preparations for the assault they were sure was soon to come. The staked mounds had been completely finished, and encircled the city fully and in strategic tiers of rings.

The Peacekeepers who had returned to answer the call, along with those already present, were patrolling the city as they had been ordered, fully armed and armored. Others manned the siege equipment along the walls. Officers reported on the hour. All throughout the city, the empress's undead thralls walked among the living soldiers, numbering fifteen to every one of them. Everything was as ready as the empress could think to devise under the circumstances. She looked on with satisfaction, confident there was more than a small chance she could outlive her foes and continue to serve the All-Keeper's intentions.

"Are you sure that you are willing to be in the thick of things, Ranoth?" the empress asked as she looked to her warlock consort. "I will not hold it against you if you choose to stay on the walls and shelter behind them if need be."

"You said yourself that I would not be as effective in serving you if that were the case, my empress. From commanding the Peacekeepers in the field to seeing to the mounds, if I will be in the best position to do so whilst in the field, then that is where I will be. You are the only one who truly matters here, Raakmathna, you and your master. If I will serve you best in the midst of the battlefield, I will do so; I do not fear death."

"Very well," said Raakmathna. "You have my utmost thanks, Ranoth. You of course know what to do, when the time comes ..."

The empress's voice trailed off as she suddenly became aware of a distant shape in the sky. In the light of the noon's sun, it was a vividly scarlet form with a golden sparkle. Ranoth, noticing it as well, drew in a sharp breath of irritation.

"That must be a Phoenix," the emperor said disdainfully. "Do you think it's allied to these Elect, or that its presence is coincidental?"

"I would not be the least surprised if it were an ally of Onu's chosen," said Raakmathna calmly.

"What should we do if it is? How much does this affect our plans? We have already–"

"Calm yourself, Ranoth. If it is with those Daughters of the East, they still cannot know the full extent of our preparations."

Raakmathna took a steady, level breath. "That said, I would like to impart to you some more of my power. Come."

Ranoth eagerly took his empress's hand, breathing deeply as he drew in the great might that Raakmathna let flow from herself and into him. The aura about the emperor glowed with striking visibility, and his eyes burned bright as coals. Raakmathna clasped the emperor's hand within hers, caressing it as she assured her consort.

"Besides, win or lose, I will have done my part for Lovaariinu, as will you and all the others with us."

"Very well, my empress," Ranoth said as the two calmly turned to descend the wall and return to the castle.

169

11/22/4030 G.M.

ALLOR strode within the central company of the marching armies alongside Lerannu and the other Daughters of the East. Xavier and Ranye were also with him, as well as the monarchs of the three allied nations. They had been marching at a steady pace for four days after landing at Kannah, making use of the highway that ran along the Sunrise River and led straight to Genverdell. They had made for the capital as quickly as possible while also avoiding exhaustion.

All the while, the King of Enmayar's heart was torn between faith in his companions and the prophecy, and dread for the battle to come. He and the others in his company had discussed and re-evaluated potential strategies time and time again as they journeyed. It had reached the point where hardly anything changed with each revisiting of the plans, including the simple fact that they could not determine with precision the tactics the enemy had in mind. Nevertheless, as maddening as it was to repeat such matters, it was either speaking of them or weathering the day's journey in silence. Both choices were taken in their measure. Neither could completely comfort Allor despite his efforts to keep faith, and he sensed in nearly everyone around him the same strife of the heart.

Following the second day of marching, Allor had noticed that the demeanors of Xavier and Ranye had seemed to grow especially conflicted between hope and melancholy. He asked them if there was anything particularly the matter.

"Nothing that isn't ultimately in service to the Elect and their mission," Xavier said quietly. "Do not trouble yourself with me or Ranye; there is much going through our minds here, but we all must keep our faith in the Daughters of the East and the One who has given them their lot, and do our part for them in turn."

Allor wanted to discuss the matter further, but judged from the taciturn resolve on Xavier and Ranye's faces that there would little, if anything, more that he would get from them. He decided not to bring the matter up with Lerannu or any of his other companions for the time being.

It was now the twenty-second of Yorparon. An hour into the afternoon, Allor and all of the alliance gave a thunderous cheer as they saw the distant, but rapidly nearing form of Mercilaar appear on the northeastern horizon straight ahead of them. Within a moment, the Phoenix descended from the skies and landed before the alliance, who maneuvered as they marched to allow the great bird to join and converse with the leaders. Soon, Mercilaar was walking majestically alongside Allor and his company, relaying to them what he was able to see from his scouting of Genverdell.

"There is, of course, no doubt that they saw me," the Phoenix said plainly, "but from what I have seen since I turned back, no one has been sent to try and pursue me or determine where I have been heading. I would presume that their plan is to hole up in and around the city and let us go to them, but at least it seems we needn't worry about a confrontation beforehand. Certainly not anything significant, anyhow."

"What could you see of their forces, though?" asked Allor.

"There were hundreds of grey-cloaks, and many-fold more their number of living dead abominations. They were all patrolling in or around the capital, or staying put in various positions around the city. There are some ballistae at choice places along the walls, but none too many. They have also set up an intricate barricade of staked mounds all around the city. As we near it, you will see that much of the nearby woodlands have been felled."

Xavier's voice suddenly rose up in a peculiar tone of concern from behind Allor. "Did you see anything at all peculiar about those barricades, Mercilaar?"

"Apart from its layout of several rings encircling the city, like a ripple in a pond, no. Why? Have you seen something about them?"

"I have seen a number of things lately," said Xavier in a ponderous tone. He then shrugged irritably. "As for the mounds, I feel there's something about them ... something more than meets the eye ... but I can't say for certain. Did you perhaps notice anything about the stakes themselves? Their design? Their placement? Anything at all?"

Mercilaar shook his head regretfully. "I fear not, my friend. However, whether or not there is anything about them that goes beyond appearances, they're going to be enough of an obstacle for us as they are."

The Phoenix then looked intently at Lerannu, Mira, and Ruth. "All of us, of course, except for the Daughters of the East. Or did that plan change while I was away?"

"No, friend," said Ruth plainly. "We're still meaning to go straight for the castle and cut off the serpent's head, if we can. It's not an absolute certainty that the demon will be there specifically, but if it means to defend its mission as much as possible, that would be the most sensible place for it to try and protect itself. If you can get us over the walls and to the castle, the three of us will do all we can to send that demon back to Raakhaal."

"Very good," said Mercilaar with stone-solid resolve. "I will do all in my power to ensure your safe approach to the castle, and continue to do whatever I can to help you do your part, if there is indeed anything else I can do."

The great bird looked back to Allor and the other monarchs in his company. "And seeing as how there is indeed a great army gathered there, I take it that you all are still set on engaging them on the field while the Elect try and take down Raakmathna?"

"Indeed," said Allor with a somber nod. "But for all our efforts to plan our attack, I fear we're ultimately unaware of what exactly we'll be dealing with. We'll bear in mind that there seems to be some additional hazard to the barricades that have been erected, along with the trouble of their hindrance itself, but other than that, we'll just have to face it as it comes."

"I suppose so," said Mercilaar gravely. "Hopefully it will be enough. If Elukus's prophecy is to be fulfilled, it will be. It must be ..."

The Phoenix turned his sight directly to Xavier and Ranye. The great bird and the Trichynay leaders gazed intently at one another for a silent moment, their eyes seeming to share some heavy knowledge that only the three of them knew.

"Whatever happens," Mercilaar concluded, "it will serve the ultimate good in the end."

Xavier and Ranye simply nodded.

The great alliance marched on through the day, stopping at sundown to take another night's long-awaited rest.

***

Allor ate his supper alongside Lerannu and Verdok, watching Ruth, Mira, and Donovan as they helped some soldiers train the volunteers from Kannah. The king became lost in thought, thinking of the shift in Xavier and Ranye's demeanor, and the look that had passed between them and Mercilaar earlier that day. Finishing his bowl of stew and tankard of beer, Allor got up and gave Lerannu and Verdok a pat on the back.

"I'm just going to see how things are with everyone else," he said. "I might have a word or two with Viktor or Xenia, or maybe Dominik or Salos. I'm not sure."

"Would you rather any of us go with you?" asked Lerannu.

"No need. I'm just looking to see how things are. I don't really have any exact points of interest. If I don't see any of you before tomorrow, I wish you all a good sleep."

Allor began to wander the camp, hoping the walk would help him clear his mind or at least tire it enough so he could fall asleep that night. He passed soldiers from around the world who ate, drank, lightly practiced with their weapons, and conversed about any number of matters. He continued to ponder the exchange between Xavier, Ranye, and Mercilaar, wondering about the fulfillment of the mission and the matter regarding the staked mounds surrounding Genverdell.

A small rock protruding from the earth suddenly tore him from his musings, tripping him and nearly sending him sprawling onto the ground. He recovered his balance, however, and found himself in front of a tent. He recognized it as Xavier and Ranye's tent, being a small one made of canvas that matched the same array of colors as the high shaman's robes. He was overwhelmed by a desire to ask Xavier about what had passed between him, Ranye, and Mercilaar, and what the shaman had sensed, however vaguely, about the barricades surrounding Genverdell. Without thinking, he approached the tent and parted the flap at the entrance. His body and heart froze in an instant, moved beyond words by the sight before him.

The high chief and shaman were on their bed cushion, holding each other closely as they made love together. They kissed and caressed one another ceaselessly, staring into the depths of their teary eyes. The haunting, mystical light that glowed from the Ecclesian's eyes illuminated the scene. It was as though sacred candles bathed the tent in light.

"I know it won't be forever," Ranye sobbed, "not if we both hold true to each other and to Onu, but ... I'll miss you so much. Your voice, your laugh, the way you speak to us and all who seek your counsel ... Your eyes, and how they always stir wonder in the hearts of those who see them ..."

The two Trichynay leaders shifted together in a shared movement, moaning gently as they tightened their embrace. Through the tears, Ranye began to laugh.

"And I'll certainly miss this."

Xavier stroked his wife's back, breathing a sound that was both a laugh and a sob. "Just stay strong. To the eternity we'll share when all has run its course, the time before we meet again will be as nothing. And we'll have all the time we'll ever want for any and every joy that we'll be able to share with Onu, with each other, and all the others who come to finally rest in the ultimate peace."

Xavier held Ranye and caressed her as he gently shifted on the cushion again, smiling affectionately as he was rewarded with another soft groan from her lips.

"And we'll most certainly have plenty of time for this again, when the time comes."

"I'll do what I can. To keep going until then."

"I know you will."

"There will still be those days, though ..."

"It's still alright to weep, if the tears aren't all that there is in your life."

"I know."

"Tell Layna I love her."

"I will."

"And Garthon."

"Of course."

Realization burrowed into the depths of Allor's heart, and tears sprang unbidden to his eyes. He berated himself for intruding upon the two for the sake of satisfying his impulsive curiosity, and sniffed loudly as he blinked the first of the falling tears.

Xavier tilted his head, looking at Allor as though he knew he was there all along. Though his face was still lined with the tears that had flowed, it bore no expression of agitation toward Allor's intrusion. Ranye looked behind her, gazing intently into Allor's eyes as she held Xavier close, her face the same as her husband's. Allor swallowed and took a deep breath before speaking.

"You ... you know that you will ..."

"Yes."

"Isn't there something that can be–"

"Not without ultimately leading to more loss than what is already to be. Besides, those who fall for Fidonhaal and the love of Onu are not truly lost."

"I suppose not. It's just ..."

"I know, Allor. Believe me, I know."

Allor nodded and stood transfixed for a moment, then remembered the silent exchange of looks that passed between the leaders and the Phoenix.

"I take it that Mercilaar knows what's to happen to you?"

Xavier nodded. "And to him."

"I ... I see."

"But what will be his lot, my friend, when all is said and done?"

Allor began to smile. "He will be reborn. Ultimately, he will never be lost."

"Such is the same fate for us, if we endure and continue our efforts toward love and faith, in Onu and each other."

"Yes."

"I will ask that you do not reveal this to any of the others. Not until it has come to pass, that is. Let's keep this between us and Mercilaar."

"Of course. I will."

Xavier nodded kindly to him. "Thank you, good King of the East. Go now and get some rest. We still have some more days of marching to go. Then we shall face the great evil of the day."

Allor nodded. "It has been a great honor, Shaman Xavier Onoraan."

"Likewise."

Allor lowered the canvas of the tent's entrance and turned away. He started and gasped at the sight of Mercilaar, who now stood wordlessly before him.

The king and the Phoenix nodded to one another in silent acknowledgement, and parted ways to take their rest.

Brought on Wings of Fire

170
12/1/4030 G.M.

VERDOK felt his heart begin to pound as the countryside grew ever more familiar. At last, after eleven days of marching from the port of Kannah, the Elect and their allies had reached the last stretch of country that separated them from Genverdell. Ahead of them hung an ominous stretch of grey clouds, threatening a chilly rain in the late-autumn breeze. All had donned their cloaks and jackets, and the air of the army was one of a tormenting clash between faith and fear.

They had passed the first of the woodlands neighboring the capital's vicinity, which were largely felled as Mercilaar had reported, and as they marched on, the army was met with no sound but that of its own pounding feet. The land, the air, and all else about them was terribly silent, and the cloud-muted light of the late morning's sun gave a melancholy glow to all things in sight.

Verdok looked at the army, striving to keep confident as he looked at the soldiers of the three nations and the willing citizens who had joined them over the course of their march. Having contended with his own inner struggles on violence, peace, and the great weight that this global horror had placed upon all involved, the high priest stayed close to Ruth's side, bracing himself for the carnage and losses that were bound to come.

At last the army halted along a grand tall hill, and word ran through the ranks that Genverdell would be in plain sight over the hill. Verdok drew a deep, shaky breath as he ran the long-discussed plans through his mind. He turned to Ruth, who stared at him with beautiful emerald eyes that sparkled with brimming tears, and held her close and kissed her.

"Whatever comes to pass," he said softly, "I love you, and am awed and honored beyond words to count myself as your husband, whether you were an Elect of Onu or not."

"And I love you," Ruth said in a quiet, broken voice, "and I count myself blessed beyond measure as your wife."

Verdok looked about as he embraced her, and saw Allor and Lerannu, Donovan and Mira, and countless other soldiers doing the same as he. From spouses and lovers to family and friends, a quick, quiet farewell was taking place through all the army. He then saw Xavier and Ranye, who, though neither embracing nor kissing, clasped both their hands within one another's, their eyes showing a love as deep as any of those around them.

He turned his sight to Allor and the other monarchs of Fidonhaal, who approached him and his companions with faces of steely resolve. Allor, having kissed Lerannu one last time, looked to his friends with a heavy sigh.

"Are we ready?" the king asked quietly.

Verdok looked all around him. "As ready as we can bring ourselves to be, it would seem."

"Then let us begin this end."

Verdok painfully pulled away from Ruth, who turned to join her Elect sisters in mounting onto Mercilaar's back. The Phoenix was staying hidden by the hill, with the plan being for him to not rise and fly to the castle until the first sounds of battle. The rest of the army began to split in two as they came over the hilltop and began to encircle Genverdell. Verdok was in the company of Allor, Donovan, Xavier, Ranye, and Roniil. They and all the soldiers accompanying them crossed road and country until they came as close to the city's south gate as the barricades of staked mounds would allow. Verdok's pounding heart felt as though it would burst out of his chest as he and his companions stood before the army of grey-cloaks and undead, who stared at their foes in utter silence.

Silence. Verdok could not escape the horrid grip in which the sheer lack of sound now held him. It was that which rivaled the grave, of the same sort they met when they were investigating Kannah, but far greater, as it was now a great city that was in this state instead of a modest port. The priest reflected on the fear he had seen from the people back then, and whispered a little prayer for their well-being and that of the people in the capital as the south gate suddenly opened.

Ranoth Windsbreath passed through the gate, an escort of grey-cloaks surrounding him. Verdok's fur stood on end at the sight of him. The former priest of Castle Genverdell was now adorned in fiendishly ornate armor and robes, and he held a wicked sword that glittered menacingly in the cloud-dulled sunlight. A glow that could only come from the powers of Raakhaal enveloped him. Ranoth and his company casually maneuvered about the barricades, with the horde of grey-cloaks and undead making way for them as they approached the allied army. At last he stood before the head of the alliance that had come to the south walls of the capital, his fiery eyes staring scornfully at those before him.

"Welcome, one and all," said Ranoth sarcastically, "to the capital of Enmayar, the beacon of order for the world of Fidonhaal."

Total silence loomed over all, from all directions surrounding Genverdell. Ranoth, noticing Allor, nodded with mock courtesy.

"The empress sends her regards," the warlock went on. "I, as her new emperor and consort, will be speaking with you and all these others in your company on her behalf. Know that—"

"Surrender her to us," said Allor with a dreadfully flat and cold voice, "and let all those in the city who are not in league with you depart from here. We will put an end to this demon's atrocities and offer all of you, even you, Sir Windsbreath, a form of justice that will offer a chance at redemption, despite ... everything."

"Allor," Ranoth said with a hideous sneer, "you know nothing of my empress's power, nor of her army or her trusted consort. *All* of Genverdell is on our side. You will find no allies here apart from those you've brought with you."

"I don't believe you," Allor said flatly. "No matter how many lies and twisted thoughts you've put out there, and no matter how many you've threatened to bow to your ways under pain of death, you have but a few who would ever truly follow you when all is said and done. Fidonity, for all its faults and sins, is not this utterly evil."

"You will see for yourself soon enough," Ranoth said plainly. "No, Allor, the time for a new era of this world is at hand. An era of order. And we will not let your challenge, or that of those allied to you, go unpunished. You may cast down your arms and follow me and my empress, or join the dissenters. Either way, you *will* serve us in the end."

Ranoth slunk back into the protective ranks of his escort and called out to all around him.

"The enemy has come and seeks to undo all the order we have labored to bring to this world! Let us waste no more time! ATTACK!"

A dreadful chorus of horns sounded all around the city, immediately drowned out by the battle cries of the grey-coats and abominable screeches of the subservient corpses. The first of the enemy charged through the openings in the barricade and began to clash with the allies. Verdok, bracing himself for the horror of battle, rallied to Allor and Roniil, who had taken up leadership of the immediate company of soldiers. Donovan, Xavier, and Ranye were right beside him. The high shaman was greatly distressed, his glowing blind eyes furrowing fretfully as he tried to make sense of something. Verdok caringly approached the high shaman and pulled him closer into the guard of the soldiers as he listened to Allor and Roniil. The first large bolts from the ballistae on the walls soared overhead, crashing sickeningly into companies of the alliance.

"The time is now!" bellowed the King of Enmayar as many of the allied soldiers began to fight and maneuver their way about the barricades and into the thick of the battle. "This is for all of Fidonhaal! Fight to the last, and—"

"The mounds!" Xavier cried out in horror as he pointed wide-eyed at the barricades. "Look!"

Verdok's blood froze as he saw the stakes shifting about in the mounds. A few of the allied soldiers, fighting near them, were taken aback and began to cry out in terror as decaying hands grasped at their ankles. Stakes began to loosen and fall from their fixed places in the mounds, and more undead began to climb out from the barricade pits.

"How many are there?" Verdok shouted frightfully. "Where did they all—"

The priest's voice lodged within his throat as he began to notice more details about the corpses pouring out from the hidden pits. Unlike the ones that were alongside the grey-cloaks, these had no uniforms or proper weapons. They were simply garbed in the tattered remains of everyday wear. The bodies also ranged from tall to small, more than a few of them being little older than babes.

And there were so many of them. More than the initial army of grey-coats or the undead they had already seen.

They were enough to fill a city. A great city. A capital.

Verdok was on the verge of crumbling to his knees in despair.

Then he heard the cry of the Phoenix and shot his eyes to the sky. Mercilaar was soaring past the walls, flying swiftly toward the castle. Verdok, still shaking, drew a deep breath, ran to his companions, and bellowed out his battle cries as the first cool raindrops of the threatening storm began to fall upon the battlefield.

"FOR ONU! FOR FIDONHAAL! FOR THE DAUGHTERS OF THE EAST!"

171

12/1/4030 G.M.

LERANNU gripped tightly to the staff lent to her by the Trichynay Tribe, doing all she could to focus her inner strength for what lay ahead. A cool drop of rain spattered hard against her face, and she soon began to feel one every few seconds as she and her sisters of fate soared over Genverdell and toward the castle. The battle clamor below was dreadful, and the mage was doing everything in her power to clear all but the mission of the Elect from her mind.

Suddenly, she felt an upward rush of air blow to her side. Lerannu opened her eyes and hunched up in as defensive a position as she could in the saddle as arrows and bolts began to fly up toward the Phoenix and his riders. They were almost at the castle. A shot from a ballista flew beneath them, missing by a wide mark.

"We're still going for the garden-side entrance, yes?" Mercilaar called out to the Daughters of the East, his voice one of grave resolve.

"Aye!" Lerannu heard Ruth say. "I can see guards at the door from here, but it should still be less guarded than the front. From what Lera's told us, that's probably going to be the best way in."

"Very well," said the Phoenix. "Hang on tightly! We ..."

Lerannu strained her ears over the rushing wind and rain, which began to fall more heavily by the moment.

"We shall be swift in descending!" said the great bird in a voice of finality.

Lerannu tucked the Trichynay staff tightly under her arm and gripped the handles of her seat until her knuckles hurt. The mage looked down at the castle and the grounds below. A squad of grey-cloaks were rushing to try and catch up with the apparent direction of the Phoenix's flight. A harsh sound issued from Mercilaar's throat and a ball of fire flew down, engulfing the grey squad entirely. Mercilaar then flew around the castle, steadily lowering his flight further and further as he prepared to land in the castle gardens. As they descended, the three women braced defensively against the arrows and bolts that flew from the walls and windows of the castle.

"This is it, my sisters!" Lerannu heard Mira call out to her and Ruth. "The fate of us and our world will now be decided!"

The three women cried out bravely, bracing for the impending battle as they prepared to land.

Lerannu noticed that the descent was getting sharper as well as faster.

"Mercilaar," Lerannu called out to the Phoenix, "I'm not sure if—"

Lerannu's heart dropped as she felt a fiery heat begin to sear the sides of her legs. She looked at her Elect sisters and saw them staring in transfixed horror at the bolt that was buried deeply into Mercilaar's eye.

They were falling, and the Phoenix, having died, was beginning to immolate.

172
12/1/4030 G.M.

DONOVAN faltered for only an instant as he reeled back from the horrors that clawed through the barrier mounds and reached for his ankles. Shouldering his longbow and drawing his short sword, the bard began to hack and stab at the rising horde surrounding him and his comrades. Seconds passed as minutes, and Donovan and his companions cut and shot down grey-cloak and undead alike as the allied army both dealt and suffered grave carnage.

Roniil and Allor fought by his side, and Verdok, not far away, was fighting alongside Xavier and Ranye. All fought with stunning ferocity. Verdok, having hardened himself to the grim need to fight, dealt stunningly agile, terrible blows to the grey-clad soldiers and fighting corpses with his quarterstaff, hands and feet. The foes fell before him as surely as those that fell to blade and arrow. Ranye, clinging to the bow lent to her from the tribal reliquary, did not bother once to reach for the blade at her hip, felling even the closest-reaching foe with either a shaft or a furious strike with her fist or the bow itself.

But for all the awe that the sight of the fighters evoked in Donovan, the sight of Xavier was truly a wonder to behold. His staff and spells struck true every time despite the physical blindness of his sight, and as taxing as his magical exertions doubtlessly were, the power of the Ecclesian was utterly marvelous. Wind, mingled with lightning, shot out from his hand one moment, and fingers of flame or piercing rays of light the next. His finesse with the staff matched Verdok's skill with dreadful ease. All the while, the battlefield was being cloaked ever more fully by the rain. The chilling drops were accompanied through their journey in the air by only the shafts fired by friend and foe, and the occasional bolt from a ballista along the walls. Had the bard not been fighting for his life alongside those around him, he would have loved to observe the scene and try to put it into verse.

Roniil and Allor, staying close to the bard, were no less amazing in their fight, which formed into a spellbinding scene of valiance and desperation. Roniil cleaved through the grey-coats and undead with terrible efficiency, aided by the sufficient swordsmanship of the King of Enmayar.

Donovan, running another grey-cloak soldier through with his blade, heard a cry of pain from Ranye. Veering his sight toward the high chief and those around her, he saw her on the ground, clutching her side as the grey-cloak standing over her began to raise a sword to finish her off. The bard swiftly unshouldered his bow, nocked and aimed an arrow, and let the shaft fly right into the grey-coat's throat. He was in the process of re-shouldering the bow and turning back to the battle before him when he felt an agonizing pain run through his left leg. Dropping to one knee, he turned and saw an armored corpse preparing to drive its spear directly through the bard's chest.

In a flash, the entirety of the undead body was swept off its feet, all above its waist flying back into the ranks of the enemy as Roniil's great axe cleaved through it. Donovan scrambled painfully back onto his feet, thanking the Trichynay warrior for his help.

Then a great ball of flame flew just over their heads, and the two looked to see Ranoth glaring hideously at them from a mere few yards away as he prepared to cast another body of fire in their direction.

173
12/1/4030 G.M.

MIRA and her Elect sisters all screamed in alarm as they began to plummet toward the earth. Though Mercilaar had reduced his altitude considerably before being slain, it was far from being a safe landing. The flames that were beginning to engulf the great bird were an even greater peril to the huntress and her companions. The floor of the garden met the trio and the burning Phoenix with frightening velocity, and the huntress flew several feet from the explosive force of the impact before landing hard on the stone pathway. Though her arm ached terribly, she knew it wasn't broken. She grunted in pain as she pushed herself up from the ground, and turned to find Ruth beating fire out of Lerannu's robes, wincing in agony each time her left hand struck the mage's clothes.

Running toward them, Mira picked up Ruth's pot-lid shield and wood axe, along with the tribal staff the Trichynay people had lent to Lerannu. None of the equipment was damaged in any noticeable way. As the huntress stood beside the knight and mage, the two extinguishing their burning clothes, she drew in a sharp breath as she realized that Ruth's left arm was clearly broken. The chilly rain was now starting to fall more heavily. When the fires on Lerannu's robes were finally put out, the mage shakily pulled out a tonic from her satchel and gulped it down, breathing heavy, steady breaths as Mira spoke to Ruth.

"Your arm's bad, Ruth. Is there anything we can do to help?"

"No," the Faithguard said through clenched teeth. "Just give me my axe and shield."

"You couldn't block with—"

"Just give them to me!"

Mira anxiously handed the axe and shield to the knight, as well as the staff to Lerannu, just as she heard two voices crying out nearby. The huntress looked over and saw two grey-clad guards stationed at the garden-side entrance to the castle, yelling into the slightly ajar door before slamming it shut again. The two soldiers then readied their halberds, staring spitefully at the three women as they began to advance toward them. Mira stayed behind Ruth as the knight made to charge, and fluidly drew her bow and fired a shot at one of the guards. The arrow struck its target, though just piercing the coat and hauberk beneath, and barely reaching the flesh. It ultimately didn't matter, however, as the shot was enough to throw the guard out of focus, and he quickly fell to a lethal, cleaving blow to the helmet and skull from Ruth.

The other guard bellowed out a dreadful war cry and thrust his halberd fiercely toward the knight. Ruth just managed to catch the thrust with her shield, only to crumple to the ground under the force of the blow. She let out an agonized scream from the shock she took through her broken arm. The grey-coat then swung the halberd overhead, making to cleave right into Ruth, and Mira frantically nocked another arrow to her bow and let it fly. It narrowly missed the opening of the guard's helmet.

Mira sobbed out in dread as it seemed that Ruth would be butchered before her eyes.

Then a lash of flame streamed out from behind her. It struck the guard, rapidly engulfing him and setting him to collapse screaming onto the stone pathway. Mira gasped and looked behind her to see Lerannu pulling fire from the burning body of Mercilaar and channeling it into a whip-like form. The mage whirled the fiery lash overhead as she surveyed the effects. Sobbing with relief, the huntress ran over to the knight and helped her up gently as Ruth continued to groan in anguish. The cold rain was now pouring harshly.

"We *need* to do something for that, Ruth!" Mira said desperately. "We can't just—"

"We can't do anything about it now!" Ruth cried out in pain, fear and frustration. "We don't have the time!"

Knowing that Ruth was right, Mira held her friend close as the two began to approach the door to the castle. She looked back and saw Lerannu on all fours, rummaging at the feet of Mercilaar's corpse, which was still aglow with lingering flames despite the pouring rain. Mira called out to her and began to head toward her, only to stop as the mage quickly got up. She put a small pouch into the depths of her satchel and quickly clasped the bag shut. Mira gave a somber smile of understanding.

"Just in case?" she asked.

"Yes," Lerannu said with a shaky sigh. "I only managed to grab a handful of it before the rain started to soak the rest of it through. Let's pray it'll be enough ... if we need it."

The three women rushed to the castle door, and before Mira could ask her Elect sisters how they thought to proceed, Lerannu planted her staff harshly onto the garden path. The mage drew back her free arm as though she were pulling the string of a massive bow, her face creased in near pain from the intensity of the concentration. She released a burst of wind so intense that it blew the door from its hinges and broke off fragments of stone from the doorway. A great commotion sounded from inside the corridor, and upon rushing in, Mira and Ruth found that a large, mixed squad of grey-cloaks and armed corpses were waiting for them. Many of them were lying on the floor, either pinned down or injured by the debris of wood and stone, while the rest were reeling from the shock of Lerannu's forceful breach.

Mira was able to down three foes with her bow before Ruth began to close in on the others. The undead still standing were quick to recover from the shock, but not quick enough. The knight cleaved the corpses down quickly, then turned to the living grey-cloaks and began to lay them low just as they were starting to recover from the jolting force of the breach. Mira shouldered her bow and drew the short blade at her side, joining her knightly sister in the melee. With those that were still standing having now been felled, Mira and Ruth turned back to examine those under the rubble. After determining which of them no longer seemed threatening, and finishing those who were, they looked to Lerannu.

The mage was leaning on one of the broken supports of the empty doorway, taking a few steady breaths as she recomposed herself. Mira patted Lerannu on the shoulder and then nudged at the mage's satchel.

"If you need to take another one of those tonics," said the huntress as levelly as she could while trying to urge her friend on, "then go ahead and take it. We need to–"

"I'm fine for now," Lerannu said with a deep, steady breath. "Let's go."

The three women strode steadily down the corridor, with Ruth and Mira working together in the lead as Lerannu followed closely behind. They felled what few soldiers they encountered, living and undead, and each admitted to one another their surprise at the ease with which they were presently advancing.

"No doubt she's saving them up for just the right place and time," Ruth said flatly between light grunts of pain from her broken arm as the trio approached an ornate set of double doors.

"This is the throne room, right?" Ruth asked. Lerannu nodded without a word, taking deep breaths and readying her staff as the knight and the huntress checked the doors. They were unlocked, and Mira and Ruth flung them wide open with ease.

They were greeted by a large gathering of grey-cloaks and undead. A heavy-set figure was seated on the throne. But it was not Raakmathna. The demonic empress was visible, however, staring down scornfully at the Daughters of the East from the railed passageway that ran above the throne room.

"So now is the time that our fates will be decided," she cackled loathsomely at the three women. "Catch me if you can, and fight me if you dare!"

The empress loudly clapped her hands once, then slunk out of sight as her guards advanced toward Mira and her companions. The large figure on the throne rose awkwardly up from its seat, and Mira's stomach reeled as she recognized the rotted, headless form dressed in the bloody, tattered remains of a salpion's robes.

174

12/1/4030 G.M.

RAAKMATHNA strode toward the royal bedchamber, relishing the distant clashes of battle from below as she prepared for what would be her final stand if necessary. She entered the room calmly and took up the Branokian steel katana that Sheeva had used to slay Salpion Lovonhaar, which she had kept mounted over the bed. She sat on the bed calmly, directly facing the entryway from the hall, and closed her eyes as she spoke quietly to Lovaariinu, the All-Keeper, whom the foolish mortals condemned as the bane of their existence.

"It may well be that I will be returning to you soon, dear Hand of Order. Should I fail, do to me as you will. Know, however, that whatever comes to pass, our efforts to show the folly of Onu surely will have resonated with more than a few of these low creatures. We have been able to show how anything about them can be used by them to bring chaos upon themselves many times before ... but this notion ... something so simple ... I feel quite confident that this new concept will bring at least *some* measure of lingering trouble to them for a very long time. Maybe someday, if not soon, they will see that such troubles can all go away when they bow to you and you alone. But if not, they can simply continue to ignore these lessons and suffer."

The empress clasped the lightly curved handle of the blade, loosening it within its sheath as she continued to steadily breathe with closed eyes.

"I will now wait, All-Keeper. We shall see what comes to be."

175
12/1/4030 G.M.

RUTH stared at the reanimated corpse of her mentor, her eyes blurring with tears of mourning and wrath at his defilement. She walked into the fray unflinching, her axe biting past the plate, chain, and padding of the armor worn by her foes, who fell before her as wheat to the scythe. From the corners of her eyes, she saw the odd arrow flying into the ranks of the enemy, as well as one sharp blast of wind and another of flame.

The grey-clad murderers and the wretched corpse-warriors all fell to the fury of the Daughters of the East, until at last Ruth found herself standing before the last remaining foe. It was the body of Owen, which now shambled horrifically toward her with a wicked mace raised to crush her skull. An arrow struck the undead salpion, causing it to reel from the impact and miss its strike. The mace instead rang against Ruth's shield, sending a wave of unspeakable agony through her arm. The pain at last broke through the knight's battle frenzy, sending her onto both knees with a throat-rending scream.

Owen's corpse had regained its footing and now gripped Ruth's hair within its putrid hand. Forcing the knight's head upwards, the corpse again raised its mace for the kill.

Another blast of wind flew over Ruth's head and tore through the undead body like a gale through fallen leaves. She saw Mira flying headlong into what little remained of Owen's body, tackling it to the ground with a great battle cry before she realized that Lerannu had already put an end to the threat.

From the wretched pain in her arm, and the sadness and anger at the sight of her mentor's violated remains, Ruth sighed out a shaky sob and wept. She felt a hand on either shoulder and looked up to see her sisters in destiny.

"Th-thank you both," Ruth said tearfully as she slowly got up from the floor. She turned to Lerannu and suddenly began to chuckle. "That's twice you've saved me from corpses with that spell, Lera."

Lerannu's eyes lit up as she recalled the incident in Bravagoth long ago. She smiled, and assisted Mira in supporting the knight as the three of them made for the nearest staircase.

"Come on," Ruth said as she breathed shakily in an effort to ignore the pain and regain her strength. "We're almost done with this. Let's finish it."

176
12/1/4030 G.M.

ALLOR bellowed out a challenging cry at the vile salpion-emperor, calling his friends and nearby soldiers to join him in focusing the attack on Ranoth. Donovan and Roniil, already at his side, hunched up as tigers, ready to pounce on the warlock at Allor's word. Verdok, Xavier, and Ranye, along with several other soldiers who managed to hear Allor over the cacophony of clashing steel, scrambled to join him. Ranoth flung another fireball at Allor, which missed him by a hair and exploded into an unfortunate cluster of allied soldiers.

Over the burning soldiers' screams, Allor pointed his sword at Ranoth and let out a piercing war cry. He and his companions began to bull their way through the muddy, rain-soaked battle and close in on Ranoth, cutting down the foes in their way and soon coming within reach of the warlock. The emperor quickly drew his sword, and with the aid of the grey-cloaks and corpses around him, he faced off with Allor and his companions in a battle to the death.

Allor and Roniil were the closest to the warlock, and they worked together in an attempt to overwhelm him. Donovan was right beside them, doing the best he could with his shorter blade. Xavier continued to throw out mighty spells into the surrounding throngs of foes, with Ranye firing shaft after shaft into those who tried to outflank Allor and those nearest Ranoth. Verdok was nimbly fighting and maneuvering his way through the battle, rushing to reach his friends.

At last, Roniil managed to strike Ranoth in the middle with his great axe, and the warlock screamed hideously as he reeled from the blow, blood flowing rapidly from the long, deep line that had been cloven into him. Allor and Roniil closed in to finish him off, but suddenly the King of Enmayar felt a great many bony, putrid hands clawing into him from behind and either side. Struggling desperately to free himself, he glanced over and saw Roniil in the same peril.

Allor began to feel a barrage of sharp, cold blades pierce him from all over. He fought desperately to free himself from the corpses and their swords so he could rush in to finish off Ranoth. He saw that Roniil was also suffering wounds from all sides by the undead that assailed him. The adopted Trichynay warrior, and the father of his love, managed to cleave his axe deeply into Ranoth's left shoulder, all but severing the arm attached to it.

But it was not the arm that held the warlock's sword, which flew forth and ran through Roniil. The sword's point protruded from Roniil's back, and the warlock cruelly pressed the hilt of the sword against his chest before withdrawing it.

Allor bellowed out in grief and rage, and lunged free of the undead that assaulted him. He managed to avenge the wound that Ranoth had dealt to Roniil as he ran his blade through the emperor in the same fashion. The warlock screeched in agony and looked piercingly at Allor with eyes like cooling coals.

The emperor swung his sword one last time and Allor felt a horridly cold bite run across his throat, followed immediately by the wet warmth of fountaining blood. Blood swiftly flooded his mouth, and the King of Enmayar crumpled to the earth, looking up with swiftly fading vision at the former castle chaplain. Ranoth finally fell to the ground, feathered by several arrows and stricken with a beam of lightning that flew overhead.

A large ballista shaft flew in the direction from which the lightning came. Allor managed to turn his head to follow its flight and saw it utterly smite Xavier, slaying him instantly while missing Verdok and Ranye by a hair.

The last thing that Allor saw was Verdok running toward him, calling back to Donovan to check on Roniil, and Ranye silently falling to her knees as she looked upon her husband's broken body.

177
12/1/4030 G.M.

RAAKMATHNA shuddered as she felt the essence of Ranoth rush back to her and flood her being. She knew that her warlock consort had fallen on the battlefield. Aiming to make the most of the situation, she drew a deep breath and relished the sensation of her freshly restored power. She slowly drew the long, curved blade out of its scabbard and braced for her battle against the damnable Daughters of the East.

She heard a distant clamor of fighting far down the corridor. It was steadily growing louder. Closer. The empress smiled grimly and gazed at the blade in her hand, appreciating the shimmer of the dark and light steel as she braced herself for the final battle.

The clamor of steel and shouting drew ever closer, at last sounding just beyond the door of her chambers. A brief silence ensued before the striking crack of splintering wood sounded from the doorway. Another splitting of the door's wood, coupled with the loud clang of a stricken lock, sounded from the other side of the door. And then another.

Finally, the door caved in and a woman stood before her wearing some absurdly ancient armor and wielding a pot-lid and a woodcutter's axe. Right behind her was a woman with a longbow that was fashioned from the wood of Terranah and Stromarus's lowly spawn. Lastly, there was a woman with a primitive-looking staff.

The empress found it impossible to veil her contempt, despite not ever intending to really attempt it. Rising from the bed with her katana drawn, she sneered at the three Elect as she prepared to battle against them.

"So," she said in a voice dripping with disdain, "here are the long-foreseen Daughters of the East that I heard about from those damn northerners."

The three women stepped carefully into the room, their eyes afire with wrath. Raakmathna snorted in derision, raising her sword in a defensive stance.

"Just how do you see yourselves 'saving' this world? Apart from your foolish rejection of order, what do you think all this will do for those who come later, once they see that even the color of their fur could be a way to–"

"SILENCE!" said the woman in front, her face grimacing in pain as she shifted her pathetic shield upwards to guard herself. "This ends here, demon. Prepare yourself!"

Raakmathna cackled scornfully, and with her blade raised, she advanced toward the trio.

"So be it," she said flatly as she made to strike at the axe-wielding woman.

The woman with the axe and the pot-lid ducked and leapt nimbly away, and suddenly the woman with the bow was standing before her, her arrow pulled back to the fullest extent. The empress tried to dodge the shot, but noticed it too late and found a shaft protruding from her breast. Unfazed by the arrow's strike, Raakmathna swung her blade with an earsplitting cry. She struck out at the woman with the pathetically improvised shield, grinning with glee when she found that striking the pot lid dealt excruciating pain to the warrior's arm. Raakmathna lashed out at her again and again, only to be sent flying back into the room by a great gust of wind issued from the gestures of the woman with the staff. The empress recovered quickly, but not quickly enough to counter the strike of the first woman's axe. Her blade, raised hastily in an attempt to block the blow, gave way easily under the force of the axe, which then went on to cleave straight into Raakmathna's skull.

The empress screeched in the most bone-chilling voice she could manage, her blade raised high as she tried to slay at least one of the three women before leaving her vanquished shell. Another arrow hit her, smiting her in the throat. Reeling from the impact, she pushed to regain the momentum of her charge. She then felt another gale of wind rush forth, striking her so strongly that the axe in her head was forced into a spin within her skull. She felt the bone of her cranium splinter and fly from her head and a great fountain of blood gush forth before being pulled from her body and into the realm of her master.

178

12/1/4030 G.M.

VERDOK scrambled desperately to heal Allor, only to see plainly that the King of Enmayar was dead. Sobbing regretfully for his fallen friend, the high priest wheeled around and came face to face with a horrid corpse, armed and armored in the same manner as the grey-cloaks. Verdok narrowly managed to evade the corpse's strike with its axe. Preparing to strike out with his quarterstaff, Verdok was taken aback as the undead horror suddenly crumbled into a pile of dust before his very eyes. He looked frantically around him and saw corpse after corpse collapse in a similar manner all around him.

An intense silence ensued, broken only by the roar of the pouring rain. The silence was followed by a great cry of victory from the allies as they realized what must have happened.

Verdok sobbed with elation, realizing that the Elect must have succeeded in taking down the one responsible for the horror that had plagued the world. The prophecy of the Daughters of the East, having been spoken by the Blind Seer Elukus Aganon nearly four thousand years ago, had at last been fulfilled.

The surviving grey-coats looked on in horrified defeat for an instant. Some attempted to flee, with a few escaping while the rest were run down or captured in their flight. Others wordlessly fell upon their swords while still others fought to the bitter end.

The priest's sense of triumph dampened, however, when his mind returned to the matter of Allor and Xavier's deaths, and the impending one of Roniil. His heart went out to Lerannu, who, if she still lived, would be greeted with two losses upon her return. Amidst the great cheers that thundered all around him, Verdok managed to catch Donovan's attention. The bard, gently lowering the dying Roniil against a nearby stone, rushed over to the priest. His winter-blue eyes bore both triumph and sadness.

"We need to let them know," Verdok said to the bard over the clamor of victory, "assuming that any of them are still alive. I don't know where exactly they'll be, but in case they haven't gotten back to Mercilaar yet, we need someone to get to them and tell them what's happened."

Donovan nodded grimly. "I'll go," he said levelly. He turned back to Roniil and passed some quick consoling words to him, and then dashed past the gate and up the hill toward the castle. Verdok turned his attention to Lerannu's father, doing all he could with the bandages and medicines he had on hand to keep the warrior alive a little longer, hoping he might live at least to see his daughter one last time. He then glanced at the body of Xavier, his heart aching at the sight of Ranye quietly weeping as she held him. Verdok was grieved at the loss of such a good and wondrous friend, but he also wished that the Ecclesian had not perished because his blessed powers could have very well saved Roniil or possibly even revived Allor.

179
12/1/4030 G.M.

LERANNU stood frozen in a state of macabre awe at the sight of the demonic empress collapsing in a bloody heap with Ruth's axe buried into its skull. Though there was no telling what the repercussions would prove to be in the future, the immediate, obvious threat was at last vanquished. All the strength within Lerannu evaporated instantly. She barely managed to stay on her feet long enough to fish out another flask of Kamgenbew from her bag and drink it.

The mage leaned against the wall, looking at her companions as they stared at their fallen nemesis. A moment passed when suddenly they heard a great cry of triumph from far below. Looking to one another, they gave each other a small smile, certain that it was their friends and allies who were now crowing victoriously outside Genverdell's walls. Having regained her sense of energy, Lerannu approached Ruth and offered the knight her hand. Ruth took it, and with Mira on her other side, the knight leaned on the huntress's shoulder. The three then carefully made their way out of the castle.

The body of Mercilaar was now naught but a pile of charred bones and drenched ashes, swiftly being washed away by the rain. The only other thing left was the unbreakable egg that had formed amidst the ashes. Mira picked the egg up caringly, though there was no worry of it cracking, and held it in a mother-like embrace as she and her sisters of fate began to descend the east hill toward the sounds of victory. They were roughly halfway down the hill when a familiar face came dashing up to them.

"Don!" Mira cried out in tearful cheer as she ran to embrace her husband. Lerannu and Ruth looked on as the huntress and the bard held and kissed one another. Suddenly, the bard noticed the egg under his wife's arm, and his ears flattened somberly against his head.

"So Mercilaar ..."

"Yes," said Mira as she gently petted the large egg. "I thought that, once we settle everything here, we might go back to Karzynhaal like you mentioned earlier and put this somewhere nice and quiet for it to hatch later."

The bard smiled and nodded, but his smile quickly faded when he looked up to Lerannu. The mage felt a horrible dread grip her heart, and she tried to brace for the worst as Donovan approached her.

"Who has fallen?" she asked in a small voice strained by threatening tears. "Al? Papa?"

Donovan nodded sorrowfully. "On both counts, my lady, yes."

Lerannu wept as Donovan took her hand.

"Roniil is still alive," he said, "though it doesn't look like he has much time left. Hurry with me, my lady, and you might still have a chance to bid him farewell before he journeys to Onu."

Lerannu looked to Ruth, who was still leaning on her shoulder. The Faithguard knight nodded.

"Go," she said, gently. "Mira and I will catch up."

Taking Donovan's hand, Lerannu ran down the hill and past the south gate. Within moments, she was in the midst of the battlefield and at her father's side.

Roniil groaned in a raspy breath, looking into the eyes of his daughter.

"L-Lera ..." he said shakily.

Lerannu looked pleadingly at Verdok. The priest shook his head and nodded to where Xavier's body lay, embraced by the silently weeping Ranye and the surrounding Trichynay warriors who gathered to grieve with her.

"It wouldn't have been a certain thing," Verdok said sadly, "but if only Xavier had made it, he could've at least tried—"

"Lera ..." Roniil rasped as he stretched his hand out to his daughter. Lerannu knelt beside him, embracing him tearfully.

"It's over, Papa," she said soothingly. "Raakmathna is gone, and now we can begin rebuilding all that has been lost."

"I'm ... so proud of you, Lera. I just wanted to say ... before I go ... that I'm sorry for all—"

"Papa," Lerannu wept, "please don't. I've let it go. Don't let that be the last thing on your mind when ... when ..."

Lerannu held her father close and wept freely. Her tear-blurred eyes suddenly found themselves roaming to Allor's body, and suddenly she remembered her satchel.

"Mercilaar's ashes! He was slain as we reached the castle, and I thought to grab some of them before the rain really started to fall. Maybe I can ..."

Lerannu fumbled about in her pack for the little pouch that held the Phoenix ashes. She opened the pouch and her heart sank into the deepest wells of grief.

"There ... there's only enough for one of them ... if that."

Lerannu despaired for only an instant before turning to Ranye.

"I could revive your husband," she said desperately as she got up to approach Xavier's corpse, "and he could try to revive them both in turn and—"

"He said that he was not to be brought back," Ranye said levelly. "He said this was simply his time. And besides, all the stories of resurrection tell of how exhausted the revived were upon returning."

"Yes, but ... I saw him heal Layna and Garthon, and Zongar told me about how ..."

"Surely you know that reviving the dead is far more than healing a wound, even for those most blessed and skilled in magic? And you saw how much it took out of him when he healed them. Healing Layna and Garthon wearied him, even though he rested soundly the night before, and healing Zongar really drained him, since he had only a few minutes' rest after a battle before seeing to our champion's stump."

Ranye chuckled sadly, patting her husband's shoulder and embracing him tightly.

"Do you really think that my Xavier, for all that he could do, can just hop right up and *revive* someone, let alone *two* people, right after being pulled from his walk toward the Great Curtain, or his brief time on the Shores of Passing?"

Lerannu breathed deeply, rasping through the tears. "You never know, and ..."

"Lady Stonefaith," Ranye said with a gentle, appreciative smile, "your intentions warm this widow's heart, but that's simply too high a gamble, especially when my husband has already declared that it was simply his time. Believe me. Let him go; the ashes are to be for another."

The mage nodded to the Trichynay chieftain, then exchanged looks with Donovan. She was at a loss with the dilemma that tore at her heart.

"If ... if he can be spared," Roniil wheezed, "use it for Allor."

"Papa," Lerannu sobbed, "I can't just–"

Roniil took his daughter's hand within his, squeezing it tenderly as he drew a deep, shaky breath.

"E-Enmayar needs him ... and he needs you. I ... I've done my part. It's time for me to go ... and settle everything with Onu. You two will be great in healing all the harm that's been done to the world, Lera. I ... I know that you'll do me proud."

Roniil shook violently, coughed, and went limp in Lerannu's arms. The mage wept, her grief quickly interrupted by Verdok.

"If we're to try to do as he asked," the priest said with an urgent voice that tried to be gentle, "we need to do it now. There's no telling how much time is left before Allor's soul passes the Shores beyond returning."

Lerannu took a deep, rattling breath, and handed the pouch to Verdok. She then crawled over to Allor's body and held him in her arms as Verdok began to place ashes on the gash in his throat and into his mouth.

180

12/1/4030 G.M.

ALLOR felt himself walking along in the dark, a barely perceptible light shining far in the distance. It seemed impossibly far away, and yet he found himself almost before it in no time. A soft, shimmering body of infinitely spanning material slightly obscured the light. As he walked on, he passed through it and the sensation of a soft, light curtain caressed his fur. He stepped past the Great Curtain and sighed in all-consuming awe at the paradisiacal sight that stretched out before him.

The great Holy Sea shimmered brilliantly, stretching into infinity with the land of Onu's home barely visible on the vast, sparkling horizon. Allor stepped lightly onto the Shores of Passing, seeing all around him countless souls waiting leisurely for passage. Suddenly, the people pricked up their ears and their tails waved from side to side with elation. The Sacred Ship was before them, landing right along the beach, and the souls hailed their two guides eagerly as the couple stepped off the ship and greeted them. Vitahla and Morinaar, whom Allor had seen in the clearing the night he and his companions fled from Genverdell, were now ushering the departed onto the ship, bound for the realm of eternal peace. Allor approached them calmly, having readily come to terms with his own death.

"I am ready," he said.

"We know," said the Angels of Life and Death in gentle unison, "but it seems you still have some time left within the realm of mortality. You still have a land to lead, a world to help heal ... and a woman to love."

Allor's heart leapt with awe. Only a very blessed few had ever been graced with a drink from Vitahla's flask. The king made to lift his hand to take the Flask of Life, but faltered as he gazed off into the distant paradise of eternity. He could see the Mountain, the Tree and its children, and all the other glorious splendors of Onuhaal clearly despite the vast distance that lay between him and the land beyond. His heart ached to simply go there and leave the pains of the world behind him forever.

"It will be alright," said Vitahla soothingly. "It's not going anywhere, and neither are we. We'll be waiting for you when your time does come, as with all your loved ones."

Allor drew a deep breath, relishing the bracing, ethereal air that filled his lungs. "So be it," he said as he again lifted his hand to accept Vitahla's flask. He was puzzled when the Angel of Life withheld it, and she and her husband began to gently laugh.

"What's this all about, then?" Allor asked with a raised brow.

"Your revival will be by the ashes of a Phoenix," Morinaar explained, "not the wine of my wife's flask."

Allor gaped with wonder. Morinaar and Vitahla quietly returned to their ship, stood at the helm, and waved a kind farewell to him.

"Until we meet again," they said jointly. The two angels then beckoned to someone behind Allor. The king turned and saw Xavier and Roniil approach. Sorrowful that the two men had passed from Fidonhaal, but joyful that they were now bound for the ultimate peace, Allor simply embraced them briefly and with no words between them. The two men boarded the ship, which swiftly sailed away. Singing and laughing echoed across the waters and into Allor's ears. The King of Enmayar breathed deeply once more, moved to the core of his being at the wonders he had seen.

He soon felt as though he was trapped within a great typhoon, and a massive, crushing weight within him pushed his spirit back into his body. A great burning sensation flared within his throat, and he felt the flesh on his neck mending.

The chilly caress of the gently pouring rain, and the familiar, warm arms of Lerannu greeted him upon his revival. His heart pounded achingly, and his lungs felt as though they were about to collapse until at last air rushed back into them.

Allor gasped and coughed intensely, and at last wearily opened his eyes.

181

12/1/4030 G.M.

LERANNU sobbed with joy at the sight of Allor's brown eyes fluttering open. Allor made no move to rise from her embrace, gazing deeply into her eyes as he clasped her hand within his. The king looked around, noticing all the familiar faces of the alliance before returning his sight to Lerannu.

"So ... we did it, I take it?" he said with a light laugh.

Lerannu nodded through her tears. "Yes, Al."

"Did all three of you make it?"

"Yes."

Lerannu kissed him, and a great cheer thundered all around her as she and Allor got to their feet. They turned to face their friends and allies, happy to see Ruth, Verdok, Mira, and Donovan together at their side. The kings and queens of the other three nations were also beside them, as was Ranye, her grief for Xavier briefly put aside. Donovan, kissing Mira, approached the king and the mage.

"A moment for the ages, my friends," the bard said cheerfully with a smile that pierced the grime and wounds that covered him. "Every soul here is blessed beyond words to have had any part in aiding you end this horror."

Lerannu and Allor nodded in agreement, at a loss for words in light of all that had passed. Ranye approached them, a small smile on her lips despite her tears.

"I take it you will be resuming your role as the King of Enmayar, Allor?" she asked.

"Of course," Allor said, "if Enmayar will have me."

"And what of the Queen?" Ranye asked as she looked squarely at Lerannu.

The mage stared levelly at the high shaman's widow, her hand gently squeezing Allor's. "If Enmayar and Allor will have me, I will take my place beside him and do what I can to lead the land and heal the world."

"So be it," said Ranye as all around them cheered once more. The high chief then approached them closely, speaking softly over the booming cheers.

"Go with Onu's blessing, my friends. Lerannu, I can tell that you will do your father proud, without a doubt."

Epilogue

182

4/7/4041 G.M.

MIRA stirred from her sleep. The light was bright outside her cottage window, shining green from the vibrant leaves of Santaru. She looked over and saw that Donovan was out of bed. That, along with the abrupt growling of her stomach, told the huntress that it was quite late in the morning. She got up, dressed, and left the bedroom, finding some breakfast that was left out for her. After eating, she stepped out into the main pathway of Plen.

She was quick to find everyone gathered together outside behind Kahle and Isaak's hut. They were sorting and preparing an array of herbs for the healer to use later, drying and grinding them as needed. Donovan was there, with Zarlin and Ona beside him as they helped their older cousin, Novon, grind several different roots into powder. Kahle and Isaak were tying together bundles of leaves to hang and dry. Ann was sorting the plants out for each group's respective task.

Xelof, the reincarnation of Mercilaar, sat contentedly beside them, and was the first to notice and greet the huntress. Her family greeted her in unison, with Ona and Zarlin getting up to hug their mother.

"Sorry I'm late," she said with a laugh as she glared at Donovan with mock severity. "Looks like nobody wanted to wake me."

The bard smiled. "You were beat from yesterday's hunt. We didn't want to disturb you."

"Well, I'm here now. What would I be most helpful with?"

"Just get that other mortar and start grinding those leaves, please," said Kahle.

Mira began grinding herbs beside her husband, children, and nephew as the Phoenix looked on. Xelof, having faint memories of his past life, was fond of all three of the Daughters of the East. With Mira and Donovan, and the rest of her family, however, the huntress liked to think there was a little more to their bond with the great bird. Xelof had visited them several times after Mira and Donovan had returned to Plen from their yearlong rest on Karzynhaal, where they had tended to the Phoenix's egg and conversed with him as he grew into a young adult. While the bird had visited all three of the Elect, Mira was quite sure that he visited her and her family more times than the others.

After a while of quietly observing the villagers' work, the Phoenix looked to Mira and asked a question.

"You all will be set to go to Genverdell ... when again? Soon, I know, but when exactly?"

"A week from today," Mira said cheerfully, "Our first night traveling will be graced with the full moon. We'll be there with a nice bit of time to catch up, and then both weddings will be held on Estonmay's Eve."

"It'll be nice to see them all again," said the Phoenix warmly. "Especially Talrah and Samuel, since it's going to be their big day. They grow up fast, don't they?"

"That they do," Mira said with a pondering sigh.

"Don't get started on that, young lady," Ann said with mock sternness as she placed more leaves beside her daughter for grinding. "It's my job to be like that; you've still got a good way to go before you should be musing on all that."

183
6/14/4041 G.M.

RUTH and Verdok walked down the corridors together, checking to see if they could find Arthur in any of the rooms. The archgeneral of the Faithguard and her salpion husband walked arm-in-arm, calling out to their son until they finally found him in the archtemple's kitchens.

"Grandma asked me to help them count out everything in the larders," Arthur explained. "I didn't forget; I was looking for you to go over the ring ceremony again, but I didn't want to say no to Grandma."

"That's fine," Ruth said warmly as she and Verdok joined him. "We'll help, too, and once we're done, we'll rehearse the ring-bearer part again."

Arthur hugged his mother, placing himself beside her so her left arm, though misshapen and not fully articulate, rested comfortingly on his shoulder. The boy and his parents then looked over the spacious and well-stocked larder alongside Sister Arza and a few other brothers and sisters of the Temple.

"Looks like we should be all set, as far as our part is concerned," Verdok said happily. "Besides, there's all that everyone else will be preparing and having wherever they'll be celebrating, and Allor and Lera have said several times that they'll manage the feast in the castle garden."

After one more quick evaluation of the larder's stock with her mother, Ruth and her family left the kitchen and began to make their way to the salpion's study. As they walked down the corridor, a young Faithguard squire jogged toward them, calling out to them as she came to a halt.

"Yes, Frelda?" asked Ruth.

Frelda saluted dutifully. "Lady Greenheart and her family have just arrived from Plen, Archgeneral. And the Phoenix is with them."

Ruth looked excitedly at Verdok and Arthur, and the three postponed their rehearsal to greet their longtime friends.

184
6/28/4041 G.M.

LERANNU stood beside her husband, King Allor Stonefaith, and their son, Roniil, as the three looked reflectively at the ornate tomb of the mage-queen's father. It was a marvelous construction of marble and the centerpiece of the gardens of Castle Genverdell, which since had become better known as the Phoenix Gardens in honor of Mercilaar. Since its renovation, the gardens had become a space that was almost always open to the public, being a memorial to Mercilaar, Roniil Tern, and all others who had perished in the dreaded war of hatred.

Today, however, the gardens were closed off for a private celebration: the wedding feast of Lerannu's stepson, Samuel, and her stepdaughter, Talrah. The twins were celebrating a joint ceremony, with Samuel marrying Orannah from the Karamus line of Sorrenar, and Talrah marrying Ifahn Bluemoon, the son of King Dominik and Queen Fida of Kellmayar. It was the day of Estonmay's Eve, the day before summer's beginning.

The time was an hour before noon, the hour at which the wedding was set to begin. Salpion Verdok, naturally, was ministering the unions, and Ruth and their son would be personally involved as well. Mira and her family had arrived a fortnight ago, along with Xelof, Mercilaar's reborn form. All of Genverdell, whose population had been renewed following the horrible slaughter of Raakmathna's last resort, now eagerly awaited the festivities.

Everyone was together again, and Fidonhaal had continued the cycle of struggling and healing as it had for the past four thousand years.

Samuel and Talrah, each dressed in their wedding splendor, looked with brightly shining eyes at the family, pulling Lerannu, Allor, and young Ron from their contemplations.

"Will we be off to the Temple soon?" asked Talrah, not wanting to spoil the serenity of their apparent reveries while also clearly being unable to contain her anticipation.

Lerannu and Allor joined hands and embraced Roniil between them as the three prepared to leave the gardens with Samuel and Talrah.

"Yes," said the Queen of Enmayar. "If you're ready, then let's go. The future is at hand. Let's not keep it waiting."

The queen and her family exited the gardens together, making their way toward the front courtyard, where the procession of carriages stood waiting. A majestic call reached their ears from the skies, and the royal family looked up in unison to see Xelof soaring overhead. Soon the Phoenix would descend to their side and lead the procession to the archtemple, representing the new beginnings that were soon to come.

Appendices

The following pages are offered to the more inquisitive reader who may wish to learn more about the world of Fidonhaal and its people than what might have been clearly provided by the tale told within this book alone. It should be noted, however, that the details comprising this story and the world in which it occurs, along with the endeavor of gathering, translating and organizing them into a form hopefully more approachable for the reader, entail more than what any one story or set of appendices can hope to completely fathom.

Furthermore, this labor has been conducted under the presumption that the reader is a fellow denizen of the world that the chronicler refers to as "Earth," and is also of the human race, being a fellow creature of the chronicler's kind. Failing that, it is presumed that the reader has, at the very least, enough knowledge of that world and species to be able to understand any references made to them for the sake of comparing and contrasting Earth with Fidonhaal, and humanity with Fidonity.

The potential shortcomings of these presumptions aside, it is hoped that the following information will be enough to sate at least some of the reader's curiosity.

Maps

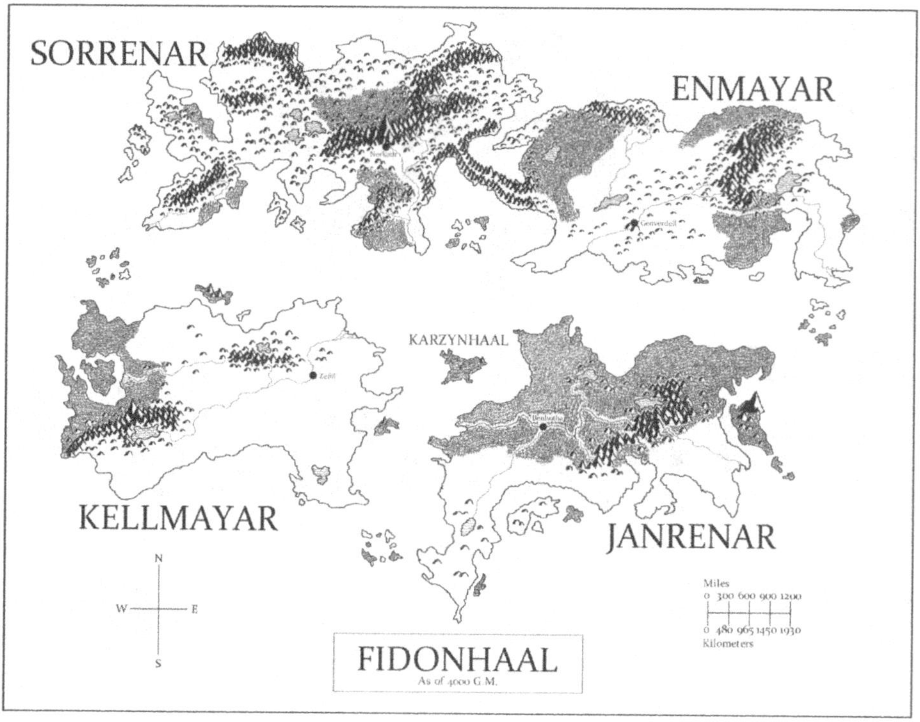
SORRENAR
ENMAYAR
KARZYNHAAL
KELLMAYAR
JANRENAR
N
W
E
S
Miles
0 300 600 900 1200
0 480 965 1450 1930
Kilometers
FIDONHAAL
As of 4000 G.M.

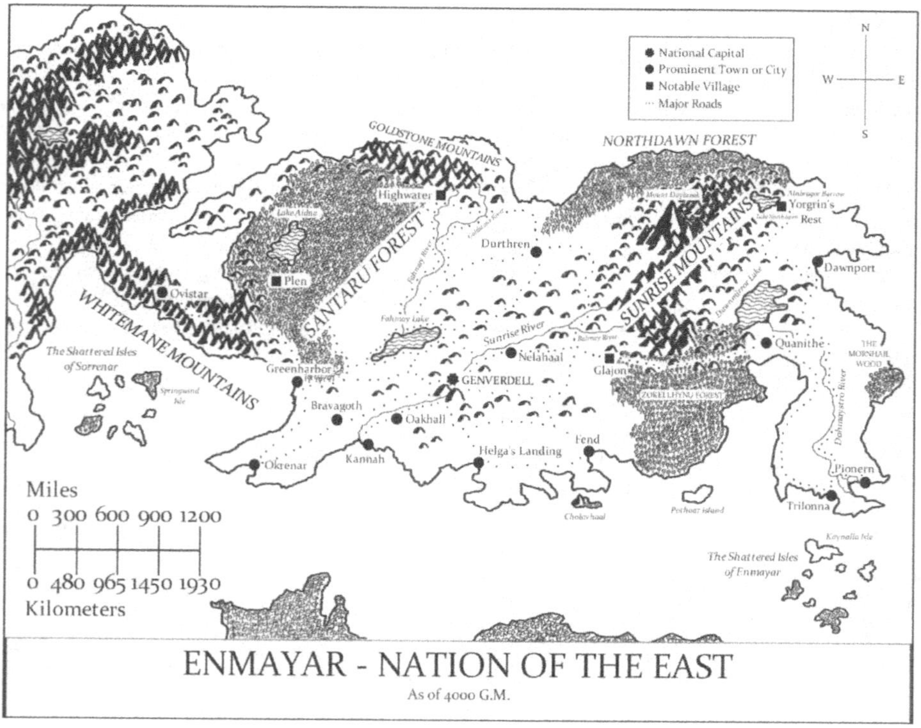
National Capital
Prominent Town or City
Notable Village
Major Roads
N
W
E
S
GOLDSTONE MOUNTAINS
NORTHDAWN FOREST
Highwater
Yorgrin's Rest
Durthren
SANTARU FOREST
SUNRISE MOUNTAINS
Dawnport
Plen
Ovistar
WHITEMANE MOUNTAINS
Fahnsey Lake
Sunrise River
Quanithe
THE MORNHAIL WOOD
The Shattered Isles of Sorrenar
Greenharbor
Nelahaal
Glajon
GENVERDELL
ZOKELLHYNU FOREST
Bravagoth
Oakhall
Fend
Helga's Landing
Kannah
Okrenar
Pionern
Trilonna
Miles
0 300 600 900 1200
0 480 965 1450 1930
Kilometers
The Shattered Isles of Enmayar
ENMAYAR - NATION OF THE EAST
As of 4000 G.M.

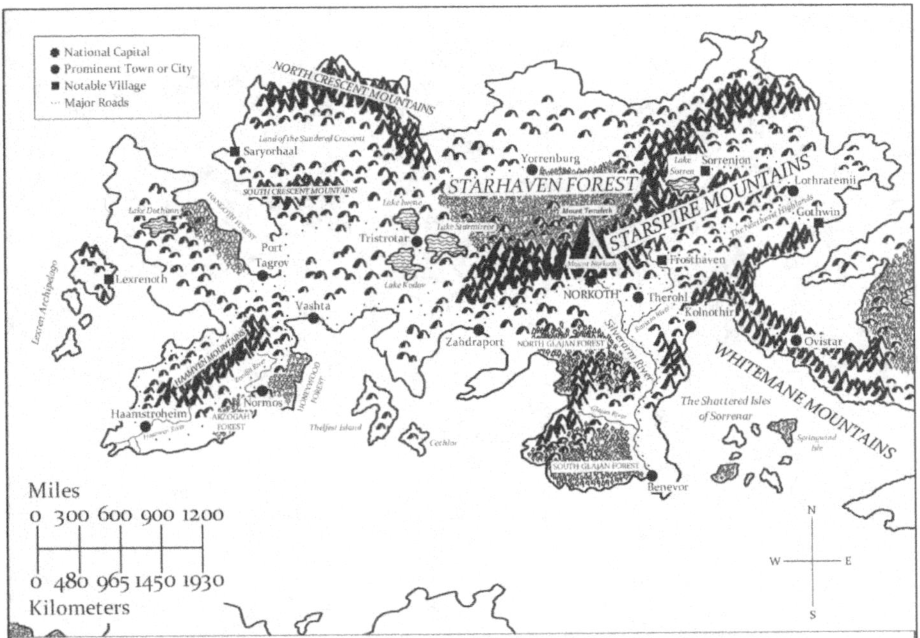

SORRENAR - NATION OF THE NORTH

As of 4000 G.M.

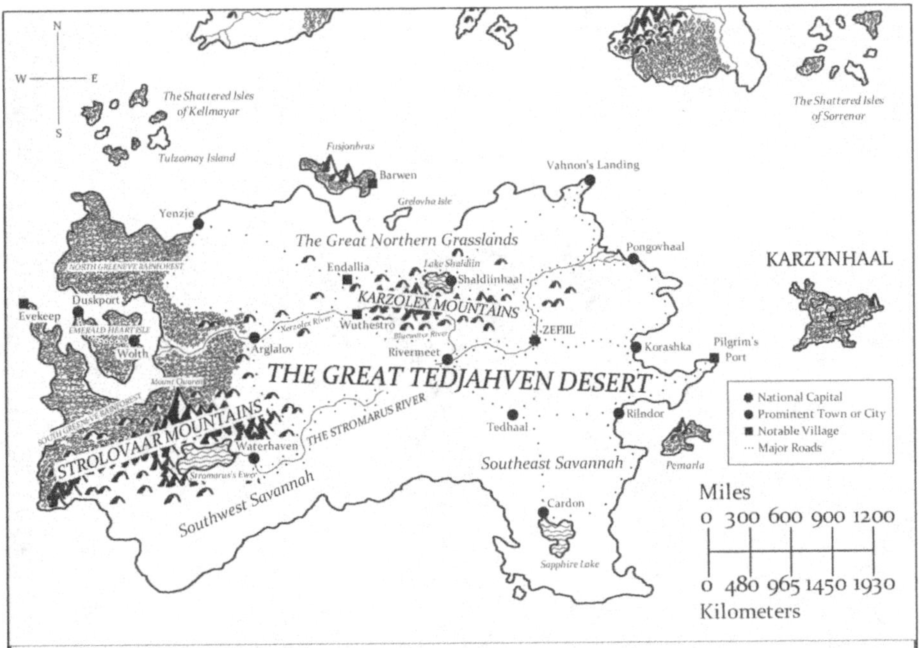

Legend:
- National Capital
- Prominent Town or City
- Notable Village
- Major Roads

Map labels: NORTH CRESCENT MOUNTAINS, Land of the Sunder of Crescent, Saryorhaal, Yorrenburg, Lake Sorren, Sorrenjon, STARSPIRE MOUNTAINS, Lothratemii, SOUTH CRESCENT MOUNTAINS, STARHAVEN FOREST, Lake Ivene, The Northern Highlands, Gothwin, Lake Dothinn, HANNOTH FOREST, Lake Svarmairese, Mount Terraloch, Port Tagrov, Tristrotar, Lake Koslov, Frosthaven, Lexrenoth, Vashta, Mount Norloth, NORKOTH, Therohl, Kolnothir, Silverarm River, Zahdraport, NORTH GLAJAN FOREST, Ovistar, WHITEMANE MOUNTAINS, Lexten Archipelago, HAMAYEN MOUNTAINS, Zenlin River, HONEYWOOD FOREST, The Shattered Isles of Sorrenar, Springwind Isle, Haamstroheim, Normos, ARZOGAH FOREST, Hamayen Bay, Theljest Island, Cethlor, Glajan River, SOUTH GLAJAN FOREST, Benevor

Miles
0 300 600 900 1200

0 480 965 1450 1930
Kilometers

N / W / E / S

KELLMAYAR - NATION OF THE WEST

As of 4000 G.M.

Legend:
- National Capital
- Prominent Town or City
- Notable Village
- Major Roads

Map labels: The Shattered Isles of Kellmayar, The Shattered Isles of Sorrenar, Tulzomay Island, Fusjonbras, Barwen, Vahnon's Landing, Yenzje, Grelovha Isle, The Great Northern Grasslands, Pongovhaal, KARZYNHAAL, NORTH GREENEVE RAINFOREST, Endallia, Lake Shaldiin, Shaldiinhaal, Duskport, KARZOLEX MOUNTAINS, Evekeep, EMERALD HEART ISLE, Kerzolex River, Wuthestro, Blaewnitra River, ZEFIIL, Korashka, Pilgrim's Port, Wolth, Arglalov, Rivermeet, THE GREAT TEDJAHVEN DESERT, Mount Owaren, STROLOVAAR MOUNTAINS, SOUTH GREENEVE RAINFOREST, THE STROMARUS RIVER, Waterhaven, Rilndor, Tedhaal, Southeast Savannah, Pemarla, Stromarus's Ewe, Southwest Savannah, Cardon, Sapphire Lake

N / W / E / S

Miles
0 300 600 900 1200

0 480 965 1450 1930
Kilometers

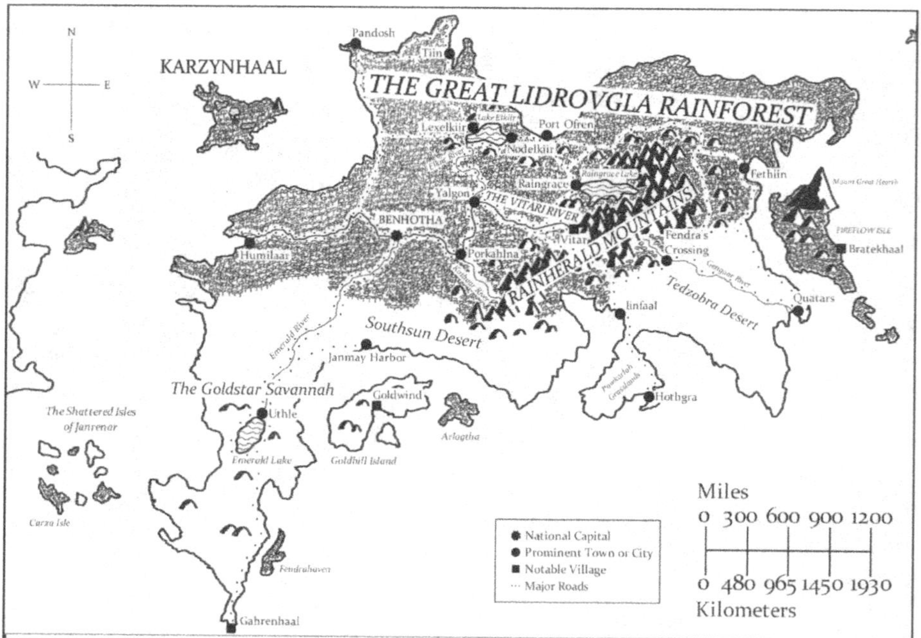

JANRENAR - NATION OF THE SOUTH

As of 4000 G.M.

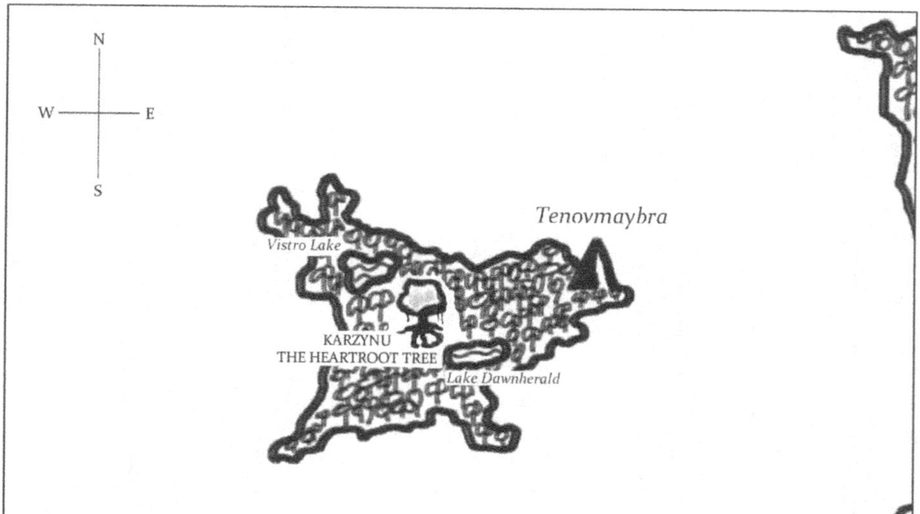

KARZYNHAAL

THE ISLE OF FIDONITY'S AWAKENING

APPENDIX A

History and Time

The saga of Fidonhaal is a great amalgam of events that span millennia. The following information gives further context to this history, as well as how the people of this world mark and record the passage of time.

Measurement of Time and Calendars

Translating the measurement and passage of time from the Fidons' perspective to that of ours is by and large a simple matter. The length of a Fidonhaal day is very much the same as one to us, so the text's usage of timespans such as seconds, minutes, hours and days mirrors how we use these units.

It is in the lengths of the months and years, however, where differences arise. In addition to the cycle of the seasons, the Fidon calendar is based on the phases of the world's moon. Fidonhaal's lunar cycle has been astoundingly consistent, with each of the four major phases, in sequence from the waxing quarter to the new moon, occurring on the seventh night of their respective week without fail in all of Fidonity's recorded history. Thus, with the Fidons basing their months on this cycle, each month, or "moon," is twenty-eight days long and segmented into four weeks spanning seven days each. The four seasons, used to gauge the span of the year, have three months allotted to each, resulting in a season spanning eighty-four days.

A year on Fidonhaal, though also twelve months long, totals only three hundred and thirty-six days as opposed to Earth's three hundred and sixty-five. This essentially makes a year on Fidonhaal about one month shorter than on Earth.

The months and days are named very simply in the Fidon tongue, with each month's name translating into the current month's number out of twelve, and the day of the week named by its number out of seven. Furthermore, months of the year have a name indicating their number, out of three, for their place in a given season, and the days of the month have an individual name based on their specific number out of twenty-eight.

To give examples, the Fidon word for the number six is *rek* and the word for "moon" (and "night") is *yor*. Since the months are referred to as "moons," the sixth month of the year is thus named *Yorrek*, meaning "Moon Six" or "Sixth Moon." The Fidon word for the number three is *tri*, and the season of winter is called *sard*. The third and final month of winter, therefore, is named *Sardtriyor*, meaning "Winter's Third Moon." The number four is *qua* and the word *may* translates to both "day" and "sun." The fourth day of any given week, therefore, is named *Quamay*, while the fourth day of each month is named *Mayqua*. Both forms translate to "Day/Sun Four" or "Fourth Day/Sun," but the specific arrangement of the words comprising the name indicate the specific context.

The following calendars represent the charting of a Fidonhaal month, along with a representation of the year and its seasons respective to the north and south hemispheres.

Monthly Fidon Calendar

ONMAY	FUSMAY	TRIMAY	QUAMAY	GONMAY	REKMAY	SETMAY
1 Mayon	2 Mayfus	3 Maytri	4 Mayqua	5 Maygon	6 Mayrek	7 Mayset
8 Mayok	9 Mayjiv	10 Maypar	11 Mayparon	12 Mayparfus	13 Maypartri	14 Mayparqua
15 Maypargon	16 Mayparrek	17 Mayparset	18 Mayparok	19 Mayparjiv	20 Mayfuspar	21 Mayfusparon
22 Mayfusparfus	23 Mayfuspartri	24 Mayfusparqua	25 Mayfuspargon	26 Mayfusparrek	27 Mayfusparset	28 Mayfusparok

Annual Fidon Calendar

1	2	3
YORON	**YORFUS**	**YORTRI**
Sardonyor in the North Hemisphere; Estonyor in the South Hemisphere	Sardfusyor in the North Hemisphere; Estfusyor in the South Hemisphere	Sardtriyor in the North Hemisphere; Esttriyor in the South Hemisphere
Mayon = Sardonmay in the North Hemisphere; Estonmay in the South Hemisphere	Mayparqua = Midwinter in the North Hemisphere; Midsummer in the South Hemisphere	Mayfusparok = Veronmay's Eve in the North Hemisphere; Kysonmay's Eve in the South Hemisphere
4	5	6
YORQUA	**YORGON**	**YORREK**
Veronyor in the North Hemisphere; Kysonyor in the South Hemisphere	Verfusyor in the North Hemisphere; Kysfusyor in the South Hemisphere	Vertriyor in the North Hemisphere; Kystriyor in the South Hemisphere
Mayon = Veronmay in the North Hemisphere; Kysonmay in the South Hemisphere	Mayparqua = Midspring in the North Hemisphere; Midautumn in the South Hemisphere	Mayfusparok = Estonmay's Eve in the North Hemisphere; Sardonmay's Eve in the South Hemisphere
7	8	9
YORSET	**YOROK**	**YORJIV**
Estonyor in the North Hemisphere; Sardonyor in the South Hemisphere	Estfusyor in the North Hemisphere; Sardfusyor in the South Hemisphere	Esttriyor in the North Hemisphere; Sardtriyor in the South Hemisphere
Mayon = Estonmay in the North Hemisphere; Sardonmay in the South Hemisphere	Mayparqua = Midsummer in the North Hemisphere; Midwinter in the South Hemisphere	Mayfusparok = Kysonmay's Eve in the North Hemisphere; Veronmay's Eve in the South Hemisphere
10	11	12
YORPAR	**YORPARON**	**YORPARFUS**
Kysonyor in the North Hemisphere; Veronyor in the South Hemisphere	Kysfusyor in the North Hemisphere; Verfusyor in the South Hemisphere	Kystriyor in the North Hemisphere; Vertriyor in the South Hemisphere
Mayon = Kysonmay in the North Hemisphere; Veronmay in the South Hemisphere	Mayparqua = Midautumn in the North Hemisphere; Midspring in the South Hemisphere	Mayfusparok = Sardonmay's Eve in the North Hemisphere; Estonmay's Eve in the South Hemisphere

Essential Historical Summary

Historians have catalogued four eras in their studies of Fidonhaal's past. A summarized list of these epochs follows:

The First Era is named *Onu Resdryn Mahze*, or Era of Onu's Creation, and *O.R.M.* is its historical abbreviation. It spans the time from the beginning of the universe and the formation of Fidonhaal to the rise of the first conscious Fidons, and is when the conflict between Onu and Raakaru began. It concludes with the event known as "The Awakening," when the First Ancestors of Fidonity's history awoke on the island of Karzynhaal fully sentient, and began learning of the world under the guidance of Onu and the angels.

The Awakening marks the beginning of the Second Era, which is named *Ontryn Mahze*, or Era of Communion. Abbreviated *O.M.* by scholars it is known as the "Lost Times," an age of unparalleled glory and peace in the world. Precious few records and relics have been recovered from that time, a few of which imply that the final few millennia of that era were marked by a curious, gradual drifting apart of the Fidons from Onu. Among the Fidons, both toward Onu and one another, attitudes shifted from trust to suspicion, and gratitude and love began to crumble to the rise of hubris and excessive self-interest. This trend ultimately led to the global collapse of the civilizations of the Lost Times, which was heralded by *Umay Zobravens*, The Day of the Flaming Winds.

On that day began the Third Era, *Nogryn Raakaru Mahze*, the Era of Raakaru's Reign. Historians abbreviate it as *N.R.M.*, and it is the time of Raakaru's conquest of Fidonhaal and enslavement of the Fidons to his will. Fidonity was reduced to barbarous, warring tribes that slew and enslaved one another in service to Raakaru and his demons, who ruled them as false and cruel gods. It was also in this time that the fell creatures of Fidonhaal, the Curse Spawn, came to be, being formed by Raakaru's defilement of the creatures of the world and Fidonity itself. Only the sacred soil of the island Karzynhaal remained untainted by Raakaru's touch, and the Hateful Heart spitefully erected a great and terrible citadel that spanned over it, cloaking it in its ill shadow.

That age of darkness ended when four Fidon warlords, having discovered remnants of lore from the Second Era and learning of their meaning from the angels' revelations, repented to Onu and became the First Elect. They began to unify the world against Raakaru, and in time played their role in the exorcism of the Hateful Heart from Fidonhaal. This expulsion heralded the beginning of *Gentryn Mahze*, the Era of Reunion, the fourth and present era of Fidonhaal's history. This is the time that has become the central point of interest for the Saga of Fidonhaal, for it tells of all the good and evil, triumphs and defeats, and wonders and horrors that have transpired within Fidonity since Raakaru's expulsion.

At the time of the story told in this book, just over four millennia have passed in this era. Great heroes and heroines, from those marked by Onu himself to those who rose to renown by their own will and efforts have come and gone throughout this age, as have the villains who served the will of Raakaru, knowingly and willingly or through their own darkness. Events wonderful and atrocious had already transpired many times over in this world and age. The tale told in this book is but another body of such persons and happenings, and is thus ultimately but one part to the Saga of Fidonhaal.

APPENDIX B

Basic Descriptions
of Geography and Climate

The lands of Fidonhaal consist of three major landmasses, with a spattering of islands across the globe and Karzynhaal, the Sacred Isle of Origin. For a more detailed view of Fidonhaal's geography, the reader may consult the book's enclosed maps.

Enmayar

The continental nation of the East is named *Enmayar*, or "The Sunrise Branch," and it shares the same landmass as the nation of the North. The two nations are joined by a mountainous isthmus that is home to the famed Whitemane Range as well as the pass that runs through it and shares its name. Enmayar is known for having the mildest temperate range of overall climates when compared to the other three nations, and has a landscape consisting mostly of rolling hills, wide flat plains and valleys deep and shallow.

Its capital city is *Genverdell*, a grand city that rests upon two great hills, the valley between them, through which the Sunrise River flows, and the land immediately surrounding them. The Sunrise River shares its name with the mountain range that births it, and the Sunrise Mountains are the site of Fidonhaal's third-largest mountain, Mount Daybreak. The great forest named Santaru, one of the largest in the world, stretches across a large expanse of Enmayar's western land from south to north.

The northernmost regions of the East are cooler throughout the year, though not to the same extent as the northmost reaches of Sorrenar. The southernmost regions enjoy warmer temperatures, with the climates ranging from subtropical to what the reader might know as Mediterranean.

Janrenar

The south continent-nation is named *Janrenar*, or "The South Star Branch." It is famous for its primarily tropical climate and massive rainforest. The forest is named *Lidrovgla*, or "Ever Green," and is the largest single forest of both its kind and the world at large, stretching across much of the continent. The long and broad Vitari River runs through the Lidrovgla Rainforest along with its tributaries. Another river, the Emerald, flows from the southern great lake that shares its name and joins the Vitari at a great intersection.

It is just before this conjunction where the majestic capital city of *Benhotha* stands, spanning the Vitari from bank to bank as a massive bridge. Two deserts, along with patches of subtropical land, border the rainforest's southmost reaches. The southernmost land of the continent is the mildest, coolest region of Janrenar, comprising of temperate grassland and hills.

Janrenar's largest island, Fireflow Isle, lies shortly off the east coast. The island forms an extensive strait with the mainland and is home to Mount Great Hearth, the world's largest volcano and fourth-largest mountain overall.

Kellmayar

The nation of the West is named *Kellmayar*, or "The Sunset/Sunfall Branch," and is home to the largest desert in Fidonhaal, which is named *Tedjahven*. The presence of this desert is the foremost sign of Kellmayar's predominantly hot and arid climate, though smaller rainforests exist in the westernmost region, and the lands spanning Tedjahven's north and south borders are home to flat and hilly expanses of savannah.

Its capital, the city of *Zefiil*, spans and is nestled on the banks of the great Stromarus River. This river, the longest in Fidonhaal, is named after the Angel of Water, who is especially regarded by the people of the vast desert, and flows from a lake known as Stromarus's Ewer. The lake rests at the feet of the mountain range called the Strolovaar Mountains, which is the home of Mount Quaren, the second-tallest mountain in the world.

Sorrenar

Sorrenar, its name translating to "The North Star Branch," is the northern continent and nation. It shares the great landmass where Enmayar also lies, being joined to it by the Whitemane isthmus. Sorrenar is renowned as the most rugged and mountainous terrain in the world, as well as the land with the overall coldest clime. The warmest regions of Sorrenar are found on the southern peninsulas, and the summers there are pleasantly mild. The northernmost lands are ever-blanketed in snow. The climate of all the land between these far reaches is a gradient from the south's mild warmth to the north's frigidity.

The North's capital is the great city of *Norkoth*, built upon (and into) the mountain of the same name and in sight of Mount Temeleth, the tallest mountain in all of Fidonhaal. Temeleth belongs to the Starspire Mountains, the furthest-spanning mountain range in the world and the source of the Silverarm River, which flows past Norkoth on its course to the ocean.

Karzynhaal

Karzynhaal is the name of the Island of Origin, the place where Fidonity became conscious and began their sentient existence according to Fidon lore. Karzynhaal's climate is tropical, for it rests along Fidonhaal's equator. However, some of the ocean's currents help moderate the general temperature of the island, making it somewhat more temperate when compared to the general temperatures of Janrenar or Kellmayar.

The island's name translates to "Home of the Heartroot," and refers to *Karzynu*, the colossal tree at the island's center, which has lived for all the millennia since Fidonity's Awakening and the likes of which is found nowhere else in the world. The Great Tree's bark is made of shimmering, interweaving bands of black, brown, grey and white, and its leaves are the green of fiery emeralds. Amongst its many magnificent boughs, there are four that are the largest, and each one points either north, east, south or west. Most of the bark on the north-pointing branch is white. The majority of the eastward branch's bark is grey. The southward bough is mostly black. The west-pointing limb is mostly brown.

When the first generations of the Awakened Fidons prepared to depart from Karzynhaal and journey throughout the world, Onu bade them to go where they pleased, stressing that they would be able to visit those who went elsewhere in due time. However, the Fidons were indecisive at first, unsure of where to journey and whether to travel all together or to go separate ways. Then they looked upon the Heartroot, and seeing the manner of the four greatest branches, they agreed to take the limb's dominant colors and directions as a sign. The majority of the first Balons journeyed in the direction of the northward branch, which led them into view of the blue North Star. The majority of the original Zarons traveled eastward, in the direction of the rising sun. Most of the first Mavons followed the south-pointing branch, which led them to the land under the golden South Star. Most of the original Kasons followed the western branch, which led them to travel to the land where the sun descended below the horizon. As a gesture of honor to the Great Tree of Karzynhaal, the Fidons named the continents they settled in memory of Karzynu's four boughs.

On the northeastern shore of the island is a volcano named *Tenovmaybra*, the Mountain of Sunfire. Its name alludes to the mountain's continuous but gentle flow of lava, along with the sight of it greeting the dawn. This view was first seen by the Awakened Fidons and has continued to be an awe-inspiring sight to those who witness it today.

The Archipelagos of the Shattered Isles

Off the coasts of the four continents, there are a number of islands of various sizes. Most of these have formed through typical geological phenomena, be that volcanic activity, the shifting of fragments from the main landmasses, or a combination of the two. However, there exist archipelagos that were formed by a cataclysm that occurred in the first days of Raakaru's tyranny. These groups of islands are referred to as the "Shattered Isles," and are so named in reflection of how they came to be.

In the days of the Lost Times, when Fidonity's bond with Onu was strongest and most pure, there were four sizeable islands that lay in the waters between the continents. These islands formed places that enabled people from the lands either side of them to easily meet and communicate. Archaeological findings have shown that great cities were built here, cities that scholars have speculated to be the original capitals of the lands.

When Raakaru seized the world in the wake of the Fidons' severance from Onu, the warlords that arose in that time sought control of the islands as key positions from which to wage their battles and conquests. The angels, their hearts broken by grief and contempt at what had come to pass, and not wanting to allow the barbarians to have such easy outposts for their globe-spanning wars, beseeched Onu to either permit them to sunder the islands or to do so himself. Onu granted their request, and in a great clash of the elements, the seasons, and day and night, the angels desolated the four islands, leaving them scorched and windblown. As the final blow, Terranah smote each isle with her great hammer, breaking them into pieces that were then sundered further by the seas under Stromarus's governance. Though the warring peoples still clamored for positions amongst the newly formed archipelagos, none could gain enough ground to enable easy forays into the lands across the seas. This kept most of the barbarous clans from significantly advancing beyond the continents on which they lived, as the myriad of opposing archipelago outposts and the hindering skirmishes on open waters kept any one group from gaining a particular advantage.

Now, in the days of the Fourth Era, the Shattered Isles of the North, East, South and West are home to various numbers of Fidons, and have had their own places in history and tales throughout the ages. Some of the islands are largely uninhabited while others are quite densely populated. The climates of the east and west archipelagos range from tropical to subtropical. The Shattered Isles of the North are more moderate, being in the Springwind Sea between Sorrenar and Enmayar. The islands of the South's archipelago are also temperate, being a fair distance from the tropics, though still warmed by the ocean currents that flow from there.

The Whitemane Mountains and Isthmus

The Whitemanes are a mountain range that span across the isthmus of the same name, joining the continents of Sorrenar and Enmayar. The winds of both Sorrenar and Enmayar blow through the pass, with the air from the north being consistently chilled and the wind from the east, though generally milder, varying by the season. Furthermore, the warmer ocean currents that flow from the south affect the air that passes between the many peaks of the land. This results in a climate that, while generally cooler than the east, is not as regularly cold as the north. Its coldest time is naturally in winter, but the other three seasons are generally not too frigid or harsh.

Prior to the unification of the continents into four large nations, the Whitemanes existed as its own domain. The kingdom oversaw the land traffic from one continent to the other, trading with those who passed by and generally assuring safe passage despite the domestic conflicts that regularly afflicted the mountainous realm. The city of *Ovistar*, which stands at the heart of the great pass, has long served as the central seat of power for the Whitemanes.

When the four continents unified into single nations, Sorrenar and Enmayar, in honor of their longstanding and mutual amicability with the Whitemane people, negotiated with them and each other to split the isthmus along the border formed by Ovistar. The land north and west of the border-citadel would officially count as land of Sorrenar, while the land south and east of it would be recognized as Enmayar's. However, the three parties agreed that the Whitemanes would retain much of its prior autonomy while still communicating with both of the nations that now shared it, in addition to receiving support from them in return for their cooperation. Thus, the warden or wardeness of the isthmus oversees the region on both sides of the border, reporting important matters to the respective nation and tending to local matters on their own and in conjunction with their subordinate officials.

APPENDIX C

Cultural Summaries of Fidonhaal

The world of Fidonhaal is a place of global culture that is both homogenous and variable. While virtually all of the information in the appendices has some sort of relevance to culture, the following summaries intend to give a broad-stroke vision of what makes up some of the more fundamental, miscellaneous aspects of Fidon life. More specific cultural elements, such as religion, magic and government, are detailed in the appendices following this section.

Common Values

The distances that span the lands and seas of Fidonhaal, along with its various climates, landscapes, and historical events, have led to the development of a number of distinctive cultures spread across the world. These cultures include the settled majority of the population, with their villages, towns and cities, as well as several varieties of "Wild-Dwellers," those who live off the land in groups that range from secluded settlements to nomadic and semi-permanent tribes and gatherings.

While the Fidons have an array of cultural "flavors," there is also a marked presence of common values and practices that can be seen across all of Fidonhaal, albeit in varying ways of expression. This has been attributed to the longstanding and constant contact that the Fidons have had with one another across the globe, as well as the common, essential belief of the Fidons' purpose in the world and universe at large.

These two factors behind the Fidons' core similarities are traced to the beginning of their sentient history, when the First Ancestors awoke on Karzynhaal. There they conversed with their creator and the angels, met one another, paired as mates, had children, and eventually journeyed and settled throughout the world to peacefully live and interact with each other for millennia. While most of the Fidons' values were lost during the Era of Raakaru's Reign (and those that weren't "lost" were corrupted for ill means and ends), they were in time reclaimed at the beginning of the Era of Reunion and have been pursued (imperfectly, but earnestly) by the majority of Fidons since.

The first of these common values is the effort of the Fidons to keep a bond with their creator, whom they call *Onu*, or simply "The One." This value plays into the very name of the Fidon race, for *Fidon* means "Faithful One" or "One of Faith" in their language, and the name of their world, *Fidonhaal*, means "Home of the Faithful Ones." This value was the driving ideal of Fidonity in the Era of Communion, the lost age of unparalleled wonder and achievement. Following its revival after the fall of Raakaru's dominion, it has once again become a paramount value for the vast majority of Fidons. This bond is believed to be the essential source and drive for a Fidon's abilities and purpose for the duration of their mortal lives, which the people hold as being to live in trust and love with Onu, one another, and themselves. By striving toward this end, the Fidons value the efforts to love and learn, and to otherwise attempt to do whatever good – great and small – they can, and aid their fellows in doing the same. Through these efforts, the Fidons maintain a communion with Onu and act out the purpose, collective and individual, that they have. This purpose, though already great within the confines of the mortal life, is nevertheless incomplete until a Fidon's time comes to die, at which time they are forever reunited in full with Onu within the holy domain of *Onuhaal*. This essential value of the bond, and the faith in which it is pursued, is also generally cited as being the ultimate source of most, if not all, other crucial values and beliefs commonly held by the faithful.

Because of the essential beliefs of the Fidons' purpose, they place great value on both the potential of the individual as well as the common good of communities, nations, and the world at large. Of course, due to many circumstances, the balance between these two values is rarely, if ever, truly equal at any one time. Nevertheless, it is an ideal that most Fidons strive to achieve and maintain as best they can. The Fidons' purpose also stresses a value in the basic sense of equality amongst all Fidons, whatever their wealth, nation of origin, occupation, sex, or other such factor. It may be argued that sexual egalitarianism is an especially important aspect of Fidon life at large, as Fidons value the roles of both men and women as equally important to the perpetuation of life, and extends this notion to virtually all other aspects. Regardless of whether a given man or woman takes part in procreation, Fidons view the pursuit of their calling as crucial to the ultimate progression of Onu's design for existence.

Thus, women and men alike can pursue education and the occupation of their choice, though exact opportunities vary by locale, present resources and other circumstances. Furthermore, Fidons generally marry who they desire out of love as life partners as opposed to social, economic, or political gain, though such things have certainly come into play at times. In most cases, the furthest extent of parental or other external influence on a marriage is typically of "strong encouragement" instead of outright coercion. This longstanding value of common potential and mutual respect between the sexes has blessed Fidonhaal with a rich history of both heroes and heroines, and their deeds (as well as villains and villainesses, for that matter). Scholars, clerics, soldiers, traders, and craftspeople of both sexes exist and work together.

While numerous other values can be seen in common, yet variable, measures across Fidonhaal, loyalty, honesty, and trust are likely to be seen as the last major values of Fidonity. These three values, intertwined with one another, apply to the individual Fidon with oneself, their spouse, their children, parents, and other family and kin, as well as their friends, community, nation, and ultimately their world at large and their God, Onu; the last two being bound together in a covenant of trust that began with the First Ancestors.

With all of this being said, as can be seen within the story told in this book, Fidonhaal is by no means an absolute utopia where these values are held universally and practiced without fail. These ideals are what *most* Fidons hold, not *all*, and they are values that the people *strive* to uphold. The relative majority of Fidons may have a decent record in their pursuit of these ideals, but they are not by any means free of vice, sin, or strife. One should not mistake any of these generalizations as unanimous and absolute. Nor should one perceive the relative lack of mentioned flaws or exceptions as an implication that such things are absent from the Fidon condition. Their past and their present have been marked by evil and struggles plenty of times.

Commerce

By the time of the accounts told in this book, the Four Nations of Fidonhaal had long established a standard currency comprised of coins minted from copper, silver, and gold. The size, weight, and amount of metal used in each are uniform throughout the world, with the only variance being the insignia on the back, indicating the nation that originally minted it. The front of every coin, regardless of the metal from which it's minted, depicts a likeness to Karzynu, the Heartroot Tree of Karzynhaal. The copper piece, or *kahdan*, is the smallest coin in size and value, comparable to a penny or the like. One hundred kahdans makes one silver piece, or *fahdan*, and it takes one hundred fahdans to equal a single *gahdan*, or gold piece.

Many of the crafts and trades of the world, especially by the time visited in this book, are an interweaving of individual pursuit and achievement alongside standards set by government, longstanding common values, and those regulated by an array of guilds and other such organizations.

Education

The pursuit of knowledge is a well-regarded value amongst nearly all of Fidonity, as it is viewed as the embracing and learning of Onu's design for the betterment of oneself and their bond with their Maker, as well as the improvement of general society. However, due to the array of circumstances and environments that a given Fidon may have experienced, the specific degree of education one may have can vary significantly.

There are resources for practically any Fidon to pursue as much education as they wish, ranging from private instructors to publicly funded schools. Furthermore, utter illiteracy is virtually nonexistent amongst the Fidons. Though some are certainly more well-read than others, nearly all Fidons can read on a basic level, typically being able to at least read and comprehend important and common information, such as what might be found in a public news bulletin.

Medicine and Disease

The Fidons' efforts in pursuing and refining medicine were being practiced even in the dark days under Raakaru's tyranny, as many barbarous warriors were wounded and mended, and the potential for disease was as present then as any other time, if not more so. The advancement of medicine became greater following Raakaru's expulsion, with many diseases, though potentially still persistent, being largely manageable at the time of the events in this book. Most populated areas, from cities to Wild-Dweller camps, have at least one doctor or herbalist relatively close by, and the international cultivation and trading of medicinal plants was long practiced even prior to the four continents becoming consolidated into the Four Nations.

One of the diseases that had still been of significant concern until the latter period of this tale was the dreaded Endallian Fever. This ailment, named after a Kellmayarn town that was long ago utterly wiped out by an outbreak of the disease (and has since been the site of a world-renowned center for medicinal studies), had been well-combated by the steady advances in medicine made over the centuries. Nevertheless, it had still been a significant cause of death on the occasions when outbreaks gave way to pandemics, even in the time of this tale, until research conducted and supported by Queen Sheeva Mivinaar produced a remedy that reduced the fever to a relatively minor concern.

Though Fidon cultures the world over greatly value and celebrate the continuation of life through procreation and birth, there is also the practice of moderating the rate of births in the form of the plant known as Fallowroot. The root of this plant is finely ground into a powder, which is then imbibed as a tea by men on an as-needed basis to temporarily neutralize their seed. Some men drink a dose of Fallowroot tea on a more or less daily basis, either as a general precaution or simply as a habit to practice unless specifically intending to sire children. However, most men, due to the Fidons' general practice of monogamy, simply take doses during their wives' periods of peak fertility, which both mates can readily account for in their routines. Its properties were discovered in the earlier centuries of the Fourth Era, and Fallowroot has since come to be cultivated across all of Fidonhaal and is largely accessible by the general population.

General Marriage Customs

The union between spouses is regarded as a deeply significant bond amongst the Fidons, with many holding it as the highest single bond that can exist between two mortal individuals. While the exact nuances and specific customs vary across the world, there are a few common elements that all cultures have developed in regards to standard marriage and courtship practices.

Most Fidons, whatever their station in society, have at least a few suitors they consider as potential mates before deciding on one. While some might be greatly encouraged by their families to marry from a certain selection, and for considerations other than just love, the concept of a marriage that is forced outright is considered a corruption of the initial purpose of the bond and has been practiced very few times in Fidonhaal's history.

The typical wedding rite has its roots in the way by which the Fidons began rebuilding their civilizations following Raakaru's expulsion. Back then, the lands were comprised of many small domains, the leadership of which was held by one who had enough wealth, martial support, or prestige to maintain their claim. Other Fidons came to these leaders, swearing fealty to them and offering whatever skills and services they could contribute to the realm's prosperity in return for security. While plenty of those who became subjects were of trades other than agricultural, the initial call by the leaders was for people who would work the land. The basic point of the Fidons' oath of fealty was to be loyal to their leader and the land, or "earth," that they held. The domain of a given leader simply shared the name of the leader's family, and those who were subjects of the realm carried that name, in addition to their own individual and family names, as a mark of citizenship.

The rite of marriage swiftly became a favored practice again, being welcomed in the aftermath of the previous era's barbarism. However, the specific practice of the rite, and relevant matters such as the adoption of one surname or the other, varied significantly from one place to another. The unions in some areas defaulted to adopting the husband's surname, while others took that of the wife, and others yet practiced the discarding of both and devised an entirely new name. It ultimately didn't take long for a common practice to begin spreading across Fidonhaal, unconfined by the many political boundaries of the day.

In several places throughout the world, Fidons looked at the oath between liege and subject, and drew symbolic parallels between this bond and that of matrimony. They likened women to the earth, or land, of a leader's domain, which, amongst other things, bore the fruit of the farmers' labors. Men, in turn, were likened to the subjects who swore loyalty to the land and its leader, then labored to ensure the land's prosperity, whether by sowing seed to produce fruit or by some other means. Regarding both women and men as equally important for life's continuation, as well as for one another's mutual potential, those who drew these parallels nevertheless devised a standard marriage rite that entailed the husband's adoption of his wife's surname, similar to how a subject adopted their liege's surname to indicate their citizenship. Word of this practice, and the reasoning behind it, soon spread beyond the borders of the realms that first practiced it. In time, it became the general custom across all of Fidonhaal, with the Temple officially adopting it as its standard rite after a few further refinements.

This is, however, only the default method, used simply as a standardized means to document marriages and track genealogies. It is not a practice that is enforced by any actual secular or religious mandate. There are couples who, for one reason or another, agree beforehand to adopt the husband's surname instead. This is more common with marriages where the husband's surname has a prominent reputation, especially for royal dynasties and similar situations. It is entirely possible, however, for the husband's surname to be adopted solely because the wife favors it.

Another longstanding practice has been the wearing of some form of jewelry to designate a Fidon as being married. Most Fidons practice the wearing of a simple ring, though a handful of cultures across the world use other jewelry to express the bond, along with other implications. Such cases are listed in the following entry.

Sexuality

Being an essential aspect of life and held as an act highly blessed by Onu, the Fidons regard sexuality and intercourse with a positivity that encompasses both reverence and frankness. It has long been treated with highly regarded ideals and standards, while simultaneously being the subject of normal conversation amongst peers as well as humor. Plenty of writings cover the matter, with one of the oldest and most well-regarded being *Benu Tryn Zolih*, or "The Blessed Bond of Flesh." It is a treatise jointly authored by two married clerics who wandered the world and documented the numerous common and nuanced stances on sexuality across Fidonhaal's cultures. Fidon literature has plenty of songs and poems regarding the matter, varying from rowdy to romantic, and many entailing measures of both. Visual and performance arts around the world include works featuring artistic nudity and depictions of copulation. No occupation, even that of the clergy, prohibits a Fidon from marrying and engaging in an intimate bond.

Monogamy, as well as abstinence until marriage, is the ideal practice across all of Fidonhaal, regardless of the exact practices and expressions found within a given region's culture. That being said, the deeply running passions pertaining to this matter are well-acknowledged and understood by nearly all Fidons. Therefore, those who have engaged in premarital intercourse, whether with only one Fidon or more, are generally not written off outright as immorally promiscuous solely by that fact alone. This is especially the case if the involved parties either commit afterwards or otherwise responsibly resolve the relationship.

The majority of Fidonhaal's cultures, regarding sexual intercourse as a blessed act between two people, generally place a value on at least some degree of privacy for the engaging couple. Some extent of agitation or awkwardness, though generally mild, are common reactions in the event of an intrusion upon a mating couple, both for the couple and the one(s) who happen upon them in the act. However, these reactions typically spring from the general sense of respect for the act, as opposed to outright embarrassment or distaste, especially if the situation is otherwise in accord with general Fidon attitudes. In addition, these reactions are only the general case for actual, live incidents of intrusion, as depictions of sexuality and nudity are present and appreciated in literature and the arts, and viewing couples through such means is not regarded as inappropriate observation.

Though there are no records of any type of sexual relationship occurring amongst Fidons other than heterosexual, the forms of both women and men are popular subjects of viewing and admiration by either sex, especially when practiced within the inclinations of a given region's culture. Most cultures hold the primarily appropriate means of such viewings as those found in the arts. However, some cultures have developed a laxer attitude in the viewing of the body and of sexuality while still valuing the general practice of monogamous commitment.

The most well-known example of such a culture is that of the Trichynay Great Tribe in the land of Kellmayar. The general nature of the Trichynay's culture and dwellings are markedly more communal in comparison to many of Fidonhaal's other cultures, with the tribespeople living in camps of various sizes that are either nomadic or semi-permanent. Because of this, while still holding some sense and appreciation for privacy, the Trichynay people are far more accustomed to seeing their fellows copulating with their spouses, along with general sights of the bare Fidon body, as they go about their everyday lives when compared to most other people. Very few of the Trichynay have any trouble mating with their spouse in potential view of those who share their tent, and often even appreciate the potential for observers, viewing the act as a commending gesture toward the couple. Furthermore, the customary ear piercings of both sexes signify their sexual (and thus typically marital) status, being symbolic depictions of the wearer's genitals in an either "active" or "inactive" state.

For most of Fidonhaal's other cultures, a traditional wedding ring represents a Fidon's status of matehood. However, a few other cultures practice different expressions. In the eastern highlands of Sorrenar, the people wear nose rings to mark their marital status, with widows and widowers bearing nose jewelry consisting of only half of the loop. In the southeasternmost region of Enmayar, the people traditionally wear ear-piercing jewelry comprised of up to two jeweled studs on each ear that express life milestones entailing some degree of sexuality. The first piercing occurs at the age of eighteen, when the Fidon is fully recognized as an adult and of the commonly viewed minimum age suitable for marriage. The second piercing takes place upon the Fidon's wedding. The third occurs on the day of their first child's birth. The fourth and final piercing takes place upon the birth of the Fidon's first grandchild.

With fidelity being such a highly valued practice by most of Fidonity, the act of adultery is considered a significant offense. It is not, however, customary to subject the offenders to severe punishment from the general public. It is held by Fidons across all cultures that it is the right of the offended spouse to decide whether to remain with the offender or dissolve the marriage. The existing accounts of such instances tell of both decisions occurring at relatively equal rates, with varying degrees of civility in regards to the matter's resolution.

Prostitution is generally regarded as degrading to both the bodies of the participants and the general Fidon view of sexual congress, that being of a blessed act for the most sacred of bonds between two mortals. It is largely held by society that prostitutes and their clients are themselves not to be regarded as loathsome or evil, given that nearly all reports of such people describe them as having resorted to the act out of some sort of despairing circumstance. Efforts have been made throughout the centuries to civilly remedy, or at least reduce, the matter as much as possible, with varying degrees of success and controversy.

Though adultery and prostitution are considered sad and weighty trespasses against a sacred bond, they are handled with far greater civility than the crime of rape. The carnal violation of a Fidon is punished far more severely, being viewed as an utterly heinous corruption of an Onu-blessed act. Though the law across Fidonhaal does not sanction the killing or genital mutilation of a rapist, such incidents have occurred in cases where authorities failed to arrest and secure the offender before vengeance-seekers reached them, and few have much sympathy for those who meet such a fate. Even when they are arrested, tried and sentenced to the sanctioned punishment, it is an ordeal of great pain as well as a case of public shame that echoes throughout the remainder of the offender's mortal life. The rapist is taken to a public space, such as a town square or city gateway, branded on the forehead with the name of their crime for all to see, and then subjected to a period of incarceration. As severe as this punishment is, such an offender, upon re-entering society, may still be largely forgiven by the general public, and even by the offended parties, in due time following the sentence's fulfillment. However, the branding ensures the deed will never be forgotten.

APPENDIX D

Religion and Spirituality

The bond between the Fidons and their Maker, Onu, is a point of paramount concern to the vast majority of the people. However, an individual's particular approach to this relationship can vary significantly due to environment, personal temperament, philosophy, and other such factors.

Aside from simply praying to Onu in private, the Fidons most commonly practice the effort of communing with Onu by attending services conducted by the Temple. Such meetings are held daily, with the number of attendants varying from day to day. Nearly every settlement has a house of worship or a space regularly used to serve such functions, as well as at least one cleric and one high cleric to manage it.

For those outside the majority of settled society, be they Wild-Dwellers or simply travelers without access to a nearby temple, there are other sources for spiritual engagement and counsel available to those who seek them. These include traveling clerics, as well as roadside way shrines to Onu, the angels, and the Exemplars. In addition, while most look to officially recognized clergy of the Temple for spiritual counsel, it is an essential Fidon belief that the task of helping others keep (or recover, as need be) their bond with Onu is a universal task in which all should help one another, though also ultimately each individual's responsibility for oneself. Thus, any who wish to dedicate themselves to the attempt of studying and counseling the ways of the soul and the holy may do so. Consequently, Fidonhaal is home to the rank-and-file clergy of the Temple, the mystic druids in the woods, and the shamans of the roaming peoples. The Hand of Onu is always open for the mortal to grasp, but the will and decision to do so, and the manner in which one chooses to take it, is for each Fidon alone to decide.

Essential Lore

The core of the Fidons' faith revolves around their creator, *Onu*, whose name simply means "The One." Onu is the sole Creator of Existence, creating the angels and the Fidons, along with all else in nature, to share Creation with them. Thus, Onu blessed each of them with their own lot of powers and abilities so they could have a role in the universe in communion with him. However, Lovaariinu, the First Angel, whose name means "The All-Keeper," sought to impose absolute order on all things, depriving them of their own will, in order to keep the mortals from possibly straying from Onu's intended purpose. This intention, though well-meaning in origin, was refuted by Onu, who told Lovaariinu that the freedom of will was indeed essential to Onu's design; for faith, love, and communion given and reciprocated willingly is true, as opposed to that acted out by mindless shells.

Lovaariinu, angered by Onu's refutation, came to resent his Maker, nurturing in his mind the thought that he was greater and more righteous than Onu, and knew better than him on how to govern existence. This gave rise to Lovaariinu's arrogant pride and wrathful hatred of all that Onu had made, and what began as the desire to control all things for their own good soon became corrupted into a desire to enslave all that he deemed lesser than himself (which is to say, all in existence apart from himself, including Onu). Whatever he couldn't subjugate, he would seek to destroy.

When Onu at last called the angels together to reveal to them the Fidons and their allotted place in the universe, Lovaariinu rebelled against Onu and became thenceforth known as *Raakaru*, which means "The Hateful Heart." Raakaru then gathered those spirits that he managed to persuade to his side and attempted to overthrow Onu and his faithful host. When the revolt failed, Raakaru and his followers fled from the holy plane of Onuhaal and went into the void, where he formed his own domain, the realm of demons, which is known has *Raakhaal,* or "The Home of Hatred." From that time onward, Raakaru has sought to spite Onu and Creation by undermining, corrupting, conquering, and destroying the Fidons along with all else of Onu's making.

In time, after millennia of peace and prosperity on Fidonhaal, Raakaru succeeded in swaying the

Fidons away from Onu. This brought a devastating collapse of the wondrous civilizations of the world that marked the great Era of Communion and ushered in the Era of Raakaru's Reign, when all of Fidonity was reduced to a race of warring barbarians. This was also the time when demons, ill magic, and horrid monstrosities came into the world. With this severance of the sacred bond, Onu and the angels left the world and its people to the fate they chose. Yet Onu did not destroy Fidonhaal or the Fidons, nor did he take away the Fidons' will to impose absolute order, for he still held that his mortal children were to have their will, and still loved them despite their sin. Thus, Onu watched his children fall into darkness for a thousand years, waiting for the day when the Fidons might be led back to the bond they once held together.

That day came when four Fidons, warlords of their lands, discovered remnants of the Lost Times. Wondering of the artifacts' significance, they learned it from Onu and the angels, who appeared to them at the utterance of their inquiries. Onu and the Angelic Host then offered them, and all the world, a chance to break free from Raakaru's grasp and try to mend the bond they once had with Onu. In time, these four rallied their brethren against Raakaru and his servants, and exorcised Raakaru from Fidonhaal. Ever since Raakaru's expulsion, the Fidons have struggled to rebuild their world and return to the blessed communion with Onu they once had.

Alas, for all the progress the Fidons made since that ill era, Raakaru's influence had by that time taken deep root into the world and the hearts of the people, thus leaving the world far from being in the blissful state that it once held. Throughout the Fidons' history since Raakaru's fall, however, many heroes and heroines have come in times of peril and strife to try and set matters to rights. Some of these were specially chosen by Onu, having been blessed and marked by him with a sacred brand. Such heroes and heroines are referred to as being of the Elect in homage to the first Elect, the four who led Fidonhaal on the crusade against Raakaru.

The Angels

Though Onu is regarded as the Ultimate Being in Fidon lore, the religion and spirituality of the people includes an array of other spiritual beings who have played a part in the saga of Fidonhaal. The greatest of these are the angels, who were given roles of governance over aspects of existence and partook in the shaping of the universe alongside Onu. Originally, there were thirteen angels, the greatest of them being Lovaariinu the All-Keeper, who rebelled against Onu and became Raakaru. Twelve angels remained following Lovaariinu's fall and have faithfully played their part in Onu's design ever since.

When Onu showed the forms of the Fidons to the angels and the wondrous purposes for the differences between male and female and the concepts of mated pairs, the angels were moved greatly and took on male and female forms with Onu's blessing. They then joined with one of their fellows as mates, and by their unions begat wondrous creatures collectively known as the Angelborn. These creatures were birthed upon the world by the angels shortly before the Fidons' Awakening, and they have since taken their own places in the history of Fidonhaal, appearing in legends, and aiding heroes and heroines throughout time.

The Angels of Life and Death are named Vitahla and Morinaar. Both have been viewed as robed and hooded figures, tall and slender, and of beauty that is both simple and grand. The light that Vitahla emanates has been described as the golden white of a diamond held to the sun, and Morinaar's glow is as shining silver. They have always appeared before mortals as a pair, ever representing the entwining of life and death. They each bear staves that are like the crooks of shepherds, and carry a flask of holy drink. The flask of Vitahla is filled with the holy wine of Onuhaal, which revives any dying Fidon who drinks it. The flask of Morinaar is filled with the holy water of Onuhaal's river, which, ever refreshing to the denizens of Onu's eternal home, sends a dying mortal peacefully to the Shores of Passing. Their children are the guardian spirits of life and death, looking over the living to ensure their safety, and accompanying the dead and dying as they depart from the mortal realm.

The Angels of Earth and Water are named Terranah and Stromarus. Representing both the might and bountifulness of the earth, Terranah has been seen as a tall woman, greatly muscular in frame while still having a highly curvy physique. Being also affiliated with flora and fauna, she has been sighted and depicted as wearing garments wrought from both hide and plant. She wields a great hammer. Her light is an immensely vibrant green. Her husband, Stromarus, being a personification of the strength of the waters, is also of tall and muscular build, and typically wears a simple, light cloth about his waist. He wields a spear. His form's light shimmers as a deep, yet bright, blue. As imposing as their forms may be, they have been described by those visited by them as being largely taciturn, though still very kindly. Their children are the Arbonyns and the merfolk.

The Angels of Wind and Flame are Vente and Branok. Vente has been seen as slender and graceful, garbed in clothing light and short. She carries a long hunter's bow. Her glow is of a light, shimmering white. Branok's form is also slender, though more muscular than his wife's, and he wears a light vest along with a kilt about his waist. His light burns a great, fiery red. Though both angels are kindly, Vente has been described as more playful and whimsical than Branok. The Angel of Flame is generally more given to sincerity and straightforwardness toward his charge, which could bring great destruction if not properly managed, and is yet vital to life and many of the tasks of mortals. Their children are the Lofons and the flamehearts. In the days of the First Elects' crusade against Raakaru's tyranny, Branok and the flamehearts showed the repentant how to craft great steel with which to combat their foes. This metal is known as Branokian steel, and it has been highly prized throughout the ages for the making of the most prestigious of weapons, armor, and tools.

The Angels of Summer and Winter are named Estvii and Sardoth. Estvii has been viewed as light and slender, clothed in a light, short toga and glowing with a bright yellow light. She holds a scythe, as her season is a time of great harvest, and also wears a crown of mature leaves and branches. Sardoth is depicted with a tall, large, barrel-chested physique, wearing heavy clothes and cloak of hide and fur, and carrying a large woodsman's axe. He also dons a crown of holly and evergreen branches. He glows an icy blue. Estvii's temperament has been described as lively, yet stately. Sardoth, though friendly and caring to mortals, is more solemn. Their children are the summer centaurs and the bearlike winter giants.

The Angels of Autumn and Spring are Kyse and Vernid. Kyse, representing the ideal bounty of autumn's final harvests, carries a great basket filled with food, and has been viewed as beautifully buxom and plump. She wears a roomy gown and a crown of aged but majestic leaves and branches, and glows a warm, orange light. Vernid, a figure of joyful vigor, carries and plays a harp while donning a short, light kilt. His form is lean and virile, and his head is crowned with tender green branches and leaves, along with newly bloomed flowers. He glows a bright, vibrant yellow-green. Both angels have been known as highly festive, though Kyse has been described as being more mellow in comparison to her vibrant husband. Their children are the autumnfolk and springlings, the kindly satyrs and fauns.

The Angels of Day and Night are Maywa and Yorun. Maywa is seen as slender and muscular, wearing a long, flowing gown and carrying a mirror. She glows a grand, golden light. Yorun, tall and lean, wears a light veil over his face in addition to light, flowing robes. He bears a lantern fixed to a tall staff and emanates a blue glow deeper than the lights of Stromarus or Sardoth. Maywa's demeanor has been described as stately, but benevolent, while Yorun has been noted as very calm and quiet. Both angels have been associated with revelations literal and metaphorical, with Maywa representing the light of day dispelling the darkness and Yorun's lantern being regarded as the light by which dreams and visions are seen. Their children are the sunwisps and the moonwisps.

Onuhaal

Onuhaal is the abode of Onu and those faithful to him. The angels and faithful spirits dwell here with their Maker when not engaging with the mortal plane, as do the souls of the repentant and faithful Fidons. The name of the realm translates simply to "The Home of Onu," and it is an eternal, wondrous place outside the confines of the mortal, corporeally tangible universe. It is a surreal place, but of boundless beauty and peace.

Upon death, the soul of a faithful Fidon passes from the body and arrives at what is called the Great Curtain, which is a supernatural veil separating the physical from the spiritual. Passing through this barrier, the soul then arrives at the Shores of Passing, where the recently departed gather and wait for the arrival of Morinaar and Vitahla's ship. When this sacred vessel arrives, the departed board it and sail to the Isle of Onuhaal. The isle is home to a great mountain and tree, as well as a river with many streams branching from it. There are peaceful groves of trees, offshoots of the great tree on the mountain, as well as peaceful fields and shorelines.

Here, all the souls of the faithful forevermore reside, communing and reveling with their Maker, the angels, and their fellows, from those they knew and loved in the mortal life to those they never met until encountering them in eternity. Each Fidon, in time, finds an eternal mate in Onuhaal. For most, it is the soul of their spouse, once both have (presumably) made their way to Onu's home. For others, particularly those who did not have such a relationship during their mortal days, they either find their soulmates waiting for them upon arrival or they need only wait a little while themselves for them to come.

The Temple of Onu

The Temple of Onu, often simply referred to as "Temple" or "the Temple," is the organized religious institution across all of Fidonhaal. Its figurehead is the *salpion*, the highest cleric, who generally resides at one of the four archtemples of the world when not abroad. Beneath the salpion are the *alpions*, who oversee the faith of the world's major regions. At the time of the accounts told in this book, the alpions number sixteen, with one alpion to each of the four wards of the four nations. Under the alpions are the high priestesses and priests, one of which can be found managing every "official" temple in a given ward. These clerics oversee the rank-and-file priestesses and priests that tend to the temple, who vary in number depending on the size of the temple and the community it serves.

The Temple's centers for worship vary in size and their general approach in practice across the world, ranging from small chapels to grand cathedrals, and places with high numbers of visitors to relatively secluded cloisters. The largest and most famous places of worship are the four archtemples, one of which is located in each of what are now regarded as the capitals of the nations. They consist of grand complexes housing many priestesses and priests, as well as several companies of Faithguard Knights, and also have quarters for visitors and residents of laity. A grand temple or cathedral serves as the central point of worship within these compounds, and are the sites of massive congregations on holy days and other special occasions.

While the essential teachings of the Temple are preached across the world, there is some variance to the exact philosophies and expressions of faith practiced. Many Fidons believe that an individual's communing with Onu is to be a direct practice, praying to Onu and pondering one's bond with him. Others have felt that, due to the deeply rooted darkness that was sown into the Fidon soul during Raakaru's tyranny, they are unworthy of appealing to Onu directly unless the Maker deems to address a mortal himself. These people have developed the practice of praying to the angels, communing with the spirits of their ancestors, or both, though neither practice is to be confused with actual worship.

By the time of the tale in this book, the Temple has largely adopted a spiritual approach that entails varying measures of these practices, with individual worship centers potentially exercising some of them more than others based on the specific local culture. Most value the respect for departed ancestors and acknowledge the angels as the most powerful children of Onu, while still seeking to form and keep their most paramount bond with the Creator. So far, only one period in Fidonhaal's history has witnessed an incident where these differences in exact spiritual views led to any severe problem, that being the time of the inquisition initiated by Salpion Gwellah Benarbu. Seen as the worst days in the Temple's history, this period was marked by efforts to further unify the faith, but led to many deaths and horrors. Though the Temple and the world have largely moved on from that dark time, the inquisition remains one of the grimmest reminders of the potential evils that can spring from good intentions.

The Faithguard and Other Orders

Though the clergy of the Temple receives training in predominantly nonlethal, hand-to-hand defense techniques, their roles are intended to be focused on spiritual concerns rather than combat, even that which is done for the defense of the good. For such instances, the Faithguard has become the Temple's answer. Being founded alongside the Temple itself, the Faithguard is a broad order of warriors trained for the defense of the Temple and its people, from the clergy to the worshippers. This intention to protect people from the forces and creatures of evil has, in essence, always extended to all Fidons who strive to live in pursuit of bonding with Onu, even if they do not specifically approach the communion as typically practiced by the Temple. This has especially been the case, however, since the aftermath of the inquisition, as reformative declarations issued by the Temple following that incident officially charged the Faithguard to defend all "faithful-hearted" Fidons.

The Faithguard was founded by Konoth Alpharon alongside Elukus and Sophia Aganon, the first salpions of the Temple. Konoth was a woodcutter and militia-fighter in a struggling village during the early years after the expulsion of Raakaru, when one day Elukus the Blind Seer and his wife, Sophia, arrived to offer spiritual guidance to the people who lived there. The first centuries following Raakaru's reign were hard and full of conflict, being a time of many small feuding domains and people both desperate and devious. Concerned by this and moved by the consoling and inspiring words of the Blind Seer and his loving wife, Konoth frantically prepared to follow and defend them from the sure perils of travel when he heard of their prompt departure. Grabbing his wood-axe and the lid from a cooking pot, and donning his heavy fighter's jacket of chain and hide, the first Faithguard knight accompanied Elukus and Sophia on their wanderings, protecting them from monsters and brigands alike.

When the Faithguard was founded, the order comprised only of those who would now be referred to specifically as the Konothian Knights, warriors who adopted the fighting techniques of wielding an axe and a small shield. In time, however, other martial styles began to be practiced by the Faithguard, and there are now numerous other orders of knights within the general order of the Temple's defenders, each focusing on a favored weapon and array of equipment.

Other orders affiliated with the faith, if not officially with the Temple itself, have arisen over the centuries. These include the *Vibonmor* ("Life and Death") Shepherds, who are wandering healers and consolers of the dying with a modest level of experience in defensive combat. Modeling the inseparable union between the Angels Vitahla and Morinaar, and their domains of Life and Death, each agent of this order is paired with another, and they embark into the world in pairs. They then do their best to heal the sick and wounded, and bring comfort to those beyond the help of medicine.

Another order, one that is heavily steeped in mystery and controversy, is that of the Yorunian Nightblades. Named after the Angel of Night, the Nightblades are a shadowy network of assassins. However, it is understood that they are not for hire by anyone, instead being a group that acts solely at their own discretion and only resorts to murder in the direst of situations, targeting the most corrupt and dangerous of individuals. Their numbers are unknown, as is the exact number of times they have acted in history. Though the Temple has constantly denied having any affiliation with them, this claim has been met with much skepticism. All that is known of them for certain are their daggers, shaped in the likeness of the crescent moon, along with their veils and robes, mimicking those of Yorun himself.

The Beldsantu

The *Beldsantu*, its name meaning simply "The Holy Book," is the primary compilation of sacred texts for the Fidon faith, being read and referenced regularly by the Temple and the average Fidon for counsel and inspiration. It contains the Fidon account of Creation, along with the lives of the First Ancestors, as well as the world's fall into Raakaru's tyranny and the following liberation by the combined actions of Onu, the angels and the First Elect. It also lists prophecies spoken and written throughout the millennia of the Fourth Era, as well as summaries of many of the ideals and lives of the Exemplars.

Prayer

The Fidon faith teaches that communion with Onu can be practiced in a variety of ways. However, prayer is naturally one of the most common ways in which Fidons pursue their spiritual efforts, and they vary from the extensive list formulated by the Temple to prayers said in the moment and from the heart of the individual.

Whatever the prayer, however, the Fidon concludes their words with the phrase, "In you I strive to trust," or "In you we strive to trust," if the prayer is spoken amongst two or more people. This closing statement comes from the words said to have been spoken by the First Ancestors, when Onu spoke to them following Raakaru's first attempt to lead them away from the Maker. Raakaru, having tried to convince the First Ancestors that Onu was neither caring nor trustworthy due to his allowance of freedom, sowed a seed of doubt into their hearts that they and their descendants would have to contend with for the rest of time. Nevertheless, when Onu spoke with them after Raakaru's departure, he told them once more of his love for them. The First Ancestors continued to commune with Onu, saying they would strive to keep their faith in him.

This conclusion to Fidon prayer is meant to reflect the honesty necessary for a true and loving bond with Onu; it is at once both a confession of doubt, even if only as much as a grain of sand, and a declaration to continue the efforts to overcome the doubt and keep the faith.

Iconography

The Fidon faith has been expressed by countless works of art and iconography throughout the millennia. Paintings, sculptures, and other forms of art depicting people and events from Fidonhaal's religious and spiritual history adorn temples, castles, and homes throughout the world, with many of these works being hailed as some of the greatest achievements of art in general.

The most vital, unifying piece of iconography for the faith, however, is the emblem of the *Uqua*, which translates to "The Four." This emblem at once represents a number of important elements from the faith and its lore. The subjects of this symbolism include the Heart, Eye, Mouth and Hand of Onu, as well as the Maker's Four Breaths, which were breathed during the first processes of Creation, by which spirit, wind, life and will were made.

The Uqua also represents the four elements of earth, flame, water and wind, as well as the four Fidons who became the First Elect and led the mortals' efforts to drive Raakaru out of Fidonhaal. Indeed, this emblem is what marked the foreheads of the First Elect and all those who have since succeeded them. This symbol is present throughout all of Fidonhaal, a universal expression of the Fidons' efforts to commune with Onu. It is the official insignia of the Temple, with pendants and talismans bearing its design, and druids and nomadic shamans carve the emblem into monoliths and other places of significance.

Exemplars

Throughout Fidonhaal's history, men and women have demonstrated ideals, and the pursuit of ideals, that have been recognized and recounted by the people. A number of these people have been designated by the Temple as "Exemplars" of the ideals associated with their lives, and have inspired generations of Fidons as they journeyed the paths of their lives in seeking to bond with their Maker.

One example of this designation is Konoth Alpharon, the first Faithguard Knight. Being cited as a warrior who did not resort to unprovoked violence and accepted his foes' surrender, he was designated as an Exemplar for Righteous Warriors. Another Exemplar is Konoth's wife, Devora, who forgave a group of brigands who raped her when she had the chance to condemn them to her husband's vengeance. She has since been cited as an Exemplar of Forgiveness, and many of even the most empathetic and compassionate Fidons have not fully matched Devora's capacity for mercy.

APPENDIX E

Magic

The craft of magic is comprised of mental, spiritual, and physical exertions by a Fidon to manipulate an aspect of existence into producing a desired effect. In addition to the exertions of mind and soul, nearly all acts of magic necessitate a gesture or array of bodily motions to direct the focus of the spell.

Be it for good or evil, magic is most commonly practiced by Fidons who pursue the occupation known as mage. Mages constitute a relative minority of the population, but are greatly respected and valued for their craft. Priests and priestesses are the next most common practitioners of magic, but are second by a very wide margin when compared to mages, especially in regards to the typical clergy of the organized Temple. Other Fidons of spiritual occupation, such as those referred to as shamans and druids, vary in their usage of magic, with some being comparable to highly skilled mages, some not troubling with it at all, and others moderately practicing it.

It should be noted that the potential for magical abilities is present within all Fidons, though most who demonstrate it are those who have a greater, seemingly inborn aptitude. It is a matter of discipline, education, experience, and energy that largely determines the success and consistency of a magic-user's abilities. Reports, albeit rare ones, tell of warriors with no prior training having a bolt of lightning fly from their blades, or having some similar experience. In addition, an injured or exhausted mage, regardless of knowledge and skill, will likely find it immensely difficult, though not impossible, to perform even simple magic.

For all that has been studied regarding magic, there remains a significant degree of mystery. Much of what is commonly practiced by mages is a matter well-known and understood by them, and even much of the common populace has a basic understanding of it, even if they themselves lack the aptitude to actually practice it. However, there are a few forms of magic that go beyond what most readily know or understand, such as magical healing, and resurrection and necromantic reanimation, along with clairvoyance and other matters of mysticism. There are also accounts of fabled, immensely rare objects that have had enchantments or curses placed upon them, as well as blessed and cursed sites that might have some form of power bound to them. Furthermore, there have been several instances in history where a great feat of magic surpassed what one would expect to be possible from even the greatest of mages. These instances are presumed by many to have been a magical act performed out of one's own will and talent. However, many more contend that such occurrences have been the result of divine or demonic intervention, or at least of some sort of guidance from one such force or another. Others yet propose that both bear a measure of truth.

The following information details a few of the more specific matters of the craft, including knowns, unknowns, and matters that lie between.

The Elements

The force and practice of magic entails a communion between a Fidon's mental and spiritual faculties, and the aspect of existence from which the spell is drawn. The prime aspects of existence that are involved in magic are the four classical elements of earth, flame, water and wind. When it comes to magic that goes beyond physical, elemental manipulation, such as healing or necromancy, the spiritual essences of a Fidon and their connection to either Onu or Raakaru (depending on their allegiance) are the determining "elements" for the magical act. Such forms of magic are significantly more complex and demanding than typical elemental magic, a matter that most Fidons, even those among the most capable, find quite taxing for the mind, body, and soul.

The Mage Society of Fidonhaal

At the time of this tale, most mages are instructed by a local chapter of the Fidonhaal Mage Society. Affiliation with this organization is not legally required for magic practitioners, but is generally very beneficial for its members as it provides great support, education, and credentials. Mages are welcome assets in virtually any and every area of society, but accredited ones are especially so, enjoying places in royal and lesser official courts as well as religious and academic institutions.

Necromancy and the Undead

It is said that Raakaru and his demonic host created the first of the undead during the age of the Hateful One's domination of Fidonhaal simply as a means to further the carnage that had been inflicted upon the world. Having successfully led the Fidons astray from their ways through the nurture of hubris and doubt, Raakaru and his minions used foul powers to possess and reanimate some of the Fidons slain by the resulting escalations in violence. These corpses were then unleashed upon the world, driving Fidonhaal into a deeper state of terror and darkness.

In time, however, the Fidons who became warlords, aligning themselves to demons to gain further power, sought this magic to bolster their armies. These brutal tyrants brought greater destruction and woe upon Fidonhaal either by making additional pacts with Raakaru's host themselves, or by gaining a wizard already aligned to such magic. Captives from enemy tribes were often sacrificed to the warlord's demonic patrons, continuously adding to their reserve of mindless soldiers.

With these origins, necromancy and the act of reanimating the dead, as opposed to resurrection by an article from a Phoenix or divine intervention, still entails the possession of a corpse by a demon, which must be purposefully summoned by a Fidon. Such an act is universally condemned by Fidonity, as it entails the deliberate communion with demons to profane a Fidon who has been laid to rest for selfish purposes. Typically, these reasons have been documented as matters such as revenge or the desire for power, but even reasons considered more sympathetic, such as wanting to reanimate a loved one despite the process not resulting in true resurrection, are condemned for their involvement of demonic powers.

The exact nature of a given occurrence of undead can vary, with some accounts telling of armies of murderous corpses while other instances tell of a necromancer having only one or two at hand. The magnitude of a particular instant involving undead depends on access to corpses, as well as the intentions of the Fidon seeking to reanimate the dead and the pact formed between them and the summoned demon. Megalomaniacal necromancers gather many bodies, or conduct their rituals in cemeteries or battlefields where the dead still litter the earth, and call on as many demons as can be summoned to possess the corpses and follow biddings of conquest. A grieving Fidon who resorts to necromancy to reanimate a departed loved one, not wishing to harm anyone but still committed to turning to such an act, will try to summon a less powerful demon, and try to keep the corpse hidden and restrained. A handful of necromancers in an army serving a heinous power or cause can raise hundreds if not thousands of undead, and a necromancer who is also bound to a demon's power themselves in the form of a warlock's pact can achieve powers even more terrible.

Magnitudes of Power

Scholars, having analyzed numerous accounts of magical acts, have speculated that the potential magnitude of a Fidon's magical power is theoretically limitless. In reality, however, due to the strenuous exertions that spellcasting requires, even the most knowledgeable and skilled of mages can typically go only so far. Some of the most powerful of mages, with enough strength and readiness, can conjure a fireball that can consume most of a squadron of foes or blow them off their feet with a mighty gust of wind. However, many of these mages will likely need to rest or consume a stimulant afterwards, especially if they are to continue performing comparable feats.

Instances such as bringing a city's wall down with an explosion of fire, however, have almost always been attributed to either holy or unholy intervention, or else have been the acts of either an

Ecclesian or warlock. These are mages who have become so strongly attuned to the spiritual aspect of magic that they can draw far greater power from themselves, and from the greater powers with which they are aligned, than most other magic-practitioners. Even for those capable of such feats, acts such as these have been done sparingly throughout history. Most Fidons, whatever their intentions, usually do not desire the level of attention to themselves that would inevitably arise from it unless they believed it was warranted.

Ecclesians and Warlocks

Ecclesians and warlocks are mages who have become so deeply bound to either the holy essence of Onu and the angels, or the unholy power of a demon, or even Raakaru himself that their magical capabilities can go well beyond that of most other mages, even some of the otherwise most skilled. Warlocks, being bound to the powers of Raakaru or one of his demonic servants, must willingly enter a pact with the entity. The origins of an Ecclesian, however, can vary. Some Ecclesians have been graced by this blessing from birth, while others gained this power by making an oath in great conviction. A few others have gained this power through reaching an immensely deep spiritual state via prayer and meditation.

Neither Ecclesian nor warlock can hope to conceal their endowment from the people unless they were to cover their eyes, for the eyes of both sorts of high-mages glow with holy or unholy light. The occurrence of either an Ecclesian or warlock is very rare, as becoming an Ecclesian is a blessing that eludes most of even the most good-hearted Fidons, and few of even the most malicious can conjure the willpower to forge such an overt bond with a being of Raakhaal.

Kamgenbew Tonic

A magic-practicing Fidon cannot cast spells indefinitely without some measure of replenishment from the intense mental and spiritual concentrations required, which translates into physical exertion and exhaustion. The extent and swiftness of such exhaustion varies from person to person, depending on factors such as the potency of the spell and the practitioner's experience, as well as how well-rested they are, their nourishment, and general state of mind. The most healthy and ideal way for a mage to stay capable of performing magic is by pacing the frequency with which they exercise magic, along with taking adequate food, rest, and meditation.

However, in situations where such means are absent, such as a battle or grueling march, there is an herbal concoction made from the ground seeds of a plant known as Kamgenbew that can replenish a magic-user's sense of energy in much the same way as a strongly caffeinated beverage. These potions can be conveniently carried in small flasks on one's person in case of emergencies that may require extensive use of magic and, consequently, extended periods of exertion. It should be noted, however, that this potion does not truly restore a mage's energy, as it is only a strong stimulant that provides the feeling of regained energy. Because of this, constant use provides diminishing returns, and long-term constant use is highly unadvised due to concerns of possible psychological dependency. A few mages outright refuse to keep any supply of the tonic, while others do their utmost to keep their store of it to a minimum, intending to mostly make do, when necessary, with less potent libations such as tea or coffee. Some Fidons make use of Kamgenbew in professions outside of magic, particularly ones requiring intensive manual labor, but most refrain from it, concerned about the potential risk of dependency.

APPENDIX F

Language

Because of the Fidons' long-standing history of connectivity and communication with one another the world over (even when warring with each other during Raakaru's reign), the people have developed and maintained a common global language that essentially differs only in matters of regional lingo, accents, and dialects.

The endeavor of chronicling this book's tale entailed both keeping numerous words and names in their original Fidon form, giving as close a translation or explanation as possible when appropriate, and translating others from the outset without elaboration. This alternating approach attempts to showcase the Fidon language while also trying to avoid alienating the reader. This method also keeps the text relatively easier to read and minimizes potential confusion when words and names of seemingly similar meaning appear, as a number of Fidon words carry more than one meaning depending on the context of a specific sentence or phrase. Thus, one encounters places with names like *Zeful* and *Quanithe* as well as ones named *Peargrove* and *Oakhall*, and people named *Lerannu* and *Verdok* appear alongside ones named *Sarah* and *Owen*, even if these names are not truly direct stand-ins of their true Fidon forms.

Sample Words and Phrases

Ag – see.

Agan – seeing/sight.

Al – great (in rank, importance, value, etc.)

Alquevyn – great story/great account/great telling; an epic, a legend, a chronicle.

Aln – evil; ill or fell in nature; bad, negative.

Anye – peace.

Ar – branch/limb/arm.

Arb – tree.

Av – bird.

Ayra – wine.

Bal – white.

Balon – White One; a Fidon whose fur is white.

Beg – born.

Begryn – birth.

Begtenov – Mountainborn; an honored title of the long-reigning monarchy of Sorrenar, referring to the circumstances of the birth of the dynasty's founder, Karanor Karamus

Beld – book/tome.

Ben – bless/blessed/blessing.

Bew – seed.

Bon – and/also.

Bra – flame/fire.

Chyn – sibling/kin; used for both literal and metaphorical terminology; "chynol" translates to "brother," and "chynay" translates to "sister."

Dan – piece/fragment; also used to name currency, such as "fahdan" translating to "silver-piece" or "silver coin."

Dell – valley.

Dod – subject of/to a concept, power, force or individual.

Dodmor – subject of/to death; mortal, used as either a noun or adjective.

Dodmorhaal – home/domain of those subject to death; the domain of mortals; the mortal plane; the Fidons' name for the physical, temporal universe.

Doh – blue.

En – rise/ascend.

Est – the season of summer.

Fah – silver; both the metal and the color.

Fi – faith.

Fidon – Faithful One/One of Faith; the name of the predominant, sentient creatures of Fidonhaal.

Frel – free.

Freld – freedom.

Fus – two.

Gah – gold; both the metal and the color.

Gen – heal/healing/restore/mend.

Gentryn – reunion/reconciliation; a bond/relationship that either has already mended or is in the process of mending.

Gla – green.

Gol – designation of something being the "most" of a quantitative quality, such as size or weight; an example of this is "golmag," meaning "biggest" or "greatest in physical stature."

Golmagstro – ocean; the greatest/largest water.

Gon – five.

Gor – serpent/snake.

Gra – love; specific meaning relies on context, as the word encompasses all potential forms of love, from that demonstrated between two Fidons simply regarding each other kindly to the love between family members and spouses.

Gwila – fruit; usage includes literal and metaphorical terms.

Gwilanay – daughter.

Gwilanol – son.

Gwilanyn – child/immediate descendant.

Haal – home/domain/place; exact meaning can refer to everything from an individual's residence to the entire world or universe.

Haam – warm.

Iin – all/every.

Jah – dry.

Jan – south.

Jiv – nine.

Kah – copper; both the metal and the color.

Kam – strong/strength.

Kar – heart; encompasses meanings both literal and metaphorical.

Karzynhaal – the home of Karzynu; the home of the Heartroot; the sacred isle of the Awakened Fidons' origins, at the center of which stands the sacred tree named Karzynu.

Kas – brown.

Kason – Brown One; a Fidon whose fur is brown.

Kell – fall/descend.

Kys – the season of autumn.

Lag – stride/sprint/run/gallop.

Lak – curse/cursed.

Lakon – cursed one; the collective name for the monstrosities wrought by Raakaru in the age of his tyranny over Fidonhaal; these creatures were initially formed by the abominable conjoining of Fidon and other creatures and objects, and continue to haunt the world from the dark recesses into which they have since largely retreated.

Larv – field.

Levstro – river.

Lex – west.

Lid – for; can be used to designate something as being "for" a certain individual, place, time, span of time, etc.

Lidrov – forever/eternal.

Lih – flesh/body.

Lof – wing.

Lov – protect/defend/keep/guard (as a verb or noun).

Lovaar – defender/keeper/guardian (a more refined title for a "guard," which can also be simply called "lov" in the Fidon tongue).

Mag – big; great in size and/or stature.

Magstro – sea; a named area of the ocean.

Mahze – era/epoch/age.

Mav – black.

Mavon – Black One; a Fidon whose fur is black.

May – day/sun.

Mor – death.

Nah – in/inside/within.

Nay – woman/female.

Nem – no/not/none; contexts of usage include general statements of refusal or denial, as well as to designate something that is in utter opposition to something else; an example of the latter is "nemresdryn," meaning "destruction," which could be translated more literally as "anti-creation;" also used to refer to the numeric value of zero.

Nemresd – destroy/unmake.

Nemresdun – destroyer; can be used to designate one who engages in any particular degree of destruction, but is especially used in reference to a murderer or as another title for Raakaru, particularly if the term is specifically "Nemresdunu," or *The* Destroyer.

Nemrov – never.

Nemvyn – nothing/nothingness.

Nod – east.

Nog – lead/rule.

Nogryn – reign/dominion.

Nol – man/male.

Nyn – person.

Ok – eight.

Omek – beast/creature/animal.

On – one.

Ontryn – communion/harmony.

Onu – The One; the ultimate power in all existence, the sole, supreme deity according to Fidon lore.

Onuhaal – The Home of Onu/The Home of The One; the name of Onu's supernatural domain, the eternal realm of love, peace and bliss; the destination of the faithful and repentant Fidons for the afterlife.

Ovis – crossing/cross.

Par – ten.

Qua – four.

Que – speak/tell/say.

Quevyn – story/account; something that is told.

Rab – drink (verb).

Rabvyn – drink (noun).

Raak – hate/hateful.

Raakaru – The Heart of Hate/The Hateful Heart; the name of the greatest evil entity in Fidon lore, who was once the highest angel in Onu's host and is now the bane of the Fidons and all of Onu's creation; formerly named "Lovaariinu," or "The All-Keeper," prior to his fall.

Raakhaal – The Home of Hate; the name of Raakaru's supernatural domain, the eternal realm of tyranny, hatred and agony; the destination of the unfaithful and unrepentant Fidons for the afterlife.

Raakon – Hateful One/One of Hate; typically refers literally to demons, though it can also be used to label mortal followers of Raakaru.

Rek – six.

Ren – star.

Resd – create/make.

Resdun – creator/maker; can refer to an artist, author, designer, and the like, but is especially used in reference to Onu, particularly if the phrase is specifically "Resdunu," or *The* Maker.

Resdryn – creation; can refer to something of anyone's making, but is especially used in reference to existence at large, as well as Onu's act of making it.

Rof – numerical designation; examples include "onrof" translating into "first" and "rofparok" meaning "eighteenth."

Rov – ever.

S – used to pluralize when placed at the end of a word; an example is "nays," being the pluralized form of "woman," hence "women."

Sal – greatest (in rank, priority, value, etc.)

Salquevynu – the greatest story/the greatest account/the greatest telling; the saga of Fidonhaal, all of Fidonhaal's historical and spiritual chronicles and lore.

Sant – holy.

Sar – the season of winter.

Set – seven.

Shan – message/messenger/herald.

Shanlof – heraldwing; birds specially trained for transporting correspondence over great distances, capable of delivering letters from one end of the world to the next.

Sor – north.

Stro – water.

T – a diminutive; taken from the first sound of "ti," the Fidon word for "small;" an example is "twin," which, combining the diminutive with the word "win," or "spirit," translates to "little spirit," which is typically used to refer to spiritual entities such as wisps.

Tar – fort/fortress/castle/stronghold/keep.

Te – earth/land.

Tek – stone.

Temii – hill.

Tenov – mountain.

Ti – small/little.

Tri – three.

Tryn – union/bond.

U – the; most often used in conjunction with the word that indicates the subject of a sentence, title, name or phrase; examples include "Onu," which translates to "The One," and "Beldsantu," which means "The Holy Book."

Ven – wind/air.

Ver – the season of spring.

Vi – life.

Vyn – object/thing.

Win – spirit/soul.

Xe – red.

Xer – blood.

Yor – night/moon/month.

Zar – grey.

Zaron – Grey One; a Fidon whose fur is grey.

Zo – of; usage depends on certain needs for distinction within a given sentence, phrase, etc.; many Fidon words and phrases have contexts that don't necessitate its use.

Zyn – root.

APPENDIX G

Government and Security

Records recovered from the lost Era of Communion concerning matters of government are far from complete or comprehensive, but seem to indicate a time of unparalleled peace, unity, and stability. The current governments of Fidonhaal are the product of an initially feudalist system that has developed into a combination of dynastic leadership and election-based representation.

Current Organization of Government

A thousand years prior to the events chronicled in this book, each of Fidonhaal's four continents unified their realms into what are now referred to as the Four Nations. Each of these nations are led in equal power by a queen and king. If their leadership and appointed heirs are deemed satisfactory by the majority of the nation, they can potentially hold the throne for life. The heirs ascend to the throne following their predecessors' deaths or retirement. Throughout Fidonhaal's history, the overwhelming majority of the monarchs have been spouses to one another, with their appointed successors being selected from their children, in-laws, or other kin. However, there have been leaders who weren't married to each other (or at all), and successors have varied from distant relatives to candidates of no known relation.

In most cases of a new dynasty's founding, particularly when such occasions have been peaceful, the first queen and king are elected by the general populace of the realm. Message relays are sent throughout the land to call for votes and inform the public of the candidates. An allotted time is given for the votes to be cast, collected, and counted at the realm's capital, and the elected candidates are then announced and coronated. The procedure is essentially the same for removing leaders, even ending dynasties, when such things are done peacefully, which has certainly not always been the case.

Below the royalty are their personally appointed court advisors and household. The wardens and wardenesses are governors of the four wards. Each of the Four Nations has four of these large provinces, which are each designated as the East, West, North, and South wards. These are appointed by the monarchy and potentially heritable like the royal office, but are subject to approval by the populace and the same election process as that of the founding members of a royal line.

The *Quaparvis*, a council of forty representatives, are assigned ten to each ward and inform the warden or wardeness of the goings-on in their respective districts, which are known as *parrofs*, or "tenths." Each of the forty council members are appointed and elected by the general public of their respective district.

The lattermost office that has jurisdiction beyond a single settlement is that of the holder. These officials manage districts called holds, which lie within their respective ward and tenth. Finally, there are the offices of mayor or chieftain, which lead individual communities ranging from cities to hamlets.

All offices below warden or wardeness, from Quaparvis representative to mayor, are elected solely by the citizenry of their respective jurisdiction and have no provisions for potentially inherited authority. That being said, the individual can still hold their position until death or retirement if their performance is generally deemed satisfactory, and more than one case has demonstrated that penchants for these offices can run in families as well.

Police and Military

Most settlements have a guard garrison for maintaining civil order that is a branch of the ward, parrof, or hold's police force. As for military matters, each of the Four Nations has a standing army and navy, though armed conflicts between the nations, following the domestic consolidations of the continents, were essentially nonexistent prior to the time of this story. These forces, though trained for the possibility of war with a foreign nation, had largely been used as support units sent to areas within their respective nation or to one of their allies in times of abnormal civil instability or other state of emergency. As a result, though none of these armies were meager handfuls of warriors, they were far from being massive forces that stood ever at the ready, nor did they have much recent experience with "true" warfare prior to the events chronicled in this book.

APPENDIX H

Bestiary

Fidonhaal is home to many creatures besides the Fidons themselves, many of which have essentially equal resemblances to creatures from our world. That being said, there are a number of creatures and entities that are unique to Fidonhaal, particularly those which have origins tied to the overarching spiritual and cosmic lore of the world.

The Angelborn

Shortly before the Awakening, the angels coupled with their mates and begat an array of creatures and entities which have since taken their place in the world alongside the Fidons, partaking in their saga. Collectively, these creatures are referred to as the Angelborn. Each of them, in some way, has at least some resemblance to a Fidon, for the angels marveled so greatly at their forms that they wished to weave their likeness into the appearance of their children in addition to taking such forms themselves. Nevertheless, they can still be clearly distinguished from a Fidon, for their appearances are further defined by their size, the incorporated likeness of some other beast, or some other distinctive quality.

They are at once not fully of the world, being born to the angels, and yet deeply bound to the world into which they were birthed. As such, a number of their qualities, particularly how they live, reproduce or else perpetuate their presence, vary from one kind of Angelborn to another. Some sorts, themselves subject to a mortal death, beget offspring of their own in one manner or other that is typical for mortal life. Other sorts do not die in the manner of mortals, and though they still seek mates and engage intimately with them, they do not birth descendants. Instead, these kinds fade away and reform at a later time, becoming a new being while still potentially holding memories from past incarnations.

Arbonyn – Known also as tree-folk, dryads or spriggans, the Arbonyns are one of the two creatures begotten from the union of Terranah and Stromarus. Though not beings of earth or stone themselves, they have taken the form of the trees that grow from the earth, coupled with the likeness of a Fidon. They can potentially be found in any forest or wooded area, and have even been seen traversing open ground. However, they overwhelmingly prefer to walk within the embrace of great forests, such as Lidrovgla in Janrenar and Santaru in Enmayar. They are known to be fairly mellow and quiet, though approachable in conversation, and generally known to have slightly peculiar speech patterns. Though they pass from the world in the manner of mortals, Arbonyns, if not met by some atypical end, can live a very long time, like the trees they resemble. They have male and female forms, and seek companionship with mates. Their manner of copulation is not like that of most other Angelborn, which largely mimics that of the Fidons and other mortal creatures. Being much like the trees, male Arbonyns bear stamen-like growths upon their extremities, which are received by the flowers bloomed by the females. This produces seeds, which the Arbonyns then bury within the embrace of their angelic mother's charge. In time, the seeds sprout and grow into saplings, which then stir and rise from the ground to wander their forested homes.

Brankar – Also known as flamehearts, these entities, appearing as average-statured Fidons wreathed in flame and warm ash, are one of two beings resulting from the union between Branok and Vente. Though they can be potentially found anywhere in the world, they generally favor hot, dry regions, and sites near volcanoes. While goodhearted, they are usually quiet and straightforward, much in the same general temperament as their father. Though they have likenesses to male and female forms, they do not mate or beget offspring. Instead, when the time comes for their present incarnations to end, their ashen bodies collapse and are carried away by the winds. The ash settles in time, and a new fire of being is kindled upon it, forming a new Brankar.

Estlagun – Also known as summer striders or centaurs, these warmhearted creatures are one of the two sorts of beings born from the bond of Estvii and Sardoth. They spend the time of their season quietly watching over the peaceful places in which their kind tend to dwell. They appear as a horse with the upper body of a Fidon. At summer's end, they quietly fade out of the world, either returning to their prior abodes upon their season's return, or else reforming on the other side of the world following the end of the opposite hemisphere's springtime. Though benevolent, they are generally a quiet and reserved lot. Estlaguns do seek mates with which to have intimate companionship, but do not beget descendants in the way typical of mortals. When they pass from the world at their season's end, they reform as beings who are new to the world while still carrying memories and particularities of lives past.

Kysnyn – Known also as satyrs, these creatures of autumn have the form of a Fidon and a deer, with the males bearing majestic antlers. They are one of two Angelborn creatures born to Kyse and Vernid. Like their springtime kin, they are a kindly and festive lot, though taking more after their mother than father, they are comparatively mellower. Like the other Angelborn of the seasons, they do not procreate as mortals do, though they do still seek mates for intimate companionship. They fade and return with the coming and going of their season, reforming as both a part of who they were and as a new being.

Lofon – Known also as winged ones, these creatures, born from the coupling of Vente and Branok, appear as sizable birds with beaked, Fidonlike faces. They can be potentially found anywhere in the world, though they favor mountains, cliffs, and places with tall trees. Friendly and whimsical in temperament, they happily greet those who happen upon them, and have been known to offer short flights to ease the fatigue of travelers. They have male and female forms, and mate and beget descendants by laying and hatching eggs. While usually long-lived creatures, potentially living as long as a well-aged Fidon, each Lofon passes from the world in the same manner as other mortals.

Maytwin – Known also as sunwisps, these entities are one of two beings that sprang from the bond of Maywa and Yorun. They appear as tiny winged beings bearing the likeness of a Fidon and emanating warm-hued glows. They can manifest themselves at any time between dawn and dusk, fading from view at sundown. Though they have a Fidonlike form, they are neither male nor female, and do not seek mates or reproduce. They are benevolent, known for things such as aiding lost travelers and the like, but do not speak. They are generally solitary, though it is not impossible to see more than one of them in a given area or time. Many places where sunwisps have appeared continue to have at least somewhat recurring visits from them, though it is not certain whether or not these wisps are the same as the previous visitors or reformed incarnations of wisps past.

Morlovaar – Also known as death guardians, reapers or valkyries, these entities are one of two beings that were born from the union of Morinaar and Vitahla. These beings appear in places and times of death, sharing their father's task in gathering those who are to make their way beyond the Great Curtain and await passage to Onuhaal. They give release to those who suffer upon the threshold of Death, and accompany them on their walk to the Shores of Passing. They bear much the same likeness to a Fidon as their father, but are neither male nor female, nor do they mate or beget descendants. It is not known if they experience any form of passing and renewal, if new ones are begotten from their father and mother's union, or if each of them are the very same as those born before the Awakening. Though compassionate, they rarely speak.

Sarmagon – Also known as winter giants, these large, sincere beings are one of two creatures born from the bond of Sardoth and Estvii. They spend the duration of their season quietly overlooking the areas they call home. They appear as tall, large creatures bearing the likeness of a Fidon and an upright-walking bear. At winter's end, they vanish from the world, reforming in the general area they were last present or appearing when winter visits a season later on the opposite side of Fidonhaal. They are kindly beings, but fairly taciturn and solitary. Like their Estlagun kin, they seek intimate partners but do not actually reproduce, instead reforming at a later time with echoes of memories and personalities of those who came before.

Stronyn – Also known as merfolk, these creatures are one of two such beings that are the product of the bond between Stromarus and Terranah. They appear as a large fish with the upper body of a Fidon, and mostly favor the waters of the ocean. However, they can potentially be found in any body of water that ultimately connects to the seas. Generally speaking, they are kindly but fairly reserved. Stories across the millennia have told of merfolk helping sailors lost at sea and even occasionally helping fishers with their labor, driving some of the sea's bounty to their nets or lines. They mate and yield descendants in a manner much like an aquatic mammal, birthing them live as opposed to laying eggs. A Stronyn is due to die as a mortal creature in time, though they can live to an age comparable to that of a long-lived Fidon.

Vertnyn – Also known as springlings or fauns, these beings, appearing as an interwoven form of a small-statured Fidon and a rabbit, are one of two creatures born to Vernid and Kyse. Taking after their father, they are incarnations of spring's liveliness and love to revel in due measure with their mates, their kin and any Fidons who encounter them. They are talkative and outgoing, and are immensely fond of music and games. Though they do not beget offspring, they do seek to pair with a mate as soon as they can upon reappearing in spring. Like their other seasonal kin, they fade from the world when the next season is due, but reappear elsewhere in Fidonhaal once their time returns as a being at once alike and different from before.

Vilovaar – Also known as guardian angels, these beings, born to Vitahla and Morinaar, appear in times and places of life. They have watched over many Fidons, gently and quietly guiding or warding them from potential harm, but only a fortunate few Fidons have laid eyes upon them. They bear much the same likeness to a Fidon as their mother, but are neither male nor female, nor do they mate or bear offspring. Like their Morlovaar kin, it is not known for certain if these beings experience a form of expiration and reformation, if more might be birthed from future couplings between Vitahla and Morinaar, or if they are all the same as those first born prior to the Awakening.

Yortwin – Known also as moonwisps, these entities are one of two beings that sprang from the bond of Yorun and Maywa. Like their sunwisp kin, they appear as tiny winged beings bearing the likeness of a Fidon, but their glow tends to be cooler in hue. They can manifest themselves at any time between dusk and dawn, fading from view at sunrise. Like the sunwisps, they have a Fidonlike form, but are neither male nor female, and do not seek mates or reproduce. They are also mute like their daytime counterparts, though they are also known for kindly and watchful acts. They are generally solitary, though one can find places where small groups of them congregate. Many places where moonwisps have appeared continue to have at least somewhat recurring visits from them, though it is not certain whether or not these wisps are the same as the previous visitors or reincarnations thereof.

The Curse Spawn

Following Raakaru's conquest of Fidonhaal, an array of evil creatures was brought into being by the powers of the Hateful Heart and his followers. Many of these beasts were simply common animals that were warped maliciously by Raakaru and his servants, and are known collectively as *Alnomeks*, or "Fell Beasts."

However, Raakaru went beyond simply tainting what already was, and taking many Fidons, he forcefully conjoined them with other creatures, or parts of the world itself, to create heinous beings that lived to hate the Fidons and their world, and work toward their destruction. These creatures, referred to as the Curse Spawn, are either the direct product of Raakaru's curses or the descendants of those initially cursed from long ago. Their continued existence is due to either biological reproduction or some form of malicious craft.

The hatred of Fidonity that these monstrosities have, along with those of the Alnomeks, must be stressed as a definite, conscious quality. Unlike a normal predatory animal, which might at times attempt to set upon a Fidon for food, the Curse Spawn and the Tainted Beasts do not attack merely out of an instinct for survival despite the fact they do indeed favor Fidon flesh and blood. Raakaru and his demons ingrained this conscious hatred into the minds of these monsters, and they live to kill and destroy to spite the Fidons and their Maker.

Loflak – Known as either a "Cursed Wing" or a harpy, the Loflak is a heinous mockery of the Lofons, first formed when Raakaru joined the bodies of Fidon and vulture. They can be found in forests thick and thin, though they generally enjoy high places with clear views. They are more often found along cliffs, mountain ridges and other high, rugged terrain when not hunting. They breed as the birds and Lofons do, laying eggs among the heights in which they linger. Their talons and beaks are sharp, and their cries are piercing and blood-chilling.

Maglakon – Their name translating to "Cursed Giant," a Maglakon is also known as an ogre or troll. They have the form of a large, tall Fidon with no fur, along with large eyes and extremely sharp claws and teeth. Like the Qualakars, these monsters are descended from Fidons who were grossly forced into their form by Raakaru's hand. Generally favoring caves, Maglakons will settle for any environment that enables them to find or create a secluded shelter, to which they retreat after slaying or capturing prey. They are mostly solitary, usually meeting and engaging only to breed, with the females promptly leaving the males after mating in order to bear and rear the offspring.

Qualakar – Their name essentially translating to "Cursed Four-Limbs," the Qualakar resembles a large, thinly furred, quadrupedal Fidon. Those present in Fidonhaal today are the descendants of the first, who were once Fidons, cursed horrifically by Raakaru's power. They are pack animals who favor caves and the dense foliage of heavily forested areas, from which they spring in ambush and into which they retreat with their prey in their jaws. Though they operate within a group, many Qualakars separate from their central pack for a time to survey their territory and hunt. All Qualakars within a pack can breed, though the alpha male and female generally spawn the majority of a pack's brood.

Strolak – Their name meaning "Cursed One of the Water" in the Fidon tongue, the Strolak is an abomination that was formed by Raakaru's conjoining of a Fidon with one of the tentacled creatures of the deep. Like the benevolent merfolk, they largely favor the ocean's waters, but can be found in any body of water that ultimately finds its way to the seas. Unlike the merfolk, however, they would never seek to aid a Fidon, instead driven to slay and devour. Unfortunate fishers have been dragged to a grisly end when a Strolak gripped their lines or upended their boats, and swimmers should be wary when entering unfamiliar waters.

Teklak – Their name translating to "Cursed One of Stone," a Teklak is also known as a golem. These horrors were formed by Raakaru's infusion of a Fidon's body with portions of earth and stone, and stories tell of the terrible harm and destruction that just one such creature can inflict. When the Fidons began to rebel against Raakaru's tyranny, many golems were slain while others managed to shelter into the depths of the earth, becoming dormant. Since then, incidents have occurred when golems have awakened, reaching the surface and causing varying amounts of destruction and death. It is believed these abominations are incapable of breeding, but their numbers from the time of Raakaru's reign are unknown, as is the number of those who managed to hide from their hunters. Furthermore, there have been accounts of a few Fidons who aligned themselves to Raakaru and managed to fashion more such monsters with vile magic. Thus, there is no way to know for certain how many golems remain in Fidonhaal, nor their exact whereabouts or when they might rouse from dormancy.

Xerrabun – Their name translating to "Blood Drinker," the Xerrabun is also known as a vampire. A winged abomination resembling a Fidon with pronounced fangs, claws and bat-like wings, these horrors prowl in the dark, rending their victims to pieces and gulping down their blood. Their jaws are vertically aligned, and their eyes are compounded and can easily see in the dark. They favor any dark and secluded or abandoned place, such as caves and forgotten ruins.

The Beasts of the Renewed Bond

When the First Elect exorcized Raakaru from Fidonhaal with the aid of Onu and the angels, they gave their lives during the fateful battle, and their following armies were filled with sorrow upon hearing of their fate. Onu, assuring the Fidons that the Hateful Heart no longer had total reign of the world and a new era of reconciliation was at hand, made two new kinds of wondrous beasts and placed them in Fidonhaal.

These creatures, their very being symbolic of the cycle of life and renewal, live up to a century at a time if not met by some violent or unusual end. Whenever they die, an unbreakable egg forms in the midst of their remains, and their consciousness enters it to form a renewed body. In time, these creatures hatch from their egg and begin their lives anew, bearing echoes of memories from all their past incarnations. Only four of each of these creatures exist, being of neither sex and incapable of mating or reproducing.

These creatures have since come to take a place within the saga of Fidonhaal alongside the Fidons, much in the same manner as the Angelborn, being present in legends and accounts throughout the millennia following Raakaru's expulsion.

Benmaggor – Their name translating to "Blessed Great Serpent," and also known as the Leviathan, the Benmaggor is a benevolent serpent of colossal size. Capable of traversing both land and water, these creatures spend the majority of their time in the ocean. When they die, in addition to their egg, their bones can remain where the Benmaggor perished for many years before crumbling to the elements, and their scaly hide remains draped upon the bones until it decays. Some Fidons have gathered some of these serpents' bones or collected a measure of their hide to fashion armor, clothing, weapons or related accessories. A few accounts even tell of Benmaggors befriending Fidons and offering their remains to them as a gesture of friendship and well-wishing. Though they don't desire violence, accounts tell of great devastation when a Benmaggor partakes in battle.

Vibranav – Also known as the Phoenix, the Vibranav, essentially translating to "Bird of Life and Flame," is a great creature of wonder and legend. They appear as birds of great stature, with feathers of red and other fiery colors, and are renowned for the healing and resurrecting properties of their tears and remains. A feather plucked or molted from a living Pheonix can cure even the most grievous wound or ailment if it touches the afflicted, and the bird's tears and ashes, in addition to healing the living, can resurrect the dead if their soul has not yet left the Shores of Passing. They can channel the power of flame into their breaths, cementing themselves as terrible foes to those who would seek to oppose the good of Fidonhaal. They are otherwise renowned for their compassion and wisdom, and have been allies to heroes in counsel as well as battle.